Holding Onto You

VOLUME 1

- KENNEDY FOX - WILLOW WINTERS - CHARITY FERRELL -
- EMILY GOODWIN - T.L. SMITH - SKYE WARREN -

Holding Onto You: Volume 1

The Two of Us
Copyright © 2020 Kennedy Fox
www.kennedyfoxbooks.com
Love in Isolation, #1
Copy Editor: Jenny Sims | Editing 4 Indies
All rights reserved. No parts of the book may be used or reproduced in any matter without written permission from the author, except for inclusion of brief quotations in a review. This book is a work of fiction. Names, characters, establishments, organizations, and incidents are either products of the author's imagination or are used fictitiously to give a sense of authenticity. Any resemblance to actual persons, living or dead, events, or locales is entirely coincidental.

Possessive
Copyright © Willow Winters

Just One Night
Copyright © 2018 Charity Ferrell
All rights reserved.
www.charityferrell.com
Editor: Jovana Shirley, Unforeseen Editing, www.unforseenediting.com
No part of this book may be reproduced or transmitted in any form or by any means, electronic or mechanical, including photocopying, recording, or by any information storage and retrieval system without the permission of the author, except for the use of brief quotations in a book review.
This book is a work of fiction. Names, characters, brands, places, and incidents are either products of the author's imagination or used fictitiously. Any resemblance to actual persons, living or dead, events, or locales is entirely coincidental.

Side Hustle
Copyright © Emily Goodwin

Kisses and Lies
Copyright T.L Smith
All Rights Reserved

This book is a work of fiction. Any references to real events, real people, and real places are used fictitiously. Other names, characters, places, and incidents are products of the Author's imagination and any resemblance to persons, living or dead, actual events, organizations or places is entirely coincidental.

All rights are reserved. This book is intended for the purchaser of this e-book ONLY. No part of this book may be reproduced or transmitted in any form or by any means, graphic, electronic, or mechanical, including photocopying, recording, taping, or by any information storage retrieval system, without the express written permission of the Author. All songs, song titles and lyrics contained in this book are the property of the respective songwriters and copyright holders.

WARNING
This book contains sexually explicit scenes and adult language and may be considered offensive to some readers. This e-book is intended for adults ONLY. Please store your files wisely, where they cannot be accessed by under-aged readers.

Escort © 2018 by Skye Warren

The Two of Us

KENNEDY FOX

Author's Note

Although the romance in this book is fiction, there are some real aspects of the pandemic mentioned throughout. Please go to the cdc.gov and who.int websites for all current information.

CAMERON
DAY 1

My heart pounds as I rush around my penthouse, shoving clothes and books into my Louis Vuitton suitcases. It's my senior year at New York University and the campus has shut down indefinitely today. Starting next week, I'll finish the semester online.

No graduation ceremony.

No saying goodbye to my classmates I've seen every day for the past four years.

No final words of wisdom from my professors.

I'm heartbroken.

With a 4.0 grade point average, I can't risk falling behind and losing my spot as valedictorian. Hopefully, this doesn't interfere with graduating on time because I've been accepted into the Master of Business program in the fall.

While I'm upset about no longer attending classes and missing out on the last few months of my final year, I'm more concerned and devastated about what's happening around the country and in the city I was born and raised in.

New York was recently declared a major disaster area. A dangerous viral outbreak has swept the world, and we're being told to self-isolate to help slow the spread, but the hospitals are already overcrowded.

When the news broke, my parents begged me to come home, but I know my mother. Clara St. James can't function without her housekeepers and personal chefs, and if she continues to let them help, she's directly breaking the basic guidelines of being quarantined. Unless her staff moves in, my parents will still be in contact with people who are carrying germs from the outside world. I love my mom, but she's the classic Upper East Side's cliché of wealth and power who doesn't follow rules because they're below her.

My family owns a billion-dollar fashion empire, so it's all I've ever known. Since I could walk, my mother has groomed me to be involved with the business. As the elite princess of the St. James estate, I'm expected and have agreed to maintain the company when they're ready to retire. I love my family, but behind our socialite status and the media's glamorized portrayal, we're dysfunctional with a capital D.

My brother, Ryan, is four years older than me and graduated from medical school last year. He's doing his residency in one of New York City's top-ranked hospitals and will work directly with patients who have contracted the virus. It's scary as hell to know he'll be there, but he's determined to do whatever it takes to help people and save lives. I'm proud of him, but I worry about his safety.

"Cameron, this is absurd," my mother says on the phone with a long sigh. "Rodrick will pick you up and drive you home."

"I'm staying at the cabin so I can focus on my schoolwork and stay inside." I repeat the same words I said yesterday. I don't tell her my boyfriend, Zane, is meeting me there in a couple of days. She's not his biggest fan because he hasn't proposed yet, but I'm nowhere near ready for marriage. I'm only twenty-two and want to finish school first. This year, we're both graduating, and we plan to move in together this summer as a trial run. So for now, she'll have to get over the idea of planning the wedding of *her* dreams.

I could've driven with him, but I was too anxious and ready to get out of the city to wait. He needed extra time to do his laundry, pack, and buy more supplies. Zane doesn't live on campus, but he slept over at my place a lot, which is why it's better we isolate together.

"Plus, I could've been exposed by someone at school. We really have no idea how many cases there are, so it's best I stay away. That way, I don't risk getting you or Daddy sick."

He has high blood pressure, and my mom smokes. Though she claims she quit, I know she hasn't.

"You two should go somewhere for a few weeks," I suggest. "Your company employees are working remote, so there's no reason to stay in the city. Visit the Hampton lake house or drive to the Tennessee resort."

"And leave all my things?" She gasps. "We'll be fine, dear. Your father and I are usually six feet apart anyway. The housekeepers will wear masks and gloves. You really should just come here so we're together." I roll my eyes as she continues to beg. For the past fifteen years they've pretended to be madly in love in front of the cameras and brush aside any rumors that my dad has a drinking problem. They want the world to think they have a picture-perfect marriage, but it's only an act.

Denying her request again, I explain how labor-intensive my online classes will be, and as nicely as I can, I remind her I'll need this time to focus on finishing my semester and keeping my grades up. She seems to buy it and tells me to check in with her daily. I make her promise to keep her distance from everyone because while she's health-conscious, her smoking puts her at a higher risk, so I worry.

After the call ends, I grab the rest of my essentials and pack my Range Rover. The back is full of enough food and water to last a few weeks. I picked up a large online shopping order today so I wouldn't have to go to the store again for a while. Just the thought of being in public gives me hives, but my mother never believed I had anxiety and didn't allow me to get help or medication. Last year, I secretly saw a therapist and finally got a prescription to help me cope.

Once I have everything, I grab Chanel's carrier and food. She's another reason I prefer not to stay at my parents' house. She's a Sphynx cat, and my mother's Yorkie barks at her nonstop, which means I'd spend the entire time trying to keep *them* six feet apart.

I load her up, take one last look around to make sure I didn't forget anything, then leave. The cabin is in Roxbury, which is three hours away, but with an overwhelming number of people leaving the city, the traffic could make it longer.

I listen to the radio as I drive, watching people rush down the sidewalks. It's complete madness. My mind wanders as I reflect on what's happened over the past few days. Schools and non-essential stores closing. No flights going in or out of the country. National parks and Disney closed. No large gatherings allowed and being told to stay six feet apart from strangers. Not to mention the masks people are wearing.

It's a culture shock and surreal how fast this happened. The sooner I get out of the city, the better.

The past week has been a blur. Between the news reports and social media posts, it's hard to know what to believe and whether our government is really prepared. I'm well aware of my family's legacy and what it's provided me. The media paints me as a privileged white girl who doesn't have to work, who has everything handed to her on a silver platter, and only has an education and future career because of the family business.

I'm an introvert and keep to my small circle of friends I trust. The media's perception is an unfair assessment, but it sells a story and gets clicks online. Reporting the truth wouldn't be as entertaining.

I've worked my ass off in school. I love learning and am passionate about business. I can't deny my closet is full of designer clothes and shoes, but it's to be expected. I wear the family collection and other designer brands my parents personally endorse. I was raised by nannies, housekeepers, and personal drivers and believed this lifestyle was normal until I got a taste of the outside world and reality. Life is different when your family is in the top one-percent richest of the population, which makes me an easy target for ridicule.

It also doesn't get me a lot of *true* friends, and it can be lonely at times.

The scene driving into town is gorgeous. Spring is a few months away. The trees are still bare, and there's a crisp chill in the air, even for mid-February. Once I turn onto our private road and see the cabin, I let out a sigh of relief that I made it. The Roxbury cabin is one of my favorite properties even though my mother hates it. It's not glamorous enough, and she feels too disconnected from her high-society friends here. But that's exactly why I love it so much.

The semi-open layout is rustic yet modern. Large windows and a wraparound deck offer the best views of the sunrise and sunset. It's a three-story cabin that sits on ten acres overlooking two ponds and the mountains. There's no better place to be, and maybe it'll distract me from what feels like the end of the world. And if that doesn't do the job, I have vodka.

"Chanel, we're here!" I sing-song as I park in the three-car garage. "We'll be safe here, baby."

The downside of traveling without Zane is having to unload this shit alone. Fortunately, my mom had the cleaning crew come out two weeks ago, so it should still be decent inside. We rent it out to family and friends once in a while, so we keep the five thousand-square-foot cabin maintained year-round.

I set the cat carrier down and open it so she can explore and get accustomed to the space. She hasn't been here since last year, so it might take her some time to remember it. She immediately sniffs around and flicks her tail, annoyed.

"You'll like it here," I tell her, then lean down to pet her. She purrs, and I smile. "I'll be right back with your litter box and dishes."

After dragging my suitcases inside, I make three more trips until every grocery bag is on the counter. I put the food and drinks in the refrigerator and pantry, then unpack my clothes and hang them in the master bedroom closet. It's the only room on the third floor and has a large window that overlooks the property. The other two bedrooms are on the second floor.

"I'm exhausted." I fall back on the bed with my arms spread out. After a moment, I feel Chanel jump up by my feet.

"What about you, Chanel?" Turning my head, I see she's curled in a ball and falling asleep. "Yeah, a nap sounds good."

I quickly text Zane to let him know I made it and will probably be out for the rest of the night.

Cameron: Chanel and I made it safely. All unpacked and just waiting for you now :) I'm gonna go to bed. Love you!

Setting my phone on the nightstand, I stand and head to the bathroom. The jet tub looks so damn tempting, but I'll have plenty of time to use it tomorrow.

After I change into my comfy clothes, I brush my teeth and wash my face.

Once I'm tucked into bed, I check my phone and frown when I don't see a response from Zane. Maybe he's on his way here to surprise me and can't text because he's driving. Before I think too much about it, my eyelids grow heavy, and I fall asleep with Chanel snuggled into my side.

Blinking awake, I sit up in bed and recall where I am.

The Roxbury cabin.

Then I remember what woke me. A loud noise.

Chanel is no longer sleeping either, which means she heard it too.

Grabbing my phone, I check the time and for any messages from Zane. It's half past midnight, and I'm exhausted. If Zane decided to come early, he would've called or sent a text to let me know.

Another deafening crash has me jumping.

"Oh my God…" My breathing picks up, and I panic.

Someone's in my house!

Looking around for something, I see one of my mother's marble statues on the dresser. It's heavy and could probably break a skull. I don't have time to think twice before I grab it and tiptoe to my bedroom door. More noise echoes from downstairs, and I know it's probably some dumb kids hoping to steal something they can sell. Joke's on them because my parents never keep any expensive possessions here.

Putting my ear against the wood, I listen for footsteps. When I hear another ear-piercing boom vibrate through the house, my heart drops into my stomach. I could call the cops, but by the time they arrived, the murderer would have me chopped into a thousand pieces and thrown into the pond.

Slowly, I open the door and poke my head out, holding the statue tight in my grip. The hallway light glows, and I check both ways before stepping out. I walk toward the staircase and yelp when Chanel rubs against my leg.

"Chanel, no! Get back here!" I whisper-hiss, hoping she'll actually listen to me. Instead, she runs down the first set of stairs, and I follow as quietly as I can. "Chanel!"

As I chase her, I keep an eye out for a potential killer. If she outs me being up here and gets us both caught, I might strangle her. When I'm on the second level, I notice the kitchen light is on, but I distinctly remember turning it off.

Gripping the marble tighter, I prepare myself to fight for my life as I walk down the final staircase. When I move closer, I see a large duffel bag on the kitchen counter and the fridge is wide open. Did someone break into a multi-million-dollar cabin to steal food?

While I discreetly scan the space, my rapid breathing is the only sound I hear until Chanel loses her shit, and complete chaos ensues.

She hisses, jumping from the floor to the island, then leaps off the countertop as a huge Doberman chases after her. A man is hunched in front of the refrigerator and tries to stand when the dog plows him over. He's unsteady on his feet and tries to catch his fall. The moment he turns toward me, I freak out and throw the statue at his face. It falls to the ground with a deep thud and surprisingly doesn't break.

"Ow, what the fuck?" a deep voice groans as he takes a hit to the cheek. Chanel is having a fit as I try to grab her.

Then to make matters worse, the Doberman barks and growls at me like I'm his next meal. Chanel hisses and runs into the living room, and the dog gives chase at a full sprint.

"Chanel!" I panic and turn toward the criminal. "Get your fucking dog away from my cat!" I beg. "I'll pay you whatever you want, just don't let him kill her!"

"Cami?" His deep voice catches my attention, and my body freezes.

I look over and finally meet his eyes that are squinting at me. Swallowing hard, I narrow my gaze at the man who's broken into my house and called me by a nickname I haven't heard in years.

Releasing a frustrated breath, I'm nearly panting when I ask, "What the hell are you doing here, Eli?"

Chapter Two

ELIJAH

"Cami?" I rub my cheek. She threw a heavy fucking statue at me that could've easily given me a concussion if she had better aim.

She narrows her eyes and exhales a frustrated breath. "What the hell are you doing here, Eli?"

I look at the woman who's haunted my dreams for ten years and notice she's as painfully beautiful as I remember. The tabloid magazines never paint her in a positive light and always snap photos when she's trying to escape or has partied too much, but I knew her before she had the snobby rich-girl reputation.

Cameron St. James is the epitome of perfection—gorgeous, smart, and an heiress.

Unfortunately, she knows it too.

A girl like her would never give a guy like me—lower class, wage-earning real estate agent—the time of the day. Though a decade ago, she looked at me like I hung the moon, and it ended as quickly as it started.

"I was about to ask you the same." Closing the fridge door, I walk over to pick up the statue that miraculously didn't shatter and set it on the island. My attention is quickly brought to Bruno who's chasing the cat. "Bruno! Come."

He immediately stops, rushes over, then sits in front of me and begs for a treat. He's a one hundred pound Doberman who's as tall as I am when he stands.

"Chanel!" Cami runs to her butt ass ugly hairless cat. She grabs her and holds it tightly. My eyes lower to her chest as her tank top slides down, nearly revealing everything.

Swallowing hard, I avert my gaze. "Uh, Cami...you might—"

"You need to leave," she snaps before I can continue. "How'd you get in? The alarm is on and active."

"Ryan said I could stay here," I explain. Her brother is my best friend and gave me the keys and security codes. "Told me to make myself at home, but failed to mention you'd be here too."

"I haven't had the chance to talk to him yet," she says. "But it doesn't matter because you're not staying."

"Yes, I am," I argue. We're in the middle of a goddamn pandemic, and as New York City is the epicenter of it, it's the last place I want to be right now. Not to mention, my three dumbass roommates aren't taking it seriously and will be exposed any day now because they're not abiding by the CDC guidelines and staying the fuck inside. All of them can work from home, but they are still going out like nothing has happened. "The cabin is plenty big enough for the both of us."

"Chanel, stop," she scolds. The hairless rat is trying to wiggle free from her grasp. Bruno just wants to play and keeping him away from Chanel will be difficult.

"Bruno, heel," I command, but he's not always the best listener. I swear he gets way too hyper around other people.

"Big or not, my boyfriend, Zane, is coming tomorrow."

"Alright, so I'll stay in my area, and you stay in yours. Problem solved." I grab my duffel bag, then step around the gigantic kitchen island.

"Like hell it is! You can't. I'm already here and made plans." She pouts, and it's stupidly adorable. Cami is used to getting her way, but she won't this time. I'm not going anywhere.

"Watch me." I flash her a toothy grin on my way toward the staircase. "I'm guessing you took the master?" I ask over my shoulder, then continue before she responds, "I'll take one of the guest rooms on the second floor, so you won't even know I'm here."

"I doubt it," she mutters.

Bruno walks behind me, and she squeals when he gets too close. "Don't worry, he only bites entitled New York princesses."

"Funny."

"It's called having a sense of humor, Cami. Did you lose yours, or is it still up your ass along with that stick that's been stuck there since we were teens?"

"You know, I could call the cops and have them remove you."

"Good luck with that. We're in a national lockdown, and they're only responding to life or death calls, so in this case, they wouldn't come to your rescue." I throw her a wink, then take the steps two at a time with Bruno next to me. Of course, I'm agitating her on purpose, but if I know Cameron St. James as well as I think I do, she's about to have a rich-girl tantrum.

"You better keep that stupid mutt away from my cat!" she screams as I reach the second floor. "Or I'll feed him to the mountain lions!"

I snort, shaking my head at her dramatics. Bruno won't hurt her naked cat, but he'll have fun taunting them both in the process. And so will I.

Once I walk inside the spare room that Ryan typically uses when he stays here, I set my stuff on the bed and look around. It's bigger than my entire apartment, and sadly, I'm not even exaggerating. There's a bathroom down the hall, and the jet tub alone cost more than a year's worth of my rent.

I sit and look around. Without knowing, you'd never suspect Ryan is a St. James. He's two years older than me and an ER doctor in the city. While doing his residency, he's smack-dab in the center of this epidemic, and that scares the shit out of me. Ryan's humble and loyal to a fault and will work as long as he needs to fight this and save his patients.

Being his best friend growing up, I know all about Cameron and their family's billion-dollar fashion company. I'm from a completely different world, and the only reason we met is because my mother was their housekeeper for years. When the sitter canceled at the last minute, she'd take me and my little sister, Ava, with her, and though we promised to stay hidden and quiet, the moment Ryan saw us, he encouraged us to play with him. I was ten years old when he showed me that money wasn't as important as kindness and compassion. A lesson the rest of his family has yet to learn.

Clara St. James didn't approve of our friendship at first but warmed up to the idea. Her husband, Bradford, was never around to be with his son, and Ryan needed a real friend because he hated his uppity private school classmates. After a while, Clara approved for my mother to bring Ava and me along. Ryan and I developed a strong bond that's lasted for fourteen years.

Cami was eight at the time and wasn't allowed to play with us—Ryan's rules. He couldn't stand his annoying little sister, but for some reason, he didn't mind Ava. Probably because she wasn't a stuck-up sass machine, but I think that's why she never wanted to play with Cami either. They were the same age but had nothing in common. As time went on, Cami grew on me, and the four of us hung out and played. It was the first time I felt included in a group.

But that was ages ago, and I'm not that boy who easily gets his feelings hurt anymore.

My mother saved as much money as she could and made sure we didn't go without even though she had nothing. I never knew my dad but didn't care much about it based on the stories my mother told me about him. When I met Ryan, he opened up and talked about how dysfunctional his family was too, which made me feel not so alone. He was the older brother I always wanted and still is.

I keep Bruno in the bedroom and head back to my rental car to grab the rest of the items I brought. Since I take the subway to the office, owning a car in the city is unnecessary. Parking's a bitch and expensive, but I got my license for random road trips.

After popping the trunk, I grab as many bags as I can. I brought enough perishables, medicine, drinks, cleaning supplies, and toilet paper to last for weeks. Of course, that was before I knew other people were staying at the cabin, so it might not last that long.

My goal is to stay quarantined for at least a month before I have to make a trip to the store. Last weekend, my roommates were out partying and could've infected me. It's why I had to get the hell out of there as fast as I could. Cami's a student at NYU, and it only shut down yesterday, which means she was around dozens of people too. So it's best we steer clear of each other, which shouldn't be an issue. This place is massive.

I have plenty of work and reading to keep me busy. Between that and taking Bruno out for walks and playtime, there's no reason to be around Cami and her tool bag boyfriend.

"What are you doing?"

She's so loud that I nearly jump out of my skin. "Jesus." I groan, shaking my head as I continue to the kitchen and set the bags down. "What's it look like?"

"Looks like you're doing the opposite of leaving."

"Very good. You're *so* observant." Pulling the items out of the bags, I start cleaning them with disinfectant wipes, then look over at her. "Why do you care if I'm here? You've done an incredible job of ignoring me for years. So, it shouldn't be a problem for you now. Right?"

She crosses her arms, tilts her head, and squints at me. "Why do you insist on always being an asshole? Is it ingrained into your DNA or something? Or do you just enjoy pissing people off?"

I hold back a smirk because I'm getting to her as much as she used to get to me. "Nah. Just you, princess."

Cami rolls her eyes, and her arms fall to her side. She's still wearing next to nothing, but I'm sure she doesn't care. She's used to people gawking.

"I already stocked the fridge," she says after I open it and try to make room.

"Yeah, I see that." I move her stuff around and shove mine in. "Except this shit will go bad in just a few days. Unless you plan on growing a garden in the middle of winter, you'll be out of food in a week."

"I have plenty of frozen meals. And I can make a grocery order and have it delivered," she states matter-of-factly.

"Out here? Not likely." I grab the boxed food and put it in the pantry. "Not to mention, they're all booked out two weeks or more with the increased demand."

She wrinkles her nose. "Guess I didn't think about that."

"Do you even know how to cook?" I ask, already knowing the answer. Cameron St. James can't boil water. She may be brilliant in school, but she's not common sense smart. I can't even place the blame on her for it, though, because it's not entirely her fault. Unless Cameron was interested or invested in something, she didn't care to learn more, and her parents never forced her to do anything for herself. It's common knowledge that she'll take over their family business, and she'll have staff who'll do her dirty work while she keeps it afloat.

Cami blinks and nervously shuffles her feet. "Well…not really. But it's not like I was going to bring a chef to isolate with me. We'll figure it out."

"I take it Zaney boy can't cook either?" I chuckle as I finish putting everything up.

"We never have to." She shrugs unapologetically about her privileged life. "It can't be that hard."

I'm unable to hold back my laughter this time, and she scowls. I'm well aware of what Cami's lifestyle includes—gourmet chefs, housekeepers, drivers, family jets, personal shoppers, extravagant *everything*. She'll never know the sick feeling of not being able to pay bills while barely scraping by.

"You're going to either burn the house down, burn yourself, or starve. The virus isn't even your biggest threat. It's your inability to feed yourself."

"Do you always have to be such a dick?" she scolds with her hands on her hips. "Are you capable of being anything other than a condescending ass bag?"

"Well, I don't know. Are you able to determine the difference between sarcasm and country club asshole traits? I'll give you a guess which one your boyfriend is," I say smugly. "And I'm ninety-nine point nine percent positive you're not with him for his *great* personality." Zane Vandenberg is the equivalent of a thirteen-year-old Justin Bieber who was just handed millions of dollars. His maturity level is the same, too.

"Ugh!" She throws up her arms, then stomps away.

"You need to get a sense of humor, Cami!" I shout through my laughter. "You'd think with all your billions, you could at least buy one! Maybe I can order you one and pay for overnight shipping?"

"Go to hell, Elijah!" she screams from the staircase.

"Don't worry, I'm already there!" I yell back. Moments later, her bedroom door slams with a loud bang.

"Well, this is gonna be fun," I mutter to myself.

I have no idea how long this crisis will last, but Cameron St. James may kill me before it's over.

CAMERON
DAY 2

I WAKE UP TO THE SUN STREAMING THROUGH THE WINDOW AND QUICKLY REMEMBER I'm at the cabin with Eli.

There's no way I'm spending weeks, possibly *months*, with him. Since we were teenagers, he's lived to torment me. Only God knows why my brother is friends with him, but if I had to guess, it's to piss me off.

I considered Elijah Ross a friend once. When his hormones turned him into the asshole of the century, he became my number-one enemy instead.

The only thing that lifts my spirits is knowing Zane arrives today. I'm not worried about being around him every minute of our isolation because of how we feel about each other. After graduation, he'll propose, and our engagement and wedding will be the event of the decade. The St. James and Vandenberg marriage will make the front page of every paper and magazine.

We're already the perfect power couple, and the media loves sharing photographs of us together.

Zane and I ended up in all the same business classes together and inevitably formed a relationship. When we started dating my second year of college, our parents were over the moon and have hinted about us getting married for years.

Deciding to get out of bed, I head to the bathroom and clean myself up before making my way downstairs. Before going down the second staircase, I stop and listen closely. When I don't hear anything, I tiptoe into the kitchen. Hopefully, that means Eli's still sleeping or is staying in his room away from me.

"C'mon, Chanel. Breakfast time," I say quietly with her following me. She rubs against my leg as she prances along the hardwood floor.

"Why are we whispering?"

Spinning around, I smack right into Eli's broad chest. When I stumble against him, he grabs my arms and steadies me. Once it's obvious I won't fall on my ass, he releases me with a smirk.

"Jesus! Don't sneak up on people!" I scold and playfully slap him. Putting space between us, I then realize he's shirtless. His shaggy, dark hair is pulled back and sweat drips down his neck. Stupidly, I lower my gaze and notice his ripped abs and that sexy V that leads below his workout shorts.

The clearing of his throat brings my eyes back to his. "You always this uptight in the morning?"

"Only when creeps refuse to leave my house," I retort, pissed he caught me staring. I don't want him thinking I was drooling, but it's hard not to when he's half-dressed and looks more muscular than I remember.

Eli pops a brow with an amused grin on his face. "You get that a lot?"

Groaning, I walk to the fridge and grab what I need. I twist the cap off Chanel's water, then pour it into her dish.

"Did you seriously just use a ten-dollar bottle of water for a *cat*?"

Technically speaking, it's more like thirteen dollars, but I don't give him more ammunition to taunt me. He already has enough in his arsenal.

"Cat has expensive taste just like her owner." He cackles.

"Why are you still here?" I ask, then get up to grab her cat food. "You need a shower."

"Thanks for noticing. I was about to before I saw you trying to Tom Cruise your way into the kitchen."

Rolling my eyes, I proceed to feed Chanel. If he thinks her water is high maintenance, he'd probably burst a blood vessel at her custom-made organic cat food. She purrs and immediately rushes over.

"Why are you sweating anyway?" It's in the thirties outside, so running shirtless outside isn't an option.

"Wanted to work out before starting this beautiful first day of quarantine with you." He beams, furthering my irritation.

"You're taking the whole *make yourself at home* thing to the next level." I grunt that he used the home gym that my mother insisted on building in the basement. Not sure why she bothered, considering she visits once a year, and it's *never* to work out.

"And for my next trick, I'm going to cook breakfast." He flicks his fingers in the air, mimicking a magician. Then he grabs a pan and sets it on the stovetop. "Or is that off-limits, too?"

"At this rate, I'd expect nothing less." I force a smile, push off the counter, and grab a mug from the cabinet.

"I'm making an omelet. Would you like one?" he asks, digging into the fridge as I mess with the espresso machine.

I raise an eyebrow. "Depends. Will it be poisoned?"

"If by poisoned, you mean it won't be some fake meat bullshit, then yes. But it'll taste heavenly." He whips eggs in a bowl, and considering my options are cereal or a granola bar, I contemplate it. Then on cue, my stomach roars and grumbles loudly.

"Fine, but at least use the low-fat cheese in mine."

He snorts. Fucking *snorts*, then laughs. "Whatever you need to make yourself feel better."

"What the hell does that mean? Do you have to make a comment about everything I say?" I shake my head.

"Only when you say things like *low-fat* cheese. Sounds gross and would ruin my masterpiece." He grabs more ingredients from the fridge. "If you're going to survive being in a house with me for God knows how long, you're gonna have to loosen up."

"Or you could just be a decent human and stop antagonizing me every second?" I push buttons on the espresso maker, and it starts grinding the beans. *Thank goodness*. I can't deal with him much longer without caffeine.

"But bothering you is the only thing on my to-do list today." He flashes a devilish smirk.

Groaning, I open the silverware drawer, grab a spoon, then slam it closed.

"C'mon, Cami. You can't be this wound up all the time. Let your hair down and relax a little."

"Easy for you to say. You don't have paparazzi following you everywhere. If I'm bloated one day, pregnancy rumors are blasted the next week. If I yell for them to stop following me, they say I'm on the verge of having a nervous breakdown."

"Sounds like you can't win either way, so why bother? Just be you, and they'll get bored."

I shoot him a death glare. "Are you inferring that I'm boring?" Turning away, I grab the sugar-free creamer, and when I spin around, Eli's standing in front of me so I can't move.

"That's not what I said," he softly states. I lower my eyes to avoid his, but he tilts up my chin, and our gazes connect. "I meant, the more you give in to what they expect, the more they'll demand it." He drops his arm, and I swallow hard. "They want to sell scandalous tales to magazines by twisting reality. You play into it, and it makes you look bad every time, so if you quit giving a shit, maybe they'll stop targeting you."

I gulp, blinking hard. Eli's split personalities give me whiplash.

"Well, that's easier said than done." I shrug. "The media portrays me in a negative light no matter what I do or say, but I've learned that if I'm presentable and look like I have my shit together, it's harder for them to make up bullshit headlines."

Eli looks around, squinting before meeting my eyes. "You don't have to worry about being judged here. No paps to follow you around, and I swear I won't take pics of you looking like a hot mess and sell them to the media."

"Do I need to get that in writing?" My shoulders fall as I release a small laugh. "Actually, the idea of being secluded and away from all that was what drew me to the cabin in the first place."

He presses a hand to his bare, sweaty chest. "Was I the second?"

"Hardly," I reply dryly, holding back a smirk, considering I was shocked to see him.

"Well, don't worry…" He steps back and mixes the meat and cheese into the bowl of eggs. "You won't even know I'm here. Bruno and I are very chill."

Furrowing my brows, I shake my head. "Somehow, I doubt that."

Once my espresso is done, I set it on the table and walk back to my room to grab my phone. Zane hasn't responded to my last text, so I send him another one.

Cameron: Babe, are you on your way? There's been a little mix-up. Ryan told his friend he could come here, so he's staying in the guest room. Just a heads-up. Let me know when you leave the city. I miss you!

I go downstairs and am immediately bombarded by Bruno. He gallops into the house after being outside, and he's in my face, sniffing me.

The dog has never heard of personal space. Another reason I love cats more.

"Okay, go away…" I shoo, stepping back, hoping he doesn't follow. Before I can say another word, Chanel charges at him, hissing.

"Chanel, no!" I scold, though she couldn't hurt Bruno even if she tried. She might piss him off, but that's about it. "Elijah, get control of your dog!" I squeal, running around the kitchen table. "Stay! Sit! Stop!"

Of course, the asshole laughs.

"Bruno, heel," Elijah commands. The dog immediately stops, goes to Eli, and sits as though nothing happened.

I'm nearly out of breath from chasing Chanel, who doesn't listen *at all*.

"Your dog…or *horse*, rather…is trying to kill my cat and eat her as a snack. Can't you lock him up or something?"

Bruno licks his chops and pants with his tongue out. I shoot daggers at him as Chanel finally saunters toward me.

"My animal listens. Yours is the prissy bitch," he states, busying himself in the kitchen.

I gasp, ready to murder them both.

"It's not his fault," Eli says, looking over his shoulder at me. "She looks like a meaty, hairless dinner."

Grabbing Chanel, I hold her tightly to my chest. "She does not. She's adorable and better for my allergies." I kiss her head, and she leans against me.

"Do you like ham?" he asks, pouring the egg mixture into a pan.

"What?"

He turns and looks at me. "Ham. Do you like it?"

I shrug. "Yeah, I guess."

"For your omelet," he reiterates. "Otherwise, I can do sausage."

"Um…ham is fine. I'm going to put Chanel in my room." I turn toward the staircase before he can say another word. Between him offering to make breakfast, our pets trying to murder each other, and his sudden subject change, I'm at a loss of what to think about Elijah being here.

When we were kids, Eli would come over to play with Ryan while his mom worked as our housekeeper. Eventually, I started hanging out with them too, and always looked forward to the days he was there. His sister, Ava, would tag along, but we were never close. As time went on, my mother's constant pressure to be classy, elegant, and sophisticated took a toll on me. She wanted me to hang out with the girls she approved of who held a specific social class. It was always about money and power to my parents, and I quickly became too *snobby* to be Elijah's friend. He wrote me off but remained best friends with my brother, who never cared about that sort of thing.

Eli made snide comments about what I wore, how I spoke or acted, and who was in my circle. Nothing I did was good enough for him. He never knew he was the only person I wanted to impress. Being friends with Elijah already pissed off my dad, so there was no way he would've allowed us to date as teenagers.

But that didn't matter anyway because he hated me as much as I hated him. The feud continued through high school, and when he'd hang out with Ryan, I was brought back to those days of him thinking less of me because of my friends.

I wasn't completely innocent, but he escalated the situations. I'm judged by thousands of people who don't know me, but to have someone I cared about have such harsh opinions of me hurt even worse.

I place Chanel on the bed and realize I forgot her bowls. "I'll be back," I tell her before shutting the door.

Once I'm in the kitchen, I grab her food and water. "I'm gonna put these in my room so we can avoid World War Three in the mornings."

"Between you and me or the animals?"

"Ha. You're a comedian now."

"Well, you are scary before your coffee." He squints, then continues, "Or is that how you are all the time?"

"Gonna have to drink mine with alcohol just to deal with your ass."

Elijah releases a deep howl. "Oh, you and me both, *princess*."

I take the stairs to my room, drop off Chanel's dishes, then go back to see Elijah dancing in the kitchen as he flips an omelet. It's amusing to watch a six-foot-something guy who enjoys the great outdoors move around like Channing Tatum. If I didn't know any better, I'd say he was a mountain man stuck in the city. I know he works in real estate, but I'm not sure exactly what that entails.

"If you ever give up on real estate, you should take up stripping. Bet you'd get lots of singles tucked into your G-string."

Eli faces me, popping a brow. "You picturing me in my underwear now? I think we're gonna have to discuss boundaries…" he taunts, and I roll my eyes.

Grabbing my phone, I notice Zane finally messaged me.

Zane: Not gonna make it.

What the fuck? I sit at the table and furiously type a response.

Cameron: What do you mean? Where are you?

Zane: Staying in the city.
Cameron: Why? I thought we were going to be together during this time.
Zane: I don't think this is working out for me anymore.

My blood pressure rises, and I grow more frustrated with each passing second.

Cameron: What the fuck are you talking about, Zane? We had plans!
Zane: I think we should see other people, Cameron. Indefinitely.

Shifting in my chair, I ball my hand into a fist and see red. How fucking *dare* he break up with me over a text message?

Cameron: GO TO HELL, ASSHOLE!

"Okay, one ham and *regular fat* cheese omelet is ready." When Elijah places the plate in front of me, the steam from the food floats toward my face. I wish I could ignore what just happened with Zane, but I'm so fired up that I'm seeing red. "Bon appétit. Do you want orange juice or just your coffee? OJ is full of calcium and vitamin C, which we need at a time like this, so I brought plenty. I'll even share it with a *princess*." He chuckles.

Eli chats as if nothing is wrong while I can't think straight because I'm in shock. I'm not heartbroken over the loss of Zane, but his text definitely blindsided me. I should be upset, considering we've been together for two years, but I'm more outraged than anything. Why are guys such pricks?

As I push back, the chair scrapes along the floor. I stand and grab my mug off the table. "Don't bother."

Instead of giving Eli an explanation, I rush to my bedroom before I have an emotional breakdown.

Zane can kiss my ass.

He made me believe he wanted a future with me, but if he's staying in the city, that means he's not alone. The bastard is probably with another chick, and considering how easy it was for him to break up with me, he's more than likely been cheating the entire time.

Fuck him.

Chapter Four

ELIJAH

WHAT THE HELL JUST HAPPENED? I scratch my head at Cameron's sudden mood change and abrupt departure. She can't honestly be *that* upset I teased her about the damn cheese. That'd be a stretch even for Cameron St. James.

"Well, I guess it's just you and me, Bruno." I shrug, setting my plate and juice down on the table. The espresso machine looks complicated, and I had planned to figure it out later, but now I'm contemplating taking a shower and going back to bed to restart this weird as fuck day.

Moments later, Cami stomps down the staircase, and I watch in silence as she marches to the kitchen. I stab a piece of meat with my fork and shove it into my mouth, keeping my eyes on her. When she's not shouting at me or having a tantrum, she's quite breathtaking. Blond hair sweeps along her face and shoulders, her shining blue eyes glance around as her nostrils flare.

"Digging out the alcohol already?" I ask with amusement as she grabs the vodka from the top shelf in the liquor cabinet. Her mood shift has me eager to find out what the hell happened because she obviously has a problem.

She ignores me, opens the bottle, and takes a long swig. My eyebrows pop up, impressed that she swallows it down so easily.

"Did I drive you to drink already?" I grin, waiting to see if she cracks.

She brings the bottle back to her lips, downing another long swig.

"Damn, killer. I made you breakfast, gave you a dance show, and pissed you off all before ten? That's gotta be a new record for me."

"It's not you," she says calmly, gripping the neck and swinging it as she walks to the table. "Zane broke up with me in a text message."

I hadn't expected that. Dropping my fork, I say, "Oh, I'm sorry to hear that."

She sits across from me and gives me a side-eye. "No, you're not."

"Actually, I am. I was hoping he'd bring pot."

Cami laughs, and it's the sweetest, most genuine sound I've heard since we both arrived. "You mean you didn't bring any?"

"Of course, I did. But I figured a rich boy like him would have the good stuff. If you want to wallow, I'll share mine with you." I flash a grin.

"How nice of you," she deadpans. "I don't smoke it with him. He looked like an idiot but did it around his stupid friends to seem cooler than he was."

That's not surprising. Zane's a fucking moron, especially if *he* broke up with *her*.

I inhale half my omelet. "I can teach you. I brought my pipe."

"A pipe? Oh, my God. What are you, eighty?" She crosses her legs on the chair. Right now, in her non-designer tank top and cotton shorts, she looks *normal*. Not at all like she'll inherit billions of dollars before she turns thirty.

"Oh, I'm sorry. Would you prefer to be classier and smoke it rolled in a joint?" I take a sip of my juice and grin.

Cami's frown turns into a full-on smile, and knowing I made her laugh gives me a small sense of pride.

"Vodka and weed. Sounds like the perfect medicine for heartbreak."

"I'll even sweeten the deal…but I'm gonna need something in return."

She waves her hand. "Like what?"

"Since I made you breakfast—a delicious one, might I add—you have to make dinner."

Cami narrows her bright eyes at me. "You're joking."

"No, really. Try it. This omelet is fan-fucking-tastic."

"Not about that," she says. "I can't cook."

That I knew. Cameron St. James has never had to cook a day in her life.

"Well, now's a good time to learn." I flash her a devilish smirk. She shoots a death glare my way, folding her arms. "Okay, okay." I laugh. "I'll *help*. Consider me your personal cooking tutor."

"That's a horrible idea," she states. "I'll probably poison us both."

"I guess that's just a risk I'm willing to take." I tap my knuckles twice on the table, then stand and grab my dirty dishes. "We'll start nice and easy."

"Like what? Boiling a pot of water?"

"Well, that'll be the first step for making pasta." I rinse my plate and mug.

Cami follows with her vodka in hand, and I watch as she takes another gulp.

"You're gonna be drunk before we make it to dinner."

"That's kinda the plan. I'd like to numb as many feelings as I can right now, so you either find more alcohol or you're a part of the problem."

Chuckling, I take the bottle from her tight grip and put the cap back on. "Go take a hot bath and relax. I'll be here to shout curse words at later."

The moment the words fall from my mouth, her shoulders slump, and guilt washes over her face.

"I'm sorry about that," she says softly.

"I know." I flash her a wink, and she groans with an eye roll. "Now, upstairs you go. Take a nap after the tub. Once you're awake, we'll cook a delicious non-poisonous meal, then smoke."

Cami snorts, and I can tell she's already feeling the vodka. "This really must be the twilight zone."

"What do you mean?"

"I'm at the cabin—one I haven't been to in ages—with *you*, and we're talking about weed. I must be dreaming."

"Well, that's very possible, but just in case…we should make sure."

Sauntering toward her, I close the gap between us and grip the back of her neck. She steps forward, and I cover her mouth with mine.

I halfway expect her to push away and slap me, but she leans in and wraps her arms around my waist. Cupping her face, I slide my tongue between her lips and deepen the kiss. Cami moans against me, and her response has my dick reacting. I'm not sure what came over me—especially since she's been single for barely a few hours—but she looked so sad and helpless moments ago, and I wanted to help her forget that asshole.

"Well?" I ask, breaking the kiss after a few moments. We're panting and out of breath.

Cami blinks and brings a finger to her mouth. "Um…" Swallowing hard, she looks up at me. "What the hell was that?"

I shrug as if it didn't affect me, but truth be told, I've imagined kissing her like that since when we were teenagers. "Guess you're not dreaming."

Cami blinks again, licks her lips, then nods. "Apparently not, though I'm unsure if I'm happy about that or not."

"Well, dreaming would almost be better because the current circumstances kinda suck."

"Oh, uh, right. Yeah, that part definitely does."

"Okay, well, I gotta shower and check in with my boss." Walking toward the stairs, I notice she's flustered, which has me grinning, but I tuck it inside. "Don't forget about our dinner plans." I point at her. "Five o'clock sharp."

"Sure. Maybe eat a big lunch in case it's a fail."

"Nah, I have faith in you." I flash her a wink. "But just in case, I have snacks."

Bruno follows me to the stairs, and I take two steps at a time, then go into the bathroom. I'm not sure what the fuck came over me, but I don't regret it. Even though Cameron tormented me for years, I still fantasized about kissing her. And it was everything I thought it'd be—searing hot and passionate, greedy even. Since Zane just broke it off, and she was in a vulnerable state, I shouldn't have taken advantage, but…Cami didn't push me away either.

Once I finish showering and get dressed, I hear the water running upstairs, and smile knowing she's soaking in the tub like I suggested. Cami's so damn uptight; she probably doesn't know how to chill out, but it makes me happy that she's trying.

"Alright, Bruno…work time, buddy." He nudges me with his wet nose, nearly climbing on my lap as I sit at the desk. "Lie down and take a nap. We'll play later," I tell him.

He's used to constant attention because one of my roommates played with him while I was at the office, but he won't be getting that here. I have to complete my tasks remotely through this crisis, which is fucking with my head.

On one hand, I need to figure out new ways to connect with clients and am even hoping to get promoted soon to an appraisal manager. But on the other, I hate pushing people to sign contracts on leases they don't need right now. Nevertheless, I still need a paycheck, and I'm grateful to receive a salary when millions have lost their jobs.

After an hour of responding to emails and following up with a few clients, I take a short break to get a drink. As I'm walking down the hallway, I hear a commotion from above and pause. I wait and then hear Cami scream followed by a loud thump.

Rushing to the third level, I knock on her door and call her name. "Cami? You okay?"

Her feet pad against the floor, and when she opens the door, she's only wearing a towel.

"Uh…" I lower my eyes, not hiding the fact I'm looking. "I heard something. Are you alright?"

"Aside from falling on my ass, I'm fine," she says, breathlessly.

"You fell?" I meet her eyes. "Getting out of the tub or what?"

She bites down on her lower lip and fidgets. "Well, no, not exactly."

Leaning against the doorframe, I wait for her to explain. This is going to be amusing as hell, I can already tell.

"I half-dried off and needed to pee, but then the fucking seat broke, and…" She hesitates, closing her eyes briefly. "I fell off."

Standing straighter, I blink. "You fell *off*?" I hide my smile, trying my hardest not to chuckle at the utter defeat in her eyes.

"Yes. The seat shifted, and I guess I was too wet and slipped."

The expression on her face is pure annoyance and shock that a toilet seat would dare to break while she's using it. Her reaction has me doubling over. I can't help myself and burst out laughing.

"Shut up! I landed on my tailbone, and now it hurts!" She steps closer and smacks me against the chest. "You're such a jerk."

I hold up my hands and grin. "I didn't do it. Why am I a jerk?"

She folds her arms over her half-bare chest and scowls. "You're laughing."

"Well, I'm sorry. But it's hilarious."

"It's not."

"No, trust me. It very much is. Considering you slipped off a toilet seat buck ass naked is the funniest thing I've heard in months. Actually, I'm going to replay it in my head anytime I need a good laugh. This moment might last a lifetime."

"Alright, asshole. Bye." She starts to shut the door, but I stop it with my foot.

"Oh, c'mon. I'm just messin' with you."

"I'm gonna have the biggest bruise." She pouts with a frown.

"It sounds like it needs to be tightened. You have a screwdriver?"

"A what?"

"Oh, God. You don't know what tools are, do you?"

"Can you not mock me right now?"

"Sorry, but you make it a little too easy." I grin. "I'll look in the garage and see if your dad has anything in there. Get dressed, and I'll help you fix the broken seat situation."

"Alright. Thanks."

"And maybe get some ice for your bruised ass," I mumble with a chuckle as I walk toward the stairs.

"I heard that, asshole."

"I know," I mock. "Be right back."

I remember seeing a basic tool set sitting on a shelf in the laundry room, probably from when they installed the appliances. Grabbing it, I notice it's never been opened, which isn't surprising. No one in the St. James family aside from Ryan would know how to use them.

Cami lets me into her room, and I follow her to the bathroom, which is fucking massive. She's dressed in casual black leggings and an off-the-shoulder sweater. With her hair pulled up and face bare, she looks so different from the pictures printed in the magazines. I much prefer this Cameron—casual and not trying to impress anyone.

Kneeling, I discover a screw on the floor. "Just as I thought. The screws were loose. See?" I hold it up. "Now you want to line it back up with the hole and twist the washer while you—"

"Huh?" she asks. "Can't you do it?"

"Yes, but it's time for you to learn, princess."

She folds her arms and narrows her eyes. "I can watch and learn."

"Nope, you've gotta get your hands dirty every once in a while. What would you do if I wasn't here?"

"Use the other bathroom."

I snicker at her immediate answer. "Not happening. C'mon. It's not that hard."

She inhales with annoyance. "Fine." She kneels next to me and takes the screwdriver. "Now what?"

I give her simple instructions, and she grunts with every step. It's quite humorous, considering it's child's play.

"Tighten it up a bit more. That way, it won't happen again."

"I'm trying!" She groans, using all her strength.

"Put a little muscle into it, geez," I tease.

Once she's done, I check and make sure they're secure, then smirk. "Not bad for an amateur."

"Har har." She gets to her feet and brushes off her knees. "I feel like I need another shower now."

"Wait until a light bulb goes out, and I make you change that, too."

"Do you have to mock me about everything?"

I put the screwdriver in my jeans pocket as I stand, then face her adorable pouty face. "Well, it *was* on my agenda for the day, but I could move my mockery to tomorrow if you'd prefer to reschedule?"

"I swear, Eli." She huffs, busying herself by picking up towels around the bathroom. "You wouldn't know how to have a serious conversation if it bit you in the butt."

"Now, that's not true." I cross my arms, ready to play her little game. "How about we talk about why you were such a bitch to me when we were teens?"

"Me?" she snaps, quickly spinning around to scowl at me. "You're the one who teased me every chance you got. Constantly made fun of me for every-fucking-thing, and you're still doing it now." She holds out her arm. "Let's talk about *that*."

"I think you have your memories twisted because you humiliated me anytime your uppity friends were around. If I recall, you started calling me trailer trash because my mom worked for your family."

"Because you called me a Paris Hilton wannabe!"

I take a step forward as both of our tempers heat. "Well, it was true. Hell, it probably still is. You can't even sit on a damn toilet without hurting yourself."

"God!" She comes for me, pushing firmly against my chest with her hands. I barely flinch, which only pisses her off further. "You're such a fucking child. Grow up." She walks around me and storms out of the bathroom.

Well, it wouldn't be a conversation with Cami if we weren't screaming or annoying the fuck out of each other, but I hadn't expected it to be on the same day I finally kissed her.

A kiss I selfishly want to relive.

Chapter Five

CAMERON
DAY 3

After a day from hell yesterday, I'm ready to start fresh. It's day three of being at the cabin, and I'm already going stir-crazy with Elijah here. Add in my boyfriend breaking up with me, and I'm a ticking time bomb. Last thing I need is to have a full-blown Britney Spears circa 2007 breakdown.

Kendall: Babe, you okay? I heard about Zane and you.

I groan, reading my best friend's text message. Of course, she did. Even during a freaking pandemic, the rumor mill is strong. I hadn't told a soul—besides Eli—which means Zane's already started running his mouth. Who knows what the hell he's telling people because he's known to exaggerate. Kendall Montgomery has been in my life since elementary school, and she's my ride or die. She also loathes my brother, which cracks me up because I believe she's secretly in love with him. While she pretends she can't stand his know-it-all attitude, Ryan makes comments about her being beauty *and* brains. They're a match made in heaven, but both are in denial.

Cameron: I'm fine. He can suck a giant bag of dicks, though.

Kendall: I can't believe he broke up with you! What an asshole. I wish we could go to the club and get shit-faced! I'd make sure you were over that bastard and under a hottie within an hour!

I laugh, knowing she would totally force me to go out and party. Her answer to everything is booze and one-night stands. Chanel startles awake and gets comfortable in a chair by the window. She's not much of a morning cat until she's ready to eat.

Cameron: Well, I started with vodka for breakfast yesterday, but that backfired on me real quick when I kissed Elijah Ross, then snapped at him.

I skip the broken toilet part because it's embarrassing as hell, but also because I overreacted after he helped me. I was frustrated about Zane and confused about Eli kissing me, and all of that mixed with vodka was a dangerous combination. After I pushed him and stormed away, I went to the theater room and fell asleep watching Netflix. When I woke up hours later, it was late, and the house was dark and silent. I ruined our dinner plans and ended up eating cereal before going to bed.

Kendall: Wait, what?! You're at the cabin with Eli? How'd that happen?

Cameron: Ryan told him he could stay without telling me, and we both showed up! Now we're stuck here since neither of us wants to be in the city. I told Eli to leave because having Zane here would be weird, but now that he's out of the picture, I kinda don't mind him here. Though he's still a jerk, and he brought his freaking dog!

Kendall: I'm laughing so hard right now. You and Eli have fought for as long as I've known you. I can't picture the two of you being stuck together. It's like a reality TV show.

Cameron: Trust me, it wasn't a pretty picture when he arrived. I threw a marble statue at his face.

Kendall: I don't know why you don't just bang it out already. Clearly, you have some animosity to work out. Now would be a PERFECT time ;)

Having her encourage me to cross that line with Eli makes me shake my head. Kendall comes from a wealthy family too, but her life wasn't thrust into the limelight like mine. The Montgomerys are old money, and she inherited so much after her grandparents died five years ago.

Cameron: Kinda ironic since I've told you the same thing.

Kendall: What are you talking about?

Cameron: You and Ryan.

Kendall: Why'd you have to ruin my day by mentioning him? If he wasn't dealing with some serious shit right now in the hospitals, I'd say some not-so-nice things.

Cameron: Your hostility toward each other is comical. Just fuck already—like you said—and work out whatever tension you have.

Kendall: That's a hard fucking pass. He probably recites medical journals in bed to stay hard.

Oh my God. That's not an image I ever wanted to have of my brother. It's hilarious she pretends she hates him when I know she's crushed on him forever.

Cameron: Ew, I just cringed. What the hell is wrong with you?

Kendall: SAME.

I laugh, and it feels good to talk to her after having a crappy couple of days.

Cameron: We should FaceTime and drink together since we can't in person. Though I need to get started on my schoolwork. So, maybe not tonight.

Kendall: Yes, definitely soon! Then you can give me all the juicy details about Eli :)

Cameron: Literally nothing to tell.

Kendall: From his Instagram pictures, he's gotten pretty buff. How does he look in person?

I roll my eyes, though it's true. I hadn't seen Eli in over a year before this unexpected reunion. He's had shaggy hair for as long as I can remember, but graduating college and getting a job has agreed with him. Eli's really taken care of himself, and it shows.

Cameron: OMG. Don't go there.

Kendall: So, are you gonna tell me about this kiss, or are you determined to make me beg?

Cameron: NO! It was a total fluke.

Kendall: Fluke or not, get some quarantine action! And you're no fun. I bet his lips were super soft and warm. Did he use tongue?

Cameron: Go away.

Kendall: That's a yes. But fine. I need to take a shower anyway, so go climb Elijah like a tree so you can give me some gossip to share that'll "accidentally" spread to Zane.

Cameron: I'm not gonna hook up with Eli just to piss off Zane.

Kendall: No, you're going to because you know you want to ;)

Cameron: Bye. Xo

Kendall: Love you!

My mood instantly lifts, and I'm determined to have a better day, which starts with apologizing to Eli. Even though he gets a kick out of teasing me, there's no excuse for how I reacted when he brought up the past after helping me. He tried to teach me something new, but I was a brat. I can't take my frustrations out on him because we're stuck here for weeks. Given the circumstances, I need to make the most of it.

I decide to message Ryan and check on him.

Cameron: Hey, big bro. You doing okay?

I watched the news last night before I cleansed my thoughts with Netflix. It was heartbreaking and depressing to see what was happening in the world and terrifying that New York City is the epicenter of the virus outbreak in the US. It scares me even more that Ryan's in the middle of it.

Ryan: I'm about to leave for a 36-hour shift. It's been pretty rough.

Cameron: The news says things haven't peaked yet and that hospitals are running out of protective gear. That true?

Ryan: Unfortunately, yes. Don't watch that, though. It'll make you more anxious.

Cameron: I'm already there.

Ryan: Exactly. How are things going at Mom and Dad's?

His abrupt subject change doesn't go unnoticed, but that's how Ryan is. Blunt and to the point.

Cameron: I didn't go home. Decided to stay at the Roxbury cabin so I can focus on my classes. But then an unexpected visitor arrived…

Ryan: Hahaha.

Cameron: I hate you.

Ryan: You love me.

Cameron: Yeah, yeah. Well anyway, he brought his big ass dog and scared the shit out of me and Chanel.

Ryan: So, where did Eli go then?

Cameron: What do you mean?

Ryan: I assume you sent him packing…

Cameron: Well, I tried. But he refused and said we could "share" the cabin. So we are.

Ryan: I'm glad you let him stay because he had nowhere safe to go. Though, I'm not sure being quarantined with you is much safer.

Cameron: Okay, jerk. I'm getting enough shitty remarks from Eli. I don't need it from you, too.

Ryan: Oh, come on. As your older brother, it's my job to pick on you. He just does it to get a rise and response from you.

Cameron: I've noticed the last ten years.

Ryan: Well, I gotta go. Glad you two are isolating together. Be nice!

Cameron: Tell that to him!

Ryan: I'll get right on that ;)

Cameron: Ha, I'm sure! Please be careful. I love you.

Ryan: Love you too, sis. Stay there so I don't have to worry about you.

Cameron: I will.

I laugh, knowing Ryan is purposely keeping things light so I don't freak out even more. Losing a sense of control as a perfectionist only fuels my uneasiness. I managed to get a refill of my anxiety medication before I left, but I'm trying to save it for when I really need it.

Once I've showered and dressed for the day, I go downstairs.

"Good morning," I sing-song when I find Eli in the kitchen and head to the fridge for the OJ. "How'd you sleep last night?"

He turns toward me, one eyebrow arched as if I've grown a second head. Fortunately, he's wearing a shirt this morning, so there's zero temptation to ogle him.

Walking around him, I reach inside the cabinet and grab a glass, then pour myself some juice. Silently, Eli closes the gap between us, and my breath hitches as he leans in closer. He places his palm on my forehead and squints.

"What're you doing?" I ask, confused.

"Checking to see if you have a fever." He steps back, dropping his hand as he examines my face.

"Why?"

"Because I'm concerned that you're sick."

I immediately touch my cheeks. Then I slide my palm down my neck to see if my glands are swollen. "I don't think so." I feel fine, anyway.

"Hmm...then perhaps you were possessed by a friendly ghost while you slept because you skipped down here way too cheerfully." He smirks, and then I realize what he's doing.

Grinding my teeth, I narrow my eyes and bump him with my hip so he's forced to take a step back. "You're such an ass. For a second, I thought I was dying."

"Yeah, I hear Jekyll and Hyde is a symptom. Better be careful."

I take a sip of juice, then scowl. "And to think I was going to apologize to you. Never mind."

Eli dramatically puts a palm on his chest over his heart and widens his eyes. "Oh, God. Don't do that. I might stroke out."

"At the thought of me saying sorry?" I ask as he moves around the space, grabbing a pan and items from the fridge.

"At you admitting you were wrong about something," he confirms, cracking an egg into a bowl.

"I never said that."

He shakes his head and smirks. "Alright. I'm all ears."

Sucking in a deep breath, I lean against the counter and mentally prepare myself for his sarcastic remarks.

"Okay, well first..." I lick my lips and watch as he continues to prepare breakfast. "I'm sorry for how I reacted after you helped me with the toilet seat. I should've said thank you and that I appreciated you checking on me when you heard me fall. I was angry with Zane and took it out on you, and it wasn't right. It won't happen again."

"Apology accepted." He grins. "You hungry? I'm making scrambled eggs and hash browns."

Blinking, I stare at him. "That's it?"

"What do you mean?"

"You're not gonna give me some smart-ass comment? Make a joke about how I'm a spoiled rich girl who uses her money to right my wrongs or some shit like that."

"Were you offering me money?"

I sigh. "Well, no, but that hasn't stopped you before."

"See, you're not the only one who can turn over a new leaf."

"So, no more snide comments?" I wait as he mixes cheese and milk in the bowl, then pours it into the pan.

"Now, I never said *that*."

Chuckling, I move to the espresso maker. "Figures."

We easily move around the kitchen, him making breakfast and me brewing coffee. Bruno even lies close and doesn't attack me, but his head perks up when he smells the eggs.

"Would you like some toast?" Eli asks.

"Sure, did you bring any bread?" I haven't had any in months.

He laughs. "Yes. But it's not the healthy no-carb shit. It's the good stuff."

"That's fine. I'll have a fruit smoothie for lunch to even it out."

Eli smirks, shaking his head as he pulls a loaf from the cabinet. "A protein smoothie would be better for you. It's more nutritious than blended fruit and is balanced."

"Is that so?"

"Yep. I drink one after my workouts as a meal replacement."

"When did you start going to the gym so much?" I ask after he sits across from me at the table and hands me two slices of buttered toast. "Thank you."

"Welcome." He stabs his fork into his hash browns. "It became a habit for me after college."

"Any particular reason?" I say before taking a bite.

"Needed a distraction."

"From what?"

"A girl."

"Oh." I swallow. "Were you together long?"

"Not really. About six months."

This is probably one of the most personal conversations Elijah and I have ever had, and it's oddly normal. I had no idea he'd dated someone, but that's not surprising since we hardly crossed paths after high school.

"What happened?"

"Found her mouth wrapped around my roommate's cock." He says it so casually as he continues stuffing his face.

I nearly choke on my eggs. "You're kidding."

"Nope." He shakes his head. "The icing on the cake is we still live together, and they started dating after we broke up."

"Oh my God, no way!" My eyes widen in horror. This chick is a straight-up bitch.

"Yep. So, it was either be in the same apartment with them after work or go to the gym."

"Wow…" I take a sip of my coffee. "Are they still together?"

"Engaged, actually."

This keeps getting worse. "Please tell me he didn't ask you to be in their wedding."

"Fuck no. They invited me, though."

"What a douche. Both of them. Seriously. I can't believe some people."

"Don't worry, karma came to play."

"What do you mean?"

"The ceremony was supposed to be in two weeks, but with the restrictions on social gatherings, they had to cancel it. They're losing their asses in the money they spent."

I laugh, smiling wide at his victory. "Good. I mean, the circumstances are awful, but at least they got what they deserved."

"I'm over it now. We weren't right for each other, but I would've preferred she break it off before sucking off one of my friends."

"No kidding." I finish my eggs that seemed to melt in my mouth. "I'm pretty sure Zane cheated on me."

"Zane's a fucking moron. For several reasons, but especially for taking you for granted."

"Yeah, he really is. I guess I was fixated on the *idea* of us, not really him. I should be more upset than I am. It's not our relationship I'm grieving, but rather the fact that he made a fool out of me."

Bruno gets up and walks over to me, setting his head down on my lap. I'm a little stunned and don't know what to do.

I grin down at him. "What do you want?"

"He knows you're sad," Eli explains, standing and grabbing our empty plates. "He's offering you himself to pet so you'll feel better."

I snicker at the way Eli talks about Bruno as if he can read the dog's mind. "Is that so? You want to be my comfort animal?"

"He's a good boy, aren't you?" Eli saunters over after placing our dishes in the sink. "I'm gonna take him out for some exercise for a bit. Wanna join us?"

I look at my phone and notice the time. "I would, but I have to start my schoolwork so I can stay ahead. Need to make sure that ho Francine Withers doesn't steal my valedictorian spot."

Eli raises his brows, amused.

"She flirts with all the professors, so trust me, the label is accurate. I'm pretty sure she slept with the dean just to get into the program."

"Wow, desperate times call for desperate measures. Well, if you change your mind, you'll know where to find me." He grins, then finishes his coffee. "My offer to help you make me dinner still stands, by the way."

Laughing, I get up from the table and grab my mug. "How sweet of you."

"I'm a nice guy, babe." He winks, then calls Bruno, and the two of them head to the front door.

I grab Chanel's food and water dishes from my room, then refill them in the kitchen. As I walk back to the staircase, I peek through the window and see Eli throwing a stick for Bruno in the backyard. He's smiling wide as he grabs it from Bruno's mouth and stretches his arm back, tossing it as far as he can. Bruno gallops like a small horse and happily fetches it.

As I watch them, a strong sensation ripples through me. I'm relieved and glad Eli's here, so I'm not alone, but he's also great company. It doesn't hurt that he cooks, too. However, he's helped keep me distracted from what's happening right now. My anxiety spikes just thinking about it, and if I were here by myself, I'd drive myself crazy watching the news. I'm not being ignorant about the extreme situation we're in, but it doesn't help to overly obsess either.

If there's anyone I have to self-isolate with during times of uncertainty, I'm glad it's Elijah.

Chapter Six

ELIJAH

Cami has given me whiplash the past couple of days, but I'm managing the best I can.

One second, she's blazing hot, and the next, she's ice cold.

Then she's apologizing.

I must be living in the twilight zone because Cameron *rarely* admits she's wrong, so I certainly appreciate her apology. Though she may not believe it, I'm actually glad she's here and keeping me company. It beats being in this big cabin alone, and if we can get along, even better.

I throw sticks for Bruno until my arm nearly gives out, then we head back into the house. I grab some bottles of water, go upstairs and take a shower, then log in to my laptop. I have a video conference with some clients and my supervisor for two hours, which is as boring as it sounds. The only bonus is the view of the snow-capped mountains in the distance and clear blue skies. Though it's a little chilly outside, it's common for Upstate this time of year.

Once I'm off the call, I return dozens of emails and decide to turn on the news.

Bad fucking idea.

Reporters show footage of doctors working in the ER in New York City under extreme distress, and it has me on edge thinking about Ryan. Though he might not be able to text me back, I message him anyway so he knows he's on my mind.

Elijah: Hope you're doing okay. Shit is looking scary on TV.

I'm shocked when his reply comes minutes later.

Ryan: It's fucking bad. Never in my life have I ever seen anything like this before.

Elijah: I can't believe it. It doesn't seem real.

Ryan: I heard you're stuck with my sister. Sorry, I didn't know she'd be there, but I'm glad you guys are together and safe. Gives me one less thing to worry about.

Elijah: Did she chew your ass out?

Ryan: Not really. She said she was worried about me so I tried to downplay things so she wouldn't have an anxiety attack.

Elijah: Does she still get them?

I knew she did in high school but wasn't sure if she still did. Since the media is constantly in her business and making up stories, she's overly private about her personal life.

Ryan: Yeah, sometimes. She doesn't always tell me, so it could be happening more than I know.

Elijah: I'll keep an eye on her. Did she tell you Zane broke up with her?

Ryan: What? No. That fucker. I'm gonna punch his pretty boy face.

I laugh, knowing he totally would too.

Elijah: Don't worry, she's taking her anger out on me.

Ryan: I believe that. Don't let her near the vodka…

I snort.

Elijah: You're a day late and a dollar short on that tip.

Ryan: Fuck. Sorry.

Elijah: Don't be. We'll be fine. She's coming around. We'll be married in no time ;)

Ryan: I'm not sure if I should worry about the virus killing you or my sister, but good luck either way!

Elijah: Be safe, bro! Keep me updated with how things are going. I'll make sure Cami is safe.

Ryan: Appreciate it, man. I gotta run. Talk to you later!

I'm not a religious guy, but I whisper a little prayer to keep my best friend safe and healthy along with his coworkers and patients.

By three thirty, I'm tired of glaring at my computer screen and want some fresh air, so I take Bruno outside. I chase him around the yard, throw the stick a dozen times, and am nearly out of breath after thirty minutes.

"Alright, let's get some water, bud." I pet his head, and we go into the house. As I reach the fridge, I spot Cami at the kitchen table with her cat lying next to her computer.

"Hey," I say as she pounds her fingers on the keyboard. Grabbing a bottle of water, I offer her one, too.

"No, thanks." She doesn't take her eyes off the screen.

I chug half of it before taking a deep breath, trying to get as much air as possible. Bruno drinks every drop in his entire water dish, and I fill it up for him. When I turn around, I notice Cami's cat is moving around the table, taking notice of the dog. To avoid another war between them, I put Bruno in my room.

"You okay?" I ask Cami when I return downstairs. "I don't think you've blinked in five minutes."

"Just working on a paper."

"You look like you're about to fire someone." I chuckle. She finally drifts her gaze toward me and shoots me a death glare. "What? You seem tense. That paper piss you off or something?"

"It's called focusing."

"Why are you down here anyway?"

"I got tired of looking at the same thing upstairs," she explains. "Plus, I needed more caffeine."

"Speaking of which, can you teach me how to use that machine? I mean, unless your plan is to make it for me every morning. And if that's the case, I'd prefer it be delivered to my bedroom." I smirk, sitting on the edge of the table.

"You have a better chance of a meteor hitting us than me bringing you coffee in bed."

"Ouch." I chuckle, placing my hand over my heart. "Why don't you take a break? Have you eaten yet?"

"Not since breakfast."

I check the time and see it's already after four. "That was hours ago. C'mon, shut down the laptop and make me dinner."

Her fingers finally stop moving, and her shoulders shake as she laughs. "You're not as slick as you think."

"Really?" I stand. "Because I think I just got you to finally smile."

She rolls her eyes with a groan. "Fine, but after we eat, I have to get back to it. This professor is a hard-ass, and instead of taking it easy on us during this time, she's *added* assignments."

"Sounds like a bitch move," I say. "But you're a genius, so I'm sure it's cake for you."

Cami flashes me a look of uncertainty. "I can't tell if you're being sarcastic or not."

I hold up two fingers. "I swear, totally genuine." Her expression softens. "You're obviously smart, Cami. You got into NYU on your own merits. You're just not…fix a toilet seat smart."

She leans back in the chair, and her arms fall to her sides. "And you're clearly not make coffee smart."

Laughing, I nod and shrug. "Right. So it's perfect. I'll be in charge of the hard labor, and you're in charge of making sure I'm caffeinated enough to do it."

Her gaze lowers to my mouth, and I wonder if she's thinking about our kiss like I am. When she licks her lips, the temptation to lean in is strong, but I refrain. The last thing I want is for things to be more complicated between us. It's only the two of us, and it's too easy to blur the lines. If we're going to stay here and get through this together, we have to be civil and respectful of each other

"Okay, deal. But don't expect room service," she teases, closing her laptop.

"Oh…" I say slowly. "So then I guess it's a no for personal lap dances?"

"Are you always this obnoxious?"

"Only when I know it gets on your nerves." I beam, staring into her crystal blue eyes. They're brighter than yesterday.

"I'm gonna need way more vodka to deal with you." She stands and pushes in her chair, then moves to the kitchen.

"Actually, I was informed to hide that."

She looks over her shoulder and glares at me. "If you know what's good for you, you won't."

I follow her, then rummage through the fridge for the meat I brought. It'll go bad if we don't eat it soon. "Do you like chicken fettuccini Alfredo?"

"Is that pasta?" she asks, leaning against the island.

Turning to look at her, I furrow my brows. "Are you serious?"

"What?" She shrugs. "I don't eat a lot of pasta." I tilt my head at her. "Okay, fine. I *never* eat pasta."

"Guess that means you're about to have the best meal of your life," I tell her, gloating. "Wash your hands."

"Why?"

"Because I'm not making this alone. Time for you to learn how to cook, woman."

She sighs and goes to the sink, then suds up her hands. "Don't get your hopes up."

I chuckle at how she exaggerates her inability to cook and grab all the ingredients for dinner. After I place the box of pasta and chicken breasts on the counter, I grab a knife and cutting board.

"Alright, you're in charge of the chicken. Cut off the fat, then slice it into long pieces. Think you can manage that?"

"I guess we'll see." She steps closer to the counter and opens the package. I hold back a smile when she grabs the chicken breast and cringes. Carefully, she places it on the cutting board as if it's going to jump out of her hands. "This is really gross."

"Dry it with a paper towel first," I tell her.

Cami does what I say, and I'm amused by how helpless she looks. You'd think she was dealing with a live animal by the way she's holding it. With her back to my chest, I lean into her ear. "Don't worry, it won't bite ya."

"Not funny," she deadpans.

I place my hands on her shoulders, and she shivers. "I have faith in you."

She inhales sharply, and I release her so I can prepare the sauce. "Wanna learn how to make homemade Alfredo sauce?"

Cami looks over at me, unamused. "Sure, why not?"

Chuckling, I grab the butter, heavy cream, garlic cloves, parmesan cheese, and parsley. Then I tell her what I'm doing as I do it. After I melt the butter in the saucepan, I add the cream, then let it simmer.

"You wanna whisk it?" I ask after I check the sauce, not wanting it to burn.

She looks over her shoulder. "Do what?" Before I can respond, she drops the knife. "Fuck!"

When I rush to her side, she's holding her finger that's bleeding. "Did you cut yourself?"

"Yes, and it hurts like a bitch."

"Let me see it." I grab her arm, turn her toward me, then grab a paper towel before holding her hand in mine. "Oh man. I think I'm gonna have to amputate."

"Stop!" she whines. "That stupid knife is really sharp."

"I think this was caused by the operator's error," I say, laughing. "It's just a small cut. But I'll grab some supplies and bandage you right up. You'll be as good as new in no time."

"You distracted me with your sauce." She pouts, looking down at her finger as I race to the staircase. I'm full-on laughing as I grab the first-aid kit I packed from my bag and bring it back to her, cradling her hand.

"Raise your arm over your head to slow the bleed." I stand in front of her and open the kit, finding the items I need to play doctor.

After a moment, I grab her hand and inspect her finger again. "Let's rinse it under some warm water for a second, and then I'll clean it with an alcohol pad before putting some Neosporin and a Band-Aid on it."

She nods, and I lead her to the sink, carefully placing her hand under the stream. She winces for a moment, then relaxes. It's a baby cut, but I think it freaked her out more than anything.

Once it's clean, I dry off her finger, then continue to help her. "There," I say, meeting her eyes and pressing a soft kiss over the wound. "All better."

She sucks in her lower lip, and I admire the way her freckles sprinkle over her face. Cami's barely wearing any makeup, but she doesn't need any because she's a natural beauty.

"Thank you," she says softly.

"You're welcome." I pat her hand before releasing it. "Perhaps I should take over this part, and you can stir the sauce."

"You still want my help?"

"Of course I do. A deal is a deal, and it's pretty hard to fuck up pasta."

"Don't underestimate me." She snickers. "We just started, and I'm already injured."

"Well, good thing battle wounds are sexy." I flash her a wink, and I swear I catch her blushing. Cami would never admit it, but I think I'm getting to her the way she's always got to me.

She continues to stir, and I show her how to make the pasta with my salt and oil trick so the water doesn't boil over and the fettuccini doesn't stick together. I bake some garlic bread, and soon, our meal is complete.

"Wow, this smells delicious," she says as I set our plates on the table. "Even the bread."

"Don't hate on bread."

"I'm not, but I don't typically eat this stuff. It'll probably put me in a carb coma."

"Maybe it'll force you to relax for a change." I smirk, sitting across from her.

"What's that mean?"

My smirk deepens. "Means you're uptight."

She narrows her eyes as she lifts her fork and stabs a piece of chicken. "I'm not uptight."

I smile when her deadpan expression breaks, and she laughs at her own statement.

"If I get anything out of this situation, it's gonna be to hear more of that sound come out of you."

"You act as if I don't know how to laugh."

"Do you? All I heard from you growing up was 'Go away, Elijah!' followed by a door slamming in my face." I cock my head, challenging her to deny it.

"Well, I'm not slamming doors now," she says, the tension in her body nearly melting away.

"No, just throwing expensive statues."

Cami playfully rolls her eyes, grinning. "I thought you were a burglar!"

"One who knows the security code and brings food…"

"Keep being a jerk. I just might change the code, and you'll be out on your ass." She points at me with her fork, trying to act all serious.

"I'm willing to risk it." I shrug, knowing she wouldn't know how to do that. You have to call and verify a bunch of shit with the security company. I know because Ryan tried to change it so we could sneak up here one weekend, but his parents busted him after they got an alert.

"So how's your sister doing?" She changes the subject abruptly, but I don't mind. My sister was one of my best friends growing up and still is.

"Ava's great." That reminds me I have to text her and make sure she's self-isolating, too. "Not exactly your biggest fan…" I mock, finding it ironic she's asking about her. "She's going to freak out when I mention the two of us are here."

Cami groans, sucking in a deep breath. "Another person I need to make amends with, I suppose."

I shrug, twirling the pasta with my fork. "Wouldn't hurt."

"If we ever get to leave and go back to civilization, I'll make sure I do. I'd rather apologize in person."

"I'm sure she'd appreciate that. I know I would."

Chapter Seven

CAMERON
Day 4

After dinner last night, we talked casually as we cleaned the kitchen and put our leftovers in the fridge. Yet again, I was reminded of how being a selfish teenager affected Eli's sister, Ava. She'd come over with him, and I could tell she was desperate for a friendship, but I had this false idea in my head of who was allowed in my life. Knowing I hurt a lot of people is something I live with and regret every day. I don't want to be that person anymore, and I'll do whatever it takes to make things right with those I treated poorly.

We said good night and went our separate ways. I still had some homework to finish but could feel my anxiety spiking. When Eli and I are hanging out, even for like five minutes, I forget that we're in the midst of a global pandemic. It's when I'm left alone that reality smacks me in the face. Uncontrollable fear resurfaces and reminds me that this isn't some nightmare I'm stuck in.

It's reality.

Chanel wakes me up earlier than usual, nudging me with her nose to feed her. It's chilly, so I wrap myself in a throw blanket and slide my slippers on before grabbing her dishes and going to the kitchen.

"Alright, alright. Calm down," I tell her as she meows louder, following me downstairs.

Bruno's asleep on the couch, and I look around for Eli but don't see him. Thankfully, Chanel is more concerned about eating than antagonizing the dog this morning.

Once her bowls are full, she follows me back upstairs to my room. That same uneasy feeling that visited last night returns, and I know a panic attack is coming. I've gotten them periodically since high school, but I haven't experienced one in months. Things are starting to get to me, and it hasn't even been a week.

Crawling back on the bed, I curl into a ball and wrap my arms around my legs, holding them tight to my body. I close my eyes and slowly count. My heart races even though I'm not moving, and my head is heavy.

After ten minutes, I stand and pace the room, unable to calm down. It agitates me more. My chest tightens, and I know the worst is still to come.

Sitting on the edge of the bed, I take deep breaths and try to picture what life was like before all of this happened. Somehow, weeks seem like so long ago.

A knock sounds on the door, and I look up, trying to stabilize my breathing.

"Come in," I say.

Eli peeks his head inside before opening the door wider. "You okay? I could hear you pacing up here."

I blow out an unsteady breath and nod. "Just working through a panic attack." Placing my hands on my knees, I slouch over and close my eyes.

"Jesus, Cami. Let me help," he says, stepping inside.

"You can't." I inhale, then slowly release it. "It'll eventually pass."

"Did something trigger it?" he asks, sitting next to me on the bed.

"I don't really know. Just…everything. All the unknowns are a lot to handle right now," I explain. "I guess it started to really hit me that this is happening. I was watching some news footage on my phone last night and read a few articles, which didn't help my anxiety. Then I started thinking about Ryan and how scared I was for him. I tried to sleep through it, but it came back in full force this morning."

Eli stands, then leans down and lifts me until my arms wrap around his neck. "What are you doing?" I squeal.

"Just hold on," he instructs as he walks us to one of the oversized chairs by the window. I'm still wrapped in a blanket, but my temperature always rises when my anxiety is high. I'll start sweating soon, but I don't care.

Eli sits and cradles me against his chest. It settles me, and when I rest my head on his shoulder, he holds me a little tighter.

"This okay?" he whispers softly.

I nod, closing my eyes and snuggling deeper into his chest.

"Remember when Ryan invited me to the Hamptons with you guys the summer before my junior year?" he asks after we sit in silence for a while.

"Yeah," I say. "Why?"

"It was the first time I saw you in a bikini," he replies, chuckling. "I was a hormonal teenage boy, thinking very dirty things about my best friend's little sister. You were only thirteen or fourteen, so I kept telling myself not to stare at you. But it was nearly impossible." He rubs a soothing hand over my arm, caressing lightly. "You had basically written me off at that point, but I was determined to get your attention any way I could. Even if it was having you tell me off."

"Is that why you were flirting with Cherise the whole time?" I quip. I brought my best friend with me that week too, and she thought Eli was cute, which I hated. I didn't want him to like her, so I kept telling her bad things about him, hoping she'd stop. It didn't work.

"She flirted with me first!" he defends. "I was innocent."

That has me grinning. "I was ready to tell her you were gay so she'd leave you alone, but then you kept spewing out sexual innuendos, and I knew she'd never believe me."

"Wow…thanks."

Looking up, I peer into his gorgeous green eyes. "I didn't want her to know I was crushing on you. She would've sabotaged me and told everyone, especially *you*."

"And why would that have been so bad?" he asks, studying the sincerity on my face.

"At the time, it would've been. Now? Not so much," I tell him honestly. "I thought you'd think I was a dumb kid, especially after all the fighting we did."

Eli licks his lips before responding. "Perhaps you weren't aware of or I hadn't made it obvious enough, but I had the biggest crush on you in high school." The corner of his lips sweep up. "I still do."

Instead of feeling nauseated like I typically would during one of these attacks, butterflies surface in my stomach and a shiver runs down my back. Our eyes connect as we sit silently, staring at each other. My heart hammers as he leans down, and I tilt my chin upward.

Before our lips can connect, Bruno barges into my room, and Chanel immediately loses her mind. She hisses at him, and he starts chasing her around the bed.

"Bruno, heel!" Eli orders, standing and carefully setting me on my feet.

Chanel runs under the bed, and Bruno has a barking fit. He loudly howls and tries to wedge himself underneath, but he's too damn big.

"Out, Bruno. Let's go…" Eli grabs his collar, pulling hard and forcing him into the hallway. A moment later, he returns, closing the door behind him. "I'm sorry about that. He needs to go outside and burn off some energy."

The whole scene has me laughing. "It's alright. He likes your attention. I can relate."

Eli pushes off the wood and saunters toward me. "You feeling okay now?"

Nodding, I flash him a small smile. "Yeah, I think so. Thanks for talking to me and helping me think about something else."

He brushes a hand through his hair and fixes it. I love when he casually throws it up like this. Eli's the exact opposite of every guy I've ever dated, but it's why I've never been able to get over my feelings for him. I've fought them every chance I've had, allowing statuses and other's opinions to affect my choices, but I don't want to live that way anymore.

"You're very welcome." He winks. "I'm gonna take the beast out. Wanna join us?"

"Uh, sure. Let me get dressed, and I'll meet you out there."

After he leaves, Chanel slowly comes out from underneath the bed and jumps on my lap. I pet her and try to calm her down because she's as on edge as I was earlier. "Bruno just wants to be your friend," I tell her, jokingly.

Once she's chilled out a bit, I move her off me and find some warm clothes. With leggings, boots, and a sweater under my jacket, I put on a hat and gloves, then go out the back door. Eli is throwing a rubber toy to Bruno who is happily fetching it. Eli has him dressed in a bright-colored coat.

"Oh, look at Bruno all fancied up." I giggle.

"Yeah, Dobies can't be in low temperatures because of their body fat percentage and short hair. He'll start shaking without it, and I can't let my boy get cold." Eli looks me over and smirks.

"Wow, I had no idea. Chanel won't move an inch when I dress her and acts like she's being smothered or something. Bruno's totally in his element." I laugh, watching him run around as though it's no big deal, and place my hands in my pockets.

He lowers his eyes down my body. "You look like you're going to the North Pole," he teases. I notice he's wearing gym shorts and a sweatshirt.

"Not all of us are natural ovens," I retort, wrapping my arms around my body. "I'm always cold, even in summer."

"So when I felt you shiver upstairs, it wasn't because of me?"

I blush, my cheeks heating at his bluntness. "You're quite full of yourself, aren't you?"

"Only when I know I'm right."

Rolling my eyes, I ignore his stare and refuse to admit it. Bruno returns, and as Eli praises him, I lean down and roll snow between my palms. After Eli throws the toy again, he turns toward me, and I throw the snowball directly at his face. He's so caught off guard, he doesn't move, and I burst out laughing at his expression.

Brushing off his face, he narrows his eyes at me. "You're *so* dead."

The moment he comes for me, I start running. Something hits my back, and when I look over my shoulder, I see he's leaning down for more snow. Bruno barks at us, chasing us both, and I keep running even though my lungs burn.

"Get her, Bruno!" Eli shouts.

"No!" I yell, laughing so hard I can barely catch my breath. "Go away!"

Of course, Bruno quickly catches up to me and is all up in my shit, giving Eli the opportunity to tackle me to the ground. He's on top of me, holding me hostage and grinning like he's won the Super Bowl.

"Payback, princess." He cups a handful of snow and holds it over my head.

"No, please, no," I beg, squinting my eyes. "I'll do anything!"

"Anything, huh?" He stops and cocks his head, amused.

"Yes! Just don't get me in the face," I plead.

Strands of his hair fall over his perfect face as he releases the ball. The scruff over his jawline reaches up to his hairline, and he keeps it nicely trimmed. It's probably a good thing he has longer hair, considering a haircut is impossible to get right now.

"Alright, I'll bite." He flashes an evil grin, and I know whatever he's gonna make me do will be torturous.

He stands and helps me up, brushing the snow off my jacket. "Tonight."

"Tonight, what?"

"You will see…"

"I don't like the sound of that," I say as we walk back to the house.

Bruno is still energized as hell as he gallops into the kitchen, bringing a trail of snow with him. Eli follows me, smirking as I remove my coat.

He walks around me, removing his boots, and looks at me. "I'll clean up my mess, don't worry."

"I wasn't." I swallow.

He snorts. "Yeah, right. I can tell when you're lying."

Furrowing my brows, I ask, "How?"

"I've known you for over ten years, Cami. And for most of that time, when you were around, I watched everything you did. Being observant allowed me to learn a few things about you."

"You're starting to sound like a creep," I tease, taking off my boots.

"Which is exactly why I didn't tell you." He grins, then continues, "Your nostrils flare."

"What?"

"When you're lying."

Immediately, I cover my nose with my hand. "They do not."

"I bet you hate that I know so much about you," he says. "But you know a lot about me, too."

He's right, I do, but I hadn't thought about it in a while. "Like how you haven't cut your hair in seven years."

"Aside from trims, that's right."

"I'm jealous it's thicker than mine." I chuckle.

"Gotta use the right products," he says, smirking. "If you're nice, I'll share them with you."

I place a hand over my chest, faking excitement. "You're *so* sweet!"

"It's not your three-hundred-dollar shampoos, but it does the job."

Crossing my arms, I scoff. "I don't spend that much."

"Go clean up and do what you gotta do. You owe me, and I want payment tonight," he says, walking backward toward the staircase and pointing at me. "After dinner."

"Well, I should be relieved you aren't going to make me cook again, but somehow, this sounds more terrifying."

He grins, waggling his brows, then turns and walks up the staircase with Bruno following.

When he's out of sight, I let out a sigh and go to the kitchen. As I make a smoothie and think about how much has changed in only a few days, I can't contain my smile. He admitted he had a crush on me—and still does—and I realized those feelings I had for him have never faded. They've always been bubbling under the surface, and I've constantly fought to keep them under control, but not anymore.

Eli made me feel comfortable and not at all like a burden when I was at my most vulnerable. It's hard for me to admit I suffer from anxiety and panic attacks, but instead of judging me, he stepped right into action. I should've known Eli would want to help, and I'm so thankful he did. My thoughts drifted away from our reality as he held me, and I feel a hundred times better now. Though the circumstances suck, I'm so damn grateful he's here with me.

Whatever he has planned for us, I'm in. If it means spending more time with him, I'd agree to just about anything.

Chapter Eight

ELIJAH

Inhaling the mountain air, I close my eyes and smile. Bruno runs around, and I laugh at his playful antics.

Four days ago, my world turned upside down, and I thought I'd go stir-crazy being here alone. Having Cami here too has changed everything.

And for once, it's changed it for the better.

Away from her high-profile life and the pressures of status, Cami's the same girl I first met before any of that shit mattered. Before she let the idea of who she was allowed to date get into her head. I resented her for a long time, even while crushing on her, but those hurt feelings are long gone. Before now, it'd been months since I'd last seen her, and being around her has only cemented the way I've always felt.

Yes, she did just get out of a long-term relationship, but I know he wasn't right for her. She was arm candy for their public appearances and played along to appease her parents. Cami might've thought they had the picture-perfect relationship, but her eyes always gave away her true feelings regardless if she smiled wide. I know her well enough to see the sparkle was missing, proof she didn't love him like everyone thought she did. Every photo printed and posted was forced and had no real meaning behind it.

Given that we're here together and we have this second chance, I'm not taking it for granted. I'll get Cami to admit she hid her feelings for me and find out if she still has them.

"What'd you make? It woke me up from my nap." She laughs.

I arch a brow. "Nap, huh? Thought you had lots of schoolwork to do."

She groans while taking a seat at the table. "I do, but I get fatigued after a panic attack."

"You feeling better now?"

"Yes, very much so. I took a hot bath and fell asleep to an audiobook."

"Couldn't have been that interesting then if it made you pass out."

"It's one I've listened to a hundred times. The narrator's voice is soothing," she explains, which I find adorable. I never thought to do that.

"Well, I made pork chops slathered in cream of mushroom soup with a side of angel hair pasta."

"More pasta." She releases a dramatic sigh. "I'm going to leave here fifty pounds heavier."

"I doubt that." I set the plate in front of her. "But even if you did, you'd still be gorgeous."

"Thank you," she says, but I'm not sure if it's for the food or compliment. Either way, I meant it. Cameron St. James is a beautiful woman, always has been.

"Wow…this is really good," she admits after she tries the meat.

I grab my plate and sit across from her. "You sound surprised."

"Well, kinda. It sounds so simple, but it's really flavorful." She shoves another bite into her mouth, making me smile.

"I'm genuinely curious how you planned on surviving here without knowing how to cook," I add with amusement. "Once the Lean Cuisines were gone…you were gonna do what exactly?"

"I hadn't really thought that far ahead. My focus was getting out of the city as fast as possible, and the shelves at the grocery store were already bare."

"Lucky for you, I brought a lot of frozen meat."

"And double lucky that you know how to cook it," she adds, grinning.

"I'm determined to turn you into a chef before we leave." I cut into my pork. "This recipe is so easy, it'd take a miracle to fuck it up."

"Don't underestimate my ability to do just that."

We chat as we eat, and the conversation's never forced or awkward. The fact that it flows so easy should be weird, but I'm soaking up every second. Once we finish, I take our plates and rinse them in the sink.

"I'd help you, but you're gonna have to roll me and my food baby off this chair," she says, leaning back and patting her flat stomach.

I chuckle. "Don't worry about it. Gonna put them in the dishwasher anyway."

"So you gonna tell me what your payback plan is?" she asks once I finish wiping the counters. "I'm getting nervous, so just tell me."

"Well…" I move around the kitchen, grabbing a bottle of Jack and two shot glasses. "It includes these things and a TV."

She squints her eyes, looking confused as hell. "Hmm…you're going to get me drunk and make me watch porn?"

I raise a brow. "Is that an option?"

Cami scowls, shaking her head.

"Alright, well then onto plan B. C'mon." I wave my hand, and she huffs.

Begrudgingly, Cami stands and follows me to the couch. I grab the remote, turn on the TV, and click to A&E.

"What are you gonna make me watch?" she asks, curling her feet underneath her butt.

"You ever seen *Live PD?*" I ask, setting the bottle and shot glasses down on the coffee table.

"No…" she answers hesitantly.

"Oh man…" I beam. "You're in for a treat."

"Why do I have a feeling I'm about to regret this?"

"Depends what kinda night they have." I chuckle. "Now, there are rules to this drinking game. You ready?"

"I suppose." She shrugs.

"We take a shot every time there's a police car chase, someone gets tased, or the cops find drugs in the car and the person says it's not theirs."

"Dear lord, we'll be tanked before the end."

"That's the point."

She laughs, and her eyes go wide as soon as the show begins. I pour the whiskey into the glasses and sit back, knowing it won't be long before this game starts.

On the very first traffic stop, an officer pulls someone over and smells marijuana as soon as the window comes down. Of course, she asks him when he last smoked it, and he denies using it. The smell gives her probable cause to search the vehicle, and then…he tells her it's his buddy's car and that the drugs aren't his.

"Oh, here we go!" I cheer. "Shot time."

"I feel like that's such an obvious lie…" She scowls. "What an idiot."

I hand her one of the glasses, and we clink them together. "Cheers."

We choke down the burn in one swallow.

"This is a horrible idea," she slurs after the third shot. "How long is this show?"

"An hour," I reply. It's only been twenty minutes. "Be glad I only listed three. There could've been a lot more."

"Did he seriously think he could drive off and get away with it?" Cami holds out her arm, getting pissed at the screen when another police chase starts. "This is why we can't have nice things." She shakes her head, takes the glass, then tilts her head back.

Cami's blinking obsessively, and I start cracking up. "You gonna be okay?"

"Oh, sure. I'm starting to see stars, but I'm totally fine."

"Perhaps we should turn this off..." I chuckle.

She stands, wobbling on her feet. "No, no. I'm fine. Totally got this." She swings out her arm and attempts to touch her nose.

"What are you trying to do?"

"A sobriety test." She lifts one foot and steps it in front of her other, tripping over the coffee table.

Quickly, I catch her arm to stop her from falling, then get to my feet. "You're gonna hurt yourself. Maybe you should stay sitting."

She turns and scowls. "I think you got me drunk on purpose."

Taking her hand, I guide her back to the couch and sit next to her. "I didn't realize you were such a lightweight."

"I'm not!" She hiccups, then narrows her eyes at me when I try to hide my smile. "Shut up."

I snort and chuckle because she's adorable. "I'll get you some water."

"Wait." She grabs my arm, then within seconds, her legs are around mine, and she's straddling my lap.

"Cami, what are you doing?" I securely hold her waist as all the blood rushes to my dick.

"Well, if I have to explain it to you, then perhaps I shouldn't be on top of you."

"I think you're drunk and—"

"Are you saying you don't want me?" She leans in closer, and the strong smell of whiskey on her breath reminds me how inebriated she is.

"I do, but not like this."

"Maybe this is the only way I can be brave enough to make a move..." she states clearly. "You're the one who said I'm uptight, so this is me being..." She pauses, thinking. "*Un*-uptight."

My face splits into a grin at her hesitation and response.

Cami sinks down harder against me, and I groan at how good it feels. She's making this too fucking difficult.

"I appreciate that, but the next time I kiss you, you'll be sober." Bringing my hand up to her cheek, I brush away her hair and cup her chin. "That way, it'll be a moment you won't forget or regret."

"Okay." She nods, contemplating my words. I can tell she's thinking about something before she moves off me. The silence draws on for a second, and I wonder if she's embarrassed. "Any chance we can pretend this didn't happen?"

I smirk. "Not a chance in hell."

She crosses her arms over her chest, but she's smirking.

Cameron St. James throwing herself at me is a moment I'll never forget. Intoxicated or not, it's something I'll always find humor in.

After helping her upstairs and into her room, I tuck her into bed and kiss her forehead. "Night."

She's snoring by the time I shut the bedroom door.

I take Bruno outside, then get ready for bed and text my sister before passing out. Ava and I were super close growing up, but as we got older and focused on school and work, we didn't spend as much time together. I miss her a lot. The same age as Cameron, she's finishing her last semester of college online since the stay-at-home order was issued. I know she's bummed about it, but everyone's suffering one way or another.

Elijah: Hey, sis. How's it going?

Ava: Fine, I guess. Bored as hell already. How's the cabin?

Elijah: You'll never believe who's here with me.

Ava: Barack Obama?

I snort. She's obsessed with the Obama family. He's why she decided to study politics in college.

Elijah: Cameron St. James. I didn't know she was coming, and she didn't know I was either. We both just showed up.

Ava: Oh my God. Did she freak out? I bet she did.

Elijah: You could say that. Demanded I leave. Haha.

Ava: Of course. I'd expect nothing less from her.

She sends an eye-roll emoji, and I laugh.

Elijah: We're getting along if you can picture that.

Ava: That's because you're in love with her.

Elijah: I can't even deny it.

I send her a shrugging emoji. My feelings for Cami have always been more than just infatuation. Being here with her has made me truly realize how much she means to me. There's no hiding that.

Ava: Well, I hope you survive the quarantine with the fashion princess. Looks like we'll be locked inside for a while.

Elijah: There goes your dating life. HAHA!

Ava: Don't be a dick! I didn't have a dating life before this.

Elijah: Good. Guys are idiots. Stay away from them.

Ava: Says the idiot.

Elijah: Yeah, yeah. I'm going to bed. Good luck with your online classes. Stay safe!

After tossing and turning for two hours, I give up trying to sleep and decide to work out in the basement. I want to stay positive during this whole situation, especially since Ryan's on the front lines, and I need to be strong for Cami, knowing she's worried about him. But the truth is, it's been keeping me up at night. Everything is so surreal that I can hardly wrap my mind around it.

There are so many people who I love and want to stay safe, which only adds to my stress. I worry about my grandparents who are both in nursing homes. My mother is still cleaning houses to pay the bills. Then my sister staying with friends in the city. And of course, for my best friend. Without him, I'd be stuck in Brooklyn with three dumbass roommates who think this is a hoax. I'm not sure how long this lockdown will be, but I know I don't want to go back there.

Being with Cami is the only thing keeping me sane, even when she's the one driving me crazy. Crushing on her from afar was one thing, but having her here, literally on top of me, is testing my willpower. I don't want to be her "quarantine hookup" or a rebound if that's all she's looking for.

I'd give her forever if she'd let me.

Chapter Nine

CAMERON
DAY 5

Before I open my eyes, I know it's going to be a miserable day. Between my head pounding and my stomach rumbling, I'm not sure I can even get out of bed.

I pull the blankets over my head and groan. Last night, I tried to make a move on Eli, and he shot me down.

Rejected.

In retrospect, it was one of the most humiliating things I've done in a long time. Not to mention, it involves the one person who already thinks I'm an uptight royal princess.

He'll never let me live this down.

Sinking further under the sheets, I want the mattress to swallow me whole. Knowing Eli, he's shirtless in the kitchen wearing a smug smirk and waiting for me to grace him with my presence. One part of me wants to get this over with, but the other part hopes I can hide in here and he'll forget my existence.

After a few minutes, the throbbing in my head worsens. I debate whether to suffer through it or search for some medicine. Then an annoying beeping starts.

God. I'm already at this stage of the hangover.

The beeping continues.

Sitting up in bed with my hair in disarray, I look around and notice Chanel's staring at me.

"Do you hear that, too?" I ask, but she blinks at me, then starts licking her paws.

The annoying sound grows louder.

"What the fuck is that?" I grumble, deciding to get out of bed. Wrapping a blanket around my shoulders, I walk across the room and listen for it again.

Opening my bedroom door, I'm convinced it's coming from downstairs.

The fuck?

Dragging my sorry ass to the staircase, I brace myself for Eli's inevitable gloating. He's going to have a field day teasing the shit outta me.

Sure enough, Elijah's in the kitchen with his hair looking sexy and perfectly messy. I imagine running my finger through his dark strands, then remember the embarrassment I felt just moments ago.

"Good morning, sunshine." His deep voice echoes against the walls, causing a shiver to run down my body.

"Please tell me you hear that noise…" I plop down on the stool behind the breakfast bar.

He spins around and looks at me—the smirk I knew was coming planted firmly on his chiseled face. "What noise?" He furrows his brows, studying my face. "Feeling okay?"

"Not really." I rest my arms on the counter and lower my head. "I swear, something is beeping in this house."

"Here…" I hear him walk closer. "Drink this."

I blink, and a glass of orange juice is in front of me. "I can't. I might puke."

"Nah, it'll help. Go slow. I'll make you some waffles to soak up the alcohol."

He shuffles around, and I try to focus on not throwing up, but the high-pitched squeal is driving me insane. I get up to walk around the dining area and living room, searching for where it's coming from.

"Are you sure you don't hear it?" I drag my blanket with me. I know I'm not imagining it.

Moving back to the kitchen, I see his shoulders shake, and soon, he's full-on laughing.

"What's so funny?"

He smirks. "You."

"Are you enjoying my pain?"

Eli arches a brow. "What pain?"

Pinching the bridge of my nose, I inhale sharply. "Can we pretend last night didn't happen? *Pretty please*, for the love of God, don't gloat about what I did either. It's embarrassing, and this fucking beeping in my head is going to make me lose it! Not to mention, I have a headache."

"You mean, the part where you crawled into my lap and begged me to fuck you?"

"Okay, I know I didn't do that…you've lost your damn mind. I tried to kiss you, not bang you."

"I remember it differently…" He beams. "You were grinding against me, trying to get my dick all excited."

I hang my head, knowing my cheeks are burning bright red. "I hate you. Shut up. Go away. I'm leaving now."

"Wait, wait, wait…" He grabs my arm and pulls me back, tightening the blanket around me.

"What?" I snap.

"You're somehow even more adorable hungover as hell, but don't be embarrassed. I wanted to kiss you last night, but I didn't want you to regret it this morning. So, if you still have the urge to straddle my lap and rub against my cock, do it when you're sober so I know it's what you actually want."

I swallow down the lump in my throat, my heart hammering relentlessly in my chest, and nod. "Okay," is the only word I can muster.

The noise returns.

"Are you sure you don't hear that?" I tilt my head.

Eli retreats slightly, dropping his arms. "Yeah, it's the smoke detector. The backup battery is going out."

I step toward him and swat his chest. "You asshole! You heard it all along!"

He chuckles, moving back to avoid my wrath, but I quickly give up. Eli shrugs with a motherfucking grin. "Sober up so I can teach you how to change it."

Narrowing my eyes, I follow him to the table. He brings me my glass of juice and then busies himself with the waffle maker.

"Why does it sound like it's in my room and down here at the same time?"

"Because the ceilings are so high, and the sound echoes off the walls."

"There are a few up there, so how do you know which one it is?"

"You're supposed to change them all at the same time. But I'm not sure how many batteries you have, so we'll have to check."

"I'm part relieved it's not just in my head, but the other part wishes it were so it'd stop when my headache disappears."

"Speaking of which, take these." He hands me a couple of white pills. "Waffles are almost done."

"Thank you," I softly say, then swallow them down with my juice. "How are you not hungover this morning?"

He shrugs. "I'm twice your size. I can tolerate more."

"Next time we play your stupid game, I'm drinking vodka."

"You'll be puking for sure. Ryan told me it doesn't agree with you."

"Ryan is a fucking tattletale." I roll my eyes. "And he shouldn't talk."

"That's true. Ryan doesn't drink enough to be able to handle more than a few beers at a time."

I slap a hand against the table. "Exactly, thank you!"

Eli brings our plates over along with the butter, syrup, a can of Reddi-wip, and silverware.

"You ready for the best breakfast of your life?" he gloats.

"What's in these?" I ask, poking at one.

"Chocolate chips."

"That's a lot of carbs in the morning."

"You won't be worried about that once you take a bite." I watch as he slathers his toppings on. "Don't forget the whipped cream."

"I'm literally going to go into a sugar coma," I say as I add everything on top of mine.

The timer on the oven goes off, and he returns to the kitchen. Moments later, he returns with a plate full of bacon.

"You made enough for an army, geez."

"I made extra for BLTs later."

Good thing I packed leggings and yoga pants because there's no way my skinny jeans will fit after eating Eli's delicious meals.

"So? Thoughts?"

"I like it! I can't remember the last time I had waffles."

"Seriously?"

I shrug. "I live off smoothies and salads. Paparazzi, remember?"

"Fuck the paps. For real. Who cares?"

"I'm starting to wonder why I did so much," I state honestly. "But when I'm unable to fit into my clothes, you have to stop cooking this junk."

Eli snorts, shaking his head and stuffing more food into his mouth. "You have a home gym, so I wouldn't worry too much. I used it this morning. We could work out together," he suggests.

"What time were you down there?"

"I couldn't sleep, so I went around one."

"Oh damn." I blink. "Why couldn't you sleep?"

"Too much on my mind, I guess. Couldn't turn it off."

I nod. "I know how that feels. Especially now. My anxiety is the highest it's ever been, which is crazy, considering my life."

"I hear pot helps with that." He smirks. "Just sayin'."

"You know…" I bite down on my lower lip. "One day, I might take you up on that. Especially if I can't get it under control."

"I only do it when I need it."

"I wasn't judging you," I whisper. "I'm always worried about—"

"The media," he finishes for me. "I know."

Nodding, I take another forkful and swallow it down. "This really is delicious. Thanks for an amazing breakfast again."

"My pleasure. It's nice cooking for more than just me for a change."

"Maybe I'll try making something for you, but don't have high hopes. It'll be something easy."

"Like what? Cereal?"

I scoff, shaking my head at him. "Nothing with that attitude."

He laughs, shoving two pieces of bacon into his mouth.

"I have been craving grilled cheese and soup. Is that weird?"

"That sounds fucking amazing actually." He pats his bare stomach. "Think you can do that for lunch?" Eli pops a brow.

"No!" I chuckle. "Don't expect anything from me today."

"Okay, fair enough." He snaps his fingers with a wicked grin. "Tomorrow then."

I groan as he stands and takes his plate to the sink. "I'm gonna see if I can find a ladder and some batteries for that detector."

"Okay, good luck. I have no idea where either would be."

Eli smiles. "That's why I didn't ask."

He takes off as I continue eating. Bruno stares at me from the floor, giving me puppy eyes. "What?"

Bruno sits up and edges closer.

"I'm not giving you anything."

He blinks, licks his chops, then nudges his nose against my hand. Groaning, I pet his adorable head. "Fine, but don't tell your daddy. He'd probably yell at me. It'll be our little secret."

I take a piece of bacon and give it to him. He gobbles it up in one bite, then begs for more.

"No more!" I stand with my plate and bring it into the kitchen. Looking around at the mess, I decide to help the best I can and rinse off all the dirty dishes. I even manage to load everything into the dishwasher and find the detergent under the sink. There are a dozen buttons, so I press a couple and hope it's right.

At least ten minutes have passed, and I'm growing concerned that Eli hasn't returned yet. I decide to look for him, and Bruno accompanies me. There's probably a ladder in the garage, so I head there first. I open the door and glance around, then see Eli on his knees with his hands to his chest. He's wheezing like he can't breathe, and his lips are blue.

"Oh my God, Eli." I panic and rush to him. "What's happening?"

He pats his chest, then bows down, sucking in air. If I didn't know any better, I'd say he's having an anxiety attack, but then he leans back, and mouths, "Inhaler."

"Inhaler?"

He nods, and my eyes widen in shock. "You have asthma?"

He nods again, and I can't believe I didn't know this about him.

"Okay, inhaler. In your room?"

He confirms, and I quickly run out of the garage, then jump up the stairs. Rushing into his room, I realize I have no idea where to look. I start in the bathroom, rummaging through the drawers and cabinets. When I come up empty, I go to his nightstand. Scattering his shit everywhere, I frantically look for it.

Spinning around, I panic as I try to figure out where he keeps it. I go to his desk and finally find it next to his laptop.

"Thank God," I mutter, then rush back to the garage.

He's in the same spot I left him, and he's bent over, taking in shallow breaths. Bruno's lying next to him as if he knows how to comfort Elijah during his attacks.

"Sorry, it took me forever to find it." I hand it over, and he quickly presses the top and sucks in the medicine. I watch eagerly for him to recover. He takes a few more puffs, and after a moment, he starts breathing regularly.

"Are you okay?"

He nods, blowing out a breath. "That was a bad one."

"How did I not realize you had asthma?"

"It's not something I've broadcasted." He gets to his feet. "Don't feel bad."

"What triggers them?"

He winces, and I step back. "What is it?"

"It's a little painful. My chest and lungs feel sore afterward, but I'll be okay. It'll pass."

I fidget with my shirt, feeling helpless and wishing I could do something to make him better.

"I think it was the dust," he states after a moment. "I found the batteries and came in here to get the ladder."

"Well, let me change them out. I'm sure I can figure it out."

He flashes me a wary look.

"What? I can. Just talk me through what to do."

"Okay, well. You gotta carry that ladder inside the house. Think you can do that?"

I look up at the wall where it's hanging. It's at least eight feet, and there's no way I'm gonna be able to lift it on my own. "Oh, definitely."

Eli chuckles and backs away. "I'll put on a mask and get it. Don't worry."

"Hey." I grab his arm and move him toward the door. "I can totally do it."

His eyes lower to my hand, and he smirks. "Alright, be my guest."

Chapter Ten

ELIJAH

Watching Cami struggle to carry the ladder is comical. She's about to take out the dining room chandelier, and no matter how many times I offer to help, she insists she's got it.

I direct her to a spot in the living room where we should check first, but honestly, it could be any one of the smoke detectors. It's too high to actually know until you're closer to it.

"Alright, here is good." I grab one side of the ladder and set it on the floor. "You climbing up or am I?"

"Nope, you stay right there. I'm doing this."

Digging into my pocket, I grab a battery and hand it to her. "Okay, here you go."

Once the ladder is secure, I hold the other side and watch as she carefully climbs it. Her face pales the higher she goes. "You're not afraid of heights, are you?" I ask.

"No. Well, maybe a little."

I snort, chuckling. "Don't worry. I won't let you fall."

"That's very reassuring when I can hear you laughing." She makes it to the second to the top step and reaches the smoke detector. I instruct her on how to remove the old battery.

"Now make sure the positive and negative are lined up correctly."

"Okay, I'm not that stupid," she retorts.

"I'm just trying to be helpful," I say, moving to the other side so I can get a better look. "But if it's wrong, you'll have to go back up and fix it."

She sighs loudly. "Fine. I'll double-check."

Once she snaps it in and secures the cover, I tell her to hold the test button until it beeps. "You did it."

"You doubted me?" she taunts, slowly climbing down. I hold the sides of the ladder even as her ass brushes against me.

"I'd never," I tease, but it's hard to concentrate with her this close.

"I think you can let go now. I can't hurt myself falling from one foot off the ground," she states as my chest presses against her back.

Releasing my grip, I step away, giving her space. "Good job," I tell her when she spins around and faces me. "Only ten more to go."

Her proud expression drops. "Are you serious?"

I grin. "Nah, you got the right one."

She smacks me, and when I cough, her eyes go wide, and she covers her mouth. "Oh, shit. I'm sorry. I forgot already."

My chest still feels a little tight, and not getting enough oxygen exhausts me, but she's been a good distraction.

I haven't had an attack of that magnitude in months, and it's a good thing we never did smoke since there's always a chance that can trigger an attack. I was caught off guard, but I should've known better. The garage hasn't been used in who knows how long, other than Cami parking her Range Rover in there, and there was dust everywhere. As soon as I moved shit around, it triggered my asthma. I typically only need my inhaler when I work out too hard or during allergy season, but I'm thankful she was here to get it for me. Her springing to action and being so concerned made me realize she cares about me more than she lets on.

"You're fine, but maybe don't beat me up right after I can breathe again."

She rolls her eyes and shakes her head. "Now you're just trying to make me feel bad."

"I'd never." I retreat, putting space between us.

"Mm-hmm. Well, it's not gonna work anyway." She takes a step toward me.

Folding my arms over my chest, I step forward. "Don't want your pity anyway, *never have*."

"Do you have to argue with me on everything?" She closes the gap between us until our bodies press together.

Leaning down, I retort, "Do you have to argue with *me* on everything?"

She narrows her eyes. "Just for that, you can haul that ladder back into the garage on your own."

Smirking, I laugh as she walks around me, and Bruno follows her. Damn dog has already abandoned me for her. Not that I can blame him. She's feisty and somehow even more pretty when she's annoyed. It's probably why I've always enjoyed pressing her buttons so much. Not to mention, it's so easy to get a rise out of her.

Once I get the ladder back in the garage, I head to the kitchen to clean the mess from breakfast and realize she already did it. I see she even figured out the dishwasher.

Well, that's progress.

I head to my room and take a shower, needing to check in with the office. My supervisor has been blowing up my phone all morning, but I've been ignoring him. Not that I ever thought it was possible, but he's somehow been more annoying than usual. I've told him as such, too, which of course he didn't appreciate, but he seriously needs to chill. People aren't spending money unless it's essential, so sales are down company-wide.

By the afternoon, I'm exhausted from staring at my laptop screen, and my stomach is grumbling from hunger, so I get up to go find something to eat. When I get downstairs, I see Bruno has betrayed me and is on the couch with Cami. I'm surprised she's down here, considering how she was feeling this morning. I figured she'd be sleeping or attempting schoolwork.

She continues messing with her phone, so she either doesn't hear me or she's ignoring me. Tiptoeing closer, I look over the sofa and notice she's on TikTok.

Leaning down until I'm in the camera frame, I smirk. "Whatcha doing?"

"Jesus, Eli!" She jumps and quickly spins around. "Stop doing that!"

"Are you making a video?" I ask with amusement. "Can I see it?"

"No, you can't. Go away."

"Oh, come on. I wanna see."

"No!"

Reaching over, I try to grab it from her hand, but she moves away.

"Stop!" She laughs when I climb over the couch and land on top of her. She holds it up above her head, trying to keep it out of my reach.

"What're you hiding? Why can't I watch it?"

"Because it's just a dumb skit, and you'll laugh at me."

"Now I definitely wanna see it." I grin. She shuffles underneath me, and I hold myself up with one hand so I don't crush her.

"Never gonna happen!"

I bring my fingers under her arm and tickle her side. "Oh my God!" She wiggles long enough for me to grab the phone from her grip, and she screams. "No!"

Laughing, I pull back until I get a better view of her screen. With one arm, I hold her back as she struggles to fight against me.

Cami sucker punches me in the gut, causing me to lean forward. She tries swiping it, but I'm faster and move it out of reach.

"Nice try," I say. "You can't hurt steel."

She rolls her eyes at the reference to my abs. "So I should aim lower?"

"God, no. Don't do that." Especially since she's underneath me and my mind is going fucking wild with ideas.

"Give it back and no one gets hurt."

"Just let me see it. How bad can it be?"

She pushes herself up, trying once again to take it, but I pull back just far enough so she can't. With my other hand, I grab her wrist and hold it above her head. Towering over her, I bring my face close to hers.

"The more you fight it, the more I want it." My cock throbs in agreement.

There's a fire behind her eyes as we stare at each other. She brings a hand around my neck and pulls me closer until our mouths connect. My body stiffens for a moment, but when she slides her tongue between my lips, I instantly relax. Cami's legs wrap around my waist, and she arches her back, grinding her body against mine.

I drop the phone, sliding one hand to her face and squeezing her hip with the other.

"Fuck," I growl when she pushes into me harder.

Her hand roams down my body, and I kiss down her jawline until my lips find her ear. "If you think this gets you out of showing me that video, you're sadly mistaken."

Trying to be sneaky, she stretches her arm and searches around the floor for it. Grabbing her elbow, I suck on her neck and stop her. "Nice try, princess."

Pinning her to the couch, I squeeze my hand around her wrists. She attempts to shuffle out of my grip, but I'm too strong.

"You can't distract me with your mouth."

"Is that so?" She licks her lips and lowers her eyes to my noticeable erection. It doesn't help that I'm wearing gym shorts.

I study her and notice the way her body reacts to me. With flushed cheeks, she gasps for air as her chest rapidly rises and falls. She might've used kissing me to get her phone, but she wants this as much as I do. Cami's just as affected as I am but doesn't want to admit it.

Instead of giving in, I grip her hips and flip her over until she's on her stomach so she can't wiggle loose. She squeals as I take her wrists again then put her arms around her back, making sure I'm being careful with her. "What are you doing?" She rests her cheek on the couch and doesn't try to get away.

"Tell me what you want me to do…" I lean down and whisper in her ear. "Did you make a move because you only wanted something or because you want *me?*"

She swallows hard and licks her swollen lips, staying silent.

"You want to use me? Then use me," I challenge.

Blinking, she clears her throat and furrows her brows, trying to look at me. "I'd never do that to you, Eli."

"Good," I say with a smirk. I release my grip, giving her room to leave, but instead, she sucks in her bottom lip and stays put.

Shifting my body, I roam my hands down her back, then slowly lift her shirt. I press my lips to the little dimple above her ass, and she lets out a bated breath. Kissing up her spine, I remove her clothes in the process. Cami releases a moan, and I nearly embarrass myself with the way my cock responds.

She puts her arms between the couch and her body, slightly lifting herself so I can bring a hand around her and cup her bare breast. The softness of her skin almost has me tearing everything off and giving in to what we both want. Pressing my head into the crook of her neck, I groan at how good she feels pressed against me. She shifts and turns slightly until her gaze meets mine. Without a word, I capture her lips with mine, and when she moans, I grab her jaw and deepen the kiss. I taste the sweetness of the syrup she ate with breakfast this morning, and we both fight for more.

My other hand slides up, and I wrap my fist in her hair, slightly tugging. The heat burning between us is so hot, I wouldn't be surprised if that annoying smoke detector started beeping again.

Then the doorbell rings.

What the fuck?

We pull apart, both gasping for air as we look at each other confused.

"Did you hear that?" she asks.

"I did." I furrow my brows. "Are you expecting someone?"

"No. Are you?"

"No." I lift off her, then straighten my shirt and shorts. Holding out my hand, I help Cami to her feet, and she adjusts herself as we stand awkwardly in front of each other. "I'll go check it out."

"I'll come with you."

She follows me as I walk to the front door. I look through the peephole, but don't see anyone. Relief floods through me until I swing it open and see a bouquet of at least two dozen roses on the welcome mat.

I step to the side and watch Cami's reaction.

"I'm gonna take a wild guess and say those are for you."

She releases a heavy sigh and grabs them. The crystal vase alone looks like it easily cost a grand, and I know I can't compete with that. They're obviously from Zane, and no matter what, he'll always have an advantage over me.

Cami takes them into the kitchen, and I shut the door, then follow her. The flame that ignited our hot make-out session has extinguished, and she notices when I walk past her and grab a bottle of water from the fridge.

"So, who are they from?" I ask bitterly, unable to look at her. Chugging the water, I keep my back to her and wait for the inevitable.

"Zane," she responds. "And he left a note."

I finish the bottle, twist the cap back on, then toss it into the trash. "Congrats."

Heading for the staircase, I call Bruno and demand he come upstairs with me.

"Wait," she blurts out.

"What?" I ask over my shoulder.

"Why are you congratulating me?"

I know I'm being a dick, but I'm so goddamn tired of trying to win her over and failing. We take two steps forward, then something like this happens—a reminder that I'll never be good enough for Cameron St. James—and we move five steps backward.

Turning around and facing her, I flash a smirk and shrug. "For getting back what you wanted."

Chapter Eleven

CAMERON
DAY 6

Staring at the vase of roses on the dresser, I wait to feel something. *Anything.*

I was tempted to throw them out yesterday, but the flowers are beautiful, and I would have felt bad for tossing them. Not because of who sent them, but because it seemed like a waste of a perfect bouquet. I didn't want to upset Eli further, so I brought them to my room

Zane has always showered me with gifts, and I was too blind to see the reason behind them. They'd make me so happy, knowing he thought of me enough to send something so pretty, and I'd forget whatever problems we were having. Then another issue would come up, he'd buy me something else, and the cycle would repeat.

I'm an idiot for not realizing this sooner and allowing this nonsense to happen for as long as it did.

But now, I look at this bouquet and feel nothing. Well, except indifference. I couldn't care less about him or that he's trying to win me back.

To my dearest Cameron:
I was stupid for breaking your heart. Please forgive me and let me make things right again.
I love you.
-Zane

If I had to guess, Kendall started a rumor about Eli and me, and it got back to him. She was never his biggest fan, and him breaking up with me pissed her off even more. I'd bet my trust fund she had something to do with his miraculous change of heart.

But honestly, fuck him.

Nothing could make me take him back nor do I want to.

In the past week, I've seen a new perspective in life, and it's nothing like the one I had during the two years we dated. For all I care, Zane can jump off a bridge and forget that I exist. The only man I *do* care about isn't talking to me and avoided me last night. I plan to do whatever I can to help push his insecurities away. I nearly melted against him yesterday, after finally giving in to my inhibitions, and he left me high and dry because a bouquet of roses that I don't even want arrived.

As I undress and get into the shower, I think back to our younger years before we fought all the time. We were close until I ruined it by picking my snobby rich friends over him. I don't even know why I did it aside from wanting to be liked by the popular girls. My mother's constant pressure to fit in didn't help either. There was no excuse for treating him the way I did, and I will make it up to him. The last thing he deserves is to feel less than because of our past because right now, I don't feel good enough for him.

Remembering the way he touched and kissed me has my body temperature rising all over again. The warm water melts across my skin as I slide my hand between my legs. I rub circles over my clit, and my eyes roll into the back of my head. Imagining Eli's fingers on me along with his bedroom eyes have me moaning until the buildup is too much. I bite down on my lower lip to keep from screaming his name. It was so intense, I stand under the stream until I catch my breath.

I dry off, get dressed, then fix my hair. For the first time in ages, I feel brave enough to finally go after who *I* truly want. Deciding to take advantage of this newfound courage, I leave my room and go to the second level.

My heart hammers in my chest as I knock on his door. Waiting for him to answer has me sweating with the anticipation of what I'm about to do, but he doesn't answer. I take the stairs and check in the kitchen, but he's not there either. There are two plates on the table and a covered dish. He made breakfast, but he's not here.

Where the hell could he have gone?

The gym.

Taking the stairs to the basement, I hear the clanking of the weights as he works out. Peering around the corner, I spot him on the bench press in a sleeveless T-shirt and black gym shorts. His hair is pulled up, and sweat's dripping down his neck.

Weirdly enough, it's fucking hot.

I'm in my leggings and NYU shirt, looking like a hot mess, but I don't care because it's comfortable as hell.

I walk in, waiting for him to finish his reps so I don't scare him. He's wearing earbuds and is breathing hard, so I know he can't hear me, but it doesn't stop me from watching. I'm completely mesmerized by his focus and strength.

Eli sits up and finally looks in the mirror across from him. His eyes shoot to mine, and he arches a brow as he reaches for his phone and pauses the music.

"Enjoying the show?"

Leaning against the doorframe, I cross my arms over my chest and grin. "Actually, I was."

He turns and faces me, then grabs his bottle of water from the floor. Our eyes stay locked as he inhales his drink, and the intensity of our gaze has me second-guessing my plan, but I'm determined to do this.

No more being a coward.

"Did you make breakfast, then bail?" I ask.

He stands and saunters toward me. "I've been waiting for you."

"Why didn't you tell me? I thought you didn't want me around after yesterday," I say shyly.

"I've been waiting for you," he repeats, closing the gap between us. "For a *long* fucking time."

I blink, swallowing down the lump in my throat. "It's only ten," I counter.

He chuckles softly, the corner of his lips turn up into a panty-dropping smirk. "Years, Cami. I've been waiting for you to finally see me, and as soon as you did, reality smacked me in the face, and I remembered you're not mine. Never have been." He brushes his arm over his forehead. "You just got out of a relationship, and I shouldn't have crossed the line, but the temptation was too hard to resist."

"I wasn't saying no," I tell him. "I kissed you first yesterday."

"I know, but—"

"But *nothing*," I interrupt, tilting my head at him. "Stop trying to convince yourself that you're not good enough for me because that couldn't be further from the truth. I'm not worthy of *you*." Licking my lips, I bring a hand to his chest and fist his shirt, yanking his face lower. "If that doorbell hadn't interrupted us, we would've ended up naked on that couch, and my only regret would've been that it didn't happen sooner."

His intense stare burns through me, and I anxiously await his reaction.

"I don't want to be your rebound, Cami. Or your quarantine fling. So unless you can say with one hundred percent certainty it's not, then I can't. Don't give me false hope. Please," he begs.

"I swear it's not like that at all," I whisper, panic building inside me. "I want you, Eli. I've always wanted you."

He clenches his jaw, not saying a word, but he continues to stare. After a moment, he blinks. "Say it again."

Butterflies invade my stomach at the roughness of his voice, demanding and sultry. "Kiss me. I want *you*, Elijah Ross."

One second, my feet are on the floor, and the next, they're wrapped around his waist. My back presses against the wall as our lips collide. My arms grip his shoulders, holding him tightly as he effortlessly supports me with one palm under my ass. Our tongues tangle together, and we're barely breathing as we desperately taste each other.

I moan against his mouth as he pushes into me, and I feel how hard he is for me. He was turned on yesterday too, and my mind went wild, imagining how it'd feel to touch.

"Fuck, Cami," Eli whispers my name with painful exaggeration before moving his lips over my jaw.

My head falls back as he sucks on my neck. It sends heat straight between my legs. I want his tongue and fingers there, but honestly, I want all of him, everywhere. *Now.*

"I need you inside me," I plead as he presses himself into me again.

"Christ," he hisses. "I want to, Cami. I really do…"

"But?" I meet his hardened gaze. "What's the problem?"

"I don't have any condoms," he responds.

Furrowing my brows, I ask, "You don't? Seriously?"

He sucks in his lower lip and shrugs. "I was coming up here to isolate, *alone*. Didn't know I'd need them."

Shit. He's right. I don't have any either because Zane was bringing his stash.

"Any chance you think Amazon would deem them essential and overnight them?"

Eli laughs. "Maybe it's a good thing. It'll force us to go slow."

"That sounds like the opposite of fun, though." I stick out my lower lip and pretend to pout.

"Ohh, Cami. How wrong you are." He releases me until my feet touch the floor, then he kneels in front of me, grabbing the hem of my leggings and pulling them down to my ankles.

"Did you forget something?" He arches a brow as I step out of them.

"No, I shaved this morning, thank you."

He tilts his head and licks his lips. "I can see that."

"Oh, no panties. That's because I came down here to seduce you," I tell him matter-of-factly and am almost embarrassed by how quickly I blurted that out.

"Jesus," he chokes out. "You're making it hard to say no."

"Then don't," I say. "I'm on the pill and always get my annual screening." If he doesn't touch me soon, I won't be able to stop rambling.

He groans, wrapping his fingers around my thighs. "Spread your legs."

I part my feet, my heart beating faster with every eager second. Eli moves a hand up and slowly brings a finger to my pussy, then slides it across my slit. "You're already wet."

"Mm-hmm," I hum, my eyes rolling. He's torturing me. "I wasn't lying when I said I wanted you."

"I guess not," he says, chuckling softly.

If I admired his facial hair before, it's nothing compared to how it feels when it rubs against my skin. It's rough and tickles, and I crave more of him. His tongue slides to my clit, and he squeezes it between his lips.

"Oh my God." My fingers curl in his hair as the sensations ripple through me. "Don't stop. Please, for the love of all that's holy, do not stop."

"Don't worry, *princess*." He emphasizes the nickname he's called me for years, except this time it sounds sweet and hungry. "I could please you for fucking hours."

My back arches as he pushes two digits inside me. The pressure feels incredible as he fucks me with his fingers and flicks his tongue against my sensitive spot. The buildup comes fast, and soon, I'm falling over the edge as he increases his pace, driving as deep as he can.

I clench my teeth, then moan out his name, breathing rapidly as I come down from the highest high I've ever had. Eli doesn't stop like I expected and continues his sweet torture.

"You thought I was done?" He flashes a cocky grin. "I'm just getting started with you." He stands and takes my hand, guiding me to one of the equipment benches. "Lie down."

My brows rise in hesitation. Eli nods his head toward it, encouraging me to oblige. Before I do, I grab the bottom of my shirt and take it off. If being naked doesn't drive him as insane as he's making me, then I don't know what will.

"Jesus fuck," he grunts. "What are you trying to do to me?" He kneels with me spread in front of him. Bending my knees, he pulls my ass closer and places his mouth back between my thighs.

Feeling his fingers and mouth on me is so damn intense that everything goes white, and stars invade my vision. I fist my hands in my hair, trying to breathe through the best orgasm I've ever experienced.

"I need you," I whimper, begging him to fuck me. "Inside me."

"Cami," he growls, wiping his mouth as he stands. "Don't tempt me."

"Don't deny me."

"I just gave you like five orgasms. There was no denying."

Laughing, I sit up and am eye level with his crotch. He's so hard; I can't stop myself from touching him outside his shorts. Thick and big. He steps back, and my hand drops.

"No."

"No? You don't want me to return the favor?" I arch a brow.

"I do. I *really, really* do, but the moment your mouth is on me, my willpower will snap."

I smirk, knowing he's struggling as much as I am. "Well, you either let me take care of that or you get to jerk off in the shower like I did earlier."

He swallows hard, groaning. "You didn't."

"I swear! The real thing, though? One thousand percent better, so let me."

"I'm walking away now. Put your clothes on and meet me upstairs for breakfast." He steps toward the doorway.

My arms drop to my sides, and my jaw nearly hits the floor. "Are you serious?"

"Cami," he pleads. "Trust me. I'm going to rub my dick raw later thinking about you, but we can't just jump into sex."

Rejected. *Again*.

Chapter Twelve

ELIJAH

Cami is the sexiest woman I've ever laid eyes on, but damn, when she's annoyed, she's somehow even sexier.

It's quite fucking adorable too how hard she's trying not to be mad when I know she is. With her shoulders squared and her nose in the air, she walks to the table and silently sits.

"Good morning," I say, holding back a smile. "I warmed this up, so it's nice and hot."

"Great," she grits out. "What is it?"

"French toast with berries."

"Sounds *delicious*," she blurts out, flashing me a fake grin. It's hard to keep a straight face when she's worked up like this. But if there's one thing I've learned about Cami, it's that she's used to getting her way.

Not this time, though, and it's killing her.

I might be getting a bit too much enjoyment out of this, but it's best for both of us that I not cave. It doesn't erase how much I desperately want her. I've always used a condom, but *when* Cami and I cross that bridge, I don't want anything between us anyway. I could tell her that, but watching her squirm is far too entertaining.

I place the syrup and butter on the table, and after she puts them on her food, I hold out a small bowl. "Powdered sugar?" I ask.

She narrows her eyes, grabbing her fork. "Sure. Why not?"

"It's tasty. Especially with the cinnamon in the mixture."

"Load me up then." She moves her plate closer.

I snort, shaking my head at her fierce determination to be bitter. "My pleasure."

We eat in silence, casually stealing glances across the table. She keeps a pissed-off expression as she chews even though she's obviously enjoying each bite by the way she scarfs it down. Once our plates are nearly cleaned, I stretch my leg underneath the table until it touches hers. At first, she flinches, but I continue until my foot reaches between her thighs.

"What do you think you're doing?" She gives me an incredulous look.

"Checking if you're still wet for me."

With the corner of her mouth tilted up slightly, she pushes her chair back until my foot falls. I watch her closely and am confused as hell when she slides down to the floor and crawls between my legs.

"Uh..." I pull back, but she grips the hem of my shorts and yanks them down. "Cami..." I lower my voice, pushing the chair out from under the table. "You better not."

Her delicate fingers wrap around my shaft, and my entire body succumbs to her touch. Fuck. Me.

She rises up on her knees just enough to place her lips around the tip of my cock, and I scramble to move away because she's testing my control. However, she digs her nails into my thigh with one hand while gripping my length with the other and halts me in place. The moment I feel her hot breath brush over my sensitive skin, I know I don't have a fighting chance to resist her.

I've wanted her for so long and can't deny how incredible it feels to have her mouth on me. Tilting my head, I watch as she devours every inch of me. I fist her hair and admire how gorgeous she looks on her knees.

"You suck me so fucking good, Cami." My eyes roll back. She twists her wrists, stroking me faster and harder while twirling her tongue like a goddamn goddess. "*Shit.*"

My arms fall, unable to concentrate on anything other than how good she's making me feel. I'm already close and about to explode. With a loud pop, Cami leans back and wipes her mouth. She flashes a wide, perfect smile, then gets to her feet.

Confused, I glare at her. "Uh…" I clear my throat, unsure of what I'm supposed to say.

"You finish inside me, or you don't finish at all."

"You know I can just get myself off, right?" I challenge, shifting uncomfortably in the chair.

"Sure, but you'll have to live with the fact that you chose your hand over my pussy."

"Cami," I growl. "Quit being a sadist and get your sexy mouth over here."

"Mmm…nah. Good luck with that." She points at my painful erection and winks, then walks away.

I'm not about to let her get her way and win, so I quickly pull up my shorts and follow her. She sees me coming and runs.

"No! Go away!" she scream-laughs, rushing up the stairs as fast as she can. Before she gets to the third floor, I grab her wrist and yank her to my chest.

We're both panting and smiling as she tries to escape my grip. "Where do you think you're going?"

"To my room. *Alone.*"

"Wouldn't you rather have some company?" I arch a brow, pushing her into the wall with my hips so she can feel my cock rub against her. If she wants to play games with me, I'll make the next move and show her who's gonna win this battle.

She glares at me, looking like pure temptation, and shrugs. "I got off. You're the one with blue balls."

Burying my face in her neck, I chuckle against her ear as I slide my hands over her body. "I have plenty of bikini images of you in my spank bank to finish what you started, but you wanna know the best part? You're not talking in any of them. I'll blow my load in less than ten seconds flat."

Cami gasps, pushing hard against my chest, and I release her. She sneers and takes off to her room, slamming the door behind her.

I can't help laughing as I make my way to the kitchen to clean up the mess. She has no idea what she's in for if she thinks I'm just another person who'll give in to her demands with the snap of her fingers. Granted, I want to fuck her senseless until we're both panting, but I'm not giving in that easily. If she wants me, she's going to have to work for it.

After everything is cleaned, I take Bruno outside for his daily exercise, then jump in the shower. I can't wipe the grin off my dopey face when I relive Cami's lips on me. That image will forever be ingrained in my mind no matter what. It's a fantasy I've had since I was a teenager, and as soon as it became a reality, it was programmed into my eternal memory.

I reply to emails and take a couple of video calls to appease my boss, but it's a waste of time, considering nothing's changed in the past few days. I'm keeping in contact with my clients and trying to prove myself, but I refuse to be annoying and pushy when so many jobs have been furloughed, and people have been laid off. I'm fortunate I can do some of my work from home and still earn a paycheck, so I'm not taking that for granted, but I'm also empathic.

I can put people first and be good at my job, regardless of what my supervisor thinks.

Checking my phone, I notice a missed call from Ryan and immediately worry. I return it, but he doesn't answer, so I text him instead.

Elijah: Sorry I missed your call. I was on a conference call. Everything okay?

Ten minutes later, he finally responds.

Ryan: As much as it can be, I suppose. Shit is freaking crazy here. Just checking on you guys. Cameron said you had an asthma attack yesterday. Are you alright?

I'm surprised Cami told him or that she's talking about me to him period. I'm tempted to ask if she mentioned the panic attack she had the other day, but I won't air her business in case she doesn't want him to know.

Elijah: I'm fine. Freaked her out, though. She nearly nose-dived the concrete running to get my inhaler.

Ryan: She would've had a royal meltdown if that had happened.

Elijah: Trust me, I saw a glimpse of that while she changed the smoke detector battery.

Ryan: You mean you got her to actually help? What kind of spell did you cast on my sister?

I'm tempted to fuck with him and tell him what else I got her to do, but I don't need him thinking I'm using her because I'm not. I also don't want a brotherly speech from him about not hurting her. He knew how much I crushed on her in high school, but he has no idea it never stopped.

Elijah: It's the quarantine, man. She even loaded the dishwasher this morning.

Ryan: Shit. I think she's cracked.

Elijah: Haha…wouldn't surprise me. She's gonna have a hard lesson in doing laundry soon.

I chuckle to myself because I'm almost certain she's gonna need to wash her clothes in a few days.

Ryan: Just don't let her near the stove. She'll burn down the cabin, and then you'll both be homeless or recovering in the burn unit.

Elijah: Considering she doesn't know how to turn it on, I'm not too worried. I've been cooking to prevent any hazards.

I feel guilty talking shit about Cami to her brother, but if I start throwing out compliments, he'll grow suspicious.

Ryan: Good. I wouldn't be surprised if this shit lasts for months, so get comfortable.

I'm torn on how I feel about that. Honestly, I don't mind being away from the city, especially with Cami here, but the consequences of an epidemic are terrifying. What long-term effects will it have on the people and our economy? Only time will tell.

Elijah: Please be safe. I worry about you.

Ryan: I'm doing my best with what we've got. Taking all the precautions I can.

Ryan: I gotta run. Love you, man. Take care over there, okay?

Elijah: Will do! Stay safe!

I set my phone down and say a quick prayer for my best friend and all the frontline workers. I've always looked up to him, but now even more. Ryan's my hero.

Though I read the news every morning before I get out of bed, I only allow myself ten minutes because the government's handling of this is a mess. No one can agree on anything, and it's like watching toddlers fighting over toys. Watching the press conferences or reading the briefings only spike my anxiety and nerves, and if there's anything I can control during this time, it's how much outside noise I allow in while keeping my ass at home.

Deciding I need a break and to leave this room, I head downstairs with Bruno, plop on the couch, and click on Netflix. I'm in the mood for something that'll keep me interested for a few hours, so I end up clicking on an original documentary about a guy who owns a tiger zoo and needs a different hairdresser. Within thirty minutes, I've asked myself *what the fuck* at least a dozen times.

"This guy is bat-shit crazy," I mutter after finishing the second episode. It's a train wreck, but I can't look away and end up clicking on the third episode.

"Who's bat-shit crazy?"

I look over my shoulder and see Cami holding her cat as she walks toward me.

"This redneck with a bleached mullet," I explain. She's quieter than usual and looks nervous. "What are you doing down here?" I assumed she'd stay in her room the rest of the night, doing homework and staying pissed at me.

She shrugs, biting down on her plump lower lip. "I got hungry, and I need to refill Chanel's water."

"I could make something," I offer. "I'm hungry too."

"Okay, thanks." She rounds the corner and sits in the recliner. "Wanna watch the first episode while I cook? Or I can give you a recap and catch you up?"

"Sure, I'll start it, and you can fill me in on the rest when you're back," she says sweetly. The tension in the room is so thick, I nearly choke on it, but we're not bickering, so I won't set her off on purpose.

I restart the first episode and smirk. "Get ready for the best shitshow of your life."

Cami shivers and reaches for a throw blanket.

"Are you cold?" I ask. "I can make a fire." One of the best things about this cabin is the wood-burning fireplace. None of that propane, press a button crap.

Yesterday, I noticed there wasn't much wood left, but maybe enough to last tonight. There might be more in the shed, but if not, I'll have to chop some so we have it for the next few weeks.

"Yeah, that'd be nice," she answers.

I get it started, and her face contorts when the first episode begins. It makes me laugh.

"This is what you've been watching?" She looks just as confused as I was.

"Hey, I'm blaming it on the quarantine. Plus, the memes I've seen for this are fucking hilarious, so I had to see it for myself. So far, it hasn't disappointed in the entertainment department."

"But why does he look like that?" She cringes, curling her legs underneath her and settling into the seat. She's more invested than she's willing to admit.

I dig through the fridge and pantry, trying to figure out what to make us. I'm in the mood for some comfort food, and when I see the can of tomato soup, I remember how she said she was craving a grilled cheese sandwich yesterday.

Grabbing all the ingredients, I put together four sandwiches and two bowls of soup, then grab a few napkins. It looks so damn good, I'm ready to dive in before I deliver it to her.

"Oh my God. That smells heavenly," she says, moaning when I set it all on the coffee table. She perks up, her mouth opening in surprise. "You remembered. Thought you said I had to make this for you?" She raises her brows.

"Sounded too good to risk you screwing it up," I tease.

She stares at me for a moment, her eyes softening as I meet her gaze. "Thank you for this."

"You're welcome." I take a seat on the couch and reach for one of the plates and bowls. "I wasn't sure if you liked extra cheese in your tomato soup, but I sprinkled some in anyway." I grin, remembering how dead set she was on eating low-fat cheese when we arrived.

"Mmm." She hums around a spoonful. "So good."

"You better calm down over there. You're getting my dick excited with all that moaning."

Cami quickly covers her mouth as she spurts hot liquid from her lips. Her shoulders bounce up and down as she laughs, trying to swallow down the soup. "Don't say shit like that when I'm eating." She wipes her mouth on a napkin.

Chuckling, I shrug. "Sorry. Don't moan like that then." Though I *really* like hearing it come from her. Especially when she's underneath me.

"I was moaning about the *food*," she emphasizes. "Quit being a perv."

I flash a smirk when she glares at me. "Don't make noises that remind me what it felt like having your mouth on me."

She blushes, and instead of throwing a retort at me, she focuses on the TV and tries to ignore me. It's cute, but this is just foreplay for me.

Driving Cami insane the same way she drove me wild is just the beginning of what I know is to come.

Chapter Thirteen

CAMERON
DAY 7

I've been at the Roxbury cabin for a week, and somehow, it feels like a month has passed. Though it hasn't been horrible, it's been a drastic change from my normal routine.

My daily schedule used to consist of two to four classes, meeting up with friends for lunch or a quick shopping trip, and then studying for a bit before Zane and I went out for dinner. On the days I only had a couple of classes, I'd work out or go to a yoga class with Kendall. We'd also do spa days every week that consisted of pedis, manis, and body waxes. Massages were a bi-weekly adventure, and my hair would get cut or colored every four weeks. If the paparazzi are going to take pictures of me, the least I could do was try to look put together to avoid their criticism, but that didn't always work. They'd catch me off guard, then blast rumors. Oftentimes, I wouldn't feel good enough based on what they wrote, and my self-esteem would take a hit. Regardless of their opinions, I took so much for granted and kinda miss my old lifestyle. I don't know if things will ever be like it was before. In a few months, I'll be graduating with my undergrad degree, then I'll start my postgraduate classes. Eventually, I'll take over more responsibility in the company while I finish my master's, and then I will shift to a higher position. I shouldn't complain, but I'm grieving everything I was accustomed to.

But it could definitely be worse, so I'm counting my blessings. I remind myself this isn't forever. It's temporary, and if Ryan and all the other essential workers can risk their lives and work on the front lines, then I can suck it up and stay here for as long as it takes.

After my embarrassing tantrum in front of Eli yesterday, I know I'm slowly losing it. Being trapped here should be fucking easy. I'm safe. I have everything I need and more, but I'm going stir-crazy without being able to see my classmates, professors, friends, brother, and parents.

I didn't anticipate the emotional aspect. I'm pretty stable, considering all the shit I've had to deal with in my life, and I just wish people knew the *real* me.

The media never highlights the positive things I do. They never talk about how I donate my time to help charities, attend fundraisers, rally for women's rights and equality for all, and I even proposed grants for underprivileged students so they could afford to attend NYU. Unfortunately, the tabloids have created a persona that's not me, and I'm not sure if I'll ever have an identity of my own. The biggest disappointment is knowing Elijah grew up thinking those things about me too. Though I haven't always presented myself in the best way, I'm still human and make mistakes. And I can admit when I'm wrong or I've overreacted.

I felt awful for the way I treated Eli yesterday, so that's why I went into the living room. Besides being hungry, I wanted to see if he was downstairs so I could apologize. Instead of ignoring me like I deserved, he brushed it off and made me the best damn grilled cheese I've ever had. As we watched his weird but equally entertaining documentary and ate our dinner, the fire crackled. It was the most relaxed I'd been in days. The setting felt romantic, but after the way things ended earlier in the day with me on my knees under the table, I was too embarrassed to sit on the couch next to him.

Eli's the most forgiving person I've ever met. He didn't force me to admit my wrongdoings, so I want to thank him and return the favor.

It won't be much, but I'm going to try to make breakfast this morning and hopefully smooth things over with him. If we're going to get through this together, we can't argue like we have the past seven days.

Chanel rolls to her back, waiting for me to give her tummy scratches. The sunlight beams through the drapes, and I know if I'm going to beat Eli to the kitchen, I need to get moving.

"C'mon, girl. We can't stay in bed all day." I pet her for a moment, then push off the covers.

As soon as I stand, I hear a weird noise. A loud, continuous thumping echoes and when I peek out the window, I see Eli by the shed chopping wood. He's in dark blue jeans, a college sweatshirt, and wearing a beanie with his hair down. Simple but somehow, so damn sexy. Bruno runs around barking, happier than ever, and buries his nose in the snow as he eats it.

I'm mesmerized as I watch Eli pull his arms back and strike the log, splitting it in half. He makes it look so effortless. Without him here, I'd be fucking doomed. Even if Zane hadn't broken up with me, we might've lasted forty-eight hours without calling our parents to rescue us. I appreciate Ryan sending Eli here more than he'll ever know. Otherwise, I'm not sure what I would've done.

I head to the kitchen and am relieved when I don't see breakfast already made. He probably doesn't expect me up this early, which is perfect. I can ace college exams and outsmart professors who've been teaching for decades but ask me how to make an omelet, and I become a freaking moron. But hell, I'm determined to learn.

Digging out the egg carton, shredded cheese, and ham, I set everything on the counter, then grab my phone to search for a YouTube tutorial. Undoubtedly, someone's made an instructional video on how to properly do this.

I'm relieved to find a decent one by an actual chef and get started. I dice the ham steak first, then crack three eggs into a bowl and whip them with a fork. The instructor says to use an eight-inch pan, and when I dig around the cupboard, there's at least three different sizes. Shamelessly, I picture Eli's cock and figure out which one is eight inches by how big he is.

Next, I turn on the stove and add the vegetable oil and butter to the pan like I'm told. "That's a lot of freaking butter," I murmur when I see how much coats the bottom.

Once it's hot, I add in the whipped eggs. It sizzles and the oil flicks up and burns my finger.

"Fuck," I hiss, grabbing a towel, then rewind the video, knowing I missed a step.

I'm confused as hell and quickly dig around in the drawers in search of the same utensil used by the instructor. Realizing we don't have one, I grab the next best thing, which looks like some kind of flipper device.

Good enough.

As I move the eggs around like he is, it splatters and burns me again.

"Ouch! Goddammit," I growl, stepping as far away from the stove as possible while still somehow reaching the pan. I keep listening to the video and try to do what he says, but honestly, this is a mini-disaster waiting to happen.

"Next, you're going to carefully flip the omelet, and while sometimes it breaks, just roll with it and flatten it out," the instructor continues.

"Yeah, easy for you to say..." I mutter, stepping closer and trying my best to flip the damn thing. It goes as expected—half flipped, half smooshed. I try to even it out so it's level and the other side can cook.

While that happens, I add in the ham and cheese, then allow it to cook for a few more minutes.

Once it looks done, I grab a plate and try to slide it on there without dropping it.

"Well, that looks horrendous." I set the pan to the side and stare at the saddest omelet I've ever seen. I add more ham pieces and cheese on top so he won't notice how badly I botched it.

Grabbing the loaf of bread, I slip two pieces into the toaster. Once it's ready, I slather on butter and set them next to the heaping mess on the plate.

Bruno comes charging in just as I place the dish on the table. Eli follows, and we lock eyes. The intensity behind them has my entire body burning with desire.

"Morning," he greets, carrying a stack of wood in his arms. "Did you…cook?" He sniffs, then grins.

"Yes." I quickly clear my dry throat. "Well, I *tried*."

He blinks, then chuckles. "Smells good."

"Hopefully, it's edible. I wanted to make breakfast to repay you."

Eli walks in farther and goes to the living room, then drops the wood by the fireplace. He pulls off his gloves and sets them on the island, noticing the huge mess I've made.

"You didn't have to do that," he says softly. "But I'm starving, so I appreciate it."

"It's on the table," I tell him. "Do you want some coffee?"

"Sure, I'd love some."

He sits down and dives in, moaning as he chews. I make him a cup of black coffee, and when I bring it to him, half of the omelet is already gone.

"This is really good, Cami," he mumbles around a mouthful. "You really made this?"

"I have the oil burns to prove it." I chuckle. "Admittedly, I had to watch an instructional video. Don't judge me."

Eli licks his lips, holding back his laughter, but there's amusement in his eyes. The whole thing is pretty hilarious. Poor rich girl who's twenty-two can't cook to save her life and has to research the simplest recipes. Regardless, I'm determined as hell to take advantage of this situation and learn some useful basic skills.

"No judging." He holds up his fork, taking another large bite. "It's delicious. In fact, now that I know you can cook, I'll be expecting this every morning."

My head falls back with laughter, but his encouragement warms my heart. It's nice to hear that it wasn't a complete epic fail.

"Baby steps," I mock. "There are one-minute how-to-cook videos on TikTok, so I might be able to learn a second dish before this is all over."

"I have a super easy one called toad in a hole. It'd be really hard to screw that up."

I furrow my brows. "Toad in a hole? Where you fry the eggs in the middle of a piece of bread?"

He confirms with a nod.

"Then you mean egg in a basket." I fold my arms, challenging his weird name. "I've never made it, but our chef did when Ryan and I were kids.

He scrunches his nose and shakes his head. "Toad. In. A. Hole," he emphasizes slowly. "Is the correct term. Fight me." He smirks.

"That doesn't even make sense. If you're going with an animal, wouldn't it be chick in a hole?"

He snickers, shrugging. "Aren't you going to eat anything?" he asks once he realizes I don't have a plate.

I cock my head, pursing my lips. "It was hard enough making one omelet. I'm not pressing my luck again."

"Cami."

"Stop, I'm fine. I wanted a smoothie anyway." I slide the chair back and stand.

"Let me make you something as a thank you for breakfast," he urges. "Please."

"No way!" I scold, walking to the kitchen island to clean up. "I made you that as a thank you. You can't thank me for thanking you."

He squints, grabs his plate, then walks toward me. "Wait, what?"

I sigh. "You've cooked since we got here, so I wanted to repay you for that. You can't in return thank me for it when I was already thanking you."

"Says who?" he challenges, setting his empty dish in the sink.

"Me," I remark. "If it'll make you feel better, I'll eat a big lunch."

"Hmm." He thinks it over, brushing his fingers over his scruffy jawline. "Alright, fine. But lunch is in an hour then."

"Oh my God." I shake my head, laughing at his persistence. I open the dishwasher and load it, add in the detergent, then hit start.

Eli silently watches me with an amused expression as he leans against the counter, crossing his ankles.

"What?" I ask. "Why are you staring at me like that?"

"Just thinking how sexy you look right now." I was certain he was going to make some smart-ass comment about me using the dishwasher properly, but I hadn't expected *that*.

I look down at my outfit, which consists of the same clothes I wore to bed. Normally, I'd never be caught wearing loungewear around anyone other than my family, but I'm comfortable around Eli. Plus, he doesn't care about any of that.

"You mean, greasy hair and an unwashed face are your kink?" I release a dramatic gasp. "Who knew?"

"Actually, I was thinking you being all domestic and shit makes me horny as fuck."

I set my hands on my hips and narrow my eyes at him. "Let me guess, you want your woman barefoot and pregnant, am I right? A traditional housewife, dinner on the table at six every night, sex on Saturday nights after *SNL*."

"Oh, there'd be sex *every* night," he retorts. "Especially if I want to keep you knocked up."

"Well, sorry to burst your 1950s era bubble, but I plan to have a career," I state matter-of-factly.

His shoulders rise and fall. "So? Have a career. You can be a mom and wife at the same time. Millions of women do."

"And what will you do? Chop wood and fix light bulbs while I raise the kids and bring home the bacon?"

He smirks. "I'll pick up the kids from school, take them to the park to play, then bring them home. I'll give them a bath, then read them a bedtime story. Once they're asleep, I'll pleasure my wife and make sure she goes to bed completely satisfied."

"Wow. Sounds like you have it all figured out."

He bobs his head back and forth, pushing off the counter. "Except for a few minor details."

"Like what? Pussy or anal?"

His cocky smirk returns as he takes a step toward me. "Is everything about sex for you?"

I roll my eyes, leaning against the island. "What then?"

"I'd prefer to marry a woman who wants me as much as I want her. I don't mind the chase, the challenges even, but I don't want to constantly second-guess her feelings for me."

A lump forms in my throat, and butterflies swarm in my stomach. His reference is about me, and the way I've been hot and cold. It's no wonder he's confused.

Hell, I was confused by the way I acted just days ago.

"So what could she say or do to help alleviate those fears?" Our eyes lock on each other, and my rapid breathing echoes between us.

"She could be honest," he states, closing the gap until he's standing in front of me.

Swallowing hard, I suck in my lower lip and feel the heat from his gaze burn into my skin. He wants a real answer—not based on just the physical aspects but the emotional too—and I've never been good at that. I've struggled with who to trust and how much of myself to give to keep from getting hurt. Growing up, I had numerous friends who I thought would be my ride or dies, but they'd use me, then toss me out like trash. That emotional wall was built to help protect myself. But if anyone's capable and worthy of protecting my heart, it's Eli.

"I want *you*," I admit. "Even through the constant arguing and teasing, I've wanted you. I convinced myself it'd never happen, so I pushed you away instead, but don't think for a moment I didn't care about you or wasn't attracted to you. I was and still am."

I inhale sharply as he palms my face and brings his mouth close. Not quite touching, but just enough to feel his hot breath against my lips.

"I never want us to stop arguing or teasing each other because that means the fire is still there. We're both a little hotheaded but at the same time, down to earth and easygoing. We share a lot of common traits but have a lot of opposite interests. I'm someone who enjoys cooking, and you're someone who enjoys eating."

"So, what you mean is we're a match made in heaven?" I smile.

He plucks the pad of his thumb over my bottom lip. "Precisely."

I gulp. "Are you going to kiss me yet?"

"I was thinking about it." His deep voice rumbles low in his throat, sending vibrations between my legs.

"What are you waiting for?" I challenge, feeling more anxious with each passing second.

"To see if you're going to change your mind."

Without hesitation, I fist his sweatshirt and pull him toward me until our mouths collide.

He tilts my head back as he deepens the kiss. My arms wrap around his shoulders, and he quickly slides his hands down until he grabs my ass and lifts me off my feet. My legs go around his waist as he sets me on the island counter and settles between my thighs.

The last time we had a heated moment was on the couch, and the damn doorbell rang, interrupting what I had hoped would turn into more, but knowing he doesn't have a condom has me wondering how far we'll go.

"I still don't—"

"I know," I say, breathing heavily. "It doesn't matter. I want you."

Eli releases a deep moan, moving his mouth lower to my neck. "I agree, but not yet."

My arms drop to my sides, and I groan in frustration. "We've waited long enough," I argue. "If you add in all the years we pined over each other, it's overdue at this point."

He pulls back slightly with a mischievous grin. "When I imagined being inside you for the first time, it's not like this. Not when I've been sweating and chopping wood all morning. I want to wine and dine you first."

"Seriously? You're worried about *that*?"

"It should be romantic," he states. "And I'll try my best, considering…"

"Okay, so how much time do you need? I can be shaved and showered in an hour."

He snickers, shaking his head. "Gimme a few days."

My eyes widen in horror. "*Days?*"

"Anything worth having is worth waiting for."

"Don't get poetic on me."

He leans in and softly brushes his lips against mine. "You're even more adorable when you're sexually frustrated."

"Imagine when I'm sexually satisfied," I counter.

His whole body shakes with laughter. "The longer we wait, the better it'll be. I promise."

"I'm willing to prove that theory wrong."

"Don't challenge me, Cami. Resisting you is something I've perfected over the years. You're at level one while I'm at level fifty. You really wanna play this game?"

"Sure, let's gamble," I say confidently. "You have to resist me while I seduce the shit out of you. If you crack, and we end up in bed together, I win."

"Technically, if I give in, we both win."

I bite my lip, grinning. "But I'll have bragging rights for life."

Chapter Fourteen

ELIJAH

I'M EITHER A GENIUS OR THE BIGGEST FUCKING IDIOT IN THE WORLD FOR TELLING Cami I wanted to wait a little while longer.

Now, it's a game to her. She wants me as badly as I want her, and she's ready to do whatever it takes to make me crack.

As much as I want to give in to what I've fantasized about since we were teenagers, I'm determined to resist her.

Cami saunters around the kitchen and prepares her smoothie. I watch carefully as she puts fruit, yogurt, and milk into a blender, and when she looks over her shoulder and winks, I know it's game on. She's not gonna make this easy, no matter what I do or say.

I help clean up the counters and wipe everything down while she pours her drink into a glass. Walking into the kitchen to find her cooking for me was a nice surprise, but I actually enjoy making her food. It's the one thing I can offer that isn't about money or status.

"You have a lot of schoolwork to do today?" I ask casually with her back to me.

"Nope. Planned to take the day off, but now it looks like I'll have nothing to do." She shrugs, then takes a sip of her drink. "Any ideas what I could do?"

Fuck, she's cute when she wants something. Who knew someday it'd be *me*?

Walking up behind her, I wrap my arms around her waist and bury my head in the crook of her neck. She instantly freezes at my touch, then melts her body against mine. "You could relax for a change and watch a movie with me," I whisper. "Cuddle, you know, that sorta thing."

"Cuddle? You cuddle, huh?" She turns and faces me, and I quickly give her a peck. She sinks into me, but I stop it before things get too heated. I'm determined to keep the willpower I've controlled around her for years.

"I'm a great cuddler. You should see for yourself," I offer with a smirk. "I'll start the fire, and we can watch something together."

"Is this your way of forcing me into another weird as fuck train wreck about gay throples and tigers?"

I push back slightly until I'm leaning against the opposite corner. "Nope. I'll even let you pick. Lady's choice."

She gives me a skeptical look, sliding her straw between her plump lips, then eyes me curiously. "Anything?"

I wave out a hand. "Anything."

She ponders and then her mouth sweeps up into an evil grin. "Alright, deal. Bring the vodka and meet me in the living room."

"Vodka?" I raise my brows. "It's not even noon."

"It's time to play *my* game. You scared?" she challenges with a cheeky grin.

I chuckle. "Very."

She saunters past me, fluttering light on her feet with a booty shake, which drives me insane. My eyes lower as I take in her curves, knowing I'm only making it worse for myself.

Once I grab the bottle and shot glasses, I find her on the couch and set everything on the coffee table. Lighting the fireplace, I create the perfect atmosphere. She turns on the TV when I settle next to her.

"Well, what'd you pick?" I ask, putting my arm around her. I'm close enough to smell the sweetness of her hair.

"I'm *so* glad you asked." She smirks, and I see a bunch of twentysomethings in swimsuits. Then the trailer begins.

"What the fuck is this?" I ask at least three times within the first thirty seconds.

"Netflix's new reality dating show about personal growth and resisting temptation. Thought you'd especially be interested in it."

"Am I really supposed to believe they don't give in? This feels like a trap…"

"Oh, Eli. I'm going to enjoy this." She chuckles as the narrator begins explaining the "experiment" and how they have to abstain from kissing, sex of any kind, and masturbation, or money will be deducted from the hundred-grand prize.

"You're withholding and not even being rewarded with any money…" she taunts, resting her hand on my leg.

"Which means, I should've gone on that island because I would've won!" I gloat.

Cami shakes her head. "You just wait."

"Wow…" I say after all the participants are introduced. "So they picked the absolute most shallow people they could find on the planet, grouped them together at a beach house with nothing else to do besides sunbathe and work out, and they have to try not to jump each other's bones?"

"The goal is to form a connection that isn't based on sex."

"Precisely what I suggested we do…" I counter.

"Yes, but they all literally just met. We've known each other for a long ass time," she argues. "So…"

"But we only kissed days ago. You can't go from hating each other's guts to getting naked in a matter of days."

She turns and faces me. "You really hated my guts?"

I look at her, frowning. "Well, I've always had underlying feelings for you, but when you called me out for being poor and made me feel like I wasn't good enough for you, it was hard to like you as a person. Yet for some reason, I couldn't get you outta my head. Or my heart, apparently."

"I was an awful teenager, I know." She lowers her gaze.

I tilt her head up until her eyes meet mine again. "We fed off each other's hostility. I don't blame you. I provoked you just as much as you provoked me. There was tension because *something* was bubbling between us that neither of us understood. But I do now. The chemistry and connection, it's real. It always has been, and I'm glad we can use this time to get to know each other better."

"Yes, I agree. But we can also have some fun while doing so."

I sigh with a small chuckle. "Okay, so what are the guidelines for your drinking game?"

"Every time a couple breaks a rule, we take a shot and mimic their offense."

"You mean, do what they did?"

"Right!"

"Cami," I warn, easily seeing right through her.

"Don't worry. We don't actually see them having sex or doing anything more than touching and kissing."

"Baby, listen…I like your intentions, but I don't trust you with this one."

Her hand slides up my thigh. "Did you just call me baby?"

"Don't interpret that as me giving you the green light to jump me," I tease.

"Fine, but you can't stop me from wanting you to whisper that in my ear while you're inside me. I'm definitely gonna be imagining that very thing while I'm in the shower later."

I grab her hand and stop her from going higher. My dick is well aware of her presence and doesn't need further temptation. "You can fantasize all you want, *baby*…" I bring my mouth close to her ear. "But that's all it's gonna be for now." Pulling away, I smirk at her pouty expression.

"You won't even kiss me?"

"I'll kiss you," I tell her. "But you can't get handsy."

"We'll see. I played your stupid drinking game, so now, you gotta play mine."

"Did that girl really just admit she's ditzy?"

"She's actually one of my favorites," Cami replies. The longer this show goes on, the more I know it's going to be painful to watch.

"The rules should be to take a shot every time one of the girls flips their hair." I snort after we meet the sorority chick who flipped hers six times in thirty seconds.

"I didn't think you'd want to be hammered by the end." She chuckles.

Taking her hand from my leg, I interlock our fingers.

"David is my reality husband, by the way. He's my number one."

"Really? So he'd be your celebrity free pass?"

"Can you blame me?"

"I mean, if rock hard abs and a chiseled jawline are your thing…" I snicker.

Cami looks over at me. "You're quite comparable."

"Am I? Would I still be in the running to win your heart then?"

"Yeah. I mean…" She shrugs casually. "Probably."

"Probably?" I remark, bringing my hands to her sides and tickling her.

"Stop!" She laughs, collapsing on the couch. I tower over her, digging my fingers under her arms.

Bringing my mouth to hers, I brush it softly without quite kissing her. "That's what you get for making me watch this ridiculous show."

She pushes me until we're both sitting again. "It's payback, so deal with it."

I smirk, knowing she enjoyed that crazy documentary even if she's denying it.

"I love how everyone's in their bathing suits, showing off ninety-five percent of their bodies, and this guy waltzes in looking like Jesus."

"Just wait till he takes off the hat…"

He finally does, and I nearly choke when he reveals his bun and starts taking it down. "So that's me? I'm Jesus."

Cami laughs. "Well, I imagine there's a lot of *Oh my Gods* in bed with you."

I nearly blush, but I don't tell her that. "I might actually like that guy." Then the scene continues. "Okay, then. Never mind…" I say when Jesus claims he doesn't believe in monogamy and wants to spread his seed to as many women as possible.

"He's Jesus on the outside, but the devil on the inside." Cami chuckles.

"Okay, this show is making us dumb, and it's only been ten minutes." I groan.

"It's about the journey. You're supposed to see their growth throughout, so of course they all look like morons in the beginning."

"The best part of this is the narrator's jokes. Even she knows it's ridiculous."

"She's actually a comedian and is pretty funny. No one is there to explain to them what's going on—that we see anyway—so they'll meet their virtual host soon," she explains.

"So how long until one of them breaks the rules?"

"Keep watching..."

More time passes, and my brain cells start to dissolve. There's a dressing room where they get ready and do their hair and of course, gossip.

"What are they supposed to do all day? What are they preparing for?"

Cami glares at me, and I shrug. I thought those were valid questions...

"Did he really just say four weeks was considered a long-term relationship? Oh my God, I can't." My head falls back in agony, groaning as we continue watching. "Wait. She climbed on his lap after just meeting him. Oh shit, now they're kissing!"

"It's technically not breaking the rules because the ban hasn't started yet," Cami explains.

"Because they just arrived!" I hold out my hand. "This is absurd."

"Have you never watched a reality show before? They go from zero to sixty in an hour. That's the whole premise, and why there's so much entertainment value in trash TV."

"During this quarantine, I'm going to introduce you to *quality* entertainment. I'll do this one little game with you, but afterward, we're onto better shit."

"We'll see, we'll see..." She grins. "You might be a fan after the eighth episode."

"*Eight?*" I raise my brows. "Seriously?"

"That's how many there are total. They're only like forty-five minutes long. We can binge the whole series by dark."

Blowing out a slow breath, I brush my fingers over my jawline.

"That dude just said, 'there are plenty more days left for her to choose the right guy,' and if that wasn't my teenage brain every time I saw you with some idiot, I don't know what was." I laugh as she blushes, and soon, we're cracking up.

"So you're saying you're the one for me? The *right* one?"

"I've known forever. Just been waiting for you to catch up."

"Am I allowed to kiss you yet?" She looks at me and bites her lip.

"Not until the contestants start breaking the rules..."

She rolls her eyes, trying her hardest to be mad.

"Okay, I think I know why that girl's your favorite," I tease after a twist in the show is announced. She immediately elbows me in the rib cage, and I choke out a laugh. "If she's challenged to wash or cook, she knows she's fucked and won't win the prize money."

"Excuse you, I *did* cook this morning! For you, might I add."

I take her hand and kiss her knuckles. "And it was delicious."

The first episode finally ends, and as we get previews of the next, I know we're gonna be taking several shots.

"Should I start pouring the vodka now?"

As expected, the first rule break comes ten minutes into the show.

"Ready?" I grab the bottle, pour the liquid, then hand her one of the glasses. We clink them together before shooting it down.

Next, I grab Cami's face and capture her lips with mine. She sinks into my chest, moaning as our tongues collide. Heat builds between us as our hands slide over each other, and I feel goose bumps cover her soft skin. Cami keeps our tongues fused as she climbs over my legs and straddles me, then wraps her arms around my neck. She rocks her hips and grinds against my cock, making me harder and desperate for more.

"Cami..." I warn, pulling back slightly. "This is a bit more than what they were doing."

"Trust me, they will be soon," she quickly retorts.

I chuckle against her mouth and somehow garner enough strength to move her off me and place her back on the couch.

"You get off on telling me no, don't you?"

I eye my crotch, and her gaze follows to the noticeable erection. "That's not the case. If my dick was capable, it'd cuss me out right now."

"Whoa...that guy totally threw his chick under the bus after initiating the kiss and even saying fuck the money. What a douche."

"Those two..." She blows out an exaggerated breath. "Drive me crazy."

"The two chicks are now making out..." I shake my head. "Another rule break." We each take another shot.

"Saddle up for kiss number two."

I grab one of the pillows and put it over my crotch before she can grind against me again.

Cami chuckles as her eyes lower. "Trying to resist temptation?"

"Trying to keep myself from blowing my damn load. These people are gonna get me drunk with blue balls."

She cups my face and kisses me, sliding her tongue between my lips. Moaning at how amazing she tastes, I deepen our connection as her head falls back. My fingers thread through her hair as I pull her closer, but before things go too far, I create space as we gasp for air.

"I think I need a cold shower."

"Nope! No self-gratification per the rules."

"You're going to be the death of me, aren't you?" I inhale sharply, then exhale. I'm really trying to take things slow with Cami so I don't fuck it up, but damn, she's making me second-guess my decision.

With the episode nearly over, the show takes a turn, and I can't stop laughing at how dramatic everyone is.

For the next few hours, we continue watching, taking shots, and making out. Honestly, it's a goddamn miracle I don't tear off her clothes.

By the final episode, there were eight rule breaks, three of which were more than just kissing. One couple had sex and another almost did, but none of that is shown, other than glimpses of a blow job.

At that point, I was eight shots deep and couldn't say no as Cami kneeled between my thighs and took me in her mouth.

And as every member of the cast who broke a rule said—it was *totally* worth it.

Chapter Fifteen

CAMERON
DAY 10

It's been three grueling days of seducing Eli and him denying me before we get too far. We watched my show and played my drinking game. There was some action in between, but since then, he's insisted on an "above the waist only" rule.

He'll kiss me and lay with me on the couch no problem, but anything more and he resists.

Eli's encouraged me to watch the "classics" with him, including *Ferris Bueller's Day Off* and *Groundhog Day*—which ironically feels like what we're living in—and I had him watch a few of my favorites like *Pretty in Pink*, *Breakfast Club*, and *Sixteen Candles*. It's been nice hanging out with him and using this time to talk. I definitely feel like we've grown closer and have created a tighter bond, but now I'm ready to jump his damn bones.

Cameron: No matter what I do, Eli still says no! Even when I basically straddle his lap and grind on his cock. And trust me, he's hard!

Kendall: Did you try just walking around naked? As someone who's seen your boobs before, there's no way he'd be able to resist them.

I chuckle, knowing she has a good point. I do have awesome tits.

Cameron: I don't know. That seems too obvious. And a little chilly, honestly.

It's been in the thirties and windy.

Kendall: There's a trend on TikTok where you walk in on your man naked and record his reaction. Most don't deny the opportunity and chase after their women. It's worth a shot!

Cameron: You're right…I'm playing to win here!

Kendall: Yes, you are! Take off your clothes and go get your man!

Cameron: I'll report back!

After I get out of bed and take a shower, I slather myself with lotion and spritz body spray. I towel dry my hair and put moisturizer on my face. Wrapping myself in only a robe, I head downstairs to find him. He's probably making breakfast, and he can stare at my naked ass while I prepare his espresso.

The moment I get downstairs, I untie my robe and prepare to take it off. I'm not going to film his reaction because then he'll know something's up, but I will seduce him until he cracks.

Eli's facing the stove, and my eyes trail down his bare back and stop at his gray sweatpants that hang low on his hips.

This asshole is testing me.

There's no way he's wearing anything underneath them either. I want to tear them off with my teeth.

"Morning," he calls out, and as soon as he looks over his shoulder, I slide the robe down my arms, and it falls to my feet. He quickly does a double take and blinks.

"Good morning," I sing-song, walking closer. "What's for breakfast today?"

Staring, Eli licks his lips and studies me as I open the fridge and grab my creamer.

"Uh…thought I'd make you my famous toad in a hole dish," he answers, then blinks. "Isn't it a little…nippy to be walking around naked?"

Fuck yes, it is. "No, I'm pretty hot actually." I go to the espresso machine and make him a cup of coffee. "*Eggs in a basket* sounds great."

I feel his eyes on me as I move around, neither of us speaking as we work. He grabs two plates, and I get the forks, then we set everything on the kitchen table.

Eli places the pan of food in the middle. "Orange juice?"

"Is there still some left?" I ask.

"For one cup."

"You have it then."

"Nah. It's yours if you want it."

I arch a brow, grinning.

"The *juice*," he emphasizes.

Dammit.

"We'll share it," I say. "Half each."

"I can live with that." He taps his knuckles on the table before going to the fridge. He returns with two glasses and sets them down. Then he leans in, grips my chin, and brings our mouths together.

I moan, loving the taste of him, and wrap my arms around his waist. Pulling him closer, I feel his cock growing hard against my chest, and know I'm getting to him.

Eli grabs my wrists from behind his back and moves them away.

"I know what you're doing, and it's not gonna work."

"I'm not doing anything. I'm out of clothes and don't know how to do laundry." I bat my lashes innocently, grinning.

"Is that so?" He leans back, folding his arms.

I shrug, nonchalantly. "Yep. So it's naked central until I can find a tutorial online."

Chuckling, he shakes his head. "I just stuff all my clothes into the washer with the detergent. I don't think it's rocket science."

"Most of my clothes are dry clean only."

"You can borrow one of my T-shirts then."

"Seems you're out of them too since you're going without one." I lower my gaze down his body, admiring how delicious he looks. He even has a happy trail going from his belly button to below his sweats. God, I want him so badly.

"Nah. Just felt like giving you breakfast *and* a show." He winks with a shit-eating smirk. He knows exactly what he's doing.

"Well, I can be your dessert if you're still hungry…"

He places a finger under my jaw, then closes the gap between us. His mouth covers mine again, but he retreats too soon. "That's tempting, it really is, but my answer is still no."

I slouch back in my chair, pouting. How the hell didn't this work? I'm fucking naked, for Christ's sake!

"I'm really digging that tattoo, by the way." He waggles his brows, and I quickly cross my arms over my breasts so he stops staring. I got a little butterfly underneath my left boob for my twenty-first birthday, and only my ex, Kendall, and the tattoo artist know about it.

"Too bad you're choosing not to inspect it further," I quip.

"I can see it fine without having sex with you. But the moment I touch you, you'll be on me like white on rice. So…" He holds up his hands. "I'll just admire from afar."

I narrow my eyes. "You're only torturing yourself, you know? I hear blue balls is painful."

"They can be. That's why I'm going to take an extra-long shower this morning."

Grinding my teeth, I growl and turn in my seat. He walks to the other side of the table with a stupid grin on his face. I grab his glass of orange juice and pour it into mine, leaving his empty. Then I look at him over the rim and scowl as he holds back his laughter. I know I'm being childish, but at this point, I don't care. Eli is purposely withholding sex to make a point, but there has to be something that'll make him snap.

And I'm going to figure out what it is.

After my embarrassing naked protest at breakfast, I take my robe and bare ass back to my room and decide if he's not going to do the job, I'll do it myself.

Chanel sits on my bed, watching me. "Don't judge me." I scowl, marching to my nightstand and finding my vibrator.

I turn it on and thank God the batteries aren't dead. I brought it with me since I thought Zane and I would have lots of time to mess around. Instead, I'm single and taking care of myself. I'll get in the tub and have my own fun.

There's a knock on the door, and I smirk, hopeful Eli changed his mind.

"Yes?" I answer.

"Thought I'd bring you a shirt, ya know, in case you needed something to wear." He grins and holds it out for me.

"Thanks, that's *so* thoughtful." I grab it and flash him a pleased grin. "Can you hold this for me?" I hand over the vibrator, and he takes it, holding back his dirty comments. I put on his T-shirt, and it hangs just above my knees. "It even smells like you." I pull up the fabric to my nose and inhale.

He reveals a smug smile. "Guess that'll come in handy when you're using this." He gives the vibrator to me.

"Too bad you don't want to help me."

"I'd be happy to assist you, but I know you wouldn't play by the rules." He takes a step back, crossing his wrists over his body, and covers his crotch.

"Well, then you could watch?" I arch a brow, hoping that'll tempt him enough to break. "That's not against the rules, is it?"

He swallows hard and shakes his head. "No."

Lowering my hands, I use one to pull up the hem of the shirt and the other to turn on the vibrator, then place it over my clit. It starts humming, and I bite my lower lip, enjoying the way it feels.

"Mmm…" I purr, my eyes fluttering closed. "So good."

"Rub it in circles," he orders, his voice gravelly.

I do as he says, forming a fast rhythm. My back arches as I slide it down my slit and feel it vibrate my pussy. It feels so goddamn good, though I wish he'd take control and do it for me.

"Mmm, yes," I hum again, bringing it back to my throbbing clit. I look at Eli and see the fire in his eyes as he tries to restrain himself. Biting my lip, our eyes lock, and I grin.

"I bet you need to come, don't you?"

"Yes, badly." I click a button and increase the speed. "God, I'm so close."

My eyes slam closed, and there's no holding back as my body builds closer to the edge.

Eli takes me off guard when he pushes me deeper into the room and backs me up against the wall. His hand wraps around my throat as he closes his mouth on mine, sliding his tongue in deep and fast. I moan, releasing a satisfying breath as he lowers his other hand and takes the vibrator from my grip.

He lowers it, coating it with my juices, then slides it inside me. I gasp at the intrusion and the delicious way it fills me. Gripping his shoulders, I lean into him to stabilize myself because my knees are close to buckling beneath me.

Eli kisses down my jaw and lands on my neck, sucking hard as he thrusts the vibrator in and out.

"When I'm inside you, you'll be screaming my name, got it? Until then, you come picturing my cock in you."

"Why don't you just fuck me now then?" I challenge. "What are you waiting for?"

"You know exactly why...patience, baby."

The way his tongue rolls the word *baby* has my core tightening, and a burst of heat soars through me. I dig my nails into his skin when he slides the vibrator to my clit, bringing more pleasure between my thighs, and soon, fireworks explode throughout. Everything tightens, and I release a loud moan as another wave of pleasure shoots up my spine. My head falls back as he licks a trail up my neck, then sucks on my ear.

"Fuck, Cami," he growls, turning off the vibrator and tossing it aside. "That was the hottest fucking thing I've ever experienced." He releases a deep groan.

My entire body feels like jelly, but all I want is to climb Eli like a goddamn tree and have his hands all over me.

"It could get *a lot* hotter. You could join me in the bathtub," I offer as he slides his fingers down, cupping my breast.

"*Shit*, that's tempting..." He plucks my lower lip with the pad of his thumb. "I don't trust your wandering hands, though."

"You're the one who can't be trusted." I eye the vibrator. "I was doing just fine by myself when you took over."

"Really? Is that so?"

"Yep," I say confidently. "I have plenty of experience going solo."

He furrows his brows. "That's sad. Mr. Money Bags didn't get you off?"

"Well, truthfully, he couldn't always *find* it."

Eli steps back and glares. "You're joking, right?"

I shake my head. "Stop, this is embarrassing."

"I'm not trying to make you feel bad, Cami. You have nothing to be embarrassed about. His number-one priority as your boyfriend should've been to pleasure and satisfy you. You shouldn't have had to do it yourself if he was doing it right."

"Not all guys think that way," I defend, shrugging. It definitely wouldn't be the first time a man hasn't been able to get me off. It's why I brought it in the first place.

"There's no way you'll be needing it once I've had you, got it?" He winks, placing his hand on my cheek. "Go take your bath, enjoy one more solo session, and then know the next time you're moaning, it'll be because of me."

"Quite confident for a guy who keeps turning me down," I retort. "Join me in the tub and give me a preview of what's to come."

He contemplates it for a moment, then says, "Alright, but on one condition." He closes the space between us. "I wear my shorts, so you can't try anything." Eli flashes a smirk, knowing I would touch him if he was completely naked.

Even though I'm disappointed at his exception, I'm still happy he's agreed to come with me. "Okay, deal."

I cup Eli's neck and lower his mouth to mine, needing to taste him. As I slide my tongue over his, we frantically move toward the bathroom as he lifts his shirt off me, and I bring my hands to his waist.

"You're not wearing boxers," I tell him as I slide my fingers into his sweatpants.

He stops my hand before it can lower to his growing cock. "That's right, shit. Okay, new plan. I watch you take a bath instead."

"That doesn't sound nearly as fun," I whine.

"Oh, it'll be pure torture for me," he says, groaning. "But I like watching you. Been doing it for years."

Chapter Sixteen

ELIJAH
DAY 12

It's been two days since our little game started, and Cami's determined to push me to my limit. One thing's for sure, she's a firecracker and knows how to tease me until my cock nearly breaks off. I've never jacked off so much in my life, but when it comes to her, this isn't anything new. But fuck, she's all I can think about, and it's consuming every part of me. Truthfully, I don't know how much longer I'll be able to stay strong and tell her no. The past forty-eight hours have been pure torture as she's pranced around in lingerie she brought for her asshole ex. Honestly, I should send him a thank-you letter for letting her go because I've been given the opportunity of a lifetime—to be with the woman of my dreams.

I walk into the kitchen, where she's making an espresso. "Good morning."

She glances over her shoulder at my bulge, then back up at me. One look is all it takes from her to have my body springing to life. Just the way she commands me with her sparkling blue eyes is enough to drive me wild, and she knows it.

I move past her, and she presses her back against my chest. Wrapping my arm around her stomach, I grab her tightly, and she pushes her ass into my already raging hard-on. She gives me an evil laugh but doesn't say anything.

I brush my lips against the shell of her ear, causing her to shudder.

"You're a monster," I whisper.

Quickly, she spins around, then loops her arms behind my neck, and seconds later, I'm lifting her ass onto the countertop. "No, I'm just a woman who knows who she wants and isn't afraid to say it."

"And what do you want?" My eyebrows pop up.

"You," she confirms, and I'll never get tired of hearing it. Our kisses are white-hot as she runs her fingers through my hair, and somehow, I put space between us. "You're trying to break me."

A chuckle escapes her as I adjust myself. "No, I just want you to break *me*. There's a difference, Eli."

"You deserve more than a quick fuck." I grab a mug from the cabinet, and she jumps down from the counter and presses all the buttons for a dark roast coffee.

She groans while I wait. "Your willpower is commendable. I'll make sure to get a trophy made for you."

Now, I'm the one who's laughing. "I want it engraved."

She rolls her eyes. "Guess I'm going to have to go upstairs and have some fun with Prince Harry."

Coffee spews from my mouth as I choke it back up. "Excuse me?" I ask, wiping off my chin.

"The vibrator that got me off when you refused a couple of days ago," she explains with a shrug. "He never denies me and always *comes* through."

I grin at her and then burst into laughter. She continued her torture by taking a bath and playing with herself, knowing I was struggling the entire time and holding back. I was tempted to get in the water with her, but I didn't trust her intentions nor did I trust my self-control. She gave me one helluva show, though.

"What kind of batteries does it take, because you might wear him down."

"Triple A, I think." Immediately, Cami opens different drawers in the kitchen and checks each one. "No. No. No."

Her eyes go wide in a panic, and I shrug. I can tell her where they are kept from when I searched for the smoke detector batteries, but this is way more fun.

"Enjoy him while you can, sweetheart. Because at some point, it'll be useless. And he can't please your clit the same ways I can." I lick my lips, and she watches my mouth, which curls up into a grin. With arms crossed, she shakes her head, and I sip my espresso, smiling over the rim. When Cami huffs, I chuckle.

"Welp, going to give myself the royal treatment." She snickers with her cup of coffee held in one hand.

"Have fun," I say with a grin and wonder if she's really going upstairs to pleasure herself or if she's fucking with me. I never know with her.

Needing some fresh again, I decided to take Bruno for a walk around the property. Well, I walked. He ran around in a full sprint with his tongue hanging out. Though I tried to play with him, he was in a mood today. Anytime I'd throw a toy, he'd run after it, then refuse to give it to me, so it got old pretty quick. He's a bigger tease than Cami.

After an hour, we go inside, and I notice Cami's asleep on the couch. The news is on, and the volume is a whisper. The silk panties and bra she's wearing leave zero room to the imagination. She's giving me everything she's got with her body and smart-ass mouth. While most guys would just fuck her as quickly as possible, I'm not like that, and Cami deserves better. What we have is more than just a physical relationship, and I want her to see that too. Our hormones are raging, and I honestly can't remember the last time a woman's made me feel the way Cami has. She's the first and only.

As I stand with my arms crossed, watching her, she stirs and mutters my name. For a moment, I think she's awake and has noticed me creeping, but then I realize she's asleep, dreaming about me. A smirk touches my lips because she's saying my name with breath as soft as butterfly wings. My willpower is quickly waning, so I force myself to walk away before she catches me and wins this game, after all. I go upstairs and pace around my room, my heart racing as I think about all the ways I'd pleasure her. Remembering the soft moans and pants that escaped her and how she bit her lip as she came have me nearly busting a nut in my boxers.

It quickly becomes more than just want, and I need to relieve myself before I have to deal with blue balls again. I unzip my jeans and push my clothes down and lie on the bed.

I tightly grip my shaft and stroke it a few times, closing my eyes. Most guys use porn to get off, but Cami has given me enough in the past few days that I won't need it for a lifetime. Her name is on my lips, on my tongue, and all I want to do is taste her again and devour her sweet pussy. Fuck, just thinking about her in that bathtub pleasuring herself as she thinks about me has me increasing my pace, but I don't want to come just yet.

A few more pumps and the next thing I know, my bedroom door is being cracked open. Cami sees me, and my first instinct is to put my clothes back on, but she walks in, flashing a devilish smile. Her eyes study my dick, and she sucks in her bottom lip. Goddamn, she's so gorgeous. "Don't stop. I want to watch you, Eli," she whispers, and I brush a finger over my chin, watching her breasts rise and fall.

Cami reaches behind her back and unsnaps her bra, fully revealing her beautiful body.

Giving me the best show of my life, she pinches her nipples and moans. I stroke myself so vigorously that I have to force myself to calm down. Slowly, she moves toward me, her perfect tits bouncing as she walks.

"Cami," I let out in a deep gruff.

"Let me ride you, Eli," she taunts and looks at me with pure desire. "I'd love you inside my tight little pussy. God," she purrs, and I can tell she's getting just as worked up as I was when I watched her get off."

"We can't," I whisper, my release growing closer.

She pouts, batting her eyelashes.

"Not yet, baby." My balls tighten, and I squeeze harder, groaning.

"Mmm. That's the sexiest fucking thing I've ever seen," she tells me. "I love watching you, knowing you're thinking about me."

She squeezes her thighs together tightly, and I can just imagine how soaked her little lace panties are right now. The thought of finally sinking deep inside her nearly takes over. After a few minutes of her gaze on me, which is one of the biggest turn-ons, Cami decides she can't handle it anymore. Because she's the type of woman who always gets what she wants, she moves forward and climbs on the bed.

"Let me help you at least," she insists. I remove my hand, and she takes over. She rubs the pad of her thumb across the top, then a second later, her hot mouth is on me, and I don't have the willpower to make her stop. It feels so fucking good that I've lost my ability to speak.

"Cami," I growl. She looks up at me with big blue eyes, humming. "Fuck, your mouth feels so goddamn good," I admit, running my fingers through her hair.

She slides her hand over my shaft as she takes all of me. When my dick touches the back of her throat, she gags but keeps going. Watching her choke on my erection is hot as fuck as her head bobs up and down. I don't know how much longer I'll be able to last as she trails her tongue down to the base, then sucks and licks my balls. She's gentle but also forceful in her own way, letting me know she's in control right now. And fuck, I don't even care. The woman is a savage and doesn't leave an inch untouched as she gives me the royal treatment. Right now, I feel like a fucking king with her mouth all over me.

My eyes roll back, and while I didn't want to cross the line like this, I have no regrets. I let out an animalistic groan as she increases the pace and pressure. Before I explode, she stops with a naughty smirk.

"Good enough?" She looks up at me with a popped eyebrow, casually flicking her tongue against me, making everything overly sensitive.

Leaning closer, I grin, already missing her mouth on me, but I don't tell her that. "Sure. I'll finish," I say, shrugging.

As I lower my hand, Cami laughs and pushes me away, then places her sweet lips back where they belong.

"Not a chance in hell. This cock is mine now, Eli. Remember that." She goes slow, which is fucking agonizing. The orgasm builds in the pit of my stomach as she devours me. Cami is a goddamn fucking pro and deserves a gold medal because she's the best I've ever had. Perhaps it's the fact that my feelings for her are more intense than I've ever had before, but everything is a hundred times better with her.

I fist the comforter as electricity shoots up my spine. She feasts on me, and I can't take it any longer and release inside her. Cami swallows with a satisfying hum, and a huge fucking smile on her face. She licks me clean, devouring every single drop like it's candy.

"You taste so good, Eli," she whispers, not taking her eyes off me. She moans with satisfaction, and I can tell she wants me. All of me. More than what she just had. God, I want to fuck her into next week, next month, next *year*.

"Thank you," I say. She gives me a seductive wink, and I don't know how any man could leave her. My sweet, seductive, sassy Cami is the whole fucking package.

Cami continues up the bed until her mouth presses against mine. "So fucking hot," she tells me, and I can't resist touching her soft skin. My palm goes straight to her pebbled nipple. Her head falls back on her shoulders, and I slide my mouth to her neck until I'm at her ear.

"Let me repay you," I whisper, and she moves away, searching my face with a grin.

"What did you have in mind?"

I love it when she's playful like this.

Rolling her off me, I slip my hand into her panties and move my fingers across her needy clit. Her body instantly reacts, and when I slide inside her pussy, she squeals and arches her back.

"Baby," I whisper as her mouth crashes against mine. "You're so fucking wet," I say between bated breaths.

"Your touch…" she says, trailing off, leaning against the pillows. "It's fucking magical."

Adding another finger inside her tight little cunt, I watch her eyes flutter closed as she sinks into me. "Make me come, Eli. I need it badly."

I love her demanding tone and that she knows exactly what she wants. With all my strength, I rip the panties off her body, and they snap in a second. She lets out a small grunt and then grins as I tuck them under my pillow as a keepsake. My mouth captures her nipple, and I palm the other while thrusting two fingers inside her hot body and rubbing circles with the pad of my thumb against her clit. The way she reacts to my touch has me wanting to come again.

She grinds against me, and I know she needs to come, but I want to put her through the same agony she put me through, so I dramatically slow to a snail's pace. Her chest rises and falls so quickly that it's obvious she's dangling on the edge.

"Eli," she pants, wrapping her hand around my neck. "Eli. *Please*."

I close the gap between us and kiss her, twirling my tongue with hers. Within just a few minutes of continuing to work her clit precisely the way she loves, her back arches, and every muscle in her body tightens as she sucks in a breath. She moans my name as she relaxes against me, and it's the sweetest fucking sound I've ever heard.

Once I pull away and lie on my back next to her, she rolls over on her side and leans up on an elbow. I can see the pulse in her neck, continuing to race, and I grin at how happy and sated she looks.

"Damn…" She chuckles before her head drops to the pillow. I bow my head down and kiss her forehead.

"Better than Prince Harry?" I quip.

"Oh yeah. He's been fired."

I laugh, cupping her cheek. "That was just the warm-up." I wink.

She laughs and perks up. "So, are you gonna fuck me now?"

"Soon."

With a groan, she playfully smacks my chest, and I capture her wrist, then bring my lips to her knuckles. "Patience."

One side of her lip curls up in disagreement. "You're insufferable."

I gently sweep away pieces of hair that fell into her face. She's even more beautiful when she looks at me with lust in her eyes. It makes it even harder to deny her.

"Now you know what you've been missing out on," I tease.

"Had I known, I would've jumped you in high school."

I snort, shaking my head. "Nah. It's been worth the wait."

Her eyes are sad for a moment, but she quickly smiles. "So what does that mean for us now?"

I lean forward and kiss her, loving how candid we are with each other. "Marriage and babies," I tell her confidently.

Her eyes widen in panic but then quickly soften. "If the sex is as good as your foreplay, *I* might be the one proposing."

"That's a deal," I say. "One I'd take any day of the week."

Chapter Seventeen

CAMERON
DAY 14

Teasing and tempting Eli the past two days has been intense, but I have to give it to him for staying strong. Today, we ate breakfast together then went our separate ways because we're both overwhelmed with school and work. Before I went upstairs, I made an espresso but have a feeling I'll need four more because I'm dragging ass. I have a pile of reading assignments and two papers to write, and Eli has meetings scheduled with clients until dark. Everything has piled up, and now I'm stressing to get it all completed on time.

We make plans to have dinner around seven, so until then, I'll be forcing myself to finish my assignments. Once I'm upstairs, I open my laptop and set it on the desk that faces the window with the best mountain view. I grab a notebook and make a task list, then figure out what will be the easiest way to accomplish it all. After I have some sort of a roadmap, I get started.

I groan when I realize I have to write a three-thousand-word paper on how to drive topline growth for large companies. It wouldn't be acceptable to tell my professors my father has an entire department to handle all of this. So instead, I pull up my digital marketing book and use some common sense, but it'll take me hours to finish this. Right now, I want to cry into my coffee. Instead, I take a sip and stare outside.

When I close my eyes, I replay the last time Eli and I fooled around. I lean back in my chair and a smile plays on my lips as I remember tasting him. I decide to text Kendall, because the girl needs an update, buts as if she knew I was thinking about her, she texts me first.

Kendall: Sex update, please! I'm living vicariously through you.

Cameron: He's determined to wait! Nothing, and I mean NOTHING has convinced him otherwise.

Kendall: Are you sure he's not gay? You're hot. There's no way he can say no to that ass of yours.

I snort-laugh.

Cameron: I have to hand it to him, though. His willpower is iron tough. I think he just wants it to be natural, not forced in any way, which I get. But still…I'm going crazy!

Kendall: That's respectable. At least you know he's not using you, so that's a plus. Sorry, my friend. Hopefully, Prince Harry can keep you company in the meantime ;) How's the online schoolwork going?

Cameron: If the batteries don't die. LOL! I'm at the point in the semester where I understand why people pay their smarter classmates to do their assignments. I have so many to do. I feel like I'm drowning. Not to mention, I'm a little mentally drained from everything going on, so it's hard to focus on it like before this all happened.

Groaning, I want to bang my head against the desk.

Kendall: Yikes. Sorry. That sucks, but just think, it's almost over, and then you'll have your degree!

Cameron: I know. Send help. And vodka. Oh, and triple A batteries.

Kendall: Haha! Next week, when you're caught up, let's have a video chat happy hour, please. My wine subscription box was delivered, and I'm bored as hell.
Cameron: Deal! Count me in!

I glance at the clock and tell Kendall I'll chat with her later because I need to get back to writing. Every word is painful, but after a grueling three hours, I finish. After a quick bathroom break, I run downstairs and grab some water, and see Eli sitting at the table looking all sexy in a button-up shirt with his hair up wearing headphones. He must be having a meeting with his colleagues because he talks about negotiations for the seller and improving online listings. Damn, he sounds so smart when he talks about sales contracts and contingencies, all which go over my head. Instead of eavesdropping anymore, I make double shots of espresso for both of us. When I deliver it to him, Eli mouths a thank you and shoots me a wink, then goes back to his conference.

As I climb the stairs, my heart races thinking about him. Honestly, he could probably write the second paper I have based on his real-world experience.

When I walk inside my room, I find Chanel lying on my chair. I pick her up and move her to the bed. She bitches with an annoyed meow, then resettles in a different spot. Her attitude makes me chuckle.

For the rest of the afternoon, I sluggishly work through my assignments, and after a while, I need a pick-me-up. I decide to hop in the shower because the hot water typically relaxes me enough to refocus.

After I dry off, I slip on a matching bra and panties set and a slinky sundress that's cute, but comfortable enough to lounge around in. When I go back to my laptop, I write the last five pages and feel so damn accomplished when it's finally done. I suck in a deep breath and glance over the screen. The sunset hangs lazily on the horizon behind the trees and mountains. Soon it will disappear, and darkness will fall. I take a moment to admire and memorize how beautiful it is. It's so different from the city views I'm used to seeing. The only thing that breaks my thoughts is my stomach growling. I check the time and see it's nearly seven. I can't believe I completely lost track of time.

After quickly brushing my fingers through my hair, I leave my room, but when I do, I see a note taped to the outside of my door. Confused, I tear it off and open it.

Cami—it's time to play a game. Follow the clues until you find me. I have a surprise.

I grin so wide my face hurts. Farther down on the paper is the first clue.

If you can't stand the heat, get out of the kitchen.
Preparing gourmet meals will have you bitching.
Open me up and have a look,
Don't worry, baby. You don't have to cook.

A chuckle escapes me, and I feel giddy. This is so unexpected and sweet. I walk downstairs, then go to the fridge and look around. Nothing. Opening the microwave, I find it's empty too. I stop and think a little harder. That's when I see the oven and notice the light is on. Inside is a tray with another slip of paper, and I hurry and unfold it.

There are only three more clues left.
So you must do your very best.
Open me up and climb inside.
I can't wait for you to take me for a ride.

I reread the clue, confused, so I repeat it out loud. The only thing I can think of is my Range Rover. Curious to see if I'm right, I head to the garage. Once I'm there, images of Eli having his asthma attack fill my mind, but I push them away as I open the passenger door. On the seat is a letter, and I snatch it, then go back inside.

Very good. You're so damn smart.
If you allow it, I'll give you my heart.
Screw me in tight, so again you don't fall.
This should be the easiest clue of them all.

"Bastard," I huff with a chuckle and walk upstairs. Somehow, he ran up to the third story while I was in the garage because I took a shower earlier and didn't see anything then. Sneaky and witty all at the same time. The note is on the back of the toilet. I laugh, remembering my ass being on the floor when the seat broke and how he came to my rescue.

I want to hold you in my arms all night.
Even after we argue and fight.
Don't worry. This hunt is almost over.
Sit down, bring some popcorn, and get your closure.

I know exactly where he is. Smoothing down my hair, I take a quick glimpse at myself in the mirror and stack all the clues on my vanity. With a permanent smile on my face, I go to the lower level, walk down a hallway, then open the door to the theater room. He's moved the seats against the walls and set up a small table with chairs to create a romantic dining area. The gigantic screen has a night sky scene playing, and the sounds of summer surround me in the low-lit room. My mouth falls open, and I see him standing with his hands tucked in his suit pockets, grinning.

"You found me," he says as I walk over to him. He hands me some paper flowers with a ribbon tied around them. Taking them, I look around the room and am overcome with emotions and shock.

"Of course I found you," I say, beaming. "How did you get…" I can't even finish my words or thoughts. I'm stunned, wondering how he got all of this together in a few hours, considering he had so much work to complete. Glancing down, I see how much care he put into each stem and petal. It's the most beautiful bouquet anyone has ever given me, and best of all, it'll last forever.

Eli places his fingers under my chin and forces me to look into his emerald green eyes. "It took some planning."

A few tears stream down my cheeks because no man has ever done anything so special for me before. Eli leans in and kisses my tears away. "What's wrong? Everything okay?"

I wrap my arms around his waist. "I'm just overwhelmed with happiness. This is all so perfect and thoughtful. Incredibly sweet. I'm just…I don't deserve all this."

"You do and more. But wait until you see what I cooked." He chuckles, and I notice how good he looks, and damn, I'm ready to undress him with my teeth.

Grabbing my hand, he walks me over to the table and uncovers two large bowls. A plate in the middle is stacked full of homemade-looking crackers, and my stomach is screaming out in protest because it smells so good, and I'm starving.

"Lobster bisque with bread crisps," he says.

"Eli," I whisper. "It smells so good."

Pulling the chair from under the table, he motions for me to sit. We might still be in the cabin but sitting under the fake stars and listening to the sounds of crickets lightly chirp is one of the most romantic dates I've ever had. This is everything I ever dreamed of, more than I expected, and I'm not worthy of this.

He fills two glasses full of wine, and I take a sip, grinning over the rim. I pick up the spoon and taste the bisque. "Yep, pretty sure I just died. This is so good." When did he make this, and how did I not smell it? The man is a pro at being stealthy.

Eli licks his lips. "I'll teach you how to make it one day."

I nearly spew out my wine. "With my current record, we better start with ramen."

"I was worried my clues might be too hard," he says with a chuckle. "I forgot how much shit I remembered over the years."

"The kitchen one got me for a second until I saw the oven light, but honestly it was the most thoughtful thing anyone's ever done for me," I admit, my temperature rising at the intensity that streams between us as he studies me. I'm nervous and unworthy of the man sitting in front of me.

"Well, there's a lot more where that came from, baby."

I chuckle at his playful wink. "I swear I'm living in a Hallmark movie right now." I bite my bottom lip, and he smirks.

"Well, there'll be no fade to black tonight." His voice is velvety smooth, and his confidence is sexy as hell. Is tonight finally the night? Butterflies flutter in my stomach, and my heart pounds at his words.

I down my wine. I'm already feeling it swarm through my body, or maybe it's Eli who's making me feel that way.

Our dinner is delicious. We talk and laugh, and everything between us feels natural and perfect. We finish eating, and I pour the rest of the wine that's left into my glass. He opens another bottle and fills his too.

"I want to dance with you," I tell him.

Eli chuckles and stands. He grabs the remote to the sound system and randomly finds a song. It's an old classic that's played at weddings—Nat King Cole's "Unforgettable." I somewhat stumble getting up, but he's by my side in a second to steady me.

Wrapping my arms around his neck, he pulls me to him, and we slowly move together. All of my exes hated dancing at the events I dragged them to and acted like it was a huge inconvenience. But not with Eli. The song ends, and another begins, and he holds me closer as if I'll slip through his fingers. I lean my head against his chest, and we sway together in harmony.

When I step back and smile, Eli's eyes are locked on me. Seductive and sexy. He dips his head down, and our mouths connect in a feverish kiss, the passion sizzling when our tongues twist. I moan against him and fist his shirt. I need Eli. He groans, and I need him right now, and I don't have to say it because he knows.

We grow greedier, more desperate, and soon, my back presses against the wall as Eli's muscular body leans into me. His touch is light and warm against my skin like a summer breeze.

"Cami, fuck," he growls, standing inches from me as his hand trails up my thighs. Eli lifts my dress, then slides my panties down to my ankles, and I step out of them. I've wanted him since the moment I saw him tonight, and the last hour was grueling as I waited in anticipation. With steady fingers, he rubs my clit, and my knees nearly buckle from how goddamn good it feels. My eyes flutter closed, and I whisper his name like a prayer, knowing it won't be long before he pushes me over the edge.

Eli has my body memorized like his favorite song, and when he gives me not one finger but two, I wrap my arms around his shoulders. His hardness presses into my stomach, and my pussy aches for all of him.

"Come for me, baby," he demands, his voice full of rasp. I hope the wall holds me up as I see stars. Moans escape me as the orgasm rips through my body. Eli wraps an arm around my waist, steadying me because the intensity nearly brings me to my knees. My breasts fall and rise as I pant, licking my lips and smiling up at him.

He places his fingers in his mouth, tasting me, then smirks. "And to think, I'd almost forgotten about dessert."

Chapter Eighteen

ELIJAH

Cami looks up at me with hooded, lust-filled eyes. Our night is just getting started, and I can't wait to give her everything she wants and deserves.

"That was one. How about we go for five?" I ask with a wink.

She raises her eyebrows. "Five? Are you trying to kill me?"

"You just wait, baby," I quip, smacking her ass, then bending over to pick up her panties. She grabs them from me and wraps them around my neck, then pulls me closer. Our mouths crash together in a hot, needy exchange, and when we finally come up for air, I interlock my fingers with hers, leading her out of the theater. Tonight, I'll please her in ways she's never experienced and will prove to her what she's been missing.

When we make it to the staircase, she can't keep her mouth or hands off me, and we nearly fall trying to get to the second floor. The wine doesn't help steady either of us, but I'll be damned if that stops me.

"Fuck, Cami," I say as I lift her and carry her to the third level, claiming her as my prize. She holds onto me, laughing as I take the stairs two at a time. Once we reach her bedroom, I carefully kick open the door, then set her on the floor. Gracefully, she takes a step back and watches as I undo each button of my shirt.

"Mmm, dinner, dessert, and a show? You spoil me," she murmurs with a grin, tilting her head to one side and admiring her view.

My shirt falls to the floor, and I move closer to her. Cami greedily unbuttons my slacks and pushes them down with my boxers, then I toss them aside. She kneels in front of me as she grabs my cock and strokes it in her palm.

I groan. Her grip feels so damn incredible.

She smacks her lips before wrapping them around the tip and sliding her mouth down my cock. I grunt, twisting my fingers in her hair and guiding her up and down my shaft. Her hot breath feels amazing, but if she doesn't slow down, I'm going to embarrass myself and come too quickly.

"Get back up here," I demand.

"I need you so fucking bad," she says breathily. "I'm done waiting."

"That's the understatement of the decade," I say, then lift the thin material of her dress from her small frame. She raises her arms, allowing me to pull it off her. I step back slightly and admire how stunning she is. Cami is a goddamn vision.

Wrapping my arms around her, I undo her bra, and her breasts spill out, giving me the perfect view. I study every part of her, taking a mental snapshot. My fingertips brush across the softness of her collarbone as I dip down and capture her taut nipple in my mouth. Her eyes flutter closed as she arches her back, and I want to ravage her sweet pussy again.

She walks backward, pulling me on top of her as she falls to the mattress. I hover over her as our mouths fuse, our hands all over each other. The sparks fly between us so violently that if I don't slow us down, we might get burned. She's hungry for me, and I've fantasized about this moment so many times, I almost pinch myself to make sure I'm not dreaming. But as Cami peers up at me with her big baby blues, nothing in my entire life has ever felt this real.

"Okay, then. This was fun," I joke, pushing against the bed and pretending to leave.

"Elijah Ross, I swear, you better fuck me like you mean it." She locks her legs around me, pulling me back down.

I laugh, but I won't be *fucking* her. Instead, I'll be worshipping every inch of her, hoping she understands how much she means to me and how hard I'm falling for her.

"On one condition," I say.

She frowns and narrows her eyes at me. "Are you serious?"

"Admit I won," I mock with a smirk, knowing she's gonna be pissed she didn't get her way for once. "I won our bet, and you lost." I bury my nose in the nape of her neck, and she wiggles beneath me, and I pull away, wanting to see her expression.

A sly smile spreads across her plump lips. "There are only winners here, but I guess I'll order you that trophy after all," she concedes, giggling. When I look down at her again, she lifts and gives me a chaste kiss.

I nibble on her ear, and whisper, "You are my trophy. Best prize I've ever had."

"Then claim me as yours already," she purrs.

While she wants me now, I prefer to take my time exploring and cherishing her body. When my fingers brush against her cheek, her pulse quickens. Cami's eyes drift closed, and her breath quickens as I feather kisses along her jawbone, neck, and down to her breasts. I give each one equal attention before sliding down her stomach and burying myself between her legs.

She's a greedy little thing and wants more. Tasting her again is all the motivation I need to devour her as if she's my last meal. I increase my pressure and pace until she yells my name with sweet agony. Her back arches, but I keep going. I slide my palms under her ass cheeks and squeeze as I sink my tongue deeper inside her tight cunt.

"Mmm, Eli. Oh my..." She doesn't finish her thoughts because I place two fingers into her glorious pussy and one in her ass. Her eyes pop open, and she gasps at the intrusion.

"Trust me," I whisper, filling her as I lightly flick and tease her clit with my tongue.

"I do," she says softly, relaxing against me.

"Mmm," I hum when I glance up and see Cami pinching her nipples. I add more pressure as her moans become more guttural.

"Eli," she gasps, and I continue finger fucking her, allowing the orgasm to build until it steals her breath away. It doesn't take long before every muscle in her body tightens, and I want to be the best she's ever had. As I watch her, it's almost as if she's about to be suspended in air, and then the release takes hold.

I kiss her inner thighs as her body seizes, then look up at her.

"Wow. Damn. That was...intense as hell," she says, coming down from her high and looking at me with satisfaction. I kneel between her legs, watching her bite her lip as she cups her breast. My cock is so goddamn hard as I lean in closer and play in her wetness, sliding my tip up and down.

"Eli," she whispers desperately. "I need you inside me."

"Don't you know the magic word is please?" I tease. In a blink, her arms loop around my neck, and she pulls me on top of her.

"*Now*," she demands, slamming her mouth to mine.

"Did you forget who's in control here?" I taunt. Kissing my way back down her body, I then shift back to my knees, spreading her legs wider.

"If I say you are, then will you *please* fuck me?" she says sweetly.

I smirk, then glance down at my bare dick.

I've never not used protection. I know it's going to be mind-blowing because it's with

Cami, but to feel her without nothing between us has me eager to fuck her raw like she's begging.

"Good girl." I waggle my brows, amused by how desperate she sounds.

I hover above her, then slowly slide inside inch by inch. There's silence except for the sounds of our shallow breaths as she adjusts to my size and takes all of me. She's so damn tight and warm, and I groan as I lift her hips to rock against me.

Cami grins as she wraps her legs around my waist, and our steady movements create an intense buildup. We escape in each other's eager lips, experiencing intimacy on a higher level than ever before. I nuzzle her neck, smelling her skin and hair, getting caught up in the emotions that swarm through me.

"It's never felt like this before," I admit, my voice a breathless whisper as I rest my forehead against hers.

"Me either. It's so good," she says with desperation in her tone. She has all of me but demands more. "Harder, Eli. I won't break."

Her confidence makes me grin, and I lift one of her thighs, then place it on my shoulder. I slide deeper, then thrust with more power than before. She gasps and drags her nails down my back as her head falls back.

"Yes, just like that. Oh my God," she cries.

"Fuck, I'm not gonna last as long as I want if you keep making those little whimpers," I tell her before crashing my mouth to hers.

"I can't help it." She chuckles softly.

Brushing my fingers over her soft skin, I cup her breast and squeeze. She brings her hands to my head and removes the ponytail, my hair falling down against my face.

"You look so sexy with your hair like this," she says, playing with my strands. "Then again, I love when you pull it up too."

"Yeah, it's a chick magnet," I tease.

"Shut up." She giggles. "No chicks better be touching or even looking at my man."

"Hearing you say that is hot as hell," I admit, lowering until I capture her lip between my teeth.

As we make love, our ragged breaths fill the silent space.

I pick up my pace, pounding faster and causing her glorious tits to bounce. We're needy and moan together, a melodic sound of audible emotions.

"Damn, baby," I groan. "You feel so good. I could stay here all goddamn night."

"Yes, yes, yes," she repeats. As the intensity builds and our releases threaten to take hold, she tugs my hair.

"Come inside me," she urges.

I pant, my heartbeat in my ears. "Cami, that's risky."

"I'm on the pill," she reassures me. "I've…never shared that with anyone before. I want it to be you, Eli."

My mouth goes dry, and I know if I continue pumping into her, I won't pull out fast enough. However, the thought of Cami pregnant with my baby has me wanting to lose all control.

With my arms on each side of her, I hold myself above her petite frame. I move my face closer to hers, twisting my tongue with hers as I ram my cock inside her tight little cunt.

Her pants quicken, and when her body seizes again, she demands I fuck her. Deep in the pit of my stomach, I feel the build. I move upright and pull her thighs toward me, ramming harder like she wants. Cami studies me, and my vision blurs as I spill inside her, releasing deep groans as the orgasm takes over. As I try to inhale, I lean down, and we exchange a searing-hot kiss.

"Wow," she blows out, satisfied, tucking her bottom lip into her mouth.

I give her a wink and then help clean her up, both of us unable to stop touching each other.

Afterward, we lie together and stare up at the ceiling. Eventually, Cami and I move to face each other. I reach over and push her hair behind her ear. I notice her cheeks are rosy red, and her lips are swollen.

"I'm speechless," she finally says, staring like she's scared I'll disappear if she blinks. "And you know how rare that is for me. I feel like we just did this soul-bonding ritual like in those fantasy books."

Laughter escapes me. "You're so fucking cute," I admit, and she leans forward and captures my mouth. I deepen the kiss, and she moans against me.

"It was intense," I admit, trying to make sense of what I'm feeling. I want to tell her how much I love her, how much I've always loved her, but I also don't want to say those words too soon and scare her away. So I keep them to myself, but I think she feels it too.

We make out like ravenous teenagers making up for lost time. When I finally pull away, we're both breathless. "Take a break, because I'm ready for more of you." She glances down at my cock.

"Are you gonna name him too?" I ask, referencing to how she named her vibrator. I place my hands behind my head and grin.

She scrunches her nose, thinking hard. "Maybe. Hmm. Zeus? That sounds like a name for something big and mighty."

A roar of a laugh escapes me. "Oh really? You're too good for my ego."

Wrapping my arm around her, I pull her close to my body, and she lays her head against my chest and listens to my heartbeat. "Do you have any idea how long I've waited to be with you like this?"

"Do you know how long *I've* waited?" she counters.

"A week?" I ask.

"Wrong," she states, peeking up at me. "You're so wrong, and you don't even know."

The words are like music to my ears as she shifts, then straddles me. She grabs my cock that's still hard, then takes every inch of me again, rocking her hips as I grip her waist. Her head falls back on her shoulders, and she takes full control. This is the Cami I love, the one who knows what she wants and takes it without apology.

With her name on my lips, I dig my thumbs into her skin, driving into her. Cami rides me until we're close to the edge, then soon we're spilling over.

"Four," she screams out as we both chase our high. She runs her fingernails down my rib cage and mixes pleasure with pain. Cami paints her mouth across mine while we're still connected, fully satiated.

"One more to go," I tell her with a smug smile.

"I'm numb from the waist down."

"Then you better hold on." Swiftly, I grab her waist and flip her on her back, then rub my fingers over her clit. It's swollen, and I can tell it's sensitive.

"Holy shit," Cami mutters as her eyes roll to the back of her head. It's only another couple of minutes until she's digging her nails in my arm and exploding in relief.

After cleaning up for the second time, I fall asleep with a smile on my face and Cami in my arms.

I've imagined what it would be like being with her, but none of those fantasies even compare to reality.

Not in a million fucking years.

Chapter Nineteen

CAMERON
DAY 15

I WAKE UP WITH SWEAT COVERING MY FOREHEAD, AND MY BODY FEELS LIKE IT MIGHT be on fire. Eli's legs tangle with mine, and I try to wiggle out of his hold. Drinking too much last night has made me feel like shit. As soon as I sit up, I know something isn't right. It's not the first time I've had stupid amounts of alcohol, but this seems different. I wobble when I place my feet on the floor, and I find some strength to move forward. My chest is tight, and I wonder if I slept weird or if our sexual activities last night did a number on me, but I've never felt this way before. On repeat, I tell myself I'm just hungover. That's all this is.

I walk to the bathroom and slip on a robe when I start shivering and coughing.

"Cami," Eli mumbles from the bed in a sexy morning rasp.

"In here," I respond. My voice sounds different, and it burns when I swallow. "In the bathroom," I say louder, but my throat is scratchy, which isn't typical for me after a night of drinking.

Footsteps lightly sweep across the floor, and he opens the door wearing loose hanging sweatpants and notices me leaning over the sink. When I meet his eyes, they go wide.

"Are you okay?" he asks, concern coating his tone.

I choke down my fear of being sick and push my hair out of my face. "I think I drank too much."

"Do you have a fever?" he asks.

I bring my palm to my forehead and shrug.

"Where's your thermometer? We need to check your temp."

I point at the cabinet between us. He comes closer, grabs it, then hands it to me. I look down at the digital stick in my hand, turn it on, and place it under my tongue. Moments later, it beeps, and when I see the result, I want to cry.

"What does it say?" Eli searches my face, but he knows by my expression that it's not good news.

I create distance as tears build in my eyes. I shake my head, trying to comprehend what this means.

"Cami? What's it say?" he repeats, his voice deep and cautious. He knows something's wrong. We both do.

I look over at him, and when he steps toward me, I hold out my hand to stop him from coming any closer. "It's 101.6. Stay back, please. If I'm sick, you're at a higher risk of hospitalization if you catch it."

Those aren't the words I want to say after the amazing night we shared. Images of his mouth and hands on my body flash through my head, and I replay all the times we kissed. If Eli gets it from me, it could kill him, and I wouldn't be able to live with myself. We've been isolated together for two weeks, which means I've been a carrier since I arrived.

Disregarding my pleas, he takes two steps forward. His voice softens. "No, let me take care of you."

"Please," I beg again. "Being near me is too dangerous with your asthma," I remind him. The episode he had a week ago is still fresh in my mind. It was traumatizing to watch him struggle to breathe.

"You don't know what you have, though. It could be anything. It's flu season, too." He tries to calm me, but it doesn't work. My gut screams that I'm not that lucky, and that this isn't something I'll get over in a few days. I was around hundreds of people before the shelter in place was ordered. People who were asymptomatic continued going to class because no one knew how bad it was until it was too late.

"A fever this high is enough warning. For your sake, we have to treat it like the worst-case scenario to be on the safe side." I choke back a sob, then turn on the faucet, holding a washcloth under the cool stream. "I'll be okay," I say more to comfort myself than him. Eli stares as I wring out the water.

"If you really have it, then so do I. It's a little too late to think I haven't caught it." He shrugs as if it's no big deal. "We kissed on the second day here and have been around each other every day since then. We'd be foolish to think otherwise."

I relentlessly shake my head in disagreement. "No, that's not one hundred percent true. We don't know, so we have to take every precaution possible."

"I'll text your brother and see if he has any advice so we can be more prepared in the coming days. He might have a few tips and tricks or something, but let me help you, Cami." He's nearly begging, and I'm not sure I'm strong enough to push him away when I just want him to hold me.

"Eli," I whisper. Panic and unease swim through my veins as my chest rattles. The morning after such an amazing night isn't supposed to be like this. I wish we could have breakfast together, spend the rest of the day snuggling, and relive last night. Instead, I have to force him to leave me alone.

He exits the bathroom, and for a second, I think I may have gotten through to him. Moments later, he returns with Tylenol and two bottles of water. He sets them on the nightstand and glances at me. "You can't get dehydrated. Take these and text me if you need anything, okay? Anything at all, even if it's just to keep you company. And if you get any worse, let me know."

I nod, wanting to lie down and cover myself with a pile of blankets. "I will. Thank you."

Once he's out of the room, I grab the thermometer and place it on the bedside table, then take the pills. The sheets are a crumpled mess at the end of the bed from rassling in them last night, and I try to fix them the best I can, but my head is too heavy. I'm scared of what the future holds, more than I've ever been before. I know Eli said he'd text Ryan, but I text him too.

Cameron: I think I have the virus. What should I do?

I don't expect him to answer me anytime soon. Having a conversation with him the past couple of weeks has been difficult. My brother's a goddamn hero, but I selfishly wish he were here with me.

Somehow, even though I'm restless, I fall asleep. My skin sticks to the sheets, but I'm cold, so I stay covered. Fever dreams capture me, and I wake up in a panic with a racing heart. I should let my parents know what's going on, but I also don't want to worry them. My mother gets irrational when it comes to her children. Considering my brother is on the front lines of this war against the illness, she's got enough on her emotional plate to deal with. But if I end up hospitalized, the guilt of not speaking up would consume me. Before I call, I take my temperature again. As I suspected, it hasn't changed.

She answers, and I know she's smiling by how upbeat she is. "Hey, sweetie. Why didn't you FaceTime me?"

I inhale a deep breath, trying to find the strength to speak. "Mom."

"Yes, dear?"

"I have a fever and feel like death. I'm terrified." My voice trembles as I try to swallow down my fear. I don't care that I'm twenty-two and nearly crying. Sometimes, I just want my mom to comfort me and say everything will be okay.

"How high is it?" The concern in her question is clear.

"When I just checked, it was 101," I say with a small cough. "I was fine yesterday, but woke up like this," I explain.

She lets out a fearful sigh. "Can you get tested so you know for sure?"

"They're not testing people like me with no pre-existing conditions who're young and healthy. Only if they have to be admitted. They'll instruct me to stay home, take Tylenol, and if things get worse, call the helpline," I repeat what I read online a few days ago, then take a sip of water.

"Did you call Ryan?" Mom asks, alarmed. "Maybe he can get you one?"

"I texted him, but he's swamped, so I don't know when I'll hear back. He'll say the same, though. I've watched the news, read all the articles, and am aware of what the process is right now." The line is silent for a while. "Hello?"

"Yes, I'm still here. I'm extremely worried about you. If you would've listened, you'd be with me so I can take care of you. I'd call the family doctor to do a house visit, and he'd get you tested."

This isn't the time for her to power play me or use our family's money to get special treatment. I'm not labeled high risk and would feel guilty when thousands of other people are being denied. "No, if I would've stayed home, you'd be sick too. Me being at the cabin is for the best for you and Daddy." I try to ease her mind, but it's no good. She'll lose sleep over this regardless of what I say.

"Promise me if your temp rises or you have trouble breathing, you'll go to the ER. The nearest hospital is only a half an hour away from you."

"Okay, Mom," I concede.

"Cameron," she pushes, not satisfied with my response. "If I need to drive there, I will."

"That's unnecessary. The entire place needs to be disinfected. I'll go if things get worse. Eli is here and will check on me, too," I reassure her, hoping to ease her nerves. We've been FaceTiming or texting every couple of days since I've arrived and when I told her Eli was here too, she had a gleaming look in her eye. She adores him.

"I should be with you," she argues with a huff.

"No, you shouldn't. Please, just stay put," I demand. "Being around me is too dangerous."

She sighs again. "Cameron, I love you. I just want you to be healthy."

"I know, Mom. I love you and Dad too. I should let you go, though, so I can rest," I say calmly, wishing it would rub off on her.

"I'll send your love. Please keep me updated," she orders, and I agree before ending the call and going to the bathroom.

I take a shower, hoping it settles my nerves. As the water runs over my body, I lean against the wall. It's almost too hot, but I breathe in the steam and flower-scented body wash. After a while, I slip on a fluffy robe and wrap a towel around my head.

As I'm walking into the bedroom, I hear a tap on the door. "Cami?"

"Yes?" I ask, going to the edge of the bed.

"I brought you something to eat. It's on a tray on a small table I moved into the hallway," he says.

I blink away tears at his sweet gesture. "Thank you."

"Are you feeling any better?"

I look down at my pruned hands. "Not really, but I just got out of the shower, so I still feel really warm. The steam felt good, though."

"Take two Tylenol every four to six hours," he says on the other side of the door, and I hate that we have to stay so far apart. It's torture after being so close to him.

"I will," I mutter. "I appreciate you cooking. Hopefully, I can get it down."

"If anything, it'll help not to take the meds on an empty stomach and give you some strength."

"Right now, all I want to do is sleep. Maybe I'll wake up better." I snort at my wishful thinking. "Are you okay so far?" I ask.

"Yeah, I feel great besides the fact that I can't be near you. I miss you already. Chanel misses you, too," he adds at the end, and it earns him a slight laugh. She must've snuck out earlier when he left.

"You can send her in," I respond, knowing how often she annoys Bruno.

He chuckles. "Nah, she's fine. The three of us are hanging out. She's spilling all your secrets, though."

Somehow, he has me smiling. Few people can do that so easily.

"Never trust a pussy. Sometimes they're liars." I grin.

On the other side, he snickers. "I'm walking away now so your food doesn't get cold. Text me when you're done, and I'll come and grab the tray."

"Okay, I will. Thanks again," I say and hear his feet shuffle down the hallway with Bruno's big paws trampling behind.

Once he's gone, I go to the hallway, and see my mother's wooden serving tray with a giant bowl of oatmeal, toast with jelly, along with more bottled water and a note.

I lift it, close the door behind me, then climb back into bed. I grab a spoon and dive in. I blow on it and then swallow, enjoying the warmth. It actually feels really good on my throat, and though I have no appetite to continue, I do anyway. Then I open the piece of stationery and smile at Eli's sloppy handwriting.

Can't stop thinking about you :)

I'm swooning.

Completely smitten by this man who's captured my heart.

I wish more than anything we could be together right now and devour each other like we both want.

I take a few more bites then look over at the bottle of Tylenol. Not enough time has passed for another dose, so I force myself to wait before taking more. They haven't kicked in yet, which means I'll have to deal with this fever the best I can.

After I'm finished eating, I place the tray outside, then change into some comfy clothes. I text Eli so he knows I'm done and feel sad when I hear him grab everything. I wish he could come in and wrap his muscular arms around me. Instead of dwelling on that, I turn on the TV, but the news is bleak, and it pushes me into a panic, so I click through the channels to busy my mind.

I don't know for certain what is wrong with me, but it's best to act like I have the virus and take every precaution to keep Eli safe. Thinking about each moment Eli and I have spent together has my heart racing and my head pounding. I'm more frightened about him getting it than I am for possibly having it.

I adjust my pillow and settle on the Hallmark channel. Though it seems impossible, I try to get lost in a movie where illnesses don't exist and all the sex scenes fade to black.

Instead of being cooped up in this room with horrible thoughts floating through my mind, I want to be on the couch with Eli watching stupid shows and playing drinking games by the fireplace. It's become my new normal, and I already miss his company.

In fact, I think I'm falling in love with him. And truthfully, I'm okay with it. He treats me well, calls me out on my shit, and wants the best for me. I've never had a man make love to me and please me in the ways Eli has. We understand each other on a higher level, and over the past few days, I've seen a side of him I never imagined. Elijah Ross is the whole damn package, and I want him in my life forever.

The movie ends, and another begins. This time, it's about a couple who grew up together, lost touch, and are now back in the same town. If I wasn't so out of it, I'd think it was cute and would be more invested in the story. However, I drift in and out of sleep and go from being ice cold to blazing hot. No matter what I do, I can't get comfortable. At some point, I wake up and check my temperature, noticing it dropped some. My phone buzzes on my nightstand, and when I grab it, I see it's my brother. I desperately answer it.

"Just seeing how you are." He sounds exhausted.

"Fever's high. Chills and sweats. I've taken Tylenol every six hours like clockwork, but it doesn't seem to do anything. Drinking water. I'm eating, though I'm not hungry," I explain.

"Seems like you're doing everything you can. I wish there was something more I could say, sis, but there's not. Make sure you try to walk around some. It won't be easy, but it'll keep your lungs functioning. You'll be tired, and your fever will probably stay high for a week, maybe a little longer, but keep an eye on it. If it doesn't go down and your coughing worsens, go to the ER." He recites it as if he's repeated that dozens of times to his patients.

I blow out a frustrated breath, feeling overwhelmed by everything he's said. "I'm going to be okay, right?" I know he can't answer with certainty, but I still want some comfort from him because he's seen different scenarios from those who've tested positive.

"I'm sure you will. If you feel like you can't breathe, try rolling onto your stomach. It's helped some of my patients," he explains. "Stay hydrated. If you're cold, don't cover yourself unless you want your fever to increase."

I laugh, kick off the blanket and pull the sheet over my body. He knows me so well.

"You're your own best advocate with your health. If something isn't right, tell Eli and call your doctor. Most are able to recover from home without major complications, just watch for signs. You know you can text me anytime, too."

"I know."

"How's Eli doing? Keeping his distance from you?" I'm sure Ryan is just as concerned about Eli as I am.

"As far as I know he's okay. Staying away from me but helping from afar." I wait a few moments. "How are you?" I ask.

He lets out a lengthy breath. "Good as I can be. Not sure how much longer my colleagues and I can keep working these back-to-back shifts, but we're short a few doctors because they ended up getting too sick to work. Luckily, we've had teams of medical staff fly in from other states to help."

That's the most I'll get out of him about his well-being and don't push any further because I can only imagine what he's seen or had to do. It's a war zone out there. Ryan has been training to save lives for years, but he wasn't prepared for a pandemic. None of us were.

"Please take care of yourself," I plead. He's my best friend, and I can't imagine losing him.

"You too, Cameron. Call me when your mind wanders and you're in freak-out mode. I'll try to calm you down. Don't forget to take your meds. It might help with your anxiety," he says sincerely. A deep voice speaks to him in the background. "I've gotta go. I'll check on you as soon as I can."

"Sounds good. Thank you," I offer. "Love ya, bro. Take care."

"Love you too."

The call ends, and I sit in silence. Uneasiness and fear build inside me, and the walls seem as if they're closing in.

I'm having a panic attack.

Lying down, I close my eyes and try to steady my breathing, trying to slow my racing heart. I count down from ten, breathe slowly through my nose, and release it through my mouth. It takes several times before I come back to earth and gain control.

My throat's dry, so I take sips of water, but even that's exhausting. Eventually, I fall asleep thinking about Eli. Though I'm not the praying type, I send one up, begging he doesn't get sick. The realization that we were never safe is like a giant slap in the face, and I wish more than anything this wasn't happening.

Chapter Twenty

ELIJAH
DAY 18

Three days have passed since Cameron started running a fever. I've wanted to do nothing but hold her in my arms and tell her everything will be fine, but I can't. All I can do is make her food, leave it in the hallway, and write sweet notes on stationery I found in the kitchen. When I go to her door, I hear her dry cough and that she's gasping for air. I want to burst inside her room and confirm she's okay, but I also understand the severity of the situation. Cami's already warned me, more concerned about my asthma than anything else, and I don't want to upset her further.

Her cough sounded worse this morning, so I called Ryan again. He didn't answer, but I know he will as soon as he can. I keep my phone on me and charged at all times, making sure the sound is up just in case Cami needs anything. She hasn't asked for much help, and I don't know if it's because she's too proud or if I'm doing such an outstanding job of keeping her stocked full of water and food that she doesn't need anything.

Sometimes, I pace in front of her room. Other times, I sit with my back against the door and just talk to her. She responds, but I can tell she's weak and tired. I've never felt so hopeless in my life.

Chanel has rubbed against my legs and jumped on my lap so many times she's learned how to guilt me into giving her double treats and wet food. She sometimes meows outside of Cami's door, which makes her laugh. Last night, she watched the news and learned some tigers in a zoo tested positive, and although there's conflicting evidence confirming that, she won't allow Chanel inside her room anymore to be on the safe side. The cat and I have bonded over being locked out, and I've tried to keep my mind busy by taking Bruno on extra walks as much as possible for fresh air. It's still cool and crisp outside, and I can't wait for spring.

When I'm sitting still is when the fear of what's going on around me settles in. Cami could have the virus. I want to constantly ask how she is, but I also don't want to be annoying.

My mind wanders further, and I can't stop thinking about the night we spent together. I've never experienced chemistry like this with anyone, except her.

Something changed between us, and we haven't been able to explore it further since she got sick. I haven't mentioned us being *together*, and the silence has me doubting everything. In the back of my mind, I'll never be good enough for her or her family's standards. I don't have the social status her parents require, and Cami's always been out of my league. I'm still scraping by financially and hope that eventually changes, but the future is unknown at this point. Even if I got promoted, I don't think her father would approve because I don't have a trust fund to pay for everything.

Just as I'm walking into the kitchen, my phone vibrates in my pocket. Thinking it's Cami, I hurry and answer, but it's Ryan.

"How is she?" he asks. His tone is rushed, and in the background, different medical codes are blared over a loud intercom.

I exhale slowly. "She's coughing nonstop, and I know she's having trouble breathing by the sounds of her wheezing. I check on her every few hours, but I don't feel like I'm doing enough," I tell him. "We FaceTimed a couple times and she looked absolutely miserable."

"All you can do is help her from a distance. Stay away from her, Eli. If Cameron has the virus, she's highly contagious, and I'm worried about what would happen if you got it. Unless her coughing gets worse or she struggles to breathe, they won't admit her with how limited they are on space and equipment. She texts me each time she takes her temp, and her fever seems to be holding steady for now," Ryan explains.

"But it's still high," I say with defeat in my voice.

"It is, but she still won't be admitted unless she's worse than—"

"Worse than what she is now?" My agitation takes over. I'm so frustrated. Not with him, but over the testing situation and how our healthcare system is overwhelmed to the point of nearly collapsing. This situation of uncertainty weighs me down, and I've never been so stressed before.

"I know you're upset. I am too. I'm also concerned about my sister, but the hospitals are complete madhouses. We can't get the supplies we need, and the staff are growing exhausted. Honestly, she's better off staying at the cabin unless her symptoms and condition worsen. She's healthy, young, and is still breathing on her own. Cameron is doing better than a lot of people right now, and she's a fighter."

"You're right, man. I'm sorry for adding more to your plate. I know you're going through hell. I'm not upset with you, just concerned, exhausted, stressed, and anxious—which I'm sure you are too. I hate that Cami isn't well and is all alone in there. I'm worried about you and my family too. Everything feels so damn heavy and uncertain right now, but I'm gonna do whatever I can for her."

"I know you will."

"Don't forget to take care of yourself too."

"I'm trying." I clear my throat, knowing his time is limited, but I don't want him to be blindsided later. "Before I let you go, I should tell you something."

He chuckles softly. "That you're in love with my sister? Because I've known that for years."

I smirk. "Yeah, but now that she doesn't want to murder me as much anymore, I think I have a real chance with her. I hope at least."

"Well, aren't you glad I offered the cabin now?" he says, amused with himself. "I'm happy for you guys. It's about goddamn time."

"Wait, you knew she'd be here?"

"My mom briefly mentioned Cameron might be going up there, but she wasn't positive. Though she never said anything about Cameron bringing Zane. Honestly, I figured if you both ended up in the same place, you two could finally talk through your issues."

"Sneaky bastard," I quip. "I haven't been able to bring it up to her yet, but no matter what, she'll always be the one for me."

"I better be the best man at your wedding," he taunts.

"Your lack of sleep is making you delusional." I laugh, though the idea of marrying Cami and making her my wife and the mother of our children makes me smile.

"I'll keep checking in on you guys when I can, but I gotta get back." He releases a deep sigh, and I can tell he's broken. Each passing day has become more tragic than the previous.

"No problem. We'll chat soon, or I'll text you."

"Sounds good. Be safe, my friend." Then he ends the call.

I stand in the kitchen with my back against the counter. When I close my eyes, I see flashes of Cami and me together. I replay her lips brushing against mine, and my firm hands on her hips. Right now, I want to kiss the freckles sprinkled across her nose and hold her tight against my chest. Dealing with the unknown while being completely isolated from reality is scary. When we were together, it wasn't so bad, but now that I'm alone, I want nothing more than to be with her.

Though I did a thorough clean of the cabin when she first got sick, I continue to re-sanitize constantly. After I grab some Clorox wipes, which are like gold these days, I wipe down every surface. Whatever I can't use them on, I spray Lysol until the space smells like my mother came over and cleaned from top to bottom.

Grabbing my inhaler and my laptop, I sit on the couch to get some work done. I answer an ungodly number of emails. Though our company's revenue has fallen by thirty percent across the board, some are still reporting to work. Each year around this time, I finalize enough contracts for my commission check to catch me up on bills through the summer. Without that, I'll struggle, even if I have three roommates who help share the bills. I try to push the thoughts away, but it's impossible not to worry. It doesn't take long before I'm surfing the web and reading more articles. I shut the screen, not wanting to see any more, not when Cami is upstairs with a high fever.

Noticing it's now lunchtime, I make some chicken noodle soup and find some saltines for Cami. I grab a few bottles of water and carry it all upstairs.

I placed a small table outside of her room so Bruno doesn't help himself to her food, though I've been keeping him downstairs as much as possible. Setting it down, I tap on the door, then walk away.

She typically waits a few minutes before opening the door to give me time to leave. I go to my room and take a shower. The warm water pounds against my skin and does nothing to soothe the uneasiness I have. The entire world is experiencing loss on such a high level that it seems like a messed-up apocalyptic movie, and I'm trying to process it the best I can.

After I change, I realize I need to do laundry. Cami probably needs clean clothes too, so I text her to leave her hamper in the hallway for me to grab. She doesn't respond, but she's probably sleeping, so I put a load of mine in the washer. Afterward, I busy myself with work for the rest of the afternoon. My stomach growls, and I glance out the window, noticing the sun is setting.

I skipped lunch, so I decide on an early dinner. I make a couple of peanut butter and jelly sandwiches and grab a bag of chips. Bruno sits at my feet while I eat, and Chanel sleeps on the opposite end of the couch. I turn on the TV and get sucked into the news. When I see images of the city with streets that are usually full of people looking like a ghost town, I shut it off. I don't know why I torture myself further by watching it. Standing, I decide to prepare something for Cami to eat and switch over the washer.

When I go back upstairs to grab the tray, I notice what I brought her earlier hasn't been touched. Worry covers me like a warm blanket as I move closer. I stand in the hallway and suck in shallow breaths, trying to hear her on the other side. She's not coughing, and I hope more than anything that she's still breathing. Knowing I shouldn't go in, but not giving two fucks, I crack open the door.

All the lights are off, and the curtains are drawn, making the room pitch black. I see the outline of her body in the bed and notice she's lying on her side. For a second, I stop and listen, and can hear each time she struggles to inhale, but then coughs a few times. My head tells me I should leave, that I need to get out, but my heart protests. Instead of being cautious, I take several steps forward, then crawl into bed next to her. She rustles as I wrap my arm around her blazing hot skin. It might be dangerous, but I just want to comfort her. Forcing her to deal with this alone isn't an option anymore. If she's ever needed me, it's now.

Chapter Twenty-One

CAMERON

I'M IN AND OUT OF SLEEP. MY THROAT BURNS, AND MY RIBS HURT FROM COUGHING SO much. I wish I could close my eyes and the next two weeks would pass by. Yesterday, I emailed my professors and told them I'm sick so they're aware of why I'm behind on my assignments. It should be the least of my worries, but keeping a perfect GPA has been high on my priority list. It's taken years of dedicated studying and late nights doing homework, but none of that matters when the world is in chaos.

This is only the beginning of feeling like shit. Ryan mentioned I'd feel worse before I got better. I've followed his instructions and have walked around some when I feel strong enough. Each time I get the strength to sit up, I check my temperature and track the doses of Tylenol I've taken, so I don't take too much. My mother has called to check on me daily, but I downplay how I am so she won't show up and try to take care of me.

I go from having the chills to my body being on fire several times a day. No matter what I do, I can't get comfortable. I've soaked in the bath, hoping it'll help with the stiffness and body aches, but it hasn't. Though my appetite has vanished, I've forced myself to swallow down food.

Eli has done his best, giving me plenty to eat and drink throughout the day, so I don't have to leave my room. I'm already going stir-crazy lying in bed, but I can't hang out downstairs with him, which kills me. Though I can't deny how much I miss Eli's company, witty banter, and the way he makes me laugh at the stupidest things. The past two weeks with him, even though they started rocky, ended up being the most memorable moments I've shared with someone. It's because he understands me on a level most don't bother with.

Most guys want me because of who my family is, with hopes to climb the social ladder. That's why I've dated those who are well off because they have nothing to gain from being with me, and they're unimpressed by my fortunes.

Eli doesn't give two shits about my social class and has always been his true self.

As I drift to sleep, I hear a light tap on the door and pick up my phone to see it's a little after noon. I'm not in the mood to eat, but I tell myself I need to at least try. Minutes turn into hours, and I don't move. Eventually, a muscular arm wraps around my stomach, waking me from a deep sleep. I press against him until I realize how close he is.

Turning my head, I panic when I see Eli snuggled against me. Every cell in my body is on high alert because he shouldn't be in here. I try to find my words, but nothing comes. I need to tell him to get the hell out.

"Eli," I say in a hushed tone. "You can't be in my bed."

My words don't faze him as he tightens his arms around me. I have a mini panic attack, knowing what could happen to him if he catches it. If I'm having a hard time breathing, what will it do to him? I've tried my hardest to stay away, but here he is, inches from me.

"Eli," I repeat louder this time, moving his arm off me and creating space between us. Just the quick movement has me breathless, but I stand my ground. "You have to leave. My germs are all over this room."

He gives me a cute smirk and shakes his head. "Nah, I don't think so. I'm staying."

What the hell is he doing? "This isn't up for discussion. You know the rules."

"Cami." He sits up, not taking his eyes off me. "It's okay. Let me hold you through this."

I suck in a deep breath, needing the oxygen and strength. "Please…" I'm nearly in tears as I beg because I don't want to be the reason that something happens to him. The guilt would kill me before the virus could. "This is too risky."

"We had sex three days ago. Before that, we kissed—*a lot*. You undoubtedly had been carrying it this whole time, considering we've been here for over two weeks and haven't been around other people since then. I've come to terms with catching it. It's just a matter of time before the onset of symptoms, so the least you can do is let me comfort you."

Sitting on the edge of the bed, I shake my head. "You don't know that for sure."

"I do. It stays in your system for days, sometimes weeks. You were fine, and now you're not. Do you regret being around me?"

His eyes pierce through me. "Hell no. You're worth it, Cami."

As I open my mouth, instead of words come coughs, the ones that make my entire body protest. I'm having a fit and can't catch my breath as I choke for air. Eli rushes toward me, and I hold up my palm, trying to keep him at arm's length. A second later, he's leaving and returns with his inhaler.

"Inhale a few puffs of this," he instructs, shaking it before handing it to me. "Just inhale and hold it in your lungs. It always helps me with the tightness."

I don't want to use his medicine, but I'm desperate for relief. Listening to him, I do what he says when I stop coughing enough to draw in some air. After I have some, my chest isn't as tight, but I'm shaky. I return the cap and hand it back.

"Keep it," he tells me. "Use it when this happens again."

"I can't do that." I sit and lean against the pillows.

"You need it more than I do." He's stubborn to the bone. "Another option is sitting in the shower with hot water and breathing in the steam. That can help loosen things up."

Once I'm settled, Eli goes to the bathroom and comes back with a cold washcloth.

Leaning over, he rests it on my forehead, and it slightly soothes me. Eli crawls back in bed with me and moves to his side, propping himself on his elbow. I wish he'd be smarter about this and keep his distance. Regardless of not taking a damn test, I have all the common symptoms, and the odds are stacked against him.

"I can tell you're uneasy about me being in here, but even if you demanded I leave, I still wouldn't."

Snapping my eyes shut, I don't want to fight, knowing he'll do what he wants anyway. "So you're okay with me living with guilt if something happens to you? That's not fair."

"I'd never blame you. The choice is mine, and I'm choosing you."

My heart flutters, and I smile. "I don't understand how you can flirt with me when I look like a zombie." It's easy to know how pale I am, along with the bags under my eyes. Every time I go into the bathroom, I avoid the mirror like a vampire.

"You're beautiful," he whispers, grabbing my hand and kissing my knuckles. I pull away.

"It's like you're trying to get sick," I reprimand.

He softly chuckles. "No, I'm not, but I've already accepted it. In the past seventy-two hours, I haven't been able to get you off my mind, Cami. I've wandered around wishing I could be near you. And I can't figure out how you did it."

"Did what?" I ask, meeting his eyes.

"Got into my head and heart so quickly," he admits. "I mean, you're still a major pain in my ass, but it's different now."

We still haven't talked about our night together. I was curious if he'd mention it, or just pretend nothing happened. I've wondered if he considers being with me a mistake, but seeing his expression is proof that he doesn't.

"You're positive I'm what you want?" I ask for confirmation. Though I feel like death, talking about this is keeping my mind off it.

Eli tilts his head. "Are you serious?"

I shrug because I'm jaded to men using me, but his confession has butterflies dancing in my stomach. "Yeah, kinda. Not sure I'm your type and all."

"And what's my type exactly?" he asks with an eyebrow arched.

Honestly, the kind of women Eli likes are beyond me, but most guys find me hard to handle or intimidating. "I dunno, perky boobs, fat lips, brunette, tan and tall." I list out everything I'm not.

He smirks at my obvious lack of confidence.

"I'm thinking about a blonde with freckles, great suckable tits, and the perfect height for fitting under my arm in bed with the best ass in all of Manhattan," he cracks. It's the first time I've laughed in days. Even when I feel like shit, he has a way of helping me escape.

"That's very descriptive. You sure she exists?" I mock.

"Oh, I'm fucking positive." He winks, beaming at me. "And just to throw all your doubts out the window, you're the only woman I want, Cami. I'm confident about that. All those years of teasing each other led us here, and there's nowhere I'd rather be. Must be the fever giving you those crazy thoughts because I thought I've been more than obvious," Eli jokes. He comes closer, pulling me into his arms until my head rests against his chest. His heart pounds as he holds me. Partly due to his confession, the other part because my anxiety spikes at this whole situation. My coughs come in waves, but they're manageable. With him near me, I calm down.

As I drift away to dreamland, my breathing steadies, and Eli shifts, waking me. "You need to eat something. You skipped lunch, and I was getting ready to make you some dinner. What would you like?"

"I'm not hungry, and nothing sounds appealing."

He softly presses his lips to my forehead. I miss his touch and wish I could kiss him. "Eating isn't for enjoyment at the moment. You need to stay nourished and hydrated."

I take shallow breaths, covering my mouth when I cough. "What about some tomato soup?"

He grins and hurries out of bed. "Grilled cheese?"

"No, maybe just a piece of toast." I rest my head on the pillow as he nods.

"I'll be right back. Don't go anywhere." He winks.

I snort and roll my eyes as I pull the sheet up to my chin. Eli walks out, and I'm still smiling. The anxiety I've felt the past few days is slowly fleeting. It's comforting to have Eli nearby, but it doesn't mean I've forgotten the risks and what's at stake—his life.

Chapter Twenty-Two

ELIJAH
DAY 25

A week ago, I went against my better judgment and entered Cami's room. I knew I was risking exposure, but I also couldn't forget how close we were just three days prior. Nothing I can do will change what happens. She's been overly cautious, covering her mouth when she coughs and is continually washing her hands. There was a point when she even talked about wearing a mask to keep me from getting sick, but the damage has already been done.

I gave her my inhaler, and she uses it when she can't catch her breath. Each day, I make her three meals, and though she doesn't have an appetite, she eats some of it to appease me. There were a few nights when I was worried as fuck about her because she sounded like she was choking, and all I could do was wait it out. I was so fucking helpless watching her, wishing I could do more but knowing I couldn't.

Each night, I lie next to her until her breathing steadies, and then she finally falls asleep. Her coughing has subsided, and lately, we've slept until the sun wakes us.

This morning, I roll over to see Cami looking at me with a sweet smile.

"I could get used to this," she says in a low voice.

"To what?" I clear my throat.

"Waking up with you in my bed," she admits, and if she wouldn't freak out, I'd kiss her the way I've imagined for the past ten days. Our lips haven't touched once, and she's been adamant about me keeping some distance, though at this moment, we're only inches apart. I watch her chest rise and fall, and I'm tempted but don't. "You hungry?"

She nods. I slide the blankets off and stand, grabbing the thermometer and handing it to her. After she places it in her mouth, we wait for it to beep. She removes it and glances at the reading, then grins.

"No fever," she whispers, turning it around to show me.

"*Finally.*" I let out a relieved breath. "You beat it, Cami."

I sit on the edge of the bed and open my arms, and she falls into them.

"What's wrong?" I ask, noticing she's upset.

She lets out a sigh. "I'm just happy and worried all at the same time. I'm feeling a little better, but I'm so goddamn concerned about you."

Gently pushing away, I carefully wipe the tear that spills down her cheek. All I want to do is comfort her. "I've been counting down the days. I might be in the clear."

"It could take longer than that." Her head lowers. "Up to three weeks sometimes."

I lift her chin with my finger, forcing her to look at me, then smile. "I'm thinking positive. And now that you're feeling like a billion bucks, let's get you fed."

"Hardy har har." Cami stands, and I notice how frail she is as she yanks the sheets and blankets off the mattress and holds them in her arms. "I need to disinfect this room."

"Don't overdo it. You've not been fever-free for twenty-four hours yet," I remind her, grabbing the linens. I snicker at the thought of her using the washing machine, and she notices.

"What's so funny?"

I shake my head as I leave her room and head toward the laundry room downstairs. "Nothing. Nothing at all."

I've done laundry a couple of times now, making sure she had clean clothes and changing out of mine twice a day to be on the safe side. One of these days, I'll make her do it for shits and giggles, but she's still not one hundred percent yet, even if she thinks she is.

Cami texts me and lets me know she's going to take a shower. I send her a thumbs-up emoji as I stuff the big fluffy blanket and sheets into the wash. Knowing she's feeling better has me hopeful that if I get sick, I'll be able to recover too. While I hope I'm just asymptomatic, I'm not holding my breath. It's not like I could anyway, my asthma wouldn't allow it, though it hasn't been flaring up as much since I've been here.

After I pour the detergent in and start the cycle, I go to the kitchen and grab a skillet and pull out the ingredients to make breakfast. The cabin still has plenty of food, probably enough to last another two weeks. While I wish we could get back to normal by then, I'm convinced it won't be that soon.

As I'm frying sausage links, Cami appears and looks around. "Wow, it's super clean in here. Feels weird to be down here after all this time."

"You know who my mother is," I remind her. "I learned a thing or two growing up. A person should never go to bed with a sink full of dirty dishes or a filthy floor."

Cami laughs. "You're close with your mom, aren't you?"

I crack the eggs in a bowl and whip them together, sprinkling in cheese, onions, and mushrooms. "Absolutely. One day, I hope to repay her for all the sacrifices she made for Ava and me. I know being a single mother wasn't easy, but she gave us the best she could, and we turned out okay." I look over my shoulder at her and wink.

"You did," she says, and I can't stop grinning. How could a woman like her even think about being with a man like me? "You were always well-mannered, too."

Turning on the burner, I put oil in the pan, swirling it around until it's covered, then dump the ingredients inside. It sizzles and pops. "Well, no, not always," I tell her. "I went to the principal's office quite a lot in high school. Trust me when I say you didn't miss much."

She huffs. "I wish I could've experienced public school. You were lucky to have a normal life. I've dreamed about what it must be like."

I tilt my head. "And there are a billion reasons people would switch places with you."

"It's not all it's cracked up to be, Eli. Money doesn't buy happiness, and it sure as hell can't buy love or normalcy. Sure, there are perks, but being a St. James has done nothing but cause me problems, honestly. Why do you think Ryan went to med school?"

I already know the answer to this question, but I stay silent.

"To make a name for himself, to break out of being more than an heir. I somewhat envy him for choosing a path outside of the family business."

This side of Cami is different, more vulnerable, and I'm sure she doesn't show it to many people. "Well, for what it's worth, I think you've handled things the best you could. And I think you're going to be kick-ass at running a business. You're smart, kind, and compassionate. Even if the media doesn't see it, I do."

"You're sweet to say that."

"I meant every word." I wink. Once everything's done, I put our food on plates, then hand one to her with a fork and napkin. She sits at the bar and slowly eats as I pour some milk into a glass.

"Thanks." She covers her lips and continues around a mouthful, "You spoil me."

"Have to keep you well fed." I sit next to her and eat too.

Her blue eyes meet mine, and she tucks loose strands of hair behind her ear. "I promise I'll repay you for taking care of me."

I laugh and waggle my eyebrows. "I can think of a few ways."

Cami snorts. "*Men.*"

"You know it, babe."

Once we're done, I rinse the plates and put them in the dishwasher.

"Oh, I thought we could watch a movie and relax for the rest of the day," I suggest.

Cami grins with a nod, and we enter the living room where Chanel sleeps peacefully. She tries to hold her like a baby, but Chanel is dead set on wiggling free. Eventually, she succeeds and jumps down, prancing away as if Cami inconvenienced her.

"Wow, what a traitor. Chanel doesn't see me for nearly two weeks and acts like she doesn't even know me," Cami says with a shrug just as Bruno runs toward her.

I yell his name and tell him to sit.

"You know it's rude to get in people's personal space. Stop," Cami says as his little tail and butt wiggle. His tongue hangs sloppily out of the side of his mouth.

"This is why dogs are better," I taunt. "When they see you, it's like the very first time. Cats don't give two shits about their humans."

"She misses me in her own way," Cami explains. "She'll come to me when she's ready."

I nod. "Whatever you say."

Cami coughs, then her face contorts.

"You okay?"

"Yeah, my chest and ribs are killing me. But I'm alive, thankfully." She looks at me with sad eyes.

"Hopefully, you'll be good as new soon."

A smirk slides across her lips. "Can we build a fire?"

"By we, you mean *me*, right?" I tease, and she playfully rolls her eyes. "Sure." I glance over at the neatly stacked wood by the fireplace and make a mental note that we'll probably need more in a few weeks. Grabbing some, I place it inside with a quick start log and light it. Once it crackles and pops, and the flames lick upward, Cami smiles. I meet her on the couch where she's already covered with a blanket.

I sit beside her and turn on the TV. Cami snuggles closer and rests her head on my shoulder. There's nothing we could watch that would take my attention off her right now. I've been dreaming of moments like this for weeks.

Eventually, we lie on our sides, spooning as she watches a murder mystery movie. I'm so comfortable, but tired, and end up falling asleep with her wrapped in my arms.

Hours pass, and I'm being woken to Cami repositioning herself. When I sit up and put my feet on the floor, I close my eyes tightly because my head is pounding. I suck in a deep breath, and my chest burns. While I try not to freak out, Cami notices.

The concern in her voice is clear as she asks me if I'm okay.

"I don't feel great," I admit, not wanting to worry her, but not wanting to lie either. I don't know if it's my asthma and a migraine, or the onset of the virus. Immediately, Cami gets up and rushes upstairs, then returns with the thermometer.

"Let's check if you're running a fever," she states, handing it to me. "I disinfected it, I promise," she says as I turn it on and put it in my mouth.

Seconds later, it beeps. When I glance at the reading, Cami leans over to see it.

"Eli." She gasps and shakes her head. "*No.* That's high."

I want to assure her everything will be okay, and that I'll be fine, but we both know what this means. All I can do is take it one day at a time and fight like hell to live if I have it.

"Get plenty of rest, and drink tons of water," she instructs, and I shoot her a look.

"I know, babe. I just took care of you, remember?"

"I'll help you, Eli. Shit, you need Tylenol," she says.

Cami gets up again and comes back with a glass of ice water and Tylenol. I swallow them down. "I kinda wanna go to bed." A wave of exhaustion hits me, and I'm not sure how bad I'll feel later, but so far, it's mostly fatigue and chest tightness.

I glance out the large windows at the beautiful mountaintops and realize the sun hasn't set yet. I've slept for a few hours, but it doesn't seem like enough. I didn't expect to wake up and be symptomatic. Every time Cami and I get some alone time, the universe claps back. But I'll be damned if I'm giving up that easily. As if this year could get any worse, it proves that it can.

I stand and go to the stairs, and Cami follows like my shadow. I go to my room, and when I turn around and look at her, I notice she's holding back tears that will fall any second.

"Come here," I say, opening my arms. "What's wrong?"

"I knew this would happen." She sobs. "I knew you'd catch it from me, and I—"

"Hey. Hey." I put some space between us so I can fully look into her eyes. "Being able to hold you when you were so beat down was worth it. I'd do it a thousand times over. Don't you forget that." I wipe away her tears. "We'll get through this. I have the hottest nurse in New York."

My words make her smile, and I take a mental snapshot of how beautiful she is, even when she's upset. Her heart is so big.

"Now, disinfect everything. I don't want you to catch this again." I suck in air, and it feels like an elephant is sitting on my chest.

"Let me grab your inhaler," she whispers, and I pull her back into my arms, wanting to hang on to her warmth because I know this might be the last time we touch for weeks. "And I'll call Ryan too," she adds.

We break apart, and I walk to the bed. "Seriously, take care of yourself, okay?" I demand. "Promise me you won't overdo it, please. You're still on the mend."

Cami looks at me, wipes away more tears that stain her cheeks, and nods. "I promise, but right now, I'm more concerned about you than myself."

Chapter Twenty-Three

CAMERON

While I'm no longer running a fever, I'm still not myself, but it's manageable. I'm not as tired, and even though the dry, unproductive cough lingers, I know I'm on the tail end of this. Thankful is the only way to describe how I feel because it's been devastating for others.

Last night, after Eli went to his room, I grabbed his inhaler. He insisted that I keep it, but I wouldn't feel okay doing that knowing how much he'll need it. It still burns to breathe, but my lungs are stronger than his.

I can't stop blaming myself, and while it's counterproductive, this is my fault. Eli came here to escape his inconsiderate roommates. Who would have thought being here was more dangerous? If I could go back and self-isolate myself for the first two weeks of being here, I would. Then again, we never would've gotten to know each other on a deeper level if I had done that, so I'm torn on how to feel.

After I jump in the shower and dry my hair, I move the small table from outside of my bedroom to his, then I go to the kitchen. Chanel rubs against my legs and meows as I place her favorite chicken and gravy food in her bowl. Taking a step back, I trip over Bruno, who's right behind me, and catch my fall. I yell at him, and he gives me sad eyes.

"I'm sorry, but you can't stand that close to me."

He takes a few steps back and watches me. "Come on, buddy. I'll feed you the good stuff." He follows me around as I fill his bowl and throw him a few treats, then bring Chanel upstairs to eat. As they chow down, I realize I'm hungry too, a sensation that's new, considering I've not had an appetite. Eli took great care of me, and I'm determined to do the same for him.

Cooking isn't my strong suit, but I'm thankful for the internet because I wouldn't have known how to scramble eggs. I put them on the plate and decide I need to become more self-sufficient. There's no reason I can't teach myself and do more.

A smile touches my lips because I actually made something else without burning down the cabin. I load the tray with everything and some bottles of water, then carry it upstairs. As I'm walking down the hallway, I hear Eli struggling. His coughs are deep, and the wheezing makes my heart drop. Helplessness overtakes me as I frantically knock on his door.

"Eli," I call out. "Are you okay?"

Instead of answering, he continues coughing. I swallow hard, set the tray down on the table, and wait for him to come to the door.

Once he catches his breath, he says my name.

"Eli?" I ask, becoming more concerned with every passing second.

"I'm fine," he finally croaks out.

"I made you breakfast," I proudly say.

"Thanks, baby." He sounds defeated. I'd trade places and experience being miserable all over again if that'd mean he didn't have to. Though I want to go inside his room and be with him, I walk away. As I'm near the bottom step, I hear the door open, then click closed.

Knowing I need to keep myself busy, I disinfected the entire cabin again. After three hours of scrubbing, spraying, and wiping, I'm finally done and sweating. Though Eli told me to take it easy, I can't stop obsessing about making sure everything's clean. I quickly take another shower, then grab my laptop and try to catch up on the previous two weeks of assignments I missed.

Several professors emailed and asked about my health, along with some of my classmates. It takes a while, but I reply to everyone and explain I'm okay. Afterward, I go through my writing assignments and finish some homework that's due at the end of the week.

I'm so distracted, and it's hard to stay focused. Bruno jumps on the couch and rests his head on my thigh just as Chanel prances by and sits in front of the enormous window. The hours pass, and I try my best to make something for lunch but resort to microwave meals. I'm sure Eli will understand, considering my cooking experience. Dinner's the same. He doesn't complain, though I suspect he's not too hungry anyway.

I text Kendall and update her on everything. The conversation isn't a happy one, and she tries her best to comfort me as she listens to my fears. I'm so thankful to have her in my life through the good, bad, and ugly.

After I eat and get some reading done, I try to fall asleep but struggle with knowing he's suffering. The virus attacked him quicker than it did for me, and I don't know what to do. I text Ryan, hoping he replies and gives me a glimmer of hope, then I force myself to close my eyes.

The next two days are the same routine. I clean, cook, and worry. The worst is still to come, and I'm on high alert, constantly checking to make sure he's still breathing.

On day four, I'm more concerned than I've ever been. The news only magnifies my anxiety.

Just as Ryan enters my mind, my phone rings. I hurry and answer.

"How are you?" he asks, sounding like he got run over by a Mack truck.

"I'm better. Not quite myself, but I'm getting there. I tire fairly quickly and still have somewhat of a cough, but mostly, I'm okay."

"I'm so glad to hear that. How's Eli?"

I pause and release a deep breath, trying to stay positive so my brother doesn't notice how concerned I am.

"He's struggling, and I'm worried he's too stubborn to say he needs anything."

"How do you know?"

"He's gasping and coughing; the kind of deep cough that's buried in your chest. He's using his inhaler, but it's not helping very much. I'm desperate."

"If he's rapidly declining, you should call the hotline and get him to the hospital. I'm not saying that to stress you out more, but to get him help before he progresses too far."

"I will as soon as we hang up," I say, knowing they won't let just anyone walk in and get tested. If I would've called for myself, they would've told me to stay isolated. Will it be the same for Eli, too?

The line is silent for a few seconds. "When this is all over, if I ever complain about working seventy-hour weeks or bitch about being too tired, you have permission to kick my ass," he orders. "Because I'd be happy to only be working that much right now."

"Same, oh my God, same," I agree, feeling bad that he's probably working over a hundred hours right now. "And if I ever complain about not knowing what to order for takeout, kick mine. I didn't realize how good I had it until delivery was no longer an option."

Ryan chuckles and agrees with me. "Did you hear Dad and Mom donated a few million to a relief fund to help the hospitals in the city get more medical supplies and the proper masks?" Ryan asks. "It's been reported on the news, and people are posting articles about it. I've had so many of my colleagues thank me with tears in their eyes. I'm kinda taken aback since I had nothing to do with it."

"Well, that doesn't surprise me. You're loved and appreciated either way." I smile, hoping he understands how true that is.

"Or rather, our parents love a great PR stunt," he mumbles. "Though I'm grateful and we desperately needed it, they could've made it anonymous and donated without the family name attached to it, you know? But they wanted the recognition, so I got dragged into it. They flashed my picture across the screen a dozen times. You know I don't want that kind of attention," he says. "I'm here doing my job because it's what I'm passionate about."

"I'm sure it wasn't like that, though. They're proud of you," I say. "I am too, Ryan. Though I worry about you."

"I'm *more* worried about you and Eli, and I'm pissed I can't be there for you guys," he says.

"Your patients need you, and I'm better now. I won't let anything happen to your best friend. I care about him a lot."

"I know you do. This weird love-hate thing you two have has been going on for years. I was wondering when you'd both get over it."

I chuckle. "Right? Too bad it took this long to realize it, but honestly, I've never felt this way about a guy before."

"Eli's in love with you," he tells me matter-of-factly. "Please don't break his heart."

Wait, what? I blink hard at his words, my throat dry for a completely different reason now. Ryan blurts that out with ease, as if he has no doubt about it.

"Hurting him is the last thing I'd ever want to do," I say truthfully. "This past month has been a game-changer for me. I'm falling for him, too."

"Honestly, it's about goddamn time." He chuckles. "Take care, okay? Keep me updated."

"I'll do my best. I gotta call and check in with Mom, too." I've been texting her because she wants to have full-on conversations, and I was too tired for that.

"Don't forget to call the hotline. See what they say based on his symptoms."

"I will as soon as we hang up," I reassure him. We say our goodbyes, then I look up the number.

Little did I know how much of a disaster it would be.

The phone rings; I'm put on hold, then get disconnected. I'm not a quitter, so I call back, get transferred again, and hung up on after thirty minutes of waiting. Four hours of my time are wasted because I get nowhere, and I'm so goddamn frustrated that I can't contain my aggravation.

I busy myself at the stove and attempt to cook hamburgers. When I remove the meat from the frying pan, it's burnt. Bruno's at my feet, and I pinch off a piece from the patty and fling it to him. He sniffs it, then walks off without eating it.

"Great," I whisper. "The dog won't eat it, and he more than likely eats poop."

I heat a frozen pasta meal, then take it upstairs to Eli.

Not like it's anything new, but I sleep like shit, tossing and turning. Once I wake up and chug coffee, I attempt to cook more eggs. After another successful scramble plate, I deliver them to Eli, then call the hotline again. Determined to get through to someone today, I'm hoping since it's earlier, I won't have as many issues. It takes two hours to speak with someone who's knowledgeable.

She asks me all the basic questions, the same ones people can find online to self-diagnose.

"I'm sure I had it the past two weeks, and now he's caught it. I'm more concerned because he's asthmatic."

"Has his fever risen above 102?" she asks.

I think back to all the times Eli has checked in with me. "No."

"Is he showing signs of improvement?"

"Compared to what?" I ask with a sigh, then continue before she can respond. "Listen, I just want you to be honest with me. What are the odds of him getting a test so we can know if it's the virus, flu, or something else?" I can only imagine how many people she speaks to daily who treat her like shit, so I try to rein in my frustration, but it's so damn hard.

"It looks like they're only testing those who end up admitted and need lifesaving equipment. They aren't testing everyone at this moment…"

"Even for someone who shows all the symptoms and has asthma?" My words come out choked and harsher than I intend.

"I wish I could give you better news. If your friend gets worse, call a local doctor to get a referral first. Otherwise, I'd stay inside and monitor him closely."

The line is silent for a moment, and I thank the woman, then end the call. Tears pour down my cheeks, and I sob into my hands. My hands are tied, and there's nothing more I can do but watch him.

The cabin's clean, the pets are fed, and now I'm lonely. I walk upstairs and knock on Eli's door, wanting his company. I sit on the floor and wait, placing my back against the wood.

"Yes?" he asks. It's not quite lunchtime yet, so I'm sure he's wondering what I want.

I rest my head against the door and look up at the ceiling, trying to find the strength to keep it together. "I miss you," I say.

He chuckles, then coughs before responding. "I miss you, too."

"I hate that you're so close, yet so far away," I admit, thinking back to what Ryan said about his feelings for me. I hear him sit on the floor too. We're back to back with only a few inches of thick wood separating us.

"Me too. What have you been doing today?" He takes several puffs of his inhaler.

"I called the hotline for you to see if we could get a test and…"

"They refused," he finishes. "Amiright?"

"Yes." I grow quiet and close my eyes, wishing this would pass soon.

"I'll be okay, Cami. I'm already on day five and am on the mend."

I smile. "You don't sound like it."

"Oh really? I heard women really like a man with a raspy voice," he tells me. "I've just been practicing to impress you."

I chuckle and shake my head, appreciating the way he's trying to lift my spirits. "I'm worried that if you recover and I get it again, then you could be re-infected. I was reading yesterday about someone who tested positive twice. We'll both just keep passing it to each other, and eventually one of us will get it bad enough to be hospitalized," I say. I know I'm being dramatic, but it's a possibility.

"When I'm better, we'll wipe down every wall, ceiling, and floor, not leaving a spot untouched. As long as we do our due diligence, we'll be okay. I just have to survive the next week," he breathlessly says.

"My cooking isn't the best, so you're probably starving," I mock, wanting to get a rise out of him. It works because he laughs. "Bruno wouldn't even eat my hamburger." I pout.

"To be fair, he's a vegetarian," he states, and I burst out laughing.

"You're such a liar." I shake my head. "It was burnt. He probably thought it was mud."

"I would've eaten it," he says. "I can't taste for shit anyway."

Chuckling, I smile and love that we can still communicate like this. If this is as close as we can be, I'll take it. And when he's better, I'll make it up to him in all the right ways. I miss his touch, his kisses, and the way he looks at me as though I'm his everything. Just the thought of losing him scares me beyond belief.

Chapter Twenty-Four

ELIJAH
DAY 35

It's been twelve grueling days of feeling like shit, but when I woke up this morning, I didn't feel like there was a pillow over my face. Though my back aches from coughing so much, I think the hard part is over, as long as I don't relapse or get pneumonia. I roll over in bed and reach for the thermometer. I place it under my tongue and wait, and I'm shocked to see my fever has finally broke. Thank fuck.

There were a few days when I was worried. My inhaler barely provided any relief, and I almost asked Cameron to rush me to the hospital, but I kept holding on, hoping my body would fight it. When I was at my worst, I told my mother I was sick too. She nearly had a heart attack, but I couldn't keep it a secret just in case something terrible happened.

Mom called Ava, who then insisted on coming to the cabin, but I told her it was best if she didn't and that I'd check in as much as I could. I climb out of bed and go to the window that overlooks a meadow. Fog bellows over the dense grass, and in the distance, I can see the mountains. Instead of going back to sleep, I take a hot shower. Though my skin is sensitive to the touch, the water relaxes me and the steam helps my breathing. Once I'm done, I realize I gave Cami all my clothes.

I forgot I asked her if she could do my laundry yesterday. I only packed one suitcase because I didn't know how long I'd be here. At this rate, I should've taken everything I owned, considering I probably won't be returning home for at least another month. Probably longer, though. Not that I'm complaining because that means more uninterrupted time with Cami.

For the first time in ten days, I leave my bedroom and walk down the hallway with a towel wrapped around my waist. I carefully take the stairs, and when I get to the bottom step, Bruno comes rushing toward me.

"Hey, boy." I smile wide as he tries to jump on me, and I tell him to sit, then pet his head. It's barely past six in the morning, so everything is quiet.

When I walk into the washroom, my clothes are in the dryer. A grin touches my lips because she actually figured it out, not that I completely doubted her. Okay, maybe just a little. I put all of my items into a spare basket and put on a pair of joggers and my favorite Yankees T-shirt. Just as I turn around, I nearly run into Cami.

"Oh my God!" she yelps, covering her mouth with her hands. "I thought you were a burglar."

I chuckle. "Who broke in to steal my underwear?"

"I came downstairs to make some coffee so I could start doing schoolwork, and I heard noises."

I look down at her hand and notice she's tightly grasping a skillet.

"And what's that for?" I point at it and grin.

"To kill you!" She swings it in the air, putting all of her weight into it. Bruno runs to her and thinks it's time to play.

I hold the basket under one arm and laugh. "Not sure if that would do the job, babe. You should stick with statues. At least they're heavy as hell."

Her eyes meet mine, then she gazes down my body and back up. A blush hits her cheek, and I smirk. "Are you feeling better?" she asks, swallowing hard.

I nod. "Much. Not fully, but I'm on the rebound. No fever."

"Thank God," she whispers, her shoulders relaxing. Cami drops the pan, then wraps her arms around me. Dropping the basket, I hold her close, smelling the sweetness of the shampoo in her hair, and never want to let her go. "I've been so worried."

"I know. Me too," I admit. "I got lucky. Didn't hurt having you take care of me." I smirk.

"It's easy to take things for granted when you suddenly realize you may never be able to again," she says, then pulls away. "I had tons of time to think about that between my fever-induced nightmares. The fear of not living is what scared me the most. But the realization that tomorrow isn't promised was empowering in a way."

I grin and pick up my basket of clean clothes. "I can relate. I thought about all the things I wanted to do and never have, along with adding to my bucket list. I've never been in a situation like this before, and I never want to be again." I cough, and suck in as much air as I can, but I end up dropping the basket, and Cami moves toward me.

"I'm fine." I gasp, trying to catch my breath. This has rapidly become my new normal for the past week and a half. While I bend over because I don't have much strength, I know it's best to stand straight to open my airway. Quickly, fatigue takes over, and I have a full-blown asthma attack.

"What can I get you?" Cami asks, panicking. I can't even catch my breath long enough to say two syllables, but she figures it out on her own. She rushes away, running as fast as she can out of the room. I feel like someone is squeezing the air out of me as the pressure of a million pounds sits on my chest. Though she's only gone for a moment, it seems like an eternity.

She hands me my inhaler, and I put the plastic up to my mouth and push down, allowing the medicine to fill my lungs. I take three more pumps, needing it to work faster than it is. Eventually, it does, but my heart is galloping at full speed, and my hand is unsteady from the medication hitting my bloodstream. Cami watches me intently with fear written all over her face.

"I'm okay," I tell her. "My asthma attacks are a million times worse right now. Go wash your hands," I remind her, knowing she touched something that came from my room.

She quickly does, and I pick up the basket, then follow her into the kitchen as she scrubs her hands under the hot water. I'm exhausted all over again, and my body aches, but I'm determined to have a little time with her today.

"You're going to make me worry to death or give me gray hair."

"You'd be sexy with some gray." I chuckle and notice how spotless everything is. "You know what would be great right now?"

Blinking up at me, she grins. "Coffee?"

"Yep. The caffeine helps with my asthma."

"Really?" She tilts her head. "That's good to know."

"Yep, I learned that in college. My doctor suggested it when I didn't have a rescue inhaler at work one time. He said coffee acts as a bronchodilator and in a pinch can help with attacks. It's a reason I drink several cups in the morning."

She nods. "Strong ass double shot of espresso coming right up," she sing-songs, using the fancy machine that auto grinds the beans. As it drips, she places a can of Lysol in my basket. "When you go up there, spray everything down, then take your linens off the bed and put them in the washer. We have some cleaning to do. I want the virus out of the cabin *forever*. We'll know we're in the clear in a couple of weeks if we're both healthy and then should just live here for eternity."

"I could definitely get on board with that plan." I'm dying to kiss her, but don't. It's too soon.

Bruno moseys into the kitchen, goes to his bowl, and barks three times. Cami looks at me with a proud smile. "I taught him to do that when he's hungry."

I nearly snort because he's been commanding me like that since he was a puppy, but it's sweet that they've been bonding, so I don't want to burst her bubble. "Nice. Maybe I should stay in my room, and you can teach him how not to get in people's personal space."

She pets his head, then grabs some food and pours it in his dish. "We made a deal. I think by the time we return to the real world, Bruno will have his act together."

"He's his own boss. But hey, you're cuter than me, so it's possible he'll listen." I shoot her a wink, then go upstairs. I take a few puffs from my inhaler and set my clothes on top of the dresser. Though I feel weak, I pull off all the sheets and blankets, and put them in a big pile before spraying as much Lysol as I can handle in the room. Considering the smallest tasks exhaust me, I sit down for a short break.

Grabbing the linens, I carry them downstairs, stuff them in the wash, and start it before going to the kitchen and lathering my hands with soap. It's weird how it's become an obsessive part of my everyday life—wash, clean, sanitize. I didn't think much about it before all of this happened, but now I can't do it enough.

Cami stands at the stove, and I admire the booty shorts she's wearing that show off her perfect ass cheeks. She's making scrambled eggs, something she recently learned how to do when I first got sick and even whipped up some pancake mix. After a second, she catches me staring and turns and grins. "Coffee's ready."

I can't stop staring as the early morning sun reflects through the window and casts a glow over her skin. Damn, she's just so gorgeous, and she's going to be mine. A small smile plays on my lips as I walk toward her, and she hands me the mug. I thank her, then grab some creamer before taking a sip. "Whoa," I say, tasting the hint of chocolate. "This is different. What kind is it?"

"Some ridiculously expensive kind Daddy enjoys," she says. "You like it?"

I nearly down half of it in two gulps. "It's incredible."

"Apparently..." She lingers, then chuckles. "It comes from cat poop."

"What?" I nearly choke, looking at her with wide eyes, hoping she's joking. "Are you serious?"

She acts like it's no big deal. "Yeah, Kopi Luwak. Some luxurious bean. I don't know. Sounds odd, but glad you like it, though."

"Rich people are so fucking weird," I murmur, and she laughs.

Cami places the eggs on two plates, covers them, then goes to a cabinet. "We have enough to last us through an apocalypse." Cami waves her hand down a shelf, and she's not lying. It's full of golden coffee bags. I lean against the counter, admiring how sexy she is. "Great. Guess we're drinking cat shit coffee for the rest of our quarantine."

She turns around and notices my gawking, then laughs. "What? Do I have food in my teeth?"

"Nope, just thinking how fucking beautiful you are and how it was torture being away from you," I say, setting my mug down. Reaching for her, I pull her into my arms, tempted to close the gap between us. Our mouths are inches apart, and all I want to do is kiss her. I've missed her so damn much, but I also don't want to re-infect her. She should have some immunity built up, considering she survived it, but there are still a lot of unknowns about this particular virus. As I'm about to pull away, she stands on her tiptoes and moves in. Taking the lead, she parts her lips and presses them against mine. I should push her away, but now that I'm tasting her, I lose all my willpower. We exchange a searing-hot kiss, and we nearly melt into one another. I can't help but grab her ass as she moans into my mouth.

"Eli," she whispers.

"Mmm," I say, plucking her bottom lip between my teeth when she pulls away.

"Our eggs are getting cold," she says dreamily, then goes in for another.

"Not the words I want to hear right now." I groan, adjusting myself.

Her hands twist in my hair, and the only thing that stops us from going any further is the fire alarm blaring through the cabin.

Her eyes go wide. "Fuck, fuck, fuck!"

I notice the burner is on with a skillet on top, and it's smoking. Immediately, I turn it off and let out a hearty laugh.

"Right when I thought I was becoming a chef." She groans. "At least I took the eggs out before walking away."

"This is true," I reassure her with a wink, opening the windows and fanning a towel to try to clear the smoke. "Nice save."

Once the alarm is off, and our ears are safe, Cami grabs another pan and pours the pancake mix inside. "I thought I'd try my hand at pancakes since the video I watched on TikTok made it look easy."

"You shouldn't make them so big. They might not cook all the way through and will be difficult to flip," I explain because I learned the hard way when I was thirteen. It always seems like a good idea, but it's not.

She turns and throws me a smart-ass look. "I've got this."

"Pretty confident for someone who nearly caught the cabin on fire," I tease.

She wrinkles her nose and snarls.

I lean against the counter and watch her. Because she's so stubborn and wants to prove her point, she grabs the handle with both hands and proceeds to flip it as though she's a celebrity chef. Only she puts too much strength into it and the cake flies in the air, then falls dough side down on the floor with a splat. Seconds later, Bruno rushes into the kitchen and gobbles it up, not caring how hot it is.

Cami frowns, then shrugs. "Good boy." She leans down and pets his head. "He's a champ at cleaning messes."

I nearly fall down laughing. "I wonder how many *messes* he's eaten in the past two weeks."

"It's our little secret." She looks at him. "Right, Bruno?"

He stares up at her, his little tail wiggling as he begs for more. "Bruno," I warn, and he turns and trots away once he realizes he's not getting it. I try not to feed him too many table scraps because it's not healthy for him.

"Let me help," I tell Cami, and she reluctantly moves over. I scoop the batter, then pour it into three perfect circles. They're palm size and don't take too long to cook before I flip them over.

She playfully scoffs. "Okay, now you're showing off."

"Pancakes were one of my favorite things to make when I was old enough to stay home alone. I remember cooking so many one time that I was nearly sick from eating them. I had a stomachache for days."

A giggle escapes her. "I can only imagine. We never ate stuff like that growing up. I would've probably killed someone for a stack of pancakes at thirteen. And now, I go between eating like a rabbit and gobbling up all the processed shit because of how strict my mother was."

"She *was* weird about sugar," I confirm, remembering the weird shit she'd try to feed me when I was playing with Ryan. It always tasted like cardboard.

She nods. "Apparently, it goes straight to your hips. So every Valentine's Day, Easter, and Halloween, I buy ten bags of candy. You'd probably throw up if I told you how much of it I eat. Then I go back to refusing carbs for a few months. It's a vicious, stupid cycle."

"Your secrets are safe with me." I make a few more pancakes and give her a stack of four, then she grabs some fancy ass maple syrup from the cabinet.

"Well, now I know the way straight to your heart. Bread, sugar, and sweets."

She nods, takes a bite, and moans loudly. "And your cock," she adds.

"That too." I chuckle. "And what's his name?"

She eyes me with a smirk. "Zeus. How could I forget?"

"Damn, I've really missed you," I admit again, imagining our night together.

"Me too." She grins with a mouthful. "I've missed having real food. It's so much better when you cook," she says.

I snicker. "Probably because it's actually edible."

"That is most definitely why."

I meet her eyes as I take my own plate to the table. There are unspoken words and stolen glances as we eat, both wanting to be all over each other but knowing we can't just yet.

We clean the kitchen once we're finished, but it takes a while since I get out of breath quickly.

For lunch, we pop a pizza in the oven and eat on the couch while we watch some new docuseries about a religious cult in Texas on Netflix. We lie around the rest of the afternoon, holding each other close, and I squeeze her just a little tighter while we watch the news.

Though it's been over a month since I left my apartment, I don't want this to end. I could get used to this. Cami's become such an integral part of my days that when this is all over, and we go back to our everyday lives, I'll probably be lost.

Eventually, she changes the channel, and we try to tune into something more comedic to take our mind off what's happening in the world. Though I have a lot of work to catch up on, one more day off won't hurt. We spend the rest of the night together, taking every advantage of this time as we can.

Chapter Twenty-Five

CAMERON
DAY 41

It's been a week since Eli's fever broke, and I'm so damn relieved. We've taken extra precautions around the house and have cleaned it top to bottom several times. I've never been this germ cautious, but I find myself washing my hands regularly.

As I look inside the freezer, I see there's only one package of chicken left. We're out of eggs, bread, juice, and other stuff. When Eli enters the kitchen, he wraps his arms around my waist and kisses the nape of my neck. My eyes flutter closed, and I lean into him as he mentions making a run to the store. I turn around and watch him as he pulls his wet hair up into a bun.

"I was thinking the same thing, but just the thought of it makes me anxious as hell."

"I know, me too, but we need stuff." He leans down and slides a kiss across my mouth, and then it intensifies to something more possessive.

"Mmm," I hum, inhaling the scent of his freshly showered skin. He slips his tongue between my lips, deepening our connection.

By the time we break apart, I'm breathless, and a cocky smile plays on his lips. As my breasts rise and fall, he glances over at the clock. "I should probably get going if I want to find the good stuff before it's all gone."

"Should I come with you?" I ask. I've lived in shorts and T-shirts for the past few weeks, but I'd change into something warmer.

He shakes his head. "You'd have to sit in the car and wait. Most stores are only allowing one person per household inside at a time," he explains.

"Well, I don't mind. I've got my phone to keep me occupied and—"

Leaning forward, he kisses me again, making me forget what I was saying. "You're too sweet, and I'll never get enough of you, but you should stay here and hold down the fort." His mouth crashes against mine, and heat rushes through my body. I try to hide my smile, but he notices.

"What?"

"Just realizing how much of a flirt you are, trying to distract me with your delicious mouth." A blush hits my cheeks as my internal body temperature rises. I can't stop thinking about him being inside me again. We've been taking it slow while we both try to recover because Eli still has difficulty breathing.

He pops an eyebrow. "You're the only cock tease in this room."

I scoff. "Seriously? You're the guilty one."

"Babe," he says. Moving closer, he traces the shell of my ear with his mouth. "I've been thinking about the way you taste for weeks and would have you for breakfast every morning if you'd allow it."

"Damn," I say breathlessly. "I'll be your breakfast every day starting tomorrow. Also, I'm pretty sure I just had an orgasm."

He tucks loose strands of hair behind my ear, and I look up at him as he smirks.

"That's all it took?" He chuckles.

"Tease!" I push against his chest, then start running when he charges for me.

"Take it back," he playfully warns as he chases me around the kitchen.

Once he catches me, he tickles me until I nearly piss myself laughing.

I keep protesting and shaking my head until his lips capture mine again. "I don't want you to go," I admit, wrapping my arms around his neck. "Don't leave me."

"Trust me, I don't want to, but we're out of shit. I'll try to get enough to last us a few more weeks at least. Make a list of things we need, and I'll do my best to grab it all. Remember, the sooner I leave, the quicker I'll return." He winks.

"Think you can pick up some toilet paper?" I ask, half-joking, knowing it's nearly impossible right now. Pretty sure it's selling for several hundred dollars a roll on the black market.

I would've never imagined a time when toilet paper would be such a hot commodity, but everyone started hoarding it the moment people started panicking. Now it's like finding the golden ticket in a Willy Wonka chocolate bar.

"I'll see if I can find some," he says. "If not, I'll teach you how to do the pee and shake."

"Gross!" I laugh.

I grab a sheet of paper from my notebook and begin to make a grocery list. Eli randomly adds stuff to it too.

"I want to make you a fancy dinner. What are you in the mood for?" he asks.

"You. On a plate. Naked." As if he needed the reminder.

Eli takes off his shirt and stands in the kitchen. "Don't tempt me, sweetheart. I'll dick you down right now." He growls, causing me to snort.

"Uhh," I say. "Did you just say *dick me down*? Is that what all the players say these days?" Laughing, I lower my gaze down his body and admire every solid inch of him.

He shrugs, putting his shirt back on. "Apparently. Heard it from one of my roommates who's addicted to Bumble and Tinder."

I giggle. "Mm-hmm, sure. How about you surprise me? I don't want to give you a meal choice because what if it's impossible to find the ingredients? I've heard some things are tough to come by. You might not find half of what's on this list." I glance down at it. Who knew in today's world there'd be struggles to get common everyday items?

"You're right. I kinda forgot about that. I haven't been out in so long, I'm not sure what to expect. I'm a little nervous being around people."

I meet his eyes. "We could place a pickup order instead? I'm not sure when we could schedule it, but it's an option if you don't want to go out."

"No, it's okay. We need these things now unless you want to eat shitty microwave dinners for the next three weeks. You brought enough, but seriously, they're kinda gross, and the chicken tastes weird after a while." He gives me a look, and I snort.

"Remember the story about my mother? She would have a heart attack if she knew how much processed food I was eating here." I chuckle.

Eli tilts his head at me. "You're such a rebel."

I finish adding things to the list, then hand it to him. "I was able to order a few masks before I came here. Do you want to take one?"

"Yeah, that'd be good," Eli tells me, and I nod. I head up to my room to grab one while he grabs his keys.

When I return, he chuckles as he reads over the list. "Cadbury eggs. Mini Snickers bars. Reese's cups. You're not joking, are you?" He arches a brow.

"Hell no," I retort, handing him the mask. "If so, buy out the store. There's no dieting in quarantine. I've decided."

He lets out a hearty laugh. "You are something else, Cami."

"A hot mess and a handful? You're welcome." I glance over at the clock and then back at Eli. "Better get going. Maybe it won't be so busy this morning, but they're on restricted hours."

"You're right," he says. Taking a few steps forward to close the space between us, he kisses me until I'm breathless, but I still want more.

When we break apart, I squeeze my arms around him tighter. "Please be careful out there."

"I will. Don't worry, I'm not fighting vampires or zombies," he teases. "I grabbed my tiny bottle of hand sanitizer. Got a mask. And as soon as I get home, I'll put everything up, sanitize the hell out of it, then strip down naked and take a shower."

"Ooh, stripping. That sounds fun. Dicking me down later on that list too?"

"Only if you're a good girl," he throws back before tucking the small bottle back in his pocket and then folding the list and putting it in the other.

I kiss him goodbye one final time. Before he walks away, I grab a handful of his ass. "Hurry back."

"If you keep that up, I might not leave."

"Get out of here." I playfully point toward the door. "And watch out for zombies."

He shakes his head and throws me a wink. I watch as he leaves and frowns, immediately missing him.

While he's gone, I pull out all the cleaning supplies and rubber gloves so we can safely unload the groceries when he returns. I'd come across a video online demonstrating the proper way to disinfect items, and I'll watch it again before he returns.

After I have the counter ready for when Eli is back, my phone rings, and I'm giddy when I see it's Ryan. I haven't been able to get him off my mind, and it's been a while since we've chatted. When I answer the phone, I'm a little too excited.

"Ryan!"

He chuckles but sounds defeated. "Hey, sis. Doing okay, still?"

"Yep, pretty much back to my old self," I say happily.

"Ahh, so back to being a major pain in the ass," he retorts.

I scoff. "That's no way to talk to your favorite sister. How are you holding up?"

"I'm making it. I wanted to check in with you. How's Eli?"

"He's better. Not coughing nearly as much. He left not too long ago to get groceries. We were running out."

He lets out a breath. "Good. I'm so relieved and happy to hear that. Hopefully, he's being careful out there."

"He is. I was really scared there for a few days. It was horrible, but he pulled through," I say.

"Yeah, me too. I've been thinking about you two nonstop. Also, have you been watching the news?"

"I haven't in a few days. It's been depressing and wasn't good for my anxiety. The stories throw me in a panic, so I've been trying to busy my mind with other things." I'm happy I can quickly turn it all off but sad that Ryan can't.

"Good. Don't. We're low on ventilators, and things are a shitshow. The governor has been begging other states to send some. Companies are supposed to be making them, but they can't keep up with the demand. They set up tents in Central Park, Cameron. There's a military ship coming to help treat those who need medical help since the hospitals are at capacity. It's like living in the twilight zone," he says, his voice flat.

"Oh no," I whisper, ignoring his orders and going into the living room. I sit down on the couch and turn on the news, and he's right. I put it on mute, but I see the images of the tents and the boat. My mouth falls open in shock. I've never seen anything like this in my life. "Ryan, please be—"

"I'm extra careful," he interrupts before I can finish. "Thanks to all the donations swarming in, we have more PPE coming in, but it's still not enough. I spoke to Mom and Dad yesterday, and she said they're donating another few million to the relief funds, but I begged her not to make it a publicity stunt again."

"Good," I say, knowing how much he hates that. "I read about a lot of celebrities and other companies pitching in, so that's good news. Hopefully, Mom and Dad are staying home, though."

"They say they're locked in the house. But..." He pauses for a moment. "Staff is still coming in and out, which is ridiculous. I've told them for weeks to stop doing that, but they're stubborn."

"I don't think they could survive without the help, though. Mom hasn't cooked since before you were born." I laugh, trying to lighten the mood, but he doesn't take the bait.

"You're right, but still. Let Eli know I called to check on him, okay?"

"I will. I love you so much," I tell him.

"I love you too, sis. I'll call you soon. Take care. Wash your damn hands. And stay inside," he repeats his orders like always.

I chuckle at his strict doctor tone. "Yes, I will. Bye." I hang up, staring at the TV in shock. Chanel prances up and crawls on my lap, purring. I pet and scratch under her chin, then seconds later, Bruno comes barreling in. He doesn't realize his size and believes he's still a puppy, so he jumps on the couch, then lays his head on my lap. Chanel turns around and hisses at him, batting at his nose. He looks so offended, and I laugh at his adorable reaction. As soon as I do, she jumps down.

"Aww, Chanel, sweetie. Come back by Mama," I coo. She glances at me as Bruno nearly crawls on top of me, looking at me with sweet, begging eyes.

"Now you've pissed her off," I tell him, and he licks my face.

"No, stop," I protest, but he doesn't listen. I eventually stand to get him off me, though it barely works. If my parents saw this big ass dog on their leather couch, I'm sure they'd shit a brick, which makes me snicker.

As I go to the kitchen and rummage through the fridge, I get a text from Kendall, and I can't stop grinning. I told her when I got sick, and I updated her when I could, but then Eli got sick, and my full attention was on him. However, I haven't had a chance to fill her in on any recent events. She went to her parents after self-quarantining in her penthouse for two weeks since she was at NYU before the lockdown. Now she's convinced it was the worst mistake of her life.

Kendall: So...this is my weekly health check-in.

I grin and immediately start typing up a reply.

Cameron: I'm great. How are you?

Kendall: Living my best life. I haven't washed my hair in two weeks, and my wardrobe consists of no bra, leggings, and witty T-shirts that drive my mother crazy. Also, wine. Lots of it.

I snort. Kendall then explains how annoyed she is that her mother keeps inviting people over to their house to socialize. I sympathize with her, and then she abruptly changes the subject.

Kendall: So, how's the Eli situation?

Cameron: He's doing good.

My heart races when I read his name. While I haven't told a soul about us having sex yet, I feel as if I'm obligated to spill it all to my bestie. I wanted to wait to see how it all plays out, but deep down, I know how happy he makes me. I swallow down my nervousness and try to find some courage. I type a few messages, wondering how to break the news that this is so much more than a physical attraction. Before I hit send, I delete it, then type it again. I'm nervous.

Cameron: I'm falling in love with him, Kendall.

I can see her typing, then the next thing I get is an emoji with heart eyes followed by nearly twenty exclamation points.

Kendall: I KNEW IT! I wish I would've bet you on it.

Cameron: Ha! Yep, you would've won.

Kendall: I mean, he is hot as hell, so I don't blame you.

Cameron: Yes, he is, but he's soooo much more. Sweet, considerate, and spoils me. Tells me how beautiful I am on the inside and out, and kisses me like tomorrow will never come. As cheesy as it sounds, it feels like we're living in a fairy tale being isolated out here just the two of us.

Kendall: Oh. My. God. I'm so fucking jealous. I wish I were stuck with a man right about now. I'd never leave the bedroom.

I giggle at her message, but this is a big deal for me. I've never felt this way about anyone before. Never. Kendall knows that too.

Kendall: Wait, did you have sex already? You never filled me in because you were so sick. HOW COULD YOU KEEP THAT FROM ME?

My cheeks heat instantly. I guess there's no going back on this conversation now. She sends another message before I have the chance to reply.

Kendall: OMG, you did. And you need to give me every dirty detail right fucking now.

Cameron: Imagine the best sex of your life and multiply it by a thousand. There you go.

Kendall: So, he's better than Prince Harry?

Cameron: Oh, hell yes. I can't even explain the things he does with his mouth. And his tongue. I swear, it has superpowers.

Kendall: Lord, I think I just came on the spot. Does he have a brother?

She has me drowning in giddiness. Though Kendall's being silly, I know she's had a crush on Ryan since we were teens, but I don't rag on her today. There's plenty of time for that later.

Cameron: No, but I do ;) Eli only has a sister. You could bat for the other team if you wanna live out one of your college fantasies?

Kendall: I love the D too much. NOT Ryan's though. But truthfully, I'm happy for you. Zane was a bag of shit, and I always knew you could do better. Can't wait to start the next rumor that he cries after he orgasms.

Cameron: So, you said something so it would get back to Zane about me and Eli. Haha! I knew it!

Kendall: What are best friends for? Shit, my mother is calling. I need to answer this before she has a meltdown.

After we say our goodbyes, I'm floating on cloud nine. I go upstairs and jump in the shower, so I'm clean and ready by the time Eli returns. As I'm towel drying my hair, I see him pull into the driveway. I hurry and get dressed, then rush downstairs. Unlocking the door, I charge toward him, but he quickly stops me.

"Cami, wait." He holds out his hand. "I need to take off all these clothes first, but then..." He lifts an eyebrow, then pops the trunk, and I pull out a few bags.

"And then?" I laugh with my hands full. "You better not be talking the talk unless you plan to walk the walk...or fuck me into tomorrow," I say over my shoulder and head inside, setting everything down on the left side of the counter, ready to explain what we need to do before we unload it all.

I wait another second and notice he's not behind me and go outside, talking shit about how I'll do it all on my own if he's gonna be a slow poke. But when my feet hit the driveway, I immediately stop. My smile fades, and my heart drops into my stomach.

Eli turns and looks at me with his arms in the air as two men point guns directly at him. One sees me and is startled. Rapidly, he turns his weapon on me. I hold my hands up as my adrenaline spikes.

"Go inside," Eli says calmly.

"Fuck that!" one man shouts. "She's staying where I can see her. Don't fucking move," he demands, his beady eyes trailing over my body. I'm more frightened than when I was in bed with a deadly virus. I tremble, unnerved by how fidgety they are.

"What do you need?" I ask. All I want is for them to go, to take whatever, then leave us alone.

The other guy speaks and looks maniacal like he hasn't slept in days. Dark circles are under his eyes, and his hair is a greasy mess on top of his head. "You bought the last of the items I need for my pregnant wife and three kids. And the only other option is to pay double in the next city over, which I can't afford."

"I can give you plenty of money," I speak up, wanting to dissolve the situation and for them to disappear.

"You can have everything in my car. All of it. Anything that'll help your family," Eli offers.

His partner looks at me. "Come here," he demands, motioning with the gun for me to move closer. I don't dare defy him and do what he says. I stop when I'm standing next to Eli, both of our arms still in the air.

"I want your wallet, cell phone, and keys," he demands, and Eli gives him what he wants. The guy turns to me. "Your phone too."

I swallow, pulling it from my back pocket and handing it over. They turn and whisper to each other, and Eli glances at me. "Everything will be okay. Stay calm. They'll take everything and leave, and we can figure out what to do. We'll be fine. I promise."

Eli is always giving positive reinforcements, but I'm so damn scared that I don't know if I can believe him this time. Panic rolls in like a storm, and my breath feels like it's stuck in my chest. Seconds later, Eli has a coughing fit, and he needs his inhaler, but there's nothing I can do.

"What the fuck? Are you sick?" one of them asks, alarmed, then coming back over to us.

"No, he has asthma," I explain. "He needs his medicine."

Their eyes are wild like they're tweaked out as they dart back and forth between us, and I wish I could read their minds.

"You both need to turn around and get on your fucking knees," he orders.

Eli wheezes, and I turn around to help him but slip on the gravel. He reaches to catch me, and then the gun goes off. The shot is so close, my ears immediately ring. It all happens in slow motion, and I see Eli collapse to the ground, and he's bleeding. There's movement and yelling behind us. When I glance over, I see one man jump into Eli's rental, and he peels out of the driveway with the other guy behind him in a truck. Looking back at Eli, I start panicking as the realization hits me.

"Eli," I whisper, seeing the dark pool of blood, and I try to put pressure on his shoulder. I'm frantic as tears stream down my face. I'm not sure what I can do, considering we don't have our phones.

He's moaning out in pain as he reaches up with his other hand, but I warn him not to touch it. The sound of his agony is something I'll never forget for the rest of my life. There's so much blood. "Please don't die on me. *Please*. Elijah," I emphasize his full name, hoping to capture his attention enough to hear me.

I take off my T-shirt and place it over the wound, putting all of my body weight on him. Thankfully, his asthma attack wasn't severe, and he's breathing okay, but I'm still scared. "Hold this the best you can. We need to get you to the hospital."

Eli groans, and I dart inside the house and grab the keys to my Range Rover. "Fuck, fuck, fuck."

I reverse out of the garage, drive as close to him as I can, then get out and rush back to him. With all the strength I have, I somehow get him to his feet, but he's so fucking weak. I get him in the passenger seat, then buckle him in. My hands shake as I shut the door and run around to the driver's side. As I place my hands on the steering wheel, I notice his blood on my hands and arms.

"Eli." I put the SUV in drive, then speed down the long driveway that leads to the main road. He's fading quickly as he groans, and I try to keep him focused on my voice by talking to him. "Please, stay awake. Don't close your eyes."

I reach over and add as much pressure as I can to his shoulder while I keep one hand on the steering wheel. I tell him how much I love him, how much I've always loved him, but I'm not sure he hears me.

"Please, baby, please stay with me," I beg.

The nearest hospital is almost thirty minutes away, and he's losing so much blood. Tears spill down my face, and I know I need to stop and focus because I have to get us there safely, but at this rate, I'm scared we'll never make it.

This can't be the way I lose him. It can't be.

Chapter Twenty-Six

ELIJAH
DAY 45

I WAKE UP GASPING, OPEN MY EYES, AND NOTICE I'M IN A STARK WHITE ROOM. Machines beep around me, and there's an IV in my right hand. Pain shoots through my shoulder, and I wince as I look around. My left arm is in a sling, and my muscles feel stiff from lying here for only God knows how long. What the fuck happened? Where is everyone? What day is it? I have more questions than answers, and it frustrates the hell out of me.

I press the call button on the remote that's haphazardly looped around the hospital bed. A woman answers and asks what I need, but my throat is so dry I can barely get out any words. "Nurse."

"I'll send someone in."

Leaning back, I struggle to get comfortable. Twenty minutes pass, and eventually, someone enters.

"Oh, you're awake," she tells me.

"Where am I?" I ask gruffly. There are so many thoughts zooming through my mind, but I try to focus. I have a feeling I'm drowsy because of the pain medicine they're pumping in me, but I also feel out of it and exhausted.

"You're at Margaretville Memorial. I'm Patricia, and I've been your nurse since you arrived four days ago," she explains. "The doctor should be in soon." She's wearing full protective gear from head to toe, and her kind eyes are all I can see, but they remind me of my mother's.

Wait. My eyes go wide. "Four days?" I ask, clearing my throat.

"Yes. It's nice to see you awake," she says sweetly.

Patricia moves to the computer, looking at the monitors around me. She types as she asks me questions about how I'm feeling and what I would rate my pain level.

The door gently opens, and a male doctor enters, wearing the same protective gear as Patricia. "Hello, Elijah. I'm Dr. Jenner," he tells me.

"Hello," I say. "Nice to meet you."

He steps toward me, checking the monitors. From what I can see on the screens, my blood pressure and heart rate all look normal.

"I was just about to tell him," Patricia interjects, then smiles at me.

Dr. Jenner nods, then continues, "Your surgery went well. Being shot in the shoulder isn't an easy wound to manage, but you're lucky. A little farther over, and you might've not been so fortunate."

"You've been *very* lucky," Patricia emphasizes. "No spiked fevers, no infections, and all your stats have been stable the past twenty-four hours."

I blink. Surgery? Then I glance at my left shoulder again and realize it's all bandaged in the sling.

"Gunshot…" I mutter as flashes of that day begin to surface, and then I remember the two men who followed me to the cabin from the grocery store.

"I was able to stop the bleeding, and with some physical therapy, you'll be as good as new in a few months," Dr. Jenner explains.

"That's a relief," I breathe out.

"Patricia will get you on their schedule, so you can meet with someone for a consultation before you go," he explains.

"Thank you," I tell him.

Dr. Jenner nods and gives Patricia further instructions before he excuses himself.

"The medicine has had you in and out since the surgery, but we started to wean you off this morning to see how you'd react."

"I feel like I could sleep for another four days," I say with a grunt.

She grins. "Getting shot and having surgery will do that to you. We'll continue to give you pain meds until you're discharged. We just have to keep an eye on your stats for another couple of days to make sure you don't have any complications arise."

Another two days? I groan at the thought. She begins talking about how PT will teach me some at-home exercises to do since the facilities are closed. But I don't give two shits about that right now. The only thing on my mind right now is Cami. Sweet Cami. Is she okay?

With the little strength I have, I reposition myself in the bed and sit taller. The nurse adjusts my pillow when she notices me struggling. "Where's the woman who brought me here?"

"You came from the ER, then the ICU, so I'm not sure. Unfortunately, the hospital isn't allowing any visitors. No one's allowed to visit."

Well, that fucking sucks. I bet she's been going crazy not being able to see me because I know I am already.

"Though, someone has been calling at least once a day asking about you but since she's unable to prove she's family, we couldn't give her any information due to HIPAA."

That has to be Cami. "Did she leave a phone number?" I ask, and she shakes her head.

I vaguely remember giving the man my wallet, phone, and keys. I think he took Cami's too. Without my cell, I don't have anyone's number memorized except my mother's, and the last thing I want to do is alarm her, considering how nervous she was when I told her I was sick. I'd call Ava, but she recently changed her number, and I don't remember it. Basically, I have no choice but to lay here and wait for Cami to call.

I move a bit and wince. The pain shoots through my body and is like nothing I've ever experienced before. Leaning back, I tuck my lips into my mouth and hold in all the obscenities I want to scream.

Patricia looks at me and notices I'm uncomfortable. "You aren't due for another dose of meds, I'm sorry."

"It's okay," I tell her, though this fucking sucks.

"Do you have any other questions?" Patricia asks when she steps away from the computer.

"No, I don't think so." I let out a sigh, hating that I'm in here with no communication with the outside world. "Thank you," I add before she leaves.

"Hit your call button if you need anything."

"Oh, could I get some water?" I quickly ask, feeling thirsty regardless of being pumped with fluids.

"Sure thing," she replies with a smile.

She leaves, and I find the remote, then turn on the TV.

Moments later, she returns with a full cup of water and another with some ice chips. Setting them on the tray, she moves it closer to me. I thank her, and then I'm left alone, just me and the constant beeping. I take a sip of water, and the cold soothes my dry mouth. I can only use my right arm, which is annoying, but I know things could've been worse so I'm counting my blessings.

As I watch the screen, my eyes grow heavy, and I end up falling asleep. All I can think about is Cami and what she's doing. I hope she's okay and those men didn't go back to the house while she was there. I wish I could remember more, but the last memory I have is Cami tripping and me catching her. Then it goes black.

◦◦◦

Two more days go by, and the hours pass in a blur. I go between sleep and watching the news, which doesn't help my nerves, but I can't seem to stop.

Breakfast is delivered, and I raise my bed to an inclined position. Once I'm settled, the phone rings. I try to answer it as quickly as I can, hopeful it's Cami, but when I do, a man speaks.

"Hello, this is Deputy Pomfrey. I'm looking for Elijah Ross."

"This is," I tell him.

"Oh, good. I've called a few times but haven't been able to get through. There was a police report made involving you, and I'd like to take your statement so we can move forward with an investigation."

Inhaling deeply, I try to recall exactly what happened. "Okay."

"Just start at the beginning, if you don't mind. Whatever you can remember," he says.

"Alright, well. I went to the grocery store, and as I was leaving, I noticed a truck followed me home. I didn't realize they had pulled behind me in the driveway until two men jumped out and held me and my…" I abruptly pause. What are we right now? Before I get too caught up in my thoughts, I clear my throat and call her what she is. "My girlfriend at gunpoint. Took my wallet, phone, and keys. They told us to get on the ground, and when I did, I started having an asthma attack. That's when she came to me, and the gun went off. I don't remember much after that," I explain, and it hurts to relive it all over again. It's all I've thought about for the past forty-eight hours, but repeating it aloud causes my anxiety to surface. I still can't believe this happened amongst everything else.

"According to Cameron's statement, one of them took off in your rental car while the other drove the other vehicle. We found yours totaled a few miles from the cabin. They ran it into a grouping of trees close and emptied it out before abandoning it."

"Great. Glad I got insurance on it," I say, shaking my head. Those two fucking idiots had to be completely tweaked out of their minds.

"Can you give me a description of them?" he asks.

"One said he had a pregnant wife and three kids. Both tall, around six feet with scruffy facial hair. Crazy eyes. They were driving a blue truck. Chevrolet. It was an older model, maybe mid-nineties." I think harder. "And the bumper had a dent in it like it'd been in a previous accident." It's coming back to me in pieces. I remembered seeing the truck in my rearview mirror as I pulled out of the parking lot, but little did I know they were following to rob and fucking shoot me.

"Any other details or information you can think of?" the officer asks.

"No, I don't think so. That's about it," I tell him.

"Great. If you remember anything else, I left my number with the nurse. I'll call you if we find them."

"It might be a while before I get a replacement phone, but I'll give you my number anyway," I tell him, then give it to him.

After the conversation is over, I set the phone down and get resettled in bed. Moments later, the door opens, and Dr. Jenner walks in.

"How are you feeling today?" he asks.

"Better. Still in pain, but mostly okay."

"Good to hear. Your stats are looking great, PT said the mobility in your shoulder was already improving, which is fantastic. I'll put in the order for your release papers so you can be discharged this afternoon."

For the first time since I got here, I smile wide. "Great. That's the best news I've heard all day."

"Figured you'd be happy to hear that," Dr. Jenner says, then explains he'll be prescribing me pain meds and some other antibiotics to take home. I thank him once again before he leaves.

When Patricia enters, she looks exhausted, and I tease her, asking if she ran a few marathons today.

"Feels like it," she says with a light chuckle. "I hear you're getting discharged today. I bet you're ready to go home." Though I can't see her mouth, I can tell she's smiling by how her eyes crinkle at the edges.

I nod. "I definitely am." I miss Cami like fucking crazy. We still haven't talked, and I'm eager as hell to get back to her. "Quick question. Are there any pharmacies close by?"

"There's one in Roxbury, but it might take them a while to fill it. They're doing curbside, I believe."

"Okay, uh. Hmm…" I grab the hospital gown I'm wearing. "What about my clothes?"

"I believe they were thrown out. My guess is they had to cut you out of your shirt, and you were probably covered in blood," she explains. "I can check if we have anything that's been left behind that might be your size. Or you can always leave in the gown."

I let out a huff. "Great. Is there a taxi that can take me around? My family isn't close."

She tilts her head. "Sure, I can call one of them."

"Thank you. You're an angel, Patricia," I say, grinning. She really has been nothing but amazing since I woke up.

Lunch gets delivered as I wait, but it literally looks like something Cami made on a bad day, which isn't saying much. I chuckle at the thought but can't force myself to eat it. Patricia enters with a pair of jogging pants and an oversized T-shirt along with a stack of papers in her hands.

"They're my son's and have been in my trunk for a while now. Might be a little big, but much better than that gown with the open back." She snickers.

"Thank you so much. I'd kiss you if I could."

She laughs. "You're welcome. You remind me of my son, so it's the least I can do."

"You're the best. Seriously," I tell her.

"I have your discharge papers finally. I'll need you to sign in a few places, then you can be on your way. I called a cab for you, and they'll be here soon. I'm leaving a mask for you to wear while you're out. Be careful with your sling while you change. Let me know if you need help." Patricia shoots me a wink, then leaves. It takes me a minute to figure out how to do it one-handed, and she's right, they're large, but I'd take this any day of the week over that itchy gown that lets my ass hang out.

While slipping on my shoes, the only items of mine that were left, I notice blood splattered across the top.

I slip the mask over my face, and when I walk out of my room, it feels weird to finally be going home.

When I pass the nurses' station, I wave goodbye and thank Patricia once again, then make my way to the elevator and go to the lower level.

Once I'm out of the main entrance, I'm shocked to see the nearly empty parking lot.

Guess that's what happens when visitors aren't allowed, and only emergency surgeries are being done. My anxiety spikes as I sit on a bench and impatiently wait for my ride. All I want to do is talk to Cami and hold her. My dark thoughts appear as the fear of what the future holds consumes me. Is she upset with me? Does she regret the time we had together? Why hasn't she reached out? Everything feels so wrong without her, and I don't know if she's still at the house or what's going on. If anything, I just hope she's safe.

Cami's the only person on my mind, and I can't stop thinking about her or us. I'm madly in love with her, and I don't know how much longer I can go on without her knowing. I almost lost the opportunity to tell her, and I don't want to wait any longer. When I see her, I'll make sure she knows how much she means to me.

The taxi takes forever, and all I want is to return to the cabin to see Cami and our pets, but I need my prescriptions. I also need my laptop, so I can order another phone and check in with my boss. After that, I'll need to decide what my next steps are. Going back to my apartment is out of the question, but if Cami is no longer at the cabin, I'm not sure I want to stay without her.

Too many thoughts are happening at once, and I suck in a deep breath, but it's shallow. I need to calm down before my blood pressure rises, but I hate the insecurities flooding through me and not knowing what I'll be walking into when I return.

After an hour of waiting, the cab finally pulls up, and I grab my papers and get inside. I ask him to take me to Roxbury and will have to find the pharmacy when we get there since I can't look it up myself. He talks to me while he drives, but my focus is elsewhere.

Cami.

Chapter Twenty-Seven

CAMERON
ONE WEEK AGO

After I rushed Eli to the emergency room, they told me I couldn't stay due to their lockdown restrictions, but I could call for an update. I was completely frustrated and angry over everything that had happened, and then not being able to stay with him made it worse.

As I drive back home, tears streak my cheeks, and I'm hysterical by the time I pull up to the road that leads to the cabin. Stains of Eli's blood are on the seat, a reminder that he's fighting for his life right now without anyone there to support him. I pull into the driveway and replay what happened just hours ago as I stare at the spot where they shot him.

When I get out of the SUV, I see the pool of dark liquid on the ground and force myself to look away before I have a panic attack. I can't stop glancing over my shoulder to make sure no one is around. My paranoia is in overdrive as I walk toward the front door and input my code on the keypad to unlock the door. As soon as I enter, Bruno barks and sniffs me. Chanel is lazily lying on top of the couch and doesn't even lift her head to greet me.

"Bruno, down," I tell him. I'm still only in my sports bra and covered in blood. I need to wash up and change. The house feels so empty without him and the fear I have over losing him consumes me while I shower. I can't stop crying as the hot water covers my skin, and I watch the red water pool to the bottom.

Once I'm in clean clothes and throw up my hair, I go to the sofa and lie there bawling for the better part of the night, hoping Eli will be okay. By the time we arrived at the hospital, he was pale and fading in and out of consciousness. Everything happened so fast that my head is still spinning.

This is the second time in a month that I've worried about losing him. My heart can't handle much more as I sob into a pillow. At some point, my tears dry up, and my stomach growls in protest because I haven't eaten in hours. I go to the kitchen and throw together a peanut butter and jelly sandwich on the last few slices of bread we have left. The groceries I brought in earlier are still on the counter, and thankfully, it's nothing but produce and boxed items; otherwise, I'd have to toss it from sitting out for so long.

I call the hospital with the satellite phone my parents had installed through our internet for emergencies, and right now, I could kiss them for it. When they told me they were getting one installed, I explained how ridiculous the whole idea was because we have cell phones. It's my saving grace, though I can't remember anyone's numbers other than Ryan, Kendall, and my parents'.

I need an update on Eli before I drive myself crazy with worst-case scenarios, and after I'm routed to several nurses' stations, I find out he's out of emergency surgery and in the ICU. Since I'm not his spouse or related to him, they tell me they can't give me much information, but that I can try calling back once he's in recovery.

I'm so unsettled that I don't even notice I'm pacing until I hang up the phone. The next person I call is Ryan. He answers the phone immediately, and as soon as I hear his voice, I burst out into tears.

"Cami, what's wrong?" He's on full alert, and I hate to throw this on him on top of everything else, but I have no choice.

"Eli got shot," I choke out as I cry.

"What?" He's nearly yelling on the other line. "Did I hear you correctly?"

"Yes. Two men followed him back to the cabin after he went to the grocery store and held us at gunpoint for our groceries. After they took our phones, one of them shot Eli in the shoulder, then they took off in his rental. There was so much blood, Ryan. By the time I got him to the hospital, he was barely conscious."

He's speechless.

"I'm worried they'll come back for me. I don't know if I should try to get back into the city or if I should wait for him to be released." Assuming he makes it out alive.

"I know this might not be what you want to hear but do not come to the city. You're safer there, trust me. As long as the security system is on, and the doors and windows are locked, no one will be able to break in. That place is like a fortress. I can't believe this happened. Dammit, Cami. You're gonna give me gray hair."

"I know. It was the last thing we expected, and then it happened so fast. I don't want to call Mom and Dad because they'll demand I come home or hire a whole SWAT team to guard the cabin. And if I tell Kendall, she'll drive out here even if I tell her not to. You're the only logical person I can talk to."

He chuckles. "I'm the only logical person you *know*. Period. Point blank."

I crack a slight smile. "I need to call the cops and make a report. Let them know what happened."

"Okay, keep me updated with everything. Send me a text if I don't answer. I'm checking my phone as much as I can," he tells me.

We say our goodbyes and end the call. I grab my laptop and report my cell phone as stolen and order a replacement. I pay extra for overnight shipping, so I'll hopefully get it tomorrow. After that's taken care of, I look up the number to the local police department and tell them what happened. I give them all the details I can remember, though it all feels like a blur as I run through it.

Recounting the events aloud has my hand trembling, and I feel the uneasiness in my body. The officer tells me they'll need to speak to Eli, and I tell him where he currently is, but honestly, I'm not sure how much Eli will even remember. Once he knows the full story, he states they'll look into it immediately. I don't care about the groceries or the items we lost, but they deserve to pay for shooting Eli. As soon as that thought crosses my mind, my chest tightens, and I feel a panic attack surfacing.

Though I have breathing exercises, they don't always work, and right now, they're not. I'll wait fifteen more minutes, and if the panic attack doesn't subside, I'll take one of my anxiety pills. Knowing how hard it'll be to get them refilled, I've used them sparingly. Time passes, and I grow more edgy. I rummage through my bag and find my meds, deciding it's time to take one.

It takes nearly an hour for the clouds to fade, and while my head isn't fully clear, I feel more in control of my emotions. After everything I've been through with us getting sick and then this, I was spiraling.

I stretch out on the couch, and Chanel jumps up and sits next to me, then starts purring. She makes me smile. Moments later, Bruno jumps up by my feet and tries to crawl on me too, but I quickly scold him, and he leans his head on my thigh instead.

"You are such a big puppy," I tell him. "But we gotta have a little chat."

He looks up at me with his big dark brown eyes and blinks.

"You're gonna have to be a watchdog while your dad is getting fixed up." My words choke because I really hope Eli is doing okay. "Like, if I say *attack*, you need to rip someone's head off, okay?"

Chanel settles in and lies down. Bruno continues to stare at me as if he's waiting for a treat.

"Got it? Bite someone's leg off or something. You're a big bad Doberman, so you better act like it if someone breaks in. Be ferocious and scary," I tell him with a firm nod. He readjusts his position, then leans his weight against me. I look up at the ceiling and suck in a deep breath.

I tell myself he's going to be okay.

He has to be because I'm in love with him, and I didn't even get to tell him.

The days have been grueling since Eli was shot. It's been some of the hardest days of my life knowing he's been up at the hospital alone, and I have no way to speak to him.

The guilt of it all eats at me, and I feel like it's my fault. If I wouldn't have turned and fell, he wouldn't have tried to catch me, and the two idiots who were holding us at gunpoint wouldn't have been startled. Each day, I've beaten myself up for putting Eli in that situation. This is the second time I've put his life in danger, and it's really fucking with my head. It feels like me being in his life is all wrong even though having him in mine is what I need.

I've called the hospital every day since he was admitted, but they're swamped, so I'm continually transferred from the operator to the nurses' station or even hung up on. Eventually, I'll get connected to Eli's room, but then he won't answer because he's passed out, then I start the process all over again to get an update on him. They won't tell me anything specific, just that he's alive.

Once my new phone arrived, I was able to keep Ryan in the loop and also FaceTime Kendall. She happily told me I looked like shit but still poured an enormous glass of wine and drank with me as I cried. It was therapeutic and helped pass the time since I don't know when Eli will be back.

Bruno has stayed at my heels, refusing to leave my side and even started sleeping in bed with me, but honestly, he's a bigger scaredy-cat than Chanel. The big doofus is growing on me, even if he takes up half of the mattress and snores like a human.

When I climb out of bed, my stomach growls more than usual, and I realize I have to stop eating cereal for every meal. When I walk downstairs, there's a chill in the air, and I glance next to the fireplace where there is only one log left. Another cold front is supposed to move through, which means I'll need more wood. Sucking in a deep breath, I walk to the kitchen and decide to make pancakes, and smile as I recall the last time I tried when Eli was home. Of course, he showed me up.

I mix the batter, heat the skillet, then pour them in the same size he did. I carefully put the spatula under them one by one and flip them over. My mouth waters as I see the perfect golden brown pancake. I wait a few more minutes for the other side to cook, then slide them onto a plate, spread butter on top, and pour syrup.

I sit at the bar with my coffee and eat, satisfied that I didn't burn them or the cabin down. I watch a handful of YouTube videos that explain the steps of how to chop wood. I know we have an ax, but honestly, I don't know if I can even swing it over my head, but I'll try.

After I finish my food, I change into jeans and boots, and just to amuse myself, I grab a plaid button-up shirt. When I walk outside, Bruno follows, being my protector. Bruno runs as fast as he can to the pond, and when he goes to jump in, I yell at him at the top of my lungs, but he doesn't listen and sloshes through it, jumping around.

"Oh for fuck's sake," I mutter under my breath. "You're going to stink like shit!" I yell. His tongue hangs out of his mouth as he runs around the property, dirty and happy as can be. Bruno sprints toward me, and I squeal, quickly moving away so he can't jump on me. The damage is done, so I don't even scold him for it anymore.

I find the ax in a stump and manage to wiggle it free, then grip it in my hand. I take a few practice swings, putting all of my strength into it. As Bruno plays, I grab a wheelbarrow and wheel it to the stack of wood on the side of the shed, and struggle to lift the pieces in. I wasn't built to carry heavy shit, but I'm trying regardless. Once I have enough, I move to the cutting area and dump them on the ground. Grabbing a log, I place it down on the chopping stump but lose my grip and break a goddamn nail.

"Are you kidding me?" I groan, shaking my head. They're long overdue for a manicure anyway, but still, that hurt like a bitch.

I try again and adjust the piece of wood. Grabbing the ax, I lift it over my head, putting all of my strength and body weight into it, and then the sharp blade crashes down and slices the log in two. I drop the ax, and my mouth falls open in shock. Soon, I'm jumping up and down with victory, then laugh my ass off. If my mother could see me doing this, she'd probably faint with shock, then ask me if I've lost my damn mind.

I repeat the steps, doing precisely as I did before until I have an entire wheelbarrow full of logs. As I'm rolling it toward the patio door, Bruno barks, and my internal alarm goes off. Immediately, I turn around, searching the surrounding areas and see him chasing after a rabbit. Placing my hand over my heart, I try to calm myself, then continue forward.

"Bruno!" I shout. That dog needs a Xanax.

I make it to the patio door, then slide it open. I carry each piece inside one by one, and neatly stack it next to the fireplace. My arms and body are so sore, and I don't think I've ever done this much physical work in my entire life. Knowing Bruno needs a bath, I go to the kitchen and grab the Dawn dish soap. If it's good enough for the ducks during oil spills, it'll be good enough for stinky dogs. I go back outside and put the wheelbarrow up and wrangle Bruno to the back patio, then grab the water hose.

He jumps all over me, leaving muddy paw prints on my clothes, and scratches me with his nails. Bruno nearly knocks me over when he gets excited like this. I try to use my best Eli manly voice and tell him to heel, but he doesn't listen, so I resort to begging him instead of yelling. Eventually, he sits, and I run water over him and soap him up real good. Once he's clean, he tries to run off, but I grab him by his collar, and he shakes himself all over me.

"You're a little shit sometimes, Bruno," I tell him, but I'm laughing about it because he's so happy. "And now I need a shower too."

I open the door, and he runs inside, hyper as can be. He chases Chanel around the living room until she's had enough and runs upstairs. Water is all over the floor as he continues shaking and air-drying. With an annoyed groan, I clean up the mess, then try to towel dry him off. I'm filthy, and my back is already aching. Tonight, I'll try to make myself dinner that doesn't include a microwave while downing a bottle of wine. I'm going to need all the luck in the world to actually make something edible.

∞

Eli's been in the hospital for a week, and I still haven't spoken to him. I think he'd be proud of how I've taken care of myself for seven days. Even I'm kinda shocked, considering I couldn't boil water before arriving here. I've chopped wood, learned to open wine with a corkscrew, and even baked homemade lasagna. Next up is learning how to change my oil and build a house with my bare hands. I laugh at the thought, but honestly, Eli is to thank for this. If he hadn't made fun of me and challenged me to do things on my own, I probably would've eaten TV dinners and ramen for a month.

Today, I slept in because I've stayed up late doing home improvement tasks after my homework assignments, trying to keep my mind busy. I hung photos that have been in a closet for years. I cleaned the cabin, did more laundry, rearranged the living room furniture, and even dusted the top of the kitchen cabinets. At some point, I won't have anything else to do but worry and waste away.

Calling the hospital is one of my everyday habits now. I'm transferred to the nurses' station, who then tells me Eli was released nearly two hours ago and left in a cab. I wish I'd known so I could've at least picked him up instead. My heart races in a semi-panic because the cabin is only thirty minutes away, and he's not here. Did he not plan to come back here? Is he mad? Does he blame me for what happened? I hate not knowing what he's thinking and hate even more that I couldn't speak to him.

While I nervously wait, I make my second espresso of the day. Another hour passes, and there's still no Eli. I know he doesn't have his phone and probably doesn't remember my number, so I text Ryan and see if he's heard from him. I don't get a response, which only annoys me even more.

I'm nervous as hell and filled with worry. He wouldn't go home without seeing me or taking Bruno, would he? Did he go to his mom's? I'm literally driving myself crazy not being able to talk to him.

My stomach growls, reminding me I skipped dinner. I pull out the macaroni I made last night and reheat it, noticing Bruno is on my heels. I feed him a few noodles and tell him to keep it our little secret.

After I eat, I sit on the couch and turn on the news, knowing it's not what I need but still wanting to know what's going on in the city. It's been almost a week since I turned it on. Before I lose myself in the scene unfolding at the hospital where my brother works, the front door opens. Bruno lets out a roar of a bark, and I jump up, my eyes wide as I spin around to see what's going on.

Eli's eyes meet mine; his hair is a shaggy mess and his arm is in a sling, but he's smiling when he sees me. My hands cover my mouth in shock as my eyes water. I rush to him, and he immediately wraps his good arm around me and presses a soft kiss against my lips. Uncontrollable tears stream down my face, and when he puts space between us, he rubs the pad of his thumb over my cheeks and wipes them away.

"I didn't think you'd come back," I whisper, swallowing down the emotions that have been bubbling inside me for a week.

He searches my face and shakes his head as he tucks loose strands behind my ear. "Why wouldn't I come back, Cami? You're all I've been thinking about. I've been going insane without you."

His words cause goose bumps to trail up my arms, and my cheeks heat. "When I called this afternoon, the nurse said you were discharged hours ago, and I thought you didn't want to be here anymore…" My insecure thoughts linger, and a small smile plays on his lips.

"I waited over an hour for a cab to pick me up. Then he drove me to Roxbury to drop off my prescriptions, then after another hour of waiting for them to be filled, I remembered I didn't have my wallet. After figuring out that mess, he got lost on his way here, but I didn't realize it at first, or it wouldn't have taken so long." He blows out a breath and shakes his head. "It's been a weird fucking day."

I feel so bad for him and wish I'd been able to help. "How did you pay for it all?" I ask.

"I gave him a handie," he jokes, and I roll my eyes. "The pharmacy is gonna charge it to the hospital, and they'll add it to my bill. The cab driver is gonna mail an invoice."

"I was so worried," I tell him. "They couldn't tell me anything about you except that you were alive, and every time I tried to call, it took forever to get through, and then you'd be sleeping. I can't believe you're here right now." Happy tears stream down my face, and I want nothing more than to hold him. I carefully wrap my arms around his neck. "I've missed you so much."

"Those words are like music to my ears, baby." He tightens his arm around me. "I've missed you too. So fucking much." He pulls back slightly until our gaze meets. "You're the only thing that kept me sane in there," he admits.

I paint my lips across his, claiming him as *mine*.

Bruno wiggles between us, clearly annoyed he's not getting any attention. "Hey, buddy." Eli kneels and pets him as Bruno slobbers all over his face.

"He missed you," I say. "And he sucks as a guard dog. He's a bigger baby than me."

Eli laughs, then grabs my hand and leads me to the couch. I look at the clothes he's wearing. "Where did you get those from?"

He looks down at the oversized T-shirt. "The nice nurse who took care of me gave me her son's extra clothes since mine were ruined. I need to write her a thank-you letter and send it with the biggest bouquet," he tells me. "She was a godsend in the midst of all the chaos."

"Hmm…is that who's been keeping you busy? Flirting with your nurse?" I tease, popping a brow.

He leans over and plucks my bottom lips between his teeth. "Nah. I'm much more into bossy blondes who can't cook," he mocks, and I want to smack him, but I lean over and press my mouth to his again. I can't get enough of him.

"I've been dreaming about that for days," he admits, cupping my face.

"Me too," I say as a blush creeps up my cheeks. "I thought I lost you."

"Never," he says. "I'm not going anywhere, baby."

Relief washes over me as my pulse increases. I know I can't live another day without telling him how I feel. "Good. I'm not sure my heart could survive without you."

"Cami," he whispers, his eyes searching my face. "I only thought about you while I was there. What you were doing, how you were feeding yourself," he says with a chuckle. "I was worried how this was affecting you."

"You were worried about me?" I roll my eyes with a smirk. "I kept thinking the worst. Eli…I—"

He sweeps his lips against mine. "I love you, Cami. I don't think I'd be able to live another day without telling you how much you mean to me."

I choke up, tears falling because he somehow stole my breath and the words I was going to say. "I love you too."

Our mouths crash together, and as we become greedy for one another, Eli winces in pain. "Sorry," I say. "What do you need? More pain meds?"

Eli smiles. "As long as you're with me, I've got everything I need."

Chapter Twenty-Eight

ELIJAH
DAY 69

It's been a month since the accident that landed me in the hospital for a week. So much has changed in that amount of time, and though my shoulder isn't fully recovered, every day I feel stronger. I video conference my physical therapist twice a week, and I do daily exercises to keep up the mobility. It often leaves me breathless and needing my inhaler. I was so used to working out but have had to take it easy.

Cami's been extremely helpful with everything, doing way more than she needs to. I can do things one-handed, but she insists. She reminds me to keep up with my PT and doesn't let me get lazy with it.

After a couple of days back, I noticed the things she did around the house and considering how much she struggled before, she's really putting in the effort to be more independent. She's definitely changed, and without a doubt, she's changed me too.

I get tired a lot faster than before, which frustrates me. Sometimes, I wish I had my old life back, the one I had before the pandemic and before getting shot, but then I remember that life didn't include Cami. I wouldn't change having her for the world. If having her means all the other bullshit had to happen, I'll happily accept it.

New York is still in lockdown with shelter in place orders. I'm kinda shocked it's lasted over two months, but then again, it makes sense with the current data. It reminds me to hold Cami that much tighter each night because I know how lucky and fortunate we are. We can help flatten the curve by doing our part and staying here as long as it takes. People like Ryan and all the essential workers are the true heroes during this crisis, so until there's a safe way to reopen the state, we'll isolate together.

After spending so much time with each other, I notice the littlest things about her. Like when she laughs really hard, her nose crinkles and sometimes she snorts, which I find cute as hell. She likes to sleep on her side, and sometimes snores like a Mack truck. When she's obviously tired, but I'm not, she'll try to stay awake to be with me longer. When she thinks I'm not watching her, she'll steal glances at me, and then I'll catch her, which makes her laugh. Cami is my rock, and I'm grateful everyday for our second chance.

I still can't believe she's fallen for me as hard as I have for her, and now I can't live without her. Hell, I've nearly died twice since coming here, but she's been the light at the end of the tunnel.

We FaceTimed my mom and told her the pleasant news that we were officially dating. My mother cried with joy, then asked us when we were getting married. I just shrugged and laughed. But honestly, I'd marry Cami in a heartbeat even though I still don't feel like I'm good enough for her.

Next, we called my sister, Ava. Cami was nervous as hell about it, but it was time they talk through their differences so there's no hostility. Their conversation lasted well over an hour, and by the end, both were laughing at my expense as they took turns telling stories about me and talking shit. Though, I don't even care because I'm just happy the air has been cleared between them.

We haven't told her parents about us yet. I've been too nervous, knowing her father would never approve of the poor kid being with his princess daughter, but Cami has assured me she couldn't give two fucks what her parents think. When the time's right, we'll tell them, but not yet. I like the bubble we're in right now and don't want anyone's outside opinions to burst it.

After another physical therapy session, Cami and I go for a walk outside. Spring is finally coming, and the weather has been much nicer. Eventually, I'd love to cook using the outdoor kitchen and watch the sunset with Cami while we eat. Though I can't buy her expensive things—but even if I could, they don't impress her—I can make memories with her in ways that count.

A few days ago, we drove to Roxbury and got more food for the next month. She went a couple of weeks ago, but only got the necessities, and now we need more to stay stocked up. We went together this time so we could double team and get out of the store faster. As we drove home, she continuously looked behind us to see if anyone was following us. I know what happened still affects her, but I'm doing my best to reassure her we're safe. The two guys who did it were finally caught, so I can breathe a little easier knowing they didn't get away with it, but we still stay alert.

Once we're back home, we unload and sanitize the groceries before putting them away, washing our hands in between a dozen times. It's become such a part of our lives that we don't even think twice about it.

We haven't been intimate in weeks. Even though she's given me all the hints, I know she hasn't wanted to rush me with my shoulder recovering, but it's doing much better now. We've been taking things slow, but right now, she's looking at me with a fire in her eyes.

"I think we should change out of our clothes and take a shower," I tell her, brushing my lips against her ear. Her head falls back, and she lets out a ragged breath as I drag my teeth against her skin.

"Yes," she says breathlessly. "Absolutely, yes."

I smirk as I take her hand and lead her to the master bathroom. Slowly, I peel off her leggings and shirt, allowing my fingertips to brush against her soft skin, and each time I touch her, her breasts rise and fall with shallow breaths. Cami watches me intently with a smile playing on her lips.

Walking toward the shower, I turn on the water and wait for it to get hot.

"You're so goddamn beautiful," I tell her, and she blushes.

"You're just saying that," she throws back, and I hate it when she downplays my compliments. "I've been in sweats with messy hair for days."

"Just how I like you," I tease, sprinkling kisses on her shoulders.

She reaches forward and helps take off my sling. I've still been wearing it daily but not for too much longer.

Cami lifts my shirt and pulls it over my head. She runs her fingers down my abs until her fingers are unbuttoning my jeans. Quickly, she slides them down my legs, along with my boxers. She stands confidently in a sexy as hell matching bra and panty set, and I take in the view before I remove them. Leaning down, I capture her taut nipple in my mouth. She arches her back and moans while running her fingers through my hair, then tugs. I release an animalistic growl, then scrape my teeth along her sensitive flesh, adding just enough pressure to drive her wild.

I move to the other, licking and sucking. She pants as I lick a trail up to her mouth and lower my hand to her pussy.

"Fuck, Cami. You're so tight," I murmur, feeling her wetness on my fingers.

Before I lose myself in her, I grab her hand and lead us into the shower. Once we're inside, she stands under the stream of water, letting it cascade down her body. She tilts her head back and gets her hair wet. I watch in awe at the gorgeous woman in front of me, waiting for me to pleasure her in all the right ways.

Stepping closer, I bring my hand down and begin stroking my thumb against her clit. Cami moans and nearly crumples under my touch. She's so damn sensitive, and seeing her like this has my dick growing harder. At this rate, I won't last five minutes inside her, but I want to go all night. She bites her bottom lip, causing me to let out a throaty moan as she writhes.

"Eli," she whispers. "I want you so badly."

"Me too, baby," I admit. "I don't want to rush, but damn, I don't know how much longer I can wait to taste you. It's been too long."

Water spills over her chest, and as I trail kisses down her body, it soaks my hair and falls into my eyes. I brush it back and lift a brow when I catch her gawking. Flashing her a quick wink, I kneel in front of her and settle between her legs, running my nose along her sensitive bud. I love the way she tastes and the soft moans that escape her as I flick my tongue against her clit.

"Eli, Eli," she whimpers, fisting my hair as I worship her body with my mouth. Cami's back arches as I wage war against her pussy, and I know she's close by the way her body shakes. As she sinks into me, I pull away with a smirk. I love how quickly she loses herself with me and how willing she is to please me in return. In the bedroom, Cami is a fucking goddess, and I plan to worship her body for the rest of our lives.

Her eyes pop open in protest. "Nooooo!"

I shrug with a laugh. "What?"

"I swear, I will bring Prince Harry in here and let him finish the job," she threatens, and I chuckle at her eagerness.

Her perky breasts rise and fall as I ease my fingers up her legs and bring my mouth back between her thighs. She's so damn wet that all I can do is smile as I taste her sweetness. She shudders under my touch as I insert one finger and then another, twirling my tongue against her clit.

"I'm so close. Don't stop," she pleads on a whisper, and while I want to tease her, my baby deserves this release. I slow my pace, allowing the orgasm to fully build before she completely unravels. Moments later, she's trembling and groaning as she loses herself. I pull away, kissing her inner thighs before standing.

She looks at me with hooded eyes, begging for a kiss. Our mouths fuse and our tongues twist under the hot stream. The emotions overwhelm me because I still can't believe this woman is mine. The way I feel about her is unfathomable. I'm never letting her fucking go.

"I can taste myself on your lips," she tells me, and I chuckle.

"And you're so goddamn delicious I'd eat you for every meal." I slyly smile as my erection presses into her stomach.

"Should we get you cleaned up?" I muse.

"No, you should fuck me."

I chuckle, reaching for her body wash.

I lather it on a loofah between my hands. "I'll make it worth your while, don't worry."

Cami narrows her eyes and pretends to sulk.

Gently, I wash her shoulders, chest, arms, and legs. Then I spin her around and scrub her back and down her ass. I wrap my good arm around her waist and lower my hand between her legs.

"You smell so good," I murmur in her ear, teasing my tongue along her neck. I thrust a finger inside her, and she tightens against me. "God, you drive me fucking wild."

Cami turns, places her palms on my cheek, and forces me to look into her bright blue eyes. "Quit being a gentleman and *fuck* me," she demands.

I pop an eyebrow, loving her eagerness. "That's what you really want?"

"Be careful with your arm, but I won't break, Eli," she says as a devious grin spreads across her face.

Cami quickly rinses before turning off the shower and stepping out. She hands me a towel, and I swiftly dry myself. While she wraps hers around her body, I charge forward, and she squeals as I chase her into her bedroom. She falls onto the mattress with a laugh as I hover over her.

"Hope you're ready for what you asked for," I taunt as she moves to the middle. My cock throbs between us, and I can't wait any longer. Grabbing her thighs, I pull her body closer and settle between her legs. Stroking my shaft a few times, I slowly ease into her, and she gasps before I pull out. I've always loved teasing her, but it's even more fun when we're naked. Then I slide back in, thrusting deeper.

"Harder," she pants, but instead, I pull out, grab her ankles, and drag her to the edge as I stand. "Oh my God," she squeals.

"Flip," I demand. She licks her lips before she gets on all fours.

With a firm hand, I smack her ass, and the sound echoes through the room. She purrs, which is a complete turn-on. I dig my fingers into her hips as I guide myself inside, fucking her hard and deep. Our skin slaps together and mingles with our moans. My dick is so goddamn hard it feels like it might break off as she arches her ass against me, screaming my name and fisting the comforter.

"Yes, yes, yes! Oh my God, *yes*," she cries out. "Eli…" Her breathlessness, combined with how her muscles tense, tells me everything I need to know. Wrapping my arm around her waist, I pull her up until her back is to my chest. I slow my pace, cup her jaw, then bring our mouths together.

Her body shakes, and she comes, moaning my name. My movements are slow and calculated, and soon, I'm losing myself too. We collapse on the bed and crawl to the middle where I hold her in my arms. Emotions pour through me, and when I look at Cami, she's flashing a satisfied smile. Cupping her cheeks, I fuse our mouths back together, unable to stop kissing her.

"Pretty sure I need another shower," she says when we break apart. "I'm a sweaty mess."

"Me too. I think we should conserve water," I tell her, and she nods, then follows me to the bathroom. I turn on the water and allow her to step in, taking in every inch of her gorgeous curves. I'm so fucking lucky.

I squirt shampoo in my palm and gently massage her scalp. She closes her eyes, and a small smile plays on her lips.

"Have I told you how much I love you today?" I ask her, grabbing her body wash and paying extra attention to her breasts, then moving down to her sensitive areas.

"Actions sometimes speak louder than words," she mutters, and I chuckle.

"I love you," I whisper against the shell of her ear as the warm water falls over our bodies. "I'll love you till the day I die."

She smiles so sweet as she plucks her lip. "I love you too, Eli."

I reach around and grab a handful of her ass until she squeals. She washes me, and then we make out until our skin prunes. We wrap fluffy towels around our bodies and go back to the bedroom.

She lifts an eyebrow as she gazes her eyes down my body. "Ready for round two?"

Genuine laughter escapes me as I move closer to her. "I'll never tell you no. My cock is yours. Prince Harry 2.0."

Cami nearly doubles over, then takes me in her hand before kneeling in front of me as she sucks me long and hard.

We make love for the rest of the afternoon, only taking breaks for food and quick naps. I hold her and make sure she knows how much she means to me, and how in love with her I am. What we have is more real than anything I've ever experienced, and I wasn't lying when I told her I'd love her until the day I die. Honestly, I can't imagine a day without her in my life; that's how quickly she's burrowed into my heart and soul.

Cameron St. James is my everything, and I'll spend forever proving that to her.

Chapter Thirty

CAMERON
DAY 90

We've officially been in the cabin for three months, but it hasn't been what I expected at all when I first decided to come here. When Eli first arrived, I was convinced it'd be hell sharing this space with him. Little did I know, I'd fall stupidly in love with him and end up never wanting to leave this place or his side.

A week ago, I got the news that my graduation ceremony was canceled, and I feel cheated as hell. I understand why, but for the past four years, I imagined walking across that stage and getting my diploma. I've been excited to give my valedictorian speech since I knew I was in the running. Though I won't be giving it in front of everyone, I still plan to record myself so they can hear it. Getting this honor was hard work, and I don't want to miss the opportunity to speak to my peers one more time. I know I'm not the only one who's missing out on events such as this right now, and even though I understand this is our new reality, it's still hard to cope with.

Eli notices my mood is off and wraps his arm around my waist as I make coffee.

"What's wrong?" he asks. Anytime he's around, my whole demeanor changes.

"Just thinking about graduation, that's all," I tell him, turning around and wrapping my arms around his neck as he dips down and presses his mouth against mine.

"Babe." He smiles, lifting my chin. "You should be so fucking proud of all that you accomplished, especially since you finished your last semester online and during a pandemic when you were sick. You are at the top of your class at one of the most difficult universities in the country. No one or nothing can ever take that away from you. Ever."

I smile and nod. "You're right. I don't want to seem like a brat. I'm just disappointed."

"You're not a brat for that. For other things, absolutely, but for that, nah," he tells me with a wink, and I playfully smack him. I love how grounded he keeps me. It's nice to have a boyfriend who isn't an elitist.

"Hungry?" he asks.

"I'm always hungry," I throw back. "For your Prince Harry."

"I thought you named him Zeus?" He arches a curious brow.

I giggle. "Not when it gets me off better than the vibrator. Then it deserves the royal name."

He laughs and goes to the fridge and pulls out ingredients for breakfast. "You're a sex fiend, but that's why I love you."

"That's not the only reason," I argue. My stomach growls just as the espresso finishes brewing. I fill two mugs, then hand him one. After I add cream to mine, I lean against the counter and admire how sexy Eli is. I can't stop staring at his bare chest and how his sweats hang low on his hips, showing that V that goes to the happiest place on earth, but I'm not referring to Disney World. Though what he does sure is fucking magical.

He catches me gawking and lifts an eyebrow, and I swear if he wasn't almost finished cooking, I'd fuck him until tomorrow. "Yes?"

I clear my throat, not even sorry he caught me. "Stop looking sexy, and I'd stop staring."

"My bad." He smirks.

"So…" I speak up to get my mind out of the gutter. "I'm going to FaceTime Mommy Dearest today."

He laughs. "Yeah?"

"I still can't believe how giddy she is about us being together," I say. I think back to a couple of weeks ago when I finally told my parents. They were so supportive that if I wasn't already living in the twilight zone, I definitely would be now. Daddy always stressed to marry a wealthy man with status who could contribute to the family name. My mom, on the other hand, always told me to marry for love. She didn't and later regretted it. It's obvious they're not *in love* and would be happier apart.

"Your mom has always loved me. Seriously, I was more worried about your dad than her."

"Really? I was worried he'd give you one of those fatherly 'you break my daughter's heart, and I'll break your neck' speeches. Or worse, they'd make you join the country club." I look down his body again. "But there's just no way you'd properly fit in," I say with laughter.

He chuckles, shaking his head. "Oh really? Don't think I can pull off a thousand dollar polo and slacks and order the servers around while I brag about my mistress?"

I roll my eyes at his mockery. "You're hilarious. Keep that up, and they'll forbid us from being together. Then again, if they would've disapproved, we'd be married right now."

"Hot damn!" he shouts ecstatically. "That's too bad because I'd marry you in a heartbeat."

He turns off the stove, slides our food onto plates, and we move to the bar. I'm sitting so close to him as we eat that I'm practically on his lap. "Did you mean it?"

"Mean what?" he asks around a mouthful.

"That you'd marry me in a heartbeat."

Eli finishes chewing, then turns and grabs my hand. We're nearly facing each other in the barstools. "Without a doubt, Cami. I've seen you nearly every day for the past ninety days, and while I hate the state of the world, I'm grateful to spend this uninterrupted time with you. I honestly don't remember what life was like without you in it, and I don't want to. You're my everything, baby. I mean it, but I do worry sometimes that I'm not good enough for you."

My eyes go wide, and I pull back slightly at his confession. "Not good enough for me? Don't be ridiculous. You're more than enough."

He shrugs shyly. "I know the *type* of guys you've dated. The money, well-known name, extravagant dates. But all I can offer you is my love."

I tilt my head and flash him a small smile. "You are definitely *not* the kind of guys I've dated in the past, and I'm grateful for that. I've never felt this way about anyone before, which isn't something I'm used to. It's different with you. Most men just want to use me to get to my parents. Status and materials don't matter to you, and when it comes to who I want, it doesn't matter to me either. You've loved me in ways I've never been loved before. It can't be faked or bought, and I hope you know that because I don't want to lose you."

"Lose me? You'll need to put a restraining order on me to leave you alone," he says with a chuckle.

I sigh, hoping he's right. "When all of this is over, and we go back to the real world, things will change. I know that, and I'm trying to prepare myself for it. Some people don't want to be in the spotlight, and I don't want the added attention to ruin what we have. It scares the shit out of me, Eli. You're the best thing that's ever happened to me, and I'm scared of losing you and everything we've built. I keep telling myself it's all too good to be true, and I don't know what I did to deserve you." I can feel my emotions bubbling, but I need him to know what's burning inside me.

"Cami," Eli whispers my name. "I've known you for a long time. I've been best friends with your brother since we were kids. I understand what you and your family go through, and I'll be there by your side, no matter what happens. I promise you with everything I am. It'll take much more than some paparazzi and gossip stories to ruin what we have. And if we go out of town, I could always hide you in the trunk of a car when we leave for the weekends just like Taylor Swift does."

I snort and laugh. "Yeah, I heard that rumor too. She was wheeled out in a suitcase and loaded in the back of a car to avoid the photographers. It's clever actually, and I wish I would've thought of it. Kendall suggested it one time, too."

"Of course she did." He shakes his head and picks up his fork. "I've waited this long, and I'm not giving up being with you for anything or anyone. Love you, baby."

"Love you more. You're mine forever, Eli."

"Forever and ever," he echoes. "I promise."

I let out a relaxed breath, and we finish eating. After we're done, I go into the living room to call my mom while Eli cleans up the kitchen. She answers, and I can tell she's in a pleasant mood by her wide grin.

"Cameron! So happy you called. Eleanor was just putting on some morning tea for me, and your father is outside playing golf on the mini green he had installed a few weeks ago," she says. She's well put together with her hair perfectly done, pearl earrings, and a diamond necklace. I wouldn't be surprised if she's wearing pantyhose as well because my mother dresses up like she's hosting a tea party every day. She's weirder than those who quarantine in jeans.

Eleanor is one of the maids who helps around the house, and it worries me that my mother has still allowed her workers to come and go. They could easily afford to pay her time off.

She clears her throat, bringing the attention back to her. "I was thinking about you this morning. I miss you dearly, sweetie. I wish you'd come home and see your father and me soon."

"Mom, I know. I miss you too, but I have no desire to set foot in the city right now. I talk to Ryan as much as I can, and it doesn't sound like things will let up soon."

"Honey, we're past the curve. That hunky governor said things are better. I'm sure life will get back to normal soon."

I roll my eyes, but she doesn't notice. He never said that. The fact that our political views don't always align can be frustrating, but I learned a long time ago to keep my mouth shut to avoid a family feud. "It won't, Mom. It may take years."

"We'll see," she says in her typical patronizing tone. I watch as she reaches for her tea that's being served on fine china. She even holds out her pinky when she sips, and I almost laugh, but hold back. "So, how's Eli? Where is he?"

I snort. "I swear you have a crush on him, Mother."

As if he was summoned, Eli comes from the kitchen and leans over the back of the couch. "Hey, Mama C! You're looking so gorgeous today," he says in an overly flirty voice.

I turn and shake my head at him. "Why, thank you, Eli. How have you been feeling?"

He takes the phone from my hand, laughing, and chats with my mom. I swear she loves talking to him more than me. I even hear her giggle, and the way he charms her has me chuckling. Popping up off the couch, I walk toward him, and he has the camera turned around facing Bruno, showing Mom how big and well-mannered he is. I shake my head. "He doesn't know how to listen," I whisper-hiss.

As soon as I do, Bruno jumps up on me. He's so heavy he nearly knocks me over, then he starts licking me to death. "Aw, sweetie. I wish you treated Coco like that. You never were much of a dog person."

Bruno is relentless, and once I push him down, I lean over and pet his head. I motion for Eli to give me the cell so we can end this conversation.

"Okay, well, I'll give the phone back to Cami. Chat soon. Bye!" Eli flashes a cheesy grin, then hands it over to me with a cocky smirk.

"He's such a nice young man. So charming and handsome. I love what he does with his hair. Perfect for you, dear," Mom gushes, and I swear I catch her blushing.

"I'm so glad you approve," I deadpan, and Eli does a little dance on the other side of the screen, completely distracting me. His fingers play on the edge of his jogging pants, and he slides them down just a tad lower, and my cheeks burn. I don't even know what my mom is saying because I stopped paying attention.

"Don't you agree, Cameron?"

I try to ignore him the best I can. "I'm sorry, what was that?" I ask, clearing my throat.

"I was saying how disappointed and upset I am that I won't get to see my little girl walk across the stage to receive her diploma," she repeats. "After all the money we spent for you to go there," she mumbles, and I suck in a long breath, reminding myself not to engage.

Nodding, I give her a forced smile. "I know. Me too."

"Well, hopefully it'll make graduate school that much sweeter for you," she says.

"Yes. It'll be extra special when I finally walk across the stage." In two more years.

Thankfully, Mom changes the subject and chats about Ryan and praises all the good work he's been doing. Then she mentions the hefty donations they gave in his name, but I don't tell her what he told me about not wanting people to know. She voices her concerns but, in the same breath, downplays the situation, which is one reason I get so frustrated speaking with her. I love my mother, but sometimes, she pushes my buttons, even if she's not trying. For decades, she's been living in her own little elite world where money can buy anything and problems don't exist, so during a pandemic is no different. Instead of going back and forth with her, I ignore it and discuss the weather and Chanel.

"I'm just waiting for things to get back to normal. I knew it was dire when fashion week was canceled," she brings it up again. I swallow down a groan. My head is about to explode if I don't get away from this conversation. "When do you think you'll come back?"

"I'm not exactly sure. Eli's still working remotely, and I think we might stay through the summer and just see how it goes before we decide." Things change every day so if I give my mother a timeframe, she'll expect me to abide by it, but if I leave it open, then she can't hold me accountable.

"Summer? That's nearly four months from now," she exclaims as I sit back down on the couch. "Surely, you can come back before then."

All I do is shake my head. "I want to, Mom, I really do. But I don't know what the future holds, so we're just taking it day by day. No telling what's going to happen in a few days, nevertheless, a few months." While some parts of the country have loosened their restrictions, the hospitals are still overflowing, and there's still no cure or vaccine. I may be in limbo with my penthouse and graduate school, but as long as Eli is with me through it all, I don't care. We'll figure it out together.

"I worry about you," she says.

"We'll be fine and can FaceTime as much as you want," I remind her.

"Cameron, you know I'm not very good with technology."

"Well, luckily, you'll have plenty of time to figure it out. But anyway, I'll let you go. I'll chat tomorrow if you want," I say quickly, wanting off the line.

After taking another sip of tea, she grins. "Okay, sweetie. I love you. Chat soon." She blows two kisses, then I end the call.

If I was home, I know she'd wrap me in a big hug and press a kiss on each of my cheeks. I let out a lengthy sigh and lean my head back on the couch, then close my eyes. When I open them, Eli is standing above me, and I jump.

"Jesus, you scared me."

His lips tilt up. "We should go for a hike today."

"Seriously?" I ask, furrowing my brows. I haven't hiked since Ryan and I were kids. "Do I look like someone who hikes?"

He licks his lips and chuckles with a shrug. "I noticed there were some trails cut out. They might be slightly overgrown, but I'd love to go check them out. Take Bruno with us and let him wander around the property for a few hours."

"Alright, I'm down, but you can't make fun of me if I trip and fall or something." Because it's a high probability.

"I can make that deal." He leans over and places his lips on mine. Wrapping my arms around the back of his neck, I smile against his mouth.

"Go get dressed," he tells me, and I notice he's already changed. When I get up, he takes the opportunity to smack my ass before I run upstairs.

I dress comfortably in one of my tennis skirts because it's so beautiful out today, then tie my running shoes nice and tight. As soon as my foot hits the bottom stair, he's grinning ear to ear, reaches his hand out, and I meet him. "You're wearing a skirt to hike, huh? Why am I even surprised?"

I roll my eyes at his little dig. "It's a thing. Google it."

He shrugs. "If you say so. I mean, I'm not complaining about the view at all."

"That's what I thought." I wink. "Now, let's get some fresh air. I'm shocked we haven't gotten cabin fever yet."

"You and me both," he retorts.

Bruno follows us, and as soon as he can get around us, he's off in a full sprint going straight to the pond. Eli laughs, and I groan, knowing that means he'll need a bath when we return. We take a trail that leads to some woods, and Eli and I walk in silence, holding hands. The wind rustles through the dense forest, and it brings me back to being kids and playing out here with Ryan. We never had a "normal" childhood, and the only time I felt like a kid was when we came to the cabin. I didn't have to put on fancy dresses or sit up straight or do any of the things my parents wanted me to do to impress their friends and the media. Out here, I got to get dirty, play outside, and be a kid.

We continue walking farther down the path, and the sunshine peeks between the trees. A smile plays on my lips as Eli squeezes my hand, then kisses my knuckles.

"I love you," I tell him. "Thank you."

"Love you too. And for what?"

"For the escape. I needed it," I say truthfully.

Eli stops walking and turns to me. The space between us disappears, and I'm getting lost in his mouth and touch. His large hand slips under my shirt, and he palms my breast. I'm panting, and all I want is him. I take several steps forward, guiding him until his back rests against a gigantic tree. We're breathless already as I untie his shorts, then fall to my knees and take him in my mouth. I look up in his eyes, and when he runs his fingers through my hair, I stroke his shaft as I suck harder. Eli breathes out deep grunts as I increase my pace until I'm nearly choking on his cock.

I slow my pace, then suck and lick his tip as I stroke him.

"Cami, fuck," he groans, and his legs begin to tremble. "Baby," he whispers, fisting my hair tighter around his fingers. I know he's close because his cock jerks in my grip, but I don't stop. After a few more moments, he tenses then releases in my mouth. I swallow it all down, not wanting to waste a drop, then stand with a smile as I lick my lips.

"Baby," he murmurs, then cups the back of my neck and fuses our mouths. I love that he doesn't even care I just had my lips on his cock and kisses me anyway. "Your turn."

I look around. "What do you mean?"

He arches a brow and lifts my skirt. "I feel like you had this planned all along," he slyly says, sliding my panties down to my knees.

I shrug. "Maybe." I'm so fucking wet from pleasuring him that it won't take much to get me off.

"Goddamn," he says as his fingers twirl on my clit, then he pushes one inside my pussy. I nearly lose my balance at how good it feels. "You're fucking drenched, baby. So smooth and tight, too."

"Always," I tell him. "You turn me on so much."

A boyish grin plays on his lips as he continues, then thrusts another finger inside. They're so big I nearly gasp as he pounds into me. Seconds later, he pushes my panties all the way down. I step out of them, and then he slides them in his pocket. It's no mystery I'm running out of underwear, considering he's always stealing them. Then he gets on his knees and loops one of my legs over his shoulder. I hang onto him as he leans in and devours every inch of me like I'm his favorite meal. He moves between finger fucking me and twirling his tongue on my clit, and I'm so thankful for this tree because I'm not sure how much longer I can hold my weight.

"Your pussy tastes so fucking good," he says. I moan out his name as the midmorning sunshine reflects through the trees. "You have such a tight little cunt."

"I love it when you talk dirty," I say between pants, and I don't know how much longer I'll last.

"Yes, baby. Come for me. Let me taste all of you," he continues, and when the orgasm builds, I nearly see stars as it rips through me. My voice echoes as my body loses complete control. Eli doesn't stop until I've fully come down from space.

"Wow..." I say, trying to catch my breath.

"You need my inhaler?" he teases, pulling it from his pocket as he stands, and my skirt falls back into place. I squeeze my thighs tightly together, not sure how I'll make it back to the cabin. I don't even think I'm on planet earth right now as my heart rapidly pounds.

"That was intense," I finally say, and a smirk slides across his lips, which is so damn adorable. I love that look on him, and it makes me crave him all over again.

"I had to return the favor." He leans forward and kisses me just as Bruno rushes up at a full sprint.

I laugh. "Do not jump on me." I point at him, and he actually sits. My mouth falls open. "Oh my God, he listened."

Eli wraps his arm around my shoulders as we walk back, enjoying the spring air and cool forest breeze. Bruno runs around, digging in the brush, and pees every thirty seconds. Watching him has me giggling because he's so excited to be outside. I've never seen a dog so damn happy all the time. We take our time walking to the cabin, and I make him promise we'll do this more often, especially since the weather has turned warm.

Bruno is filthy, so before we go inside, we rinse him off with the hose, and immediately after, he shakes, getting me completely soaked. Eli knew it was coming and was smart enough to step away, and he cracks up at my face.

"Every single time!" I shout with a groan. "Bruno, you're a jerk." He comes up to me and licks my hand, and I almost feel bad for raising my voice.

"You should go upstairs and hop in the tub," he tells me when we walk into the house. "Relax a bit. I'll bring a glass of wine up for you."

I look up at him in awe because that sounds amazing right now. "Why do you spoil me so much?" I ask, then kiss him.

"Because you're hot." He winks, then goes to the kitchen.

After I head upstairs, I take off my clothes and run the water, then add some bubble bath. When it's half full, I get in and immediately sigh in relief. Like clockwork, Eli comes in with a glass of wine.

"You're a saint. Thank you." I grab it and smile. I'm so relaxed already. Eli sits on the edge of the tub with a grin.

"Want to get in with me?" I ask, waggling my brows.

"I'll take a rain check. I need to get some work done this afternoon," he says sweetly. "But tempting." He stands, adjusting his groin. "*Extremely* tempting."

Eli tells me he'll be back later, then leaves. I sip my wine and stare out the big window. I nearly drink the entire glass, and when I get out, my eyes are heavy with exhaustion. I text Eli and tell him I'm going to take a nap, not wanting to bother him while he's working. He responds with how much he loves me and to sleep well.

By the time I wake up, I can tell it's late afternoon. I pick up my phone and see I slept for nearly five hours. When I walk downstairs, I smell something delicious and see Eli's busy at the stove.

"Babe," I say, and he nearly jumps. "Sorry, didn't mean to startle you." I walk closer. "Whatcha making?"

"I know how upset you were about graduation, so I thought I'd make you a special dinner to celebrate."

My face lights up. "Wow, seriously?" I glance over and see the table's set with one of Mom's lace cloths. The crystal wine glasses and fancy china from the cabinet are set out on it. I look back at him in shock. He wraps a hand around my waist and pulls me close. "I can't believe you did this."

"Of course, baby. Nothing but the best for you." He kisses my forehead. "I made lobster, sautéed spinach, and gratin potatoes. And your mother sent a bottle of Dom Pérignon Rose Gold."

"She sent a fifty thousand dollar bottle of champagne?" I gasp.

His eyes widen as if he hadn't realized the value, though neither of us should really be surprised at my mom's gesture. Everything about her is over the top. "She insisted. Only the best for her *princess*."

I grin and roll my eyes at the way he emphasizes the word. Then my smile spreads wider when I realize he's wearing a suit and tie, looking sexy as hell. Taking a step back, I study how good he looks and know I'm the luckiest woman in the world. He treats me like a fucking queen and makes me extremely happy, but this is beyond incredible.

"You didn't have to go through all this trouble, baby," I say, looking at the spread of food and how hard he's worked while I napped.

"Yes, I did. I wanted to make it special for you as best as I could."

I wrap my arms around his neck and crash my mouth on his. The kiss deepens when he slides his tongue inside, and now I'm tempted to skip dinner and have him instead.

"You already have," I tell him, pulling away slightly. "More than you'll ever know."

Epilogue

ELIJAH

It's been eighteen months since Cami graduated, and things have been crazy ever since, but there hasn't been a dull moment since we both arrived in Roxbury. She's my everything and being able to wake up next to her every morning has been the highlight of my life. Growing up, I never imagined I'd be good enough for her, and each day, she proves to me I'm more than enough.

The cabin holds a special place in our hearts now that we ended up staying there for eight months. We returned to the city last October when the state lifted the lockdown orders, but certain things were still restricted. No large gatherings over fifty people, limited business hours, and social distancing was encouraged. All schools and universities continued with online learning programs for their students. It felt a bit safer to return to the city, especially after Ryan said they were no longer struggling to get what they needed for their patients. The curve was flattening, and things were slowly going back to some kind of normal.

Cami was determined to buy a new penthouse, one that we could decorate and make a home together, but it had to have a view. Of course she paid for it, and I contributed by negotiating a great deal on an incredible sky rise. Working in real estate helped us find a place that we now call our own. We make love with the blinds open, allowing the skyglow of the city to light the rooms without worrying that anyone can see us.

Four months ago, I planned a weekend getaway at the cabin for her birthday with just the two of us. I surprised her with flowers, balloons, and a chocolate cake I made from scratch. And of course, we brought Bruno and Chanel. After we had a candlelight dinner and she blew out her candles, I got down on one knee and popped the question after telling her how much she meant to me. I was more nervous about asking her than I'd been about anything else in my life. When she said yes and cried, I picked her up and carried her upstairs, and we made love until the morning. It was the best day of my life.

We made the announcement to our family and friends a couple of days later after we went home. Everyone was so damn happy and supportive and were ready to add the big day to their calendars. However, until the lockdown was completely lifted, we weren't able to set a date. Though, two months ago, a vaccination was finally approved for mass distribution, and we immediately started planning every detail.

Sometimes when I wake up in the mornings, I don't know how this is my life, or how someone as sweet and funny as Cami is going to be my wife. Now in less than three weeks, it'll be official, and we'll be married the first weekend of December. A winter wonderland wedding is everything Cami's ever wanted, and I'll do whatever it takes to make sure it's perfect for her.

I glance over my checklist of things that still need to be done while Cami is at school. Since everything is now open, she was able to finish her last semester of graduate school on campus. Better yet, she'll finally get to walk across the stage and receive her diploma. Knowing there's quite a lot to do, I decide to call her best friend and maid of honor. I was going to ask my sister since she wants to be involved too, but I know she's busy with work through Christmas.

"Hi, Kendall," I greet her when she answers.

"Hey! How's it going, groom-to-be?" she asks in her typical bouncy voice. The girl has so much energy that sometimes she exhausts the piss out of me.

"Just getting some final touches together before the big day," I tell her with a smile.

"Of course. Give me all the tasks."

"So, since Cami wants to spend two weeks at the cabin to relive old times, I want to make sure it's completely stocked and ready. Any way you can pick up enough food and things to last us that long?"

She snorts. "Is Ryan gonna help me? I might need some strong muscles."

I shake my head. "I think I can arrange that," I murmur, knowing I'll have to coax my best friend into taking off work, and even though he's more than willing to do whatever we need, I feel guilty for asking. He's not been the same since the pandemic started. He's the strongest person I know, but it broke him.

"Then absolutely," she says matter-of-factly. "Food for two weeks. Enough booze to have you drunk 24/7 and a case of lube. Got it."

I can't even hold back the laughter, and I'm sure as hell not going to argue with her. "Whatever you say, Kendall. You know what Cami likes."

"Oh, then I can't forget chocolate, sparkling water, and shitty microwave meals."

I think back to when we were quarantined in the cabin together and all the unhealthy processed shit she brought to eat. Kendall knows her as well as I do.

"Extra wood, too," I tell her, knowing that'll be Ryan's job. "Maybe some holiday decorations." We'll return five days before Christmas Eve, so it'll be nice to have the tree and stuff up while we're there.

"I've got this, Eli. I was basically born for this task."

I chuckle. "Alright, great."

"I think I can make it happen this weekend. Check with Ryan and see if he's down, then we can carpool up there on Saturday."

"Will do," I say, and we end the call. I was ready to give Cami a glamorous, over-the-top, super-expensive honeymoon, but she didn't want our first moments as husband and wife to be captured by the paparazzi. She knew if we went anywhere public, they'd undoubtedly find us, and our privacy would be gone.

Moments later, Cami walks through the door with a smile on her face.

"Hey, baby." She pulls me into her arms and presses her lips against mine.

"How was class?" I ask as we settle on the couch. Cami reaches over and lights the fireplace with a push of a button, then kicks off her shoes.

"Great. Getting a little stressful with exams coming up, but then it'll be the wedding, and we'll officially be married! Then I'll graduate, and we can finally start our forever without interruptions." She leans her head back on the couch and looks at me with a smile.

"We're almost there, babe. Everything's gonna work out," I tell her encouragingly.

"You're right. I'm just getting antsy now that it's all coming up."

I grab her hand and kiss her knuckles. "So, um. I called Kendall," I say, and she immediately perks up.

"For what?"

"Well, since we're staying at the cabin after the ceremony, I asked if she could go up and stock it for us beforehand and get it all nice and ready. That way, you don't have to worry about it since you're studying for finals."

"What'd she say?"

"She wants me to see if Ryan will join her. Give him the hard tasks."

A big smile fills Cami's face, and she nods. "Mm-hmm. I bet she did."

It's no secret that Kendall has the hots for Ryan because of the comments she's made. But Cami's convinced her brother has a major crush on her best friend even though he denies it and acts like he can't stand her. Honestly, he's never mentioned anything to me before, so I don't want him to think I'm playing matchmaker because I'm not. That is Cami's area of expertise, not mine.

"I'll call him and make sure he joins her," she says with a chuckle. "You know, so they can get fully *acquainted*." She lifts her hand to give me a high five. "Come on, don't leave me hanging."

I scoff. "I don't know why we're high-fiving. Leave me out of this."

"Because you found the perfect way to hook up my brother. He's in love with her, Eli. I swear he is, but he's just too damn stubborn to admit it."

I let out a groan. "Great, he's going to think I'm in on this."

"He basically set us up, so we're just repaying him," I remind him. Ryan sent Eli to the cabin knowing there was a chance I'd be there. The sneaky shit knew what he was doing. "I'll call him and pull the little sister card. He will not deny me during my special time. Don't worry about it." Cami stands, grabs her phone from her backpack, then starts texting Ryan. I can't see what she's typing, but she's got an evil grin on her face, and I know that means she got her way.

"He'll join her on Saturday." Cami snorts. "This is too easy. Like feeding candy to a baby."

"You are so wrong," I say. "So, *so* wrong."

She shrugs. "They need to just bang it out, fall in love, and get married so she can be my sister already. I've got it all planned out, and now you've helped."

The weekend quickly comes, and on Sunday, I'm waking to a phone call from Ryan.

"Dude, I think we're stranded here," he says.

I sit up in bed and look outside to see everything is coated in white. Last night when Cami and I were watching the news, an arctic blast was mentioned, but I didn't think anything of it. Upstate probably got it even worse than the city.

"There's no alternative ways out?" I ask, knowing there's only a single highway that leads to and from the cabin.

"No, the main road is snowed over. It's so bad they won't be able to get the plows out for a few days, and apparently, the news said they expect more snow to come. I had to take a few emergency vacation days from work. We got twenty inches so far, and it's still coming down. The wind is brutal, so it's just fucking blowing everywhere. Even if the roads were open, I wouldn't be able to see shit."

"Holy fuck. Man, I'm sorry. I didn't think it'd be that bad." I brush a hand through my hair, pushing it back off my face.

Cami rolls over and looks at me. She sits up and grabs her phone, noticing it's six in the morning and then gives me an annoyed look that we're up this early on the weekend. I mouth her brother's name, and she perks up.

"If you need anything, let me know, okay? I'll try my best to help you out."

Ryan lets out a huff. "Thanks. I just wanted to let you two know so you don't get worried about us. Hopefully, we don't lose power. With my luck, an ice storm would make its way here too."

"God, let's hope not. Well, I appreciate the update. Take care of yourself and Kendall," I tell him.

"Yeah, she's a fucking trip." He groans, and I hold back my laughter.

"Good luck," I say before we end the call.

Cami looks at me as I lower my phone. "So!"

"There's a huge blizzard in Roxbury, and they're stranded at the cabin until the snow lets up. Apparently, it's worse up there, so it might for a while, depending on when the roads clear," I tell her.

"Yes!" She claps her hands. "I knew it."

"Knew what?" I ask, tilting my head and watching her excitement.

"That the cabin is lucky and helps people fall in love." She comes closer and wraps her arms around me.

"You think so, huh?" I ask as we exchange a heated kiss.

"I know so," she says matter-of-factly. "Look at us. How else do you explain what happened?"

I smirk at her happiness. She does have a point.

CAMERON
6 MONTHS LATER

Eli and I have been married for six months, and it's been pure bliss. I can't imagine my life without him, and every day, I'm thankful for what we've been through to get where we are today. He's my best friend, biggest supporter, the voice of reason, and the love of my life. I honestly don't remember how I survived without him. While the circumstances that brought us together were awful, we were able to find love in the midst of it.

Our wedding ceremony was beautiful, and while my parents wanted it to be an elitist event, I refused and planned it my way instead. We got married in front of close friends and family only. I made them all promise not to leak any of the wedding details to the media because the last thing we need to deal with is the paparazzi following us all day. I got so spoiled living in the country that when I returned to the city, it was a wake-up call for Eli and me. But just as he promised, none of it affected our relationship. If anything, it brought us closer. Honestly, I love seeing the printed pictures of us together because it's proof to everyone that he's mine. It also doesn't hurt that my exes saw too. Eli doesn't care for the attention and has even come up with creative ways for us to escape without being seen. I have yet to sneak out in a suitcase, though. The thought makes me giggle because who knows, maybe someday I actually will.

I roll over and see the early morning light peeking through the windows, but the side of the bed is empty. Reaching over, I feel the sheets, and they're cold, which means Eli must be up working. He got promoted in his company and now works mostly from home unless he's doing showings or meeting with clients over drinks. He's worked so hard for it, and I'm so incredibly proud of him.

After I go through my morning routine, I put on a fluffy robe and walk into the kitchen where Eli is sitting with his laptop. I study him, admiring how handsome he is with the scruff on his chin before he notices me. As soon as his eyes meet mine, he stops typing, and stands to kiss me good morning.

"Coffee?" he asks with a cheesy grin, pouring me a mug and adding a splash of creamer until it's the color I like. I take it, then sit at the barstool next to him at the island.

He glances over at me. "Hungry?"

"You should just automatically know the answer to that by now. I will never turn down a meal. Especially from you," I tell him.

"Breakfast coming up," he says, pulling food from the fridge. He chops veggies and throws them in the skillet, and when they're sautéed, he cracks a few eggs on top with cheese. After he plates it and grabs two forks, he brings them over, and I immediately take a bite.

"You didn't drink your coffee..." He looks at the mug that I haven't touched, then glances back at me.

I swallow and tuck my bottom lip into my mouth. I can't hold my secret in much longer, especially when it comes to not drinking caffeine. It'll be the most suspicious thing about me.

"No. I think I'm going to have to stop drinking it for a while," I say casually, taking another bite of food with a knowing smirking.

His face contorts. "Why? Are you hopping on some weird no-caffeine trend?"

I laugh because I live off coffee and fashion. "No, just pregnant," I say it so nonchalantly with a shrug, I wonder if he'll comprehend it or not.

Eli takes a bite, then hurries, and swallows it down. His eyes go wide as a smile sweeps across his perfect lips. "Wait, what did you say?"

"We're having a baby."

He stands so fast the barstool falls over, and I laugh at his excitement. I get up as he wraps his arms around me.

"Wow, babe. This is the best news I've ever heard," he says, and when I pull away, I see tears of joy waiting to spill over, which makes me an emotional mess. I start crying too, and then we're laughing and hugging and kissing.

"You'll be an amazing dad, you know." I wipe my cheeks. Considering he never knew his dad, I know he'll give our baby everything he or she needs along with tons of love.

"I hope so. Either way, I know the kid will be loved unconditionally, and if your parents have any say, completely spoiled rotten." He grins.

"Very true."

"Have you told your parents yet? When did you find out?" he asks.

"No, no one. Just you. When you were at the office yesterday, I felt a little weird and realized I was over a month late, so I got a few tests. Each of them were positive. I was shocked, but then was so exhausted and fell asleep before I could tell you."

He's grinning from ear to ear. "We're going to be parents." Eli kneels in front of me, then lifts my shirt and kisses my stomach.

"I can't wait to see you barefoot and pregnant." He winks up at me, and I burst out laughing at the very thing I mocked him for.

"Elijah Ross, we are not having ten babies, though, so get that thought out of your head," I say firmly.

He winks. "We'll see."

Groaning, I shake my head at his stupidly cute smile. "And to think just last year, it was only the two of us," I say, running my fingers through his hair.

Looking up at me with bright blue eyes, he chews on his bottom lip. "And now we're starting a family. Maybe it'll be twins." He waggles his brows.

I snort. "Maybe."

Eli stands, wraps me in his arms, and slides his lips gently across mine. Even after all this time, my heart gallops when he touches or kisses me. It always feels like the first time with him.

"I love you, Eli," I tell him.

"I love you too, Cami. So fucking much. You've made me the happiest person alive."

I shake my head and laugh. "Impossible because I'm the happiest person alive, and it's all because of you."

This concludes Elijah & Cameron's romance and we hope you enjoyed it! Don't worry, you'll see glimpses of them soon. Curious about what happened with Ryan and Kendall being stuck in the cabin for two weeks? Find out next in their story in *The Best of Us*!

About the Author

Brooke Cumberland and Lyra Parish are a duo of romance authors who teamed up under the *USA Today* pseudonym, Kennedy Fox. They share a love of Hallmark movies & overpriced coffee. When they aren't bonding over romantic comedies, they like to brainstorm new book ideas. One day, they decided to collaborate under a pseudonym and have some fun creating new characters that'll make you blush and your heart melt. If you enjoy romance stories with sexy, tattooed alpha males and smart, quirky, independent women, then a Kennedy Fox book is for you! They're looking forward to bringing you many more stories to fall in love with!

Find us on our website:
kennedyfoxbooks.com

Subscribe to our newsletter:
kennedyfoxbooks.com/newsletter

Possessive

WILLOW WINTERS

Some men are born with a black heart and a tainted soul.

It's in my blood and in my bones. In every impure thought and desire.

I tried to walk away from my past.

But then she came back into my life.

Stumbling toward me and looking up at me as if I was the one she'd been looking for all this time.

As if I could be her savior and take her pain away.

If only she knew.

She brings out what I hate most about myself.

Selfish, ruthless, *possessive*.

I tried to be a good man. To be cold and distant and warn her away.

She should have taken the hint and run.

She didn't …

And now she's *mine*.

Preface

ADDISON

It's easy to smile around Tyler.

It's how he got me. We were in calculus, and he made some stupid joke about angles. I don't even remember what it was. Something about never discussing infinity with a mathematician because you'll never hear the end of it. He's a cute dork with his jokes. He knows some dirty ones too.

A year later and he still makes me laugh. Even when we're fighting. He says he just wants to see me smile. How can I leave when he says things like that? I believe him with everything in me.

My friend's grandmother told me once to fall in love with someone who loves you back just a little more.

Even as my shoulders shake with a small laugh and he leans forward to nip my neck, I know that I'll never really love Tyler the way he loves me.

And it makes me ashamed. Truly.

I'm still laughing when his bedroom door creaks open. Tyler plants a small kiss on my shoulder. It's not an open-mouth kiss, but still it leaves a trace on my skin and sends a warmth through my body. It's fleeting though.

The cool air passes between the two of us as Tyler leans back and smiles broadly at his brother.

I may be seated on my boyfriend's lap, but the way Daniel looks at me makes me feel like I'm alone. His eyes pierce through me with a sharpness that makes me afraid to move. Afraid to even breathe.

I don't know why he does this to me.

He makes me hot and cold at the same time. It's like I've disappointed him simply by being here. As if he doesn't like me. Yet there's something else.

Something that's forbidden.

It creeps up on me whenever I hear Daniel's rough voice; whenever I catch him watching Tyler and me. It's like I've been caught cheating, which makes no sense at all. I don't belong to Daniel, no matter how much that idea haunts my dreams.

He's twenty-one now and I'm only seventeen. But more importantly, he's Tyler's brother.

It's all in my head. I tell myself over and over again that the electricity between us is something I've made up. That my body doesn't burn for Daniel. That my soul doesn't ache for him to rip me away and punish me for daring to let his brother touch me.

It's only when Tyler speaks to him that Daniel looks away from me, tossing something down beside us.

Tyler's oblivious to everything happening. And suddenly I can breathe again.

My eyelids flutter open, my body hot under the stifling blankets. I don't react to the memory in my dreams anymore. Not at first, anyway. It sinks in slowly. The recognition of what that day would lead to growing heavier in my heart with each second that passes. Like a wave crashing on the shore, but taking its time. Threatening to engulf me as it approaches.

It was years ago, but the memory remains.

The feeling of betrayal, for fantasizing about Tyler's older brother.

The heartache from knowing what happened only three weeks after that night.

The desire and desperation to go back to that point and beg Tyler to never come looking for me.

All of those emotions swirl into a deadly concoction in the pit of my stomach. It's been years since I've been tormented by the remembrance of Tyler and what we had. And by the memories of Daniel and what never was.

Years have passed.

But it all comes back to me after seeing Daniel last night.

Chapter One

ADDISON
The night before

I love this bar. Iron Heart Brewery. It's nestled in the center of the city and located at the corner of this street. The town itself has history. Hints of the old cobblestone streets peek through the torn asphalt and all the signs here are worn and faded, decorated with weathered paint. I can't help but to be drawn here.

And with the varied memorabilia lining the walls, from signed knickknacks to old glass bottles of liquor, this place is flooded with a welcoming warmth. It's a quiet bar with all local and draft beers a few blocks away from the chaos of campus. So it's just right for me.

"Make up your mind?"

My body jolts at the sudden question. It only gets me a rough laugh from the tall man on my left, the bartender who spooked me. A grey shirt with the brewery logo on it fits the man well, forming to his muscular shoulders. With a bit of stubble and a charming smirk, he's not bad looking. And at that thought, my cheeks heat with a blush.

I could see us making out behind the bar; I can even hear the bottles clinking as we crash against the wall in a moment of passion. But that's where it would end for me. No hot and dirty sex on the hard floor. No taking him back to my barely furnished apartment.

I roll my eyes at the thought and blow a strand of hair away from my face as I meet his gaze.

I'm sure he flirts with everyone. But it doesn't make it any less fun for the moment.

"Whatever your favorite is," I tell him sheepishly. "I'm not picky." I have to press my lips together and hold back my smile when he widens his and nods.

"You new to town?" he asks me.

I shrug and have to slide the strap to my tank top back up onto my shoulder. Before I can answer, the door to the brewery and bar swings open, bringing in the sounds of the nightlife with it. It closes after two more customers leave. Looking over my shoulder through the large glass door at the front, I can see them heading out. The woman is leaning heavily against a strong man who's obviously her significant other.

Giving the bartender my attention again, I'm very much aware that there are only six of us here now. Two older men at the high top bar, talking in hushed voices and occasionally laughing so loud that I have to take a peek at them.

And one other couple who are seated at a table in the corner of the bar. The couple who just left had been sitting with them. All four are older than I am. I'd guess married with children and having a night out on the town.

And then there's the bartender and me.

"I'm not really from here, no."

"Just passing through?" he asks me as he walks toward the bar. I'm a table away, but he keeps his eyes on me as he reaches for a glass and hits the tap to fill it with something dark and decadent.

"I'm thinking about going to the university actually. To study business. I came to check it out." I don't tell him that I'm putting down some temporary roots regardless of whether or not I like the school here. Every year or so I move somewhere new … searching for what could feel like home.

His eyebrow raises and he looks me up and down, making me feel naked. "Your ID isn't fake, right?" he asks and then tilts the tall glass in his hand to let the foam slide down the side.

"It isn't fake, I swear," I say with a smile and hold up my hands in defense. "I chose to travel instead of going to college. I've got a little business, but I thought finally learning more about the technicalities of it all would be a step in the right direction." I pause, thinking about how a degree feels more like a distraction than anything else. It's a reason to settle down and stop moving from place to place. It could be the change I need. Something needs to change.

His expression turns curious and I can practically hear all the questions on his lips. *Where did you go? What did you do? Why did you leave your home so young and naïve?* I've heard them all before and I have a prepared list of answers in my head for such questions.

But they're all lies. Pretty little lies.

He cleans off the glass before walking back over and pulling out the seat across from me.

Just as the legs of the chair scrape across the floor, the door behind me opens again, interrupting our conversation and the soft strums of the acoustic guitar playing in the background.

The motion brings a cold breeze with it that sends goosebumps down my shoulder and spine. A chill I can't ignore.

The bartender's ass doesn't even touch the chair. Whoever it is has his full attention.

As I lean down to reach for the cardigan laying on top of my purse, he puts up a finger and mouths, "One second."

The smile on my face is for him, but it falters when I hear the voice behind me.

Everything goes quiet as the door shuts and I listen to them talking. My body tenses and my breath leaves me. Frozen in place, I can't even slip on the cardigan as my blood runs cold.

My heart skips one beat and then another as a rough laugh rises above the background noise of the small bar.

"Yeah, I'll take an ale, something local," I hear Daniel say before he slips into view. I know it's him. That voice haunted me for years. His strides are confident and strong, just like I remember them. And as he passes me to take a seat by the bar, I can't take my eyes off of him.

He's taller and he looks older, but the slight resemblance to Tyler is still there. As my heart learns its rhythm again, I notice his sharp cheekbones and my gaze drifts to his hard jaw, covered with a five o'clock shadow. I'd always thought of him as tall and handsome, albeit in a dark and brooding way. And that's still true.

He could fool you with his charm, but there's a darkness that never leaves his eyes.

His fingers spear through his hair as he checks out the beer options written in chalk on the board behind the bar. His hair's longer on top than it is on the sides, and I can't help but to imagine what it would feel like to grab on to it. It's a fantasy I've always had.

The timbre in his voice makes my body shudder.

And then heat.

I watch his throat as he talks, I notice the little movements as he pulls out a chair in the corner of the bar across from me. If only he would look my way, he'd see me.

Breathe. Just breathe.

My tongue darts out to lick my lips and I try to avert my eyes, but I can't.

I can't do a damn thing but wait for him to notice me.

I almost whisper the command, *look at me*. I think it so loud I'm sure it can be heard by every soul in this bar.

And finally, as if hearing the silent plea, he looks my way. His knuckles rap the table as he waits for his beer, but they stop mid-motion when his gaze reaches mine.

There's a heat, a spark of recognition. So intense and so raw that my body lights, every nerve ending alive with awareness.

And then it vanishes. Replaced with a bitter chill as he turns away. Casually. As if there was nothing there. As if he doesn't even recognize me.

I used to think it was all in my mind back then. Five years ago when we'd share a glance and that same feeling would ignite within me.

But this just happened. I know it did.

And I know he knows who I am.

With anger beginning to rise, my lips part to say his name, but it's caught in my throat. It smothers the sadness that's rising just as quickly. Slowly my fingers curl, forming a fist until my nails dig into my skin.

I don't stop staring at him, willing him to look at me and at least give me the courtesy of acknowledging me.

I know he can feel my eyes on him. He's stopped rapping his knuckles on the table and the smile on his face has faded.

Maybe the crushing feeling in my chest is shared by both of us.

Maybe I'm only a reminder to him. A reminder he ran away from too.

I don't know what I expected. I've dreamed of running into Daniel so many nights. Brushing shoulders on the way into a coffee shop. Meeting each other again through new friends. Every time I wound up back home, if you can even call it that, I always checked out every person passing me by, secretly wishing one would be him. Just so I'd have a reason to say his name.

Winding up at the same bar on a lonely Tuesday night hours away from the town we grew up in ... that was one of those daydreams too. But it didn't go like this in my head.

"Daniel." I say his name before I can stop myself. It comes out like a croak and he reluctantly turns his head as the bartender sets down the beer on the wooden table.

I swear it's so quiet, I can hear the foam fizzing as it settles in the glass.

His lips part just slightly, as if he's about to speak. And then he visibly inhales. It's a sharp breath and matches the gaze he gives me. First it's one of confusion, then anger ... and then nothing.

I have to remind my lungs to do their job as I clear my throat to correct myself, but both efforts are in vain.

He looks past me as if it wasn't me who was trying to get his attention.

"Jake," he speaks up, licking his lips and stretching his back. "I actually can't stay," he bellows from his spot to where the bartender, apparently named Jake, is chucking ice into a large glass. The music seems to get louder as the crushing weight of being so obviously dismissed and rejected settles in me.

I'm struck by how cold he is as he gets up. I can't stand to look at him as he readies to leave, but his name leaves me again. This time with bite.

His back stiffens as he shrugs his thin jacket around his shoulders and slowly turns to look at me.

I can feel his eyes on me, commanding me to look back at him and I do. I dare to look him in the eyes and say, "It's good to see you." It's surprising how even the words come out. How I can appear to be so calm when inside I'm burning with both anger and ... something else I don't care to admit. What a lie those words are.

I hate how he gets to me. How I never had a choice.

With a hint of a nod, Daniel barely acknowledges me. His smile is tight, practically nonexistent, and then he's gone.

Chapter Two

DANIEL

My father taught me an important lesson I'll never forget.
 Never let a soul know what you really feel.
 Never express it.
 Only show them what you want them to see.

I hear his voice as I slip my hands in my jacket pockets and keep walking down Lincoln Street with my heart pounding in my chest and anxiety coursing in my blood. Two more blocks and I'll wait there. The alley is the perfect place to wait and collect myself.

Until then, my blood will pound in my ears, my veins will turn cold and my muscles will stay coiled. But I won't let anyone see that. Never.

I remember how my father gripped my shoulder when he looked me in the eyes and gave me that advice.

His dark stare was something no one ever forgot. It was impassive and cold. I lived many days wondering if my father loved me. I know my mother did. We were family and his blood, but he would never show any emotion and after that night, neither would I.

I was fourteen years old. And standing only a few feet away from the body of someone I once knew. I don't even remember his name. A friend of my father's. He worked in the business and gave the wrong person the wrong impression.

When you reveal that fear, that anger, that emotion, you give someone a hint of how to get to you. And that's what my father's friend had done. When someone gets to you, you end up dead.

My shoes slap on the concrete sidewalk as I slow down at the intersection, as if I'm merely waiting for the cars to stop at the red light so I can cross. It's not a busy night, so only a few people are walking down the street. A man to my right lights up a cigarette and leans against the brick wall to a liquor store.

I make my way around the block, replaying what happened in my head. It was supposed to be a simple, easy night. Another night of waiting for Marcus to show for the drop-off or waiting to hear word about what's going on with the deal between my brother and the cartel.

She caught me off guard.

Addison Fawn.

She's always been able to do that. She gets to me in a way I despise.

She makes me remember.

She makes me weak.

Another step and I see her face. Her high cheekbones and piercing green eyes. I love the way her hair falls in front of her face. There's always something effortless about it, like she doesn't put an ounce of work into looking as fuckable as she does.

The cool night air whips past me as I round the corner. The next alley will take me where I want to go. Directly across from the lot where her car must be. It's the only parking lot on this street for three blocks.

I swallow thickly, checking my phone again. It's been three minutes since I've left.

Three minutes is more than enough time for her to pay the tab and walk off.

I don't know if she will though.

It's been years since I've felt like I've known who she is.

Years since I've heard her say my name.

The corners of my lips turn up in a smirk as I hear the hesitancy in her voice replay in my memory and I let it. Like she was scared to say my name out loud.

It echoes in my head as I lean against the wall of the dark alley and gives me a thrill I haven't felt in a long time. *Too long.*

The alley is narrow, the type of passageway built decades and decades ago before the world knew better. Before humanity realized they were inviting sins in the night with small spaces like these.

My phone vibrates in my pocket, and I take a quick look around me before pulling it out.

There are four cars parked in the dirt lot. The streetlight on the right side illuminates the area easily, as do the headlights of a passing car.

My eyes flicker to the text on my phone and the amusement from only moments ago leaves me instantly.

Who's the girl? Jake texted and I'm reminded that I upped and left as if she mattered. As if her existence would cause an issue.

And of course it does. More than anyone could know.

My shoulders rise as I draw in a deep breath and let it out slowly, releasing the anger from letting her get to me and I focus on regaining control. Control is everything.

No one, I write him back but think better of it. It's obvious she's someone to me and Jake needs to be reassured. *My brother's ex,* I add.

My body tenses as I wait for him to respond. I keep my posture relaxed, although I'm anything but.

Off limits? Jake must have a fucking death wish.

I can't help the way my teeth grind as I text a response and then delete it before finally firing off a quick message.

For now. If Marcus comes tonight, tell him I'll be back late. I'm smoldering with rage as I realize how stupid it was to risk missing the meet with Marcus all over a quick emotion I couldn't suppress. Shock, anger ... fear even. She's only a girl. Inwardly, I can hear myself seething.

Alright, Jake messages me, making the phone vibrate in my hand. I almost ask him if Addison is still there. My fingertips itch to push for information.

But it's not needed.

Even as Jake continues to text me about the drop-off, I watch the skirt sway around Addison's hips. It's the color of cream and loose on her, not giving me any hints of how her ass looks right now. But her legs are on full display.

I've always thought of Addison the same way, even after everything that went down. From the first day I met her until this very second. She's a sad, but beautiful girl. You can see her pain in every bit of her features when she doesn't know someone's looking. Like I often did. From the way her full lips pout delicately, to the way her eyes seem to stare off in the distance, even when she's looking right at you it's as if she can see through you.

Those eyes have haunted me. The beautiful shades of green and brown are like the sunset over a forest. Like flecks of light peeking through and enhancing the darkness that's soon to come.

She runs her hand over her soft porcelain skin and through the modest waves in her thick dark hair. Even those slight movements and the swing of her hips as she walks carry a sadness with them. It never leaves her. It defines her. But it suits her well.

More than sad, and more than beautiful, Addison is memorable. *Unforgettable.*

Her car beeps as she unlocks it, a shiny new black Honda from the looks of it, and the sound echoes in the alley. She's parked in the third spot in the row of cars lined up under the streetlight. She looks to the left and right, cursing as she drops her keys in the gravel.

My dick stirs in my pants, straining against the fabric and I let out a low groan at the sight of her bent over. Her hair is swept to one side and the strap of her top is falling off her shoulder, giving me a view of that soft spot in the crook of her neck.

I adjust my dick and memorize the curves of her hips and waist until she opens up her car door and slips inside.

Every second my breaths come in heavier. The air around me feels as if it wants to suffocate me. Her tires kick up the gravel in the lot and I have to take a step back into the alley to avoid her headlights as she turns out onto the street.

I tell myself it's only out of instinct that I take a picture of her license plate as she drives off.

Well I try to, but I'm a poor liar.

When she's gone from view, I step back out onto the concrete sidewalk, staring down the desolate street and letting the brisk night air cool my hot skin.

Addison is back.

The only question on my mind is what I'm going to do with her.

Chapter Three

ADDISON

I'VE HATED DANIEL FOR A LOT OF THINGS. I'VE NEVER REALLY TALLIED THEM UP before.

The silent drive back to this tiny apartment provided plenty of time to recount each and every moment that bastard has made me feel inadequate, embarrassed … undeserving.

I take in a deep, calming breath then toss the keys onto the small kitchenette table and head right for the wine.

This day was going so well.

The thought settles me as I open the fridge and quickly grab a half-full bottle of red blend. I use my teeth to pull out the cork and pour the wine into a bright yellow coffee mug with sunflowers engraved on it. It's the closest thing to me and all my glasses are still packed in boxes.

It'll do fine to hold the wine, I think as I take a small sip. And then a large one.

I don't have a buzz yet, but in fifteen minutes I'm sure I will.

As I lick the sweet wine off my lips, I stare aimlessly at the glass bottle. I have to be careful not to fall into old patterns. It's been a long time since I've needed wine to sleep. But I can see myself relying on that bad habit tonight. *That's what some memories will do to you.*

I take a good, hard look at the bottle. It's more than halfway empty as it is. I'll be fine.

Leaning against the counter, I let the past flicker in front of me and trace the outline of the flowers on the mug.

Each memory is accompanied by another gulp of wine, each one tasting more and more bitter.

So many times Daniel's left me feeling less than. And it's my fault.

Even the first time was my fault.

The sudden memory of Tyler both warms my heart and makes my vision blur as my eyes gloss over with tears. I can't think of him for long without feeling a deep pain in my chest.

He was my first. My first everything.

Just like his brother Daniel and just like the rest of the men in their family, Tyler Cross was stubborn. And he didn't let up until I finally caved and said yes to being his girlfriend.

I told myself he was nice and that it felt good to be wanted. And my God, it did. When you're an orphan, you learn rather quickly people don't want you.

It's a hard thing to unlearn.

And at sixteen years old and in my fourth foster home, I didn't believe Tyler wanted anything more than a kiss, or to cop a feel. To get into my pants. Just like the previous foster dad wanted from me. He was a rotten bastard.

I run the tip of my finger along the edge of the mug, remembering how Tyler didn't give up on making me feel wanted. I only stayed with the Brauns, my fourth foster home in three years, because of how Tyler made me feel.

I didn't want to move to another school district.

I finally wanted to stay somewhere.

The Brauns would get their check and I would be a good kid, I'd be quiet. I'd put up with whatever it was I had to do in order for them not to send me back.

All because Tyler genuinely made me feel wanted. Even if it was obvious the Brauns, like the other foster parents, only wanted to get paid. Having to watch over a teenager with hormones and homework wasn't on their wish list.

Looking back on it now though, I don't much mind Jenny and Mitch Braun. They were okay people. Maybe if I hadn't run away when everything happened, I'd have a relationship with them. Or a semblance of one.

They didn't like Tyler though. They were probably the only people on the face of the earth who didn't like that boy. I can't blame them, since he did in fact want to get into my pants when they eventually met him.

I cover my mouth with my hand as I let out a small laugh at the memory.

He had to meet my guardians before I'd go anywhere near his house.

I have to give Tyler credit, he put up a good showing.

And then I had to face his family.

There was one big difference though. One massive separation between what he had to do and what I had to do in our little agreement.

Tyler had a real family.

That was so obvious to me. Actual relatives. Like I had once. It's an odd feeling standing in a room with people who belong together. Especially when you don't, but you want to. You desperately want to.

It was wrong of me. Every reason I had for staying with Tyler was selfish.

I was young back then. Young and stupid and incredibly selfish.

I know that now and it only makes the shame that much worse.

I remember how I could hardly look at anyone as Tyler wrapped his arm around my shoulders. Like he was proud of me and I belonged to him.

His mother had died years before, something Tyler and I had in common. His father was in the leather recliner in the living room, seated in front of the television although I'm certain he was sleeping.

Tyler told me his father worked late nights, but I could read between the lines. I knew the type of family the Crosses were. I knew by the way people spoke in hushed voices around them with traces of both fear and intrigue. And I heard the whispers.

There were little clues too. Tyler and his brother Jase were always being handed money under the cafeteria table and making quick exchanges. Certain people avoided them, certain red-eyed and scrawny potheads, to be exact.

It didn't matter to me.

In fact, I liked that their family was doing some type of business that meant his father would be asleep when I was forced to meet them all. Five boys in the family and Tyler was the youngest.

One less male to have to endure was fine by me. Declan, the middle boy, gave the impression of being disinterested in life in general. Let alone his brother's girlfriend. He was the first of Tyler's brothers I met, and even he seemed to be kind, if nothing else.

And that continued as I met his other brothers. They all welcomed me. There was no hidden agenda, no sneers or snide comments about where I was from or what the Brauns did at the local tavern two weeks ago.

That's one thing people liked to gossip about at school when I first got there. Foster parents aren't supposed to be drunks. Funny how that type of talk died when Tyler staked his claim on me.

Yet another reason I stayed and gave more and more of myself to a boy who could never have all of me.

It was so obvious that he never would. Especially that first day he brought me home.

The moment I thought I could relax, I met the last brother.

Daniel.

Tyler knocked on the door to his room, tapping out song lyrics and telling him to open up.

I remember exactly the way my polish had chipped on my thumbnail. I'm a nervous picker and I was busy chipping away at it when the door opened.

"What?" The word came out hard and my body stilled. I could feel the anger coming off of him from being interrupted.

He gripped the doorframe, which made his shoulders and height seem that much more intimidating. It was his toned muscles and the dark stubble lining his upper throat and jaw that let me know he was older.

And the heat in his stare as he let his gaze wander to where I stood that let me know I wasn't welcome.

That was the first time Daniel made me feel the same way I do now.

And the first time I knew I'd never love Tyler the way he deserved.

But I stayed with him. Deep inside I know it's because a very large part of me wanted Daniel to want me back. I wanted Daniel to want me the way that I instantly wanted him.

Chapter Four

DANIEL

The back door to Iron Heart Brewery is propped open a couple inches with a brick. There's a small stack of them next to the dumpster and I've seen a few of them used for a number of things.

The door creaks open slowly as I take a look to my left and right. It's pitch black out now and deserted. It's been four hours since I left. Enough time to pass for me to get my shit together and figure out what it is that I want and how I'm going to handle this.

The entire town is quiet now that everything on Lincoln Street is closed.

I sneak in the back, hearing the clinking of glass around the corner and past the stockroom. The fresh scent of hoppy beer in this place never gets old.

I've only been here a couple months and I thought I'd get bored fast. So far there's not much action or competition. For a college town, it's surprising. But feeling out this area and waiting on information about future deals for my brother hasn't been the pain in the ass it usually is.

Other than Jake. He's not good for a damn thing other than asking for a beer or who comes around here when I'm away. He knows this place is used for drops, but that's as far as our relationship goes.

Jake's got his earbuds in, he's not paying attention in the least. My shoulder leans against the wall closest to the far end of the bar, and just enough so I can see the table where Addison sat earlier today.

I let the memory linger for a moment before speaking loud enough for Jake to hear over the music blaring in his ears.

"Marcus show up?" I call out and Jake startles, hitting his lower back against the counter and dropping a glass to the ground.

It breaks, cracking into a few large pieces rather than shattering.

Pushing off the wall, I take a few steps closer to him.

"Shit, dude," he tells me as he slowly lowers himself to the floor, catching his breath, and starts picking up the shards. "You scared the shit out of me." He starts to ask, "How did you get—" before stopping and looking past me to answer the question himself.

"Sorry," I offer him and crouch down to pick up the single piece of broken glass that's left. It's a solid piece a couple inches long with a sharp tip. I slide my finger along the blunt, slick side of it, toying with it as I talk to him. "Didn't mean to startle you." It's hard to keep the grin off my face, but it's easier if Jake is somewhat relaxed. He needs to know to fear me, but only so much that he doesn't do anything stupid. So long as he's easygoing, so is everything else that goes down here. He can keep looking the other way and I can keep everything moving as it should.

"No worries, man," he says as he stands up and deposits the chunks in his hand into a bin under the counter. He's still shaking and instead of reaching out for the piece I'm holding, he takes out the rectangular basin and offers it to me.

I hold his gaze as I toss it in to join the rest of them.

"What's going on?" he asks as he sets it back into place and pretends that he's not scared. That he doesn't look like he's going to piss himself.

"How long was the girl here?" I ask him and take a look around the counter. This section of the bar is small and narrow. There's a lone window on the other side and it's cracked open, letting in a small breeze.

"Addison?" he asks, saying her name out loud and I don't trust myself to speak as the anger swells inside of me, so I wait for him to look at me and give a short nod.

"Not long," he answers and gets back to wiping down a few of the glasses still lined up on the far side of the sink. "She left right after you."

"What was she here for?" I ask him and pray it wasn't for a meet. They're all done here. It's the perfect place, in the perfect town. Any necessary conversations can happen right here. And any arguments can be settled in the back ... with those bricks. But this city may be more useful and profitable. Time will tell.

"Just coming in for a drink."

I nod my head and remember how I've found a few guys I know sitting at the bar, completely oblivious to what was going on around them. Like Dean. He had no idea; he was too wrapped up in his own story to realize what was happening here.

"Who is she?" Jake asks, interrupting my recollection.

"A girl," I answer and then go back to being the one asking the questions. "She come in with anyone?"

"Nope, she's single. She didn't say she knew anyone or that she was looking for anyone." He replies with the information I was hoping for. It was just a coincidence that she was here. But the way he answers it doesn't quite sit right with me.

He's a funny kid and a good guy in some ways, but he's the type who looks the other way and likes to pretend everything's friendly and fine and nothing fucked up is going on.

I don't have any problems with him. *Yet.*

"Is that so?"

"Yeah, she's looking at going to the university. New to town. You know, that kind of thing."

"Hey Jake," I start and wait for him to look up at me. "How do you know her name?" My body's tense and tight, even though I don't think he has a clue how badly I'll fuck him up if he hit on her. He's a flirt, young and carefree. He gets plenty of action from girls coming in here to get a drink and drown out their problems with alcohol.

The fucker looks up at me like it's a given and says, "From her credit card."

I don't like his tone, or the ease with which he talks about her. But my body's relaxed, and the smile on my face grows as I tell him, "Of course. Sorry, she's got me a little wound up."

"I could tell." My back stiffens at his confession. "I mean I get it, she's hot," he says, completely oblivious to how my hand reflexively forms a fist. He shrugs and dries off the last glass. "You want me to keep tabs on her?"

The correct answer is no. But it's not the word that slips from my tongue. "Yes," I reply and it comes out harder than it should, with a desperate need clinging to the single syllable.

Jake pauses and takes in my appearance.

"I have a soft spot for her," I tell him and inwardly I hate myself. Both for the lie and for the hint at the truth. He nods his head and hangs up the dish towel in his hands.

"So she's going to the university?" I ask him and he returns to his normal easy self.

"I didn't get much information from her. She'd just gotten here and Mickey was at the bar."

"Well, don't worry about it. But if she comes in here again, text me."

"No problem. You need anything else?" he asks and I remind him of my earlier question.

"Did Marcus come?" I already know the answer. He hasn't shown up yet. Carter, my brother, messaged me to let me know not to waste my time in the bar tonight. But I know Marcus is a lot like me. He likes to know people's habits and if I tell him I'll meet him, I want him to know I'll be there.

This isn't my first run-in with him. Last time it took weeks before he finally showed.

There aren't a lot of men I'd wait on, but Carter says this is important and Marcus and I have history.

"He didn't. I don't know why he—"

"Looks like you're almost done," I cut him off with a trace of a smile on my lips. "Sorry to keep you."

"Not a problem," he says to my back as I turn and leave the bar.

The bright light of the Iron Heart sign casts a shadow beneath my feet as I walk toward the barren parking lot with only one thing on my mind—how to find little miss Addison Fawn.

Chapter Five

ADDISON

Daniel's a prick.

Why is it that the assholes stay in your head, rankling and festering their way into your thoughts while the nice guys are passed over?

I went shopping on the strip downtown to distract myself. I spent a pretty penny on décor for this apartment and on the softest comforter I've felt in my life.

One tweed rug, two woven baskets and a dozen rustic wood picture frames later and my living room is acceptable. Snapshot after snapshot I post the different angles on Instagram, where I have my largest following and where I sell most of my photos.

But it's all done absentmindedly. And it's not like these are for sale, just pictures that serve as an update to let my followers know I've found a new place.

I don't have an ounce of interest flowing through me.

I came here to settle down. To finally give myself a reason to stay and possibly take formal classes to breathe new life into my business.

And instead I've been pushed back to when I was only seventeen.

No home.

No life.

No reason to do anything at all.

My throat tightens and my eyes prick, but I refuse to let a single tear fall.

It's all because I'm still not worthy enough for Daniel fucking Cross.

My phone pings and I go into the messenger app on Facebook to see who it is.

Another person wanting me to photograph their wedding.

I don't do functions.

I politely message back that I don't do shoots. I only photograph the things around me and tell my own story. Not other people's. In other words, I'm not for hire. Photography is my business, but also my therapy. I photograph what I want and nothing else. It's the only way I've survived and I won't compromise that.

That's how I've made a living for the past few years. Little sales here and there. Enough to keep my head above water and to keep moving from place to place.

Searching for Something is what I eventually called my business.

Not that it started as a business. I was just taking pictures of every little thing that reminded me of Tyler.

All I had was my camera, the only present my last foster mother had ever given me. Tyler told her she should get it for me for Christmas. He said if she wouldn't, he would. He would've given me anything.

And so it started with me wanting to take a photograph of the snow around his old Chevy truck that couldn't run anymore. The rusted-out hood. The flat back left tire.

I started taking pictures of everything, obsessively. It was something Tyler and I had done together and it made sense to do at the time.

I needed something and although I didn't know what that something would be, I took photos of everything on my way to find what I was looking for.

Something to take the guilt away. Something to make me smile the way a boy who loved me in a way I didn't deserve had.

Searching for Something.

What it turned out to be was profitable.

A myriad of photos all priced ridiculously high. In my opinion, at least. But that's what everyone else was doing. The competition's pictures sold for hundreds. And mine looked like a steal simply because of the price tag.

I adopted the "fake it till you make it" strategy. And it's been working. But I don't know shit about running a business.

The random person on Facebook shoots back an apology and I don't bother to respond. My customer service isn't the best either.

Some days are better than others.

Some days are filled with reminders of the past. And those days are the worst for me personally, but the best for the things I see and can capture with a lens. And they sell well. Not just well, like serious money.

The shots I've taken today don't tell my story. It should be a part of my journey, but the pretty images of wooden frames and white tweed with pale blue accents are what I wanted before last night. Before I went to Iron Heart and ran into that asshole.

This is a décor shoot for a new life with new roots. It'll look pretty on Instagram with a soft filter, but that's about all it is. Just a series of pretty pictures.

My phone pings and pings with updates and I put it on vibrate before heading to the kitchen, where I place it on the table.

Next week is the kitchen makeover.

For now, it's all black and white with pops of cherry. A red teapot sits untouched on the stove as I shove my sunflower mug into the microwave to heat up water for tea.

I doubt I'll ever use that teapot.

My phone vibrates yet again, rattling the table just as the microwave beeps. A heavy sigh of irritation leaves me, but I know it's not the messages, nor the headache from stress and exhaustion.

It's because of Daniel. Just like years ago, I'm losing sleep over the asshole. Back then I never said a word. I let him treat me how he wanted, and I cowered away.

I'm older now and last night I should have said something. I should have gotten up and slapped him for being such a dismissive prick. Well, maybe that's taking things a little too far. But he deserves to know how much it hurt me. How I still struggle with what happened and how him treating me like that only makes the pain that much worse.

As the tea bag sinks into the steaming water, an idea hits me to search for Daniel on Instagram.

If not Instagram, then Facebook. Everyone is somewhere online now.

With my feet up on the chic glass table and the mug in my right hand, I search both on my cell phone.

And when both of those prove useless I try Twitter.

The steady, rhythmic ticking of the simple clock across from me and above the little kitchenette gets my attention when my search proves to be futile. I stare at the second hand that's marching along, willing it to give me an answer.

But time's a fickle bitch and she's never helped me with anything.

I take another sip of the now lukewarm tea before getting up for another cup.

As I wait for it to heat, I decide to search Iron Heart Brewery on Church and Lincoln Street.

Slowly a grin forms on my lips. Jake Holsteder stares back at me from a black and white photo where he's holding up a beer in cheers. The bartender from last night is apparently the owner. Jake has links to his social media accounts.

And more importantly, Daniel knows Jake.

It's a stretch, but I send a message to Jake on Facebook and then prepare my second cup of tea.

Nice to meet you last night. Sorry I left early.

It's a simple message and if he doesn't respond, I can always go back to the bar. I'm vaguely aware that I'm chasing after Daniel. After the man whose very existence brings back the ghosts of my past. But I don't care. I live off instinct and everything is telling me that I need to find Daniel. If for no other reason than to tell him he knows damn well who I am.

I add more sugar to the cup this time than last and the spoon clinks against the ceramic edge of the mug as my phone vibrates.

No worries. You leave for any reason in particular?

I chew on the inside of my cheek at his message.

Just had to go. But I wanted to come back and try that beer. I don't even remember what the hell the beer was called, but then I add, *I'd love to take pictures of the place too if that's okay?*

I purse my lips and tap my thumb against my phone before finally sending the message.

Pictures? That's all he answers.

I send him a link to my Instagram and then text, *Your place gives me so much inspiration.*

NICE!

Even if he's only being polite, I appreciate it. *Thanks!*

He writes, *Seriously, these are beautiful. You should try selling them.*

I do. It's what I do for a living and I'd love to take some pics in your bar. The whole place gives me a ton of inspiration. Maybe we can chat too?

He takes a moment and then another to respond. Each second makes my heart beat a little faster and I find myself picking at my nails. *You come by looking for him?*

Him? I play coy.

I thought maybe you knew Daniel? he asks me although it's a statement.

I did, but I haven't seen him in years. I send the message without checking it. Maybe I gave away too much.

You should stay away, Jake warns me and although I know he's right, it pisses me off. All the kids at school told me that about Tyler too—well, more about his family than him specifically, and he was the only good thing I've ever had in my life. And I really don't like people telling me what to do.

I didn't go to your bar looking for an old friend. I pause before adding, *I'm here to make new ones.*

It feels like a hand's squeezing my heart in my chest as an anxious feeling comes over me. The only sense I can gather from it all is that I know I'm only doing this to piss Daniel off. And that's something I shouldn't do; I've done it once before and the memory makes me feel weak.

You can come by anytime. What's your number? he asks me and although it's forward, I send it over. Jake knows Daniel. So maybe I can get some intel at the very least.

Daniel was always the possessive type. Even if he hated me, he hated anyone who showed me any attention more. So maybe finding out Jake has my number will piss him off. I can only hope.

I feel petty as I walk away from the phone, listening to it vibrate in time with the ticking of the clock.

As I peek out of the sheer white curtains and down onto the street below me, an eerie feeling washes through me. It slowly pricks along my skin until the hairs on the back of my neck stand up.

It's a feeling like someone's watching me. I'm slow as I turn so I'm facing my living room. There's no one else here in my studio apartment. Not a soul.

My hand wraps around the hot mug and I pull the curtains shut. It's only the memory of Tyler that's brought this back.

I couldn't go anywhere without feeling him there. Watching me. A shudder runs down my spine as I remember each day. Each photo I took as I whipped around, expecting to find someone lurking in the shadows. There was never anyone there. It was only my shame that followed me.

I hate Daniel even more in this moment.

It took me years to get to where I was days ago. And with one look, I've gone back to being the girl I was trying to leave behind.

Chapter Six

DANIEL

"It's been long enough, hasn't it?" my brother's voice asks on the other end of the phone.

My eyes close as I try to push down the irritation. Madison Street is busy today in the quiet town. Cars pass and I can hear the hums and rumbles with the windows opened in the diner as I lean back in the booth. The vinyl coverings protest as I lean forward and wave the waitress away before she can offer me another cup of coffee.

"We go through this every few months, Carter." I close my eyes again as I continue, "Do you really want to have the same conversation again?"

Across the street is a coffee shop. And inside it, Addison. She's hunched over in the corner with her laptop on a small circular table as she sits cross-legged in a chair. Some things never change.

I watch her from a distance in the safety of the diner. I'm within view; she could see me if she wanted to. But that's the thing about Addison. She never wanted to see me.

"How long are you going to keep this up?" Carter asks me. He's older than me by a year, almost on the dot. Irish twins, so to speak. I don't bother answering him and instead I remember the details of her address that Marcus gave me.

Funny how he can't show up to deliver the package from the Romanos. But one encrypted message from me to him with Addison's license plate number sparks enough interest for him to respond.

I suppose he hasn't forgotten. Marcus has a good memory.

"Whatever, I just need the package." Carter sighs on the other end of the phone. "I need to know what we're getting into before we decide..."

He doesn't continue, but I know what he's getting at. It's best not to speak those things where others can hear.

"He'll show. You know how he is."

"He's a pain in my ass."

The corner of my lip kicks up at his comment. "So many things are a pain in your ass, Carter. It's hard to believe you can sit down without wincing," I joke as I watch Addison take a large drink from her coffee cup. It's the tallest size the shop has and it looks like she's almost done.

"You're fucking hilarious, you know that?" I laugh at Carter's comment even though he says it with disdain. He runs the family business now. What started as a way for my father to make extra cash became an empire formed from ruthless and cutthroat tactics. Carter's the head, but I do his bidding more from a vague obligation that we're blood than anything else.

"Are you coming home after this? As soon as this package arrives? There's no reason for you to stay away and we need you here."

Her name is on the tip of my tongue. *Addison*. I may deal in addiction, but she's the only addiction I've ever had and the only one I desire.

"Well?" he presses.

"I'm curious about something," I answer my brother.

"What's that?"

"Something of personal interest," I mutter and the words come out lower than I intend them to. He's quiet for a long moment. And my focus is momentarily distracted. A man in a thin leather jacket walks past the coffee shop slowly, but his gaze is on Addison.

My eyes narrow as he stops in his tracks and glances inside the place. I shake off the possessive feelings. I'm only projecting.

Carter's voice brings my attention back to him. "With that shit your friend Dean pulled, there's too much heat around you." He ignores my earlier comment and I decide it's for the best. There's no need for anyone to know what I'm doing.

I'm quick to answer him. "Which is exactly why I need to stay. Leaving would raise suspicion."

A line of cars pass on the street in front of me, temporarily blocking Addison from my view. At their movement, she peeks up through the large glass windows of the shop.

Her hair brushes her shoulder and falls down her back as she takes a break to look out onto the street. Her pouty lips are turned down. They always are. There's a sadness that's always followed Addison. It's only a matter of whether or not she's trying to hide it, but it's always there.

Her green eyes are deep and even from this distance they seem to darken. Her hand moves to the back of her neck, massaging away a dull ache from sitting there for hours now. With each breath, her chest rises and falls and I'm mesmerized by her. By all of her.

More so by what she does to me.

The hate and anger I felt toward her years ago has numbed into something else each minute I sit here.

Curiosity maybe.

"Just get the package from Marcus. You've been gone long enough and we could use you here."

"I don't know if I want to come back," I tell him honestly and flatly.

"It's not a matter of want," he replies but his words come out hollow and with no authority although he wishes he had it. "We're your blood." He plays the only card he has that can get me to do his bidding.

"You never fail to remind me."

My phone vibrates with a message and I'm more than happy to end this call.

"I've got to go." My phone vibrates again. "I'll update you when I can." I don't wait for him to acknowledge what I've said, let alone tell me goodbye. I've never been close to my brothers. Not like they are toward each other. I'm the black sheep, I suppose.

I crack my neck as my phone vibrates for a third time. Before checking it I glance back at Addison only to see she's gone, although her laptop is still there. My heart stills and my body tenses until I see her by the counter, ordering something else.

Annoyance rises in me as I realize how much pull she has over me in this moment. I've turned back into what I hate. My teeth grit as I pull up my texts and that annoyance grows to an agitation that makes me grip the edge of the table to keep me from doing something stupid.

Three messages, each from Jake.

Marcus isn't coming tonight. He said there are complications.

I have your girl's number though if you want it.

And I think she's coming here tonight.

Jake wants to die. That's the only explanation. He literally wants me to kill his ass.

My glare moves from the cell phone in my hand back to the coffee shop across the street.

Addison's cardigan dangles loosely around her as she moves back to her spot. Her jeans are tight and I can just imagine how they'd feel against my hands as I ripped them off of her. It'd be difficult, but I would fucking love it.

"Do you ..." I hear a small, hesitant voice next to me and I have to school my expression before I can look back at the waitress.

She's an older woman, with soft lines around her eyes. A stray lock of dark hair with a line of silver running through it falls from her bun and into her face as she offers me a smile and holds up a pot of coffee. "You're all out this time," she says, like it's a reason to have another.

"Sure," I say and smile politely as she fills the cup.

The hot coffee steams and I stare at it as she leaves me be.

So Addison is giving her number out.

I wonder if she would have given it to me. I replay that scene in my head and instead of leaving, I slip in beside her.

I don't deserve Addison. That's a given.

But I'll be damned if I let some asshole like Jake get his hands on her.

Chapter Seven

ADDISON

It took three days to actually go through with it and go back to Iron Heart Brewery.

Three days and this feeling in my gut that won't leave.

Three days of fiddling with images in Photoshop and hating each and every one because I can't focus.

And worst of all, three nights of not sleeping.

Every night I keep dreaming of the bar and every time the scene ends differently. It starts out how I'd have liked for it to have gone. With him giving me the time of day. With him offering to get me a drink. But then it turns dark and wicked. Daniel grabs me. Or worse. I hear Tyler tell me to stay away.

And I wake up shaken.

I feel just like I did that winter I ran away.

And I hate it. I hate Daniel even more for making it all come back. And if I can find that asshole I'm going to tell him exactly how he makes me feel. Not just the way he made me feel the other night, but also the way I felt all those years ago.

Part of me wants to run. But I already did that. I can't keep running forever.

I open the heavy glass door to the bar with the buzz of the late traffic behind me. This is an old town, but on weekends everyone is out and about.

I'm immediately hit with the aroma of pale ale lingering in the air and the chatter of everyone in here. The air outside was crisp, but only two steps in and the warmth lets me slip off my cardigan.

"Addison," Jake says my name from his place behind the bar. It carries over the hubbub and a man seated on a stool by him turns to look back at me.

Jake's smile is broad and welcoming as he gestures to an open seat at the bar.

For a small moment I forget the churning in my gut. I think that's what really happened these past couple of years. I slowly forgot. And if that isn't a tragedy, I don't know what is.

"You alright?" Jake asks with his forehead creased and a frown on his lips.

"Sorry," I tell him and shake my head as I fold the cardigan over the barstool and then slip on top of it, resting my elbows on the bar. "Been a long few days."

"What's bothering you?" he asks while passing a beer down the bar to an old man with salt and pepper hair and bushy eyebrows that are colored just the same.

The man waves him a thanks without breaking his conversation. Something about a football game coming up.

Letting out an easy sigh, I pull the hair away from my face and into a small ponytail although I don't have a band, so it falls down my back as I talk. "Oh, you know. Just moving and getting settled." I smile easily as I lie to him. "So, how's it been going for you?"

Even as I ask him I'm almost painfully aware of how I couldn't care less. I'm eager for information and that's all I want. I rest my chin in my hand and lean forward, pretending to give him my full attention even though my mind's on all the questions on the tip of my tongue.

How often does Daniel come here?
Do you think he'll be here tonight?
Do you know where I can find him if he doesn't come?

Instead I smile and laugh politely when I'm supposed to; all the while Jake chitchats about the bar and points to the pictures on the wall. Occasionally he answers his phone and texts or gets someone a beer.

Although it's crowded and I'm having a real conversation for the first time since three nights ago, I've never felt more alone.

"So we go around from place to place, collecting all of them we can find," Jake wraps up something he said that I was only half listening to and then takes a seat on his side of the bar.

"What's really bothering you?" he asks and it catches me off guard. My simper slips, and my heart skips a beat.

"What do you mean?" I ask him as if I haven't got a clue and then quickly follow up with, "I'm just tired." It sounds phony to my own ears, so I'm sure I sound like a bad liar to him too.

"You seemed a little shaken the other night," Jake says softly, leaning forward. Someone calls out his name and he barely acknowledges them, holding up his hand to tell them to wait. "Maybe you came in looking for something?" he asks me with his eyes narrowed.

The playfulness is gone, as is the sound of all conversation in the busy bar. In its place is the rapid thumping of my heart.

"Or someone?" he says as somebody else calls out his name again, breaking me from the moment. I turn to the man with the bushy eyebrows as Jake tells him, "One minute!" in not the most patient of tones.

"So what is it?" he says and waits for me.

"I didn't come in here looking for anything or anyone." I tell him the truth. My voice is small, pleading even.

"But you found something," he prompts.

I only nod my head and he pushes off of the bar, standing up and making his way back to the draft beers to satisfy the old man's order.

"If you don't want to see him again, you should leave now," Jake speaks without looking at me and then smiles and jokes with the man at the end of the bar.

"Why's that?" I call after him, my voice raised so he can hear me and the bar top digging into my stomach as I lean over it to get a good view of him.

Just as Jake opens his mouth to answer me, the door to the bar opens and I can feel the atmosphere change.

No one else stops talking. No one else turns to look over their shoulder.

But I do. I'm drawn to him and always have been. It's like my body knows his. Like my soul was waiting for his.

Daniel's always had an intensity about him. There's a dominance that lingers in the way he carries himself. A threat just barely contained. The rough stubble over his hard jaw begs me to run my hand against it. The black leather of his jacket is stretched over his shoulders.

Thump ... thump ... my heart ticks along and then stops.

Daniel's dark eyes meet mine instantly. They swirl with an emotion I can't place as they narrow, and I can't breathe until he takes a step. We both hang there for what feels like forever. He must know I've come here for him.

I watch as he moves, or rather stalks toward me. Each movement is careful, barely contained. Like it's taking everything in him just to be near me. I know he wants to appear relaxed, but he's faking it.

And with another step toward me, I can finally tear my gaze away.

I look forward, my back straight and my eyes on the beer in front of me as he walks behind me. I can hear each step and the scratch of the barstool on the floor directly to my left as he pulls it out.

I remind myself I came here for him. No, not *for* him. To see him. To clear the air.

I came here to this small town for me because I finally had my life together.

And he ruined it. The memory of his cold reception and dismissal hurts more and more with each passing second. I'm not a little girl for him to shove aside anymore and treat like I'm some annoyance.

The thought strengthens my resolve and I turn sharply to the left just as he takes his seat. He's so close my breasts nearly brush his bicep and it forces the words to a grinding halt as I pull back.

I'd forgotten what he smells like, a woody scent with a freshness to it. Like trees on the far edge of a forest by the water. I'd forgotten what it feels like to be this close to him.

To be too close to what can ruin you is a disconcerting feeling.

"Addison," he says and although his voice is deep and masculine, in that smooth cadence my name sounds positively sinful. The irritation in his tone that was constant in my memory is absent.

"Daniel." I barely manage to get his name out and I clear my throat, slowly sitting back in my seat to grab the beer in front of me. "I was wondering if I'd find you here," I admit and then peek up at him.

A genuine grin grows slowly on his handsome face. I swear his teeth are perfectly white. It's a crime for a man to look this good.

"You came here looking for me?" he asks me with a cockiness that reminds me of a boy I once knew and again, for the second time, my confidence is shaken. As I lick my lower lip to respond, I fail to find the words.

"Do I intimidate you, Addison?" he asks in a teasing voice and I roll my eyes and then lift the beer to my lips. I assume he'll say something else as I drink, but he doesn't.

As I set the glass down, I look him in the eyes. "You know you do and I hate it." There's a heat between us that ignites in an instant. As if a drop of truth could set fire to us both. I can barely breathe looking into his dark eyes.

"Do you now?" he asks again in that same playful tone. "So you came here looking for me because you hate me?"

"Yes," I answer him without hesitation, although it's not quite truthful. That's not why, but I'm fine with him thinking that.

His brow raises slightly and he tilts his head as if he wasn't expecting that answer. Slowly he corrects it, and I can feel his guard slowly climb up. It's this thing he always did. It's odd how I remember it so well. For only moments, only glimpses, I swear he let me in. But just like that it was gone, and a distance grew between us, even if we hadn't moved an inch.

"Don't do that," I tell him as soon as I sense it and his eyes narrow at me. "I don't hate you. I hate that you were rude to me."

"I wasn't rude."

"You were a dick." My words come out with an edge that can't be denied and I wish I could swallow them back down.

"I'm sorry," he tells me and he looks apprehensive. It's weird hearing him say those words. I can't think of him ever speaking them to anyone before. "You came looking for an apology?"

"No, not really," I tell him and shrug, wanting to take a step back from the tense air, but my ass is firmly planted on this stool. He turns to his left and I look back at the glass while I continue, just wanting to get it out of me before he's gone again.

"I just wanted to talk." The words finally come out, although they're not quite right. I want to spill every word that's inside of me. From the last night I saw him all those years ago, to everything that's happened up until this moment. There aren't a lot of people who can relate to what we've gone through.

He still hasn't said a word. His gaze is focused on me as if he's trying to read me, but can't make out what's written. If only he'd ask, I'd tell him. I don't have time for games or secrets, and our history makes up too much of who I am to disrespect it with falsehoods.

"Are you going to run off again?" I ask as he only stares back at me.

"Do you want me to?" he asks me in return.

"No," I answer instantly and a little too loud. As if what he'd said was a threat. I'm quieter as I add, "I don't want you to go." The desperation in my voice is markedly apparent.

"Well what do you want then?" he asks me and I know the answer. *I want him.* I take in a breath slowly, knowing the truth but also knowing I'd never confess it.

"I haven't been able to sleep since the other night," I confess and my gaze flickers from the glass to his eyes. My nail taps on the glass again and again and the small tinkling persuades me to continue. "I had a rough time for a while, but I was doing really well until I saw you." I don't glance up to see how he reacts; I'm merely grateful the words are finally coming to me. "When you didn't even bother to look at me, much less talk to me ..." I swallow thickly and then throw back more of the beer.

"It was a shock to see you." Daniel says the words as if he's testing them on his tongue. Like they aren't the truth, although I'm sure they are. I look into his eyes as he says, "I didn't mean to upset you."

"What did you mean then?" I ask him without wasting a second.

He hesitates again, careful to say just what he wants. "I didn't know what to say, so I left."

"That seems reasonable." Or at least that seems like the version of Daniel I remember. I take another sip of beer before I say, "It hurt though."

"I already said I was sorry." His words are short, harsh even, but they don't faze me.

"I wasn't looking for an apology. I only wanted you to know how you make me feel."

He responds quickly this time, still looking over my expression as if he's not sure what to make of it. "And how do I make you feel now?"

I swear his breathing comes in heavier, and it makes mine do the same. "Like I have someone to talk to."

That gets a huff of a laugh from him. A disbelieving one. "I'm sure you have better options for that."

I shake my head and answer before taking another sip, "You'd be wrong then."

It's never felt pathetic before. The fact is I don't talk to many people and the one friend I have is thousands of miles away. But admitting that to him and seeing the trace of the grin fall on his lips makes it feel slightly pitiful.

I muster a small smile although it's weak, and time grows between us. The seconds tick by and I know I'm losing him, but I can't voice any of the things I'm feeling.

"It's been a while," he says and I nod my head as I answer, "Since the funeral."

I don't think I've ever said it out loud and it's the first mention of Tyler between us. The air turns tense but not in a way that's uncomfortable. At least not for me. I even have the courage to look back at him. I can see hints of Tyler in Daniel. But Tyler was so young and he looked it. Still, there are small things.

"You remind me of him, you know?" All while I speak, Daniel stares at my lips. He doesn't hide the fact in the least. I think he wants me to know. I swallow and his gaze moves to my throat, then he leans in just slightly before correcting himself. The hot air is tense and as he finally looks me in the eyes again, the noise of the bar disappears from the pure intensity of his stare.

"You do the same for me, I think."

"You think?" I ask him to clarify.

"You bring back certain things," he says icily, so cold it sends a chill down my spine.

My shoulders are tight as I straighten myself in the seat, again looking into the glass of beer that's nearly gone as if it can save me. Or as if I can drown in it.

It's only the sound of him standing up that makes me look back toward him. "Are you leaving?" I ask him like an idiot and then feel like it.

He only nods and I'm sure he's going to walk off, but instead he steps closer to me. He shoves a piece of paper in front of me onto the bar and then grips the barstool I'm sitting on with both of his hands.

He's so close I can feel his heat as he whispers to me, "I'll see you soon, Addison."

Chapter Eight

DANIEL
Five years ago

The wind howls as it whips past us. We're all dressed in black suits, but the shoes we spent all last night shining are buried beneath the pure white snow. The ice melts and seeps between the seams, letting the freezing cold sink into what was once warm. It's fitting as we stare at the upturned dirt in front of us.

We're the last ones here. We stopped on our way back from the dinner since the sun has yet to set, and there's still a bit of light left.

The sky beyond us is blurred and the air brutally cold, the kind that makes my lungs hurt each time I try to breathe.

One of my brothers cries. It's a whimper at first but I don't move to see who's the weakest of us. My muscles coil at the thought, hating how I've judged. Hating how I view strength. I'm pathetic. I'm the weak one.

Jase, the farthest from me, sniffles as his shoulders crumple and then he covers his face.

He was the closest to Tyler but now he's the baby, taking Tyler's place. The air turns cruel, biting at the back of my neck with a harsh chill as his cries come to a halt. My throat's tight as I try to swallow. It makes me bitter to be standing here, knowing I need to leave and can't stay here. That I'm the one who gets to continue breathing. That fate chose to take one of the good ones, and leave the ruthless and depraved behind.

Five brothers are now only four.

Four of us stand over Tyler's body. Six feet in the ground.

All of us will mourn him. The world is at a loss for not knowing him. I finally get the expression about how it's better to have loved and lost than never to have loved at all.

Tyler was good through and through. He would have lived his days making the world a better place. He'd try to start a conversation with anyone; just to get to know them, just to make them laugh if he could.

All four of us lined up and saying our final goodbyes will never be the same after losing our youngest brother.

But only one of us knows the truth.

Only one of us is guilty.

The worst part is when I leave. I'm the last of us to finally part from Tyler's grave, but when I leave, my gaze stays rooted to where her car was. Where Addison had parked. My memories aren't of my father crying helplessly against the brick wall of the church, refusing to go in when he couldn't hide his pain. The images that flash before my eyes as my shoes crunch against the icy snow aren't of all his friends and teachers and family who have come from states away to tell us how sorry they are and how much Tyler will be missed.

All I can think about is Addison. How she stood so quietly on the fringes of the crowd, her fingers intertwined, her eyes glossy. How even as the wind ripped her scarf from her shoulders, carrying it into the distance and leaving her shoulders bare, she didn't move. She didn't even shudder. She was already numb.

The picture of her standing there motionless, staring at the casket is what I think about as I leave my brother.

I didn't know then how dangerous that was. Or maybe I did and I didn't want to believe it. But Addison would haunt me long after that night, as do so many other things.

She's only a girl. One small, weak girl.

Her red cheeks and nose and windblown hair made her look that much more tempting. Everything about her is ruined. At least she appeared to be that night. But I knew she had more left in her. More life and spirit. More emotion to give.

I may be cruel and unforgiving, but I'm right. I'm always right.

Chapter Nine

ADDISON

The night Tyler died, I saw it all happen.

I was there and I heard the tires squeal.

At the memory, I can practically feel the cold raindrops from that night pelting my skin. I turn on the faucet to the hottest it can go and wait until steam fills the room. I step into the shower, ignoring how the sounds of water falling are so similar to the rain that night as I stood outside the corner store. He called my name. My eyes close and my throat feels tight as I hear Tyler's voice.

The last thing he said was my name as he stepped into the street.

It takes a lot to leave someone because you fell in love with somebody else. Somebody who would never love you back.

It takes even more of your heart to witness the death of someone who truly deserved to live. More than I'll ever deserve it.

And to know that they died because they were looking for you ...

God and fate are not kind or just. They take without reason. And the world is at a loss for Tyler being taken from us.

I thought I was doing the right thing by leaving Tyler. I didn't know he'd come looking for me. If I could take it back, I would.

The water hits my face and I pretend like the tears aren't there. It's easier to cry in the shower.

I was fine until I saw Daniel again. It took me years to feel just okay. That's the part I can't get over. Maybe this is what a relapse is? One moment and I've lost all the strength I've gained over the years. All of the acceptance that I can't change what happened and that it'll be okay. It's all gone in an instant.

I lean my back against the cold tile wall and sink to the floor. The smooth granite feels hard against my back as I sit there, letting the water crash down on me as I remember that night over and over. Just a few moments in particular. The moment Tyler saw me, then the moment he spoke my name and moved toward me.

The moment I screamed at the sight of him stepping into the road.

The car was right there. There was no time.

It didn't matter how I threw myself forward, racing toward him even as the car struck him.

I swear I acted as fast as I could. But it wasn't good enough.

My head rests on my knees as my shoulders shake.

Life wasn't supposed to be so cruel. Not to him.

"Deep breaths," I tell myself. "One at a time," I say, brushing at my eyes even though the water is still splashing down.

Standing up makes me feel weak. The water's colder, but the air is still hot.

Just breathe.

As I open up the shower door to inhale some cool air, I hear something. My heart stops and my body freezes. The water's still on but my eyes stare at the bathroom door.

The mirrors are fogged even though I left the door open slightly. A second passes and then another.

My body refuses to move even after I will myself to reach for the towel. My knuckles turn white and keep me where I am. I know I heard something. Something fell. Or something was pushed. Something beyond the door. *Something*. I don't know what, but I heard something.

I force myself to take one step onto the bath mat, and then another onto the tile floor.

I keep moving. I take the towel in both hands and then wrap it around myself although I can't take my eyes off the door.

Water drips down my back, but I don't bother with drying my hair. I make myself open the door and it groans in protest as I do.

The second it's open wide, I feel foolish.

It's only a picture I'd put up with hanging tape strips. It's fallen and the paint on the wall where it was hung, a Tiffany blue, is marred.

I should have used nails or screws to hang it.

Even as I pick up the picture and roll my eyes, my body is still tense; my heart still races. The frame is cracked and broken. When I place it onto the dresser, I catch a glimpse of the piece of paper Daniel gave me. It's a ripped portion of something—maybe a bill, I'm not sure. But on it is his number. The number I texted so he would have mine and to ask when we could meet. The number that didn't answer, even though the message was marked as read.

I leave the paper there with the broken frame and head back to the bathroom to finally turn off the water. But I stop just shy of entering.

Peeking at the door to my bedroom, a chill travels down my spine.

I don't remember leaving it open.

Chapter Ten

DANIEL

I would say I don't have time for this shit, but I do. I really do.

I would make time for it if I didn't already have it in spades.

I'm cradling my chin while I drum the fingers of my other hand in a rhythmic pattern on the sleek mahogany tabletop. The soft sound doesn't even reach my ears, mixing with the chatter and hum of small talk and the clinking of silverware in the restaurant.

The Madison Grille has gotten a facelift recently. It's obvious. From the new wood beams that make the place smell like cedar, to the industrial lighting with exposed bulbs. I deliberately chose a place that wasn't too expensive or elegant so this wouldn't seem like a date. But it's better than a bar. There's privacy here that I'm eager to take advantage of. I waited to message her until only hours ago. Last night took a lot out of me, but once I decided, there was no turning back.

"Would you like anything while you wait?" The waiter already has his pad out and pen ready to go. There are a lot of things I'd like right now. Addison bent over the table, for one. Simply for inviting me back into her life. She may not know how much she taunted me, but she's smart enough to know the attraction was there and still she teased me.

"A whiskey sour and two waters," I tell him and he waits for more, but a tight smile sends him away.

Again my fingers drum as I think about each and every curve of the woman I'm waiting for.

Addison is all grown up.

And that look in her eyes is one I recognize. Desire. My blood feels hotter with every second I sit here thinking about what I wanted to do last night. And what I plan to do tonight.

I can imagine those pouty lips of hers wrapping around my cock and the sounds she'd make as I shoved my dick down her throat.

If nothing else, I can finally get a piece of what I wanted when I first laid eyes on her. Just the thought makes my dick harden and I stifle back a groan as the zipper of my jeans digs into me.

It took everything in me not to take her last night.

When she looked at me like she could see right through me.

When she told me to stop, as if she could command me.

When she spilled her little heart out as if I was the one meant for those words.

I'll be damn sure to make the time for Addison. Finally having her is worth all the fucking time in the world.

Sheets of rain batter against the large front window of this place and crash noisily on the tin roof.

I hate the rain. I hate what it does to me. The memories it brings back.

Addison is out there in the rain right now. Feeling it beat against her skin. Listening to the familiar sound.

And the unwanted memories that come with it.

I should feel a good number of things with the memory of Tyler besetting me right now as I wait for Addison. Shame, maybe even disgust. Swallowing thickly, I replay the memories, but this time focus on *her*. How she looked at me and shied away. How she couldn't talk to me while looking me in the eyes. How she blushed every time she caught me staring. Her reaction to me and only me was everything.

It was never about Tyler and I stayed away back then for him. It was always about Addison.

My thoughts are interrupted by the drinks I ordered being set on the table in front of me.

"Will you be dining tonight?" the waiter asks and I shake my head no and reply, "Just drinks."

"Let me know if I can get you anything else." With that he's gone and I'm left sitting alone at the table in the back. Staring at the entrance and waiting.

The soft lighting is reflected in my watch face as I turn my wrist over, showing the time is nearly ten minutes past the hour. She's late.

My eyes narrow as I look back toward the entrance, willing her to walk through the doors. There's a mix of worry and fear that I'm vaguely aware of. Fate's been a cruel bitch to me and I wouldn't put it past her to take the one thing I've always wanted. The one person I'm so close to getting.

Before I can let the unwanted emotions get the best of me, the door opens and Addison steps inside, huddled under an umbrella that she's quick to shake out over the mat and close. The hostess greets her as I sit paralyzed, watching Addison.

It's still surreal to see her here. I don't know how to react to her.

My fingers long to help her slip out of her jacket, but instead they grip onto the table.

I frown at the sweet smile she gives the hostess for helping her with her things. Addison hasn't given me one. In fact, it falls as she's directed toward me.

The happiness so evident only a second ago is gone as she walks over.

It makes my blood heat to a simmer but I stand anyway, pulling out the chair across from me for her to sit.

"Hi," she offers politely and the scent of her shampoo wafts toward me.

I don't trust myself to say anything, so I only offer her an inkling of a smile. I'm better than this. I know better too. "Thank you," she says softly as I retake my seat.

"I didn't know what you'd like to drink," I tell her even though I know she'll order a red wine. On the sweeter side.

"Oh, I'm fine with anything," she says agreeably and just like that, the bits of irritation slowly ebb and start to fade. She offers me a hesitant smile as she adds, "I'm glad you texted me."

Her smile broadens and she takes a sip of water before the waiter comes by again. And she orders cabernet. She's a creature of habit, little Addison.

"You wanted to talk?" I sit back easier in my seat now that she's here.

"I do, but I don't know how."

A genuine smile creeps onto my face. Little things like her innocent nature have always intrigued me. "Just say whatever you want, Addison."

"Do you hate me?" she asks me quietly. The seriousness is unexpected and catches me off guard.

"No, I don't hate you." I hated that I couldn't have her. But that was then.

"I feel like you should," she tells me although she's staring at her glass. She does that a lot. She looks down when she talks to me. I don't like it. My chest feels tighter and the easiness of tonight and what I want from it tangle into a knot in my stomach. I reach for my drink, letting it burn on the way down.

The words to ease her are somewhere. I know they exist, but they fail me now because the truth that begs to come out is all I can focus on.

I'm saved by her glass of cabernet that she accepts from the waiter graciously.

"Tyler did mean a lot to me, you know?" she asks me as if my acceptance means everything. As if I couldn't see it in her eyes back then. Every fucking time I saw them together it was obvious. He was all she had and I think she hated that fact, but loved him for simply being there for her.

"That was never a question," I tell her with a chill in my voice. One that I can't control.

"I just feel like," she pauses and swallows, then takes a sip of wine. With her nervous fidgeting, she's clearly uncomfortable and it's pissing me off. "I'm just afraid of what you and your brothers think. Your dad, too."

"My father died two years ago," I tell her and ignore the twinge of guilt running through me plus the pain of the memory. The knot seems to tie tighter.

I went home for the first time in years only to watch him being put in the ground next to my mother, just twenty plots down from Tyler's grave. And I haven't been back since. It's funny how guilt spreads like that. How it only gets worse, not better.

"Oh my God," Addison gasps and reaches her small hand out on the table for mine. "I'm so sorry." One thing I've always admired about Addison is how easy it is to read her. How genuine she is. How honest. Even if the things she was thinking were less than appealing.

"My father liked you, so he told Tyler that you would come back." I don't know why I tell her that. The memory doesn't sit well with me and the conversation isn't going where I'd like it to. Uncomfortable is an emotion I don't often experience. I suppose it makes sense that I am now though. Yet again ... that's Addison's doing. But I allow it. It would be easy to get up and leave, to not have to deal with this conversation. But having Addison tonight is worth it.

Barely catching a glimpse of the starched white shirt of the waiter, I hold up my hand just in time to stop him.

"Yes?" he asks and I order two rounds of black rose shots, which are a mix of vodka and tequila and the restaurant's drink of choice. Plus another whiskey sour. I greatly underestimated this conversation and the need for alcohol to go along with it.

"Anything else?" the waiter asks and Addison pipes up. With her hands folded in her lap, she orders the bruschetta.

It's only once the waiter's left that she leans forward, tucking her hair behind her ear and says, "I didn't eat much today."

"Get whatever you'd like," I tell her easily and keep my gaze from wandering straight down her blouse. It's only a peek. Only a hint at what's under the thin cotton, but I can see the lace of her bra and it begs me to look.

"I have to get this off my chest." Her words distract me and looking at the serious expression in her eyes I'm irritated again, but I keep my lips shut tight. It will be worth it when it's over with. It better be.

"I just ... even that day when I left, I didn't want you to think that I didn't appreciate everything."

She has no fucking idea. How is it even possible that she could be so blind?

She lived under our roof. It was off and on for nearly a year while the two of them dated. Tyler insisted. And the nights she didn't stay felt off toward the end. Each and every time she left I thought it was my doing.

But she always came back.

Tyler wasn't one to make demands, but he wanted her there with him. He wanted her protected and cared for. And when he told us why, when he told us what she'd been through, my father agreed.

It wasn't just that she had a tragic backstory. That she'd lost her parents and had no one.

It was the story of her previous foster father that changed my father's mind.

You could see it in the way Addison shied away from everything and everyone. And how she didn't want to go back to a stranger's house and hope nothing like that ever happened again.

She was safe with us. Even if she felt like she was intruding, every one of us wanted her there.

Even more so after we paid that sick fuck a visit.

It wasn't in Tyler's nature to want to hurt someone. Addison had a good way of bringing out a different part of him. She's good at that, at bringing out facets of your personality that were dormant before.

Carter was the one who decided when and how we'd take care of the asshole who'd touched her the year before. He was forty years old with a fifteen-year-old girl under his care.

Carter decided all five of us would go together while Addison was at class. The drive was only three hours away. Too long to do it at night, because she'd have noticed. But we had plenty of time during the day.

Carter always has a plan, and I was supposed to go around the back. Which is right where the asshole was raking up leaves.

I'd never killed anyone with gardening equipment before. I still wonder what it would have been like had I used the sharp tines of the metal but the damn thing broke in half. The spike of the splintered wooden handle worked well enough.

He got out one scream, if you can even call it that. More of a pathetic cry.

My family may have sheltered her.

I killed for her.

Tyler should have told her back then, and I have a mind to tell her now. But I don't break promises, not even to the dead.

So I keep that little bit of our history to myself.

The memory gives me the strength to look her in the eyes as I tell her, "You care a lot about what other people think. You'd be happier if you didn't."

"I'm not sure I would be," she answers softly with the corners of her lips turned down.

Again, the alcohol saves the conversation. The shots hit the table one by one.

"I think you need a drink."

I sure as fuck do. I didn't have her come here for a heart to heart. This isn't going how I'd planned. Wine and dine and fuck her is what I wanted. The first two I could take or leave, but the last I've needed for so long.

"I could use one ... or six," she jokes and pulls her hair over her shoulder, twirling the dark locks around her finger.

Addison's entire demeanor changes as she watches the dark purple shot swirl in the glass.

"Thank you," she says as she smiles up at the waiter.

"Cheers." I tilt my shot toward her in jest and down it before she can say otherwise. No salutes to the dead, or to anything else for that matter.

When my glass hits the table, Addison's is just reaching her lips.

Everything about the way she drinks it turns me on. From the way her slender fingers hold the glass, to the way her throat moves as she swallows.

A million images of how she'd look as she sucks my cock are going through my head until she speaks again.

"You make me feel …" she trails off and hesitates to continue.

"Scared?" I offer her. I'm used to making certain people feel that way. Only when I need them to remember what I'm capable of.

"No … unworthy." I'm struck by her candor.

"If you think that, it's because you've come to that conclusion on your own."

"You've always made me think that. Even back when I was with Tyler." My spine stiffens hearing her bring him up so casually this time. Like it's easy to use his name in conversation.

"Your bruschetta," the waiter says, setting the plate down in the center of the table. I've never wanted to kill a waiter for delivering an appetizer before. Not until this moment.

He starts to speak again and I cut him off. "We're good here, thank you." My words are rushed and hard and I pray for his sake he takes the fucking hint.

My gaze moves from him to Addison, and her expression makes me regret it.

"You made me think that when I got here." Addison looks as if she's debating on eating. I guess the topic has ruined her appetite. It takes me a second to remember what she even said … *unworthy*.

"You were late."

"I got here as soon as I could," she protests weakly. As if she's truly apologetic and the part that pisses me off the most is that I know she is.

"If you don't want me to be angry, then don't make me wait." I'm wound tighter and tighter by the second. It's amazing how a girl like Addison can tempt my self-control.

"You didn't have to wait. You can go," she retorts, saying each word while staring straight into my eyes. Daring me.

I smile. "I don't want to leave."

The anger in her features softens at my response. "I just hit traffic."

A heavy breath comes and goes as I settle back in my seat, watching for her reaction. This tit for tat is different for me. "It's fine," I tell her, hoping to end it. And move back to the plan.

"Why do you look at me like that?" she asks me and I still.

"How is it that I look at you?" I ask her to clarify. It's usually so easy to manipulate others into seeing me how I need them to. But Addison is observant beyond measure. She always has been. And she's always been different.

"Like you don't trust me. Or maybe you don't know what to expect from me."

I shrug. "I don't trust anyone. Don't take it personal."

She laughs and her shoulders shake slightly. "Maybe that's because of the people you hang out with?" she suggests and quirks a brow at me.

"I don't hang out with anyone." I answer her simply, with no emotion. Merely stating a truth.

She hums a response and reaches out for a piece of the toasted bread. As she bites into it, the bread crunches loudly and diced tomatoes fall into her hand. She actually blushes, and after she swallows she says defensively, "You should eat some, it's weird with you just watching me."

I let a rough chuckle vibrate up my chest. "I'm not hungry."

"I hate being rude and eating it all myself, but the alcohol is already hitting me."

Good. I don't say the thought out loud.

As she wipes her hands on her napkin, I ask her, "What is it that you want from me,

Addison?" My hands clench under the table as I wait. I know exactly what I want from her. To fuck her out of my system. To be done with an obsession from long ago.

She shoots me a sweet, genuine smile and the blush grows hotter on her face. "I think it's the alcohol talking."

Her smile is addictive and I feel my own lips twitch up into a lopsided grin. "Why's that?"

"Because I want to tell you I've always wondered what it would be like to kiss you."

I feel myself swallow. I feel everything in this moment. Watching her blush and smile at me like that, I want more of it. I don't know if it's the vodka, the tequila or the wine. Maybe a combination of the three. But whatever's making her blush, she needs more of it.

My heart beats rapidly and my cock hardens to the point where it's nearly unbearable.

As she covers her face with her hands, the waiter walks by casually and I reach out, fisting his shirt and stopping him in his tracks.

The look on his face is a mix of shock and fear. But I'm quick to loosen my grip and tell him, "More shots."

Chapter Eleven

ADDISON

When I'm drunk, I have some odd thoughts. Some do make sense. For instance, how many shots did we have? That one seems like a logical thought, and I'm not sure of the exact answer, but at least three. Which is probably three too many but with how tense and awkward I was at the start of dinner, maybe three was just the right number.

Also, what happened to my car? I should be concerned about that. But I'm drunk, so walking seems smart. I keep my feet moving, one after the other even though I sway slightly. Only slightly though.

The thought that matters the most and the one I keep coming back to is whether or not Daniel can see how my hands keep trembling.

I'm sure the heat in my cheeks is obvious. And the butterflies in my stomach aren't staying where they ought to. They fly up and mess with my heart. Fluttering wildly and with an anxiousness that makes it feel like they're caged and trying to escape.

Maybe it's normal for what I'm doing.

When you want to kiss someone who's obviously a dick, it makes sense that your body would feel anxious and like you should run, right? Not to mention I'm sure he's still dealing. When your family's business is crime, you don't exactly walk away from that life. This heated nervousness won't leave me. I can't stop fidgeting with my hands and I'm sure it's ridiculous, but what else could be expected of me?

And then there's the fact that he's my ex's brother. An ex who's gone. And in many ways, it's because of me. It should make me feel worse than I do. But in a lot of ways, it feels the same way as running has. Only this time, I'm running to Daniel. A man I've dreamed for so long would comfort me and tell me these feelings were alright.

Obviously, that never happened. And I'm not sure it ever will.

There's a part of my mind that won't stop picking at that fact. A part that wonders how Daniel can even stand to be around me. A part that wonders if he's only toying with me. Like he's waiting to get his revenge and tell me how he truly feels.

And that's the part that scares me when I look up at him. I don't care how many times he'll tell me that no one blames me. How could they not?

I don't know what's happening, but I'm too afraid to stop, because I really want to find out. I'm too eager to finally know what it feels like to be wanted by him.

"You're so nervous," he says as if he's amused.

"Aren't you?"

His smile dims and he runs his hand through his hair, looking to his left at the stop sign. "Let's go to my place."

We're standing on the corner of Church and Fifth and I know I just need to go six blocks and I'll be two streets over from my apartment building ... I think. There are bus stops everywhere in this college town. So even if I get lost, I could find my way back home by just hopping on a bus.

"Your place?" I question him while squinting at the signs. I'm more than a little tipsy. But everything feels so good.

"Let's go," he answers and then takes my hand in his, pulling me across the street even though the sign at the crosswalk is still red.

"Still a rule breaker," I tease and I think that one is from the alcohol. I must find it funnier than he does though, because once we're on the other side, I'm the one smiling at my little joke while he stands there. Staring at me like he's not sure what to do with me.

"So you aren't nervous?" I ask him, daring to broach the subject again. I don't mind what he does to me. I crave it. And I'll be damned if he tells me he doesn't want me. I can see it in his eyes.

But what exactly he wants me for? That I have yet to know for sure.

A good fuck seems to be first on the list though. And I can't argue with that.

"I don't get nervous."

"Everyone gets nervous." The words slip out of my mouth and I tell him about a study my friend Rae told me about. She's a psychology major and she told me about public speakers and how even professional public speakers' adrenaline levels spike when they get on the stage. Everyone gets nervous. "There's no denying it."

"If you say so, Addison." That's all I get from him as the night air seems to get colder and I shiver. That's when I notice he's still holding my hand.

"This doesn't make you nervous? It doesn't make you question if ... if we should be doing this?" I lift up our clasped hands and he lets me, but he doesn't stop walking.

"Why shouldn't we?" he responds, but I hear the hard edge in his voice. *He knows.*

"There are so many reasons," I tell him and look straight ahead.

"Can I tell you a secret?" he whispers and the way he does it makes me giggle. A silly little girl giggle that would embarrass me if I wasn't on the left side of tipsy.

"Anything," I breathe.

"I was jealous that Tyler got to have you."

I nearly stumble and my smile slips. That erratic beating in my chest makes me want to reach up and pound on my heart to knock it off.

He continues once I get my footing back. "You were too young and Tyler got to you first."

I walk with my lips parted, but not knowing what to say or do.

Daniel's arm moves to my waist as his steps slow and I look up to see a row of houses. Cute little houses a few blocks from the university campus. They're the type of houses that come equipped with white picket fences and for the second time in fifteen minutes, I nearly trip.

"How drunk are you?" Daniel questions with a serious tone.

"Sorry, not that drunk," I answer him as we walk up the paved drive to the front door of a cute house with blue shutters. My heart won't knock it off, but I ignore it and change the subject. "This is your place?"

"Just renting."

I nod my head and as much as that makes sense, it's also one less thing to question. And now I find myself on the front steps of Daniel's place, with his hand on mine. Drunk after I've confessed to him how I feel.

Not the smartest thing I've ever done, and not the best decision I've made in my life.

But maybe I'll wake up in five minutes, and this will just be another one of my dreams.

My breathing comes in pants as Daniel lets his hand travel lower down my back and I instantly heat everywhere for him. My heart pounds and my blood pressure rises. I'm almost afraid of how my body is reacting so intensely. He has to see it, but if he does, he doesn't let on.

I don't need Rae or a shrink or anyone to tell me I'm going to regret this. I know that already.

Maybe I can blame it on the alcohol.

Or the sudden flood of memories.

Sleep deprivation, that's a good excuse too.

I don't care what I blame it on. So long as it happens. I wanted him for so long, even if it was from a distance. An unrequited and forbidden lust, not love. I refuse to believe it was love.

I lost the chance long ago to have what I always wanted. There's no way I won't push for it now.

I watch as Daniel reaches for the doorknob but stops, dropping his hand and directing his gaze to me.

"What are you thinking?" Daniel asks me and instinctively I look up at him, swallowing hard and licking my lips. I love how his eyes flicker to them and I hesitantly reach up, spearing my fingers through his hair.

And he lets me.

He lowers his lips and gently brushes them against mine although he doesn't kiss me yet. The lingering scents of whiskey and vodka mingle with my lust and love of bad decisions, giving me a heady feeling.

"I always knew you were bad for me," I whisper against his lips as he bends down to kiss me. To actually press his hot lips against mine this time. His tongue demands entrance, licking against the seam of my lips and I grant him his wish. The heated kiss is short-lived and I'm left breathless.

I can feel his smile as he pulls away, taking the key from his pocket and licking his lower lip. I love how he does it like that. Slow and sensual and like he's hiding a secret that thrills him to no end.

"Bad for you doesn't even begin to cover it, Addison."

Chapter Twelve

DANIEL

BARELY CONTAINED.

Everything about me is barely contained. All I can think about is ripping off Addison's clothes and finally getting inside her tight cunt. I know she wants me. She's sighing softly every time I let my skin touch hers, filling the night air with her little pants of need.

Tiny touches. It started out as a way to tease her as we walked back to the house I'm renting. Little caresses that made me smile at her desperation.

She's so responsive. So needy.

I can't fucking stand it.

I've always known I was selfish. It's something my father said I inherited from him. He looked at me with pride when he said it too.

Tonight I'm going to take advantage of that particular trait of mine.

The front door swings open and it's pitch black inside. I don't waste my time stumbling for a light in the foyer.

I'm fucking her in my bed. I've already decided that.

"Daniel—" Addison gasps my name as I pick her up with one arm, forcing her legs to wrap around my hips. The door slams shut and I lock it as I crush my lips against hers.

My name. She's gasping my name. She'll scream it too. Hearing that hauntingly sweet voice say my name as if it's the only word meant to fall from her lips is everything I've ever wanted. Fucking music to my ears.

She moans into my mouth and then pulls away to breathe, her neck arching as I press my stiff erection against her heat, pushing her into the door and nipping at her neck.

"Upstairs," I groan against her hot skin although she doesn't have a choice in the matter. I've only said it to remind myself that I'm not fucking her here.

Not just yet. Only seconds away. Only seconds.

I take the stairs two at a time, making her cling to me. My heart feels as though it's losing control, beating chaotically. All the blood in my body must be in my dick. Her lips crash against my neck over and over and her nails dig into my shoulders through my shirt.

"Daniel," she moans and my name on her lips is a sin. I kick the bedroom door open and moonlight is shining through the blinds, giving me everything I need to see all of this.

I want to remember every detail. I can barely breathe and the alcohol is coursing through my blood, but I will remember every fucking detail of this night.

The bed groans with her surprised gasp as I toss her onto it and pull my shirt over my shoulders. She's still trying to get her balance as I kick off my pants and crawl on the bed to get to her. My breaths are coming in short and frantic. I'd be embarrassed, but Addison is just the same. She's just as eager and there isn't a thing in this world that could make me feel more desire than the way she stares back at me with nothing but lust.

Something tears as I pull at her dress, ripping it off her shoulders and down her body. Before I take her panties off her to join the puddle of clothes by the bed, I cup her hot pussy as I kiss her again. And this time it's me that moans into her mouth.

My dick is already impossibly hard, and precum is leaking from me at the feel of the silken fabric beneath my fingers, hot and damp with her arousal.

I don't bother to take them off gently. But I never thought I would either. Shredding them with my hands, I ignore her gasp of surprise and quickly lower my mouth to her cunt.

She falls back onto the mattress, spearing her fingers through my hair as I lick her from her entrance to her clit.

So fucking sweet. Sweeter than the shots. Sweeter than the trace of wine on her lips as she kissed me.

There's not enough time in a single night for everything I want to do to her. I barely pull myself off her clit to shove two fingers inside of her. I'm not gentle as I finger fuck her, thrusting as deep as I can go.

Her back arches, threatening to pull her pussy away from me, but I pin her hip down and curl my fingers up to stroke against her front wall. The sweet, strangled moans are everything I need and everything I've ever wanted.

I pause for only a second to watch her reaction. How her eyes are half-lidded but she's staring at me. Her dark green eyes meet mine and I press my thumb to her swollen nub to see her throw her head back in pleasure. Her pussy clenches around my fingers with need.

"So tight," I say with reverence.

"It's been a while," she breathes out while writhing.

I almost ask how long. *Almost.*

There's a small voice in the back of my head that keeps hissing that she doesn't belong to me and when she utters those words, I'm acutely aware of how my brother had her first.

He might have been her first, but I'll ruin her.

I'll make her mine and make her forget about any other man who's touched her.

My dick throbs with a nearly unbearable pain from the desire to be inside her. To thrust into her and take her exactly how I've been picturing since I saw her four nights ago.

My fingers wrap around her throat, and at the same time I palm my dick.

"I want you to look at me," I tell her although I'm breathing heavily. I feel her swallow against my grip and then she nods. Lining up my dick, I press the head between her folds and she shudders beneath me.

Her soft moan vibrates against my hand and then I slam all of me inside of her. Every bit of me, and I watch her eyes widen and her mouth drop open with a sharp gasp.

Fuck! She feels too good and she immediately spasms around my dick. I can't move or breathe. If I do, I'll cum with her without a second thought.

It takes every ounce of control I have to keep my eyes on hers. To watch her so I can remember this forever.

Her body trembles as she tries to bow her back, but I'm holding her down, making her take it all. Her hands reach up to her neck. Her nails are digging into my fingers as I thrust again and again, tightening my grip but still letting her breathe. *Yes!* I love how she lets me own her body. *Mine. All mine.*

Her cunt tightens around my cock to the point where it's fucking strangling me the way I am her. The room is filled with the noises of me fucking her relentlessly.

I loosen my grip as I pound into her and she sucks in a deep breath. Feeling her pant and struggle against me, my lips slam against hers. With her chest pressed against me, I can feel her heart beating just as hard against mine.

Her nails rake down my arms and I can tell she isn't sure if she wants to cling to me for dear life or shove me away. I lift my lips from hers to breathe and she screams out my name with reverence. Her reaction only makes me fuck her harder, with every ounce of energy in me. *Mine.*

My fingers dig into her hips as I keep up my ruthless pace, each stroke taking me higher and higher to a pleasure that nearly makes me cum. My toes curl and I struggle to breathe, but I put every bit of energy into looking into her eyes.

As she screams out my name, her teeth clench and her heels dig into my ass. Her nails break the skin at my lower back as she cums violently on my dick.

My body begs me to give in and bury my head in the crook of her neck as I cum inside of her, but I can't. Not yet.

Mine. The word slips from my lips as she screams out my name again. Her back arches while she struggles beneath me, shoving against my chest.

"Look at me," I command her as I shove myself deep within her, all the way to the hilt, pausing for the first time since I've entered her. My dick slams against the back of her warmth, stretching her and forcing her lips to make a perfect "O."

Her eyes meet mine, dilated with a wildness to them I've never seen. I brush my pubic hair against her clit, angling just slightly and rocking. Just to see how much she can take.

"Daniel," she whimpers my name as she thrashes her head from side to side, cumming again even though I've stilled inside of her. Her pussy clenches and tries to milk my cock. And I groan from deep in my chest at the sensation. "Fuck," I mutter then hold my breath and tense my body.

Not yet. I can't cum yet.

It's only once her release has passed and her body is still that I move again.

One more. One more is all I can take.

My forehead rests on the mattress above her shoulder and I gently kiss her soft skin although she flinches from the sensation. Even that's too much for her. She's already cumming again.

I ride through her orgasm, pounding into her heat and with each thrust the word mine escapes between my clenched teeth.

Even as I cum deep inside of her, not breathing, not moving with the only exception being the pulsing of my dick. Even in that moment I whisper the word against the shell of her ear. *Mine*.

I've never been able to sleep well.

Some people aren't meant to be heavy sleepers.

So instead of trying to sleep, I watch Addison in the dark. My eyes adjust easily and with the moonlight shining through the slats of the blinds, I can see every feature of hers clearly. I can see the gentle rise and fall of her chest with her steady breathing and the little dip in her collar that begs me to kiss it.

I'd forgotten how badly I wanted her all those years ago. The thrill of having her near and the desire to hold on to her outweighed the memories. But seeing her beauty so close and the beast inside me sated, there's no denying the attraction.

No one has ever held my attention like Addison. No one makes me forget like she does. Nothing else matters when she's near me. Only the need to make sure she knows that I see her, that I feel her, that I want her.

And now I have her.

A deep rumble of satisfaction leaves my chest. Addison mirrors me in her sleep, a sweet moan slipping through her lips as she nuzzles closer to me. But then she stiffens.

My body tenses at her reaction.

I watch her lashes flutter and the realization show in her expression. Shock is evident on her face as she slowly lifts up her body, bracing herself on one palm. Covering her chest with the sheet, her lips part and her forehead pinches. She clenches her thighs and I've never been so proud in my fucking life.

There's a warmth in my body, knowing how I took her as if her body was mine alone to ruin.

It's been hours, hours of me simply watching her so close to me and memorizing the curves of her body. And she can still feel me inside of her.

With the ghost of a whimper on her lips, she slowly slips off the mattress, ignoring how it dips and could wake me. As if she wouldn't mind me waking.

My heart stutters and the hint of happiness in my expression falls. She's leaving? The fuck she is.

"What are you doing?" My voice is sharp in the still night air and it startles her. But only enough that she turns to face me. With one hand splayed across her chest and the other covering her bare pussy, she looks from me to the pile of her clothes on the floor.

Seeing her naked, and even better, trying to hide that nakedness from me makes my spent dick hard in an instant. I'm already eager for more of her. The slit of my cock is wet with precum and my thick shaft twitches at the thought of taking her again. I can keep her here. She'll stay. I fucking know she will.

"I have to go," she speaks softly, her words a murmur.

"You don't have to do anything but get back in my bed," I command her and then let my eyes roam down her body, making sure she knows exactly what I want. "Lie down."

She hesitates, but only for a moment. And then she lowers herself slowly, first leaning on her elbow and then nestling into the covers. That warmth comes back as soon as she's back where she belongs. The trace of the fear of losing her and the sickening feeling that she's leaving are both still present, but muted.

As soon as she's settled, staring up at me in the darkness with the moonlight highlighting her face, I lean down and kiss her on the lips. Not a gentle kiss, and not a goodnight kiss either.

She's breathless when I pull back and my own chest heaves for air, but I speak calmly, with the control I've come to expect.

"Spread your legs for me," I tell her and before her back is even settled, she does as she's told. Her thighs part so easily as a blush covers her skin and her eyes shine with the same hunger I remember from so long ago.

I take her by surprise, shoving my hand between her thighs and thrusting my fingers into her cunt. Slamming my lips down on hers, I silence her screams. Her back bows and she squirms under me, trying to get away from the intensity.

Pinning her hip down, I keep her where I want her and finger fuck her until she's screaming into my mouth. My teeth sink into her lip and then nip along her jaw, all while I'm enjoying her cries of pleasure and how tight her pussy gets when it spasms around my thick fingers. With my thumb on her clit, I don't stop until she's breathless and can no longer make a sound as she cums on my hand. Her body's still trembling when I finally thrust myself deep inside of her.

And it's my name on her lips.

My dick wrapped in her warmth.

My bed she sleeps in.

All mine.

Chapter Thirteen

ADDISON
Five years ago

I know I should stop this. My belly aches with this disgust. I hate myself for it.

For using Tyler as a distraction.

We go out every day, taking pictures of all sorts of things. The project is over, but he keeps asking if I want to go. And I never tell him no.

It's better than going back to the Brauns' place.

"Let's go over there," Tyler says and points toward a run-down path in the woods behind the park. We're at the far end of the park and I know this area. In front of us is the creek and if we go left and walk half a mile or so, we'll end up at the highway line and can follow that back to the parking lot. There are running trails along the way too. Although I don't like to run. I just walk and take pictures. I like doing that with Tyler.

One step to follow him. Two steps and he reaches for my hand.

I slip mine inside of his and he squeezes tight when he holds it. It's a little thing, but he really holds my hand like he means it. And that sick feeling in my stomach feels like nothing compared to the bittersweet sensation in my heart. I'm not sure if it's really pain or what it is.

I want more of it though.

A part of me knows it's selfish. That part's quiet as fallen branches crack beneath our weight and we stop at a clearing on the edge of the creek.

"It's beautiful," I whisper, staring out at the bubbling brook. It's the softest shade of blue although it gets darker where it's deeper.

"Like you," he says and gives me a charming smile. When he lets go of my hand to take his jacket off and lays it on the ground, those feelings mix, and the resulting brew is something I don't know how to handle.

But Tyler knows my secrets, and he's seen me in those moments I wish I didn't have. The ones where I cry and sometimes it's hard to know what's caused the outburst.

I swear I used to be happy. I used to be normal. But I'll never be normal again.

Although Tyler's jacket is laid flat, he sits next to it in the dirt and beckons me, patting the fabric and looking up at me with big puppy dog eyes. He doesn't ask much of me, but I can't help feeling like today may be different.

My shoulders hunch in a little as I sit down and tuck my hair behind my ear.

It takes everything in me to look at him. To look at Tyler and try to gauge his intention.

"Do you want to sleep with me?" I ask him bluntly.

He lets out a bark of a laugh and rests his forearms on his knees as he looks out onto the creek. Looking back at me he answers, "I read once, I think in a biology book, that teenage guys are horny as fuck."

I can't help the smile that cracks on my face at his joke. That's the way Tyler handled anything serious. He'd just make a joke and deflect.

"Seriously though," I say then wipe the palms of my hands on my knees instead of looking at him as I continue, "I don't get why you keep coming out with me."

He shrugs. "I like spending time with you," he tells me.

"So you don't want to get into my pants."

"I definitely want to fuck you."

I'm shocked by his candor. Tyler's ... careful around me. I feel like he considers each word carefully before speaking to me. Like if he says the wrong thing, I'd run. And that's not too far from the truth.

"You haven't tried anything ... though."

"Don't confuse my patience for a lack of interest." The second the words slip from him, Tyler lets out a genuine laugh. "Of all the dirty things I could say, that's what gets you to blush?"

It's only then that I feel the heat in my cheeks. It matches other places too.

Minutes pass with both of us taking small glances at each other, watching the sunset descend behind the forest with shades of orange and red in the clear blue sky. He even tosses a few twigs and rocks into the creek. He tries to skip them, but he's not very good at it.

"I think you'd like it if I kissed you here." He almost mumbles his words when he catches me staring at him. They're spoken so low and nearly absently.

His lips brush along my neck and desire sweeps through my body unexpectedly. Both of my hands move up to his chest and I push away from his overwhelming touch with my lips parted, my breath stolen.

He blinks away the lust in his gaze and slowly a smile forms on his face. "I knew you'd like it."

As I bite my lip, he leans forward cautiously, judging my reaction and then he does it again. His lips kiss over every part of my neck and up to the soft spot behind my ear.

***

And that's why I slept with Tyler. He said and did everything that made sleeping with him feel like it was right and meant to be.

As soon as we started walking back to his truck, that sick feeling returned. And I began to think that tomorrow he'd be different. That he'd gotten what he wanted, so he wouldn't want to be with me anymore.

But I was wrong again. He held me tighter. Talked to me sweeter. And loved me harder than before.

Tyler was patient. He didn't look at me as if I was broken, but he treated me like breaking me would be the worst sin in the world.

I could never tell him no.

Even if I still thought of his brother in ways I shouldn't have.

***

You shouldn't compare lovers.

Certainly not brothers.

It was a fantasy come alive to feel Daniel's skin against mine. To finally know what it's like to writhe under him.

But that's all he can ever be. A fantasy.

One that I'm prolonging by letting the days blend together in a whirlwind of alcohol and sex. He messages me where to meet and I go. We drink. We fuck. There are no more awkward conversations of our past, but the reminder stays deep in the pit of my stomach.

I'm not stupid. Daniel's no good. And this thing between us is merely two people giving in to a pipe dream we had long ago.

It's all-consuming and I wouldn't have it any other way.

But the moment this cloud of lust and bliss dissipates, I'll be left with the sobering truth.

I've given myself to a man who's only ever seen me as a plaything.

I've slept with someone who should truly hate me for being the reason his brother is dead.

And the events I've allowed to occur are something that should shame me for a lifetime.

There's no getting around those hard facts. But it's nice to ignore them for a while and in the moments when Daniel's with me, it feels different. It feels like nothing else exists.

And when your world is made of nothing but painful memories you're constantly trying to outrun, it's a relief for nothing else to exist.

Well, nothing but this flutter in my chest and this ache between my thighs. I love it. I love feeling this way even if nervousness and tiny bits of fear creep in.

It was better than I ever could have imagined. Even when I woke up alone in the morning. Even as I took the bus home with my hair a mess and still in the clothes from the night before.

A walk of shame had never felt so fucking good.

I bite down on my lip to keep the smile on my face from being too smug.

It was something I know I'll regret, but right now all I'm going to do is love this horrible mistake.

Over and over again.

The spoon clangs against the ceramic mug as I stir in the sugar for my tea. I need caffeine badly. I've slept soundly for the past three days, two of them in Daniel's bed, only to be woken up on occasion and fucked into the mattress. It feels good to be back at my apartment though, where I can rest undisturbed. He had a meet last night so I slept alone, which is a good thing. I'm too sore for any more of Daniel right now.

A smile graces my face as I lift the mug to my lips.

I blow across the top of the mug, breathing in the calming smell of the black tea and avoiding the hot steam. With my eyes closed I feel like I could go back to bed right now.

My little moment is interrupted by the sound of my phone going off. It's a distinct noise and I know exactly who it is by the tone. It's from an app that allows you to text people overseas for cheap. Which means it's Rae.

The mug hits the counter a little more aggressively than I'd like, sloshing a touch of tea on the counter as I reach for my phone.

"Shit," I mumble under my breath, but I don't bother with it. I need to talk to Rae.

How are you love? Miss you.

She always calls me *love*. She says things like *cheeky* and *cow* too. I love the diction of the United Kingdom and their accents. A very big part of me misses her and the small farm town she lives in. But it will never be home for me.

I message her back, *Miss you to pieces. How's your mom?*

I wait with my eyes on the screen and my lips pursed. She doesn't write back quickly so I busy myself with cleaning up the spill and having another sip of tea. Rae's mom is going through some health issues. I know it's been a pain in the ass for both of them. Or *arse* if it's Rae talking about it.

Mum's fine. Happy for now and enjoying the time off work. How have you been?

I start to text her everything from the very beginning, but then delete it. And then I try once more, but the words don't come out quite right. Before I can even message her anything, she texts again.

I'm thinking of going back to that bar in Leeds and having another go at the boy bands there. Made me think of you.

The reminder makes me smile and spreads a sense of warmth and ease through me. Enough that I reply simply, *I think I'm seeing someone. But I'm not sure if it's good or bad.*

"Seeing someone" might be a stretch. It's just fucking. I'm smart enough to know that.

She writes back quickly this time. *Spill it.*

You already know him. Well, of him. It's Daniel.

I feel a momentary pang of guilt, like I've betrayed him. As if saying what's between us out loud will ruin it. Because no one else will understand.

Tyler's brother?

I stare at her response and feel that spike of chagrin and shame I should have known was coming.

Yes.

It's all I can write back. The mug trembles slightly in my hands, but I ignore it, taking a drink although now the heat feels different on my lips. Less soothing and less comforting. Even if it isn't lukewarm yet.

Seeing him? she questions.

I put the mug back down and gather up the courage to try to make her understand. She knows everything. Including how I left Tyler because of what I felt for Daniel. What I thought was one-sided and an indication of how awful a person I was. All I had to do was love Tyler back. Instead I ruined what we were over dirty thoughts I couldn't stop.

We ran into each other. And I told him how I felt about him.

A moment passes, and then another. And that feeling in my gut and heart keeps at it. Twisting and squeezing until I feel wrung out. I wish I could say I don't care what she thinks about this. But she's the only person I have left. I'm careful not to get too close to anyone. Everyone I love dies. So it's best I don't let people in. Rae is the only exception.

How do you feel about it?

I let out a single chuckle, like a breath of a laugh at her response. I text back, *You sound like a shrink.*

You sound like you might need one.

Her response makes the small bit of relief wash away. *Maybe I do.*

I just worry about you, she texts me and then adds, *I know it has to bring back memories and other unpleasant things.*

It does. But it also feels like a relief in a way. And so much more than that.

Are you dating? she asks.

I roll my eyes at that question. She knows better. *I don't date.*

She sends back an emoji rolling its eyes and a genuine snicker leaves me.

Just take care of yourself, will you?

She's a good friend and I know better than to think she'd be anything other than concerned.

You burst my bubble, I tell her and I really mean it.

Five years ago

Tyler's lips slip down to the crook of my neck. He knows just the spot that makes me wet for him.

My palms push against his chest and the motion makes my body sink deeper into the mattress beneath him.

"Spread your legs." He gives the command against my skin, making me hotter ... needier. But my eyes dart to the door and then back to him.

"But your brothers," I whisper as if my words are a secret.

Tyler pulls away, breathless and panting with need. He always makes love to me wildly. Like it's all he needs. Each time is quick, but he takes care of me first. I bite down on my bottom lip as he hovers over me and then looks over his shoulder at the door.

"They don't care," he tells me and I can only swallow the lump in my throat.

One brother cares. I know he does. He looks at me like I'm a whore whenever I stay over here. And I haven't even slept with Tyler under the Cross roof yet.

"I don't want them to think I'm staying over just so we can have sex."

"They don't think that." Tyler smiles and brushes the hair from my face as I pull the covers up closer around me. I still have my nightgown on; Tyler's just pulled the fabric up around my waist.

"What if they think I'm using you so I don't have to go back home? Like I'm spreading my legs just so I can have a place to stay." I heard a girl say that at school a week ago and the thought hasn't left me. It's true I don't want to go back. But I'm not a whore either.

"I have to fucking beg you to stay here, Addie. They can hear that. They know that. And we've been dating for how long now?"

Almost six months to the day he first tapped on my shoulder in science class.

The uneasiness still doesn't leave me and I stare at the door until Tyler's hand cups my chin.

"We can be quiet," he whispers and lowers his lips to mine.

My eyes close and I let myself feel his warmth and comfort.

"Just kiss me," he tells me as he slips his hand between my legs, parting my thighs for him.

I keep my eyes shut and try to be quiet. My muffled moans carried through the walls though and so did the unmistakable sounds and steady rhythm of Tyler fucking me.

I know because of the way Daniel looked at me late that night when I snuck into the hall to use the bathroom.

My hand was on the doorknob when he opened his bedroom door. Caught in his heated gaze, I couldn't move; I couldn't breathe. He let his stare trail down my nightgown before looking back into my eyes.

I'll never forget the way my body heated for him and how my heart pounded. I thought he was going to punish me, to pin me against the wall and make me scream. That's the way he would have fucked me. The kind of sex where you can't keep quiet.

Instead of doing or saying anything, Daniel turned around, going straight back into his room.

I sat in the bathroom for the longest time, feeling like the worst thing in the world. Like a whore and a fraud and an ungrateful bitch.

I snuck out in my nightgown, with my clothes clenched into a ball in my hand and drove home as quickly as I could.

I didn't go back to the Cross house for weeks. And the next time I let Tyler fuck me in his bed, I wasn't quiet about anything.

Chapter Fourteen

DANIEL

It's cute how she keeps looking at me like she's waiting for me to walk away. Like how yesterday she was surprised that I told her to come over. I'll never forget the shy look on her face. How her eyes scanned mine and she was hesitant to come back in.

So long as I'm in this small town, she needs to be in my bed. Every second I can have her. Our one-night stand turned into one week ... turned into two.

I've waited for so long to have her. Did she think I'd have my fill of her so quickly?

As she stretches on my bed, the sheet slips and reveals more of her back, along with the curve of her waist.

I could get used to this. Waking up with her in my bed, going to sleep alongside her.

If I could keep her here forever, I would.

"That was nice," she whispers as she rolls back over and lays her hand on my bare chest. Her finger traces up to the dip below my throat then moves lower, and lower still. Stirring my already spent dick back to life.

"Be careful what you ask for," I warn her in a rough timbre as I hold back a groan.

I can feel her smile against my shoulder and then she laughs sweetly.

"I think I need a shower first," she says.

"You'll need another when I'm done with you." I don't miss the way her legs scissor under the sheets at my comment.

"Shower first," she says as if she's decided. Had I slept well at all last night, I'd slip my tongue between her thighs and convince her otherwise. But the meeting location changed yesterday and then again. It seems the message I've been waiting on Marcus to deliver has changed as well and Carter's on edge with what's coming our way.

The unwanted thought is what motivates me to get up. I've been in a daze with Addison. She's a distraction.

I crack my neck and stretch my arms before getting out of bed with a twisted feeling in my gut.

With my back to Addison, she traces the small scar on the bottom of my shoulder. A scar I've long since forgotten. There are a few really, but they're faint. Only one is easily seen.

"How'd you get that?" she asks me and I clench my jaw as I stand up.

She always liked my father. He was a good man ... to her at least. And maybe the family business wouldn't have survived if he hadn't been so hard on Carter and me.

"I popped off to my father," I explain, keeping it short and simple as I get off the bed and grab a pair of boxer briefs from the dresser. My voice sounds strained even to my own ears.

My dick's already hard and wanting more of her, but the unpleasant reminder of my childhood makes me want to bury myself in work. I have an encrypted file I should look over with details for a big shipment coming in next week. It includes a list of new hires and Carter always gets wary when it comes to new people unloading stock.

"You popped off?" she asks and I turn around to the sound of her saddened voice. My stomach twists when I see her expression. Like she can't believe my father would have ever struck me.

She has no idea.

"I should have known better." My words don't do a thing to change the look in her eyes and when they move from the thin scattering of silver scars on my back to my own gaze, all I see is sympathy. And I don't fucking want it. Not from anyone, and sure as fuck not from her.

"Leave it alone, Addison." I move back to the dresser for pants and a shirt, opening one drawer and slamming it shut before moving to the next.

"What did you say?" I hear her ask softly as I shut a third drawer, still not finding what I'm looking for. The fourth drawer slams shut harder than I intended.

"It doesn't matter." My response doesn't faze her.

"I wouldn't have thought he'd ever–"

"He saved that side of himself for Carter and me," I say, cutting her off sharply before I can stop myself. Apparently the anger is stronger than I thought. Up until now I assumed the animosity was buried with him when he died.

"I'm sorry," she says softly and it only amplifies my agitation.

The air is tense in the bedroom as I slip on a t-shirt and pajama pants, an old plaid flannel pair.

"Pass me one?" Addison asks, apparently ready to move on from the revelation that my father wasn't the saint Tyler made him out to be.

I almost toss the black cotton Henley toward the bed, but instead I walk it to her. Letting her take it from me and when she does, her slender fingers brush against mine.

There's nothing sexier than watching her pad around this place in nothing but my t-shirt. Her occupation means she can work anywhere, which means her ass is staying right here with me. *For now.*

Gripping her hand as she takes the shirt, I pull her closer to me and steal a quick kiss. And then another as I release her.

She props herself up on the bed, getting onto her knees and deepening the small kiss. As she bites gently on my bottom lip, she tangles both of her hands in my hair. I let myself fall forward, bracing my impact with one arm on either side of her.

She doesn't open her eyes until she gives me a sweet peck right where she bit me. Her green eyes stare back at me for only a moment before she closes them again and brushes the tip of her nose against mine.

My fucking heart is a bastard for wanting to believe the kiss has anything to do with the conversation we just had. But it flips in my chest as if that little nudge and the fact that her eyes were closed meant everything in the world.

I've always had a bastard heart when it comes to her.

"I have to work," I tell her and quickly bend down to plant a quick kiss on her temple. I'd better leave before I wind up doing nothing but staying in bed.

"So you don't want to come with me to check out the campus?"

"I'm not sure there's a polite way to say this, but fuck no." It amazes me how easy it is to be candid with Addison. Maybe it's because just like now, she isn't offended or taken aback. She simply takes what I have to give and smiles.

"So you think I shouldn't go here?" she asks and from her tone I know it's a loaded question.

"Why would you?" I offer in rebuttal.

She breaks eye contact and shrugs, picking at a thread on the comforter. "It seems like a business degree would make sense."

"You already have your business set up and it's successful, isn't it?"

"I'm doing well. How'd you know? You look me up?" she asks playfully, but I ignore her and the twinge in my chest.

"Then why bother?"

She peeks up at me over her shoulder with a defensive look on her face. "Well, why do you bother?"

Leaning forward, I lower my voice to answer her. "I don't. I'm not staying."

"You're going home?" she asks and the very idea of home doesn't quite sit right with me, but neither does the expression on her face. The hurt one that she can't hide although I'm not sure she would bother even if she was aware of how transparent her emotions are.

"I'm working and that might lead me back to where we grew up."

As I lower myself back onto the bed slowly, I question being so honest with her. The coy and curious nature I've come to enjoy from her turns timid. Like she's walking into dangerous territory.

"Should I ask?" Her voice is quiet and she doesn't look me in the eye.

"That depends on what you want to know." She hasn't asked a single question since we've started hooking up. She's smart enough to know. Maybe smart enough to know not to ask too.

Finally, her gorgeous green eyes look back at me and she presses, "Would you tell me the truth if I did? Tyler never did."

"Tyler wasn't ever involved in anything serious." I ignore how everything in me turns cold at the mention of his name. Being with Addison ... knowing he was her first. It hurts to swallow as she keeps talking. Especially after the memory of my father. *I don't like to remember.*

She answers me, "Your version of serious and mine are different, I think."

The time passes as I fail to come up with a response. She doesn't need to know about any of this shit. It would be better if she didn't.

Another second. Another thought.

"Is that why you left him?" I ask her and although it hurts deep down in my core, I need to know if her idea of what he did for work is what made her leave him. I don't say his name though.

"I don't want to talk about that night." Her answer comes out sharper than I expect. With a bite and a threat not to question her. It only makes me that much more curious.

"The night you broke things off?" I ask her to clarify. That night isn't the one that haunts me. That's not the night that's unspeakable to me.

Addison stands on shaky legs with her back to me. Finding her packed bag and unzipping it as she speaks.

"I just don't like thinking about how the last couple of times I saw him I was turning him away," she says with a tinge of emotion I don't like to hear. The kind of emotion that's indicative of love.

A love I know for certain he had for her.

"You weren't the first seventeen-year-old girl to end a high school relationship," I remind her and also me. It was puppy love. That's all it ever was.

"Yeah well, I didn't know what it would lead to," she says and her voice trembles as she slips on a pair of underwear and sweatpants.

I'm not sure I want to know the answer, but I have to ask. "So if you could go back?"

Addison's quiet at my question and I walk toward her although her back is still to me. "If you could go back, you'd still be with him?" Her hesitation makes my muscles tighten. My fist clenches as a tic in my jaw spasms.

I've been kidding myself to think otherwise. Of course she'd be with him and not me. My breathing comes in ragged as she answers.

"If he were here now—" she starts to say, but I cut her off.

"He's not, and he never will be." The anger simmers. Everything that's been pushed down for so long rises up quickly. All the years of control and denial.

The hate that my brother was taken from me. And the pain of knowing it was my fault and that I've never told a soul. I could tell her now. But I never would. It's too late to confess.

Addison turns to face me with wide eyes. "Don't say that."

Maybe it's the denial, the guilt that plagues me. But I sneer at her, "You think it's easy for me? You got over his death far easier than I did."

I don't see the slap coming until the sting greets my cheek. My hand instinctively moves to where she's struck me. I flex my jaw and feel the burn radiate down the side of my face.

Her beautiful countenance is bright red with anger and her eyes are narrowed. I've never seen her this full of rage. Never.

Her hands tremble as she yells at me.

"You don't know how many nights his death haunted me!"

I do.

Her voice wavers and I know she's on the verge of tears. The kind that paralyze you because they're so overwhelming. But instead of giving in to grief, she screams at me.

"You don't know how I blamed myself to the point where I begged God to just kill me and let me take his place." She takes each breath in heavily.

I do.

Adrenaline rushes through my blood. The hate, the shame, and the unrelenting guilt surge within me. And I can't say anything back. I can't have this conversation with her.

When I don't say anything, when I feel myself shutting down, she snaps. "Fuck you," she tries to yell at me but her voice cracks as she grabs her bag and storms out of the room.

She doesn't have her shoes on and she's not wearing a bra under my shirt.

"You're not leaving?" It's meant to be a statement but the question is there in the undertone. All because I said she got over his death easier than I did? It's a fact. I fucking know it is.

"Yes, I am," she snaps as she turns around just as I walk up behind her. I have to halt my pace and take half a step back as she cranes her neck to bite out, "How dare you tell me that it was easy for me."

"You don't know-" I try to tell her that she has no idea how well I relate to her pain, but she doesn't let me finish.

"Leave me alone."

She angrily brushes under her eyes as she quickly descends the stairs with me right behind her. The front door is right there and she makes a beeline for it.

She's out of her fucking mind if she thinks I'm letting her leave here like this. "Addison. Wait a fucking minute."

"Don't tell me what to do," she yells back and tries to whip open the door. My palm hits it first, slamming it back shut.

"You're not leaving like this," I warn her. My muscles are coiled, but it's the fear making me wound so tight. She's leaving. And she's not coming back.

I can feel it in every inch of me.

"Yes, I am," she replies, though with shaken confidence.

"The fuck you are." My words are pushed through clenched teeth.

"If you respect me in any sense of the word, you will let me leave. Right now."

"Addison, don't do that."

"I mean it, Daniel. I need to be alone right now."

"I want to be there for you." I don't know how true the words are until I've said them. And oh, how fucking ironic they are.

"Well, you can't." She shuts me down.

Her green eyes stare up at me and all I can see is the same look she'd give Tyler when he was being clingy. The look that so obviously said she needed time and that she was overwhelmed. I get it now why he always hovered.

I'm afraid if I let her go now, she's never coming back. I can't lose her. Not again.

"I'm coming by tonight." I give her the only compromise I'm capable of.

I lower my arm but she doesn't respond. With a swift tug she pulls the door open and walks out, bare feet and all.

I stand in the doorway and watch her reach in her bag for flip-flops then put them on at the corner of the street.

She keeps looking over her shoulder, maybe to see if I'm coming for her.

And I am. She knows better than to think otherwise.

But I'll let her get a head start.

Five years ago

He hovers. Constantly hovering.

We all know why. It's so fucking obvious every time he brings her around.

She's waiting to run.

She's cute and sweet, but there's something about her that makes it almost painfully apparent that a kid like Tyler could never hold on to her. It would take a man to keep that cute little ass.

Just thinking that as I stand in the kitchen, watching the two of them in the dining room makes me feel like a pervert. She's only sixteen, although her curves make her look like more of a woman and less of a girl.

He gives her little touches as they sit next to each other watching something on his laptop. Her laugh makes him smile.

He's foolish to think she'll stay with him. Girls like that don't stay with men like us. He can keep pretending if he wants to. He can keep bringing her home and cuddling up with her because he doesn't know how easy it is for people to shove you away.

She'll shove, she'll push, she'll leave. And I can't blame her.

Her shoulders shake as she laughs and leans into him. His broad smile grows and like the kid he is, he wraps his arm around her shoulders.

The smile dies when Addison leans forward and away.

He doesn't know she needs space.

It's not his fault though. Tyler has a lot to learn. Hard life lessons.

Like the ones I've had to endure.

Cancer took our mother and left us a bitter father who likes the belt a little too much. Not to mention a pile of bills that a single person couldn't possibly afford. It's taken years to turn my father's small-time dealing into a thriving business. Years of destroying what little life I had left.

"Let's not," I hear Addison say and when I look up her eyes are on me. Caught in her gaze, I hold her there, but it doesn't last long. Tyler's always there to reclaim her attention.

A sense of loss runs through me, followed by disgust.

I haven't been a good person in so long, maybe I've forgotten how. Or maybe I never was a good person to begin with.

"You and Carter going out tonight?" my father asks as he interrupts the view I have of Tyler and **his** girlfriend.

It's only ever Carter and me. Never my other brothers. We're the oldest, after all. The ones who need to pick up my father's slack. The ones who pay these bills and make the business what it is.

We're the ones who have to shoulder the burden. And really it's Carter's hard work and brutal business tactics that make any of this possible. It sure as fuck isn't my father. He's good at hiding his pain. But every time he remembers my mother, I know he copes with a different addiction. One that makes using that belt easier.

Only ever for Carter and me though.

"Yeah," I tell him and wait for him to hint that he wants us to bring some of the supply back for his personal use. Friday marks four years since our mother's been gone and I know a relapse is coming. He'll disappear for days, maybe even weeks. It was worse when she first passed. I guess I should be grateful that he's better now than he was then.

"Be careful coming home. I heard there's a patrol on the east side so maybe come up the back way after you get the shipment."

A second passes and then another before I nod.

Some days I wonder if he cares for me anymore. He was always a hard man. But when Mom passed, he was nothing but angry. The years have maybe changed him to be less full of hate. But it doesn't mean he has anything in him to take its place.

I give him another nod and look past him as the sound of Tyler and Addison getting up from the table catches my attention.

My father glances over his shoulder in the direction I'm staring and then turns back to me. He only shakes his head and makes to leave, but I hear him mutter, "She isn't yours."

I hate him even more in this moment. Because he's right.

The sad, pretty girl doesn't belong to me.

No matter how much I think she'd take my pain away.

Chapter Fifteen

ADDISON

I wonder what the girl I used to be would think of me.

The girl who still had both her parents and a life worth living for.

I think she'd make up excuses for my poor behavior. She'd say I was sad, but she has no idea how pathetic I am.

Grief isn't static. It's not a point on a chart where you can say, "Here, at this time, I grieved." Because grief doesn't know time. It comes and goes as it pleases, then small things taunt it back into your life. The memories haunt you forever and carry the grief with them. Yes, grief is carried. That's a good way to put it.

I pull a pillow on the sofa into my lap and stare at the television screen although my eyes are puffy and sore and I don't even know what's on.

Playing with the small zipper on the side of the pillow absently, I think about what happened. How it all unraveled.

I think it started with his scar, the past being brought up. But just like scars, some of our past will never leave us. The old wounds were showing. That's what it was really about.

I always knew Daniel was broken in ways Tyler wasn't. But I didn't know about his father. I didn't know any of that. I don't even know if Tyler knew.

But what happened between Daniel and me, that ... I don't even have a word for it. It was like a light switch being turned off. Everything was fine, better than fine. Then darkness was abrupt and sudden, with no way to escape.

My eyes dart to the screen as a commercial appears and its volume is louder than whatever show or movie was playing. I sniffle as I flick the TV off and look at my phone again.

I'm sorry. Daniel messaged me earlier and I do believe he is, but I don't know if that will be enough. My happy little bubble of lust has been popped and the self-awareness isn't pretty.

I'm sorry too. It's all I can say back to him and he reads it. But there's nothing left for either of us to say now. I wonder if this will be the end of us.

We can't have a conversation about the bad things that have happened. That's the simple truth. It's awkward, tense. And we can't escape the moments coming up in conversation. There's no way getting around that.

It's easy to blame it on my past. On things I had no control over and things I can't change.

It's a lot like what I did when I left Dixon Falls. But really I was running, just like I had been since the day my parents died. Tyler was a distraction, a pleasant one that made me feel something other than the agonizing loneliness that had turned me bitter.

And then there was Daniel. He left me breathless and wanting, and that's a hard temptation to run away from.

I'm woman enough to admit that.

So sure, I can blame it on our past.

It's easy to blame it on grief, but it's still a lie. It's because neither of us can talk about what happened.

I startle at the vibration of the phone on the coffee table.

My heart beats hard with each passing second; all the while a long-lost voice in the back of my head begs me to answer a simple question. *What am I doing?*

Or maybe the right question is, *What did I expect?*

My gaze drifts across each photo on the far wall of the living room and it stops on three. Each of the photos meant something more when I took them. There are a little more than a dozen in total. Each photographed in a moment of time when I knew I was changing.

I keep them hung up because they look pretty from a distance; the pictures themselves are pleasant and invoke warm feelings.

More than that, the photos are a timeline of moments I never want to forget. I refuse to let myself forget.

But the three I keep staring at are so relevant to how I feel in this moment.

The first photo was taken at my parents' grave. Just a simple picture really, small forget-me-nots that had sprouted in the early spring. There was a thin layer of snow on the ground, but they'd already pushed through the hard dirt and bloomed. Maybe they knew I was coming and wanted to make sure I saw them.

In the photo you can't even tell they've bloomed on graves. The photo is cropped short and close. But I'll always remember that the flowers were on my parents' grave.

Tyler was with me when I took it. It wasn't the first, second or even the third time we'd gone out. But it was the first time I'd cried in such a long time and the one friend I'd met and trusted was there to witness it. I thought I was being sly asking him to drive to a cemetery hours away. Back to where I'd grown up. I hadn't been there in so long, but on that day when Tyler said we could go anywhere, I told him about the angel statue at the front of a cemetery I'd once seen that would be perfect for the photography project.

I didn't tell him that my parents were buried there, but he found out shortly after we arrived.

Part of me will forever be his for how he handled that day. For letting me cry and holding me. For not forcing me to talk, but being there when I was ready to.

Like I said, I never deserved him.

The second is a picture of the first place I'd rented after I ran away from Dixon Falls. I went from place to place, spending every cent I'd gathered over the years and not staying anywhere any longer than I had to. Until I found this farm cottage in the UK and met Rae.

She's such the opposite of me in every way. And she reminded me of Tyler. The happiness and kindness, the fact that she never stopped smiling and joking. Some people just do that to you … and because of it, I stayed. For a long time.

She's the one who took me to the bar in Leeds where I kissed another boy for the first time after Tyler's death.

She's the one who showed me how to really market my photography and introduced me to a gallery owner. She made me want to stay in that little cottage I'd rented for much longer than I'd planned. But feeling so happy and having everything be too easy felt wrong. It was wrong that I could move on and it made me feel like what had happened in the past was right, when I knew without a doubt that it wasn't.

It would never be right and that realization made me see Tyler everywhere all over again. I needed to leave. It was okay to remember, but it wasn't okay to forget. And I did leave. Each place I stopped at was closer and closer to Dixon Falls. At first I didn't realize it. But when I picked this university, I was keenly aware that I'd only be hours away.

The third picture is only a silhouette I took in Paris.

I don't know the people.

It's the shadows of four men standing outside of a church with a deep sunset behind them. From a distance, all I could see were the Cross boys. And I took picture after picture, snapping away as quickly as I could. As if they'd vanish if I stopped. I wanted them back badly. I wanted them to forgive me and tell me it was alright. After all, they were the only family I had for a long time and just like my parents, I lost them.

That picture hurts the most. Because there should be five people in the shot. And because when the men did leave the hilltop behind the church and come closer, they weren't the Cross boys and I knew in that moment I'd never see them again. Daniel was never going to show up for me to stare at from a distance. It would never be them, no matter how much I prayed for it to happen.

Three pretty pictures, mixed in with the others. All hues of indigo, my favorite color, and all seemingly serene and beautiful. But each a memory of something that's made me the person I am.

My phone vibrates with the reminder of the most recent message. It's Daniel, of course. *Come over.*

I need to work, I text him and snort at his immediate response. *No you don't.*

I do, in fact, need to work. I could easily work at his place. That's what I've been doing and I actually enjoy it. I love it when he kisses my shoulder and tells me what he thinks of the photo I'm working on. He makes me feel less alone and he understands how I see the pictures and why they mean so much to me.

I want to apologize.

You did and I get it, I tell him even though it makes the ache in my chest that much deeper.

Please, just give me another chance.

Please is another word I'm not used to hearing from Daniel and as much as I want to give in, I need a little time.

I really do have to work. We can meet up next week. As I press send, I realize I'm caving in. Simply prolonging what is sure to end. But then I remember the men by the church. If I could go back in time and make them stand there forever so I'd never have to face the fact that they weren't the Crosses, I would.

It hurts deep in my chest. Denial is a damning thing.

And that's what this is, isn't it? Just a futile attempt to deny that we could ever exist without our past tearing us apart.

The phone sits there silent, indicating no new message from him although I know he sees my response. Picking up a tissue from the coffee table, I dry my nose and pick myself up off the sofa.

Life doesn't wait for you. That's something I've learned well.

Before I can take a step toward the kitchen to toss the tissue, a message from Daniel comes in. *I promise I will make it up to you.*

I don't know what to write back. There's no way to make this right.

So instead I focus on the work that's waiting for me and choose not to respond.

I've barely been active online for a week now. Instead I've been taking pictures. Lots of them. Some of Daniel in abstract ways. Others of little things that remind me of him from when we were younger. I haven't posted those yet though. I'm not sure I will either. No matter how beautiful I think they are.

I haven't answered messages or sent out any packages. I don't even know how my sales are going. When you run a business all by yourself, you can't afford to take time off. For years I've buried myself in my passion and work, although really I'd just been running from reality. From my past.

Staring at the message from Daniel, the black and white text that's so easy to read, I can't answer the one question that matters.

What am I doing?

Six years ago

"Hey ... hey ..."

I hear a persistent voice but I ignore it. No one in this school has said a word to me. At least not to my face.

With a tug on my shirt, I'm forced to turn around and face a boy. A boy who's nearly a man. He doesn't have a baby face, and I can tell he shaves, but there's a kindness about him that makes him appear young. And likable. Which is something I haven't felt in the last two years.

"What are you doing?" he asks me and my forehead pinches.

I lift the pencil in the air and point to the chalkboard in science class as I say, "It's called taking notes."

The handsome guy laughs, a rough chuckle that forces me to smile. Some people's happiness is simply contagious.

"No, I mean tonight."

I don't bother to respond other than to shrug. I do the same thing every night. Nothing. My life is nothing.

"My brothers and I are having a little party."

"I don't really do parties," I answer him and nearly turn back around in my seat, but his smile doesn't falter and that in itself keeps my attention.

Shrugging, he says, "We can do something else."

"I don't really do much," I tell him honestly. I don't really feel like doing anything. Each day is only a date on a calendar. That's all they've been for a long time now.

"What about the assignment for art class? We could take some pictures for the photography project?" It takes me a moment to place him, but now that he's mentioned it, I think I did see him in the back row yesterday in art class.

"It's not my day for the camera." The budget for the art department is small, so we have to take turns checking out the equipment.

"I've got one we can use—well, it's my brother's."

"Your brother?"

"Yeah, his name's Daniel." It all clicks when he says his brother's name. I've seen him. It must be him. I've watched as this boy I'm talking to waits outside at the entrance to the school and another boy picks him up. Except he's not a boy. There's no question about that. Daniel is a man and it only took one glimpse of him to cause me to search him out each and every time the bell rings and I'm waiting in line for the bus.

"Now I know your brother's name, but I don't know yours."

"It's Tyler." I repeat his name softly and when I look at him, I see traces of his older brother. But where Daniel has an edge to him, Tyler is warm and inviting.

"I'm Addison."

"So what do you think, Addison?"

"I think that sounds like fun. I wasn't doing anything anyway."

Maybe fate knew I wasn't going to be able to keep Tyler. It was going to take him from me. So it gave me Daniel to keep me from loving Tyler too much.

I don't know for sure and there's no point in speculating.

All I know for certain is that Daniel will consume me, chew me up and spit me back out. I need to end this before I get hurt ... well, before it gets worse than it already is.

Chapter Sixteen

DANIEL

I'M LOSING IT.

I can feel myself slipping backward into a dark abyss.

Addison and I are alike in more ways than she knows. In ways I'd never dare to whisper out loud. She's lying to herself when she says she needs space.

She doesn't.

She needs me, just like I need her. She's the only thing that takes the pain away and I do that for her too. I know I do. I can feel it. I can see it in her.

The light from the computer screen is the only thing that saves the living room from being in complete darkness. I've been staring at it, waiting for him to see I've been logged in for hours.

I'm trying to stay away from Addison. I'm trying to do what's best.

It's been a long time, Marcus finally responds. It's not his name or his alias in this chat. But I know it's him.

Three years now, I answer, leaning back into my seat with my laptop on my thighs and trying to ignore the shame that rings in my blood. It's been three years since I've logged into this black market chat and sought him out. Three years since I've felt the urge to watch over Addison every second of every day. Three years since I've had a hit of my sweet addiction.

What brings you back? he asks me and I swallow thickly.

She came back into my life. But you already know that.

She, as in Addison? he asks me to keep up this charade.

The keys beneath my fingertips click faintly as I type. It's odd how I find it comforting, the soft sounds tempting me to confess my sins.

I wasn't stalking her or trying to find her. The first time was a coincidence.

How many times have there been? he asks me.

A lot, I admit but then add, *but she's been with me this time. It's not me hiding in the shadows. She sought me out.*

Do you think that makes it healthier? The text stares back at me on the brightly lit screen and I want to answer yes. Of course it is. This time isn't anything like what happened years ago. He doesn't wait for me to answer before he poses another question.

If she knows, does that make it okay to allow your interest to grow to obsession?

Obsession may be the wrong word. I think possessive is better. She's mine. My reason to move on from what happened before. My desire for more. My only way to cope.

It's different this time. This time she wanted me there.

Wanted? he presses, and the shame of why I'm even here in this anonymous chat makes my chest feel tight. *As in past tense?*

She asked me for time apart and I'm having difficulties. I'm slipping back into old habits.

It's called stalking, Daniel.

I'm aware of that, Marcus.

I use his name, just like he uses mine. No one else knows it's him, but I do. Because years ago, when I watched Addison finally sleep without crying, when she could say Tyler's name with a sad smile instead of barely restrained agony, he was there for me. All those years ago when she moved on and I was still struggling to cope with the guilt of Tyler's death, Marcus is the one who stopped me from pulling the trigger with a gun pressed to my head.

It took nearly two years before it came to that point. A year and a half of following her, of watching her and living out my pain vicariously through hers. And months of slowly losing myself and any reason not to end it.

She kept me sane in a way she'll never know as I watched her grieve with the same pain I had.

But as the months went by, she started to smile again.

It made me feel worse than the day Tyler took his last breath.

She got better, when I didn't. Every laugh, every bit of happiness made zero sense to me. I could only cope through her sadness. I understood it; I needed it.

Does she know about the past? he asks me.

She'll never understand, I type into the chat box, but I don't send it.

I shake my head, remembering how I followed her everywhere after Tyler's death. How I watched her run and that alone was enough to take my pain away. She loved him after all and felt responsible like I did. And if she could move on, so could I. But I could never move on from Addison.

Five years ago

I tell myself the only reason I'm on this train is to speak to her.

To tell her it's not her fault and I'm the one to blame.

That's the reason I've followed her, stalking her in the shadows and silently watching her as she struggles with what to do.

I tell myself that, but I don't move. I'm struggling too.

The train comes to another stop and my grip tightens on the rail as I wait to see what she does. Where she goes, I'll go.

I need to make sure she's okay, that she doesn't have the same thoughts I do. I'll protect her.

Her hoodie is up, hiding her face as she leans against the wall of the train. Unmoving.

My body tightens, wanting to go to her. To hold her, to check on her and make sure she's still breathing. She saw him die like I did. That changes you. There's no way to deny it or to recover.

It will forever be with us.

Chapter Seventeen

ADDISON

It's funny how time moves.

It crawled along for years before and after Tyler came into my life. Each day's only purpose was to be a box on a calendar I could cross off with a deep red marker. If I bothered to even count.

But the days with Tyler, when I was really with him? They flew by. Because time is quite like fate, it's a bitch.

And the same thing happened with Daniel. The days were whirlwinds of moments that made me feel like everything was alright. Like it was okay to simply live in his bed and sleep in his arms. Like the selfishness of ignoring everything else was how life is supposed to go.

But the past few days without him … it's been worse than the slowest pain. There's a coldness that feels like it's just below the surface of my skin. As if my blood refuses to heat. And the nights are filled with memories designed to play on my weakest moments.

Knock. Knock. Knock.

My focus is shifted to the front door of my apartment as I sit cross-legged on my sofa with my laptop cradled on me. The screen's gone black and I don't know how long it's been like that.

He knocks again. There's only one person it could be. *Daniel.*

Every day and night since we last talked I've thought about him. And about what I need to do. Each text he sends is met with a short response that makes the pain in my chest grow.

I'm no longer in denial. It's time to move on. That means moving on from everything, including Daniel. And that hurts. But it's supposed to.

My neck is killing me from bending over the computer for hours. I have a standing desk; I should really use it, but I don't. I spend hours a day sitting on the sofa with my computer in my lap while I Photoshop my pictures. There are at least three dozen more I want to edit and post before going out and searching for my next muse. Although I don't know if I'll find it here. Maybe it's time to move on already.

My sore body aches all over when I stand, but that pain is temporary, so I don't mind it.

Each step to the front door makes me feel like I'm running in the opposite direction from where I was going days ago. I've come to the only logical decision there is and I've never liked breaking up with anyone. The way Daniel made me feel is unlike anything I've ever felt. Wild and crazy, I suppose. Thanks to the late night sex and not caring about anything, not even our next breath so long as our skin was touching and our desires seeking out refuge in each other.

Pausing with my hand on the doorknob, I let out a deep breath. He'll understand. He's probably here to do the same. This thing between us could never last.

I feel like I'm being stabbed in the heart, but the moment the door is opened, the pain dims and that other feeling, that fluttering sickness I have trouble describing takes its place. The kind of pain that I want more of, but it scares me.

"Daniel." I whisper his name as his dark eyes meet mine and then soften. His leather jacket creases as he puts his hand on the doorframe and leans in slightly.

"You still mad at me?" he asks with a deep timbre to his voice that speaks to vulnerability and I answer him honestly, shaking my head.

"I'm not mad at you." Forgiving others is easy. It's forgiving myself that's hard.

Daniel lets out a breath and starts to come in, but I can't do this. It's better to stop it now and not do the easier thing. Which would be to fall back into bed with him and numb the pain with his touch.

It's not healthy.

My palm hits his chest and his expression turns to confusion, but he stops just outside the threshold.

"I've been thinking," I start to tell Daniel and he tilts his head, his eyes narrowing.

"This sounds like the *we have to talk* conversation." There's a trace of a threat in his voice.

"It kind of is," I say softly and the pain in my heart grows. "I've just been thinking about every way this is going to end."

"End?" he asks incredulously, moving forward and closing the distance between us. He's standing on the threshold now.

It's hard to speak, but I have to be honest with myself and him. I have to protect myself.

"I'm not sure we should do this at all."

Stunned is how I'd describe the look on Daniel's face, and it surprises me. "It doesn't make sense for us to continue this-"

"You don't want me?" Daniel asks, cutting me off in a voice devoid of anything but sadness. I've never heard the sound from his lips before. The tone pains my heart in a way nothing else ever will. I know it for a fact. Some things simply break a piece of you that can never be mended.

"That's not what I meant. Not at all. I didn't anticipate this happening," I try to explain. What I thought would be a simple conversation ending with Daniel leaving me behind escalates to something I hadn't anticipated. "I didn't think you would care." My words come out rushed.

"You thought I wouldn't care that you're done with me?"

"I'm not done … I could never be done with you. But this," I gesture between us, "this is something I know is going to hurt me. And both of us know will never last."

"I'm not Tyler. That's why?" Daniel's words should be cutting. They should hurt me. But I only hurt for him. How could he think that?

I have to swallow hard before I can tell him, "I want you." I almost say Tyler's name. I almost tell him how I wanted the love Tyler gave me and how I wanted to love Tyler back but never did. But I can't. I can't bring him into this. "It's not that at all, Daniel. I've wanted you for the longest time and I hated myself for it. We can't even have a simple conversation about anything before…" I swallow hard, the lump in my throat refusing to let any more words pass.

"You hate yourself for wanting me?" The sadness is gone and anger quickly takes its place. Suddenly I'm suffocating, finding myself taking a step back and then another although he stays in the doorway, radiating a dominance barely self-contained.

"You're scaring me," I whisper and Daniel flinches. The emotions cycle through him one by one. The anger, the shock, the frustration from not knowing what to do.

And I've felt them all, I've also suffered the torture of not knowing what to do for so long. Every day that I felt loved by Tyler but knew I loved Daniel more. I know his pain as if it was my own. But there's no way to make this right. And the sooner this is over, the better.

"I want you Daniel, but it's wrong."

"It's not wrong," he says and his words come out strangled, his breathing heavier. He almost takes a step forward and then stops himself, gripping the edge of the doorframe and lowering his head, hanging it in shame. I'm reminded of the day I first met him and that makes the agony that much worse. "I don't know how to …" he trails off and swallows thickly.

"There's no way this is going to be more than … than what we were doing."

His head whips up and his dark eyes pin me in place. Daniel's always been intense, always been dangerous. For others, I'm sure it's similar. But they'll never feel *this*. Not the way I feel for Daniel.

"Why does it need to be *more* right now? Why can't we hold on to what we have?"

"It's not good for either of us, Daniel," I whisper and wrap my arms around my chest. I don't know how else to explain it and how he could fail to understand that.

The silence grows. All I can hear is my own breath as Daniel stands there stiffly, staring at the faded carpet beneath his feet. Finally, he looks me in the eye again and the intensity and pain there shatter me to the very center of my soul.

"I know that you belonged to Tyler first, as much as I hate to admit that. I hate to say his name. I don't want to imagine what used to …"

"Daniel, please don't," I say and reach for him, my heart hurting for his and I hate myself in this moment. Why did I have to do this?

"We can't change the past, Addison. I wish I could. But it's over now. And right now I want you."

There was never a point in my life where I thought I'd hear those words from Daniel. And the shock, the sadness, and the conflict of not knowing how to protect myself and what I should do keep the words I'm desperate to say trapped in my throat.

I want to believe what he's saying. But he's already said the words I need to hold on to the conviction of leaving him. *There will never be more.*

"You know where to find me if you want to see me." Daniel's last words are flat, with a defeated tone.

I can't form a coherent thought as he turns his back to me and walks off. This isn't what I wanted or how I'd planned for it to go. "I didn't mean for this to happen," I say, but my choked words are barely audible to me, let alone Daniel as he disappears in the distance.

I worry my bottom lip and a storm brews inside of me. A storm that feels as though it's never left, like it was only waiting in the darkness. Preparing for when it could come out and destroy the little piece of me that remains.

It's not until Daniel's gone that I close the door, lean my back against it and fall to the floor on my ass.

I've made a mistake. More than one. But I can't keep going on like this, making mistake after mistake and running from them.

Helplessness overwhelms me and I've never felt weaker. Why is it all so complicated? Why can't love and lust be one, and right and wrong easier to decipher?

Chapter Eighteen

DANIEL
Five years ago

Every small movement makes the pain spread deeper. I shouldn't have called him a drunk. I shouldn't have yelled back when my father yelled at me. I know better. I brought this on myself.

I let out a deep breath, but even breathing hurts. Carter will cover for me. He always does. I swallow thickly as I hear heavy footsteps coming to my door and my heart pounds for a moment, thinking it's him. Thinking I fucked something up.

Like I did last night, losing thousands of dollars. Thousands and thousands of money and merchandise are gone. Stolen off the truck. And it's my fault. I'm the one who opened it, getting the fucking CD Addison left in there and not remembering to lock it back up.

This is all because of her.

There's only a slight bit of relief when I hear Tyler yell out my name as he bangs on the door.

I struggle to put my shirt back on, but do it through clenched teeth while wincing. It was only a belt, I grit out with the part of me that thinks I'm pathetic. That I deserve all of this and more.

I open the door without thinking of the cuts on my back and the pain sears through me.

"Why do you have to be such an asshole all the time?"

Tyler's question is met with nothing from me. Not a single emotion that I can give him.

"You don't have to make her feel like she's not welcome."

Anger makes me swallow hard. I still don't respond.

I'll never tell him how I feel about her, but at least now I know how she feels about me.

"Are you going to say anything?"

My lips part and I want to give him something, anything. But the fact that I went out of my way for her last night … maybe that's why. Maybe she knows I want her. The idea hits and steals my words from me.

"She's a good person," Tyler tells me as if that's why I stay away from her.

"I love you, Tyler. God knows it. But you're a fucking idiot."

I should have kept my mouth shut, but everyone has their limits.

"She loves me and she's not going anywhere," he tells me with a confidence I've never seen in my baby brother.

My baby brother who's oblivious to what we really are and what goes on here.

My baby brother who's never been struck once by my father.

My perfect baby brother who wants to make everyone around him smile because he's never known pain like I have.

"She only loves you because she has no one else who loves her." My gaze pins him where he is as I say the words. "Remember that."

Loneliness is a bitter pill to swallow. I know I've brought it on myself, but still. A sarcastic, humorless huff leaves me as I grab the bottle of whiskey and take a swig.

It must be karma.

I left Addison to her loneliness so I could survive.

Now she's leaving me to mine to ruin me.

Touché, little love.

The whiskey burns as I take another heavy drink. And with it every possibility of where I lost her flashes in my mind. The times from back when we were younger and I held back so much, to only moments ago when I didn't hold back a damn thing.

I lick my lower lip and then pick the bottle back up, but a timid knock stops me from chugging back more of the amber liquid.

"Daniel," I hear Addison's voice from beyond the door. Hope flickers deep inside of me, flirting with a darkness that's nearly consumed me.

My heart pauses. So do my lungs. It's only when I hear her again that they both decide to function again. She's here. *She came to me.*

My blood buzzes as I stand up and make my way to the front door. All while I stride to the door the alcohol sets in, and I hear her call out again. "Please open the door, Daniel."

She's mid-motion of knocking again with her mouth parted and more to say when I pull the door open. She looks shocked and even flinches slightly.

"Daniel," she says my name with a hint of surprise, but quickly her expression and tone change. "I wanted to explain."

And that right there is why I didn't let that hope grow. The coldness in my chest puts out the small flame. It's hard to school my expression. It's hard to hide it from her. But a part of me is screaming not to. To let her see what she's doing to me. To make sure she knows she's destroying me bit by bit.

"Explain?" The question comes out with a bit of anger and I have to readjust my grip on the door and look away from her for a moment.

"You don't owe me anything, Addison," I tell her and turn to walk down the hall, but I leave the door open. I let her come to me willingly.

When I hear the door shut and her following me inside, a smile slowly forms on my face. It's only a trace of genuine happiness. But at least I know she can't let me go as easily as she thinks she can.

"Daniel, please," she says as she catches up to me in the living room, gripping my shirt and making me turn to face her.

"What is it you want to explain?" I ask her and almost call her little love. Almost.

"I didn't think that you wanted anything but a good fuck." God, she does something to me when she talks like that. When foul and dirty words come out of that pretty little mouth of hers.

My own indecent thoughts keep me from responding quickly enough. So she storms over to the leather chair in the corner of the room and sits down angrily, crossing her legs and then her arms.

Of course that's what she thought. It's what this started out as. But she's fooling herself if she thinks what we have could ever be anything so shallow. Even I can admit it. "I'm not leaving until you talk to me," she demands and it's cute. She's so fucking adorable thinking she can make demands like that. My bare feet sink into the rug as I make my way to the chair opposite hers.

With the blinds closed, the only light in the room is that of the tall lamp in the corner.

"Say something, please. I feel awful. I didn't expect you to react the way you did." She leans forward and grips the armrests of the chair. "The last thing I wanted to do was hurt you," she confesses and I know she's telling the truth. Addison isn't a liar.

And that gives me hope.

"I don't know what I want, other than you." My voice comes out rough as I lean forward and put my elbows on my knees so I can sink down to her eye level.

"What does that mean?" she asks breathlessly. Her chest rises and falls as if my answer is everything she's ever needed. The only thing she's ever desired.

Licking my lower lip, I stare into her eyes but the words don't come. I don't know how else to say it. I want her.

I want her to be mine. It's all I've ever wanted.

Not just in my bed. I want her touches, her kisses, her intentions. Moving forward, I want each piece of her. Every little piece. I want them all.

More than that, I want her to give them to me.

Her words spin chaotically, as do her emotions. "I need something to hold on to, Daniel, and this, this is intense and overwhelming and emotional-"

"But do you want it?" I cut her off, asking the simple question.

"Why did you come get me in that bar? Don't lie to me. You knew I'd be there, didn't you?" she asks me and I don't know if she knows more than she should, or if she's just that damn good at knowing who I am.

I lean back in my seat and decide to be careful with my words as I slowly say, "I wanted you for so long."

"So that's all this is? You wanted to fuck me, so you finally did?"

"You already know that's a lie." My words come out like a vicious sting and she drops the act. "I know you feel this too." I finally speak the words that feel as if they'll break me. But they're true. "There's always been something between us."

Addison's expression is pained.

"I know you feel guilty admitting it, Addison. I do too. I'm just as much to blame." She doesn't know how true those words are.

Time wears on and more than a moment passes. Addison pulls her knees into her chest and all I want to do is grab her ass and pull her into my lap. But my fingers dig into the leather, pinning me where I am until I have the only answer I need from her.

"Do you want me?" I ask her.

"It's not that easy," she whimpers. Torn between the desire she feels and the guilt she won't let go of.

My body tenses and the rage from knowing the past may forever darken my future takes over as I lean forward. "The fuck it isn't."

I have to close my eyes and focus on what I want, what she needs to hear. I speak so low I'm not sure she can hear me, but I pray she can. "I can't tell you what will happen a week from now, but I know I'll still want you." I open my eyes to find her watching me intently as I continue, "I've always wanted you. It's not going to stop, and I don't care about anything that happened yesterday as long as I get you tomorrow."

"When did you turn into this man?" Addison's question is quiet, but full of sincerity. "I don't remember any of this from you."

The answer is right there. So obvious to me.

Because she wasn't mine and couldn't be.

"You were young, and belonged to someone else." I can't bring myself to speak Tyler's name. The alcohol and thought of losing her if he comes up again is too much.

Before she can respond to the omission I ask her the only thing that matters, "Do you want me?"

Her green eyes shine with sincerity as she barely whispers the word, "Yes." She bites down on her lip as I rise from my seat and make my way to her. Slowly and carefully, with each step knowing I'm so close to keeping her.

"If you stay here Addison, I swear I won't let you leave." I swallow thickly and clear my throat when she searches my eyes and knows I'm speaking the truth. "This is your last chance to run from me." I owe her that at least. One last chance to run.

"I've never wanted to run from you." Her words are laced with raw emotion and she reaches up to cup my face. "We're doing this?"

"You can't leave me, Addison. You have to promise me, no matter what happens," I say and hope she can't hear the desperation in my voice. "No matter if we fight." I start to say more, but I choke on the obvious. *No matter if Tyler comes up again.*

I can barely breathe as she strokes the stubble of my jaw with her thumb and whispers, "I promise."

She falls into my lap so easily. Her warmth and soft touches light every nerve ending in me on fire. But so much more than that too. The pounding in my chest. The need to be close to her. To be skin to skin and show her she's mine again.

I'm dying inside, needing to take her, but I move so achingly slowly. Cherishing every second of something I almost lost. Every second of *her.*

"Daniel?" Her voice is hesitant, but raw. As if the question itself will break her as I kiss the crook of her neck and let my fingers barely graze her skin, just a whisper of a touch.

"Addison?" I answer her with a playful air and smile against her skin when she breathes easily.

"I'm scared," she whispers into the air and when I pull away from her, her face is toward the ceiling with her eyes closed tight. Her fingers dig into my shoulders as I nudge her chin with my nose to get her attention.

"I won't hurt you," I whisper when she doesn't respond. My heart races, though not in a steady rhythm. But when she lowers her gaze, her green eyes finding mine, it steadies and slows. It's lost without her.

Addison nods, a small nod of recognition, but the hesitancy is still there. Her slender fingers pull at my shirt and I help her, leaning back and pulling it off. Then I remove hers, and move lower. We strip each other slowly, each movement met with the sound of our breathing. Kisses in between each garment being tossed to the floor, each turning more desperate, more breathy. *More.*

And when I finally slip my fingers between her folds, she's soaking wet with need and rocks her hot pussy into my hand. Her eyes are still closed as she rides my palm and my thumb presses against her clit. Groaning against her throat, I grab my dick and push myself inside of her until I can let go and grab her hips as I fill her tight cunt.

Sucking in a breath, her fingers move to my shoulders, her blunt nails digging into my flesh.

Her wide eyes meet mine and I'm entranced.

Every thrust up, I dig my fingers deeper into her shoulder. My abs burn as I fuck her like this over and over, as deep as I can while I stare into her eyes.

The need to kiss her is all-consuming. But I can't break her gaze either.

Her lips part just slightly as her pussy flutters and then spasms on my dick. My name slips from her lips as a strangled moan. And it's only when she shudders and an orgasm rips through her that she breaks my gaze. She falls forward in my arms as I keep up my pace, riding through her climax.

I kiss her shoulder, her neck, her hair, every bit of her ravenously, worshipping her as she grips on to me for dear life.

My release comes in a wave so strong, I'm not ready. I'm not at all ready for this to end. But I swear I hear her whisper against my skin, her hot breath sending a chill down my spine as the intense pleasure rocks through me. I swear I hear her whisper as her lips graze my neck.

I love you.

My arms wrap around her and I don't move; I don't let her move either. I can't say the words back. And I don't know if she'll say them again. But I swear I heard them.

I swear I heard her say those words to me.

To me.

Chapter Nineteen

ADDISON

Daniel Cross is my boyfriend.
How high school. But still ...

That's all I sent to Rae this week. I'm used to giving her long descriptions of where I'm going next. It's all I've ever considered and she loves to hear stories of what new places are like. But this town brought me Daniel and I don't want to share a ton of details. He's mine.

A snicker makes me lean back from the laptop as I read Rae's response to my email.

How big is his dick? is her opening line. Leave it to Rae to relieve the tension.

I've been worried about what she's going to say. And knowing that she isn't judging me makes everything so much easier to accept. She even said, *As long as you're happy, I'm happy.*

That's all I wanted. As I click out of the email, ready to close the laptop, I see my subject line again. *Daniel Cross is my boyfriend.*

I cover my smile with my hand as I pull my heels up onto the sofa. With my pillow snuggled up close to me, I'm in for a night of binge-watching housewives and reality television.

But I couldn't really care less about any of that. I can't get into a show to save my life—or work, for that matter. All I keep thinking is that Daniel wants to be ... mine.

It's been over a week and that's still the case. Nights of hanging out, watching TV or looking over photographs I've taken. It's almost normal.

Those stupid butterflies in my stomach won't quit and it makes me feel childish and giddy. But even in the eye of the storm that surrounds us, I want him and he wants me.

That should be all that matters, right?

As I reach for my glass of wine sitting on the coffee table, I can't help but feel like the bottom is going to fall out from under us. Like there's something waiting on the edge of all this. I can feel it with everything in me.

Life doesn't work like this. You don't get what you want simply by asking for it.

I swallow a sip of the wine and the sweetness I was feeling only a moment ago tastes bitter with the last thought.

Daniel feels like everything. Like there was nothing before him even though I'm fully aware there was. There's no way with our history that there will be more between us, no matter what he says and how well we play house together. There won't be any family dinners with his brothers or any sense of normalcy in that respect.

No matter how much I wish that were the case.

Every day I'm waiting for Daniel to tell me he was wrong and it's over. Or that he's ready to go home and that I'm not welcome there. I like to think that my guard is up and that it won't hurt when he does it. But each day that passes is another crack in that armor.

He fucks me like he owns me. He holds me at night so tight; like if he lets go, he'll lose me forever.

And he kisses me like he's dying for the air I breathe.

We don't talk about the one thing that plagues me. About how we're supposed to just ignore our past. He thinks we've said enough, but if that were the case, I would be able to sleep without the memories haunting me.

It's hard to explain how I feel. I want to be happy and grateful. But it's obvious I'm being naïve. This is too good and I know good things always come to an end.

"You want anything while I'm out?" Daniel asks, interrupting my thoughts as he steps out of the hall to the bedroom and strides toward me. It's odd seeing him in my apartment still. I'm more used to his place, but tonight he'll be gone for a while and I need the space.

The fresh smell of his body wash follows him into the room and I find myself humming in agreement although I didn't quite hear him. He's too distracting when he's dressed like this. Black jeans and a crisp white button-up with one sleeve already rolled up while he works on rolling the other. Freshly shaven with his high cheekbones and strong jaw on display, it almost makes me wish he was always cleanly shaven. But that stubble …

Either way, he looks like a fucking sex god. He fucks like one too. *My* sex god.

"I might be out for a while, but I can bring back something for breakfast if it's too late."

I watch the muscles in his forearm as he rolls up his sleeve and as I do, the desire is slightly muted by his comment.

That's another thing we don't talk about. We don't talk about what he does late at night. I was quiet whenever Tyler would leave to go do something early in the mornings or skip school because he had to do something for "work."

But we aren't children anymore, and what Daniel's involved with isn't a high school game.

"Is this stuff for … back home?" I'm careful with my words as he grabs his keys off the kitchen counter. The jangling is the only sound in the room.

Well, and the ever-present clicking of the clock.

"Back home? As in, the family business?"

My gaze is on the tile in the kitchen. Soft gray with dark gray grout. It's nothing special, but I can't bring myself to look at Daniel and meet his gaze that's obviously on me, so I keep my eyes right where they are.

He works for his brother Carter. Dealing drugs and God knows what else.

He'll leave one day. Soon. He keeps mentioning it. The one question I ask myself every time he leaves is simple. Do I stay? Or do I go with him?

"Yeah, that's what I was asking."

"You know better than that, Addison," Daniel reprimands me and that's what gets me to look at him.

"Better than to be careful about who and what I involve myself with?" My tone dares him to question that logic.

"You already made your choice, didn't you?" The way he speaks to me simultaneously strikes a bit of fear in my heart and heats my blood with lust.

"There are lots of choices, Daniel." I know in my mind he's right. I've already decided I'd go with him. I don't want to be alone again and I crave the feeling of family and acceptance I once had with the Cross brothers. But that was then, and this is now. I don't know what it would be like to face them knowing I'm now with Daniel. It feels like a betrayal of the worst kind.

"Only one when it comes to me. Don't forget that you're the one who started this. You're the one who came back to the bar. You're the one who came to my house after you ended it. I don't like being played with."

"Funny, because you sure do like being the one doing the playing."

My comment rewards me with a charming smirk on his lips.

"With you?" he questions as he stalks toward me and grips my chin between his fingers. "Always."

My eyes close as he plants a kiss on my lips. Mine mold to his and my body melts. It's over too soon and I find myself sitting up a little taller to prolong it just slightly.

Daniel keeps his grip on me and a crease forms on his forehead as he looks down at me with a question in his eyes.

"Are you thinking of leaving me?" he finally asks and I reach up to take his hand in mine.

"No," I tell him, practically rolling my eyes and getting more comfortable in the corner of my sofa.

"Good," he says although he still eyes me curiously.

"If I hadn't come to your place, would you have let me leave you?" I don't know why I feel so compelled to ask in this moment. Maybe I already know the truth and I just want to see if he'll tell me or not.

His dark eyes seem to get darker, although his voice stays even as he answers me, "I would have tried."

I chew the inside of my cheek and look away at his response.

"Why does that disappoint you?"

"Can't you feel it?" I barely whisper the words. He makes me feel weak and foolish. But admitting there's something undeniable that pulls you to someone like it does no one else isn't weak at all. It takes every bit of strength in me.

Daniel's eyes leave mine for a moment and I begin to doubt myself. I can barely swallow until he says, "I said I would try. I didn't say I was capable."

My eyes close and I wish I could will all of this overwhelming emotion away. But that's what Daniel's always done to me. Overwhelmed me.

"I'll keep you safe. Always."

My heart soars and plummets with his words. That's how it feels and the relief on my lips falls with it.

"I just know … your job … is dangerous." I hate how my throat feels tight as I speak. "I knew what I was getting into. It's different when you wait at home alone wondering …"

"But I'm a dangerous man, Addison. I know what I'm doing."

I search his dark eyes for reassurance and it's there, but still I can't help adding, "Don't die. Everyone I love dies."

"What if it's more like anyone who loves you dies?" he questions and it doesn't help me feel any better at all. He shrugs and points out, "Then I'm dying anyway, so you might as well love me back."

Although I realize the words were spoken in a lighthearted way, the acknowledgement is there. That there's something more between us and we both feel it. We both recognize it for what it is. I don't dare to speak it again. I'm too caught up in those flutters in my chest. The ones that hurt in the best of ways. My eyes start to gloss over and I shove all the emotion away.

"Just be safe, my dangerous sex god." My voice is playful and nonchalant as I reach for the remote, ending the conversation. It's too much, too soon. But it feels like everything that's always been missing. It feels right. It feels like home. And I'm so afraid to lose it.

Daniel chuckles and leans down to cup my cheek and plant a soft kiss in my hair. "I'll be back as soon as I can," he whispers and it tickles me enough to make me pull away and snatch a kiss from his lips myself.

It's only been weeks, but this is everything I've ever wished for.

As the door clicks shut, leaving me alone in my apartment, I remember a certain saying.

Be careful what you wish for.

Chapter Twenty

DANIEL
Five years ago

I knew something was off when I walked in at 4 a.m. and the dining room light was on. The yellow glow carries into the kitchen and I follow it to see Tyler at the end of the large table, head in his hand staring at the screen to his laptop.

I expect to hear something, maybe see him watching a video. But the screen has gone black and that's when I see his expression. Defeated and exhausted.

"You still up?" I ask him, which is a stupid question. It gets his attention though, although his exhaustion makes him blink several times before he can answer me. It's then that I see his eyes are puffy, not with sleep, but with something else.

"Yeah, couldn't sleep," he answers and then visibly swallows as he closes the laptop.

My jacket rustles as I slip it off and hang it over the chair in front of me. I still feel like an asshole for snapping at him the other day. Of everyone living under this roof, Tyler's the last person who needs my shit. "Everything alright?"

He sits back and lets out a heavy breath, but instead of answering verbally, he only shakes his head no.

"You want to talk about it?" I ask as I grip the back of the chair and prepare myself for the answer I know is coming. Addison isn't here and Tyler can't sleep. She left him.

"You were right," Tyler says and then turns away from me.

"I was an asshole who was trying to be an asshole. I'm never right. You know that?"

He lets out a huff of a laugh and wipes under his eyes.

"What happened?" I ask him.

"She said it's too much for her. That she needs space."

I nod my head in understanding. "Nothing wrong with a little space," I say and try to make it sound like it's not a big deal.

"I know her, Daniel. I know it's her way of putting distance between us so I'll be the one to leave."

The legs of the chair scratch along the floor as I pull it out and take a seat. A heavy breath leaves me as I put my elbows on the table and lean closer to him. "Girls are hormonal," I say to try to make him crack a smile. He's the one who's good at this, not me.

"I think she's done with me, but I don't know why."

"She loves you," I tell Tyler although it makes a spike of pain go through my heart. She does love him. I know it by the way she kisses him. It's obvious she does.

"I don't know," he says in a whisper, shaking his head.

"Just give her a day or two, cut class if you have to. Give her time to miss you." I hate that I'm giving him this advice. But I hate to see him like this more.

"What did Mom used to say, huh? If you give someone love, they'll love you back. Right?"

He nods his head, although he still doesn't speak. It's been a while since I brought up Mom. And it still doesn't feel right, but Tyler was her baby boy. He may have been younger when she got sick, but it hit him hard. He didn't understand.

"I promise you," I tell him as I pat his back. "Come with me for the next two days. I have to make a trip to Philly for a shipment. Come up with me and let her miss you."

He's reluctant for a moment but then he nods. "I could use the distraction, I guess."

"Perfect." I stand up quickly and leave him be as fast as I can. "Get some sleep," I say over my shoulder and I don't stop walking or respond when he tells me thanks.

As I climb the stairs to go pass out, loneliness settles in my chest.

The idea of Addison never coming back hits me hard. The possibility of never seeing her again.

It's very obvious to me in this moment that I don't like it.

More than I don't like how she's younger than me.

More than I don't like how she looks at me the way I look at her when I know she's not looking.

More than I don't like that she's Tyler's.

Every day there's a memory I've forgotten. Haunting me. Showing me how I could have stopped the inevitable. Or at least changed our fates.

Late at night, holding Addison as she sleeps, I wonder if Tyler would still be alive if I had done something different. Or if I'd be the one buried in the ground now.

Fall has arrived and each step I take down Rodney Street is accompanied with the crunch of dead and withered leaves. My steps are heavy tonight because I know Marcus is going to be here.

He's finally come with whatever it is Carter's been waiting for. I know Marcus' patterns. He spends weeks scouting out a place and making sure you go to one location he has constant eyes on. And when he's found where he's comfortable, he delivers.

He's found that place at the park on the corner of Rodney and Seventh.

After tonight I have no reason to stay here. Addison will either come with me, or leave me. It's too good right now to think she'll refuse me, but she's run before and it's entirely possible she'll do it again.

I glance down the side street to see what block I'm on and my heart freezes.

The man in the black leather jacket, the one who stopped to look at Addison. That first day I watched her in the coffee shop and saw him staring at her. It's him. I swear I saw him melt into the shadows down the street.

"Hey!" I call out, more to see if he'll move than to actually get a reaction. But there's only silence. I barely glance to my right to check for cars as I run across the street. The cool air does nothing to calm my heated skin or the anxiety rushing through my blood.

I'm ready for a fight when I get there, but the shadowy corner is only a dead end. And no one's there.

A chill flows over my skin and I look all around me. It's no one. There's no one here.

It's hard to swallow as I walk back across the street. *It's just paranoia*, I tell myself. It's nothing. But still, all of my thoughts lead back to Addison. To her being alone.

She's messing with my head.

I think about every way she's consumed me with each step I take.

I can't see anything other than her when she's around me.

Every breath she takes depletes the air from my lungs.

I hated her for it back then, back when she was with Tyler. When she smiled at him instead of me. She tempted me, and I couldn't do a damn thing about it.

But time changes everything.

Every step she takes closer to me makes my fingers itch to grab on to her and never let go.

Fate simply waits for men like me. So it can fuck us over until we fall to our knees and admit there isn't a damn good thing about us.

Addison has no idea what she does to me.

She'll be the death of all that's good in me. I would lose focus of everything just to have a miniscule piece of her attention. I'd steal for her. I'd kill for her. I already have.

Goosebumps still cover my body as I get to the empty park. It's in the back of a small church that's surrounded by woods. I guess for Sunday school.

My gaze scans the perimeter of the park, but there's no one there. It's empty.

Marcus is never late. I check my watch and make sure I'm on time.

A minute passes as I walk toward the church and then back. It's not a good look to loiter and I don't need anyone getting suspicious.

Another minute and my anger and anxiety start to get the best of me.

A flash of white catches my eye as the breeze goes by; the squeaks of the swing's rusty chains make me turn toward them.

A note. I walk toward it without hesitation. Marcus and his fucking games.

There's a message on the swing.

Another address.

Tomorrow night. Check the mailbox. That's all you'll need.

Gritting my teeth, I hold back the urge to scream out toward the forest in anger. I know that fucker's in there watching. Making sure I got the memo.

The paper crumples in my hand as I stare out into the forest and wonder why he didn't meet in person.

Marcus always meets me in person. I've heard tales of him not showing and only leaving notes. Everything is fucked after. Marcus doesn't like to meet with you if he knows you're about to be fucked over.

A chill runs down my spine.

The only guess I have is that it has something to do with Addison. She's the only thing that's changed.

He knows everything. He knows about what happened the night Tyler died. He knows about my obsession. And he knows she's back.

My eyes flicker to the woods, searching him out but coming up with nothing. Every small sound of a branch breaking or the wind rustling the leaves reminds me of that night, the images flashing in front of me.

The night that Tyler died.

I'd just finished a meet with Marcus. It was an easy transaction for a hit we needed. He seems to like those better than being a messenger. He responds faster.

He knows that on my way home, I saw Addison in the diner.

I saw him across the street watching me after I'd sent the message to Tyler. She was in pain and I knew Tyler could take it away.

Marcus followed me as I followed Addison. I couldn't leave her, knowing Marcus saw me watching her. I didn't trust him. So I followed her from place to place. The diner, the bookstore and finally the corner store. And Marcus was there, every step of the way. I told myself it was only to satisfy his sick curiosity.

And worse than anything, Marcus was there; he was the closest when Tyler died right in front of us.

Marcus knows everything and he's not coming to see me in person. That leaves a bad taste in my mouth.

Deep breaths come and go.

This doesn't have anything to do with her. It's about Carter. It has to be about Carter and not about the shit Marcus knows about Addison.

Part of me questions if I should confess to her and tell her the truth before someone else does. She blamed herself for so long and I know she did. But I'm the one who sent Tyler after her.

He knew where she was because of me.

He went to see her because I told him he should.

It's all my fault. It was never hers.

Chapter Twenty-One

ADDISON

IT'S BEEN STRANGE.

My fingers hover over the keys and I delete my last words. I don't know how to tell Rae what's going on. I shift on my sofa, feeling uneasy. This whole day has felt different. Daniel hasn't touched me since yesterday morning. And things have been off since he got back from his meeting. It's also when the word "love" was said. Maybe he didn't realize he'd said it until after he left.

I've gotten short kisses, but nothing else. It feels different.

It's a way that makes me feel uneasy.

It's a way that makes me feel like the end is here and I was right all along.

All the flutters stop and the butterflies fall into a deep pit in my stomach.

That's the way he's making me feel.

The hall light flicks on and Daniel's large frame takes up the opening of the narrow passage. He doesn't look at me as he strides to the kitchen, walking right behind the sofa. He's not talking to me, but he doesn't want to leave either.

I can't take this. I prepare myself to type up the email telling Rae what I'd like to say to Daniel. Before I can even type a word I get fed up and slam it shut, turning sideways to face him. All of my frustration and nervous feelings snowball together into nothing but anger.

This time he's looking right at me.

"Something's wrong." That's all I can say and instead of answering me, Daniel reaches for a mug from the cabinet.

"Could you give me something?" I ask him with all this pent-up frustration and shove the laptop onto the coffee table. "You've barely looked at me, spoken to me, or touched me. Something happened or something's wrong, and if it's us I need to know."

Silence. I get silence in return. "If it's just work, you can tell me." My voice cracks and I hate that I'm so emotional while he gives me nothing.

It would be easy for him to simply say it has nothing to do with us. I can accept that. But he doesn't and that's when the sick feeling that's been twisting my gut all day travels to my heart.

I'm already halfway to him, determined to get some answers when he finally says something.

"I have to leave tomorrow night."

My bare feet stop on the cold tile floor in front of him. "That quick?"

"Either then or the next morning at the latest."

I swallow down my heart and breathe out somewhat in relief, but it's short-lived as I cross my arms over my chest. "You have to leave?" I ask him that question because the other one is too scared to leave me.

What happens to us?

He answers the unspoken question. "I want you to come home with me."

"Home?" I say the word with a humorless huff and pull out one of the chairs at the kitchen island. I don't know where home is. Taking a seat, I tell him, "Are you sure they'll even want me there?"

It's hard to swallow when I look at him. I can say goodbye to the idea of college, or at least this college, easily. But facing his brothers? That's something else entirely.

"They'll be happy to see you again." He says the words with compassion, but there's something there, something else that he's holding back.

"When did you find out you need to leave?" I ask, prying for more answers.

"Last night." He clears his throat and adds, "It's not my brothers that I'm worried about. It's you ... deciding to leave me again."

"Stop it," I snap at him and then correct myself. "Why would you even say something like that?"

"I've done some things," he says and then leaves the empty mug on the counter. It's quiet and all I can hear is the sound of my heart beating as he takes a seat on the sofa in the living room. Although I know something bad is coming, I follow him, taking the cue to sit next to him.

"You're scaring me again," I whisper to him with a pleading voice and wait for him to look at me.

With his elbows on his knees, his head is just a smidge lower than mine as he turns to look at me and says, "It's because I'm a bad man. That's what bad men do. They scare people."

"I told you to stop it," I tell him as I reach up to put a hand on his broad shoulders. His shirt is stretched tight, making him seem caged beneath it. "You're a good person inside. I know you are."

"You think I'm good?" he says with an air of disbelief and then he turns to look straight ahead. When he speaks again, it's as if the words aren't directed at me. "I'm sure you think you can see the good in everyone."

"I don't like you talking like this. Seriously. You need to stop." I find myself struggling to speak. "I don't know what's making you say these things, but you have to stop."

"I think I should tell you something." Daniel speaks as he runs his finger around the lip of the coffee table in front of him. He focuses on it as the silence stretches out and I wait.

"Whatever it is, you can tell me." My heart flickers, the light going out for a moment. Maybe from fear, or maybe from knowing it's a lie I've spoken. There are so many things Daniel could say that would destroy me. But he knows that already.

"You're so breakable, Addison."

I huff a laugh, although it's drowned out by relief. "Is that the big news? Because I knew that already."

His dark eyes lift to meet mine and the intensity swirling within is something I haven't felt for a long time.

"No, that's not the news, but it's why I don't want to tell you."

My shoulders rise with a heavy breath. "If you have something to tell me, then I want to hear it."

Daniel relaxes his posture, sitting back and sinking into the cushion of the sofa as he stares at me. His hands are folded in his lap and I can tell he's deciding. Judging. And I allow it.

Because he's right. I am breakable. And the last person I want to break me is him.

He clears his throat, bringing his fist to his mouth and then looks at the decorative pillow that's next to him. I suppose it's just so he doesn't have to look at me. He runs his thumbnail over the fabric of the sofa as he talks, busying his hands. "When Tyler died, you left and didn't say goodbye."

I nod my head and ready myself to answer, leaning forward and even scooting slightly closer. He has to know how ashamed and riddled with guilt I was. I could barely speak to anyone.

I wanted to tell them all goodbye, but I couldn't even look them in the eye.

My words are halted when Daniel continues, not waiting for a response from me at all.

"And when I went to your house," he pauses and licks his lips before moving his gaze to mine. "I could lie to you here, and say you were already gone."

My heart beats hard and my breathing halts from the danger that flashes in his stare.

"But you hadn't left yet and so I watched you pack. I wanted to pack too. I didn't want to stay where Tyler had just walked, just sat. Where I'd just listened to him tell me about that beat-up truck he wanted to fix but never would." Daniel runs his thumb along his lower lip as his eyes gloss over. "I wanted to run like you wanted to, but I didn't think I would be capable until I saw you do it."

"You watched me leave?" I ask him, not knowing where this is going, but fearing what he has to say because of his tone and bearing. Because of how the air thickens and threatens to strangle me. As if even it would rather I be dead than for Daniel to destroy me with the history between us.

"I wish it were as easy as that," he says with a smile that doesn't reach his eyes. "I watched you board the train with that heavy suitcase, and I got on too. I watched you check in to a motel four cities over. And I requested a room next to yours."

Every word he says makes my heart feel tighter.

"I watched you for days before finally breaking myself away from you to call Carter and tell him I wasn't coming back. I'd decided to spend my time doing one thing." The heat in his eyes intensifies at the memory and his gaze feels like fire against my skin. "Watching you."

"You stalked me?" I ask him although the words stumble over each other and barely come out as a croak. I can't deny the fear that begs my body to run, but I'm frozen where I am, waiting for his confession to release me.

"I watched you because I needed to. You blamed yourself and your pain was so raw and genuine. So full of everything that I didn't have. Of course I hated every bit of who I was because Tyler had to die, while God chose to let me live. I wanted to cry and mourn like you did. A very large part of me wanted you to cry harder as you hugged your pillow to your chest in the dark. Some nights you couldn't even stand long enough to make it to the bed."

He cocks his head as he looks me in the eye and asks, "Do you remember how you'd sleep on the floor even when the bed was so close?" His last words come out as a whisper and I can't answer. I can hardly breathe as tears leak from my eyes.

"I thought about picking you up and putting you in the comfort of your sheets–"

"You came in?" I cut him off and suck in a deep breath. "You broke in to my room?"

"Addison, I couldn't be away from you." His admission elicits a very real fear that makes my body tremble as I shy away from him. Scooting farther away on the sofa, but not quite able to run.

"Not until you started getting better," he adds and then stands up. I cling to the cushion, cowering under him and backing away when he tries to touch me.

The tears fall freely as the extent of my fears from so long ago is realized. I swear I heard things. I heard someone walking in my room in the darkness. I swear I felt eyes on me. "I thought it was him," I cry out and cover my burning face. I thought Tyler was with me for so long. And it took me years to think that it wasn't because he wished me harm. I thought he hated me and wanted me to be scared. And then I loathed myself that much more for thinking so poorly of such a good soul.

"I needed to watch you, Addison. I'm sorry."

I stand up quickly, and I'm close to him. So close I nearly smack the top of my head against his chin as I stand. "I need to get away from you," I sputter, crossing my arms over my chest and walking around the sofa although I have no idea how I can even breathe, let alone speak and move.

I can barely see where I'm going, but I know where the door is.

Gripping the handle, I swing it open and face him. My legs are weak and I feel like I'm going to throw up. He made me crazy. It was him all along.

"I never did anything to hurt you, Addison, and I didn't want to." Daniel speaks calmly, the other side of him starting to emerge. The side that's okay with Daniel dropping his defenses. The vulnerable side that wants me to understand and isn't pushing me away. But that's exactly what I need to do right now. I need to shove him far away.

"I want you to leave," I tell him and sniffle, swiping under my eyes aggressively, willing the tears to stop. I'm shaking. Physically shaking.

"You need to go," I tell him because it's the only truth I know. My mind is a chaotic storm and everything I'd been keeping at bay, all the fear and sorrow are screaming at me until I can't hear anything. I can't make out anything. The exception being the man standing right in front of me who's the cause of my pain.

"Who did you think I was, Addison?" he asks me as if this is my fault.

And maybe part of it is.

"You knew I wasn't a good man back then, and you know that now."

"Get out." They're the only words I can say.

"It was years ago."

"I said get out!" I scream at him, but he only gets closer to me until I shove him away. He can't hold me and make this right.

"You stalked me." I can barely get the words out. I'm in disbelief and terrified, although I'm not sure which reaction is winning.

"You had hope," he says back hard as if it justifies everything. "You had happiness. You had everything I wanted. You were everything I wanted. You can hate me for it, but you can't deny that. It's the truth."

"I want you to leave."

"Please don't make me leave," he tells me as if it's only just now getting through to him. He looks at the open doorway and then back at me. The hall is empty and cold and a draft comes in, making me shudder.

"Get. Out." I can't look at him as he stares at me, waiting for me to say something else.

"Addison-"

"Out!" I yell as loud as I can. So hard my throat screams with pain and my heart hurts.

Even over my rushing blood I hear each of his footsteps as he walks away from me.

"You said you wouldn't leave me," Daniel grits between his teeth as he stands on the threshold of my door.

The words leave me as I slam the door shut in his face. "I lied."

Chapter Twenty-Two

DANIEL

The heavy pit in my stomach is why I don't give people a damn piece of myself. That sick feeling that I swear is never going to go away is why I play it close to the vest.

I thought she was different.

I close my eyes, swallowing although my throat is tight and listening to the busy traffic on Lincoln Street. I'm close to the address Marcus gave me. Close to being done with this town and having no reason to stay.

It's only when the street quiets that I open my eyes and force myself to move forward. Going through with the motions.

She *is* different. She does know better. She knows who and what I am.

She just doesn't want to accept it.

And how can I really blame her? I don't want to accept it either. I didn't even get to tell her all of the truth. I didn't get to take her pain away from thinking she's to blame.

And that makes everything that much harder to swallow.

Passing a corner liquor store, I make sure I track the movements of the few people scattered around me. I keep to myself, heading south down the street. It's late and only the moon and streetlights illuminate the road ahead of me. But dark is good when you don't want to be seen.

I try to focus, but with the quiet of the night, I can't help but to think of Addison. She's always comforted me in the darkness.

I finally had her. Really had her. I felt what I always knew there could be between us. And I let her get away. I lost her by confessing.

Maybe that's why it hurts this fucking bad. She loved who I am, but hates what I've done. And there's no way I can take it back.

She saw the truth of what I was, but I could have sworn she knew it all along.

Maybe I should have just hinted at it. And let her ask if she wanted to know more.

You can't change the past. If anyone knows that fact all too well, it's me.

Give her time. I close my eyes, remembering the advice I gave Tyler once. If only it was that easy.

The chill in the autumn air is just what I need as I steady my pace with my hands in my jacket pockets. The metal of the gun feels cold against my hand as I glance from house number to house number.

55 West Planes. In the mailbox.

That's what Marcus said. Simple instructions. But an easy setup if he's planning one.

They say he's a man with no trace, no past, and nothing to use against him. A ghost. A man who doesn't exist.

He knows everything and only tells you what he wants when he wants to deliver it. But he's a safe in-between for people like us to use. Because if Marcus tells you something, it's because he wants you to know it.

And that's a good thing, unless he wants you dead.

I brush my hair back as I glance from right to left. There's a group of guys on the steps of an old brick house across the street and on its mailbox is 147.

I cross the street after passing them, so I'm on the odd-numbered side. The block before this was numbered in the two hundreds. So one more block.

The adrenaline pumps in my blood and I finger the gun inside my jacket pocket.

I have to will away the thoughts of Addison, no matter how much they cling to me and plague me every waking second.

My father taught us all to pay attention. Distractions are what get you killed.

A huff of a laugh leaves me at the memory of his lesson.

I guess when you don't care if you live or die, the severity of his words don't send pricks down your skin like they did when you were a child.

Tyler wasn't with me that day. I wonder if my father ever bothered to give Tyler that advice. Addison was as big of a distraction to him as she was to me.

With the tragic memories threatening to destroy me, I halt in my tracks, realizing I wasn't even looking at the numbers.

And I happened to stop right at 55. The mailbox is only two steps away.

The cold metal door of the mailbox opens with a creak. The sound travels in the tense air and the inside appears dark and empty. I dare to reach inside and pull out only an unmarked envelope. Nothing else.

My forehead pinches as I consider it. It's thin and looks as if it's not even carrying anything. But it's sealed and this is the right address.

All of this for one little envelope.

Slamming the door to the mailbox shut, I walk a few blocks, gripping the envelope in my hand and looking for a bus stop.

I text my brother even though I don't want to. I don't want him to know it's done. That I have what he's been waiting for. *It's just an envelope.*

It's marked as read almost immediately and he responds just as quickly.

Good. Come back home.

Staring at his text, that pit in my stomach grows. I'm frozen to the cement sidewalk, knowing I have to leave and hating that fact.

I know I need to move and not stay here, lingering when Marcus will be watching. But with the phone staring back at me with no new messages or missed calls, the compulsive habit of calling Addison takes over.

The phone rings and rings and goes to her voicemail.

I haven't stopped trying and I don't intend to.

I stayed as long as I could outside her door. I listened to her cry until she had nothing left. I don't know if I should have tried to talk to her and made her aware that I was still there wanting to comfort her, or if it would have only made her angrier.

A heavy burden weighs on my chest as I slip the envelope into my jacket, careful to fold it down the center and keep moving in the night.

I have no choice but to take this back to Carter. There's no way I can stay.

For the first time in a long time, I feel trapped. Suffocated by what's coming.

I can't leave her again.

I can't watch her walk away, and I can't leave her either.

But it was never my choice.

It's always been hers.

Chapter Twenty-Three

ADDISON

I can't count the number of times I swore I was haunted. Not the hotels I stayed in or the places I moved. But me. A Romani woman in New Orleans once told me that it's not places, it's people who are haunted.

And since the day Tyler died, I swore up and down that he decided he would haunt me as I ran from place to place, never finding sanctuary.

From the creaks in the floorboards, to small things being misplaced. Every time I tried to find meaning in those moments. Each time I thought it was something Tyler wanted me to know and see.

There were so many nights when I cried out loud, begging him to forgive me. Even when I couldn't forgive myself.

I wonder if Daniel heard my pleas.

My phone pings on the coffee table and out of a need to know what he has to say this time, I reach for it. I haven't answered a single call or message from him. I don't know what to tell him.

It's fucked up. He's fucked up.

He hurt me beyond recognition.

I should tell him how I couldn't move for days on end. But the bastard knows that already.

I truly loved him, but a lie from years ago makes me question everything. He could have helped me heal. He could have shouldered the burden of my pain and I would have done the same for him. But just like when Tyler was alive, he was silent. He gave me nothing.

I'm surprised by the hurt that ripples through me when I see it's Rae and not Daniel.

It's a shocking feeling. And it takes me a moment to realize what I really want. I want him to beg me to forgive him. I want him to know my pain.

I let the idea resonate with me as I ignore Rae and click over to Daniel's texts. Six of them in a row.

I'm sorry.

I was wrong.

I couldn't help myself.

If I wasn't with you and watching you it was too much for me to take.

I wish you would understand.

I would never hurt you. I never will.

I read his texts and the anger boils as I text back. *You'll never know how much it hurt to go through that alone. And you made it worse for me. You sat in silence while I was in pain. How could you ever think I'd forgive you?*

I realize I'm more disturbed that he didn't try to help me than the fact that he stalked me. I guess that's not so different from what he did when I was with Tyler.

I press send without thinking twice. And then I click over to Rae, who wants to know how it's going. *Fucking priceless*, I think bitterly.

I roll my eyes, letting a shudder run through my body and tears roll down my cheeks. Instead of answering her, I move to the kitchen for a bottle of wine.

I still haven't unpacked my wine glasses and I know it's because part of me was already envisioning leaving with Daniel. I knew he wasn't staying long and I'd go anywhere with him. I would have done anything he wanted to be by his side.

My phone pings again as I bend down and grab a bottle of merlot by the neck from the bottom shelf of my wine rack. I pretend I'm going to let the phone sit there, but I'm too eager to see what he has to say. I'm a slave to his response.

He writes back, *Because I was in pain too. And I'm sorry. It wasn't to hurt you. It was only to distract me from the guilt I felt.*

Pain and guilt and agony and death make people do awful things. But it's no excuse.

I write back instantly, *You used me.*

I did.

I hate you for it. I stare at the text message and with the pain in my heart, I already know it's not hate. It just hurts so much that he watched and did nothing.

Can you love me and hate me at the same time?

I'll never forgive you.

He types some and then the bubbles that indicate he's writing stop. And then they continue, but suddenly stop again. All the while I grip my phone tightly.

Instead of waiting, I write more. My hands shake and the anger in me confuses itself for sorrow.

I needed someone and I had no one. I wanted you, you had to know. I blamed myself for everything when there was no reason to think otherwise. You could have helped me, but you only watched. You made my pain so much worse than it needed to be.

I send it to him and although it's marked as read, nothing comes. Minutes pass and the ticking of the clock serves as a constant reminder of every second going by with nothing to fill the gaping hole in my heart.

The moment I set the phone down on the counter and reach for the corkscrew, the phone beeps. I have to read it twice and then reread the message I'd sent him before the sob escapes me.

That's the way I felt every time you kissed him.

My shoulders shake so hard that I fall to the ground, my phone falling as well, although the screen doesn't shatter. I cover my face as I cry, hating myself even more and not knowing how to make anything better.

My phone pings again, but I can't answer it for the longest time. Even though it feels pathetic, I cry so hard it hurts every piece of my heart. The piece I gave Tyler when I gave myself to him. The piece I thought I'd left behind when I walked away from him. The piece that left me when he was laid to rest, and the piece I gave Daniel. There are many pieces. Pieces from years ago, from only days ago and the very big piece he just took.

I want him back instantly. I want him to hold me. There's a part of me that knows it's weak and pathetic to feel this desperate need for someone else. But deep inside I know I'd live my life happily being weak and pathetic for him. Isn't he weak for me just the same?

Sniffling and wiping at my face, I somehow get up, bracing myself against the counter and reaching for the faucet. My face is hot and I can still hardly breathe.

I don't think you ever get over the death of someone who's taken up space in your soul. It isn't possible. There are only moments when you remember that you're a pale imitation of what you could be if they were still with you. And those moments hurt more than anything else in this world.

As I turn off the faucet, I swear I hear something behind me and I whip around, a chill flowing over my skin and leaving goosebumps in its wake.

It takes every ounce of strength in me to lower myself to the ground, although my eyes stay on the skinny hallway where the noise came from.

It's silent as I pick up the phone, barely breathing, and quickly message Daniel. *Are you here now?*

It was a long time ago. I promise you. I wasn't well. I'm sorry.

I stare at his answer, feeling a chill flow over my skin and the hairs on the back of my neck raise.

So it's not you? I will myself to keep my eyes on the hallway, my back to the counter as I type. I can barely breathe.

Someone there?

I don't answer him and a series of texts come through. Ping. Ping. Ping. Each another sound that echoes down the hall.

Without looking at the messages I text, *I'm fine.*

His answer comes through before I look back to the hall. *I'm coming over.*

At his response I push forward, forcing myself to walk down the hall and to the loft bedroom. There's only one door and I push it open, telling myself it's nothing as the phone pings in my hand again.

It pings again as I take in the bedroom, cautiously stepping forward until I see a picture has fallen from the collage on the far side of the room.

My phone pings a third time and I can finally breathe. It's only a photo that's fallen.

I read his latest text and roll my eyes. *Answer me.*

My heart nearly jumps out of my chest as the phone rings and I drop it on the floor. It takes the entire time it's ringing for me to catch my breath and when I do I pick up the phone to text him. *It was only a picture falling.*

I'm on my way.

Don't come here, I text back while I'm still on the floor and I hope he can feel the anger that's still there. I add, *I don't want you here.*

It hurts me to tell him that. Partly because it's a lie. It hasn't even been twenty-four hours and I can already see myself forgiving him.

Addison please. Don't shut me out.

It took us long enough to admit what we needed.

I miss you. I need you.

If you're scared I need to be there.

With the fear and regret and everything else that's tortured me today, I just want to give in to him after reading his rapid-fire texts. But I won't.

I just need sleep, I reply and then add, *Don't come.*

Please forgive me, he finally texts and I can't respond right now, so I shut the phone off and fall onto the bed. I don't know how long I stare at the wall or at what point I decide I have enough energy to clean up the fallen picture, but I know it's longer than I'd like.

The command tape is stuck to the wall this time. I swear I'll never use it again.

Just like I'll never let myself give in to Daniel again.

Some people you're meant to miss.

They're just no good for you.

I think the words, but I don't know if I really feel them.

With that thought in mind I move to where the picture frame lays facedown on the ground and lift it carefully. Luckily there's no broken glass.

I almost feel okay as I turn it over to inspect the frame.

But then I see the picture that fell. One I took myself, five years ago.

A still life of Tyler's rusty old truck.

And that's when I lose it all over again. I'm forced to come to terms with the fact that some wounds never heal. And they aren't meant to be forgotten.

Chapter Twenty-Four

DANIEL

The phone rings and rings as I throw a zipped up bag into the corner with the rest of the luggage. I've packed light for years, but it's never bothered me before.

Looking at the small pile that comprises everything I own, I've never felt so worthless. Or so tired. I didn't sleep at all.

The phone goes silent and instead of calling Addison again, I scroll to Carter's number and call him. I could easily text him to let him know I'm on my way, but I don't want to. I want him to hear the defeat in my voice. And I need to talk to someone. Someone real. I'm losing everything, slowly feeling it drain from me.

I need someone. Desperately. I stayed awake outside Addison's apartment all night. I had to make sure she was okay. But time doesn't wait, and I had to pack ... and now I have to leave.

It only rings twice before he picks up, greeting me with my name although it comes out as a question. And I know why he'd be confused to see I'm calling him.

I don't call anyone ever. I don't care to talk to him or any of my brothers, and they're the only ones alive I love. *My brothers and Addison.*

"Do you miss him?" I ask Carter without prefacing my question. "Not like Mom and Dad, where we knew it was coming and it made sense." Carter tries to talk on the other end of the line, but I keep going, pinching the bridge of my nose and sitting on the end of the bed. It protests with my weight. "The kind of missing someone where it feels better to pretend they're coming back? The kind of missing where you talk to them like they can hear you and it makes you feel better?" I know why I don't go home. It's because he's there in my head. I know what home is, and he's there. I refuse to accept otherwise. I can't.

I tell him I'm sorry every time I'm reminded of him. I hate going south, too many old trucks. I could never tell the difference, but they were Tyler's thing. He was an old soul like that.

"Every day," Carter says as I sit there quietly.

"I did something," I start to confess to Carter but stop myself. I'm too ashamed, so I settle on something else. "I ran into Addison." Her name leaves me in a rush, taking all the air in my lungs with it.

"Tyler's Addison? That's what brought this up?" he questions me and I nod my head like an ass, as if he can see.

"Yeah," I almost repeat, *Tyler's Addison*. But she never belonged to him. As much as I love him, she was always mine. Maybe he was meant to be her first, but I'll be her last. My throat tightens and my heart hammers in my chest. She's not his anymore. She's mine. And telling Carter feels like a betrayal of the worst kind. It feels like I'm telling Tyler. And as much as I thought it would be easy to admit it, I don't want them to hate me. They have to understand.

"And?" Carter presses and I'm not sure where to begin.

"When I left ... after Tyler died five years ago ... when I left you and the family, I followed her." The words spill from me. "Watching her cry made me feel normal. She gave me hope that I wasn't broken, because she felt the same way. But she stopped crying, Carter. She moved on without me."

"Daniel," Carter warns and I hate him for it.

"You'll listen to me," I seethe with barely concealed anger. He will listen and accept it. There are no other options. I can't have it end any other way. "I have no one."

"You chose no one. You left us."

"You know why." They gave Tyler's phone to Carter after the dust settled. Carter saw. He never spoke it out loud. But I was there and I know he saw that I was the one texting him.

I'm the one who led Tyler to his death.

"You didn't have to go." His voice is sincere, but soft and full of sympathy.

"Well I'm coming back now," I tell him.

"Does she know?" he asks me and I answer him with, "I shouldn't have told her."

"She knows you followed her? Is she going to press charges?" he asks and I huff a humorless laugh and then stare at the ceiling fan that's perfectly still.

"I don't think so," I say and it's only then that question becomes a possibility. I've only been thinking about what I can do to make her forgive me.

"She has to forgive me," I tell him with words stronger than I feel.

"She doesn't have to do anything," Carter answers me and the silence stretches as my disdain for him grows.

"What did she say?" he asks me just as I'm ready to hang up.

"That she hates me." It doesn't hurt me to say the words today like they hurt me yesterday. There's hope, only a small piece, but it's there. "She didn't mean it," I tell him.

"Did you do anything else?" Carter asks me with a tone that's cautious, like he already knows.

"I've done lots of things, brother."

"With her. With Addison." My gaze wanders to my shoes by the bed and I bend down to put them on and lace them while I tell him, "I tried to stay away from her, but she sought me out ... before she knew."

"Did she fuck you?" he asks me and it strikes me as if he's said it backward.

"I fucked her, yes." The irritation gives me strength and I stare at the pile of shit next to the door that I'll take with me back home and nearly leave it behind. It's all meaningless.

"Is she ..." Carter hesitates to ask.

"She's mine." The words leave me quickly, whipping out as if they're meant to lash him, hating how he questions it. *She's always been mine.*

I almost tell him that she'll forgive me, but the doubt in me stops the words on the tip of my tongue.

"I'm coming home. I've been running away for a long time."

"If you bring her, tell me so I can tell the others."

"Why tell them?" Although I don't give a shit what they think, I know Addison will.

"She was like a sister to us, Daniel. She didn't just leave Tyler, she left all of us."

She didn't just leave us once. She left us twice.

When I heard her break up with Tyler in the kitchen, I could hear every word. I stood by the window, watching her leave.

I can't let her leave a third time. I can't let her go.

Before I can stop myself, I speak into the phone, "I'll let you know."

Staring at the closed door to this rented house, I can see Addison so clearly all those years ago. Driving away and I never bothered to stop her or tell her how she wasn't allowed to leave.

She could never leave.

She was meant to be there.

Not with Tyler, but with me.

Maybe if I had bothered to tell either of them that, Tyler would still be here and none of this would have happened.

Chapter Twenty-Five

ADDISON

This coldness won't go away. It follows me everywhere. Even burying myself under the blankets doesn't take the chill away.

I can't sleep. I can only wait for updates from Daniel. He texted me all night. He's really leaving.

It all feels so final and I have no time to process anything. There's a heaviness in my chest and a soreness in my lungs that I'm so painfully aware of. They won't leave me alone.

Another message, another plea from him.

Please meet me, he begs. *I can't lose you again.*

Looking at his message stirs up so much emotion. I don't want to lose him. That's the worst part of all of this. It's the fact that I don't want to be alone and without him again.

But how can you forgive someone for watching you suffer when they knew they could save you?

I'll wait outside. I'm on my way and I'll wait for you, but I can't wait long. Please Addison.

The seconds tick by as I stare at his message.

Tick-tock. Tick-tock.

It's early in the morning; the sun is still rising. A new day.

I can tell him goodbye. Just one last kiss. A kiss for the love we had. The love we shared for another too. A final goodbye that I should have had years ago.

I can pretend that's what this will be, but I already feel myself clinging to him.

Some people you're meant to say goodbye to, and others you aren't.

I don't text him back. Instead I head to the bathroom. I look exactly how I feel, which is fucking awful. I half question getting myself somewhat put together to see him.

But I don't want him to remember me like this if it really is the last time I'll see him.

I take a few minutes, each one seeming longer and longer even though hardly any time has passed. And when I look up, I see a pretty version of me, with mascara and concealer to hide the exhaustion. I can't hide the pain though.

I'll try to let him go and move on.

Because that's what I'm supposed to do. Isn't it? It's what a sane, strong woman would do.

The zipper seems so loud as I close the makeup bag, as does the click of the light switch. There's hardly any light from the early morning sunrise as I make my way out and down the stairs to the side entrance of the apartment.

Each step feels heavier than the last and my heart won't stop breaking.

It's a slow break, straight down the center. My heart hates me, but yet again, it's something that seems so fitting.

There's a large window on the side entrance door and I'm staring out of it, looking for Daniel's car when I push it open. He isn't here yet. Not that I can see.

I want more time before I have to say goodbye and it makes it painfully obvious that I don't want to speak the words. But I can't be weak and I don't know that I can forgive him.

The cool air hits my face as the wind whips by and I walk slowly down the stairs. I take my time, not wanting this to end but knowing it's so close and there's nothing I can do to stop it.

The second I hit the bottom step and see Daniel's car pull up to the curb, a large hand covers my face at the same time that I'm pulled back into a heavy wall—no, a man's chest.

A man. Someone's grabbed me. The realization hits me in a wave. I didn't see him coming. I still can't see him.

A scream rips up my throat as I try to swing back and hit him. Daniel! I try to scream, but I can't. The man whirls around and my vision is blurred as I hit a brick wall, my arm scraping against it.

I don't stop screaming; I don't stop fighting with everything I have. My knee thumps against the brick wall as the man sneers at me to be quiet, the black leather glove on his hand making my face feel hot. I kick off the wall with the fear, the anger, and the knowledge that if I don't scream for Daniel, he won't know. He won't be able to save me.

My knee burns with pain as I shove my weight into the man and push at the same time, falling to the asphalt and breaking free for only a split second.

I scream out for Daniel, although I don't know if he heard me. I can't breathe as a man in a black hoodie with bloodshot eyes shoves his hand down on my face so hard that I think he broke my nose for a moment. The pain radiates and tears stream from my eyes.

I always thought the worst thing you could see when you die was the face of someone who loved you, but couldn't help you.

Staring into the black eyes of this man, I question that.

But relief comes quickly.

Through my blurred vision, I see a boot slam into his head, knocking him off of me although I struggle to get myself free and scramble away.

Bang! Bang!

I hear gunshots and I scream out again out of instinct, falling onto my side and huddling into a ball. *Bang!*

One last shot.

One heartbeat.

Another.

Silence.

And then I look up to see the man lying still, but Daniel clutching at his chest. He breathes heavily and then stumbles.

"No!" I cry out as blood soaks through his white cotton t-shirt and into the open button-up layered over it.

"Daniel," I cry out with fear gripping my heart.

He screams at me, even though the strength is gone. "Get inside!"

My body refuses to obey as he pulls his hand away from his chest. There's blood. So much blood.

Daniel's expression only changes from worried for me to angered as he stares at his hand. His focus moves to the man lying motionless on the asphalt and he points the gun at his head, firing.

Bang! Bang! Bang! Each shot makes my body tremble. The man's body doesn't react. His face is one I don't recognize as he stares lifelessly at nothing.

My gaze shifts from his dead eyes back to Daniel as he hunches over and grips his chest, falling to his knees on the ground.

That's the moment I can finally move again. And I run to him as fast as I can with one thought running through my mind.

Everyone I love dies.

Every.

Single.

One.

Chapter Twenty-Six

DANIEL

Fuck. Hot blood pours from my wound and soaks into my shirt as I lean against the brick wall, feeling sharp, shooting pains run up and down my spine. I apply pressure to the gunshot to try to stop the flow.

I can barely breathe through my clenched teeth at the pain.

"Go inside," I try to yell at Addison as she hovers over me. "Now," I grit out and my words come out weak.

"Daniel, get up. Get up!" she yells at me. And it actually makes me smile.

As I try to stand, with her pulling on me and attempting to aid me, I look back down at my hand. It's bright red, not black. That's the first good sign. But when I look down to my chest and see how much it's still bleeding, the lightheadedness nearly makes me collapse.

"Come with me," she begs. "We have to go to the hospital."

"No, no hospital. No cops." I'm still okay enough to know better than that. "You can't stay here; the cops will be coming. You have to go."

"I'm not leaving you," she yells at me with disbelief. "Just stay with me. Hide in my apartment. Let me help you, please," she begs me and that's the only reason I let her wrap an arm around me and guide me back to her apartment.

Thank fuck it's so early in the morning and everything went down in the back alley.

Dark alley.

A man who knew where to be and when.

Someone with information.

Not Marcus ... but it's someone who must know Marcus. My gaze moves to Addison's pale face as she opens the door to her apartment. Someone who wanted her. Someone who wanted to hurt me. And Marcus had to have told them. He's the only one who knew I was with her and what she meant to me.

"Come on." She tries to push me into her apartment and for a moment I hesitate, but if Marcus or someone else is after Addison, I have to be beside her.

It's too late for me to say goodbye.

I feel breathless as my gaze darts from the door behind us to the counter, then to the window. I have to tell Carter. At the thought a pain shoots up my back and down my shoulder, making me grit my teeth.

Fuck! Holding my breath, I put more pressure on the wound.

My steps are wide as I walk in and head for the kitchen. To the tile floor where it will be easy to clean up.

"Was there blood in the alley?" I ask Addison in a pained voice that I can't control and look behind me as I walk. Nothing's spilling onto the floor. Not a drop. My shirt is soaked with blood, but hopefully there's nothing that will lead the cops up to Addison.

"A lot of it," she answers me as she rips open the cabinet door and pulls out a roll of paper towels.

"Did it lead up the stairs?" I ask her breathlessly and then wince from the pain. *Fuck! Make it stop. Please.*

She looks at me wide-eyed before realizing I was talking about my blood. Not the asshole who dared to put his hands on her. She visibly swallows while shaking her head frantically. "No, nothing." She winds the paper towels around her hand before giving me the bundle of them. Her hands are still trembling. My poor Addison.

I take a quick look, as quickly as I can. Looks like the bullet exited cleanly. The wound isn't the problem. It'll bleed, but it'll heal. It's the infection that'll kill me if I don't have one of the guys take a look at it.

"Come sit," she tells me while also reaching for my shirt. "Sit down," she commands again. Her hands are shaking and her voice trembles, but she's trying to be strong.

I reach out and grab her hand to stop her. My blood smears on her soft skin. "I'm fine," I say to try to comfort her.

Addison shakes her head with tears in her eyes. "Sit down and let me take care of you." She swallows her tears back and adds, "If you won't go to the hospital, it's the least you can do."

A breath leaves me and makes me feel weak.

Another and my hand releases hers, but she doesn't look at it. She doesn't even wipe the blood away; she's still searching my eyes for approval.

Nodding, I take a step back and push the chair at the kitchen island far back enough to sit.

I watch her face the entire time she helps me pull my shirt off. She cares about me still. I know she does. *She'll forgive me.*

"Didn't you say you'd hate me forever?" I ask her. Maybe I'm delirious. I don't know why I push her.

"I said I'd never forgive you," she tells me flatly and doesn't look me in the eyes. Instead she pulls the wad of paper towels away, which are mostly soaked with blood and she quickly balls up more and presses against the wound.

"But you came down to see me," I say without thinking. "It had to mean something." The hope in my chest falters with her silence.

And when she does speak, its light dims.

"It means I was ready to say goodbye."

"I don't believe you," I tell her without hesitation and she looks up at me teary eyed.

"Don't cry," I command weakly. "I didn't want to upset you."

She sucks in a breath and blinks the tears away, but pain is clearly written on her face.

"I'm sorry," I whisper as she wipes the tears from her eyes. "I didn't mean for this-"

"Oh, shut up. You couldn't have known that this …" her voice breaks before she can finish and she closes her eyes and struggles to calm her breathing.

"It's fine, Addison," I try to reassure her, reaching out even though it sends a lance of pain through my chest. I run my hand down her arm and then pull her in closer, positioning her between my legs.

"It's okay," I whisper into her hair and then plant a small kiss on her temple as I hear sirens outside. She opens her eyes and looks to the far side of her living room, where the alley is just below.

"They may knock, but you don't have to answer," I tell her softly, and she only nods once, her eyes never moving.

"I'm sorry. I can't say goodbye to you," I tell her as I wish I hadn't ever come back to the bar. I wish I hadn't brought this on her. She doesn't know. I'm sure she thinks it was a random mugging or attempted rape. She has no idea. But I know there's no way it's a coincidence.

"I wish I could say goodbye to you again. I wish I could tell you I'll let you go, because it really is what a good man would do."

"Here you go with words about good and bad men when you don't even know the difference." Addison's tone is flat but there's the hint of a smile waiting for me. I can feel it.

"Thank you for taking care of me," I speak as she pulls the wad of paper towels away and there's less blood. I try to take a deep breath, but it hurts and I wince.

"Let me clean and bandage you," she says although I'm not sure she really wants a response. I swallow thickly and let her work. She can do whatever she wants to me, since I'm just grateful that she's here for me.

I don't deserve her. I know I don't. And that's all I can think about as she tapes the sterile gauze in place. Even as she poured rubbing alcohol over my wound I barely felt a thing.

"I need you to go lie down." Addison speaks with authority although she looks like a beautiful mess herself.

The desperate need for sleep begs me to listen to her, although Carter is expecting me. He knows I'm coming.

As if reading my mind Addison says, "It can wait. You can't drive right now anyway."

"Will you lie down with me?" I would give anything to feel her soft body next to mine and hold her right now. The thought sends a warmth through me, but it vanishes when I look up.

Her sad eyes meet mine with something they haven't before. Regret, maybe? Or denial? I'm not sure, but I'm certain she's going to tell me no.

"Please," I add and my voice trembles. "Even if it's only a little while?"

She's reluctant to nod, but she does and my throat closes with a pain that's sure to haunt me forever.

At least I have one more night. But I know in my heart, it's only one more night.

Chapter Twenty-Seven

ADDISON

I don't want to wake up. I don't want to move.

Because right now I have a man I desperately want, and it doesn't make me weak to be with him. But when this moment is over, that's what I'll be. It's not about forgiving him anymore; it's accepting who I am if I'm with him.

I'm not sure how long we've been in bed, but the knocks at the door from the cops came and went. And at least hours have passed, because my eyes don't feel so heavy, only sore.

"You're awake." Daniel's deep rumble makes his chest vibrate. And it's only then that I realize how close to him I am, how I'm curled around him and his arm is behind my back, holding me to him.

I roll over slightly, only enough so my head is on the pillow and not his chest. There are so many things to say. And so little time.

You can want a person but know they're bad for you. That's the person Daniel's been for me since I've met him. And it's not going to change.

Daniel lifts the sheet and checks his gunshot wound. I can only see a faint circle of blood and I try to gauge his reaction, but he doesn't say anything.

"Are you going to be okay?" I ask him and try to swallow down my worry.

"Are you going to leave me if I say I'll be fine?" he asks, turning his face toward me and his lips are only inches from mine.

I huff a small laugh and a trace of a smile is there for a moment, but the pain of the unknown is quick to take it away. The smile on my lips quivers and I have to take in a deep breath.

"I don't know where we go from here." It's hard to tell him the truth.

I hear him swallow and then he looks up at the ceiling, rather than at me.

"I still want you," he says in a whisper although I'm not sure he meant for it to come out that way. "I can't let go of you," he says and puts his gaze back on me, assessing my reaction.

I can't explain how it feels to hear him say the only words I want to hear. I want to beg him not to let go of me because I'm so afraid to lose myself with him, but I don't ever want to be apart.

A second passes, and then another. And I don't know what to do or think or say. I only know time is running out.

"I'll never stop watching you, Addison. My heart thinks you belong to me and it always has. Whether I want it, whether you want it. It doesn't matter—I'll always feel this need to watch over you."

"It's not the watching part," I try to tell him and then shake my head. My hair slides against the pillow and I struggle to speak, but somehow I do. "It just hurts."

"I'm sorry." He says the same words as before, but the pain is so much more real now as he turns over slightly and puts his hand on mine.

"Do you want me?" he asks me and then adds, "Do you want to come home with me? I'll make it better. I swear I will."

He squeezes my hand and I don't know what to say. I just want everything to feel better and to not hate myself for running back to him.

"I don't want you to come with me because you're lost or lonely or scared. If you want me, I want you. I can't help it and I can't stop it. I tried and when I finally let go of you, there was nothing left of me."

My heart aches for him and for me. I know exactly how he feels. Tears prick my eyes and I can hardly breathe.

I can't answer him, so instead I tell him what I'd planned on saying when I was ready to say goodbye.

My words come out in shuddered breaths. "If you'd come to me back then, I would have let you in. Instead of watching me in pain, I would have loved you for being there for me and I would have been there for you too."

"You're blind to how you were back then. You may have had feelings for me. But you loved him."

"I loved you too though." My voice cracks as I protest and I heave in a breath.

"You wouldn't if you knew the truth. It was my fault-"

I cut him off, pressing my finger to his lips to silence him. "I'm done with the past, Daniel. I don't need to know every horrible thing you once did. I only wanted you to know that I would have let you in." I almost add, *just like I am now*. I can feel myself falling back to him after nearly losing him. After almost seeing him die. There's no way I can let him go again.

Something lifts in my chest. A lightness that gives me more room to breathe. It's the truth, and knowing that makes me feel anything but weak.

He pauses, considering what I've said and looks past me at the window to the bedroom before speaking again. "You think you would have, but I couldn't take the chance that you'd turn me away. I never had a chance, Addison. Even after he was gone you still loved him, and I hated myself for even thinking about taking his place in your heart. I don't care anymore. I already hate myself, but at least I can have you. I can love you better than anyone else."

He swallows thickly and adds, "I can promise you that."

"Love is a strong word." I'm still afraid to tell him I love him. I don't want him to die. More than anything else, I can't lose him. I know deep down inside, I love Daniel Cross and always have.

"It's the right word for what we have, but we can pretend to go slow?" he questions as if I've already forgiven him. As if I've agreed to go back home with him.

"So you think I'm yours again?" I ask him as I wipe under my eyes and sniffle. "Just like that?"

He holds my gaze as he tells me, "You've always been mine."

And I don't have any words for him in return.

It's true.

Daniel says that he's the one who never had a chance back then.

But the truth is Tyler never did.

I was always Daniel's and I don't think I had it in me to say that out loud. Because I don't know if Tyler could have ever forgiven me if he knew.

Daniel leans closer to me with the intent to kiss me. But just before he can cup the back of my head, he winces in pain.

"Shit," the word leaves my lips quickly and I hover over him. "For the love of God, lie down and rest." I pull up the sheets to check on the wound, but it looks the same.

"No, I need to kiss you," he says softly and when my eyes meet his, he smiles weakly and pleadingly.

"I need to kiss you too," I whisper and tears prick my eyes.

I lean down to press my lips to his. I mean it to be soft and sweet, but it deepens instantly and naturally. One of his hands cradles the back of my head, his fingers spearing through my hair. The other grips onto my hip, holding me there as his tongue sweeps over mine and his hot breath mingles with mine.

My body heats, feeling completely at home in his embrace.

"I need you," he whispers against my lips with his eyes closed. My pussy clenches at his words and it's then that I feel his erection against my thigh. The agony breaks and I wipe under my eyes.

"You're hurt," I tell him as I weakly shake my head and cup his strong jaw in my hand.

"Doesn't matter, I'll always need you. Always want you."

My heart pounds and pounds again. Recognizing how true it is, because it's the same for me.

"I love you," I say the words in a whisper even though they frighten me. "I can't lose you."

"I love you more," he tells me and I lean down to kiss him again and shut him up before he makes that pain in my heart grow even more.

Chapter Twenty-Eight

TYLER
Five years ago

I feel so fucking stupid.
    I don't know how I didn't see it before.
    It took him texting me where she is for me to realize it.
Daniel's in love with Addison.
And she's in love with him.
It all makes sense now.
    I check the map on my phone to make sure I'm going the right way, although every step makes my heart hurt more.
    He doesn't know that I know. Neither does she, but I can do them both a favor and tell them. I want to kiss her one last time though.
    I know it's wrong. But it's just a goodbye kiss. Something to remember her by. Something to let her know that it's okay. That I'm okay with her loving him. I just want her to be happy. She needs it more than anyone. I can see it in her eyes.
    My throat feels tight as I walk past Fourth Street. The rain starts coming down harder and it feels fitting.
    I pull up my hoodie around my head and listen to my sneakers squeak on the sidewalk as I make my way closer to heartbreak.
    I thought her telling me that she couldn't be with me anymore was the worst thing I'd ever feel.
    But knowing she loves my brother and wants him more than she wants me? Fuck, it hurts. It hurts so fucking much.
    My phone vibrates and I look down to see a text from Daniel. She's gone into the corner store now and Daniel said it looks like she's been crying. She's been doing it at school too. But she won't let me near her this time. She won't let me comfort her when she needs it so badly.
    This isn't the first time she's dumped me. My brothers don't know because I'm too ashamed to tell them.
    But each time she did, I'd find her crying somewhere and she'd let me hold her to make it feel better.
    I just loved her, hoping she loved me back. And I know some part of her does. But I never thought she didn't love me fully because there was someone else.
    I thought it was just the way she is. That she just pushes people away and that I would have to handle her more gently. I should have known by the way she avoided Daniel and the way he asked about her.
    How was I so fucking stupid?
    Do you want me to go to her? Daniel texts me and I stop one block over from where she is. Where both of them are. So close, I can see the window of the store. The light is dim in the sheets of rain. So close, but so far away.
    I should tell him yes. I should let him go to her. I bet she'd let him comfort her.
    But I just want one last kiss. Just one more time before I let her go.
    It's all I want. Just one last kiss before I let her go.

Chapter Twenty-Nine

ADDISON

"I don't think I can breathe."

"I'm not inside you right now, so you should be fine," Daniel quips as the car door shuts behind us. He leaves his black Mercedes in the paved horseshoe driveway as we step up to the Cross estate. The stubborn asshole wouldn't let me drive. The painkillers definitely helped him. But I'm looking forward to someone taking a look at him. Someone who knows what they're doing.

"It's different from the other house," I state, ignoring Daniel's joke and how easy this is for him. It's not just different. It's massive. They used to live in a small house off the backroads. This is … something else.

"Home looks different when you're different," he tells me and walks forward, leaving me standing in the shadow of the large white stone house. Is it even a house? It looks like a mansion.

"Who lives here?" I ask Daniel and he wraps his arm around my waist. "It's for all of us."

I haven't seen any of his brother's since the funeral and on that day, I couldn't look any of them in the eye. I could barely speak to them. I could barely do anything because the guilt was so strong. My pulse quickens as he pushes me forward.

"I don't know …"

"I know you can. And you'll feel better when you do. Both of us will feel better when we go in there." His eyes plead with me—not just to go in for him, but to be *with* him.

He holds out his hand for me, leaving it in the air until I finally grip on to him.

"Don't leave me," I whisper and stare into his eyes.

A tight smile is the response I get, followed by him leaning down to kiss me once on the lips.

His hot breath tickles my skin in the crisp fall air as he lowers his mouth to the shell of my ear. "I know this isn't …" He trails off and I can hear him lick his lips. "This isn't a fairytale. But there's nothing for me in there if it isn't also for you," he finally says and then pulls back.

My heart clenches with a pain that I think I love. A pain of a shared past, but of knowing we can have a future together.

Standing in front of the estate, with his thin black cotton shirt stretched tight across his shoulders, a shade of black that almost matches the darkness in his eyes, how could I deny him?

"They know you're coming. They know you're mine." He speaks with a conviction I feel in my soul.

It's not the first part of what he said that comforts me. It's everything in the second part. I want to be his, and they know that I am.

I swallow thickly and ignore the churning in the pit of my stomach as we walk up the stairs to the entryway.

It's safe. Everything is alright. I'm with Daniel.

The thoughts are comforting enough to give me the strength to breathe as he opens the large front door and leads me inside.

Each step is harder to take and I feel myself pulling away from him. I don't want to face his brothers. I'm too afraid of what they'll think. I'm afraid of their judgment and hate. Because I've only ever had love for them. Not the kind of love I had for Tyler, and not what I have for Daniel. But love nonetheless. They gave me a home when I had none. They were my family.

And right now … I can't bear for them to send me away.

"It's okay," Daniel says and holds me in the quiet foyer. "It's going to be hard at first. The memories are the hardest part, I think, and there are a lot between us all."

"I don't know if I can do this," I admit to him, wiping under my eyes to see a blurry vision of mascara smeared on my fingertips. I sniffle and then wish I hadn't come.

"We'll have good days and bad days, like everything else. And if it gets to be too much, we'll leave for a while, however long we need. We can go wherever you want to go. We don't have to stay here. I'm fine as long as we stay together. All that matters is that you stay with me." His eyes search mine as we hold each other.

I'll stay with him. Daniel is where my home is. "I'm not going anywhere."

"I've wanted you for far too long to not have you forever now."

"I'm yours," I promise him.

"You've always been mine."

The sound of footsteps is drowned out by a voice that echoes down into the open space. It's grand to say the least, but I can't take it in. I can only watch two men walk into the foyer.

"Addison," one of them says, catching me by surprise. It takes me a long time to realize it's Jase. I almost cry when I do. He looks so much more like Tyler than Daniel does. They always looked alike. Daniel tightens his grip on me as my voice cracks. "Jase."

I clear my throat as Jase stands tall in front of me.

"You look so different," Jase tells me.

"You don't," I say quickly but then take it back. "I mean you do, but you don't."

He smirks down at me and runs his forefinger and thumb over his chin. "Funny, I don't remember you being this shy."

I can only shrug; I don't trust myself to speak and I can hardly keep eye contact as I remember all the memories together. Jase and Tyler were close. The closest. And unless Tyler wanted privacy, Jase was there. Like an annoying brother.

Part of me is still aware that I'm holding on to Daniel with a white-knuckled grip. And that part of me wants to let go, so I can hug Jase.

"It's good to have you home. Everyone else thinks so too, trust me."

"Do you-" I falter and pick worriedly at the pocket of my jeans with the hand not being held firmly by Daniel. The questions I have are all begging to come out at once.

Do you hate me for leaving him?

Do you blame me for what happened?

Do you forgive me? That's the one that lingers. That's the only one that matters. "I'm sorry-" I start to say, but the words are tainted with a small cry.

"Addison." A voice to my right startles me before I can gather the strength to chance the apology. "So how'd you get him back here?" a deep voice asks me and I know immediately it's Declan.

Daniel pulls me in closer, planting a small kiss on my temple in front of both of them as we stand in the foyer. It's all too much, but none of them seem taken aback. Neither of the brothers is looking at me as if anything is off.

As if I'm not a reminder of what they've lost. Not an outsider. Not an enemy.

My lips part and I'm not sure what to say, but I'm grateful. I'm so grateful that I'm welcome. And that I get to see them again.

I never thought I would.

"Where's Carter?" Daniel asks Declan, wrapping his arm around my waist and pulling me in more just slightly, but still easy and casually. His thumb hooks into my jeans and gently caresses my hip as he talks to both brothers.

I try not to make it awkward.

It takes everything in me not to cry upon seeing both of them.

I'm surprised when Daniel loosens his grip on me and whatever they were talking about comes to a halt.

I'm even more surprised when Jase leans in close.

"It's good to see you, Addie," Jase says and hugs me hard, so hard that Daniel has to take a step back. Finally letting my hand go as Jase pulls me to him. It's been a long time since someone's called me Addie. They all did back then. All of them but Daniel. I was always Addison to him.

The hug is short-lived and I'm still numb from it along with the shock of everything when Daniel asks for a minute. As soon as his brothers turn away, I press my palms to my eyes and try to calm myself down. It's emotionally taxing to see those you've mourned because you thought you'd lost them forever.

"I'm okay," I tell Daniel weakly as he rubs my back.

"I promise I'll love you forever." Daniel whispers words that frighten me. Words that threaten to take him from me one day. I hesitate to say it back and he adds, "Just stay with me."

It's a plea from the lips of a man who could destroy me.

Sometimes when you walk into a darkness, a place filled with both what terrifies you from the past and what will forever haunt you in the future, you get a sick feeling that washes over you.

Like you know bad things are coming.

"I love you too," I whisper to Daniel and let him take my hand.

He squeezes lightly as I step further into the Cross estate.

It's brightly lit, but it doesn't fool me. The darkness is here.

There's a certain feeling in the pit of your stomach. I felt it when Tyler brought me to his home all those years ago.

It's a feeling that tells you you're doing something wrong. Something you know you shouldn't, but it tempts you and whispers all the right things; it promises you that you're meant to be here.

Not unlike what I've felt since the moment I met Daniel. This force of needing to be with him. Of knowing I was supposed to be his all along.

Even if the very thought of being his was enough to send a chill over me each time he dared to breathe near me.

That feeling is supposed to warn you, to keep you safe.

Daniel kisses the underside of my wrist as I let the feeling settle through me.

Sometimes that feeling is terrifying.

Sometimes that feeling is home.

Chapter Thirty

CARTER

I'M NOT USED TO THE ANXIOUSNESS RINGING IN MY BLOOD.

But times have changed and until this shit is settled, I'm going to be on edge.

I need all the help I can get.

And judging by the way Daniel can't take his eyes off of Addison, he's not in the right mindset.

But the important thing is that he's back.

Daniel cranes his neck to look up at me from where he's seated with her in the den.

Addison Fawn. I never thought I'd see her again. I thought I'd lost her when I lost my brother.

"Do you have a minute?" I ask him, getting their attention. Addison glances between Daniel and me, and I give her an easy smile. I've barely spoken to her, but it's only because of everything else. The war that's starting. That's what has my attention. That, and whoever decided to fuck with us.

Whoever decided to touch Addison and fuck with Daniel.

It's only a matter of time before we know who. Although the thought of Marcus being involved sends a chill through my blood.

Daniel winces as he stands, reminding me of the gunshot and rekindling that anger inside of me. He bends at the waist to kiss Addison. My eyes stay on her, noting how she pulls back slightly, but his hand on the back of her neck keeps her there. Her doe eyes look back into his and he brushes the tip of his nose against hers. And then she reaches up to kiss him this time.

I don't know what she did to my brother, but it's been a long damn time since I've seen him care about anything other than himself.

It's a good look for him.

"I was wondering when you were going to come for me," Daniel says as we walk back to the office. I keep him in sight even as he looks over his shoulder to check on her.

"You think she's going to run off?" I ask him jokingly, but it only makes his expression harden. Maybe he's still blind to it. But it's obvious she loves him. It was obvious five years ago too.

Silence escorts us until I close the door to the office with a loud click.

Daniel takes a seat in front of the large desk and rather than sitting at the head of it, I take the seat across from him, feeling the worn brown leather beneath my hands.

"I need that package," I tell him and wait for whatever the hell it is. He's already been here for hours, but Addison needed him for a little while. I could afford them that.

With a nod, Daniel slips the envelope from his back pocket. My teeth grind against one another. Hundreds of thousands of dollars in trades and a war between drug lords are on the line over whatever the fuck the Romanos are offering us.

And it's only a thin envelope, folded and creased down the center.

Our fingers brush as he hands it to me, but he doesn't let it go.

With my arm outstretched I look back at my brother, waiting for what he has to say, but nothing comes. A second ticks by and he releases it, sitting back in his chair but still not saying a word.

"What's gotten into you?" I ask him. Ever since Tyler died, Daniel's been a shell of who he once was. Until recently. Until she came back and brought him with her.

"She reminds you of Tyler?" he asks me.

"She reminds me of what you were like when he died," I answer him without thinking. And it's true. "You were on the edge of going one way or the other back then, but it looks like you've come back around."

"What do you mean?"

"I thought you were going to take care of her back then." I bite my tongue, wondering if I should tell him what Jase told me when Addison broke up with Tyler. When she said her goodbyes, she could hardly even look at Tyler. Instead she kept looking upstairs toward Daniel's room.

Everyone knew how Daniel felt about her. She was only seventeen and we had bigger and better shit to concern ourselves with. But that day it was more than obvious why she was leaving.

It was only the three of them who were blind to it.

Daniel shakes his head as if what I'm saying is ridiculous. Even after all these years he can't admit it.

"It doesn't matter. You're back, and she's with you. I don't care about anything else and neither does anyone else."

It's quiet for a long moment and Daniel runs his hand down his face, letting his head fall back and looking at the ceiling before he breathes in deep.

"Do you think he'd ever forgive me?" he asks me.

"Tyler forgave everyone," I answer him and it's true. He was the only good one of us. Of course he's the one who died young. "And Tyler wanted her to have a home. To have a family."

He nods his head, although it takes him a long moment before he looks back at me.

"It feels too good to be true," he says softly and I know why.

"Did you tell her the truth?"

"The truth?" he asks as if I don't know.

It only takes me glancing at his side where he was shot for him to understand my question.

"She has no idea. She thinks it was random. A coincidence."

"Is it Marcus?" I have a bad feeling in my gut, but he's the only person that this leads to.

"Yeah." His answer is quick and met with a simmering anger that I recognize from him. There's the brother I know and love. "I told him about her. I needed his help."

"You told Marcus. Who else?"

"He's the only one I told. It had to be him or someone he told."

"Why did you tell him anything?"

"I had her license plate and nothing else."

My thumb rubs in circular motions over my pointer finger as I take it all in.

He adds, "I couldn't lose her again." I know he could have told Jase. Jase could have looked up her information. But I don't remind him of that. He holds on to guilt too much.

I have nothing but silence as I think of any reason that Marcus would come for us. He's not a man I want as an enemy, but I'm also not certain it's him.

"It wasn't supposed to happen like that. It will never happen again." He strengthens his resolve and leans forward, daring me to object. And I do.

"And what if she leaves you again?" I ask him and he stares back at me, his chest rising and falling with determination. "What if she finds out something she shouldn't?"

He doesn't say what I expect him to, that she won't. Instead he merely answers, "Then I'll follow her."

My breath leaves me slowly, words failing me.

"She's mine," he says as if nothing else matters. And maybe it doesn't.

I nod my head once.

The hands of the clock in the office are all I can hear as I run my thumbnail under the flap of the envelope and stare back at my brother. "She's changed you."

"How's that?" he asks me. Again he's on the defensive, and it makes me smile. I like to see him showing something that's real.

"It's hard to pretend when you'd do anything for someone you love."

His gaze flickers to the envelope in my hand and he stares at it as he says, "I didn't come here for a heart to heart, Carter."

"You didn't open it?" Although the words come out with disbelief, the corners of my lips kick up with amusement. He's so consumed with Addison he didn't give a fuck about the one thing I've been losing sleep over.

"Marcus said it was a message of what's to come," he tells me as I finally open it. The paper tears easily and inside I'm surprised to find only a one-by-one-inch square photo. It falls into my palm facedown and I toss the crumpled envelope onto the desk, then flip the small piece of photo paper over.

"I went through all that shit for that?" Daniel asks, but I ignore him, too drawn to the picture.

I trace the curve of her porcelain face. I let the rough pad of my thumb run along the edge of the photo as I note her beautiful smile and the way her dark hair is lit with the sunshine in the image.

My heart pounds hard and I can't hear what Daniel's saying. I can't hear anything but the conversation I had with Tony Romano in the basement cellar months ago. The man who I've been avoiding, and the man who reached out to Marcus to deliver the message rather than tell me himself.

The dimly lit, cold and dark room was as unforgiving and unmoving as I was when he made his case and I turned him down.

Then he started bartering with things that didn't belong to him.

With women the Talverys were shipping off. His enemies. He wanted me to help him in a war against the Talverys and he was offering their property as payment. There was no way I'd ever accept.

"What it is?" Daniel presses, barely interrupting my memory.

"The gift from the Romanos." I don't know how the words come out strong as I gently place the photo onto the desk. "They want us on their side of this war they're starting."

I remember the way the heavy knife felt in my hand as I picked it up from his desk and stabbed it down onto the splintered wood in front of him. The sharp tip struck the paper in front of him.

The photo of the enemy family.

"If you give me any woman to start a war, it better be this one," I sneered in his face. I remember the stale stench of whiskey and cigars as I turned my back on him, leaving the knife where it was. With the tip of it stabbing the shoulder of the enemy's daughter. The shoulder her father's large hand was clenched around tightly.

His pride and joy, and one and only heir.

I didn't think he'd ever have the balls to take her and offer her to me.

"A gift?" Daniel questions with his brows raised and then picks up the photo.

"Yes," I answer him impatiently, quick to hide my depravity.

The photo of the one thing I asked for—Aria Talvery.

"In exchange for a war … she's mine."

The End.

Carter's story, *Depraved*, is next.
Keep reading for a sneak peek …

Depraved — coming May 15th

There are a lot of things a man like me shouldn't do.

A ruthless man with a past to hide doesn't let a soul close to him.
A coldhearted man at war doesn't risk anything for anyone.
A depraved man with a beautiful woman at his mercy … he doesn't fall for her.

She was only a bargaining chip. Now she's my property.
I *own* her.
Nothing has thrilled me more than the thought of taking her how I've always wanted to.
To break her and make that soft voice of hers whimper with a strangled moan as I ravage her.

I know better than to give in to temptation and let her distract me from everything that's at stake.

No matter how badly I crave *more* of her.
No matter how much the sordid thoughts plague me.
No matter if it's the one thing that I've always wanted more than anything else …

About the Author

Thank you so much for reading my romances. I'm just a stay at home mom and avid reader turned author and I couldn't be happier.

I hope you love my books as much as I do!

More by Willow Winters
WWW.WILLOWWINTERSWRITES.COM/BOOKS

Just One Night

CHARITY FERRELL

Prologue

WILLOW

"**What the fuck have I done?**"

I've never had a one-night stand, but I'm positive those aren't the first words you want to hear the morning after.

I twist in the warm yet unfamiliar sheets and can taste last night's whiskey in my mouth.

I lick my lips—*wrong move*—and regret it when the flavor of him hits my tongue.

Him.

The man pacing in front of me with his head tipped down while wearing only boxer briefs that show off his bulge.

I've lost count of the number of times the word *fuck* has fallen from his mouth.

I don't know what to say.

Don't know what to do.

"How the fuck could I have done this?" he continues.

My heart rams into my rib cage, just as hell-bent on escaping this situation as I am.

I'm stupid.

So damn stupid.

I drag the sheet up until it hits my chin, and he runs a hand through his thick bedhead hair, tugging at the roots the same way I did last night when he went down on me. He doesn't know I am awake and can hear him, but that doesn't make the wound any less severe.

His head rises when I jump out of bed and start scrambling for my clothes. The sheet drops from my body at the same time I frantically pull my dress over my head.

I have to get out of here.

Our eyes meet as I yank my panties up my legs. Apology and torture spill across his clenching jaw. The tears are coming, warning me to look away so that he won't see my humiliation, but I can't. I stare and silently beg him to change the outcome of this morning. The string to our stare down is cut by the sound of my name, a mere whisper falling from his loose lips.

I dart out of the bedroom, snag my purse I drunkenly threw over the arm of the couch, and rush toward the front door, not even bothering to search for my heels.

I refuse to glance back, but I hear him. No, I *feel* him behind me.

"Willow, please," he pleads to my back with a strained voice while I fight with the lock.

I slam my fist against it. *When did they start making these things so damn difficult?*

"Don't cry." He blows out a stressed breath. "Just give me a fucking minute, okay?"

Relief hits me when the lock finally cooperates, and I slam the glass door in his face at the same time he repeats my name. I nearly trip on my feet when I jump down the porch steps.

I pause when I make it to the last one.

One more.

Against my will, I turn around for one last glance.

He's staring at me in agony with the door handle gripped in his hand. For a split second, I'm stupid enough to think he'll fix this. Stupid enough to believe he'll say something, do something to make this right.

But he doesn't.

He drops the handle, spreads both palms against the glass, and bows his head.

That's my cue to get the hell out of here.

Fuck him.

Fuck whiskey.

Fuck my stupid decisions.

This is what I get for sleeping with a man mourning his dead wife.

Chapter One

WILLOW
Three Months Later

I SHOULD'VE NEVER ANSWERED HIS CALL.

"Have you been smoking crack?" I screech into the phone. "I'm telling Stella to break up with you. I can't have my best friend screwing a dude who does crack." I'm deleting him from my Contacts as soon as the call ends. I can't associate myself with someone this batshit crazy.

Hudson sucks in what sounds like an irritated breath. "No, Willow, I'm not smoking crack. It'll be the icing on the cake if you show. She misses you."

"You know I can't come back there." My throat tightens, the memory of that night crashing through my mind like a horror movie that keeps you up late at night. Hell, he does keep me up at night.

"It's not like you're fucking blacklisted. You've chosen not to come back. I emailed you your flight information. See you in a few days."

The line goes dead.

Asswad.

I grip my phone, ready to call him back and tell him to shove that ticket up his ass, but I can't.

I can't because he's proposing to my boss/best friend at her surprise birthday party. Stella deserves this—deserves love, happiness, and her best friend in attendance for one of the most important nights of her life. So, I'll put my hate of the small town aside and risk seeing him—the jackass whose bed I fled from after our very drunken and very regrettable one-night stand.

He'll be in attendance, given it's his brother doing the proposing, which means I have to put my big-girl panties on, keep them on, and refrain from smashing a wine glass over his head.

All while keeping the biggest secret of my life.

While staying sober.

This will be interesting.

Some people believe in soul mates.

I believe in champagne and cupcakes.

The problem tonight is that I can only binge on one of the above, and it's not the one I prefer.

I get a whiff of Stella's signature rose perfume before she cages me in for a hug. I squeeze her tight, a silent sorry that I've been a sucky friend, and we're both nearly gasping for breath by the time we release each other.

Damn, I've missed my best friend and how I could always confide in her without judgment. That's changed now. My secret will destroy her relationship.

"I can't believe you came," she cries out with a red-lipped smile. "How did Hudson convince you? Buy you a mini pony? Promise to kick Dallas in the balls?"

I laugh. "Two horses actually. And I didn't consider the second option, so thanks for the idea. I'll add it to my list of demands next time."

I snag her manicured hand to admire the glistening princess cut diamond sitting beautifully on her finger. It's perfection and so Stella—nothing too exuberant or obnoxious but still flashy.

"I have to give it to the corn-fed, small-town boy," I go on. "He did a kick-ass job in the ring department."

She stares down at her finger, her smile now nearly taking over her entire face. "He did, didn't he?"

Hudson threw her a great party. He invited the few family members she talks to, his family, and everyone on the cast and crew of her show. There's food galore, confetti sprinkled all over the white-tableclothed tables, and a *Happy Birthday* banner hangs in front of the empty DJ booth.

Stella is not only my boss, but also childhood star turned Hollywood's princess. I'm her assistant. That's how I met Mr. Wrong One-Night Stand. We worked together for years until he quit to move back home, and Hudson took his job.

Hudson couldn't give Stella mansions or fancy cars, but he did shower her with enough love and happiness to make up for it. She moved from LA to Blue Beech, Iowa, after convincing a producer to shoot her new show here. I tried to resign, but she wasn't having it and agreed to let me do all my work from my apartment in LA.

Her hands rest on her hips over the black designer dress. "Are you staying with us tonight? I just put a new smart TV in the guest room, and we know how much you like your classic movies."

I grimace. "That's a giant *hell no*. The last thing you need around on the night of your engagement is Willow, the giant contraceptive. I'm crashing at Lauren's."

Lauren is Hudson's and Mr. Wrong's sister.

She groans. "Fine, I'll settle for that because you showed up. That's a big deal, and you did it for me."

I crack a smile. "I also came for the cake." That comment results in her pushing my shoulder.

Her face turns serious. "Have you seen him?"

The mention of him gives me a nasty taste in my mouth. "Who?" She crosses her arms at my response, and I scoff, my heart racing, "Oh, you mean the bed evacuator? Nope."

That's a lie. He was on my radar as soon as I walked in—for precautionary reasons, of course. I saw his back first, the one I assaulted so much, I ruined my manicure, and worry snaked through me. I cowardly fled the scene when he spun around and saw me.

"Hopefully, he's ducking underneath tables, so we don't have to face each other," I say.

She smirks. "We both know Dallas is not a man who ducks underneath tables."

"Looks like I'd better start then."

"Don't you think it'd be a good idea if you talked? Cleared the air?"

"I need to talk to him like I need anal bleaching. Both of them would be a pain in the ass and are never happening."

She laughs, snagging a bubbly glass of champagne from a waiter walking by, and thrusts it toward me. "Here's some liquid courage. Just don't drink too much that you land in his bed again."

I swat the drink away. "Not happening, and no, thank you."

She stills and studies me. "Since when do you turn down champagne? Alcohol is always mandatory in these situations."

"I'm trying out a new diet."

"You might want to wipe the icing off the side of your mouth if you want to keep up with that lie."

I scrub away the remnants of my sugar binge and lick my finger. Thou shall not waste buttercream frosting. "It's this new craze diet where sugar is the main source of nutrition and alcohol is bad. *Very bad.* It's called the good decision-making diet." I start fake picking lint from my dress, so she doesn't see the untruth in my eyes. The black dress is ugly and shapeless, and I bought it specifically for tonight to hide my body and secrets.

"So, you're not drinking because he's here?"

Shit. That would've been a more believable excuse than a damn diet. I nod, feeling bad for lying to her, but I can't break the news here. It'd ruin her night.

"Does that mean, the chances of letting him rip off your panties for round two is likely?" She sets the glass down on the table behind her and bounces in her heels, like me banging Dallas again would cure world hunger.

"Calm down, matchmaker. Studies show that alcohol gives you shifty eyes." I point to my hair. "Shifty eyes don't look good on redheads."

"Bullshit. You can't deny you had a connection. Neither one of you is the casual banging type. Talk. Maybe there's a spark that'll lead to a firework."

More like a wildfire breakout.

"The only *connection* we have is that he stuck his penis inside me once. That's it. Nothing more. Now, it's time to move on."

She pushes my shoulder when I go back to my fake lint-picking. "Okay, what the hell is going on with you?"

"Nothing," I blurt out, shifting my neck from side to side like I'm sore. "Jet lag is a bitch."

"Liar."

I wave off her accusation. "It's your engagement party. Tonight is all about you."

"If that's the case, then I want answers."

I chew on the edge of my lip while her dark eyes study me. I get the opportunity to look away when music starts to blare through the room. I glance at the DJ booth and then to the makeshift dance floor in front of it and almost gag at his first song choice.

Boyz II Men? Really, dude?

Looks like we're getting served cheese with these cupcakes.

The sight of Hudson hurrying over to us relieves me. He wraps his arms around Stella from behind and squeezes her hips, his mouth going straight to her ear.

"Dance with me," he attempts to whisper, although I'm sure everyone in the state heard him.

Stella melts at his touch, like it's the first time they've ever had physical contact, and my heart hurts. This is what real love is. This is something I'll never have. She groans, and I know my best friend well enough to know she's going to turn him down to continue our conversation.

"Go dance with your *fiancé*," I insist. "We'll talk later."

A smile accompanies her next groan. "*Fine,* but you're not leaving this town until you spill the tea."

"I wouldn't imagine it any other way."

Hudson kisses her cheek, snags her hand in his, and sweeps her toward the dance floor. The crowd cheers, and people jump up from their seats to join them.

I release a deep breath, happy I dodged that conversation, and decide to reward myself with another cupcake. I grab a chocolate one with strawberry icing and huddle myself into a corner at the farthest end of the room. Shame sinks through me when I do another once-over of the party to search for the man who screwed me in more ways than one.

One more glance. That's it.

One more view of the man who gave me the best night of my life and the worst morning.

My throat tightens when I spot him sitting at a crowded table in the middle of the room with the entire Barnes family. His daughter, Maven, has his full attention as she grins wildly and dramatically throws her hands up in the air while telling him a story. His head tilts back in laughter, causing my knees to weaken. That's the smile I longed for that morning.

God, he looks sexy.

More delicious than these cupcakes.

Too bad he isn't as sweet.

Dallas Barnes is tall, dark, and handsome but also scarred, rough, and broken down by burdens. He's the man of your dreams who has been through hell and hasn't risen above it yet.

Tingles sweep up my neck as flashes of our night together come crashing through me harder than this sugar rush. I drink him in like the glass of champagne I can't have while he runs his strong hand over the stubble of his dominant jaw. The same hand that ignited nerves in my body I never knew existed. His hair, the same color as the whiskey we threw back, is freshly cut on the sides and grown out on top.

I rub at the sudden ache in my neck while begging my mind to forget, to stop feeling *something* every time I see him. Hell, every time I think about him. It's always hate laced with desire.

We were two lonely and heartbroken souls who connected over a night of drinking our pains away. When the alcohol proved not to be potent enough to heal, we tried to fuck it away.

Fucking and feelings do not go together like macaroni and cheese.

I used him. He used me. I thought I was okay with that until reality smacked me in the face when he kissed me for the first time. That was the moment I turned greedy and wanted more than just a quick fuck. The problem is, he didn't.

As if he senses me watching him, his deep-set charcoal eyes move in my direction, and my back stiffens. I hold in a breath when he scoots out his chair, gives Maven a quick peck on the top of her head, and walks toward me.

Oh, shit.

Shit. Shit. Shit.

The first few buttons are undone on his chambray shirt, exposing the top of his broad chest, and the sleeves are tight around his muscular arms. He's not fit from spending seven days a week at the gym. No, he's naturally buff, and the manual labor he does now only amplifies it.

Was driving me crazy his goal tonight? No doubt Hudson told him I'd be here.

I move my gaze from one side of the room to the other, desperately searching for the nearest exit, as he gets closer. I'm his chosen target. I bite my lip at the realization that I'll have to walk past him to leave. The determination on his face assures me that I'm not going anywhere until he gets what he wants.

I shove the remainder of the cupcake in my mouth and silently give myself a pep talk to make it through this conversation without plowing my heel into his balls. I stupidly run my hands over my dress after swallowing down the last bite and then cringe at the pink frosting smear.

Real smooth.

So much for appearing cool and collected.

This hot-mess look won't make him regret kicking you out of his bed.

I tense when he reaches me, and he shoves his hands into the pockets of his jeans, staring at me with affliction. The thread around his shirt buttons stretches when he leans back on his heels and waits for my response.

"Willow." He releases my name like an announcement, and the familiar scent of him drifts up my nostrils, a mix of regret and whiskey with small notes of cedar.

It's comforting at first since I've always felt a sense of security when he is around, but then I remember what he did.

I settle my hand against the wall to keep me from falling on my ass. "Dallas," I reply with a sneer. "Fancy seeing you here."

"It's my brother's engagement."

My mouth slams shut, and my gaze drops to the floor at my stupidity. "Oh, yeah … right."

Silence passes.

I don't look at him when I lift my head back up. Instead, I avert my attention to the people dancing, laughing, and having a good time in the room, wishing it were me.

Hell, three months ago, that would've been me. I cast a glance to his mom and dad. *Do they know what we did? That he screwed my brains out one night?*

He clears his throat to gain my attention again. I give in and focus on his broad-jawed face. He's staring at me in gentleness, almost pity, which surprises me.

"How long are you in town for?" he asks.

"Two days." My initial plan was to fly in and out within the same day, but Hudson begged me to stay longer for Stella.

"Get breakfast with me in the morning."

His question startles me. The breakfast offer is a little too late. That should've happened on our morning after.

"I'm not much of a breakfast person."

He scratches his cheek. "Grab coffee?"

"I don't drink coffee." This is the truth. Never been a coffee fan. Never will be.

"What the hell do you do in the morning then?"

"Sleep." *Get sick. Roll around in my sheets, wishing I could turn back time.*

He pulls his free hand from his pocket and slides closer into my space.

Way too close.

His steadfast eyes meet mine. "*Please.* I want to make shit right. My brother is marrying your best friend. I'm the best man. You'll no doubt be the maid of honor. We need to be civil and stop dancing around each other if we don't want everyone to know something happened between us."

There's the answer I was looking for. I wince, unsure if he's more worried about our tension ruining the wedding or that people will find out about our one-night stand.

I wave my hand through the air, careful not to hit him in the face. "Consider that night forgotten. I already have."

"Don't bullshit me. We've known each other long enough for you to be honest with me."

I hold up my hand in anger, the need to spew out something terrible snapping at me. I want to strike him with pain that consumes him like he did me. "In case you've forgotten, *you* kicked me out of your bed. What do you want from me? A friendly hug? A casual conversation with fake smiles? Not going to happen, so quit wasting both of our time. You stay out of my way. I'll stay out of yours. Agreed?"

"I didn't kick you out of my bed," he hisses. "You ran out my front door faster than a speeding bullet."

I forget we're not alone and edge closer until my chest hits his. "You jumped out of bed like *you* were dodging a speeding bullet." I grit my teeth to gain control of myself. "That was before you said that what we did was a mistake, *over and over again*, like your lips were a broken record."

His face burns like I didn't just hit him with the verbal truth, but also a physical one. He lets out a hard sigh, giving me a small sampling of the whiskey and frosting lingering on his lips. Tightness forms in my throat, and I clutch at my stomach. Just like his cologne preference, I'm sure the taste of him hasn't changed.

"I'm sorry. I overreacted," he replies. "I tried calling to apologize, but you wouldn't take my calls."

"Nor will I ever."

"Fuck, Willow, how many times do I have to say this until you forgive me? I was in a dark place and was out of line." His voice lowers even more, and I barely make out his next words. "I didn't regret that it was *you* in my bed. I was pissed at myself for even letting it happen, for putting you in that situation."

His answer doesn't make me feel any better.

I slide against the wall to move away from him. "It's done. I'm over it."

"Twenty minutes and a pastry," he pleads. "Give me that, and I promise I'll never bring it up again."

I take a deep breath. This is Dallas Barnes. A man I worked alongside for five years. A man whose job was to protect Stella and me. Tragedy changes a man. Loss changes a man. This isn't the Dallas I knew. This is a new man, a man who lost himself when he lost his wife.

I sink my teeth into the inside of my cheek. "I'm sorry, but I can't. I'll be civil for Stella's sake, but I won't spend a minute longer with you than I have to." This is for the best. I want him to hate me. I want him to want nothing to do with me in case he ever finds out what I'm keeping from him.

The anger in my words shocks him, and he runs his hand over his face.

"Daddy!"

He stumbles back at the sound of his daughter's voice. She's barreling our way, and her brown pigtails soar through the air. She runs right into his leg with a *humph* and giggles when he catches her.

"Come dance with me!"

Affection fills his face when he peeks down at her with a smile and twirls a pigtail around his finger. "Give me a second, sweetie. I'm talking with Willow, and then I'm all yours."

"But this is my favorite song ever." She pouts.

I force a laugh, seeing my perfect escape plan. Dancing seems to be my savior tonight. "You can't deny a dance with a girl that adorable," I say, shooing them away. "Go. I need to make a call anyway."

Maven jumps up and down, clapping her hands in excitement, and Dallas stares at me with concern before leaning forward.

"I never had any intention to hurt you," he whispers.

But you did, I mouth back.

Damn, did he.

"Daddy!" Maven whines. "The song is going to be over!"

He gives me a nod before walking away.

I don't let the tears fall until I see his back.

The fuck?

I'm not this overly sensitive chick.

These hormones are messing with my hard-ass persona.

I brush them away, sniffling, and dash toward the exit. I need to get out of here and away from these people. I need silence, a moment to sulk about how I made a stupid decision for the millionth time.

I'm almost out the door when I nearly trip on my feet. My arm is grabbed, and I'm pulled down a dimly lit hallway. I attempt to swat the connection away, but it doesn't work, and I'm not released until we land in a small utility room.

"What in the flying fuck is going on with you?" Stella demands, crossing her arms. "And don't you dare try to feed me some new diet bullshit. Diets don't make you cry."

"Nothing," I stutter out, wiping my warm cheeks in an attempt to rid myself of the evidence.

"Bullshit." She pauses, waiting for me to let out my secret, but I stand my ground. "I'll keep us in here all night." She narrows her smoky eyes my way. "Do you want to be blamed for keeping a girl away from her engagement party?"

Guilt trips. Stella excels at giving them.

"I'll tell you later. I promise."

She shrugs, pops a squat on the carpeted floor, and stretches out her legs.

I let out a dramatic breath. "*Fine.* But you have to promise, it won't leave this room."

"All of your secrets are safe with me. Always have been."

"This is bigger than hacking into Brett's phone or when I pissed myself after we drank too many Skinnygirl margaritas."

"You could've killed Brett, and I wouldn't blab."

"Promise me."

"Jesus, Willow, *did* you kill the bastard?"

My heart thunders in my chest. I'm on the verge of passing out, so I sit down across from her. I can't take these words back. The secret won't be mine any longer, and she'll be thrown into a difficult position.

"Someone you care about will get hurt if I tell you."

Her voice fills with worry as she hunches forward. "Is it about Hudson?" She relaxes when I shake my head. "Then, what is it?"

"I'm pregnant." The words feel heavy when they fall from my lips for the first time.

She silently stares at me, stunned at my response, and then her face brightens with fake excitement. "That's great! Congratulations." She's won an Emmy, but even she can't fake enthusiasm about this. "I didn't know you were back with Brett."

Brett. My asshole of an ex who's out on bail and awaiting trial after driving drunk and hitting a family of four.

"We're not. I haven't seen him since we broke up."

"Then, who's the father?"

I wait for her to come up with the answer, so I don't have to give it to her.

Her mouth drops open, a gasp escaping her. "Holy shit. Dallas is the father?"

"Yep, and I don't know what to do."

"I take it, you haven't shared the news with him?"

"Nope."

Her gaze lands on me in expectation. "But you're going to before you leave, right?"

"Not exactly. I was, uh … thinking about, say, never?"

"What?" she screeches. "Have you lost your mind?"

"It's for the best."

"You can't do that." She leans forward to take my hand in hers. "Don't see this as me being unsupportive, but that's fucked up. And that's coming from a girl who faked a relationship with a douche bag for months."

"It's for the best. I'm going to raise this baby on my own."

"Why?" She shakes her head, rolls her eyes, and sighs at the same time. "And I suppose you want me to keep quiet?"

My voice cracks. "Yes. *Please*."

"If I do what you're asking, I'll be hurting Dallas. I'll be hurting the man I love. It'll ruin my relationship with everyone in their family if they ever find out." Her eyes start to water.

This is the first time I've ever doubted my trust in her.

"What they don't know won't hurt them. If the truth does come out, I'll tell them you had no idea."

Stella turns around at the same time my attention goes to the door when it opens. Hudson is staring at us with a bloodthirsty expression on his face.

"Excuse me for interrupting," he huffs out. "I was searching for my bride-to-be."

Did he hear our conversation? The look on his face confirms he heard *something*, but how much?

"I wasn't eavesdropping ... at least, not at first," he goes on. "Some words of advice: when you have a conversation about fucking someone's life up, you might want to lower your voices."

My heart thuds in my chest. "Hudson, please," I beg. "Please don't tell him."

He moves into the room, closing the door behind himself, and thrusts his finger my way. "Don't you fucking dare ask me to keep this from my brother." His piercing stare goes to Stella. "And please tell me you weren't going to agree to it."

Stella's eyes swell as she throws her arms out toward me. "She's my best friend!"

"And he's your soon-to-be brother-in-law who deserves to know!" he yells. "That'll be my niece or nephew. Did you even wonder how keeping this to yourself would hurt me and my family?"

Talk about a fucking loud mouth.

"Keep your voice down," I hiss in warning.

His face hardens, almost appearing sinister, and sweat builds along his forehead. "I swear on everything that I will hate you if you do this. You don't pull shit like this on a man, especially one who is as good of a father as Dallas. He's not some piece-of-shit, deadbeat dad."

I squeeze my eyes shut in an attempt to not only stop the tears, but to also block out the view of Hudson's disgust. "It has nothing to do with him. It's what's best for me."

"Bullshit. It's you being selfish."

"Hudson," Stella snaps. "Enough!" She pulls herself up from the floor and helps me to my feet. She doesn't release my hand until I'm stable. "What are you so afraid of, Willow? What's the worst that could happen?"

Fear does the Macarena in my stomach. I can't tell them the truth. "Everything," I release. "He's a grieving widower who regrets touching me."

Stella's face softens. "This secret will add to his hurt when he finds out later."

"That's *if* he finds out." I peek over at Hudson, the anger still manifested everywhere on his body.

He locks eyes with me and shakes his head. "Un-fucking-believable. You fucking do this to him, Willow, and I will never speak to you again." His glare goes to Stella. "Good memories of our engagement night, huh?" He turns his back on us and slams his hand against the wall before opening the door and storming out.

"He's going to tell him, isn't he?" I ask.

"I'm sorry," Stella replies. "I shouldn't have pushed you, but you have to tell Dallas before Hudson does. Maybe this baby will bring some joy into his darkness."

"I'll tell him. Just give me a few days, okay?"

She nods. "As much time as you need. I can't say the same for Hudson though. You know how close they are."

"Fuck!" I scream, grabbing the ends of my hair and pulling it.

"That's what put you in this situation." She smiles when I flip her off.

"I need another fucking cupcake."

Chapter Two

DALLAS

I open the fridge with more force than necessary and snag a beer. My brain pounds when I pop the cap off, take a long yet unsatisfying drink, and set it aside for something stronger.

Nothing will be potent enough for me tonight.

But that won't stop me from trying.

Maven is at my parents', so I have no responsibilities tonight.

To say surviving the party was a challenge is an understatement. I wasn't sure I'd be able to make it through and good thing I didn't have to do it sober. I should be glad my brother found happiness, but I'm an asshole living in a dark hole, avoiding the sunlight. I'm only happy I managed not to stand up and object to him asking Stella to marry him.

Marriage isn't the answer, I wanted to scream out. *Don't let yourself get wrapped up in someone so much, you don't know who you are when they're gone.*

I pat myself on the back for keeping my mouth shut. The glass bottle feels chilly when it grazes the bare skin of my neck.

Then, I saw Willow. Hudson gave me a heads-up that she was coming, and even if I had tried to argue about it, nothing would've changed. She's Stella's best friend … and the only other woman I've slept with since Lucy died. Hell, the only woman I've slept with other than Lucy.

I decided I was going to talk to Willow and make things right between us. The problem was, I wasn't expecting my chest to ache at the sight of her walking in … or my hands to grow sweaty as I wondered how her skin felt underneath that black dress.

Is it still as soft as it was that night?

Does she still smell like strawberries?

Taste as sweet?

My plan to make shit right went out the window. All I thought about was asking her to come home with me and let me make up for my asshole behavior. I haven't touched anyone in months, haven't had the desire to, but seeing Willow made my heart race and my dick stir. Hell, it was a full-time job stopping myself from staring at her every three seconds.

I asked her to breakfast, and she looked at me like I was scum beneath her shoes. I had done a shitty thing, but I've tried to man up to it on more than one occasion, and she keeps shooting me down. So, I'm still a lonely asshole who only gets turned on at the thought of his dead wife and a woman who hates him.

I reach up to the tallest cabinet above the fridge and pull out the bottle of Jameson, my good friend who doesn't judge me when we hang out too much. I owe this motherfucker thousands of dollars in therapy. The liquid burns but feels almost euphoric, seeping down my throat.

Lately, all I've done is pretend—pretend that I'm okay in front of my family. I put on a brave face and make it through the day for my daughter … and then I go to bed, wanting nothing more than to rip myself out of my skin.

I flinch when I hear my front door slam and take the bottle with me to investigate. I stumble back at the sight of the last person I expected to show up at my door tonight.

"Yikes, what the hell are you doing here?" I ask. "Stella decide to leave your ass already?"

Hudson snatches the bottle from my hand with a snarl. "We need to talk."

I put my hands in the air. "If it's about me cornering Willow, I only did it, so we'd be civil during your wedding festivities."

He lifts the bottle to his lips and takes a sip. "I, uh …" He takes another. "I have a feeling the two of you are going to have to learn to be civil long after my wedding."

His response doesn't make sense, but I'm blaming it on the alcohol. "I won't be an asshole again, okay? I tried to apologize, but the chick wasn't having it." Not that I blame her. I pulled the biggest dick move out of all dick moves … because all I was thinking with was my dick.

"Willow is pregnant." He grinds the words out, the air in the living room shifting to something I don't recognize.

I blankly stare at him. "Okay?" My heart sinks that she's found someone else. No wonder she wanted nothing to do with me. She's found a man who isn't a broken asshole. Good for her. I would've only ruined her.

"Willow. Is. Pregnant," he stresses.

I'm not catching his drift. What does he want me to do? Throw her a baby shower? "I'll be sure to buy her a gift."

The coffee table shakes when he pounds his fist against it. "Willow is pregnant with your goddamn baby, you fucking dumbass. I thought you'd be smart enough to put two and two together."

Good thing he grabbed the bottle from me. This would've been the moment it crashed on to my hardwood floor. "You're fucking with me."

His straight face answers my question. He can't give a DNA test with his eyes, but I believe him.

"Why would you assume it's mine? We slept together once."

"I overheard her telling Stella."

I digest his news and swallow a few times before grabbing my keys. A picture cracks when I throw them across the room as I realize I'm in no condition to drive.

"I need a ride."

"The fuck you do. In case you forgot, I got engaged tonight. I've already missed a few good hours because I couldn't think of pussy when I knew I was keeping this from you."

"How very noble of you," I mutter, wincing when he slaps the back of my head. "Stella's vagina doesn't have a curfew. Take me to Lauren's."

"Hell no. Stella will bite my dick off the next time I ask for a blow job."

"Take me to Lauren's, or I'll walk."

"Get in my fucking truck."

Chapter Three

WILLOW

Bang! Bang! Bang!
I'm having a nightmare where a psychopath is pounding on the door of Lauren's apartment. I'll be murdered, and my skin will be worn as a coat. I don't realize I'm awake until I hear the familiar, masculine voice.

"Willow!" he screams on the other side of the door.

Bang! Bang!

"I know you're in there! Open up!"

My heart races, and I slap my hand over my mouth, not sure if it's because I don't want to make a peep or I'm close to puking.

"Lauren!"

Bang! Bang!

"One of you had better open this door before I break it down!"

Oh, shit.

Shitty-shit-shit!

I should've known Hudson couldn't keep his fat mouth shut. He probably went and tattled as soon as he got the chance.

I rub my eyes when the lights turn on. Lauren comes rushing into the living room, tying a purple robe around her waist in frustration.

"I hope blood doesn't make you queasy," she bites out, stomping her feet.

I raise a brow.

"Because I'm about to castrate my brother."

If only she had done that sooner.

I pull myself into a sitting position, resting my back on the couch, and shrug like the shitshow about to happen isn't my fault.

Curse words fly out of her mouth with every step she takes while he continues his tantrum on the other side of the door.

"Jesus, fuck, Dallas!" she yells, swinging the door open. "You'd better be getting a bedroom ready at your place for when I get evicted."

He bursts into the living room without paying her a glance. His sharp eyes cut straight to me, demanding answers, and his pain-stricken face confirms what I was afraid of. He's as terrified as I am.

"Is it true?" he blurts out.

Lauren slams the door and storms into the living room. "Is what true?"

His attention doesn't leave my face. "Are you pregnant?"

I have no words. I'm frozen in place—unable to move, unable to talk, unsure of where to go with this.

"I'm confused as to why that's any of your business and why you felt the need to show up here like someone is about to blow the place up," Lauren replies for me.

He doesn't answer her. His attention stays fixed on me, as if Lauren weren't even in the room.

"Answer me," he demands.

I clear my throat, about to cave in and tell him but chicken out and nod instead.

The anguish on his face amplifies. "Is it mine?"

This is the moment.

This is where I have to decide not only my future, but also my baby's.

"Wait … what?" Lauren screeches.

Chapter Four

DALLAS

My head spins like I've been beating it against a wall all day. Not one rational thought has climbed through my brain since Hudson broke the news. He'd been thrown into a tough spot. He either had to betray the woman he loved or his blood.

He chose me. He chose the truth. Instead of fucking his fiancée senseless the night of his engagement, he came over and spilled her best friend's secret. I would've never forgiven him had he kept it from me. Pure ice sinks through my veins as I just think about it.

Lauren is behind me, firing off question after question, but my attention is pinned on Willow. Her green eyes, filled with conflict and scorn, narrow my way.

I take a calming breath as an attempt to help us both relax. "Is the baby mine?" I ask again.

All eye contact shatters when her gaze drops to her lap, and she fidgets with her hands. Sure fucking sign of lying. I stupidly pull out the pregnancy test I forced Hudson to buy at the pharmacy before coming here from my pocket. I can't decipher if the gasp coming from her is from surprise or anger.

The snarl of her upper lip answers my uncertainty.

"You brought a freaking pregnancy test?" she shrieks. "Have you lost your fucking mind?"

A reaction. Finally, I get *something* from her.

Hudson warned me she'd go Muhammad Ali on my ass when she saw the test, but as I mentioned before, my brain isn't functioning at its finest.

I stumble forward when Lauren pushes my back to gain my attention.

She signals between Willow and me. "Why would you assume the baby is yours if she's pregnant?" Her hand flies to her mouth. "Holy mother of God, you two are banging?"

"No!" Willow yells, as if the thought horrifies her.

That puts a damper on a man's ego.

I grit my teeth. This isn't a conversation I want to conduct in front of my baby sister. "Lauren, some privacy, please."

She scrunches up her nose. "In case you've failed to notice, this is my apartment. Where do you expect me to go at three in the morning?"

"Your bedroom."

She rolls her eyes. "Whatever. You suck."

"And be sure to put on earplugs," I call out to her as she heads down the hallway.

She twists around on her heels with a smirk. "And miss this conversation?"

I give her a look, one that tells her I'm not fucking around, but that only grants me another eye roll. Her bedroom door slams shut, and I know she's not going for her earplugs.

The air is heavy.

I'm staring at Willow.

She's staring at me.

A scarlet flush rides up her high cheekbones.

I've never had a staring contest last so long.

Willow has the face of an angel with light freckles scattered along her nose and cheeks.

Her personality-matching fire-red hair is pulled back into a ponytail with loose strands flying in every direction. I've never had one negative thought about her until tonight. She has a huge heart and bends over backward to help others, often putting them before herself. She smiles as if she's never been hurt, but I know she has from the many times I saw her dip out of rooms with tears in her eyes after an argument with her ex-boyfriend. She acts hard but is a softie.

She's also cautious with letting people in. This is going to be a challenge.

"Put that pregnancy test away before I shove it up your ass." Her cold tone startles me.

It takes me a few attempts before I manage to push it back into my pocket. She flinches when I move in closer and drop to my knees in front of her. Pain coats my throat as I clear it.

"If you're pregnant," I say, blowing out a breath. It takes me a second to continue. "If you're pregnant and I'm the father, we need to come up with a plan."

There.

That's me stepping up and being a man even though I want nothing more than to throw myself out the window. No matter how broken I am, no matter what hell I'm going through, I could never turn my back on my child.

Willow shakes her head, swatting her hand through the air, as if dismissing what I said. "Dallas, don't worry about this, okay? You're going through a lot. I can do this on my own."

"If there's one certainty I have for you, it's that, that's not fucking happening, do you hear me?"

She sighs, rubbing her forehead. "*Fuck.*" An annoyed laugh leaves her full pink lips. "You storm over here at the ass crack of dawn after one of the most exhausting days of my life and demand I make a plan?" She snorts. "That's not what's happening right now, *do you hear me?*" She lies back down on the couch and pulls the blanket up her body. "I'm going to sleep, and you can go back to doing whatever it is you were doing … as long as it's not drunkenly waking up the entire building while waving pregnancy tests through the air."

Fuck. She has a point.

Lauren interrupts us by walking back into the living room and holds both hands in the air. "Don't get pissed at me, but, Willow, take my bed. I can't have a pregnant chick crashing on my couch."

A slight smile hits Willow's lips. "I appreciate the offer, but I'll be fine." The smile collapses when her attention goes to me. "As long as it's quiet."

That's Willow—accommodating everyone else and always putting herself last in line.

"You sure?" Lauren asks, and Willow nods. "Okay, let me know if you change your mind or need anything." She tells us good night and goes back to her bedroom.

"What are you doing?" Willow asks when I grab a blanket and pillow from a closet.

I throw them on the floor next to the couch. "You're exhausted. I'm exhausted. Let's get some rest and talk in the morning."

"You have a bed *at your home*. Go sleep in it."

I squat down and fluff the pillow. "I'm crashing here. End of discussion. I can't risk you sneaking out on me in the middle of the night and flying thousands of miles away before talking. We'll be having a conversation about this tomorrow."

She sends me one last glare before shifting on her side and giving me a view of her back. I switch off the light and make myself as comfortable as I can, resting my arms behind my head and staring at the ceiling.

A baby.

A baby with another woman.

I fight every day to hold Maven and myself together. How am I going to do this?

It'll be a struggle, but I'll figure it out.

I made Lucy a promise to be a good man, and I plan on keeping it.

Chapter Five

DALLAS
The Past
Three Months Ago

The good people of Blue Beech visit the Down Home Pub for three reasons:
#1: To forget.
#2: To feel alive.
#3: A live band is playing, and they don't have shit else to do.
I'm number one.

It's a hole in the wall, the only bar in the county, and it has been here longer than I've been alive. It's not fancy, and it doesn't carry top-shelf shit, but I feel more comfortable here than any upscale club in LA.

I've been a regular since my twenty-first birthday, but in the past ten months, I've become almost a part-time resident the two days a week I don't have Maven. My parents demand they get plenty of time with their only grandchild. I tend to come during the week when the people who don't like conversation are here.

It's a full house tonight, which is why I didn't want to come. I hate crowds. Hate the flashes of pity men give me after sucking down another shot of cheap whiskey. Hate the women who take turns coming over with the belief that food and attention will heal me.

A fucking casserole isn't going to restore this empty soul of mine.

I walked into the bar to find Lauren and Willow sitting at a table in the back. Lauren ordered a round for everyone and did her best to get us to get up and socialize, but neither one of us was having it. Willow eventually convinced her to bail on us and have fun on the dance floor.

Thank fuck.

My sister goes overboard when she tries to pep me up and give me a good time.

How Willow ended up here is a mystery to me. Pubs aren't her thing. She sips champagne, does yoga, eats chocolate with fancy-ass names. She flew in for Stella's crew party, so the only reason I can come up with is, she's trying to stay away from Stella and Hudson's lovefest.

I lean back in my chair, balancing the neck of my beer bottle between two fingers, and stare at her as she gives the bar a once-over. The pendant light above us shines over her head like a halo when she starts peeling paint off the table. Her weariness surprises me. I've always thought of her as a chameleon—someone who adapts to any situation she's thrown into.

I set my beer bottle down and wipe my sweaty palms against my jeans. "What's Tinder?" *Really? This is what I say to break the ice? It's all I could think of.*

My question surprises her, and she lifts her gaze to me. "Tinder?" She scrunches up her face like she didn't hear me correctly.

"Yeah, what is it? Lauren has been up my ass all week, insisting I join it."

She laughs, a smile cracking at the side of her lips. "Really? You've never heard of Tinder?"

"Trust me, I wouldn't be sitting here, feeling like an idiot, if I had." I grab my beer and take a long draw, finishing it off. "Looks like I'm the only one lost on the Tinder subject."

"It's a dating app." She pauses. "Let me correct myself. It's a booty-call app. Swipe right; swipe left. Let's bang; let's not."

"A booty-call app." I snort. "It's sad when your sister cares more about you getting laid than you do."

"I seem to have the same problem with everyone *but me* worrying about my vagina getting the business." She laughs again, the sound of it putting me at an unfamiliar ease—something I haven't felt in a long time.

I want to hear that laugh again. A woman this beautiful doesn't deserve to be sitting in the back of a run-down pub with sadness in her eyes.

"Hudson told me about the bullshit your boyfriend pulled," I say.

Her ruby-red lips frown, and she runs a nervous hand down her dress. I pinch the bridge of my nose, regretting my words. Bringing up her douche-bag ex isn't going to get me another laugh.

"Hudson has a big mouth," she mutters. "And *ex*-boyfriend."

"Sorry 'bout that. Hudson told me what your *ex* did."

"What he did was fucked up and the final straw of our relationship."

"Did the kid die?" I pause, the question hitting too close to home. I have a daughter. That could've been Maven. I can't imagine what those parents are going through.

"Fortunately, no. Unfortunately, he has severe brain damage and will never be the same."

Fucking jackass. Shows how one stupid decision can impact the lives of others. I only met her ex a handful of times, but I instantly knew he'd never be a friend of mine.

"And him?"

"He's out on bail, and his trial has been postponed until he completes physical therapy."

"You shitting me?"

She shakes her head. "The perks of being the son of the town mayor."

"I'm sorry," I whisper.

"It makes me sick that I loved someone who did something that bad."

She snatches the drink Lauren ordered her and downs it. My lips slightly turn up when her face twists into something that resembles disgust.

She sticks out her tongue and points to the glass, like it's poison. "Is your sister trying to kill me? What is this shit?"

"Jameson," I answer, feeling my lips tilt up again—something they haven't done with anyone other than Maven.

She stares at me, blinking.

"Whiskey."

She pushes the glass up the table with both hands. "Well then, that's my first and last time drinking whiskey. I'm more of a wine-slash-champagne-slash-give-me-something-fruity kind of girl."

"Whiskey is stronger on the heart than champagne. You can't go wrong with trying to forget with whiskey. I promise you that."

"In that case, order me another." She pauses to wag her finger at me. "Wait, if it's such a heart-mender, why aren't you drinking it?"

I shrug. "I planned on being good tonight with beer."

She holds her empty glass up. "I planned on champagne. If I'm drinking it, so are you."

I smile for what feels like the first time in months and hold my hand up to tell the bartender, Maliki, we need another round.

"This'd better work," she says when Maliki drops off our drinks. She knocks the whiskey down like a pro, inhales a deep breath, and squints her eyes when it's gone. "Shit, that one was even stronger."

"It'll help. I promise." I tap the table before draining mine. It burns as it goes down.

"Do you miss her?" she asks out of nowhere, as if the question had been on the tip of her tongue all night.

My jaw flexes. I'm surprised at her question. "Every fucking second of the day." My honesty shocks me. I've shut down every conversation my family has tried to have with me about Lucy. "Do you miss him?"

"Every fucking second of the day, and I hate myself for it. I can't stop missing the parts of him that weren't terrible."

Maliki, like he can read my mind, brings us another round. She takes another long drink, and I still in my chair, all of my attention on her while I wait for her to go on.

She scoffs, "This is *not* a conversation I thought I'd be having tonight. No one brings him up, for fear I'll want him back if they mention his name."

I nod, a cloud of grief passing over me. I want to be mad that she's complaining about losing someone she can take back at any second because I don't have that option. I'd be irate, pissed, and ready to spit out fire if anyone else had said that to me.

But not with Willow.

I grip my glass and watch her take another sip of her drink. The strap of her green dress hangs off her shoulder, giving me a glimpse of the light freckles sprinkled along her pale skin. I've never looked at her, *really seen her*, until tonight. Her red hair is pulled into two tight buns at the top of her head, a few spirals of perfect curls falling out of them.

"How about we make a toast?" she asks.

I hold up my glass. "To what are we toasting?"

"To getting wasted. To going numb. To forgetting."

I like the way she thinks. "To drinking the pain away." I tap my glass against hers. "Let's drown our sorrows."

We drink our pain away. We forget our troubles. Hell, we forget everything and everyone around us.

My brain isn't functioning when I ask my next question. It would've never happened if I were sober.

"So, have you tried it out? Had a booty call with this *Tinder*?"

Chapter Six

WILLOW

I HAVE TO PEE.

The bathroom is across the hall, only steps away, but I can't go. I'm fake sleeping, and I have been for what feels like days. My muscles hurt. My head aches. As soon as Dallas leaves, I'm off Lauren's couch, out of this town, and on my way back to California.

Even though my back is to him, I can sense him watching, his eyes slicing into my skin, hoping to cut answers out of me. He'll end up empty-handed because I have nothing for him. My goal is to exhaust him with silence until he gives up.

What happened last night runs through my mind. I've never seen Dallas so angry and intense.

In an attempt to go back to sleep, I close my eyes, but my plan is ruined when it hits me. I nearly trip over him when I jump off the couch and race down the hall, straight to the bathroom.

Un-fucking-believable.

Why now?

I make it to the toilet just in time as everything I shoved down my throat last night comes up. It's disgusting. I'll never get used to this morning-sickness hell. I flinch when a cold hand moves along my neck to attentively grab my hair and hold it behind my shoulders. He silently kneels next to me and keeps his hand in place until I finish.

"Good ole morning sickness?" His voice is soft and comforting—the complete opposite of what he gave me last night. He must've slept off the asshole.

I flush the toilet and slide away from him, my butt hitting the cold tiles, and I rest my back against the bathtub. He waits until I get comfortable and hands me a bottle of water.

"Thank you," I say, taking a long drink. "It seems morning afters aren't our thing."

"I'd have to agree." He slumps down against the closed door and stares at me, doing what I knew he'd do—wait for answers. His foot brushes against mine when he stretches his legs out. He's in the same clothes as he was last night, his jeans unbuttoned, and his hair is messy.

I cock my head toward the toilet. "You want a go at it now?"

His thick brows squish together. "Huh?"

"I figured it was your turn to puke your guts out. You had to have been wasted off your ass to tell yourself that showing up last night was a sound idea."

He chuckles. "I'll admit, that was a stupid decision. I'd been drinking, but I wasn't wasted, and I'm sure you understand the shock I was feeling."

"No," I reply sarcastically. "I can't relate at all."

He found out I was pregnant. I'd found out I was carrying a physical being in my body by someone I couldn't stand.

He scratches his cheek. "How long were you planning on keeping this from me?" And he jumps right in.

Eighteen years. My entire life if I could've gotten away with it.

"To be honest, I have no idea."

He links his hands together and holds them in front of his mouth, trying to come up with the right words. He blows out a ragged breath. "You don't like me. I get it. And, to be honest, you're not exactly my favorite person right now either for keeping this from me. But I have to get over it, just like you have to get over what happened between us." He points to my stomach. "Because that? *That* changes shit."

"It doesn't change anything. I'm not expecting anything from you. I can do this on my own."

He holds his hand out, looking shocked. "Let me get this straight. I'm an asshole because I had a minor freak-out after we had sex? What does that make you for your secret? You've known you're pregnant for who knows how long, and you didn't think it'd be right to let me in on that tidbit of information?"

"You have a halfway good point," I mutter.

Okay, it's a full good point, but I won't give someone credit when I don't like them.

He clicks his tongue against the roof of his mouth. "Make yourself comfortable, sweetheart. Looks like we're about to have that talk."

I snort. "Not happening. I can still taste puke in my mouth. I'm not doing anything but brushing my teeth and getting in the shower." I narrow my eyes at him. "So, don't make yourself comfortable. We're postponing the talk."

"Okay, *princess*. Tell me when it's convenient for you. This afternoon?"

"Tomorrow."

"You'll be on a flight tomorrow."

"And? Lucky for you, they've invented this thing called a phone. I'll call you when I get home."

"I'd rather do it face-to-face."

"Then, we can FaceTime."

He pulls out his phone. "What time is your flight leaving?"

"Why?"

His eyes are on his phone as he starts typing and scrolling his finger down the screen. "Lucky for me, Hudson booked your flight and sent me the information this morning."

"Fucking snitch," I mutter.

"Looks like I'll be joining you. Hopefully, I can pay off the poor soul who's stuck next to you, and we can talk about it all the way back to California." He gives me a cold smile. "It'll be fun."

If he thinks his behavior is going to make me *work with him*, he has another thing coming.

"You're joking."

"Do I look like I am?" He holds his phone out, so I can see his screen. "Would you look at that? They have seats available."

"Don't you think that's creepy? Following me around? Stalking me?"

"Not stalking you. Asking for answers. This conversation will happen whether you like it or not. I'd prefer not to chase you around the goddamn country, but if that's what it takes, I will."

I cross my arms with a snarl. "Fine, I'll talk to you later."

His dark eyes level on me. "Promise you won't bail."

I force a smile. "I promise."

He hesitates before getting up and taps his knuckles against the door. "I'll be seeing you soon, *Baby Momma*."

"I hate you!" I yell to his back.

"I'm pissed at the both of you for keeping me in the dark about this," Lauren says, placing her glare on me before switching it to Stella, who ditched Hudson this morning to show up here with muffins and a list of everything she wanted to know about what had happened with me and Dallas last night. "I have so many questions right now."

Lauren hasn't let me do anything since she woke up this morning. She's a nurse, so you'd think she knows that carrying a baby doesn't make you disabled.

"Questions I won't be answering," I mutter. "No one, except for Stella and Hudson, knew about that night. I was hoping it'd stay that way."

"One question, and I'll shut up," Lauren pleads.

"I'm not talking about having sex with your brother," I argue.

Her face pinches. "Gross. Not where I was going with this, creep."

I lean back in the barstool. "You'd better make it a good one because that's all you're getting."

She settles her elbows on the counter and eagerly stares at me from across the island. "How did it happen?"

I wag my finger at her. "I'm blaming it on you."

She takes a step back and shoves her finger into her chest. "Me? I might get messy drunk sometimes, but I don't recall telling you to take your panties off and give my brother the business."

I frown. "Fine. Let's blame it on the whiskey and lack of entertainment in this town's only bar."

Her mouth drops, satisfaction twinkling in her eyes as she puts two and two together. "The night at the pub?"

I stubbornly nod.

"Holy shit. I am to blame."

Stella scoots in closer. "They're the last two people I imagined screwing."

"Screwed," I correct. "A one-time thing."

"Have you decided what you're going to do?" Stella asks. "You do know, Dallas isn't going to let you freeze him out."

"No." I was so hell-bent on keeping this a secret, I never thought about what would happen if the truth came out. "We're talking later."

Stella perks up. "Like, a date?"

Lauren cracks a smile. "Survey says they've surpassed dating. She's carrying his baby."

I flip her off, and my throat tightens while I prepare myself to ask her a question I've been trying to avoid. I stare at Lauren. "So, you're not mad at me?"

Dallas's family's reaction is another reason I wanted to keep this private. They loved his wife, Lucy, like she was their own, maybe even more than Dallas. He'd started dating her before he even knew his dick could get hard, and I'm some random one-night stand crawling in to replace her.

"Why would I be mad?" Lauren questions. "As long as you're not screwing the same man as me, I couldn't care less, and inbreeding isn't my thing." She skips around the counter to wrap me in a hug. "It's no secret that I loved Lucy, but I understand the circumstances. I want my brother to be happy. He *needs* to move on." She pulls away and settles her hands on her hips. "Now, my answer would be different had you kept this from him."

She's acting cool but also letting me know where her loyalty stands. If she has to pick a side, it won't be mine. If she thinks I'm the one Dallas needs to move on with, she's out of her mind, but like so many other times, I choose to keep my mouth shut.

Chapter Seven

DALLAS

"Now, there's a sight for sore eyes."

Hudson's voice sends a rumble through my skull. I had too many drinks and bombs thrown at me last night. The way he sluggishly climbs up the stairs and collapses into the red rocking chair next to me tells me he didn't get much sleep either. Hopefully, for a better reason than mine.

"You're on my shit list," he grumbles.

I point to his rib cage that's exposed by his cutoff T-shirt. "Those scratches of anger or pleasure?"

He holds up his arm and inspects the skin with an amused, almost boyish smile. "Pleasure. Most definitely pleasure."

I never thought I'd see him happy again after his ex dumped him for his best friend while he was stationed overseas, but Stella came along and changed everything.

"Then, I beg to differ that I'm on your shit list. Had you slept on the couch, I'd feel sorry for you, but from those marks, I'm positive you didn't. End of discussion." I hand him the extra cup of coffee I poured while waiting for him to show up, certain he'd make an appearance this morning.

"Not end of discussion. Stella ran off at the ass crack of dawn to gossip at Lauren's because you knocked up her best friend."

"Fine, I owe you one. I'll mow your grass. Work one of your shifts."

"You going to tell me what went down?"

I snort. "I see Stella isn't the only gossip enthusiast in your home."

He scratches his unshaved cheek. "She's rubbing off on me."

I drum my fingers against the wooden arm of my chair. "Willow didn't deny she was pregnant, so I'd say that confirms it."

The words *I'm pregnant* never left her mouth, but she would've been hell-bent on denying it if it weren't true. She's spent years working with Stella's publicist, making up stories to clean up gossip about Stella. She would've had a good-ass comeback if it weren't true. Hell, I'm surprised she didn't have an excuse already laid out, waiting for when shit hit the fan.

"And?" he pushes.

"There's a possibility I'm the father."

"A possibility? She seemed pretty damn sure about it last night."

She still does.

"What if it's not mine though?"

"You and I both know, Willow isn't like that or a liar. Stella swears Willow hasn't slept with anyone but you in months." He chuckles. "Trust me, from the look on her face, she wishes it were someone else's."

I scrub my hand over my face, hoping it'll help clear my head. "That's what I'm afraid of."

He laughs. "Get prepared, brother. This is happening whether you like it or not."

"We're talking today, figuring shit out."

"The first shit should be, figuring out the living situation. That was my biggest struggle with Stella. Blue Beech was out of her comfort zone, and LA was out of mine."

LA was once my home. I didn't mind leaving Blue Beech years ago when Lucy asked, but that's no longer an option. Maven needs to be here with my family. *I* need the support from them. Willow, on the other hand, is stubborn. I can't picture her packing up her life and moving away from the chaos of the city life.

"Stella changed," I argue, trying to convince myself that it could work.

"She did, but that doesn't stop Willow from begging her to move back every time they talk."

"Fuck," I hiss. I'm going to have my work cut out for me.

Hudson slaps my shoulder and gets up. "Good luck. Let me know if you need anything, but try to wait a few hours, okay? I have a beautiful fiancée waiting at home for me, hopefully wearing nothing but her engagement ring."

"What do you mean, she's not here?" I ask, standing in Lauren's doorway and feeling a sense of déjà vu from last night. It seems like I've done nothing but chase Willow around since Hudson broke the news.

"I mean, she's not here," Lauren repeats, shuffling backward to let me in.

"Goddamn it," I mutter, rushing into her apartment like a madman.

My first pit stop is her bathroom to pull back the shower curtain. All clear. Next is Lauren's closet. Then, underneath her bed. No sign of Willow.

"She promised," I repeat over and over again while checking the linen closet. "She fucking promised."

Lauren meets me in the living room with an apologetic face. "I'm guessing she called a cab and bailed while I was in the shower."

I collapse on her couch and drop my head back. Lucy never fought me like this. Our relationship was always easy. She was mine. I was hers. No power struggles existed.

"Maybe she went for a walk?" I ask.

The couch dents when Lauren sits down next to me. "Her bags are gone, and I doubt she's taking a walk with them."

I slowly lift my head, and she bends forward to snag her phone from the coffee table. She sucks in a breath a few seconds later and ends the call. "Straight to voice mail."

"Same with me. That's why I came over."

Willow promised.

Promised we'd talk.

Promised she'd stay.

She's nothing but a goddamn liar.

I'm not letting her run.

I won't let her shut me out.

Chapter Eight

WILLOW

I'M A RUNNER.

Not one who runs 5Ks for fun.

A runner from situations I don't want to face.

I shut my phone off when it rings for what seems like the hundredth time and slip it into my bag. I'm not ready for this—for the reality of what's about to become my life. I don't want to engage in conversations about childbirth, epidurals, and midwives. And definitely nothing about moving.

Call me selfish, but I refuse to move thousands of miles for a man in love with another woman. A man who'll *always* be in love with that woman. A man who, even though he irritates me to no limit, made me feel beautiful and wanted one night.

He gave me an intimacy I'd never had. All I'd gotten in the past was a boyfriend who lied and cheated like it was his job. The more time I spend with Dallas the more those memories of how he made me feel that night will pop up.

I check the time on my watch and relax in my seat, my shoulders drooping. It never fails that I choose the worst in the penis pool. Millions of men in this world, and somehow, I manage to always pick the screwed up ones who see me as nothing more than a disposable fuck.

"Did you think it'd be that easy?"

I tense at the sound of his sharp voice. It's as if a knife has been jabbed into my throat. I'm terrified to face him. I can sense his eyes tearing into my back, feeling the pain as if they were breaking flesh.

I should've taken the Greyhound or hitchhiked. I probably shouldn't have headed straight to the most obvious place—the fucking airport.

"You had enough balls to run away. Don't be a coward now. Turn around and look me in the eyes," he demands. "Tell me you're not only selfish, but a liar as well."

His bossiness and cruel words set a match to my already shitty mood.

How dare he judge me. How dare he act like he understands what I'm going through.

"Willow." My name sounds like a threat, assuring me he's not leaving until I give in.

I pull myself up from my chair with a dramatic moan and jerk my purse over my shoulder. The airport is no LAX, but there are plenty of people around with curious eyes.

Dallas's face is challenging, like he's ready to close a business deal. He did nice, and I took advantage of it. Now, he's giving me something else.

I made a promise and broke it. He has every right to be pissed.

I'm ashamed it takes me a minute to square up my shoulders, to show him I'm not someone who can be scolded like a child.

"We're not doing this here," is all I say.

He sweeps his arm out. "After you, your highness."

Since I'm not that familiar with the airport, I head to the women's restroom, uncertain if he'll follow me.

He does.

"This is a better place to do it?" he questions, locking the door behind us and leaning back against it when I nod. "Suit yourself."

I throw my arms down to my sides with a huff. "What do you want from me, Dallas?"

"What do I want from you?" He lets out a mocking laugh. "I want you to act like a responsible adult. It might be hard for you to realize, but this isn't only about you."

"I know."

"So, why run?"

"I'm scared!"

"And I'm assuring you, there's no reason to be." He comes closer as a long breath releases from his broad chest. "I know your trust in me is shit." He signals between the two of us. "I'm not asking you to marry me or be with me or, hell, even like me. I'm sure we can both agree that a relationship is out of the question. You can think I'm a shit person all you want, but I'm not a shit dad, and you fucking know it."

He's hitting me with all the truths. You'd think someone would break entirely when the love of their life died. Lucy's death shattered Dallas, but she left scattered pieces, so he'd be able to take care of Maven. She knew their daughter would be Dallas's savior when she was gone.

He goes to grab my bag. "Come on. Lauren has a twelve-hour shift. We'll talk, and then you can have her apartment to yourself for the night."

I hold my hand out to stop him. "I'm getting on that plane."

His lips press into a white slash, and he tiredly rubs his face.

"Scooby is waiting for me."

He blinks. "I'm sorry, *who* is waiting for you?"

"Scooby."

He folds his arms across his chest and kicks his legs out. "You two hanging out in the Mystery Machine with Velma?"

"Scooby is my cat, smart-ass," I snap, jutting my chin out.

"Why you named your cat Scooby is a conversation for another time, but we'll be having some serious talks about the name of our child. I won't have a Shaggy Barnes running around."

My hand falls to my chest at the sound of a knock on the door. Dallas holds a finger to his mouth. The knocking stops, and I open my mouth to tell him that I'll see him later when it starts back up again. The person on the other side must really need to go because the knocks get louder and faster.

"Out of order!" Dallas finally yells. "Go somewhere else."

The knocking subsides, and I narrow my eyes his way. "You do know, this is the women's restroom? They're probably going to security."

I shrug. He can't badger me if he's in jail.

"Then, let's make this quick."

"My mom is watching Scooby for me. I told her I'd be back by tomorrow. I also need to tell her about the whole becoming-a-grandma thing."

Family—Dallas's weakness.

I realize I chose the right words when his face falls into an apology.

"Why didn't you tell me that?"

I wrinkle my nose. "If you haven't figured it out by now, I'm not the most open person."

"That makes two of us. What a pair." He gives me a gentle smile. "Go home, Willow. Tell your mom, but keep in contact."

My shoulders slump. "I will."

"Promise me." I open my mouth to do what he asked, but he stops me, scowling. "Actually, don't bother. Promises don't mean shit to you." He unlocks the door. "If you don't answer my calls, the next time you see me will be when I'm standing on your mom's doorstep, introducing myself."

"I don't know why you won't let me keep him," my mom whines while running her fingers through Scooby's thick white hair.

A few strands stick to her hand because he sheds like no other. We have the whole let-me-keep-Scooby talk every time she cat-sits.

I flew into LA, got my car from my apartment, and then drove to my mom's house. She lives in the same house I grew up in, in a small suburb three hours out of LA. The ride gave me time to figure out how I was going to break the news to her.

"Mom, you bought him *for me* as a present."

After Stella moved away, he was a birthday gift to keep me company, but I think she used me as an excuse to buy herself an animal.

"You're out of town so much, and you don't give him the attention he deserves," she goes on.

She's right. I'm not much of a cat person, but I couldn't ask her to return him to the animal shelter. Scooby came from a good place. I only wish she'd chosen something that needed less upkeep—like, say, a goldfish.

"You seem to enjoy spending time with your grandcat," I reply. "I'm doing you a favor by traveling so frequently."

She lifts her chin. "When are you going to move home, find a good man, and settle down? Stella is doing it. Maybe you should follow her example."

Here we go again.

This is why the majority of my visits with her are when she's Scooby-sitting.

"Men and I aren't on the same page right now." *I have a feeling we'll never be.*

"If you'd quit looking in all the wrong places, they'd be. Come to church with me tomorrow, honey. They expanded, and traffic is booming! God-loving young men are scouring the place for a good wife to start a family with."

I can't stop myself from scowling. "Men scouring the place for a wife? Not my type, Mom. That sounds not only desperate, but also scary." I'm sure those men wouldn't approve of me carrying someone else's baby out of wedlock.

I drag my phone from my pocket when it beeps. I turned it back on when my plane landed but have yet to reply to the seventy-eight text messages from every citizen in Blue Beech.

Dallas: You make it to your mom's okay?

I set my phone to the side, ignoring it, and then pluck it back up. His threat wasn't empty, and the last thing I need is him showing up here.

Me: Just got here. Talking to her.

Dallas: You break the news yet?

Me: I need to loosen her up with a glass of wine first.

Dallas: Good luck.

Me: I should be the one telling you good luck. She'll probably take it better than your parents.

Dallas: I haven't told them yet. I'm waiting for you to be here. Consider your mom practice.

Me: Not happening.

He's eating bath salts if he thinks I'll be attending that shitshow. Dallas's family is as traditional as it gets. They're nice people, don't get me wrong, but super old school.

Dallas: We'll talk about it.

We'll talk about it?

The hell kind of answer is that?

I toss my phone onto the pillow next to me on the couch. "How about we go to dinner at La Vista tonight?"

―※―

My plan of liquoring my mom up, so I could spill the beans wasn't as bright as I'd thought it was an hour ago.

She wisps her hair, the same color as mine, away from her eyes to better stare at me. She's been eyeballing me since our drink order was placed five minutes ago. I'm doing my best to avoid direct eye contact with her, scared she'll read my mind.

The restaurant is packed. It always is on Saturday nights, given it's the nicest place in our suburb. A few of my mom's friends stopped to talk to us while we waited for our table, their eyes scrutinizing and judging me for the wrongs my ex-boyfriend did to a young kid who was the star of his little league baseball team.

"I take it, you have something to tell me," she says.

A knot ties in my belly. "Huh?"

"You've been nervous since you got home today. You then bring me to La Vista and order a glass of wine for me before the waiter even got the chance to introduce himself. You bring me here whenever you have news you don't want to break to me."

Come to think of it, she's right. I brought her here when I decided to move to LA, when I got back with Brett, and then when I told her I'd officially broken things off with him.

I lower my head in shame and blurt out my confession, "I'm pregnant."

She takes a long drink of wine before giving me a response. Her brows pull in as she carefully chooses her words. "This isn't some April Fool's Day joke, is it?"

"It's June."

I'm trying to read her, but I can't pinpoint what's going on in her mind. She's not happy, but she's not unhappy.

"How do you feel about this?"

My heart thrashes in my chest, and my chin quivers. "Like an idiot." An idiot for not using protection. Go figure, my ovaries are the .01 percent that gets pregnant while taking the pill.

"Do I know the father?"

"It's not Brett's."

A rush of relief releases from her lips. "Thank Jesus."

"It's Dallas Barnes."

"Stella's old bodyguard?"

I nod. "And Hudson's older brother."

Mortification floods her face. "Isn't he ..." She grabs the glass of red wine and chugs the remainder of it down, her emerald eyes wide. "Isn't he married?"

Oh, fuck. She's afraid I'm a homewreckin' ho.

"His wife passed away almost a year ago."

She nods slowly, digesting my answer, the familiarity of it flashing across her face like a burn. "You didn't tell me you two were dating."

I can't distinguish if she's asking a question or giving a warning. My mother knows the nightmare of never getting over your first love—a memory that bites at every inch of your body until your last breath.

"We're not dating," I answer. "It was a one-time thing. Too much whiskey, not enough thinking."

I take a sip of water, a breath of courage, and proceed to tell her everything minus the details of the actual baby-making, and I am unable to stop the tears from falling from my eyes … and hers.

She stretches her arm across the table to grab my hand in hers. "If Dallas wants to be in the picture, give him a chance." Her voice is soft, caressing, a vocal hug. "He's a father, a single one at that, who knows the responsibility of taking care of a child."

"I'm strong, Mom." My throat is dry, causing my words to come out raspy. "I can do this on my own."

"Honey, I'm not denying you can, but I know from firsthand experience, it isn't easy, doing it alone. No mother can replace the void of a father. We can both agree on that."

A knife slashes through my heart. The reality of what I did smacks me in the face, like I've been unconscious this entire time.

I was that child, the one without a father. It was by choice for the first fifteen years. He didn't decide he was ready to be a dad until he was diagnosed with stage five colon cancer. My mother welcomed him with open arms. I didn't.

He passed away at the young age of forty-one when I was sixteen. My mother forgave him at his deathbed. I didn't. I couldn't. The bitterness was still wrapped in my heart. I couldn't forget all the times I'd been a jealous-filled child when I watched my friends have fathers.

Everyone has choices in their life. He chose to leave. You can't take that shit back when you find out your time is limited, and you have no one to help you through it.

She drops my hand and sits back in her chair, the wine now relaxing her. "Your father always wanted grandchildren."

I want to tell her that I don't care what he wanted. My mom has gone through hell since he left her … both times.

"I doubt that dream included a love child," I mutter.

"A grandchild is a grandchild. A blessing. No matter what the situation."

Chapter Nine

WILLOW

Dallas: You break the news yet?

The text was sent two hours ago. My phone stayed in my purse throughout dinner, and when we got home, we spent the rest of the night bingeing on popcorn and Matthew McConaughey movies.

Me: Sure did.

I change into my pajamas and slide into bed. My mom kept my room how it was when I moved out. The same sponge-painted yellow walls and pictures of me at different school events on the dresser. I zero in on the prom picture of Brett and me and tell myself to toss it and any others with him into the trash tomorrow.

The phone rings, and I freeze up and stare at the screen for a few seconds when his name flashes across it. We've talked on the phone before, for business, so why am I terrified of answering?

I inhale a breath of courage before accepting the call. "Hello?"

"How'd she take it?" Dallas asks.

Hello to you, too.

I chew on my nails. "Not bad. I did crush her hopes on if I'd decided to move home and find a husband though."

"You dream crusher, you."

I smile.

"Did she ask about me? About who the dad is?"

"She knows who you are."

A brief silence passes.

He met my mom at Stella's Christmas dinner one year. I brought her as my plus-one after Brett went missing for forty-eight hours on a drinking binge. He and Lucy were there, and Mom talked about how their relationship was beautiful on our way back to my apartment.

"She's happy I at least got knocked up by a decent man."

"Good." He pauses for a few seconds. "I need to ask for a favor."

"If it's being present and accounted for when you tell your parents, that's gonna be a hard no."

"Let me correct myself. I need to ask you for *favors*."

"You're really pushing it, you know that?"

"Come to Blue Beech."

"I was just in Blue Beech, remember? Hudson having a big mouth, three a.m. wake-up call—all of that jazz."

"Damn, Ms. Difficult, *stay* in Blue Beech. Give it a try. A trial run, if you will."

"Didn't we have this talk in the bathroom?" I ask, exasperated. *No way in hell is that happening.* "We decided we're not moving in together, getting married, or any of that forced nonsense."

"Whoa, whoa. Pump your brakes, sweetheart. I promise, this is *not* a marriage proposal. It's a moving proposal, so we can do this as a team."

"Why can't we do it as a team in LA?"

It's his turn to let out an exasperated breath. "I have a daughter here who adores her friends and family. My business is here. Hell, *your* job is here. Any other points I need to throw out? You belong here, Willow."

I grow quiet, and he lets out an irritated groan.

"Fine, I'll come to you if I have to, but prepare to explain the reason to my family. I won't be pushed away from this, and I am not a man you can play games with. I'm a man who will fight for what he wants and the people he loves. You might not have given birth to our baby yet, but that doesn't mean I don't care for it."

He has a point. Maven has already lost her mom. It'd be greedy of me to ask Dallas to move her away from her home and the family she has left.

"Where am I supposed to stay? On the streets?"

"You can stay at my place. I have a guest room."

"Not a chance in hell."

"Stella's?"

"Shack up with the lovebirds? Again, not happening."

"We'll find you a rental then."

I yawn. This conversation is getting too dangerous, sounding too final. "Let me sleep on it. I'll talk to you tomorrow."

I'm reading another article of what having a baby does to your vagina when the doorbell rings. My mom left for church an hour ago, so yelling for her to answer it isn't an option. I throw the covers off me before slipping out of bed with a groan. It rings again as I trek down the stairs.

I'm cranky. Heartburn and headache made an appearance and decided to stay all night. Heartburn was the consequence of overeating pasta, and the headache was from the regret of possibly agreeing to move to Blue Beech.

I swing the front door open, and my temples throb at the sight of the world's biggest asshole standing on the porch with white roses in his hand like he's picking me up for prom.

"Nuh-uh, not today, Satan!" I yell before slamming the door in his face and locking it.

Someone must've spotted me at La Vista last night and told him I was in town.

Brett bangs on the other side. "Willow! At least talk to me!"

"Fuck you!" I yell back. "Go give those to one of the fifty women you fucked behind my back."

"I have a key," he warns. "Don't you make me use it!"

"I have a baseball bat. Don't you make me use it!"

He knocks a few more times. "I'll be back. Don't think I won't. Every fucking day until I break you down."

"That's what they make restraining orders for!"

He knocks again. "I'll be back."

And then silence. Not surprising. Brett is one of the laziest men I know. He doesn't like to work for anything, but he'll try to sweet-talk me like he did every time I took him back in the past. Dealing with him is the last thing on my to-do list. Actually, not even on the list. He's lazy but also irritating when he's not getting his way. I'm guessing the woman he was cheating on me with got a glimpse of the real him and bailed. That means, he's ready to run back to me.

Maybe I do need to get out of California, get some fresh air, and clear my head. I lean back against the front door as frustration builds in my head. I'm mentally cursing myself when I head back to my room.

I snatch my phone from the nightstand, nearly ripping it from my charger, and hit Dallas's name, praying to God I don't regret this tomorrow.

Me: Blue Beech. A trial run. That's me compromising.

My phone beeps seconds later.

Dallas: Thank you. You have no idea how much I appreciate this.

I exit from his name and hit Stella's.

Me: Hello, new neighbor!

Stella: YES! Team Stella for the win! You're staying with me, BTW.

Me: Not happening, BTW.

Stella: Why? Don't tell me you're crashing at Dallas's? How romantic.

Me: Are you nuts? I'm renting a place.

Staying with Dallas is not an option.

What would he tell his daughter? That I'm homeless and then—surprise!—I'm carrying your sibling?

Chapter Ten

DALLAS

"But ... but Auntie Lauren lets me have it," Maven whines.

I snatch the coffee cup from my six-year-old, who is under the impression she's a grown-up, and replace it with an organic apple juice box. "I'll be having a conversation with Auntie Lauren."

My sister's idea of a well-balanced diet is iced coffee, margaritas, and deli sandwiches from the hospital's vending machine.

She sits down at the table with a un-caffeinated frown at the same time I place a bowl of strawberry oatmeal in front of her. I promised Lucy that Maven would be taken care of, and that means making her eat balanced meals.

My days have gone from traveling the world with Hollywood's elite to packing nutritious lunches, attending dance recitals, and reading the same bedtime stories for months on end.

But I wouldn't trade it for the world.

Time is valuable. Hug your children. Kiss your wife. Make life your bitch because you never know when it's going to turn on you.

I grab my phone and sit down next to Maven.

"What are you doing?" she asks before taking a bite of her oatmeal.

"Texting your aunt."

"Tattletale," she mutters with a frown.

Me: Mom and Dad paid for four years of nursing school, and you don't know that kids shouldn't have coffee? Your license needs to be revoked.

My phone beeps a few minutes later.

Lauren: Relax, old man. Unbeknownst to your caffeine-fiend spawn, I give her decaf. She wants to be my mini me, which I approve of.

My family has been the key to my survival. Lauren stepped up to be a mother figure to Maven when Lucy passed.

Me: That's scary. Is the apartment underneath you still vacant?

The struggling musician who lived underneath her got evicted last month for playing music all day and night. She threw a party in celebration when he left.

Lauren: Depends on why you're asking. If it's for a dude in a band, then no.

Me: Give me your landlord's number.

Lauren: WHY?

Jesus, they might be my backbones, but they are damn nosy.

Me: I need to find a place for Willow.

Lauren: Holy shit! She's moving here? The apartment is open. I can't wait to have a front row seat to your guys' drama!

Me: Send me the damn number.

I grab Maven's backpack, and she gets into my truck at the same time Lauren sends me the number. I wait until I drop Maven off at my parents' before calling Lauren's landlord, Fred. He gives me the good news that the apartment is vacant but is unwilling to put a hold on it for me, so I drive to his office and pay the security deposit.

The apartment comes fully furnished, but I decide to take a peek at it before Willow moves in. I'll do anything in my power to make sure she's comfortable here.

It's a damn good thing I did.

"I need help," I tell Hudson when he answers my call.

"With what?" he asks.

"Getting Willow's apartment together. I'll also need some input from Stella."

He takes a deep breath, almost sounding surprised. "So, you're really doing this, huh? Moving Willow here?"

"Did you think I wouldn't?"

"No, I thought *she* wouldn't. I'll believe it when I see it."

Chapter Eleven

WILLOW

Lauren pops the trunk and steps out of her over-the-top pink Mustang when I walk out of the airport. The car is hideous yet has a certain appeal to her.

"You know, I'm confused," she says, helping me with my bags and then throwing her hands on her hips in question, as if I can read her mind as to what she's confused about.

One thing I admire about Lauren is her inability to bullshit. She might just barely be grazing five feet, but she'll ask you straight up instead of gossiping behind your back.

I slam the trunk shut. "Confused about what?"

She doesn't answer my question until we're in the car. "On why you'll screw my brother but refuse to let him pick you up from the airport."

It's a three-hour drive to Blue Beech, and I asked Lauren to pick me up instead of Dallas, so I wouldn't have to spend hours alone with him, answering questions. I have the impression it might not be much different with his sister.

I fix my glare on her. "Haven't you ever had a one-night stand?"

"I live in a town with a population of six hundred. Half of the men were married off before their balls dropped. There's no one to have a one-night stand with." She pauses to give me a side-eye. "I guess I can't speak for everyone."

"Oh, kiss my ass," I grumble, rubbing my eyes.

Sleep hasn't been my friend lately, and I had an early flight. I doubt I'll be able to unwind when I get to Blue Beech either.

"Did he do that, too?" She laughs when I flip her off. "You kinky kids, you."

"I wish you had never found out," I grumble.

"Secrets don't make friends," she sings out, gearing the car in drive.

"They sure can keep them though."

She tips her thumb toward my growing belly. "That, *my friend*, would be a mighty hard secret to keep."

I made a list of lies when my first pregnancy test came out positive. IVF treatment. Secretly adopted a baby. A one-night stand, and I didn't get the guy's name. The last one is technically only a half-lie.

I slump down in my seat. "I can't believe I'm doing this."

"Doing what? Moving to the best place in the world and being surrounded by delightful company? We're going to be neighbors. That, my dear, will be the highlight of your life."

"No, I can't believe I packed up and moved to a town void of takeout sushi but also where I'll be labeled a widower-chasing tramp. Might as well pin a scarlet letter to my chest and call it a day."

"You can't be serious." She peeks over at me, her amused smile fading into concern. "Willow, no one is going to call you a widower-chaser. I mean, not to your face at least." She pauses to give me a cheesy grin. "Although it does have a nice ring to it. Willow the Widower-Chaser."

"That's it. Turn this pink puss car around."

I yelp at the sound of the door locking. "Prepare for a three-hour drive filled with prying questions and nineties hip-hop. I hope you're a Snoop Dogg fan."

"Wow, this is a nice place."

I drop my bag onto the mahogany wood floor and explore my new apartment. It's an older building with a floor plan similar to Lauren's, except mine is a two bedroom and has more space. Something like this would cost a kidney in LA. My mom told me I was choosing to live in rich-people poverty when I moved there.

A fresh coat of taupe paint covers the walls, and an exposed brick fireplace is at the front of the living room with a flat screen TV mounted above it. The furniture is new, and decorative touches are scattered throughout the living room and kitchen. A red-and-black-checkered throw is thrown over the back of the couch, and succulents are placed on the end tables to each side of it.

"Thank you for talking to your landlord, putting down the deposit, and getting everything in order on such short notice," I say to Lauren, pulling my purse up from the floor by the strap. I rummage through it in search of my wallet. "How much do I owe you?"

Her hand goes up, stopping me. "Put your wallet away. Thank Dallas. This was all him."

I give the apartment another once-over. "What? How?"

Blame it on the loser I dated for nearly a decade, but my mind can't wrap around a man doing this for me. I guess Stella wasn't lying when she said small-town guys were a different breed.

"Ask him. In the meantime, get yourself settled in. I have a double shift in a few hours and need to hit the shower. Text me if you need anything, *neighbor*."

I smile. She made a six-hour round trip to pick me up and then has to pull a double. "Have fun. Thank you for the ride. I owe you one."

"I got you, girl," is all she says before winking and waving good-bye.

I scoop up my bags and take them into the bedroom when I hear the door shut. Just like the rest of the apartment, the bedroom is spacious. Settling my suitcase on the cream-upholstered king-size bed, I start to unpack.

I let my mom watch Scooby for a few weeks, so I could get settled in and check with the landlord if pets were allowed. Only a few bags came with me on the flight, and I'm having my other stuff and car shipped. I have a baby on the way and am not handing an airline my savings to have a few extra bras.

I drop the shirt I'm hanging up at the sound of the doorbell.

"You forget something?" I ask, opening the door. I stumble back when I don't see Lauren.

Dallas is standing in front of me, shoulders broad and square, wearing a red-buffalo-plaid flannel that nearly matches the throw on my couch, dark jeans with holes in both knees that hug his legs, and brown boots. My heart races, and I can't stop myself from running a finger over my lips.

Shit. Pregnancy hormones are making an appearance. They seem to be well acquainted with him.

Dallas has the efficacy to pull off attractiveness with this casual demeanor better than any man wearing an expensive suit. My ex was a hipster wannabe who regularly sported holey jeans, beanies, and flannels. He was a generic version of the real thing—Dallas. He's no wannabe. He's this rugged, down-to-earth man who has no idea how wet he makes my panties.

I smooth down my hair and shyly smile. "Hey," I say in nearly a whisper.

Tension bleeds through the air like an open wound. Our last face-to-face conversation wasn't exactly pretty.

His thick lips curl up. "If it isn't Blue Beech's newest resident."

"*Temporary* resident," I correct, scooting to the side. My back brushes against the wall as I give him enough room to step into the apartment and shut the door.

His scent, a light evergreen that reminds me of a vacation lodge deep in the mountains where you never want to leave, hangs in the air like smoke as he skims the living room. "You getting settled in okay?"

A few inches separate us, and I play with my hands in front of me, nervousness climbing up my spine. We haven't been alone like this since that night with the small exception of the women's restroom at the airport, which has the privacy that's equivalent to one in prison.

"I haven't had a chance to find a place for everything yet, but the apartment is gorgeous. I can't believe you did all of this. Thank you."

He stares over at me, his eyes flashing with victory and satisfaction. "Thank you for moving here."

I draw in a sharp breath when he edges closer into my space, standing in front of me, as if he's geared to tell me a secret. Being too close for comfort seems to be his thing, which I find completely unnecessary. This isn't L.A. *The square footage is out of this world, dude.*

"You have no idea how much I fucking appreciate it."

I shrug off his gratitude and laugh. "I needed a getaway for a while anyway. Nothing like a vacation before delivering a baby."

He chuckles lightly. "Just a vacation, huh?"

I nod.

He runs his boots back and forth over the hardwood floor. "I stopped by to make sure you showed up and weren't planning on bailing again."

I hold out my arms. "I'm here, in the flesh, breathing and everything."

"I also wanted to see what you might be doing tomorrow night."

Like I have big plans here?

"Most likely, unpacking."

"Perfect, you're free. I'm taking Maven to the fair tomorrow. Come with us."

Is he nuts? He wants me to hang out with not only him, but also his daughter?

"The fair?" I scrunch up my face. "Like vomit-inducing, spinning rides and honky-tonks?"

"No." He pauses. "I mean, yes to the rides, no to the honky-tonks. You watch too many movies."

"I work for movie stars. Watching their movies is part of my job."

"I'll pick you up at six."

"I'll have to pass."

"Come on, who doesn't like the fair?"

"I've never been to one."

His lips tilt into a half-smile, and he opens the front door, patting the inside of it. "I'll pick you up at six."

"Wait!"

"Have a good night, Willow."

The door slams shut behind him.

Chapter Twelve

WILLOW
The Past
Three Months Ago

"Want to dance?"

Dallas and I both flinch at my question.

Did those words leave my mouth?

This whiskey shit is messing with my insanity. I shouldn't want to dance with Dallas. I definitely shouldn't be feeling this weird pull between us after only a few hours of drinking together.

Lauren stopped by our table earlier to give me a ride back to Stella's, but I wasn't ready to end my time with Dallas. Turned out, neither was he. He offered to walk me back to Hudson's on his way home. Surprisingly, Lauren didn't find it weird and took off.

The place is close to empty, except for the few lone rangers at the end of the bar, and the band left with their armful of groupies. The music has been downgraded to static-infused country songs coming from an old jukebox in the corner of the room.

He stares at me with hooded eyes, and I wave my hand in the air as rejection slaps me in my stupid, drunken face.

"Forget it," I rush out, beating him to the punch. "Of course you don't." This will mortify me when my senses come back in the morning.

He holds his fist to his mouth and lets out a shuddering breath. "I'm not really up for dancing."

He jumps up from his stool, and I avert my eyes to the tabletop.

This is where he bails. Do they have Uber around here?

His tall frame towers over me, and I jump when his strong hand grabs my chin to tilt it up.

Our gaze meets, latching on to each other's in a strong hold, and he lowers his voice. "But I will for you."

His fingertips smooth over my chin as he waits for my answer, and my brain goes fuzzy. Every person and every noise disappears around us.

"Never mind," I stutter out, not sure if my words are even audible. "It's okay. I'm a terrible dancer anyway."

His hand disappears, and he bends down, so his lips are at my ear. "Get up, Willow."

I shudder at the feel of his breath against my skin, goose bumps popping up my neck.

"You've been answering my Tinder questions and listening to me be a miserable bastard all night. I owe you a dance."

"Are ... are you sure?"

"Positive. Hell, I need it as much as you."

I take his hand and slide off my barstool. "Lead the way."

His grip is tight. Secure. I keep my eyes downcast, so I don't see the expressions on people's faces when they see him dancing with someone who's not *her*.

Judgmental eyes won't ruin my night.

My heart races when his hand leaves mine, and he swoops his arm around my back, looping it around my waist. His hand settles on the arch right above my ass, and he starts moving us to the beat of the music.

"What song is this?" I ask.

"'Hurt' by Johnny Cash."

He shuts his eyes, holding me closer, and I take in the lyrics. Dallas didn't choose this song, but God, does it fit his life right now.

The jukebox is giving me a warning. *Run! Run! You naive girl. This man will only end up hurting you.*

A sharp pain fills his eyes as he stares down at me. "You have no idea what you brought out of me tonight." He blows out a ragged breath. "What you gave me tonight, Willow. I've never opened up like this to anyone."

Even Lucy? is the question I want to ask, but I bite my tongue. *Me either* are the words I want to say next, but again, I don't, for fear he'll run away.

Almost a decade with Brett, and never did emotions drum through me like this.

Is this what it feels like—falling for someone? Is this why people who've experienced love crave it so much?

Love.

I gulp down a thousand feelings. I'm overthinking this.

I can't fall for a man after one night of conversation and a dance.

"I've never danced with anyone like this," I admit.

Instead of pulling away, he draws in nearer, pressing his mouth to my ear. I shiver as his crisp breath hits my sweaty skin. "Like what?"

"Without grinding my ass against someone while Lil Jon plays in the background."

Proms. Frat parties. Clubs. Those are the only places I've danced with men. Never so slow, so personal, so gentle. Never like *this*.

He chuckles—not only surprising me, but also making me smile. "I'm taking your virginity of how a real man dances with a woman."

My response is resting my chin on his shoulder and losing myself to the music as he takes me into another world. We stay silent in our moment, but it's a comfortable silence, something that feels necessary right now. I expect him to pull away when the song ends, but he doesn't. We dance into the next one with my arms nestled on his rugged shoulders as we feed something we shouldn't.

"Last call!" a voice yells in the distance, snapping me out of my powerful trance. I'm unsure of how many songs we've danced through. "Five minutes until closing time!"

I attempt to pull away, but Dallas tightens his hold, silently asking me not to let go yet.

"Give me that five minutes," he pleads.

"Of course," I whisper, slipping my hands down his back. "I'll give you however long you need."

He nods his thank-you. Time slows. These five minutes feel like a lifetime. Our embrace grows tighter, our sway to the music slower and the connection sharper.

"Dallas, man, I hate to do this, but I have to shut this shit down," the guy who screamed out the last call warns.

I lose our connection when he retreats a step, my arms splaying down his sides and then falling to mine, and he gives me an apologetic look.

"Sorry," he whispers to me before turning his attention to the bartender. "You're good, man. Enjoy your night."

The bartender, the same man who was making our drinks, gives him a thumbs-up and a smile. "It was good seein' ya!"

His gaze lowers to mine. "You ready to go back to Stella's?"

No! No!

I'm debating on asking the bartender how much he wants for this bar, so we can stay longer.

I force a smile. "I have to be, considering we're getting kicked out."

He grabs my hand, interlacing our fingers, and holds them against his shoulder. "It's beautiful out tonight. How 'bout we take the scenic route? Might be a good idea to show you the beauty of Blue Beech since Hudson says you hate it and refuse to move here with Stella."

I tilt my head to the side. "Hey now, did he tell you to give me a good time in an attempt to change my mind?"

"You know me better than to think I'd take commands from my baby brother. *But*"—I knew that *but* was coming—"that doesn't mean I won't try to convince you Blue Beech is a good place, and you should really consider moving here."

"I'll keep that in mind." *Especially if I can get another night like this.*

He bows his head. "Thank you."

"I didn't make any promises."

"Not thank you for allowing me to show you around. Thank you for making me forget I'm a miserable man missing half of who he is. Thank you for not treating me like a broken fucking object that needs fixing."

I hide my face on his shoulder to conceal my smile. "You've done the same for me." With my mouth pressed against his denim shirt, my face hidden, I take a risk that could go horribly wrong. "You know somewhere I haven't seen in Blue Beech?"

"What's that?"

"The home of Dallas Barnes."

Don't judge me.

I know what I'm doing is wrong, but bad ideas sometimes lead to good things, right?

Chapter Thirteen

WILLOW

One of the biggest things I've learned about Blue Beech so far is real-life county fairs are nothing like the movies.

Dallas texted me this morning to remind me of the time he was picking me up and told me to have an appetite. The impulse to decline spilled through me, but the thought of experiencing something new prevented it.

I mean, who doesn't want to find out what the fair hype is all about?

Dallas parks his truck in a grassy field converted into a parking lot. The amount of cars surprises me. *This many people live here?*

He helps Maven out of the truck before circling to my side. "Thank you for coming," he says when he opens my door. He grabs my hand and assists me out of the lifted truck. "It's all Maven's been talking about today."

I nervously laugh. "Guess it was time to pop my fair cherry." I grimace at my word choice. *No, Willow. No flirting with the widowed asshole.*

He smirks. "Honored to be the one to do it."

I nod, relieved he didn't shut down on me but scared it'll happen sometime tonight. Like me, Dallas is a pro at freezing people out at the snap of his fingers.

Maven is spinning in circles with her arms out in the air. Her hair is pulled back in two French braids that are finished off with furry pink bands holding each one in place. *Did Dallas braid them for her?*

I swing the strap of my cross-body bag over my shoulder while Dallas scoops Maven up and spins her around one last time. He takes her hand and leads us toward the flashing lights and white tents. When we hit the dusty pathway, I peek down at my feet, wishing I'd chosen different shoes. Everyone is in boots or sneakers while I'm sporting studded black flats that are going to be ruined by the end of the night.

"I want to ride that one!" Maven exclaims, pointing at rides as we make our way through the crowd. "Then, that one. And that one."

"Dinner before rides," Dallas replies, casting a glance my way. "What's your fair poison?"

"My what?" I ask.

He peeks down at Maven with a smile. "This is Willow's first time at the fair," he explains, as if I were the only person who hadn't done such a thing.

Maven giggles, her face lighting up. "Really?"

I nod, and she reaches out to connect her hand with mine. My chest tightens when I squeeze my hand around hers, a sadness sinking through me. We resemble the other families here—mom and dad treating their eager daughter to a night full of games, candy, and fun.

"My absolute favorites are elephant ears and cotton candy!" she says.

"Hey, I've had cotton candy," I argue.

"But have you had *fair* cotton candy?" Dallas counters, causing Maven to burst out into more giggles. "*Blue Beech* cotton candy?"

I glance over at him. "Wasn't aware there was a difference."

His dark brows rise. "Oh, there most definitely is."

We stop at a table underneath a blue tent, and Dallas insists on getting our food. Maven takes the seat next to me, her legs bouncing up and down in excitement.

"Did you know Daddy said I get to ride big-kid rides this year?" she asks with a burst of energy I wish I had every morning. "Last year, I wasn't tall enough, but I've grown *lots and lots!*"

"No way!" I reply before holding my hand up in the air. "I had to wait until I was *this* big before I got to do that."

Her head tilts to the side. "I thought you'd never been to a fair?"

Girl is smart for a six-year-old.

"I've been to Disney."

She bounces in her seat. "Me, too! Mommy and Daddy took me for my birthday. I had lunch with Princess Jasmine!"

I place my hand over my heart and gasp. "Princess Jasmine? That's so cool. Is she your favorite princess?"

She nods repeatedly. "Who's yours?"

"Ariel." I point to my hair. "Have to support my fellow redhead."

"She's my second favorite!" She claps her hands. "Maybe, next time, you can come with Daddy and me and meet Princess Jasmine!"

I nod timidly. "Yeah, maybe."

Our conversation stops when Dallas gets to the table with drinks in his hands and plates lined up his arms, like an experienced waiter. I slide out of my seat to help him set everything down.

"Are you feeding the entire town?" I ask.

"I promised to give you the full fair experience," he says, sitting down across from me. He points to the plates the same way Maven did with the rides. "Tenderloins are Maven's and my favorite. I also grabbed some fried chicken, shish kebabs, and pizza in case you wanted to play it safe. Then, we have some elephant ears and cotton candy. Drinks are an option of a lemon shake-up, water, or soda."

I snag a lemon shake-up. "So many healthy choices."

He chuckles. "We're splurging tonight."

Maven sticks out her tongue. "It's better than broccoli. Daddy makes me eat gross broccoli."

Dallas points his fork at her. "Give a man some credit for adding cheese to it for you."

Maven picks up a shish kebab and waves it through the air. "Not better than cotton candy! Pink is the best!" she sings out.

The nauseating smell of meat smacks me in the face, causing my stomach to churn, and she sets it back down on her plate. I close my hand over my nose and mouth—not only to block out the stench, but also to stop myself from vomiting in front of a crowd of people.

Dallas drops his sandwich. "Everything okay?"

"The meat," I choke out underneath my hand, shaking my head. "None of that."

He gets the hint, grabs it from Maven's plate, and tosses it in the trash. "Sorry, honey," he tells her. "Bad meat."

She nods and moves on to a tenderloin.

I move my hand and take a deep breath, whispering, "Thank you," to him.

His lips tilt up in a smile, a real one, something I haven't seen from him since I've been here. My breathing hitches. My heart skitters.

"Any weird cravings yet?" he asks.

"Cupcakes. Cake. Brownies. Sugar in general."

He laughs, another authentic one, making me happy I came. "I'll remember that."

My lips curve into a smile, meeting his, and I snack on a slice of cheese pizza while Maven takes over the conversation of how excited she is to leave for summer camp in a few days. She shoves her plate forward after the last bite and focuses on Dallas in determination that is too intense for a kid whose age hasn't reached the double digits yet.

"Time for rides, Daddy!" she declares. "And don't you forget, I get to ride the *big-kid* ones. No more kiddy zone for me."

Dallas holds his hand up. "Hold it, youngster. Only the ones you meet the height requirement for, remember?"

"Is she trying to talk you into letting her bungee jump again?"

Hudson's voice catches me off guard, and I turn around to see him and Stella coming our way. The sight of her eases me. Hudson … not so much. I'm not sure how he feels about me. Stella insists he holds no grudges against me, but I don't believe her.

"I'm not old enough for that *yet*," Maven says.

"Or ever," Dallas corrects. He stares down at Maven, shaking his head. "You, my dear child, are going to give me a heart attack before forty."

"Hey, brother," Hudson cuts in. "Which will be worse—the day she wants to bungee jump or date?"

"Dating," Dallas answers without hesitation. "I will bungee jump at her side before I agree to dating."

"Gross, I don't want to date," Maven chimes in with disgust.

Dallas taps the top of her head. "That's my girl."

"You want to ride roller coasters with me, Uncle Hudson?" Maven asks. "Willow is coming!"

Pregnancy and carnival rides don't go together.

"Oh no," I moan out. "I get motion sickness."

I'm not sure when Dallas is going to break the news that she's going to be a big sister, but I most certainly don't want to be in attendance. Lord knows the questions she'll have.

Maven's smile morphs into a pout. "My mommy did, too, but she was always okay."

I regret looking at Dallas at the mention of Lucy. His body goes still, and I'm confident his heart is beating faster than anyone on a roller coaster here. The lightness of our time together has been extinguished, a whirl of unease stepping through. He scratches his neck, and I notice a vein popping out from it.

"How about I go with you? I love roller coasters!" Stella quickly offers up, lying to the poor girl.

"Thank you," I whisper to her while Maven waits for Dallas's permission.

His eyes are vacant, his face cloaked with pain. He's checked out.

"I'll make sure the two of them stay out of trouble," Hudson says. "You keep introducing Willow to coma-inducing foods and sell Blue Beech to her."

Dallas pinches the bridge of his nose and nods. I grab my lemon shakeup and suck it down without even bothering to argue with Hudson about the "sell Blue Beech to her" comment. The thought of Dallas showing me around makes me queasier than the meat.

Stella grabs Maven's hand, and the three of them take off through the pack of people. I'm struggling to find the right words. I want to console Dallas, but I'm not sure if it's a good idea. It might push him away more.

Isn't that what I wanted when I found out I was pregnant?

Now, I'm thriving for more from him.

For as long as I can remember, I've admired his love for Lucy. His commitment to her, even when half-dressed women threw themselves at him in hopes of seeing Stella.

Seeing their relationship made you believe in love again.

And that's why I can't get close to him.

He'll never give me that.

You don't get love like that twice in a lifetime.

You can't awaken those emotions back out of a broken man.

I need to back off and quit trying to make strides with him that'll only end up stomping on my heart when I'm forced to face the devastation that he's just around me because I got knocked up by him.

I don't realize I'm staring until his hollow eyes meet mine. His Adam's apple bobs while he piles the plates on top of each other and disposes them into the trash.

He fraudulently smiles down at me. "You ready for your Blue Beech pitch?"

I grab a bag of cotton candy. "I'll listen, but I'm not someone easily convinced."

"Oh, Miss Andrews, I can be a very persuasive man." He must've given himself a pep talk on his way to the trash because his excitement meter has risen a few notches.

I shove a handful of cotton candy into my mouth before getting up. We walk in silence, side by side, passing annoyed parents yelling at their children and people spending their paychecks on games that are scamming them.

Everyone stops and stares when we walk past them, like we're the show animals. A few women have pulled out their phones to record us. We appear as platonic as it gets. Hell, maybe more like strangers, considering we're not saying a word to each other.

No story here, people.

Don't twist it into something it's not.

Because it's way more complicated than us having sex.

"How about a game?" Dallas asks, breaking my attention away from the crowd of women pointing our way.

I throw them a dirty grimace and set my eyes back on him.

We've stopped in front of a ring-toss game with giant animals hanging from the roof of the tent.

"The chances of me winning that small stuffed animal is one in a gazillion, and it will cost me a couple of hundred bucks. I'd rather save my money and buy a new handbag." Or a crib.

"I like your style." He laughs, shaking his head. "I've blown so much money on those stupid things. Lucy loved them." He tilts his head toward the flashing lights and spinning rides. "Ferris wheel?"

"I see you live on the wild side."

"Risky is my middle name. Be right back."

I combatively stare at him while he jogs over to the ticket booth without waiting to hear my answer.

How do I tell him I'd rather blow my life savings on a game than be stuck in the air with him?

As bad as I want to, I can't. It's hard for me to give him shit when it looks like someone ran over his dog.

So, I wait in line.

He hands the bored attendant our tickets and helps me into the car. It's cramped as we sit across from each other. I blush each time our knees brush in the tight space.

"You make a doctor's appointment yet?" he asks when the wheel starts to move.

I sigh playfully. "This was your plan, huh? Get me hundreds of feet in the air, so I can't bail when you ask me complicated questions?"

He holds his hand up, a smile cracking at his lips. It's not as real as the one he gave me at the beginning of the night, but it's better than the artificial one earlier. "Convenient timing, I swear." He pauses, the smile still flickering at his lips. "Subconscious smart move on my part, considering your history of being a runner."

His jeans rub against my bare leg when I situate myself on the metal seat. Like my flats, shorts weren't the best fashion choice.

"Awkward conversations aren't a favorite pastime of mine," I mutter.

"You mean, making adult decisions aren't?"

"I'm twenty-six." I mentally slap myself. *That's my argument?*

"Last time I checked, twenty-six was an adult."

"I mean, I don't have much experience in making adult decisions that don't only impact my life."

When I graduated from high school, I moved to LA for college and have lived my life without answering to anyone. I travel regularly for my job and don't have to worry about anyone other than my boss controlling what I do. My personal decisions have never impacted anyone else's life before.

"You'd better get over that shit *fast*. We're about to be making some big decisions together," he says.

My chest feels tight. I haven't come to terms with having a long-term relationship with Dallas, and I don't feel like diving into the reality of it now. "I haven't made a doctor's appointment yet. I have no idea where to go, but I'd prefer an office not close, considering the town doctor probably delivered you." *And Maven.*

"That's true."

I throw my arms out. "Exactly!" *Does it make me a sucky person that I don't want the same doctor Lucy had? God, I sound like a jealous brat.*

"Dr. Riley's son recently graduated from med school and moved back to work at the practice. He said he'd see us on the low until you're ready to tell people."

On the low? Like I'm going to be pushing a royal baby out of me?

"You're positive he won't tell anyone?" I ask.

"Positive. I have plenty of dirt to easily blackmail him."

"Good. Blackmail away. I'd rather not have any more attention brought to us."

He chuckles and leans forward to scan the crowd below. "I take it, I wasn't the only one noticing all the prying eyes?"

"Sure weren't."

"Ignore them. Something new will come up, and they'll forget about us."

"Doubt it. You're like the bachelor of Blue Beech, and I'm sure they want you to give a rose to a *local girl*."

"Other people don't decide whom I spend my time with."

They might not decide, but that doesn't mean they won't talk shit about it.

I point to my stomach. "In other news, I need to find more creative ways to hide this. I'm showing more, and I don't want people to find out."

"We're having a baby, Willow. It's eventually going to come out. You're struggling with the reality of it, and that's why I'm holding back on saying anything, but you'd better come to grips with it soon. I need to tell my daughter and parents before you go into labor."

Dallas isn't a bullshitter.

He shoots it to you straight. Been that way for as long as I've known him, which is something I'm not used to. The guys I date tend to be liars who whisper sweet nothings into your ear and then do the opposite. I've never had a guy … a *man* like Dallas.

He clears his throat. "And, since I have you hostage, I'd better ask the question that's been bugging me."

Oh God. What now?

"Tell me the truth. Why did you hide this from me?"

I look around. *How long does it take for us to get back to the ground?*

"Willow," he says, practically growling my name. "Give me a clear answer, not something half-assed. I want real. The truth."

I lean in and take a deep breath. *Here goes. He wants it. I'll give it. He's not going to like it.*

"I remember every second of our night together." My pulse races like a freight train is about to hit me. "You made me feel special, like I could have someone other than a cheating scumbag. You made me feel alive." *Am I really going to do this?* I want to sound strong, but my voice cracks. "At least temporarily." I stop to inhale another breath, chickening out.

"What happened that makes you question our night wasn't special?"

His gaze is fixed on me, intense, and he settles his elbow on his knee. His free hand rests on my thigh.

"You called me her."

I thought I had his attention before, but my admission kicked it into overdrive.

His head jerks to the side. "What?"

"You called me her ... *Lucy*." Tears bite at my eyes, breaking the hold I've been trying to keep. *There. I said it. I gave him the truth.*

His face contorts with a mix of pain and disbelief. "What? No way. You're lying."

"I'm not lying."

I regret it every day. Regret not slapping him in the face or screaming when it happened, but I couldn't blame him. I couldn't blame him because my intention of having sex with him was the same—to forget the person I longed for. I wanted to erase Brett. He tried to erase Lucy.

He scrubs his hand over his face. I've spent the last decade reading a man who lied for years, and Dallas isn't lying about not remembering.

He scoots in closer to clasp my chin in his hand. "Fuck, Willow. I'm sorry. No wonder you hate my fucking guts and can barely stand to look at me. I'm sorry. God, I'm an asshole."

He runs his hand over my cheek while apologizing repeatedly. I draw in the trace of cotton candy and cinnamon on his breath.

The end of our ride is getting closer, and I wish I had a panic button to freeze us in place.

"You're the only woman I've kissed other than Lucy," he says, his lips inches from mine. "The only woman I've touched. The only woman I've ever had in my bed."

I relax into his touch, into his words. *Should this admission turn me on? Should it make me want to straddle him and get a public indecency arrest?*

"And it's not for lack of trying," he goes on. "This will make me sound like an arrogant jerk, but I've had women knocking on my door daily, but I've never given them a second look. Replacing Lucy with a quick fuck wasn't my intention. I could've done that with anyone. I might've said her name, but I swear to you, I knew who I was inside of, and it wasn't her."

I breathe heavily and take in the callous palm roaming over my cheek.

"We were both missing other people that night. We can agree on that."

I nod at the truth. "What do you want from me?" I whisper, my lips nearly hitting his.

"I want you to move here permanently. I want you to raise our baby here. I don't want you to leave."

His eyes soften, and I dart my tongue over my lips without even realizing it.

God, the desperation of wanting to kiss him, of wanting to screw him, of wanting his touch anywhere on my body is all I'm feeling right now.

"What do you want from me, Willow?"

To wrap my hand around your cock again. To feel you inside me one last time. To love me like you loved her.

"I … I don't know," I answer breathlessly. I can't concentrate on anything but us.

He takes in a sharp breath. "Why can't I stop thinking about you?"

I make my move, unable to stop myself, and crash my lips against his. He tastes more like cotton candy than he smells. He groans while moving his hand from my face to the back of my neck, diving into my hair and drawing me in closer, opening his mouth so that our tongues meet.

His mouth is soft and forbidden. Him only kissing me is going to send me over the edge. He scoots in closer to use his knee to separate my legs more and slides his hand up my thigh, stopping where my shorts end.

"What are you doing to me?" he mutters, taking me deeper into his mouth and inching his hand underneath the fabric, his fingers spreading apart.

I moan and tilt my hips up, permitting him to keep going. His fingers crawl to my middle, right over my panties, and he rubs his thumb across it.

"Fuck," he groans. "You're soaked."

I close my eyes as he moves my panties to the side.

"Okay, who's next in line?" the operator yells.

Dallas's hand disappears in seconds, and his back hits the seat, his breathing labored. "Fuck. I'm sorry. That shouldn't have happened."

I straighten my shorts, rub my hands over my hair to fix it, and curl my arms around my stomach. No doubt I would smack him in the face if we weren't in a public place.

"You're right. It won't happen again," I whisper.

The operator winks at us when the car stops, and we get out.

"It happens all the time, man," he says, smirking. "Figured you wouldn't want to keep up your show in front of everyone."

Oh, hell. He saw us.

I stumble forward, my legs feeling weak, and Dallas rests his hand on the small of my back to stabilize me. We're back to silence, like he didn't have his hand in my shorts only minutes ago, like he wasn't about to get me off in a Ferris wheel car. He guides us straight to Stella, who's waiting on Hudson and Maven to finish up a ride.

Our conversation ends.

Our connection ends.

My hope for him ever touching me again ends.

I can't get attached. I can't let Dallas Barnes in again.

In my head. In my vagina. In my heart.

Chapter Fourteen

DALLAS

My hopes of taking Willow to the fair, so she'd change her mind about staying here blew up in my face.

All because me and my dick.

All because my lack of being laid.

And the fact that she looked so delicious, so damn sexy, sitting there, that I couldn't stop myself. I nearly lost it when I felt how wet she was for me. I wanted to prove to her that I wasn't an asshole whose mind was on my dead wife when I slept with her. I fucked up. I'll be the one to blame when she packs up and leaves.

We'd started to break ground, begun building something, and then my dumbass took a wrecking ball to it. My night with her had been incredible. Touching her had been incredible. What I had done that morning was fucked up and is one of my biggest regrets.

I called her Lucy.

Humiliation and stupidity crack my core.

I don't blame her for hating my ass and keeping her distance.

Had the roles been reversed, had a woman called me another man's name in bed, I would've stepped away … and most likely kicked her out of my bed.

I want to change. To be the man who can rise through the flames stronger than ever, but I can't.

That's why what happened tonight scares the shit out of me.

My goal at the bar had been to drink away the pain, the memories. I hadn't been searching for someone to talk to. Nowhere in my mind was the idea of having a one-night stand. It all took a turn when Willow spoke to me. My attention was all hers as soon as we had our first drink together. I wasn't going to leave that bar unless it was with her.

Tonight has proven it wasn't only a drunken attraction that brought us to my bed.

That fucking terrifies me.

Maven is passed out in the backseat, exhausted from going on every ride multiple times, and Willow hasn't said one word since we got in my truck.

Man, I wish my daughter would wake up and start rambling about random shit like she usually does. I gear my truck into park when we arrive at Willow's apartment and unclip my seat belt to open the door for her, but she's faster than I am.

"Well, uh … good night," is all she says before opening the door and jumping out of the truck like it's on fire. "You don't need to walk me up." She slams the door, races up the steps, and goes inside.

I shut my eyes. "Good night, Willow," I whisper even though she can't hear me.

I wait to pull away until I see the light come through her windows.

I get Maven changed when we get home, tuck her into bed, and start to pick up around the house. If I slack on the housecleaning, my mom comes over and not only plays maid, but detective as well. She checks the fridge to make sure we're consuming all the food groups and goes through my mail and underwear drawer.

I grew out of letting my mom make my bed over a decade ago—the reasons different now than before. I'm not stashing porn and condoms underneath my mattress. It's more her searching for evidence that I'm getting laid or seeing someone. She's resorted to leaving information about online dating and schedules of all the social functions happening in town.

No fucking thank you.

I finish cleaning up the aftermath of Maven's sleepover with her stuffed animals last night. It happens when I go into my bedroom. I tried to hide all the pictures once. Picked them up and shut them away in the attic. Ten minutes later, I returned them.

I like to see Lucy when I'm having a bad day, when I need someone to understand me, when I need to tell her about all the crazy stuff our daughter does. I grab the picture from my nightstand and trace my fingers over her wedding dress, her tan face, her blonde hair, and then her pink lips.

"You always were the best at giving advice," I whisper, setting the frame down to twist my wedding ring. "Tell me what I should do."

I shut my eyes and remember her last words. Lucy knew what I needed before I knew it myself.

"Find someone to love," she demanded.

"That's not ... that's not possible," I whispered.

"It is. I promise you, the day will come." I opened my mouth to argue, but she placed her finger against the crack of my lips. "You might not see it now, but it will. Your heart will make the right choice to move on with someone who loves you and Maven. Don't be scared, my love. Give it a chance. Heal and let her help you do it."

I kiss my fingers, press them to her picture, and turn off my lamp.

Sleep doesn't come to me.

Chapter Fifteen

DALLAS

Maven grins at me with her gap-toothed smile, a clear sign she's up to no good. Two bags are set at her feet, waiting for me to load them into my truck.

"Daddy, I need your phone this week. Pretty, pretty please."

"For what?" I ask.

"In case I need anything," she answers in annoyance, as if it were a reasonable request for a six-year-old.

"Nice try. You're not taking my phone to camp."

She huffs and stomps her feet. I've already vetoed her iPad making the trip. *Damn kids and electronics.* They act like it'll kill them to spend a weekend in the wilderness without Wi-Fi.

"What if I get lost in the woods and can't find my way back?"

"I've pointed out the North Star to you several times."

She frowns. "What if I see a big ole mean bear?"

I laugh. "Having a phone will be the last of your worries. If you see a bear, slowly back away, and don't make eye contact." *I thought I wasn't supposed to deal with this shit until her teenage years.*

She crosses her arms and gives me her best pouty face. She knows how to pull at my heartstrings. Her perfected pouty face has landed her a gerbil, a goldfish, and the iPad.

"Don't act like you won't miss me," I tease.

Her pouty face turns into an annoyed one.

"Now, grab your sleeping bag, and let's get going," I instruct.

This will be the longest we've been away from each other since Lucy passed. It was different when she was here. I lived states away, traveled frequently, and only came home a few times a month. I regret having that long-distance relationship. I thought I'd have more time, but it just goes to show you that time is never guaranteed. Live each moment and hug the ones you love because you don't know what can happen tomorrow.

"What are you going to do when I'm gone?" she asks as I strap the seat belt around her.

"Work. Do grown-up stuff."

I shut the door and jump into the driver's seat. The camp is about an hour drive, and I made a playlist for us to enjoy during the trip since we have the no-electronics rule. Maven is going to hate it … at first because I usually let her listen to her teenybop bullshit, but I want to introduce her to something new today.

"One Direction, Daddy!" she yells as soon as we pull out of the driveway.

"Oh, man, I forgot to tell you."

She scrunches her face up. "Forgot to tell me what?"

"Now that they broke up, their music can't be played anymore. It's banned."

"Since when?"

"Yesterday. It was all over the news." I peek back at her silence to see tears running down her face. *This can't be for real?* "What's wrong, May-Bear?"

"They're gone," she cries out, her pouty face intact.

Jesus Christ. "Let me double-check. It might have changed."

I switch to Maven's favorite station and groan when a One Direction song conveniently comes blasting through my speakers.

So much for Bob Dylan.

My little girl always wins.

Kids are jumping out of cars, backpacks strapped to them, and running toward the group of others congregated in front of the clubhouse. Maven has already said her good-byes and taken off with her friends.

I lean back against my truck and slide my hands into the pockets of my jeans. My parents sent us kids to Camp Maganaw, and I never failed to have a blast. My attention goes straight to Bear Claw Cabin. It's been updated with a fresh slab of paint and a new door, but the memories I have in that cabin will always be there. Lucy and I had our first kiss behind Bear Claw after sneaking out one night.

"Dallas, how are you holding up?"

I briefly glance over when Cindy stops at my side and copies my stance. Cindy and I went to high school together, and she was Lucy's hairdresser. She married the quarterback, had a baby, and then divorced the cheating drunk a few years ago.

I move dirt with the toe of my boot. "As good as I can be, I guess."

A breath bursts from her lips. "I get it. It's hard. I never thought I'd be with anyone other than Phil, but I've learned that the best way to heal is by moving on."

I ram my heel into the ground as anger flushes through me. "A divorce and death are not fucking worthy of comparison," I grind out.

I bite my tongue to stop myself from telling her what wants to come out. Cindy was one of the casserole-and-muffin-making chicks who checked up on me daily in the weeks after losing Lucy. I finally had to put a stop to it after the third week.

If she believes finding someone else with help, more power to her, but I won't be the man to do it … and she sure as hell isn't replacing Lucy.

"You know, you're a jackass. I'm sorry if my concern for you and your daughter eating makes you so rattled," she snaps.

"I told you I appreciated the meals, but they weren't necessary. I don't need help feeding my daughter. We both know your *concern* wasn't making sure we had hot meals twice a day."

She slumps back against the truck. "So, it's true then?"

"What's true?"

Her *concern* has switched to annoyance. "You and the new chick in town have something going on?"

My eyes stay pinned to her.

"Stella's friend," she clarifies, annoyed.

"The hell you hear that?" I ask with a scoff.

"We all saw it at the fair—to my surprise, considering, months ago, you made it clear you weren't interested in dating, *period*."

"I'm not dating anyone." I pause and pinch my lips together. "Not that it's anyone's fucking business."

A rush of red storms her cheeks. "Asshole," she mutters before turning around and stomping to her car.

Two days have passed since the fair fiasco, and communication with Willow has been limited and vague. Phone calls go unanswered. Text messages consists of one word. I've never received so many *K* and *Cool* responses.

That's changing today.

It's our first doctor's appointment. I texted Willow the details after scheduling it and waited for the argument I knew was coming, but surprisingly, she agreed … with a fucking *K*.

I park my truck and wait until she walks out of her apartment before jumping out and joining her on the sidewalk.

"Nuh-uh," she says. "I'm driving myself."

"No one is driving," I reply. "It's a five-minute walk. I thought we'd enjoy the stroll."

She pinches her lips together, and her shoulder smacks against mine when she bursts past me and down the sidewalk. "I'll pass."

She pushes when I pull.

I pull when she pushes.

One of us is always resisting when the other comes forward.

I speed-walk to keep up with her. "Come on. The weather is perfect. Let's save the environment and conserve gas, not pollute the air. Walking with me will save the world."

My humanity-saving argument doesn't stop her, and I nearly miss her mocking me, an uneven smile on her lips. I don't hold back my shit-eating grin when she passes her car and keeps walking. I stay a few steps behind and let her believe she's getting her way until it happens.

I rush forward when she trips on her feet, falling forward, her knees almost hitting the concrete while her lips are close to kissing the sidewalk. I stretch my arm out to capture her around the waist, and she yelps as I steady her. Instead of breaking my hold when she's stable, I tighten my grip, my fingers sinking into the cotton of her *Girl Power* T-shirt, and stare down at her.

I wait for her to pull out of my hold and tell me never to touch her again. She does none of that. She stays still, catching her breath, and shakes her head.

"Really?" she mutters. "So damn cliché. I fall, and you catch me."

I can't help but chuckle at the actuality of her words. "Just like in the movies."

I release my hold on her waist but move my hand to her elbow just in case.

"You're nervous," I say.

I run my hand up and down her arm in an attempt to calm her nerves. I don't know what has her riled up more—her almost fall, us touching, or this appointment.

She pulls out of my hold with a grimace and runs her hand down her long hair. "No shit, Sherlock."

"Anything I can do to help?"

"Not come."

"Anything I can do *but* that?"

Her hands start shaking, and I turn so that I'm standing in front of her. She attempts to maneuver around me, but I take a step over. She tries the other side. I do the same thing.

"Breathe. Relax." I inhale and exhale a few times in hopes that she'll follow my lead. She does. "Everything is going to be okay, I promise. If you feel uncomfortable, we'll leave."

We do this for a good five minutes, and she sniffles while calming down. "These damn pregnancy hormones are going to be the end of my sanity."

I smile. "I wish I could say they get better, but from what I've witnessed, they don't." I move out of her way and settle my hand on the arch of her back when she starts walking again.

"Then, I'd be careful not to piss me off."

"That's been my goal since day one."

I've been sucking ass at it though.

She sniffles again. "You need to work harder."

Thought confirmed.

I move my arm up and wrap it around her shoulders, bringing her to my side, hoping she doesn't pull away. This isn't sexual. It's something you do to a friend having a bad day.

"Come on, I can't have you showing up to the doctor in tears. My mom would have my ass if she found out. Give me something I can do to calm you down."

"Punching you might work."

I break our connection to move back in front of her and start walking backward. "If being your punching bag helps, then have at it." I throw my arms out and gesture for her to take a swing.

I'm the one stumbling this time when she pushes me back. "God, you piss me off."

"What? Why? I'm giving you what you want."

I've never had complications like this with a woman. Granted, my experience is limited to one woman, so that doesn't say much in itself. I don't remember learning Lucy's quirks because I grew up with them. They were instilled in me before I knew how to spell my name.

She scowls. "What I want is for you to stop being so damn nice."

"What? Why?" I repeat, confused as fuck.

If I'm an ass, she's pissed. If I'm nice, she's pissed.

"Because you're making it difficult to hate you right now."

"That's a bad thing?"

"Yes!"

I'm doing everything in my power to fix this, to make her feel comfortable, so she doesn't run away again, but it's killing me. I'm very rarely the fun guy. My role has always been the serious and overprotective brother. Hudson was the Marine who thrived on having a good time, and Lauren was the mischievous one I caught sneaking out on too many occasions. I was the big brother who made sure everyone was okay and protected.

I stop us in front of the restored yellow Victorian home. "And we're here." Perfect timing before we get into another argument, and my goal of distracting her has somewhat succeeded.

She assesses the building and glares at me like I'm fucking with her. "This …" She does another once-over. "This is a house. Where's the office?"

I point to the sign with the doctor's name.

"This isn't some midwives shit, is it? Not to be judgmental, but I'm not having my baby in some old home's bathtub."

"We'll go to a hospital when you give birth, and so will the doctor. Give Dr. Riley a chance. If you hate him, we'll go to the city."

Compromise. Compromise. Fucking compromise. Marriage taught me that compromise is what keeps you going when the tides get rough.

She sighs. "Let's do this then."

Chapter Sixteen

WILLOW

The door chimes when we walk in, and the nurse behind the counter jumps up from her chair to greet us. Her smile collapses when she notices Dallas behind me. She has the perfect sun-kissed blonde hair and a summer tan. She reminds me of Lucy. Dallas's type.

She tucks a strand behind her ear. "Dallas … I didn't see you on the books today."

"Hey, Fiona. I'm with Willow Andrews. We have an appointment with Aidan," he explains, keeping his focus on me.

Dallas wasn't lying about there being an office inside. It's not modern, like the one I went to for my first pregnancy test. First professional one. I'd taken fifteen at-home tests and then finally gone to the doctor because I was in denial and determined they were all defective.

A few chairs sit in the waiting room across from the wooden front desk A photo of an older man with his name underneath it is centered on the wall, and a corkboard covered with flyers is hung next to it.

Get your flu shot!

Join the bowling league!

Fire department fundraiser this Friday!

The nurse's red lips dip in surprise as she stares at me in curiosity the same way everyone did at the fair. "I see. Let me collect the paperwork your doctor sent over this morning, and then I'll show you to your exam room."

Dallas tucks his hands into the pockets of his jeans. "Is Rick in today?"

"No, he's out hunting. Won't be back until the weekend. We have a light schedule today, even with Aidan here." She laughs. "Everyone remembers all the trouble he got into when you guys were younger, and they aren't sure if they trust him with needles yet."

I jerk my head to glare at Dallas. *The hell? Is he bringing me to some quack?*

"Aidan knows what he's doing," Dallas says, reassuring me. "We can't all stay the kids who drank behind my parents' barn or nearly lit the town square on fire."

Fiona slaps his shoulder. "I miss those days." She taps it next. "How have you been doing?"

He nods, scraping a hand through his hair, and his face tightens. "Fine."

"You let me know if you need anything, all right?"

"Thanks," he replies flatly.

Well … this sure is fun.

"So, where to?" he asks.

She leads us to a room at the end of the hallway. The door isn't numbered but does say *Dr. Aidan Riley* across the top glass.

I sit on the exam bed while Dallas scoots his chair next to me. I don't realize I'm tapping my feet until he rests his hand on my thigh, causing me to flinch. I surprise myself by not moving it. He might piss me off, but his touch relaxes me. That still doesn't stop me from scowling at him though.

There's a knock on the door, and Dallas moves his hand like a kid caught with it in the cookie jar when the doctor walks in.

The first thing I notice shouldn't be how attractive he is, but he's definitely a looker. Blond hair cut short in almost a frat-boy style but more sophisticated and an oval face with perfect features. I was expecting a dude in overalls. Now, I'm stuck in a room with two men I wouldn't have a problem screwing. My OB-GYN and the off-limits man who knocked me up.

He holds out his hand with a smile. "Willow, pleasure meeting you. I'm Dr. Riley, but call me Aidan, considering my father has the same name, and I'm not an old goat."

I smile back, and his attention goes to Dallas next, worry crossing his features.

"Dallas, you doing okay, man?"

My smile collapses. I feel bad for Dallas. His loss follows him everywhere. He will forever be known as the man who tragically lost his wife too soon. And I'll forever be known as the woman who screwed the heartbroken widowed man and got knocked up.

Dallas's attention stays on me as he answers, "Sure am, Doc."

Aidan sits down on the rolling stool and comes closer. "The doctor who gave you your initial pregnancy test sent over your records. It appears, you're around twelve weeks. Good timing for your first ultrasound."

"Right ... right now?" I ask. I knew he'd want to run tests but figured he'd want to ask more questions before diving straight in.

"We can do it another time if you'd like," Aidan replies.

"No." I clear my throat. "Today's fine." I want to see my baby. I peek over at Dallas. "You probably don't want to be in here for this."

He kicks his legs out and makes himself comfortable in the chair. "I'd like to be. That cool?"

Fuck no.

Aidan opens a cabinet and pulls out a cup before handing it to me. "You think about it. Meanwhile, I need a urine sample." He tips his head toward the other side of the room. "Bathroom's right there."

I shut the door behind me and am washing my hands when I hear their conversation.

"Your mom know about this?" Aidan asks.

"No," Dallas answers. "Just Hudson, his girlfriend, and Lauren."

"Is she ..." Aidan pauses. "Are you two ..."

"Are we dating? No. It was a one-time thing."

Aidan chuckles. "Oh, man. Good luck, my friend, and congratulations on the baby."

My head flies up, nearly colliding with Dallas's, and I'm struggling to keep my breath.

"Twins?" I yell. "Did you ..." My gaze flicks to Dallas, who looks in as much shock as I am. "Did he ... did he say twins?"

"Sure did," Aidan answers with a wide grin. "My first prenatal patient, and we're having twins. *Yes!*"

"Don't take this the wrong way, Doctor, but you're new at this, right? Are you sure you know how to read these correctly? They're probably more ancient than what you worked with in med school."

Aidan is still smiling, not offended. "I read these things for years when I shadowed my father. I clearly see two fetuses." He puts his finger on the screen. "Here's baby one." Then, he moves it over. "And baby number two."

Holy shit. Holy shit.

Dallas is sitting up straight, mouth open, and staring at the screen like he has to memorize it for a test tomorrow.

I can't think straight. I was scared shitless when I thought I was having one baby. Now, I'm having *two*?

Double the responsibility. Double the diaper-changing. Double the expenses. Double the help I'm going to need from Dallas. Double the time we'll be spending together.

～

"Let's get lunch."

I stop in my tracks and coldly gape at him. From now on, I'll be placing all of this pregnancy blame on him because it's too much for me to carry two babies in my body along with the responsibility of our choice on my shoulders.

He knocked me up. I'm the one who has to push the babies out, so he can deal with the blame for the pain and fear I'm experiencing. It only makes sense.

"Lunch?" I repeat. "Don't you mean, let's find a safe, pregnancy-approved Xanax? Or let's go to yoga? Or find a stress-management class? Did you hear what Aidan said? I have two babies inside me."

We found out we're having twins, and he wants to get fucking lunch? Surely, I can't be the only one in shock.

Lucky for me, Fiona was on break and unable to witness the panic in me when we left the exam room.

He stares at me with unease. "I heard him loud and clear. Two babies make feeding you even more important."

"Are you not fucking terrified?" I shout.

We're on the sidewalk outside the doctor's office, which isn't too far from the town square where most of the people hang out and gossip. There's a chance someone might hear us, but I don't care right now.

He takes a deep breath. "Nervous? Yes. But it's nothing I can't handle." He takes the step separating us and runs his hands over my arms. "You can do this. *We* can do this. You're going to be a great mother. When the babies come, your instincts will kick in, and you'll have it figured out. Hell, I've seen you do shit for Stella that's more demanding than children. So, yes, I'm nervous and surprised as fuck, but I'm relieved, knowing our twins will have a kick-ass mother. I trust you. I have faith in you. It won't be easy, but we'll make it work."

I scrunch up my face when he snorts. "What's so funny?"

"I bet you're glad you didn't hide this from me now. Admit it. You're going to need my help."

"You're changing all the diapers, by the way. That's your daddy duty."

"Whatever you need, I'll be here." He rubs his hands together. "Now, how 'bout that lunch?"

"Lunch together? Like, in a public place?"

He chuckles. "Yes, together. There's a diner down the street that serves the best sandwiches and pies you've ever had."

I fake a yawn. "Thanks for the invite, but I'm pretty exhausted."

I used to feel comfortable with spending hours with Dallas. We traveled together for weeks straight at times and ate meals together, and it never felt weird. *So, why does it seem like such a big deal now?* We slept with each other, for God's sake.

"Come on." He places his hands together. "*Please.*"

"Fine, but a quick meal, and that's it." It's hard to turn down this man.

He grins in victory. We pass small shops and bakeries before stopping in front of Shirley's Diner. Large windows line the front, and I see the prying eyes before we even step foot inside. My anxiety triples when I follow him to a booth at the front of the diner sitting along the window.

"You okay?" he asks when we sit down.

I lean in and lower my voice. "They're staring at me like I'm from a different planet."

"They're just curious." He rests his hands on the table. "Say the word, and I'll get up from this table and tell them to stop."

"You'd do that?" I grab his arm when he starts to get up and let my fingers linger around his muscle before slowly peeling them away. "No!" I spread my napkin across my lap in an attempt to calm my nerves. "Forget I said anything."

An older, dark-skinned waitress comes to our table. "Dallas, it's nice to see you. I was afraid you'd been cheating on me with a new diner."

Dallas chuckles. "You know I'd never betray you, Shirley. I've just been busy."

She waves off his response with a grin. "You know I'm only giving you a hard time." Her lips form a sincere smile when she glimpses at me. "And I see why you've been busy. What can I get for you, sweetie? Iced tea? Lemonade?"

"Lemonade." I hold the menu up and set it back down. "And whatever today's special is."

"I'll have the same," Dallas tells her.

Shirley grabs our menus. "Coming right up."

"She's nice," I comment when she scurries over to the booth across from ours.

"Blue Beech is filled with nice people," he replies.

"I'm assuming you meant to say nosy people." *How bad will it get when news about my inhabited uterus gets around?*

"Yes, they're nosy, but they'll lend you a helping hand without asking for anything in return, feed you, take care of your pets when you're out of town, and always make sure you're doing okay when something tragic happens. They're only staring because they want to get to know you."

"Or because they're not used to seeing you with someone who's not Lucy."

A hint of a frown hits his lips, and his shoulders stiffen. "You could say that. I've been the town's brooding bachelor for a minute now, who's never been seen with another woman."

"They see you as a traitor. You're finally seen with a woman, and she's an outsider." I stop when I catch my words, my brain scattering to backtrack them. "Not that we're, uh … more than friends. Just *friends* sharing a meal."

"They're well aware we're more than friends sharing a meal." He relaxes in his seat. "They're really going to find out when you start to show and wear clothes that don't swallow you up."

"I'll tell them I got fat."

"And then lost all the weight, and we suddenly have two babies?"

I shrug. "Sounds legit to me."

Shirley interrupts us and winks while dropping a turkey bacon club and our drinks in front of us. "You two enjoy."

"You ready to come up with a plan yet?" Dallas asks when I take my first bite.

"Nope," I answer after chewing.

He nods, telling me the conversation isn't over but that he'll save it for later. "What's your favorite food?"

I look up from my plate. "What?"

"Your favorite food. We can't sit here in silence, and I figure we'll ask each other questions we never did when we worked together."

I tell him it's a tie between sushi and tacos. His is his mom's carrot cake. We throw questions at each other back and forth while we eat. Having a normal conversation with him feels right. It's comfortable. It doesn't feel like first-date awkwardness because this is definitely not a date.

My dream vacation is staying in one of those tiki huts in Bora Bora. His is Yosemite. Black-and-white movies are my thing. He's not much of a movie buff, but we both agree that anything with Tom Cruise is overrated.

Shirley collects our plates and comes back to set a delicious piece of blueberry pie in front of me.

"Oh no, I didn't order this," I say.

She smiles. "It's on the house, honey. First slice for a newcomer is always free."

"Thank you." I take a bite and groan at the deliciousness. "Shirley is officially my favorite person in this town."

He smiles in amusement. "She's bribing you. The first piece is never free."

"What do you mean?"

"Don't think I'm the only one hoping you stay in Blue Beech."

Chapter Seventeen

WILLOW

"**G**uess who's back, back again. Willow's back, tell a friend," Stella sings when I slide into the passenger seat of her BMW SUV.

My best friend might've shut the door on the celebrity lifestyle, but that doesn't mean she gave up her love of expensive handbags and foreign cars or that she doesn't stop gifting those cars to her favorite personal assistant.

She's grinning, her eyes pinned on me, and her charcoal-colored hair is pulled back into a high ponytail that shows off her Spanish features.

I buckle my seat belt while groaning. "I'm officially putting my two-weeks' notice in."

It's my first day back at work since moving to Blue Beech, and it feels good being around Stella again. We went from spending endless days side by side to communicating through video conferences and text messages.

Her lips curl into a smile. "You'd miss me too much, but you can bet your ass I'll be giving you maternity leave for as long as you'd like, and then you can bring the cute munchkin to work."

No one knows we're having twins yet, and Dallas promised to keep it that way until I was ready. I need time to wrap my head around everything in my life being multiplied.

"Paid leave, right?" I ask.

"Duh." She wiggles in her seat before shifting the car into drive. "So … does this mean, you're staying?"

I've lost count of the number of times Stella has asked me to move here—before and after the Dallas situation. I would've been fired for refusing to relocate if I worked for anyone else.

"Undecided. I'm giving it a chance, but I can't make any promises. I still need to come up with my single-mom plan."

We don't leave the parking lot because she puts her car back in park to give me her full attention.

Her face fills with worry. "You're not a single mom, Wills. You have Dallas."

I'm single. I'm going to be a mom. Hence, single mom.

"Not sure that makes a difference," I mutter.

Her hand tenderly brushes against my arm. "If you're worried about that, I can assure you, Dallas will be there for your baby … *for you.* He'll change diapers and wake up when the baby is screaming bloody murder in the middle of the night. He'll help financially. If that's not someone supporting you, I don't know what is."

I snort. She has a point, but I still want to see him as the jackass I thought he was that morning.

"Why are you so uneasy about a man being a *good man?* If I recall correctly, you were jumping my ass when Hudson and I were going through a rough patch. It's your turn to listen."

I hate when my actions come back to bite me in the ass. "Different circumstances."

"How are they *different circumstances?*"

"Hudson had cheating fiancée baggage. He wasn't a single dad who lost his wife. What's Dallas going to do? Have sleepovers with Maven at my apartment? I won't be stepping foot into his house after what happened there."

She rolls her eyes, her understanding moving into aggravation. "Grow up. He was going through a rough time."

"He didn't seem to have a problem with me in his bed when we were screwing—only when it was time to face his mistake."

"He doesn't see you as a mistake."

"You didn't see his reaction. The way he still looks at me."

"I'll pay better attention today."

"*Today?*"

She shrugs casually with a mischievous smile. "We're bringing them lunch."

"We?" I turn around to view the backseat. "Do you have someone shoved in your trunk?"

"You and me. *Us*. We're bringing the guys lunch."

"They're grown men. Can't they feed themselves?"

I've texted Dallas a few times on the phone, but I haven't seen him since the diner. I'm still in the process of getting comfortable with him when we're alone. Hudson and Stella breathing over our shoulders won't make it any easier.

Chapter Eighteen

DALLAS

I wipe my hands on a shop towel and toss it to the ground when my stomach growls. "Shirley's for lunch?" I ask Hudson. "I'm fucking starving."

I've been here since five in the morning, finishing up an engine on a tractor for my father's friend who needed it done yesterday. One of our biggest battles of working with agriculture and construction customers is that they're seasonal. They want their equipment done the moment they drop it off, or they're losing money.

Good for our pockets.

Bad for our stress levels.

He shakes his head. "Nah, Stella is bringing me food."

"Ah, yeah. Forgot about your little lunch dates." I smirk. "Cute kids, you. Reminds me of when I was in third grade, trying to convince Lucy to kiss me by bringing her pieces of Mom's pie on the playground."

"Asshole." He throws his towel at me and slides off a stool. "Want to join us? She brings enough to feed an army."

"I'll pass."

He returns to putting all of his tools up, and I snap my fingers to gain his attention.

"And don't forget, we have the auction tomorrow. What time do you want me to pick you up?" I ask.

That gets his full attention. "Shit, I forgot about the auction." He narrows his eyes at me. "Now that you bring it up, I told you I couldn't go."

"Nice try, jackass. I would remember you trying to bail because I wouldn't have let you. They have an excavator going through that I know we can get a kick-ass deal on."

We're in the process of expanding the family business my grandfather started decades ago. Our dad is ready to retire after twenty-five years and wants us to take over.

"I have plans with Stella."

He runs a hand through his hair, which is lighter and longer than mine. All of us Barnes children look alike with a few exceptions. I don't sport as much facial hair as Hudson. I'm convinced he does it to hide his jaw since mine is stronger than his, but he won't admit it. He argues that the few inches he has on my height counts for more than good bone structure.

"Your fiancé will be fine without you for a day."

"She'll be fine … because I'll be with her. Go alone. You're a big boy."

I frown. "It's an eight-hour round trip."

"It'll give you time to reflect."

"Reflection and I aren't a good match. Trust me." I fucking hate being in my head.

He winces, shocked at my response, and I'm positive I've won this discussion. "Ask Willow to tag along."

And I'm wrong.

"She can hardly stand spending twenty minutes around me at a doctor's appointment. I doubt she'll be jumping at the idea of a road trip."

He shrugs, his mouth curving into a sly smile. "Looks like we're about to find out."

"The fuck does that mean?"

I whip around at the sound of a door slamming. The shop is twenty minutes out of town. The only people who come around are employees, customers, and us. I like it—the quietness, the peace.

I follow Hudson out of the garage to find Stella coming our way while holding up a bag.

"Lunchtime!" she yells, stomping across the gravel parking lot.

Willow circles the car, slowly dragging her feet in our direction, making it clear she'd rather be anywhere but here.

Hudson slaps me on the back. "Would you look at that, brother? Perfect timing." He jogs forward to meet Stella halfway and plants a kiss on her lips.

I follow his lead but trail a few feet behind in hopes of sparing myself from their lovesick hellos.

I'm a miserable bastard, but that doesn't mean I'm not happy for my baby brother. He went through a messy-ass breakup. His ex fucked him over by screwing his best friend and used their scheduled wedding date to marry the so-called friend. Hudson ditched town, took over my job as Stella's bodyguard, and somehow convinced her to fall in love with him.

"I'm starving, babe," he tells her with another kiss. "Did you bring enough for my pain-in-the-ass brother?"

Stella throws me a look with a smile. "Sure did. I also brought a friend." Her chin tips toward Willow when she makes it to us. "Do you two know each other?" She slaps her knees. "My bad, you knocked her up."

"Funny," Willow grumbles, throwing her a dirty look. "You remember that two-weeks' threat?"

"You have anything going on tomorrow, Willow?" Hudson asks.

She peeks over at Stella. "No. Stella said I have the day off." Her green eyes flash between the couple in confusion.

"You do," Hudson replies. "You're probably going to be pretty bored, so I have good news for you. Dallas has to go out of town for work and needs some company. You feel like tagging along?"

She bites her lip and shoves dirt around with her shoe, dirtying them up. "I have a busy day. I need to unpack."

"Weird. You told me you were finished unpacking yesterday," Stella says, exchanging a glance with Hudson, confirming this isn't some last-minute idea.

Willow shoots her a death stare. "I have baby books to finish reading."

"Read them on the way," I suggest.

She sucks in a breath at the sound of my voice and finally acknowledges me.

"As a matter of fact, how about you read them to me?" I go on.

My jump into the conversation has shocked everyone, including myself. Making an eight-hour round trip alone sounds like a fucking nightmare.

Willow's mouth presses together in a grimace. "You can't be serious."

"Sure am. I'll bring the doughnuts. You bring the baby lit." I grin. "I'll be there at eight."

Chapter Nineteen

WILLOW

I spent last night drafting texts to Dallas that I never sent.

The keeping-my-distance plan I made at the first positive pregnancy test is backfiring in my face. I can't stop myself from reaching out and clasping on to every hand he holds out even though I know he'll do nothing but drop me at the end. My heart is begging for a repeat of that soul-to-soul connection we shared.

Dallas gets me in a way no one else seems to. He understands what it feels like to have your heart ripped out and torn to shreds. He understands the way love can throw you into a pit of denial. He wouldn't come to terms that Lucy was sick until it was too late, and I couldn't grasp that my boyfriend since high school had been cheating on me for years.

Our hurt is the polar opposite. I know losing someone is nothing compared to a breakup. My pain doesn't even register on the scale of his. His hurt snuck up on him, wearing him down on short notice, and I'm terrified he'll drag me into the dark place with him.

We run from the truth because it's easier to live a lie than face the monster. I was content with living with my struggles … until that positive test. I won't allow my babies to be raised by two broken people. One of us has to be strong, and I can't do that with Dallas Barnes playing with my heart.

The doorbell rings at eight sharp. Like me, Dallas is punctual. You learn to be that way when you're working with tight schedules and dealing with celebrities who have no regard for time. I've had to drag people out of bed, brush their teeth for them, and even buckle them up in their private jets.

"I'm surprised you didn't run off this morning," he says when I open the door.

Me, too, buddy. Me, too.

Three red travel cups are stacked in one hand, and a white paper bag is clutched in the other. A pair of heels is tucked underneath his armpits. I reach out to help him with the cups when he slides past me to get into my apartment. I inhale his woodsy scent while following him into the kitchen.

He drops the bag on the counter and then holds up the familiar black peep-toe heels. "These belong to you."

The shoes I left at his house.

The ones I thought I would never see and didn't care to see again. He'd be on my mind every time I slipped them on. *Where did he keep them? Did Maven see them?*

I grab them from him and toss them onto the floor. "Thank you." I take in all of the cups. "Someone joining us today?" I sound more disappointed than I should about having a third-wheeler on this trip.

He shakes his head. "All I know about your morning drink of choice is coffee is a no-go, so I had to get creative and bring options."

"By creative, you mean …"

"Asking the woman behind the counter at the doughnut shop."

I lean against the wall. "And what did she suggest?"

"Hot chocolate, decaf green tea, and passion fruit something." He counts off the list with his fingers. "I have no damn clue what the last option was, but she said health nuts have been going crazy over it. Thought I might as well give it a go."

His answer is so Dallas.

"Green tea for one then, please."

He frowns. "Well ... fuck."

"What?"

"I didn't take you as a green-tea lover, so I chugged it down on the way here."

"*A green-tea lover?* I don't see you as one either, considering you once told me not liking coffee was an abomination."

"It truly is." I keep staring at him until his lips crack into a smile. "I'm only fucking with you. Green tea is in the middle cup." He snags the doughnuts. "We'll eat on the way. Let's hit the road."

"I like the shirt today," Dallas says.

We've been on the road for about an hour and have covered the weather, the latest news, our ideas for where Stella and Hudson should get married, and what the best movie that came out this year was.

Everything but baby talk.

Which I'm totally okay with.

I pull at the bottom of my *You Had Me at Tacos* tee. Graphic tees are my thing. "I thought I'd give you a hint of what we're having for lunch."

"Can we delay that until dinner? There aren't that many stops on the way, and I doubt any of them serve quality tacos."

I nod. "I can settle for dinner."

It's not like I have anywhere to be. It's either hang with him or sit, bored, in my apartment. You can only watch so much Netflix before you're ready to pull your hair out.

"I'll find you the best damn tacos you've ever had for tagging along today." He grins while peeking over at me. "I woke up this morning, expecting a text from you, bailing."

I cast a curious glance from my seat. "Disappointed I didn't?"

"Hell no. I told you I'd enjoy the company."

I study his driving position. He's leaned back in the seat, right arm stretched out and steering. It comes across so casual, so laid-back, and I never thought I'd be so turned on by the way a man drove.

"What made you change your mind?"

His question smacks me out of my eye-fucking-him moment. "A change of scenery sounded nice."

He chuckles, faking offense. "Not the company?"

I bite the side of my lip. "I haven't decided on that yet."

"I admire your honesty and pledge to give you the time of your life, so you can make that decision at the end of this trip. The drive is beautiful. We won't hit any of that bullshit LA traffic you're used to."

"How long are we talking?"

Now that I think about it, I should've asked more questions before jumping into his truck. It seems I have a habit of jumping into things with this man without considering what could happen first.

"Eight-hour round trip. We'll be at the auction for an hour or two. My eyes are only on one piece of equipment, which will be at the front of the line. I bid and fill out the paperwork, and then we'll be back on the road."

"Sounds like a whole process. How often do you do this, and why do you do it?"

"Once or twice a month, depending on what they have for sale. Hudson and I buy machinery that needs to be updated. We fix it up, modernize it—that kind of stuff. Then, we sell it to farmers and construction companies around the area."

Interesting. I knew he and Hudson did some type of machinery work but never knew what exactly it was.

Stella's explanation consisted of, "They fix stuff and sell machines," which wasn't as thorough as his answer.

"How did you get into it?" I want to draw out every detail of his life that I can.

"My grandfather started the business decades ago. My dad ran it after he passed and while I was in LA and Hudson was in the military. He's ready to retire, so he asked us to take over. Since we're home for good now, we figured it was the perfect time. We've already expanded the business and doubled our clientele."

"So, you bid on the machines you want and then take them to the shop if you win?"

"Most of the time, I bring a trailer and tow the machine with my truck, but today, I'll have a contractor pick it up and deliver it to the shop."

I squint my eyes at him. "Why not tow it today?"

"It's not only uncomfortable, but also a longer trip when towing a piece of heavy machinery. I want you to be comfortable."

Dallas might have had parts of his heart shattered, but fragments are still shoved in there, beating. He's kind even though he's heartbroken. He's miserable, but he manages to consider other people.

"I've been on eighteen-hour flights and gone straight to work without sleeping for another twenty-four," I tell him. "It's nothing compared to traveling with Stella."

"You get paid for that. You're not getting paid for this, and quite frankly, even if you were, I'd still want to make it comfortable for you." He shakes his head and whistles. "I sure don't miss traveling with Stella."

I nod in agreement. "At first, it was a blast, but it's not always glitz and glam, working for Hollywood's finest."

His fingers close around the steering wheel, and he stares at the road. "Seemed like a good idea then, but I have my regrets."

"Regrets about working for her or not moving back when Lucy did?"

"Both, to be honest." The ease of his laid-back mood evaporates. We've moved from the weather to an intimate conversation. "Moving to LA was Lucy's idea. I was fine with staying in Iowa, but she wanted a change."

I've been curious about Dallas's story since he started working for Stella. She filled me in on small details, and I picked up information here and there, but we never ventured into personal conversations, never let our real life seep through the cracks of our professional one.

"You moved for her?" I ask.

"I loved her." So much was said in those three words.

"Why did you stay when she moved back?"

Dallas had been working for Stella for three years when Lucy moved back home. Stella was a stressed mess, worried about finding a new bodyguard as good as him, but he decided to stay, relieving us both.

Sadness. Regret. Tension. All of those emotions pass over his face. "I offered, sometimes even begged when the loneliness of missing my family barreled through, but Lucy insisted

I stay. The money was too good to pass up. Our plan was to save enough money, so I could move home after a few years. We'd be able to live more comfortably." More waves of sadness smack into him, and he pauses. "Fuck it."

I stay quiet, not sure if he's going to shut down or break down.

He expels a long breath before going on, "I've never told anyone this, not even Hudson. We ..." He hesitates again. "We were trying for another baby. Maven was unplanned, so we wanted to do things the right way. Expand our family. Funny how life works. We could conceive when we weren't ready but couldn't when we were. Her doctor suggested IVF, which costs a fucking fortune, so we decided to save money and try it in a few years."

Wow.

My heart breaks at his confession. He was desperately trying to have another baby with his wife and failed. Then, I got pregnant after a one-night stand with him. His wish for more kids has been granted but with the wrong woman.

"You regret not coming back," I say, my voice thick, my throat hurting.

"Every fucking day of my life."

I wanted his reality, his secrets, but I now wish for a dead end. This road is too heartbreaking, and I'm roaming along the sidewalks of guilt. He has to go through all of the motions with me now even though he wanted to do them with someone else.

"You don't expect to lose your wife that young," he continues. "You don't expect your daughter to be motherless at six. We were fucking robbed, and I didn't take advantage of spending all my time with her, protecting her, until life broke in and took her from me."

His vulnerability shocks me. It's comforting to see a flash of something other than anger spark out of him. His hurt opens up emotions in me, and I'm holding myself back from bursting into tears at the sight of this broken man. I'm fighting back the urge to reach out and console him. To let him know everything will be okay.

But I can't, for fear of falling harder for a man who's unavailable. When I fall in love, I fall hard, and that's my weakness. People that love as deep as I do get their hearts shattered harder when it all falls apart.

He blows out a stressed breath and focuses on me in pain. He tilts his lips up into a forced smile. "And here I said I'd give you a good time."

"You're fine. I like this Dallas," I answer, honestly.

He rubs the back of his neck. "You like me being a miserable bastard?"

"I like you being real," I correct. I've never evoked emotions like this out of anybody.

"This is as real as it gets. This is me, and I wish I could be someone better for you."

"What you're giving me is enough." *He wants to be a better father, not a better lover, not a better man for me.* I repeat that to myself over and over in my head, hoping it'll drill the reality through. "I mean ... what you're giving the babies."

"I hope that never changes."

Chapter Twenty

DALLAS

"Woohoo! We won!"

I can't stop my lips from breaking into a smile, watching Willow jump up and down in excitement after the auctioneer yells, "Sold," and points to me.

The men around me are either staring at her in annoyance or desire, and I want to slap all their thoughts from their heads.

I've managed to snag the excavator and got a better deal than I planned. An overweight man wearing a business suit had me worried for a minute when he started driving the price up, but lucky for me, he gave up early.

I know his kind. The men who are only in business for profit and for retail-fucking people with no concern about how they bust their asses every day to keep food in their families' mouths. Barnes Machinery and Equipment isn't like that. We give a shit about people, about their checkbooks, never high gross.

Willow insisted on tagging along with me at the bidding yard. I offered to let her wait in the truck or hang out in the coffee shop across the street since there's a lot of standing and waiting around for your item to come up. She wouldn't have it and refused to decline a ticket into my world.

She hasn't complained once, which doesn't surprise me. She's a hard worker, who scored a job with one of the most prestigious celebrity PR and assistant firms in LA at twenty-one. She worked with Hollywood's elite and impressed Stella so much, she hired her full-time. Even though Stella isn't as hard on her, Willow works her ass off to make things easier for her boss.

Hell, most of the time she goes above and beyond what is asked of her. She works long hours, does the shit no one else wants to do, and fixes any problems that come along.

"How about some jams?" Willow asks when we get back into the truck.

I paid for the machine, filled out all the necessary paperwork, and scheduled the delivery. We'd gotten lunch before the auction started, and now, my goal is to find her some kick-ass tacos for being such a good sport.

"You be the DJ," I answer.

Music comes blaring through the speakers when she turns the radio on. I haven't used it since dropping Maven off at camp and cringe at the same time she bursts out into a fit of laughter. Since her laugh is contagious, I can't stop myself from doing the same.

"Whoa," she says when she catches her breath. "Didn't peg you as a Bieber fan, Barnes."

I turn down the volume a few notches. "I'm not. *Maven* is a Bieber fan."

"Blaming it on the kid, huh? How convenient." She smacks her palm against her forehead. "Oh. My. God."

I lift my chin. "What?"

"My baby daddy is a Belieber."

"A what?"

"A Belieber. A member of Justin's fan club."

For fuck's sake.

Not only do I have to listen to this shit, but now, Willow also thinks I'm his biggest fucking fan with posters of his mug splattered all over my bedroom wall.

"I'm not, let me repeat, I'm not a member of his fan club."

"I believe you." A smile still dances on her moist lips.

"Appreciate it."

"You're the President of it."

I can't stop myself from smiling as a light chuckle echoes from my chest. "Oh, come on, you honestly can't believe I listen to this shit."

"The evidence is clear, counselor. His music is on your radio."

Thunder roars through the sky so loud, I can't hear Bieber, and rain smacks into my windshield. *Fuck.*

"And look at that. God knows you're lying, too."

"Or the weather predicted a seventy percent chance of thunderstorms, but I hoped it'd be in our favor."

At least it waited until after the auction to pour hell down.

The windshield wipers squeak when I shift them to high, and Willow turns down the music, reading my mind so that I can focus better on the road. My headlights shine brightly as the sky turns a deep shade of black even though it's only after six.

I lower my speed and get better control of my view on the road when a loud pop rings out, and my steering wheel starts to shake. The ride gets bumpy, and Willow hangs on to her seat belt for stability.

I pull the truck over and park it before slamming my hand against the steering wheel, causing the horn to blare out.

"Motherfucker," I mutter.

"What?" Willow asks.

"We have a flat."

She stares at me as if it's not a problem. "You know how to change a tire, right?"

I nod. "It helps if you have a spare though."

Her jaw drops. "You're kidding me."

"I wish I were." I feel like a defeated asshole.

This puts a damper on our almost perfect day. We're stranded in the rain, and instead of tacos, I'll be giving her Maven's fruit snacks as the final course.

"No big deal. We'll call a tow truck. I've been in bigger messes than this in my sleep."

"One problem with that." I pull out my phone to show her the screen. "No service. Tell me you have something."

She snatches her purse from the floorboard and rifles through it before finding her phone.

Horror takes over her face when the screen comes to life.

"For real?" she shrieks, throwing her hands up in the air. "We're in the ass crack of no-man's-land stranded with no spare tire. This is straight out of a horror movie." She turns around and lays her gaze out the back window. "Swear to God, if a meat-truck-driving serial killer pulls up, I'm making a run for it."

I grind my teeth, my heart crashing with anguish and guilt from putting her in this situation. I gave my dad my spare last week and forgot to replace it.

Her face softens when she peeks over at me. "Shit, sorry," she whispers over the pelting rain hitting the windshield. "That was too dramatic for this situation. I tend to do that at times."

"You're fine. I'll take dramatics over you wanting to kill me." I turn around in my seat and snatch a jacket from the backseat. "I'm going to see if I can manage to get service in the field over there."

She points out the window. "It's pouring. There are no streetlights. We should wait until the storm calms before going out."

I put the jacket on. "What if it storms all night?"

She starts to unbuckle her seat belt. "Then, I'm coming with you."

I stop her and snap it back in place. "The fuck you are. Stay here, and I'll be back in a flash."

I jump out of the truck despite her protests and hold my phone in the air while sprinting toward the field. The rain comes at me sideways while I wait for the service bars to light up on my phone.

Come on! Come on!

I jump, nearly losing my phone, when a crack of lightning bites through the dark sky. I can barely make out the truck in the downpour and am still messing with my phone when I notice the bright shine of headlights getting closer.

My attention snaps away from the car to the truck at the sound of a door slamming. I scream her name and race toward her when she starts running to the side of the road, waving her hands in the air. The car flies by, splashing her with water, and her shoulders slump in failure.

Fear and anger splinter through me like the storm.

"Have you lost your mind?" I scream, snatching her by the waist from behind and swinging her into my arms. I hover my body over hers to protect her from getting more soaked and tighten my hold on her shivering body while walking us from the street back to my truck. "They could've run you over!"

My breathing halts, dying in my throat, and a chill colder than the rain zips down my spine when she rotates herself in my arms. My hands stay on her wrists as she glares at me before jerking out of my hold with a huff.

"I was flagging them down for help!"

"You running out in the street, waving down some stranger, does not fucking help me. You keeping your ass in the heated seat in the safety of my truck is what helps me."

"It was worth a try!"

The way her voice cracks makes me feel like shit. We lock eyes. She's staring at me like she's searching my soul, assessing the situation in my eyes, unsure of what my next step will be.

I suck in each breath she expels, inhaling her sweet scent, nearly panting at the sight of her dripping wet in front of me, neglecting the shitty situation we're in. Her shirt is soaked to her skin, her hard nipples peeking through the thin tee, and I lick my lips, mentally tasting her.

My next step should be getting her inside the truck, out of this chilly ambush of rain, but goddamn it, I can't break away. I run a hand through her hair and smooth it down before lowering my fingers to her cheek. She shuts her eyes and relaxes into my touch.

I inch forward, my chest brushing against hers, and she lets out a soft moan. The sweet sound runs straight to my dick.

"Dallas," she whispers, eyes still closed, "what are we doing?"

I can't stop myself from chuckling. "We're standing in the rain."

"No," she croaks out. "What are *we* doing?"

Chapter Twenty-One

DALLAS

Willow's question shakes me back into reality, and I drop my hand from her face.

She wants to have this conversation now.

In the pouring rain.

I chuckle.

This situation sums up our relationship.

Bad timing. Unexpected. Not sure what the next move is.

I run my hands down her arms when her teeth start to chatter. "We need to get you in the truck," I say, squeezing her shoulders.

I move around her to open the door. She nods timidly, her front teeth biting into her soft lip, and turns her back to me to climb in. I stand behind her, helping her up, and make sure she's secure.

"I managed to get one bar in the middle of the field. I'm going to try to get in contact with a tow company, so I need you to refrain from leaving the car. I don't give a shit if a parade starts coming down the street." I nod my head toward the dashboard. "Turn the heat on high. I have clothes in my gym bag in the backseat for you to change into."

"Got it. No getting out of the car." I go to close the door, but she stops me. "What if a serial killer is running toward you with a knife?"

This woman and her fucking questions. *Where does she come up with this shit?* "You lock the doors and let me deal with it."

"I'm trained in martial arts, you know. I was a junior green belt. I would be a great help."

"Look at you, badass. Keep your eyes out for killers and promise me you'll stay in here." I can't believe I'm standing in a fucking storm and taking the chance of getting struck by lightning to entertain this conversation. Willow gets me swept up into her world, her words, and I can't seem to walk away. "Promise me you'll stay in here."

"My promises don't mean shit, remember?"

"Make them mean something."

I slam the door shut and let out a sigh before jogging back to the field. I ignore the rain as I hurry back to the same spot and dial the number as fast as I can, hoping that not only the service stays connected, but also that Willow keeps her ass planted in the truck.

I make it through and give the tow company our location. Then, I shove my phone into my pocket. I stop to search the dark sky and twist my wedding ring while rain drips from the tips of my fingers to the mud underneath my boots.

I don't move. I only think.

My mind hasn't been fighting back the painful thoughts of missing Lucy today. I haven't felt like a failure of a husband since I knocked on Willow's door this morning. I haven't cursed the world for my loss. The constant guilt and anger didn't seep through me when I saw the happy family in the booth across from us at the small diner we ate lunch in.

The presence of Willow blocks out that dark tunnel in my brain and gives me a way toward the light and out of my hole.

I open the back door when I get back to the truck, toss my mud-covered boots in the backseat, grab my tennis shoes from the floorboard, and slide into the driver's side.

My attention shoots straight to Willow. She's still in her wet clothes and slipping her fingers through the strands of her dripping hair. She sighs, grabs her purse, and digs through it until she scores a hair tie.

I gulp as she lifts her hair up, exposing her long, sleek neck.

Fuck, she's breathtaking.

"You good?" I finally ask.

She bashfully runs a hand along her pale cheek. "Sorry about that. Minor freak-outs tend to be my thing during stressful situations."

Her answer is a shot of relief. Relief of not scaring her away. Relief she's not broaching the conversation she started outside.

"Don't worry about it. Tow truck will be here in ten to fifteen minutes."

"They'll take us back to Blue Beech or fix the flat?"

"Depends. If he can change it in the rain, he will. If not, he'll take us to the closest repair shop. Flats typically are a quick fix."

Minutes of silence pass through the cab until Willow says something. "We missed you when you left, you know." She snorts, and I'm unsure of where she's going with this conversation. "The temps they sent when you left were terrible, and Hudson was a total asshole for the first month."

I perk up in my seat. She's talking about when I quit working for Stella. I didn't give much notice. I left a day after Lucy told me the diagnosis.

"He was mending a broken heart," I say, sticking up for my brother.

"Hmm, so is that what happens when men are *mending a broken heart*? It justifies them acting like assholes?" Her face is playful, but her tone isn't. It's built up in hurt, betrayal, and also confusion.

Fuck. Where is this tow truck? I should've offered more money to get it here sooner.

"You trying to insinuate something?" I brace myself for the impact she's about to give me.

"Damn straight I am."

I swallow down my guilt. "Care to elaborate?"

"People get their hearts broken. People lose people. No offense, but it happens every day. Every minute. That's no excuse to act like a dick. You were a dick to me. Hell, *all* men are dicks if you're not letting them give you theirs. That's when they're nice and comforting."

"I'll apologize again for my dickdom. Hurt people don't always intend to hurt other people. That's not my intention. Trust me, I'd never want anyone to go through the hell I'm going through."

Her attention moves to the back window as headlights pull up behind us. Perfect timing to end this conversation. Intimate conversations with Willow are high risk for me. I'm a man of few words, and it seems I always choose the worst ones with her.

I grip the door handle. "Don't get out of this truck, headlight-chaser."

I meet the man in the middle of our trucks. He's sporting a parka and black boots.

"Nice day out here, huh?" he asks, thrusting his hand my way.

"For a duck," I mutter back, shaking his hand.

"It's about to get worse for ya."

Of course. The day goes more to shit.

Instead of asking why, I wait for him to elaborate.

"I can't work in this weather," he says. "It's dangerous, and they're talking about possible tornadoes." He whistles. "Half of the town's power is out due to the storm. Our mechanic went home to his family 'cause of it, but I'll ask him to come in first thing in the morning to fix this."

"Fuck. You've got to be kidding me."

He takes a step closer while chewing on a toothpick. "Wish I were. If it helps, I can give you a ride to the motel a few blocks down from the shop."

I slap him on the shoulder. "Appreciate it." I nod toward his truck. "You happen to have an umbrella in there?"

"Sure do."

"Thanks, man."

I jump back into my truck with the umbrella in my hand, ready to hear Willow rip my head off when I tell her we'll be having a sleepover tonight. I open my mouth when reality cuts through me. *How am I going to handle a sleepover?* I grind my teeth. This is a small town. They'll no doubt have more than one room available. I jumped the gun with the thought that we'd be sharing.

She's relaxed in the leather seat with her bare feet resting on the dashboard. I can't stop myself from giving her a once-over. Her soaking T-shirt has been replaced with a rose-colored lace tank top that showcases her cleavage. Her breasts are small, but that doesn't mean they don't excite my dick. They fit perfectly in my hands that night.

"Everything okay?" she asks.

I jerk my chin up, my throat tight. "He's giving us a ride into town."

"Perfect. How long will it take them to fix it?"

"Till tomorrow."

Her legs drop from the dashboard faster than Maven comes running when I mention ice cream. "What?" she shrieks. "Where are we supposed to sleep?"

"There's a motel a few blocks down from the repair shop."

"Can't we take an Uber back home and then pick it up in the morning?"

I smirk. "Ubers don't go to Blue Beech, babe."

⁓

"Sorry, but we only have one room available."

Go fucking figure.

Stranded. Check.

Having to share a room. Check.

What else can happen that's not going to make Willow wish she'd never stepped foot into my truck?

"We're always booked up on auction days. It's even worse today," the woman with steel-gray hair says in a hoarse, cracked voice while shaking her head at us like we're in the principal's office. "People don't want to travel in this mess. Here's a piece of advice for next time: book in advance."

"Thanks for the tip." I don't give two shits about her advice. She's our last resort. "We'll take it."

I grunt when Willow edges into my side to push herself in front of me. She faces the woman with a *Harriet* name tag.

"That's a room with two beds, right?" she asks.

"Sorry, honey. All we have is one queen." Harriet releases a bland smile. "Again, book in advance next time."

Sharing a bed. Fucking check.

Willow shoots me an innocent smile. "This will be interesting."

Chapter Twenty-Two

WILLOW

If Dallas believes I'm calm, I'll be asking Stella for a job tomorrow because I deserve an Emmy.

I'm doing everything in my power not to freak out right now.

We've shared a bed before.

Granted, we fucked each other, but no alcohol will be present tonight. We'll keep our hands to ourselves and build a pillow wall to separate us, and everything will be okay.

No touching. No sex. Fingers crossed he won't freak out tomorrow morning and leave me stranded.

On the bright side, we can't do anything stupid enough to make a baby again.

Shit. Babies. My mind still hasn't wrapped around that.

Dallas plays with the room key in his hand, circling it around his thick fingers, while we stand in front of room 206.

"What are you thinking?" he asks.

This seems to be our go-to question.

"That we have no other choice," I answer, signaling to the door in a hurry-it-up gesture. "This is our only option unless we decide to be a pain in the ass and have someone pick us up, and then they'll have to drive you back tomorrow to get your truck." I scowl at the door like it's my worst enemy. "Open sesame. Let's do this."

He obliges in what seems like slow motion while I look around. It's not exactly the Ritz, but I don't see any vermin running about, so that's a plus.

As Harriet pointed out with her stupid, smug smile, which I wanted to slap off, there's only one bed. What she failed to mention was that she's a liar because the bed is not a queen. It's a full, which means I have even less room to build my cockblocking fort. I briefly wonder if Dallas would be opposed to sleeping in the bathtub.

It's a standard room with a fake-wood-paneled bed topped with a generic comforter, a desk complete with a Bible and phone, and an older flat screen TV. I shuffle into the room, as if I were on my way to lethal injection, and Dallas stands in the doorway, his hypnotic eyes trained on me.

I sit on the edge of the bed and chew on my nails. "Oh, shit," I say. "Where's, uh … Maven?"

This is only now hitting me. *Jesus, am I going to be one of those mothers who forgets her kids at the supermarket?*

He chuckles while stepping into the room, and I tense at the sound of the door clicking shut. It's official. We're slumber-partying it up.

"I didn't forget about my daughter, if that's what you're thinking. She's spending the week at summer camp," he answers.

"Camp? Like on *The Parent Trap*? That's a real thing?"

"It looked real when I dropped her off." He tosses the key on the desk.

What hotel still uses actual keys these days?

"Which side of the bed do you want?" he asks.p

"It doesn't matter."

He points his chin at where I'm sitting. "I'll take that side. It's closer to the door, and you'll be closer to the bathroom."

He opens up the desk drawer, shuffles a few papers around, and shuts it. His next destination is the nightstand. He does the same thing and drags out a piece of paper ripped on both sides.

He blows out a breath. "Room service menu is tempting."

My stomach growls at the mention of food. I'm eating for three, and my appetite hasn't done anything to make me doubt it.

"I'm apologizing in advance for not feeding you quality tacos, but you have some superior choices here."

I bet. "And what would those be?"

He starts to read them off while fighting to keep a straight face. "Ramen noodles—"

"There's no way it says that," I interrupt.

"I'm not shitting you." He holds out the wrinkled piece of paper for me to read. Sure enough, ramen noodles is on there. "The other world-class options include grilled cheese, corn dogs, tomato soup, and sloppy joes." He frowns. "I'm not a picky person, but none of these sound exactly appetizing."

I agree. "So many options, such a small stomach." That's not *exactly* true.

The bed descends when he sits next to me. "Again, I'm sorry about this."

"Don't be. This will be a good story to tell our kids one day."

He smacks the paper. "So, what'll it be?"

"A corn dog might be my safest option."

"I owe you plenty of taco nights after this," he mutters, shaking his head. "Fucking corn dogs."

"Hey now, I have nothing against corn dogs."

He doesn't need to feel guilty about this. Shit happens that's out of your control sometimes. It's not like he planned to get a flat in the middle of nowhere.

He hands me the paper. "Anything else you want?"

I skim my finger down the page. "Might as well add some French fries while you're at it."

"Got it." He gets up from the bed and picks up the phone connected to the wall with a cord. "Room service, please." He orders my food and throws in ramen noodles for himself.

My stomach grumbles again, and I throw a pillow to get his attention, smacking him in the head. "I'll take some of those, too!"

He nods, rubbing his head. "Make that two ramen noodles." He hangs up. "Dinner is ordered. Get comfortable. I'll grab some drinks from the vending machine I spotted on our way in."

He snatches the keys from the desk, and I pull my phone out of my purse to see three missed calls and texts from Stella, asking how things are going and when I'll be back in town.

Me: Not until tomorrow. This is me officially calling in late. We're stranded because of a flat.

My phone beeps seconds later.

Stella: Stranded where?

Me: Neverland, for all I know. I'd say thirty minutes from the auction. Doubt it's on a map.

Stella: You need us to pick you up?

Me: No. Dallas got us to a motel. We're okay for the night.

My phone abruptly rings.

"Hello?"

"You're staying the night together?" she shrieks. "This is the best day ever."

"You damn liar!" I hear Hudson yell in the background. "You told me the same thing last night when I made you orgasm four times in a row."

"Ignore him," she mutters. "Sooo … what are you guys doing?"

"Dallas is raiding the vending machine, and I'm sitting on the bed. No excitement over here." My response is along the lines of pathetic.

"You can always make it exciting."

I sigh. "I'm hanging up now."

"Call us if you change your mind and need a ride."

"I will. See you tomorrow."

"Damn straight you will. I'll be sitting on your doorstep, waiting to drag every detail out of you."

As I'm ending the call, Dallas walks in with drinks in his hand and a duffel bag draped over his shoulder. He sets the cans on the desk to hold up the bag on display.

"You didn't take me up on my clothes offer earlier, but I keep my gym bag in my truck. You need something to sleep in?"

"Are they dirty or clean gym clothes?" Not that it matters. I'll gladly sleep in anything that smells like him—dirty, bloody, stained, you name it.

"Filthy. Dirty. Sweaty." He chuckles, and I fake a horrified look. "I'm kidding."

I blush at the thoughts running through my head. "I know."

He drops the bag next to me on the bed and starts to rummage through it. "What's your preference? Pants? Shorts?"

"Shorts, please."

He holds up a pair of blue shorts with a red stripes down the sides. "These okay?" He pulls out a T-shirt next.

"They'll work." I play with the fabric in my hand when he hands them to me. "I'll go, uh … change in the bathroom."

I'm getting my pervert on when I shut the door behind me and smell his shorts. Fresh linen. I never knew what that smell was until my mom bought me the scented candle for Christmas. It was my favorite scent until I got a whiff of Dallas's *fresh linen*.

Even with my growing stomach, I have to tie the drawstring tight around my waist to keep the shorts from falling to my ankles. I grab the shirt and contemplate taking off my bra. It's usually the first thing I dispose of when I walk through the front door, but I'm not alone.

I unsnap it, snap it back, hesitate, and decide to leave it on. I pull the shirt over my head and pause to take in my reflection in the mirror before going back out. I grimace and smooth my hands over my hair. Rain turns it into a frizzy mess.

"Dinner is served," Dallas announces when I walk out. "It didn't take them long to microwave it."

I laugh. "Gourmet ramen at its finest."

He scoots out the desk chair, so I can sit down, and he places the corn dog, French fries, and the Styrofoam bowl of noodles in front of me.

"I lived off this stuff when I moved to LA and was looking for a job. Hell, even after I found a job, I ate it more than I should have because I was lazy." I grin and kick his foot when he sits down on the bed. "Meanwhile, your lucky ass got to live in Stella's guest suite that was complete with a gourmet chef."

He hooks his thumb toward his bowl. "This might be giving him some competition, and don't act like Stella didn't invite you to move in every month."

"That's true, but I wanted my own place, you know? My own space. Believe it or not, I'm an introvert at heart."

Stella also despised Brett, and they couldn't be in the same room for five seconds without wanting to rip each other apart.

"Makes two of us. Lucy was the extrovert to my introvert. She could make conversation with anyone in the room. Me? I was cool with standing to the side and people-watching."

I stiffen in my seat. *Lucy.* Her name always sends a bolt of mixed emotions through me.

Guilt from sleeping with Dallas. Jealousy that she was the one he adored, the woman he loved and shared a bed with without freaking out in the morning.

I nod and slurp a noodle into my mouth, attempting to appear relaxed. Dallas sets his bowl on the nightstand and slides to the edge of the bed until he's only inches from me. I slurp my noodles louder and faster, sounding obnoxious, and act like I don't notice how close he is.

He stays quiet until I swallow down my bite. "I was in a dark place then."

I drop my spoon into the bowl. "What?" *Why is he bringing this up? Abort mission. Please.*

"That morning. Hell, for months."

I fish the spoon out of the bowl, and my heart sinks at the pained expression on his face.

"Sometimes, I still am." He scrubs his hand over his face. "Sorry for sneaking this shit on you after the nightmare of a day we've had, but I can tell it bothers you when I mention her."

It's only fair I'm honest back. "Hearing her name makes me feel guilty."

He pats the space next to him, and I take the invitation, sliding between the small space between us and sit down next to him.

"If anyone should feel guilty, it's me," he says.

"I obviously played a part in it."

He didn't fuck himself.

"And today was not a nightmare. I enjoyed myself," I add.

"You don't have to lie to make me feel better."

I smack his arm. "You know I wouldn't lie about that. I'll take every chance I can to bust your balls."

"Point made. I enjoyed myself, too. To be honest, lately, the only time I seem to be in a happy place is when I'm with you." He lets out a heavy breath. "You took me out of my stressed out, broken world and gave me a good day. Same with the night we spent together. I like myself when I'm with you. I forget about the loss and the hurt. You make me feel alive again."

I nod. He misses Lucy and will always miss her but is opening up a portion of himself for me to discover.

Keep going.

No, stop. Red light. Don't drag me down this tunnel if it ends in hurt.

Keep going.

Why can't I think straight? I need to think with my head, not my heart.

"If I could take it back, I would," he goes on.

"Take us back, sleeping together?"

"No, take back my behavior. I might've not been all there, but I didn't bring you to my home for a simple fuck. I promise you that."

I bump his shoulder with mine. "It's my turn to say you don't have to lie to make me feel better."

"Babe, no bullshit. The opportunity for a quick fuck has been open to me several times, but I've never succumbed to any advances. Not one. Drunk. Sober. Horny as hell. It wasn't only my dick that felt a connection with you. I didn't want to admit that to myself that morning." He shakes his head. "I'm still having trouble with admitting that you pulled something out of me."

I wring my hands together. "Yes, there's an attraction between us, but that's as far as our relationship can go." I refuse to be second best to another woman.

He rests his hand on my knee and sucks in a breath. "I know. We'll stick to staying friends and co-parents. I didn't say that in hopes of having sex again. I said it, so you'd know I never meant to disrespect you, and what happened that night seems to be what makes us uncomfortable most of the time. I don't want that."

"Me either," I whisper.

"Good. Then, it's settled." He wraps his arm around my shoulders. "We're new besties."

It's almost midnight.

Even though we had the no-more-awkwardness conversation, it has yet to leave the building. Everything was fine while we finished eating, when we had to share a toothbrush because there was only one in the vending machine, and even when we watched endless episodes of *Cops*, which I learned is his favorite show.

Our problem now is going to bed.

We have to make ourselves comfortable and slip underneath the sheets. The lights will go off. There's intimacy involved in this whether we like it or not.

"You ready to admit, you're tired?" Dallas asks when I'm on my eleventh yawn. He chuckles. "Come on, go to sleep. You're not going to miss anything exciting here."

"Fine," I groan out. "If you insist." My shirt rises when I slide down until my head hits the rock-hard pillow. The air in the room grows thinner when I peek up and notice his eyes pinned to my exposed stomach.

He lifts his hand. "Can I?"

I nod in response since I'm struggling for words. My stomach flutters at the same time he presses his steady hand against it. It dawns on me that he's never touched my stomach like this before. Not even during the ultrasound.

His touch comforts me, the opposite of what I thought would happen, and I settle myself on my elbows to watch him. He's gentle, treating me like I'm expensive china, and he cradles my skin with his hand in awe.

"I can't believe we have two babies growing in here," he whispers.

I smile when he shifts, so he's eye-level with my stomach.

"It's beautiful." He lifts up to focus on me with compassionate eyes. "You're fucking beautiful." He lowers his head and places his lips against my stomach. "Fucking perfection."

I miss his touch as soon as he pulls away and makes himself comfortable on his side. The smile that's been plastered to his lips since I gave him the okay is still there while he stares down at me.

He's waiting for me to tell him not to call me beautiful, to make a sarcastic comment, because that's what I do when conversations get heavy.

"What are you thinking?" he finally asks.

That your touch calms me more than a lavender bath and an expensive massage. That I wish we hadn't agreed to keep things platonic because the things I want to do with you right now are far from that.

"I'm thinking ..." It takes me a second to come up with something. "I'm thinking today is officially the weirdest day of my life."

He cocks his head to the side. "That's what's heavy on your mind?"

I gulp. "Yep."

"You seemed to be in deep thought about that," he argues, running a finger over his chin.

"It's a deep subject." *Oh, hell. Let's put our attention back on people getting arrested, please.*

"Fuck, I wish I could read your mind right now, but I'll run with your answer."

I scrunch up my brows in question.

"I'll act like I'm convinced with the weirdest-day-of-your-life lie." A grin plays at his thick lips. "Today was weirder than the time one of Stella's stalkers broke into her house, dressed as a housekeeper, and begged her to wear black lipstick while going down on him?" He chuckles. "And, if I remember correctly, you tasered him before I even made it into the room."

"Asshole deserved it," I mutter.

He bursts out in laughter. *Real laughter.* I feel like I've hit the jackpot every time I get that from him.

"I'll have to call it a tie between the two."

"I'll take that and agree that getting stranded with you has been eventful. The plus is, I'll always remember this. We've formed a stronger relationship and learned more about each other in a day than we did throughout years of working together. So, thank you for the good memories and not bailing on me. Eating ramen noodles and watching a *Cops* marathon all alone wouldn't have been nearly as much fun."

I lower my head to hide the cheesy smile biting at me. He needs to stop talking like this if he wants to stay on the just-friends level. I lift my gaze when he scoots in closer, wiping out the small distance between us, and his eyes soften as he drinks me in.

I play with the chain of my necklace. "What are you thinking?"

It's my turn to ask the questions. Hopefully, he won't lie like I did.

His jaw flexes. "You want to know the truth?"

"Of course."

"What I'm thinking is, how bad I want to kiss you right now," he answers with no hesitation.

Anticipation drives through my body and straight between my legs, but I keep a calm face. "Then, what's stopping you?"

Adios, platonic, co-parenting plans. Hello, making shit complicated.

At least it'll come with an orgasm. Hopefully.

He grins. "Good point."

My tongue darts out to wet my lips at the same time he presses his mouth to mine. He sucks on the tip of my tongue before dipping his into my mouth. I've never found the taste of generic toothpaste so delectable. Our lips slide against each other, as if we'd been doing this for years.

My heart pounds when he lifts up to move over me, keeping our lips connected, and I open my legs to allow him enough room to slide between them. I take in a deep breath when his mouth leaves mine to trail kisses down the curve of my neck.

He's slanted over me, careful of my stomach, and all I'm staring at is his erection straining through the thin gym shorts. My pulse races when I remember how big he is and how electrifying he felt inside me last time. No time is wasted before he rubs his fullness against my core to hit my most sensitive spot. I'm close to having an orgasm before we've even started.

It won't take much. I haven't been touched in forever, and if he's telling the truth, neither has he. We need to take this slow if we want it to last.

Unfortunately, what I need isn't what my body wants.

I need to get off.
I need this to last longer.
Why does this man constantly seem to drag out mixed emotions?
"More," I beg and squirm underneath him. *So much for wanting this to last longer.* "I need more."

More touching. More kissing. More of him everywhere.

My back arches when his mouth returns to mine. This kiss is different than the soft one before. It's greedy. Untamed. Eager.

"Where do you want more?" he asks against my lips.

"Everywhere," I moan out.

He groans deep from his throat when I run my foot up and down his leg and start moving into him more aggressive than what's appropriate. I shift until his cock hits me in the perfect spot, and then I grind against him.

He uses a single finger to untie my shorts, and I wiggle out of them in seconds, desire blazing through me. He doesn't bother removing my panties. Doesn't see them as a challenge.

Instead, he pushes the lace to the side and gives my clit the attention I've been dying for, rubbing it with the pad of his thumb.

I gasp when he slowly slips a finger inside me while still giving me the feel of his cock. His thick finger gracefully moves in and out of me. Not how I want it. I move against him harder to tip him off on how I need it.

"Slow down, baby," he says with a laugh. "You keep doing that, and my dick is going to explode. You probably want this to last longer than a few minutes."

"I don't care how long it lasts if I get what I want," I mutter.

He chuckles and shoves another finger into me without warning. He gives me rough. "That better?"

"God, yes," I moan out in response.

"I have something you'll enjoy even more."

He dips his fingers out of me in order to grab the strings of his shorts.

Finally. This is what I need.

The sound of a phone ringing startles me.

His hand drops from his shorts, and he curses under his breath. My heart beats wildly when he places them in his mouth and sucks on them on the way to his gym bag. I can't stop staring at the outline of his swollen cock when he opens the bag and grabs his phone.

We were right there.
Right freaking there.
My vagina does not deserve this.

He checks the caller before answering.

"Hello?" He drops down in the chair and expels a stressed breath. "Hey, honey. How's camp?" he croaks out. "What's wrong? You're feeling homesick? That happened to me my first time there, too." He pauses. "I promise."

I catch my breath when he falls quiet again.

"You know what helped me? I wrote my parents a letter, telling them all the cool stuff I was doing there. I'll ask your counselor to mail it out for you, and I should get it before I pick you up."

I pull my shorts up at the next pause. We won't be finishing this.

"Good. I'll be waiting for the postman every day."

I sit up on the bed.

"Call me if you need anything, okay? Good night. I love you."

He ends the call and tosses the phone on the desk. His eyes are pinned to the floor while he sits there, looking tortured. His chest heaves in and out, and the only sound is coming from the police sirens on the TV.

"Dallas," I finally whisper.

He lifts his head, and my chest aches at the unease on his face.

"Shit, Willow. I'm fucking sorry."

He pushes out of the chair, his erection not as visible as before when he was about to screw me but still there, and then he storms out of the room.

Tears slip down my face.

Another rejection.

I'm done lying to myself.

I'm done thinking he'll change.

Fuck Dallas Barnes.

Chapter Twenty-Three

DALLAS

I deserve the rain pouring down on me in front of our hotel room. I deserve to get sucker-punched in my fucking face, mugged right here on this sidewalk, and stabbed in the back for how I treated Willow *again*.

My cock is hard. The taste of Willow's sweet pussy is on my tongue. My head is not only blasting with thoughts of how turned on I am, but also of how terrible of a man I am.

I did it again—treated her like shit and walked away while in the moment.

Willow deserves someone better than me, someone who isn't a mess. But why does it kill me to picture her having that someone? Why can't I get her out of my head and stay in this miserable place, as I promised myself I would months ago?

I shake my head in agony. What would it look like to Lucy if I fell for someone else? That would hurt her memory, show I was a shitty husband, make it seem like she was replaceable in my eyes.

I bang my palms against the motel's brick wall. *But, Jesus, fuck, what about me?*

I clench my hands and stalk back and forth, depicting a serial killer.

Would it hurt Lucy if I moved on?

She's gone.

Hell, knowing Lucy, she's probably smiling down at me. She begged me to find someone else to love and made me promise I'd eventually move on, for my daughter's sake and mine. I agreed, lying to her on her deathbed.

But who wouldn't when time was running out and you didn't want to waste your last words arguing about giving your heart to another woman?

I never thought it was possible. The thought of touching another woman made my skin crawl.

Until Willow.

Can I stay confined in my miserable bubble? Keep my heart in reserve because I'm terrified of losing someone I care about again?

I tilt my head up to stare at the dark sky.

"Lucy, baby, tell me what to do. Am I making a wrong move or being a fucking idiot?" I whisper while a million thoughts rush through my mind.

The bed is empty when I walk back into the motel room. I look at the window first, like a dumbass, considering the window is right next to the door, and I would've seen her leave. The bathroom light shines through the bottom of the door, and I hear the shower turn on.

Lucky for me, the door isn't locked. My hand is shaking when I open it while taking a deep breath. I make out her breathtaking silhouette through the thin shower curtain at the same time I hear her crying.

Damn it! I'm a fucking asshole.

I take a step into the room and say her name.

She doesn't reply.

I repeat it, louder this time.

Silence.

I strip out of my wet clothes, and when I climb in across from her, she pushes me back.

"What the hell, Dallas?" she shrieks. "You scared the shit out of me."

"I'm sorry," is all I can muster. Sorry for scaring her, for turning her down, for acting like an asshole. *Why am I always fucking up with her?*

Her tears get lost in the water. "I'm sick of your *sorrys*. I'm done, Dallas." She throws her hands up. "Done with your bullshit games. I refuse to be some toy for you to play with when it's convenient for you."

She winces when I stretch my arm out to move her fiery-red hair from her face, so I can see her beautiful green eyes better.

Today was a good day. We had fun. I told her shit no one else knows. I felt our babies in her stomach for the first time. We kissed. I had my hand in her panties and fingers in her pussy.

Then, I fucked it all up.

"No more bullshit," I whisper. "I promise."

"Your promises don't mean shit," she says with a snort, throwing my words back at me. "It only makes you look like more of a jackass each time."

I am a jackass.

"Tell me what you want me to do. How can I make this right?"

"Let yourself live!" she shouts. "Get it through that thick skull of yours that it's okay to move on, for your sake!" She stabs her finger into my chest. "For your daughter's sake!" Her finger moves to my stomach. "For my fucking sake!"

I cup her cheeks with both hands. "I've tried," I ground out. "I've tried telling myself I shouldn't do this with you, but maybe that's where I'm going wrong. I'm not supposed to be fighting it." I caress her soft skin. "Neither one of us is supposed to be fighting it because the only thing that feels natural is this. Us together."

"No," she breathes out. "You only fight shit that you don't want to happen."

"Trust me, fighting it means, it's *all* I want to happen." She shakes her head, and I wipe away her tears. "Say the word. Tell me you don't want me. Tell me you want me to leave this shower."

She breathes in deep breaths and stays quiet.

"Do you want me to leave?" I stress.

She pinches her lips together and won't answer.

"Or would you rather I did this?"

She gasps when I fall to my knees and inch her feet apart. I run my hand up her leg and straight to the opening of her pussy.

"Answer my question," I demand.

Instead of pushing me again, she slips her hand into my hair and moans. "That. I'd rather you did that." Her nails dig deep into my scalp before I make another move. "Keep going."

And that's what I do.

I situate one of her legs on the edge of the bathtub, and her body trembles at the first swipe of my tongue.

The taste of her is sweet.

Fucking heavenly.

I could eat her out for the rest of my life and never go hungry.

I apologize with my tongue.

Own her with it.

Beg her not to turn her back on me and plead to her to give me another chance.

If my words aren't convincing enough, I hope my tongue can do the trick.

"Shit, that feels so good," she mutters when I drive two fingers into her pussy and flick my tongue at her opening at the same time.

My dick stirs when I peek up at the image I'm getting. I'm on the verge of combusting from the view of Willow grinding her pussy into my face. I don't stop until I know she's on her way to falling apart.

"I'm close," she chants over and over again. Her foot arches off the edge, and she holds the back of my head in place as she lets go, her juices running onto my tongue while she moans out her final release.

So fucking gorgeous.

So fucking delicious.

My cock is hard as a rock. I'll be taking a cold shower and jacking off to thoughts of what happened in here when Willow goes to bed.

"Does that at least make up for some of my dickness?" I ask, looking up at her.

She spreads her fingers a few inches apart and massages my scalp. "A little. You still have some making up to do. I can take payment with your tongue a few more times."

I stand up, rub my hands down her sides, and then squeeze her hips. "Lucky for you, I don't mind paying interest."

She laughs. "Good to know."

I jerk my head toward the outside of the shower. "You ready to hit the sheets? It's late, and I know you're beat."

She nods. "You did just lick all the energy out of me."

I grunt when she wipes her mouth, and my hands are shoved off her hips. This time, she's the one dropping to her knees.

I stop her when she opens her mouth and bobs her head toward my dick. "No, this was about you."

I've turned down blow jobs on more than one occasion, but my body has never physically ached when I did, like it is doing now. I eye her full lips, the way she's licking them and staring at my cock like she can't wait to taste it.

"Trust me," she says. I tense and moan when she licks the pre-cum from the tip. "Me sucking your cock is just as much for me."

Her lips wrap around me before I can even come up with a response. My cock twitches, growing even harder, and I let her set the pace even though I want to plow my cock in and out of her mouth, fuck it until she can't breathe.

She takes me in, sucking me hard, and adds her hand to stroke me.

I throw my head back. "Shit, Willow. This is amazing."

She devours my cock, not stopping to catch her breath once, as water pours down over us. I thought the sight of pleasuring her with my tongue was my favorite, but her on her knees, sucking my cock, is running in close second.

I can't wait to fuck her again.

I know that'll be number fucking one.

"So fucking good."

My plan of not controlling her speed annihilates when I feel it coming. I jerk my hips up, and she moans against my cock, exciting it more.

"So good." I swipe the hair away from her face, so I can see every inch of her and give her a warning when I come, but she doesn't pull away.

The water turns cold at the same time she swallows my cum with a smile.

Chapter Twenty-Four

WILLOW

"And then what happened?" Stella asks, nearly jumping off the couch in eagerness.

I'm back at work, and we're hanging out in her over-the-top trailer while she's making me do *another* rundown of what happened last night. She knows everything but the part where we dry-humped each other and had an oral face-off.

She'll get that story another time. It's still fresh in my mind, and I don't want questions to ruin the image yet.

Nervousness is an understatement of what I felt when I woke up this morning. The bed was empty. A bad sign. I grabbed my phone, and my heart settled when I heard the shower running. Joining him crossed my mind, but I'm not as gutsy as him.

When he got out, he said the truck was ready to pick up, and a shop employee would give us a ride there.

An hour later, we were back on the road.

No more kissing, hugging, or talks of what went down, *literally*, last night. It gave me relief yet also fried my brain at the same time. I'm concerned. Scared. Terrified.

We made light conversation. He told me about Maven's call last night. She was homesick and wanted to hear his voice. We listened to the radio, and I let him choose the music. It was *not* Justin Bieber.

"You know what happened," I answer.

Stella gives me a puppy-dog look. "No, I don't," she whines. "More happened than what you're telling me. I know you better than you believe."

I throw my arms out and fall back on the couch. "You've pulled every detail out of me. What more do you want? I can start making stuff up if it helps your weird imagination. We got married. Adopted kids to go with the baby on the way. Bought a house with a four-car garage. Surprise!"

She rolls her eyes. "No one copped a feel while you were sleeping *together*? Surely, the two of you are horny as hell, considering you've both been celibate for a minute. There you were, stranded in the rain, cold and lonely. How romantic."

"Now, you're making shit up. We weren't cold and lonely."

She clips a dark strand of hair behind her ear. "Work with me here." She narrows one eye at me, studying, like the answer she wants is marked across my skin. "You have every side effect of an orgasm."

"Side effect? Since when did you get into the pharmaceutical business?"

"I haven't seen a smile that bright on your face in a long time. Your skin is glowing. You look like you've been wandering around Wonderland all day."

"Pregnancy gives me mood swings. I could get crazy angry in three seconds."

She jumps up from the couch to lock the door, and I squirm in my seat when she joins me again.

"Uh, what are you doing? Keeping me hostage until I give you what you want?"

Her lips curl up. "How'd you know?"

I rub my hands together. "You have to promise you won't tell Hudson."

"Jesus, Willow," she moans out, her smile collapsing. "Do you not trust me anymore?"

My cheeks burn. "The whole scenario at your party scares the crap out of me."

She sucks her cheeks in before answering, "The only reason Hudson found out was because he was eavesdropping, not because I told him. I would've kept your secret."

She rises from the couch again. I'm afraid I've pissed her off when she unlocks the door and sticks her head out the door.

"Hudson?" she yells, looking around before slamming it shut, the lock clicking back. "No fiancé in sight. Half of the cast and crew have left for the day. You have my word that my lips are sealed."

I inhale a long breath before giving her the real rundown of what happened. She squeals, claps her hands, and is on cloud nine with every word.

I snag my phone from the nightstand when the doorbell rings. No missed calls or texts, and I didn't make plans with anyone.

Dallas texted earlier, asking me to go out for tacos, and I declined. Getting stared down while eating isn't on tonight's agenda. It's getting more difficult, hiding my baby bump. I'm going to have to get more creative.

I throw my post-shower wet hair into a sloppy ponytail and peek through the peephole when I reach the door. Dallas didn't give me a heads-up that he was coming, which is irritating because my baggy gray sweatpants and three-sizes-too-big T-shirt isn't the most attractive outfit to greet the guy who gave you a fantastic orgasm the night before.

He moves into my apartment with grocery bags covering half of his face. His muscular arms are securely wrapped around the bags, and he nearly runs into me when I stand in the middle of the doorway because I can't take my eyes off them.

"What are you doing?" I ask when he sets the groceries on the kitchen counter.

"You didn't want to go out for tacos, so I brought the tacos to you." He winks. "I promised tacos, so they're coming your way, and you can bet your ass that they're better than anything you'd get at a restaurant."

Shit. Fingers crossed he's not expecting me to help him.

We'll be eating grilled cheese by the end of the night. Burned grilled cheese.

I watch him while he digs out the groceries and starts moving around my kitchen as if he were my roommate. He sifts through the cabinets before pulling out pans and bowls.

"You know how to cook?" I stupidly ask.

He cuts open the hamburger, drops it in the pan, and turns a burner on low. "I'm a single dad."

"Good point," I mutter.

This soon-to-be mom had better take some notes. Takeout has always been my main food group, but that doesn't mean I eat like shit. I get healthy takeout—at least, I did before, but there's not a big market for that here.

"I cook dinner every night. Come over and eat anytime you want."

That's a big hell no. Any appetite I build up will be lost when I step into his house, and the memories of his freak-out flood me.

I take in my T-shirt and pull at the bottom. "I wish you had told me you were coming over."

He snags a cutting board and starts cutting the bell peppers. I slide into his spot, pushing him away and causing him to grin, and take his place. I start slicing the peppers, the simplest task for me to take over, without saying a word.

"You would've bailed," he replies.

"No, I wouldn't have." That's the truth. I bailed on going out to dinner but would've been up for his company. "I would've made myself not look like a train wreck."

"You look gorgeous." He nods toward my belly. "You've been hiding it well. Anyone know about the twins yet?"

I shake my head. "You spill the beans to anyone?"

"I'm waiting for you to give me the green light. You do know, we have to tell everyone sooner or later, right?"

"I do, but why does it feel like it's shock after shock? Guess what?" The knife waves through the air when I dramatically throw my arms up. "I'm pregnant. Guess what? It's with twins!"

"Put the knife down, Mike Myers." He laughs while peeling an avocado and then mashing it in a bowl. "You realize, life is full of surprises as you get older. You grow wisdom with age."

I click my tongue against the roof of my mouth. "Appreciate the insight, *old man*."

"Whoa, who are you calling old?" He smirks and bumps his hip against mine. "You want to be on dish duty tonight?"

I slide the peppers off the board and into a glass bowl. The lettuce is my next victim. "I'm calling *you* an old man."

"Sweetheart, we're six years apart."

"Six years is a long time. You were in kindergarten, learning how to write your ABCs, when I was born."

"You seemed to find this *old man* attractive enough to sleep with."

"Eh, let's blame it on the alcohol."

"I'll keep waiting for you to admit it."

I drop the knife. "Admit what?"

"Admit this so-called *old man* made you feel better than any *boy* you've been with your age." He rests the spatula on the stove, and his eyes fix on me. "You lose a taco for every lie you tell, so I'd suggest you stick with the truth if you have an appetite."

Fucking tacos.

Are they worth honesty?

My stomach growls.

Hell yes.

"I don't have much to compare since I've slept with only two men. Brett cared about pleasing me in the beginning." I sigh. "That changed in the end. He'd get off, slap my ass, thank me, and then go back to his video games."

"Shit, you dated a fucking loser," he grumbles. "LA is saturated with men, and you stuck around with him? I never understood that."

"That's what everyone says."

"Why'd you stay with him then?"

"I don't know. Convenience?"

"That's a piss-poor excuse to stay in a relationship."

"You're telling me, you've never stayed with someone because starting over sounded too rough?" My voice is filled with defensiveness. I'm not alone on this.

"Fuck no. I'd never be with someone I didn't love. I stayed with Lucy for so long because my life would've been a nightmare without her. I loved her more than my own air. I would've given my life for her, taken her cancer, given her my health."

"It might not be with Lucy, but you're doing it now." I shift around him and go to the fridge for a bottle of water.

My response *really* catches his attention.

"What was that?"

I take a drink and slowly swallow it while he stares at me in confusion.

"Nothing," I mutter. I place my water on the counter and go back to my chopping duty.

He plucks the knife from my hand. "Not so fast. Tell me what you mean."

Here goes nothing. "You're doing the same thing!"

He raises a questioning brow and reaches back to turn the stove off.

"You've accepted being alone because the thought of starting over without Lucy seems too rough. *Convenience.*"

My eyes pierce his, and I wait for him to turn around and leave me with a half-cooked dinner. I should feel guilty about what I said, but I don't.

His shoulders draw back while he takes a pained breath. "She was my wife. You're not supposed to get over the love of your life."

My mention of Lucy has put a damper on taco night, but it needed to be said. His answer will tell me if last night was just sex or if he's ready to open his heart and try something with me.

"I'm not saying you have to get *over* her but more of coming to terms that she's gone. I stayed with Brett because the thought of something new scared the living shit out of me, and you're doing the same. Don't throw stones at glass houses."

He wipes his hands down his jeans. "How'd you do it then?"

The fact that he's still standing here shocks me. "Do what?"

"Let your heart move on."

"It wasn't easy. It was one of the hardest decisions I'd ever made."

His jaw twitches, and his eyes are downcast on me. I suck in a breath. "I'm trying, trust me. I'm fucking trying for you." We're so close, I can feel his heart beating against my chest. "You've opened up what I feared for months. It doesn't seem as fucking scary, exploring with you."

I point my fork at my plate. "This is delicious." Screw those fancy taco joints. Dallas Barnes kills anything they serve. "Seriously, the best guacamole I've ever had."

He showed me how to make it step by step. I'm in charge of taco night next time.

"Told you I knew my way around a kitchen," he says proudly and then takes a drink of water.

I offered to run upstairs and grab a beer from Lauren's fridge for him. Tacos always taste better with beer. He wouldn't let me because it wasn't right for him to drink when I couldn't.

"How was work today? Stella drill you about our trip?" he asks.

Yep, drilled me as hard as his tongue did in the shower. I give him my best *duh* impression, and he laughs.

"Hudson pulled the same shit with me."

"They're more invested in our relationship than their own." I scrunch up my face. "I can't blame them though. I did the same thing with them."

"I'll admit, it's fun when you're on the other side." He tilts his water glass my way. "Did I thank you for the company the night we got them back together?"

A while back, Stella and Hudson broke up after the tabloids went after their relationship. I called Dallas, and we set up a plan to get them back together. It worked, and Hudson and Dallas flew to New York to surprise her.

I didn't want to be a cockblock during their making up, so I hung out in the lobby. That was where Dallas found me. We spent the night tasting food at every food cart, and I showed him my favorite spots in Times Square.

"You gave me my first good night in a while," he says. "No matter how shitty I'm feeling, you seem to always bring me back to the light." He runs his hand over his jaw. "Since we're talking about fixing relationships, about last night …"

"I know, I know. It was a mistake," I rush out, sensing his regret. *Did he make tacos to soften up the blow?* "We were tired, not thinking clearly, horny *again* because we hadn't been laid in months."

"Whoa, hold up. I wasn't tired, and my mind was crystal clear." He stretches his shoulders back and grins. "Although you hit the nail on the head with the horny part."

What's he saying?

"I didn't eat your pussy last night just to get off. I don't do pity sex or pity *oral sex*." His tone turns serious. "In fact, I thought my sex life was over, but then you sat your perky ass across from me at the bar with your sexy-as-hell red hair pulled back to show off your contagious smile." He chuckles and leans in to rest his elbows on the table. "So, let's quit using the horny-and-not-thinking excuse."

Why do my words always come back to bite me in the ass? I'm judging him for pushing me away yet doing the same.

"In case you forgot, I was there in the morning," he continues.

"'Cause you were stranded."

Why can't I stop pulling away? Rejection still scares me.

"That was part of the reason, yes, but the other was you."

"Good. So, we can confirm we're both sexually attracted to each other. Maybe we should explore that and leave our feelings to the side for now."

"You want this to only be about sex?"

I nod.

"You sure about that?"

"Positive."

We'll screw for now and get each other out of our systems. In my head, I want to believe the only reason I'm pursuing him is that he gives me the best orgasms I've ever had. I want sex, and then we can worry about a relationship later. The opposite of what I was taught as a kid, but whatever.

He wipes his mouth, throws the napkin on his plate, and gets up from the chair. "Let's see if I can change your mind." He holds his hand out to me.

I stare at him in shock. I wasn't expecting this to go down now. "What?"

His eyes grow wilder every second he stares at me. "A warning, sweetheart. Don't challenge me and then be surprised when I rise to it."

I take his hand and let him pull me up. He doesn't give me a chance to take another breath before he hungrily captures my mouth with this. I moan when his tongue slips into my mouth. The kiss makes it clear that he's going to make me regret saying that all I wanted was his cock. It explains he'll make me beg for it until I admit that I want more.

I gasp for those lost breaths when he grabs a handful of my ass and draws me in closer. I waste no time in pushing his shirt up and over his head. I didn't have the chance to thoroughly appreciate his body last night in the shower. His tongue between my legs consumed my every thought.

My mouth waters at the sight of his firm chest, muscles galore, the six-pack finely sculpted. He's right about one thing. He might be older, but his body and his cock outweigh Brett in every way. He tenses when I run my lips down his chest and flick my tongue against his nipple. His cock swells under his jeans, him *rising for the challenge*, if you will, and I drop to my knees to frantically pull it out.

I'm taking control before he gets the chance to.

Blow jobs have never been my thing. I saw them as a chore with Brett, but everything is different with Dallas. The thought of his hard dick inside my mouth excites me. Pleasing him pleases me.

I wet my lips, drinking in the sight of his large erection twitching in front of me, pre-cum dripping from the tip. His head falls back when I take the full length of him in my mouth. He's so big, it stabs me in the back of my throat. I bring my mouth back, drawing his dick out to catch my breath, and then eagerly suck him back in.

"Fuck, that mouth, Willow," he croaks out when I sink my nails into his ass to blow him better.

His hand dips down to wrap around his cock, and he jacks off in sync with my mouth. The hottest fucking thing I've ever experienced. I take him in, more excitedly.

He's close, I can tell, and I can't wait to taste his cum again.

Can't wait to swallow him down but still have the taste of him lingering there.

I wait for it, my mouth moving faster, but he pulls away right before we reach the finish line.

The hell?

His face burns with desire as he stares down at me on my knees. "I'll never get the sight of this out of my mind. It's better than anything I've imagined while jacking off."

Chills climb up my spine. "You think about me when you're jacking off?"

His hand is still wrapped around his cock, and he goes back to slowly stroking it. "Every fucking time," he grits out.

"Let me finish the job then," I say with a pout.

He shakes his head. "I'm going to finish the job in your tight pussy. I know you enjoy sucking my cock, but that'll be nothing compared to sliding inside you." He catches my chin between his thumb and forefinger. "Now, stand up, so I can put you on this table and eat you as my dessert."

I shyly bite my lip. "How can a girl deny that?"

"You'll never want to deny me when I give you this dick again. You'll be coming back for more."

He picks me up underneath my elbows and settles me on the table. I open my legs the second my ass hits the edge. I'm ready for this. I *need* this.

"Put your hand over my mouth before you start," I breathe out.

He cocks his head to the side. "Didn't know you were into that."

I shake my head and laugh. "We have to be quiet. Your sister lives right above me, and the walls are thin."

"I don't give a shit. I want to hear you scream my name."

My sweatpants and panties are off in seconds, and he disposes of my bra and T-shirt. He licks his lips when he takes in my breasts. He cups them and leans down to draw a nipple into his mouth. He sucks hard and releases me, and not another word leaves his mouth before he drags my legs over his shoulders. My breathing hitches when he falls to his knees.

The first lick sends jolts through my body, and I would fall off the table if he wasn't holding me in place. His tongue is an expert, dipping in and out of me, before he slips it out to suck on my clit. When he uses it to separate my folds for a better angle, my toes arch toward the ceiling.

Ache blossoms through my chest, and the need for an orgasm pushes at me even harder. His hands move up and down my legs as he pleasures me, and I make sure I'm balanced well enough before reaching down and pushing a finger inside myself. I work in sync with his tongue the same way he did when I was sucking him off earlier.

Our connection is what ends me. My back comes off the table, my legs buckling against his shoulders, and I never want to come down from this orgasm as it shoots through me.

"Say my name," he groans, still working his tongue in me.

I do as I was told—not screaming it at the top of my lungs, but repeatedly gasping it out.

He slowly releases my legs with a shit-eating grin on his face. "Damn, I love the sound of that when my face is shoved in your pussy."

He gets up and goes to help me down from the table, but I stop him.

"I want to fuck you."

He's shocked at my outburst. "Don't worry, sweetheart. I fully plan on doing that—*multiple times*—but let's save the table sex for another time. I want you in your bed."

I grunt when he picks me up in his arms, newlywed-style, and he races to the bedroom. As badly as I want this, I still have nervousness riding through me like a hurricane. We're taking a big step here.

This isn't a quick blow job in the shower.

This is *sex*—something so intimate for the both of us. Neither one of us sleep around, so this is a big deal, especially for him.

I don't want him to freak out this time and feel like he's betraying Lucy by sleeping with me.

"Are you sure about this?" I ask when he carefully lowers me onto the bed.

He doesn't respond until I give him full eye contact. "I've never been surer." He situates himself between my legs, and his cock impales me with no warning.

I constrict around him while he gives me time to adjust to his size. I know the situation I'm getting into with his first thrust. His first moan tells me I'm not making the wrong decision.

He starts out slow, which frustrates me. This is something I've wanted for months. I tilt my hips up to give him a better angle, excite him, and hint that I want more.

Harder. Faster. More.

It works.

He pounds into me rougher, sweat building up along his forehead, and groans with every stroke.

"Say my name," I whisper. "Tell me who you're in bed with." It's my turn to show ownership.

"Willow," he says, his eyes drinking in my face … my body.

We slow down when he stretches forward to take my lips with his, and he devours my mouth.

"I'm in Willow's bed, fucking Willow, and Willow is about to make my dick explode."

I kiss him until he pulls away to fuck me harder. That's when I place my hands over my stomach to hide it. I've never been an insecure person, but I've gained weight. *A lot of weight.* My stomach is no longer flat. I see myself as less attractive.

"Don't," he demands in a raspy voice. "Let me see what we did together."

I slowly drag them away, and he grasps my hands in his, placing them over my head and tightly holding them.

I shudder underneath him, coming undone, and scream out his name again.

There's no doubt everyone in the building heard that one.

He jerks and gives me two more thrusts before releasing himself inside me.

"Fuck," he grunts, breathing as hard as I am. "That was fucking amazing."

I'm still catching my breath when he collapses next to me. We're a sticky and sweaty mess. Pretty sure I've burned off every calorie of those tacos.

I turn my focus on him. "You work an appetite back up?"

He smirks. "I had a very filling dessert."

His answer makes me tingle. *Tingle*. This is the first time I've ever felt myself do that.

"I'm starving, and I don't like eating alone if I don't have to. Lucky for you, I have a pantry full of ramen noodles."

He chuckles. "Fucking ramen noodles."

I'm falling for this man who is broken, a little ruined, a bit of a disaster ... and who gave up on love.

Chapter Twenty-Five

WILLOW

I tense when the bed shifts behind me.
 He yawns.
 Then, he heads to the bathroom.
 What happens now?
 God, why am I so paranoid every morning after?
 We went back to the kitchen last night and didn't have ramen noodles. Instead, we had ice cream, and then he did fuck me on the table after licking our dessert off my chest. We were exhausted, and I'd reached my exercise goal for the month, so he suggested a movie. I introduced him to my favorite black-and-white film, *Casablanca*, and we passed out before reaching the end. He carried me to bed, kissed me good night, and wrapped his arms around me. It felt good to be held, relaxed me, and I was back to sleep in seconds.

His next move this morning will tell me everything I need to know about our relationship—or possible lack thereof. Him not bailing at the hotel doesn't count, doesn't ease my mind, because he had an obligation to stay with me. He didn't have a working car, and Stella would've kicked his ass if he'd left me stranded.

I brace myself for whatever is about to happen when he comes around the bed and drops to one knee, so we're eye-level.

His lips curl up as he edges closer. "I didn't want you to assume I was sneaking out. I have to pick up Maven from camp."

I smile. "Do you mind if I come along?"
 What the hell am I thinking?
 "You up for another road trip with me?"
 "Why not?" I want to spend all my time with him.
 My smile grows when he kisses my forehead.
 "All right, get dressed, and we'll be on our way. I'll grab my clothes from the truck."
 I hop out of bed like I'm ten and it's Christmas, and I scurry to the bathroom.
 Our relationship shifted into something last night—something that exceeds friends but isn't quite into the whole relationship thing yet.
 Friends with benefits?
 Co-parenting with benefits?
 Sex, not love?

"Oh my gosh, this is so cute," I say when we pull into the camp parking lot. "It's not like the movies but still cool."

Dallas cocks his head toward my stomach. "Can't wait for our little ones to join Maven here in a few years."

"A few years? You mean, six?"
 "I started coming here in Pampers."
 I slap his shoulder. "You are such a liar."

Maven comes running our way as soon as we get out of the truck.

"Daddy!" she screams. "You brought Willow! This is the bestest day ever!"

I lose a breath when she rushes into me and wraps her tiny arms around my waist.

"Hey now," Dallas says, coming up behind her and peeling her away from me. "What am I, chopped liver? You haven't seen your dad in a week, and you roll right past me."

She giggles and jumps into his arms. "You know I missed you, Daddy!" When he releases her, she pulls a stack of papers from her bag. "I made all of these for you and wrote letters like you said!" She snatches the top piece from Dallas's hand and holds it out like she can't wait for me to see it. "This one is for you."

"Wow, thank you," I say with a smile. It's a hand-drawn picture of her and a tall redhead holding hands and walking around what resembles lights. "It's so pretty."

Her eyes sparkle with pride, and she bounces on her tiptoes. "It's us at the fair. I had *sooo* much fun and can't wait to do it again next year!"

I squat down and give her another hug. "Me either. Maybe, next time, I can gain some courage and join you on the rides."

"I would love that so much!" She turns around. "Daddy! Willow said she'd get on the big-kid rides with me next year!"

Dallas smiles and winks at me. "Oh, really? We'd better hold her to that."

"Dallas, I thought that was you," a feminine voice calls out.

Maven loses my attention when I see a woman walking our way. A pretty blonde dressed similar to what Lucy used to wear, and she gives me a once-over, sizing me up to see if I'm competition.

Sure am, sweetie.

She thrusts her hand in my face when she reaches us, and I can't stop myself from rolling my eyes. Her face scrunches up into a sneer to assure me it wasn't missed.

"You must be Willow. It's nice to finally meet you. You're all everyone in town has been talking about."

Her eyes drop down to my stomach, and I pull my arms around it to block her view.

Really? I cross my arms. *Let's see her squirm.*

"Like what?"

I've only gone to the fair and the diner for lunch once. The only other times I've left my apartment is to go to work, and Stella's show is filmed thirty minutes out of Blue Beech. I've kept to myself, but I'm sure she's heard about me from the videos taken at the fair.

My question surprises her. I don't mean to be rude, but the way her eyes scrutinize me is rude in itself.

She signals between Dallas and me. "That you two have been spendin' an awful lot of time together." Her smile is bright and phony. "You're from the big city, like Hudson's little fiancé, right?"

"Sure am. I'm her best friend and assistant."

"I see," she clips. "How long do you plan on staying here? You probably miss LA. It's pretty boring around here."

"Cindy," Dallas warns.

She whips around to smile at him. "What? I'm only introducing myself to the town's newest …" Her attention moves back to me. "Visitor? Resident?"

"Resident," he growls to her back. "Willow is a new *resident* of Blue Beech, so you march on and relay that to your gossip club and quit interrogating her."

She throws me a flat smile, turns around to give him her attention, and slides her hand across his chest. He jerks away.

"You want me to make y'all dinner tonight? I can bring that fried chicken of mine you love so much." She glances down at Maven with a faker smile than she gave me. "Didn't you say it was your favorite, honey?"

Maven shakes her head. "My grammy's fried chicken is my favorite."

Dallas glares at Cindy. "As much as I'd love to chat and deny your company, we have places to be. Enjoy our day."

"Call me," she sings out to him.

This time, she wraps her arm around his, and he pulls out of her grip, narrowing his eyes on her.

"Stop." He gives her his back and grabs Maven around the waist. "You ready to go, sweetheart?"

I throw *Cindy* the dirtiest look I can manage before getting into the truck.

She brings him dinner? He said he cooks every night.

Dallas gets into the truck and leans into my space. "Don't let your head go there. Give me the benefit of the doubt, and we'll talk about it."

I nod. My heart aches with jealousy, terror, and betrayal.

Dallas starts the truck with fire in his eyes.

"Walkers! Walkers! Walkers!" Maven chants twenty minutes into the drive home. "Daddy, you promised!"

Dallas pats my thigh. "You hungry?"

"The waiters are rude to you at Walkers!" Maven says. "It's *so, so, so, so* funny! They told Daddy he had a nose bigger than a rhino's horn one time."

I laugh and twist in my seat to smile at her. "No way." I fake lower my voice and place my hand on the side of my mouth. "I totally see what they're talking about though."

Maven bursts into a fit of laughter.

"Hey now," Dallas cuts in. "That's supposed to be the part where you stick up for your dad and argue that I don't have a nose like a rhino." His hand moves to rest on my leg this time when I turn back around. "You cool with stopping?"

"I'm not passing on this, rhino man."

Maven and Dallas sit across from me in the booth.

Walkers is an old-fashioned diner where the waiters wear ridiculous uniforms with unusual, most likely made-up names.

The waitress tells me I'm cheap when I order a water. Maven cracks up.

She says Dallas isn't man enough for real beer when he orders a root beer. Maven cracks up.

She gladly takes Maven's order for a milkshake without saying a word. Maven still cracks up.

At least they're nice to kids.

Not only does Maven take over all the conversation, telling us everything she did at camp, but she also takes my mind off what happened with *Cindy*.

Fucking Cindy. I can't be pissed at Dallas for hanging out with another woman when we're not officially anything. I can't call dibs on him just because I'm carrying his babies.

Wait ... yes, I can.

I can because, last night, he was in my bed.

I'm calling dibs.

I'm stuffed after lunch, but Maven insists we share a dessert.

"My birthday party is next weekend," she tells me, scooping up a bite of the brownie sundae. "Will you come? Pretty, pretty please with cherries on top?"

I swallow my bite down. "Sure." My attention goes to Dallas. "I mean, if that's okay with your dad."

"I'd love for you to come," he answers.

"It's at my grammy and grampy's," she continues. "They have a giant yard, and Daddy promised to get me a princess bounce house, so all my friends can play in it. Didn't you, Daddy?"

Dallas ruffles his hand through her static-filled ponytail. "Sure did."

"A princess bounce house?" I say with high enthusiasm. "I can't say no to that."

Maven bounces in her seat. "Yay! I'm so excited!"

We finish our dessert, and Dallas leaves the table to pay the bill.

"Do you have any kids?" Maven asks as soon as he's out of earshot.

I nearly spit my water in her face and cough a few times before managing to swallow it down. It takes me a second to get over the shock and tilt my lips into a smile.

"I don't," I croak out.

Chapter Twenty-Six

DALLAS

Fuck, it's been a day.

After I dropped Willow off, I helped Maven unpack her bags. We went through all of her painted pictures, letters, and worksheets she'd created. There were several she had drawn with her family doing activities she enjoyed. I flipped through them with a smile, and my heart crashed into my chest when I got near the bottom of the stack.

She and I are standing together, holding hands, and a blonde angel is flying above us. *Lucy* is flying over us.

The next one was a picture of us with Willow.

My daughter is confused.

Willow is confused.

Shit, I'm confused as a motherfucker.

Cindy's comments when I picked up Maven didn't help. Dinner went well until I went to pay the check. After that, Willow froze me out.

I can't wait to collapse on the couch and go over all the shit I need to fix. I need to clear up the Cindy situation with Willow before shit falls apart.

My day gets even more complicated when I finish Maven's favorite bedtime story and tuck her in.

"Willow is nice," she says. "I'm glad she's coming to my birthday party."

I kiss her forehead. "Me, too, honey."

"And she's really pretty."

I nod, hoping I can make it out of the room before she starts her favorite game of a million questions.

"Is she your girlfriend, Daddy?"

She never fails to catch on to something.

I shake my head and fake a laugh. "Now, that's a silly question."

She frowns. "It's not a silly question."

"Your daddy can't have a girlfriend."

I need to tread lightly here. I can't get her involved in something that could break her heart. I'm already growing attached to Willow, constantly thinking about her. *But can I throw my daughter into the mix?* I'm more worried about her heart getting broken than my own.

"Why not? Mommy told me, when she was gone, you'd someday get a new girlfriend who'd be a good mommy to me. Willow would be a good mommy, don't you think so?" She sighs. "Maybe I'll ask her."

Oh, fuck. Holy fuck. This is heading into territory I'm not ready for. Territory Willow isn't ready for.

I squeeze her sides over the blanket. "Honey, Willow is just Daddy's friend."

"*And* my friend," she corrects.

"And your friend."

"She rubs her belly a lot. Marci's mommy did that all the time when she had a baby in there. Does Willow have a baby in there?"

And shit just got even more complicated.

Chapter Twenty-Seven

WILLOW

"You're overthinking this," Stella says on the phone. "You can't seriously believe Dallas is messing around with some other chick named fucking Cindy. I've never heard of a Cindy, which means she doesn't get thought of around here."

I thought the night at the hotel was a crazy one.

That's nothing compared to today.

I spent a morning with Dallas. We hung out with his daughter. A woman told me he'd been hanging out with her. Maven asked me if I had kids, and I somewhat lied to her. I don't have kids … yet.

"She said he's been eating her food. Fried chicken, to be exact," I argue.

"And?"

"And?" I shout. *Why does she not agree that this is a problem?*

"Does eating her food mean eating her vagina or something? Is fried chicken a code phrase I don't know about?"

I slump down on the couch and groan. "I don't know. I just …" *Just don't want him falling for another woman.* I'd better start whipping up some food Betty Crocker-style to compete with this chick's fried chicken. Time to call KFC for their secret recipe.

"Trust me, you're the only woman I've seen Dallas hanging out with. Shit, even talking to."

"You not seeing it doesn't mean it's not happening. You don't see me witnessing you screwing Hudson, but I know you guys are."

"Holy shit," she bursts out.

"Holy shit what?"

"You're falling for him, aren't you? This isn't about your hook-up the other night or about you wanting to get along for the baby. You're into him."

"What?" I yell. "No! Absolutely not!" I'm getting good at this whole lying/denying-my-feelings thing.

"Oh, come on. It's obvious. You've been hanging out, having dinner, giving each other oral before having sex, and picking up his daughter from camp. All that is falling-for-each-other stuff."

"It's not *obvious*." I take a deep breath to change the tone of my voice to sound more self-contained. "Don't take me making sure my baby daddy isn't a psychopath for me falling for him."

She sighs dramatically. "You owe me a hundred bucks when you two become official. I can take it out of your paycheck. I'll ask Hudson if anything is going on with Dallas and fried-chicken chick."

I snort. "Like he'd tell you. Dallas is his brother. Bro code."

"I can be very persuasive with my man. Trust me."

I stretch my legs out and measure my stomach—something I've been doing every night to track my progress. "I'm beginning to second-guess my decision of forcing the two of you to get back together. All this lovey-dovey crap makes me sick."

She laughs. "It's the morning sickness making you sick. I can't wait until you and Dallas admit you're in love, and I can throw all of this back in your face. I'll be the one rolling my eyes at your lovey-dovey shit."

"Whatever. Dallas is in love with his wife, who passed away." I'm acting like a brat, feeling sorry for myself, but this is where I start to push him away again. My heart is ready to go back into solitude. You can't have your heart broken if you don't give it out. "He'll always be in love with her, and I doubt that's going to change anytime soon."

She expels a long breath. "People move on. He can still love her *and* you."

"People can move on, yes, but a man in love as deep as Dallas was? No." A call beeps through, and I pull my phone away to check the caller ID before she keeps up with her argument. "Let me call you back. I have a call coming through."

"Is that call from Dallas?"

"Good night, best friend."

She's laughing when I end the call to answer his.

"Hello?" I throw my hand over my mouth, regretting taking the call. I haven't prepared myself for this conversation yet. I have to get myself together.

"Hypothetical situation," he breathes out, sounding stressed. "What would you say if I told you Maven knew you were pregnant?"

I don't even have time to *think* about what I would say before I screech out my reply, "I'd say you were out of your mind, and there was no way she'd know unless someone—say, her *father*—told her."

"Another hypothetical situation. What would you say if I told you Maven knew we were having twins?"

"What?" I shriek. *Him and his big mouth.* "You've lost your mind!"

He groans. "I couldn't help it! My six-year-old is apparently the damn baby whisperer. She asked me if you were pregnant because you rubbed your belly like fucking Marci's mom."

"Marci's mom? Who's that?"

"Another pregnant woman, I'm assuming."

"Let me get this straight. She asked if I was pregnant because I rubbed my stomach like another pregnant chick?"

"Correct."

"And you felt it was important to confirm it?"

"Correct again."

"Are you nuts?" I scream.

"I didn't know what to do. I can't lie to my daughter."

The hell he can't. I'll be lying to my children all the time about stuff they have no business knowing yet.

"Oh, really? So, you've told her Santa Claus isn't real and the Easter Bunny is you?"

He chuckles but tries to keep his voice serious. "You know what I mean."

"Well, you could've maybe, I don't know, changed the conversation to fucking Barbie dolls or something? Asked her to have a tea party? Talked about anything but my uterus."

"We can't have tea parties before bedtime," he explains.

"That fake caffeine is bad for children and their stuffed dogs after the streetlights come on, huh?"

"Smart-ass," he mutters. "I don't see why you're pissed. You should be thanking me. This saves you from having to be there when I planned on telling her."

"At least one good thing to come out of this." My heart stammers, and confusion flickers through me. Why am I upset that I wasn't there? Why am I sad I didn't get to see her reaction?

"You still pissed?" he asks a few seconds later.

"Not pissed. Shocked."

"If it makes you feel better, I made her promise she wouldn't tell anyone until I told her it was okay."

"I'm not sure how much I trust a promise coming from a six-year-old."

"It helps when you add an extra birthday gift as a hush bribe. Some parenting advice to a mommy-to-be—nothing works better than bribery with extra doll clothes."

"Bribery is okay, but lying is off the table? Makes sense. I'll have to keep that in mind." *While mine is going fucking crazy right now.*

"Now that I know you're not pissed, *just shocked*, I need to ask for a favor."

Seriously? This co-parenting relationship with benefits is getting demanding.

"Haven't you thrown enough at me tonight?"

"This one will be a fun one."

"Shoot." I cross my fingers that it doesn't involve any more pregnancy announcements.

"Will you go shopping with me for Maven's birthday present? Lauren planned on going with me, but she's been pulling double shifts to save up for a house. I don't want to put more stress on her."

"Maybe you should ask *Cindy*. You can go shopping, and then she'll feed you some fried chicken casserole." I'm acting petty, but this is how I bring up my problems. I use my sarcasm to tell people how I feel.

"What?"

"The smiley chick who came over when we picked Maven up." *Is clarification needed?* "The one who thought her fried chicken was the best thing since sliced bread."

"Wow," he says with a laugh.

"What?".

"Surely, you don't believe I'm hanging out with her?"

"No," I stutter out. "I mean, I don't know."

He sounds like he's enjoying this now. "Would you be upset if I were?"

"Nope. Not at all. Eat her fried chicken. Get heart disease. It's all good."

"Willow," he draws out in warning, "would you be upset if I were?"

"Would I upset? Nope. Pissed? Yes. Will I have sex with you again if you are? Definitely not."

"I'm not hanging out with her, I swear. She came around and dropped off food when Lucy passed but hasn't been around in months. Even then, it was nothing. I accepted the food, so my daughter wouldn't starve until I got my shit together. When I managed to perfect grilled cheese, I put a stop to it."

I roll my eyes. "Whatever."

"You're the only woman I'm hanging out with. Hell, other than my sister and mother, you're the only woman I even talk to. So, now that that's done, when do you want me to pick you up for shopping?"

"We're not going anywhere in town, are we?"

"No. I figured we could take a trip into the city. She asked for an American Girl doll?" He says it like he's unsure if that's the right name.

"Oh, I had one of those, growing up. Which one does she want?"

"Uh … one that looks like her? They have a store in the mall near the airport."

"Another road trip, huh?"

"Seems to be our thing. My mom is taking Maven to her bake sale, and then they're going shopping for her party decor on Saturday. That okay?"

"My Saturday looks open." Like almost every day.

Stella is on break from filming and hasn't been asking much of me, so getting out of my apartment sounds refreshing.

"Then, it's a date."

I grin. "It's a date."

Chapter Twenty-Eight

DALLAS

"Do you remember the doll I want, Daddy?" Maven asks for the umpteenth time.

I tap my finger on the side of my head. "Sure do." I have it written in my phone notes. I pulled up the doll website last night, and there's a shit-ton of options. I pause and cock my head to the side. "And you don't even know if you're getting a doll."

Yes, she does.

She bounces from foot to foot. "I *really, really, really* hope so." She skips up the steps to my parents' porch to meet my mom standing outside. "Grammy, don't I need an American Girl doll?"

My mom draws her into her side. "Of course you do, sweetie."

Maven wags her finger my way with a smile on her lips. "You have to listen to your parents, just like you tell me."

"Oh, honey, your daddy was not a good listener when he was your age," my mom replies with a laugh. She squeezes Maven's shoulders. "Now, go wash up for lunch, and we'll go to the bake sale and then shopping for your party decorations."

"Yay! Princess Jasmine all the way!" she shrieks. She pulls the door open and disappears into the house.

"Thank you for watching her, Ma," I say.

She nods. "Anytime. You going to the city to get the doll?"

I scrape my boot against the steps. "It's what she wants."

She can't contain her loving smile "And her daddy always gets her what she wants."

"It's the least I can do. She lost her mother. She deserves the world."

Her smile drops. "You're getting her a doll in the hopes that she won't be sad every day?"

I grew up with parents who refused to sweep shit under the rug. If there was a problem, we talked about it. If they wanted to know something, they asked and expected honest answers. I grew up, facing my challenges, but this isn't a problem easily fixed. No amount of parenting or life lessons could've prepped me for losing Lucy.

"That's not the ultimate reason, but it has something to do with it," I answer. "I want her to heal and enjoy her childhood. If that means spoiling her right now, then that's what I'll do. Whatever my daughter needs to put a smile on her face, I'm willing to do it."

A tear slips down her cheek. I hate seeing my mother upset. I take the few steps up to wrap her in my arms. She sniffles for a second before she continues her impending lecture.

"It'd help her much more if her father started working on the healing process as well," she says when she slips out of my arms.

I clear my throat to bring out my kindest warning voice. "Ma …"

She wipes her eyes and then places her hand on my shoulder. "Dallas, honey, I loved Lucy. We all did. We all miss her, but she's gone."

"She was my *wife*." I'm using all my power not to get pissed with her. "You'd be lost without Dad."

"I would. The difference between you and me is, I'm in my sixties. I have thirty years on you, son. A whole life is waiting for you. Happiness is out there, but you're never going to find it if you're blocking it out. Find someone for Maven. Find someone for *you*."

My mother is the best person I know. She's beautiful. Selfless. Caring. There will never be another woman with a heart as kind and nurturing as hers. She raised us to be strong, fearless, and independent.

Her age doesn't show, and Lauren is the spitting image of her. They're both short and have long brown hair. Lauren keeps hers down most of the time while my mom's stays in a bun. They also have a personality with enough spark to light up a city. Mom doesn't make it easy to get upset with her.

"Can we talk about this another time?" I ask.

"Of course." A smile plays on her lips. "Are you going shopping by yourself?"

I shake my head. "Willow is coming with me."

"Stella's assistant?"

I nod, and her lips form a sly smile.

"Word on the street is, you've been spending an awful lot of time together. Beautiful girl, I must say. The few times I met her, she was such a sweetheart."

"I see the Blue Beech gossip is still alive and kicking," I mutter.

"You go have fun, honey. If it gets too late, stay there, and have a nice dinner. I've already told Maven she could spend the night, so we have plans."

"You spoil her too much."

"That makes two of us." She pulls me in for another hug. "Now, I'm ready for some more grandchildren. I don't know why my children are taking so long to give them to me."

Oh, shit.

She's about to be surprised.

The American Girl store is packed with moms and daughters, and I have no idea where to make my first move.

Willow cracks up before grabbing my hand. "Come on. I'll try to lead the way the best I can. It's been about two decades since I had one of these dolls, but surely, not that much has changed."

We don't lose our connection and dodge people while migrating through the loud crowd.

"We're looking for one that resembles her!" I yell over the noise, as if it were normal to be hunting for the incarnation of your child.

I scan the aisles and stop her each time I think I've found it, but Willow shakes her head and continues her search.

Good thing she came with me, or I would've grabbed the first doll I saw and bolted out of here. Lauren most likely wouldn't have had the patience to deal with this crowd either. She didn't play well with dolls. She drove my mom crazy because she popped all the heads off them, so she could play outside with Hudson and me.

Unlike us, Willow is thorough. She'll assess every doll until she finds the perfect fit.

We've been in the store for thirty minutes when she spots the one and clutches the doll to her chest for me to see. "What do you think?"

It eerily resembles Maven. The dark brown hair, a bow clipped to the side of it, bright purple sunglasses, and a checkered dress.

I tilt my head toward the doll. "Sold."

"Now, we need to find clothes for her."

I point to the doll. "She has clothes."

"She needs more than one outfit. *Geesh*." She pulls on my shirt. "Do you live with only one outfit?"

"No, but unlike this doll, I'm a living, breathing human."

"She needs outfits." She pivots around, and I follow her into another section.

Willow picks out three outfits for the doll, and a sense of happiness jerks through me when she demands to pay for the clothes. I've been terrified of letting someone else around my daughter. I didn't want her to feel neglected or jealous. I didn't think another woman could make Maven feel as loved as Lucy did. But Willow thinks of my daughter, smiles with my daughter, enjoys her company. And my daughter enjoys hers.

"One more stop, and then we'll head home." I snag her hand after paying for the doll and hope I'm taking her in the right direction. I haven't been here since Lucy was pregnant.

"I'm in no rush." She's more at ease in this crowd than she's ever been in Blue Beech.

She stills when we reach our destination, and I'm not sure if it's a good or bad thing. It's a baby store, the largest one in the state, and it has everything you need from clothes to furniture to supplies.

"I thought we could look around. See if there's anything we like," I tell her. She nods in hesitation, and I throw my arm out. "After you."

"Are you sure we're ready for this?"

"One hundred percent."

"Is it bad that I have no idea what some of this stuff is?" Willow asks. "I've read every baby book I could get my hands on. Researched for hours and made lists of every necessity needed, but this all seems too overwhelming."

I still have Maven's nursery furniture in the attic. We kept it in hopes of having another baby and saw it as a good-luck token. As much as I want to pull it out, along with the memories, it wouldn't be right for me to do that to Willow.

"It is at first. I Googled everything of Maven's to figure out how to use it." I point to the cribs on the other side of the store. "One thing we know our little tykes will need for sure is somewhere to sleep. Let's start there, and we'll work our way through the store."

She grins. "Sounds good."

Chapter Twenty-Nine

WILLOW

Dallas leans against the doorway to the guest room I'm converting into a nursery. "There's still time to change your mind and set the cribs up at my place."

"Yes, you've mentioned that several hundred times," I reply.

Our shopping adventure ended with bags of baby items. We spent three hours shopping and had to get two of everything. Dallas shoved my card away when I tried to pay and nearly threw my wallet out the window when I tried to give him half of it in cash when we got in the truck.

He wraps his arms around my waist from behind and drags me into his firm body. "I'll give you the master and crash in the basement. I'll be the nanny. I'll get up in the middle of the night and change diapers. Feed them. Bathe them. Whatever you want."

"*Give you the master.*"

The room where he freaked out on me.

No freaking thank you.

It'd help me physically with the babies but not emotionally. It'd obliterate my heart. Two babies is hard work, but I'd rather risk being sleep-deprived than take him up on that offer.

I'll fuck him but not walk through his front door.

I'm a hot mess.

He scrapes his hands together. "You want to start setting everything up?"

"Can we leave that for another day? I'm exhausted, my feet hurt, and I'm sore everywhere."

"You want me to give you a massage?"

"Can you do it with your tongue?"

He smirks. "I'd love to."

※

Stella sits down next to me with a plate of cake in her hand. "Hudson said Dallas spilled the baby beans to Maven."

We're at Maven's birthday party, and she's started opening gifts. I showed up early, sat down so that the table would hide my stomach, and haven't moved since.

Maven's face lights up with excitement as she opens each gift, and she thanks the gifter before moving on to the next. Dallas is saving ours for last. I peek over at him and smile at the happiness on his face as he watches her.

He's a good dad.

He might be broken, but he managed to repair part of his heart and opened it up for her. I'm hoping he'll do the same with our babies.

Half of Blue Beech's population is here, eating the food Rory, Dallas' mom, made—which is enough to feed the entire NFL—chasing their screaming children around, and staring at me like I have a nip slip. Maven has attempted to drag me to the bounce house dozens of times, and it looks like Disney vomited everywhere.

"She figured it out herself," I answer.

"No shit?"

"Apparently, I rub my stomach like some other pregnant chick around here does. She put two and two together." I laugh. "Dallas broke the news because he couldn't handle fibbing to a six-year-old."

"Damn, kids are getting smart these days. I was still under the impression storks dropped babies off on doorsteps when I was her age."

Maven squeals and jumps up and down when she opens Dallas's gift. She screams again when opening mine, and then she runs over to give me a tight hug. "Thank you!" she yells, still jumping up and down. She sits down next to Stella and starts ripping open the doll box and all of the accessories.

Stella bumps my shoulder with hers. "You sure you don't want to take a run in the bounce house? It'll be a first time for me."

"You've never been in a bounce house?" I ask, looking horrified. *Who hasn't been the kid who fell down and tried to get up while the others bounced harder to stop them?*

"Nope. My mom considered having a childhood was an abomination, and all I needed to do was work." She puts her hands together. "So, *please*."

I point to my stomach. "No sudden movements, remember?"

"Oh, crap, I keep forgetting about"—she pauses and nervously looks around—"*that*."

"She can't go into the bounce house, Aunt Stella!" Maven shouts with a gasp. "She has to be very, very careful because there is a baby in her tummy." She stops to correct herself and holds up two fingers. "I mean, two babies in her tummy because she and Daddy are having twins!" She slaps her hand over her mouth. "Uh-oh." Her gaze sweeps over to Dallas with wide eyes. "Sorry, Daddy. I broke our secret. I'm so, so sorry!"

The noise in the backyard comes to a halt, and Rory's cup falling to the ground is the only sound I hear before I freak the hell out.

Chapter Thirty

DALLAS

*H*OLY FUCK.

This isn't how I imagined this going down.

Willow looks like she's about to vomit. My mom looks hurt. My dad looks like he's ready to lay into my ass. Hudson is grinning like a motherfucker.

I clear my throat, ignoring every set of eyes on Willow, and bolt her way. I kiss my daughter on the top of her head. "It's fine, May Bear. Why don't you go show your new doll the bounce house, okay?"

"I'm sorry, Daddy," she says again. "I've just been so excited." She throws her hands out. "It just blurted right out of my mouth."

I kiss her forehead. "It's okay."

Willow jumps out of her chair when her eyes start to water. She doesn't want anyone to see her cry. "If everyone will please excuse me for a second." Her voice breaks. "Or a few minutes. Possibly a few hours … or days."

She turns and dashes into the house. Stella jumps up to follow, but I stop her.

"Let me have this one, okay?"

She stares at me with a hard look and hesitation before nodding.

As soon as I leave the crowd, I can hear the voices erupt into chaos. Question after question is being fired off, one after the other, to my family. I feel sorry for leaving them to the Blue Beech gossip wolves, but I have to make sure Willow is okay.

I find her sitting on the bed in my childhood room with tears in her eyes. I shut the door and bend down in front of her. I take her chin in my shaky hand and lock eyes with her.

"I'm so fucking sorry, do you hear me?" I whisper. "I made a mistake."

She tries to pull away from my touch, but I don't let her.

"Please," I hiss. "Please don't fucking run from me because of this."

Willow is a pro at helping other people with their problems but terrible at facing her own. It's easy for her to turn her back on situations she doesn't want to deal with.

She sniffles. "This is humiliating. Did you see their faces? All the jaws dropping?"

"They were surprised, which we expected. I mean, we haven't exactly been forthcoming about your pregnancy or *this*." I signal between the two of us. To be honest, I'm relieved it's out there. I wish it had happened in a better situation, like us sitting my parents down and spilling the news, but at least the secret is off my chest now.

"*This?*" she questions, scrunching up her face and reenacting my movement. "What do you mean, *this?*"

I get up and sit down next to her on the bed. "We're doing something here. I'm as confused as you are about it, but we are. You're the only woman I've looked at since I lost Lucy. I can't …" I pause. "I can't stop thinking about you. Whenever I leave your apartment or drop you off, the excitement from when I get to see you next keeps me high. Hell, I can't wait until the next time I even get to talk to you. You're something I look forward to every day. The thought of seeing you, talking to you, and spending time with you gives me so much fucking happiness." My revelation only makes her cry harder. "What can I do to make this better? Anything. I'll do anything."

Except let you walk away.

Please don't fucking walk away.

"Turn back time to months ago," is all she whispers.

Fuck. I want to beg her not to go there.

"Tell me you don't mean that. You might've thought that at first, which I don't fucking blame you, but tell me, after all this time we've spent together, after seeing the beautiful babies we made on that monitor, that you don't mean that."

She sighs. "I … I don't." She covers her face with her hands. "I thought I would. Sometimes, I wish I still felt that way. I thought it was the end of my happiness when I found out I was pregnant after our night together, but now … now, I can't think of a time when I've been happier. A time when I thought I was doing something so right." She rubs her stomach. "These past few months have changed my life, too."

"These past few months have dragged me out of the darkest hole I thought I'd never escape." Not all the way. I'm still there, and I'll never be the same man, but Willow has brought out parts of me I thought would never come out again. And I can feel myself healing as the sun rises each day.

I drop down to my knees to take in the sight of her and show her the honesty in my eyes. "You brought me to the light. We might not have expected this, but it's somehow made us stronger, brighter, happier."

I cringe at the knock on the door that interrupts us. Stella pokes her head in, apology on her face, and takes in the scene in front of her.

Me on my knees in the begging position, and Willow crying.

Willow wipes away a tear and nods her head, silently permitting Stella to come in and shut the door behind her.

The door opens again seconds later, this time without a knock, and Hudson appears with brows knitted in concern. "I know this is bad timing, brother, but Maven is in the bounce house, crying, and insists on only talking to you or Willow."

"Fuck," I snap, averting my attention to Willow. "Will you be okay for a minute?"

She nods. "Go ahead. I'll be fine." I get up, but she grabs my arm to stop me. "Actually, I'd like to come with you, if that's okay?"

"I'm not sure you'll be ready for eyes on you," Stella says.

"How about I try to get her to come in here?" Hudson asks, leaving the room before waiting for our answer.

Willow sniffles again. "That's a good idea."

Stella starts to go toward the door but stops and darts over to Willow. "I love you," she says with a hug. "Know that I'm here, no matter what, and I love you."

This brings a small smile out of Willow. "I love you, too."

Stella pokes her shoulder. "And you know you have some explaining to do. *Twins?* You couldn't even let a girl know she's having two godchildren now?"

"I was waiting for the right time," Willow replies.

The door opens again, and a sobbing Maven comes running into the room and crashes into my arms. "Daddy, I'm sorry!"

I keep my arms around her and rub her back. "It's okay, May Bear."

She turns around, still in my arms, and shyly peeks over at Willow. "Are you mad at me?"

Willow's eyes go soft, and her tone turns soothing. "Of course not, honey. Just shocked, is all."

She composes herself, gets up, and runs a hand down her dress. I can't stop myself from grinning at the sight of her stomach showing through. Fingers crossed, she'll let it be on display more now. "I need another slice of cake."

I grab her elbow to make sure she's stable and dip my mouth to her ear. "You sure you're okay with going back out?" I ask. "We can leave, if you want?"

"We'll have to face them sooner or later," she says.

"We'll be out in a few minutes," I tell Hudson. "Tell people no questions until we're ready."

Maven wraps her hand around my leg. "I know you promised extra doll clothes if I kept our secret." She pushes her lower lip out. "Do I still get to keep them?"

Willow snorts before bursting out into a fit of laughter. "God, I needed that."

Chapter Thirty-One

WILLOW

"I KNOW MY SON DEMANDED NO BABY TALK, AND I RESPECT THAT, BUT CAN I GIVE you a hug?" Rory asks.

I nod, and she pulls me into her tight, patting my back. "Congratulations, dear. I am incredibly grateful for you. So is John, who's around here somewhere, waiting to corner his son and lecture him on keeping secrets from his mama." John is Dallas's father.

The majority of the crowd has ventured home, but a few people are still hanging around. Since we came back, Dallas stayed by my side until minutes ago when I finally convinced him to go to the bounce house with Maven and her doll. Some people have been pretending not to stare at me, others have refused to acknowledge me, and the rest have shamelessly watched every move I make.

"Don't worry about them," Rory says when she pulls away. "If anyone asks too many questions, you let them know they'll have to deal with me." She grabs a slice of cake and hands it to me. "You deserve this. I told Dallas to give you my number. Don't hesitate to call if you need anything."

I nod. "Thank you."

She throws me another smile, pats my shoulder, and then walks over to a table of women hunched over while talking in hushed voices. Most likely about me.

"Holy shit," Stella gasps, wrapping her arm around my shoulders. "That was seriously something out of a movie. I need to use that in a script."

"No benefiting from my problems for your career," I mutter, leaning into her.

"How are you feeling?" she asks when we sit down at a secluded table.

"A million things at once. Mortified that this is how everyone found out. Relieved that we no longer have to hide it."

She smirks. "He's a good dad, Willow. He'll be good to you and your baby." She winces and pouts. "I mean, *babies*. Why do I feel like I'm not your first call anymore?"

"Sorry. It's just been so overwhelming. I'm still digesting it myself. There hasn't even been a call to anyone else." I shake my head. "Hell, all of these people found out before my mom did."

"You'd better call her. Blue Beech news makes national news."

I laugh. "I saw the town's newspaper. The front page was about some ribfest cook-off. I'm sure my mom subscribes because who can go about their day without finding out Sandy May's special recipe?"

"Sandy May makes killer ribs. I'd never even had ribs until Hudson dragged me to that festival."

"I'm sure there's a plan in Dallas's head to drag me to the next one."

"It'll be fun." She pokes my side. "Now, if you get any more baby news, you'd better let me know. If I find out you're having quintuplets from another six-year-old, I won't be happy."

"Maven didn't tell you? It's actually sextuplets. We're waiting for another party to shock everyone."

"Very funny." She glances around. "By the way, I'm pretty sure Rory is over there, planning your baby shower."

"God, her reaction was dramatic. Her fruit punch fell to the ground in slow motion. I thought she wanted to kill me for not telling her."

"Oh, that was just the shock. You didn't see the bright-ass smile on her face after you left. She's not pissed. She's fucking elated." She laughs. "The only people who weren't over the moon were the women who wanted to be the one Dallas had knocked up. You got knocked up by Blue Beech's finest bachelor. You go, girl."

"So, the news is out," Dallas says.

"The news is out," I repeat slowly.

Maven is passed out in the backseat, snoring like a man in a nursing home, and it's almost eight o'clock. She apologized to me countless times for her outburst, but I couldn't be upset at a girl sporting a *Birthday Girl* tiara and sash.

"You want to come over?" he asks. "Hang out for a bit? I have leftover cake."

Jesus, does everyone think all I eat is cake?

The thought of spending more time with him excites me, but the problem is, going to his house doesn't. It terrifies me. The memories from our night together might slash a hole in the connection we've been making. We've already been through enough today. Reliving those memories isn't something I want either one of us to do.

"Not tonight," I answer. "I'm exhausted."

"You sure?"

I nod at the same time he pulls up to my apartment building, and I stop him from unbuckling his seat belt. "Don't wake her up. I can walk myself in."

"Okay. I'll wait out here until I see your light come on, and you call me to let me know you made it in okay."

And that's what he does.

It's seven in the morning, and someone is banging on my door.

"What is up with your family knocking people's doors down at the butt crack of dawn?" I ask when Lauren walks in.

"Good morning, my future sister-in-law," she sings out while walking into my apartment. "I brought doughnuts and green tea."

Seriously?

"What do you want?" I mutter in my best cranky voice.

"You didn't believe it'd be that easy to dodge me, did you, neighbor?" She plops down on a barstool at the island. "I was upset enough that I got called into work and missed my niece's birthday party, and then I find out you're having *twins*, and you didn't tell me." She crosses her arms. "As the girl who lives above you, I am extremely offended."

I take a gulp of the green tea. *Yummy.* "We were waiting. No one knew."

"Except the six-year-old."

"Except the six-year-old," I mutter. "Your brother apparently can't lie to his daughter."

"Yeah, he sucks at saying no to her. She's got him wrapped around her finger. Now, if it's a girl, I'd like her name to be Lauren."

I side-eye her. "It's too early to argue about baby names."

"It's never too early to hash it out over baby names. *Trust me*. I've heard stories from the maternity ward nurses about the kind of drama and chaos families have over baby names."

"I'm naming them after my pet goldfish—Goldie and Nemo."

She rolls her eyes. "Now that we've got Lauren Junior covered, what's going on with you and my big bro?"

My brows lift. "Other than the fact that we're having twins together, nothing."

"His truck was here the other night when I got home at *four in the morning*. It seems to be here pretty frequently, if you ask me. Since we know you weren't discussing *baby names* at four in the morning, what were y'all doing?"

"Discussing nursery decor."

"You suck," she grumbles.

I perk up. "You love me."

"I do. But can I say something serious?"

"I don't think I can stop you."

"Don't hurt him."

This really catches my attention. "Huh?"

"You know exactly what I'm talking about. Don't hurt my brother. He's been through too much to lose someone else he loves."

Deflection time. "I've made it clear, I won't ever keep the babies from him."

"I'm talking about *you*, girlfriend." She annoyingly shakes her shoulders while drinking her smoothie through the straw.

"Your brother most certainly does not love me."

She grins. "Not yet. From what my mother tells me, it's getting pretty damn close, and my mama knows everything."

Chapter Thirty-Two

DALLAS

The excavator I bought from the auction is kicking my ass. Even though I do my due diligence the best I can, you never know what you're going to get when you buy an item as is.

It's an easy fix but fucking time-consuming, and Hudson ran off for a staycation with Stella for the day—whatever the fuck that is—at the local bed-and-breakfast. I tried to fight him on it, telling him they could eat Cheerios at their kitchen table, and then he could come into work, but he agreed to give me as much time as I needed off when Willow had the babies.

Almost a week has passed since Maven's birthday party, and I've talked to Willow on the phone a couple times a day but not in person.

The machine loses my attention when the music is cut off.

I look down and grin. "This is a nice surprise."

Willow holds up the cooler in her hand. "Thought I'd bring you some lunch."

Good. I'm fucking starving, and I was planning on skipping lunch, so I wouldn't have to spend time driving into town and then back today.

I carefully move down the ladder and wipe my forehead with the back of my arm while coming her way. I laugh when she licks her lips while brazenly eye-fucking me at the same time I'm eye-fucking her.

She's not wearing her usual baggy clothes today. I'm not sure where she got the maternity clothes, but she's breathtaking in her jean shorts and T-shirt that says *Tacos for Two, Please.*

Her and her tacos.

I run my hand down my sweaty chest. I have the air on high, but I get hot, no matter what, when I'm working on machine engines. "You like what you see?"

She lifts her gaze back up my body and grins playfully. "Oh, I *love* what I see."

"You know, I'm more than just a hot, lean body."

I curl my arm around her shoulders to pull her into me and plant a kiss on her lips. She doesn't even flinch. Us touching has become so natural. Not only does it feel good, having her here, but she also showed up without my asking. She took the time to make lunch and came to surprise me. She can deny it all she wants, but she's falling for me.

"I'm starving. What did you whip up for us?"

She glances around the room. "It's a surprise."

I gesture toward the other side of the garage. "We have a table and shit in the office, if you want to eat in there, or we can go outside?"

"Outside. I've been quite the hermit lately. I could use some sun."

"You know the remedy to that problem?"

She wrinkles her cute nose in annoyance. "Funny. I'll start venturing out of my apartment when the time is right."

"I hope it's before our kids turn sixteen."

She shoves my side and pulls away when we reach the picnic table underneath two weeping willows. My grandfather built the table decades ago for when my grandmother would bring him lunch.

I rub my hands together when we sit down. "So, what have we got?"

Her eyes widen in reluctance. "They say it's the gesture, not the gift, right?"

Did she bring cheese and crackers? A Snickers bar and Sunny Delight?

"I'll enjoy whatever you brought."

She draws in a breath when I open the cooler and start dragging out its contents. There are plastic bags with sandwiches in them.

"I love me some peanut butter and jelly," I say upon further inspection. The next item is a bag of tortilla chips large enough to feed Maven's entire preschool and then a covered bowl. I open it and can't stop the cheesy smile from hitting my lips. "And guacamole."

"I'm giving you a run for your money on the best guac in Blue Beech."

"Let's taste-test it, shall we?" I open the bag of chips and dip one into the guacamole.

It's good, definitely not as good as mine, but I can tell she worked hard on it. She analyzes me chewing it likes she's a contestant on *Top Chef*.

"You killed it. I'll bring over my trophy for you later this evening."

She raises a brow. "You're just saying that because we're having sex."

"There are better things I could say to you to get laid than"—I stop to fake a smoldering gaze I saw on *The Bachelor* once—"Hey, girl, you make excellent guacamole. *Let's fuck in a bed of guacamole, have it served at our wedding, and name our children Guac and Mole.*"

She throws a chip at me while trying to contain her laughter and then slides the sandwich in front of me. "Now, eat your PB and J and shut up. I slaved all day, making this."

I scarf down the two sandwiches she made me and make sure I moan with every bite of her guacamole.

She looks from side to side. "So … is there anyone else here?"

"No. Just me today. I'm sure you know, Hudson is feeding Stella strawberries in bed."

She laughs. "I booked the room for them. Stella's been coddling me since our secret came out. I couldn't handle it any longer."

"What secret?"

She leans forward. "You know."

"Which one? I believe we have a few."

She narrows her eyes my way. "You know exactly which one I'm referring to."

"The one where we're having twins?" I give her a shit-eating grin. "Or the one where I've been eating your pussy?"

She blushes. "You've been doing that? I think I'm in need of a reminder."

I smirk. "Oh, I see what's going on here. You thought you could come here and butter me up with PB and Js to get laid?"

She shrugs. "Just a little."

I point to my chest. "You do know I'm sweaty as fuck?"

"Let me make you even sweatier," she whispers with a wink.

I surge to my feet. "You don't have to ask me twice."

Willow slips off her seat and speed-walks to the garage. Her mouth crushes to mine as soon as I lock the shop door behind us. Adrenaline speeds through my blood as she demands more of me, pressing her tongue into my mouth. I'll never be disappointed to come to work again. This memory will hit me every time I walk in.

I grunt when I'm pushed back against the wall, and she kisses me harder, owning me, as our tongues slide together. She consumes me. The need of wanting her takes over every thought in my mind. I seethe at the loss of our connection when she runs her lips over the line of my jaw.

She's running the show.

She needs this.

And I'm a willing participant—anytime, any-fucking-where, any way.

My hands trail down her body to cup her perfect ass and lift her off the floor. I spin us around, so I have her against the wall now. She wastes no time in grinding against my cock. I do the same against her pussy.

"God," she whispers. "Please fuck me. I need it."

"Where do you want it?" I grit out.

She jerks her chin toward the parked car on the other side of the garage. "There."

We don't usually work on cars here, but I'm doing it as a favor for a buddy.

He's the one doing the fucking favor now.

"You want me to fuck you on that car, baby?"

Her breathing is labored, and she has to speak between breaths. "Yes"—inhale—"right"—exhale—"there."

"You want it hard or soft?"

"Hard. Really hard," she says against my mouth.

Heat radiates through my chest when her teeth graze my tongue, and she bites it.

Oh, yeah. She wants it hard. Rough. Dirty.

We fumble around until we're both naked, and I race across the garage and lower her bare ass on the '67 Chevelle.

I brush her hair back from her face and don't make another move until her eyes meet mine. "Willow, you're beautiful."

A bright grin spreads across her mouth when she hears her name, and I tense when her soft hand wraps around my aching cock. My heart hammers against my chest when she guides me into her. My head throws back as a roar rips through me.

The first move is made by her tilting her waist up, slowly taking in the length of me, and I'm close to losing it when my gaze drifts down to our connection.

Her pussy juices cover my cock. Her legs are open wide as she takes me in again and rolls her hips in the process. Nothing describes the feeling of watching the girl of your dreams lying on the hood of a car and taking your cock like she owns it.

"Fuck, you feel good," I grind out.

No more taking it slow. I grab her ankles, pull her down the car until she's on the edge, and slam inside her. She clings to my shoulders and rests her weight on me.

"I'm there," she says, her body going weak. "Oh God, I'm there."

I keep my focus on her to watch her face. Her mouth opens, a loud moan escaping her, and she clenches around my dick.

The view of her getting off sets me off.

My body shakes when I bury my face between her breasts and release inside her.

We stare at each other, breathing heavily, and she cracks up laughing.

"Not the best reaction after someone gets you off," I say, unable to hold back my smile.

"I so buttered you up with my guacamole."

I join her laughter.

Willow Andrews isn't just working her way inside me. I'm also falling in love with her.

Chapter Thirty-Three

WILLOW

Two paint samples are in my hand as I hold them against a wall in the nursery.

Red or yellow?

I want to go with a neutral theme since we don't know the sex of our babies yet. I drop them onto the floor when my phone rings.

"Hello?" I answer.

"Hey," Dallas says on the other line. "You busy?"

"Nope, just unpacking the rest of the stuff we bought for the babies and trying to decide what look I'm going for in the nursery." I balance the phone between my shoulder and ear. "What's up?"

"Maven's preschool called. She's sick. I'm swamped at the shop, and my parents aren't available until this evening. Any way you can pick her up and hang out until I get a break from here?"

"Sure, that's no problem."

He lets out a relieved sigh. "Thank you. I shouldn't be any later than five. There's a spare key under the planter on the porch. Make yourself comfortable. There's plenty of food in the house. Let me know if you need anything, okay?"

"Okay."

I throw my hair up in a ponytail, change into shorts and a T-shirt, and hop into my SUV. I don't realize what I'm about to do until I pull into the parking lot of Maven's preschool.

I'm going to his house.

Holy shit. I should've told him I'd bring her back to my place.

Stepping foot in his house again is something I've been putting off even though he's invited me countless times.

I take in a breath. *I have to get over this fear, right?*

There's no way I would've gotten away with it for too much longer. At least it won't be in front of Dallas in case I have a panic attack.

~

"Hello. You must be Willow," the older woman behind the desk greets me when I walk through the front door and into the lobby. "Dallas said you'd be picking up Maven." She picks up the phone and tells the teacher I'm here.

I look up at the sound of heels coming down the hallway. I recognize the woman from Maven's birthday party but don't recall seeing her again after the pregnancy outburst.

She stops in front of us and rests her hands on Maven's shoulders. "Hi, Willow." She gives me a red-lipped smile and holds out her hand. "I'm Mrs. Lawrence, Maven's teacher."

"She's my aunt Beth," Maven corrects.

I freeze up and blink a few times, noticing the similarities between her and Maven … and Lucy. Mrs. Lawrence—*Beth*—squeezes Maven's shoulders.

She nods. "That I am." Her voice turns soothing. "I'm Lucy's sister."

I shake her hand. "It's nice to meet you."

Damn, Dallas has thrown me so many curveballs today, I'm dizzy. I'm meeting the sister of his dead wife *and* going to the house he shared with said wife.

"She's had a fever for the past hour. Thank you for picking her up. It seems everyone is busy or out of town today, and I couldn't find a sub to come in for me."

"It's fine. I was, uh …" *Getting a nursery together for my babies with Dallas.* "Off work today."

"I feel no good, and I'm sleepy," Maven whines, rubbing her eyes.

Beth kisses her cheek before releasing her. "Get some rest, sweetie." Her attention moves to me. "Please ask Dallas to keep me updated, and don't hesitate to call if she needs anything."

I nod, pressing the back of my hand against Maven's forehead. She's warm.

"Of course."

I help Maven into the backseat of my car, and she falls asleep the first few minutes into the short drive to Dallas's house. Even though I haven't been back inside of the house since that night, I know where it is. We've driven by it dozens of times, and Maven has pointed it out to me.

I admire the large white farmhouse he restored years ago. There are large gray shutters on each side of the windows and planters under the ones next to the front door. It's perfectly landscaped with bright pink roses and daisies. It's a beautiful home.

The key is under the planter, like he said, and I follow Maven through the front door.

"Mommy and Daddy always let me sleep in their big bed when I no feel good," she says, stomping down the hallway. "It's right down here."

Oh, honey, I know where it is.

I gulp when she opens the door. This is the moment of truth where I find out if I can go forward with Dallas or if I can't get over him loving another woman. This is where I find out if I'm a quick screw because he's horny. You don't have to love someone. Hell, you don't even have to like them to fuck them.

The familiar whitewashed wood bed sits in the middle of the large master bedroom. The plaid comforter is the same as it was that night. The scent in the room smells like him. Nothing has changed. My hands are on the verge of shaking as I help Maven into the bed.

That's when I see it.

The picture of him and Lucy on the nightstand. There's another of Lucy by herself on the other nightstand. Her … or another woman's perfume is sitting on the dresser next to a white jewelry box with her name branded on the front. There's a chair in the corner with a woman's sweater draped over it.

Was that Lucy's?

Or is it Chicken Chick's?

"Will you put on cartoons for me?" Maven asks with a yawn.

"Sure." I snag the remote from the nightstand and flip through the stations until I find her favorite cartoon.

She slides underneath the blankets and relaxes against the pillows.

I tap the bed as my heart thumps against my chest. My throat grows tight, and the room feels warmer than Maven's forehead. "You let me know if you need anything, okay?"

"Will you stay?" she asks. "And watch with me?"

I nod even though all I want to do is abort mission and hang out in my car until Dallas gets here. I take off my shoes and sit down next to her, over the covers. That night haunts me as the opening of the cartoon lets out some annoying song. Maven snuggles into my side.

"Willow," she whispers, hesitation layering her voice.

"Yeah?" I ask.

"Will you be my new mommy?"

I blankly stare at her, fighting off the desire to flee the room, and try to give her the most comforting smile I can manage.

"You're going to be my brother or sister's mommy, so maybe you can be mine, too, since my mommy is in heaven."

A knife digs into my heart, and I take in a deep breath to stop the tears. Maven looks just as upset as I feel.

I kiss the top of her head and then smooth my hands over her hair. I don't know what to say. I don't know what to do. I don't even know my name at this point because my brain is spiraling out of control. "We'll talk about it when you feel better, okay, honey?"

"Okay," she whimpers.

She only lasts five minutes into the show before she dozes off. I slowly and quietly pull away from her and get out of the bed to grab my phone.

I catch my breath when I make it into the kitchen and drop onto a chair. I glance around the kitchen. More pictures of Lucy on the refrigerator. Another one by the coffeemaker. A grocery list that's not in Dallas's handwriting is stuck under a magnet on the fridge.

Will I always think everything is Lucy's here? That Dallas wants to keep and display every part and memory of her, so he won't forget … so he won't move on?

It's petty of me to think these things. He wants to keep those memories of her alive because he was a good husband.

But I can't stop myself.

That's why I need to take a break from him. Why I need to consider the consequences before throwing myself into a situation this serious. His daughter asked me to be her new mommy. That's big. *Huge.* A little girl's heart is on the line, and I can't break it if everything doesn't go well with Dallas.

I grab my phone and text Stella.

Me: You busy?

She got home from the bed and breakfast yesterday, and nothing was on her schedule for the day.

Stella: Nope. Just going over some scripts. What's up?

Me: I picked up Maven from school for Dallas because she was sick, and now, I'm not feeling so hot myself. Would you be able to watch her until Dallas got home, so I could get some rest at my apartment?

Stella: I'll be there in 15. You need anything?

Me: I'm good. Thank you.

Her answer slows down my heart rate. Now, I need to make sure she doesn't notice anything is off with me. I need to put my actress face on and hope the actress herself doesn't find out I'm a fraud.

I'm still in the kitchen when Stella walks in. She rushes into the room and falls down in the chair across from me.

"You feeling any better?" she asks with concern.

"Not really," I mutter. "I just need to lie down. I've been working on the nursery all morning, and I think I overdid it. That, or the twins are pissed that I fed them a healthy breakfast this morning."

She laughs and gets up to wrap her arms around my shoulders. "You take care of yourself, girlfriend. Call me here soon."

Chapter Thirty-Four

DALLAS

It's been a hell of a day.

The shop's phone has been blowing up all day with people wanting maintenance on their machines that weren't scheduled in. I took them, of course, but I'm feeling overwhelmed.

I can't wait to get home to my girls. Willow texted me a few hours ago when she picked up Maven, but I haven't heard anything from her since even though I've tried calling. I'm guessing they fell asleep when Maven made her put on cartoons.

I wasn't sure how Willow would react when I asked her to take Maven to the house, but she didn't seem to have a problem, which is a fucking relief. I don't want her to feel like she can't step foot through my front door. I don't want her to feel uncomfortable in my home. I want her to feel so fucking good there that she decides to move in.

I start my engine and then kill it a few seconds later.

Fuck. She's going to see them.

She's going to see all of Lucy's stuff. I haven't built up the courage to move anything related to Lucy. Her toothbrush is in the holder, her clothes are in the closet, her touch is everywhere. I haven't moved anything because it's comforting, knowing there's a part of her there. I can't forget about her if her bracelet is still on the kitchen counter. I can't forget her if I see her favorite pink top when I open the closet.

I don't want that to change. I don't want to forget the woman I loved. I don't know if I can move her things yet, but I have a feeling that Willow won't be comfortable until I do.

I call her again. No answer. I text her next.

Me: You doing okay over there?

I start my truck again and head home. She still hasn't answered when I pull into the driveway, and instead of parking next to her car, I see Stella's red BMW. I walk in, check in on Maven sleeping in my bedroom, and then meet Stella in the kitchen. She's at the table going over scripts.

"Hey," I greet, tossing my keys onto the counter.

She presses a finger to her lips. "We don't want to wake her up. She's been knocked out for a few hours."

I nod, lowering my voice. "Where's Willow? I've tried calling her a few times but no answer." Anytime Willow goes MIA, I go into nervous-wreck mode.

"She texted me and asked me to come hang out because she wasn't feeling well. She wanted to go home and lie down."

I lean back against the counter, resting on my elbows. "Huh. I wonder why she didn't mention anything to me."

She chuckles. "You know Willow. She doesn't want to inconvenience anyone."

"You heard from her since she left?"

She shakes her head. "She seemed like she couldn't wait to get out of here. I wish I had more for you, but she's been distant with me lately. It most likely has something to do with her fear of sharing anything with me since it will get back to you because my fiancé has a big-ass mouth."

"Fuck, sorry 'bout that. I don't want to come between the two of you. If it helps, I don't expect anything from you. Your loyalty is to her."

They've been close for years, and I hate that she has no one to turn to right now.

She gets up. "No worries. She's used to dealing with shit on her own. Brett made her that way. She kept all of their problems inside because she was sick of us telling her to break up with him every day. It's hard to vent to people when they agree the guy you're venting about is an asshole."

"I get it."

"I have to head out. I have a reading for the new season of my show in an hour." She kisses my cheek. "Let me know if you hear from Willow, okay? And I'll do the same for you. I'll call her on my way to set and ask if she wants to come with me. Maybe I can get something out of her."

I hug her. "Thank you for watching Maven. Be careful, and keep me updated."

"You're welcome, and of course."

Maven is sound asleep and snoring when I go to check on her again. She insists on sleeping in my bed if she coughs the wrong way. Some might find it annoying, but I enjoy that she considers my space a healing place.

I turn off the TV and do a once-over of the room.

Then, a twice-over.

Willow didn't run because she was sick.

I was right.

She ran because Lucy was everywhere.

Chapter Thirty-Five

WILLOW

Even though I don't know where I'm going, I packed an overnight bag. All I'm sure of is, I need to get out of Blue Beech for a minute and clear my head.

Is it sad that Lucy's stuff upset me?

I've been second best to Stella for years. Her assistant. The second choice to hang out with and only when someone wants to get closer to her. People have looked past me to see the celebrity. I can handle not being the star in the spotlight, but being second place in someone's heart isn't an option.

My SUV's sunroof is open. The music is up while I drive down a deserted road. I didn't turn on my GPS. I'm just driving. I'm blurting out the words to my favorite song when a sharp pain shoots through me, causing me to buckle forward. I swerve to the side of the road when another one hits me just seconds later. Tears well in my eyes, and the pain overtakes me. This isn't a baby kicking or morning sickness.

It's something else.

Something I haven't been expecting.

Something I haven't read about.

Something not normal.

I dump the contents of my purse out in the passenger seat to find my phone and then power it on.

Please have service. Please have service.

One bar. All I have is one bar.

I dial the three digits as tears start crawling down my cheeks.

"Nine-one-one, what's your emergency?"

"My name ..." My voice trembles, and I struggle to come up with the right words. "My name is Willow Andrews. I was driving." I stop and double over, holding my stomach and groan. "I'm pregnant and having severe abdominal pain."

"Okay, ma'am," the woman says on the other side. "Do you know your location?"

I urgently search for a street sign, mile marker, anything that can help them. *Nothing.*

"I ... I'm not sure. There's hardly any traffic." I open the Maps app on my phone to get the exact location and recite it to her.

"Thank you. We have an ambulance on the way. Stay with me, okay? Take deep breaths, Willow. Are you experiencing any bleeding?"

I'm sobbing louder. "I'm not sure." I'm not proud of this, but I dip my hand into my panties and gasp when I drag it back out. There's not much of it, but it's there. And it's bright red.

Tears fall down my face faster.

"You doing okay, Willow?" she asks.

"Yes," I croak out, the words barely audible. "Yes, I'm bleeding."

I should hang up and call Dallas. Call Stella. Call my mom. *Somebody.*

But I can't move. I'm frozen to the spot, imagining every nightmare that could happen.

Please let everything be okay with my babies.

Please let everything be okay with me.

Please. Please. Please.

Chapter Thirty-Six

DALLAS

I'VE BEEN PACING THE FLOOR IN MY KITCHEN FOR WHAT SEEMS LIKE HOURS. I FED Maven dinner, and she passed back out an hour ago. Her fever has gone down, which is a relief.

I've tried calling Willow countless times. At first, it was going straight to voice mail. It's ringing now, but she's not answering, so I get her voice mail again.

When my phone rings fifteen minutes later, I quickly hit the Accept button without even looking at the caller ID. "Hello?" I rush out.

"Dallas!" Lauren screeches. "You need to get to the hospital right now."

"What?" I stutter out. "What's going on?"

"Willow is here. They brought her in about ten minutes ago."

My stomach drops. "How do you know? Did she call you?"

"Oh, gee, I don't know, maybe because I work here. Get here fast, and I'll explain everything. I've got to get back to my patients."

"I'll be there as soon as I can."

I hang up, and my hands are shaking when I dial Hudson. "You busy?"

"Nope, just parked on the couch, watching sports and waiting for Stella to get home. You want me to come hang out with you and my sick niece?" He must've not heard the urgency in my voice.

"Can you come watch Maven for me?"

He catches on now. "What's going on?"

"Lauren said Willow got admitted to the ER."

"Fuck," he hisses. "What for?"

"I don't know. Lauren wouldn't tell me over the phone." *That means, it's not fucking good.*

"I'll be there in five, sooner if I can."

"Thank you."

I call Willow's phone again. It rings. Then, voice mail. A million reasons why she's there flash through me. If it were contractions or something small, Lauren would've told me to ease my mind.

Why didn't Willow call me? Why didn't she let me know what's wrong with our babies? It's just as much my information as it is hers.

Because she's fucking selfish, and I'm fucking pissed.

Thirty minutes later, I'm pulling into the hospital parking lot. A bad taste fills my mouth as I run through the sliding glass doors. The last time I was here was when I said good-bye to Lucy.

I nearly collide with the front desk and ignore everyone standing in line, cutting straight to the front. "Willow Andrews," I blurt out. "I'm looking for Willow Andrews. Redhead. She's pregnant."

The middle-aged woman stares up at me in annoyance. "You family?"

"The father of the twins she's pregnant with. My sister is a nurse here and will vouch for me. Lauren Barnes." Never thought I'd use that to my advantage of getting in somewhere.

The way her face falls confirms it's not good news. She picks up the phone. "Will you please tell Nurse Barnes her brother is here?"

The doors open, and Lauren comes sprinting into the waiting room. "Dallas!" she calls out, nearly out of breath, and waves her hand. "Come with me."

We speed-walk through the crowded hallway, and she knocks on a door before opening it. Willow is lying in the bed, tears and mascara running down her face, while the nurse checks her vitals. Her eyes are puffy from crying. She's exhausted. Broken. Worn out. Like she's been through hell. I'm positive I'm about to go there, too.

I rush over to her side, take her shaking hand, and slowly massage it with my thumb when she starts to cry harder.

"I don't know what happened. I was driving down the road, and all of a sudden—" Her free hand flies to her mouth, stopping any words from exiting.

"All of a sudden what?" I ask, swallowing hard, my voice breaking, my heart breaking.

The nurse hits a few buttons on the monitor and scurries out of the room. Lauren shuts the door and leans back against it.

Willow moves her hand, so I can understand her. "All of a sudden, I got these sharp pains in my stomach." She plays with her admittance bracelet over my hand and glances at Lauren in torture. "Can you … will you …"

Lauren takes a step forward with a pain-stricken face. "They did an ultrasound. It's the first thing we did when the EMTs brought her in."

My eyes pierce hers. "The EMTs. An ambulance brought you in?" I've already heard more than I want to, but I know it's only going to get worse.

"There was only one heartbeat," Willow whispers.

A knot forms into my stomach, tightening every muscle, and I gag, positive I'm about to vomit. I squeeze her hand before pulling away to sit down.

"One heartbeat? What do you mean, one heartbeat?" I ask, practically begging for the answer I want even though I'm not going to get it. "We have two babies. *Twins*. I saw them with my own two eyes at our ultrasound!" My lip trembles, and I lock eyes with Lauren. "Tell them to do it again." My tone is demanding.

"I already had them do it again. They showed me ten times!" Willow cries out. "I begged them to keep doing them, so I could prove them wrong. There were two heartbeats during our last ultrasound. I swear there was!"

"There was," I gulp out.

"They did multiple ultrasounds," Lauren says, wiping her eyes. "Trust me when I tell you, they wouldn't put an expecting mother through this unless they were positive about it." She moves across the room to rest her hand on my shoulder. "I'm sorry, but the second baby is gone."

"The fuck you mean, the second baby is gone?"

There's a knock on the door that gains our attention, and Lauren tells whomever it is to come in. I've been to too many doctor visits and had too many hospital stays with Lucy to know when a doctor is about to deliver bad news, and the doc that walks in is about to deliver some bad news. I prepare myself for the blow.

He shoves his glasses up his slender nose. "Hello, I'm Dr. Jones." I stand up, and he holds his hand out for me to shake. "I'm deeply sorry for your loss. I've talked to Willow, but I wanted to come back when you arrived in case you had any further questions for me."

"Sure do," I reply. "Where's my other baby?"

He doesn't seem surprised at my aggression. No doubt, he was expecting it. "We performed an ultrasound on Willow. She immediately told us she was pregnant with twins when she was brought in, but we could only find one heartbeat. I double-checked. Another doctor did, too." He looks over at Lauren. "Your sister did also."

Lauren's face falls.

"Willow experienced symptoms of a miscarriage. She lost one of the fetuses from what appears to be vanishing twin syndrome."

She lost a baby.

One of our babies is gone.

Gone. I'm so sick of that word.

If I could set that word on fire and kill it, I would. Risk doing time. Risk going to hell. Risk anything not to hear that fucking word again.

Everything good in my life gets taken from me.

"What about the other baby? There's a heartbeat?" I rush out.

"Yes, there is a heartbeat for the surviving fetus."

"And everything is okay with that one?"

"So far, yes. The prognosis of the surviving twin is hopeful, but it can be more difficult since she's in her second trimester."

"So, what do we do now?"

"The ultrasound didn't show any remains of the lost fetus, so we won't have to perform any additional procedures. Again, I'm sorry for your family's loss." He hands me a card. "If you have any additional questions, please feel free to call anytime. Day or night."

I grip the side of the bed from my chair and stare down at Willow when the doctor leaves. "How did this happen? Where were you?"

She hesitates before answering me, looking deflated and hugging herself. "Taking a drive."

Lauren moves to Willow's side to kiss her on the forehead. "I'm going to give you some privacy. Let me know if you need anything."

"Taking a drive?" I ask. "I thought you didn't feel well. Why were you taking a drive when you were sick?"

This stops Lauren from leaving, and she whips around to stare at me. "Dallas, none of this is Willow's fault, so don't you dare go there. There was nothing she could've done to stop the miscarriage."

"I'm not blaming her," I hiss.

I'm blaming myself. I'm fucking blaming everyone and everything.

"Well, you're not convincing me of that," Willow fires back. "Sure sounds like it."

"All I asked was, why you were out driving in who the fuck knows where when you knew you were pregnant, and you told Stella you were sick!" I reply.

Her face lights up with anger, and she jabs a finger in my direction. "Don't talk to me like that. Don't you think I'm hurt about this? I lost a baby, too!"

"Okay, *now*, I'll give you two some privacy," Lauren says. She points to me before leaving. "Don't be a dick."

When Lauren shuts the door, I stare at it for a few seconds to calm down. Arguing with Willow isn't going to help either one of us. It'll only make shit worse.

"What happened?" I ask softly. "Why did you leave my house? I could've been there for you."

She blows out a breath. "I needed to clear my head. Get some air."

My voice starts to break. "Why?"

"I just did. It was all too much. Too much was happening, and I couldn't keep up. Stella said she could watch Maven, and I needed to get out of there."

I can tell she didn't mean to say that last sentence.

"You needed to get out of there?" I repeat.

She nods.

"Are you going to tell me why?"

"It doesn't matter."

I rub my eyes to fight back the tears. "It was because of Lucy's stuff, wasn't it?"

"That was one of the reasons, yes." She's not shocked I knew what it was. She knew I'd know.

This is my fault. If I had picked up Maven myself or taken down Lucy's stuff or told Willow to take Maven to her place, this might've never happened.

"Fuck. I'm sorry. It didn't even cross my mind before I asked you."

She shrugs. "It's fine. She's a part of your life. She was your wife. I get that now."

"What do you mean, you get that now?"

"I understand the loss of someone you love. I now understand, sometimes, you can't get over it." She rubs her stomach as the tears fall. "I know I'll never get over this, just like you'll never get over Lucy. I don't blame you for it. I'm not mad."

"What are you saying?" I ask, simmering with fear.

Her eyes are vacant. Dull. She's here physically, but she's not *here*.

"I'm saying, we should spend some time apart."

I feel my pulse in my throat. "Are you … are you saying you're done with me?"

She shakes her head and rubs her forehead, like I'm stressing her out. Like it's the last conversation she wants to have.

Me, too.

"I can't be done with you. We're having a baby together, but we should take a step back from everything else."

I can't be hearing her right. I lost Lucy. I lost one of my babies. Now, I'm losing her.

"Take a step back from the relationship we've been building? Take a step back from feeling happiness? Take a few steps back from making love?"

She cringes. "Don't call it that."

"Don't call it what?"

Her jaw clenches in anger. "Making love. We don't *make love*, Dallas, because we don't love each other. We fuck. That's it. You and I both know it."

"You know that's not true!" I grind out, fighting the urge to raise my voice. "If I were only interested in *fucking* someone, do you think I'd do it with the most complicated woman in the world?" I shake my head and lean in. "I do it because I'm falling in love with you. Not for a quick fuck!"

"Oh, shit!"

I stumble back at the sound of Stella's voice and look at the doorway to find her standing there with my parents.

"Bad timing?" Stella asks regretfully, tears lining her eyes. "Sorry, I suck at knocking."

Tears are falling down my mom's cheeks. My dad has his fist against his mouth to fight his own hurt.

They know before even asking questions.

I stride across the room to hug my mother, rubbing her back as she lets out her hurt, and then move to my dad next. He's not much of a hugger, but he keeps a tight hold on me, understanding my pain.

I lean back on my heels. "Will you give us a moment?"

They nod, and I'm back at Willow's side when they're gone. I scrub my other hand over my face and try to control my breathing. "You honestly can't believe I'm not in love with you. I've been trying to show you how damn good we are together."

Her chin trembles as she prepares herself to break my fucking heart. "I might be younger than you, but I'm not stupid, Dallas. We have fun together. We like each other. We're attracted to each other. But your heart isn't ready for anyone else. And my heart isn't whole enough to give someone a piece I'm not sure I'll get back. We were caught in the moment, moving too fast, even though we told each other in the beginning that a relationship was off the table."

"That was before I brought you into my life, before you showed me how wonderful you were with my daughter, before you showed me what it was like to be happy again."

She stares down at her stomach without saying another word. She said what she needed, and now, she's done.

"So, this is it, huh? Where you want us to go? I've lost two people in my life that fucking meant something. No, make that three if you walk away from me."

She keeps her head bowed and grimaces.

"Please, look at me. Goddamn it, look me in the eyes and tell me you don't want me."

She appears almost frail while slumping down on the bed. "I understand you're upset about our baby, but please don't try to act like you're hurt because I'm asking for space. We would've never worked because you're not ready to open your heart to me."

"Glad I know where I stand with us." I push off the railing on the bed. "I need some air."

I speed out of the hospital without stopping to talk to anyone else, get in my truck, and slam my fist against the steering wheel, taking all of my anger out on it. The pain hits me like a brick. I let the tears fall freely, and I'm certain my heart is dying in my chest.

My tears were finally starting to dry from losing Lucy.

I'm back at square one.

My life keeps falling apart.

Chapter Thirty-Seven

DALLAS
The Past
Eleven Months Ago

You don't know what you have until it's gone.
    It's a bullshit cliché.
    But fuck me if the reality of those nine words isn't smacking me in the face.
I knew what I had.
I cherished what I had.
But I sure as hell didn't plan on it getting ripped away from me at thirty-one years old.
The beeping of the machines next to Lucy is the only noise in the room. I have a love-hate relationship with them. They're her helping hand, her strength, but they won't be here much longer.

And neither will she.

A relentless surge of panic rips through my veins like a drug when I grip my hand around hers. Watching someone you love die is like your flesh torturously being stripped from your bones, inch by agonizing inch, baring the most vulnerable parts of yourself.

I wipe away my tears with the back of my arm, pissed at them for blurring my limited view of her. I haven't cried like this since I was in Pampers.

I'm a Barnes boy. We're known for our resilience, for our strength in the most desperate times. Emotions don't bleed through our skin. We hide them underneath and let them eat us alive.

At least, that's what I thought until I had to shoot myself with the truth. She is going to die, and there is nothing I can do. No one can fight. No amount of money I can pay to stop it.

That shit does something to a man.

I tilt my head up to painfully stare at the tiled ceiling and wish it'd cave in on me. Her lips are a bruised blue when I bore my eyes back to her.

Metastatic breast cancer.

It spread fast, too fast, and was caught too late. There was nothing we could do. Chemo didn't work. Praying didn't work. Her liver is failing. Her body is shutting down.

I've followed her wishes. This is where she wanted to do it—not at our home where our daughter lays her head. Here, with just the two of us, so that's what I'm giving her.

"Take me," I plead to the good man above. "Take me, goddamn it!" My chest aches, my lungs restricting airflow, and I pound my fist to my chest. "Let her fucking stay! Take my last breath and give it to her!"

My throat is scratchy and sore, like I've been screaming my pleas, but they've merely been coming out as a whisper.

I tighten my grip on her, wishing I could be her lifeline, as she starts to let go. I gulp down the urge to beg her to hold on, beg her not to leave me, but the thought of her enduring more pain kills me just as much as losing her. I have to let her go in peace even if I selfishly don't want to.

I don't know how to live without her.
I sob as the radiant eyes I fell in love with dim.
No!
Take my light! Take it all from me!
Let her keep shining!
I slump down in my chair like a fucking coward when the machine starts to fire off.
And, with her last breath, she takes me with her.

Chapter Thirty-Eight

WILLOW

Gone. I was on the verge of a panic attack when they brought me to the hospital. I cried. Man, did I cry. I'm shocked I have any tears left. I didn't know what was happening—if I was miscarrying, if it was something serious, if I was overreacting. The pain told me something was off, and I was hoping that it wasn't the something that happened.

I shrank into my bed, a cry escaping my lips, when they couldn't find the second baby's heartbeat. They checked it once. Checked it twice. Nothing. Blame wrapped around me like a blanket when Dallas walked in. I shouldn't have been on the road in the middle of nowhere. I shouldn't have been stressing myself out over a man when I had babies to worry about.

At first, I blamed myself.

Then, that blame shifted to Dallas.

He shouldn't have asked me to go to his house.

It's not my fault we lost the baby.

It's not his fault we lost the baby.

But, sometimes, you want to blame someone because you can't handle knowing they're just gone. Even though I haven't been pregnant that long, I've already started to fall in love with my babies, and now, one of them has been taken away from me. My heart is hurting, like someone stuck a knife inside and is twisting it until every part of me has ruptured.

I still have a baby relying on me. I'm not going to put myself into any other stressful situations. I won't be worried about Dallas's heart because I'm only going to focus on keeping mine sane for the baby, and trying a relationship with him isn't going to do that.

I need space. I need to step away. I stare at the door, wondering if he's going to come back or not, and tense up when a knock comes.

Stella peeks her head in. "Cool if I come in?"

"Yes," I answer. I need someone right now.

She smiles and sits down in the empty seat next to me. "Have you called your mom yet?"

I shake my head. "I honestly don't want to tell anyone. She'll want to fly here and take care of me, which is what I don't want. I need time to breathe on my own, to accept this, to take it in." I rub my stomach. "Can you give me a ride home when they release me?"

She squeezes her hand over mine. "Of course." She opens her mouth and then shuts it. She wants to talk about Dallas, most likely wants us to patch things up, but that's impossible right now.

Like I told Dallas, I understand now. I know how it feels to lose someone you love so much, someone you thought you'd spend years with.

And I understand never wanting to let them go.

Three days have passed since Stella brought me home from the hospital.

I'm sore. Exhausted. Hopeless.

Calls and texts have gone ignored, and the only reason I've seen Lauren is because she has a spare key to my apartment and lets herself in, uninvited. I'm selfish because they're worried about me, but I want to be left alone. I asked Dallas to give me some space, and except for a few texts, he has. But no words, no lecture, nothing will stop me from feeling some blame in this. I was too stressed. I wasn't eating right. I should've been resting more. The guilt that my body is the one that lost my child kills me.

I called my mom the day I got home. We cried. She prayed. She begged to fly out here to be with me, and I begged her not to.

I'm reading another article on vanishing twin syndrome when I hear my front door open. I turn around on the couch and shut my laptop at the same time Lauren walks in, wearing her scrubs, going straight to the kitchen like she owns the place.

"Hey, girl," she calls out when I meet her. "I hope you have an appetite." She starts the oven and begins pulling out containers of prepared food. "Tacos are on the menu for tonight."

I do a scan of all the items laid out on the counter. Meat. Lettuce. Cheese. Salsa. Guacamole. "You made all of this?" I ask. "Didn't you have to work?"

She laughs, removing the lid from the meat and pouring it into a pan. "Sweetie, you know my cooking is shit. Although my reheating game is pretty good." She turns the burner on. "Dallas did all of this last night before going to work and asked me to bring it over."

I snort. "Why? Is he scared I'm not feeding myself well enough, and we'll lose the other baby?" The words come out before I can stop myself.

She narrows her eyes at me. "No. And we both know he doesn't think that, so quit acting like a brat."

"Excuse me?" I snap.

"You heard me," she says, her attention going back to the stove. "Quit acting like a brat."

I huff. I puff. I want to kick her out of my apartment, but she keeps going, "I get you're going through pain, but don't forget you're not the only one experiencing this loss. So is my brother."

I press my finger to my chest. "He's the one who tried to blame me for losing the baby."

"Did he say those words?"

"Well … not exactly."

"The only thing that's exact about your argument is that he never said you're to blame. Not once. You're pissed at him because you have no one else to be mad at—because no one is to blame. *No one.* You heard the doctor. The miscarriage would've happened, no matter what."

"I don't blame him for the miscarriage."

"But you blame him for what occurred before the miscarriage. You need something to blame for losing the baby, so you're blaming it on Lucy's stuff at his house."

"Don't do this, Lauren," I mutter. "I'm not talking to you about this."

"Then, don't talk to me. Talk to him. *Please.*"

"I have. We've texted a few times."

"Maven has a sleepover tonight. Let him come over."

"I can't," I whisper, and my voice starts to crack. "It'd be too hard."

"Going through a hard phase in life is a lot more difficult with no one at your side. It starts getting softer, gentler, when you have someone else with you. Trust me."

Dallas knows food is the way to my heart. The tacos and the slice of blueberry pie he sent over are making me reconsider seeing him. Lauren's right. We've barely said a few words to each other since our argument at the hospital. I've run our exchange through my mind hundreds of times, staying up late because I can't sleep, and I've tried to dissect every word that fell from his lips.

I shut my eyes and remember what he said.

"Take a step back from the relationship we've been building? Take a few steps back from making love?"

He said *making love*. I corrected that and said we were only fucking.

I'm the only one being honest with myself, with our relationship. We were both in a sensitive place the night of our one-night stand, and I'm afraid we're only pulled to each other because of that and my pregnancy.

But bad days, bad months, don't last forever, and eventually, we'll get over our bad times and realize we were only using each other as a Band-Aid until we healed. He'll go back to being a widower mourning his wife but still be getting laid. And I'll go back to being a woman who doesn't want anything to do with love but still getting laid.

We're having sex for the need of it, the connection of it, for desire. Not for love, like he said. I gulp. Not for love on his part because the more time I spent with him, the more I knew I was falling into the pit of somewhere I didn't want to go. A hole of falling for a man not interested in falling for me other than in the sheets. I'm afraid to admit, I'm in love with this broken, beautiful, loving man.

There's a knock at the door when I'm taking a tray of cookies out of the oven. Dallas cooked for me, so I wanted to return the favor. Making the cookies has also helped keep my mind off everything I'm going through. Granted, I used a premade box mix, but a girl has to start somewhere.

Dallas said he'd be over after dropping Maven off for her sleepover. I take a deep breath and don't bother looking through the peephole before answering the door.

"What the hell are you doing here?" I yell.

Brett is standing in the doorway with flowers. *Yes, fucking flowers again.*

His blond hair is swept back in a baseball cap, and a T-shirt and jeans cover his tall and scrawny body.

My asshole ex has a history of bad timing—having a girl in our bed when he thought I was out of town, sending dick pics without putting a password on his phone, being on a date with another woman when I ran into him at the frozen yogurt shop.

I stumble back when he takes a step forward and shuts the door behind himself.

"I heard about what happened to our baby."

"I'm sorry. What did you just say? Our *what*?" I'm dreaming. I have to be dreaming. This isn't happening.

Brett is out on bail. He shouldn't even be leaving the county, let alone the state.

He tilts his shoulder in a half-shrug and walks into the living room, placing the flowers in the middle of the coffee table and sitting down. "I've gotta say, I'm unhappy you kept this from me, but I'll forgive you ... for the sake of our family."

"Have you lost your mind?" *Does jail make you imagine things?* I take a step closer to look him in the eyes. He has to be high to consider this to be a good idea. "Are you on drugs?"

"No, Willow, I'm not on drugs," he mocks in annoyance.

"You need to leave."

"I'm not leaving until we talk about our dead baby."

"There is no *our* baby, dumbass."

My breathing labors, and my fist itches to connect with his face. He just referred to my baby as *dead*. He gets up and struggles to grab my hand, but I fight him off.

"Leave before I call the cops. You know this baby isn't yours. I haven't touched you in almost a year."

"I don't care. I'll take on the responsibility if it's another man's because I love you." He arrogantly looks around the room. "I don't see anyone here to help you. What'd you do? Get knocked up by some random dude while traveling with Stella?" He clicks his tongue against the roof of his mouth and shakes his head. "You know, that's why I said I didn't trust you working with her. You'd get mad at me for cheating when I knew you were doing the same."

That's a lie. He was always jealous of my job.

"Fuck you. Do you honestly believe I'd ever have a baby with you? You almost killed a child."

He points to my stomach. "I want a paternity test on the one that's still alive."

God, could his words be any more horrible?

"Excuse me? You admitted the baby wasn't yours seconds ago."

"No, I didn't."

I don't have the time or the patience to deal with this asshole today. Or ever. "Screw you. I just had a miscarriage, for fuck's sake, and you thought it would be a good idea to fly thousands of miles and harass me?"

We look at the door at the sound of a knock. Brett goes to answer it before I can stop him. I make it at the same time Dallas walks in, bumping into Brett on his way, and his attention bounces between Asshole and me.

"Did I miss something?" he asks.

"Stella's old bodyguard?" Brett spits with a bitter laugh. "The fuck is he doing here?"

"The better question is, why are you here?" Dallas fires back, moving into his space.

"Stop!" I hiss. "I have neighbors!" I gesture for Dallas to close the door behind him. I can't lose my apartment because of this.

Brett points to my stomach again. "This is my baby, and I've come to take care of my family."

Dallas looks straight at me. "What is he talking about?"

"How do you even know about the baby?" I finally ask Brett.

"My father told me after your mom asked the church to pray for you. Your mom wouldn't tell me where you were, so I took matters into my own hands. I figured you were still working for Stella, stalked her social media, and found you." He shrugs like that's not creepy at all and then throws his arm out toward a fuming Dallas. "You never answered my question. What are you doing here, bro?"

"Don't fucking call me bro," Dallas snarls.

He smirks. "Jesus, fuck, this is the dude you're banging? This is the dude trying to take you and my baby away from me?"

Dallas takes a step closer. "You better get the fuck out of here before I throw you out."

"So, you were cheating on your dying wife with her? You guys have been fucking around this entire time." He laughs. "This is fucking perfect. You're not such a good man, are you? You walked around like you were this perfect husband who then left his job to take care of his dying wife, but you were cheating on her and fucking my girl." He glares at me. "You're nothing but a lying cunt."

I jump when Dallas punches Brett in the mouth. Brett pushes him back. Dallas wraps his hand around Brett's neck and traps him against the wall.

"What the fuck, dude?" Brett struggles to breathe out, wiggling to get free. "I'm pressing charges!"

"You're not even supposed to be here!" I yell. "Call the cops, please. Let them take you back to where you belong—behind bars."

We don't have to call the cops because they knock on my door seconds later.

"Blue Beech Police Department!" one yells.

Dallas moves his hand from Brett's throat to open the door, and Brett dramatically collapses on the floor, holding his throat and fake choking.

Two officers step in. A young guy and an older gentleman.

"Hi, I'm Officer Barge," the older man says.

The younger cop tips his head forward. "Officer Layne." He surveys the room. "We received a noise complaint about two men fighting." His eyes cast a look straight to Dallas. "What's going on, man?"

"He punched me!" Brett screams, stumbling to his feet and sticking out his chest. He's a badass now that there's protection. "I want him put in jail."

"I punched him," Dallas says. "Because he was harassing her. She's pregnant with my baby, and he was giving her trouble. He's out on bail, and he shouldn't even be out of California."

"That true?" Officer Barge asks.

"No," Brett lies.

Officer Layne holds out his hand. "Let me see some ID."

Brett flinches. "Are you going to ask him for ID? He's the one who assaulted me!"

"Already know who Dallas is," he answers and then tilts his head my way. "I know who she is. Now, how 'bout you let me get acquainted with you?"

"I'll tell you who I am. I'm the son of a mayor in a very affluent California town."

"Cool story, man," Officer Layne replies. "But this ain't California, hipster boy. I don't care if your father is the president. Let me see some ID, or I'm going to have to bring you in for failure to cooperate."

Brett pulls out his wallet and reluctantly hands his driver's license over.

"I'll go run this," Officer Layne says while Officer Barge keeps his eyes narrowed on Brett.

The officer and Dallas make small talk until Officer Layne comes back.

"It appears you broke the stipulations of your bail. We're shipping you back to that *affluent* town of yours where you can enjoy your time in a cell." His upper lip snarls in disgust. "I can't believe they even gave you bail for what you did."

Brett throws every name at me while they cuff him and force him out of my apartment. "He doesn't love you!" he screams before the door shuts. "He'll always love that dead bitch!"

Dallas stalks out of my apartment, ready for round two, but the police officer stops him from getting to Brett.

"Let it go, man," Officer Layne says. "He isn't worth it." He looks at me. "Congratulations on the baby, you two."

Dallas slaps him on the back. "Thanks, man."

He hands me a card. "Willow, you let me know if he gives you any more trouble."

Dallas's defeated gaze focuses on me after he shuts the door, and his jaw twitches. "That fucker telling the truth?"

"Huh?" My brain is so exhausted, I don't catch the severity of his question.

"Is he telling the truth about him being the father?"

My heart races. "Are you kidding me? You believe him?"

"I don't know what to believe. He seemed pretty damn adamant about it."

"If you want to believe him, be my guest. Leave. I planned on doing this by myself from day one, and I have no problem going through with that plan. I don't need you or Brett. I'm a woman who has her shit together. I have a good job and don't need to fucking baby-trap a guy." I shake my head. "Fucking trust me, it would've been much easier to do this on my own."

"Don't say that," he growls.

I cock my head toward the door. "Leave. I'll take care of this supposed illegitimate baby on my own."

"Don't." He grabs my hand in his. "Don't say that. You can't be pissed at me for asking. I asked, you told me the truth, I believe you."

I release his hold and shove him away from me. "The fact that you even doubted me is bullshit."

This is too much to handle right now. My hands are shaking in anger. I should've punched Brett in the face.

Dallas throws his arms in the air. "I'm sorry. It's been a rough fucking week. I came over to make things right with you, and that asshole was here."

"He showed up, unannounced! It's not like I invited him."

He grabs my hand, leads me across the room, and situates me on the couch. I hold my breath when he falls next to me and then drags me into his chest. I relax against him, and my heart calms when he starts massaging my neck.

"Why does it seem like the world's against us?" I whisper.

"It's not." He places a kiss on my neck. "People go through trials and tribulations, but we'll be okay. We can get through this because we have each other to lean on. It fucking killed me for you to think I blamed you for losing our baby. I was hurt. Upset. Expressing my emotions isn't something I excel at." He chuckles. "Those words came from Lauren, not me."

"That makes two of us."

I drop my head back on his shoulder to see him, and my body relaxes when he kisses away the tears hitting my cheeks.

"How about we start the night over?" he asks. "Let's act like your douche bag of an ex with bangs longer than yours didn't come here."

I reach up to circle my hand around his neck and bring him down for a kiss. "You have no idea how great that sounds."

I planned on telling him we needed to stick to being friends tonight, but that's all changed. Brett slapped some reality into me. I could turn my back on Dallas and have to deal with more men like Brett because I'm too scared to get close to someone capable of love, or I could spend my time with a man who has a heart.

Things might not work out with us.

Things might go wrong.

But being with him feels much better than being alone.

We stay on the couch and talk about everything that's happened since we last saw each other. Maven is feeling better and is back to her usual self. She's been asking hundreds of questions about where I am.

Dallas tucks me into bed and turns around to leave.

"Are you not staying the night?" I ask, disappointed.

He smiles. "Hell yes, I am. But I need to get rid of those ugly-ass flowers first."

I can't help but laugh. I needed that.

He comes back with an even brighter smile on his face, and I arch my brows in question.

"You baked me cookies," he states.

"Tried to." I frown. "They're a little burned."

"You do like me."

We spend the rest of the night eating burned cookies in bed.

"Maven misses you," he whispers in my ear.

It's morning, and the faint ray of sunlight peeks through the windows as we lie in bed. My hand is in his. My legs are a wild mess across his. It feels good to have him back here.

I shut my eyes. "I miss her. Tell her I'll be seeing her soon." His hand tightens around mine, and I sigh. "So, this is what grief feels like."

No wonder Dallas was so miserable when Lucy died. This pain is what he was feeling. This void in my heart is what he was going through.

"Losing someone isn't fun." His breathing slows. "I just wish we could've met him even if it was for only a minute."

His eyes are on me when I shift to rest my chin on his warm chest and smile up at him. I sag against his body when his arms wrap around my back, and he settles me next to him, his fingers tracing my spine.

"Him?" I ask.

He chuckles. "Is it bad I was convinced we were having a boy?"

I can feel his thick breathing when I stroke his chest. "I was so convinced we were having a girl, I had a name picked out."

"Is it Daphne?" he asks, and I can feel his laughter through his chest. "She can hang out with Scooby, and they'll chase ghosts together."

An even bigger roar of laughter comes from his chest when I pinch his nipple. "No!" I follow his lead, feeling it coming from the bottom of my stomach, and damn, does it feel good for something other than pain to consume me. "Can I ask you for a favor though?"

He nods.

"Let's wait until we have the baby before choosing a name. I don't want to get my hopes up and then have something happen."

His arm tightens around me. "Nothing will happen."

I reach up and run my fingers over the stubble on his cheeks. "Just in case."

"We'll wait. And, when you have our baby and it's a girl, we'll go with the name you choose. If it's a boy, we'll go with mine."

I smile. "I like that idea."

"Now, can I ask you a favor? You don't have to answer right away. Think about it and get back with me when you decide."

Damn it. Him and his favors.

"What?"

Sincerity takes over his features. "Consider moving in with me. I'll do anything to make you comfortable there. Sleep on the couch. Crash in the basement. Sleep in my truck if I have to."

"It didn't end well the last time I was at your house. I feel like too much of an outsider."

"I'll make things right. Make you happy there. Give me a chance."

I slowly nod. "I'll think about it."

"And …" he draws out. "Just one more serious question."

"What more can you want?" I ask, faking annoyance.

"Why did you name your cat Scooby? Letting you name our child worries me."

"My grandfather had a cat named Scooby. No one understood why, and he never told us." I narrow my eyes at him with a smile. "So, consider yourself lucky to hear my reason."

"And what would that be?"

"Because my grandfather named his Scooby."

He nods. "Let's keep the cartoon names to our animals."

Chapter Thirty Nine

DALLAS

I remember the day I told Maven that Lucy had died.

I sat her down and broke the news, and she didn't take it well. For weeks, she cried and lashed out. Trying to explain death to a six-year-old isn't easy. All I could tell her was that Mommy had gone to heaven, but she took that as Mommy had left because she was mad at her. We went to counseling with our preacher. I stayed at home for days, built pillow forts, and had tea parties with stuffed animals.

Telling her about losing one of the babies terrified me, thinking that she'd revert to that sadness. We'd lost too many people. Gone through too much hell. Maven had started suggesting names from her favorite books. Everyone we passed on the street, at the grocery store, at her preschool had heard her boast and brag about how she was going to be a big sister.

I took advice from my family and set her down last night. As badly as I wanted Willow at my side, she'd been through enough. Maven cried but is more understanding of death now. She said her mommy was taking care of the baby in heaven.

It's been a week since I asked Willow to move in. She hasn't brought it up again, and I know what I need to do before she does. And today of all days is when I decide I have to do something that will hurt me.

I didn't want to get out of bed today, but I had to pull my shit together and do it.

Today is a day I used to celebrate. Now, it's a day of darkness. My mom offered to watch Maven before I even told her my plans.

I take the drive I haven't made in a few weeks. I haven't told her the news, I've been afraid to tell her, but I can't be anymore.

I sit down in front of her gravestone and place the pink tulips, her favorite flower, in front of it.

"Hey, Lucy-Pie," I whisper. "Happy birthday." I chuckle, sitting back. "Big thirty-two."

I sigh. "I know I haven't been here in a while. I'm sorry. And I know you like me to be honest, so that's what I'm going to give you. I've been consumed with guilt, feeling like a trader, a bad husband, like you'd be disappointed in me. It was a dumbass thought because I know your heart. You'd probably want to slap me right now and tell me to get it together. You'd lead the way for me when I didn't know which way to turn. Tough love is what you called it."

My eyes water. "I'm having a baby. We were supposed to have two, but we lost one. It was like going through hell again. Maven wants you to watch over her baby brother or sister. Can you do that for us?"

The sun beats down on me, and a tear falls down my cheek. "I lost the baby like I lost you, and I was so mad. So damn mad. I felt sorry for myself. I was pissed at everyone … at everything. But my anger and fear is only going to make me keep losing people."

I sigh and slip my wedding ring off my finger. I stare at it one last time before digging a small hole in the dirt with my fingers. My hands shake while I bury it next to the tulips. "I realize now why you made me promise. I had no problem promising to be a good father, and that's what I'll do to both of my children. I reluctantly promised to find love again, and I hope you'll be proud of me when I say I have." I tell her about Willow, about our babies, about how excited Maven is to become a big sister.

I wipe my nose. "And, while you're up there, will you give our baby a hug for us?"

I won't forget about Lucy.

I won't try to replace her.

But I will let myself move on.

Chapter Forty

WILLOW

It's been a month since we lost the baby.

A long and gruesome month.

There hasn't been a day that's gone by that I haven't gone over the things I should've done differently to stop the miscarriage from happening. I've read article after article and talked to Aidan about it at every appointment.

So, I've been doing everything I can to take it easy, attempting to stay on bed rest, like the doctor suggested, but I'm going stir-crazy.

The uncertainty of another miscarriage has been the only thing on my mind.

Dallas hasn't brought up his offer for me to move in with him. I don't know if it's been retracted or if he's scared of the rejection.

Stella insisted I do most of my work from home, and when I do visit her on set, she practically caters to me like I'm her boss. Lauren stops by before every shift. Rory and my mom regularly check in with me, and Dallas and Maven are here nearly every day.

Lauren is right. Having a good support system helps.

I sit on the couch and stare at the doorway to the nursery. Something I do every day. I haven't been back in it since I lost the baby. Dallas keeps asking if he can put the crib together or start painting, but I can't bring myself to say yes.

It's not that I don't want this baby to have a nice nursery.

It's that I'm terrified I might lose this baby, too.

The front door opens, and Maven comes running into the living room. Dallas is behind her with a bag of takeout.

Her smile beams when it lands on me. "Can I ask her now, Daddy? Can I *pleeease* ask her now? I can't wait any longer!"

I tried to stop it, Dallas mouths to me.

She plops down next to me on the couch, and I play with her hair.

"Ask me what?"

"Um …" She opens her mouth but chickens out and slams it shut.

Well, that's new.

She whips around to look at Dallas. "Will you do it for me, Daddy? You say it much better."

He slowly nods, and I know what he's about to ask isn't going to be easy on me.

"Maven will be starting kindergarten soon. Tomorrow is Parents' Night."

"Will you please come with me?" Maven chimes in. Her spunk is back. "Pretty, pretty please? It'll be *so, so* much fun. They'll have snacks, and you get to meet my teacher! I'm going to big-kid school!"

I don't know if Maven told him she'd asked me to be her new mommy, but he hasn't mentioned it. And I don't plan to tell him. That's a secret between the two of us.

Dallas leans back against the wall and fights a smile on his lips. "There was no way I was going to stop her from asking you. You know she doesn't take no for an answer very well. Plus, I could use the company."

"Please," Maven continues to plead. "Everyone else is going to have their mommy there."

The air leaves the room.

"Maven," Dallas says, his voice almost sounding shaky, "you know Willow isn't your mom."

"I know, *but* she'd be a good second mommy." She closes her eyes in sadness. "She doesn't even have to be my new mommy. I just want her there, so I won't feel left out."

Dallas rubs his hands over his face. "I'm sorry. I wasn't expecting all that."

I wave off his answer, seeing the hurt on Maven's face, recognition hitting me. I was the girl without a father at everything. I understand her hurt, the pain she's going through.

"Maven, I'd love to go," I answer, shocking myself and Dallas.

She springs off the couch. "I told you she'd say yes, Daddy!" She wraps her short arms around me and jumps up and down.

My heart warms. I'm doing the right thing. Going to her Parents' Night will help me just as much as her.

We devoured our dinner, and Maven fell asleep on the couch while watching cartoons.

"Want to talk?" Dallas asks.

I'm not reluctant this time. I'm not going to blow him off. I lead him to the kitchen.

He blurts out his apology as soon as we sit down. "I don't know where the hell the mommy thing came from. I'll break the news to Maven and tell her you had something come up."

"I'm going," is all I reply, but so much is said in those words.

"You don't have to do it if you don't feel comfortable. You looked like she'd asked for a kidney."

"It surprised me, is all. I want to go. I know what the need feels like to have two parents at functions because I was the little girl whose father never showed up. It was heartbreaking, and if me doing something as small as showing up makes that little girl feel better, I'll be there."

He leans forward and presses his lips to mine. "Thank you. You have no idea how much this means to me."

"You're going to love my school!" Maven squeals when we pull into the parking lot of the elementary school.

I run a hand down my stomach. No more hiding the baby bump. No more hiding my affection for Dallas and his little girl.

Maven's class is small, and we take a table in the back. Parents fill the room, greeting each other and spewing off question after question.

Everyone knows everybody.

Except for me.

But that doesn't mean they don't know *of* me.

"Oh, you're that actress girl's friend, right?"

"So, Dallas, this is the woman you've been spending all your time with?"

"I heard about what happened at the birthday party. That sounds so tragic to have the news come out like that."

If they're not asking ridiculous questions, they're staring.

There are a few exceptions though. Not everyone is nosy and rude. A few have introduced themselves without fishing for gossip, and they seemed genuine.

Dallas took Maven up to select her cubby, and my body tenses when someone sits down next to me.

"I was hoping you'd come," Beth says in a soft voice. "My daughter and Maven are in the same class this year. They're going to have a blast together." She smiles. "This is the first time I've seen you since you picked her up from preschool, so I haven't had the chance to congratulate you on the baby, and give my condolences on your miscarriage."

I flinch.

"I hope you don't mind that Maven told me, but I promise, your business is not mine to tell."

"Thank you," I whisper.

"How far along are you?"

This isn't an interrogation. She's not asking me this question out of spite. There is not a doubt in my mind that she's truly happy I'm having this baby.

"About five months," I answer, giving her a smile back.

"I remember the anticipation as the date gets closer. You're nervous the baby is going to come anytime."

I smile and nod. *I'm more nervous of losing my baby.*

Our attention is caught at the sound of Maven laughing. Dallas is down on one knee, helping her decorate her cubby with stickers and stuffed animals.

Beth tilts her head toward them. "He's a good man. A broken one, yes, but still a good one."

"He's been a good friend to me."

"Just a friend?"

I shrug. "Our situation is … complicated."

She pats my shoulder. "I hope I'm not overstepping my boundaries here, but there's something I want to give you." She opens her purse, and I notice the water in her eyes as she places a folded piece of paper in my hand. "My sister wrote this before she passed and asked me to give it to the woman Dallas fell in love with." She closes her hand around mine as a tear passes down her cheek.

I jerk it back to her. "You're mistaken. Dallas isn't in love with me."

"Read it. It'll help you understand how he loves you."

I don't mention the letter to Dallas.

I keep it tucked in my pocket and constantly check to make sure it hasn't fallen out all evening. The meeting doesn't last much longer after Beth leaves, and Dallas and Maven convince me to go out for dessert before going home.

Other than doctor's appointments, which Aidan started sneaking us through the back door for, this is my first time stepping out with Dallas since the miscarriage. I've been so terrified of getting judged, of people staring, of hearing vicious things coming out of their mouths, but I'm done with that now.

Tonight has made me feel comfortable.

Tonight hasn't made me feel like such an outsider.

Maven doesn't hesitate in unbuckling her seat belt when Dallas pulls up to my apartment. They've been here more than their house lately. She heads straight to the couch and drags out the crayons and coloring books I leave for her in the coffee table drawer. Her tongue sticks out as she colors, and Dallas makes each of us a cup of tea.

We watch a movie until she falls asleep with a crayon still in her hand. He kisses me good-bye, and they leave. I'm picking up the mess when I remember the letter. I take a deep breath, not knowing what I'm getting myself into, and lie back on the couch before opening it.

To the lucky woman who reads this.

Hello,

My name is Lucy. I'm sure you've heard about me. Possibly seen my pictures, my belongings, traces of me in the home we shared. You might've even known me.

I was Dallas's wife. And, since you're reading this, I'm no longer here.

Dallas is a difficult man. Always has been. He'll be even more difficult after my death, but please don't give up on him. If he's opened up his heart enough for you to receive this letter, you have something extraordinary. Receiving this letter means he's in love with you. I'm sure he's fighting it because he wouldn't be a Barnes boy if he didn't fight the reality that's right in front of him.

Watch his actions. Those are what speak his love. He's not the best at words, but the more you let him in, the more he opens up for you.

Don't be afraid. We've all had other loves. Don't think he can only have one because you've proven that wrong.

Please don't give up on him because he won't give up on you. When you make your way into his heart, he'll fight to keep you there. He's the strongest man I've ever known.

Thank you for loving my family and give Maven a kiss for me.

Lucy

I'm in tears when I finish, and I hold the letter to my heart.

Chapter Forty-One

DALLAS

WILLOW: WE NEED TO TALK.

Her text isn't the only thing that worries me. She sent it at three this morning. The early hours of the morning are when your brain is working the hardest, going over important choices, the shit you want to forget but can't.

Is this a good or bad we need to talk?

Should I be heading to the airport?

After I drop Maven off at school, I call Hudson and let him know I'll be late today, and then I drive straight to Willow's apartment. Fingers crossed it's not empty when I get there.

I take the stairs three at a time and find her sitting on the couch. My chest gets heavy when I notice the moving boxes scattered everywhere. Some flat, some put together, some taped up with scribbled words on them.

She nervously glances back at me while I trudge across the room. I don't take my eyes off her

like it's the last time I'll get to see her. Her naturally plump lips that fit perfectly around my cock are puckered as she watches me. The hair I love twirling my fingers around is down in loose curls. The woman I've fallen in love with is going to walk away with the remaining pieces of what's left of me.

"Hey," she says. "You never texted me back. I wasn't sure if you got my message."

Why? Was she trying to get out of here before I showed up?

I snatch a half-filled box and dump out the contents. I need physical evidence that my life is going to change. That I'll be going back to the miserable asshole I was before she took me over.

"What the hell?" Willow screams, sliding off the couch in frustration.

I scowl at the items on the floor. Clothes. Shoes. My eyes zero in on the shoes she left at my house that night. Her gaze goes to me, then to the pile on the floor, and back to me.

Where did this sudden change come from?

We spend all of our free time together, and from what I believe, we've been enjoying it. No arguments have occurred. Every prenatal appointment has gone well.

What happened? Where did it go wrong?

"You going somewhere?" I ask.

Her brows scrunch together. "The moving boxes give it away?"

"Sure did." I struggle to keep my voice calm.

Stress is bad for the baby. We can't risk another miscarriage. I won't argue. Won't fight it. She's calling the shots. I'll move if that's what she wants, get a job bussing tables in LA if I have to, turn my life upside down to keep her.

Her head cocks to the side. "I thought this was what you wanted?"

I grit my teeth. "That's never what I wanted. Not once have I told you to pack up and ditch us. Just so you know, what you're doing is going to leave my daughter and me broken. Do you understand? You're not supposed to turn your back on us because we fell in love with you. I fell in love with you." I shake my head, my voice breaking. "And we don't want another person we love to leave us."

She blows out a breath and smiles.

The fuck?

"Did you bump your head? These boxes are for me to move in *with you*."

Her answer melts the burden off my chest. "What did you say?"

"I said, I've been packing my stuff because I'm accepting the offer of moving in with you, dipshit."

Damn, does my girl have a mouth on her.

Stupidity rails through me. So much time has passed since I asked her to move in, I figured it wasn't an option.

She's staying. Halle-fucking-lujah.

I crack a smile while she blankly stares at me.

"So, now that you know I'm not leaving your ass, promise me you won't do that anymore," she says, her tone turning emotionless. "If you want me to move in with you, you can't go around, saying things you don't mean."

I cock my head and stare at her in confusion. "What don't I mean?"

"That you love me." She throws her hands down to her sides. "We get along great, the baby will have two parents, but don't get my hopes up. I've made my mind up to move in, so you don't have to lie to me."

Oh, shit.

The L-word hasn't left my mouth again since we lost the baby. In fear of her running away, I've stopped myself every time. Now, my dumbass has blurted it out and ruined any chance of her moving in with me.

I draw nearer before she kicks me out, and I walk her back until her back hits a wall. I press a hand to her cheek, and hers wrap around my neck, massaging the built-up tension. I look down, searching for eye contact, but she's not giving it.

"Look at me," I whisper. My voice turns raw. Raspy. My breathing falters when she does. "I'd be lying if I said I didn't love you."

I didn't bring her home with me that night, expecting to fall in love. I never thought that having surprise babies, going on road trips, getting stranded, and then surviving a miscarriage would bring so many emotions out of me. That it would warm my cold heart. That'd it bring me closer to her.

She's managed to do that.

She makes me want to be a better man.

A man who believes in love again because he's in love with her.

She's a strong woman with a heart of gold, who brought a flashlight in my darkness to show me the way to happiness when I was fighting not to find an exit.

I won't lose her.

"Tell me you feel it, too," I say.

Worry is evident on her face. The hesitation tells me she's insecure about getting hurt again if she says it. My pulse quickens. The same feeling is driving through her. She wouldn't have agreed to move in if it wasn't.

"I'm scared of feeling it," she finally replies. "I'm scared that loving you is reaching for something that'll never be mine. A lifeline I can't reach because you're in love with someone else."

I look down at her, unblinking. "I'll always be your lifeline. You'll always be able to reach me because you have my heart. No matter what you're going through, I'll be at your side, helping you hold on."

Tears fill her eyes. "You can't love me like you loved her."

"You're right. The way I love you is different than the way I loved her. I've fallen in love with you in different ways, for different reasons, than I did with Lucy. I've fallen in love with finding love, learning your tics, how to make you smile, hearing your fears, and getting to know the deepest parts of your soul. I loved Lucy. I'll never stop loving the memory of her, but I can love you right along with it."

I grew up with Lucy. I loved her for as long as I can remember, but I don't remember *falling* in love with her because I knew everything about her. This is something new to me. A different love but still love. You don't love the same every time.

I squeeze Willow's hips and hope my next question isn't pushing the limit. "You ready to admit you love me yet?"

She shakes her head.

"Then, why are you crying?"

"Hormones," she croaks out. "Fucking hormones."

"You can blame it on that for now." My mouth finds hers, giving her a long kiss, before pulling away and pecking the tip of her nose. "But I'll be asking again later."

"What are you doing?" she asks when I move across the room and pick up a box.

"Helping you pack your shit. You can keep the apartment for as long as you want, but I'm going to take as much time with you under my roof as I can get."

Chapter Forty-Two

WILLOW

Dallas and Hudson are moving the few boxes I packed for my trial run at Dallas's.

I'm doing this.

Really doing this.

I stop on the porch before walking through the front door. I jumped down these stairs, barefoot, with tears running down my face. I stare at the door, remembering my last look of Dallas that day. *Let's hope history doesn't repeat itself.*

I haven't been back in the house since Maven was sick. Maybe I should've taken a tour, made sure I was emotionally stable to handle more than three hours here.

I'm going to walk in there, be strong, and do what's right for my heart.

For my baby. For *us*.

The excitement of spending more time with him and Maven is what keeps me walking. I love spending time with them. I'd go to bed, wishing Dallas were there to hold me, to kiss me, to share the moment when the baby kicked.

Dallas is still a man who struggles, but that only makes me fall more in love with him. Lucy's note sparked something inside me, an insight I never thought about when I shut myself down after considering a future with him. Dallas might be a little broken, but he knows what love is. He sacrifices for love, for his family—something Brett never did with me.

I'd rather have a broken man who knows how to love than a man with no scars who's never loved anyone but himself.

Dallas squeezes my elbow when I walk through the front door. "If you're not cool with this, let me know, okay? I'll call a realtor, and we can look for another property."

I stare at him, unblinking. "Are you talking about buying a new house?"

He practically built this house with his own two hands. He loves this home.

"If that's what makes you comfortable." He slides in closer and gently pushes a fallen strand of hair from my ponytail out of my eyes. His hands then rest on my hips. "This is your home now, do you hear me? *Our* home. I want you to be able to relax, to be able to touch me, to feel okay with having sex with me here." He chuckles. "Because we know that's going to be happening a lot as soon as our little one is born."

I smile. "You have no idea how much I've missed that." Especially with him. It's hard to go from having sex with fuck boys to Dallas and then being told you're on bed rest and that you need to refrain from sex. It's like tasting an expensive cupcake for the first time after years of eating cheap candy, and then it gets taken away from you.

His hand moves down to brush between my legs. "I might not be able to fuck you yet, but I promise I'll do something for you tonight."

I rest my hand on his chest. "I have something to look forward to."

"You most certainly do."

"All right, kids, take it to the bedroom," Hudson says, walking in. "And, speaking of bedroom, is that where you want me to put this stuff?"

I take my time while Dallas waits for an answer. "Yeah," I stutter out. "Sure."

I follow them down the hallway and into the bedroom, not sure if I'm truly ready for this. I take in a heavy breath and wait for the blow of bad memories and heartache to hit me, but nothing does when I walk in.

The furniture and bedding is new. I try not to make it too obvious that I'm searching for the signs of Lucy I saw last time I was in here, but they are now missing. The perfume bottle, the pictures, the clothes—it's all gone.

Hudson sets the box down on the floor and leaves the room.

"You got rid of her stuff?" I ask Dallas, guilt seeping through me. Forcing his hand to do this wasn't what I wanted. "I swear, my intentions weren't for you to erase her."

"I didn't erase her."

He holds his hand to his heart while mine pounds. He's no longer wearing his wedding ring. Hasn't been for a few weeks, but I haven't questioned him about it. I wasn't sure if he did it to make me happy, or because he wanted to for himself.

Now I know it's because he wanted to.

"No matter what, Lucy will always have a spot in my heart," he goes on.

I nod. I don't want him to lose that either.

"It was time I did it. I can't keep living in the past, especially when it was destroying my happy future. It was hell, don't get me wrong, pushing myself to do something I should've done months ago. I waited until I was ready, so thank you for giving me time to do that. I went through everything with Maven. She chose the stuff she wanted to keep, and then Lucy's family came over for their own keepsakes."

I sit down on the bed and trace my fingers over the new white bedspread. "Just don't kick me out of this bed, okay?"

He smirks. "Sweetheart, the only reason I'd kick you out of this bed is to fuck you on the floor."

I stand up to wrap my arms around his neck. He did all of this for me. Opened his heart back up for me. He wants to make a home with me and have a family together because he loves me.

I love him.

I'm tired of running from it. Tired of fighting. I have to be strong and honest for our baby, for ourselves, for the six-year-old girl who made me a *Welcome Home* sign, which is displayed on the front door.

"I love you," I whisper into his mouth.

"There it is." He grins. "And I love you."

Chapter Forty-Three

DALLAS
Four Months Later

THE EAR-BLASTING CRY IS MUSIC TO MY EARS.

A sound I was afraid I wouldn't hear. I put the sadness that there should be two in the back of my mind. I won't let that loss interfere with the bliss of this moment.

No surprise to me, Willow was a fucking trooper. She spent ten hours in labor and didn't complain once. All that was on her mind was the excitement of meeting our baby mixed with worry that it might not happen. I stayed by her side the entire time, not moving once, because I didn't want to miss a thing. She needed to know I was with her on this all the way.

Our life has turned into a whirlwind of changes. Willow has moved in, but nothing has changed in the Barnes' household. It feels like she's been there forever. I was anxious at the beginning, given our history there, but losing our baby has taught us to cherish every moment.

Fuck the petty shit.

Fuck running.

Fuck being afraid.

His wails calm when Aidan hands him, wrapped in his blanket, to Willow. My breathing halts when she situates him in her arms, already comfortable with how he likes to be cradled, and she plays with his tiny hand while whispering to him.

I stare at them with compassion. With happiness. With love.

As much as I want to have my turn, I wait until she's ready. She deserves this.

My heart thrashes against my chest when she stares up at me with wet eyes. She moves her arm, shifting toward me, and I waste no time in scooping him up. He's perfect—from his full head of dark hair to his button nose—and he's squirming like a fish out of water.

I'm ready to take him home. To show him the nursery we've been working on for months. To give him love every day.

Aidan heard a heartbeat during every ultrasound, but the thought of losing our baby still hung over our heads daily.

The chance of another miscarriage was high. There could have been problems at birth.

Those burdens have fallen off me. That worry is gone. He's here, healthy, and staring up at me with sleepy, dark eyes that resemble Maven's.

He owns my heart already.

It's been a rough journey, but like our road trips, we've seemed to make them enjoyable, memorable, crazy. Our turns and detours made us stronger, made us love deeper, made us appreciate each day.

We name him Samuel.

After my grandfather.

Willow and Maven love his name just as much as I do.

Samuel Logan Barnes.

Eight pounds and four ounces of fucking adorableness.

My son. My new sidekick. More happiness brought into a life I thought was over.

I didn't know what I was going to get when we walked into the hospital this morning. My heart surged with fear with every step I took. Bad news had been a constant for me here. I'd experienced so many losses within these walls.

That ended today.

This place will no longer be a reminder of loss.

I lost people I loved here.

And I've gained someone I love just as much.

Chapter Forty-Four

WILLOW

I AM A MOTHER.

I whisper those words to myself again. *I am a mother.*

This job, this role, means more to me than any I've ever had.

I tried to stay positive before Samuel was born, but it was hard because the doctor telling me there was a chance I'd never be able to hold him was a constant worry.

"Jesus, someone had better give me some Tylenol to cure this baby fever," Stella says while rocking Samuel back and forth, cooing.

Our friends and family have piled into the room, all of their attention on Samuel.

Samuel. I've only known him a few hours, but he already has my heart gripped in his tiny fingers.

My mom flew in a few days ago and has been staying in my apartment along with Scooby. She's fallen in love with Dallas and Maven, and we're already in talks of her moving here. I've caught the Blue Beech initiation bug.

Samuel has taken his first selfie and had his first diaper changed by me, and people rock-paper-scissored over who got to hold him first.

Hudson throws his hands up. "I'm all for making a baby. Tell me when and where, babe." He slaps Dallas on the back. "Congrats, big brother. You might be one ugly dude, but you make some cute kids."

Dallas laughs and punches him in the arm.

That gorgeous smile hasn't left his face since I handed him Samuel for the first time. Stella gives Samuel back to him as the baby-holding circle starts again from the top.

Dallas cradles him and rocks from side to side. "That's my boy."

Maven tugs at his shirt. "And my little brother!" she announces. "I'm a big sister now!"

We've had to nearly pry Samuel from her arms every time she's held him. She made a list of requests, and the top one was him sleeping in her bed. There's some explaining to do when we get home. Samuel can't be thrown into strollers and tossed on the floor after changing his diapers, like she does with her toy babies.

I'm exhausted by the time the room clears out, and Dallas is sitting on the edge of my bed. He gently climbs in next to me and laces our fingers together.

I close my eyes and sigh when his lips hit mine.

"We did it," he says. "We made a healthy baby."

I lean up for another kiss, making it last longer, and hold my hand against his cheek. "We did it." I stretch my legs out and drum my fingers along his skin. "A year ago, this is so not where I thought I'd be."

He chuckles. "Oh, sweetheart, it's a hell of a lot better than where I imagined I'd be." He situates himself to look at me better. "You saved me, Willow. You saved my daughter. And not only did you save us, but you also gave us Samuel as a bonus. I've been lifted from fires I never thought I'd escape because of you." He disconnects our hands to circle his around my wrist. "And, someday, you're going to let me put a ring on this finger." His lips graze my ring finger.

"Oh, man, did we go backward on that one," I tease. "First does not always come marriage."

"We do our own thing at our own pace."

"That we do."

Epilogue

WILLOW
Two Months Later

I STRETCH OUT IN THE SHEETS AND YAWN WHEN DALLAS COMES WALKING BACK INTO the bedroom with Samuel in his arms. I watch the silhouette of him with the help of the sunrise creeping into the morning sky. He's shirtless, wearing only a pair of loose gym shorts, and I lick my lips when he climbs back into bed.

"Dirty diaper," he explains with a grin. He pokes Samuel's belly. "You know our little man can't handle a dirty diaper."

Dallas is the only man … hell, the only person I know who enjoys changing diapers.

"Thank you," I whisper.

We agreed to take turns in getting up with him at night, but that hasn't happened. Dallas is a lighter sleeper and never wakes me up when it's my turn. He does whatever Samuel needs and comes back to bed without uttering one complaint.

Moving in with him was the right decision. My initial worry that it'd hurt our relationship is gone. It's only fueled more attraction and love between us.

Our bond is tighter, our love stronger.

"Daddy?"

Maven's voice catches me off guard. She's standing in the doorway with her blankie. Dallas or Samuel must've woken her up. She rubs her eyes and sluggishly stomps into the room. I scoot over and pat the space between Dallas and me, and she climbs right in. I smile when her head rests on my shoulder, and she snuggles into my body.

The cartoons come on.

We eat breakfast in bed.

This is my family.

One night changed my life.

One night gave me life.

Other Books by Charity Ferrell

TWISTED FOX SERIES
(each book can be read as a standalone)
Stirred
Shaken
Straight Up
Chaser
Last Round

BLUE BEECH SERIES
(each book can be read as a standalone)
Just A Fling
Just One Night
Just Exes
Just Neighbors
Just Roommates
Just Friends

STANDALONES
Bad For You
Beneath Our Faults
Pop Rock
Pretty and Reckless
Revive Me
Wild Thoughts

RISKY DUET
Risky
Worth The Risk

About the Author

Charity Ferrell resides in Indianapolis, Indiana with her future hubby and two fur babies. She loves writing about broken people finding love with a dash of humor and heartbreak, and angst is her happy place.

When she's not writing, she's making a Starbucks run, shopping online, or spending time with her family.

Subscribe to my Newsletter here
www.charityferrell.com

Side Hustle

EMILY GOODWIN

Chapter One

SCARLET

For as long as I can remember, there's been an emptiness inside of me. The more I try to ignore it, the deeper it sets into my bones, seeping down, deep down, until it becomes part of me. It's easy to blame the emptiness on my shitty upbringing. Having to give up my dreams of a future to take care of my brother and sister. Growing up with an addict for a mother and being the one who found her cold, stiff body after an overdose.

But I felt it before then, and sometimes I wonder if the emptiness isn't empty at all. Maybe it's darkness, and it's always been a part of me. And when you have darkness inside of you, you have two choices: hate yourself for it or embrace it.

I chose the latter.

The bathroom door closes with a heavy thud, and I step up to the mirror, pulling out cherry red lipstick from my purse. I carefully apply it, fluff my hair, and stare at my reflection, avoiding the tiny bit of judgment my moral compass is giving me. That thing's been broken for years anyway.

I close my eyes and think of homeless puppies, conjuring up images from those heartbreaking commercials I usually fast-forward through. It doesn't take much to make myself cry fake tears. If my cards had been dealt a different way, I'd be one hell of an actress.

Fake crying? No problem.

Real crying? I haven't done in years. Crying means feeling, and feeling isn't a luxury I can afford. My life is such a mess that if I stopped and looked at it—really looked at it—I'd be a blubbering mess.

Tears well in my eyes, and I let a few fall, smearing my mascara, before heading back out to the bar. It's a little after noon on a Tuesday, and the bar just opened up. It's inside a swanky hotel, and I can afford exactly half a watered-down whiskey here.

Spotting my target, I take a seat at the bar and order a vodka tonic with top-shelf liquor. I'm getting cocky, perhaps, but I didn't wear this uncomfortable-as-fuck pushup bra for nothing today.

I slowly sip my drink, crossing my legs and leaning back on the bar stool. I squeeze my eyes shut, and more tears roll down my cheeks. Setting the glass down, I angrily wipe them away, looking down at my phone and shaking my head.

"Excuse me, miss," the man in the blue Armani suit says, striding over. He extends a designer monogrammed handkerchief, flashing his Rolex at the same time. "But I have to ask who made a pretty thing like yourself cry?"

I'm not a thing, asshole. I'm a human-fucking-being. "Thank you," I sniffle, taking the handkerchief. I blot up my tears and turn to him, doe-eyed. "My boyfriend is here on business and I thought I'd surprise him. But when I got to the room…he wasn't alone." I turn away, waterworks in full force. I wish I could give myself an Emmy.

"He's a damn fool," Blue Suit says, taking a seat next to me. I can feel him eye-fucking me. "You're exquisite."

I shake my head. "Tell him that." I pick up my drink and down it. "I just want to forget him."

Blue Suit signals the bartender and orders us two martinis. "Here's to forgetting," he says, sliding the drink in front of me. I angle my body toward his and reach out, putting my hand on his bicep.

"Thank you," I say slowly, giving his arm a little squeeze. Blue Suit narrows his eyes and grins.

"Drink," he orders, eyes dropping to my cleavage. I know his type, and I can't fucking stand them. Relatively young for making so much money, they usually hail from trust-fund families to begin with. I bet Blue Suit posts selfies with his Lamborghini at least twice a week on Instagram and has to constantly remind people of how much pussy he gets.

Overly full of himself, he thinks wearing that fitted suit makes him the living embodiment of Christian Grey. Sorry, buddy. I'm not going *Fifty Shades* on your cock today.

"I hardly ever drink," I say, making my voice a little breathy after I take a big swig. "I'm such a lightweight."

His thin lips pull into a grin again, and I wish I could take the toothpick from my drink and stab it into his dick. I'll be doing all women a service from this snake in a suit.

"Well, sweet thing," he starts, leaning in and brushing my blonde hair over my shoulder. "That'll work in both our favors."

I giggle, doing an impressive job of hiding my cringing on the inside. I sip at my drink again, purposely spilling it. A little stream of alcohol runs down my chest, and I make a show of wiping at my breasts.

Like a hungry dog, Blue Suit has sunk his teeth into me, but it's only a matter of time before I walk out of here as *Best of Show*.

"I'm such a mess right now."

"You're too sexy to be a mess."

I mentally roll my eyes. *You're a beautiful mess* was a much better line, dude. "I'm so embarrassed. It's been one hell of a day, and I get a little flustered around attractive men. Oh—" I bring my hand to my face, and right on cue, my cheeks flush.

He chuckles and moves in. I rub my hands up and down my arms, shivering. Blue Suit takes off his jacket and drapes it around my shoulders, smoothing it out just so he has a reason to touch me.

"You're such a gentleman," I coo, pulling the jacket around my slender body. I can feel his wallet press into my side, and it only takes another few minutes of small talk for me to reach inside and pull out his cash. It's not the first time I've done this, but I always get a little rush. I'm right there literally in front of him, picking his pocket under his nose. I've yet to be caught, but there's a first time for everything, I suppose.

I fold the bills up in my hand and reach for my phone with my other. Sandwiching the money between my palm and my phone, I tell him I need to use the bathroom. I leave his suit jacket hanging on the back of the bar stool and slip right out of the bar, through the lobby of the Four Seasons and fall into step with the fast-paced Chicago foot traffic.

"This'll cover what insurance doesn't." I hand over crisp one hundred dollar bills, silently cursing the woman behind the counter. She holds each bill up to the light, making sure they're real, and proceeds to ring me up.

"You need to confirm the address for delivery." She slides the paperwork to me, and I can feel her judgment digging into me like a knife hot out of the fire. I'm still in my strappy Valentino dress, still showing more cleavage than your average street-corner hooker, and still have mascara smeared across my cheeks. I wiped it up the best I could, but I really don't give a damn right now. I changed out of my heels for two reasons: I'm down to one pair of designer shoes, and they're not the most comfortable to be trekking along the south side of Chicago in.

I'm now wearing a pair of worn-out Nikes and have twisted my hair into a messy bun on the top of my head. I had to hurry to get to the medical supply store in time to put in the order and have it delivered with tomorrow's shipment.

I've had this wheelchair on hold for weeks now, and after arguing with insurance for days on end, I knew it was either make my father suffer in his current ill-fitting chair that pinches his thighs and causes sores on his lower back or do whatever I can to get the money to get him this new one before the sores open up and turned into pressure ulcers. Again. We've been down this road before and it almost ended his life. The sores get infected and he's too old and too weak to fight off another infection. It would take me weeks if not months to earn enough from my waitressing job to cover this expensive as fuck wheelchair.

I confirm everything, making double sure the wheelchair will get delivered to the nursing home and then the right patient tomorrow afternoon. The cashier throws out a catty, "Well, you could be there if you're so worried," that I respond to with a glare and a roll of my eyes. I don't have time for her shit.

The wind picks up, carrying a cool fall breeze with it. It's the end of September, and it's been unseasonably warm all week. Not that I'm complaining, though. The lake-effect snow will be here before we know it, and I'll be trudging through it to work and back.

But today, though it's nice enough out to walk, I have enough leftover cash from Blue Suit to take public transportation and buy myself something for lunch. I put on my headphones and sit at the back of the bus, ignoring the world around me.

I get off a block away from the nursing home, intent on grabbing a taco from a hole-in-the-wall Mexican place. My stomach grumbles, and the last remaining twenty is burning a hole in my pocket. I round the corner a little too fast and almost step on a homeless woman sitting close to the side of a building. Her eyes are red and glossed over, but not because she's high. It's because she's been crying.

A sleeping toddler is tucked under her arm, wearing dirty clothes. They're both in desperate need of a bath, and suddenly tacos seem irrelevant. I come to a stop, digging the twenty out of my purse.

"There's a church three blocks over that'll take you in for the night," I tell her. I know this because I stayed there before years ago, back when it was me, Heather, and Jason against the world. "They'll have clothes for her too."

The woman takes the twenty from me, bottom lip quivering. "Thank you. My boyfriend…he got arrested, and we've had nowhere to go." She starts to get to her feet, struggling to keep her child nestled against her body and pick up her shit at the same time.

"Want some help?"

The woman eyes me suspiciously, and if you're going off my looks, I can't blame her. Two-bit whores aren't known for their generosity.

"I've been in your shoes," I offer.

"You have kids?" The woman gets to her feet and grabs a duffle bag full of baby clothes. She only has a backpack full of stuff for herself.

"Not my own, but I looked after my siblings for a few years." I take the duffle from her and lead the way down the street. We walk in silence, and when we get in front of the church, the woman tells me a tearful and heartfelt thank you.

I hike back to the nursing home, sweating by the time I get there. Dammit. This dress is dry clean only. The smells of body odor, urine, and bleach hang heavy in the air, mixed together like some sort of stomach-churning perfume. I turn down the hall and head in the direction of my father's room. I slow, seeing the curtain pulled around his bed.

The nursing assistant behind the curtain hums "Don't Go Breaking My Heart," and I hear him plunge a washcloth into a basin of water.

"Hey, Corbin," I say, knowing who he is without having to look.

His shoes squeak on the tile as he steps over to peer at me. "You pulling tricks again, hooka?"

"Magic tricks," I say, snapping my fingers. "And for my next act, watch that new wheelchair appear tomorrow."

"You didn't."

I raise my eyebrows. "I did."

He waggles a finger at me. "Girl, you are something else."

"How's he doing today?"

"We've had some good moments today, haven't we, Mr. Cooper?"

I perch on the edge of the other bed in the room, not wanting to go behind the curtain. My father's been in this shithole of a nursing home for the last several years, thanks to heavy drinking in his youth, a brain injury acquired during a bar fight, and most of all, early-onset Alzheimer's.

"Good."

"I'm going to take him down to Bingo after I get him cleaned up. He got a little messy during lunch."

"How'd that happen?"

"New CNA. Let him alone with a bowl of soup."

I let out a sigh. You can't leave food out around Dad. He'll try to feed himself and will end up spilling it everywhere. I pull my phone out of my purse, checking the time. I'm going to have to cut my visit with Dad short today if I want to make it over in time to see Heather, which I need to do. It's been a few days, and I have to make sure she's staying out of trouble.

Once Dad is up and dressed, I wheel him down into the cafeteria and sit him at a table along with a few other residents. I stay through one round of Bingo and then give him a kiss on the forehead and rush out, getting to the prison with only minutes left of visiting hours.

I've gone through the process of signing in and going through security so many times I could do it in my sleep.

"Hey, Scarlet," C.O. Benson says as I pass through the metal detector. "Looking good."

I flash him a smile and bat my eyelashes, just enough to keep him hanging on. "You too. Have you been working out?"

"I have," he replies with a wide smile. "Starting some new supplements."

"Keep it up. I can tell." I grab my purse, holding the smile on my face until I turn away. He's not a total loser but isn't my type. And by that, I mean, I'm not into guys who live in their parents' basement and find taxidermy a fun way to pass the time. But I know how helpful it can be to have that flirty relationship with someone in his position, and I never know when I'll have to ask for a favor.

For my sister, that is.

I get seated in the visitor area and lean back while I wait. My mind starts to wander, and I quickly reel that fucker in. *Don't think. Don't feel.*

"Scar!"

I look up and see my sister quickly walking over.

"Jesus Christ, Heather." My eyes widen, and I shake my head. "What the fuck did you do to your hair?"

She flops into the chair with a huff. "I knew you'd hate it."

Reaching over, I run my fingers through the rough cut. A natural blonde like me, Heather has butchered her long locks into a terrible above-the-shoulders bob with streaks of black and red throughout.

"It looks like a prison haircut."

"Well, it is a prison haircut. I'm in fucking prison, Scar," she spits out, nostrils flaring. We glare at each other for a few seconds and then burst out laughing. She reaches over the table and gives me a quick hug, ignoring the C.O. telling us not to touch.

"How are things?" she asks.

"As good as they can be," I say with a shrug. "I got Dad the new chair, and Jason was able to call home a few days ago."

Heather's face lights up. "God, I miss that little shit."

"Me too." Two years ago, our younger brother shipped off to the Middle East with the Army. I hate that he's away, but I'm proud of him for making something of himself. He's the only Cooper to do so…so far. We're a dysfunctional family, but we care about each other something fierce.

"Hey," she says, lowering her voice and leaning over. "I was talking to one of the girls in here."

I raise my eyebrows, knowing what comes next. It's usually a harebrained idea like all of her ideas are and never ends well for her. Hence why I'm visiting my baby sister in prison.

"And?"

Her lips curve into a smile. "I have a job opportunity for you."

Chapter Two

WESTON

"**D**AD, CATCH!"

I make a wild dive, over-exaggerating everything to humor my son. He throws the football, which only makes it a few feet before hitting the ground. I slide on the grass, making Jackson laugh.

"I won! I won!" Jackson chants, jumping up and down.

"Ouch!" Owen shouts from the patio. "Did you break something, old man?"

With a dramatic roll on the grass that makes Jackson laugh even more, I grab the football, pop up, and throw it at my younger brother. He's holding a beer in one hand and lazily reaches out with the other to catch it and misses. Luckily our sister, Quinn, is standing next to him and catches it before it crashes into the house.

"Seriously, guys?" She laughs and tosses the ball to Jackson. Shaking her head, she goes back to her fiancé, who's holding their sleeping baby. Emma looks so small in Archer's arms, reminding me of when Jackson was that little.

They really grow up so fast.

"Try to catch me!" Jackson shouts and takes off through the yard. I don't know where this kid gets his energy from.

"How about Uncle Dean come and chase you around?" I ask loudly so both Jackson and Dean hear. Jackson loves the idea and runs over to Dean, grabbing his hand and pulling him off the bench. Logan steps out of the house, carrying two more beers. He hands one to me and cracks the top back on the other, and we both find a place to sit on the patio with the rest of our siblings.

It's a rare afternoon when we're all off together, and while my parents don't usually have us over for a big dinner on a Tuesday, we couldn't pass this up. It's nice out for late September and might be one of the last times we can grill and eat outside before the cold sets in.

"How's wedding planning?" I ask Quinn, watching my sister-in-law, Kara, out of the corner of my eye. She's still harboring resentment toward Quinn for going into labor on her wedding day and has said more than once she doesn't see the point of Quinn and Archer having a big wedding when they already have a kid.

It's made for some awkward get-togethers, but hey…at least I'm not the only one with a wife not everyone in the family is crazy about. Though other than the stupid wedding drama, no one has an issue with Kara. She's been good for Dean in a sense as well.

"Good. Disney makes things easy." Quinn smiles and rests her hand on top of Archer's. "I ran into Mr. Pickens today," she starts. "And he thinks you should up your game. We all know you'll win if we give this one-hundred percent."

I shrug off her words and take a sip of beer, turning and watching Jackson run around the yard with Dean. All four of my mom's dogs are following, barking and yipping and thinking Jackson is running around solely for them.

"I couldn't even if I wanted to," I say.

"So you do want to?" Logan asks.

"I guess." I haven't wanted to admit it to myself that yes, I'd fucking love to be Sheriff of our little county. I've been an Eastwood cop for years, and I always planned on moving up in the ranks. I officially threw my hat in the ring and am currently running for sheriff, but as we get closer and closer to the election, I'm feeling more and more inclined to drop out. It's weird to get close to a long-time goal like this and want nothing more than to pull out. To stop trying before you fail, or worse, you win, and the results aren't what you expected.

And I did expect this. Well, maybe not being sheriff, but being more than a run-of-the-mill cop in this small town. But then Daisy up and left when Jackson was just a baby, putting a screeching halt on all our plans. Jackson is—and always will be—my first priority. He comes before anyone else, even if that means passing up on what I used to call my dreams.

My dreams have changed, and all I want in life is to see him grow up, happy and healthy.

"Having a brother as a cop around here has gotten me out of a few jams," Owen starts. "Having a brother who's the Sheriff…now that could come in very handy."

Quinn laughs. "Maybe you should just stay out of trouble."

"Where's the fun in that?" Owen counters and finishes his beer. Out of the five of us, Owen has the biggest sense of adventure. Which is a nice way of saying he has a lot of growing up left to do.

"You'd be great at it," Quinn goes on, being the voice of reason. "I know the crime rates around here aren't staggering or anything, but being in a position of political power—no matter how small—can have a big impact on the community."

Watching Jackson throw the football as hard as he can, I think back to when he was a newborn and I sat in the hospital room, talking to him as Daisy slept. I promised him the world, and so far, I've done a damn good job giving him everything he needs. But I'd love to be able to give him more.

"He'd be proud of you," Quinn says softly, knowing exactly what to say to get under my skin, not that she does it to upset me. Like our mother, Quinn is freakishly perceptive when it comes to her family.

"I know," I agree. "But…think about it…if I were the Sheriff, I'd be responsible for the whole county, not just Eastwood. It's hard enough now trying to figure out who can watch Jackson when I'm at work."

"You know I'm happy to help," Mom says, listening to our conversation from inside the house. "Jackson is a great little helper when I'm at the office."

"Thanks, Mom. But what if I'm called out in the middle of the night or can't make it to pick him up from school and you're out on location for a job?" I look at Archer. "You get what it's like being on call."

Archer, who's a surgeon at a nearby hospital, nods. "I couldn't just leave, either. But Quinn is there to watch Emma," he adds almost guiltily.

"You need a hot nanny," Logan and Owen say at the same time. They're identical twins and do that quite often.

"It's not a bad idea," Archer says, earning a quizzical look from Quinn. "She doesn't have to be hot, but I mean, that won't hurt."

Quinn rolls her eyes. "I used to work with several people who had live-in nannies. That way they're always there, which would solve the issue of being called out to a crime or whatever."

"A live-in nanny?" I ask dubiously.

"We talked about this," Quinn reminds me. And we did, several months ago. The only way for me to be the Sheriff around here requires having someone at home to watch

Jackson, and while I agreed to it back then, I'm having second thoughts. "It sounds more pretentious than it is." She tips her head toward Archer. "You know we're willing and ready to contribute to our town by enabling you to be our Sheriff. Just say the word and we can move forward."

I take a long drink of my beer, not answering, but not saying no either.

"I want absolutely nothing to do with this." I put my arm around Jackson, who rests his head on my chest. I rake my fingers through his hair, dark and slightly wavy like mine, and hope I remember to take him to get a haircut this weekend. He needs it. Then again, so do I. I've grown used to having longer locks, and it's one less thing to worry about. Maintaining a short cut requires too much work.

"I'll handle it," Quinn promises, nursing Emma with one hand while she opens her computer with the other. "Bethany from my old job swore by this site, and so did the CEO of our company."

"Sounds expensive," I grumble. Having invented and sold an app to Apple and then taking a high-paying position at a prestigious software company, Quinn has plenty of money. She cut back her hours of work now that she has Emma, but she's engaged to a surgeon for fuck's sake.

Quinn waves her hand in the air, dismissing me. "Think of this as us investing in our beloved community. Lots of people give big donations to the city, you know."

"If I don't like this, you're dealing with it," I go on. "Which means firing the nanny."

Quinn does a good job of ignoring me. In her defense, when we talked about this the first time, I was much more open to the idea. But that was because it was so far in the future I was able to not actually think about it. "Jackson is in school Tuesday and Thursday, right?"

"Right."

"Okay." She types away with impressive speed for someone one-handed, and a few minutes pass before she looks up, smiling. "I put up your profile and, in a day or two, we'll get applications from nannies who are fitting."

"And then what?"

"I'll screen the applications—Owen made me promise I'll let him help, which we both know means he's going to pick the prettiest one." She looks up from her computer with a hopeful smile. "Which really isn't a bad thing. Who knows what could happen?"

"You too?" I ask dryly.

"What?" She shrugs, acting like she has no idea what I'm talking about.

If Jackson weren't here cuddled up with me, I'd remind Quinn—again—that I'm technically still married. I haven't seen Daisy in years, which means she hasn't signed any divorce papers. I know I could push the issue, file something with the courts, and could be a single man in a few months. But what's the point?

Daisy was my high school sweetheart. Yeah, we broke up and got back together several times over the years, and I know my deployment was hard on her, but if over a decade of dating wasn't enough to see we weren't right for each other, then nothing is. I'm done dating. Done with women.

I've gone back and forth on my feelings for Daisy since she left that morning. She put us all through the wringer, worrying about her physical and mental well-being. I scoured the county for her, leaving our newborn with my parents while I drove around in a panic looking for her.

Her sister hadn't heard from her.

Her parents hadn't seen her.

Something terrible had happened. I was sure of it.

And then I found out she was partying in Chicago with a group of friends she met online in some sort of chat room.

She told me she didn't want to be tied down. Being a mom wasn't her thing. She spent years living on a military base, away from friends and her family, and felt like she deserved time to herself. She even thought I should give her credit for not cheating on me while I was overseas.

I spent the first year of Jackson's life hating her. Cursing her name. Wishing I could forget everything related to her—except Jackson, of course. She showed up on his first birthday, played the part of perfect mother for a few days, and we haven't seen or heard from her since.

"All I'm saying is having a good-looking woman around might not be a bad thing." Quinn readjusts Emma, who's done nursing now and is pulling on Quinn's hair, and closes her computer.

"I second that," Logan says, coming into the living room. His eyes meet mine and he gives me a tiny nod, knowing how much I can't fucking stand it when Mom and Quinn get on me about dating again. He sits next to Quinn and takes Emma from her arms, holding her up and making a silly face. "And while you're feeling generous, Quinn, how about hiring a maid for me?"

"I think most of them prefer to be called house-cleaners now, and no. Owen's capable of cleaning."

Hearing his name, Owen rounds the corner. "Are you insinuating that I'm the messy one?"

"We all know you are, Uncle Owen," Jackson quips and makes us all laugh. He pushes himself up and wiggles his way in between Logan and Quinn, cooing and talking like a baby to Emma.

"Ready to head home, buddy?" I ask Jackson, knowing he's going to protest. We have about half an hour before we have to get home, and I'm buying my time to avoid a meltdown. We've gone back and forth a lot this week, and while my parents and Jackson enjoy the time they get to spend together, it would be nice to keep him home during the week, especially now that he's in preschool.

Admitting I need help has never come easy for me, but I know deep down that this might be exactly what we need.

Chapter Three

SCARLET

I pinch the bridge of my nose, gripping my phone so tight in my other hand I think it might break. I sink down on a creaky kitchen chair, looking at the bills laid out on the table. I'm behind on everything, like usual, and I don't have enough to cover the bare minimum this time.

Trying to get Heather the best outcome possible, I skipped the public defender and hired a lawyer, who was able to cut her sentence in half. But the lawyer fees weren't cheap, and I've been without TV or internet all month, making me go over on my data plan, but hey— that bill's not due until next month. The next to go will be my electric and water, though not by choice.

And now I'm dealing with insurance, who randomly decided to stop covering several of Dad's medications that he's been taking for the last three years. I've been on the phone for over an hour, mostly on hold, of course. I rest my head in my hands, zoning out as I continue to listen to crappy elevator music through the speakers on my phone.

Finally, I get through to a new person, whose accent is so thick I can hardly understand a word they're saying. I argue some more, but in the end, there is nothing I can do. The insurance company no longer deems the blood pressure medication necessary and will no longer cover it.

I hang up and let my phone clatter to the table. The fall is cushioned by the million bills covering the surface. Seething, I close my eyes and clench my jaw. I want to beat someone up, preferably Steve at the insurance company who has as much empathy as a pile of dirt.

"I am so fucking sick of this," I mutter. I'm sick of taking one step forward and two back. I'm tired of never having enough. I'm tired of everyone else's shit always falling on my shoulders.

I want out.

Out of the ghetto. Out of poverty. Of working my ass off for measly tips and dealing with rude customers who see me as that trashy girl from the south side. I want to make a life for myself. I want to do better.

Picking pockets will only get me so far. I need to do something big, something like I used to do before, and get enough money to finally start the life I know I deserve. Picking my phone back up, I log onto a caregiver site. I have a profile on here, though it's been a while since I used it.

Two years ago, I was a live-in nanny for a rich couple, looking after their entitled asshole children. Mostly I saw them off to school, spent the day hanging around the pool, and picked them up after school. I made sure they did their homework, but they each had separate tutors for their different subjects.

My biggest job while working there was constantly turning down advances from the children's father. He was a decent-looking guy, ten years older than me and working the salt-and-pepper hair hard. He was funny, cultured, and totally infatuated with me. He started sending me gifts, which is how I acquired a few designer items.

Then the gifts turned into dinner dates, and after a night where he flew me to New York

City on his private jet, I drank too many mini bottles of vodka and took things a little too far with him. I threw up before we actually had sex, but that night opened up a whole new window of opportunity for me, not that I'm exactly proud of it.

Afraid I'd tell his wife of what almost happened, he started giving me cash in exchange for my silence. I had photographic evidence of him shoving his tongue down my throat, after all. I quit working for his bratty-ass children and was able to live off hush-money for a good six months. Then he got caught cheating on his wife with someone else and she left him, so my silence wasn't worth paying for anymore.

Not letting myself think about how deplorable I am, I make my account active again and update my resume a bit. I don't think Mrs. Milton ever knew about me, and to be honest, I don't care if she did. She was an awful woman who didn't deny marrying for money and openly admitted the only reason she had children was because she saw it as a way around the prenup.

Still, her name looks good as a reference. I'll leave it. I spend a few more minutes tweaking my resume, not exactly lying but making myself sound way better than I really am. I submit it to the site for review and answer a few questions to see if I can still pass a background check. Luckily for me, background checks don't go into my family history.

"You make sure Jason does his homework, you hear?"

I press my lips into a thin line. "Dad, Jason isn't in high school anymore. He's in the Army now."

Dad gives me a blank stare and tries to get out of his wheelchair. The new one is much more comfortable than the old one, but I guess I was overly optimistic that he'd keep his ass in this new chair better than the last. He's too unsteady to be up walking on his own.

"And you tell your skank-ass whore of a mother to stop drinking my beer."

"Mr. Cooper," Corbin scolds as he comes around the corner. "Now I know your pretty little daughter didn't take that nasty old bus and then walk two blocks in the rain to get her ass badgered by you." Corbin stops in front of my dad's wheelchair and pops his hip, holding out one hand.

Dad grumbles something I can't discern but hefts back in his chair with a sigh. I mirror his actions, letting out a breath of frustration.

"He doesn't mean it. You know that, right?" Corbin tells me, leaning against the wall.

"I know."

"It can be hard to see family like this, but it's the nature of the disease. Don't take it personally."

"I don't," I tell him, blowing a loose strand of hair out of my face. "He wasn't very involved when I was a kid. It's not like I have all these good memories of him to tarnish."

"Maybe that's a good thing."

"I should have been there," Dad says in a rare moment of clarity. "I should have been there for you and Heather and Jason. I should have made your mother get help. I'm...I'm sorry."

I close my eyes, shoving all my feelings aside. "You're here now, Dad."

Corbin pushes off the wall. "Anyway, Mr. Cooper. It's time for dinner. You coming, Scarlet? I can get an extra plate for you."

"What are they having today?"

"Sweet potatoes and fish."

I try not to cringe. "I'll take some sweet potatoes, but I'll pass on the fish."

"Smart choice," he mouths and unlocks Dad's wheelchair. I follow behind as we head to the cafeteria, pulling out my phone to see who just emailed me. It's a response to the nanny position I applied for a few days ago, which specific one is beyond me. I applied for any and all that I could.

I quickly skim the email, looking to see who sent it. The email was sent from a work account, and the name *Quinn Dawson* is at the bottom as an e-signature. Once I get to the table next to Dad, I enter her name in a Google search.

"Holy shit," I say out loud, earning a nasty look from the uptight nurse passing by. Quinn's made quite the name for herself, and she's younger than me. I find her on Instagram and creep through her photos. She has a baby, and it looks like she's either married or engaged to a doctor. I already hate her.

I don't care what the job description is. This is exactly the type of gig I need.

Corbin comes over with two plates of nasty-looking salmon that reeks like it's been left out on the counter all afternoon. Yep, I'm only eating the sweet potatoes. Swallowing the little bit of morality I have left, I turn to Dad and look into his eyes.

"I'm going to get you out of this shithole, I promise."

I feel like I'm drowning. Like I'm madly treading water just to stay afloat. I'm gasping for breath, but every time my lungs fill with air, it feels wrong. Like I shouldn't be breathing.

Like I should drown.

But like a cockroach, I keep coming back. Pulling on the cross necklace that's hanging from my neck, I push my shoulders back and step into the coffee shop.

We're meeting in The Loop, near Quinn's place of work. She already ran my background check and said she called my references, and it's a miracle she hasn't been scared off yet. I spot her sitting at a table in the back, typing on a laptop. There's an iced coffee next to her, and I can tell from back here her purse, clothes, and shoes are designer.

Her brunette hair is pulled into a braid that's perfectly messy, and she's not wearing much makeup. She's pretty and has a kind face. You can tell she's a nice fucking person just by looking at her, and I can't let myself fall into a trap.

I need money. Specifically hers.

My phone rings right as Quinn looks up, and our eyes meet for a fleeting moment before I glance down at my cell in my hand. It's the nursing home, and I hesitate before answering. They called this morning to tell me Dad was out of the medication insurance stopped covering and asked if I would be able to provide it until something was worked out.

I'm trying.

I silence the call and look back at Quinn, plastering a fake smile on my face.

"Hi," she says, standing up to shake my hand. "I'm Quinn."

"Scarlet. Nice to meet you."

"Do you want anything to drink? This new caramel frap is to die for."

"Uh, sure. Thanks."

Leaving her computer on the table with me, Quinn gets up and gets in line, returning a few minutes later after putting in an order for me.

"So," she starts, fidgeting a bit as she talks, "I've never interviewed anyone like this before. Sorry in advance if I'm a little awkward. And don't feel like you need to put up a front or anything. I'm not looking for Mary Poppins. Just someone who can help with basic household chores and make sure a four year old makes it to see another day."

Dammit, I kind of like her. "I think I can do that." My phone buzzes, and I glance down, seeing a text from Corbin. *Shit.*

Wait. Did she say a four year old? From my internet creeping, I only saw her with a baby who couldn't be older than six or seven months old. Doesn't matter. I'd rather take care of a four year old than a baby anyway. Changing diapers isn't my thing.

Quinn goes on to describe the job, and I hear her say the house is in a small town in Indiana, about an hour and a half away. I smile and nod as she explains the rest, not really paying attention because I'm trying to surreptitiously read Corbin's text. And when I see the words *your dad fell again*, nothing Quinn says stays with me.

The faster I can get to Quinn's husband, the better. I need to find a way to blackmail him into giving me money so I can move my dad to a place that's better equipped to handle someone with memory issues.

We go over pay, where I'll stay, and how my time off will work. She's pretty fucking generous and even offers to arrange a car to come get me since I don't own one myself. I can start tomorrow, and I have no doubt things will work out just fine. Being able to accommodate anyone is just one of my superpowers. Though, really, I don't see why it's all that hard. Find out what people want and embody it. Compliment them. Make them feel important.

And then you've weaseled your way into their lives enough to reach in and take whatever you want. Hey…I never claimed to be a saint.

"Miss Cooper?"

My eyes flutter open, and I blink in the bright sunlight. "Yeah?"

"We're here."

"Oh, uh, thanks." I unbuckle my seatbelt, feeling a little disoriented. I had just slipped into deep sleep and am having a hard time pulling myself out of it. I smooth out my hair and pop the top button on this ridiculous pink sweater. It's not at all my style but gives me the image I want to portray. Squeezing my eyes shut to try and focus my vision, I open the car door before the driver has a chance to come out and open it for me. I'm capable of opening my own doors. It's just weird to sit here and wait for someone else to do it.

I blink once. Twice. Three times. "This is the house?" I ask, looking up and down the street. There's a good chance the driver took a wrong turn and accidentally drove us onto the set of a Hallmark Channel movie. We're parked along the curb of a postcard-worthy small town road, with well-maintained houses lining either side of the street. A handful even have white picket fences.

Forget Hallmark. There's an even better chance this is a horror movie and I've just been hand-delivered to a serial killer who spends her days knitting and offs her unsuspecting victims by poisoning their lemonade. Which she made. By hand.

"Yes," the driver tells me, coming around to get my bags. "This is the address Mr. Dawson provided."

"Oh, uh, okay." I hike my purse up over my shoulder and grab the handle to one of my suitcases. This isn't what I signed up for. The house I saw on Quinn's Instagram is brand new and big, with curved double staircases greeting you from the oversized foyer. This house in front of me looks like a century-old farmhouse, safely nestled into the historic district of this small town.

The fuck?

I know I tuned out most of what Quinn was saying the other day at the coffee shop. I looked at her and saw nothing but dollar signs and was willing to watch two sets of hyperactive triplets if it meant getting a shot at some of her money.

But this…this has to be a mistake. On her part. Not mine. Because I didn't sign up for this.

"Uh…thanks," I tell the driver as he sets my last suitcase by the porch steps. I stand there like a deer in fucking headlights, taking in the perfectly groomed lawns on the surrounding houses and how nearly everyone is already decorated for fall. If I don't pull myself out of this living Pinterest board now, I fear I never will.

I'm about to turn around and leave, walking to the nearest bus station and pulling whatever trick I have to do to get enough money to get me back to Chicago. And then the front door opens. If anyone else stepped out of the house, things might have turned out differently. But the moment I lay eyes on *him* all I can think is, "Oh shit."

Tall and muscular, the man standing before me is just that: a *man*. His presence is intoxicating, intimidating, and impressive all at the same time. He has messy dark brown hair that's pulled away from his face, and the darkest navy-blue eyes I've ever seen.

His face is set, and I can tell just by looking at him that his guard is up, and for a damn good reason. Takes one to know one, I guess.

"Scarlet Cooper?" he asks, looking me over. His gaze slowly wanders over my body, but he's not checking me out. He's inspecting me, looking for flaws in the system and signs of obvious damage.

It's there, hiding in plain sight, but all he sees is a pretty blonde woman in a white skirt and a stupid fuzzy pink sweater.

"Yes. Nice to meet you, Mr. Dawson." I plaster a pleasant smile on my face, freaking out on the inside but otherwise appearing level-headed and cool as a cucumber. With practiced grace, I ascend the porch steps and shake Mr. Dawson's hand. His grip is strong and firm, and the skin on his palm is just rough enough to make me think he must work with his hands.

That thick skin would feel so good slowly making its way up my—stop. Get it together so you can get the fuck out of here, Scarlet.

His furrowed brows give way to a more friendly expression as he grips my hand for a moment before releasing it. He lets out a breath and his whole body relaxes. There are pounds of muscle under his black T-shirt, and it makes my body react purely on its own accord.

"Weston. But call me Wes," he says and steps aside. "Come in."

Suddenly, I can't move. This guy—Wes Dawson—isn't the surgeon I assumed I'd be working for. Is the con artist getting conned? Is the universe finally catching up to me, and this is its way of giving me the middle finger while laughing out a big *fuck you*? I have no idea what is going on or what I'm going to do, but I know one thing for sure. If I go into that house, there's no going back.

Chapter Four

WESTON

Scarlet stands on the front porch, vivid blue eyes wide. Her blonde hair falls in waves around her face, and I can't help but notice how beautiful she is. Everything about her is soft and delicate, but there's a hardness to her I immediately recognize. Blinking, I sweep my hand up and over my hair, pushing it out of my face.

I don't know what I expected—Mrs. Doubtfire perhaps?—but I certainly didn't expect a blonde bombshell. Though really, Owen got the final say in who Quinn interviewed after she narrowed it down to her top five choices. Still…this woman before me belongs on the pages of a magazine, not living in someone else's house looking after strangers' children.

She freezes, looking around as if she has no idea what the fuck is going on, and then recovers fast. She blinks, puts on a smile, and comes up the porch steps. Scarlet is the definition of a hot nanny, even in that stupid fuzzy sweater. Perky round tits bounce underneath it as she walks, and it doesn't look like she's wearing a bra.

My dick jumps, and I turn away. She's been here all of a minute and I'm already reacting to her. Dammit. I don't even want her here, let alone want to find her attractive. She's here for Jackson, and he's all that matters.

He'll always be all that matters.

I don't move, and we stand there in a weird stare-off. My face is set, and my mind is made. Letting her into my house means I can't do it all, and that's not something I've admitted to myself. When Daisy left, I swore I didn't need her. That I didn't need anyone. Jackson was more than enough, and I have to be enough for him.

Knowing I can't stand here staring at Scarlet forever, I take a step forward. She smells amazing, like fresh flowers and clean laundry and sunshine. Impossible, right? I fucking wish it were. She sweeps her eyes over me, inhaling quickly. Her lips part, and we both reach for the same suitcase at the same time.

Her nails catch on my skin, and she jerks back.

"Sorry." She makes a move to grab my hand but stops, holding hers awkwardly out in front of her. "Did I hurt you?"

"No," I say gruffly, fully aware how easily a woman like her could hurt me. She shuffles back, and I grab her two big suitcases with one hand, pinching my fingers between the handles but wanting to get them inside so we can move off the porch. I'm suddenly sweating, and I'm blaming it on the hot sun.

Hah.

Once inside, she leans over to unzip her boots, and I get a clear view of her tits behind that sweater. She's definitely not wearing a bra. She's well-endowed, and I can't help but imagine what those gorgeous tits would feel like in my hands.

Obviously, I'm still attracted to women. Very attracted. But being married due to a technicality complicates the shit out of things, and even more pressing is not wanting to get Jackson's hopes up.

He's still too young to fully grasp what happened, but he knows his mother left him. I'm certain he doesn't actually remember her, but he understands the idea of a mother and asks every now and then if either his mom is coming back or if I'll get married again. I can usually sidestep those questions with an "I'm not sure" or "Mommy is busy," but what really gets me is when he asks why his mommy doesn't love him.

Because I don't fucking know why.

That kid is my moon and stars. He's my reason for getting out of bed every morning. He's everything to me, and the only reason this Scarlet woman is even here is to offer him a sense of stability that I can't on my own.

Everything I do, I do for him.

"So you talked to my sister yesterday," I start, stepping into the living room.

Scarlet's eyes zero in on me, and she takes a few seconds to study my face. She makes no attempt to hide it either, and her brazen move to check me out throws me.

"Quinn is your sister?" she asks, tipping her head to the side a bit. Why does she sound surprised?

"Yeah, she is."

Scarlet's long eyelashes come together as she blinks. "Oh. I thought she was your wife. You, uh, have the same last name."

I let out a strangled laugh. "No. She's my baby sister, and she won't be a Dawson for much longer anyway."

Scarlet's lips part, but no words leave her mouth. Then she smiles again and looks me over once more. "I can see the similarities."

I shrug. Dean and I look alike, Logan and Owen are obviously identical, and Quinn holds a resemblance to us all. Only prettier. "I guess. This whole thing is her idea," I add. I want to keep pretending I can do it all, play the role of perfect father and devoted police officer to our town, but dammit, I can't. Sticking to a schedule will do Jackson a world of good, especially now that he's in school.

"Oh." Scarlet brings her arms in, looking a little unsure of herself. The gesture throws me, and it takes me a few seconds to realize why. Her body language says she's shy and uncomfortable—expected in this situation, of course. But her face is set with determination, and she has a distant look in her eyes that reminds me of a huntress on the prowl.

I hate that I find it so fucking attractive.

"She was supposed to explain everything."

"Yeah," Scarlet says without missing a beat. "She did." She smiles and grabs the remaining bags, bringing them from the foyer and into the living room. I know they're heavy and she's struggling under the weight, but she doesn't let on or ask for help.

"But we can go over it again." She sets her purse down on the coffee table and looks around. The determination in her eyes gives way to a moment of panic, but she hides it well. I wouldn't be able to see it if it weren't something I've experienced myself.

"Jackson is watching cartoons in his room. He's excited to meet you." I give her another few seconds to look around. The house is historical and has been fully restored and professionally decorated. Buying and fixing up this place was a dream Daisy and I shared back when we first started dating, and we saved for years to have enough to do things right.

"Your house is beautiful," she says but almost sounds disappointed.

"It's haunted," Jackson quips, appearing at the top of the stairs. "The Tall Man comes into my room at night."

"Jackson," I scold, hoping Scarlet doesn't go running out the door. Though on second thought…nope. This is for Jackson. I can grin and bear anything for that boy. "We talked about this. Ghosts aren't real."

"The Tall Man isn't a ghost. He's a zombie!"

Scarlet smiles, going over to the base of the stairs. "Well, you're in luck. I just happen to know that zombies don't like cinnamon. All we have to do is put a little pinch of it by your door and he won't be able to come into your room anymore."

"Really?" Jackson's face lights up.

"Really."

Jackson comes down the stairs. "Are you my nanny?"

"I am. My name is Scarlet."

"I'm Jackson. I'm four years old. Did you know that babies grow inside their mommy's tummies before they pop out of their belly button?"

Scarlet smiles. "I didn't, but I do now."

I close my eyes in a long blink. It's Dean's fault Jackson won't stop talking about where babies come from.

"Want to see my room?" Jackson takes Scarlet's hand. "I got a new PAW Patrol blanket for my bed. I have a big boy bed!"

"Hang on, buddy," I tell him. "Let's show Scarlet around the rest of the house first and give her a chance to get settled."

Jackson makes a face but agrees—as long as he can hold Scarlet's hand during the tour. He's a friendly kid, loving pretty much anyone who'll give him the time of day. I try to remain pleasant for his sake, but this whole thing is pissing me off.

And for some reason, having Scarlet be as pretty as she is makes me even angrier. I don't want a nanny. And even more so, I don't want to *need* a nanny.

I give Scarlet a hurried tour of the house, ending with the small guest room upstairs. It has a tiny bathroom attached to it, and the entire room is rather plain in comparison to the rest of the house. The door to this room hasn't been opened in months prior to today.

"I'll bring up your bags," I say and turn to go down the stairs. Jackson starts to go in with Scarlet, but I call him down, telling him I need his muscles to help me carry Scarlet's stuff up.

She's sitting on the bed when we return and gets up to take the suitcases into her room. Her hand brushes across mine as she grabs the handle from me, and I'm taken aback by how soft her skin is. Has it been that long since I've felt the touch of a woman?

"Thank you."

"I'll, uh, give you some time to get settled. Jackson," I call, not wanting to leave him alone with this woman. Not yet. "Help me make dinner."

"I'll do it," Scarlet offers.

"It's fine. We got it tonight."

Jackson protests the whole time, wanting to stay and play with Scarlet.

"She's pretty, isn't she, Daddy?" he asks as I lift him onto the kitchen counter. On the evenings I'm home, we always make dinner together. It's never anything fancy, and tonight we're making spaghetti and meatballs. The meatballs are frozen and won't take long to heat up in the microwave. Like I said…we're far from five-star fancy around here.

"Sure," I say, not wanting to lie to my son but for some reason finding it impossible to verbalize out loud that this woman might be the prettiest person who's ever walked into this house.

"She looks like Elsa!"

I shrug. "I guess." I grab a box of spaghetti noodles from the cupboard and hand it to Jackson. He likes to pick at the cardboard until it opens. Grabbing a pot and filling it with water, I put it on the stove to boil and bring Jackson off the counter. He sets the table while I stick the meatballs and sauce in the microwave.

Hopefully Scarlet can cook.

My mind wanders back to her pert breasts under that sweater, and as if she can read my mind, the floor creaks under her feet.

"Hey," she says almost shyly, and this time her timidness seems genuine. She changed into black leggings and a gray T-shirt, and her long blonde hair is twisted into a bun at the nape of her neck. "Would you like any help?"

"No, thanks."

Jackson's in the living room, too distracted with his toys to notice that she came down into the kitchen. Scarlet sits at the kitchen table, body angled out toward mine.

"So, Wes," she starts. "Quinn told me about Jackson but didn't tell me about you."

"I'm not that interesting," I reply dryly.

"What do you do?"

I add the pasta to the water and turn to steal another glance at her pretty face. "I'm running for sheriff of our county, but who knows how that'll turn out. For now, at least, I'm a cop."

Chapter Five

SCARLET

A *cop.*

I'm a con artist posing as a nanny for a fucking cop. What the hell did I get myself into? I can feel the blood leave my face at a dizzying rate. Stay calm. Freaking out won't do me any good now. I need to hold it the fuck together.

I squeeze my eyes shut. How did I get things so wrong? I wasn't paying attention, but how did I miss this? Surely that Quinn chick mentioned she was hiring me for *her brother*.

Her apparently-single brother who just happens to be irritatingly sexy with that whole dark and brooding thing going on. I can tell he doesn't want me here, that he's reluctant to accept help, and I'm trying really hard not to find that attractive.

"Have you always been a nanny?" he asks after a beat of awkward silence passes between us. Sweat rolls down between my breasts.

"No," I say with a shake of my head. "I was a waitress for a while." I swallow hard, carefully calculating my next move. It's not too late to back out and find a family that has money to blow. I could be gone in the morning and put this whole thing behind me. Move onto a bigger and better target.

Or I could stay and actually work as a nanny. You know. Do the job I was hired to do. But that's not my style.

"How long have you been a cop?" I ask, body going on autopilot.

"A while," he tells me, turning away from the stove just long enough to look at me. "I was in the Army before then and served two tours in Afghanistan before joining the police force."

"My brother is in the Army," I blurt, breaking one of my cardinal rules of *don't get personal*. "He's overseas right now. I haven't seen him in a few months."

Wes's brows push together, and his gaze drills into mine. "Next time you talk to him, tell him I thank him for his service."

Suddenly flustered, I bring my hand to my chest, tugging at the T-shirt. Why is it a million degrees in here? "I will."

"How long has he been in?"

"He joined a year and a half ago and has been somewhere in the Middle East for the last five months. I'm not exactly sure where he is."

"He probably can't tell you," Wes goes on, turning back around. His whole demeanor has changed, and I know his mind is taking him back to the days when he was overseas too. I've been soured by corrupt cops before, but I have the utmost respect for our military, especially soldiers since Jason is one.

God fucking dammit. Now's not the time to get a conscience, Scar.

"Jackson seems like a great kid," I say.

"He is." Wes grabs a wooden spoon from a drawer and stirs the spaghetti. My heart is beating with fury inside my chest, so loud I think it's going to give me away. I can't think, I can't feel. I just need to focus on the job at hand.

And that job is hustling every penny out of Mr. Weston Dawson that I can.

I sit on the edge of the bed, running a comb through my damp hair. The window is cracked behind me, letting in a cool breeze. Everything is silent. Freakily silent. No one is yelling or drunkenly arguing with a street lamp outside my window. The walls aren't shaking from the Chicago L going by, and I haven't heard a single gunshot all night.

It's eerie as fuck.

Weston put Jackson to bed a few hours ago, and I basically just watched, getting familiar with their routine. It was pretty standard, I suppose, but wasn't something I've seen before.

My own parents didn't give me the time of day, and I suppose they couldn't even if they wanted to. Mom was drunk, high, or in jail throughout my youth, and Dad didn't enter the picture until I'd already dropped out of high school in order to take care of Heather and Jason. He stuck around long enough that time for me to go back and graduate the next year.

The family I nannied for in the past didn't have children out of love, and that love didn't foster and develop slowly over time as the children aged. I can't recall a single time either parent went out of their way to do anything for those kids, which only furthered my belief that loving and caring families only exist in movies.

But what happened tonight is shaking everything I've built my life on.

After dinner, Weston went over letters and numbers with Jackson and then gave him a bath. He read him a few books before tucking him in and stayed in the room with him until Jackson fell asleep.

Wes might seem a little cold and callous, but there is no denying he loves his son.

Pulling my hair into a braid, I wonder what happened to Jackson's mother. She's probably dead, because I can't see how anyone could leave that sweet little boy…or that beast of a man.

He's unlike anyone I usually work with—well, if you can call what I do work. It enables me to bring home money to pay bills, which is what work is, right? But Weston…he's closed off, and if he even has any weaknesses at all, he's not going to let me in on them.

I set my brush down and lay back in bed, grabbing a yellow stuffed unicorn. I've had the thing for years, and I'm well aware how weird some people think it is that I'm a grown-ass woman sleeping with a stuffed animal. But the thing brings me comfort, which is something I desperately need most nights. The mattress is comfy, and the quilt is thick and warm. I should be able to pass out, sleeping soundly, but I can't. I'm unnerved, but I'm not afraid. Wes won't hurt me, and unless the neighbors actually turn out to be Stepford wives, I'm as safe as I've ever been.

After an hour of tossing and turning, I'm risking a run-in with my conscience. Normally, I'd toss down a shot of whatever's cheapest at the corner liquor store, but I didn't bring any booze, and I can't exactly go downstairs and start raiding Weston's alcohol stash. Assuming he has one, that is.

Nevertheless, I get up to go downstairs for something to drink. I slowly open my bedroom door and look into the dark hall. Red light from Jackson's nightlight spills into the hall, but he's not in his bed. I panic for a brief second, thinking I lost the kid my first night on the job, and quickly tiptoe down the hall.

Weston's door is cracked open, and I can just barely make out his form laying in the bed. All rigid and muscular, he's a hard shape in the dark, and nestled up against his chest is Jackson.

I'm fairly certain the kid didn't have a nightmare. He was still in his bed after I got out of the shower, and the only reason he's in here, still fast asleep, is because Weston went in and got him, not trusting me enough to let Jackson sleep in his own room tonight.

Without meaning to, I find myself smiling. Wes is smart. Maybe too smart. The smile wipes off my face fast. I'm one wrong move away from being arrested and thrown into jail. Whatever I do next, I must proceed with caution.

The stairs are creaky, and long shadows are cast on the walls in front of me. Going slow so I don't trip, I hold my hands out in front of me and feel for the wall leading into the kitchen. I slide my hand up and down it, feeling for the switch.

I pour myself a glass of orange juice and slowly sip it, wishing for some vodka. Sitting at the farmhouse-style table, I look out into the dark backyard. It's illuminated just enough by the back porch lights to see the outline of a swing set, and the whole yard is enclosed with a white picket fence.

Freaky, indeed.

Finishing my orange juice, I put the glass in the sink and kill the light, taking another minute to stare into the dark and void my mind of all thoughts. Suddenly, the lights flick back on, and I jump.

"Jesus!"

"No, not Jesus. Just me." Weston stands in the threshold of the kitchen, eyes narrowed as they adjust to the light. He's only wearing navy blue boxers, and all the self-control in the world can't keep me from sweeping my gaze across his muscled torso, down to his defined abs, following the happy trail of hair that leads right to his—

"What are you doing?" he asks, diverting his eyes. Looks like I'm not the only one having trouble tonight. I'm wearing white underwear and a gray Columbia University shirt that barely covers the bottom of my ass.

"I came down to get a drink."

"In the dark?"

"I had the lights on, and then I turned them off."

Weston raises an eyebrow, bringing a hand up to push his hair back. I want nothing more than to run my fingers through it and see if his body feels as hard and chiseled as it looks. I want to slam him up against the wall, putting a crack in that shield he has around himself.

"What are you doing?" I shoot back.

"I heard something."

"Oh, I didn't mean to wake you."

"You didn't." He scrubs his chin with his hand.

I go back to the fridge and grab the orange juice again, pouring him a glass. I set it on the table and take a seat. Wes stares at the drink like I just poured poison in a glass and added a skull-and-crossbones warning for good measure.

"Can't sleep?" He finally takes a step and my god, men like him aren't supposed to be real. They're supposed to exist on the cover of romance novels or in magazines, digitally altered and giving us all a negative complex about the way we look.

"No," I reply.

"I suppose it's weird being here."

"A little. It's very quiet."

"I've never been a fan of big cities."

I shrug. "I've never lived anywhere else to compare it to."

His long fingers wrap around the glass of orange juice, but he doesn't pick it up. Maybe he *is* worried I poisoned him.

"Did you go to Columbia?" His eyes fall to the faded letters across my chest. I'm not wearing a bra, and it's chilly down here. I'm not ashamed to use my body as a weapon, but the flush that comes to my cheeks happens on its own accord. I lie to pretty much everyone I meet, and yet I find myself unable to lie to Wes. And more importantly, I don't want to.

"No, I didn't. Well, I've set foot on campus but not as a student." I fold my hands in my lap. "I didn't go to college." If he looked at my resume, he already knows that.

He picks up the glass and drinks all the juice and then gets up to put his glass in the sink. He has a scar on his back. It's faded considerably but hangs on to the red anger that was inflicted years ago. I can't tell what caused the scar…maybe a burn? My eyes drop to his tight and firm ass. The man does his squats and he does them well.

"You should go back to bed," he says, voice gruff again. "It'll be loud tomorrow once Jackson is up." And without so much as a look back, he crosses the room and disappears up the stairs.

He's brazen, a little rude, and it unnerves me. Wes Dawson is the last person I'd try to con, and not just because he's a cop. He's not looking for a hookup. He's not desperate and needing to prove something to himself.

Though deep down, everyone wants something, and finding out what drives Wes is key to getting what I want. I'll crack him eventually…as long as he doesn't crack me first.

Chapter Six

WESTON

I sit back at my desk and pull out my phone, logging onto the security company's app and checking the cameras inside the house again. For the fifth time. This hour. It's not that I don't trust Scarlet, it's just…I don't trust Scarlet.

She's well aware of all the security measures I have in place at our house, and I haven't given her the codes just yet. The only place she's going today is the backyard with Jackson, and there's no need to arm the house just to be outside.

The cameras aren't at all nanny-cams and show the front, back, and side door, as well as one looking down the steps with a view of the foyer. I can just barely see Scarlet and Jackson in the backyard. She's chasing him around with her arms outstretched, dragging one leg as she stumbles through the grass.

I can't help but smile, knowing exactly what she's doing. Jackson is currently obsessed with zombies and loves to be chased by them.

"Who are you sexting?" Officer John Wilson asks me as he passes by my desk on the way to his.

Another officer laughs. "The day Dawson sexts is the day we bust an underground crime ring in Eastwood."

"Fuck you," I shoot back. The guys never back down from a chance to hassle me about my sex life, or technically lack thereof. "And don't fucking jinx us."

"Come on, don't tell me you don't wanna bust a crime ring?" Wilson goes on. He's a good cop, got his degree in law enforcement from a community college, but has never been in combat. Not the way I have.

"It'd give us something to do," I say with a chuckle. Movement flashes across the screen of my phone again, and I look down just in time to see Scarlet pull her sweatshirt over her head. She has a tank top on underneath, but I still feel like I just witnessed something I wasn't supposed to.

And fuck, I want to see it again.

A minute later, we're called out to a domestic dispute, which is probably the most excitement we'll see all day. I shouldn't complain, though. Eastwood is a safe, small town, and I couldn't think of a better place to raise my son. It's not to say nothing bad ever happens here. Our biggest problem is drugs, and given the rural setting of many of our residents' houses, we've shut down a surprising number of meth labs over the years.

Last year's big bust was arresting Marty McMillian, Eastwood's resident redneck, for threatening and harassing a gay couple. When we got to his house to take him in, hundreds of guns were laid out in his living room. Turns out he'd been stealing them for years and selling them on the black market.

We have a few burglaries and break-ins every year, but in my time on the force, I've yet to be called out to a murder. There was a body found two years ago, but it turned out to be a man from Newport who got drunk and stumbled his way into our township before passing out and succumbing to the elements.

It's obvious what's going on as soon as we pull up to the farmhouse. It's the second time we've been out here in a month.

"Here we go again," Wilson huffs and gets out of the squad car.

"Mr. Green," I start and shut the driver's side door. "I see you've been drinking again."

"Drinking!" his wife shouts. "He's been doing more than just *drinking*! Tell them, Earl, tell them what else you've been doing. Or *who* you been doing!" She's holding a shotgun and has it pointed in his general direction. And I do mean general. Her hands are too shaky to take a clear shot.

The neighbors across the street are on their porch, and it looks like they've got popcorn. This is high-quality entertainment here.

"Put the gun down, Grace," Wilson says, holding up his hand. "We'll cart his ass back to the station."

I really don't want to put Mr. Green in the back of my car. He always ends up puking. But clearly, he's going to be spending at least the day sleeping this off.

"You take him, and you keep him!" Grace, Mr. Green's wife, pumps the shotgun.

"Come on now, Grace." I go around and take Mr. Green's wrist. If I can lead him away, Grace will start to diffuse. "You don't want to come down to the station with us."

"We'll put you in the same cell," Wilson goes on.

"Good!" Grace shrieks. "I'll beat him. I'll beat him to death this time!"

I wave my hand in the air, dismissing her. It's the same old song and dance, and it happens two or three times a month. The Greens have a daughter, but she can't be bothered with her parents anymore, not that I blame her. Mr. Green has been an unfaithful drunk for as long as I can remember.

I get Mr. Green around my car, and he doubles over and pukes on the grass. Score for me. I hate when we have to ride back to the station with a car full of vomit. I make sure he's done before putting him in the back, and Wilson deals with Grace and her shotgun.

Just a typical day on the job…which makes me want to run for sheriff even more.

Owen: Getaway tonight. Drinks on the house.
Me: You always say that, yet I always end up paying my tab.
Dean: WHAT!? YOU'RE ACTUALLY GOING OUT?
Me: No.
Logan: Isn't the hot nanny there?
Dean: I'm sure she is, and that's why he's not going out.
Owen: If I come over and misbehave, will she spank me?
Me: Grow the fuck up.
Dean: I take that to mean she's as hot as her photo made her seem.

I roll my eyes, silencing my phone. Another slew of text messages come through that I ignore. My brothers and I have had an ongoing group text for years that we mostly use for hurling insults or sending crude GIFs to each other.

Putting my phone in the top drawer of my desk, I take care of the rest of the paperwork and grab a coffee from the breakroom. After leaving the Green residence, we had one minor car accident, teenagers trying to shoplift at one of the two gas stations in Eastwood, and ended the shift by helping Betty Perez round up her goats that broke out of their pasture.

I close the file and take it to Sergeant Lopez's office, dropping it off on her desk. Sipping my coffee, I get my phone out to check on the house once more and see I have fifteen missed texts from my brothers and one from Mom. Knowing the texts in the group message Owen named *Bros before hoes* are most likely bullshit anyway, I ignore them for now and see what Mom had to say.

Assuming she's asking about the nanny, her words almost take me by surprise. She wants to make sure I'm okay and not sad…and I have no idea why. Usually she'll text me and ask me that same thing—in the exact same wording every time—when the subject of Daisy is brought up. But we haven't talked about my almost ex-wife recently, nor is it our anniversary or any—oh shit.

Today is Daisy's birthday. It wouldn't have crossed my mind if Mom hadn't texted me. I respond back to her, telling her I hadn't even realized what day it is and yes, I'm fine. I put the phone down again, thinking that it's time to move on from this and file the paperwork after all.

Chapter Seven

SCARLET

Come on, get it together. I inhale and open the fridge, trying to find something to make for dinner. My first day as Jackson's nanny is almost over, and it did not go as planned at all.

Today wasn't miserable. Time didn't crawl, and I didn't want to claw my eyes out or drown myself in a bottle of wine. Instead—dare I say it—I had fun. I didn't expect to like Jackson. I hoped to mildly tolerate him while I formulated a plan on how to con his dad out of a large sum of money, but events unfolded differently.

Jackson isn't a spoiled and entitled brat. I can tell teaching Jackson manners is important to Wes, and even though he comes off as a mean old grump, I sense he's a gentleman at heart. After only a day, the kid is growing on me, and I need to press pause—if not rewind—on this whole situation and go back to not giving a shit.

But, dammit, I can't.

"Do you want help making dinner?" Jackson asks, little feet slapping against the hardwood floor behind me.

"Uh, sure. What do you want?"

"Chicken nuggets and mac and cheese and pickles and maybe a cupcake for dessert."

I laugh. "Well, we can do the mac and cheese for sure." I grab butter and milk, setting them out the counter. "Pickles too," I add when I see the jar. I preheat the oven, glad there's a bag of dinosaur-shaped nuggets in the freezer.

It's not exactly a home-cooked meal, but the kid's not going hungry tonight. That has to count for something, right?

As the food is cooking, Jackson asks me to sit down and color with him. I bring a coloring book and a big box of crayons to the table.

"I'm going to draw a picture for Daddy," he tells me. "And one for you."

"Thanks, buddy." I carefully tear out the pages he wants and take one for myself, absentmindedly coloring Mickey Mouse in different shades of pink.

"Are you from Chicago?" he asks.

"I am."

"Aunt Winnie lived there. I went there before. We took a train!"

"I used to take the train a lot. It's pretty cool." Cool if you like the smell of piss and dealing with the assholes that always seem to be on the same route I am.

"It wasn't like Thomas the Train."

"No, I guess it's not." I trade my light pink crayon for a darker one.

"Actually, I'm going to give this picture to Emma."

"Who's Emma? A friend?"

Jackson shakes his head, and hair falls into his eyes. He looks so much like his father.

"My cousin. She's a baby."

A baby cousin? Must be Quinn's. I just smile and nod, not wanting to know any more about the Dawson family. Don't know, don't care. Once I get enough money to take care of Dad, I'll be out of here and won't give them a second thought.

"Emma and Uncle Archer have the same birthday."

"Mh-hm." I need to tune this out.

"And Uncle Archer cuts people open. For his job!"

"Wow, that is cool. He's a surgeon, right?" Dammit. I already know too much.

"Right. And he really cuts people open!" Jackson says slowly, eyes wide. "He saved me from the pool once. I almost died."

I stop coloring and look at Jackson. "You almost died?"

He nods and puts on a terrified look. It's fake, but he knows he's supposed to be upset when he talks about this. Smart kid. "I fell in and water got inside my breathing. I had to go to the hos-able!"

It takes me a second to realize "hos-able" is hospital. "That's scary. I'm glad you're okay now or else I wouldn't get to play with you all day."

He nods and starts coloring again. "Daddy was scared. I think he cried. Don't tell him I said that. Daddy doesn't cry. Not even when Mommy left."

"Your mommy left?"

Abort. Abort. Stop asking questions. The less personal info you have about Wes, the better.

"Daddy doesn't know where she is."

"Oh, um…" I have no idea what to say to that. I'm no good at this.

"She didn't love me enough to stay here." A line of worry forms between Jackson's eyes, and I hurt for him. I put my arm around his shoulders.

"That's not true. She must have just, uh…uh…had something else to do." It's a good thing I'm not posing as a counselor. The gig would be up on that one within minutes. "I'm sure she loves you in her own way."

"I don't know what she looks like. Maybe she's pretty like you."

"If she's lucky." I give him a wink.

He goes back to coloring, telling me about something that happened on an episode of *PAW Patrol*. I wrestle with my mind, and my mind ends up winning. So Jackson's mother left him when he was little, too little to remember her. Why? And how?

It. Doesn't. Matter.

Water boils over from the pot on the stove, hissing as it reaches the burner beneath. I jump up and turn the heat off, hoping I didn't ruin something as simple as boxed macaroni and cheese. Jackson keeps coloring as I drain the water, testing a noodle. It's a little overdone but isn't terrible.

I make the mac and cheese, cover it, and take the nuggets out of the oven. Weston should be back from work soon, and I suppose we can all eat together. My phone rings, and I know it's my sister right away.

"Hello?" I answer, waiting for the automated voice asking if I'll accept a call from an inmate.

"Hey, sis," Heather rushes out. "You didn't come visit me today. What gives?"

"I started a new job." Looking at Jackson, I step out of the kitchen. "I probably won't be able to come for a while, actually. I'm in rural Indiana."

"What the fuck are you—sorry, I won't swear anymore," she says to a guard. "What are you doing there?"

"I'm a nanny again."

A few seconds of silence pass, and I can only imagine Heather's stunned face. "Why?"

"I need money."

"But I had a job for you."

"I'm not doing that," I spit out, blood pressure rising. "No fucking way."

"But you've been all flirty with that C.O. He has it bad for you. Asks about you all the time."

"That doesn't mean I'll bring—just no. I keep him favorable in case you need an extra snack or if I ask him to look the other way if—no, when—you do something stupid. Like this. But I can't flirt my way into or out of this."

"You underestimate the power of your pussy."

"Heather," I start, pinching the bridge of my nose. She sounds manic, and she just went through a cycle a few weeks ago. "Are you taking your meds?"

"Yes! Jesus, Scar, stop trying to be my mother and be my sister for once, why don'tcha?"

"Trust me, I'd love nothing more." Unfortunately, I've been a mother to her since the day she was born. "I just…I just want you to get through your time and get out of there. No more talking with shady people who promise you protection in exchange for business, okay?" I step out of the kitchen and out of earshot. "Just keep your head down and behave."

She grumbles something but doesn't push the issue, mostly because she can't. Not over the phone. But even still, I'm not bringing drugs into a prison. I'm no Mother Teresa, but even I have my limits.

"So is this nannying gig going to turn out like the last one?" she asks.

"If I'm lucky."

"You *are* lucky, Scarlet. You're beautiful, and the world loves beautiful people."

"It's more than that." I sink down on the first step, feeling the threads I keep tightly wrapped around myself start to loosen. I tighten the threads back up until I can hardly breathe.

Not today, Satan.

"I have to go," I tell her. "Call me the next time you can, okay? And please, Heather, just keep to yourself."

"That's not how it works in here, sis. You gotta find a crew or you'll get eaten alive."

"You're in minimum security, Heath. Is it really that bad?"

"You have no idea," she says in a voice so icy it sends a chill through me. "Love you, Scarbutt."

"Love you too, bitch."

I end the call and close my eyes. She's in minimum security now, but I have a sinking feeling it's only a matter of time before she's sent to max. Dad's dying. My sister is in prison. Jason is overseas.

I'm so alone, and I just want my family back…though deep down I know I never really had one in the first place.

Chapter Eight

WESTON

"Daddy!" Jackson comes running, throwing his arms around me. Coming home to my son is the best part of my day. I never realize how much I miss this kid until his skinny little arms are wrapped around my neck. Scooping him up with one hand, I stand, pretending to drop him.

Jackson lets out a dramatic yell and then laughs hysterically. I do it again and get the same reaction.

"We made dinner!" he tells me excitedly, taking my hand as soon as his feet hit the floor. "Come eat!"

"Give me one minute, and I'll join you."

"It's just nuggets and mac and cheese," Scarlet says almost apologetically. She's still wearing the denim shorts she had on earlier but has added a button-up flannel shirt over her tank top. Her blonde hair is in a messy braid, with loose strands hanging around her face. Even a blind man would notice how gorgeous she is.

"Some of our favorites," I say and take off my shoes. I'm still in uniform with my gun strapped to my utility belt around my waist. I go upstairs to lock it up and change into gray sweatpants and a white T-shirt.

Scarlet is bringing plates to the table and does a double take when she sees me. I can't get a good read on her, and I don't get why everyday things seem surprising to her. Maybe it's a sign this isn't going to work out and I should let her go after the weekend is over, saying we're just not a good match.

Though that would be one hell of a lie. There are plenty of things I'd like to do with Scarlet where I think we'd be a match made in heaven.

"How was your day, buddy?" I ask Jackson, tearing my eyes away from Scarlet as she sets the final plate down on the table. Her shorts are tight in all the right places, and it's a battle of willpower not to steal another glance at her fine ass.

"It was so fun!" He puts his chicken nugget back down on his plate and bounces with excitement. "First, we played dinosaurs. Then Scarlet chased me around like a zombie!"

"Sounds like you had a pretty fun day." I smile, heart warming at the sight of his happy face.

"It was more fun than when I spend the day with Grammy, but don't tell her that." Jackson hunches his shoulders in as he speaks, making both Scarlet and me laugh.

"Your secret is safe with me," Scarlet promises.

Jackson takes one small bite of his food before starting up again, going through every single detail of the day. It sounds like he really did have fun, and it's nice knowing he was up and active and not stuck in front of a screen all day. Not that Mom gives him her phone with YouTube videos all the time or anything, but sometimes she has work to do and that's the only way to get shit done.

"Are we going to Grammy and Papa's this weekend?" Jackson asks.

"Yep," I reply and then flick my eyes to Scarlet. "We go to my parents' house for dinner almost every Sunday."

"That's nice." She pushes her mac and cheese around on her plate before taking a bite.

"Can Scarlet come too?" Jackson asks, eyes full of hope.

"Uh," I start, not knowing what to say. Scarlet lives with us—for now—but she's not part of the family. She has no obligation to do anything other than take care of Jackson, and Sunday is technically her day off. "If she wants to, she's welcome to come."

"Yay! Did you hear what my daddy said? You can come!"

"If she wants to," I stress.

"Please!" Jackson begs her. "Please oh please say yes!"

Scarlet laughs. "How can I say no to that face?"

Jackson gets so excited he jumps out of his chair and runs around the table to give Scarlet a hug.

"Eat," I gently remind him. "We have to go over letters and then get a bath in."

"We already did letters," he says, giving me a know-it-all look.

"Excuse me?" I raise my eyebrows.

With a dramatic sigh that he learned from Dean no doubt, he points to Scarlet. "We already did letters, Dad."

"He showed me his workbook and asked if we could do a page. He got lowercase 'b' and 'd' mixed up a few times, but other than that, he did a good job."

I'm not sure how to feel about this. Can this woman teach Jackson as well as I can? It's not like I'm an overqualified child educator, but he's my son.

"Thanks," I say.

"Can we go to the park then?" Jackson asks.

"Yeah, we'll have time before bed now."

"Yay!" Jackson drops his fork and starts clapping. I shift my gaze from him to Scarlet, taking in the slight smile pulling up her full lips. "Will you come too, Scarlet?" he asks.

"Of course!" She beams at him, and he jabbers away about his favorite things to do at the park the rest of dinner. I take Jackson upstairs to change into something a little warmer. The evening air takes on a chill once the sun goes down.

The park is two blocks away, and Jackson usually rides his bike while I walk behind. He still needs training wheels and struggles a bit when the sidewalk is uneven.

Scarlet changed into black leggings and a long-sleeve T-shirt and is walking in step next to me. I turn my head, unable to help but notice the way her breasts bounce with each step even though she's wearing a bra.

"You don't have to go to dinner with my family on Sunday," I start. "Don't feel pressured by Jackson. He'll get over it."

She gives me a pleasant smile. "I don't mind, really. I have nothing else to do. But if you don't want me there—"

"No, that's not it," I say quickly. Why do I care about offending her? I shouldn't.

I don't.

"They're a bit overbearing," I warn. "And there's a lot of them."

"Jackson was talking about an Uncle Archer."

I nod. "That's Quinn's fiancé. She's the youngest of my siblings and has a baby. Then there's Logan and Owen—they're identical twins—and then Dean and his wife, Kara."

"Four siblings and two more by marriage?" She laughs. "I can hardly handle the two I have."

"It's a lot, but I like it," I admit. "It's always loud and crazy, but that's the way it's always been."

"You must be close to Quinn."

"We're all pretty close." We stop at the edge of the street, and after making sure Jackson remembers the concept of looking both ways, we cross and make it down half the block before either of us speak.

"So," she starts, voice soft. She pushes a loose strand of hair from her face and turns to me, blue eyes sparkling in the fading sunlight. "Jackson mentioned his mother. He didn't go into detail, but I don't know how you want me handling the situation. He seemed a little upset."

Well, shit. I didn't think this fun piece of conversation would come up already. Out of the mouth of babes…

"We don't talk about her." I set my gaze forward, watching Jackson peddle his little heart out. Indiana is relatively flat all around, but there's a slight incline on the way to the park that he sometimes needs help with.

"Oh, okay. I'll just try to change the subject."

I let out a sigh, knowing that sooner or later, this is going to all come out, and I'd rather have Scarlet hear it from me than anyone else.

"Jackson's mother left a few weeks after he was born. She came back once, stayed a few days, and that's the last time I've seen or heard anything from her. When Jackson asks, I tell him Daisy had other things to do." I shrug. "It's not the best response, but nothing is a good response in that situation."

"I'm sorry," Scarlet says, and I brush off her words. I don't want pity. I get along just fine, and raising my son on my own for the last four years allowed us to bond in a way we couldn't if Daisy was still in the picture.

"Slow down," I call out to Jackson, who spotted one of his friends at the park. We have one more street to cross. Picking up the pace, I catch up to him before he zooms across the street. We wait for a pickup to go by, and then he rides as fast as he can to the playground, dumping his bike to the ground and pulling at his helmet strap as he runs to the swing set.

I wave to Mrs. Hills, the mother of Jackson's friend, and motion to a park bench. Scarlet follows, eyes wide as she takes it all in.

"What part of Chicago are you from?" I ask.

"The South Side." She gives me a lopsided smile. "Yes, the ghetto."

Nodding, I decide that's enough information to share for one night. She's my employee, after all. The wind picks up, blowing in the scent of rain. Scarlet shivers and pulls her arms in around herself. The faint outline of her nipples becomes visible through her shirt, and I take off my jacket to give to her.

"Thanks." She slips her arms inside the sleeves, thinking I'm being chivalrous. Really, I'm helping out my dick.

"Dad! Scarlet!" Jackson yells from the top of a slide. "Come watch me go down the slide. It's super fast!"

We both get up, going across the playground to watch Jackson go down a twisty slide. He grabs Scarlet's hand and leads her up the playground steps. My phone buzzes in my pocket, no doubt more texts from my brothers.

"Good evening, Officer Dawson," Mrs. Hills croons, sauntering over. She got divorced last year and makes sure everyone knows just how single she is every time she talks.

"Hello, Mrs. Hills."

"Please, call me Terry. Our boys go to school together. We're practically family at this point."

I force a smile, realizing that running for sheriff means having to put up with bullshit small talk and pleasantries. Maybe I don't want to do it after all.

"I can't help but notice your companion," she goes on. "Finally free?" She wiggles her eyebrows hopefully.

"She's Jackson's nanny," I reply, sidestepping her question. Sometimes I hate this small town as much as I love it. Everyone knows Daisy ran out on us and I haven't petitioned for a divorce yet.

"Well, she's very pretty."

"I suppose so."

"Are you coming to the kids' fall party at school next week?"

Motherfucker. It's next week? "I'm not sure. We'll see how much crime happens that morning."

Terry laughs like it's the funniest thing in the world, and Scarlet snaps her head around. Her eyes flit from me to Terry, taking a second to watch us before turning back to Jackson.

"Well, I'm in charge of snacks, and if you want, I can bring you something extra. Maybe something a little sweet?" She angles her body toward mine, inhaling so her breasts rise up in front of me. "Or do you prefer salty?"

Doing everything I can not to physically recoil from her, my phone ringing at that exact moment is welcome.

"It's my sister. Gotta take this," I say.

"Quinn? Tell her I said hello!" Quite a few people in this town were quick to judge Quinn when they found out she was pregnant and not married. Then they remembered she was rich and suddenly are her best friend again.

"Hey, sis," I say into the phone.

"Hey. So…how'd it go today?"

"The day isn't over yet."

"Uh-oh. Is that a bad thing?"

I watch Scarlet run in slow motion as Jackson and his friend chase her around, pretending to be the zombies this time. "No. Jackson seems to really like her."

"Good! She was really nice when we met at the coffee shop."

I don't feel like getting into it with my sister tonight, but we've all tried to explain to her that just because someone seems nice doesn't mean they should be trusted. But that's just Quinn for you, always finding the good in everyone.

"We'll see how it goes. I'm still not sold on this, you know."

"Make up your damn mind. If you want to pull out of the race, just do it already. If not, we need to amp up your campaigning."

"I thought you were certain I'd win," I tease.

"I am. But people need to know you're running against that sexist old Sheriff Turner so they can vote for you."

Chuckling, I agree. "Okay. Give me to the end of the week. If this works out, we'll go all the way with this."

"Yay! Oh, shit. Emma just puked all over Archer and he was on his way out the door to do an emergency appendectomy."

"I don't miss those days. See ya later, sis."

"Love you. Give Jackson a kiss for me!"

"Will do."

Chapter Nine

SCARLET

I PULL THE BLANKETS TIGHTER AROUND MY SHOULDERS AND BRING MY LEGS UP under myself. It started raining not long after we got back from the park, and it dropped the temperature by twenty degrees. A damp chill took hold of the house, and while the heater is on and running, I haven't warmed up yet.

Which has nothing to do with my cold heart, I'm sure.

Wes put Jackson to bed, and knowing that he actually *wants* to spend time with his son is charming. Wait, no it's not. There's nothing charming about him. Nope. Not at all. And he certainly didn't look good in those gray sweatpants. And offering me his jacket wasn't a smooth move or anything. And putting my arms in the sleeves of said jacket and feeling the heat from his body was a turn-off. Big time.

He's closed off but not socially inept, and his charm isn't lost on the people of this town. Ms. Soccer Mom at the park was flirting with him, and we got stopped three times on the short walk home. Two more single women just "wanted to say hi" and find out who I was, of course. His next-door neighbors are an elderly couple, and they thanked him for helping mow their lawn a few days ago.

He's the golden boy of this town, and pulling any sort of trick on him will probably cause the townspeople to grab their torches and pitchforks and march after me while singing "Kill the Beast."

I roll over, debating if I should get up and get socks or if moving out of the covers will make me even more cold. I cuddle my unicorn close to my chest and make myself into a little ball, too lazy to get up.

Someone softly knocks at the door, and I shoot up, thinking it's Jackson.

"Scarlet?" Weston calls, voice low. "Are you awake?"

Suddenly, I'm nervous, and it's not because I don't want him to come in here and make an advance. It's because I do.

"Yeah, I am." I get up, pulling the top quilt from the bed and wrapping it around my shoulders. Ignoring the urge to smooth out my hair, I open the door. Weston is standing there, wearing a white T-shirt and plaid PJ pants. The look is casual, completely appropriate, and not at all sexy. So why do I feel heat rushing through me?

"I never opened the vents in here." He motions to something on the ceiling. "I just remembered."

"Oh, um, how do you open them? I'll do it."

"I got it." He doesn't look at me, and for some reason, it annoys me. "You probably won't be able to reach it." Stepping aside, I flick on the light and pull the blanket tighter around my shoulders. "It's cold in here. Sorry," he mumbles and walks through the room, reaching up and opening the vents. Warm air rushes down on me. He turns to leave and spots the unicorn on my pillow.

"You sleep with that?" he asks, lips pulling up with a bit of amusement.

"Every night. His name is Ray."

"Interesting name," Wes says.

The half smile turns into a real smile and, dammit, it's doing bad things to me. I sit on my bed and pick Ray up. "He's yellow, like a ray of sunshine."

"That makes sense, I guess."

I shrug. "I've had him forever. I know it's weird."

"There are weirder things to have in bed."

I raise my eyebrows. "Speaking from experience?"

"Unfortunately, no."

"I suppose that's good to know," I laugh.

Weston smiles, holding my gaze for a few seconds, and I see the man under the tough exterior. He's a bit damaged, like me, and the strangest feeling takes over, making me want to comfort him. Then he stiffens, inhaling deep and pushing his shoulders back. I watch his chest muscles rise and fall, feeling so little next to him.

"Goodnight," he says and walks right past me out the door. He doesn't shut it behind him, and I watch him disappear down the hall. Jackson is in his own room tonight, and Wes closes his door halfway, probably leaving it open to be able to hear if I get out of bed and decide to kidnap his son or something.

I close my door, twisting the knob before it clicks into place, silently shutting it. Then I get back in bed, still cold but feeling hot and flustered inside. Along with having little experience with good parents, I have little experience with good guys. My track record is unimpressive, and I haven't had anything serious since I broke up with Tommy three and a half years ago.

I can feel warm air filling the room, but I'm still chilled. I get up and grab a pair of socks from my suitcase—no, I haven't unpacked yet and probably won't until I've worn everything at least once and doing laundry is a necessity. Hunkering back down into bed, I curl up with Ray and fall asleep.

It shouldn't surprise me that I dream of Weston. Of his large, rough hands running up the back of my thighs. Of his lips against mine as he kisses his way down my neck, over my breasts, and down my stomach. He yanks off my panties and dives between my legs, and his warm tongue against me is the best thing I've ever felt.

I wake up with my hand between my legs, body begging to go back to sleep and finish the dream. Rain patters against the window, and I let out a breath, no longer cold. I close my eyes and try to get comfortable, but I'm too hot and bothered to peacefully fall back asleep.

What am I doing wrong here? Well, besides wanting to cheat an honest man out of money—don't judge me on that. That's a topic for another day, one that will require confession, ten Hail Marys, and hours of community service.

Weston isn't a wealthy asshole with money to burn. I can't convince myself I'm a sexy Robin Hood with him, stealing from the rich to give to the poor—aka me. I can't take anything from him. I don't want to.

I hoped to get through to him, to knock down his walls and see what makes him tick. But I think he's going to get to me first…and he's not even trying.

I plunge my hands into the warm, soapy water. I didn't sleep well last night, and around five AM I gave up and came downstairs to start breakfast. Wes works today and said he leaves the house around seven.

So far, I've made blueberry muffins, cooked an entire package of bacon, and have eggs whipped up and ready to scramble once the boys come downstairs. They're best fresh out of the pan and don't take long to make. I've piled the bacon onto a plate and put it in the oven to stay warm. The muffins are neatly arranged in a bowl on the table. I even found a white cloth napkin to put in the bowl first, making it look all fancy and proper.

And now the dishes are almost done, and the table is already set. Show me an attractive single dad and suddenly I turn into Betty fucking Crocker.

What.

The.

Fuck.

Compartmentalizing and not dealing with my feelings is my thing. My claim to fame. The only reason I've been able to get by this well for so long. My deck has always been stacked a few cards short, and in a dog-eat-dog world, I've never had the chance to stop and think about a better life.

And I mean really think.

Like muffins and bacon kind of thinking.

Opening the oven, I grab a piece of bacon before making a pot of coffee. The smell of French roast fills the air, and something inside me relaxes.

"Morning," Wes says when he comes into the kitchen. He's dressed in his uniform, and he looks so good I don't think I'd be surprised if someone started playing "Hot in Here" and he started taking off all his clothes in a private strip show just for me.

I'd grab the bacon, sit back, and watch.

"Morning," I say back, going to the cabinet to get him a coffee cup. Assuming he'll have his coffee the same way he did yesterday, I fill the cup and add just a little bit of cream and sugar. "Do you want eggs? I was just about to make some."

Wes's brows move together, and he looks around the kitchen as if I finger-painted the furniture, not made him breakfast.

"Sure."

"Okay. Have a seat. It'll only take a few minutes." I already preheated the pan. With my back to him, I focus on the eggs, doing my best not to turn around and make small talk, because I know if I look into Weston's dark eyes, there's a good chance I'll turn into a pile of goo on the floor.

And then who's going to finish making breakfast?

"You didn't have to do all this," Weston says in a level tone. "We usually eat cereal or Pop Tarts in the morning."

"I was up, and that's the kind of thing I usually eat too. Something hot for breakfast sounded nice."

I turn down the burner and risk a look back at Weston. He's pulled his hair away from his face and is leaning back in the kitchen chair. He looks right at me, and something burns behind his stormy eyes.

"Yeah, a hot breakfast is nice every now and then."

He's literally agreeing with words I just spoke, yet I'm feeling flush like he's filling every syllable with a secret innuendo. And dammit—I want him to. And now there's no denying that Weston Dawson has done the impossible: gotten under my skin and is weaseling his way into that dark cavity in my chest that some call a heart.

Chapter Ten

WESTON

Goddammit. Bacon and eggs and blueberry muffins have never tasted so good. Scarlet piles bacon and eggs on her plate, fills a mug halfway with coffee and then tops it off the rest of the way with creamer. She dumps a spoonful of sugar in it as well, bringing her food over to the table. Her hair is pulled up in a messy bun, and the loose strands that fall around her face are begging to be pushed back.

She's wearing black leggings and a tight black T-shirt, with a loose-fitting red-and-black flannel shirt over top. She's effortlessly beautiful, and I can't find a single thing about her to complain about.

"Blueberry muffins are cliché." She reaches for one, setting it on her plate. "But it was the only kind I could make. You guys must like blueberries."

I smile as I finish chewing a piece of bacon. "Jackson eats them like candy."

"That's good. Better than eating candy like candy." She laughs at herself, realizing what she said. "You know what I mean."

"Yeah, I do. And I agree. He's always been a good eater in that sense."

She picks up a piece of bacon. "I can relate to that."

A few minutes of silence go by as we both eat our breakfast. It's still gray and cloudy outside, but Scarlet is brightening up the whole room. "When does Jackson usually get up?" she asks.

"Eight-thirty or nine if he's able. Usually when I work on a Saturday, I take him to my parents' and have to wake him up early. He'll be happy to sleep in today."

Scarlet nods, finishing her bacon and eggs. She goes for the muffin next. "Are your parents retired?"

I shake my head, picking up the coffee. "No. My dad's a contractor, and my mom works with him running the office aspect of the business."

"What do your brothers do? Are any of them cops as well?"

I laugh at the thought of Owen or Logan in uniform. "No. Dean works with our dad, and Logan and Owen own a bar called Getaway."

"In town?"

"Yeah. It's pretty much the only good bar around here, and I'm not just saying that because my brothers own it."

"I've only seen quite literally two blocks of this town, but I'm guessing there's not much to it?"

"Eastwood isn't huge, but we have more than you'd think…I think." If she's used to Chicago, then she's not going to be impressed by our little town. "We're not some podunk town in the middle of nowhere," I go on. "If the weather clears up, I can show you around."

She smiles. "I'd like that. Better get used to things here, right?"

I open my mouth but can't make the word come out. It's easy. One syllable. *Right*. But saying that one word feels like I'm saying a magic spell that seals our fate. She's here. To stay. Which means there's a good chance of winning this race, which of course is the end goal. But that means being away from Jackson more, and it's suddenly hitting me like a punch to the face.

"Yeah," I finally force myself to say and get up for a refill of coffee. Scarlet's almost done with her muffin by the time I get back.

"You eat a lot for someone of your size," I blurt, needing to fill the silence with something.

She smiles, finishing the last bit of her muffin. "I do a lot of bad things, and I think the guilt inside of me burns a lot of calories." Her eyes meet mine for a second, and I laugh.

"I didn't realize that was the key to dieting."

She winks. "It's a secret. Don't tell anyone."

Still smiling, I clear my plate from the table. "Thanks for breakfast. Jackson will be thrilled to have bacon when he gets up."

"Should I wake him up at any particular time?"

"No, you can let him sleep in. He might wake up when I go say bye to him."

Scarlet gets that surprised look again. "That's sweet you tell him goodbye."

"I always do."

She drops her gaze to her hands, blinking rapidly. I fill a to-go mug with coffee, fully aware of my caffeine addiction, though I think a caffeine addiction is almost a requirement when you're a parent, let alone a single one.

Quietly, I go into Jackson's room and pull the blankets back over him. The kid sleeps like an octopus, and his pillows, blankets, and stuffed animals always end up on the floor.

"Love you," I whisper and kiss him on the top of the head. "See you tonight, buddy."

∞

"I have no idea where Jackson is," Scarlet tells me, raising her shoulders in a dramatic shrug. The pile of blankets behind her on the couch moves, and Jackson giggles from inside.

"Oh no," I say back. "Where could he be?" Jackson laughs again, and I take off my shoes and stride to the couch. "I'll go look for him after I sit down for a bit." Perching on the edge of the couch, I slowly lean back against Jackson. "This pillow is lumpy." I pretend to fluff it, and Jackson pops up from under the blankets.

"Boo!"

"What?" I lean back, eyes wide. "I didn't know you were there!"

"I tricked you, I tricked you!" Jackson chants. He jumps into my arms, and everything is right in the world.

"What did you do today?" I ask, though I already have an idea. Scarlet texted a few photos throughout the day. It rained all morning, and they built a pretty epic fort in the living room. She was laying down inside it next to Jackson in one of the photos she sent. Jackson's face was scrunched up, eyes closed with a toothy smile.

Then it seems they played with Jackson's farm set the rest of the day, which is his current favorite thing. The handmade, wooden barn was mine when I was a kid, and Jackson thinks it's extra special knowing I played with it when I was his age.

Jackson tells me about his day, and Scarlet goes back into the kitchen. I can't see what she's doing, but it sounds like she's chopping vegetables. We don't have vegetables. Well, not fresh ones anyway. I desperately need to go grocery shopping, but Jackson's been a pain in the ass to take with lately, and I'm ready to bang my head against the wall by the time our shopping trip is over.

"Can I play at Dillan's house after dinner?" Jackson asks. Dillan lives across the street. His sister is in Jackson's preschool class with him, but girls currently have cooties, and Jackson wants nothing to do with her. Which is fine by me.

"Maybe for a little bit."

"Until it gets dark?"

"You can see if he wants to play here," I offer, liking it better when Jackson brings friends here as opposed to him going to a friend's house. I can keep a better eye on them...which is probably what every parent on the face of the earth thinks.

"Yay! Thanks, Dad!" Jackson gives me a hug and jumps off the couch.

Scarlet peeks out of the kitchen, knife in hand. Yep. She was chopping something. "You still need to go pick up your farm toys, buddy," she tells him. "You promised you'd pick them up before dinner."

"Okay," Jackson says without so much as a glare or a stomp of his little foot. He hurries up the stairs, and I look back in Scarlet's direction, thinking I hired a witch instead of a nanny because there's no way Jackson agrees to cleaning this easily.

Once the shock wears off, I go into the kitchen to make sure Scarlet is cooking dinner and not chopping up frog legs or eye of newt and adding it into a cauldron.

"Hey," she says with a smile, looking up from the cutting board. She's chopping carrots and adding them to a Corningware dish.

"Where'd the veggies come from?" I ask, bypassing telling her how spellbinding she looks with her hair in messy waves hanging around her face, wearing a simple black tunic and gray leggings.

"Ms. Hills *accidentally* bought too much at the farmers' market today." Scarlet raises her eyebrows. "Imagine that."

I plow a hand through my hair, smiling. "Yeah, she's...uh..."

"Totally hot for you?"

"That's not how I'd phrase it, but...yeah...I suppose so."

Scarlet chops up a few more pieces of the carrot and adds them to the dish. "I can't blame her." She flicks her eyes up, a small smile playing on her lips. Inhaling deep, Scarlet's breasts rise and fall beneath her scoop-neck shirt.

"What are you making?" I ask, trying to steer myself back into PG territory. Because my cock is making this conversation want to go into the *adults-only* section.

"I'm not really sure," she admits with a laugh. "I found this recipe on Pinterest." She grabs her phone to show me what she's making.

"Looks good."

She grabs an onion and starts slicing. "How was work?"

"Slow today, which isn't a bad thing."

"No," she agrees. "Not at all." She turns her head, blinking fast. "Oh my god. It really does burn your eyes."

"The onion?"

"Yes." Laughing, she sets the knife down and squeezes her eyes closed. "My eyes are watering like crazy!" She opens her eyes again only to shut them a second later. She wipes at them with the back of her hand, still laughing at herself.

"It can't be that bad," I say and stride over to cut up the rest of the onion for her. But the second I get next to the cutting board, my own eyes start to burn.

"Okay, you're right. This has to be the strongest onion in the world."

Laughing, she turns away and takes a step forward and walks right into me. Her supple breasts crash against my chest, sending a wave of heat right to the tip of my cock. She bounces off me, and I reach out, hands landing on the gentle curves of both her hips to steady her.

With her eyes still closed, she reaches forward with one hand, flattening it against my chest. Slowly, she trails her hand down until it's resting just inches above my belt. Her lips part, and my heart speeds up. I wonder if she can feel my pulse racing, if she knows what her body close to mine is doing to me. If she brought her hand lower or moved just a tiny bit closer, she'd feel it. My fingertips dig into her flesh, soaking up all the warmth I can through her shirt.

She smells like lavender and strawberries, an intoxicating scent on its own, but so welcome over the smell of the onion. I want to move close and breathe it in, but getting close to Scarlet is a bad fucking idea.

Clearing my throat, I tear myself away before this semi turns into a full erection.

"How are you able to keep your eyes open?" she laughs, blinks hers open for just a few seconds.

"I have superpowers."

"Well, then use them and chop up the rest of the onion." That smile looks so good on her, even with the red, watery eyes. She goes to the sink, washes her hands, and rubs her eyes. "Okay…that's a little better. But, oh my God, I had no idea it got that bad!"

"Have you never chopped an onion before?"

She shakes her head. "It's been a while. And I'm not the best cook, so don't hold it against me if dinner tonight sucks."

"I'm not a good cook either, so I won't." Besides…there are other things I want to hold against her. Swallowing hard, I take one last look at her before tearing my eyes away and going upstairs to change.

"Dad, look!" Jackson calls when I walk past his room. "I cleaned up!"

"You did a great job, bud!" I go into his room, impressed by how thorough the kid was.

"Do you think Scarlet will be proud of me?"

"I know she will be. I am."

"Really?"

"Of course!"

He makes a face. "You're just saying that because you're my dad."

I laugh. "Well, I suppose I am a little biased. But you are a good kid. Most of the time."

"What am I the other times?"

"Rotten. And a stinker."

Jackson laughs. "No, I'm not!"

"Yeah, you are," I tease and poke at his sides, making him erupt in giggles. He climbs onto my lap and runs his finger over my badge.

"I love you, Daddy," he says softly.

"And I love you."

I dozed off putting Jackson to bed and woke up not knowing what time it was. Or what day it was. Or my name. Napping always does that to me. All I know is it's late, and I'm way too old to sleep contorted in a twin bed around my wiggling four year old.

Light from the living room TV filters up the stairs. Scarlet is huddled on the couch, knees drawn up to her chest. She's wearing a baggy sweatshirt and tight black shorts. Her hair is piled on the top of her head, and her eyes are wide.

The bottom stair creaks under my weight, and Scarlet jumps, knocking a pillow off the couch.

"Jesus!"

"Again, just me," I say with a cheeky grin. "You're jumpy." I flick my eyes to the TV. "And now I see why."

"Have you watched this?" she asks, picking up the remote and pausing the horror show she's watching.

"Not all of it. I'm up to episode four."

"I'm not even through the third episode and I don't know if I can handle the rest."

"It is creepy. They did a good job with this show."

She picks up the pillow and stretches her long legs out on the coffee table. "Want to watch it with me? You can hold me accountable not to chicken out."

"Should I indulge you with junk food too?"

A smile plays across her face. "I'm starting to think you get me, Mr. Dawson."

"You know you can call me Wes, right?"

The smile gets bigger. "It makes me feel like I'm on the *Titanic*."

"What?" I ask, my own lips curving into a half-smile.

"Seriously?" She pushes up on the couch and leans forward, and God help me, I can see down her shirt. She's dressed for bed and not wearing a bra.

"I'm not following." I run my hand over my face, needing to physically block out the sight of her perfect breasts.

"Isn't that part of the reason you named your son Jackson, so you could call him Jack Dawson?"

I shake my head again. "He's named after my grandfather."

"Oh. Well then, never mind." She leans back only to round on me again. "So you're telling me you've never seen the movie *Titanic*?"

"Can't say I have."

"We can't be friends now," she says seriously.

"That puts a strain on this whole situation, doesn't it?"

"It does." She slowly moves her head back and forth and picks up the remote again. "If only there was a way to solve it."

"You want me to watch *Titanic*, don't you?"

Laughing, she nods. "Not tonight, though. Tonight, we need to find out why angry spirits are haunting this family."

"Go ahead and keep watching," I tell her and cross the room. "I've already seen this episode."

Several minutes later, I come back with popcorn, Oreos, and a bag of chips.

"You delivered on that junk food," Scarlet says, folding her legs up under herself, freeing space on the couch. She pats the seat next to her and I can't move. Usually, the floor is lava and Jackson and I are jumping off it onto the couch, but right now it feels like it's the other way around.

"Do you like horror movies?" I ask, forcing myself to take a step forward and place the food on the coffee table.

"I do. I have a slight fascination with paranormal stuff. What about you?"

"They're okay. Most are lame nowadays, though. I miss the old slasher flicks from my childhood."

She tips her face up to me, eyebrow raised. "You watched a lot of slashers when you were a kid?"

"Actually, no. I watched them at a friend's house when I'd spend the night and then would have to lie about why I was so scared when I came home. My parents were kinda strict."

"Mine weren't." She grabs the bowl of popcorn, and I'm still standing there, eyeing her down like she's Kryptonite and I'm Clark Kent. "My dad wasn't around much until later." As soon as the words leave her lips, she leans back, almost as if she's surprised with herself for the confession. Seeming a bit flustered, she shoves a handful of popcorn in her mouth and grabs a blanket off the arm of the couch.

I go around the coffee table and sit on the couch, moving a pillow in between us.

"The flashbacks threw me," I say, wanting to break the silence. "I'm not good at remembering names in shows."

"Yeah, it took me a minute to get it too."

I watch her face, knowing a rotten body is going to fall out on screen when the closet door opens. Scarlet's eyes widen, but she doesn't jump.

I did.

"This house is old." She turns to me, pulling the blankets tighter over her shoulders. "But it's not haunted, is it?"

"I've never seen anything. And even though Jackson says he does, I don't really believe him. I'd think he'd be scared if he saw a real ghost."

"So you believe in ghosts?"

"I haven't seen enough to sway me either way."

"Smart man." She takes another handful of popcorn, and by the way she shuts down, I have a feeling she has seen something to sway her. But not necessarily a spirit. Something more real. Something that can hurt you in a way a ghost can't.

We finish the rest of the episode in silence, and then the next one starts. I'll admit, this show is creepy. There's something about weird shit happening to everyday people to get you thinking and make you become paranoid…which is exactly what the writers of this show wanted. They succeeded.

Halfway through the new episode, I reach for the chips the same time Scarlet does. My hand brushes over hers.

"Your skin is freezing," I say, using it as an excuse to take her small hand in mine. I splay my fingers over hers, sandwiching her hand between both of mine. Her skin is cold but so smooth and soft. Blood rushes through me, and the tip of my cock tingles, imagining that small, soft hand wrapping around it.

"My feet are even colder." She shifts her weight and pushes her freezing cold feet underneath me, laughing. "They get cold at night. I used to want a dog just so I could have them lay in bed and keep my feet warm."

"That's a good reason to get a dog."

"I know, right?"

I let go of her hand and move mine to her feet, cupping them both against my palm.

"You're so warm," she says quietly and leans back. I start to rub her feet—to be helpful, of course. There's no need to make her be cold.

"I tend to run warm. I'm always hot."

"I'm the opposite. I get cold easily and my hands and feet feel like ice if the temp drops below eighty."

I laugh. "I can tell."

She lays back, throwing the blanket over her legs. I don't mean to keep rubbing her feet, but I do, making sure she's properly warmed up. She twists, laying on her side but keeping her feet on my lap. I swallow hard, tempted to run my hands down to her thigh and see if the skin on her calves is as smooth and soft as I think it'll be.

She inhales deeply, slowly moving her feet against my thigh, and I can't help but think she's doing it on purpose. Does she know the effect she's having on me? Certainly a woman like Scarlet is well fucking aware of what she can do to a man.

Episode four ends and five begins, and Scarlet's legs are still draped over me. This episode is even freakier than the last, and Scarlet does jump a time or two. When episode six starts, we're both too far down the rabbit hole to stop. Scarlet gets up to use the bathroom, hurrying down the hall during the opening credits.

"I was convinced someone was going to jump out of that closet and bring me into the spirit world," she says when she gets back, taking her spot on the couch. Instead of leaning against the arm on the opposite side, she moves the pillow between us and scoots closer. "Feel." She holds out her hands, and I freeze, mouth going dry as I raise my gaze to her face.

Her blue eyes are wide, and red-and-blue flashes from the TV illuminate her face. A slight flush colors her cheeks, and her full lips are parted. She's so damn pretty it hurts.

"I think you were taken into the spirit world." I wrap my hands around hers. "You're even colder than before."

"Time probably stopped for you out here, and I was in there for like an hour at least, getting my soul sucked out by demons."

"That is the most likely explanation." Before I can stop myself, I push a loose strand of her hair back out of her face. She shivers, closing her eyes in a long blink and then inches closer. "I'll turn up the heat. Jackson runs hot too."

"He gets it from you."

I nod, eyes falling from hers to her breasts. "My brothers are the same way. My mom and Quinn were always freezing, but they learned to deal," I add with a laugh. Goosebumps break out along her arm, and I slide my hand up, feeling each tiny bump covering her flesh. My heart hammers loudly in my chest as I fight against every fiber in my being.

I want to pull her close. I have the perfect opportunity screaming at me. It's like the universe is throwing me a bone, trying to make up for the shit I've trudged through before. There's no denying the attraction between us, and maybe I'm out of practice, or all together too damn hopeful, but I feel something with Scarlet.

Something I haven't felt in a long, long time.

Something I never even felt with Daisy.

But I can't. She's Jackson's nanny. She's here for him, and he's the only thing that matters.

Chapter Eleven

SCARLET

I forgot about conning this man. I forgot about wanting to squeeze every penny I could and leave without so much as a look back. I forgot about my old life, about the shit I have to deal with on a daily basis.

For the last four episodes of this scary-as-shit show, all I've been able to think about is 1.) we are probably going to die at the hands of evil spirits tonight and 2.) Weston is so big and so warm and it's taking every ounce of self-control I have not to move over and lean against him.

I want to feel his hands on me. His lips against mine. I want to at the very least press my hand to his muscular chest and see if his heart is racing, because mine is. And it's not only from being scared of this show.

It's because I know I'm walking a fine line, one that puts me at risk. And I don't take risks, not like this at least. When my heart is involved, I'm out. It hasn't been an issue for me before, because I've come to believe my heart is shriveled and small like the Grinch's, but unlike a children's story, no amount of singing and kindness can make mine grow and start beating inside my chest.

It can't.

Because beating hearts get broken.

The floor creaks above us and I tense, turning to Wes with wide eyes. "Please tell me you have a cat I don't know about."

Slowly, he turns his head to look at me, eyes vacant. "No cat. Just the Tall Man." He looks at me, unblinking. My heart speeds up. I swallow hard, waiting for him to crack.

He doesn't.

"The Tall Man's coming for you," Weston whispers, almost scaring me before he starts to laugh.

I throw a pillow at him. "Jerk!"

"I totally got you," he says, still laughing.

"Not funny!"

Wes picks up the pillow and tosses it back at me. I tuck it behind me and scoot a little closer to him.

"But really...what was that?"

"When the heater kicks off it causes the whole house to creak. There's a lot of sounds you'll get used to. The pipes rattle when someone is in the shower. Or the dishwasher is running. If you open the windows upstairs, a draft comes down the stairs and blows the front door shut, and sometimes when you turn on the back porch light, it makes the hallway light come on."

"And you say this house isn't haunted."

Wes laughs again, and dammit, I need to look away. Because this man is beautiful when he smiles. "It's faulty wiring and a drafty old house with poor insulation."

"Keep telling yourself that, mister."

He leans back and puts his feet up on the coffee table. "It's three AM. You're sleep-deprived and it's making you paranoid," he teases. "We should probably call it a night."

I grab his arm before he gets up, and the moment my fingers touch his warm skin, I regret it. Because now I know he's as warm as I imagined, and I'm drawn to him like a moth to a flame.

Though, unlike the moth, I know what will happen if I succumb and fly right into the bright light. I don't feel like burning to a crisp today, so I pull back.

"We have two episodes left. I won't be able to sleep until I know how this ends. Stay with me?" I meant to say *stay and watch it with me*, but somehow the other words got lost on the way out.

Wes is standing above me, with the light from the TV illuminating his back. He's so big and so tall, and with his long, messy hair hanging around his handsome face, it's like I'm sitting before Thor himself. I swallow hard, lips parting, preparing myself for him to go up to bed.

Alone.

Which would be a good thing. The *right thing*.

For him.

For me.

And for Jackson.

But I've never been good at doing the right thing.

"Sure," Wes says, and I watch his beautiful lips curve into a smile. My body is reacting *hard* to him, and I have to reel in my libido. Trying to convince myself his physical attraction is the only thing that's pulling me to him, I put a pillow in my lap and tuck my legs firmly underneath myself.

Wes settles back onto the couch, and the TV show cuts to a scene of a bright and sunny day, contrasting with the dark and gloomy mood of the rest of the show. The light illuminates Wes's face, and I take a few seconds to study him.

It's the middle of the night. We're both tired, and if he's anything like me, he's questioning the existence of ghosts and demons right about now and feeling very vulnerable.

Very human.

He rests his head against the back of the couch, and this is the most relaxed, the most *real* I've seen him with the exception of the moments he's with Jackson. Right now, sitting here in the dark, the walls have been lowered, and he's not resisting the fact that I'm here. I get not wanting to admit you want help, but what I don't get is why Wes seems resentful of the fact that he needs a nanny.

Maybe it has to do with Jackson's mother, who walked out on them?

"I didn't see that coming," Wes says, pulling my attention back to the TV. I look away from his face, and it takes me a few seconds to catch up to the twist that was revealed.

"That's fucked up," I mutter, shaking my head.

"Yeah, it is. But it explains why the shadows always followed her."

"Ohhh, it does."

Tiredness grips me, and if I were to lay down and close my eyes, I'd be asleep in minutes. I want to see how this show ends because I know once I get up and walk up to my room, I'll be awake enough to lay there terrified the shadows cast by inanimate objects will manifest into dark spirits.

And I like being here next to Weston.

It's weird. It doesn't make sense. We're not talking. Not touching. Yet his presence is calming, and the faint scent of his woodsy cologne clings to his muscular body, and I know if I were to inch close and snuggle up, resting my head on his chest so I could count his heartbeats, the smell would fill my nostrils and I'd be a goner. There's something about an attractive man who smells good that makes them irresistible.

I'm so comfortable right now and feel so safe around him. I close my eyes for just a minute.

"Scarlet," Weston whispers. "Scarlet."

My eyes flutter open, and I realize I've fallen to the side, drifting to sleep. Wes is looking down at me, his face dangerously close to mine.

"You're falling asleep," he says with a chuckle. "Go to bed."

"No way." I stretch out, moving closer to him. "We're too far in to give up now. I don't take you to be a quitter."

Wes laughs again. "I'm not, though I never looked at turning off the TV because it's now almost four AM as quitting."

"We've got, what, one episode left? It's quitting in my book."

"Well, I guess we have to watch until the end." The smile is still on his face as he leans back, but the second he relaxes, he gets up again, moving in between the couch and the coffee table, reaching over to get the blanket that fell onto the floor. He grabs it and spreads it over me.

My heart speeds up, and suddenly I feel like I'm in a rickety boat, being tossed about in stormy water. Not because Wes scares me, but because he does the exact opposite.

You're walking the line of dangerous territory, I remind myself. He's my boss. Sleeping with your boss is never a good idea.

"Thanks." I smooth out the blanket and sit up, fixing the pillows. "Is it just my imagination or is it colder in here now?"

"It's colder. I have the heat set to go down a few degrees between midnight and five AM. It goes back up at six-thirty, around the time Jackson gets up." His brows furrow. "Though I suppose I can change it to seven-thirty now since he doesn't have to get up so early anymore."

I nod, knowing what he's talking about. They used to leave the house around seven in order to drop Jackson off at Wes's parents' before Wes went in for work.

"Are you cold?" I ask him, swinging my legs over the side of the couch and offering to share the blanket.

"I'm okay," he says and kicks his feet back up on the coffee table.

"Really?" I ask dubiously and reach out—against my better judgment, of course—and press my hand against his bicep. "You are warm." I push up and eye him suspiciously. "Are you really a shifter?"

"Huh?"

I shake my head and laugh. "Shifter. Or werewolf. In paranormal romance books, any sort of were or shifter is always described as being warmer than normal humans."

Wes raises an eyebrow, looking amused. "I didn't know that."

"I'm a little weird. Maybe I should have warned you."

Slowly, he angles his body toward me and brings one arm up, resting it on the back of the couch behind me. "I like weird."

"Well, you're in luck."

Our eyes meet and my heart flutters. This is the most real I've seen Wes, and this is the most real he's seen me. Because right now, I'm not Scarlet, the con-artist, scourge of the South Side. I'm just Scarlet, the quirky blonde who reads smutty vampire and werewolf romance novels in her spare time and gets way too wrapped up in scary TV shows.

Wes's fingertips brush against my shoulder, and I shiver. I tip my head towards his, lips parting. He moves his head down toward mine.

He needs to stop.

I need to look away.

But I don't.

And he doesn't.

Our eyes meet again, and I know he's feeling the exact same thing as I am. My heart flutters in my chest, like it's taking flight before it starts flapping its wings as hard as it can, beating away like a drum inside my chest.

He sweeps his hand down, and his fingers trail along my arm. His touch is gentle, making me want to lean in and feel more. He's doing it on purpose, knowing exactly what kind of reaction he's going to get from me.

I don't know if I should be mad at him for it or not. Swallowing hard, I take my bottom lip between my teeth and slowly lean in. He brings his hand up again and pushes my hair back behind my ear.

He's going to kiss me.

The little bit of logic that hasn't left me is screaming to stop, because if he kisses me, things won't end there. I'll climb into his lap, press my core against him, and feel his cock harden beneath me. I'll wrap my arms around his neck and buck my hips back, rubbing his cock against me once, maybe twice, before going in for another kiss. His hands will settle on my waist, pushing under my T-shirt, feeling the soft skin on my back. He'll shift his weight, rubbing himself against me until the top of his boxers dampens from the glistening tip of his cock.

He'll press his lips to mine again, and I'll push my tongue into his mouth. We'll fall back on the couch, kissing with fervor as we peel off each other's clothes. He'll want to carry me upstairs, but I'll be too impatient to wait even half a minute to feel his big, rough hands sweeping over my body, moving down my thighs, parting my legs, and rubbing over my clit.

If I let him kiss me, I'm going to end up sleeping with him. And nothing good ever comes from sleeping with your boss.

My heart flutters again, and the little bit of logic dissolves into nothing.

He's going to kiss me.

And I'm going to let him.

Chapter Twelve

WESTON

If there was ever a rational part of my brain, it's now dead and buried six feet under. My cock has taken over, and right now it's screaming at me to kiss Scarlet. To take her in my arms, feel her breasts crush against my chest, to put my lips to hers and see if she tastes as good as I think she will.

It plays out before me, and I imagine her in my lap, legs wrapped around my waist, pulling my shirt over my head. My cock jumps at the thought, and I inch in closer and closer.

Somewhere in the back of my mind, I know this is a bad idea. She's Jackson's nanny and hasn't even been here that long and I'm already trying to make a move on her. But it's not like she's uninterested, and I can tell by the way she's biting her bottom lip and is moving toward me that she wants this too.

We shouldn't. We really fucking shouldn't.

But dammit, I'm tired of holding back, of going to bed alone. I've spent the last four years convincing the world that I'm not lonely, but you can only lie to yourself for so long before the smoke and mirrors gives way for the bullshit it really is.

I'm going to kiss her.

I bring my hand to her face, cupping her cheek. Her skin is so soft, and her long hair tangles around my fingers. I want to take a fistful of it, pulling it gently as I kiss her hard.

Scarlet's tongue darts out, wetting her lips. I'm officially a goner now. No logic is left, and I move forward, bringing my other hand to her waist. My fingers rest on the curve of her hip, and she tenses for a second before melting against me, bringing a hand up and resting it on my chest. She tips her head up, lips parting.

I inhale, heart beating faster and faster. I take one last second to look at her pretty face, to admire the sapphire blue of her eyes, the light freckles on her cheeks that she covered up with makeup the first time I saw her. I brush her hair back, moving it out of the way.

My heart is beating so fast I can hear it echoing in my ears, and I wonder if Scarlet can hear it. She brings her free hand up, placing it over my hand that's cupping her cheeks. Her thumb rubs over my palm, and she leans into my touch.

My cock is hard, pulsing, begging for me to get this show on the fucking road. To kiss her, bring her close, and feel the heat of her pussy hovering over me. She pushes herself forward, and the softest whimper leaves her lips.

God, this woman. If I don't kiss her now, I'm going to implode. I tighten my grip on her waist and pull her close. Her breasts crush against my chest, and she slides her hand up and over my shoulder.

And then I kiss her.

The moment our lips touch, desperation sparks between us, and she holds me close, pressing her body against mine. I run my hand down her waist and down to her ass, lifting her up and bringing her onto my lap. She straddles me, slowly easing herself over my cock, gasping slightly when she takes in the length, feeling it through my pajama pants. She stops kissing me for a brief moment, looking down in my lap, and the lust in her eyes paired with the shock does me in.

With an animalistic growl, I flip her over, moving on top of her. She curls her legs around my waist, rocking her hips so she rubs against my cock. Fuck, it feels so good even with clothes on I could come right now, dry humping her like a horny teenager. I haven't been with a woman since Daisy left, and the desperation is getting to me.

Scarlet grabs the hem of my shirt, but right as she goes to pull it off, the bottom stair creaks.

"Daddy?"

Jackson's little voice comes from behind us, and I move off Scarlet so fast I fall off the couch, hitting my shoulder on the coffee table.

"Dammit," I mutter, rubbing the spot where the corner of the wooden table hit. Scarlet scrambles up, smoothing out her shirt.

"Hey, buddy." She rushes around the coffee table. "What are you doing down here?"

"The Tall Man is back."

Scarlet glances over her shoulder at me, flicking her eyes to my cock. She knows I can't exactly stand up right now.

Sitting on the bottom stair, she pulls Jackson onto her lap and brushes his hair back. "Is he still there?"

"No. He went into Daddy's room, and then Daddy wasn't there. I thought the Tall Man got him."

"We were watching a movie," Scarlet says, wiping away a tear. I push myself up onto the couch. "No Tall Man down here. Let's get you back to bed, okay?"

"Okay," he says and pulls out of Scarlet's arms to run to me. "Daddy, will you tuck me in?"

"Of course, buddy." I wrap my arm around him and kiss the top of his head. Scarlet turns on a light, and I pause the TV, knowing watching even a few seconds of this show will make him have nightmares. In the light, I look at Scarlet. She meets my eyes and then looks away.

What the fuck was I thinking?

She's here for Jackson. Not me. We're lucky Jackson had a nightmare and stopped us before we got in too deep. Because getting in deep was exactly what I wanted to do. This can't happen again. It *won't* happen again.

Scarlet's bedroom door is closed when I get up Sunday morning. Technically, Sundays are to be her day off. Unless some big crime happens in Eastwood and I have to go in, I'm always off on Sundays. It was discussed with her before she even started, but seeing her door shut like that makes a bad feeling form in the pit of my stomach.

Not that I'm in a rush to see her either. Because...what the fuck will I say? Hey, last night *almost fucking you* was fun? That I want to do it again but know we shouldn't. That my will is paper-thin at best and avoiding each other is ideal, but that won't work because *you fucking live here*. God, what the fuck did I do?

She's. Jackson's. Nanny.

"What do you want for breakfast?" I ask Jackson, plugging in the coffee pot.

"Can you make bacon and eggs like Scarlet does?"

"Sure," I say, internalizing my grimace. I'm no master chef, but I do try to eat healthy, and I want Jackson to grow up with good eating habits like I did. And it makes working out worthless when I eat like shit anyway, so the Pop-Tarts and cereal mornings should be over.

Jackson watches cartoons while I cook, and I'm putting his plate on the table when

Scarlet comes downstairs. Her hair is messy, and she has pillow creases on her face. My mind immediately jumps to her waking up in my bed, rolling over with that bed-head in my face. I'd slip my arm around her and bring her close, not ready to get up.

"Morning," she says with a small smile and crosses the kitchen, going right for the coffee.

"Morning." I pull the creamer out of the fridge. Her fingers brush over mine as she takes it from me, and the small touch is enough to send a jolt through me, going right to my cock. I need to get it the fuck together.

"How'd you sleep?" she asks Jackson, looking over her shoulder as she prepares her coffee.

"I stayed with Daddy. He kept me safe," Jackson replies between bites of bacon. "The Tall Man didn't come back, but I did see him standing outside your door."

Scarlet's face blanks. "Well, I'm going to be sleeping well tonight."

I laugh, wishing I could give her a similar offer. My bed is open to anyone scared of the dark tonight.

"Are you still coming with us to Grammy's tonight?" Jackson asks Scarlet.

She flicks her eyes to mine, and in that half-second, the room fills with tension so thick it's hard to breathe.

"Yeah," she tells him with a smile. "I wouldn't miss it." Taking a sip of her coffee, she keeps her eyes focused on the floor in front of her. I pile bacon, eggs, and toast onto my own plate and take another down from the cabinet for Scarlet.

"Hungry?" I ask.

"I'm always hungry in the morning." With a smile, she sets her coffee down and starts to walk over to the stove. Her perky tits bounce slightly under her T-shirt, and I need to turn around and stop looking for my own good.

"Want to play zombies after breakfast?" Jackson asks Scarlet.

"Today's Scarlet's day off," I remind him gently. "She's here but not really here."

Jackson tips his head. "Huh?"

Scarlet laughs. "It's okay. I don't really have any plans other than showering and reading a chapter or two from my book."

"Are there zombies in your book?" Jackson's eyes widen.

"Actually, yes." Scarlet fills her plate and joins us at the table. "It's a romance set in the zombie apocalypse. It's really good."

"Can you read it to me?"

"When you're older." She smiles and then digs into her food. We eat in silence, and I'm a little jealous of the innocent way Jackson is completely oblivious to how fucking awkward things are right now.

"After breakfast, let's go grocery shopping," I tell Jackson, who groans in response. I'm sure Scarlet would appreciate a little time to herself, and Lord knows I need some time away. Or a cold shower.

Probably both.

Once everyone is done eating, Jackson goes back to his cartoons and Scarlet clears the table. She's at the sink washing dishes, and I'm a few feet away from her cleaning the grease off the stovetop that splattered when I made bacon.

I need to say something. I pull the burner apart and wipe it down. *I really need to say something.* I put the clean burner back on and move onto the one behind it. Once that's cleaned, I put the grates back on and start on the other side, even though it's clean. I'm being fucking ridiculous. Has it been that long since I've had any sort of a connection to a woman? I can't remember how these things go.

And I've also never almost slept with someone and then had to see them like this in the morning. It's like some sort of tight-rope version of the Walk of Shame. I need to suck it up and tell her I enjoyed last night, I like her, but we have to keep things professional for Jackson's sake.

"So, last night," I start and at the exact same time she asks,

"Should I bring something to—sorry, what?"

I shake my head. "Go ahead."

"Should I bring something to your parents' tonight?"

"Nah, you don't have to. I never do."

She smiles and scrubs at the pan, trying to get the baked-on eggs off. "I've never done a family dinner like this before. I don't know the etiquette."

I know our family isn't the norm. There's seven of us, plus a few spouses and children now, and the fact that we get together once a week goes above and beyond what a lot of people do. But hearing her say she's never done a family dinner takes me by surprise, and I know she's not exaggerating the use of "never" like so many people do.

She really hasn't gone to a big family dinner before.

I look away from the stove, not prepared for the sadness I see in her eyes. She forces a smile and pushes her shoulders back, a move I've seen her do before. It's a move I know, one that might fool the world but starts to break down over time. You can't lie to your own heart, after all.

"You're not close to your brother?"

"Oh, I am. I pretty much raised him. He's nineteen, so the nine-year age difference made me feel more like his mother than anything else, though I guess you get that. You're the oldest."

I nod because I don't know what else to do. Quinn is eight years younger than me, but I never felt like a parent to her. I probably annoyed her growing up—and still to this day—by being an overprotective older brother, but that's all I was. Her *brother*. I never felt like I had to raise her or step in and fill a role.

"I have a sister too," she goes on, turning her head down to look at the dishes she's washing. "She's twenty. We didn't get along growing up much either. For the same reasons."

"What about now?"

She laughs. "Sometimes." She rinses the pan and sets it on the counter to dry. "My mom wasn't the best, and my dad wasn't in the picture until I was fifteen."

"Oh, I'm, uh, sorry."

She waves a hand in the air. "It's water under the bridge. What doesn't kill us makes us stronger and all shit, right?" She goes back to washing dishes, closing the conversation about her family. I know there is more to be told, and I know emotional scars when I see them.

"We can bring wine," I suggest. "My mom likes wine."

Scarlet looks up with a smile. "That's something we have in common."

I laugh. "You're off to a good start."

Chapter Thirteen

WESTON

I'VE NEVER ONCE BEEN NERVOUS BRINGING A GIRL HOME TO MEET MY PARENTS. AND Scarlet is far from *my girl*. Still, my heart is beating faster than normal when we get into my Jeep. Scarlet is dressed in a simple black dress. It's long-sleeved and ends above her knees, with a scoop neckline that shows off her large tits just enough to cause me to want to stare. She curled her hair and put on makeup, looking perfect as usual.

But the way she's clutching the bottle of wine makes me think she's nervous too.

"Is there anything I should know about your family?" she asks as I back out of the garage and into the alley that runs behind our house. "Any dark secrets or things?"

There really isn't. Daisy's betrayal is the only dark secret in the Dawson family…that I know about, at least. We might not be the most exciting bunch, but I wouldn't trade my family for anything.

"Don't bring up cats," I tell her. "Quinn is almost married and successful, but still very much a crazy cat lady at heart. If she starts talking about cats, she won't stop."

"Cats? Well, I wasn't going to bring them up, but now I'm terrified I'm going to. You're putting too much pressure on me. Don't get mad if I start meowing at the dinner table."

"Funny." I steal a glance at her, heart hammering even faster when I see her smiling.

"I'm serious. I don't know if I can handle this kind of pressure right meow." She looks at me with a straight face. I roll to a stop at a stop sign and stare right back at her. We hold each other's gaze for a few seconds before we both start to laugh.

"So that's your family's deepest, darkest secret? Your rich and successful sister is a crazy cat lady?"

"I never said she was rich."

Scarlet's cheeks flush. "I kinda assumed so from meeting her. Not that she was stuck-up or anything. She had a lot of designer items."

"Oh, I guess." I turn down the main street that runs through Eastwood. "I don't pay attention to that stuff. And she is, so you weren't wrong. And yeah…I guess that's the worst of it. Quinn's fiancé is my brother Dean's best friend. There was some drama there for a while, but everyone is over it."

"Ohhh, falling for her older brother's best friend. That is good drama."

"And Dean's wife is kind of a…a…" I trail off, not wanting to badmouth family.

"A bitch?" Scarlet finishes for me, mouthing the word so Jackson doesn't hear.

"You said it, not me. But yes."

She smiles again. "Your secret's safe with me." She turns her head, looking out the window. She hasn't seen any of Eastwood yet, and now I feel like an ass about it. I'm off tomorrow as well, and I'm going to make it a point to show her around town.

"Do you like dogs?" I ask, turning off the main road and heading toward the outskirts of town.

"I'm more of a cat person. I think I'll get along well with your sister." Her cherry-red lips pull into a smile. "Why?"

"My mom has four dogs. Now that we're all grown, she's a *dog mom*."

Scarlet laughs. "She's one of those."

"You know the type?"

"I do."

Jackson looks up from the backseat. "I like dogs."

"I know you do, buddy," I tell him. He's been asking for one for a while now. I briefly considered letting him take home one of the kittens Quinn's been caring for once it's old enough, but I wasn't home enough to feel like it'd be fair to any animal. Though now that Scarlet's here…

"I like dogs too," Scarlet tells him. "But I like cats more. They're elegant and so mysterious."

I laugh. "You are going to get along with my sister."

"How's everything going?" Quinn whispers, giving me a hug.

"Pretty good," I say, unable to keep the smile off my face.

Quinn leans back, eyebrows going up. Damn her and her ability to read me like an open book.

"Not like that. Jackson is happy, and I think I can trust her around him."

"She's hot, you know."

I unzip my coat and shake my head at my sister. "Having you tell me she's hot doesn't make me want to date her. She's Jackson's nanny. You and Mom need to get off this, okay?" My words come out harsher than I mean to. I'm yelling at myself, not at my well-meaning baby sister. "Sorry. I just—"

"It's fine," Quinn says, green eyes flashing. "I want you to be happy, so shoot me."

Like Dean, Quinn has a flare for dramatics when she's angry or hurt. "I know," I say gently. "And thanks. Just…let me find happiness on my own?"

"But playing matchmaker is so fun."

"Play it for Logan and Owen."

"I said 'matchmaker,' not 'miracle worker.' Which is what they need."

We both laugh, and I turn around to introduce Scarlet to everyone. We're the last to arrive, and I'm pretty sure the only reason Logan and Owen got here before us is because they knew Scarlet was joining tonight.

"Hi, Quinn," Scarlet says, bending over to unzip her boots. Oh God, I shouldn't have looked. The feel of her breasts pressed against my chest is seared into me like muscle memory, and I can't go down that road right now.

"Hey." Quinn drops to her knees to hug Jackson. "How are you liking it here so far?"

"So far so good," Scarlet tells her and flicks her eyes to me. "Everyone has been very welcoming. Though I haven't seen much of the town yet."

Quinn eyes me, and I smile guiltily. "It's supposed to be nice tomorrow. We can walk around downtown in the morning."

Jackson grabs Scarlet's hand and pulls her through the foyer. My parents' house is also historical and fully restored, but on a much bigger level than mine. This place was a dump when we first moved in, and my brothers and I might have had fun teasing Quinn about how haunted it was since it looked like something out a horror movie.

Slowly over the years and in between projects for clients, my dad did most of the renovations himself. He taught us all how to be handy, and there aren't many home improvement projects I can't handle myself because of it.

"Your parents' house is gorgeous," Scarlet says, looking around with wide eyes. "I feel like I'm going to a dinner party with Chip and Joanna."

"Who?" I ask, following after her and Jackson.

"I'll tell you later," Scarlet says over her shoulder. The whole family is gathered in the kitchen, like always. This place is really the heart of the house, and the custom-built island is always a topic of conversation. It's huge, long enough for us all to have a seat at, and is the perfect place for everyone to converge, eating, talking, and drinking.

I watch Scarlet's face as we enter, and she does her little trick again, inhaling and pushing her shoulders back, acting like she's ready to take on the world. Emma, who's being held by my mom, coos when she sees Quinn and extends her chubby little arms for her mother.

"Hey, sweet pea," Quinn says and takes her baby. Jackson runs through the kitchen, excited to see everyone. And then all eyes fall on us. Scarlet stays close to me, holding the bottle of wine so tight in her hands I fear the bottle might break. I'm comfortable around everyone in this room. My siblings, obviously. Archer feels just like another younger brother since he and Dean have had a serious bromance going on since they met their freshman year of college, and Kara's been part of the family for the last four years.

We don't bring home dates unless it's serious, and I need to keep reminding myself that Scarlet isn't my date. There's nothing going on between us, and there never will be, even though I very much want it.

"This is Scarlet," I say, putting my hand on her shoulder. She's nervous, and her words come back, echoing through my head. She's never been to a family dinner, and while this doesn't seem like anything special to the rest of us, it's probably overwhelming to her.

"Hey, I'm Owen." My little shit of a brother gets up, flashing her a charming smile, and shakes her hand, taking the wine from her. "It's nice to meet you."

"You too." Scarlet returns his smile.

I spread my fingers over her shoulder, and the warmth of her skin through the material of her dress feels like fire. It's burning me, but I can't remove my hand.

"And that's Logan," I say, pointing to him. "Don't feel bad if you can't tell them apart."

"I'm the better-looking one," Owen says with a grin as he opens the wine.

Scarlet laughs and looks from Logan to Owen. "Logan's in the black, and Owen's in the blue. I'm good for now at least."

"That's Dean, his wife Kara, and Archer, Quinn's fiancé." We take a few steps forward into the kitchen. "This is my mom, and my dad is somewhere."

"He's getting Nana," Mom tells me, striding over. "It's nice to meet you, Scarlet."

"You too," Scarlet says with a sweet smile.

"Nana?" I question, trying not to grimace. Our Nana has a few screws loose and suffers from what we've dubbed Old Lady Syndrome, meaning she's lost her filter and it's gotten worse since last year.

"It's been a while since we had her over," Mom reminds me. "How are you liking it in Eastwood?" she asks Scarlet. "You're from Chicago, right?"

"I am," Scarlet answers. "And it's nice here. Very quiet."

"Quinn lived in Chicago for a few years, and I used to enjoy going for a visit. Though a visit is all I could stand. I was born and raised here. I like my yard and my privacy."

Scarlet laughs, nodding in agreement. "I could see that. I'm used to hearing the L and the constant chatter of people on my street."

"The L?"

"It's a train, Mom," Quinn answers, sitting down next to Archer.

"Oh, right." Mom nods. "Anyway, welcome to Eastwood." She looks down at Jackson and smiles. "And I hope this little guy is being a perfect gentleman."

Jackson giggles. "I always am, Grammy!"

"He has been perfect," Scarlet agrees.

"Just wait," I warn her with a wink. "He's still in the honeymoon phase, trust me."

Scarlet smiles down at Jackson. "I think I can handle it."

Owen comes back over with two wine glasses, offering one to Scarlet and keeping the other for himself.

"We got that for Mom," I deadpan. Owen gives me a look and then gives Mom the glass.

"I prefer beer anyway," he says.

"What happened to that moonshine you were raving about?"

Logan snorts a laugh. "Yeah…what did happen to it?"

Owen glares at Logan, and I motion for Scarlet to sit with me at the island. "I'd rather not talk about it," he mutters.

"You don't have to." Logan takes his phone from his pocket. "I have evidence."

Mom shakes her head. "I don't think I want to see this, do I?"

"No one wants to see it," Owen interjects, going over and trying to steal Logan's phone. Mom shakes her head and goes into the living room to play with Jackson. Giving up trying to get the phone, Owen takes Emma from Quinn and pulls a silly face, making her laugh.

"Your baby is adorable," Scarlet tells Quinn, taking a drink of her wine.

"Thanks," Quinn and Archer say at the same time. All the bar stools are taken now, so Quinn sits on Archer's lap. He wraps his arms around her and leans in for a kiss.

"Get a room," Logan teases.

"Don't encourage them," Dean replies dryly.

"Upstairs is free," Owen goes on, blowing a raspberry on Emma's cheek. She lets out a shriek of laughter. "They need to have another baby for me to play with."

"You could have your own," Archer counters.

Owen's eyes widen, and he shakes his head. "Nope. It's not for me."

"Not yet," I tell him with a laugh.

"You and Quinn can have the babies. I like being an uncle."

Kara flicks her eyes up from her phone. "Are you going to have another?" she asks.

"Not soon," Quinn answers, looking into Archer's eyes. "I want to be able to drink at our wedding and go on all the rides at Disney. Ideally, I'll be pregnant by the time we come back from our honeymoon."

"Gross," Dean mumbles.

"Stop envisioning it," Archer teases.

Dean gives him a dead stare. "I'm still scarred by that time I walked in on you two."

"Dean!" Quinn squeals, eyes wide. If looks could kill, he'd be dead on the floor.

Logan laughs. "When did this happen?"

"A long time ago. Before Emma was born," Quinn laughs, burying her head against Archer.

"At least he never saw the picture," Archer whisper-yells to Quinn.

"Picture?" Owen asks, cuddling Emma against his chest.

"No," Quinn says, putting her hand up to Archer's mouth to silence him. Everyone laughs, and I lean back in my chair to look at Scarlet. A small smile is on her face, and she's watching us almost as if she's in a lab observing our behavior. Rufus, the biggest and oldest of Mom's dogs, jumps up at the back door, startling Scarlet a bit.

Dean gets up to let him in. I'd already moved out and was overseas when she got him, but he's the family dog to the rest of the family. Without thinking, Dean opens the glass doors, and all four dogs come barreling in. Most are friendly, but Rufus can be finicky with new people. He's a German Shepherd mixed with a Malamute and is big and intimidating.

Scarlet tenses, bringing her wine glass to her lips and taking a big sip. I slip off the stool and take a hold of his collar as he sniffs her.

"This is Rufus," I say. "He's a cranky old dog but will leave you alone."

"Hey, Rufus," Scarlet says and holds out her hand for him to sniff. His fur raises for a few seconds, and then he decides she's not a threat.

"I found my wedding dress," Quinn tells me, looking over Archer's shoulder. She beams, and I'm so damn happy for her. She's my baby sister, one of the nicest people in the whole fucking world, and I want nothing but the best for her.

"When are you getting married?" Scarlet asks.

"June. At Disney World!"

"Ohhh, that sounds awesome. Have you picked out the rest of the wedding, uh, stuff?"

Scarlet's trying, and I give her props for that. She doesn't have to. It doesn't really matter if she gets along with my family. She's Jackson's nanny...*not my girlfriend*. I've never really cared if my boss's family liked me before. It actually never even crossed my mind.

"Most of it," Quinn tells her. "Disney takes care of a lot of stuff, which makes it easy. All I'm really concerned about is having good food."

Scarlet smiles. "I think that's how I'd be too. Do you have a picture of your dress?"

"Of course. Want to see?"

"Heck yes!"

Quinn moves off Archer's lap. "I don't want to risk him seeing."

"Oh, definitely." Scarlet gets up and follows Quinn into the living room. The moment she steps out, my brothers round on me.

"Dude," Owen starts, still holding Emma against his chest. "What the fuck?"

I shake my head, playing dumb. "What?"

"Your nanny is fucking hot."

"Shut up," I snap.

Owen raises an eyebrow. "You disagree?"

"I don't agree or disagree."

Logan chuckles. "Spoken like a true politician. Has this election gone to your head already?"

"Funny," I tell him. "Yeah, she's good-looking. But she's here for Jackson so I can work."

"Of course she is." Dean raises his eyebrows. "Why else would she be here?"

"Sorry," Archer starts. "I know Quinn had a secret agenda hiring her. She means well."

"I know," I tell him. "She does. And so far, Scarlet is great with Jackson. But it's only been a few days so..."

"Who knows?" Logan finishes for me. I meet his eyes and nod.

"Right." I get up and go to the fridge to get a beer. And who the fuck knows? I return to my seat and suck down a few gulps of the beer. I'm on edge, fighting my own attraction to Scarlet, and I feel like everyone can see right through me. That's the only downfall of having a close-knit family like this.

The garage door opens, and Dad and Nana come in. Things get rolling after that, and Jackson throws a little fit when I tell him to wash his hands before dinner. I look at Scarlet.

"Told you so," I mouth, and she laughs. She picks him up off the floor and takes him to the bathroom to wash his hands. Finally, we're all seated around the table. Scarlet's at my side, and Jackson ended up across the table by Mom. I've introduced Scarlet to Nana twice now, and she's staring at her, questioning who she is for the third time.

"I'm Scarlet, Jackson's nanny," Scarlet says sweetly.

"What the fuck happened to Daisy?" Nana asks, trying to steal Logan's beer. He takes it from her and slides her water glass into her reach. She bats his hand away and goes for the beer again.

"Mom," my own mother scolds. "We don't swear at the dinner table."

"Daisy is my mom," Jackson says slowly, as if he's not sure of himself. Silence falls over the table, and it's taking everything inside me not to pound my fist before getting up and storming out. I'm not mad at my nana. Her mind has been going at a scary rate the last few months, and she doesn't remember much of what's happened recently.

I'm mad at Daisy and what she did to Jackson.

No one speaks, and each second that ticks by gives Jackson more and more time to think, to let his own mind question *what the fuck happened to my mom?* Dean opens his mouth only to snap it shut again, and Dad looks just as stunned as the rest of us.

"So, Quinn," Scarlet says, reaching for her wine. Well, what's left of it. "I hear you like cats."

Chapter Fourteen

SCARLET

"Yes," Quinn says, eyes meeting mine. I can see the relief on her face and, more importantly, the relief on Weston's face. Poor little Jackson is still sitting there with a spoonful of mashed potatoes hovering on his spoon in front of his face, not knowing what to think. "I do."

"How many cats do you have?" I flick my eyes to Wes's not knowing if I should be apologetic for going into forbidden territory or not. He meets my gaze and offers a small smile.

"Eight."

"Eight?" I echo.

"One or two might be temporary."

Quinn's fiancé, Archer, raises an eyebrow. "Only one or two?"

Quinn smiles guiltily. "They're all so cute."

"I want a cat!" Jackson says, face lighting up. He eats his mashed potatoes and bounces in his seat. "Daddy, can we take Dobby home?"

"We'll see," Wes tells him, and I know it's a firm *no* from him.

"Please! I want a pet." Jackson drops his spoon and glares at Wes, crossing his arms. I don't mean to laugh, but the over-the-top dramatics are a little cute.

"Dobby is really nice," Quinn goes on. "And will be able to leave in a few weeks."

Dean shakes his head, looking at Archer. "I can't believe you let her keep the others. Eight cats? That's crazy."

Archer's eyes fall on Quinn, and the way he looks at her makes me want to turn around and throw up. But mostly because I'd give anything to have someone look at me like that. On its own accord, my head jerks toward Wes.

Nope. Can't happen. He's my boss. And he'd never go for someone like me…the real me.

"I have a hard time saying no to Quinn," Archer says, and I want to gag.

"That's why they have a baby out of wedlock," Wes's grandma says. Everyone at the table rolls their eyes and ignores her. I'm guessing this isn't the first time she's brought it up, and neither Quinn nor Archer seem bothered by it. "Though I can't blame her. I do like a man who's good with his hands. You know, doc, I'm overdue for my annual exam." She winks at Archer. Archer shakes his head and turns his face down to his food, concentrating really hard on cutting his steak.

I turn to Wes, trying not to laugh. He leans over, shaking his head.

"She hits on Archer every time they're together. Don't judge us."

"I'm not," I say honestly, and for the life of me, I can't come up with a single judgment against the Dawsons. And trust me, I'm trying. But they're all nice. Caring. No one tries to impress each other or puts up a front. Logan cuts up his grandma's steak for her, and Owen takes Emma again when she gets fussy so Quinn and Archer can eat a meal in peace. Mr. and Mrs. Dawson love each and every one of their children and grandchildren equally, and I can tell just from this brief interaction how proud they are of them.

They're the perfect American family, and I'm convinced they are the real deal. That families can be functional.

And I'm not sure if I hate them or love them for it.

Thinking big family meals like this don't exist made it easier for me to handle knowing we were nowhere near perfect. Get-togethers with homemade food only happen in the movies. Thinking it wasn't real helped me deal with the fact that there was a huge part of me missing.

Because I want a family. I want this. But I can't have it. People like the Dawsons would never want the likes of me sitting around their dinner table if they knew the truth.

I'm Scarlet Cooper, a thief from the South Side with no college education, a former drunk for a father, a sister in jail, and heir to a fortress of lies.

I sit on the living room couch next to Wes, a hot mug of coffee in my hand. His dad and his brother Dean are in his dad's study going over something for work, and the rest of his family is still in the kitchen.

"Have we scared you off yet?" Wes asks, leaning against the arm of the couch. "We can be a little loud and overwhelming."

"Not overwhelming. Your family is super nice. Well, except for Kara. You were right about her being a bitch."

"I never actually said that."

"You didn't have to. It's written all over your face."

Wes laughs and shifts his weight, moving a little closer to me. Things should be awkward with him, but they're not anymore. Being around him is as easy as breathing, and while he still holds up walls around him, they're starting to turn more into windows, letting me see inside.

"Hey," Logan says, stepping into the living room. Or maybe it's Owen. Shit. Who was wearing blue again? "You guys want dessert?" He eyes Wes, smirking. Owen. It's Owen. He's the smartass of the two, and it's oddly endearing.

"Yeah," Wes says quickly before Owen can slip in a line about Wes getting dessert elsewhere. We both know it's coming.

"Scarlet!" Jackson stops running around the kitchen and gives me a hug. "Will you do the Baby Shark Challenge with me?"

"Sure," I tell him. "But what is it?"

"What?" Wes's hand flies to his chest as he fakes his shock. "You don't know what Baby Shark is?"

"You're lucky," his mom says, raising her eyebrows. "It'll get stuck in your head for days."

"So it's a song?" I ask.

"And a movie," Jackson tells me.

"It's more like a music video. For kids," Wes says and shakes his head. "And you gave me crap for not seeing *Titanic* and here you are never having seen Baby Shark."

I laugh, heart skipping a beat when I look into his eyes and see that smirk on his face. "You've had years to see it, mister. Baby Shark can't be that old."

He laughs before shrugging. "You got me there." Motioning to the dining room, he puts his hand on Jackson's head and tousles his hair. "And we'll do one song after dessert. Then it'll be time to go home and get ready for bed."

"If you make me leave, I'm going to throw a fit," he threatens. His face crumples, and he tries to make himself cry but stops when Emma lets out a shriek.

"She's all yours," Dean says, handing the crying baby to Archer. "I think she pooped."

"You're welcome to change her diaper, Uncle Dean," Archer tells him, laughing. I look around the kitchen as this cute-as-hell family and might start throwing a fit like Jackson when it comes time to leave too.

Though getting back to late-night TV with Wes sounds nice...

"I think it's time to eat cake," I say, dropping down to Jackson's level. He beams and grabs my hand, hopping as he leads me into the dining room. I have another glass of wine and the best chocolate cake I've ever had in my entire life. Turns out Kara is a really good cook, which is probably one of the reasons Dean's with her. Or at least that's one theory I have.

"Scarlet," Quinn starts, looking at me from across the table. "Would you guys want to go to the farmers' market with us on Tuesday? It's supposed to be nice out and we can walk from Wes's place."

"Sure," I say, looking at Jackson, who nods excitedly. "I've never been to a farmers' market. Are they like the ones in movies?"

"This one isn't as big. Especially now that it's fall. I need some mums for our porch."

I don't know what a mum is, but I smile and nod anyway.

"And there's a local winery that sells the best sweet red wine and blueberry cider. Now that Emma is eating solid food I can half like an ounce of wine at night once she goes down."

"You had me at sweet red wine." I scrape the last bit of icing off my plate and wonder if it would look bad if I picked it up and licked it. This stuff is like crack. We stay for a bit longer after that, and I hang out with Jackson in the living room while Wes talks about the campaign with his dad and brothers.

It's dark when we go to leave, and I stop short in the driveway.

"You okay?" Wes asks, unlocking his Jeep.

My head is turned up to the sky. "I've never seen this many stars before." I exhale, and my breath clouds around me. "It's beautiful."

"Yeah," Wes agrees, and I can feel his eyes on me. "Beautiful."

"I could see them from my house, but not like this. It's...it's incredible. It makes me feel so...so..."

"Small?"

"No." I shake my head, unable to tear my eyes away from the heavens above. "Connected. It makes me feel so connected and grounded at the same time. It doesn't make sense, I know." I shake my head and shiver. I didn't put my coat on, not thinking I'd need it for the quick walk from the house to the Jeep. "Forget it," I say with a laugh. "It's stupid."

"I don't think it's stupid." Wes steps close next to me. Jackson's opening the back of the Jeep and climbing in. "When I was deployed, I'd look up at the sky and take comfort knowing I was under the same blanket of stars as the people I loved. The people I missed. So I get what you mean about having it make you feel connected."

I tip my head down, eyes meeting his. My lips part, and another chill goes right through me. Ignoring the fact that I'm dumbly holding my coat in my hands, Weston takes off his jacket and drapes it around my shoulders.

Dammit, Wes, stop being such a nice guy.

A nice guy who loves his son more than anything, has a family I wish could adopt me, and who may or may not be making me feel things I didn't think I was capable of feeling.

I'm in over my head here, and it won't be long before the waves crash against the shore and pull me out with the undertow. But being washed out into dark waters isn't scary.

It's that I want it to happen.

Chapter Fifteen

WESTON

I push Jackson's hair back, feeling bad that I forgot to take him for a haircut—again. It's hard juggling everything, but now it should be easier. Scarlet is here to help with housework, make dinner, and most of all, to care for the single most important person in my life.

"Love you," I whisper and kiss his forehead before quietly slipping out of his room. Light pours into the dark hall, coming from Scarlet's room. She's sitting on her bed, with one hand pressed to her forehead and the other holding her phone. I can tell right away she's upset.

"Yes, I'm fully aware he needs that medication, but insurance denied it. I've been working on it and will pay out of pocket if I have to." She pauses, listening to whoever is on the phone. "Sure. If the doctor thinks he needs it, then yeah." Another pause. I should go and not listen to her conversation, but I'm fighting hard against myself and the urge to go comfort her. "How many falls does that make this month? Fuck—sorry. It's just…I didn't realize he'd fallen so many times."

She exhales, and I turn away, giving her privacy. I head into the bathroom to shower and then put on sweatpants and a T-shirt. Mom packed a plate of leftovers, and it's calling my name. The light is off in Scarlet's room when I step back into the hall, but her door is open, leading me to believe she's downstairs.

But she's not.

She's nowhere to be found, and I actually go back up and peek in her room—she's not there—and she's not in Jackson's room, either.

"Scarlet?" I call quietly when I get to the bottom of the stairs. I'm starting to get concerned when I see her sitting on the back porch, arms wrapped tightly around herself and her head tipped up to the sky. She's not wearing a coat and has to be cold.

Grabbing a blanket from the living room, I put on my jacket and step onto the porch.

"Hey," she says, flicking her eyes to me for a nanosecond before looking away.

"It's freezing out here."

"I know." Her breath leaves in silver wisps, hanging in the air. "I didn't mean to stay out here for so long."

I go to the steps and sit next to her. "Here."

"Thanks," she says and takes the blanket from me. She wraps it around herself and looks back up at the sky.

"Do you believe in aliens?"

"Kind of," I admit. "I think there has to be other life forces out there, and I do enjoy the *Ancient Aliens* show on the History Channel."

"Nerd." She bumps me with her elbow and smiles.

"What about you?"

"Not in the traditional sense. I don't think little green Martians are going to come abduct us and probe our butts, but I agree that we can't be the only life in the universe."

I laugh. "Not probing butts is a good thing."

She turns her head down and meets my eyes. "Well, sometimes it can be a good thing."

Dammit, Scarlet. Leave it to her to turn a tender moment borderline erotic. Though she could read the phone book and I'd get turned on.

"It's so quiet here," she says and rests her head on my shoulder. I clench my fists, trying to keep my hands to myself.

I know how good her lips feel against mine.

If I touch her, I'm going to kiss her again, and there's a good chance we'll make love right here on the stairs.

"It is."

"I thought downtown would be a little louder than this."

I chuckle. "Main Street is, and we're three blocks away. Though everything shuts down around ten or eleven. There are a fair amount of festivals in the summer, though, and we have one twenty-four-hour diner. And, of course, Getaway, my brothers' bar is open until two or three. Friday and Saturday nights are a different story, though once the weather starts to turn, it does quiet down a lot."

"Do you like it here?"

"I do. I was born and raised here, so maybe I'm biased. But it's a good town with good people and it's a safe place to raise a kid."

She nods and gently touches a scar on the back of my hand. "What is this from?"

I swallow my pounding heart. "Dean threw a glass bottle at me when we were kids. I needed a ton of stitches, and he got grounded for a week. I was the one who told him to throw the bottle in the first place, but I never told my parents that."

She laughs. "I'm surprised he forgave you."

"I was able to convince him it was all his fault, and he felt bad about it for like a year. I milked it for all it was worth, of course."

"I would too."

"Do you have any scars?" I hear the words leave my lips but don't know where they came from. Clearly, my upstairs brain has checked out.

"I do. Nothing too interesting, though. I have a cigarette burn on the back of my left shoulder."

"How'd that happen?"

"My mom fell asleep with a cigarette in her hand, and it dropped on me."

"Damn."

"Yeah." She takes her head off my shoulder and raises her eyebrows. "I think I had an entirely different childhood than you."

I'm not quite sure what to say. I know Scarlet isn't one to want pity. She said what she did factually and only because I asked. She's not trying to make me feel bad for her.

"Oh!" She jerks up and points to the sky. "I think I saw a shooting star!"

"Make a wish." I look up, breath catching just a bit when I see how sparkly the night sky is above us. Then I look at Scarlet, and my breath does more than catch. It stops.

Her eyes are closed, lips curved into a slight smile, and her head is tipped up to the sky.

"You should make one too," she whispers.

I look back at the stars and wish for self-control. Because Lord knows I need it tonight. Scarlet gathers up the blanket and lays back, eyes fluttering shut.

"What do you do if you're hungry in the middle of the night?"

"What do you mean?" I lick my lips, watching her breasts rise and fall beneath her shirt as she fixes the blanket around herself.

"Does the diner deliver?"

"No. I'd just go get something from the kitchen." I raise an eyebrow. "You can't possibly be hungry."

"Oh, I'm not. I'm preparing for future nights. Sometimes I have a hard time falling asleep, so I get up and eat my feelings."

I'm usually good at reading people, but I'm struggling with Scarlet. Because she spits out her truths like they're lies, saying serious things so casually it's like a joke.

"Make sure to keep the fridge stocked," I tease and lay back with her, scooting closer, but only so I can see the stars. Not so I can feel her against me. "What'd you wish for?"

"Wes Dawson," she scolds. "I can't tell you."

"Right. It won't come true if you do."

"Oh, I didn't think of it like that. I was going to be cliché and say if I tell you I have to kill you, but you're so big and tall. It'll be such a pain to chop you up and bury your body."

I laugh, and her hand brushes against mine. "You're different than I expected."

"Is that bad?"

"No, it's perfect."

She turns to me, face inches from mine. Suddenly, the humor in her eyes goes away, and I see darkness reflected back at me. I get a glimpse of her, and if I hadn't felt the same thing when I came back after my first tour overseas, I wouldn't have noticed.

She's struggling, fighting tooth and nail to stay afloat in choppy waters.

And then she blinks, and the moment is gone. Slowly, she reaches out and runs her finger over the scar on my hand again.

"Remember you said that," she whispers. Her eyes fall shut, and she turns her head away, sitting up and pulling the blanket tight around her shoulders. "Want to finish that ghost show?"

I do, but now that I've seen inside, and it was like looking into a mirror, I can't. "Maybe tomorrow." I get up and extend a hand. "I'm pretty beat, and I have work tomorrow night."

"Right." She gives me a tight smile and takes my hand, letting me pull her to her feet. "Then you should get to bed."

Chapter Sixteen

SCARLET

I sit on the couch, twisting Ray's yarn mane through my fingers. It's worn and frayed by now, but the sensation still gives me comfort. I cheat and lie for a living but still take solace in a stuffed animal I've had since I was a child.

Psychologists would have a field day with me.

After going out for breakfast at the cutest little mom-and-pop diner this morning, Wes showed me around town, and we ended the tour at the library. Jackson likes to play there, and we left with an armload of picture books, as well as a few paranormal romances for me.

One of the books is on the coffee table next to me, and I intended on reading it. Jackson fell asleep pretty quickly tonight, and once he was down, I took a quick shower, changed into my PJs, and came downstairs to have a cup of tea and read.

It's so domestic it's weird.

It's not me at all, and yet I'm finding myself liking this more and more. It's putting me in the middle of an existential crisis that I certainly don't have time for. My whole life, I've identified as Scarlet from the hood, the girl who had to grow up too fast, who had to raise her siblings as well as take care of her inebriated mother, cleaning up vomit and dragging her inside when she passed out in the yard. Some days she'd be covered in frost by the time I found her, and I'd spend my morning carefully soaking her fingers in bowls of warm water to try and prevent frostbite.

I wasn't always successful.

The simple fact that I like this—putting Jackson to bed, straightening up the house, and sitting down with a cup of fucking tea and a book—is rocking my whole sense of identity right now. I never understood why some people criticized women who chose to stay at home and look after their household. If that's what they want and aren't being repressed into anything against their will, then it's no different than a woman going out and getting a job. She's doing what she wants. What makes her happy.

I didn't realize this could make me happy.

"It's only been a few days," I tell myself and stand, needing to reheat my tea by now. Before I make it into the kitchen, the alarm beeps, and Wes steps into the house. I get to the keypad first and punch in the code to disarm the system.

"Hey," he says, closing the door behind him. I open my mouth to say hi back, but the words die in my throat. I was not prepared to see what I'm seeing.

Weston is wearing a fitted suit, and dear God, it's worse than if he were standing naked before me. I want to throw myself at him, wrapping my fingers around his sleek black tie and using it to pull him up to the bedroom with me. His hair is neatly pulled back away from his face, and a slight five o'clock shadow covers his strong jawline.

And I thought he looked good in his uniform.

"Look at you," I say, raising my eyebrows. "Looking all GQ."

He smiles and looks down at himself, almost as if he forgot what he's wearing. Fuck, it's adorable.

"I had a debate tonight."

"For the race?"

He nods and takes his suit jacket off. "Yeah, and then I had a meet-and-greet." His face tightens, and he shakes his head. "I don't like this part of it. I just want to do my job as the Sheriff and not convince Mr. and Mrs. Johnson why they should donate to my campaign over anyone else's."

I smile at him, body still tingling. He hangs his jacket on the back of a kitchen chair. Then he starts to roll up the sleeves on his button-up dress shirt.

And now I'm dead, lying motionless on the kitchen floor.

"That's why you'll be good at the job," I say, words coming out thinner than I'd like. I tear my eyes away, trying to convince myself that Weston looks like the homeless man who used to sleep in our crawlspace instead of Chris Hemsworth at the Met Gala.

It doesn't work.

"You want to do the job for the job. Not many people in politics are that way."

He chuckles. "It doesn't feel that political, to be honest. I'll be the Sheriff of our county, not governor of Indiana."

"You'd be good at that too." I put my mug in the microwave.

"How'd Jackson do at bedtime?"

"He was good. I ended up reading like four extra stories. Maybe I'll get used to saying no when he asks for another with time, right?"

Wes smiles. "I have a hard time saying no to books, too. Someday he's not going to want me to sit in bed with him and read."

"Right. They don't stay little for long."

He holds my gaze for a moment too long, and blood rushes to my cheeks. He goes upstairs to change, and I take my tea back to the living room. I read a few pages, and already I'm imagining the alpha werewolf in my book to look like Weston.

Dammit.

"I have something for you," he says, coming back down the stairs. He's wearing black athletic pants and a Chicago Bears hoodie. I'm not a big sports fan, but I do support my city.

"You do?"

"Well, kind of." He crosses the room. "Grab your coat."

Setting my book down, I get up and hurry after him. "If it's a cat, you should have waited until Jackson wakes up."

He gives me a playful glare. "It's not a cat."

"Darn."

We put our shoes on, and I grab my coat, following him to the back porch. There's a telescope standing on the sidewalk, pointed up at the night sky. I pause, suddenly forgetting how to move my feet.

"So you can see the stars." Wes is standing by the telescope, a smile on his face. He takes a cover off the lens and wipes away dust. "It was mine when I was a kid. It's been at my parents', and I grabbed it on my way home. I have no idea if it still works, but it's not like these things go bad, right?"

I fumble with the zipper on my coat, and for some reason, I'm still unable to move. I stare down the telescope feeling the weirdest sensation prick at the corners of my eyes. And an even weirder one inside my chest.

Wes holds my gaze, waiting for me to come down the stairs. To say something. Anything. But I'm still standing there like a statue.

"Anyway," Wes goes on, bringing his hand up to his hair. He pulls the band out and lets his long locks fall around his face. I can feel his eyes on me, and I know he's waiting. The longer I go without reacting, the more he's going to think I don't appreciate the gesture or that I think it's stupid.

Which couldn't be farther from the truth.

He went to his parents' house, which I know isn't on the way home from anything. They live on the edge of Eastwood, away from the police station and the town hall where the council meetings are held.

No one has ever done anything like this for me before.

"Jackson might think it's cool at least," he says, and I shake myself.

"It is cool." I inhale, finally get my zipper to go up, and dash down the stairs. I stand close to him, feeling the heat radiating from his large body. I look into eyes, seeing the stars reflected before me, and want to tell him just what this means to me. Attraction aside, this was the most thoughtful thing he could have done.

"How does it work?"

"I have to put a different lens on," he starts and opens a bag. "We might have to watch YouTube tutorials on this."

I laugh and use the sleeve of my coat to carefully wipe the dust off the metal. It takes us a while, but we finally get the thing ready. Wes goes inside to quickly check on Jackson and to turn off the back porch light.

"You know," I say when he comes back. "We could totally spy on your neighbors."

He raises his eyebrows. "Why do you think I wanted to get one of these in the first place?"

"Seriously?" I laugh.

"No. I went through a phase where I wanted to be an astronaut. Like all kids, I suppose."

"Not me." I bend over and put my eye to the focuser. "I wanted to be a professional mermaid."

"That's a thing?"

"Yeah. You swim around at aquariums or shows."

"Shows?"

"Yeah." I carefully move the telescope until I see the fuzzy bright light of what I think is a star. "Like carnivals."

"You'd be a mermaid carnie," he snickers.

"It sounds not as fun when you say it like that. But yeah…and come on. It sounds like a sweet deal. I'd get to swim all day, wear pretty seashell bras, and have lots of glittery makeup on my face."

He laughs and helps me adjust the telescope. "When you put it that way, maybe I'll be a professional merman."

"We could make a career out of it, traveling the country together."

"Clearly I chose the wrong profession." His hand drops from the telescope, and he inches closer. I swallow hard.

"Oh, I see the moon!" I spend a minute adjusting everything, and it comes into focus. "Holy shit, this is amazing." My heart hammers away in my chest, and a chill goes through me, but it's not from the cold. I stare at the moon, and that weird feeling comes back. It's so overwhelming I break away, telling Wes he should take a look as well. His large frame leans over, and he looks at the moon.

"Now I want to be an astronaut again," he says after looking up at the moon for a moment. "It's incredible."

I'm looking at him when I agree. "It is."

He straightens up and reaches back into the bag. "There's a map of the stars. I never was able to make much sense of it."

Another chill goes through me, and I'm unable to hide the shiver.

"Cold?" Wes asks.

I shake my head, not wanting to go in just yet. "I'll survive. Let's try to read this map."

He unfolds the paper and gets out his phone to use as a flashlight. His lock screen is a recent picture of Jackson, and I just about die all over again.

"I can see the Big Dipper," I say, pointing to the sky. "And that's it."

Wes smiles, still looking at the sky. "Same here." We stand there in silence for another moment, looking up at the stars. Something streaks across the sky.

"Did you see that?" I gasp.

"I did." He tips his head down to mine, and there will never be a more perfect moment for him to kiss me. It's like we're floating amongst the stars and nothing matters. Not the past. Not the mistakes I've made.

Just this moment.

But he doesn't kiss me.

Instead, he folds the map and puts it back in the bag. "It's cold out here, and I have an early morning tomorrow. And Jackson has school."

"Right." Back to earth I go, free falling from outer space. "He picked out his outfit for tomorrow," I go on. "With approval, of course. He has really cute clothes."

"I enjoy shopping for him," Wes admits. "So does my mom."

"I can tell."

Wes picks up the heavy telescope with ease, putting it on the back porch for the night. I don't think theft is a worry around here. We step back into the house, and the warm air feels hot against my cheeks.

"You're all set for the morning?" he asks, taking off his shoes. He's nervous about me driving Jackson, and usually something like this would annoy me. I'm capable. Trustworthy, well, that's questionable, but this time there's nothing to worry about.

"Yes. His bag is ready to go, and you showed me the drop-off and pick-up procedure twice today."

He laughs. "Sorry. He's only been in school a few weeks, and I don't know if he's used to his new routine or not yet."

"Don't be sorry. I'd rather see you be a little overprotective than too carefree with him. I know you love him, and you're a good dad."

"Thanks," he says, almost as if my statement caught him off guard. "It's not always easy, ya know, doing things alone." He goes to the fridge and grabs the plate of leftovers. Jackson helped me make chicken enchiladas tonight, and while I don't mean to toot my own horn, we both went back for seconds.

"This looks good," Wes says as he sticks his plate in the microwave.

"I enjoyed it. Jackson did too." There's still nearly a minute left on his food, and suddenly the silence feels awkward. I go into the living room, fold the blanket I was using, and grab my tea to reheat again.

I add another spoonful of sugar to it, stirring it, and stick it in the microwave once Wes's food is done heating. We both sit at the table.

"Do you have campaign stuff tomorrow too?"

He shakes his head. "No, just the gym and then work. I'll go grocery shopping on the way home. If there's anything you want, I can grab it for you."

"I do like chocolate an awful lot."

He smiles. "Noted. Any kind or something special?"

"I guess any kind. But not dark chocolate. That shit is nasty."

Wes laughs, cutting into another piece of his food. "Agreed. And you know you don't have to make dinner every night. I'll do it the nights I'm home."

"I don't mind," I say honestly. And really, I want to stay busy. Being busy keeps me from thinking.

"Oh, and I'm off all day Wednesday, so if there was something you want to do, feel free."

"I might go visit my dad and my sister," I tell him. And I really should, especially since Dad fell again yesterday. As soon as I get paid, I'm going to burn through half my money just buying medication for him. Since my food and lodging are figured into my pay, I'm more or less living here for free. I *could* send all my money over to Dad and Heather. Yeah, I want stuff for myself. But I don't need stuff.

Wes nods. "I'm sure they'd like that."

"Yeah. I think so." Heather will, at least. Dad might not remember who I am. I finish my tea, put the mug in the dishwasher and wipe down the already-clean counter just so I have something to do. Wes is done now, and we both look at each other in an awkward stand-off.

He has to be thinking the same thing I am. We kissed, and it was a damn good kiss. I felt his hard cock against me. My breasts pressed against his firm chest, and we both wanted more. If Jackson hadn't come down the steps, we *would* have had more.

And then what?

Would we be in an even more awkward situation than we are right now? I've never had someone resist me like this, and it sucks. Only because I want him something terrible…and not just physically, as much as I don't want to admit that to myself.

I should hate him, but I can't. Because, without a doubt, Weston is making me feel.

Chapter Seventeen

SCARLET

"I THOUGHT MAYBE YOU FORGOT ABOUT ME NOW THAT YOU'RE A WORKING GIRL AND all," Heather says, sitting back in the plastic chair. Her hair is even worse than before, and she has a bruise on her cheek.

"What happened?" I ask, ignoring her subtle jab.

She shrugs. "Kickball got a little rough in the yard."

"You're allowed to play kickball?" I shake my head. "That's not the point. Please don't get in fights."

"Seriously, Scar? Like I want to get in fights?"

I let out a breath. "Sorry. I didn't mean it like that. Just…don't get into fights."

Heather rolls her eyes. "How's the new job? Are you ready to slit your wrists yet?"

"No. It's not bad at all. I kinda like it."

Heather cocks an eyebrow. "You hate kids. This guy must be loaded for you to say you like being a nanny for a rich, spoiled brat."

Her words piss me off, and I try hard not to let myself recognize it. Because you only get upset when someone insults someone you care about. "He doesn't have the money I thought he did. And the kid isn't spoiled or bratty at all. He's sweet."

"Are you fucking him? He must have one magic cock for you to hang around now."

I want to be fucking Wes. I have no doubt his cock *is* magic. "Nope. Not sleeping with him."

"You mean not yet, right? That's how you pull your tricks, isn't it? Sex and blackmail are like your claim to fame."

"They're not," I say, fully aware of another visitor eavesdropping. I get it, our conversation is unorthodox at best, but geez, be a little discreet.

"So what are you going to do? We need money."

"My job."

Heather's eyebrows push together, and she stares at me for a good few seconds. "Wait. You took a job as a nanny for a rich couple so you could con them out of their money, but you're just going to be a fucking nanny and earn minimum wage?"

Hearing her say it out loud makes me realize how terrible a person I am. "I'm doing the job I was hired to do. And it's not a rich couple. Wes is a single dad."

"Ohh, his name is Wes. You must be hot for him or something. Because my badass big sister doesn't work petty jobs."

I roll my eyes. "Stop bragging about me to your prison friends, okay? You're going to get me caught or something."

"Please." She runs a hand through her butchered hair. Fixing it is the first thing I'm going to do once she's out of here.

"And I don't get hot for people. I think all that love shit is that just that: shit."

Heather drums her fingers on the table. "Have you seen Dad lately?"

"Yeah. I saw him before I came here."

"How'd he look today?" she asks apprehensively.

"Okay. He has a big bump on his head from falling face first out of his wheelchair. I guess he was reaching for something and hit the floor." I rub my forehead, feeling a headache coming on. "I was able to talk to the doctor today about switching medications. I don't want him to be drugged up, but something needs to change so he doesn't bust his head open."

"Yeah, we need to get him into a better place with more staff."

"Oh, that would help for sure. But places like that are expensive."

Heather looks down at the table, dropping her *I don't give a shit* attitude. She knows the stunt she pulled that got her arrested took away a lot from Dad. I spent money on her lawyer, and she obviously can't work and contribute to the medical bills anymore.

"Why do you have so many scratches on your hands?" she asks.

"Kittens."

"Awww, I want a kitten. Are they at the house?"

"No, Wes—my boss—has a sister who really likes cats. We hung out yesterday." I say it almost like a confession, because Heather knows how far from normal this is for me. After picking up Jackson from school, I met Quinn and Emma at the farmers' market downtown. I really like her, which surprised me more than anyone. Never in a million years would I think I'd be talking and laughing with someone like Quinn.

"You're really making yourself at home. I thought one of your cardinal rules was not to get involved and make personal attachments or whatever."

I shake my head, stomach tightening. "This isn't my usual situation. I told you, Wes doesn't have a trust fund. I don't know…" I pick at the lint that's stuck to the sleeves of my sweater, angling myself away from the chick who's still looking at me. Judge away, bitch. You can't be much better considering we're both visiting someone in prison. "I'll figure it out."

Heather lets out a huff. "Do it fast. I'm almost out of money, and I really like being able to buy snacks."

I can't help but laugh. "I'm glad you have your priorities in check."

⁂

"Is everything okay?" Wes asks softly. We just finished dinner, and I've hardly said a word throughout the meal. Going back to the south side, seeing my sister and my dad, and walking down the streets I've haunted since I was old enough to venture out on my own…it reminded me who I am.

Of the shit I've done.

And all the thoughts I've wrestled down are fighting to come up. To remind me how shitty of a person I am.

That there is no such thing as redemption.

"Yeah, just…just thinking." I force a smile.

"Okay." He doesn't believe me, but he's not going to press it. His phone buzzes again, and I eye it.

"You're mister popular tonight."

He flips it over and glances at the text. "It's my brothers trying to get me to go out to the bar tonight."

"On a Wednesday?"

"Yeah. There's a twenty-first birthday celebration going on, and it's always entertaining to watch."

"You should go," I tell him. "I'm here to look after Jackson after he's asleep."

Wes considers it for a whole two seconds. "Honestly, I feel bad going out."

"Don't. I'm here, and if you put Jackson to bed, then it's not like you're missing out on time with him, which is what I think you feel bad about, right?"

He smiles. "Right. They have been bugging me for ages. And I'll only stay for an hour."

"Stay as long as you'd like. I have a wild night planned, and having the law here is going to cramp my style."

Wes laughs. "Then maybe I should stay."

I gather the plates from the table and take them to the sink. "It's going to get crazy up in here. It'll start with me singing off-key to Def Leppard and will end with tea and a few more chapters of a rather steamy werewolf-vampire romance."

"You like Def Leppard?"

"I do. Motley Crue, KISS, and Skid Row will be on repeat as well." I turn on the sink to rinse the dishes. "You sound surprised. Are you judging me, Mr. Dawson?"

"I am. I am judging you hard, and I will admit you do not look like someone who'd be a fan of 80s hair bands."

"Looks can be deceiving."

"Apparently so."

I laugh and start loading the dishwasher. "Don't be mad if I teach Jackson the words to 'Pour Some Sugar on Me.'"

"Oh, he already knows them."

"Seriously?"

"Seriously." Weston comes up behind me and grabs a plate from the sink to put into the dishwasher. "Add in Bon Jovi, Poison, Van Halen, and Ratt and you've pretty much named my whole playlist."

"Did we just become best friends?"

"You like 80s rock and you made a *Stepbrothers* reference? It's like you're not real."

I laugh, finding twisted humor in his words. I've never been this real with someone before.

"I'm not. You're imagining everything right now. It's all a dream."

"At least it's a good one."

Dammit, Weston…if only you knew.

His phone rings, and he wipes his hands on a towel with a sigh.

"Your brothers really want you to go out."

"They won't stop until I do."

"It's cute, you know. And nice to see you all still be close as adults."

"So close I'm going to send this call to voice—oh, it's my mom. Never mind." I finish loading the dishwasher as he talks to his mom, and it sounds like she's stopping by to drop something off.

"Remember how I said my mom likes buying Jackson clothes?"

I start the dishwasher and grab a rag to wipe down the counter. "Yeah."

"She's bought 'a few things' and is bringing them over."

"Awww, that's so sweet."

"Hey, Jackson!" Wes calls, and Jackson comes in from the living room. "Grammy is bringing you something."

"A kitten?"

I can't help but laugh.

"No, not a kitten."

"Oh, man!" Jackson throws his head back dramatically. "But I really, really want one."

"You should let him get a kitten," I say, flashing Wes a sweet smile. "We played with them yesterday, and they're so sweet."

"I'll think about it," Wes says flatly, and Jackson starts jumping up and down. He runs back into the living room to look out the window for his grandma.

"The kittens are cute," Wes agrees.

"They are so stinking cute, and oh my God, your sister's house is huge," I blurt, and it feels good to finally say it out loud.

Wes laughs. "Yeah, it's…it's something."

"She has enough room for more cats."

"Don't encourage her," he chuckles and goes to get the vacuum. We work together to get the kitchen cleaned up, falling into a rhythm without even meaning to. The front door opens, and Mrs. Dawson steps in, carrying two large shopping bags.

"Hi, Scarlet," she says, setting the bags down. Jackson drags one into the living room and dumps it out, sorting through his clothes. There are new figures for his farm set at the bottom of the second bag, and Jackson races up the stairs to put them in his barn.

Wes's phone starts buzzing again, and this time it is his brothers.

"Who's texting you so much?" Mrs. Dawson asks, trying to look over Wes's shoulder at his phone. He's too tall to get a look.

"Dean, Logan, and Owen. They've been annoying me all night about going out with them."

"You should!" Mrs. Dawson says right away. "Both of you should. I'll stay and put Jackson to bed." She looks at me and smiles. "He told me you're more fun, but I do miss that little rascal."

"It's a school night," Wes counters.

"I know. I can get him to bed. You should go out. You don't," his mom says gently. "And you should."

"You're encouraging me to go to a bar on a weekday. Such good parenting, Mom."

Mrs. Dawson laughs. "Take that as a sign of how much you need to get out of the house. And I'm sure Scarlet would appreciate it too, right?"

"Uh, right," I agree, even though a quiet night alone not being able to sleep due to excessive amounts of guilt was what I had on my agenda. "I'm curious to see this bar too."

"Fine," Weston huffs. "But only for an hour. I do have to work tomorrow."

"Let me go get changed," I say and dash up the stairs. Usually, if I go to a bar, I'm pulling out all the stops. But tonight, I'm brushing through my messy hair, putting on just enough makeup to look presentable, and am wearing leggings.

Scratch that. I'm wearing a v-neck black sweater dress that hugs my curves and shows the perfect amount of cleavage. I do enjoy dressing up for myself every now and then. Not wanting to keep Wes or his mom waiting, I hurry out of my room.

Wes and Jackson are coming up the stairs right as I step into the hall.

"He wants me to give him a bath," Wes says before he sees me. He does a double-take, and I'd be lying if I said it didn't feel good to see his reaction.

"Oh, okay."

"I'll try to be fast. Give us twenty minutes."

Jackson races ahead, already stripping out of his clothes. Twenty minutes is all I need to put on more makeup and curl my hair. I finish getting ready a few minutes after Wes and Jackson are downstairs.

"Wow!" Jackson says when he sees me. "Your hair is so bouncy."

I run my hand over a curl. "Yeah, I guess it is. Do you like it or is it too bouncy?"

"I like it! You look like a princess!"

"Thank you. And you look super cute in those Mickey Mouse jammies."

Jackson narrows his eyes. "I'm not cute. I'm handsome."

"Ohhh, I'm sorry," I say with a laugh. "You are very handsome."

Jackson beams and looks at Wes. "Like Daddy."

I can't disagree. Wes *is* very handsome. He changed too, and the dark jeans and gray Henley shirt look so good on him.

"We won't be out too long," Wes tells his mom, dropping down to his knees to give Jackson a hug and a kiss. "Be good for Grammy. And don't stay up too late. You have school in the morning."

"Yay, school!" Jackson throws his arms around Wes, hugging him goodbye. I grab my coat and put on my favorite over-the-knee boots and follow Wes outside.

"You look nice," I tell him, looking over my shoulder at him.

He looks a little surprised by the compliment. "Thanks. And you…you look beautiful." The headlights of the Jeep flash as he unlocks it. I turn around, twisting the strap of my purse in my hands, and look at Wes. There's an undeniable hunger in his eyes, and I know it'll only take one move to be devoured.

I part my lips, eyeing Wes up and down. He steps in, loose stones on the pavement rolling under his feet. The chill in the air starts to disappear the closer he gets, and I want so badly to reach out and pull him to me. He hesitates, holding my gaze for a moment.

And then he steps around, going to the driver's side of the Jeep. I exhale heavily, just now realizing that my heart is racing. What the hell is wrong with me? It's not like it's been that long since I've had sex that I'm desperate to hook up with the first attractive man I can find. He's my boss. We can't just hook up and go on like everything is fine and dandy the next day.

And really…I don't want to hook up with him. I want more, but I know Wes wouldn't date someone like me. Not the real me.

"Something tells me he's not going to make it through the first three shots, let alone the twenty-one he wants to do," Logan laughs, wiping up a spilled drink from the wooden surface of the bar.

"People still try that?" I ask.

Logan nods. "They do. We'd cut them off before they get close, but I've never seen anyone get past four shots in a row like that." He shakes his head. "It wasn't pretty."

I wrinkle my nose. "I actually never thought about that before. You probably have your fair share of vomit to clean up."

"We really try to cut people off before they get to that point, but it's not always possible. Luckily most people somehow get outside and puke in the parking lot. It's easy to hose away."

"Glamorous."

Logan laughs and steps away to take drink orders from two girls who just walked up. Wes is throwing darts with Dean, and I turn around to watch for a minute. The bar is pretty crowded for a Wednesday, even without the birthday party. The bar itself is amazing and much bigger than I imagined.

"Do you want a drink?" Logan asks, coming back over.

"Sure. Do you have wine?"

"We do."

"Give me a glass of whatever's cheapest," I say

"You don't want what's cheapest. It's shit."

I laugh, looking Logan over. Physically, he looks exactly like his twin. They wear their hair the same and probably share clothes. But there's a distinct difference between the two, with the biggest being how obviously Logan is crushing on fellow bartender, Danielle. I've been watching him flirt and get flustered when she's around, and she's giving it right back.

"You work for Wes. I'll put it on his tab." Logan steps away and returns a minute later with a glass of sweet red wine.

"This is good," I say after I take a sip.

"It is, isn't it?" Logan looks across the bar at Danielle, spacing out for a second before turning back to me. "What's it like living with my brother? He can be very, uh, uptight at times. Though he's dealt with an unfair amount of shit in his life."

"He's great. Jackson too."

"You can be honest," Logan jokes.

"Really," I laugh. "We get along well, which is nice. I'm there for Jackson, but it helps, ya know? We eat dinner and watch TV together and it's not weird."

"That's good. Going and living with someone would be weird on its own."

I nod and take another drink of wine. "It takes a while to get used to. I know he wishes he didn't have to have a nanny for Jackson." I look over at Wes again. "He'll never admit it, but I think he feels guilty for being away."

"He does. My big brother might be a tad prickly at times, but nothing is more important to him than family."

"I can tell," I say as my gaze drifts back to Wes. "It's a very admirable quality, and if I'm being honest, it's not one I see too often."

"Right," Logan agrees.

I can't help the smile that pulls up my lips or the flush that colors my cheeks. I'm still looking at Wes, and Logan catches me watching.

"So your place is really nice," I blurt, feeling almost as if I'm having an out-of-body experience. The last time I was at a bar, things went very different. I actually can't remember the last time I went to a bar just for fun like this. This isn't me. It's so far from the version of myself I usually am it's jarring.

But I like it.

Chapter Eighteen

WESTON

I put my squad car in park and get out, stepping into the quiet night that surrounds my house. It's been a long week, and I'm looking forward to having the weekend off. The living room light is on, and I can see the fuzzy outline of Scarlet sitting on the couch through the sheer curtains.

Several pumpkins and a few pots of mums are on the porch steps, and it looks like she and Jackson finished putting up the little graveyard scene in the lawn today, finally decorating for Halloween. She's been here for two weeks now, and we've fallen into a good routine.

A good routine that involves awkwardly avoiding the very obvious fact that we're both extremely attracted to each other.

We eat meals together whenever I'm home, and on the nights the sky is clear, Scarlet goes outside to look at the stars. I've joined her a few times, but it's harder and harder to keep my hands to myself and my heart in my chest whenever I'm around her.

Jackson loves her, and having the stability has already made a difference in his behavior and mood. He's always a happy kid, but not having to get up at the crack of dawn makes a huge difference on the kid. He's not a morning person.

My life has been simplified in some aspects as well, and not having to try to fit in cleaning and making dinner has been a huge relief. I shouldn't be as tired as I am, but I've had a hard time falling asleep knowing Scarlet is just down the hall. I wake up almost every night after dreaming of her, cock hard and heart racing.

She's beautiful, but it's more than that. She's good with my son. Takes care of him and makes him happy. The rare times I'd let my mind wander and would think of dating again, I always came back to the same issue: Jackson.

Dating isn't easy. Dating with kids is even harder. Not only do I need to find someone who is fine with me having a kid, they'd have to bond with Jackson before I considered moving into anything serious. It's almost like things have been done in reverse with Scarlet. She came here for Jackson, and I know he'd approve if we—

"Stop," I say out loud to myself. It's not going to happen.

A gust of wind blows through, rattling the trees. Misty rain begins to fall, and I hurry into the house. I take off my shoes and coat, and head upstairs to lock up my gun for the night.

"Hey," Scarlet says, looking up from her phone. "How was work?"

"Work was fine. The meetings…" I shake my head. "They went all right too. But you know how I don't like them."

"I do." She sets her phone down on the coffee table. "Jackson polished off the leftovers, but I can make something for you if you want."

"Thanks, but I'm good. I picked up fast food on the way home." I pat my stomach. "I undid my workout from this morning, I know. But those fries were worth it."

Scarlet laughs. "I admire your dedication." She stretches her legs out in front of her. "I was just about to start the new season of *American Horror Story*. Want to watch it with me?"

We haven't sat on the couch like this since *the incident*. I think we're both afraid of what might happen if we stay up late and sit in the dark together again. And good Lord, I want it to happen again. I've been able to use work as an excuse before. I can't stay up late because I have to get up early, and obviously working the night shifts prevented any such offerings.

But tonight…tonight I have no reason to say no, and I do want to watch the show. I'm off all weekend, and so is Scarlet. She's going to Chicago to see her dad again tomorrow. I haven't asked, and she hasn't said anything, but I get the feeling her dad is sick or something. I've heard her a few times on the phone, talking about treatments, and once she seemed close to tears while arguing with insurance about getting a medication covered.

"Yeah," I tell her. "I'll watch it."

"Great. So you said no to food, but what about popcorn?"

"I never say no to popcorn."

Scarlet smiles and gets up to make some while I change. She's still in the kitchen when I come back down. Her phone is set to silent and is still on the coffee table. It vibrates, getting my attention. A text comes through from someone named Corbin. Two black hearts follow his name, and I divert my eyes, not wanting to so much as read a word he's saying.

I never really thought about Scarlet dating, and I assumed she was single from 1) taking a job where she moved two hours away from home and in with another family and 2) that kiss was pretty intense the other night.

Scarlet comes back, smile on her face, and sits on the couch next to me. There are three cushions on the couch, and there's an unwritten rule of leaving the middle one free when two people who aren't romantically involved sit together. But Scarlet ignores the rule and puts the popcorn in her lap.

Her phone vibrates again, and as soon as she reads the texts, her smile disappears and a line of worry forms between her eyes. She hands me the popcorn and texts back, making sure her phone is angled away so I can't see it.

With a sigh, she sets her phone down next to her and picks up the remote. Her face is tight as she turns on the TV.

"Everything okay?"

"Yeah," she says back without missing a beat. She puts on her front again, pushing her shoulders back and lifting her eyebrows just enough to cover the worry. She holds that stance for a while, and I wonder if it's subconscious or if she's really good at understanding body language and is doing it on purpose.

Either way, something is upsetting her, and it upsets me. I don't want to pry, because I know Scarlet isn't throwing out the "it's fine" line just to see if I'll keep digging. She wants me to believe things are fine so I don't pressure her.

"Okay. If you need anything…just let me know," I say quietly.

Her smile trembles for a quick second. "Thanks. And I will. Actually, I'll probably leave early tomorrow to beat the traffic."

"You can take my Jeep," I offer, knowing she's been Ubering to Chicago and back. It's not cheap.

"Don't you need it?"

"I don't plan on going anywhere tomorrow, to be honest, and I have my squad car if I absolutely need to leave the house."

"You're sure?" she asks again.

"Yeah. This might be a stupid question, but do you drive a lot in the city?"

"Where I lived, yeah, I did. Well, when I had a car. I sold it for drug money."

I raise an eyebrow, waiting for her to laugh so I know she's joking. She doesn't.

"Drugs for my dad," she goes on, seeing the blank expression on my face. "And not illegal drugs. Prescription. My dad is…" She lets out a breath and, at the same time, lets go of the air she's putting on. Her shoulders sag forward, and her smile is nowhere to be seen. "My dad is sick."

"Shit, I'm so sorry."

She pulls her arms in around herself. "He's been sick for a while, and the medical bills won't pay themselves."

"It's bullshit how much healthcare costs."

"Yeah, you're telling me." She pushes her hair back and lets out a deep sigh. "We missed the beginning." Turning her attention back to the TV, she rewinds the minute or so we missed. Halfway through the episode, Scarlet's rests her head on my shoulder. Only a minute or two later, she's asleep.

Guess I'm not the only one having a hard time sleeping at night.

Chapter Nineteen

SCARLET

"I don't get it," I say, cutting apart a piece of chicken. Well, if you can consider this over-processed mess chicken. "If the issue is he wants to get up and walk, then why can't someone walk with him?" I stab a small piece of chicken on the fork and feed it to my father. "He wouldn't fall then because someone would be helping him, right?"

"Girl," Corbin says, feeding two patients at once. "We are so understaffed I'm thrilled if we get through our shower list. You're right, and it's not fucking fair, but it's all I can do just to get two aides to cover the south wing with me."

"It's not your fault," I say, making sure he knows I don't hold any blame on him. Corbin works his ass off, as do many of the others here. The problem is there aren't enough of them. This place is a dump, and nobody wants to work here. Unfortunately, most of the residents here have similar financial situations to mine and can't go anywhere else.

"You need to get out of here," Corbin says quietly, as if he's reading my mind. "I'm trying to, and I have an interview at the hospital next week." He looks around the table and shakes his head. "I don't want to leave these guys, though."

"You deserve better," I tell him.

"So do they."

I give Dad another bite of chicken. "This fucking sucks."

"I know it." Corbin shakes his head. "It's lose-lose no matter what we do."

I let out a sigh. "Yeah, it is." I pick up the water and put the straw to Dad's lips. He swats my hand away.

"I can feed myself, Wendy."

It's not the first time he's called me by my mother's name. Once upon a time, before the meth and the heroin, my mother and I shared a resemblance. I remember looking through her high school yearbook once and thinking she was the most beautiful woman in the world.

Ignoring my father, I move the water away and wait a few seconds before trying again. This time he takes a drink.

"So," Corbin starts. "You pulled up here in a Jeep Wrangler, not a Caddy. Did the new job not work out?"

My stomach tightens. I'd moved past conning Wes, and dare I say I almost forgot about it? I didn't, not by a long shot, but a girl can dream, right?

"I'm still working as a nanny, but in the traditional sense this time."

Corbin gives me a quizzical look. We never hang out, but he's the closest thing I have to a friend. He's one of the least judgmental people I know, and there's just something humbling about the guy who wipes my dad's ass and gives him a shower. There are two people in this world who know the nitty-gritty details of my life. One is my sister, and the other is Corbin.

"But you don't like kids."

I shrug. "This kid isn't so bad." I smile. "He's great, actually. And his dad—my boss—is a great guy too. His whole family is great, and now I've said great like a million times."

"They must really be great."

I roll my eyes at Corbin. "They are, though, and it's been nice hanging out with them," I say, lowering my voice. I'm not sure what state of mind Dad is in, but there's always a chance he'll hear me, and I don't want to make him feel bad.

Not that his behavior is excused. He and Mom had a tumultuous relationship that imploded when Mom cheated on him. Dad always drank too much but spiraled after that. He left us, and Mom went into a depression. She wasn't without her vices before, of course, and things got worse from there on out. We never realized how much Dad tried to keep Mom clean until he left.

He wanted to leave her, but he also left us. When he showed back up in our lives, I refused to talk to him for half a year. I caved only because I wanted to go back and graduate high school.

"And his wife?" Corbin asks, raising his eyebrows.

"He doesn't have one."

"Ohhhh."

"It's not like that." I shake my head and trade the fork for a spoon and test the soup before giving some to Dad. It's not terrible, but it is lacking a bit in flavor. I add some salt, stirring it up. "They're just good people. Maybe they'll rub off on me. They all get together on Sundays for dinner, and by all, I mean my boss and his four siblings. At their parents' house. Like a TV family."

Corbin shakes his head. "Perfect families like that freak me out. Lord knows what's hiding in their closets."

I smile and laugh, but I know the Dawsons aren't like that. They're perfect in my eyes. But they're not without their faults.

Maybe we're not so different after all.

"I thought they misspoke when they called my name." Heather's arms are crossed tightly over her chest, and she's sporting a new bruise on her temple. I'm not even going to ask.

"Funny, Heather."

"It's been, what, two weeks since I've seen you?" She cocks her eyebrows and stares me down as if she just caught me with my hand in the cookie jar.

"That's not my fault."

"What's that supposed to mean?"

"It means the reason I haven't seen you is because you're in jail." My words come out harsher than I meant. Trumpets will sound the day she grows the fuck up and takes responsibility for her actions. "I've been busy."

"Too busy to see Dad?"

"I saw him today."

"And that was the first time since you came out this way last?"

The woman who obviously eavesdropped on our conversation the last time I was here comes into the room. Her eyes fall on me for a few seconds before she moves in and takes a seat at a nearby table.

"No, I saw him last week."

"And you didn't come see me?" The pitch of Heather's voice goes up. Dammit. She takes things too personally, and I know she has to be miserable in here. Knowing I was in the area but didn't stop by stings, but it's not like that.

"It's a two-and-a-half-hour drive from here to Eastwood, and I was tired. Plus, I needed to get back for...for dinner."

"You couldn't come see me so you could fucking eat dinner? It better have been a damn good meal."

"The food was good," I admit. Though the company is even better. "What happened to your face?" I change the subject, knowing asking about her injuries will piss her off too, but at least she'll be pissed off for a different reason.

"This is what happens when you try and stay out of trouble." She motions to her face. "But it's been handled."

"Handled?"

Heather lets out an exasperated sigh. "It's hard to explain unless you've been in here, okay?"

I nod. "Okay. I just want you to come home."

"Do we even have a home anymore? Aren't you living with some rich family in East-something-or-other."

"Eastwood, and I told you, he's a single dad and not rich."

"So that's *your* home. Where am I going to go?"

I shake my head. "I'll figure it out."

"What if I get out tomorrow?"

She won't, so that's not even a concern. "I'll come get you."

"And then what?"

"I'll take you back with me."

She lets out a snort of laughter. She's angry at something else and is taking it out on me. "And I could stay in the house you're living at?"

"No, I don't think Wes would be okay with that," I say honestly. "But we'd get you a hotel room until we could set up something more permanent."

"We?"

"Yes, I know Wes would help me. He's a good guy."

Instead of coming back with a sassy comment, Heather smiles. "You really like this guy, don't you?"

"I do like him, but not in the way you're insinuating. He's a good guy."

"Yeah, you said that."

Heat rushes through me. "Okay, yeah…he's attractive, and if I wasn't his son's nanny, I'd make a move. Another move, since Jackson kind of cock-blocked us the first time." I shake my head. "But he's a *good guy*, Heather. One of the rare, really good ones. And I'm, well, not. I took the job as a nanny with the intentions of conning money out of him. I'm a horrible person."

Heather laughs and reaches across the table, taking my hands. "Scar, don't even say that. You're not a horrible person. We've all done things we're not proud of. And this orange jumpsuit proves it on my end." She gives my hands a squeeze. "So what are you going to do about it?"

"Nothing."

"Nothing? That's not my older sister talking."

"He's my boss. What if we hook up and then it's weird? I live with him and his son."

"But what if it's not weird?"

I shrug. "I don't know. He doesn't strike me as the kind who would be okay with a fuck-buddy type of relationship. If we hooked up, things between us would go to the next level."

"Isn't that what you want?"

God yes. I'd love to be Weston's girlfriend. To go out together and actually cuddle on the couch as we're watching horror movies, staying up way too late and then crawling up to bed together. We'd be so tired but unable to keep our hands off each other, and we'd have sleepy, lazy sex that only couples who have reached a deep level of comfort have.

"I wouldn't mind," I tell my sister. "But then I'd have to disclose personal info, and I don't know how he'd feel about me if he knew, well, everything."

"That you've been conning people for years, Dad was a drunk, Mom died with a needle in her arm, and your baby sister is in jail?"

"Yeah. That."

"Just brag about Jason a bit first."

I give her a lopsided smile. "I already have. It doesn't matter. He won't understand where we came from, and more importantly, I'm not going to sleep with my boss."

"You're in love with him."

"No. I don't believe in love." The words escape my lips and feel like a lie. I *didn't* believe in love, but now I'm not so sure. Being in love meant having a heart, and I convinced myself mine stopped working long ago.

But now when I close my eyes and the world becomes still, I feel it fluttering back to life.

Chapter Twenty

SCARLET

"What about this one?" Jackson races forward to the biggest pumpkin he can find.

"I think that might be a little too heavy," I laugh. It's late Monday morning, and Jackson and I are at the pumpkin patch with Quinn, Archer, and Emma. "How about this one?" I point to a round, white pumpkin.

"It lost all its color!" Jackson's eye widen in shock, making both Quinn and I laugh.

"It's supposed to be like that," Quinn explains, adjusting Emma in the baby carrier she's wearing. "Ohh, a cat!"

"Don't even think about it," Archer says, slipping his arm around Quinn's waist. "Pretty sure it belongs to the orchard."

"I didn't say I was going to take it."

Archer gives her side a squeeze. They're gag-worthy cute together, but Quinn is quickly becoming a friend, so it doesn't bother me like it normally would. "I know the way your mind works."

"Look at this one! It's all bumpy!" Jackson laughs, looking at the pumpkin with a look of disgust on his face.

"You don't like it?" I ask.

"It has warts!"

"It does?" I make a move to touch it, and Jackson grabs my hand, laughing.

"You'll get warts too!"

I take Jackson's hand and lead him to another row of pumpkins. He goes to a large, oval-shaped one that has to be heavy.

"I like this one!"

"I think it's perfect," I tell him.

Archer picks up the heavy pumpkin for us and puts it on the wagon he's pulling. We make it through the rest of pumpkins, grabbing a few more little ones along the way. Jackson and I grabbed pumpkins from the store not long ago, but this is way more fun. I've never been to a pumpkin patch like this before. We go into a big barn to pay for our pumpkins and to get apple cider. The sun is out in full force today, making the fifty-degree air comfortable.

I'm having fun, and while I'm working, it doesn't feel like it. I really care about Jackson, and seeing him light up and have fun makes me happy. We get our cider and take it outside, enjoying what could very likely be one of the last warm days this fall. Archer's loading the pumpkins into the back of the SUV when Quinn's phone rings.

"It's Wes," she says, brows coming together. Weston is at work today, and his call isn't expected. "Hey, Wes. What's up?" She waits a moment, listening to her brother. "Oh no. Yeah, yeah, we'll be right there." Another pause. "Archer's with me. I'll let him know."

Archer, having heard his name, looks up. Once he sees the worry on Quinn's face, he comes over. "What's wrong?"

Quinn shakes her head. "Thanks, Wes. Just, uh, keep him calm if you can. We'll be right there." She ends the call and readjusts Emma on her chest. "It's Bobby."

Archer's face falls. "Is he…is he…"

"He's alive," Quinn answers and starts to take Emma out of the carrier. "Wes has him."

"Where is he?" Archer asks, fumbling with the last pumpkin. Obviously, something is going on and Bobby has significance to both Quinn and Archer.

"Wes has him."

"Jackson," I call, taking his hand and leading him over to Quinn and Archer. "Is everything okay?" I ask Quinn.

"No, it's Archer's brother, Bobby. He's an addict, and Wes found him passed out in the park. He's been clean for the last few months." She lets out a sigh and shakes her head. "I guess he relapsed."

"Oh my God, I'm so sorry."

Quinn frowns, looking at Archer as he hurries to put the wagon away. "He'd been doing so well."

I swallow hard. That's something I know all about, and the disappointment crashes down on you hard.

"How long had he been clean?"

"A couple months, which is the longest ever." Quinn starts to take Emma out of her carrier. "Archer really thought it was for real this time."

"It's hard," I say with too much emotion. Quinn catches on and tips her head slightly, flicking her eyes to mine. "You said Wes has him…did you mean in jail?"

"No, and thank God it was my brother who responded to the call about a drunk in the park. He took him to a cafe that's like five minutes away and got him coffee instead of taking him to the station."

"Is he supposed to do that?"

"Probably not, but he knows how hard Bobby's been working…and how much this means to Archer."

I feel a tug on my heart, pulling it up from the dark pit I shoved it in, bringing it closer to the spot it's supposed to be in.

"Do you need to go get him?"

"Yeah. We can take you home first."

"No, you don't have to. You said he's only five minutes away, so we should go."

"Are you sure?"

I nod, words of truth bubbling inside of me. I know what it's like to have a family member be an addict, and I want to tell her that she and Archer are good fucking people. And Wes too, but dammit, his goodness is so bad for me.

"Yeah, and I can hold Emma for you if you need help."

"Thank you."

It's a tense ride to the diner, and when we get there, Jackson says he has to go potty. Emma is asleep in her car seat, and Quinn carries her in. Wes is sitting in the back, looking all gorgeous and heroic in his uniform.

"Daddy!" Jackson calls and runs to him. Wes gets up, face tight but smiling as soon as he sees his son. Jackson throws his arms around Wes's neck, and my ovaries explode.

Then I notice the guy who's sitting at the table with Wes. He looks like Archer but is dirty, tired, and worn. It's a look I know, one I used to see on my own mother's face.

Archer rushes forward, and Bobby stands, face falling. Tears well in his eyes.

"I'm sorry, Arch."

"It's okay," Archer tells him, pulling him into a hug. Quinn sets Emma's car seat on the table and puts her hand on Archer's back. Bobby breaks away and looks at Quinn and then Emma. His face falls, and he hefts back into the booth, covering his hands with his face.

"Hey, buddy," I say, dropping down to Jackson's level. "Do you still need to go potty?"

He does, and I take him into the bathroom. When we get back, Bobby is drinking coffee with Archer, and Quinn is talking to Wes near the door. Jackson goes to his dad, and Wes scoops him up. I slowly make my way over, giving them some space.

"Thank you, Wes," Quinn tells him.

"It's no problem." Wes pats Quinn's shoulder. "I'm glad I was the one who responded."

Quinn nods. "Me too. The last thing we need is for him to get arrested again."

I watch them and then look back at Archer. He's ordering food for Bobby, who is still very much drunk and overly emotional.

"Do you guys have this?" Wes asks his sister.

"Yeah. We'll order him some food and take him home. The Joneses are out of town this week, and we thought Bobby would be okay on his own. We'll bring him home with us and look into rehab again."

"Can I get food too?" Jackson asks.

"Of course you can," Quinn tells him with a smile. "But you have to share your fries with me."

"No!" he laughs. "Order your own!"

"I will. But I'll still steal one of yours." She smiles, and Wes looks up at me. His navy eyes meet mine and, Lord have mercy, that man is fine. Out of the corner of my eye, I see Quinn look from Wes to me and back again. "Can you join us for lunch?" she asks him.

"Yeah, I'm not doing much else, and I eat lunch around now anyway."

"Can I show you my pumpkin?" Jackson asks Wes. "It's so big!"

"Sure, on our way out," Wes tells him, setting him down. Jackson takes my hand and pulls me over.

"Hungry?" Quinn asks, giving a guilty smile. "Sorry if this isn't how you imagined your day would go."

"It's fine," I assure her, though she's right. This isn't how I thought my day would go. I didn't think I'd see Wes and Quinn deal with a sensitive issue with nothing but concern and care.

Maybe there's hope for me after all.

Chapter Twenty-One

WESTON

I zip up my coat, feeling chilled despite the warm sun beating down on me. Maybe I shouldn't have ignored the fact that I woke up with a sore throat. But the day is over, and I'm looking forward to going home and having dinner with Jackson and Scarlet.

I call Quinn on the way and check on Bobby. He's at their house and has been sleeping it off for hours. I remember the first time Archer stayed with us while he and Dean roomed together in college because his brother got himself into trouble with drinking. They've been trying to help Bobby get clean for so long. It's starting to get hard to think he ever will.

Scarlet and Jackson are outside when I get home, and she's chasing him around like a zombie again. He fakes a fall, dramatically rolling through fallen leaves. Scarlet sees me first and stops dragging one foot with her arms out in front of her. She smiles, and I have to work hard at ignoring the rush that goes through me, making my cock jump.

Her hair is a mess and leaves are stuck to the back of her sweater. Knowing she was rolling around in the leaves with my son makes her all the more attractive, and after the dream I had about her last night, I'm going to have a hard time looking her in the eye.

"Hey," she calls, giving me a wave. Jackson gets up, smiling, and starts running again for Scarlet to chase him. "Your dad's home," she tells him, but he doesn't stop. "Jackson," she calls again, and this time he stops.

"Hi, Dad!" He gives me a quick wave and turns to Scarlet again. "Can we keep playing now?"

"Dinner's ready and waiting," she reminds him. "I know it's not Tuesday, but we're having tacos."

"Sounds good." I stop a few feet from Scarlet, and suddenly everything feels so fucking weird. We function like a couple but don't touch each other. She takes care of my son, and he's enamored with her. She's a little odd, but it's one of the many things I find so damn attractive about her.

And that kiss we shared her first weekend here…there's no denying we have chemistry.

"Have you heard from your sister?" Scarlet asks, brushing leaves out of Jackson's hair. "I was going to text her and see how things are going but didn't know if that would be overstepping."

"I don't think it would be, and yeah, I did. Things are going as well as they can, considering."

Scarlet nods. Her concern is genuine, and her friendship with my sister makes this even weirder. No one in my family liked Daisy much. They tolerated her for my sake, but she never even made an effort to hang out with Quinn.

"That's good, I guess. It's hard when you think someone is doing well and then things go right back to the beginning." She gets a distant look in her eyes, and I get a feeling she's speaking from experience. "And Wes…"

"Yeah?"

"What you did for him was really nice."

"Bobby's not a terrible person, and arresting him is hard on Quinn and Archer."

"You really care about your family. It's not something I see too often." A slight flush colors her cheeks. She pushes her hair back, finding leaves at the end of her long locks, and shakes her head. "We should get in and eat."

"Yeah," I agree. We all go into the house, and by the time I get changed and back down, the table is set, and Mexican music is playing from Scarlet's phone.

"We're having a fee-yes-ta," Jackson tells me, proud of himself for learning a new word. He takes my hand and leads me to the table. There are chips and salsa already out on the table, and Scarlet brings over two margaritas.

"They're virgin, obviously, since there's no tequila in the house."

"I have one too!" Jackson picks up his plastic up and wants to "do cheers" with everyone. Dinner is good, and Jackson tells me about his trip to the orchard. My sore throat gets worse, and by the time I get Jackson bathed and in bed, I have a bad headache.

"Not feeling well?" Scarlet asks when she sees me get a bottle of painkillers from a cabinet in the kitchen.

"I think I'm getting sick," I admit.

She sets her book down on the table and gets up, coming right over to me. She doesn't stop until her small frame is lined up with mine, and she presses the back of her hand to my forehead. "You have a fever."

"You don't know that."

Pursing her lips, she turns around and gets the thermometer and swipes it across my forehead. "See?" She flips it over to show me my temperature. "One hundred and one point seven. You are sick."

"I'll be fine in the morning."

"Hopefully. You should go to bed and try to rest."

I make a face. "I'll go to bed later. I want to watch TV for a while."

She raises her eyebrows. "You sound like a child."

"And do you go to bed at eight-thirty when you're sick?"

"Oh, of course. And I drink extra water and always make sure to take my vitamins."

"Don't give up your day job to pursue stand-up comedy."

She laughs. "But my witty sarcasm is everyone's cup of tea." She sets the thermometer down and goes back to her book. "Do you want to continue *American Horror Story*?"

"Sure," I say, and we go into the living room together. I make it through one episode before I start to feel worse, and as much as I want to stay on the couch and imagine taking things farther with Scarlet, I go up to bed.

I feel even worse when I wake up in the morning. Scarlet is already downstairs making Jackson breakfast.

"How are you feeling?" she asks, cutting up an apple.

"I've been better."

She trades the knife for the thermometer and takes my temp again. "Your temp went up. You should stay home."

"I'll take some Tylenol and my fever will go down. I'll be fine."

―⁂―

"Wes?"

The kitchen light turns on and I look up, blinking. Scarlet stands in the threshold, hand still on the light switch, eyes narrowed as they adjust to the dark.

"You okay?"

I pick up the pill bottle I dropped, head throbbing so bad it's hard to function. "A little shitty," I admit. I felt like shit when I came home from work, and the fever never went away. I don't get sick often, but when I do, it's usually bad.

And right now, I feel like I'm dying.

She crosses the kitchen, stopping in front of me and putting her hand on my cheek. "Jesus, you're burning up." She grabs the thermometer. "One-oh-three point four. That's really high, and you've had a fever for over twenty-four hours. Maybe you should go into the ER or something. You could be dehydrated."

"I don't need to go to the ER."

She takes the pill bottle from me, looking worried. "Trust me, I'm not one to suggest going to the hospital, like ever, since they rip you off on bills." She rolls her eyes. "It's bullshit, but having a high fever for this long isn't good for you."

"Are you worried about me?"

"Maybe."

She takes out two pills and hands them to me. I grab a glass and fill it with water.

"No need to worry." I try to smile, but the lights above me are making my headache worse. I'm not entirely sure I won't throw up. "I'm gonna go back to bed."

"I'm going to come check on you in twenty minutes," she says seriously, "and make sure your brain hasn't fried."

Bringing my hand to my forehead, I nod, wincing from the movement, before dragging my ass back up the stairs. I crash into bed, closing my eyes and praying for the Tylenol to bring down this damn fever and make the headache go away.

It doesn't.

I toss and turn, trying to get comfortable, which is hard to do since every bone in my body is aching now. Scarlet softly knocks on the door.

"Wes?" she whispers. "Are you awake?"

"Yeah." I sit up, squinting in the dark. I can see the glow of the thermometer in her hand as she draws near. She sits on the edge of the bed and brushes my hair back. Her touch is soft and gentle, instantly comforting me.

"You still feel warm."

"It's been twenty minutes already?" I mumble.

"Eighteen. I've been timing it."

My eyes fall shut, and I smile. "You really are worried, aren't you?"

"I am." She takes my temperature. "And I have good reason to be. Your fever went up."

"That's probably because I'm covered up."

She presses her lips into a thin line, not convinced. "You can get brain damage from high fevers."

"They have to be higher."

"Wes," she stresses, hand falling to my thigh. I've imagined her here, in my room…in my bed…touching me so many times before. But not like this. Still, having her here is nice. "It'd be one thing if you woke up with a really high fever and we waited it out. But this has been going on for over a day. You probably have the flu. People die from the flu. And you could give it to Jackson."

Dammit, she knows exactly what to say to make me bend.

"Fine. If I still have a fever in the morning, I'll go in to the doctor."

"Thanks." She brushes my hair back again. "Lay down. I'm bringing you a wet rag and some cold water."

"You don't have to," I tell her, though that sounds heavenly right now. "And I don't want you to get sick."

"I'm already exposed. Jackson too."

"He's probably the one who gave this to me," I say with a smile. Then my headache intensifies, and I squeeze my eyes shut, laying back down. Scarlet leaves, coming back a minute later. Ice clinks against the sides of the water glass, and she makes me get up and take a drink before gently pressing the wet rag to my forehead.

I don't remember the last time someone took care of me like this. Daisy was never very maternal—obviously—and while she cared and really did love me for a while there, so much of our time was spent fighting or ignoring each other that it's hard to remember the good times.

"Do you have another thermometer?" she asked, picking up the rag and flipping it to the cool side. "Because the forehead one won't work now."

"Yeah, there's one in Jackson's bathroom."

"It's not a rectal thermometer, is it?" she jokes.

"That's actually the kind I prefer."

She laughs and runs her fingers through my hair. I'm feeling a little out of it thanks to the fever. I'm not going to kiss her again because I'm sick, but I wouldn't be surprised if I confess what I'm feeling.

Because right now I know that I'm starting to fall for her.

Chapter Twenty-Two

SCARLET

The bed frame creaks, and I startle awake. I sit up, goosebumps covering my arms, and blink in the dark.

"Wes?" I whisper, feeling the mattress shake beneath me. I didn't mean to fall asleep in Weston's bed. I'm on top of the covers and he's underneath, and we're on the opposite sides of this king bed.

The sheets rustle, and I see the outline of Weston's large body moving. Red hot fear pulses over me, and my heart immediately starts racing. I reach for Wes, hand landing on his shoulder.

"Scarlet?" he croaks, throat dry. "What's wrong?" He sits up too fast and winces. I squeeze my eyes shut, having a hard time blocking out the memory.

"I thought you were having a seizure." A chill rips through me, causing me to tremble.

"Why would you think that?"

The words want to come out, and the fear I had before of him judging me, of being looked at differently—as unworthy—is gone. "When my sister was little, she got really sick with a bad fever." I wrap my arms around myself, shivering harder. "Our mom was too drunk to care or take her to the doctor. Her fever got so high she started convulsing. It still scares me to this day."

It's hard to read Weston's expression in the dark. He feebly sits up and puts his hand on my arm.

"You're freezing."

"And you're still hot."

"Come here," he whispers, pulling back the blankets. My fingers shake as I move in, sticking my feet under the warm sheets. Wes wraps his arms around me, and his warmth goes right down to my very core. "That's why you're so worried."

"Yeah," I say in a small voice.

"I'm sorry."

"Why are you sorry?" My eyes flutter shut, and I put my hand on top of Weston's, apprehensively bringing it around me. He wiggles in a little closer while keeping a careful distance at the same time. If I scoot back a mere inch or two, my ass will press against his cock. My body craves it, but now's not the time. He's sick and needs to rest.

"If I would have known you were scared like that, I would have gone to the ER."

"Just to appease me?"

"Just to put your mind at ease."

I close my eyes before I run the risk of having them get glossy. "Thank you," I whisper so quietly I'm not sure he can hear me. "And be warned, if Jackson spikes a fever, I'll be even more paranoid."

"I will too," Wes agrees, tightening his grip on me. "That's one ER trip you won't have to pressure me to take."

"I should check your temperature again," I say but don't make a move to get up. "I don't even know what time it is. I didn't mean to fall asleep."

"It's three-thirty, and you need to sleep. There's a good chance you're already sick and it's just a matter of time before the symptoms hit you."

"I have a pretty strong immune system," I tell him. "That's one good thing that came out of having a drunk for a mother. She wasn't a good housekeeper, and I think it helped me build up a strong immunity."

"I don't know if you're joking or not," Wes admits.

"You know what? I don't either." I open my eyes, looking around the dark room. I can't see Wes, and even if I roll over and look him in the eyes, his expression will be hard to read. It doesn't make sense, but there's something safe about the dark. It hides the truth, and sometimes the truth hurts. "I say things like that with sarcasm and dark humor, but it's not really funny, is it?"

"Sometimes you laugh so you don't cry."

"I think that's what I've been doing my whole life."

"You don't have to anymore," he mumbles, lips brushing against the back of my neck as he talks. "At least not for tonight."

I roll over in his arms and brush his wavy hair back out of his face. His cheeks are warm, and his forehead is even hotter. If it really is three-thirty, then he should sit up and drink some more cold water and take another dosage of Tylenol.

But his arms are locked around me and he's drifted back to sleep. I bend my leg up, hooking my ankle over his calf, and run my fingers through his hair, lulling myself back to sleep.

"Daddy?"

My eyes wake up before my mind, and I can't make sense of the small figure standing before me for a good three seconds. I'm still in Weston's bed. His arm is still draped over me.

And Jackson is standing at the side, looking curiously at the both of us.

"Hey, buddy," I whisper. The sun hasn't fully risen yet, and I'm so tired. I want to go back to sleep. "What are you doing up so early?"

"I had a bad dream."

"Want me to tuck you back into bed?"

He shakes his head. "I want Daddy."

"Daddy's not feeling too well," I softly explain.

"Is that why you're in bed with him?"

It is one-hundred percent why I'm in bed with him, but I still cringe. "Yeah. I've been taking care of him."

"Is Daddy okay?"

"He will be."

Wes stirs behind me, and his hand slides along my side.

"Daddy?" Jackson asks, climbing onto the bed.

"Jackson," Wes murmurs, eyes fluttering open. "Shit," he says under his breath. Shit is right. We're in bed together, though I don't think Jackson is jumping to conclusions. He has no idea what being in bed together can imply.

"Can I watch videos on your phone?" Jackson asks.

"Yeah, this morning you can."

"Thanks, Daddy."

Wes feels around his nightstand for his phone, unlocks it, and gives it to Jackson, who takes it back into his room.

"Don't judge me."

"That's the last thing I'll do," I tell Wes. "You're sick. A little screen time isn't going to hurt anything." I sit up. "Do you want me to leave?"

"No." Wes blinks a few times, face tight. I can tell he doesn't feel well. I reach over and grab the thermometer to take his temp again.

"Still high."

"How high?"

"Hundred and two point eight."

"Dammit," he mumbles.

"I should probably take you to the doctor now." I grab the glass of water and hand it to him. He takes a drink and shakes his head.

"It's not open yet. Doctor, not ER, remember."

"Oh, right. Lay back down then."

"You too." He sets the water down and snakes his arm around me, pulling me back to him. We lay back down, and I rub his back until I fall asleep, not waking for another hour. I slip out of bed and into my room to change out of my PJs and into black leggings and an oversized gray sweater. Jackson fell back asleep, and I carefully take Wes's phone from his hands, turning it off as I walk back into Weston's room.

I gather up the damp rag and the water glass, take them downstairs, and then go back into my room to run a brush through my hair and brush my teeth. Going back into Wes's room, I slip under the covers with him, heart going a million miles an hour.

I'm worried about Wes. Whatever virus he has is hanging on strong with no signs of leaving. But I'm also feeling more for him than I have before. Realizing how scared I am of something bad happening to him, of him being really sick, makes it pretty much impossible to deny that I more than like him.

He's making me believe in love, and I think I'm falling for him.

"Thanks for coming over," I tell Owen, shutting the door behind him.

"No problem," Owen says, looking concerned. "Wes must be really sick to willingly go into the doctor."

"He's had a high fever for three days now."

"Oh, shit." Owen unzips his coat and steps out of his shoes. Jackson is finishing his breakfast and gets so excited when he sees his uncle he almost spills his milk.

"Hey, Jackson!" Owen calls. "Ready to have some fun?"

"Yeah!"

"I'm going to teach you all about cars and picking up women." Owen's face tightens when he sees Wes sitting at the table, hunched forward with his head in his hands.

"Thanks for getting up and coming over," Wes mumbles.

Owen pulls out the chair next to him and sits, looking at his oldest brother with worry. "Of course. And you look terrible."

"I still look better than you."

Owen laughs. "You wish. Take care of yourself, bro. And I get to have some fun with my favorite nephew. We don't spend enough one-on-one time together, do we, buddy? What do you want to do first?"

"Brush teeth after breakfast," I suggest, and Owen nods. I grab the keys to the Jeep and put on my coat and shoes. Wes moves slowly on his way to the car, and I keep looking over to check on him as we go to the clinic.

Wes rests his head on my shoulder as we wait, and when the nurse calls his name, I look at Weston.

"Do you want me to stay out here?"

"It doesn't matter to me," he says. I don't think much of anything matters to him right now. He's pretty damn sick. I loop my arm through his and walk with him into the examination room.

Not surprisingly, he's dehydrated, and the doctor wants to send him to the hospital for a bag of IV fluids and monitoring until his fever goes down. Wes doesn't even argue, which lets me know just how shitty he's feeling at this point.

"How far is the hospital?" I ask, unlocking the Jeep as we walk through the parking lot.

"About twenty minutes," he tells me, moving slow.

"Can you tell me how to get there or should I program it into the GPS?"

Wes gives me a look. "I'm sick, but I still know how to get to the hospital."

"Just making sure," I say with a smile and try to rush forward and open the car door for him, but he beats me to it. "Are you going to call Owen?"

"I'll text him. Hopefully this shit doesn't take long," he grumbles. "I'd be fine if I went home, you know."

I start the Jeep and shake my head. "Why must you perpetuate the stereotype and be so difficult? Though you're not complaining nearly as much as the average man."

"Being sick is too time-consuming."

"I totally agree. It's a huge inconvenience. But taking care of yourself—like going to the hospital—will speed up your recovery. Who knows? Maybe by tomorrow, you'll feel a lot better because you got treatment. And if you didn't…"

"I would have suffered miserably for weeks."

"There's that overdramatic attitude I was looking for." I take my eyes off the road to look over and see the small smile on his face. He's quiet the rest of the way to the hospital, and we end up waiting over half an hour before we're taken back into a room in the ER. Things drag again after that, and it's been over an hour before he's finally given an IV and meds.

"Thanks for coming," Wes says, looking into my eyes for a quick second before diverting his gaze to the floor. "You didn't have to."

"I know," I say softly, shifting my weight. I'm sitting in an uncomfortable chair next to the bed. "But I'm glad I did."

"Me too." He starts to reach for my hand but is stopped by his IV line. My heart skips a beat, and I get to my feet, words burning in my throat. Words that want to come out. Words I'm not entirely sure I know the meaning of.

"Scarlet," he starts and pushes himself up. My lips part and my heart pounds away in my chest, so loud I'm sure Wes can hear it.

"Weston," I say back with a smile, shuffling closer. I take his hand, and he links his fingers through mine. He circles his thumb along the soft flesh on the inside of my wrist. I bring my free hand forward, brushing his hair back behind his ear.

There's nothing romantic about this moment. We're standing in a crammed ER room while Wes gets IV fluids due to dehydration. And yet I've never felt something more intimate. Then again, I know nothing about love.

I bring my hand down and cup his face. Wes closes his eyes and leans his face into my palm. He tightens his grip on my hand, and I can feel his heart racing along with mine.

And then someone knocks on the door. I drop my hand that's on Weston's face but keep a hold of his hand.

"Hey." Archer pulls back the curtain, and Wes takes his hand out of mine. "I saw your name in the system. How are you feeling?"

"I've been better," Wes tells his almost brother-in-law.

"I'm surprised you didn't say 'fine,'" I tease.

"I didn't read your chart," Archer says. "What's going on?"

"He's had a high fever for three days and finally let me take him to the doctor this morning." I give Wes a telling look and then smile.

"There's a nasty virus going around," Archer tells us. "The ER has been busy." He pulls out the little rolling stool I've always been too afraid to sit on. What if the doctor came in and yelled at me? "Are you being admitted overnight?"

"No," Wes says. "And I won't stay even if they say I should. I'll be fine at home."

Archer and I give Wes the same dubious look.

"This virus is serious. It's put a few people in the ICU already. Take care of yourself so you can take care of Jackson," Archer tells Wes, using his *you better listen to me because I'm a doctor* tone. Wes just grumbles in response, and Archer tells him he'll check back later if we're still here. He's off to perform another surgery.

"Oh shit," Wes says after Archer leaves.

"What?"

"I didn't tell him not to tell Quinn."

"You think he will?"

Wes raises an eyebrow. "I know he will."

"That's not a bad thing. They're concerned about you because they care." *Like I do.*

"Once Quinn knows, she'll tell our mother."

"That's not a bad thing, either," I press. "It's nice the way you guys all look out for each other."

His eyes meet mine, and something passes between us, something unsaid, something I can't describe, but it's in that moment it's like he knows.

He knows I'd give anything to have a family like his.

"I know," he says softly. "It's really nice, and I shouldn't complain about it. I don't like people doting over me."

"Well, you're still a big, strong man even when you're lying here in the hospital, you know."

His eyes narrow into a playful glare, and then he sighs. "I know. It's more that I don't want to burden others."

"Taking care of people you care about isn't a burden. People like doing it, and it makes you feel good."

"Does it make you feel good?"

My mouth goes dry, and I forget how to breathe for a second. If his hand was still surrounding mine, there'd be no way to deny just how good this is making me feel.

"Yes," I whisper. "It does. Because I care about you." I swallow hard and inch closer to the bed. The moment is becoming too intense, and suddenly I'm hot and sweat breaks out along my hairline.

Someone else knocks on the door, and this time I'm thankful for the interruption. Because I'm feeling things I've never felt before, and I'm not sure what to do with all these fucking feelings. Moving back to the chair, I pull out my phone and text Corbin, asking for an update on Dad.

The nurse leaves, telling Wes to try and rest and she'll be back in half an hour to check on him.

"You don't have to stay," Wes says, looking tired.

"I'll probably wander around and see if I can find something to eat." He'll be more likely to fall asleep if I'm not in here. "Are you allowed to eat?"

"No one told me no."

"I'll bring you something." Standing, I fight back the urge to go to him, brush his hair back, and kiss his forehead.

"Hey," Wes says, catching my hand as I walk by. His fingers walk up my wrist, and a shiver runs down my spine. I inhale sharply, knees weakening. How can he affect me so much with just his fingers on my wrist?

"Yeah?"

"Thank you, Scarlet, for everything."

I put my free hand on top of his hand and close my eyes in a long blink. "Of course, Wes." I look into his eyes. "Get some rest so you get better. We still have Netflix to binge."

His lips curve into a small smile. "That's good motivation."

I take a drink of ice water, debating pouring it over my head while I sit in the middle of the hospital cafeteria. After practically running out of the room, I hid in an elevator with my back against the wall until my heart stopped pounding.

I don't know what is happening to me...even though I really do.

But I won't say it. I don't believe in love. My heart isn't capable of it.

My phone buzzes in my purse, pulling me out of the reverie I was in. It's Quinn, and I'm sure she's calling to check on Wes.

"Hello?"

"Hey, Scarlet. Are you with Wes?"

"Not currently. I went to the cafeteria to get some food."

"Oh, okay. How's he doing?"

"He's looking better."

"Thanks for taking him. Wes doesn't go to the doctor willingly."

I lean back and smile. "I noticed. Did you happen to call your mom and tell her Wes is sick?"

Quinn laughs. "I know better."

"Wes said she freaks out a little."

"That's an understatement." Emma starts crying in the background. "I gotta go, but thanks for looking out for my brother. Can you text me an update later?"

"Yeah, I will. Give Emma a hug for me."

"I will. Bye!"

I hang up and finish my food, then grab a drink and a snack to take up to Wes. He's asleep, so I quietly slip in and try to get comfortable in the chair next to the bed. The nurse comes in a few minutes later, looks him over but doesn't wake him, and then all is quiet again. I read a book on my phone and end up drifting off, not waking until the doctor comes back in to look Wes over.

His fever went down to a manageable level, and Wes can go home.

"You're still sick," the doctor tells him. "Rest the remainder of today and take it easy tomorrow."

"I will," Wes agrees, eager to get out of here. The doctor leaves, and a few minutes later a nurse comes in with discharge paperwork.

"Is your girlfriend driving you home?" the nurse asks, going over the standard questions.

I look at Wes, who hesitates but doesn't take the time to correct her. Maybe it's because he's too tired to bother, or maybe because he's pretending we're together too, like I am.

I grab Wes's coat, taking it to him once the nurse leaves.

"Thanks again," he tells me.

"You're welcome. You look better already."

I text Quinn as we're walking out, letting her know Wes is on the mend and is heading home. Logan is at the house along with Owen. They're both wearing jeans and gray T-shirts, making it hard to tell them apart.

Jackson has his play doctor kit out on the coffee table and immediately leads Weston to the couch for a check-up.

"Did you mean to dress alike?" I ask the twins, going right to the bathroom to wash the hospital germs off my hands.

Logan and Owen look at each other and then down at their own clothes.

"I didn't even realize it," Logan admits with a laugh. "It's a twin thing, I guess."

"That's funny and very interesting at the same time." I join everyone in the living room, sitting on the edge of the couch. Wes bends his legs up, giving me more space.

"Well," Owen says, giving his twin a look. Logan widens his eyes and ever so slightly shakes his head. "You're in good hands here. We gotta head out and get the bar ready for tonight."

"Thanks, guys," Wes says, sounding like he's about ready to fall asleep again.

"No problem." Logan gives Jackson a hug goodbye. "Take care of your dad, okay?"

"I will," Jackson promises.

"Thanks for looking out for Wes," Owen tells me quietly before they leave. Jackson cuddles up with Weston on the couch, and I slip upstairs for a quick shower. When I get out, I hear voices coming from downstairs. I pause by my bedroom door, recognizing Mrs. Dawson's voice. Towel drying my hair, I quickly get dressed and go downstairs.

Wes is still on the couch, looking tired and a little annoyed by his mother's presence. She's fussing over him, taking his temperature and removing the blanket Jackson had covered him with.

"Hi, Mrs. Dawson," I say.

"Scarlet, hi." She stands, setting a Tupperware bowl on the coffee table. She comes over and gives me a hug. "Thank you so much for making my stubborn son go to the doctor."

"You're welcome. I wanted him to go yesterday, but he swore he'd be better."

"I would have been," Wes counters, and I laugh. Mrs. Dawson looks from Wes to me and back again.

"I brought chicken noodle soup. Is anyone hungry? I can heat it up."

"I am, Grammy!" Jackson exclaims but makes no move to get up and away from the cartoons he's watching. Mrs. Dawson goes into the kitchen, and I move closer to Wes.

"Make her leave," he whispers.

"She's just worried."

Wes rolls his eyes. "I have the flu, not a rare jungle disease. I'll be fine, really." He sighs. "I'm tired."

My heart lurches in my chest, and I want nothing more than to crawl under the blanket with him, run my hands up and down his muscular arms until he falls asleep.

"I'll try to speed things up," I promise.

"Thanks."

Going into the kitchen, I plug in the coffee pot.

"Tired, honey?" Mrs. Dawson asks.

"Yes. I was worried about Wes and didn't sleep much through the night," I admit before I realize how that sounds. He's my boss.

Instead of looking shocked, Mrs. Dawson's face lights up. "I'm glad you're here for him."

"For Jackson?"

"For them both." She takes the lid off the Tupperware. "Weston's always been the strong, responsible one. The last few years haven't been easy on him, though he'll never admit it. It's nice seeing him happy again."

Is she saying what I think she's saying? "Well, I'm sure it's because he doesn't have to worry about Jackson's schedule as much anymore."

Mrs. Dawson gives me a wink. "Sure. That's all it is."

Yes, she is saying what I think she's saying. And dammit, I want it to be true. In fact, I've never wanted anything more in my whole life.

Chapter Twenty-Three

SCARLET

"You could take another day off," I tell Wes, looking up from Jackson's bed. I'm stripping the sheets and replacing them with new ones. Wes slept pretty much all day after we got home from the hospital and took it easy the next day. Now he's ready for a long day of work.

"I don't need to," he tells me, leaning against the door frame. "I don't have a fever anymore. And you and Jackson are fine, so the virus is gone."

"Don't you dare jinx us. Those things can lay dormant for days."

"If you get sick, I'll take care of you."

The elastic slips out of my fingers, and the fitted sheet pops off the mattress. Heat rushes through me, and my pussy quivers at the thought of him *taking care of me*. Yesterday, the three of us lounged around and watched movies for most of the day. It was more than just nice.

It was perfect.

Well, except how fucking horny Weston makes me. We get along. He makes me laugh. And I want him so bad I'm going to have to change my underwear the moment he leaves. My body craves him, making it physically hard to *not* touch him when we're near.

Just to see what will happen.

He kissed me once. I'm sure he'll do it again.

I kneel on the mattress, bending forward to stick the corner of the fitted sheet back on. My ass is in Weston's direct line of sight, and part of me hopes I'm driving him as wild as he drives me.

Because this is really un-fucking-fair.

"I'm sure you will," I say in a tight voice. "Though if I do get sick, it'll be your fault, for one, bringing home the virus, and two, having just jinxed me like a minute ago."

Wes laughs and steps in, grabbing the other end of the sheet. He helps me make the bed and gathers up the laundry Jackson left on the floor. He adds it to the laundry basket in the closet.

I could sit back and watch him clean all day.

"When will you be home?" I ask, crossing my arms tightly across my chest.

"Around nine."

"Okay. I'll keep a plate of dinner in the fridge for you."

"Thanks."

He's in uniform, looking hot with his hair pulled back. The color is back to his face, and he looks better. Though a proper inspection is probably a good idea. "Hot in Here" plays in my head again as I imagine him stripping naked in front of me. I'm getting so wound up and sexually frustrated. I need to stop.

"I'll see you tonight."

"Right," I say. "Tonight."

"Time for bed, buddy," I tell Jackson, eyeing the time.

"Aww man," he says, throwing his head back. "But we just got the farm all set up."

"I'll tell you what. Let's leave it out until morning and we can play again after breakfast."

"Okay!"

I get up and offer him a hand. He lets me pull him off the ground—and I mean literally pull him up—and we go into the bathroom to brush his teeth and go potty before bedtime. We read a dozen books, and I'm starting to drift off during the last one.

"Lights out," I yawn. Jackson starts to freak out the moment the light goes off. "What's going on?" I ask.

"The Tall Man might get me in the dark. Can you leave the light on?"

"The Tall Man isn't here. Are you scared of the dark tonight?"

He nods, and I flick the bedside lamp back on. "Hang on a second. I have something for you. Stay here."

I get to his door before he scrambles after me, following me into my room at the end of the hall.

"This is Ray," I say, taking my scruffy unicorn from my bed. "He was mine when I was a kid, and he kept me safe. He'll keep you safe too."

Jackson looks at the stuffed animal, not sure whether to believe me or not. A few seconds pass and he hugs Ray.

"Can you feel his protection powers?"

"I do!"

"Good." Taking his hand, I lead him back into his room and into bed. I shut off the lights and pull the blankets back up, gently tucking Jackson in. He cuddles the dingy yellow unicorn against his chest and closes his eyes for half a second before opening them again.

"Are you still here?" he asks, voice thin.

"Yes," I assure him. "I am."

"Can you sleep without Ray?" He eyes the unicorn, face tight. "You can have him if you need him."

"He's yours now," I say with a smile. "I think he'll have more fun hanging out in your room with your other toys than he did sitting alone on my bed."

Jackson nods. "And you're kind of old to have toys."

I laugh and lean forward, kissing his forehead. "I suppose I am. Try to get some sleep, buddy." Smoothing out his blankets, I get up to leave.

"Scarlet?" Jackson sits up right before I close the door.

"Yeah?"

He twists the frayed yarn that makes up Ray's mane through his fingers. "Will I always be scared of the dark?"

"No," I say with a shake of my head. I go back into his room and sit on the edge of his bed. "You won't be. I used to be scared of the dark, you know."

"You were?"

"Yeah. But I'm not anymore."

"How do you stop being scared of the dark?" His eyes meet mine, and something pulls on my heart. I look at him and see everything a child should be. Innocent. Playful. Pure. Kind-hearted and carefree. It's then I realize that I'll do anything to keep him that way, to make sure he lives the best life he can, the life he deserves to live.

It's then that I realize I love him.

"I don't really know," I start. My eyes flutter shut, and I think of my own life, of the darkness that grew around me, suffocating and deafening at the same time. The darkness that spread so deep within, it turned everything inside of me black, and the numbness took over, like poison ivy twisting on vines, wrapping around my head and eventually my heart.

I think of the numbness that was so vast and hollow it reverberated through my soul with an emptiness that hurt more than anything I've ever experienced. That isolated me and made me feel alone even when I was standing in a room full of people. That made me do bad things just so I'd feel anything other than nothing.

I open my eyes, and Jackson clicks on his flashlight. The tightness in my chest releases, and it's here, in this moment, I realize how I stopped being afraid of the dark.

"You stop being afraid of the dark when you learn how to make your own light."

Jackson tips his head. "Like my flashlight."

"Yes," I say, tears pricking the corners of my eyes. "Like your flashlight."

"Can I keep it on all night?"

"Of course. And I'll be just downstairs in the kitchen. I have dishes to wash. But if you need me, call for me and I'll be back here."

"Okay. I love you, Scarlet."

I smile, heart pounding inside my chest. "Love you, too, buddy."

Chapter Twenty-Four

WESTON

Fuck. Me. I'm in trouble.

It's Friday night, and while I'm still not at one hundred percent, I agreed to go out with everyone to Getaway tonight. And I mean everyone. Logan and Owen are there already, of course. Dean and Kara are going, as well as Quinn and Archer. Quinn invited Scarlet to hang out with her and her friend Jamie, and I can tell Scarlet's looking forward to it.

"Ready?" Scarlet asks, coming down the stairs as if she has no idea she looks like a temptress. Swallowing hard, I shift my weight to hide my hardening cock. It's going to be one hell of a night. She curled her hair and is wearing a simple, curve-hugging black dress and heels. My mind jumps ahead, and I imagine myself pushing her up against the wall. I can almost feel her legs around me as I inch the hem of her black dress up and over her ass.

Dammit. Now I have an erection.

"Just a second," I mumble and go into the kitchen, clenching the muscles in my thighs to try and get rid of this thing. I open the fridge, pretending to dig around for something to eat until my cock goes down.

"Are you seriously eating again?" Scarlet asks, voice coming from behind me.

"I'm always hungry."

She laughs. "We literally just ate."

And we did. I put the food away while Scarlet brushed her teeth upstairs. I waste some more time before grabbing an apple and closing the fridge. Feeling like a teenage boy at the risk of popping a boner just from looking at a hot girl, I grab my coat and hold it in front of me as we walk to my Jeep.

"It was nice of your parents to watch Jackson tonight," she comments.

"Yeah. I think my mom misses having him around even though it made it hard for her to do her job."

"I can see that. He's a great kid."

We get in, and we both reach for the radio at the same time. The slight feeling of Scarlet's skin against mine sends a jolt right to the tip of my cock. She took such good care of me when I was sick, balancing helping me out but not being overbearing. Every minute I'm around her puts me more and more at risk for spilling my guts. Or maybe I'll cut through all the verbal nonsense and kiss her.

Again.

But this time I won't stop.

"Strike out already?" I ask Logan, taking a drink of my beer.

"Not as bad as you," he fires back, pulling out a chair and joining me at the table. "Though we think you're holding out for your new nanny."

I shake my head, flicking my eyes to Scarlet. She's sitting at the bar with Quinn, Kara, and Jamie, sipping a vodka tonic and laughing at something Quinn just said. "She's Jackson's nanny. I'm not getting involved with her."

"I'll get involved with her," Owen says, coming up behind us. He's on his third—maybe fourth—beer already.

"No," I say a little too sternly. Dammit. "Besides...you seemed to be getting involved with the chick in the leopard skirt."

Owen grins. "Yeah, I am." He motions for Logan to follow him. "Her friend thinks I'm hot, which translates into thinking you're hot. Kind of. We might look alike, but I have the winning personality."

Logan brings his beer to his lips and doesn't say anything. Owen stands there, looking at Logan as if there's something seriously wrong with him. I lean back, always amused by these two.

"Nah, I'm staying here." Logan rests his arms on the table, taking another swig of beer.

"What the fuck?" Owen's eyes widen.

Logan shrugs. "I'm not feeling a one-night stand tonight." He flicks his eyes to mine, knowing I understand where he's coming from. With Dean married and Quinn engaged and planning her wedding, thoughts of settling down are hanging heavy above him too.

"Are you sick?" Owen sinks into the chair next to Logan. "Should I get Archer?"

Logan rolls his eyes. "Fuck you. Don't you want something more?"

"As long as I'm getting laid, I'm happy," Owen says, and I believe him. Sometimes I wish I could be as carefree as him, but having a kid changed all that. Jackson is my world, and I won't even think about bringing anyone new into our lives unless it's the real deal.

Logan shifts his gaze to the girls Owen was talking to. "Don't you want someone a little more...uh...cultured?"

"She's cultured, all right," Owen says and holds up his hand. "Pop-cultured. I bet she knows everything there is to know about the Kardashians."

"Go get em', tiger," Logan says, making a shooing gesture with his hands. Owen mumbles something incoherent and wanders off. Dean and Archer, who've been playing pool since we got here, come over and join us at the table.

"You're not out there on the prowl?" Dean asks Logan, grabbing his beer from the table and taking a swig.

"Nope. It's more fun sitting here giving Wes shit about his hot nanny. He says there's nothing going on between them."

"Her name is Scarlet, and there's nothing going on between us."

"Don't lie to us, man." Dean raises his eyebrows. "We've seen you two flirting and giving each other fuck-me eyes. You're sleeping with her, aren't you?"

"Nope."

"Why not? You two obviously want each other."

I shake my head. "Just because I want her doesn't mean I should go for it." Everyone looks at me like I'm crazy. With a sigh, I pick at the label on my beer. "What if things don't work out? I wouldn't just be losing a friend, I'd be losing a nanny, one Jackson really likes and one I actually trust."

"But what if they don't?" Archer says, and all eyes fall on him. "Trust me, I understand where you're coming from. I waited years to tell Quinn how I felt because I was afraid of what would happen when I finally did." He looks across the bar at her and smiles without meaning to. "I'll spare you the details since she's your sister, and you guys know how happy we are. But I do regret the time I lost every now and then." He looks back at me. "If you like her, tell her. At least you'll know one way or another."

"She's into you," Dean goes on. "I can tell. And she already lives with you and knows what a tyrant you can be."

"I'm not a tyrant," I say, and both my brothers give me dubious looks. "It's not the right time."

"Weston," Logan starts, and I know whatever he has to say is going to be seriously simply by the fact that he called me by my whole name. "You can date again. You can hook up again. You can have no-strings sex with anyone who wants to participate. And you should. Daisy is gone, and if she comes back, she's going to know she's not welcome."

I peel the label down the bottle and nod. "You're right."

"What?" Logan asks, blinking. "Did I hear you correctly?"

"Yeah," I say with a laugh. I look across the bar at Scarlet again, and my heart lurches in my chest. "You're right. Daisy is gone, and it's time to move on." I look my brother in the eye. "And this time, I want to."

"That was fun," Scarlet says, looping her arm through mine. We're leaving the bar, and I think she's a little drunk. I swallow hard, soaking in the warmth of her skin. I'm carrying a take-out bag full of burgers and fries for us to eat once we get back to the house.

"It was," I agree, aware of the way my heart speeds up as soon as she's near. "I haven't gone out like that in a while."

"I know. Quinn told me. She's really talkative when she drinks."

I laugh. "She drank tonight?"

"She had one glass of wine and it was more than enough to make her loopy." Scarlet tightens her hold on my arm, having a bit of difficulty walking through the uneven gravel in her tall heels. "This was her first time going out and having a drink since before she got pregnant, but something tells me she's always a lightweight."

"She is, but Dean's worse. Don't tell him I told you."

Scarlet laughs, clinging to me after her ankle almost twists. We get to the Jeep and she lets go of my arm, walking around to the edge of the parking lot. It butts up to a cornfield, and a big half-moon hangs high above it. Stars dot the black sky, and the night is quiet.

"What are you looking at?" I ask her, setting the food down on the hood of my Jeep and unzipping my jacket. She has a black sweater over her dress but no coat. I take mine off and drape it around her shoulders.

"Thanks," she says quietly and pulls the coat tightly around herself. "And nothing."

"Nothing?"

"I'm looking at nothing. And I like it." She tips her head back and reaches for me. My heart pounds, and I think back to what was said in the bar. I like her—more than like her. I step forward and wrap her in my arms.

"I never thought I'd end up in a place like this," she says quietly. I'm behind her, with my arms wrapped tightly around her waist. She leans back against me.

"Like this?"

"Quiet. Safe. A place I'd like to call home."

"You can call it home," I say without thinking. "I mean, you're here for a job, I know, but once Jackson is too old for a nan—or if you want to leave or…or—"

"You're cute when you get flustered." She smiles as she turns around to look at me. "And maybe I will." She takes a few steps out in the dirt that leads to the cornfield and holds out her hands. "Look at this. I'm behind a bar and don't feel threatened for my life. Partly because you're with me."

"Was it really that bad where you lived in Chicago?"

She turns around and nods. "Yeah, but you learn how to deal. Don't go out at night alone…carry something that either is a weapon or looks like a weapon…avoid certain streets and places after dark." She shakes her head and puts on her mask again, pretending everything is okay. Looking up at the sky again, she becomes completely still for a moment. "I think I saw a shooting—wait, it's an airplane."

I laugh. "We do get a lot of flyover traffic to the Chicago airports."

She takes a few steps back, and I find myself moving toward her. My arms fold around her slender waist and my cock jumps. I turn my head to the side, fighting with myself. I want to kiss her and tell her how I feel…but she's more than a little tipsy.

I'll wait.

"The food is probably getting cold," she says, eyeing the bag. "And those fries smell amazing."

I unlock the Jeep and open the passenger door for her, then quickly go around and get in. Scarlet turns up the heat and plays with the radio as I drive us home, stopping on a classic rock station. "Living on a Prayer" is playing, and she looks at me with a smile before cranking the volume. We belt it out together, laughing and dancing in our seats. I don't realize it until a car comes up behind me, but I've slowed down, going less than half the speed limit on this country road.

Speeding up, I glance over at Scarlet, watching her move her seatbelt to the side so she can take off my coat. Her dress gets caught when she pulls it off, and the low-cut neckline of the dress moves to the side, exposing part of her lacy black bra. Fuck, she's gorgeous.

I clench my jaw and grip the steering wheel, keeping my eyes on the road the rest of the way home. Parking in front of the house, Scarlet and I walk up the sidewalk together. She stops a foot before the porch and looks up at the sky again.

"It's so beautiful, isn't it?"

"Is it making you believe in aliens?"

She laughs, and the way her face lights up is even more beautiful than the sky above us. "It's starting to convince me."

I pull my keys from my pocket to unlock the front door.

"Can we eat on the porch?" Scarlet asks. "So I can look for shooting stars?"

"I can do you one better."

"Careful." I hold out my hand, planting my foot down on the shingles of the roof. Scarlet steps through the open window, gripping my hand tight.

"I'm not really scared of heights," she starts, holding onto the window frame. "But I'm afraid of falling from heights."

"I won't let you fall."

She looks me right in the eye. "You sure about that?"

"I'll catch you."

Her lips curve into a smile. "You better."

"You can trust me."

"I know."

She steps onto the roof, and I help her down a few feet. We're on top of the covered back porch, and while the roof still angles down a bit, it's level enough to sit. Once she's settled, I reach back inside and grab a blanket and the food. I take a seat close to Scarlet, draping the blanket around both of us.

Scarlet opens the take-out bag, and we eat together in a silence that's anything but awkward. Once we're done with our food, I gather up the wrappers and toss them along with our empty water bottles into the house through the open window.

"You know Jackson is going to come out here once he's older, right?" Scarlet says, resting her head on my shoulder.

"I'll nail the windows shut before then." I slip my arm around her.

She laughs. "I'd be out here every night if I were a kid."

"Just wait until winter."

"I can tough it out."

She could, and she would just to see the stars. "Have you been to the Alder Planetarium?" I ask.

She shakes her head. "I've always wanted to go, but I haven't been. I used to take my brother and sister to the Field Museum, though. It was within walking distance of our house. Well, a long walk. We'd make a day out of it. Then when my dad came back into the picture, he'd meet us there." She closes her eyes and rests her head on my shoulder. "I haven't been in a while. A long while. I haven't even thought about it but now I really miss it."

"Do you want to go? We can take Jackson and drive up next week."

She lifts her head up and looks at me. "Really?"

Her smile is making me smile. "Yeah. I haven't been since probably high school, and Jackson's never been. You could invite your dad and sister, if you want."

She stiffens, and the smile is gone from her face. "They…they won't be able to come."

"Shit, right. Your dad is sick. How's he doing?"

With furrowed brows, she turns to me. "I need to tell you something."

Chapter Twenty-Five

WESTON

"You can tell me anything," I say. Unable to help myself, I put my arms around her again. Scarlet tenses, and for a moment I think she's going to pull away from me. Then she relaxes in my arms, leaning back against me. Holding her is one of the best feelings in the world.

"My dad is sick, but it's not the kind of sick he'll get better from."

"I'm sorry."

"Don't be. He more or less did it to himself. Years of heavy drinking and getting into fights takes its toll on the body." She inhales, breath catching. I hold her closer, pressing my lips to the back of her neck. I can tell this is painful for her, and the confession is like pulling the bullet out of the wound. It hurt going in, and it'll hurt coming out, but once it's gone, the wound can begin to heal.

"He's in a nursing home, a really shitty one at that, but it's the best I can do. And my sister can't join us because she's in jail."

I blink but don't say anything. I was not expecting any of that. Waiting for her to go on, I run my fingers up and down her arm.

"Why is she in jail?"

"She got caught up with the wrong crowd." She shakes her head. "She's so desperate to fit in she went along with this stupid idea to rob a store and got caught. Her friend had a gun, and even though my sister didn't, she still got charged with armed robbery."

"Damn."

"My sister and my dad…they're not bad people, though. They've just…they've made bad choices. Hell, I've made bad choices."

"Haven't we all?"

She turns, eyes glossy. "You have no idea." Slowly, she twists in my arms and cups my face with her hands. "You're a good person, Weston. A good dad, a good brother, a good cop. I used to think people like you only existed in fairytales."

I rest my hands on the curve of her hips. "No one has ever compared me to a fairytale before."

"Well, they should have. You're everything I could have—"

I can't stop myself any longer. I pull Scarlet to me and kiss her. She melts against me, arms flying around my neck. Everything disappears in that moment, and it's like it's just us and the stars.

Scarlet's lips, soft and warm, press against mine with a passion that matches my own. I slide one hand down to the small of her back, feeling the heat of her skin. The blanket falls from her shoulders and she shivers, pressing herself closer to me. The desire I've been trying to ignore, trying to convince myself isn't there, comes rushing back, and my need to be inside her is the most intense thing I've ever felt.

"Scarlet," I say, breaking away and not having my lips on hers feels like I've dived underwater and have no air. "You were a little drunk when we left the bar. Are you sure you want to do this?"

"I was a little drunk then," she says, holding tightly to my shoulders. "But I'm not now. And yes, Wes, I want to do this. I've wanted to do this pretty much since the moment I saw you."

Her brazen confession turns me on even more. I kiss her again and forget we're on an angled roof. Scarlet pushes up with the intention of moving into my lap but slips and starts to fall. I grab her around the waist, pulling her against me.

"You did catch me," she whispers.

"I told you I would." I press my foot down on the roof and steady her. "Let's go in."

She nods and turns, reaching for the window frame. She gets in first, and I follow behind, tossing the blanket in behind us and closing the window. We're in my bedroom, and light from the hall spills in.

"Scarlet," I say again, heart still racing. Blood rushes through me, and every nerve in my body is alive. "Are you sure you—"

She doesn't give me a chance to get the rest of the question out. Her lips meet mine again, and it's all I can do not to throw her down onto the mattress. I kiss her hard, tongue pushing into her mouth, and run a hand through her hair, over her back, and down to her supple ass. Heat rushes through me, and the tip of my cock tingles with anticipation. She puts one of her hands on my chest, slowly raking her fingers down until they rest above the button of my jeans.

I pull back, needing to look at her, needing to make sure this is real. I've dreamed about this more times than I can count since the first time I saw her. Taking her chin in my hand, I tip her head up and kiss her, eyes falling shut. My tongue pushes into her mouth, and I slide my hands down her back.

Scarlet fastens her arms around me, standing on her toes to better kiss me. She presses herself against me, and her desperation is almost enough to undo me. *Almost*. It's been a long time since I've been with a woman.

I'm going to take my time with Scarlet. Make her feel, pleasuring her until she's screaming my name, writhing on the bed beneath me. I take a tangle of her hair in my hand, kissing her harder.

"Are you ready, Scarlet?" I pant, barely taking my lips off hers. My cock pulses, begging to be inside of her. "Are you ready for me to fuck you?"

Chapter Twenty-Six

SCARLET

If my arms weren't wrapped around Weston's neck, my weakened knees might have given out. He's standing before me, with one hand wrapped in my hair and the other planted on the base of my back, fingers inching down my ass. His legs are slightly spread, hips close to mine.

I open my mouth to tell him I've been ready for him to fuck me, but no words come out. I'm breathless before him, excited and intimidated all at the same time. Tingles are running rampant through my body, and I'm as hot as I am cold from the chilly night air.

He steps forward, closing the distance between us. His hard cock presses against me, and holy shit, that thing is big. I shouldn't be surprised since he towers over me. Every aspect of Weston is big, and his cock is no exception. I bring my hand down, fingers trembling, and feel its length through his pants. Wes grunts, pushing himself forward. It will be a tight fit inside of me, and the thought of having him push that big dick all the way in makes a shiver run down my spine.

"Do you want this?" he says, voice low.

"Yes." The word escapes my lips in a single breath. Wes brings his head back down to kiss me again. The desperation is here again, and I can't get enough of him fast enough. But this time is different. This time we're not going to stop. We're going to go all the way, and Lord help me, I want it.

I want him.

I've never wanted anything more in my life.

Desire for him swells inside of me, growing hotter and hotter. It'll only take a spark to start this fire, and I know we're going to burn hot and bright together. You can tell a lot about a person from the way they kiss, and I knew the first time Weston kissed me that he's the kind of man who takes his damn time.

I push up against him, lips crashing against his. His fingers press into my ass and a guttural growl comes from deep inside his throat, vibrating against my lips. I moan, growing wetter by the second.

There's no going back after tonight. We can't ignore this kiss like we did last time. We're in too deep, feeling too much. Wes picks me up as if I weigh nothing and strides forward, pressing my back against the wall. His cock is so hard beneath me, fighting against his jeans. I slide my hand up the back of his head, running my fingers through his hair, and buck my hips against his.

I'm so wound up and turned on, but it's more than that. The connection is emotional as well as physical, and my heart is yearning for his to beat along with mine just as much as my clit begs to be touched. I don't want to think about it and risk ruining the moment, though something tells me nothing could ruin this moment. Zombies could be scratching at the door and I wouldn't be fazed. Not when this monster cock is rubbing over my clit, nearly bringing me to come right here and now.

He grinds himself against me, and my dress bunches up around my ass. I'm so wet that if he reaches down, he'll be able to feel it through my panties. Taking his lips off mine, he kisses my neck, sucking at my skin in a way that drives me crazy. Pleasure shoots through me, going right to my pussy. It pulses, needing to be touched. I rub myself against him again, needing to come before I explode.

"Wes," I pant, letting my head fall to the side. I don't know how he's standing so steady, supporting all my weight nonetheless. His hands are under my ass, fingers digging into my skin.

As suddenly as he picked me up, Wes puts me back on my feet. For a split second my heart stops, thinking he's having second thoughts and is going to pull away, taking his body away from mine. It would be as painful as sucking all the oxygen out of the air, which is basically what he does to me anyway.

He takes it all away and the only way to breathe is to put my mouth on his and inhale him all in. I swallow hard, pulse bounding, and stare at him. My lips are parted, and I've never felt so empowered and so helpless at the same time. This beast of a man is standing in front of me. I'm so small compared to him, yet I know he's as much of a slave to the desire to lose ourselves in each other as I am.

Suddenly, he drops to his knees, pushing my dress up to my stomach. I lean back against the wall, gasping. My breasts rise and fall rapidly, and I look down, watching him slowly slide a hand up my leg.

He starts at the inside of my knee, touching my soft flesh with only his fingertips. I shiver from his touch, and every single nerve in my body is humming with pleasure. My eyes flutter shut, and I surrender to him.

I'm usually the one who stays in power, who always has to be on top. But not tonight. Weston won't allow it even if I tried, and being with a man who's as gentle and caring as he is domineering and demanding is throwing me for a loop, and it feels so fucking good.

Slowly, he slides his hand up the back of my thigh, pushing his fingers up inch by inch until they're right below my entrance. I'm burning hot for him and don't know how much of this teasing I can handle before I bring my foot up, push it against his chest, and force him back so I can climb on top.

No one has ever made me this wound up before, and I'm entirely sure it's because no one has ever made me feel this much outside of the bedroom before. Wes has done something to me, damn him. He didn't mean to, didn't set out to get under my skin and into my heart.

But he did, and now I want him in every way possible.

He pushes his hand up to my ass and brings me to his face. I'm trembling with anticipation, almost nervous to take things to the next step with him. I've been with my fair share of lovers, but no one compares to Weston. He's uncharted territory, and the thrill of setting sail in unfamiliar waters is shadowed only a bit by the fear of not being enough for him.

I want to offer him everything. I want to give him all of me.

"Ohhh," I moan when his lips gently brush over my stomach. He kisses me softly, and my entire body hums in rhythm to him. He moves closer, parting my legs, and I reach out, grabbing the edge of his dresser to steady myself.

And then he moves in, slipping his hand up under my panties and pushing them to my side. There's no easing into it. No warning. His tongue lashes out against my clit and my mouth falls open, but I'm unable to make a sound.

He licks and sucks, speeding up and slowing down, going at me hard and soft and he's paying attention to my reaction the entire time, taking note of what I like better, and then he does it again. And again. And again.

I feel the orgasm coiling tight inside of me, and he brings his free hand up, nails dragging over the flesh of my ass and pushes a finger inside of me. He rubs against my inner walls, finding my g-spot. He pushes against it, holding the pressure there for a moment before releasing. *Holy shit.* I press my head against the wall behind me. This feels so fucking good.

He does it again, moving his fingers in more of a circular motion. It's a different stimulation, one that sends another wave of pleasure through me. Part of me thinks it's going to all come crashing down soon, and I'll be left with female blue-balls. Because this build-up is too good. And things that are too good to be true usually are.

"Ohhh my god," I moan, and everything inside of me becomes alive. Weston sucks my clit, while at the same time he flicks his tongue against it. He continues to finger-fuck me, rubbing my g-spot with two fingers. If my eyes were open, they'd roll back in my head.

My mouth is hanging open, and I grip tighter onto the dresser, feeling my knees threaten to buckle. If I fall, he'll stop, and having him take his mouth off my pussy would be a sin right now.

I need to come.

He knows it, and as soon as I'm close, he pulls back.

"Wes," I growl, trying to find my voice. I reach down with my free hand and take a tangle of his hair, keeping his head against me. "Weston Dawson," I say, forcing my eyes open. "If you stop—"

"What?" He looks up with so much lust in his eyes I could drown. "What will you do if I stop?"

Holy fuck, this man. I arch my back, pushing my pussy forward and in his face.

"If you stop, I'll be forced to finish myself while you watch, and then I won't let you lay a finger on me."

Wes inhales and dives back in with an open mouth. He licks and sucks with fury, and only a minute later I'm hardly able to hold myself up. The orgasm rolls through me, slow at first and then crashing in with fury. It floods every part of me, making my toes curl and my ears ring. I come so hard wetness spills from me.

"Holy shit," he pants, wiping his face.

"Should I be sorry?" I pant as stars dot my vision.

"Hell no. You are so fucking sexy, Scarlet."

I rapidly blink, still floating on ecstasy. I pitch forward, hands landing on Weston's broad shoulders. He stands, scooping me up. I'm like a rag doll in his hands. He brings me to the bed, gently laying me down. He moves on top of me, parting my legs and moving between.

I'm still fully dressed, with damp thighs and wet panties. He brushes my messy hair back, kissing me so that I taste myself on his lips. I feebly reach for the hem of his shirt, trying to pull it up over his head. It's a moot point; I'm not fully functional yet. My pussy is still spasming from the intense orgasm he just gave me, and we're not even close to being done.

"Weston," I breathe, so quiet I'm not sure if he can hear me.

"Scarlet," he whispers back, holding himself over me. I swallow hard and bite my lip.

Reaching down, I undo the button on his jeans, freeing his massive cock. The sheer size of that thing is hardly contained by his boxers, and it feels so fucking good in my hand. I push his pants and boxers down enough to free his cock. I let my eyes fall shut, waiting until my heart stops racing to sit up. I plant my hands on Weston's muscular chest and give him a shove. He's so big and so solid he doesn't move.

Instead, he takes my hands, moves them aside, and flips me over onto my stomach. With a slap to my ass, he gathers the hem of my dress in one hand and slips the other under the band of my panties. I arch my back, making it easy for him to pull them off me.

"Sit up," he grunts, and I obey without question. Licking his lips, he eyes me up and down. I push onto my knees, looking at his cock in all its massive glory. Precum wets the tip, spilling down the thick shaft.

Weston grabs the hem of my dress and pulls it over my head. He groans with want when he sees me. He inches closer, running a hand up and over my breasts. The dress I was wearing required a pushup bra, and I'm looking all cleavagey right now, with my tits pushed up and together. He brings his head in to my breasts, kissing his way up along my collarbone. With deft fingers, he unhooks my bra.

I hold the cups against me, slowly letting the straps fall down one at a time. Weston waits, licking his lips with anticipation. I smile coyly, watching his face as I let my bra fall to the mattress. He sweeps his hands over me, thumbs circling my nipples.

"You're beautiful," he says and moves back to me, kissing me with fervor. I'm on my knees, naked before this man, but I'm anything but shy. I push him back, wanting to level the playing field. He needs to be naked too.

Biting my lip, I inch forward, hands going to his pants. I pull them the rest of the way down, after struggling to get them over his ass, Wes gets impatient and yanks them off.

"Your shirt," I say, leaning back a bit. "Take it off."

Wes looks me right in the eye and gives me a devilish smile before pulling his shirt over his head.

I want him to go down on me again, make me come so hard the entire world falls off its axis again. But there's another thing I want more than coming so hard nothing else matters.

Him.

I want to feel him push inside me. I want to join together, even briefly, and exist as one. It's fucking lame, I know, but dammit, I'm craving him like a starving man craves food.

"I need you," I whisper, body coming alive at the thought of that big, muscular man lying down on top of me. "Now."

"You're sure?" he asks, and having him make sure I'm good with this is such a turn on.

"I've never been more sure of anything in my whole life."

He lets out a growl and moves on top of me, spreading my legs as wide as they'll go and lining his cock up to my entrance. He pauses, kissing me first, and then pushes that big cock inside of me.

He fills every single inch, and I cry out with pleasure as he pulls out only to push back in. I bend my knees, hooking a leg around him. He rocks his hips, thrusting in and out slowly at first and then speeding up his movements. He's doing everything he can not to come right now, and I'm getting closer and closer to coming again myself. My eyes are shut, and my head is to the side. I have one hand on Westin's ass, feeling him drive that big dick in and out of me.

The other hand is gripping the sheets beneath us. Because I've never felt anything this intense in my whole life. I'm not just having amazing sex with Weston. We have a connection, and being together like this only furthers that.

I squeeze the leg that's wrapped around him, bringing myself up against him. Wes moans, head falling forward. He buries it in my neck, teeth nipping at my skin. Then he pushes in balls deep, biting at my neck as he comes. Feeling his cock pulse inside of me pushes me over the edge, and I dig my nails into his skin as I climax again.

Weston holds himself in me for a moment and then moves back, holding himself above me just enough to look into my eyes. Brushing my hair back, he kisses me softly and pulls out, lying down on the mattress next to me.

We're more than aware of the mess we've made, but neither of us cares. Weston pulls me into his arms, spooning his body against mine. We stay like that for a moment, neither of us wanting to move. But I have to pee, so I force myself up and hurry to the bathroom. I clean myself up and dash back to bed. Wes pulled the covers down, and I climb in next to him.

Moonlight spills in through the window, illuminating Weston's face. I sit up, sheet falling off my shoulder, and gently brush his hair back. My heart is still hammering away in my chest, breasts rising and falling. I've never felt so much with anyone before.

I've never let myself.

I've been afraid, though laying here next to Wes, I don't know what I was afraid of.

"Tired?" I ask him, snuggling back down against his muscular chest.

"Not really." He folds me up in his arms, and it's like I'm where I'm supposed to be. Where I'm meant to be. Soon enough, the effects of the intense orgasms he just gave me will wear off and the gravity of the situation will hit me.

Whether or not I'll survive impact is still up in the air.

But I do know I *want* to survive it. Even though I've stayed in the same place for so long, I've spent my whole life running. Trying to escape what was right in front of me, and it's not until this very moment that I realize I was running in circles.

"Are you?" His lips brush against the back of my neck as he talks.

"No, but I don't plan on getting up any time soon." I roll over and hook my leg over his. He sweeps his hand across my waist, splaying his fingers over the small of my back. I push one arm under his pillow, pulling myself closer to him. He kisses my forehead, and I close my eyes, relishing his warmth.

"We should have done this the first time I kissed you," Wes says softly.

"We're quite good at it," I say, nuzzling my head against him. "We could have been doing it the whole time. But that's okay because we get to keep doing it now." I don't realize what I'm saying until it's said. I'm implying we're taking thing to the next level, that we're in a relationship more than boss and employee now.

He's my boyfriend.

Previously, the thought would have made me go running for the hills without a look back. But now…now things are different. Wes is different.

He made me different.

Or maybe…maybe he brought out exactly who I always was. Who I was always meant to me. He showed me that there's nothing to fear, that surrendering to someone isn't scary. It's exhilarating. It's freeing.

That admitting I'm happier with him doesn't make me weak. It makes me stronger, and having my heart beat right along his is the thing I was missing my whole life. He makes me want to be a better person and leave the past behind me. He even makes me think it's possible to move on and start over.

Simply put, he makes me happy. Nothing will bring me down from the high I'm on right now.

"Scarlet, we need to talk."

Chapter Twenty-Seven

SCARLET

THE WAY HE SAYS MY NAME MAKES MY HEART SKIP A BEAT, BUT NOT IN A GOOD way. I tense and sit up, suddenly cold now that I'm away from his body heat. He swallows hard, doesn't look me in the eye, and pushes himself up on the mattress. Moving his pillow behind him, he leans against the headboard.

"You regret sleeping with me?" I blurt.

"Fuck no." He shakes his head and reaches for me. I tense, heart hammering away and feeling like I might throw up. I open my heart to a man for all of half a night and he's already dropping the *we need to talk* line.

What is wrong with me? Why did I think things would be different with Wes? I've been burned by love so many times in the past, starting with my own mother. Love isn't real, and I need to pull away now before I die in a sea of flames.

"Scarlet," he says again and takes a hold of my waist. He's stronger than me and he knows it, but I'll be damned before I let him get the best of me.

"I can just go if you want me to." I pull away and start to get out of bed.

"What?" he rushes up, moving toward me. "No. I don't want you to leave. Please."

I stop, turning around and looking at the man before me. He's so big, so muscular and strong. And yet he looks so vulnerable right now. Letting out a shaky breath, I inch closer. "I'm no good at this, Wes," I admit. "I usually avoid my feelings and try not to let myself get attached to anyone or anything. It's hard for me to trust people, and you're freaking me out."

"I know," he says, snaking his arms around me again. I should protest, but dammit, it feels so good to have his body against mine. I cave and let him pull me close, and I snuggle up with my head on his chest. "That's why I need to tell you something."

"Okay." I run my hand up his side, bracing myself.

"Maybe I should have told you before I slept with you."

I sit up, eyes wide. "You're not helping your case."

He nods and closes his eyes in a long blink. "I'm still married," he says and waits, expecting the bomb to go off.

"Oh. That's it?"

His eyebrows go up. "You're not mad?"

I shake my head. "I already knew that."

"You did?"

"Quinn told me at the bar tonight."

His brow furrows. "Oh, well that's good I guess."

I smile. "So does that solve our issue?"

He doesn't look at me. "It feels unfair to you to start something when I haven't ended things with Daisy."

"Do you want to end things?" I ask carefully, afraid of his answer. My heart is on the line here, and one word can change everything. I inhale and brace myself for the worst. That he doesn't want to end things. Daisy is Jackson's mother, after all.

"I wanted to end things before she left," Weston admits, and his words throw me.

"Really?"

He nods and looks away. "We were together for a long time. Being with her was easy because it was familiar. But that didn't mean we were meant for each other, and we kept waiting for things to get better. Obviously, you know how that turned out. So, yeah…I want to end things."

"Why haven't you?"

"I didn't see the point. If I dated again at all, it wouldn't be for a long time. I can't do that to Jackson…bring someone into our lives and risk them leaving."

"But didn't you want to date?"

"Of course I did. And I do. But Jackson comes first." He flicks his eyes to me, and my heart skips a beat. I look at this beautiful man before me, realizing now more than ever that he's everything I never knew I wanted. I used to think my dream man had to be a rich alpha asshole, but now I know how wrong I was.

My dream man is kind and caring, fiercely protecting those he loves. He's willing to put his own happiness on hold for the sake of another. He's brave and stands up for the right thing. My dream man values his family, doesn't get caught up in petty drama and…and is sitting right next to me.

"How long has she been gone?"

"She left when Jackson was almost two months old."

"Oh, wow. I mean, I'm sorry. Can I call her an idiot? Because she is to leave both Jackson and you."

Wes smiles, and the tension leaves his face. "Yeah, you can call her an idiot."

"I'm not sure how the laws work in Indiana, but I know some places have abandonment of marriage rules or whatever they're called so you can get a divorce without her signature."

"I know. I've thought about it but never saw the point. But now…"

My heart flutters, and he takes me in his arms again. "Now?"

"Now I want to." He holds me tight against his chest and brings one hand up, combing his fingers through my hair. "I didn't think I'd find someone who'd fit."

"Fit?"

"Into our family," he says quietly. "Someone who I want to be with and someone who's good with Jackson."

I blink rapidly, keeping tears at bay. I'm not a crier. Damn you, Weston.

"You think I fit?" I ask, each word coming out a little stronger than the last.

"Yes," he says.

I close my eyes and lose my battle with the tears. One slips out, cascading down my cheek and landing on Weston's chest.

"Scarlet?" He tips my head up to him. "Did I say something wrong?"

"The opposite of wrong."

He hugs me tight and presses his lips to mine. Another tear falls, and he wipes it away with his thumb as he cups my face. I inhale deep, trying to calm myself down. This is everything I wanted and now that it's happening, I'm already panicking about it coming crashing down around me.

"If it's too much pressure to date someone with a kid, I understand," Wes starts.

I stop fighting my tears and kiss him. To anyone else, maybe this isn't a big deal. It's not like a marriage proposal or anything, but to me, this means so much.

He looks at me and sees something more than the girl from the ghetto.

"So," he goes on, kissing me once more. "I'm going to talk to a lawyer. Tomorrow."

I can't stop smiling. "I think that's a good thing."

He rolls over, pinning me between his large body and the mattress. Heat rushes through me and my pussy contracts. I can still feel him in between my legs, as I'm sure I will in the morning. I curl my legs up around him. His cock jumps and knowing I'm turning him on just from my slight touch makes me horny all over again.

I buck my hips, rubbing myself against him. The tip of his semi-hard cock rubs my clit, and I let out a moan. I do it again, feeling his cock get hard as I use him like a sex toy. Wes takes hold of his cock and rubs it against me, not stopping until I'm squirming against him, mouth falling open as I come.

I'm still riding high, unable to form a coherent thought or even lift my head off the mattress. Wes doesn't wait, doesn't give me time to come down from the high. He moves to the edge of the bed, grabs my ankles, and pulls me toward him in one swift movement.

He stands before me, eyes full of hunger as he looks me over. I'm still panting, breasts rising and falling rapidly. Wes leans forward, precum pooling on the tip of his cock, and slips his arms around me. I think he's going to pull me to him and kiss me, but instead, he flips me over and grabs my ass, bringing his cock to it.

Breathing hard, I push myself up, looking behind me at this beast of a man. He has one hand on his cock, face set, and slips his free hand down between my thighs, spreading my wetness along my opening. His finger sweeps over my clit, sending another jolt through me.

Guiding his cock to me, he slowly pushes into my pussy. Taking a hold of my hips, he thrusts in hard, pulling back until only the tip remains. He pauses, leaving me waiting with bated breath to feel him fill me, every single inch of me, again. Pushing in slow, he teases me, and it hurts so good.

And then he lets loose, fucking me hard and fast. My eyes flutter shut, moaning loudly as I'm overcome with pleasure. Wes's breathing quickens, and I know he's close to coming. His fingers press into the flesh on my hips and he pitches forward, hitting me at a new angle. He slides one hand down my hip, going between my legs. He moves his fingers in circles over my sensitive clit, and my god that man is good with his hands. He's balls deep inside of me, moments away from coming, and he's reacting to me as if he can read my mind and knows exactly how to touch me.

My muscles tense, and I feel the orgasm building inside me. My mouth falls open, but no sound comes out. My breath hitches, and the orgasm rolls over me, coming in waves. The first feels amazing. The second knocks me senseless. I collapse down onto the mattress, pussy spasming tightly around Wes's cock, wetness spilling onto the sheets beneath us.

Wes pulls out, hand going to his cock, pumping his dick as I fall back onto the mattress. He dives on top of me, falling between my legs, and kisses me as he enters me again. I can hardly kiss him back, and I'm not even going to attempt lifting my arms to wrap around his neck. I know I can't.

Stars dot my vision, and my ears ring. Wes buries his head against my neck, pumping in and out of me faster and faster until he lets out a guttural growl as he comes. He lowers himself to the mattress, panting.

"That was incredible," I breathe, blinking open my eyes.

"I am incredible." He smirks and rolls over, getting out of bed to grab a towel from the bathroom. I clean myself up and snuggle up with him. "Not to ruin the mood," he starts. "But we didn't use protection."

"I don't have anything," I tell him. "And I'm assuming you don't, either."

"Right. But I don't want you to get pregnant."

"It's a fat chance. But we should probably use protection or pull out just to be safe."

"I can do that."

I could easily fall asleep right now, but I don't want to miss a minute with Wes.

I wake up to the smell of coffee and bacon wafting up the stairs. I'm still naked in Weston's bed. My heart is still soaring as I get up, use the bathroom, and put on a robe. I brush my teeth, twist my hair into a messy bun, and go downstairs.

Wes is standing at the oven, flipping pancakes. He's wearing just a pair of boxers, and seeing that muscular man making breakfast does me in and I'm ready for round three.

"Good morning," I say, smiling as I step into the kitchen.

Wes looks away from the stove. "Morning. Are you hungry?"

"Starving. You wore me out last night."

He smirks. "I plan to wear you out again if you're up for it."

I drop my eye to his crotch. "I'm sure you'll be."

"Don't tease me. The bacon might burn."

Laughing, I cross the kitchen and go to him, wrapping my arms around his waist. Wes turns down the burner and twists in my arms, taking a hold of me. He picks me up and sets me on the counter.

I rake my fingers through his messy hair, pressing my forehead to his. He steps in, fingers inching down my spine.

"Bacon," I whisper, knowing if we start kissing, we won't be able to stop. "Is breakfast almost ready?"

"Yeah." He doesn't step away, and the bacon on the cast iron skillet starts to sizzle and pop. It takes a joint effort to separate from each other. Wes goes back to the stove, and I get out plates and fill two glasses with orange juice, sitting at the table and admiring him cooking.

He serves the food on the plates and brings them over to the table. We eat a few bites in silence, just enjoying each other's company.

"So," I start, picking up my glass of orange juice. "Now what?"

"We keep eating?" Wes says, cocking an eyebrow.

"I plan to, but I meant with us." I look down at my plate, suddenly feeling a little shy.

"Last night wasn't a one-time thing for me," he says with no hesitation. "I meant what I said. You fit with us, and I really like you, Scarlet. I want more."

"Me too." I look up and smile, resisting the urge to reach across the table and take his hand. I refuse to be one of those couples. "This means we get to change our Facebook statuses, right?"

He laughs. "I don't have a Facebook account. Shocking, right?"

"I got rid of mine." I wrinkle my nose. "My life isn't that interesting." That part is true, but another reason I took myself off social media was because I didn't want to be easily found. Being unrecognized comes in handy when you're conning people.

"But I do like the idea of being able to show off my hot new girlfriend." Wes wiggles his eyebrows. "We'll have to get T-shirts instead."

"Ohhh, I do like obnoxious couples' T-shirts. I'm going to get you at least a dozen T-shirts that say *Property of Scarlet Cooper*."

He chuckles. "If being your property means we get to do what we did last night again, then I'm okay with it."

"I can be a very selfish lover," I warn. "I expect you to pleasure me at least once a day and always be enthusiastic about it."

"I don't think I'll have a problem with that. In fact," he says and stands, chair scooting out fast behind him. "I'll pleasure you right now."

"Here?" I ask, trying to keep the school-girl-in-love smile off my face. "At the table?"

He grabs my chair and turns me around. Tingles make their way through my body. Wes leans forward, eyes full of lust and hunger. "Yes, Scarlet," he growls. "I'm going to fuck you right here on the table."

And, Lord have mercy, he does.

"Hey, Mom." Wes sits up, pulling the blankets down with him. After breakfast, sex, and a shower, we got back into bed and passed out. "Yeah, I just woke up." He pauses. "No, I'm not sick again. Just tired from working night shifts all week."

I'm half asleep and don't want to move, but I'm cold. I wiggle closer to Wes, and he lays back down, wrapping his arm around me.

"I'll get dressed and come get him. Is that Quinn in the background I hear? Tell her we'll be over." He looks at me with a smile. "And that I'm considering letting Jackson take one of the kittens."

I sit up, eyes flying open, and nod encouragingly. The only pet I had growing up was the raccoon who lived under our stoop for a few weeks. I named him Ringo—original, I know—and fed him scraps. He started waiting for me at dusk, and it still makes me sad to think back to the evening I went outside to feed him and he never came.

"Yeah, you too," Wes says and ends the call. He puts his phone on the nightstand and pulls me on top of him. We're both naked, and his cock starts getting hard against my stomach.

"Again?" I ask, raising my eyebrows. "I'm gonna go back on my multiple-times thing and add in spacing it out."

Wes laughs and kisses my neck.

"Well, maybe I can make an exception."

"Should I be sorry?" His hands wander over my body. "You're beautiful…and it's been a long time since I've been with anyone."

I push up so I can look him in the eyes. "You haven't slept with anyone since your wife left?"

He shakes his head. "I'm still married…technically, I mean. But it felt wrong. Like I was cheating."

I push his hair back. "You're a good man, Weston Dawson. And she's been gone for four years. It's not cheating at this point."

"It doesn't feel like it. I don't feel like I'm married," he tells me. "But legally we still are."

"Is she still on your insurance and everything?"

"No. I took her off the first time she left me. She did take a car that was in both our names."

"What about the house?" I ask, not sure if I'm overstepping. He's my boyfriend now, I suppose I should know some of this stuff.

"It's in my name. I bought it before we were married."

"That's good." I brush his hair back. "Do we have to go get Jackson?"

"Yeah, we should. It's ten-thirty. I didn't realize how late it was."

"Ten-thirty is late?"

He laughs. "For me it is. We should—dammit."

"What?"

He rolls off and grabs his phone. "I want to talk to Mr. Williams. He's in his office sometimes on Saturday."

"Is he the lawyer?"

"Yeah."

"You go. I'll get Jackson. You said Quinn was there? I wouldn't mind hanging out with her a bit."

Wes smiles, blue eyes sparkling. "I like that you two are friends."

"Me too."

It takes us a few minutes to untangle, and the moment we do, I miss him. "So…I'm guessing I shouldn't give Quinn the gritty details of my night."

Wes laughs. "I don't think she'd appreciate it. And now I kinda get why Dean acts like such a baby about Quinn and Archer." He shakes his head and gets out of bed. I admire his muscular ass for a moment before reaching over the bed for Wes's T-shirt I'd been wearing. "But if you're asking if I want to keep our relationship secret or anything…no."

"What about Jackson?" I ask quietly, getting back into bed. I'm cold already. "Do we tell him?"

Wes shakes his head. "Honestly, I'm not sure how to go about that. There are guidelines and rules, but most of them have already been met since you already live here, and I know you get along." He shakes his head.

"Do kids his age understand dating? He knows what it means to be married, well, kind of."

"If I told him you were my girlfriend, he'd know it was important. He doesn't really seem to get that Quinn and Archer aren't married yet since they live together." Wes shakes his head. "Sorry I don't have a better answer."

"Don't be sorry. It makes me feel a little better for being clueless. In the movies, they always do things slow. Date for a while, make sure things are getting serious before the kid even meets whoever is dating their mom or dad. But like you said, Jackson already knows me."

Wes pulls on boxers, and I'm disappointed to see that gorgeous ass covered up. "As much as I like to have a plan and know what I'm doing, I think we should wing it." He turns, smile on his face. "We kind of already function like a couple."

"Yeah, we do." I smile right back.

Wes dives back onto the bed, snaking his arms around me, tickling me and making me laugh. He presses his lips to mine. "But now I get to do this whenever I want."

Chapter Twenty-Eight

WESTON

Scarlet and Jackson are back at the house by the time I'm done talking with Mr. Williams. I'm not officially divorced yet, but the process has started. And it feels so fucking good.

My heart lurches in my chest, and I can't stop smiling when I step onto the porch carrying a pizza. Jackson's sitting on Scarlet's lap on the couch, and she's reading him a book. His eyes are heavy, and he looks like he'll fall asleep at any minute. They haven't noticed me yet, and I stop to watch them through the window for another few seconds.

Jackson rests his head against Scarlet's shoulder, and she brings her hand up, running her fingers through his hair. His eyes start to flutter closed, making me almost feel bad for coming into the house and waking him up. It's impossible to sneak in and out with our current alarm system, which is why I have it set up the way I do.

I unlock the front door and step in. Scarlet smiles the moment she sees me, and Jackson is more excited about the pizza. I set it on the coffee table and tell Jackson to go wash his hands before we dig in. The second he runs into the bathroom, I pull Scarlet into my arms.

Feeling her body against mine sends a rush through me, and I can't kiss her fast enough. She hooks her arms around my neck and leans in, lips parting. I bring my head down, lips crashing against hers. Once I start, I can't stop. My cock jumps, and I want to carry her upstairs, stripping her out of her clothes and burying my cock inside of her.

"I take it things went well with the lawyer?" Scarlet asks. Her arms are still around me and my hands are still firmly planted on her waist. Jackson will be out of the bathroom at any second, but even one more second with my lips on Scarlet's is worth it.

"Yes," I growl and go in for another kiss, which isn't the smartest idea because I'm starting to get a hard-on, and now I'm thinking of how good it feels to make love to her. As if she can read my mind, she brings one hand down, sweeping it over my chest, and cups my balls.

"Jackson is pretty tired. He was up late at your parents' last night. I think an early bedtime would actually do him some good."

"It'll do me good too." I push my pelvis against her hand and she closes her eyes, moaning. "You're killing me, Scarlet."

"That's all part of my master plan."

"Oh, is it now?"

"Mh-hm."

I raise an eyebrow. "What happened to me being too big to chop up and bury?"

"Now that it's getting colder out, I'll wrap you in a tarp and keep you in the shed."

"I'd rot and would start to smell in a few days. It's not cold enough yet."

"Dammit." She shakes her head. "I forgot you were a cop and know how these things work. So tell me, Officer, what's the perfect murder?"

I laugh, but before I can get any words out, Jackson calls for help.

"What's wrong, buddy?" I ask.

"I had to go potty, and I missed."

Scarlet slides her other hand down my chest. "Good thing you're home."

"Fine. I'll clean up the pee."

"You're a good dad." She gives me a smile and steps away, going into the kitchen to get plates and drinks while I clean up the floor as well as Jackson, who requires new underwear, pants, and socks.

Finally, we gather in the living room, eating pizza while watching a movie. When we're done eating, Scarlet scoots closer to me on the couch, and I drape my arm around her. Jackson gets a blanket and sits close to Scarlet, leaning against her. Scarlet helps him fix the blanket, draping it over both their legs.

"Are you comfortable?" I ask Scarlet, aware of how uncomfortable it can be when Jackson decides to use you as his personal pillow. Though at the same time, having him close like that is the best thing in the world. There really is nothing like snuggling up with your child.

"Yeah," she says, turning her head to look at me. I sneak in a quick kiss, pressing my lips to hers. She puts her hand on top of mine and leans back against me. Sitting here with Scarlet and Jackson is such a simple thing, yet it means so much. We just admitted our feelings last night, finally hooking up after weeks of ignoring the spark. It's not like we're going out and getting married tomorrow, but I know I want her to be part of this family.

"Every time the weather turns, I question why I live in the Midwest." Scarlet zips up her coat. We just got to my parents' for Sunday dinner, and freezing rain is falling down on us. "And it's not even winter yet."

"I used to want to move out west. Though spending years in the desert kind of changed my mind. I like snow."

Scarlet makes a face. "Not me. It's too cold."

"Come sledding with us this winter and maybe I can change your mind."

She opens the back door to the Jeep, getting Jackson out of his car seat. She puts his coat on before he's even out of the car, zipping him up and making him wear his hood.

"We're walking fifty feet from the driveway to the house," I tease. "We're not going to die of hypothermia in that time."

"You never know." She snaps the top button on Jackson's coat and takes his hand. She's so good with him, and he's so responsive with her. Seeing them together makes me so fucking happy, and I can't stop smiling right now.

I let out a snort of laughter when I see the magnet on the back of Owen's truck that reads *Big Truck, Small Penis*.

"What's so funny?" Scarlet asks.

"Owen and Logan must be at it again," I tell Scarlet, pointing to the magnet. "They put ridiculous and usually vulgar magnets on each other's cars and see how long it takes before the other notices."

She laughs. "That's actually hilarious. I wonder how long that's been on."

"No clue. A few months ago, Logan drove around with a big smiley-face magnet that said, 'I have herpes' for four days before he noticed."

"Can we get a magnet like that for your car, Daddy?" Jackson asks, and his innocence pulls on my heart.

"Sure," I tell him. "Something similar but not the exact same."

"Yay!"

We hurry into the garage, shaking off the slushy rain from our coats before stepping in and being bombarded by my mom's dogs. Logan and Owen are in the kitchen at the big island counter, eating chips and salsa. Meat for tacos is simmering on the stove, and tequila and margarita mix sit out on the counter next to the fridge.

"Hey," Logan says, and Jackson rushes over, getting excited to see his uncles. He flicks his eyes to Scarlet and then me in question, and I know he's thinking about what we discussed back at the bar Friday night.

"Hi, Logan," Scarlet says, pointing to him. "And Owen. I got it right this time, didn't I?"

Logan nods. "Right, but it's not hard. I'm much better looking than he is."

Scarlet laughs and takes off her shoes and coat. "You dress alike, and even your mannerisms are the same."

Jackson slides out of Owen's lap, wanting to show him the farm set-up he worked on while he was here yesterday. Logan starts to get up to follow them, but I stop him.

"Does he know Charlie is engaged?" I ask in a hushed voice.

"Charlie's engaged?" Logan's eyebrows go up. Fuck. Owen doesn't know.

Scarlet takes a seat next to Logan and pulls the bag of chips over. "Who's Charlie?"

"Owen's ex who he's not over," Logan tells her. "He won't admit it, but we all know he still has feelings for her."

"Poor guy." Scarlet shakes her head.

"How'd you find out she's engaged? Last I heard she was living in New York," Logan says.

"I met with her dad today," I tell him, and he puts two-and-two together right away.

"Are you free?" His lips curve into a smile. "Can I pour a round to celebrate?"

"What are we celebrating?" Mom asks, coming into the kitchen carrying an armload of Mason jars. "Oh, hello, Scarlet. It's so good to see you again."

"It's nice to see you too. Need any help?"

"No, but thank you. I'm canning tomorrow and just brought these up from the basement." Mom puts everything in the sink. "Is there really a celebration? I'll drink to it if there is."

"You'll drink to anything," Logan quips.

Mom nods. "That is true. I do enjoy wine, though tonight I'm having a marg to go with my taco."

"Don't call it a marg, Mom." Logan shakes his head.

"Why not?"

Logan laughs. "Just don't. And Wes said he talked to a lawyer today. So I'm assuming that means..."

"I petitioned for a divorce," I finish, feeling a huge sense of relief as soon as the words come out of my mouth. "Given the circumstances, how long Daisy has been gone, and the fact that she hasn't provided any sort of support for our son, Mr. Williams thinks he can have things handled fairly quickly and I'll be granted full custody of Jackson."

Mom gasps and claps her hands together. "I have been praying for this!" She pulls me into a hug.

"You know how weird it sounds to admit you've been praying for me to get divorced?"

Mom laughs, giving me one more squeeze. "Oh, stop it. I want you to be happy."

"I am, Mom. I am."

The garage door opens, sending the dogs running in a frenzy. Quinn and Archer make their way in, trying to make it to the kitchen table without being tripped by the dogs. Archer sets Emma's car seat on the table, folding back the blanket she's covered with. Somehow she stayed asleep through all the noise.

"Hey, guys," Quinn says and notices Mom's watery eyes. "What's wrong?"

"Nothing," I assure her. "Mom's being overly emotional."

"Shocker, right?" Logan laughs.

"About what?" Quinn goes right for the tequila and unscrews the lid.

"I finally filed for a divorce," I say.

Quinn reacts just like our mother, running over to hug me. "Yes! Can you make her take her maiden name back too? I don't even want her to be a Dawson anymore."

"Having your name be Daisy Dawson forever is almost a punishment," Logan says.

"It's pretty awful," Archer agrees. "Sounds like a cheap porn star." He yawns, and I notice he looks dead on his feet.

"Long day at work?" I ask.

"I had a nine-hour surgery and then spent forty-five minutes arguing with a patient's insurance company." He shakes his head. "I don't know if want to punch someone or take a nap."

"Have a drink first," Quinn says, going back to the margarita. "Then take a nap."

"Why are you here?" Logan asks, grabbing another chip. "I'd be passed the fuck out if I did anything for nine straight hours."

"I'm hungry," Archer says, and we laugh. "And it's nice coming here and being together. It means a lot to Quinn."

"You're so whipped," Logan teases.

"I don't mind it. Not one bit." Archer watches Quinn mix him a drink. Gaining my approval to date my baby sister isn't easy. But Archer's a good guy, and I know he really cares about her.

"I think it's sweet," Scarlet says with a smile. "And it is nice that you all get together like this."

"I love it." Quinn pours way too much tequila into the drink, making Logan wince. "I missed it when I lived in Chicago." She mixes up the drink and pours it into a glass. "Anyone else want one?"

"Let me take over, sis." Logan gets up, patting Quinn on the shoulder and takes the margarita from her hand. He smells it and shakes his head. "Are you trying to get Archer drunk?"

"Kind of. Then I'll ask for another cat." She flashes Archer a smile. "Kidding. Eight is enough."

"More than enough."

"Actually," I start, sure I'm going to regret this. "If you still want to get rid of one… Jackson keeps asking."

"You guys need a pet," Mom says, taking Emma out of her car seat. "But dogs are much friendlier."

"Cats are easier," I counter. "I'm not home enough for a dog."

"But Scarlet is," Mom goes on.

Scarlet wrinkles her nose. "I'm more of a cat person."

"I knew there was a reason I liked you." Quinn beams, going over to the chips and salsa. Dad, who was grilling corn on the covered patio, comes in. He's a die-hard griller and will stand out there in the middle of winter.

Owen and Jackson come back to the kitchen, ready to eat. Dean and Kara aren't here yet, and we all try to convince Mom to let us go ahead and eat without them. Right when we've just about got her to cave, we see Dean's car pull into the driveway.

"I need to update Jackson's forms at school," I start, turning to Logan. "I'm putting you as an emergency contact after Scarlet. I had Quinn on there, but now it's easier for you to get over to the school than it would be for her with Emma."

Logan nods. "Okay."

"I can be an emergency contact," Owen offers, and I make a face. He'd do a good job looking after Jackson, I know, but it's fun hassling him.

"You're the last person I'd put on the list," I tell him. "Quinn is first, and then Logan, then Dean, then Quinn's cats, and then you."

"You're so fucking hilarious," Owen says dryly.

"Finally! We're starving," Quinn says dramatically when Dean and Kara step into the house.

"Sorry." Dean unzips his coat. "We couldn't leave with the dishwasher going." He rolls his eyes. Kara shakes her head, clenching her jaw. I can tell they were fighting, and I don't think the dishwasher was the only issue.

"It might leak," Kara says through gritted teeth. "Like it did before."

"I fixed it," Dean spits.

"Hey!" Quinn blurts, trying to be the peacekeeper. "Wes has good news!"

"Yeah, I do." I put my arm around Scarlet. I look into her beautiful blue eyes and smile. "I filed for divorce, and Scarlet and I are dating."

Chapter Twenty-Nine

SCARLET

I've never felt more welcome, more at home, than I do with the Dawsons. Everyone was thrilled when Wes told them we were dating. I think I smiled the entire time we ate, the whole way home, and while I straightened up the house when Wes put Jackson to bed.

"I have to work in the morning," Wes reminds me when I get into bed next to him.

"I know. You're leaving at seven, right?"

"Yeah. And then I have some campaign shit to do." He turns off the bedside light and takes me in his arms. "I want to stay home with you."

"I'd like that too." I curl a leg up around him.

"Is it presumptuous to open that box of condoms now?" he asks with a cheeky grin.

"No. Not at all."

He kisses my neck and moves on top of me. "So, we had sex," he starts.

"We did? When?"

"Just now. You didn't feel it?"

"Ohhh, that's what that was." I laugh, and he nibbles at my neck.

"What I mean is, we had sex without protection. I know you said you don't think you can get pregnant, but...well...are you sure?"

"Yes. If you knock me up, it would be a miracle."

"What do you mean?"

I let out a breath. "I don't think I can have kids." As soon as I say it out loud, I wish I could take it back. What if Wes wants another kid? Is that a deal-breaker? Thinking of him not wanting to be with me is like a stake through the heart.

"Why do you think that?"

"The last time I saw my OB, she said I only have one functioning ovary and my cycles are extremely random. Like I only have a few periods a year."

"Oh." Wes's face is unreadable. He's thinking, but I can't tell what he's thinking about. "I'm glad an unplanned pregnancy isn't likely, but, uh, sorry? I don't know what to say."

"I don't either. But I really like how honest you are." A twinge of guilt hits me. I'm honest with him now, and I plan to be from here on out. But I wasn't, and thinking back to the woman I was when I stepped out of the car, remembering the disappointment I felt when I realized he wasn't some rich asshole I could charm money out of...it makes me hate myself.

"Does that change how you feel about me?"

"No, of course not."

"Good." I let my eyes fall shut and realize how fast my heart is beating. "Do you want more kids?"

"I don't know. I used to. Coming from a big family, I thought I'd want that too. But things didn't work out as I expected, and I'm happy. Now more so than before. What about you?"

"I think I've always wanted kids," I admit, not letting myself stop and think. "But I didn't want to raise them in the same situation I was in when I grew up."

"You've never mentioned your mom," he says carefully. "Is she out of the picture?"

"Yes. She's dead."

"Oh, fuck. I'm sorry."

"I'm not." I'm speaking my truths. Why stop now? "It sounds terrible, I know. But she was a terrible mother who had me young and should have given me up for adoption and gotten her tubes tied. She died of an overdose, and I'm the one who found her. The worst part wasn't her dying. It was having to tell my sister and brother." My eyes fill with tears, and all the emotions I've denied myself of feeling over the years come rushing back. "I dropped out of school to take care of them." Hot tears roll down my cheeks. "I wasn't able to go back to school until our dad came back." I break off, choking up.

"It's okay," Wes soothes, gently wiping away my tears.

"But it's not. You're such a good person, Wes. I'm not. I've done so many things I wish I could take back. My life sucked but that's no excuse. I could have done better. I should have. You need to know this if you want to be with me. That's who I am. Scarlet Cooper: South Side trash with a dead mother, a sister in jail, and a father who poisoned his own brain with drugs and alcohol."

"That doesn't define you."

"But that's the thing." More tears spill from my eyes. "Nothing defines me. I…I don't know who I am."

"You're Scarlet Cooper," he says slowly, looking right into my eyes. "A little quirky and a lot amazing. You like shifter romance and classic rock. A certain four year old who I happen to think is the coolest kid in the world really likes you."

I smile.

"And I do too."

"I've done bad things, Wes." My jaw quivers and I want to tell him the truth as much as I don't. I want to start fresh, confess everything.

Because I'm in love with Wes Dawson.

"It's okay," he says like he believes it. "It's in the past."

"But I still did them."

His brows pinch together. "We live by going forward, not backward." He wipes away a tear.

I sniffle, turning my head to the side to mop up my messy face. This is only part of the reason why I hate crying. "I wish I could see myself the way you see me."

"You'd see how incredible you are."

"Weston," I start, ready to tell him everything. But he cuts me off with a kiss, and I give in, surrendering myself to him.

<hr />

"What's your excuse this time?" Heather asks before she even sits down at the table. I haven't seen her in a while, and I feel bad about it. But I'm here now, right? The last few weeks have passed in a whirlwind. A wonderful whirlwind, but they've been crazy nonetheless.

The closer we got to the election, the busier Wes was, and he's barely been home this week. Logan and Owen came over to pass out candy yesterday so I could take Jackson trick-or-treating. Wes made it home in time to do the last two blocks with him, and we pigged out on candy as soon as we got back to the house.

"Things have been busy at home."

"You call it home now?" Heather's sporting a fresh cut on her lip and has more bruises on her cheek and arms.

"What the hell is this?" I reach forward and push up the sleeve of her shirt.

"Nothing." She smirks. "You should see the other guy."

"This isn't funny, Heather. I want you out of here." I close my eyes and let out a breath. There's no point in arguing with her. I don't know what it's like to be in her shoes. My knowledge of how prison is run is limited to what I've seen on *Orange is the New Black*.

"Home?" she questions again.

"It feels like home," I admit. And it does. Everything I own is there. It's filled with people I care a lot about. I'm sleeping in Wes's room every night, even when he's working nights.

"You look different." Heather eyes me up and down.

"How?" I ask, looking around the visitation room. That one annoying woman isn't here, thankfully. She listened in on my conversations with my sister and just gave off a bad vibe.

"You're not wearing black, for one."

I look down at my wine-colored sweater. "I don't always wear black."

"Nine times out of ten, you do." Heather shrugs. "But it works for you."

"It's the color of my soul. What can I say?"

"Sure. Keep telling yourself that, sis." She shakes her head. "It's almost like you're glowing. You had sex, didn't you?"

"Maybe."

"With your boss?"

"He's my boyfriend now." A smile takes over my face.

"Seriously?"

"Yeah." I lean back, heart swelling in my chest. "He's…he's amazing."

"You're so in love with him."

"He's a good guy."

"Who you *love*," Heather presses.

"I care a lot about him."

"Oh my God, Scar, just say it."

"I don't want to jinx anything," I admit. "Because I'm happy. Things are finally going right in my life, and I'm terrified they're going to crash and burn. That tends to happen to me, you know."

"Because you're usually the one causing the crash. And then pouring gasoline on the fire. I love the shit out of you, big sis, but you're a bit self-destructive at times."

"I know," I admit with a sigh. "I'd rather end things on my terms…do whatever I can to stay in control." Shaking my head, I lean back. "Is it crazy to think things can work out for me?"

"No, not at all." She puts her hand on mine. "You deserve to be happy, Scar. I've had a lot of time to think in here—shocking, I know—and I realized how much you gave up for us. You dropped out of school, and you fucking loved school. You were such a nerd."

"Yeah," I say with a smile. "I was. I still am."

"And everything you did to take care of Mom and me and Jason…it was a lot to put on you. No one asked you to do any of that. You just did it. And then you did it again when Dad got sick."

"It had to be done."

"Yeah, and you never once complained. You've always taken care of us. Now someone is taking care of you. And I don't mean just financially."

I wiggle my eyebrows. "You mean sexually?"

Heather laughs. "That's not what I meant, but it's good to know he's adequate in all aspects."

"Very adequate." My heart skips a beat, and warmth floods through my veins at the thought of Wes.

"I want you to be happy. You deserve it, Scar, so much."

"Thanks. I...I don't feel like I do," I admit. "I've been thinking a lot too, and I want to do better. Wes makes me want to be a better person."

"And you say you don't love him."

"I didn't say that I didn't love him."

An inmate a few tables over stands up, yelling at her baby daddy. Heather and I turn, distracted by the drama.

"That's Jasmine," Heather whispers. "She's not sure if he's really her baby's father or not. It might be his cousin."

"Damn. And you say jail time is boring. It's like a real-life soap opera."

"Oh, I could write a sitcom with all the shit I've seen and heard. Half of which no one would even believe. Like the chick a few cells down from me." Heather shakes her head. "She had a cell phone up her snatch for over a week."

"Ew. And ouch. But mostly...how?"

Heather slowly shakes her head. "No clue. But can you imagine the smell? And rumor has it, it was an iPhone."

I shudder. "I have all sorts of questions, but I don't think I even want to know."

"I've learned not asking is the way to go."

I lean back in the uncomfortable chair. "I talked to Jason yesterday."

Heather's eye light up. "How is he? Is he coming home anytime soon?"

"He said he's doing good, and he sounded like it. I think he's a little homesick and he's hoping to be able to come home in January."

"If he does, please bring him to see me! I miss that little twerp."

"I don't think he's a twerp anymore."

Heather laughs, wiping her eyes. Unlike me, she's emotional. Cries during commercials and during certain songs no matter how many times she's heard them.

"And I will."

"What else did he say?"

A few more visitors shuffle in and the room gets louder. I fill Heather in on everything Jason told me, which isn't much.

"I should get going," I tell Heather, feeling bad. "It's a long drive back to Eastwood." I go to stand, and Heather reaches forward, taking my necklace between her fingers.

"You're wearing a cat charm?"

"Oh, yeah. I almost forgot. It's a joke."

"A joke?"

"Wes's sister, Quinn, is kind of a crazy cat lady, and their mom is very much a dog person. Their house is more divided than Bears and Packers fans living under the same roof."

"So you've sided with Team Cat."

"I do like cats."

Heather laughs and stands with me, giving me a hug before I leave. I spot that one annoying eavesdropper on my way out. I wouldn't think much of it, but she won't stop looking at me. I put on my coat and glance her way.

She's not just staring at me. She's glaring, seething with hatred.

Chapter Thirty

WESTON

"You're officially a heartbreaker, Weston." Scarlet turns away from the stove, setting down a wooden spoon. I just got home from work and the house smells amazing.

"How so?" I ask, amused. I take off my shoes. "And what is that?"

"Spiced cider. We can add rum to ours if you want."

"That sounds good." It's a cold and windy day, and I spent the last hour and a half of my shift outside in it, dealing with a car accident. No one was seriously hurt, but both people involved had flaring tempers, which made everything take twice as long. I unzip my coat, longing to feel Scarlet's warm body pressed against me. "How am I a heartbreaker?"

Scarlet strides over and wraps her arms around my neck. I slip a cold hand under her shirt, making her shriek and squirm away. I hold her tighter, laughing.

"Your hands are like ice!"

"It's cold out."

"Don't you have gloves to wear?"

"Yeah, but I didn't wear them."

"Obviously," she laughs. "And Mrs. Hills stopped me when I picked up Jackson from school today. She was very upset to learn you were off the market."

"How did that even come up?" I slide my hands to Scarlet's ass. She's wearing leggings, and I don't think she has panties on underneath. I bring my head down, lips going to her neck.

"My dress blew up in the wind and she saw my *Wes Dawson's tight end* panties."

I laugh. "That's what I figured happened." I kiss her neck, and Scarlet arches her back, pressing herself against me.

"Really, she said she saw us at the diner last week and we seemed close."

I step in, widening my legs. "Well, we are." We kiss, and just seconds later Jackson comes down the stairs. He runs over for a hug, and I scoop him up, pulling Scarlet to me with my other arm.

Things are so fucking perfect.

"Is dinner ready?" Jackson asks.

"Let me check it." Scarlet gets a pot pie from the oven. "It's done. It needs to sit for like five minutes to cool first." She taps her chin, looking at Jackson. "I wonder what we could do in that time? Oh no. I think the zombies are back!"

Jackson wiggles out of my arms and takes off, laughing and screaming as he starts to run around the house. Scarlet and I both chase after him, and we run around the house for more than five minutes.

I go upstairs to change while Scarlet cuts into the pot pie and has Jackson help set the table. We function so well together. I don't want to get ahead of myself, but I'm already thinking about the future.

Never in a million years did I think I'd want to get married again, but my mind has drifted to proposing to Scarlet. I want us to be a family.

"What are you guys looking at?" I ask, coming down the stairs. Scarlet and Jackson are peering out of the blinds in the living room with the lights off.

"That white car has been by twice," Scarlet says. "And Jackson told me it was stopped in front of the house earlier."

"Really?" I go right to the front door, not bothering with socks.

"Wes, wait!" Scarlet springs up and comes after me, telling Jackson to stay in the house. "Shouldn't you go back and get your gun before you go up to a creepy car?" She grabs my arm.

The car goes from *park* to *drive* and moves down the street. People do stop along the side of the road sometimes, whether to text or mess with something in their car. But if Scarlet has seen this car before, and they left as soon as we stepped onto the porch, something is up.

"That's weird, isn't it?" Scarlet says, and I wrap my arm around her, keeping her warm. I watch the car go down the street, stopping and making a turn onto a one-way road.

"Yeah. That is a little weird. Let's go in." I lock the door behind us and pull my phone from my pocket, arming the house.

"Hopefully the crust is cooked through this time," Scarlet says as we sit down. "I undercooked it last time." She wrinkles her nose and looks so damn adorable.

"I liked the mushy-crust," Jackson tells her.

"You were the only one," I loudly whisper.

"Hey now." Scarlet gives me a pointed look and we dig in. After dinner, I give Jackson a bath and put him to bed. Scarlet is sitting on the couch when I come back down, wrapped in a blanket. She's holding a cup of tea in one hand and her book in the other.

"Want me to make a fire?" I ask, eyeing the brick fireplace that we rarely use. Call me paranoid or overprotective, but it makes me nervous to have the fire going with Jackson around. The fireplace is original to the house, and the entire hearth gets pretty warm when a fire is going.

"That would be amazing." She puts her book down. "And a little romantic."

I wiggle my eyebrows and go to the couch first, needing to feel my lips against hers before I go outside and get firewood off the back porch.

"Do you want any tea?" she asks as I work on getting the fire going. It's not as easy as it looks.

"No, but I will take some of that spiked cider."

"Ohh, right. I almost forgot! I'll heat us both a glass."

I have a small, rather pathetic fire going by the time Scarlet comes back into the living room, carrying two mugs of steaming cider. We sit together in silence, drinking our cider and watching the flames.

"I could do this every night until summer," she says, putting her mug down and snuggling up against me.

"Me too." And then do it again next fall. And the one after that…and the one after that…

"Quinn asked if we wanted to double-date with her and Archer to dinner and a movie tomorrow. She already talked to your parents about watching both of the grandkids."

"Yeah, that'd be fun. Are Dean and Kara going too?"

"She didn't say they were. Is that weird to go and hang out with Archer when he's Dean's friend?"

"It's not weird for me. Archer's like another brother. But Dean can be possessive," I say with a laugh. "I haven't gone to see a movie that wasn't G-rated in years."

"I haven't seen one in a while, either. And just to warn you, I'm probably going to hog the popcorn, which has to have extra salt and tons of butter."

"That's the only way to eat movie-theater popcorn."

"I'll text Quinn back now before I forget." She grabs her phone and fires off a text.

"You and Quinn seem to really get along."

Scarlet smiles. "She's great."

"She is." I put my empty mug on the coffee table. I don't drink very often, and I think Scarlet put too much rum in the cider. Or maybe I'm feeling buzzed because I'm with Scarlet. "Having Jackson and Emma will be interesting."

Scarlet laughs. "I think your parents can handle it. And Jackson loves Emma."

"He does because they're not together all that often. And he's been difficult lately."

"Yeah," Scarlet agrees. "He was difficult today a few times."

"What'd he do?"

"Nothing serious. Just defiant and I had to tell him multiple times to pick up. And I pretty much ruined his afternoon by giving him a green cup instead of a blue one."

I chuckle and shake my head. "Don't be afraid to discipline him," I remind her. We went over ways to handle his bad behavior from the start, but I know Scarlet still feels a little awkward. I don't want her to, especially with the way things are going.

"I know. And after his meltdown at the grocery store the other day…" She shakes her head. "I got this."

Fuck, I love this woman. "You do."

She climbs into my lap and rakes her fingers across my back. It drives me crazy and she knows it. "I know it's borderline arctic outside, but it's a full moon. Want to look at it with your telescope with me?"

"Why does that sound dirty?"

"Everything sounds dirty to you."

"That's your fault," I tell her. "I think about your pussy all damn day."

"Weston," she exclaims, faking shock and bringing her hand to her chest. "I'm a lady. How dare you speak like that in front of me."

"You were not a lady last night when you had me pull your hair and fuck you from behind."

A little moan escapes her lips. "Fuck that was good."

"We can do it again."

"Oh, we will. But…the moon."

"Yeah, let's go look at it."

I check on Jackson before we go outside. He kicked off his blankets and is covered in goosebumps. After fixing the covers and adding one more blanket to make sure he's not cold, I grab socks and a sweatshirt from my room and meet Scarlet in the kitchen.

"It's not *that* cold," I tease, seeing her bundle up like it's the middle of winter.

"Promise you'll warm me up later?"

"You know I will."

We go outside onto the back porch and bring the telescope into the middle of the backyard, trying to get a good view of the moon. Trees and the roof of the house obstruct our vision. I pick the heavy thing up and lug it around to the front, even though Scarlet protests and says I shouldn't go through any trouble.

But doing anything to see her smile will never be trouble for me.

"I'm starting to really love this quiet," she whispers, looking up and down the street. It's dimly lit from a few street lamps and porch lights. I set the telescope down on the sidewalk and adjust it until the moon comes into view.

"It's really bright tonight. It looks awesome," I tell her and step aside so she can have a look. A car drives by on the street perpendicular to ours, rolling through the stop sign. Things are pretty quiet downtown once night falls, but it doesn't become a ghost town.

"It's amazing," Scarlet whispers, and I find myself smiling as I watch her. "I can see so much detail."

I zip up my coat and stick my hands in my pockets, turning around. It feels like someone is watching us, and unease creeps over me. After years as a soldier and then a cop, I know to trust my gut. I take a few steps away from Scarlet and look down the narrow stretch of grass that separates my house from the neighbors'. I don't see anything…and then I remember that we went out the back door and walked around to the front.

The back door is unlocked.

Jackson is inside.

"I'll be right back," I say and start forward, only to stop. "Come with me."

Scarlet looks up from the telescope. "Where?"

"Inside. The back door is unlocked."

"Oh, shit. Go lock it." She waves me away and bends her head back down.

"Come in with me. Please?"

"I thought you said this was a safe town."

"It is." I inch toward the house. "But I'd feel better if you came in with me."

She looks up and sees the worry in my eyes. "Yeah, I'll come in. I need more warm cider anyway."

I run around the house and leap up the porch steps. The door is still closed, but that doesn't mean anything. I don't stop until I'm in Jackson's room, seeing him safely sleeping in bed.

I sit on the edge of his bed, resting one hand on his back. I used to sit up with him like this when he was an infant, making sure he was still breathing. I still do this when he's sick. I'll probably always do this.

"Everything okay?" Scarlet whispers, appearing in the doorway.

"Yeah." I pull my phone from my pocket and log into the alarm system app, checking the activity. Other than me opening the door less than a minute ago, the last time the back door was opened was when Scarlet and I left the house. "I worry about him."

"I know." Scarlet comes into the room and perches on the bed next to me. "I do too." She takes my hand and brings it to her lips. "He's lucky to have such a caring father."

I give her hand a squeeze. The words are burning in my mouth, wanting to come out.

Wanting to tell her I love her.

Chapter Thirty-One

WESTON

"Are you getting nervous?" Scarlet asks, pouring herself a cup of coffee.

"No."

She looks at me incredulously. "Not at all?"

"Honestly, I'm looking forward to election day so this campaigning bullshit will be over."

She laughs. "I don't blame you there. You'll know if you won that night, right?"

"In theory."

"I have a good feeling about this. Come Tuesday night, I'll be calling you Sheriff."

"Even if I do win, I won't be the Sheriff until the term ends."

She sits at the table next to me. It's early Friday morning, and she woke up when my alarm when off. Instead of going back to sleep, she came downstairs with me for breakfast.

"I'm still calling you it. And I'll make sure to be a bad girl who needs to be arrested and appropriately punished."

"It is my duty to uphold the law."

She takes a sip of her coffee, smiling. "I'll make sure you catch me jay-walking or something."

I laugh. "Living on the edge."

"I'm a regular criminal."

"Please. Like you've ever broken a law."

She chokes on her coffee, eyes going wide.

"Forget how to drink?" I raise my eyebrows.

"Went down the wrong pipe," she says between coughs. "And it's hot."

"You okay?"

"Yeah. And I have broken laws before."

"Really?"

She casts her eyes down. "Yeah. What if I told you I did some bad things but never got caught?"

With one question, she's back to being hard to read. I think she's joking, but she says it seriously. Her body language changes as well, and she's still looking down at the table. Before I can question her, my phone rings.

"It's the station." I answer, talk to my boss for a minute, and then stand. "Gotta go."

"Already?"

"Yeah. We got a lead on a meth lab in a garage."

"Be careful."

"I will." I grab my plate and carry it to the sink. "We bust meth labs more often than you'd think around here."

"Is it like *Breaking Bad*?"

"Most aren't that cool-looking."

"Sounds dangerous, though."

I nod, not one to sugarcoat anything. "I know what I'm doing."

"Good. Because I need you home tonight."

I'm tempted to tell her I love her again, because I never really do know what the day will bring. I suppose the danger is there for anyone who leaves the house: car accidents claim the lives of many every day, but it's a little different when you're leaving the house to go running into danger.

"I'm gonna go give Jackson a kiss goodbye," I tell her and hurry up the stairs, sneaking into his room so I don't wake him. I pause in the doorway, looking at his handsome little face. We finally took him to get a haircut, and the shorter locks make him look older. He's four and a half already. Time is fucking flying by.

"See you later, buddy," I whisper. "I love you."

If Scarlet weren't here, I would have had to wake Jackson up already, fight with him to eat breakfast and get dressed, and probably deal with a tantrum or two as I get him to put his shoes on and get buckled into his car seat. I'd drop him off with my mom before heading into the station, tired and most likely irritated from dealing with his attitude. It's inevitable that all parents feel frustrated with their own children. I still get frustrated with him. But having him on a solid schedule where he's developed a routine and gets plenty of sleep has been so good for us.

"Can you call me when you're done?" Scarlet asks before I head out the door. "So I know you're okay?"

"Yeah. I will."

"Thanks." She brushes her blonde hair over her shoulder. "I'm going to sit here worrying, you know."

"I do. And not that I want you to worry, but it's nice knowing you are. If that makes any sense at all."

"It does. You know that I lo—that I care a lot about you."

Was she going to say she loves me? I look into her blue eyes and my heart hammers away. Fuck this. Life is too short to live cautiously when it comes to matters of the heart.

I stride over, take her in my arms, and plant a big kiss on her lips.

"Scarlet?"

"Yeah?" She fastens her arms around my neck.

"I love you."

Her lips curve into a smile and her eyes get misty. "Are you sure about that?"

"Yes," I chuckle. "I'm very sure. I am in love with you, Scarlet Cooper."

"I didn't think I'd ever love anyone, because I was convinced love didn't exist." Her eyes flutter shut, and my heart starts to beat faster and faster. "Then I met you, and I realized that love is real, and I don't just mean romantic love. You have so much love for your son... and your family...every one of you." She swallows hard, having a hard time with the words. Tipping her head up, she locks her eyes with mine. "I love you, too, Weston."

We kiss, and my heart explodes with happiness. For the first time in years, everything is perfect.

⁂

"Look at him," Scarlet whispers, leaning in. "He totally wants her!"

"Do you think she knows?" Quinn whispers back. We're sitting at the bar at Getaway, and are currently watching Logan painfully try to get out of the friend-zone with fellow bartender, Danielle.

"She messes with her hair when they talk." Scarlet slides her drink in front of her and looks at Danielle. "And they're so flirty, you'd think so. How long has she worked here?"

"I think like a year," Quinn answers. "Or at least that's about how long ago he started mentioning her. As his friend, of course." She slides her drink in front of her and takes a sip. "I have to pee. Want to come with me?"

"Sure." Scarlet slides off her bar stool and follows Quinn to the ladies' room. Dean ended up joining us after the movie, and he and Archer are playing pool. I grab Quinn's drink, not wanting to leave it sitting on the bar unattended and join them.

"Ditching the girls already?" Dean asks, glancing up from the pool table.

"They went to the bathroom together."

"Oh. Scarlet and Quinn have become good friends."

"Yeah," I say, not meaning to smile as much as I do. "It's nice."

"I guess," Dean says flatly, and I look at Archer and roll my eyes. We both know what he's getting at. Kara is—for some stupid fucking reason—annoyed at the new friendship. If she weren't so uptight, we could all hang out together and it'd be fun. Though I suppose when I stop and think about it, it's kind of a weird situation.

Archer and Dean have been best friends for years. Quinn is marrying her brother's best friend. My girlfriend is now good friends with my sister, so when those two hang out and we double-date, Archer comes with.

Whatever. We're all family now.

"How's Bobby?" I ask Archer.

"He's doing all right. Supposedly he made a breakthrough during group therapy yesterday. Like he did the last time he was there. And the time before that."

"I'm sorry, man. That's rough."

"You can't help someone who doesn't want to help themselves." He moves around the pool table. "Speaking of help…you are taking a cat, right? Quinn mentioned that you wanted one for Jackson."

"I did, and I'm considering it. Scarlet would like it too."

"Getting her a pet already?" Dean trades his pool stick for his beer. "Are you ready for that type of commitment?"

He's joking, but my answer is serious. "Yeah. I am." I look in the direction of the bathrooms, hoping to see Scarlet walking out. "She's perfect."

"It's nice seeing you happy," Dean tells me. "We all like Scarlet, which is a welcome change from—what the fuck?" He cuts off and almost drops his beer, eyes going wide. "Daisy."

He doesn't have to say the words for me to know. The look of horror on his face says it all. Daisy is here, and I turn just in time to see her stop in her tracks. We make eye contact, and she doesn't so much as smile. Then she turns and makes a beeline to Scarlet.

Chapter Thirty-Two

SCARLET

"I SWEAR TO YOU, IT BURNED MY MOUTH," QUINN SAYS, AND WE BOTH LAUGH. "I told Archer I would never go down on him again if he eats spicy food. I know he likes it, but for the sake of a blow job he'll give it—what the fuck?"

She grabs my arm and comes to a dead stop.

"What's wrong?" I face Quinn. Her green eyes are wide, and it's like she just saw a ghost. Following her line of sight, I turn and do a double-take. The annoying eavesdropping woman from the visitation room at the prison is standing a few feet from us.

Is this a strange coincidence or is she—

"What the fuck are you doing here?" Quinn demands, and a darkness that I've never seen before comes out in here. "Get the hell out of here before I beat your ass."

The annoying lady puts her hand on her hip and shakes her head. "Nice to see you too, Quinn."

Wait a minute. She knows Quinn?

"Get out of here," Quinn says through gritted teeth. "Now."

"Or what?"

"I'll force you outside myself."

Annoying Lady leans in. "We both know you don't have it in you."

"But I do." Logan rushes forward, putting himself between Annoying Lady and Quinn. "This is my bar and I can kick whoever I want out. So get out."

"That's no way to treat a lady."

"You're not a lady," Logan spits. "Get the fuck out of my bar, Daisy."

Daisy? I blink. Once. Twice. She's still there. Owen and Archer are coming over, and Dean is standing in the back of the bar, hands raised a bit as he tries to talk down Wes.

And now it makes perfect sense.

The Dawson siblings are ready to tear this woman apart because she's Weston's wife. She's Weston's wife who sat next to me while I poured my fucking heart out to my sister. While I admitted every bad thing I've done and planned to do.

I can't breathe.

"Babe, you okay?" Archer puts his arm around Quinn's shoulder, trying to turn her away. She's still seething with anger, ready to throw the first punch.

"Archer Jones?" Daisy tips her head. "Wait a minute—you two are together?" She laughs. "I did not see that coming. How'd Dean take it?"

"Stop acting like you know us," Logan warns. "And get out before I call the cops."

"But one is already here." Daisy smiles. "I'd like to talk to my husband now." She looks right at me. "You do know you've been sleeping with a married man, right? Though I suppose breaking up a marriage is a cake-walk for you."

She knows. She fucking knows.

The world spins around me, threatening to swallow me whole at any second. And I think this time I'll let it.

"You okay?" Owen puts his hand on my shoulder.

"Yeah." I blink and shake my head. "Shocked, that's all."

"You knew about her, right?"

I move my head up and down, unable to force out more words. Owen gives me a gentle nudge, leading me away. My feet don't want to cooperate, and part of me knows that if I walk away, anything is fair game.

She'll tell Weston what she overheard.

He'll know the truth. Know what a horrible person I am.

And he'll hate me for it.

I squeeze my eyes shut, trying to block out the noise. My mind races, going into self-preservation mode. There's no reason for Weston to believe a word this bitch says, right? I'll tell him she made it all up. I'll admit to some of the less terrible things I did, like steal a few bucks from assholes who got a little too handsy at the bar.

And then we can go on like nothing happened, because it *has* to go on like nothing happened. I love this man so much. And I love Jackson.

I can't lose them. I won't lose them.

But maybe I should.

I'm obviously not the woman Weston thinks I am. I love him. I really, truly love him. I don't want to live the rest of my life lying to him.

"I'm not your husband anymore," Wes says, and hearing his voice makes me feel sick, because I'm already thinking of losing him, of never hearing his deep voice again. Daisy whips around, and I see the remorse in her eyes the second she looks at Weston.

She messed up big time, and she knows it.

We already have one thing in common.

"What do you mean?" she asks.

Wes sidesteps Daisy and puts his arm around me. "I mean I filed for divorce."

"But I didn't sign anything." She smiles again, trying to look victorious. Really, she's terrified that she just lost the one angle she thought she could play.

Which is bad news for me.

"Doesn't matter. The papers are already being processed. It'll be official soon enough."

"Why, Wes?"

"I haven't seen you in three years, Daisy. What did you expect?"

She lets out a breath and shakes her head so fast it looks like a nervous tic. "I want to see my son."

"No."

"You can't keep my son from me."

Wes's grip on me tightens, and I know he's working hard to keep calm. I can't imagine how pissed he is. "You can take it up with the court. You haven't seen him for over three years. You haven't provided any sort of support for him since he was two months old."

"He's *my* son."

"He is. And he's a fucking awesome kid. It's a damn shame you missed out on him."

"I want to see him."

Wes slowly shakes his head. "He doesn't even know who you are."

Daisy's eyes fill with tears that she angrily wipes away. She looks at me. "There's a lot of that going around."

Feeling like I might puke, I turn in toward Wes. "She's not worth it," I whisper, unable to make my voice any louder. We need to get away. Maybe she'll disappear again, and we can go back to how things were before.

Because things were perfect.

"Let's go," I tell him.

"Yeah." Wes brings his arm down and takes my hand. "Let's."

"Wes, wait. Please," Daisy pleads.

"You heard him," Dean says through gritted teeth. "He doesn't want to talk to you. None of us do, so do yourself a favor and get the hell out of here. And don't stop until you're out of Eastwood."

"I have a right to be here." Daisy pushes her shoulders back, trying to hang onto what's left of her dignity. There isn't much to hold onto. "And I have a right to see my son."

"You forfeited that right when you abandoned him," Logan interjects. "As my brother said, take it up with the court if you want to see him again. Though if you really care about Jackson at all, you'll stay away. He doesn't know you. Best to keep it that way."

"He can get to know me," Daisy pleads. I watch her body language, breaking her down as if she were a potential client to scam. She's desperate all right, and I think some of it is genuine.

"For how long?" Wes spits. "How long before you take off again? It won't be any different than the last time."

"It might be," Daisy goes on. "I deserve a chance."

"Not with me." Wes shakes his head and squeezes my hand. "And not with Jackson. We're leaving, and if you even think of coming to the house and seeing Jackson, I'll arrest you for trespassing myself."

"Wes, stop! Let's just talk."

Wes turns, pulling me with him. Logan and Owen move in, blocking the way so Daisy can't chase after us. Wes storms out of the bar, letting go of my hand the moment we get outside. He's upset, and I should comfort him.

Better yet, I should tell him the truth. It will sound better coming from me than from that crazy bitch. All I need to do is open my mouth and confess. Just get this over with.

But I can't.

We get into the Jeep and Wes pulls out of the parking lot. Now's another good time to come clean.

But I don't.

"I'm so sorry, Scarlet."

"Don't be," I tell Wes, reaching over and putting my hand on his thigh. I close my eyes, clenching my jaw to keep my teeth from chattering. If anything, I'll blame it on the cold. "It's not your fault."

"I feel like it is. I have no idea why she showed up."

I do. She showed up because she heard me running my mouth about this nanny job I took, thinking I could con money out of my new boss. She showed up because I talked about her soon to be ex-husband and son.

I was careless, thinking it was damn near impossible that someone would overhear me and know exactly who I was talking about. It has to be fucking fate. The universe is finally giving me the middle finger, getting back at me for all the shit I did.

Just a few days ago, she heard me say I was in love with Weston, and now she's here. Which only means one thing.

She's here to break us up. She's here to tell him everything she knows about me.

Chapter Thirty-Three

SCARLET

"Wes?" I ask quietly. We're at a four-way stop and need to turn left to get to his house. There are no other cars around us, and we're still sitting there. I take my hand off his thigh to turn on the heater. The cold has crept through me, going straight to my heart.

I want to shove it back down into the hole it crawled out of. But it's beating strong inside my chest, making me feel so much. Too much.

I can't do this.

Not to Weston. Not to Jackson.

My jaw trembles, and I think about how far I've come, how much I've changed. *How happy I've been.* Weston has given me everything without even offering. He showed me love, real, unconditional love.

"Wes," I start again, voice breaking. I bring my hands into my lap and swallow the lump in my throat. I need to say it. Now. Get it out. One way or the other, Wes deserves to know, doesn't he? I'm not stupid. These things have a way of coming out when you least expect it, and even if Daisy goes away and never returns, I can't live with this hiding in the closet.

His phone rings and Logan's name pops up on the display screen on the dash.

"Daisy just left," Logan rushes out as soon as Wes connects the call. "And she said something about finding Jackson one way or another. We think she's headed to Mom and Dad's. Owen's on the phone with Mom now. Dean, Quinn, and Archer went after her."

"You let Quinn—never mind." Wes grips the steering wheel. "I'm headed there now. Thanks, Logan."

Wes hangs up, and I know I can't drop a bomb on him now. Though maybe it would be a good time. He's more distracted with Jackson that what I did might not seem so—God, listen to me? I'm going into self-preservation mode again.

And then it hits me. Hard. Harder than the thought of Daisy telling Wes that I took the nanny job thinking I'd sleep with him and would blackmail him into paying me for my silence or something.

She might try to kidnap Jackson.

"Drive faster," I say through clenched teeth. Wes doesn't say anything but steps on the gas, jerking the Jeep forward. We make it a few miles before I speak again. "Should you call this in or something? Get a squad car to go to their house?"

"I can get there faster."

I'm so tense the rest of the way that my back hurts by the time we peel into the gravel driveway of the Dawsons' farmhouse. The kitchen light is on, as is one upstairs. Quinn and Archer's Escalade is parked in front of the garage, and they're just now getting out. Wes really did drive fast.

Wes kills the ignition and rushes out of the Jeep, running to the garage.

"I already disarmed it," Quinn says, face illuminated by light from her phone. She has to be freaked out almost as much as Weston. I know she loves her nephew fiercely, but Emma is inside too.

Wes pushes the door open, and the five of us rush in. Mr. Dawson is in the kitchen, wearing plaid pajama pants and a white T-shirt. He was obviously settled in for the night and is already putting on a pot of coffee.

"He's upstairs sleeping," Mr. Dawson assures Wes, knowing he's going to go up there anyway. "Mom's in the room with him. Emma just finished a bottle and went back to sleep too."

"Thanks, Dad," Quinn says, shrugging off her coat. She sets it down and wraps her arms around herself. "I'm still shivering."

"It's from adrenaline and nerves." Archer steps in, wrapping her in a tight embrace. Wes disappears up the stairs, needing to see Jackson for himself.

"Well, now you've met Daisy," Dean says, pulling out a bar stool. He sits, letting out a heavy sigh. "She's lovely, isn't she?"

"She seems great." I force a smile, feeling myself slipping back into the shadow of Old Scarlet. It feels weird, though familiar, and I don't like it. I wasn't a happy person before I met Weston. I barely got by, and I don't just mean with money.

Every day was a struggle to keep my head above water. Some days, just waking up and facing the day was hard to deal with. I had no purpose, no drive…no meaning. Life sucked and that was just the way it was. I didn't think things could ever get better.

That I'd actually be happy.

And yet here I am, feeling it all slipping out from underneath me like sand being washed out with the tide.

"Do you really think she'll show up?" Quinn asks, sitting down on the floor to pet the dogs. The biggest one—Rufus, I think?—pushes into her lap, and she nervously twists his long fur around her fingers.

"Who knows?" Archer takes a seat next to Dean and shakes his head.

Mr. Dawson gets out coffee cups and sets them on the island counter. I'm still standing awkwardly in the hallway leading into the kitchen, feeling unworthy of sharing the company of these people.

"I always knew she'd show back up again," Mr. Dawson says. "Thank God Wes filed for divorce and primary custody of Jackson a few weeks ago." He looks at me and smiles. "We have you to thank for that."

It's like the real Scarlet checked out and took a first-class ticket to hell, being forced to watch things unfold before me with no control.

"Yeah, I did push him a little," I say with a smile. *But it's my fault she's here in the first place, and it'll be my fault when Wes learns the truth.* Hurting him is the last thing I ever wanted. Even when I hoped he was a rich asshole, I didn't necessarily want to hurt him. Teach him a lesson in fidelity maybe, but not crush his heart with my bare hands.

And Jackson—oh my God, Jackson. Tears fill my eyes, and I pull my boots off, knowing Mrs. Dawson has a strict no-shoes rule, and start to cross the kitchen, mumbling that I needed to check on Jackson too. I've never been upstairs in this house, and each wooden plank creaks slightly under my feet.

Daisy is in town, adamant about seeing Jackson. Most kidnappings happen when a non-custodial parent takes the child. We have a recipe for disaster and I have no idea how long the danger will be there. Everyone is freaked out enough right now, making me think there's a good chance Daisy will actually try to do it.

Suddenly, the thought of dropping Jackson off at school on Tuesday terrifies me so much dizziness crashes down on me. My heart hurts and I can't bear the thought of anything bad happening to that sweet little boy.

"Scarlet?" Mrs. Dawson calls softly. I blink away tears and look up the stairs. "Is that you?"

"Yeah." I dash up the rest of the stairs and step into the dim light spilling out of the open bedroom door. Weston's large frame is bent over a bed. He kisses Jackson's forehead and pulls up the blankets.

"Come here, honey." Mrs. Dawson picks up on how upset I am right away and pulls me into a hug. If only she knew…

"Do you really think she'll do it?" I whisper, not needing to explain what I'm referring to.

"I don't know." Mrs. Dawson pats my back, stepping away and motioning for me to follow her. She steps into the room across the hall, going right to the window which looks out at the street in front of the house. "I'll be honest and say I never really liked Daisy, not even when she was just a teenager. I questioned her faithfulness to Wes while he was deployed, but that's not the issue at hand." She lets the curtains fall shut and turns back around to face me.

"Motherhood isn't easy, and I'll be the first to admit that. There were times when the idea of running away seemed like a dream come true. But never forever. A childless vacation can be a welcome—and needed—escape, but the thought of being away from my children…" She shakes her head. "I don't understand how she did it. We thought maybe it was post-partum depression, and Wes did everything he could to find her the first time she left. They weren't on good terms, but he was worried sick. And then she showed up at Jackson's first birthday party, acting like nothing happened."

She lets out a heavy sigh. "I've accepted that there are certain things you'll never understand. People do unspeakable things for reasons that make sense to them and them alone. I've stopped seeking answers for questions that shouldn't be answered."

"That's…that's very wise." My throat feels thick. Like I might burst into tears or puke or something.

"And don't worry, honey. Weston cares deeply for you. He's been smitten from the start. It was pretty obvious."

I smile, wishing I could close my eyes and erase my past. "Yeah, it was obvious." The stairs creak, and Quinn stops in the threshold of the room. She's holding a phone, and the screen is glowing.

"Do you know the passcode to Wes's phone?" she asks me.

I shake my head. "Why?"

"His motion sensors are going off." She holds it up, and I see the alerts.

"Try Jackson's birthday," Mrs. Dawson suggests.

Quinn looks down at the phone. "Wes wouldn't be that predictable—well, I guess he is."

She opens up the security system app, impatiently tapping her fingers on the back of the phone case as she waits for it to load.

"Oh shit. It's Daisy."

"What?" Mrs. Dawson rushes over.

"She's just sitting on the front porch. Looks like she's waiting for someone to answer the door." Quinn shakes her head. "She did say she wants to talk to Wes." With a sigh, Quinn turns and goes down the hall.

And I'm back to not being able to breathe.

My heart beats loudly, echoing in my ears. I clench my fists, digging my nails into my palm. Wes's deep voice comes from the hallway, and the second he comes into view, I spring forward, wrapping my arms around him.

"Maybe if you ignore her, she'll go away?" I say, attempting to make a joke. I'm shaking, and Wes holds me against his firm chest. Even now he's calm and collected.

"I wish."

"Then we should." I don't want to let him go. If I let him go, he'll talk to Daisy. He'll find out everything.

"Come get some coffee and something to eat," Mrs. Dawson says softly. "Jackson and I made chocolate cake that I could use some help eating."

"That sounds good," Quinn says. She peeks in at Jackson before turning down the stairs. Mrs. Dawson goes down with her.

"You okay?" Wes asks, running his hands down my arms. "You seem freaked out."

"Well, it's not every day your boyfriend's ex-wife storms back into town and under-the-table insinuates she's going to kidnap her son."

"I'm sorry."

"Don't be," I interrupt before he can go on. "This'll blow over, right? It has before."

"Yeah." He lets out a deep sigh. "Fuck, it's weird seeing her."

"Yeah, that would be. Was she like this the last time she showed up?"

"No, not at all. The last time was even more fucked up. I came home from work and she was just there in the kitchen making dinner like it was something we did every night."

"That is fucked up."

"Yeah." His eyes fall shut for a few seconds. "I don't have feelings for her anymore. I need you to know that."

"I know you don't."

He cups my face. "You're the only one I want."

Tears burn my eyes. Thankfully it's too dark in the hall for Wes to see them. He puts his mouth to mine, kissing me hard and desperate.

"Do you want cake?" I ask, stepping in closer.

"Yeah." He rests his head on mine for a moment. Then he steps back, takes my hand and goes downstairs.

The kitchen isn't nearly as tense as it was a few minutes ago. Mrs. Dawson is talking to one of the twins on the phone, and Dean and Archer are very animatedly telling a story to Quinn about something that happened back in their college days. I can tell by the look on her face this isn't the first time she's heard the story.

Mr. Dawson brings Wes a cup of coffee and pats his back. God, this family is perfect, and their faults and flaws are exactly what make it so.

"What's the plan?" Mr. Dawson asks Wes.

"I don't know." Wes takes a drink of coffee. "She's not going to leave until I talk to her, so I should bite the bullet and just do it. I'll give her copies of the papers I filed so she knows what's going on. Part of me doubts she'll even fight for Jackson."

Mr. Dawson nods. "I agree. Lay everything out so she knows exactly what's going on and then tell her if she wants to see or talk to you again, she'll have to go through the legal system."

Wes pinches the bridge of his nose. "This is the last thing I need right now."

Shit, I almost forgot amidst all this chaos that the election is only days away. He told me he wasn't nervous or stressed over it, but I know better.

"It'll be okay in the end," Mr. Dawson assures his son. "She's been gone his whole life. There's no way she can take him away from you."

"Right." Wes doesn't look convinced. He takes another drink of coffee. "All right. Time to get this over with."

I step forward, thinking I'm going with Wes. His face says otherwise.

"I think it'd be best if I go alone," he tells me.

No. He can't go alone. Because if he's alone with her, there's no telling what she'll say. I won't know. I'm slipping into panic mode, and part of me wants to run for the hills, seek cover, and never come back up to see the light of day again.

"Are you sure that's a good idea?" I put one hand on the counter to steady myself. "I can stay in the car or go inside."

"It's late. Stay here. And I'll grab some things and come back." Wes frowns. "I don't want to wake up Jackson and worry him. I'm staying with him tonight."

"Good idea." I swallow hard, doing everything I can, not to freak out. My life as I know it might be over in a few short hours. "So you're going to wait until morning to talk with her?"

"No, I'll go now. Or else she'll be on the porch all night and I don't want attention drawn to this matter. The quieter I can handle this, the better it'll be for Jackson's sake."

"Are you two staying?" Wes asks his sister.

"If Emma wakes up, we can stick her in her car seat and head home," Archer says. "But I don't want to wake her up either." He rests a hand on Quinn's shoulder.

"You guys can come stay with us," Quinn says, looking at Wes and then me. "Daisy might not know where we live yet, and I think she'd have a tough time sneaking around or breaking into our house."

"Right," Archer says dryly. "We'll throw a cat at her. We have enough of them."

"No one is throwing my cats. I was referring to the upgrades I did for our home security system."

Quinn and Archer's house is more secure than Fort Knox, and I wouldn't be surprised to find out they have a panic room.

"Thanks," Wes says. "But we'll be fine at home. I'll talk to her and try to diffuse the situation. If we're lucky, she'll be gone by morning."

Poor Wes. He looks so tired, and I want nothing more than to go home together, taking advantage of an empty house. We'd have sex—and I wouldn't have to muffle my moans—and then I'd rub his back until he falls asleep.

But after Wes talks to Daisy, there's a chance that'll never happen again. And it will be totally my fault.

Chapter Thirty-Four

WESTON

This is the last fucking thing I want to be doing right now. I used to hope Daisy would show up like this just so I could serve her with divorce papers, but things are already in the works and can get taken care of. I'll have to call Mr. Williams tomorrow and see how her showing up like this affects my case.

Exhaustion hits me, making the short drive from my parents' house to my house challenging. All I want to do is take Scarlet up to bed, fuck her senseless, and pass out naked next to her.

We have a good thing going, and I can't help the sick feeling that's forming in the pit of my stomach that all this soon-to-be ex-wife drama is too much for her. I'm terrified of losing her, of having her decide this isn't what she signed up for and take off running for someone with less baggage.

I know events unfolded in such a way tonight that anyone would be shocked, but there's something different about Scarlet. I don't know what it is, but it has something to do with Daisy showing up announced. I suppose I can't blame Scarlet if she doesn't want to be involved with all this.

Just the thought of her leaving makes me feel sick to my stomach. I don't like very many people, and I love even fewer. Scarlet is one of those people who I like a whole lot and also love with my whole heart.

She's the perfect fit for our family. We just click, as lame as that sounds. I get her, and she gets me. She and Jackson get along perfectly, and she's been more of a loving mother to him than Daisy ever was. Actually, Scarlet has been here for nearly two months. That's longer than Daisy stuck around after Jackson was born.

I slow at a stop sign and see a shooting star streak across the dark night sky. My mind immediately goes to Scarlet, and I can hear her honey-smooth voice whispering *make a wish*.

I don't believe in wishes. You make your own dreams come true, and it has nothing to do with a wish. But right now, I'm desperate. I close my eyes. "I wish Daisy would go the fuck away and Scarlet, Jackson, and I can get back to being a family."

Feeling stupid, I open my eyes and shake my head at myself. I let off the brake, and the Jeep inches forward, getting closer and closer to home.

Daisy is still on the porch when I pull up in front of the house. A white car is parked in front of me. It's the white car we saw the other night. Fuck, that makes me even more pissed. She was driving around spying on us.

"Wes, you came." Daisy stands, stiff from the cold, and comes over.

"Stop." I close the Jeep door behind me and hold up a hand. "I'm not here to be won over or any of your other bullshit. I'm here so you'll go home."

"Can I at least come in? I'm freezing."

"Fine. But when I say we're done, we're done."

"Fair enough." Daisy goes up the porch steps and picks up the doormat. "You got rid of the key?"

"That was an obvious place to hide the key. I took it out the day you put it there, but you weren't around enough after that to figure it out, were you?"

"Wes, I'm…"

"Save it." I use my body to block her line of sight when I punch in the alarm code and turn off the system.

"I'm sorry."

I wasn't expecting an apology this early on in our conversation. She wants something, I'm sure of it.

"Wow." She looks around the living room. "It's different yet the same."

"What do you want?" I ask her. "It's late, and I'm tired and want to get this over with."

"How's Jackson? He's at your parents, isn't he?"

"Maybe."

"Oh, please, Wes. I know you and know you'd only trust your mom with our son."

I don't like hearing her say *our son*. It's what he is, and I'm well aware she's his mother, but it sounds so wrong. She hasn't raised him. Hasn't been here to sit up with him when he's sick. To calm his fears in the middle of the night.

"What do you want?" I ask again, taking a seat on the stairs.

"I want to give us another shot."

"No." I shake my head. "Daisy, I don't love you anymore. I stopped being in love with you before you left and we both know that. You didn't love me either. We had issues from the start and should never have gotten married to begin with."

She folds her arms over her chest, and I look at her, really look at her for the first time. We were freshmen in high school when we met. She was a cheerleader and I was a football player. She went to Greendale, another small town in this county and Eastwood's rival when it comes to high school sports. We dated on and off throughout high school, and I proposed before I left for my first tour overseas. We got married shortly after that, and she moved around from base to base with me until my time in the army ended.

We should have broken things off then, but we wanted to give it one last shot. Daisy's mother was the one who put the idea in her mind that we'd magically fix things if we had a baby, and neither of us expected it to happen the first time we tried.

The moment we knew we were having a baby, things changed. For me. Daisy didn't want a kid, and I'm sure the resentment started there. I hoped things would change when she gave birth and held our sweet, tiny son in her arms, but it didn't.

Not everyone is cut out for motherhood, she told me just a few days after Jackson was born. I chalked it up to pain and exhaustion. It was a red flag of a warning. Several weeks later, I came home from work to find Jackson screaming and crying in his crib and Daisy nowhere to be seen. Judging by how dirty his diaper was, we guessed she'd been gone at least half my shift, having left poor little Jackson alone in his crib.

The raw, painful emotions come back with a vengeance, and I remember it all too well: sitting in this living room, holding my crying baby to my chest and having no idea what the fuck I was going to do. I didn't know anything about babies. How was I going to raise one alone?

"You left us," I say slowly. "And now we've started a life. A *good* life. Why do you want to take that away?"

"I don't, Weston. We were happy once. We can be again."

"It's not that easy."

"It can be." She walks through the living room, going to the photos hanging on the wall. She stops before one of Jackson, and her face pulls down with emotion. "He looks just like you."

"Luckily."

She turns, eyes brimming with tears. "Wes," she pleads.

"Don't."

Sniffling, she wipes her eyes and looks back at the photos. "Whose baby is this? One of your brothers'?" She's looking at a family photo we took over the summer, and Jackson is sitting front and center with Emma on his lap.

"No."

"Quinn?"

"Yes."

Daisy turns, eyebrows raised. "Wait…she and Archer?"

"Stop, Daisy. It doesn't matter. You left us," I repeat. "All of us."

"I miss your family."

I let out a sigh. "They don't miss you." She's been gone for so long but still knows about us. I wish I could take the memories back. I just want her gone.

"I'm really sorry."

"You already said that." I rub my forehead. It's been years, but the same round-and-round arguments are certain to take place. "Look, Daisy…I'm sorry too." I get up and step around the stairs. "I'm sorry for the way things worked out. But you made your choice and now you have to deal with it. You can't come back into our lives and expect everyone to just accept you."

"But a girl can dream, right?" She unzips her coat and lets it slide to the floor. "You're even more handsome than I remember." Running her eyes over my body, she advances, wrapping her arms around me and trying to go in for a kiss.

"What the hell?" I push her away.

"Wes," she cries. "You were the first man I slept with. I want you to be my last."

"No." I shake my head, wanting her out of my house. "What don't you get, Daisy? I. Don't. Love. You." I reach into my jacket pocket and pull out my wallet, getting out enough cash to cover one night at the local motel. "Here, get a room for the night. This isn't happening."

"We were good at it."

"It was the only thing we were good at." And it wasn't all that great, if I'm being honest. "I don't want this. I don't want you." The words sound harsh coming out of my mouth, but she needs to hear them. "I love someone else."

"That blonde whore?"

"Don't talk about her like that."

Daisy laughs. "Like she's so innocent."

"She's perfect just the way she is, and we're happy. All three of us are happy."

"Sure you are. How well do you know this woman? Maybe I don't want her around my son."

"Then you should have stuck around so you'd be able to make such decisions. It's late and I want to sleep. It's time for you to leave."

"One more thing, Wes, and then I promise I'll leave."

"Fine. One more thing."

Chapter Thirty-Five

SCARLET

I pull the blankets tighter around my shoulders, unable to stop shivering. Wes has been gone for nearly an hour now, and I haven't heard from him. Every minute that passes makes me more anxious.

I've shut down, told everyone I was tired and wanted to sit in silence on the couch. Dean went upstairs to sleep, and Quinn and Archer left about half an hour ago. Emma woke up crying, and after nursing her back to sleep, Quinn was able to slip her into her car seat and leave.

Mrs. Dawson walks out from the kitchen to check on me, and I close my eyes and pretend that I'm asleep. I have no idea what will happen. I'm in the middle of nowhere at their farm. While this place feels safe and I trust the Dawsons as if they were my own family—actually I trust them more than my own—I want out of here. Because shit is going to hit the fan at any minute and I don't think I can stand to see the disappointment in Mrs. Dawson's eyes.

My phone vibrates in my hand and I shoot up. It's Weston, and for a split second, I'm scared to answer.

"Hello?" My voice is shaky and thin.

"Hey." He's not yelling. Not telling me to fuck off or run away and never return. "She's finally gone…for now. I'm changing into pajamas and will head back. What do you want me to bring for you?"

Wait, what? He's not mad. Does he not know? Did I get a Christmas miracle in No-fucking-vember?

"Scarlet?"

"Sorry," I rush out. "I'm tired. Um, just my toothbrush and some leggings and a sweatshirt or something for the morning. I don't really care."

"Any preference?"

"Something black."

I can hear Weston walking down the hall and into my room. My clothes are still mostly in that closet. "That's easy. About ninety percent of what you own is black."

"It's a flattering color."

"Anything is flattering on you."

I close my eyes and lean back, eyes filling with tears. He doesn't know. I will live to see another day.

"Just pick the first thing you grab and get back here. I miss you."

"I miss you too." He zips a bag and moves through the house. "I'll be there soon. I love you."

"I love you too." I hang up, too relieved to realize Mrs. Dawson has come back into the room.

"Is everything okay, dear?" she asks.

"Uh, yeah. I think so." I pull the blankets up and cast my eyes down, trying to cover up how emotional I am right now. "Wes is coming back. He wants to stay here just in case."

"I figured he would. I can show you to the guest room upstairs if you'd like."

"Yeah, sure. Thanks." We go upstairs.

"This used to be Quinn's room, and when she lived in Chicago, she'd come and stay for the weekend. There should be face wash and soap in the bathroom if you need any."

"Thank you."

Mrs. Dawson looks at me and smiles. "And thank you, Scarlet, for making my Weston happy again."

Don't thank me yet, lady.

Wes rolls over and pulls me to him. The rough skin on the palm of his hand slides under my shirt and over my stomach, and I inhale deeply, not opening my eyes. It's early in the morning, and we're still at his parents' house.

He didn't talk about what happened when he came in last night. He looked tired and worn and not even his mom questioned him on it. I've been dying to ask, but I'm going on the whole *no news is good news* thing.

Once we were in bed together, Wes kissed me hard and made love to me. I know he's worried this whole mess with Daisy will send me running, but he has nothing to worry about. The expectation of finding someone with no baggage, with nothing from their past that could come back to haunt them, is ridiculous. We've all done things we're not proud of. We've all had the best-laid plans come crashing down.

It's not the past that makes up who you are. It's how you continue forward with your life. Which is why I know we can work out. I'm not the same girl I was when I first laid eyes on him, when my only thought was *oh shit*, both because I knew he was the right amount of brooding and gorgeous to get under my skin and because he wasn't the rich asshole I thought I'd be working for.

And even if I had started working for Quinn and Archer…I don't think I would have gone through with things. They're both good fucking people. Quinn is my friend now.

I swallow hard and let out a shaky breath. I fell in love with Weston, but it's deeper than that. There's Jackson, of course, and the rest of the Dawsons. I love that whole family.

The toilet flushes in the jack-and-jill bathroom, and I sit up, peering in. Jackson steps onto a stool at the sink to wash his hands. He doesn't know we're here. I wait until he's drying his hands to whisper his name. He does a double-take and then runs in, jumping on the bed.

"Shhh," I whisper. "Your dad is still sleeping."

Jackson hugs me and then squirms out of bed, running back into his room and returning with Ray, who's looking more tattered and worn as each day goes by.

"He told me he gets lonely," Jackson says, situating the unicorn under the covers with us. He's sandwiched between Weston and me, and Wes wakes up with a smile.

"Hey, buddy."

"What are you doing here, Daddy?"

"I missed you too much." Wes wraps his muscular arms around his son, making Jackson look so small nestled against Wes's large frame. "Did you have fun with Grammy and Papa?"

"Yes! We made cake, and I helped change a poopy diaper," he says proudly. "And I was the only one who got Emma to stop crying."

"You're a good cousin," I tell him, pulling the blankets up over all of us. We lay in bed for a few more minutes. Then Jackson says he's hungry and gets crabby when Wes tells him to let us go back to sleep.

"Go find Grammy," Wes mumbles, turning over. "You're at her house."

"I want you," Jackson whines.

"I'll take him down," I offer.

"You don't have to," Wes grumbles. "Jackson, it's early. Lay back down."

That starts a crying fit, and Wes gets up with a huff. It's not even seven AM yet, and the house is quiet. Well, until we go into the kitchen. Then all four dogs come running, thinking we're going to feed them breakfast. Wes lets them out and plugs in the coffee pot.

"Want any?" he asks, getting out a mug.

I shake my head. "I'll have tea instead if there is any."

Wes puts on a kettle and turns on cartoons for Jackson, who cuddles up with a blanket on the living room couch and isn't interested in breakfast anymore. But we're already up, so we might as well eat.

"Morning," Mrs. Dawson says, coming into the kitchen a few minutes later. She looks at the cereal we're eating and shakes her head. "I'm going to make you a real breakfast."

"You don't have to," I tell her, rather enjoying my Crackling Oats.

"There's no point in arguing," Wes whisper-talks. "Food is love in Mom's eyes."

"Food is comforting, and I figured after last night you could use a little extra comfort." She pulls eggs and bacon from the fridge and looks at Wes, waiting for him to explain things.

"Yeah. In that case, make me lunch and dinner too."

"Is she coming back?" I ask quietly.

"I'm sure, but I think I made it clear I'll only handle this through a lawyer. I'm not making deals or promises with her." Wes takes a long drink of coffee. "I don't know what to do." He sets his mug down and puts his head in his hands. "He's her son too."

"It's a hard situation," I agree, putting my hand on Wes's shoulder.

"You said your dad wasn't around when you were a kid, right?"

"Right. I was glad when he came back into our lives, but mostly because my mom was a dead-beat drug addict who left me to raise my brother and sister."

Mrs. Dawson turns away from the stove to look at me, but her eyes aren't full of judgment. She feels bad for me, which is almost worse than being judged. I don't want anyone's pity.

"Jackson has you," I go on. "So it's a totally different situation."

"She's never been a mother to him," Mrs. Dawson says, and I know she's fighting hard not to scream profanities and curse Daisy's name. "Thank God you're in the process of being granted full custody of Jackson."

Wes nods. "She is his mother, but she's left him. Twice. I'm not risking him getting to know his mom only to have her leave again."

"That's smart," I agree. "She'll have to earn the right to see him. He's a great kid." I look into the living room, only able to see the top of Jackson's head from where I'm sitting. "I can't imagine leaving him like that."

Mrs. Dawson beams at me. "I've always been a believer in things happening for a reason. Sometimes the reason takes years to manifest, but it's there."

The tea kettle starts to whistle, and I get up to get it. Mrs. Dawson's words echo in my head, making me think I've been looking at this all wrong. Maybe everything in my shitty past happened to push me here right now.

I never would have met Wes in the South Side. And I never would have come to this small Indiana town. The only reason we met was because I took a job thinking I could con my new boss. If I didn't have such shitty moral character before, I wouldn't be where we are right now.

I'm happy.

Weston is happy.

Jackson is happy.

Maybe this did happen for a reason.

Chapter Thirty-Six

SCARLET

"What's all this?" I ask, looking at the papers and boxes cluttering the living room. We just got back to Weston's house. In the daylight, things never seem as scary as they do in the dark. And the more I think about the universe wanting me to meet Weston, the better I feel about this whole situation.

"Family heirlooms. Jackson, don't touch them," he adds quickly.

"Why are they out?" I take off my coat and move to the couch, curiously picking up an old book.

"You-know-who wore her mother's wedding dress at our wedding." He looks uncomfortable talking about it. "She wanted it back and I wasn't sure what box it was in."

"Oh. This stuff is cool."

"You like Civil War history?" he asks, looking a little amused.

"If I'm being honest, I don't know much about it. But I love antiques. Wait, all this stuff is from the Civil War?"

"Some of it is. Not all is that old. It's been in the Dawson family for years and gets passed down to the oldest son. Jackson will get it someday."

"Can I see it?" Jackson asks, peering into a box.

"Sure," Wes says, and we all sit on the floor together. There are books, handwritten letters, a World War II Army uniform, a saber, and a silver tea set that looks like it has to be worth a pretty penny.

"Can we use it?" Jackson asks as I carefully look at the teapot, feeling like I should be wearing those white gloves you see museum workers wearing when they handle artifacts.

"I don't know if it's safe to drink out of," Wes says, looking at the sugar bowl. "It might have traces of lead in it."

I gently set the teapot down and grab my phone, doing a Google search for more info on the tea set.

"Holy shit—I mean, shoot. But holy." I turn my phone around, showing Wes the value of the tea set.

He takes my phone from me, eyes going wide. "These aren't in as good of condition."

"They're tarnished, which can be cleaned. That's crazy, though."

Wes nods. "It is. I had no idea."

"That sword and the uniform are probably worth a lot too."

"I know the saber is," he tells me. "And we know the personal history of it." He sorts through a box for a minute, pulling out a photo of great-great-great Grandpa Dawson holding the exact sword.

"Wow. That's incredible."

"It is pretty cool," he agrees. We spend another half an hour looking through the stuff before putting it away. Wes tries to get Jackson to sit and watch a movie with us since we're tired. Any other time this kid would jump at the chance to watch TV, but since both Wes and I are dead tired, of course he wants to paint instead. Everything is fine at first, and then

Jackson paints his face in the one minute Wes and I turned our backs, talking in hushed voices about being extra careful at preschool pick-up with Daisy back in town.

Wes takes Jackson upstairs for a bath, and I start cleaning up the paint mess on the table. Wes's phone is on the counter, and it vibrates with an alert from the motion sensor on the doorbell. Wiping my hands on a dishtowel, I rush through the house and see Daisy standing at the front door.

Anger surges through me, and I storm out of the house before thinking it through.

"You are not welcome here," I say, clenching my fists. "Leave before I call the cops. Or better yet. Watch Wes cart your ass off to jail."

"Please." She rolls her eyes. "And it was you I wanted to talk to."

Oh shit. I cross my arms, trying to stay calm and keep warm. It's cold out here, and I'm not wearing shoes or a coat.

"You have two minutes."

"This won't take long. Good thing I already know all about you, Scarlet Cooper."

I try to swallow my fear and keep my cool. "What do you want?"

"I want my family back, and I want you out of the picture."

"That's not happening."

She laughs. "That's what you think. Come on, we both know Wes will kick you out when he learns the truth. And not just about you coming here to rob him blind, but about all the other cons you pulled. I think my favorite was the time you convinced a Fortune 500 CEO to donate thousands to a bullshit charity you made up."

The blood drains from my face. How does she—dammit, Heather. She was bragging about me to her prison friends, who relayed the message to Daisy.

"I'll tell him you're lying."

"I knew you'd say that." She bats her lashes and gives me a smile. "So I did some digging, and your sister has been so helpful. I should really send her a thank-you note or something." Daisy reaches into her pocket and pulls out a piece of paper with a name and number written on it.

Deven McAllister.

My old boss. The one I blackmailed into paying me for my silence. Shit. Shit Shit Shhhiiitttt.

"Why would you do that to Wes?"

"Because I want him back." Daisy shakes her head like it's obvious. "And you're going to help me get him back."

"Fuck that."

Daisy holds up her finger. "The election is coming up soon, isn't it? It'd be a shame if something were to happen."

"You wouldn't fucking dare."

"Oh, I will if you push me." She takes a step forward, and I feel like I'm standing at the edge of a slippery cliff, desperately trying to keep my footing. "Star County is small and full of closed-minded, simple people. If you haven't noticed, not everyone here is as open and understanding as the Dawsons. One little rumor about candidate Wes Dawson dating a known con-artist with a sister in jail, a mother who died of an overdose, and a father who drank himself into a stupor and, well…it's not something I'd risk."

The girl from the ghetto comes out, and I don't even think as I take a tangle of Daisy's hair and yank her to the ground.

"Stop!" she screams. "Or the article will go out now!"

I freeze, breath leaving in ragged huffs. "Article?"

"My sister works for the *Star County Post*. Ask Wes if you don't believe me." She scrambles up from the ground. "It's already written and ready to go out in the morning."

"They why would I do anything for you?"

"If you tell Wes he should give his wife, *Jackson's mother*, another chance and then get the hell out of here, I'll have her yank the article. And if not…you know what will be on the front page of the Sunday paper…two days before the election."

"You're a horrible fucking person."

"Like you're much better," she snorts. "How many people have you fucked over? Actually, I'm curious. How many other married men have you slept with? Wes can't be the first."

"He's not married to you anymore."

"It doesn't matter. He was mine first. And I want him back." She taps her watch. "Tick-tock. You don't have much time before the front page is drafted up. And even if you took your sorry ass out of here after that, there's nothing I can do to stop it."

With a triumphant smile, she turns and leaves, walking across the street and getting into a white sedan. I never stopped and thought about what the people I was conning felt. They were asshole men trying to pick me up at a bar, not even attempting to hide the fact they were married. They deserved it, or at least that's what I told myself. Maybe I deserve to have my happily ever after ripped away, but Weston doesn't.

I came here with the intentions of taking everything from him, and instead he took the one thing I thought I lost years ago: my heart. He taught me how to love, not just other people but myself. Leaving him will hurt, but having everything he's worked for fall apart will hurt worse.

And if he lost his job…nope. I can't even think about it. He has worked so hard to build a life for himself and Jackson. I won't let anyone take that away.

Chapter Thirty-Seven

WESTON

"What about this one?" I ask Jackson, picking up a pink teapot with little purple flowers painted along the base.

Jackson shakes his head. "Scarlet isn't really a girly girl, Dad."

"Good point. It's too pink for her. Too bad I didn't think of this around Halloween." I push the cart forward, browsing the shelves of a home decor store. We needed to go grocery shopping, and Scarlet said she wasn't feeling well. Telling her to stay home and rest, Jackson and I set out.

Something is off with her, and I'm sure it has to do with Daisy showing back up. I don't want Scarlet to think that old feelings came back the moment I saw my wife. It did the opposite, and if there was any good that came out of this, it's knowing that I can look at Daisy and feel absolutely nothing.

Scarlet is the only one I want.

"That one!" Jackson leans out of the cart and narrowly avoids knocking a glass candle holder off the shelf. "It has a skull on it."

Smiling, I carefully move things out of the way and find what has to be leftover Halloween-themed dishes. This teapot is pink too, but instead of flowers, it's decorated with skulls.

"It's perfect. Good eye, buddy."

Since Scarlet heats up her water for tea either in a saucepan or in the microwave, I get a kettle as well. We check out, go to the grocery store, and pick up Chinese takeout on the way home.

Jackson says he's tired, which is music to my ears. Maybe after lunch, we can all take a nap. And by that, I mean Jackson nap in his room and I take Scarlet into the bedroom. I think about it the whole way home, missing her already even though Jackson and I have only been gone for a few hours.

"Can I give Scarlet her tea set now?" Jackson asks when I get him out of the car. I look up and down the street, making sure Daisy isn't lurking about before I let go of his hand to reach inside and grab the bag.

"Soon. Let's get the groceries unloaded and eat lunch before we do." Keeping a tight hold of Jackson's hand, I take him inside. The house is still and quiet, making me think Scarlet is upstairs sleeping. "Stay right here on the couch," I tell Jackson, giving him my phone to watch YouTube. He doesn't get to watch it that often, so his butt will be glued to the couch as long as the phone is in his hands.

Hurrying back to the car, I bring the bags of groceries up to the porch, setting them all in front of the front door. I lock the Jeep once the last bag is out and rush to the house. Jackson hasn't moved, and I grab the three bags with the cold stuff to put away first.

I get the first bag completely put away before I notice the note on the counter. Setting the milk down, I grab it.

Wes-

I'm so sorry. I love you and Jackson more than you'll ever know. I didn't want to do this, but I have no choice. This is for the best.

Love always,

Scarlet

I blink, not understanding what I'm reading. Shaking my head, I refuse to understand it. The note floats to the floor, and I rush upstairs. Scarlet's room is empty. There are no clothes in the closet. The bathroom counter is free from her neatly cluttered makeup.

I exhale, feeling dizzy, and sink down onto her bed. What the fuck is happening? Why did she leave? And I still don't understand her note. She didn't want to do this? Then why did she?

Pain hits me hard in the center of my chest, spreading throughout my whole body. Is this what it feels like to have your heart break all at once? I dig my fingers into the mattress, fighting against everything inside of me not to feel.

"Dad?" Jackson calls from downstairs. I'm not sure how long I've been sitting there, zoning out, flashing between grief and anger. My foot has fallen asleep, and I can hardly move it.

"Yeah?" I call back, voice coming out weak.

"Someone is on the porch."

Inhaling, I push up, shaking my foot to get some feeling back to it. "Don't move. I'm coming down."

Blinking a few times, I realize my eyes are watery, and only get worse when I see Jackson. He put the phone down and carefully got out the tea set, arranging it on the coffee table. What the hell am I supposed to tell him? I don't even know what's going on.

My heart leaps in my chest, thinking maybe it's Scarlet at the door.

"Jackson, go up to your room," I say as soon as I see Daisy.

"Why?"

"Now," I say, and my tone scares him enough to grab the phone and run.

"Shut the door."

"Is it a bad guy?" he asks, looking down the stairs.

"Kind of," I say, knowing I shouldn't tell him that his mother is bad, but I need him to stay out of sight. Once his door closes, I throw back the front door.

"What the fuck do you want?" I bark.

"Nice to see you too, Wes. Can I come in?"

"No." I grab my coat that I left hanging on the banister and step outside. "What the fuck do you want?" I repeat.

"I came here to talk." Her brows push together, and she looks confused. "Didn't Scarlet tell you that we should—"

I rush forward. "Scarlet?" It's making sense now. "What the fuck did you do?"

"Nothing."

"Bullshit." I'm raging, wanting to turn around and put my fist through the windows on the front door. "Goddammit, Daisy," I say too loudly. There are people walking their dog down the street in front of our house, but I don't fucking care right now.

Daisy showed up and Scarlet left. It has to be why. Scarlet wouldn't just leave.

Trying to recover, Daisy puts a hand on her hip, ready to come at me with some ridiculous blow, just like she did back when we lived together. "Well, if she didn't tell you *that*, then I'm guessing she didn't tell you how she took this job thinking she could con you."

"What the hell are you talking about?"

"Yep. That little snake. I knew she wouldn't confess."

"Confess what? You're not making any sense."

"Your girlfriend, the woman you left alone with *our son*, is a con artist."

"No, she's not." I shake my head and point to the street. "Get off my porch, Daisy. You're sounding crazier and crazier by the minute."

"It's true."

"And how the hell would you know?"

"A friend got arrested and spent time at Cook County with someone named Heather Cooper. Ring a bell?"

I blink. Scarlet does have a sister in prison.

Daisy's lips curve into a smile. "I take your silence as a yes. Anyway, when I've been going to visit my friend—she shouldn't have been arrested, but that's not the point—and of course I noticed the bombshell blonde coming in. Everyone noticed her. I mean, how can you not?"

Daisy inches forward. "I didn't pay her much attention after that, until I heard her mention Eastwood. You know how it is when you hear something familiar. Turns out, she has quite the reputation with the inmates. You see, her sister thought bragging about her would earn her cred or something. Boy, the stories I could tell you. But back to you, Wes. Your darling Scarlet thought some rich couple was hiring her. And then she showed up at your place. There was one thing I couldn't figure out, but now that I know Quinn and Archer have a baby, it's them."

There's no way Daisy would know Quinn and Archer are actually the ones who hired Scarlet instead of me unless she really did overhear Scarlet talking. But everything else she's saying isn't true. It can't be.

"I know you won't believe me, so I got the name of the last couple she was a nanny for. Turns out, she seduced a married man and forced him to buy her expensive clothes and handbags in order for her not to tell his wife."

"You're making that up."

She digs a folded piece of paper from her purse. "Call him. Ask about Scarlet."

Could it be true? Did Scarlet take the job thinking she'd con money out of me? But then why'd she stay? I love her…and I know she loves me.

"What did you say to her?" I ask, rounding on Daisy, whose smile disappears. I don't know what she thought would happen. I'd take her in my arms and up to bed and we'd wake up like everything was fine?

"I didn't say anything."

"Then why did she leave?"

"She left?" Daisy acts shocked. "Wow, can't say I'm surprised. Better make sure nothing valuable is missing." Her face softens. "I miss us. And now that Scarlet is gone, we should try again."

"You did something to make her leave, didn't you?" I shake my head. "Did you think you'd come here with bad news and I'd welcome you home?"

"No, but I…I…" She squeezes her eyes shut.

"Let's just say everything you said was true. It wouldn't change things between us. You left me alone with an infant. And then you showed up again only to do the same thing. I'm not stupid, Daisy."

"I know, Wes, I know you're not."

"And now you're here again, telling me these things only to hurt me."

"Wes, no. You need to know the truth about her. I'd never hurt you."

"Really?" I question, and her face crumbles. "It's always been about you, Daisy. You need to leave."

"Wes, please."

"No. Get. Off. My. Porch." I open my clenched fists and go inside, slamming the door shut behind me harder than I meant to. It rattles the whole house and probably scared Jackson. I lock the deadbolt behind me and stride forward to go upstairs and check on Jackson.

And then I realize the boxes of valuable family heirlooms aren't in the living room anymore.

Chapter Thirty-Eight

WESTON

I can't move. Not yet, not while my mind is going a million miles an hour. Scarlet wouldn't steal them. She's not a bad person. She's not a con artist or a thief. She's Scarlet, a quirky girl from Chicago who likes paranormal romance, drinking tea, and looking at the stars.

She's the woman I love.

But the boxes…I shake my head and move through the small foyer, going to the other side of the house. The boxes came from the basement, and maybe she put them back. I run down the stairs, getting hit with cool, musty air, and pull the string light at the bottom of the stairs. The basement is cold and damp most of the time, typical of older houses in this area. We use it for storage, and the washer and dryer are down here too. I go around the stairs to the storage section and see the boxes neatly put away. I pull one out and open it. Everything is inside.

And now I'm feeling bad for even doubting her. I put my head in my hands and let out a breath. What the hell am I doing?

"Daddy?" Jackson's voice echoes through the house. Shaking myself, I go upstairs and find Jackson in the kitchen.

"Can we eat now? I'm hungry."

"Of course." Having forgotten about our food, I heat it up. Jackson only wants an egg roll anyway and asks for a piece of toast with peanut butter on it instead.

"Is Scarlet still sleeping?" he asks. "Can I bring food up to her?"

I never lied to him about his mother, and I don't want to lie to him about Scarlet either. But—fuck—what do I say?

"She had to go visit her sister," I blurt the first thing that comes to mind.

"When will she be back?"

I swallow the lump in my throat. "I'm not sure."

I put the groceries away while Jackson eats. I should be hungry, but my appetite is gone. I can't get Daisy's words out of my head. I don't know what to believe, and the best thing is to ask Scarlet. I call her and get her voicemail.

"Scarlet, it's Wes…call me. Please."

I put my phone down and pace around the kitchen, feeling more and more anxious as the minutes tick by. It's like history is repeating itself and I'm damned to live through this again and again.

To be left over and over.

But this time, it's different. This time, I'm in love with the woman who left me. This time, there was no small relief in knowing she was gone, that our constant arguing was finally over. Daisy and I should have separated long before she left. I wouldn't change a thing that would take Jackson away, but if things came about differently…if we at least talked about the issue we ignored and hoped would go away things might have been a lot better for all of us.

Which is why I'm not going to sit back and hope things fix themselves. Not this time around.

I push open the door to Getaway, and bright sunlight spills into the dimly lit bar. Logan's car is parked out front.

"Oh, hey, Wes," Danielle, one of the other bartenders, says, looking up from behind the bar. It's Saturday, and the bar doesn't open for another few hours, but one of my twin brothers is always here getting things ready for the night.

"Is Logan here?" I set Jackson down and look around for him.

Danielle shakes her head. "No, we had an issue with our hard liquor delivery, so he ran to Newport to pick it up himself."

"Oh, bad timing on a Saturday."

"You're telling me. Owen is here, though. He's in the office. Want me to get him?"

"Yeah, thanks, Danielle."

She gives me a smile, looking a little concerned. I've never come in here during the day like this, so it's obvious something is up. Danielle disappears into the office behind the bar to get Owen. I was hoping to talk to Logan because he's a good voice of reason, but maybe Owen's the better one to give advice on this situation. We're the least alike, and hearing what he'd do could do me some good.

"Hey," he says, hurrying over. "What's going on?"

"You got a minute?"

"Of course." He looks at Jackson. "Is everything okay?"

"I'm not sure."

Danielle comes around the bar. "Hey, Jackson, want to play pool with me?"

"Thanks," I tell her, and she takes Jackson's hand, leading him across the bar to the pool table.

"You're freaking me out," Owen says, going to the bar. He grabs a bottle of top-shelf whiskey and pours us each a shot. I take mine and sip it.

"Scarlet left."

"What do you mean, she left?"

I finish the shot, feeling like I need another. "Daisy showed up at the house today."

"Oh, shit."

"Yeah. And she wouldn't admit it, but I think she said something to Scarlet and that's why she left." I pinch the bridge of my nose, and Owen fills the shot glass again. "But that's not all...Daisy told me Scarlet is a con artist and only took the job because she thought she was working for a rich couple—Quinn and Archer—and wanted to con money out of them."

Owen blinks. Once. Twice. "The fuck? Daisy's crazy. How would she even know that?"

"Supposedly, she has a friend who's at the same prison that Scarlet's sister is at and overheard them talking."

"Scarlet has a sister in prison?"

"Yeah, she does. I knew that already, though."

"Does she look like Scarlet? Is she single? You know I love bad girls."

For once, I'm thankful for Owen's smartass attitude. It makes me shake my head but smile. "I've never seen her."

Owen takes his shot and then slides the second one he poured for me over. "Tell me everything."

I take another look at Jackson, making sure he can't hear. He's distracted with Danielle, thankfully. Taking a deep breath, I tell Owen everything.

"I need a minute to process," he says, reaching around for more whiskey. "Do you think she's a con artist?"

"I don't want to, but I…I don't know."

"Okay." Owen nods, thinking. "Say everything is true. She took the job thinking she'd con some rich couple out of money. But she didn't. She stayed with you and Jackson and did her job. Really well." He wiggles his eyebrows. "Right?"

"She was great."

"You dog."

"Shut up," I say flatly. "She was a great nanny and did the job she was hired to do."

"Isn't that all that matters?"

I shake my head, unsure.

"Hey, Danielle?" Owen calls. "I have a moral question for you."

"Uh, sure?" Danielle looks up from the pool table.

"Two guys walk into the bar—"

"Are you forgetting little ears are present?" Danielle puts a hand on her hip and stares at Owen.

"It's not a dirty joke," he deadpans. "Two guys walk into the bar, both with the intent to rob the place at gunpoint. The first guy doesn't go through with it, even though he walked in the doors with the intention of doing it. The second guy does rob the place."

"Okay…what's the moral question?"

"Who's worse? Or are they both as bad since they both intended on doing the same thing?"

"The guy who actually robbed the place is worse. Though I suppose you'd need to know *why* the other guy didn't go through with the robbery. If it was for self-preservation, like he knew he couldn't get away so he decided to wait until another night when the bar was less crowded or something, then I suppose he's still as bad as the second guy. But if he didn't rob the place because he had a change of heart, then he's not as bad."

"Does that help?" Owen asks.

"I think so." I rub my forehead, feeling a migraine coming on. "What would you do if you were me?"

The smirk fades, and Owen unscrews the lid to the whiskey. "I wouldn't let her be the one that got away."

"You'd go after her."

"I'd run after her." He refills our shot glasses. "If she was going to con you, she would have. And once she realized you weren't who she thought she was going to work for, she would have left and moved onto another couple to con. But she stayed because she had a change of heart."

"But you don't know that."

"No." He shakes his head. "I don't. Just like you don't know she didn't. Where is she?"

"I don't know."

"Did she have a house back in Chicago?"

"No. She lived in an apartment and gave up her lease to take this job."

"Maybe Quinn can hack into her phone. Track her location or something."

"No, I don't want her involved." I don't want anyone else in the family involved, but that goes without saying to Owen. He'll tell Logan, I'm sure. They claim to have a hard time lying to each other, saying it's a "twin thing" and non-twins don't understand.

"I know where her sister is." I sit up. "And she'll know where Scarlet is."

"What are you waiting for?" Owen asks. "Go!"

"I can't just drive up to a prison and ask to see a random inmate."

"But you're a cop." He gives me a blank stare.

"I know, but it doesn't work that way. Though I might be able to get her on the phone." I pull out my cell to look up the number for the prison. "I'll have to make a few calls." I open the internet and type in the name of the prison. "I get no service here."

"I know. It's become a dead-zone after the old cell tower was replaced by a different carrier."

"What's your wifi password?"

"Shit. I don't remember. Quinn set it up...try *I love cats* or something."

"Even Quinn wouldn't be that obvious." Still, I try a handful of guesses, text Quinn for help, and wait a whole two seconds before getting frustrated with her lack of reply.

Owen gets up. "What do you need info on? We can look it up on the office computer."

"I'll be in here," I tell Jackson and Danielle, motioning to the office. He's using his hands to push in the balls on the pool table and is excited to be "winning." It'll be okay. I'll get Scarlet back. For me and for him.

Owen puts in the password and steps aside, letting me sit in the desk chair. "Are you in love with her?"

"Yes." I don't hesitate, don't try to hide my feelings. There's no point. I do love Scarlet, and I love her fiercely.

"Then you've got to do this, man. You have to go get her. Take it from me," he starts but doesn't finish. I write down the prison's phone number and address, closing the internet browser and letting out a breath. I'm so tense my shoulders are killing me. Standing, I turn to Owen.

"Thanks."

"No problem. But I do think we should mark this date down in history as the day you came to me for advice."

"I was actually hoping Logan was here."

"Fuck you."

I laugh. "He probably would have said the opposite."

"No shit. He plays it too safe." Owen shakes his head. "He's going to miss his chance with her," he says, meaning Danielle. "But what am I—"

He cuts off when he hears Danielle loudly tell someone the bar isn't open yet.

"Ah, shit. I bet that's Bart again."

"Your resident drunk?"

"Yeah. Poor bastard's drunk more than he is sober. We started giving him protein shakes and saying they're full of vodka. He drinks them at least. Hopefully it'll help him put on a few pounds before winter."

"Owen!" Danielle calls, and both my brother and I run. Danielle is standing behind the pool table, holding Jackson's hand. Her eyes are wide and full of fear, and Jackson looks confused.

"Daddy!" he yells and tries to make a run for me. But she's faster.

Daisy grabs Jackson, and he immediately starts to struggle, just like I taught him in the event someone tries to kidnap him.

"It's okay, I'm your mom," Daisy tells him, and he freezes.

"Daisy." I rush over, blood boiling. "Put him down."

"Dad?" Jackson asks, looking back and forth between Daisy and myself. "Is this Mommy?"

"Yes, baby!" Daisy hugs him and drops to her knees, tears falling from her eyes. "I'm your mommy."

"Let him go," I tell her. "You have no right to be here."

"He's my son! I have every right that you—"

"Legally," I interrupt. "You have no rights. Let him go and leave."

"No." She stands up, holding Jackson's hand. She looks down at him, smiling. "Want to go get ice cream? We can catch up."

"Okay," Jackson says, not too sure of himself.

I clench my fists. I could easily stride over and shove her away, but I don't want Jackson to see me lay a finger on Daisy. And I don't want to hurt her. Deep down, I feel bad for her. She's missing out on the greatest kid in the whole fucking world.

"No. Let him go," I say again in a calm, level voice. Out of the corner of my eye, I see Owen pull out his phone and start recording a video. I know exactly what he's doing: getting proof of Daisy trying to take my son. Thank you, Owen, for thinking two steps ahead for once.

"You have no legal standing to take him," I repeat. "You gave up custody when you left us four years ago. Let him go."

"No," she says again and shuffles back. "I'm taking him and you can't stop me."

"Should I call the cops?" Danielle asks, voice trembling a bit.

"Yes," I tell her. "Tell them exactly what's going on. Jackson's non-custodial mother is trying to take him."

"Daddy, I'm scared." Jackson tries to pull away, and Daisy tightens her grip. I rush forward, and she picks him up, holding him so tight she's hurting him. He kicks and hits a table, knocking a few glasses onto the ground. They shatter, and glass crunches under her feet. If I try to wrestle him out of her arms, she could drop him or fall, and he'll get cut.

As she shuffles away from me and toward the door, I advance, going around a table and blocking the exit.

"Get the fuck out of my way!" Daisy struggles to keep a hold of Jackson. The kid is only four, but he takes after me and is solid.

"Put him down," I say again. If she gets out the door, she's going to take him. She came here to kidnap him, though she won't see it that way. But it's exactly what it is. There's no way I'm letting her out that door.

Or walk out of here free.

"Ow!" Jackson cries, twisting as he tries to get out of her arms. She adjusts him against her, gripping his arms so tight his skin is turning red.

"For God's sake, you're hurting him!" I yell. That's it. I'm getting Jackson back. But before I can make a move, Daisy puts Jackson down, takes a death grip on his wrist, and pulls a can of pepper spray from her purse, pointing it at me.

"Jackson, it's okay," I say, swallowing hard. She's really come unhinged. Or desperate. I don't know which is worse right now.

"You can't keep him away from me."

"Daisy." I hold up my hands, heart racing. Pepper spray is far from lethal, but I don't want Jackson to go through the pain of getting it in his eyes or inhaling it. "We can work something out. Just let Jackson go."

Jackson starts struggling again, crying and calling for me. "It's okay," I tell him again. "Daisy, think about this. Is this how you want to start a relationship with your son?"

Daisy's face goes slack, and she looks down, realizing what she's doing. She lets go of Jackson, and he runs to me, crying. Having him in my arms again is the best feeling. I scoop him up, never wanting to let go.

Daisy starts crying, and Owen rushes over. I hand him Jackson, heart aching a bit not to have him in my arms. I rush forward and take the pepper spray from Daisy.

"Don't do this to me," Daisy says, looking up.

"I'm not. You did this to yourself." I inhale and hear sirens in the distance. Thank fucking goodness. I didn't want to be the one to make Daisy's official arrest.

Chapter Thirty-Nine

SCARLET

I sit up, eyes waking up before my mind. I'm uncomfortable with stiff legs and an aching back, and for a split second, I think I fell asleep sitting up on the couch. Then I blink and realize my eyes are still sore and swollen from crying.

Yes, crying.

The room is dark, and I sit up, stretching my arms over my head. I didn't mean to fall asleep in the stiff armchair next to my father's bed at the nursing home. After leaving Weston's house, I walked into town, took Eastwood's only taxi to Newport, and was able to get an Uber to drive me up to Chicago.

I didn't know where else to go other than the nursing home. Dad was having a bad day and just sat in his chair not really paying attention to anything. So, for the first time in my entire life, I spilled my guts. Said everything I ever wanted to say. Confessed the bad things I've done as well as admit just how deep my love for Weston goes.

And Dad just sat there, staring blankly in my general direction. A little empathy would have been nice, and advice on how not to farther fuck up my life would have been welcome.

But I got nothing.

Rubbing my eyes, I get up, moving slowly in the dark. My phone is in my purse, and it's dead.

"Dammit," I mutter. I have no idea what time it is, and I think I left my phone charger in the kitchen at Weston's house. I left in such a rush I wouldn't be surprised if I left more behind. Moving slow so I don't wake up my dad or his roommate, I go into the hall, blinking from the bright lights.

"Oh!" a nurse exclaims, surprised to see me. "I thought you left."

"I fell asleep." I rub the back of my neck, trying to work out a knot. "What time is it?"

"A little after two AM."

"Shit. Sorry. I'll, uh, I'll go."

The nurse shakes her head. "Stay. It's late, and I know you walk back to your place. Just this one time, though, you hear?"

"Thank you." I go to the bathroom and then back to Dad's room. The nurse put an extra blanket on the chair for me, and I'm grateful. These rooms are fucking freezing.

"Scarlet?" Dad is sitting up in his bed.

"Dad." I rush over, clicking on the light over his bed so he can see me. "It's late. You should go back to sleep."

"You listen to me," he starts. I don't have the emotional bandwidth to deal with one of his flashback rants right now. "You're a Cooper, and Coopers don't give up."

"What?"

"You love that boy?"

I blink, unsure if I'm hearing him correctly. "Weston. Yes. I love him a lot."

"Then what the fuck are you doing here?"

"I…I…" I don't know what to say. "I had to leave or else his ex-wife was going to publish an article about him that made him seem unfit to be the county sheriff. It would have ruined his chances of winning, and he was so close. And besides…once he hears what I did—what I used to do—I don't think he'll see me the same."

"So you're running away with your tail tucked between your legs? I might not have raised you, but I know that's not the type of girl you are. You have more Cooper blood in you than that."

"I just…I…" I shake my head. Dad's having a rare moment of clarity, and I've been honest all night. Why stop here? "I'm scared. Scared to hear him tell me he doesn't want me. Scared to see the look of anger or disgust on his face when he sees me. I left to save his career but also to escape rejection."

"I've been waiting to hear you admit that." Wrinkles form around Dad's mouth as he smiles. "I was scared to come back to you for the same reason."

"Really?" I perch on the edge of the heater vent next to his bed. The air coming out is room temperature, which is why this place is so fucking cold.

"Yeah. I was sure you'd hate me."

"I did hate you."

"Only for a while." Dad yawns and looks around the room. "What time is it?"

"Two in the morning."

He yawns, and I know his mind is going to start slipping back into whatever fog it's usually in. He'll forget about our conversation in the morning. Memory is such a wondrous and confusing thing.

"You should get home. You have school in the morning. We'll talk about the boy tomorrow."

"Okay. Thanks, Dad."

"It will work out." He nods and reaches forward to pat my shoulder. His balance is off, and I don't want him to fall out of bed. I stand, moving closer. "If he's a decent boy at all, he'll see you for what you are."

"I hope so," I whisper and gently push Dad back down. I don't know what I am…but I know what I want to be.

I want to be with Weston and Jackson. I want to go back to Eastwood. I want us to be a family.

I tuck my legs up under myself, trying to get comfortable. About an hour after I got Dad back to sleep, his roommate woke up and has been in bed hollering for pain meds nonstop ever since. The nurse came in, told him he's not due to have any more for another few hours, and told me that he does this pretty much nightly.

Great. Just fucking great.

I put on my winter coat and folded up the blanket, trying to use it as a pillow. My suitcases full of all my possessions are cluttering up the room, and every time I see them my heart sinks even lower into my chest. It's going back to that dark crevice it clawed its way out of, and it hurts more and more the lower it gets.

I thought about Dad's words and see truth to them. But I'm still scared, both for myself and for Weston. I'll take his anger and disappointment in me any day over the possibility of ruining everything he's worked for. I'll get over it. Somehow, someway.

I know Jackson will someday face adversity in his life, but if I can keep him innocent and carefree, I will. Weston does a good fucking job hiding his trouble and stresses from the kid. But there's only so much he can handle. Having Daisy come back, finding out my dark past, and losing his job…nope. I won't have it.

I doze off for about an hour and wake up with terrible cramps in my legs. I roll my big suitcase over and stretch out my legs, trying to get comfortable again. I'm so tired, physically and emotionally. I close my eyes and drift to sleep, dreaming that I'm back at Weston's and everything is perfect.

Dad's roommate wakes me up. He gets out of bed, and some sort of alarm goes off. And off. And off. Finally, I get up, pull back the curtain that divides the room in half and see the guy sitting on the edge of his bed, about to face plant on the floor.

"Hey," I say to him, but it's no use. He's even farther gone than my own dad, and I don't think I'll get lucky with another moment of clarity. I duck into the hall, looking for someone to help me get him back into bed. There's no one in sight. Grumbling, I spend the next fifteen minutes trying to get him to lay back down.

Once he's down, I get my toothbrush and go to the bathroom, brush my teeth, and come back to the room. I pull my messy hair into a bun and grab a new sweater to change into. Dad is still asleep and should be getting up for breakfast soon. My stomach grumbles at the thought of food. There's a crappy diner that serves crappy food not far from here, and they open at six AM. I know this because I used to work there until I got laid off.

I grab my purse, shove my luggage into the corner of Dad's room and hope no one steals it while I'm out, and step into the cold November air, keeping my head down as I walk the streets.

I make it to the diner with only a few catcalls and one offer to take a ride on some guy's pogo stick. Not bad considering how hellish I look right now. I'm in no mood to talk to anyone I used to work with, and of course luck has it out for me again.

"Scarlet, hey!" Trisha, another waitress, says. "Haven't seen you in a long time. How've you been, girl?"

"Good." I put on my fake smile.

"You left for some fancy nanny job, right?"

"Right."

She raises her eyebrows. "But you're back. We're not hiring, hun."

"I'm visiting my dad. I just want breakfast."

"Oh, gotcha. Sit in section one and I'll get you."

I force a smile. "Okay." I slide into a booth, wishing for my phone to distract myself with. Instead, I pull out a paperback of a book that I've already read three times. It was at the top of my suitcase, and I didn't want to rustle through my stuff for another. The floor in the nursing home is gross and sticky. Risking my clothes falling out onto it isn't something I want to do.

I order tea, bacon, and French toast, and hunker down in the booth, not wanting to be disturbed by anyone or anything as I contemplate the next step in my life. After getting out of the slums the first time and living in the ritzy part of Chicago, it was hard coming back. It's even harder after Eastwood.

I love that little town.

I have no job now, and with it getting closer and closer to the holidays, I probably won't be able to find one. With Dad's medical bills, I'm going to need money. So I guess it'll be back to the old ways. Just the thought of it makes me feel sick.

Though I'm not as hungry as I should be, I force myself to eat every last bite of food on my plate. Who knows when I'll get out for lunch, and if I'm going back to Old Scarlet, it's going to take some time to get on my feet. I won't have money to burn. Mentally groaning at wasting money on a hotel room for the night, I finish my tea and zip up my coat, leaving Trisha a decent tip.

I trudge my way back to the nursing home, using everything I have inside of me not to think or feel. How did I do this so easily before? Every step hurts, as every footfall reverberates through my heart, jostling the broken pieces. The sharp edges hurt all over again as they slice into me.

Cold rain mists down on me, and I flip the hood up on my coat. Tears well in my eyes, and this time I make no attempt to keep them from falling. I'm sad, really fucking sad, and it's mostly my fault.

If I could take everything back, I would. I'd accept the nanny job in good faith and show up to actually do the job I was hired for. Crazy thought, right?

Wiping at my eyes, I enter the nursing home. My feet are sore from walking, and my fingers are cold and numb. I forgot my gloves at Weston's house as well. They're in his Jeep, I think.

The entrance of the nursing home opens up to the cafeteria, and right now the smell of coffee and breakfast masks the usual sickening odor of this place. I look around for Dad. He's not as his regular table, and for a minute, I think he'd been forgotten in his room. It wouldn't be the first time.

Corbin comes down the hall, pushing Dad in his new chair.

"Ohhh girl," he says, coming to a screeching halt.

"I know, I know," I say with a shake of my head. He's obviously seen my luggage in Dad's room. "I'll explain later. I just…I don't even know." I push my hood back and sigh. "I can't right now."

Corbin cocks an eyebrow. "Well you better, because there's a gorgeous hunk of man-meat looking for you."

"What?"

"Some guy named Weston is here."

"What?" I say again. This is a dream, right? Wes wouldn't…he couldn't…

"I told him to wait in the nurses' station. It's the least stinky place here."

"Yeah…good idea," I say, still in disbelief.

"Aren't you going to go to him? Because if you don't want him, I'll take him."

Weston is here. He came here for me.

"Scarlet?"

I shake myself and inhale, suddenly nervous. Did he come here to yell at me? No, that doesn't make sense.

"How do I look?"

"You've seen better days," Corbin says honestly. "But you're still hot."

"Thanks." I wipe my eyes and pull the tie out of my hair. Running my fingers through my messy locks, I hurry down the hall, fingers trembling.

Wes is standing in the nurses' station with his back to me. The moment I see him, tears spring to my eyes again. He turns as if he can sense me coming.

"Scarlet."

My name on his lips is the best thing he can say. His brow pinches together with emotion, and he strides forward, long legs bringing him to me. He doesn't speak, doesn't question me or raise a finger and start lecturing.

He envelops me in a hug, and I've never felt more at home than I do wrapped in his arms. It's safe. Familiar. Where I'm meant to be.

"What are you doing here?" I ask, fighting back tears.

"I came to find you."

"Why?"

He runs his hand over my hair and steps back, tipping my chin up. Leaning down, he kisses me, and a tear rolls down my cheek.

"Partly to do that."

"And the other part?" I slide my hands to his forearms, scared to let go. If I do, he might vanish into a puff of smoke.

"What the hell is going on?" His navy-blue eyes hold back a storm. "You left us."

As soon as he says it, I realize I did exactly what Daisy did.

"I'm so sorry," I say, voice breaking. Tears fall like rain, and Wes brings me to his chest, cradling me against him. "I didn't want to leave, but I had to."

"Why? Why did you have to leave?"

I sniffle, trying to compose myself. "Daisy came to the house when you were giving Jackson a bath. After he got paint on himself," I remind Wes. "She threatened to have her sister publish an article in the paper about me that would hurt your chances of winning the election."

"I knew she did something. She came by thinking you'd convinced me to give her another chance."

"That was part of her ultimatum, but not even I could go through with that. So I left, and I'm sorry. I just…I couldn't…"

"It's okay."

"No, no, Wes, it's not. What I did…who I am…" I squeeze my eyes shut.

"So it's true." He lets go of me, and my heart falls to the floor. "You really are a con artist."

I can't look at him. My heart is already shattered into a million pieces on the floor. If I see the disgust or disappointment in his eyes, my soul might break too.

"Yes."

"And you took the job thinking you'd be able to con me?"

"Yes."

"But you didn't."

I shake my head, hands shaking and breath coming out in huffs.

"Why?"

Lips quivering, I look up at Wes. "I fell in love with you. And Jackson. I think he stole my heart first if I'm being honest. I tried to resist you as long as I could." He doesn't say anything back. His jaw tenses, and he looks away. "Do you hate me now?"

"No. Maybe I should, but I don't." He takes a step away, bringing his hand to his forehead. "I need some time to think about this."

"I understand." I turn to walk away, going back toward Dad's room to hide from the world.

"Will you come home with me while I think about it?" Wes asks before I get too far.

I whirl around, blinking as if that would make me hear him more clearly. Because I must have misheard.

"Are you sure you want me to come home with you?"

"Yes. I missed you a lot last night. Jackson did too. And I have to work the night shift and could really use a nanny."

"You still trust me?"

"I don't know. I think so."

"That's fair." I swallow hard. "I'm not going to scam you."

"I know. I don't have much for you to take, anyway." He gives me a half-smile. "You stayed that first night when you realized I wasn't a rich doctor. Why?"

I shake my head. "For one, I had nowhere else to go. And from the start, as much as I didn't want to admit it, there was something about you and Jackson. You two are the perfect family…and then when I met the rest of your family…" I trail off, eyes filling with tears again. "I've wanted a family like that. I didn't think families like yours actually existed outside of Hallmark movies or fairy tales. You…you made me a better person, Wes. And even if you don't want anything to do with me ever again, I'll always be thankful for that."

Wes takes another step forward, and I can tell he's fighting against himself not to come any closer.

"Wait," he says, shaking his head, and I think he's going to take back the invitation to go home with him. "You left so Daisy wouldn't publish an article in the paper?"

"Right."

"What was the plan for after?"

"I don't know. Hide here and cry until I figured out something better to do."

Wes frowns, exhaling heavily. He looks so tired and worn.

"Do you want to go get some coffee?" I offer. "You look exhausted."

"I am. I didn't sleep well at all last night."

"I'm sorry."

"It is your fault." He steps in and takes both my hands in his. "I got used to sleeping next to you already. Please come home."

"You don't have to ask me twice."

Chapter Forty

WESTON

I reach over and take Scarlet's hand. We're headed back to Eastwood, and though I should probably be a dozen other things, I'm happy. Scarlet is coming home with me.

"Why did you start conning people?" I ask, giving her hand a squeeze.

"I realized I could," she confesses. "It wasn't like a dream I had when I was a little girl to grow up and be a con artist."

"What did you want to be when you grew up?"

She shakes her head. "I don't know. For a while there, I wanted to work at a zoo, but then things changed and I realized I didn't have options. Especially after I dropped out of high school to take care of Heather and Jason."

"You did go back, right?"

"Right. My dad showed up again and was able to look after them. Luckily, because our mom died shortly after." She looks out the window, and it hits me how different our childhoods were. "I've always worked. I had to. Hell, someone had to, and it sure wasn't Mom. I busted my ass for my family, and when I realized I could get more money doing something as harmless as flirt with a guy…I still shouldn't have done it, but, well…"

I rub my thumb against her hand. I don't want to judge her. I don't want to look at her any differently than I did before. "How'd you pick people to scam?"

"Well, my go-to scam was to hang out in bars at expensive hotels. Men—usually married men away on business trips—were easy. I mean easy to con. Not easy to sleep with. I didn't sleep with them. I just took their money and left. Which was supposed to sound better but, fuck, I'm terrible."

I laugh, giving her hand a squeeze. "Honestly, I find this all really interesting."

"Well, that's good, I guess. And to answer your question, I'd read the room. Find a guy who had something to prove. The more desperate, the easier they were to take money from. And you'd be surprised at how distracting a low-cut top and a good pushup bra can be. I picked a lot of pockets after 'accidentally' spilling a few drops of whiskey down my cleavage."

"Yeah, that would be distracting. Even for me."

She smiles, but I can sense her discomfort. I don't approve of what she did, of course. It's illegal and I'm a cop.

"I used to think of myself as a version of Robin Hood who kept the money I hustled instead of giving it to the poor. My family was poor so it kind of makes sense." She shakes her head. "The people I conned were rich assholes who were more than willing to cheat on their wives. Losing a couple hundred bucks here or there wouldn't have hurt them and maybe it taught them a lesson in cheating. Instead of getting a sexy one-night stand, they got stood up and got their cash stolen."

"That's a way to look at it."

"It doesn't make it right. I know. If I could take it back, I would. There's a lot of stuff I'd take back, and I'm not just talking about cons."

"I've done things I'm not proud of too." She looks cold, so I take my hand from hers and turn up the heat. "I've never conned anyone, but there's plenty of things I'd do over. Specifically, my marriage."

"Has she been back?" Scarlet asks hesitantly, and I debate on telling her what happened at the bar yesterday. She's already upset.

"Yeah. She showed up at the house, and I told her to leave. Then Jackson and I went to Getaway—"

"You took Jackson to a bar?"

"During the day. They weren't open yet."

"Oh, that's better. I was going to say you really fell apart on me and I was only gone a day."

"I did fall apart. But anyway…we went to talk to my brothers, and Daisy followed. She tried to get Jackson to leave with her."

"Oh my God. What happened?"

"I had her arrested for an attempted kidnapping. Her parents got a fancy lawyer right away and she was released. We're supposed to have family court in the near future, so nothing will happen until it's reviewed then."

"Are you fucking serious?"

"Unfortunately."

"So she'll be back."

"Yes, but hopefully the next time she does, I'll be officially divorced and will have all the paperwork I need to legally have full custody of Jackson."

Scarlet nods and falls silent for a few minutes.

"Do you still want to be with me?"

"Yes." I slow, getting stuck in construction-zone traffic. The clouds are starting to give way to blue skies.

"Are you sure? I'm not a good person, Wes."

"What you've done and who are you are different from each other. You're not a bad person, Scarlet, and I believe that with my whole heart. I've seen you, the real you, and over the last few weeks, I fell in love with you. I never thought I'd love anyone again."

"And I never thought I'd love anyone at all." She pulls her arms in toward her body. "Not even myself."

I turn away from the crawling traffic to look at her beautiful face. Tears well in her eyes and she's working hard to keep them from falling.

"Loving you and Jackson came easy," she whispers. "But loving myself…hell, it was hard to remotely like myself most days."

"You're worthy of love, Scarlet. Admitting your faults isn't easy to do, and you have."

Scarlet nods, wiping away her tears. "Thank you, Weston."

"For what?"

"For believing in me. My past is dark, but the rest of my life doesn't have to be."

I take her hand again. "It won't be."

I lug the biggest suitcase to the top of the stairs. Scarlet is behind me, carrying her other bags. I pause at the top of the stairs, looking down the hall at the guest room. My bedroom is on the opposite end, and even before this whole mess, Scarlet kept her stuff in the guest room closet.

She dozed off on the way home, giving me time to think. I've always been cautious. Too cautious. I married Daisy because it made sense. We'd dated long enough to warrant a proposal. I loved her because she was safe and familiar, and look how that turned out.

I trust Scarlet when she says she wants to change. She did nothing to make me question her judgment before, and I know the worst thing you can do to someone who's trying to better themselves is to constantly remind them of the mistakes they made.

I'm done being cautious when it comes to love. I'm letting my heart guide me this time.

"Where are you going?" Scarlet asks when I take her stuff into my room.

"I love you." I set her suitcase on the floor by the bed. "I want us to be together and I want to make sure you know I'm not going to hold the past against you. We can't move on and enjoy the present if we're constantly looking backward. And I want to move forward with you."

Scarlet drops her bags to the ground. "I love you, too." She steps forward, closing the distance between us, and it's like I can't get enough of her. I grab her and throw her on the bed. I move over top, settling between her legs. She rakes her fingers up over my back, and I'm turned on already. I press my hardened cock against her, and she bucks her hips against me.

I bring my head down, kissing her hard before moving my lips to her neck. She reaches down, fumbling with the button on my jeans for a moment before popping it off and shimmying them down my legs. She pushes me to the side, hooking one leg over me and taking hold of my cock. I look down, groaning when I see her long and slender fingers wrapped around my dick. She pumps her hand up and down, swirling her thumb over the tip and spreading precum down my shaft.

Then she lets go and moves down. With a swift movement, she yanks my pants the rest of the way off and takes a hold of my cock again. But instead of moving back up to where she was before, she takes me in her mouth, tongue flicking the tip of my cock.

I let out a moan, falling back onto the mattress. I spread my legs, watching her suck my cock. She moves slow, teasing me, and then speeds up only to slow again. Fuck, she's good at this. My eyes flutter shut, and I enjoy her mouth on me for another minute before pushing her away.

"I wasn't done yet," she says coyly.

"You're going to make me come already."

"That's the plan. I want to take care of you."

I sit up, grabbing her by the waist. "Letting me fuck you is taking care of me."

She moans and falls back against the bed, one arm landing above her head. "I'm okay with that."

I kiss my way down her torso and pull her leggings down, dropping them on the floor. Then I trail kisses up her thigh, stopping right next to her tender core. She tenses, anticipating what's coming—which will be her in just a few minutes.

I put my mouth over her, letting out a breath of hot air and teasing her through her panties. Slowly, I stroke her, though so gently she's pressing herself against me.

"I need you, Wes," she groans, reaching down and taking my hand. "I need you to make me come."

She doesn't have to tell me twice. With a growl I move back up, kissing her lips as I slip my hand inside her panties.

"You're so wet," I moan.

"You made me wet," she replies, and I might come right here without her even touching me. "Now make me come."

I circle her pussy with a finger, inching closer and closer to her clit. Her entire body is tensing as she waits, and as much as I want to keep teasing her, I know I can't hold out much longer. I stroke her clit, soft and gently at first. She's easy for me to read, but that's only because we're so in tune with each other while we're making love.

Going off her cues, I speed up my movements, rubbing her clit faster and faster until her body stiffens and she loudly cries out. With her pussy still spasming, I move down, removing her wet panties and parting her legs.

I put my mouth over her and flick her clit with my tongue.

"Oh, God," she moans, squirming against me. Her hands go to my hair. I lash my tongue out again and again, not stopping until she's coming so hard the sheets grow damp beneath her.

My cock is dripping, pulsing so hard and begging to be inside of her. Her head is to the side, mouth still open. One of her hands is gripping a handful of my hair so tight it's painful, but the pain feels good. I move up, cock going right to her center.

"Weston," she pants, feebly wrapping her arms around me. I push in, rocking my hips slow and steady. It feels so fucking good to be inside of her. I push my big cock in deeper, feeling my eyes roll back and an orgasm build inside me.

She curls one leg up, and I hit her at a new angle. Her pussy tightens around my cock, and my pleasure hits a peak. I come so hard my vision darkens, and I collapse on top of her, sweating and breathing hard.

I roll to the side, reaching for my boxers for her to use to wipe herself up with until she can get into the bathroom. I didn't mean to come inside of her, but I was too caught up in the moment to grab a condom.

Scarlet uses the bathroom and comes back to bed. I pull the blankets over us both, and she snuggles in.

"Where's Jackson?"

"Quinn and Archer's. It's safe there with all their alarms, and Archer is home today."

"Good." She rolls over and cups my chin with her hand. "I love you, Weston Dawson."

"And I love you, Scarlet Cooper." I kiss her again and lay down, pulling her onto my chest.

I didn't play it safe. I listened to my heart instead of my head this time around, and right here in bed with Scarlet is exactly where we're supposed to be.

"Wes?"

"Yeah?"

"What if Daisy does run that article?"

"I don't think she will. Blackmailing me like that will look bad in family court. I reminded her of that when she was in handcuffs."

"But if she does anyway? Your family will hate me."

"They won't hate you," I assure her, though I am a little anxious about them finding out the truth. Dean can be judgy and Mom can hold a grudge like it's nobody's business. Dad is more practical, which is where I got it from, and while he might not have an easy time trusting Scarlet for a while, I don't think he'll object to us being together.

"I really like your family."

"They like you too. But," I start, being honest. "Finding out the truth from an article will be a hard pill to swallow."

"Maybe we should tell them. Now."

"Now?"

"Just in case."

I trace the curve of her hip with my finger. "I really don't think we have to. And if the people in the county can be that easily swayed in who to vote for, then maybe I don't want to be in charge of keeping them safe."

Scarlet laughs. "I'll still feel terrible."

"Don't. If losing the race means I get to be with you, then I've won."

Chapter Forty-One

WESTON

"Hey, buddy!" I step past the dogs, holding the bag of takeout a little higher to keep Rufus from sniffing at it.

"Daddy!" Jackson comes running. "We have to be quiet," he says loudly. "Emma just fell asleep."

"Okay," I whisper back, shuffling into the kitchen. Archer got called in for surgery, so Quinn and the kids came over to our parents, just to be safe.

"Hey, Jackson." Scarlet takes her coat off, smiling down at him.

"Are you still sick?" he asks her, taking her hand. Both Scarlet and I pause for a moment until I remember telling Jackson Scarlet wasn't feeling well and that's why she wasn't home.

"She's better now," I tell him. "Are you hungry?"

Mom is sitting at the island counter, which is covered in blueprints. "You didn't have to bring fast food." She raises her eyebrows. "I could have cooked."

"I thought Jackson would like a Happy Meal," I say, and Jackson gets excited. "I got one for Quinn too."

Mom laughs. "She'll like that I'm sure."

I hand the bag of food to Scarlet, who gives me a little nod before ushering Jackson to the table.

"Mom?" I ask. "Can we talk in private?"

"Of course, honey. Is everything okay?"

"Yeah." I inhale slowly. Scarlet was right: it's better if the truth comes from me, no matter how uncomfortable this conversation will be. Mom follows me into the sunroom. We walk past Quinn, who fell asleep on the couch in the living room with Emma on her chest. "It's about Scarlet."

"Is she all right?"

"She is." I pace toward the windows overlooking the backyard. God, this is awkward. But I know it has to be said. I want to build a life with Scarlet, and we can't have this lingering. Well, she can't. I'm fine with letting the past be in the past.

"She told me she used to con people."

I can feel Mom's eyes on me. "What?"

I turn around, swallowing hard. "She used to be a con artist and would hustle money out of men at bars."

Mom doesn't say anything for a few seconds. "But she seems so sweet."

"Yeah, she does." I run my hand through my hair. "She wanted you all to know in case it ever came up again later."

"Does she still con people?"

"No."

Mom sinks down onto a lounge chair. "Why did she tell you?"

"Now that's a funny story." I pace to the other side of the room. "She has a sister…who's in jail."

"You're kidding."

"No. She said her sister got caught up with the wrong crowd and tried to rob a store."

"Jesus Christ, Wes!" Mom's eyes widen. "Scarlet is a con-artist and her sister is a robber. And you trust her with Jackson?"

"Yes," I say seriously. "I do. And I love her."

Mom's lips pull into a thin line. "Are you sure you're not too infatuated with her to see clearly?"

"I'm sure. She's had a hard life, Mom. Her own mother was an addict, and Scarlet dropped out of school to raise her brother and sister. She was only able to go back when her alcoholic father showed up, and then her mother OD'd and died. Scarlet is the one who found her and had to tell her siblings she was dead. Her father is in a shithole of a nursing home and she's the only one taking care of him."

Mom falls silent, and I pace back and forth, waiting to hear from her.

"Mom?" I finally ask. "Say something."

Mom flicks her eyes to mine. "Poor thing. She turned out better than most in her situation, I suppose." She leans back, rubbing her forehead. I'll leave out the part about Scarlet planning to con me for now.

"Do you think differently of her now?"

"Yes," Mom answers honestly. "But it doesn't make me like her any less. I feel bad for her, but I don't think being a victim of circumstance excuses poor choices."

"I don't either, and Scarlet will agree. She doesn't want that life anymore."

Mom, who's patience and understanding has always amazed me, looks up and smiles. "I don't think that's a problem now, is it?"

I smile back. "No. Her life is here now." With a sigh, I sit next to Mom. "Do you believe people can change?"

"Yes, but only if the change comes from within. You can't change a person, but they can change themselves. Do you think Scarlet wants to change?"

"I know she wants to. And she has. Who she is now…that's who she's meant to be."

Mom puts her arm around my shoulders. "You've changed too."

"I have?"

"For the better."

I look through the sunroom doors in the general direction of the kitchen. "We have Scarlet to thank for that."

Chapter Forty-Two

SCARLET

"I think Salsa is a good name." I give Jackson an encouraging nod.

"It is cute," Quinn agrees.

"Do you think Daddy will let Salsa come home with us?" Jackson picks up the kitten and kisses her head. Wes got a little nervous around the time he was supposed to go into work. Instead of having Jackson come back here, I went over to Quinn's. Jackson and I are staying the night here, and Wes is coming by in the morning.

Even though Daisy was arrested and released with potential charges, we have no idea if she knows I'm back. And once she finds out her plans to sabotage the race, drive me out of town, and get Wes back didn't work, she'll be pissed. She might do something crazy.

Though if she's smart, she'll be on her perfect behavior so she can try to convince a judge that she's worthy of any sort of visitation rights with Jackson, which seem unlikely considering she basically tried to kidnap him.

Still, I'm worried. Worried she'll hurt Jackson and worried she'll ruin Weston's career. His parents know—more or less—of my colorful past, and while I can tell his mom was trying hard not to hold it against me, I know she doesn't fully trust me yet.

And I don't blame her.

At least she didn't come after me with a pitchfork or get the stake ready for a burning. The twins already know, which just leaves Dean, Archer…and Quinn. I don't want my boyfriend's sister to hate me. And I don't want to lose the woman who's quickly becoming my best friend.

"We'll work on it." I smile and pet the kitten. "He is very friendly. Are they ready to leave their mom yet?"

"They are, but don't tell Archer," Quinn whispers. "I'll miss them."

"Maybe we can take two," I say. "Then you'll be able to visit, and you can keep the others, right?"

"I'd like it."

"You have enough space."

"That's what I said!" Quinn laughs. We're sitting in her living room, and five of the eight cats are in here with us. Emma laughs when a fat orange cat comes over and rubs his head on her. He lazily saunters off, and she crawls after him.

"She's fast!"

"I know." Quinn gets up to grab her baby. "Too fast. I'm already getting anxiety about the balcony looking over the living room. I wake up in the middle of the night thinking she fell over."

"That's so unlikely to happen," I tell her. "Lots of people have fancy catwalk thingies like that in their houses."

"I know." She wrinkles her nose. "I told Archer I want to line the floor with mattresses just in case."

"You'll encourage her to jump," Archer teases, coming into the living room. "I would have if I were a kid."

"Don't give him ideas," Quinn whisper-yells, but Jackson is too enthralled in the kitten he's renamed Salsa to hear anything. I yawn and look at the clock. Thank God it's almost bedtime. I'm wiped out.

It's been a long fucking day, which I feel like is a summary of my life. Well, until Weston, that is. Things changed the moment I stepped foot on his front porch, and I think I knew, deep down, that I wanted that change.

I needed that change.

Emma slips as she's crawling and hits the floor. Her two little bottom teeth puncture her lip, and blood starts spilling out of her mouth. Quinn has a moment of panic, picking up Emma and going back and forth between checking her mouth and wanting to comfort her baby. I run into the kitchen to get a towel, and Archer calmly sits on the floor and tells Quinn it's okay.

"The blood is mixing with her saliva and it looks like she's bleeding more than she really is," he says.

Jackson gets freaked out, and I take him into the kitchen to avoid seeing the blood. Emma is screaming and crying, and he's upset that his cousin is hurt and upset. It's pure chaos for a good five minutes, but then we get everyone settled down and up to bed.

Half an hour later, I shut the door to the guest room, sneaking out. Jackson fell asleep fast tonight, and while I could lay there and snuggle with him, I know if I didn't get up, I'd end up falling asleep too.

"Should we have cake with our tea?" Quinn asks. I wash out the pink skull tea set Weston and Jackson got for me as a surprise.

"Of course."

"Good. Because I made one earlier today. I was craving Funfetti cake bad."

"Craving?" I raise my eyebrows.

"I'm not pregnant. Or else I better not be. I really want to go on Tower of Terror on our honeymoon," she laughs. "But I am dying to have another."

"You're a good mom. You should have at least one more."

"We want three or four." She opens the pantry and all the cats come running, circling her feet and meowing.

"I take that back. Maybe you shouldn't have this many cats."

"Their meowing is like singing." She looks at Archer, who's sitting at the large island counter eating. "Isn't it, babe?"

He rolls his eyes. "It's music to my ears."

I laugh and reach down, picking up one of the kittens. "Are you Salsa?"

"That's Binx," Archer says. "I mean, not like I can tell them apart or care or anything."

"He really likes Binx," Quinn loudly whispers.

"I guess you're staying then, huh, little guy?"

"He is."

Quinn sets the cake down, shoos the cats off the counter at least a dozen times, and heats up water for our tea. Archer goes upstairs to bed, saying he has early surgery in the morning, leaving Quinn and me downstairs to eat and talk until we go to bed as well.

I cut into my cake and sip my tea. I look at Quinn, excited to have someone I can actually call a friend. And she's my boyfriend's sister, which makes things ten times better.

Well, almost.

"Quinn?"

"Yeah?"

"I need to tell you something."

"Sure." She adds more sugar to her tea. "What is it?"

"It's more like a confession. Promise you won't judge me?"

"I promise."

And she doesn't.

The mattress sinks down next to me, and my eyes flutter open. I'm too tired to realize the body next to me is too large to be Jackson, and I lazily push myself up to tell him I'll be right up.

But then I see Wes, and my heart flutters.

"Morning, sunshine." He smiles down at me. He's in his uniform, and holy hell that man is fine. I sit up only to pull him down on me.

"What time is it?"

"Seven AM. I came here instead of going home. I don't think Quinn was too happy about having to let me in." He kisses me, brushes my hair from my face, and sits up. He's wearing a utility belt around his waist, which isn't comfortable to lay down on.

"We were up pretty late talking." I sit up again, resting my head on Wes's shoulder. "I told her everything."

"Everything-everything, or the version of everything I told my parents?"

"I was going to tell that version, then I drank half a bottle of wine."

Wes smiles. "And?"

"She didn't kick me out."

"That's a start."

I nod, not wanting to get up, but I have to pee and I'm pretty close to keeling over and dying of thirst. "Right. She might need some time to process, but I feel better. I want to start fresh."

"You are." He goes in to kiss me again, but Jackson comes in, excited to see his dad. I use the bathroom and we all go downstairs. Quinn is in the kitchen, and all the cats are following her around meowing.

"You really are a crazy cat lady, sis," Wes chuckles.

"Thank you." Quinn looks up with a smile. Her eyes meet mine, and the smile wavers. Shit.

"Once you're done feeding the beasts, can I talk with you?" Weston asks.

"Yeah, of course."

She gives Emma a few more Puffs and then feeds the cats. I pour Jackson a cup of milk, and we both get excited when we realize Wes brought us all donuts.

"What's Daddy talking to Aunt Winny about?" Jackson asks.

"I'm not sure," I tell him, though I have an idea. I set his milk on the table and see the paper under the donut box. My fingers shake as I reach for it.

My picture isn't on the front page. Or the second. Or third. Jackson laughs watching me thumb through the paper as fast as I can.

"We're good," Wes says, coming back into the room. He knows what I'm looking for.

"We are?"

Quinn takes Emma out of her highchair and sits at the table. "Yes." She meets my eye. "We are good."

"You've already looked through it," Wes says, coming up behind me. It's Monday morning, and I keep going through the paper just to be sure I didn't miss anything. "There's nothing incriminating in there."

"Thank God." I exhale. "One more day."

"Yes, and I'm telling you, most people have already made up their minds when they wake up Tuesday morning."

"You're going to win."

"I might. Or I might not."

I pour myself a cup of coffee and join Wes at the table. Jackson is still sleeping, and Wes's alarm went off on accident this morning. He doesn't have to work today, but he forgot to turn off the alarm. Once he was awake, he came downstairs for breakfast. I was going to go back to sleep but got too anxious to see the paper.

"I'm going to talk to her today," Weston says. "I'm assuming she's at her parents'. I'll call over there and see."

"What are you going to talk about?"

"How we'll proceed with things. Actually," he says and stands up, "I'll call them now. Who cares if it's early?"

"So Jackson's other set of grandparents aren't involved at all?"

"They send him presents for his birthday and Christmas, but that's it."

"That's so weird."

Wes nods. "They feel like they have to side with Daisy on it. I think it's easier if they pretend like he's not here."

"Their loss."

"Yes, and a big one." He gets his phone and calls Daisy's parents. "Well, that's shocking," he says sarcastically when he hangs up.

"What?"

"She skipped town already and is back in Chicago."

I shake my head in disbelief. "Wow, though it is refreshing to hear about someone who makes worse choices than I do."

Wes sighs. "I don't know if this is good or bad. But I think I should call Mr. Williams and let him know what happened."

"Good idea. Get everything on record."

"Yeah, it'll come up again, I'm sure." He comes back to the table. "In the meantime, I got us tickets to go to the planetarium today."

"No way."

"Yes. And I thought maybe when we're done, we could visit your dad."

"You want to take Jackson there? My dad can be a little unfiltered."

Wes cocks an eyebrow. "You've met my nana, right?"

I laugh and reach for Wes. He takes my hands and pulls me to my feet. "I love you, Weston."

"And I love you."

Chapter Forty-Three

WESTON

I put my arm around Scarlet, smiling as we watch Jackson tear into his Christmas presents. The three of us are wearing matching pajamas, which was Scarlet's idea. Not mine. She said she bought them as a joke, but was rather insistent on all of us wearing them and taking a picture together last night on Christmas Eve.

No sooner than Scarlet gets comfortable against me, she jumps up.

"Salsa, get out of the tree." She grabs the black kitten and brings him to the couch with her. He stays for half a second and jumps down, pouncing on the pile of discarded wrapping paper.

Midnight, the mother cat to all the kittens, curiously walks over, batting a plastic bow across the living room. We were only going to take the kitten, but the mama cat really likes me for some reason. She's a bit annoying, really, and rubs her head all over me purring almost every night when I go to sleep.

Scarlet laughs, watching the cats have almost as much fun as Jackson with the presents. I take her in my arms again, stealing a kiss before Jackson moves onto the next present.

"I love you," she whispers, running her hands through my hair.

"I love you too," I tell her, and we settle back against the couch as Jackson finishes opening his presents. It doesn't take long. That kid could win an award for fastest present opening.

Once he's done, I deal with the aftermath of the wrapping paper, torn boxes, and toys scattered throughout the living room. Jackson plays with a new remote control dump truck, "helping" me clean up the mess.

The smell of cinnamon rolls fill the air, and Scarlet turns on Christmas music. She comes back into the living room with a cup of tea in her hand, stopping in the threshold of the room with a smile on her face.

"Breakfast will be ready soon," she says, taking a drink of tea. She sets her cup down and pulls Salsa from the tree again. I stashed all our breakable ornaments when Jackson was a baby, replacing the pretty glass balls with shatterproof plastic ones that actually look just as good as the others. I almost dug them out of the basement this Christmas, and I'm glad we didn't.

"Then I need to shower so we can get ready to leave."

I scoop up another armload of wrapping paper and add it to the big gift bag a toy came in. We have a lot of stops to make on the way to my parents' for their big Christmas party.

The first stop is to Eastwood's Senior Care Center, where Mr. Cooper now lives. We were able to get him a room there around the first of the month, and it's been a big weight off Scarlet's shoulders. The old nursing home was a dump. I didn't want to say anything and make Scarlet feel worse, but I was shocked when I walked in, and not in a good way.

The second stop we have to make won't be fun. It'll be awkward and uncomfortable, but it's something I couldn't rightfully refuse to do.

Daisy's parents want to see Jackson on Christmas. They got him presents and asked if he could come over for lunch. Scarlet and I are going with, and I'm not sure if Daisy will be there or not. The judge let her off easy, and she's going to court-ordered therapy. I haven't seen her since she left the last time, and now all the paperwork is official and filed.

I'm not married to her anymore. I'm free to remarry anyone I want, and that person is standing in the living room with a squirming kitten in her hands. Quinn suggested I propose while we're all at Disney World together after her wedding. Scarlet's never been and is just as excited as Jackson to go.

It's a damn good idea and would be magical and fitting for Scarlet, but I don't know if I can wait that long. I love her, and I know there will never be another who fits with us as well as she does.

Things were awkward for a while after we told the rest of my family the truth. I was good with not ever bringing it up, but Scarlet insisted she come clean and start with no secrets. Dean and Archer had the hardest time with it, convinced she wasn't trustworthy. Owen already knew, of course, and told Logan later that day after I left the bar. And Mom and Dad didn't know what to say, though I think they were both so relieved to hear that I was finally free of Daisy they didn't care who I was dating now. Dad didn't understand how I could be so understanding and forgiving, and when I tell the whole story, it surprises me too.

But Scarlet isn't that person anymore. I don't think that's ever who she really was in the first place. She's a good person, and I know one day soon she'll make a good wife.

"Merry Christmas!" Jackson shouts, running through the kitchen. He's on the lookout for more presents.

"Hey, Sheriff," Owen says, piling more cookies on his plate. Ever since I won the election, that's all he'll call me. He knows it annoys me.

"Hey," I say back, letting it go this time. "Save some for the rest of us."

"You should have gotten here sooner."

Mom comes in, shooing Owen away with her hand. "Those are for dessert. We haven't even had dinner yet." She gives me a hug and moves on to Scarlet.

"You look lovely, dear. And I love your necklace."

"Thanks," Scarlet says, hand going to her neck. "Wes got it for me for Christmas."

"He has good taste." Mom smiles and goes to the stove to check on dinner.

"Yeah," Scarlet says with a smile. "He does." The necklace is a little star, encrusted with diamonds. I know how much she loves to look at the stars. I fill a plate with appetizers and take Scarlet's hand, going into the living room to find my other siblings. We're early, but soon my extended family will shuffle into the house and things will get loud.

"Logan brought Danielle?" Scarlet whispers, slowing before we get into the living room. "I thought they were *just friends?*"

"That's what he tells us."

No one believes them, and if they really are just friends, then they're both missing out. I don't know Danielle well, but she seems nice enough and gets along with Logan better than anyone I've seen him with.

He brought her to Thanksgiving too, which threw us all for a loop. He's never brought anyone home for a holiday. He claims it was because Danielle's at odds with her family right now. They're rather conservative and had a whole plan laid out for the rest of her life that she had no say in. She basically ran away from it all last year, coming to live at her grandfather's farm here in Eastwood.

"Quinn and I had an idea and we think—"

"No," I say with a laugh. "We shouldn't get involved. And you know by now how much my sister likes to play matchmaker."

Scarlet smiles and gives my hand a squeeze. "Maybe just a little push?"

I shrug, not seeing how any harm can come from that. "Fine. But nothing more than a little push."

I don't see how the push can hurt, and if one of them confesses how they really feel they finally won't be able to deny it anymore. I want my brother to be happy, and I know he'll be happy with Danielle.

A push could be a good thing.

Unless they're pushed too far.

"Merry Christmas," Quinn says, coming into the room. She's holding Emma, who's dressed like a little elf.

"Oh my God," Scarlet coos, going over. "This is the cutest thing I've ever seen!"

"She's adorable!" Kara agrees.

"Does it make you want one?" Quinn teases.

"Nope. No way."

Scarlet takes Emma from Quinn's arms, cradling her against her chest. Her eyes meet mine and I know what she's thinking, because right now I'm thinking the same thing.

It's making us both want a baby.

"Did you get everything you wanted for Christmas?" Archer asks Jackson, scooping him up.

"I did!" Jackson says excitedly and goes on to list all the new toys he got. I step next to Scarlet, putting my arm around her shoulder. I got everything I want too.

Scarlet's phone rings, and she scrambles to get it from her purse. Her brother is supposed to be calling today and was trying to call around this time. He's stationed somewhere new and it's looking like he'll come home in January.

I go into the kitchen, finding Owen stealing more cookies, and take one too. Mom comes in and shoos us both away. Scarlet is in the dining room, and I want to give her some space while she talks to her brother. I go back into the living room with the rest of my family, hanging out and talking until it's time for dinner.

Scarlet, Jackson, and I are stuffed and tired by the time we get home several hours later. I changed Jackson into his PJs and brushed his teeth at my parents, knowing he'd fall asleep on the short ride home. I carry him upstairs and lay him in bed.

"Dad?" he grumbles, eyes fluttering open.

"Yeah?"

"I love you."

"I love you too, buddy."

He closes his eyes and reaches for the yellow unicorn. "And I love Scarlet."

"That's something we both have in common." I run my fingers through his hair and kiss his forehead. The kid is wiped out and falls asleep within minutes. I tuck him in and go downstairs to find Scarlet.

Only, she's not in the house. This time, there's no panic or worry. I know exactly where she is.

Grabbing a blanket from the couch, I find her on the back porch steps, looking up at the clear sky above us. I sit next to her, draping the blanket around our shoulders.

"This is perfect," she whispers, wrapping her arm around me. "I'm kind of sad Christmas is over."

"We'll get to do it again next year."

She looks at me with a smile. "Are you sure you want that?"

"More than anything. I want *you* next year. And the year after that. And the one after that. Actually," I start and get up, extending a hand. Scarlet takes it, eyes sparkling with amusement. "I love you, Scarlet Cooper. This isn't how I planned it, because I don't even have a ring yet, but you're right. This is perfect."

"Wes, what are you—"

I get down on one knee. "Will you marry me?"

The blanket slides off her shoulders and tears fill her eyes. She stares at me in disbelief, and for a moment I think I asked too soon.

Then the biggest smile takes over her face. "Yes! Yes, of course I will marry you!"

I get up and pull her into my arms. "I love you. Today, tomorrow, and every day after that. I will always love you."

Epilogue

SCARLET
Seven months later...

"Thank you so much," Quinn says, pushing her messy hair out of her face and taking Emma from my arms. "With Archer's parents up in Michigan visiting Bobby and my own consumed with construction on the hospital, I'm dying."

"It's no big deal." I look down at Jackson. "We had fun. Emma was perfect."

Quinn raises an eyebrow in disbelief. Now that she's over a year and is walking, Emma is a handful. And poor Quinn has been puking nonstop pretty much since the day she conceived her second child. She said she went through the same thing with Emma, making me question her sanity on getting pregnant again.

"Is Archer going to be home soon?"

"Yeah, thankfully." We move into Quinn's house, which is far from neat and tidy like it usually is. I hope when I'm finally pregnant I don't get hit with morning sickness like this.

Right after Wes proposed we started trying in a sense. I knew it would take a miracle to knock me up, but I was hopeful. We had a small but beautiful wedding on Valentine's Day, and then I had a sit down with my OB to talk about what was really wrong with me. After a slew of tests, I've been taking fertility drugs and we've still had no luck.

I know many couples try much longer than we have, but it's starting to really weigh on me. Jackson is dying for a sibling.

"How's your sister?" Quinn asks, sinking down on the couch in the family room. Three of her six cats are in here, lounging around.

"She's doing pretty well, actually. I think the group home is a good adjustment for her. She got a job last week at a bookstore."

"That's great!"

"Baby steps, but a step is a step." Heather got out of prison last month. Around the New Year, she started going to a church group with a few other inmates, and it actually turned her around. She still goes to church and is currently living in a group home for troubled young adults with mental health issues. She's still in Chicago, but we try to see each other at least once a week.

"When will your belly get big?" Jackson asks, looking at Quinn's stomach.

Quinn puts her hand on her belly. "You'll probably notice a baby bump in a month or so. I've heard you show sooner with the second."

"You're totally going to be one of those pregnant ladies who's all belly and boob, aren't you?" I ask.

Quinn smiles. "I was last time." She makes a sour face and then gets up, rushing to the bathroom to throw up. Jackson and I stay a little longer, waiting to leave until Archer gets home. He thanks me as well for helping out with Emma today so Quinn can rest.

"Are you tried?" I ask Jackson when we get home. "I'm tired. Emma wore me out."

"I'm not tired," he says with a yawn. "Can I go play now?"

"Yeah, that'd be great. Dinner will be ready in about an hour."

He goes upstairs and I have every intention of starting dinner, but I fall asleep on the couch, not waking until Wes comes home.

"You feeling okay, babe?" he asks when I get up.

"Yeah, I've been tired all day. Maybe I'm coming down with something."

Wes raises his eyebrows. "Or maybe…"

"I wish." I shake my head. I've been pretty good about waiting until after my period is supposed to begin before taking a test.

"You've been tired all week."

"That's just one symptom," I remind him, though after watching poor Quinn puke her brains out I just kind of assumed I'd be like that too and I'd know with absolute certainty that I was pregnant.

Still, Wes's question hangs over me throughout dinner. And dessert. And bedtime. So much so that I break a rule and bust out a test.

Jackson is fast asleep, and Wes is watching TV downstairs. I said I was going to change into PJs and be right back. Taking one test won't take long. And I have to pee anyway.

My hands shake, and I close my eyes, talking myself down. Flipping that test over and seeing a big fat negative is more disappointing than I ever expected.

But this time…

"Wes!" I blink. Once. Twice. "Wes!"

I hear him running up the stairs. "What's wrong?" he asks, pushing open the bathroom door. I'm standing in front of the sink, too stunned to talk. I hold up the test.

Wes looks at it, at me, and back at the test again. Then he pulls me into his arms. "You're pregnant!"

Kisses and Lies

T.L. SMITH

Other Books

Kandiland
Pure Punishment (Standalone)
Antagonize Me (Standalone)

Twisted (Flawed #2)
Black (Black #1)
Red (Black #2)
White (Black #3)

Distrust (Smirnov Bratva #1) FREE
Disbelief (Smirnov Bratva #2)
Defiance (Smirnov Bratva #3)
Dismissed (Smirnov Bratva #4)
Lovesick (Standalone)
Lotus (Standalone)
Savage Collision (A Savage Love Duet book 1)
Savage Reckoning (A Savage Love Duet book 2)

Distorted Love (Dark Intentions Duet 1)
Sinister Love (Dark Intentions Duet 2)
Cavalier (Crimson Elite #1)
Anguished (Crimson Elite #2)
Conceited (Crimson Elite #3)
Insolent (Crimson Elite #4)
Playette
Love Drunk
Hate Sober
Heartbreak Me (Duet #1)
Heartbreak You (Duet #2)

I met Marcus at a crematorium.

That should have been my first clue to keep away.

He was nothing I wanted. Yet, everything I needed.

He was dark, dangerous.

And I couldn't stay away.

Even when I wanted to.

We made a deal—just our bodies.

But lines got blurred.

I asked for more than one night—I ended up asking for forever.

What a mistake that was.

What a mistake he was.

Sometimes love burns.

And sometimes kisses and lies are all you get.

Chapter One

ROCHELLE
Now

My hand grips the glass tightly, my breathing picks up as I watch Marcus Stone in action. I can see his skin glistening under the cold night as each stroke grows more powerful, one after the next. My eyes are glued to his body as he comes up for air. His strong jawline opening then closing with each powerful breath.

How can watching someone swim turn you on?

I'm not sure, but it can. Somehow, it turns me on.

Bringing the glass to my lips, I take one more drink, finishing the contents and feeling the burn as it goes down. I need the liquid courage. I need it to face him.

Marcus turns, his strokes finally stop when he looks at me. The light from the kitchen is not helping to obscure me while I sit in the dark, stalking.

My breathing stops as his two powerful eyes lock on mine, his strong hand lifts and strokes his fingers through his hair. I'm helpless, compelled to watch as the muscles in his arm flex during the simple action. His hazel eyes narrow in on me.

"Rochelle…" Marcus says my name as easily as the water drips from his body.

It makes me even madder.

The drink in my hand feels like it could smash any second with the pressure I'm applying to the glass. He pushes himself out of the water, his body glistening as he comes to a stand not too far away from me. Reaching for a towel, he wipes his body. His hazel eyes, now darkening, lock on me when I don't answer him.

"I'm leaving you," I say with a smile when my breath doesn't hitch at those words.

"This is what you want?" Marcus asks.

No fight.

No argument.

Nothing.

"Yes. I'm leaving you," I say it more to myself this time. Perhaps to help me believe it.

He chuckles.

The asshole chuckles.

"Off you go, then."

With as much strength as I can muster, I throw my glass at him, just missing his head when he ducks out of the way. When he stands taller, I know that was a mistake. But I honestly don't care. I can't care anymore.

Pushing myself up from the lounger where I was reclining while working up the courage to tell him I am leaving, I step forward and come just under his chin.

Marcus is tall.

I hate that about him.

I hate a lot about him.

But then again, I also don't.

"Is that all you've got to say?" I arch an eyebrow.

Marcus arches one back. "Yes." Then he pushes past me, not caring that he almost knocks me over as he heads inside.

I follow. I shouldn't, but I can't help myself.

"You sleep with her… when I'm not here… in this house," I yell.

He halts, turns, and smirks. "I do," Marcus says, the towel now dropping. His swimwear is sitting low on his hips. "And I fuck her hard… all the ways you hate and I love." His lips turn up, waiting for me to say something in return.

"I hate you," I spit at him.

"I know you do."

"I hate you sooo much."

"That's okay. You can leave now."

"Is she coming over?" I yell.

Marcus turns, his hand touching the railing that leads up to his room.

I've never really lived here—I was simply a visitor. No one important. Just a person in this man's life. No one can penetrate him. I feel sorry for the person who finally does get through his impervious walls. They will either be very stupid or love him more than anyone else ever has.

"She will be now. I have steam I need to work off." He takes the steps two at a time and disappears, leaving me standing in the foyer with my hands clenched as I look around for my things. Luckily for me, I never moved out of my house. What a mistake that would have been if I had.

But worse, what a mistake Marcus was.

While rushing around and grabbing my things, I hear a ding. Looking over to the countertop, I see his cell light up. For some reason he doesn't have it locked, so I slide it open and up pops a girl's name.

Misha
I want you to spank me so bad, baby.

I gag, then throw his phone at the floor, hard enough that it shatters.

Fuck him and his cheating ass.

Picking up my bags, I walk to the door and step through, pushing it hard behind me so it slams. Again, fuck him and whatever he thinks.

My car is parked out the front where I left it when I arrived to break this nightmare off. I knew I'd have to make a quick getaway.

I need to get away from him.

He's poison.

Toxic.

A virus that has inserted itself in my system and won't leave, sucking me dry.

Now is my chance to extract that poison.

I have to for my own health.

For my own good.

Marcus Stone is not good for me, that much is obvious.

Throwing my bags in the car, I look back at his house, and when I look up, I see him standing on his balcony staring down at me. Marcus' hands are on the railing, his eyes locked onto mine.

"Fuck you," I say under my breath as I walk around and get into my little red car.

The car creaks, and I wonder if it can hear my own heart doing the same.

Chapter Two

ROCHELLE
Before.

I PULL AT MY CURLS, MY FINGERS THRUSTING IN MY HAIR, WANTING TO PULL IT OUT. It has to come out. "This can't be happening," I silently scream, as I watch my parents walk into the crematorium.

How is this happening?

This is *not* happening.

It's a mantra that screams in my head over and over again.

On repeat.

I am a twenty-four-year-old woman who doesn't believe in death. I don't want to believe in it, therefore it's not true. I hate it. With a passion so bright I wanted to light the fucking world on fire.

Letting go of my hair, I sit in the hot sun rocking back and forth. This is going to be over soon. It has to be.

I don't know why they brought me here.

Damn it! Why on earth am I here?

I feel like a child, but I am anything but.

I do have trouble functioning as an adult lately.

One week to be exact.

Laying my head back on the concrete, the ground beneath me warms my cold body. It's October here in Australia and the sun's starting to become hotter and hotter.

If I continue to lay here, the makeup I am wearing will melt off my pretty little face.

It will soon be Christmas time.

Fuck! Christmas time.

A loud hiccup leaves my chest as I squeeze my eyes shut against the harsh sun.

I don't want to be here.

This is *not* happening.

My two most favorite people on this planet have left me. It was sudden. It was crushing. I am shattered I didn't even get to say goodbye.

No one understands me like they did, not even my parents. Don't get me wrong, I love my parents, but the love I have for my grandparents is my favorite kind of love. Not a day would go by when I didn't speak to them. Not an event would pass that they didn't attend or know about. They were there for me, for everything and anything, and I'd like to say I was the same with them.

They were my world.

They were my everything.

My grandfather—my protector.

My grandmother—my confidant.

My hands clench, and I reopen my eyes. When I do, an involuntary scream leaves my mouth. Standing above me, looking down, is the most beautiful man I've ever seen. He has designer glasses covering his eyes so I can't see them, but his dark hair is cut short, revealing his perfect face—square, clenched jaw, thin lips, angular cheekbones—and he's watching me. When I realize he means no harm, I look away and stand, but his eyes track my movements as he continues to watch me. I know the eyes behind those glasses are locked on me, following me. I know it as much as I know I am breathing.

"You scared me," I say.

There's a small, fake smile playing on my lips, and he says nothing in return, simply stands there like a statue.

"Sorry for screaming." I blink a few times, but again, not a word is spoken. I look around and see no sign of my parents. Damn them, I shouldn't have to be here dealing with this by myself. Where are they? I know they have to be here somewhere.

"Okay, well, you can go now." I turn back around and drop to the ground. My mind and body not wanting to deal with him, even if he is the most gorgeous man I've ever seen.

Taking a deep breath, my hands run through my hair again, a nervous habit I've never been able to stop. One day I will pull out all my hair and then wish I did try to prevent myself from doing it.

Sighing, I lay down. And when I look up again, I squeak.

He's still there.

Standing above me.

Watching me.

I didn't hear him leave, but in reality, I wasn't really thinking about him. At all.

My mind is elsewhere.

Hand to my heart, I look up at him from my spot on the ground. "You can't do that to people. Gosh, dude…" I wait for my heart to slow. *At least it's beating*, a voice inside my head screams at me. *Yes, at least it is beating.*

"Rochelle…" Pushing up on my elbows, I see my mother is at the door. She looks at the man standing behind me, then to me. "Come inside."

"No," I answer quickly, then lay back down.

I hear the door close again, knowing she went back inside the crematorium.

Looking up, he's still standing there, his glasses firmly in place as he looks down on me. I feel his eyes roam over my body, but he still doesn't say one single word.

"It's creepy, you know. To stand there and stare at someone without saying anything."

He harrumphs, and I smirk. Then when I realize I'm smirking, I put a stop to it and close my eyes.

"Why are you out here?"

My eyes fly open at his words. His voice is strong and has a hard tone. It sends shivers all over my body, in a good way. Not even bothering to get up, I answer him with the sun glaring on my face and my hands down by my sides. "Two people I love very much are in there," I say, referring to the crematorium.

I don't want to go in.

I can't.

"And…" he says it as if I should know. As if I shouldn't care.

"I can't go in there. I don't want to go in there. They aren't alive in there." When the words leave my mouth, I look up to see him staring off in the distance, as if he's thinking about what to say next. My eyes skim him and come to a stop at his hands. One hand has a skull tattooed on it, making me shiver.

"They aren't alive out here either." He starts moving, so I sit up and watch him go. His trousers are black and hug his ass, showing off the nice curves. He's wearing black boots and a crisp, white shirt.

"Hey..." The man stops as he reaches the door, but it's not the same door my mother poked her head out of, this is a side door. "What's your name?"

Distraction—it's good for the heart.

I think he's going to answer me because his lips move a fraction, but then he turns and walks in through the doorway, not looking back as it shuts hard behind him.

Sighing, I lay back down, my heart breaking inside my chest. It cracks and continues to crack further, so loudly I wonder when the pain will stop, when it will all go away.

"They say death changes people."

"Oh God!" I yelp at my mother's voice, not hearing her approach. She sits next to me, her hand sits on my thigh and she gives me a reassuring pat, and continues, "A significant death."

"I don't want to talk about it." It's my way of coping, and yet, at every chance, my mother reminds me they're dead. Like I need to be reminded. I fucking know. I'm not stupid. But it doesn't mean I want to accept it. She simply doesn't get that fact.

"It's changing you. You're becoming more distant." I look to her to see her eyes are lost, then she looks down at me. "Who was that man?" she asks, changing the subject. Mother's good at that, getting lost in her own thoughts.

"A man," is all I can manage to reply.

I hear more footsteps and sit up. My father walks toward us with his hands in his pockets. It became his burden to deal with it—they were my mother's parents and my grandparents. Though, I have to admit, I saw them more as my parents and, quite simply, my best friends.

My heart, it cracks again.

"It's time we go."

"I'm going to catch a cab," I say to Father.

He nods in understanding.

My mother stands. "No. We can drive you. Don't be silly," she says as if it's obvious.

I look up to my father for help, but he shakes his head. His hand goes to my mother's back, touching her softly, and she instantly moves into his touch.

"No. I'm not getting in the car with you."

"Rochelle, really?" Mother says.

"Yes, I'll ring you later. I might even walk home. It will do me good."

"Gosh." My mother shakes her head and walks off.

I lie back down on the concrete and close my eyes as I hear their car take off.

To live in this world is to hurt, I don't care what anyone says. It hurts. It hurts so fucking bad that I'm struggling to breathe. Sitting up, I drop my head between my legs and a strangled cry escapes me. My eyes begin to water, and my heart beats so fast I wonder how this pain will ever go away.

"Stop thinking. It helps."

Wiping at my face, which is covered with snot and tears, I finally look up. The man from earlier is standing in front of me again. There's a bag slung over his shoulder, a very large bag, and he's looking down at me.

"I don't want to," I reply.

I need the pain—it's a reminder of who they were to me.

Every-damn-thing!

"Your loss." He starts walking while I wipe angrily at my face and stand, my black boots clicking on the ground as I follow him to a large, black truck.

"Can I have a ride?"

His brows pinch together, then he turns and opens the back, throwing in the large black bag before he shuts the truck and leans against the door to stare at me.

"You're asking for a ride at a crematorium? I could be a murderer."

I shake my head—I couldn't care at this moment. "I need a ride."

The man doesn't answer me.

"Can you give me a ride?" I ask him again, my hands going directly to my hips.

"Do you want to see them?"

What? His words surprise me. I'm unsure of what to say. And before I can think, he reaches for me, gripping my wrist, and starts pulling me to the side door of the crematorium he came out of. I don't argue, the words are completely stuck in my throat, and I am unable to move of my own volition. He pulls the heavy door open and we head inside. My breath leaves me and makes a whooshing sound when we get to a glass window. That's when I see it—both of them. Their heads are visible, but their bodies are covered by a white sheet.

"Oh my God." My hands fly to my mouth as I step closer to take in the sight. "Oh my God," I say again, as one hand reaches out and touches the pane of glass in front of me. I start sliding back down, my heart full of pain and shattering into pieces. It hurts. It hurts so much. Hiccups leave me while I sob, and soon my grandparents are no longer visible as my knees touch the floor. The man leaves me there and steps back slightly so I can cry by myself while my treasured grandparents lay on cold metal slabs on the other side of the glass.

He stands there, not saying a word, until I manage to gather myself enough to stand. My eyes don't glance in the direction of where they lie.

An angry hand reaches up and snatches his glasses from his face. He doesn't flinch, simply stays still as if he was expecting it.

"You are a real asshole," I say, with as much venom as I can muster. Stepping closer, my finger touches his chest, and I stab it at him. His chest is hard as a rock. "Asshole." His hazel eyes lock onto me. Then he reaches for my wrist again, pulls hard, and walks me back out the same way we came in.

When the sun hits my skin, I pull away. He stops, turns, and reaches for his sunglasses, sliding them back in place before he leaves.

My feet are unable to move, that is until I scream at myself to head straight for his truck, open the passenger side door, and slide in.

"Don't kill me," I say, reaching for the seatbelt and buckling myself in.

He shakes his head and pulls out of the parking lot onto the main road.

Chapter Three

ROCHELLE

The man stops at a gas station first, gets out, fills his truck, and then comes back. When he slides back in, he hands me a bottle of water without saying a word and pulls out into traffic once again.

"Do you want my address?" I ask.

I watch as one hand sits on the steering wheel while the other rests on his leg.

"Figured you'd tell me when you want to go home," he says, his voice distant and definitely not warm. More like frigid and aloof.

"Where are you going?" My voice is uncertain as I speak.

"Nowhere." And he does just that. He drives nowhere with me for at least an hour. Doesn't stop, just drives. I know all the places as he cruises around because I've lived here my whole life. My mind's tired and my body is exhausted.

"You can take me home now," I state, and give him my address.

He turns the truck around and starts driving in that direction.

"Why were you at the crematorium?" I ask as we get closer to my house.

"I work there," he tells me.

"You work…" I shake my head, trailing off. Of course, I would be stuck in a truck with a guy who could easily kill me and dispose of my body without anyone knowing. What the actual fuck! Didn't *Law and Order* teach me anything?

I'm addicted to those crime shows on the television.

"Second-guessing getting in a stranger's car now, aren't you?"

At first, I think he's joking, but when I turn to look at him, his face is stoic. He's deadly serious, and I've just told him where I live.

Fuckity, fuck, fuck.

"If you wanted to kill me, you would have done it by now," I say, hoping and praying it is true.

"Or I could have just waited for you to give me your address, so I can come back when you're sleeping." His words hang in the air. "I bet a girl like you lives by herself too."

Oh God, he's right. But I am *not* going to validate that. No way does he need to know what my living arrangements currently are.

Grief got the best of me today, but it won't kill me too.

He comes to a stop out the front of my small home, which is my pride and joy. I bought this by myself, and with my own money. Reaching for the door of his truck, I turn back to look at him, his eyes are covered by those glasses, and one hand is firmly on the steering wheel.

"Laters," I say, sliding out and shutting the door.

He doesn't drive off when I walk down my driveway to my front door, which I find a little creepy, but continue on anyway.

I love everything about my home. It's a sandstone brick home, with floor to ceiling windows along the front. A small veranda juts out from the front, and on the porch is an outdoor seating area with a glass table and two lush chairs. I like to sit out here and read when the sun shines in the morning, with a coffee in hand. The house has three bedrooms and an open plan living area.

As I reach the door, I unlock it. Glancing over my shoulder, I see he's still there watching me.

It's definitely creepy, that stare he has going on.

Just because he's beautiful doesn't mean I should have trusted him.

What an idiot I am.

Locking the door and sliding the chain firmly in place, I wait to hear if his truck leaves. It takes a few minutes, but eventually he drives off.

I head to the window to look out, and the breath I was holding finally escapes me in a sigh of relief.

"You have to go to work," my mother says the next day when she comes over to visit.

"Not today."

And I don't.

I don't want to.

"Today is the day. Are you ready?" my mother's voice chimes into the phone.

It's my grandparents' funeral today, and I have to remember my heart can take it. That my life still goes on, with or without them in it.

"I'm pulling up now. Goodbye, Mother." Turning left, I drive into the crematorium parking lot—behind it is where the funeral will take place. I park in the same spot he was parked in the last time I was here. When I look around, I don't see his truck.

He didn't come to murder me, so maybe he isn't as bad as I had assumed. Walking out the back, I spot all of my family who is gathered and ready for the service to start. My mother wraps a hand around my shoulders and holds me to her. I sometimes forget that even though I was their granddaughter, she was their daughter. And her hurt is probably as great, if not more, than mine.

The service is beautiful, everything you'd expect from a loving family, and maybe even more. My mother grips me to her the entire time, and I do everything in me to not break down as I have been the last few nights as I fall asleep, with my eyes covered in saltwater and unable to see. My pain is now only seen in my sleep, no one else will witness it.

"Honey, how you holding up?" My father pulls me from my mother's tight grip and pats my back. Then he pulls back and pushes my sunglasses down so he can see my eyes. I know what he sees—heavy dark eyes that are withholding tears.

"I'll be okay."

"I know you will."

I push away after the service, waving goodbye as I head back to my car. When I do, I see him there again—he's walking out with his bag over his shoulder, and his truck is parked directly next to mine.

"You carry bodies with you every day?" I joke.

He stops, turns, and I know his eyes are narrowing in on me. "You're back. You're either stupid or—"

"Or?"

He shakes his head then continues to walk.

I unlock my car, reach for the door, then pause. "Want to go for a drink?" I ask, not looking his way.

"Are you dumb?" he asks, as I turn around to see him now standing in front of me, the bag no longer thrust over his shoulder. He's dressed much like he was the day before.

"Pardon?"

He reaches up, taps my head. "Does this have a brain?"

"Well—"

"Did your mother ever teach you *not* to take rides from strangers?"

"Well, yes. But I met you yesterday," I say.

"What's my name?"

I bite my lip. Damn! I don't know, but I don't because I never bothered to keep asking after the first try.

"Rochelle…" My aunty calls me, and I turn my head to glance over my shoulder, but then look back to him.

"Come for a drink, please?" My voice is desperate.

"Meet me at Johnny's in thirty." He slides into his truck as my aunty gets closer, then he drives off. Johnny's is in the heart of town, so it's a short drive to meet him.

"Who was that man?"

I don't answer, simply offer her a smile before I get into my car and drive away.

Heading straight to Johnny's, I don't detour or stop. I want to know more about this man.

Taking my black jacket off, my singlet, which is multi-colored, sits nicely with my black pants and boots. Walking in, I order myself a drink and sit by myself at the bar.

"One of those days?" the bartender asks, handing me my gin and tonic.

"One of those weeks," I whine while rolling my eyes. "Better make me another. I don't plan to walk out of here anytime soon." The bartender smiles, and for some reason it makes me smile back. He's younger than me, probably early twenties, and I can see in his face that he doesn't know hurt. Hurt is such an awful thing to carry around with you day after day.

"Here you go, beautiful." Handing me a drink, the bartender walks over and turns on the jukebox, winks, and goes back behind the bar. There are only a few other people in the room, and most are too involved in conversation, they don't even care about the music playing in the background.

My phone starts ringing, and without even looking at it, I know it's my parents wondering where I am. They're having a function after the funeral, and Lord knows I do *not* want to attend that.

"You should answer that, they will want to know where you are." The stool next to me slides out and he sits.

Who is he, though? A stranger who has danger written all over him. A stranger I'm highly attracted to and can't seem to stay away from. Even when I know I should. His hazel eyes stare at me, waiting for me to answer.

"I'll message them." And I do exactly that. I message my mother, telling her I'm not going to make it. I leave it at that, with no further explanation. Sliding my cell back into my bag, the bartender walks over, but when he does, he doesn't hold that soft smile he gave me before. Instead, his lips form a thin line.

"What can I get you?"

My stranger's fingers tap on the bar. "Water," is all he says, which in turn, surprises me.

"You aren't going to drink with me?"

"Why am I here?" he asks.

I bite my lip and look down.

"Do you not have any friends?"

Lifting my drink to my lips, I hiccup before taking a sip. "Yes, but—"

"But what? You want to fuck?"

I almost choke on the liquid that was in my mouth as I turn to face him.

He's serious. He isn't playing.

At first, I thought it had to be a joke. But I'm slowly learning this man doesn't joke.

He's serious.

Deadly serious.

Intense.

And I should probably stay away.

But what can I say—I'm a broken woman.

"You didn't…" I trail off, not really knowing what to say, but knowing I heard correctly. And what he said is true. "Do you have a girlfriend?" I ask.

"No."

"Wife?" I raise an eyebrow.

"No."

"Well, then, yes, that's exactly what I want to do."

He stands, offers me his hand, and I put mine in it. "How many drinks have you had?"

"Two," I say, nodding to my two empty glasses. "Why?"

He starts walking, out of the bar and straight to his truck, opening the passenger door. "Because when I fuck you, you will want to be sober."

I smirk at his words as I climb into his truck, and he watches my ass as I do. When I turn back around, he shuts the door and walks around to his side, jumps in, starts the truck, and slides on his sunglasses.

"I've never done this."

"Hmmm…" is all I get in response as I watch him drive. His strong arms show veins I want to lick. Large hands I want to roam all over my body, grip onto the steering wheel. Shaking my head, I turn away from the natural curls in his hair and focus on the road, and not the way his lips will feel against mine.

Knowing the way to my house, that's where he goes. I was hoping we were going to his.

I still don't know his name, so I build up the courage to ask, as he's not offering it. "What's your name?"

"Now you ask?"

I shrug. "You didn't tell me."

"I didn't expect to see you again," he says, then continues with, "Marcus."

"I don't picture you as a Marcus."

His fingers tap on the steering wheel at my words. "I didn't picture you stupid enough to get into cars with strangers, yet, here we are."

"You aren't a stranger," I say, smiling. "Well, kind of, I suppose." Damn it! I cringe, because he *is* a stranger. But there is something about Marcus that pulls me in, and I want to know what.

"I am. You know nothing about me." Marcus comes to a stop out the front of my house and doesn't make a move. He just sits there.

"You're coming in, right?"

Marcus looks up at my house, then back to me. "Are you sure it's a smart move?" He removes his glasses and his hazel eyes pierce me. "Have you had sex with a stranger before?" An eyebrow raises, waiting for me to answer.

My hands fall to my lap as I start to play with the material of my pants. "No, but I need a distraction. And you're the perfect one," I tell him honestly.

Marcus nods and opens the truck door. Breathing a sigh of relief, I follow him. He lets me lead the way to my front door with him close behind until we're inside. His eyes scan my house, the living room is part of an open space and we walk into it. He looks directly at my black leather couches and then the television hanging on the wall. Just past the couches is my kitchen, which I really need to clean.

"Undress," he directs.

I turn to face him as my eyebrows pull together.

Marcus shows no sign of waiting, and my nerves all of a sudden take flight through the roof at his one-word command.

"How about a drink?" I ask as I walk to the kitchen.

"No. Undress, Rochelle."

My hand touches my kitchen bench, and my heart takes off at a speed my body can't keep up with, making me dizzy. Not looking his way, I blink a few times to bring me back into the now and reach for my top, pulling it over my head. Then I proceed to drop my pants, my hands shaking as they pool on the floor. Before I can turn around to see where Marcus is, I feel his front pressed against my back, his cock coming to rest at the top of my ass as he stands there touching me. He reaches for my hair, brushing it away from my shoulders.

"I will ruin you." He breathes the words on my neck. His tongue darts out and touches me, sending a shiver I didn't know I was capable of spreading out all over my body.

What am I doing?

"I want you to ruin me," I say back to him.

"You don't want to be ruined by me, pretty girl." His breath is hot as he rains kisses on my neck, and then he disappears, leaving me cold in his wake. "Go and lay on your bed, naked."

Turning around to face him, when I look at him again, I have to remember to breathe. His eyes are slightly slanted, broody, as they penetrate through every fiber of my being. His dark shirt and broad shoulders stand tall, taking me in.

Marcus makes a clicking sound with his tongue, and I manage to move in the direction of my bedroom. Taking a deep breath, I remove the rest of my clothing, then lay down on my bed. As I do, I hear the click of a door, so I wait.

And wait.

With each breath, I am dying with anticipation more than the last.

And then nothing.

My breathing returns to normal and my hands, which were shaky, are now steady.

"Marcus." I look up and don't see him.

Getting off the bed, I walk down the hall and see he isn't in my house anymore.

He's gone.

Chapter Four

ROCHELLE

Marcus plays on my mind. I know nothing about him, but somehow, he consumes my every thought. To an extent, it makes me wonder if I'm normal. Or is it my depression that's causing me to feel this way? Losing two people who I loved dearly, am I clinging on to anything right now in the hopes of feeling that type of unconditional love again?

Maybe clinging to a man I don't know isn't healthy.

The week goes by fast, and I make a decision to go back to work. My work consists of being employed by a man who smells most of the time, and the smell is not pleasant, but he pays well, hence the reason I stay there. Being a lawyer's receptionist isn't my idea of great employment, but it pays the bills, and I don't dislike it every day. Just some days. Like today. I want to go home. I'm tired. So fucking tired.

"Rochelle, you filed those forms?" Martin is scratching his head as he walks past me. He stops when I don't answer and pivots to look at me. "Rochelle…" he says my name, gaining my attention.

I look up and sigh. "Yes. Filed and ready for when you need them."

"Okay, good. I guess you can go." Martin resumes scratching and continues to walk off. I gather my things and head to my parents' house. I've been avoiding my mother all week, and now I can't do that any longer. It's her birthday today, so I have to see her. My father has already called and messaged me three times to make sure I'm coming.

As I drive to their house, I consider bypassing the crematorium, which I've been avoiding all week, thinking it will help. But as I drive by, I see his truck in the exact same area it was the last two times I was there. My heart rate picks up, and I have to tell myself, *'do not turn in, you don't need to see him.'*

Marcus knows where I live, but I haven't heard from him.

And believe me, I want to hear from him.

Marcus is perfect in an imperfect kind of way.

Deciding it's not a smart move to go near him—even if I desperately want to—I keep going. My family is all there when I arrive. My sister, Kat, who has her baby on her hip, is the first person I see when I walk inside. She smiles and leans in for a cuddle. I take my niece from Kat's hands and focus on her as my parents come out from the kitchen.

"Rochelle, you're late," my mother chides while shaking her head. "But I made your favorite, chocolate brownie." She claps her hands as she reaches for my niece in my arms. "Come to Grandma, baby."

"Mom, no chocolate," Kat yells out to her, to which my mother doesn't reply.

My father walks out, hands me a glass of wine, and walks away. "So, who's the mystery man?"

Putting the drink to my lips, I look over the edge of the glass at my sister. We look much alike—the same strawberry colored hair and blue eyes. We are two years apart and not as close as we should be, but I am trying.

"What, man?" I play dumb. I wasn't aware Kat saw me with him at the funeral. Then again, I wasn't paying much attention to anyone on that day.

"Oh, come on… that tall, dark, handsome man." she waves her hands around. "Tell me."

"I don't know him."

She raises an eyebrow.

"You don't know him? But you got in the car with him?" she asks, then shakes her head. "Please don't tell Mom that. She will hands down die."

"I wanted a one-night stand." I shrug.

"Well, I had that… and look where it got me," Kat says, referring to my niece.

"Annabelle is perfect," I say in my niece's defense.

"Of course she is, but her father has never contacted me. Didn't even care that I was pregnant. And I told him to wear a condom." She rolls her eyes. "All I'm saying is… make sure you watch him slip that sucker on before he slips in you."

The baby starts crying and Kat walks off to retrieve her.

Finishing my glass of wine, I get up to pour another when my mother walks back out.

"Dinner is ready. You weren't leaving, were you?"

"No." I sound more defensive than I meant to with that one-word answer.

"Good. Good." Mother nods her head, and then because it's her birthday and her parents are dead, she starts crying. Wiping at her face, she tries to hide her tears.

I step up closer, wrapping my arms around her. "It's okay, Mom. It's okay."

"I miss them. Do you wish it were me instead?"

"No," I say automatically. "What?"

"You always wanted to be with them. Never me." She's not wrong, but it's not in the way she's thinking. My grandparents simply got me in a way my mother never has.

"I love you, Mom. Come on, let's have a good night, shall we?" I pull back, smiling at her. "It's your birthday."

She nods.

And I try to keep my smile on my face for as long as I can, so she knows I do want to be here celebrating with her tonight.

Marcus is still there, his car's parked in the same spot. I almost missed it, but as I pull up, I sit in my car and wait. He has to come out soon, and when he does, I want to know why. Why he walked out on me. Opening my cell phone, I lock my car from the inside, turn it off, and crack a window slightly to let some of the cool night air in.

I sit there for a few minutes before a knock on my window startles me. Turning, Marcus' dark eyes are staring right at me. The green is gone from them under the night's sky and they look darker, almost black.

"Did you not hear the part where I said I would ruin you, pretty girl?"

I shrug.

Marcus leans down, and I wind my window down farther, so I can see him better.

"What do you want?"

"Why did you leave?"

"You aren't ready for someone like me. I know it, so it was easier that way." His words make me shake my head.

I reach for my keys, taking them out of the ignition, and push on the door to open it. Marcus' hand holds it, so I can't push it open all the way.

"You aren't this stupid. Tell me you aren't this stupid?" He steps back, letting me open my door. As I get out, I slide my keys into my pocket, then lean against my car.

"I'm allowed to be stupid this week."

"It's been over a week."

"Okay, I'm allowed to be stupid when I damn well choose."

Marcus shakes his head at my words.

"I wanted to see you," I tell him, the words falling from my lips as easily as a lie. Except these aren't lies. I do want to see him. So badly in fact, I can't seem to stay away.

One hand goes to reach for him. He looks at it when I cling to his shirt. Stepping forward so my hands are now both on his chest, I look up at him and he's watching me with intent.

"I'm working," is all he says.

"I can watch you work."

Marcus' head drops to the side. "You think that's smart? I work in there." His head nods to the side, indicating the crematorium. A shiver runs through me from the last time I was in there and what I saw.

"I want to watch you work."

Marcus leans down until his lips almost touch mine. "Would you like me to fuck you on the table too, with a cold, dead body touching yours?" His breath is hot and it sends shivers all over me. "Would that turn you on?"

It doesn't, not at all. But he does. So, I think it's best I don't answer his question.

"I want to watch you," I breathe, as my eyes stare at his lips, waiting in anticipation for them to touch mine.

They never do.

Marcus pulls away, the distance between us is not something I'm fond of. My fingers twitch with an urge to pull him back down to me.

Marcus cocks his head to the side. "Maybe this will keep you away." He starts walking, and my feet step one in front of the other as they follow him back inside the crematorium.

It's dark when we enter. He touches the switch, and once everything is illuminated, I can see everything. There's a dead body covered by a white sheet in the room that he walks into. He holds the door open for me and waits for me to cross the threshold. My hands start sweating and I wonder if I should turn and run. It would probably be the smart thing to do.

Marcus is not what I usually go for in a man. I prefer a man who likes to talk. Usually the beach boy look, with tanned skin, blue eyes, and blond hair.

Marcus is the exact opposite of everything I am normally attracted to. Maybe that's why I'm so captivated by him, or maybe I have issues? I haven't quite worked that one out yet. But right now, the draw I have to this man is undeniable.

Irrefutable.

Unequivocal.

I just want a taste.

But Marcus keeps leaving me at every turn.

"Pretty girl?" he questions.

My heels click on the white marble floor as I follow him. He shuts the door behind me, locking us in, and walks over to the dead body.

I watch as he puts on an apron, followed by a face mask which is clear as well as gloves. And then there's a gasp so loud that I don't think it comes from me, but I'm sure it does, when he looks up at me with a saw in his hand.

"You can still run, pretty girl." Marcus is giving me my out.

I *should* run, but like I said before, there's something about Marcus I just can't seem to walk away from.

And for me to run, that would be weak. I don't consider myself weak. And I want what

I want, and what I want is him. So, here I stand, in a place I never want to be, all because I want the man attached to the saw.

Marcus watches me, saw in hand and a smile tilting on his lips, and I cement myself to the spot.

"I'm glad it's not white you're wearing."

And then he does the unthinkable—he starts cutting off the man's hand. The minute I hear the saw slicing through flesh, I have to turn away. But the sound—fuck, I can still hear the sound.

It's a sound like I've never experienced in my life. To describe the sound of flesh being torn apart, then the crack when it hits the bone, well, I have no words. I cringe and wish I had run, wish I was not a brave girl today, and didn't want what I want.

My hands cover my ears, and I silently scream for that noise to stop. Turning, going toward the door, I reach for the handle but it's locked. The sound penetrates my ears, and this time I do scream, but he doesn't stop. Not even when I lean against the white door screaming a little bit louder to rid my ears of that sound. My screams intensify and drown out the sound of the flesh tearing apart.

When my throat becomes dry, I look back up.

Marcus has his mask off and a smile is playing on his lips. "I warned you, pretty girl."

"Unlock the door," I say, with more strength than I thought I could manage right at this moment.

"Don't you want to fuck now, pretty girl?"

My head starts shaking. "No. Open the damn door."

He smiles as if he's won this round, and he did. I knew he was unlike anyone I have ever met. But this? This I do not understand.

Marcus removes his gloves, takes off his apron, and starts walking toward me. My back goes against the door as he gets closer. When he reaches me, that smile is still playing on his lips. He leans down and his lips connect with mine, hard, unforgiving, and breathtakingly spectacular. He tastes like peppermint and something else I can't quite name. My body, which was tense, relaxes as his lips torture mine. Then as I go to reach for him to pull him even closer, that's when I hear the click of a lock and the door is open behind me.

Marcus stands tall, smirks, and walks back to the body. I watch him, unsure of what just happened, and stand there shocked.

"You better leave before I remove the other hand, pretty girl," he says, putting his apron, mask, and gloves back in place. I look up at him to see the saw in his grip. And just as he lowers it, I turn and leave.

Only looking back once to see him watching me exit.

That sinister smile never leaving his lips.

Chapter Five

ROCHELLE

To say I forgot all about Marcus over the next month would be a complete lie, but I have avoided driving near the crematorium as much as humanly possible, especially at night.

That kiss! That kiss will not leave my head. No matter how hard I try.

"Barbecue. Come on, Rochelle, get fucking dressed," Tanika yells at me.

I flip her off and quickly get changed into a swimsuit and a cover dress. Tanika is waiting out the front in her car, the music blaring and head-bopping as if she's a teenager, which makes me cringe. Car parties used to be our favorite thing, cranking the music and dancing around like idiots while the people next to us would simply stare. I outgrew it, Tanika never has.

"It's late, should we really be going now?" It's a Saturday night, and my plan after working all week was to do fuck all. Literally.

"You've been doing fuck all for ages. It's been too long since I saw you. Live a little, girl. Plus, there are people I want you to meet tonight."

"Oh no, who have you fallen in love with today?" I ask with a moan.

Tanika is a hopeless romantic. She puts the 'L' in love, even if her preferred victim at the time does not see it that way.

Tanika flicks her long, black hair behind her ear as we pull up at the lake. There's a park and a few barbecue areas scattered around.

"Gosh, how many people are here, Tanika?" She switches the ignition off and smiles at me. "And why are there so many motorcycles?"

"Well, about that…" She doesn't continue, just gets out of the car. I follow her, then walk around to meet her. Tanika's eyes are set on where everyone is standing or sitting. The sun is starting to set, so I can't see them clearly.

"Tanika."

She bites her lip, then her eyes flick to me. "Just don't judge, okay? But they are a biker gang." She turns away from me, grabbing a bag and throwing it over her shoulder.

"A biker gang?" I hiss at her. She loves some stupid people, but this? Holy fuck. "What is their name?"

She starts walking, so I have to follow her. "Exile MC."

I stop.

She stops.

She looks back at me. "What you hear about them isn't all true, Rochelle. Please, give them a chance."

"They've been under investigation for a month now. I know because I work for one of the lawyers who's trying to prosecute them, Tanika."

She waves her hand at me. "It won't stick, you know that. Now, come on and have some fun with me." Tanika grabs my hand and skips toward the music. I follow behind her, watching as we get closer, and their eyes turn toward us despite the music blaring. Somehow, they can still hear us or know we're coming.

"Girl." A man stands, walks over and picks Tanika up, and spins her around. He's a large man, not in that he has a belly or anything, he's simply large—larger than life. And by the looks of it, all fucking muscle. If he wasn't smiling right now as he spins Tanika, I would be terrified.

"Snow, put her down," a voice booms from behind him.

I look toward that sound and hear the man now known as Snow drop Tanika back to the ground.

He looks past her to me. "You brought a friend?" he asks, eyeing me with curiosity.

"Why, Snow?" I ask him straight up. He chuckles, and Tanika groans and covers her eyes. Before I know it, he reaches for his pants, undoing the zipper, and his dick is flopped out, white hair surrounding it. It's quite an impressive dick.

"My birthmark makes my hair white. First woman I fucked called me Snow and it kind of stuck." He puts his cock back in his pants and winks before throwing an arm around Tanika, leading her off to the group sitting at a picnic table.

Tanika bounces to the middle of the table. All the men are sitting around it, most of them in vests with their logo on the back and a name on the front. The one Tanika slides in next to reads 'Blaze,' then under that is 'President.' I don't bother sitting, as the music is turned up, while Tanika leans down whispering in his ear. Blaze's eyes lock on mine, and Tanika kisses his neck before she bounces her way over to me.

"Blaze doesn't really like strangers," she says. Looking back over her shoulder at him, she offers him a wave, then pulls off her dress and nods to mine. "Come on, let's go for a swim."

Looking back, his eyes are on me as I pull my slip off and turn away from him and those assessing eyes to walk to the water. The water is not clear these days. It used to be when I was child, but then flooding happened and it made our river dark in color.

"Why are you hanging with them?" I ask. Glancing back over my shoulder, they can't hear us now, but they're all at that same table, which is covered in drinks and God only knows what else.

I sit in the water, which comes up to my belly button, as Tanika swims farther out and turns back to look at me. "I met them out one night. I like him. But don't want anything more than what he can give me. He's…" She looks over at the table where Blaze is sitting with his dark hair and a slight scar on his eyebrow. He's attractive, in the very dangerous kind of way. "He doesn't do relationships anyway. And well, me, I need to stop doing them. Live a little as they say. So, Blaze, he's fun and he gets me."

"Does he, though?"

"Do I what?" That voice makes me yelp. Blaze's standing near me, his feet not quite in the water, but his eyes are now on Tanika as she floats with her tits out of the water, just barely covered by little triangular scraps of fabric.

"Rochelle is just worried for me," Tanika says. There's no shame in her voice at all, and she doesn't stop floating or look our way.

"Is that right?" Blaze asks, not moving from where he stands.

I look up at him—the sun has fully set and the water's warm—his dark and dangerous eyes are set on me.

Turning away from him, I look over at Tanika. "I need a drink, Tanika." I stand.

"Blaze, are you coming in?" Tanika asks.

He watches me as I walk past him, and keep walking to where Tanika laid our bag down to search for my phone. Looking back, I watch as Blaze kicks his shoes off, followed by his vest—which he carefully places with great respect carefully on the sand. His back is covered in ink as he pushes into the water and goes straight to Tanika. I can hear her giggle from here.

"She talks non-stop about you. You must be all right, huh?" Snow stands next to me, his eyes dropping straight to my breasts. "I mean… you have a nice rack and all." He winks.

I smile up at him. I like him. He's easy to be around, not as tense as the rest. A little more playful in his mannerisms.

"I'm all right," I say with a smile. He hands me a drink of beer and I take it with greedy hands.

"They…" I pause, thinking about what I want to ask and then nod out to Tanika. "How long has *that* been going on?" Snow looks down at me and smiles.

"Your girl not tell you everything?"

I look to the ground. "I've been, well… someone close to me died. I've not been with it lately."

Snow's face softens. "I'm sorry, girl."

I shrug. Nothing can be done about it now. The pain is still there when I close my eyes, but it's lessening, and I'm trying to work out how to live a life without them in it. Which is very unfair.

"They've been seeing each other for at least a month, but if you ask them, it's just sex." Snow chuckles. "Never seen prez so smitten before."

I look out to the water and watch as his arms go around Tanika and he lifts her up from the water and throws her backward. She laughs as she rises and swims back toward him.

"So, what's your story?"

"I'm more interested in yours," I reply, drinking down the last of my beer.

Snow grips my waist and turns me around. "Come and drink with us, and I'll tell you all about my wild ways." He winks, walking over to the table where Blaze was previously sitting. Snow smacks one of the dudes over the head, which makes him move, making room for me to sit. A few guys stare at my breasts without one bit of shame.

"Guys, this is girl."

I laugh at his silly introduction. "It's Rochelle."

"Okay…" Snow turns and looks at me. "Girl." He laughs and turns back to the group.

Shot glasses line the table with a bottle of rum in the middle.

"What are you playing?"

"Take a fucking drink," one yells. His jacket reads 'Prospect.' He was the one Snow hit to move.

"Basically, we ask you a question. If we think you're lying when you answer, you have to take a drink."

"That doesn't sound great…" My eyebrows pinch together. "That sounds a lot like a drinking game." As I speak the words, another carload pulls up with some girls and guys. A few make their way straight to the river while a girl with white-blonde hair walks over to us. Her hand goes around Snow's neck and she kisses him on the cheek.

"Sis, this is, girl."

She smiles at me and nods her head.

"It's Rochelle, actually."

"Semantics." Snow waves me off. "This is Harper. Harper, be nice to girl. She's Tanika's friend." Harper gives me a smile so large, I can't help but return it.

"My brother annoying you?" she asks, rubbing her palm over her brother's head. For some reason he takes it and only smiles as he starts pouring shots.

"Never." I smile, and then someone calls her name.

Harper offers us a wave before she runs off.

"Okay, girl, you're up first." *Of course, I am.* "When was the last time you had anal?"

"What happens if I don't answer?" I ask.

"You have a double shot."

"Okay, double shot me."

Snow throws his head back and laughs, then pours me two drinks. He goes next, and it's the prospect who asks him a question. Snow slides the drinks over to me, and I shoot them fast, feeling the slow burn of the rum on the way down.

"Snow, when was the last time you got hard from a girl?"

Everyone goes quiet, puzzled by his question.

Then a hand goes around my shoulders as he answers, "Right now. From staring at girl's tits." Then he proceeds to look down at my breasts.

I don't even bother covering them up, nor does it embarrass me for some reason. It's simply funny. "They are mighty fine, right?" I reply, smiling up at him.

A truck pulls up and I recognize it. My heart starts to beat faster and I reach for Snow's shot, downing it in one hit.

"Girl, you stealing my shit." Snow laughs, pouring another one. He doesn't need to have one, everyone believes his words, but he takes one anyway.

Harper runs up the hill and throws her arms around a pair of shoulders I recognize.

Snow turns and looks where I am then back to me.

"You know, Reap?" Snow asks.

I turn to him, confused by his words. I don't know him as that, maybe I'm drunk. I must be. Turning back, I listen to the next one in the game, but my eyes keep flicking to where he's located. Harper clings to him, and I wonder why he allows it.

"No," I manage to answer, realizing I never did answer if I know him.

"You sure, girl, you're staring pretty hard his way." Snow pauses, turns, and yells. "Reap, get your ass over here."

I hear Harper giggle as they turn while I try to hide behind Snow as they come closer, hoping he won't see me and I won't be able to see him.

But of course, I have no luck.

"Pretty girl," the name he likes to call me drips from his lips.

Oh fuck.

Chapter Six

ROCHELLE

Snow turns, and there's a smile still on his face, but I don't look toward that voice. Instead, I reach for another shot, downing it before I tap my fingers on the table, hoping and praying Tanika comes back soon so we can leave.

"You know, girl here, Reap?" Of course Snow asks Marcus that.

"Girl?" he says, confused.

I still don't look his way, then someone next to me moves, and I know it's him that slides in because his smell is something I've dreamed about for weeks. Dark and musky, just like him. "You must be mistaken, it's pretty girl, right, Snow?" he jokes, and I look up at Marcus. And right at that moment, I wish I didn't. I wish I pretended he never existed in the first place, because when I look up into his hazel eyes staring at me, and his dark curly messy hair as if he's just showered, I want to run my hand through the locks and pull them so his lips smash against mine.

"Reap?" I ask, watching him for a reaction.

He smirks, and my heart beats hard in my chest.

"The boys call me, Reap," he answers coldly.

"Damn right we do." Snow cheers and throws his hand over my shoulders, pulling me back to him, snuggling me under his arm.

"Reap, why don't you come for a swim?" Harper walks over, and I stiffen under Snow's arm.

"No," he answers, his eyes glued to Snow's hand touching me. "Remove your arm from her, Snow."

Snow straightens over me, but his arm is still around me.

I turn to look at Marcus. His lips are thinned as he sits there with his hands clenched and a look of death to match his hand tattoo as he stares at Snow, who doesn't remove his arm.

Harper looks between us, unsure of what to do.

"You claimed her, Reap?" Snow asks, his voice has lost all its playfulness, and I get the feeling you never want to be on the bad side of Snow.

"Yes. Now tell him, pretty girl. Who do you belong to?"

I pull away from Snow. Sitting up straighter, I look at Marcus and smile before standing. He watches me with intent, but makes no move to stop me as I head straight to where Tanika has her arms wrapped around Blaze while they bounce around in the water.

"Tanika…" I call out. She looks up from the water at the sound of my voice. Blaze doesn't even look my way, he simply keeps on kissing her neck.

Before I can utter another word, my feet are lifted from the ground and I'm pressed against a hard body. I know who it is straight away. Marcus turns me in his arms, as if I weigh nothing, so now I'm pressed against his taut muscles.

"Why are you here, pretty girl?"

"Let me go."

Marcus holds me tighter, and I can feel him everywhere. He starts walking me backward until I feel the cold of the water touch my feet.

"Why?" he asks as if it's a serious question.

"Because..." No other words leave my mouth. I don't have an excuse, because I don't need one. And somehow, I have become that girl who loses her train of thought around a beautiful man.

"Do you want me to kiss you again?"

My ass is submerged in the water as he keeps on walking. He's fully dressed, but that doesn't stop him.

"No," I reply, my hands by my sides.

"Rochelle..." My name is called, but I don't turn to look at Tanika. My eyes stay glued on Marcus'—and what pretty eyes they are. Haunted, possessive, and gorgeous.

"You do, but you now realize I'm bad for you. Don't you, pretty girl?" He says what I am thinking.

"Yes." I don't bother lying.

"But you were persistent." Marcus smirks. He lowers his hands so he isn't gripping me anymore and grabs my ass cheeks, holding me to him. I wrap my legs around his waist in the water, not thinking as we stare at each other.

Body heat makes me boiling hot, despite the coolness of the water, the intensity of his gaze, which is turning me on.

"Now I see the light," I say, smiling.

One hand leaves my ass and snakes up my front until he touches the strings of my bikini and pulls at them.

"If I didn't care about sharing you, I would pull this so I could stare at your pretty tits. I bet your nipples are the perfect shade of pink."

I blush at his words and say, "Don't you dare."

Marcus moves me, just a fraction, and I feel him between my legs, and my pelvis pushes forward on instinct. He smiles when I do this.

"I'm afraid now you're back, I won't be able to say no tonight."

"Just tonight?" I ask him.

"You're so needy. I wonder if you're the same in bed." Marcus pushes back on me and I do the same. Soon, my body is moving up and down on his cock, even though his jeans are still on, and so are my bikini bottoms. But that doesn't stop us, the friction making my eyes roll to the back of my head as my head drops, my hair skimming along the water as I come close to the perfect amount of friction.

Marcus' hand slides between my breasts, and then he pinches my nipple through my bikini. My hips don't stop moving, my body taking from his what it wants, what it's wanted from Marcus since the moment I met him. It happens fast, and my hands leave him and grip my hair, but before I can open my mouth to scream, I'm lifted, and lips hot as fire burn me as he takes control of my head and my mouth.

There's no use pulling back from him, it's completely useless. Because as I come down from my dry humping orgasm, I want him back on me, and more importantly, in me.

I'm becoming addicted.

It's a bad thing.

He breaks the kiss. "You are the most beautiful thing to watch when you come."

"Rochelle..." I turn my head away from Marcus to see Tanika staring at me in question. I suppose I've kept some things from her too.

Pushing away from him, I head to the water's edge and Tanika follows. Now alone in the water, looking back over my shoulder, he watches me but makes no move to come to me.

"Who is that?" she asks.

"Can we go now?"

"But they're just about to cook the food, and I want to get to know your friend, who you quite conveniently happened to not tell me about."

Fuck!

The food is cooked, and I stay seated next to Tanika, not looking for Marcus, even if my eyes try to find him when I tell myself no.

"Eat, girl, the food is delicious." Snow shoves a plate in front of my face, smiling.

I look down at the salad and meat and start picking at it. When a hand touches my thigh, I jump and look up to see Marcus now seated next to me. I attempt to push him away but have no luck, he simply moves his hand closer until it's touching between my legs.

Goosebumps tickle my skin as he leans in closer to me.

"I bet I can make you come again." I shut my legs, squeezing them tighter. He chuckles next to me and removes his hand.

"So, how do you two know each other?" Tanika asks, looking between us.

"It was a bad mistake," I tell her.

"I warned her, over and over again," he says. "But she never listened."

Tanika looks at me with her eyebrows squeezed together as she takes in my reaction.

"Maybe she doesn't want the Reap," Snow says, laughing.

Tanika looks over to Marcus. "Why do they call you, Reap?" she asks.

I cringe.

"I own the crematorium," he replies.

What? I look at him, surprised, having no idea. "You own it?" I question.

"You've never asked." He shrugs, turning away.

"And sometimes Reap works for us," the prospect says, which earns him a smack across the back of his head from Snow.

Everyone goes quiet after such a few words being exchanged. Tanika plays with her food on her plate as I stand. Marcus stands with me. I turn away and reach for my bag, pulling out my cover-up and sliding it over my arms. Marcus watches my every move.

"Do you want me to take you home?" he asks. I look back at Tanika to see her leaning on Blaze, and I know she won't want to leave anytime soon.

"Yes, please." Marcus smiles at my words, reaches for my bag, and starts to walk away. I head over and hug Tanika from the back. "I'm going home. You stay." She turns, but I shake my head. "It's okay. I'll message you when I get back home."

"You leaving, girl?" Snow calls out. I smile and nod my head. "Come back again, okay?"

"Will do." Turning and walking away, butterflies fly freakishly in my belly as I walk toward him. Marcus is leaning on the passenger side with his door open and waiting for me to get in. My bag's already inside.

"I never took you for a gentleman," I say to him, climbing in.

The window is down, so when he shuts it, he leans inside. "I'm no gentleman, I can assure you. A man like me is not a man you take home to meet your parents, pretty girl. I'm the one you fuck in the back of your car and then go on your way." He leaves me with those words as he pushes off, rounds the truck, and slides into the driver's seat.

He takes off in silence, only a slight hum from the radio can be heard as he drives.

When we get closer to my house he speaks, and I turn to give him my full attention, "You shouldn't be around them. You should stay away."

"You're around them."

"You're a good girl. Good girls get ruined."

"There you are with that phrase again, *good girl*… you give me a headache." I turn back and stare out the window as he drives down my street. As he comes to a stop, I climb out without thanking him, and he leans across but speaks from the driver side, "Aren't you going to invite me in?"

I flip him off, not even looking as I go inside. Reaching for my cell, I text Tanika to let her know I'm home and she replies instantly.

Tomorrow, I expect to know the REAL details of you and Reap.

I laugh at her words.

His name is Marcus, and I will tell you everything over breakfast, your treat BTW.

Her reply is almost instant.

Marcus, shmarcus. Who cares? DEETS WOMAN!

Lying in bed, all I think about are his lips and the way his body makes me feel—more alive than I've ever felt in my life.

Chapter Seven

ROCHELLE

Tanika rocks up at my house before I'm even out of bed, a coffee in each hand and a smile that could light up the skies.

"You are way too happy for this early," I say, rubbing my eyes while putting on the last of my clothes. Pulling my hair back into a high ponytail, I take the coffee and drink it as if it holds magical powers.

"I had a great night… and great sex," she says, her eyes not quite meeting mine.

"Blaze?" I ask, she smiles. "What is the deal with you two? Snow said it's been going on for about a month now?" Tanika's face pulls some worry lines on her forehead, and she looks down. "Tell me, I want to know."

"I kind of ran into them, at a bar. And, well, I just haven't been able to stay away. We aren't exclusive, and I told him whatever this is, is just sex. I don't want anything more. I fall too hard and fast, you know this," she says with an eye roll. Her last guy she was engaged to within a month, the one before that she let move in after a week. She loved them all, she tells me, but I am not so sure how true that is—lust maybe.

"So, you aren't in love with this one?" I ask as we walk out and head for breakfast. We climb into her car and head to the café around the corner.

"No, don't jinx me either. I like him. A lot. But he's way too dangerous for me, too much for me."

"How?"

"Blaze knows what he wants, that scares me."

We walk into the café and order straight away, knowing exactly what we want—pancakes and berries for me, and waffles for Tanika.

"What about Marcus? And don't tell me you don't like him. I saw you two together. Fuck, we all saw it… it was fucking hot." She fans her face. "The way he grabbed you, kissed you, tasted you."

I smile at her words. "He's trouble," I say, sitting back, crossing my arms over my chest.

"Did you meet him at the funeral?" she asks, saying the last word in more of a whisper.

"No, before it, actually."

Her eyebrows pinch together. "How?"

"He was there when Mom and Dad were organizing the proceedings."

Tanika's hand reaches for mine, covering it and giving it a gentle squeeze. She pulls back when the food arrives.

"You like him, don't you?" Tanika takes a sip of her drink.

"No, of course not. He's—"

"Oh, you suck at lying. Totally suck." She laughs.

"No, I don't."

"Is it because he's nothing like your exes? Not a surfer-looking dude who tells you everything you want to hear simply to sleep with you?"

Damn, this girl knows me well.

"I tried to sleep with him. Twice, actually. It failed both times."

"Oh my God… well, that doesn't explain yesterday, then."

I shrug. "I don't even understand yesterday. I didn't even know Marcus was going to be there. I've avoided him for over a month."

"Was that painful for you?" She chuckles, and I withstand the urge to throw my food at her head, but it's a difficult internal battle to refrain.

"He's, well, let's just say… what he does, isn't something I am all that comfortable with."

"You mean in the crematorium?" I nod. "Okay, but you met him there. What did you expect?"

I place my fork on the plate, my appetite now completely gone. "He took me inside, to scare me off."

"Okay, so…"

"He started cutting a hand off one of the dead bodies while I was there." I watch as she puts her fork down too. Her elbows come to rest on the table as her head is placed on her hands, and I wait before she speaks again.

"Holy shit, Roch, that's…" she takes a deep breath. "That's fucked-up."

"Try being me. That shit was fucked-up to see."

"So, you don't want him?"

"Oh, no…" I shake my head. "That's the problem, I do want him. No denying that. It's just he's so dark. So damn intense. Not one thing about him is light."

We get up to leave and pay the account, leaving a tip in the payment folder on the table. Quickly, we walk back to the car, heading back to my house.

"So, I guess the question is… can you have him without wanting that part of your life with him?"

"Like just sex?"

She nods. "I don't know if I want him for more than sex. Definitely not a relationship, which I doubt he would want anyway."

"The boys told me about him." I turn in my seat as Tanika drives. "And let's just say, they warned me to stay away from him. Snow said he has demons bigger than the devil himself."

I sigh. Of course, he does. Of course.

"Ummm… Rochelle, is that him?"

Looking up, I see his truck parked out the front as he stands at my door, one foot crossed over the other while waiting. Marcus' hands are in his pockets, and he has on a white, long-sleeved shirt rolled up to his elbows with black pants.

He's fine.

So fucking fine.

I wonder what he looks like with that shirt off. As a matter of fact, all of it off.

"Yep."

"Okay, well, do you want me to come in?"

I reach for the door handle.

I am unsure. *Should she?*

"No. I got this. Thanks for breakfast." Pushing out of the car, he doesn't move until I reach him.

"Marcus. Or should I call you Reap now?"

He pushes off from leaning against the wall and steps closer to me. I can smell him, and my body instantly wants to gravitate toward him for him to touch me.

"I prefer Marcus coming from your lips."

I cross my arms over my chest, defiantly. "Why are you here?"

"You grew on me."

"Did I?" I ask, raising an eyebrow. "Pity, I've outgrown you."

"You have not. I bet…" he steps closer, his hand coming to my hip, "… if I touched you right, I could make you beg for it. I could taste you, and you wouldn't be able to stop me."

He's right, but I don't care. He doesn't need to know that. Fuck him.

"Don't you touch me." I step back, putting distance back between us.

He smirks, and I want to wipe that smirk off with a slap. The man is infuriating and he knows he's right, and I've just confirmed it.

"I came to invite you out. The boys are having another party tonight. This time at their clubhouse…" He pauses. "Your friend will be there. But she isn't allowed to invite anyone. I, on the other hand…"

"Go with you?" I scoff. "You did hear the part where I don't want to be around you anymore, right?"

"Oh, you mean the part where you outgrew me?"

"Yes! Yes, that part."

Marcus touches me, and it's soft and subtle, but it still burns all the same. Pulling my arm away from his touch, he smiles as if he knows what it does to me.

"Come… I promise to show you a good time."

"Like the last time? No. I think I'll pass and stay away from all things dead, and that involves you." I go to sidestep him to unlock my house, but he comes up behind me and pushes himself on my back. Then he goes to my neck again and breathes heavily—he's always at my neck. It's my kryptonite, and he seems to know it.

"I won't show you anything that's dead. Come with me."

"No, I have a busy night."

"You don't. You suck at lying." Pushing my door open, I turn to face him once I've stepped inside. "I'll wait here all day until you say yes."

"I don't want to come with you."

"You do. Now, say yes and I'll be back to collect you at eight."

"No."

Marcus nods and then pushes inside of my house. He heads straight for my leather couch and sits on it, crossing one leg over his knee. "I have all day, as you know. My work is only at night."

I shudder at his words. "You need to leave."

"Call your friend. Ask her if she will be there."

I huff at his words. Placing my purse on my kitchen countertop, I say, "I don't want to because I don't want to go."

"You do. You need to live a little, and I can make you do that."

"You can, can you?" I chuckle at his words while shaking my head.

"Yes, and I can make you orgasm, which we've already established. So, say yes and I'll leave." Marcus' lips quirk and he knows he will win.

"Yes." I smile at him.

He stands and walks over to me. Touching my chin, he lifts it and leans down. "I will be here, and if you aren't here, I *will* find you." He places a brief kiss on my lips before he walks out the door, shutting it behind him.

Fuck!

Grabbing my cell from my bag, I ring Tanika straight away.

"Well, I take it you didn't fuck him, considering you're calling me."

"Is there a party tonight? One that you will be at?"

She goes silent.

"Tanika?" I ask, thinking she's hung up. Pulling my phone away from my ear, I look and see the line is still connected. "Tanika?" I say, louder.

"I'm not sure it's something you would want to go to."

"Marcus invited me."

"Of course he did." Tanika huffs into the phone. "Look… I can't invite you. It's not something strangers walk into, and I'm not a member of the club, so everything about it is off-limits. I have to be asked by a member. But I know Reap can ask, so come. Come, hang out with me."

"You said that last time, and the whole time you were with Blaze."

"I like him," she says.

"I know. Okay, I'll come."

"Yeah," she screams. "Oh, and dress sexy. This place… well, most girls wear nothing." She pauses. "Okay, bye." She hangs up, not giving me an opportunity to question what she's just told me that *most girls wear nothing?*

Chapter Eight

MARCUS

"She's coming, so tell *him* to stay away," I say to Blaze who pulls a cigar from his lips.

"No. You want her, that's fine, I'll respect that. But Snow wants her too." He smirks.

"You're my brother, asshole." I shake my head at Blaze. "Snow's my life brother, you are my blood. There is a difference." I clutch my fists together and take a deep breath. My cell alarms, informing me it's almost time to go collect my newest little number.

We had different fathers growing up and I'm older than him, but that doesn't mean he doesn't think he's boss. He always fucking does, and he always fucking lets me know.

"Reap…" I turn to his nickname for me that's stuck over the years and has become my biker road name. "If you kill him, it will make me very fucking mad," he says, lighting the cigar again.

"Good, I like it when I have someone to hit. What better opponent than you?"

"Asshole," he says with a shake of his head as I walk out.

I don't hang around to see what else Blaze has to say. Driving to her house, I make it there in record time. Rochelle's lights are on. I slide out of my truck just as she reaches the front door. She's wearing a short skirt, showcasing her perfectly tanned legs, her stomach is on display from a shirt that stops above her belly button, and there's so much cleavage that I want to get lost in.

Cracking my neck from side to side, I step up to her. "Go and get changed."

"No."

"Change," I demand.

"No. Take me or leave me." Her hand goes to her naked hip, and she smirks.

"Fucking take you, all right," I mutter, stepping away, wondering why on earth she makes me this way. How can this little redhead inflict such strong reactions and emotions from me—I've never felt this way.

"I heard that," she says, breezing past me smelling like fucking flowers. *Fucking flowers.*

Opening the truck door for her, Rochelle climbs in, and when she does, the bottom of her ass is on display. The woman is trying to kill me. She's only wearing a G-string, and my cock immediately strains in my trousers.

"You will be the death of me," I say, shutting her door.

When I slide into my side, she turns to me, her pale pink lips smiling. "At least then you won't have to deal with tearing your body to bits like you do to all the other bodies."

"I don't do that to all of them," I say while putting the car in gear and pulling out into traffic.

"Oh, so I got the special treatment?" She gags.

"Yes… I knew it would scare you. It worked. You're too pretty for this ugly world. But yet, here I am, wanting to drag you down the rabbit hole with me, pretty girl."

"What a fucking rabbit hole," she mutters back to me.

"I heard that."

"Good, I meant for you to." Pulling away, she fidgets as she sits there, and I can feel she's doing everything possible to avoid me. To evade looking my way.

"How was your day?" I ask.

Rochelle starts laughing and then she snorts.

I can't help the smirk that pulls on my lips just from that single action.

"Really, you're asking me about my day?"

"It's either that or I pull over, yank you out of the truck, and fuck you up against it," I answer her with a shrug.

"Okay, yeah." She nods her head. "Well, my day was fine."

"You sure you don't want the other option? Because I'm up for it." I ask, raising my eyebrows.

"No. No, I do not."

Pulling my truck to a stop at the lights, my eyes rove over her legs, which are bare.

"Your outfit says otherwise."

Angry eyes turn on me, and my dick twitches at the sight.

Fuck, she's hot.

And too good.

She's too good.

The girls I fuck are dirty. I prefer them dirty because they know what to expect.

Nothing.

"Oh, so you are one of those assholes, are you? Where if I wear something short, that immediately means I'm asking to be fucked?" Angry eyes stare at me.

When she says the word 'fucked' it takes everything in me to not do just that—

fuck her into the middle of next week.

"No, what I'm saying is you know I want to fuck you. So, you wear an outfit that makes me want to fuck you ten times more. It's really unfair to my cock, which is straining against my fucking pants right now."

Rochelle's eyes drop to my pants as I start the truck again.

"I've seen enough cocks to last me for this weekend. Do not get that thing out."

Her words make me sit up straighter.

"Who's fucking cock have you seen?"

"Snow's." She answers as if it's obvious.

"If you fuck him, I'll kill him," I tell her, pulling up to the acreage where the party is going to be held. *Again, where the fuck is this possessiveness coming from?* "And you know I can get rid of the body easily," I say, throwing the door open and walking off, leaving her in my truck.

I'm angry and I'm unsure why.

Chapter Nine

ROCHELLE

THE BASTARD STORMS OFF SO FAST, I GET WHIPLASH, BUT REMAIN IN THE TRUCK. I see everyone sitting on hay bales, girls walking around with no tops on, and men reaching for them, touching their tits as if they have the luxury to do so. I don't want to be here and I told him that. Yet, here I am, in his truck as he storms off like he has a rocket up his ass.

Getting out of the truck on my own, because clearly he isn't going to help me, I stand and watch him. Marcus comes to a stop, and soon I see his body tense and his fist flies towards someone's head.

Blaze stands and pulls Marcus back, and then proceeds to push him.

Blaze notices me and waves me over.

I walk but my feet feel heavy with each step. When I finally reach them, Marcus' lips are curled in anger, his fists are clenched on each side of his body. Looking past him, Blaze turns, his eyes are blazing in fury at me.

"Calm him the fuck down." Blaze pushes Marcus, and Marcus doesn't move at the gesture. Blaze simply shakes his head and walks off.

"What the fuck was that?" I ask. Confused, looking back, I now see it was Snow he punched. "You hit Snow? Why would you do that?"

His eyes are angry slits, his lips are turned into a snarl while he simply glares at me.

I take a step back, not knowing if I am next, while he runs his hand through his hair, looking away.

"I need to fuck someone."

I throw my hands up in the air and take a step back. "That ship has sailed here, don't look at me."

"You don't want me to drive my cock into your wet pussy, pretty girl?"

"No," I answer immediately.

"Your loss." Marcus walks back to Snow and he passes him a beer, and they both sit as if nothing happened.

I check around, unsure of what I should even do. This place is a good twenty minutes out from my house, and no Uber drivers will come this far. My best bet will be a cab. Then I look up, searching around for Tanika who's meant to be here.

Walking in a little farther, Marcus doesn't look my way, but Snow does, nodding his head to me before he turns back to the conversation. I feel overdressed when I see everyone else and what they have on—which is next to nothing.

Pushing my way through the girls, some giggle, and some even stare at me wondering what the hell I am doing here. I'm wondering that too. Long, black hair sits in the corner, and I make my way to her. Tanika has her back to me, and when I reach her, she turns around with a smile.

"You came." Her arms go around me and I can smell she's clearly drunk, the alcohol permeating from her is that strong. "I missed you so much," Tanika purrs, touching my hair. I left it down thinking it would look sexy. Now I wish I had it up as she strokes it. So strange.

"How do I get out of here?"

"Girl, you leaving?" I turn with Tanika hanging off me.

Blaze walks in, picks up Tanika, and throws her over his shoulder.

"Where are you taking her?"

Blaze stops, his shoulders tense with a giggling Tanika hanging there, her hands touching his ass.

"She's going to bed," he says, then walks away.

"He hates me." I cringe.

"Aww… it's 'cause you're confusing his brother is all." I look up at Snow, confused. *Is he talking about Marcus?* "No, no girl, not me. The one with the dark locks." Snow chuckles and points his beer to where Marcus is sitting with a girl on his lap. I shiver just looking and turn back to Snow.

"How do I get out of here?" I ask. Snow holds up his hands, beer in one of them, and backs away. "You're hot and all, but I like not tasting my own blood." Snow chuckles, then walks off.

Deciding how long it would take me to walk home, I contemplate it for a while, but then decide it's ridiculous. I didn't want to come in the first place, and yet here I am. Dragged by a man who I should have known better than to follow.

Walking over to Marcus, I stand directly in front of him. He doesn't have a drink, but the girl that's sitting on his lap does. And to make matters worse, she death glares me when she looks up and I have my arms crossed over my chest. "Take me home!"

Marcus says nothing, in fact it's tits that speaks. "Get the fuck out of the road."

"No. Now get off my fucking ride, so he can take me home."

"Bitch… what did you just say?" She stands and takes a step toward me at the same time as I take a step toward her, but my hands are shaking.

"I said, get the fuck off of him, so he can get his fucking ass up and take me home, bitch. Did I stutter? Was I not clear?"

She throws her drink to the ground, and I see it in her eyes when she decides to lash out at me. Luckily for her, I grew up with male cousins and duck just in time. Then I get straight back up and hit her hard in her pretty, overly made-up fucking face, making her fall back on his lap. She screams and comes at me again, but this time Marcus grips her waist and holds her back.

My hand is hurting, but adrenaline is pumping through me and I am more than a little angry. "Take me fucking home, you asshole," I say with my hands clenched to my sides while staring him down.

The girl screams something I don't quite understand, and Marcus lifts her to the side, depositing her onto someone else's lap before he stands in front of me.

"I think I just fell in love."

What the fuck!

His words make my fists unclench.

What did he just say?

"Come to think of it… I don't fucking love, I just want to fuck you." Marcus leans down and whispers, "Want to fuck all that adrenaline out of your system, pretty girl?"

I push him and turn, walking toward his truck. His footsteps follow, and I still hear that bitch screaming at me, but it becomes quieter and darker and darker the closer we get to his truck. When I reach it, he's directly behind me; his hands come to my arm, and he turns me. Then his body is pushed against mine, his lips slam onto mine, and I moan. Despite being angry at him, I fucking moan at the feel of him, and I can't help it. I step up on my tippy toes so I can feel him right there, as his fingers slide down and lift my skirt until his hand cups my sex, then he slips one finger in. Pushing it in and out, he devours my lips.

"So fucking pretty…"

I ignore his words and let him fuck me with his fingers. Marcus pulls back, and I reach for him straight away, my hands going to his shirt and lifting it, so my hands can touch his bare skin. I feel like a crazed animal as I touch him, sliding my nails down his chest and pulling him straight back to me. He pulls his cock free, then grips both my hips and lifts. I reach between us, pulling my G-string to the side as he lowers me, and in pure fucking ecstasy he slides straight in.

"Fuck."

"That's right, pretty girl, ride my fucking cock."

I do. I fucking slide up and down, my hands leaving his bare skin and pulling at his shirt until it bundles at his neck. He drops one hand away from me and slides his hand out then followed by the other, the whole time his movements never stop.

Each thrust and push is filling me so much, like I've never been filled before.

My nails dig into his bare skin as I drop my head on his neck. I lick him just to taste him—he's salty and sweet—then I bite and suck. So many emotions are fucking with me as he takes me. He doesn't apologize either for his fingers digging so hard into my hips that I know they will bruise, or the way when we're both close he pushes me back so my head slams on the truck and I feel the vibration run through me.

I don't care, though.

I don't fucking care.

I come, my hands leaving him as he grips them both, my legs are wrapped tight around his waist as he pins me to the truck, pushing me, so my back hits the edge of the hood and I lay there lost, in ecstasy, as he finishes.

That was, quite simply, the best sex of my fucking life.

"Knew your pussy would love my cock."

And he's ruined it.

Sitting up, I slide up the hood of his truck and away from him.

"Take me home, Marcus."

"I was planning to." He smirks, tucking his cock back into his pants, then reaches for his shirt, sliding it over his head, not even bothering to look at me again.

―

We don't speak. What's the point? I have no words for him, and he clearly got what he wanted. But then again, so did I. I wanted to fuck him that first time, and now I have. My G-string snapped and is ruined but it still sits around my waist. I don't want to take it off until I am in my own home.

"I'd like to do that again," he says, coming to a stop.

I scoff and get out, not even bothering to answer that ridiculous statement.

"Tomorrow, then," he yells out, and I know he's teasing me.

"Fuck you."

"You did that, pretty girl. And soon, you will again."

When I get to my door and unlock it, I slide my G-string from under my skirt while he watches me from the darkness of his truck, and then I take a step out of it.

"This can be your reminder of me." I look down at my G-string, then back to him. "And forget where I live," I say, closing my door and locking it.

Running up to my room, I look out through my window. It's in complete darkness so he can't see me. Marcus gets out of the truck, steps up my porch while my heart races as he does, but he doesn't stay long. Just enough time to pick up what he wanted and walk back to his truck while sliding my G-string into his pocket before he takes off.

Maybe that wasn't the smartest move.

Then again, I've not managed a lot of smart moves lately when it comes to him.

And I don't even know his last name.

Chapter Ten

ROCHELLE

I don't see him Sunday, and for that I'm thankful, because if he came to me and touched me, I know I'd want a repeat of what we did. Despite how much I *don't* want to want him, I know I *do* want him. Damn, that's confusing. He's the leading man in every one of my dreams, stealing me and making me his.

Staying inside on Sunday, locking my house up was my best option, and I needed time to get my head semi-straight.

The rest of the week after that goes slowly, and I don't hear from Tanika until Thursday. And even then, it's just a message asking me how the rest of my weekend went. I bet she doesn't even remember seeing me that night, she was that drunk.

Martin annoys me almost all week while I help him work on a case. I've contemplated studying law myself with how much I have learned from him, and how much of the work I actually do for him as well. Also, I really love law, it stimulates my mind.

"Send this to the papers," he says on Friday, dropping a written-up script in front of me. I briefly run my eyes over it and freeze at the names.

EXILE MC—IS OUR CITY SAFE?
PRESS RELEASE

The Exile Motorcycle Club has been under investigation now for over two months for murder and missing persons. We suspect they're also dealing in drugs. Is our city safe with this outlaw motorcycle gang running free in the area…

What the fuck! The article goes on and on about what the club has supposedly done and how unsafe the community feels. Honestly, they can't print this or make a story out of this if it's not true. Standing, I walk into Martin's office. He has a coffee cup to his mouth and he looks up with cream all over his top lip. *Goddamn, what a waste of space.*

"Can you say this without evidence?" I ask him.

Martin wipes his face. "Do you have an issue, Rochelle? You know our job is to make the suspects look as guilty as possible."

Damn if he isn't dodgy—he couldn't lay straight in bed if he tried.

"Is anything in this article true?" I ask again, waving it around like it's burning my fingers.

"The client says it is."

"Who's that?" I ask because I know all of his clients. I'm the only person stupid enough to work for him. So it must be something he is doing on his own.

"Is this your job now… questioning your boss?" Martin asks as his hand slams down on the desk. If I didn't have a house to pay for, I would quit here and now. But I do.

"No, I was just wondering."

Martin waves a hand at me. "Get lost, Rochelle. Unless you have a conflict of interest you need to tell me about?" I freeze at his words. "Well?" he asks.

"No, I just want to know their story."

"If you know what's good for you, you will stay far away from them. They *are* bad news."

Shutting the door, I walk back out to my desk and tear the paper up before I close down my computer to leave for the day. I can't send that out—there has to be some truth in it for the papers to publish it.

"Pretty girl," I yelp when I hear that name whispered at the entrance to my office. Marcus is standing there dressed in black jeans and a white shirt rolled up to his elbows. Why does he have to look so good? And why am I excited to see him?

"For someone who pushed me away at the start, you sure as shit show up a lot," I say, shaking my head and turning as I try not to look his way.

"Maybe I woke up and smelled the pretty girl on me."

"You mean the roses, right?"

"If you say so. I mean, I haven't tasted you yet, so I don't know if it's more along the lines of roses or tulips."

I groan at his words.

"Can I help you?" Martin asks, standing at his office door.

Marcus doesn't answer him, so I do while Martin simply stares at him.

"He's here for me. I'm just finishing up," I say.

Martin stands taller, and I shake my head at him and reach for my stuff, then walk over to Marcus who doesn't move until I reach for his hand.

"See you Monday, Martin." I wave backward over my shoulder, pulling Marcus with me.

"You will," is all Martin says before we get out the door.

The minute we're out, I drop Marcus' hand and turn to face him. He's already watching me. "Why are you here?" I unlock my car and throw everything in, then turn to face him again. Marcus takes a tentative step toward me and pushes me against the car, it feels like déjà fucking vu.

My hands push him back and he smirks, but he does step back.

"I think we need a repeat."

"You're serious right now?" I ask.

"Yep, I want you. No denying that." Marcus looks down to the tent in his pants, and I roll my eyes.

"I'm busy. No time for you this weekend. At all."

"Where are you going?"

"To the Gold Coast with my sister. All weekend."

"I can come. Meet you there?"

I laugh at him. "You're joking, right?"

Marcus scratches his face, and the look that takes over it, it's as if he's just realized what he's said.

"Yes, I fucking am." Then he walks away.

Leaving me standing there confused as fuck.

～

"You aren't wearing that, are you?" my sister Kat asks, eyeing me up and down as she holds Annabelle in her arms. I look down at my dress, which has a slit up the side and leaves nothing to the imagination.

"Maybe you should live a little, let me take Annabelle and you go out tonight. And let me dress you," I say, showcasing my leg a little bit more.

"No, last time I did something stupid…" she trails off and looks at Annabelle. "Well, I got my best gift from your mistake. But I also learned my lesson, thank you very much."

Kat pulls Annabelle up on her hip. "You just have to play it safer." She eyes me.

"You know I speak to Tanika, too, right?" Kat's blue eyes look at me. They're the same color as mine. "I know you aren't playing it safe with a particular man, whom I want photos of by the way."

I wave my hands at her face. "No can do. That ship has sailed, and it's over."

"Was it fun, though?"

"It was a headache and a nightmare, plus the best orgasms I have ever had."

"What I wouldn't give for one of those." Kat laughs.

We get seated on the boat. Annabelle falls asleep in her mother's arms as the boat starts, and servers come around to serve our first course.

"Let me take her, you eat first."

"No, I like it when she's like this. It tells me she will always love me, no matter what." Kat kisses the top of her head, and I start eating as she begins using one hand. Not once complaining or asking me to take her. By the last course, I take Annabelle despite Kat's protests, and Annabelle stays asleep in my arms.

"Tanika said he's one fine specimen. What's so wrong with him?"

"Don't you mean what's right with him?"

Kat laughs and shrugs. "That too."

"He's confusing for one, and he isn't relationship material. It's obvious. I want kids one day… I don't think I could ever have kids with a man like him," I tell her the truth.

Kat looks to Annabelle then back to me. "Don't base a relationship, or even fun, on what you think you want. Wants change. Needs change. I never wanted a child, and now I'd be lost without her." Kat takes Annabelle back from me and I smile. Because she's right. Kat never wanted kids, yet here she is, one of the best mothers I know.

"I don't think he's safe to be around. I mean, his brother is the president of Exile MC for God's sake." We stand as the boat comes to a stop and make our way off. Our hotel is right on the water, so we don't have far to walk.

"Okay, stay away. Far, far, away. I heard about those boys. They're dangerous."

"Tanika is obsessed with the president."

"Of course she is. Tanika loves dick," Kat says with an eye roll.

I bump her shoulder slightly because she has Annabelle still in her arms. "Hey, be nice."

Kat and Tanika have a weird relationship. Kat likes her but thinks she's not stable. I think we balance each other out.

"I am. I'm nice to Tanika because you love her. No more, no less."

"I love you more, though," I say, leaning my head on her other shoulder as we make our way to the room. When we reach the room, we swipe in, and I see my cell ringing on the table. I forgot to take it with me, and when I pick it up, Tanika's name is flashing on the screen.

"Hey."

"Ohhh, so now you answer," she slurs into the phone.

"Tanika…"

"Yeah, yeah, don't say my name like that. What? You better than me all of a sudden?"

I look over at Kat who lays Annabelle down in her bed. She mouths to me 'what's wrong?' I just shake my head and step out on to the balcony.

"Are you drunk?"

"Of course, I am. Amongst other things," she whines.

"Why?" Tanika never used to be like this. Granted, she likes to drink, but she didn't do it often, and I hate to think what 'other things' actually means.

"Because my heart is fucking broken and this is the way to fix it," she screams.

"Tan, put the phone down and go to bed," I hear.

"Who's that?"

"Oh, Blaze. He thinks he's my knight or some shit. But he won't fuck me anymore, now he found out why I wanted to fuck him so bad."

None of her words are making any sense, at all.

"Can you pass Blaze the phone, please?"

"What, you want to fuck him too?" she snipes, and then she disappears, and I hear her speaking, "My friend, Rochelle, wants to fuck you. Tell her no."

"Hey."

"Blaze," I say his name, but he doesn't speak. "What's wrong with her?"

"If you were around, you'd know." Then he hangs up on me. I look at it, not knowing what he's talking about. Tanika and I always share everything, granted the last month or two maybe not so much, but still.

"What's going on?" Kat asks, coming out from behind me and hugging her arms around my waist.

I shrug. "It's Tan. I don't really know. Can't make heads or tails out of that phone call."

She sighs. "I told you. It's always something." Then Kat walks away.

I try calling Tanika back, again and again.

Finally, it's picked up.

"Pretty girl."

I gasp and look back at the phone to check the number I called. "Where is she?"

"Blaze handed me the phone and said I need to take this call. Wasn't going to until I saw your pretty face all over the screen…" He pauses, his breathing is heavy into the phone. "I've been thinking about your sweet cunt squeezing my cock. Have you, pretty girl? Want a repeat? I'll drive to you."

Butterflies take flight in my stomach. He knows where I am, as I told him, which is just over an hour away from home.

"No."

"You don't sound so sure. I can be quick. I need a taste."

"Find someone else," I tell him, just then a girl giggles into the phone.

"I have someone else on my lap right now, pretty girl, but it's you I want."

"Where is Tanika?"

"My brother put her to bed. Seems he has to do that a lot lately. You should pay closer attention to your friend. She's screaming for help, and this isn't the place she should be looking."

"Where should she be looking?" I ask.

"Anywhere but here." My hand grips the railing. "My offer stands, I can be with you soon, just say the word."

"Is she okay?"

"Is that your word?" I stay silent. "Yes, my brother looks after her. God only knows why."

"Thank you." I end the call, and when I turn around, Kat's standing in the doorway.

"Do you need to go?"

"Tomorrow. I'll go tomorrow."

Kat only nods as we head back inside and climb into bed.

Chapter Eleven

ROCHELLE

I head straight for the clubhouse. It's quiet when I pull up, but the large gates open for me. I feel out of place, like I shouldn't be here, but I need to talk to her.

Why didn't she tell me anything last weekend when we were together? Knocking on the barn door behind the bar area, I wait. No one comes, so I knock again, this time harder until I hear footsteps. Eyeing the door, I see the crest that's similar to the one on Blaze's back—a tiger with a snake wrapped around it and then coming out of its mouth. A girl with white-blonde hair pulls the door open, and I recognize her as Harper, Snow's sister. She looks me over and crosses her arms over her chest.

"You can't be here."

"You're here," I say, raising my eyebrows.

Harper holds up her hands as I cross my arms over my chest.

"I don't want to fight you, but you really shouldn't be here. No one is allowed, but the wives and girlfriends. Snow asked that I make you go away."

"Look, I don't want trouble, but I am also not leaving until I have Tanika with me." She looks behind her, and I hear a noise, her name being called. She shuts the door a fraction then looks back at me.

"I'll see if I can get her. Please, just wait here by the bar and don't make a sound." I nod because I really don't want trouble. I just want to get Tanika, and see what the fuck is going on.

Moving back, I wait and hope she comes soon.

"You are going to be trouble for me, aren't you?" I turn to see Blaze standing there with a cigarette hanging from his lips. My hands tighten, and I look back to the door then to the floor.

"I came for Tanika, nothing else."

"Your friend has demons. Big ones."

"So I've been told."

Blaze pulls the cigarette from his lips, drops it to the floor and steps on it, then looks back up at me with his lips curled.

"Take her, and don't come back. I don't want to see *you* around here again. You've been allowed in on the privilege you are with my brother, nothing more."

"I don't plan on coming back," I argue, pushing myself off the stool.

"You think you're better than me, girl?" He shakes his head. "You may have my brother fooled, but I know better. A girl like you doesn't fall or care for someone as fucked-up as he is." As he's speaking, the door opens and Harper yelps when she sees Blaze, who walks off in a different direction. Tanika rubs her eyes but leans on Harper, so I take her, and we start walking to the car. Opening the door, we both get her in.

I look back to Harper.

"Thank you, for this."

She shrugs. "It's okay. Oh, can I ask you something…" She bites her lip.

I nod, walking to my side of the car.

"Are you and Reap a thing?"

Reap? That's right, Marcus.

I look past her to Blaze, who's watching us from the door.

"No, we're nothing."

Then I get in and drive the fuck out of there and take Tanika back to mine.

Tanika doesn't talk until I help her out of the car and into my house. She falls onto the sofa and curls herself into a ball and starts crying.

"Tanika, what is going on?"

She won't answer me. Just keeps crying. I grab a throw and place it over her and manage to get myself on the sofa as well, hugging Tanika from behind. It takes a while, but she finally stops crying, and when she does, I hear her soft breathing.

A knock on the door makes me move, and I'm careful not to wake Tanika when I get up to open it.

Damn, I wish I looked first.

"Marcus." He looks past me and then steps back for me to step out of the house, which I do, shutting the door behind me. "If you ask me for sex, I may just junk punch you right here and now." I push my red hair behind my ear as I look up at him while he watches the movement, then his eyes flick back to me.

"She was on trips all night. She will be coming down hard," he tells me.

Fuck! Really? I look back at her and see her sleeping.

"You would know, right?"

Marcus' eyes pin me. "I don't touch the fucking shit. You forget what I do for a living, pretty girl? Drugs are high on the death list around here. Especially in a small town with nothing to do."

"So they say. Yet, here I am not having touched it."

"Yes, here you are, pretty girl." Marcus eyes me up and down, making me feel dirty. Dirty as in I want him to touch me even while my friend is on the couch coming down from God knows what. *How fucked-up is that?*

"Is that all you need?" The words barely form as they fall from my lips in a whisper.

Marcus steps closer to me. "No. I've come to invite you to my home tomorrow night. Shall I pick you up at seven?" His hands are in his pockets as he watches and waits for me to answer.

"I have to work the next day."

"Bring your clothes, I don't expect to let you go." His words send shivers all over my body.

"I'll have to let you know. It depends…" I look back to Tanika, who still hasn't moved.

Marcus reaches forward and slides his hand into my top. I go to tell him off and swipe his hand away, until he reveals my phone, pulling it out. He calls himself then slides it back into my bra.

"I'll call." Marcus turns and walks out to his truck.

Something comes over me, I don't know what it is. Could have been my talk with my sister, but I think I want to go, dive headfirst and see if I can swim.

I really hope I can fucking swim and don't drown in him.

My feet hit the pavement and I reach for him, turning him around so our lips smash against each other. I kiss him and then pull away, both of us breathless. Looking up into his hazel eyes, I smile.

Then I walk back to my house, and when I get to the door, I turn to see him smiling at me, one hand on his truck and the other in his pocket.

I'm unsure if I will survive Marcus.

His specialty is death.

My chances of survival are slim.

"You're awake," I say to Tanika as she sits up. She's been asleep all day. I've waited for her, not wanting to leave her.

She rubs her eyes and pulls her legs up, tucking them under her ass as she pulls the blanket up, covering herself.

"Tanika, what's going on?"

"Nothing. Everything is fine."

I cringe at her lie. How didn't I see it before? I move to sit next to her, placing my hand on her thigh. "You're lying. What's wrong?"

Tanika wipes at her nose and shakes her head. "Nothing," she lies again.

"I didn't think you'd ever lie to me, not like this. Not straight to my face."

Her eyes go wide, they're bloodshot and look so sore. "You don't…" she stops, shaking her head. "You don't understand."

"Help me understand. I want to understand," I say, turning to face her fully.

"I can't, it hurts too much." Tanika reaches for her chest and holds it, clings to it tightly, like it might break right in front of me.

"Then tell me why you're hanging out with those bikers. Tell me, Tan?"

Her eyes look up to me. "They help me escape, and they don't judge me."

"I wouldn't judge you if you just told me."

She shakes her head again. "You don't understand," she repeats.

I pull my hand back from her and stand from the couch. I start pacing in front of her, but she doesn't even move.

"Do you owe them something?" I ask, trying to guess at what, I don't even know.

"No."

"Okay, does your family?"

"No," she answers, then stops breathing, holding her breath, then she pushes one out.

"I was assaulted, Rochelle, and they help me forget."

I pause.

Look to her and see her gripping at her wrists.

"What?" I ask, confused, and sit back down next to her. Pulling her to me, I hug her hard while she cries into my hair.

I hold her. I hold her for as long as she needs to be held until she realizes she's safe and she can let go.

When she does, she looks up at me.

"You don't have to tell me everything if it hurts you too much to say the words."

"I was out… it was the night after I met Blaze. I like him. If you got to know him, you would see he's good, despite his gruff exterior," she says, offering me a shy smile.

"I'm sure he is."

Tanika laughs. "He doesn't like you. He thinks you aren't a good friend."

"Blaze knows what happened?" I ask, not even answering that friend part. I know I haven't been a great friend over the last month. I've been shit, actually. But she still could have come to me. Regardless, I would have been there for her. If I'd have known.

"He didn't. Well, not until after that day in the lake." Tanika shrugs. "He suspected, but I never confirmed it. I guess I did that night."

"Are you comfortable to tell me what happened?"

"I was out. You were…" she pauses, "… well, you were grieving, and I went out with some new friends. I ended up leaving them early." She hiccups, wiping the snot from her face with the back of her hand. "I don't remember it all. He came up from behind, pushed me to the ground and started tearing at my clothes. He got my pants down and I could feel him…" she visibly shudders. "I could feel him… down there. And, somehow, I managed to push away, and when I did, I just ran. I ran so hard and fast that I went straight home. When I got there, my feet were bleeding and I had no clothes on down below." Tanika's visibly shaking now, tears streaming down her face, probably matching mine.

I reach for her and she comes over, lays her head on me and cries. She cries for what happened to her, and cries for a loss I didn't even know she had lost. I hold her. I hold her all day and night, and we don't talk again until the next day.

"You need to go to the police," I tell her.

"I did," she says, reaching for the water I put in front of her. Tanika takes a sip and looks up at me. "They told me they would 'look into it.'"

"We can go back."

She visibly flinches at my words. "No, Blaze said he would handle it."

"You don't want to be involved with how they… a biker gang… will handle it," I say, thinking of all the things I've read about them.

"You don't know them. I was hoping you would see the good in them, but you don't do you?" she asks, pushing up from the seat.

"You've been doing drugs with them, Tanika." My hands go up in the air, incredulous. Anger radiates from me. How can she not see that they're not good for her?

Walking over to the sink, she places her drink in it. "It's my escape, okay? I need to escape. You don't understand."

I stand and walk to her, stopping her from going anywhere. "No, I don't understand, having never been through this. But I will be here for you. Drugs are never a good escape. Tell me you get that, Tanika. Tell me *you* understand," I say, on the verge of shaking her, but also with a tear falling down my cheek at the anguish and pain I am feeling for her.

She pushes past me, not caring, and reaches for her shoes that are on the floor. When she speaks, she doesn't look back at me, "I can't. I can't deal with this right now. I'll call you," she says, heading outside. I hear a motorcycle, and when I look out to where she's gone, Tanika's placing on a helmet.

The rev of the motorcycle is so loud and deafening I wonder if she will be all right ever again.

Chapter Twelve

ROCHELLE

I TRY TO CALL HER ALL DAY THE FOLLOWING DAY, BUT NOT ONCE DOES SHE ANSWER. I completely forget about Marcus coming to get me until I pull up in my driveway and he's there, standing out the front, dressed in all black. Straight away my tummy starts to flutter at the sight of him.

Why is he so beautiful?

So fucking beautiful.

Dropping my head to the steering wheel, I take a deep breath. And before I can even sit back up, my door is flung open, and a hand is on me. I jump and scream. And a small smile tugs at his lips.

"You have everything?" Marcus asks as he looks around in the back of my car, then back to me. He keeps a hold on my arm as I get out.

"No, I have nothing. Because quite simply… I forgot," I say, pulling my arm back from his grasp and tucking my hair behind my ear.

Marcus steps up, so my back hits the car and his front is pressed into me. My red hair falls back into my face, and this time, he reaches up to replace it with a brief touch of his fingers as he looks at me.

"I'll make you forget your own name by the end of the night, and the only thing you will be calling me is God."

I want to chuckle at his words. How idiotic they sound, but, somehow, I don't think he's lying.

"I need to get my things."

"You really don't need anything. I plan to keep you naked."

"I have work tomorrow," I say, as his body doesn't leave mine.

"But do you?" he asks, as his hand runs over my lips and down my neck.

Marcus' touch makes me breathless, and I almost give myself to him right now.

I need strong willpower around him.

"Tanika spoke to me yesterday, told me everything," I say, and his hand drops away. His lips thin out. "And your brother told me to stay away."

"Tanika needs more help than you can offer. My brother is an over-protective asshole."

"I thought you were the older one."

"I am. Can we go? My night isn't planned to go this way. I don't want to talk about my brother when I plan to fuck you."

"I need to get my things." Marcus steps away, and he waves his hand at my house as if for me to hurry up. Passing him, he doesn't touch me again. Quickly, I move to my room and grab everything I think I'll need, including toiletries. I stop one step from my front door and see him waiting out there for me.

What the fuck am I doing?

Sex. It's simple. I want this man.

There's no denying that. Even with his questionable morals and what he does for work. For some strange reason I still want him.

Stepping out, he looks up, and all my worries that I had disappear as he stares at me.

Marcus wants me. That in itself is a power trip.

He holds the truck door open and I look back at my own car.

"Will you bring me back for it?"

"In the morning."

I nod and step to him. He takes my bag and waits for me to slide into his truck. I pause, second-guessing as my thoughts run rampant.

I should turn around and go back inside.

This isn't a smart idea.

He's not your forever.

He will only ever be a plaything.

Just as I take a deep breath and think about telling him to give me my bag back, he kisses me. It's quick, efficient, and shuts my thoughts down fast. I lean into it, and I know right now, in this moment, that I will go anywhere he asks as long as he does that.

And thinking he has that power frightens me. It scares me so much.

"I can see your thoughts churning in that cute head of yours. Get in the truck, pretty girl."

"I am," I say, stepping up. He shuts the door behind me, gets in himself, and starts to drive. He's not giving me another chance to escape.

"Where do you live?" I ask, realizing I should have asked that to begin with. Marcus keeps on driving through town and out onto the highway.

"Alone," is all he replies.

Giving me nothing, he takes a turn along a gravel driveway while neither of us speaks.

I don't see anything.

No houses.

Just bush.

I cringe thinking about the spiders and snakes that could be out here. I stay in the city because the likelihood of me seeing a snake is slim, unless I go to a museum. Spiders are multiplied in numbers further out. That's Australia for you, I guess.

The lights from his truck shine on something and I see a house. It's hidden all the way off the road, down the back of the property. Green grass surrounds it, and there's a large pool as well. Finally, he comes to a stop and climbs out. I do the same. Marcus already has my backpack in his hands as he opens the large wooden French doors to his house and all the lights flick on automatically.

"This is your house?" I ask, surprised. It's very large, and nice. Oh, and I should mention very pricey. I could never afford a house like this. This place is for the rich, and he's obviously got loads of money to afford this rich person's home. The large wooden door looks like it should be on a castle, and there are glass windows so large it gives it an almost whimsical look. I come from a humbler background. You know, not rich but comfortable.

"Yes."

My hands run along the white walls as my heels, which I haven't removed, click on the wooden timber floors. It's bare, but beautiful. Only the essentials seem to be placed in various locations. The kitchen area has a massive glass door, which pulls back and leads out to an infinity pool that looks out over the bushland. I can only see a coffee machine on the countertop, other than that it's bare. The kitchen is all stainless steel and white.

The living room has plush gray couches stacked with white fluffy cushions. There are a few pieces of art on the walls, and at a quick glance, I think they are originals. A massive television screen is on one of the other walls, and under it is a large fireplace.

Everything almost feels clinical, impersonal, sterile like a hospital. It's so clean and untouched.

"This is stunning." I hear something fall and turn around quickly to see it's my bag he's dropped to the floor. "You live here all by yourself?"

He nods. Stalking toward me now, his hand clasps his black shirt, and in one swift move, it's off over his head.

Angry red scars appear on his chest, like small cuts that have risen and healed.

Before giving me the opportunity to inspect his gorgeous body too much, his hand goes to his pants and he pulls the belt free as he reaches for me, dropping it to the floor.

"I'll give you the first option… kitchen or floor."

I'm confused and can't stop staring at his body. It's painfully beautiful. My mind can't seem to make my mouth move.

He clicks his tongue impatiently. "Your choice, pretty girl. Quick. Decide now."

"Floor," I say, letting the word drop from my mouth.

Marcus smirks and steps forward, his hand goes to the back of my neck, cupping it. Sliding his hand through my hair, he pulls so our mouths collide. He kisses me longer than usual, and soon I'm pushing myself up against him so I can feel him. Marcus groans into my mouth and reaches for my dress, which is the only thing separating us, so he can peel it from my body. He makes quick work of removing it, and then his hands touch me again, pulling me to him.

"Marcus," I say, in between his lips kissing mine.

He pulls his mouth back, but doesn't stop his hands from roaming all over my body. "What," he practically growls.

"This is just sex, isn't it?" I ask, my eyes falling into the back of my head at his simple touch.

Marcus' hand slides straight into my panties. "Yes," he replies impatiently, and pulls my panties down so I'm bare.

I make quick work of dropping my bra and wrap my hands around his neck. He kisses me again, this time lowering me to the floor with him. Marcus cradles my head and I swoon, just a little. Then his knee is between my legs, pushing them apart, separating them as he disappears. Kisses trail my body with a hot tongue following before he reaches the top of my pussy. Hot breaths tickle me and I arch up with anticipation.

A finger slides between my lips and pushes in, then is gone just as quickly as it was there, sliding to my clit and circling it. There's nothing to grab hold of as I lay on the cold wooden floor. I'm about to pull him up to me, but before I do, his tongue touches me, right there, right where I need it to be. Instead, my hands lay on the floor, my nails scraping as he shows me exactly what he can do.

One lick to the clit, a circle, then back down to where his fingers are penetrating me. His tongue is at the top of my entrance before he goes back up circling my clit again, and again. The teasing is building up until I can no longer take it anymore. I feel myself tightening around his fingers, and as that beautiful fucking wave of ecstasy hits me, he doesn't stop. He doesn't even stop when I come down from it. His tongue keeps assaulting my pussy until I reach for his hair, pulling him up to me.

Marcus wipes at his lips. "I could get addicted to that taste," he says while my hands hold on.

I reach between us to feel him near my entrance. He's rock hard and I want him in me. Now. My hand grips his cock and I smile at the size of it. Pushing my pelvis up to meet him, he smirks.

"Needy, pretty girl?"

I am. I need him in me. He pulls back just as I feel him there. My hand drops, and I go to reach for him again, but he grips my hands and pulls them above my head. Then he lays on me, his cock right there, right fucking there. Damn him.

After a few moments, he pushes in, just the tip, then goes back out.

"In," I say through clenched teeth.

Marcus smiles and does it again, just the tip, making my body crazy with need.

"In," I say again, this time more desperate than the first time I said it.

He leans down and kisses my lips. I pull them away desperately while trying to arch my hips, but he's lying on me so it does no good.

"Do you want me…" he pushes in again, but not far enough, "… to go in?" Then pulls back. I try to pull my hands free, and with the third tug Marcus lets me. I push at his chest, and he moves as I pull away from under him. Standing and hovering over him, so my pussy is in his face while he sits there with his cock hard and ready. My body's dying in anticipation, it's ready and wanting his dick in me.

Desperately.

Frantically.

My hands grip his head, and I wonder how he can be so composed. Isn't he hungry with need like I am? Lowering myself down, I run my hands through his hair, then one hand comes between us reaching for his cock again as I position it between my legs and lower myself on it.

"Needy little bitch," he says.

I don't argue because I know I am very fucking needy. And the minute I'm on him my body rejoices in my neediness. And soon my hips start rocking, taking from him what I need. His hands, which were by his sides, grip my hips painfully and start rocking with me faster and faster. My legs wrap around his waist while our bodies are so close I can feel the sweat that's between us.

Marcus bites my neck as I throw my head back, his teeth scraping along my skin, and I shudder on top of him. I start to slow as the pressure builds and I know I'm close again, but he doesn't allow me to orgasm. I lift my head back up and wrap my arms around his neck, pulling our bodies so dangerously close that all that's moving now is my hips with his guidance.

I come. And I come hard. On top of him. My body exhausted and fully sated as he rides out his own release, only relieving some of the pressure on my hips as he stays holding me.

"Is this when I go home?" I ask, unable to move.

"No. This is where you stay, so I can fuck you all night." Marcus stands up and takes me with him. He slides straight out of me and lifts me higher with my legs still around his waist as he starts walking up a set of stairs.

"I'm tired," I say with a yawn.

"It's okay, I don't need you awake," he teases, and it makes me laugh. "But I will be tasting paradise again." I manage to lift my head and smile.

"You like me," I say.

He throws me onto my back on the bed and stands at the end. Now I get the opportunity to get a good look at him naked. My eyes roam with appreciation. Somehow the scars on his upper chest make him even more attractive. His tanned skin, messy curly hair from my hands roaming through it, and his jaw, which is set in a hard line, define his gorgeous face.

This man is perfection.

A god.

"I like your pussy. Don't get the two things mixed up. This is just sex. Tell me you know this is just sex, pretty girl," he says, then crawls over the top of me.

I don't know if what he said should affect me, I'm to fucked to care. When I don't answer, he taps me on my nipple making, it sting.

"Tell me you understand."

"I do. Just sex. Is it a deal?"

"Deal," he murmurs.

Then he proceeds to do all the naughty things to me all over again.

And again.

Chapter Thirteen

MARCUS

Rochelle's hand lays on my chest as she traces the lines of a few scars, not once does she ask or question why they're there.

I like that about her.

And I don't like a lot of things.

Actually, I like very little in life.

Except her.

Blue eyes look up to me, and her hand stops moving over my heart. I fucked her twice, ate her sweet pussy, and still want more. I have to have more of her.

"Who are you, Marcus?" she asks.

Such a weird question from a beautiful girl.

Pushing her strawberry curls back behind her ear, I smile down at her. "Whoever you need me to be," I reply.

She doesn't need to know who I am. It would do neither of us any good to discuss it. She would run if she knew how fucked-up I really am. The only one who knows is my brother, and that was not by choice.

"I should have expected that answer from you, right?"

"Right." I smile again.

"Why the crematorium?" she asks.

And that question takes me by surprise. No one has ever asked me why I do what I do.

"The dead don't speak," is all I reply as her blue eyes stare up at me.

Questions swirl in her eyes, and I wait for what she has to say next.

"You don't like people?"

"No. And I especially don't like talking." Pulling away so she falls onto the bed, I stand and look down on her. "You know what this is, right?"

"Sex," she answers.

"Yes, just sex."

"What's your last name?" Rochelle sits up, her beautiful, perky tits on full display.

"Stone."

"Well, Marcus Stone, it's a pleasure to fuck you." She gets up and starts reaching for her clothes. I brought her bag up when she was in the bathroom, and now she's riffling through it looking for clothes.

"Pleasure was all mine. But what do you think you're doing?" I ask.

She pulls out a dress and slides it over her body. I walk to her, placing my hand on her shoulder to stop her from going any further.

Rochelle pulls back. "I'm going. Don't worry, I'll call a cab." Reaching for her bag, she turns to leave, but I grab for her just in time.

"Stay?" I ask her.

"Why?"

I grab her hand and place it on my cock. "Stay."

Rochelle drops her bag. "I'm only here for that." The lie falls from her lips easily, and we don't bring it up. Then she reaches up on her tippy toes and kisses me.

She's demanding. I like that about her. Some women don't know what they want. She does, and she takes it with no regrets. As she drops to her knees, her dress falls past her tits and touches the floor, making her naked once again, just the way I like her. She wastes no time wrapping her mouth around my cock and sucking. Her tongue feels like fucking heaven as she brings it to the top, circles my head, and takes me again.

I grip her strawberry-blonde hair and fuck her mouth. She lets me take control and soon she's a puppet with lips so sinful taking me in.

When I come, she goes to pull away, but I keep her there and push every last drop into her mouth. When I am finished, I lift her with my finger under her chin.

"I work there because I like to cut the dead." Rochelle's eyes go wide at my words. "Some people have a hobby of dancing, mine is bodies, in all shapes and all sizes. I like to see what their insides are made of," I tell her the truth.

"You…" She shakes her head. "You're all kinds of fucked-up."

"I told you this." I make no lie of who I am. "But you're only here for sex, and that's all I will give you of me."

Lies.

"Sex," she mutters, then walks to the bed, pulling the covers back and getting in. "I need sleep too." Rochelle rolls over, giving her back to me, and I'm tempted to tell her to go to the spare room. The last person who slept in the same bed as me is dead.

And it was the last person I ever loved.

My mother.

Chapter Fourteen

ROCHELLE

I wake to someone nudging me, pushing me, and I try to ignore it, but it won't go away.

"Fuck off!" I yawn, turning away, hoping it will help.

"Feisty in the morning."

I sit straight up at that voice.

"Oh, she wakes."

Marcus pulls the blankets away from me. "You have to be at work. Get up."

Then he rushes around, puts my bag on the bed and walks out. He's fully dressed, somehow, even down to his black boots. He's like a whirling dervish and it spins my mind.

I search around for my cell and find it at the bottom of my bag.

Fuck, I have an hour to get to work.

Getting up, I slide my work skirt and shirt on, use the bathroom, and apply mascara before I pull my hair back into a bun. Sliding on my heels, I look back at his messy bed and don't see anything I've left behind.

Walking down the steps, I see him standing in the kitchen, a paper in hand as he holds a coffee. He looks up at me, slides a coffee over, and goes back to reading.

"I didn't know people still read the paper," I say, taking a sip.

"I know what to expect coming into the crematorium this way." The coffee burns as it goes down, then I look up at him. "Are you ready?"

"Yes."

He closes the newspaper, reaches for his keys, and nods toward the door. I follow and climb into his truck.

"I'd like to see you again."

"Not this week," I say, remembering it's my sister's birthday, and I really let the ball drop on that last weekend.

"Why?"

"I have plans."

He nods.

After a drive, we pull up out the front of my house. Marcus doesn't make a move to get out.

"Well, thanks for the sex," I say with a smile.

His lips twitch as he watches me, those sunglasses are back on his face again.

"Pleasure was all mine," he says, as I shut the door and walk straight to my car.

Pleasure was all mine?

What the ever-loving fuck.

Tanika stands at my door the following afternoon, her hands covering her chest as she looks at me in my car. I look around and don't see her car anywhere. Grabbing my bag, I walk up to her. She doesn't look me in the eyes before she speaks. "I can't stop," she says, shaking. "I sold my car… for drugs."

I groan. "What the fuck, Tan? Come inside." I touch her, and she flinches. "Tan?"

"I don't want to go inside with you," she screams at me, drops her hands to her sides, then throws them up in the air. "I want to die. I want to escape. What I do not want to do is go inside with you."

"Okay." I hold my hands up. "Okay, we can do whatever it is you want."

Sad eyes look up at me. "I want money."

"You just sold your car," I point out.

She scratches at her arm, and that's when I see track marks from needles. I reach for it, pulling it up for closer inspection. "What the fuck is this, Tan?"

She pulls it back from me and shakes her head. "Just give me some money."

"No," I say, crossing my arms over my chest. "You need help. And if you need money for that, I will come with you to pay."

She bites her lip at my words. "Fuck you. You're always so up yourself. Do you know that? What, you think because you work for some hotshot lawyer and have your own house, you're better than me?" she screams.

"I don't think I'm better than you, Tan, and you know this."

Angry eyes search my face before she steps closer to scream at me, "I'm going to fuck your man. I bet he won't want you after I fuck him."

"I don't have a man," I tell her.

"Reap. You like him. And I'm going to fuck him." Black hair swings when she turns to walk away. I reach for her, and she swings back and hits me across the face, knocking me over so my ass lands on the grass. When she looks down at me, I wonder who she is. "If you ever touch me again, I'll kill you. Or better yet, I'll make sure Blaze kills you."

Too shocked to stand, I watch as she picks up my keys that fell to the ground and she walks to my car.

"Get out of my car, Tan," I say while standing. She smiles, closing the door, then locking it. I stand behind the car, so the only way for her to get out is to run me over, but she starts it and revs it, then she puts it in reverse and pushes me slightly.

I don't move, my body now touching the car. "Get out of my car." I reach for my cell and dial the police. "Last chance before I call the police on you, Tan. Don't make me do this."

She revs it again and pushes me harder this time, so I have to take a step back with the car, otherwise I will fall and she will more than likely run me over. Just as she does it again, hands touch and lift me.

I grip the hands, trying to get free.

"Stop it, you crazy woman."

Then I'm placed back down on the ground. Marcus walks over to the driver's side door and in one hit smashes my side window. I groan at how much that's going to cost me to fix. Marcus reaches in, turns the ignition off, and takes the keys, throwing them my way before he opens the door and takes a crazy Tanika from the car while she screams at him. It's then I notice his truck is parked behind my car, stopping her escape anyway.

Walking over to her while he holds her still, I look up at her. "That was a shitty thing to do, Tan," I say.

She spits in my face.

Wiping it away, I step closer to her. "I'm not going to hit you because I love you, and I can clearly see you need help."

"I don't need help."

"It's sad that you think that way."

"Pretty girl, reach into my pocket."

I do as Marcus says and come out with his cell.

"Ring my brother."

"She needs to go into a facility. She needs help." His eyes pin me.

"Ring my brother. Now," he demands.

I do as he says and hear Blaze's rough voice come through.

"It's Rochelle," I say, as he says, "What's up?"

"Why the fuck do you have his phone?"

I stifle an eye roll. "Look, asshole…." Marcus raises an eyebrow to me, "… your brother asked me to ring you. Not that I thought it was a good idea."

"What the fuck is wrong with him, that he needs his pussy to ring me?"

"Because he's currently holding down my friend as if he's a prison officer."

"Shit." I hear movement and voices being raised. "Where are you?"

"My house," I say, and he hangs up. I look back at Marcus' cell then back to Marcus who's still holding a struggling Tanika. "Your brother is a real dick, do you know that?"

"No, he's not. But I bet you I can ride this dick," Tanika says before she pushes back and starts rolling her ass over Marcus.

He makes a sound of disgust, and I laugh.

It makes her stop.

She lowers her eyebrows and squints at me.

"Marcus doesn't like people much, and my bet is he doesn't like you either," I tell her.

He looks at me with a furrowed brow.

"What? You said it." I shrug my shoulders.

"Oh, but he likes you, Miss I'm-too-good-for-everyone."

"Lord help me, can we tape her mouth shut already?" I ask Marcus, who still has a hold on her but also watches me.

"Your friend," is all he says.

"I could make you forget her." Tanika tries again.

The rev of a bike comes down the street.

"What will he do with her?" I ask Marcus. "I won't just give her to him."

"He has access to a facility. The mother of one of the guys is a nurse at a reputable one. Blaze can get her in, clean her up, and get her help with what's happened." I stare at him, his dark curly hair is messy today, but somehow it still looks like it was meant to be that way. His eyes continue to watch me as he holds her down.

What are we?

We can't be just sex.

This can't be just sex.

"Why now?"

"He tried to get her to go, but she wouldn't."

"Now she won't have a choice," Blaze says, walking over to where we stand. He takes Tan from Marcus' arms as if she's nothing, and Tanika starts crying the minute his arms go around her.

"I want to know where she'll be."

"You will," Blaze says, walking with her. She's a complete mess now. He gets her to the bike, then he shakes his head while putting the helmet on her head.

Hands that are rough touch my face, making me turn away from Tanika as he strokes my cheek.

"You need ice," Marcus says.

I brush his hand away. I can't have him being gentle, I don't want him gentle. I want to keep him the way I see him in my head.

Bad. Very bad.

Just sex.

"What are you doing here?" I ask him while crossing my arms over my chest. Exhaustion is settling in, and I try not to let my body slump.

"I called you today, but you never answered."

I was busy all day, and I've hardly had time to check my cell.

"I was busy," I say, grabbing my bag and walking up the stairs. My face hurts and I know it's going to bruise. "I don't want sex, Marcus. I want to sleep."

"What on earth were you thinking standing behind that fucking car," he suddenly blurts out. I turn to face him, and he's scratching his face like he can't believe he just said that, but he waits for me to answer him all the same.

"She wouldn't have hurt me."

Marcus laughs, shaking his head. "Of course she would have. The woman's on drugs, has been for a while now. Her thoughts aren't her own." He walks over to me, takes the keys from my hand, and walks to his truck. I watch as he pulls it up on the grass, then walks to me and places his truck keys in my hand, and walks back to my little red car. "Take my truck to work." Then he gets in and backs out, taking my car with him.

Too tired to argue, or even bother, I walk back inside and go straight for the bathroom. Looking at my face, I see it's starting to purple already. Getting some ice, I lie on my couch with it pressed to my face and pass the fuck out.

Maybe tomorrow I'll wake up to this being all a dream.

Or maybe not.

Chapter Fifteen

ROCHELLE

My eye is purple, and no matter how much concealer I put on, it still shows through. Walking out, I see his truck still parked where he left it, and my car gone. Sighing, I get into it and go straight to work. When I arrive, there's a man standing at the door waiting for us to open.

"Hi, we don't open for another hour."

His hands fidget in his pockets as he looks around.

"Can I help you?"

His eyes dart around as he bites his lip. He's dressed in a suit, and I would guess in his late thirties.

"Sir?"

"Martin. I'm here for Martin."

"Are you a client of his?" I ask. I know most of Martin's clients but not this one.

"Yes."

Eyes lock onto mine, and I have an instant feeling of wanting to get away from him. Martin walks up the stairs, his eyes lock onto mine. He obviously notices the bruise and he whines.

"That boy of yours hitting you now, Rochelle?" He shakes his head and looks to the man standing near me.

"Dave, you aren't meant to be here."

"I have more news."

Martin's eyes flick to me.

"Rochelle, why don't you go and get us some coffee?"

I nod, unlocking the door and they walk in. The coffee shop isn't busy, and when I return the door is cracked, and I lean in to hear what they're saying.

"You don't understand, the restraining order will do no good once he knows."

"Dave, you pay well. But there is only so much I can do to keep them away from you."

"I'll pay more," he says, sitting straighter in his chair.

Martin shakes his head. "You hired me to go after them. Your case was strong. They paid what you asked, but you still want more. I don't know what else you want me to do?"

"I want them gone," he hisses.

Martin sighs heavily. "Can't you get them in more trouble? Make the police go after them again. They need to be put away."

"You have no evidence it was them who burned down your house. Apart from that one video, which they paid for your silence, which you requested."

"I need more money."

"You have no more evidence," Martin says again.

"They burned down my fucking house," he screams.

"You also bought drugs from them. Which you told me you owed them a lot of money for."

Well, that explains it.

I knock on the door and push it open, handing them their coffees and then step back out. Going straight to my seat, I search for recent house fires and one pops up.

House Fire—Arson Suspected
There are no suspects as of yet.

"Your boss is a real money stealing prick," Dave says, walking out of the office. He fidgets again and it reminds me of Tanika yesterday. When I don't answer him, he looks down at me. "You look familiar."

Again, I don't answer him.

"Rochelle, come in here," Martin yells out.

I look up to Dave, who shakes his head and then walks out. When he's gone, I walk into Martin's office as he sits at his desk.

"It's best you don't deal with him. If he's here, you tell me."

I nod, then walk out.

What the fuck is that about?

⁂

My red car is waiting right next to his truck in the parking lot when I leave work. When I walk over, Marcus dangles my keys in front of me. I look at the window and see it's brand new.

"Thank you. How much do I owe you?"

He shakes his head in reply and then says, "I sent you a text where your friend is located. They ask that she have no visitors for up to seven days." Then he climbs into his truck and drives off.

⁂

"What the fuck happened to your eye?" My sister reaches for me and inspects me closer. The bruising is fading now, but it's still slightly there in a more yellow tone. "So glad Mom and Dad aren't here to see this." Kat walks out of my bathroom where I'm putting on my makeup, then comes back with something. "This concealer hides everything." She applies it to my face, and when she is finished, I look and don't see any marks.

"Thanks."

"Oh no, no way. Tell me now why you have that bruise on your face."

I cringe, not wanting to tell her.

"It's that guy you like, right? Gosh, really, Rochelle, you should know better."

"It's not a guy who did this," I say, defending Marcus.

Kat's hands go to her hips, and I watch her thinking as she stares at me. "Tell me then, who hit you, and don't even try to make up some lame shit excuse."

A knock is heard on my door, so I walk past my sister to get it, but she stops me with a hand to my arm.

"You're not lying. A man didn't do this, did he?" she asks, concern laced through her voice.

"No. I swear he didn't."

Kat turns and goes to my door before I can, and when she opens it, Blaze is standing there. She takes a step back, and his eyes lock onto her.

"Who the fuck are you?" she asks.

I stifle a laugh. I guess it's not only me who doesn't like him.

I appear behind her, and he looks at me. "Your sister, I'm guessing."

"Guessed right." I smile.

"Of course," he mutters.

My sister doesn't move, and I stay where I am behind her, waiting for what Blaze wants to say.

"She's asking for you. You can visit her soon. Your name is on the list." Then he turns and walks away, but I go after him.

"Is she okay?"

He stops, his helmet now in his hands. Blaze looks past me to where I'm guessing my sister is standing, then back to me.

"She's as good as can be expected."

"Thank you," I say, and I mean it. I don't know what I would have done if he hadn't helped.

"Just be her fucking friend. She needs one." Then Blaze gets on the bike and looks back my way over my shoulder again before he takes off.

"Who the fuck is that," Kat says, coming to stand next to me. "And who were you talking about?"

"Tanika... she isn't well. He helped."

"She the one who hit you?" she asks, nodding to my face.

"Yes."

"It's drugs, right?"

I arch an eyebrow at her words.

"Please. Everyone knows. The town has been gossiping about her for weeks now."

"She came here and went crazy," I say, shaking my head. "I didn't know what to do. Marcus helped, and so did Blaze."

"Marcus is that guy you're seeing, right?"

"Yep."

"So, what are you two?"

"Nothing. We made a deal. Just sex."

Kat rolls her eyes, walks back inside my house, and we continue to get ready.

"You've never done 'just sex' in your life."

"Hence why I'm trying it," I say, reaching for my dress.

"Invite him tonight, I want to meet him."

"It's not that kind of relationship," I tell her, getting undressed and sliding on my dress.

"Call him," she says, pushing my cell into my face.

I press call, and he answers within two rings. "Do you have any plans tonight?" I ask him, my sister watching on.

"Depends. What do you need?"

"Do you want to come to a party with me?"

"No."

"No," I say back.

"Sex, pretty girl. That's all."

"Bye," I reply, hanging up.

Kat looks at me, tilting her head.

"That's, odd."

"He isn't like normal guys, Kat."

"So, what do you like about him?" she asks, slipping her heels on.

We're going out drinking and dancing for her birthday while our parents watch Annabelle.

"A lot. He's mysterious. I like that about him." I shrug.

"And?"

"And he doesn't ask for much, as you can see."

"No. No, I don't see because it seems he's using you for your body."

"That's exactly what we're doing, using each other. I am fucking him the same way he's fucking me, Kat."

"Okay, are you exclusive?"

Umm… shit! I didn't think to ask that question, and it's quite important.

"Message him, I can see you don't know."

Are you sleeping with other people, or just me?

I wait for him to answer, but instead he calls. The phone vibrates in my hand making me squeak as I answer. "This isn't a relationship. I see you because I like the way you feel. I like the way you taste."

He says it as if it's that simple.

"So, are you seeing anyone else?"

"No."

I breathe a sigh of relief.

"But we aren't exclusive. That just means I haven't found anyone else I wish to fuck."

Well, fuck.

"Does this bother you, pretty girl?"

"I don't know." I hang up.

"Well, what did he say?"

"We aren't exclusive," I tell her. That's all that I can manage to get from my mouth.

"Okay, so no feeling guilty, then. If you kiss someone else tonight," she says with a shake of her hips.

I won't be kissing anyone.

Okay, so I lied, I am kissing someone. And it feels awful. Drunk lips smash together, and I have to pull back to remember where I am.

Kat's grinding on someone on the dance floor, and I pull away from my kisser, which I might add, is the worst kisser I have ever experienced—all tongue and slobber.

"Where you going?" shitty kisser yells over the music.

I wave him off and keep walking to my sister. Kat's singing at the top of her lungs with a guy holding onto her hips.

I tap her shoulder, making her turn around. Her smile is so big, and I remember it's her first time out since she had baby Annabelle.

"We should go."

She pouts at me. "No, really?"

I'm drunk. So intoxicated I know I should be going before I make another mistake.

"Yes. I need fast food and bed."

"Go away, bitch," the guy says who's holding my sister and grinding against her.

Kat pushes back from him and shakes her head. "You're a real dick."

I giggle at her words and we walk away. Well, I should say stumble away as my feet do not know where they're going. "You should call that handsome man of yours for a ride." I give her a puzzled look. "The one who was at your door. He's very handsome."

Oh no.

"No, no, no, Kat. Stay away from him."

She waves me off. "I only want to touch his peen, not to have his baby. I did that to a dick already."

"Lord," I say as we walk out into the warm night time air. It's almost Christmas time, and the weather is becoming hotter.

"Hey, isn't that him?" I look to where she's pointing and see a few bikes parked on the street. I knew this town was small, but come on.

"Hey, asshole," my sister yells—and I mean yells—so loudly, everyone in the street turns to her voice. "Show me your cock."

Blaze stands, and I groan, holding her up, or we're both holding each other up, which one I'm not sure.

"Oh, look, he's coming. Think he has a big one?" Kat doesn't say it quietly, and I know he hears because his mouth twitches as he gets closer.

"Hey, you coming back in? We aren't finished, are we?" shitty kisser asks as he steps outside.

"Go the fuck away," I say to him, shaking my head.

Blaze now stands in front of me. "Who's this?" he asks, nodding to the guy who's going back inside.

"Just someone I kissed," I reply.

Why, oh why, did I say that?

"I want to kiss you. Let me kiss you," Kat says, going to reach for Blaze.

I pull her back and step away. "No. We are going home."

Blaze looks to me. "Yes," he says, his eyes are dark. "You should go home. Out here is where the monsters come to play." He leans in. "Marcus being the worst of them all." Then he turns and walks away.

Chapter Sixteen

ROCHELLE

My head hurts, and I smell. Gosh, what did I do last night? I roll over and feel a body. Sitting straight up, I freak the fuck out until I see it's Kat passed out in my bed. She doesn't move as I sit and manage to stand to go looking for some Advil. I need something to help my head from throbbing. It hurts so bad. Clutching it, I walk to the kitchen, and when I get there, a scream rips from my throat.

"What the ever-loving fuck?" My hand clutches to my heart as I look at Marcus sitting on my couch with one leg crossed over the other as he watches me. "Why are you in my house?" My eyes skim to the clock on my microwave. "At ten o'clock."

"I knocked. You didn't answer."

Shaking my head, I get a water and down my Advil, then turn back to him. "What do you want?"

"You."

"Get out."

"When can I see you next?" he asks.

"You sound almost desperate," I say back to him with a little cockiness in my voice. It's nice to know he wants me as much as I want him. Though him showing up in my house isn't the way I thought this would go. Then again, Marcus Stone is anything but normal.

"I am desperate for your body. Make no mistake, pretty girl. It's your body I want, it's your body I crave." He stands, walks over to me, and touches my bare thigh with his fingers, brushing them along ever so slowly. His words ring true, but something is telling me he's lying as much as I do to myself about him. "Last thing I got addicted to, I owned." He leans in. "Can you guess what that is?"

"Your work." I already know this will be his answer.

"Correct." Marcus' lips touch my neck. I look down and realize I'm wearing only a shirt. It's a large *Harry Potter* one, which I have worn over and over again. It's seen better days.

"You won't own me, I'm not property you can buy," I say back to him.

Slow, needy kisses scroll down my neck, and I have to remember it's just my body he wants. Not me.

"I need to have you enough times to remove my addiction of you from my mind."

"Kisses and lies," I say, pulling back from him.

His brow furrows as he looks at me.

"You give me nothing but kisses and lies, Marcus. And sometimes I wish you would give me more than simply the surface of you. Because I know you keep things locked away so deep you would need an excavator to get to them." I step back so his touch doesn't burn me any further. "I'll call when I need *you*. How does that sound? Stop dropping by. For someone you aren't interested in, you sure do show a lot of interest."

A hand goes to his dark curls, and he rakes his fingers through them. "You're right." Then he turns and walks out the open door, shutting it behind him as he leaves.

Walking back up to my room, my sister is sitting on the bed looking at me.

"Wow! You two are confusing as fuck."

"You're telling me," I say, reaching for some fresh clothes. I want to shower, then I plan to climb back into bed and sleep my day away.

We both are woken again later on when my mother's at the door with Annabelle in her arms.

"Do you know what time it is?" She pushes her way inside and hands me Annabelle, I take her as she smiles in my arms.

"Hello, beautiful," I whisper, which earns me a bigger smile. Annabelle giggles and reaches for my nose, pulling it as I hear my mother waking Kat.

"Gosh, will you go away," I hear Kat complain to my mother.

They don't get along. And the only reason I think they talk is because Mom is so good with Annabelle, and it is Kat's only way to have a normal life with the help my mother supports her with.

"I brought your daughter back. A thank you wouldn't be hard to say, now would it?" I hear her say.

I walk up to my room with Annabelle on my hip, who when she sees her mother, claps her hands to get to her.

Kat's sour expression changes immediately and she smiles so widely I forget she's hungover.

"Come to Mama, baby."

I pass Annabelle to Kat, who snuggles straight into her shoulder.

"Thank you, Mother," Kat says, looking up at our mother.

"You're welcome. She's a pleasure." Then she walks out, and I follow behind her, leaving Kat and Annabelle on my bed.

"You brought food?" I ask as she places the bag down, pulling out containers on my countertop.

"Yes, I made you two your favorite mince chow mien."

I walk up and cuddle her from behind. She tenses then relaxes into my touch, tapping my hands holding her.

"We love you, Mom."

"I know, it's just been hard."

I drop my hands from her, and she turns around smiling at me.

"Any boys I should know about?"

Change of subject.

"Nope."

"Are you sure?" she asks again.

"Nope."

"What about girls? You know I would be fine with either as long as I get grandbabies."

"No, to girls as well."

"Okay, okay," she says, throwing up her hands. "You're in your mid-twenties now, Rochelle, you have to start thinking about these things before it gets too late. I had you at twenty-one."

"I know, Mother," I say in a sarcastic tone, as I reach for the water and one container of food, taking it to my couch.

"Don't you 'Mother' me. How was your night last night?"

I'm about to answer her when she reaches for something on my coffee table. "Lord Rochelle, you need a cleaner. Why do you not have a cleaner?" She shakes her head and walks to the kitchen.

"She doesn't need a cleaner for the same reason I don't need a cleaner, and our night last night was great." Kat smiles at me, and it's then I remember Blaze.

Oh Lord, does she remember seeing him? I wonder. The things she said. My eyes go wide at her, and she just blushes.

"Good, good, you're a mother now, so I don't expect you to have crazy nights."

"I'm a mother, yes. But I am not dead," Kat says, sitting next to me and placing Annabelle between us, then taking my food.

"True, okay." Mother walks to the door, her bag in hand, and she looks back to us. "Love you, bye." We wave as she walks out, and I immediately turn to Kat, but she's faster because her finger is in my face. "Don't you dare mention it."

"You asked to see his cock." I giggle. "A biker. You asked a biker to show you his cock." I giggle even louder, covering my mouth as I double over.

"Oh, for fuck's sake, Roch, I was drunk."

Annabelle starts clapping between us, and I laugh even harder. Kat throws a cushion at my head when my laughter doesn't stop.

The week comes and goes quickly. The time for me to visit Tanika is finally here. And when I see her, my hands are shaky. My bruises are completely gone from where she whacked me one, and my hands stay clasped in front of me. She's sitting in a recliner when I walk into her rec room. Shy eyes look up at me, and a soft smile plays on her lips.

"Hey," I say, sitting opposite her.

"Hey," she says back.

I look around to see a few others playing board games and interacting with each other. There's no television. The facility is a fair way out from where I live, but the drive is worth it. She is worth it.

"This place seems nice." She lifts her hands and starts to bite her nails.

"It's a private rehab, it costs a pretty penny," she says between bites.

"That's nice of Blaze," I say back to her.

"Yeah, it is."

"How are you?" I ask, reaching forward, my hand touching her leg briefly. She looks down at it, unsure, and then back up to me.

"I'm sorry about your car." Tanika looks back down. "And your eye."

I shrug. "It's okay. These things happen."

Her head begins to shake. "They don't. And I don't know if I will be able to go back to who I was. I don't know who that person is anymore."

"You had something terrible happen to you, Tan. It's okay to not be yourself," I say to her, as she bites her lip.

Sad eyes look up at me. "It's just so hard. So fucking hard. If I could right now, I would get high. It takes away the pain, it makes it better. It helps me forget, even if just for a little while." She starts scratching at her arm.

I change the subject.

"I told Marcus he's being too needy of my time," I say, smiling.

She stops scratching and looks to me. "You did?"

"Yep. He says he doesn't want me. Just my body. But I see him as much as I would someone who I would be in a relationship with."

"Blaze says he's all kinds of fucked-up," Tan says.

"Yep, he is," I agree.

"But you want him all the same."

I nod at her words. "I do."

"Do you think you want more?"

"I do, but he doesn't. So, I haven't asked."

"You should. Because you're going to get hurt. Call it off, Rochelle. Especially if he doesn't want you."

"He does," I say in my defense.

"He wants your body. There is a big difference."

I smile at her. "When did you get so smart?"

"I just know what hurt does to you. You lock yourself away."

She's not wrong. I'm good at hiding when I need to. The last time I did it, after my grandparents died, I was trying to hide with Marcus.

"I have to go," I say, standing, then I lean down to cuddle her. "Can I come back next week?" I say into her shoulder.

Tanika tenses but relaxes at my touch. "Yes, I'd like that."

I smile down at her. "It's good you're getting help, Tan. It takes a strong woman to do that."

Sad eyes look back up at me. "You wouldn't call me strong if you knew what I had planned to do." A tear leaks free from her eye and slowly rolls down her cheek.

"But here you are."

"Here I am," she repeats my words, trying to smile for me.

I give her a small wave and off I go.

Looking at my cell for any missed calls from Marcus, I see none. It's been a week now, and I know I said I would be the one to call, but I was silently hoping he would.

Chapter Seventeen

MARCUS

"Do it," Blaze yells next to me.

"Will you shut the fuck up," I argue with him.

"If you had done it already, we wouldn't be arguing," he yells back.

"Well, if you shut the fuck up already, it would be done."

"Fine, call me when it's done."

"Nope."

"Arghh… just fucking ask her."

"Nope."

I can hear him grunting into the phone. "Ask her."

"No," I argue back. He won't win, and he knows it. But that doesn't stop him from trying.

"Just ask, you owe me this."

"Nope. Now, I have to get back to work. So, fuck off." I hang up on Blaze, pulling my mask back down and working on the body in front of me.

My brother once asked me when I was eighteen and he was seventeen, did I know what I wanted to do with my life.

At that time, I didn't.

It wasn't until our drugged-up mother had an overdose, and we had to go view her body at the crematorium, that I knew exactly what I wanted to do.

There was a viewing room and a man who showed you the bodies. I stayed well after everyone was gone. I sat in the dark corridors and watched him work. I was fascinated. I could see myself doing what he did, and when he placed my mother into the fire, it was then I knew it was my calling.

I loved my mother once, so fiercely despite all the bad. I loved her. It was the last time I swore to be blinded by a woman's love.

My mother never once cared for us. We were irrelevant to her. Just a check which I ended up taking to feed Blaze and myself.

Blaze fell into a gang.

I fell into the dead.

Ironic.

It was poetic justice, really.

A loud bang comes on the door, and I know who it is straight away. Pulling my mask off, I walk outside to see Blaze. He's leaning on the side of the building with a cigarette to his lips.

"Is she single?"

"Aren't you with the other one… in rehab?" I argue back at him. He wants to know about pretty girl's sister. I haven't spoken to pretty girl for at least a month now. She hasn't called, and I haven't bothered.

My need for her is fucking strong, though, and it takes everything in me to stay away. So, I've taken on extra work. And extra workload from Blaze too.

"Yes, I just want to fuck her. Nothing more."

"You sound like me," I say, shaking my head and walking back inside. He hates this place. Hates it with a vengeance, so much so he hardly ever walks inside, always stands at the door.

"It's because you showed me how to be this way," he yells, as I get further in. "Just call her. You know you want to. You haven't been with anyone else, maybe she will be good for you."

"Love and relationships are never good for anyone," I yell back at Blaze.

I look up and see him step through the door, just a fraction, so he can see me better. He wipes at his forehead and thins his lips—I know just coming in here this far is killing him.

"I'll go see her, tell her how much of an ass you've been."

"You'll do no such thing, and if you do…" I close the door to the fire, "… I'll put your ass in here and watch you fucking burn."

Blaze waves off my threat and walks out. Pulling off my gloves and mask, I go straight out after him, but he's already on the back of his bike with helmet in hand.

"At least fuck someone else. You're a moody cunt." He pulls the helmet on over his head.

"Who says I haven't."

Blaze starts the bike and revs it loud. It's pitch black, close to midnight, and no one is around.

"You haven't. I know you haven't." Then he pulls away.

I hate that he knows me so well. That he's the only person on this earth who knows my fucked-up ways and still stays around.

❦

They say love is something that suffocates you. That love is a permanent weight that will never lift you up, and forever hold you down, in that one spot you don't wish to stay in. People are blinded by love and lose themselves in it. Some will take a fist to the face, a knife to the throat, and call it love.

My mother had a love like that. She was stuck in a state where she couldn't escape, and I watched her time and time again trying to escape from such a love.

But love is like a tornado. No matter how many times you try to get away, it will spin you back right where you started.

I watch from my truck as Rochelle walks out of her work, her skirt is extra short today. Shorter than yesterday's skirt, anyway. She smiles at a man as he walks up to her car, but I can tell it's forced. Rochelle is someone who's sweet, and far too pretty. She's too good for the ugly that lurks just around the corner.

The only form of death she has known is the most recent one of her grandparents.

Someone like Rochelle doesn't know what death is really like, only the outside of it.

She doesn't know what pain is like—only the emotional kind.

A part of me despises Rochelle. I want to not want her. Actually, I want to hate her. But as I sit here watching her back away slowly from a man, I see I also want to protect her, and hold her, and most of all, fuck her.

She's becoming my second addiction.

And I'm not sure how I feel about that.

How I feel about wanting her so much when she's so good.

Pretty girl isn't right for me, but that doesn't change the fact that I want her.

And I usually get what I want.

Chapter Eighteen

ROCHELLE

I met Marcus over four months ago, slept with him twice, and haven't seen him for two months. But as he stands out the front of my house leaning on his truck, I wonder why I stayed away. My hands start sweating, and my stomach lifts, full of butterflies. This man is attractive, and I hate the fact that something inside of me calls for him with a need I can't fully comprehend. Taking the steps one at a time, I walk to him, keeping distance between us. It's safer that way.

"Marcus." His name falls from my lips. His stupid sunglasses cover his eyes, as usual, and as he stands there, he has his hands in pockets. His posture is relaxed as he watches me. "What can I do for you?" I rub my hands up and down my arms.

"How was your Christmas?" he asks, as casually as asking someone for a coffee.

Honestly?

What the fuck?

"How was my Christmas? Is that really what you came here to ask?" I look back over my shoulder and then back to him.

"Is someone in there?" he asks, nodding to the door of my house.

"None of your business." I wave my hand around at him. "Now, I ask again, what do you want?"

"You."

"You've had that. Now try again."

He pushes himself off the truck and stands to his full height, his hands clasp behind his back. "I want you."

"I am not something you can have when you please."

"But you want me too," he says with some authority in his voice.

He's right, he knows I want him.

There is no denying that.

I don't need to air it to him, though.

"You can't even argue with me that you don't."

"Arguing with you is pointless. Or better yet..." my hand goes to my hip, "... maybe I should. Maybe that will make you run away from me again for longer this time."

"I didn't run."

"Really? Because not seeing or hearing from you for two months sounds a lot like running to me."

"You told me to wait for your call."

Damn him for bringing that up.

He's right, I did.

But I expected him to call.

After all, I was proving a point, and I was right.

"Again, what do you want?"

"Again, I told you. *You.*"

"And I told you... you *can't* have me."

"Why is that?" Marcus makes a move to step closer to me, but I step back.

A car comes into my line of sight, and I groan when I see who it is.

My mother's eyes pin me with a stare as she gets out, and then they flick to Marcus, who's standing awfully close to me.

"Hello. Who is this, Rochelle?" she asks, offering her hand to him.

He takes it, shakes it, and steps away.

Mother's eyes go from me to him. "Is this your boyfriend?"

"No."

"Yes," he says at the same time.

My mother's eyes bounce from me to him. "Why don't you come out with us? To celebrate Rochelle's birthday. Is that why you're here?"

Marcus turns to me at my mother's words. "It's your birthday?"

"Tomorrow. So, there's still time to buy her a present. She likes Gucci." My mother waves off and heads toward the house where I know my sister is inside, and more than likely watching all this while laughing her head off.

"I don't like Gucci."

"You don't?" he asks.

"Well, I do. But it's expensive, and I have better things to spend my money on," I say honestly. "Oh, and you're not invited. I rescind the invitation. Please leave." I turn to walk back up to the house, but I hear his footsteps behind following me.

"Your mother invited me. It would be awfully rude not to accept her invitation."

"It wouldn't. Because you aren't my boyfriend. Now... leave," I say, turning back around just as I see my sister standing at the door.

"Marcus, was it?"

I groan. He must nod, because she continues, "Good, we were just getting ready to leave. Rochelle can go with you, if that works?"

"I'm going with you," I say to her.

"Oh no, don't have the room. Sorry."

I reach the door, grab my heels, and wonder if I can stab her in the eye with my stiletto.

"Looks like you will be with me, pretty girl."

My mother and sister walk out, handing me my bag and shutting my front door. They smile as they walk past and get into their cars, driving off and leaving me with *him* standing behind me. I haven't been able to look back at him yet.

"I'll walk."

"No, you won't. Now, get in my truck and tell me where to go."

I sit on my step like a petulant child and look up at him. Marcus steps forward and reaches out to me. I go to pull away, but he's much bigger and faster than me, and he picks me up as if I am light as a feather. He turns, walking to his truck which is out the front, clicks a lock, and goes to the passenger door.

"Happy birthday, pretty girl."

"It's not my birthday," I say. My eyes are glued to his lips as he puts me in the truck.

"But it will be." Then he shuts the door, walks around to his side, and slides in.

I tell him where to go, and the whole drive my leg bounces in the seat. Nervousness is racking through my body.

"This is weird. Whatever deal we had is over. So, why are you here?"

"I'm willing to try a new deal with you."

"No, it won't be a deal. People who enter into new friendships or relationships don't count it as a deal, Reap," I say, using his name that everyone else seems to call him.

He removes his sunglasses and looks to me.

"I'm not Reap to you."

"Why? Is that side of you scary and too much for me?"

"Yes. Way too much for you. We've already established that."

"I'm not some innocent girl," I say.

"Yes, you are. And I like that about you." He says the first nice thing to me, ever. *He likes me.* This man, who never gives me much, tells me he likes me.

I shouldn't be happy about that, I should be upset and telling him to go away. Yet, here I sit, staring at him as we pull up to the restaurant to have dinner with my family.

"You can still run," I say to him.

"Tried that already, look where it got me." Marcus gets out and walks around to my side.

My family is already inside. I can see them through the window as they wait for me to come in. Marcus clasps my hand in his as we walk in, and I try to pull it away but he doesn't let me go. My father's eyes zoom in, but my mother leans in, whispering something to him, then smiles up at us.

"Sir," Marcus says to my father.

"Please, call me Tom," my father offers Marcus.

"So, Kat tells me, Marcus, that you've been seeing Rochelle off and on for a while?" my mother says.

My face turns red at her words.

"Mother," I chastise her, and hope she shuts up sometime soon.

I try to pull my hand free, but Marcus doesn't let go until we sit, and then his hand goes to my thigh. This whole thing makes me angry that Marcus thinks we can go back to where we once were.

No, we fucking can't.

As I push his hand away under the table, Kat starts speaking, "So, you like my sister?"

"Yes," he says, as she looks to me as if to say 'thank you.'

"But why do you like her?"

Marcus' hand goes to my thigh again. "Why is the sky blue?" he answers, and Kat smiles, then nods.

Annabelle starts crying in her highchair and Kat grabs her. She sees me and tries to leave her mother's arms to get to me. Kat giggles as Annabelle reaches for Marcus because he's in the middle, and I watch as he freezes. His hand leaves my thigh, and he takes her as if she's fire, carefully holding her away from his body and passing her to me as quickly as he can. She claps my cheeks when I have hold of her, then I turn her around and sit her on my lap.

Protection from his wandering hand.

"Annabelle loves Rochelle. Do you want kids one day?" Kat asks him.

All eyes go to Marcus while we wait for him to answer.

He looks at me when he answers, "I never really thought about kids. My childhood wasn't great, and it was certainly one where kids should never have been raised in."

"Oh, hunny." My mother's hand goes to her heart.

I look at him and see his eyes are on Annabelle and me. It's like he's trying to work something else out in his mind while I sit here shocked that I just learned something about him that I didn't know.

"I'm sorry you were brought up that way. You must have some cake."

I look back at my mother. How she manages a conversation is beyond me. Cake? Really? Marcus only smirks at her words, and, thankfully, my sister changes the subject direction.

Dinner goes smoothly. Annabelle climbs back over to Kat halfway through, making

Marcus go tight and causing me to laugh. His hand stays on his own lap, and he answers questions that are thrown at him. All the questions are very basic, asking him if he's from here and if he has any family. He tells them it's just him and his brother.

I know about Blaze, but I also didn't know that's the only family he has left.

When we leave, my mother grabs me and whispers in my ear, "I like him. He looks at you like you're special."

I scoff at her words and don't say anything.

"Goodnight, Marcus. Please get my daughter home safely," my father says, shaking his hand as they leave.

When I turn to face him, he's already watching me.

Marcus has his hands in his pockets, standing tall and refined. There's a smile on his lips.

"They like me," he boasts, and it's as if he can't believe it. "No one likes me," he says as if I needed to know that.

"I like you," I say.

Marcus slides his hands from his pockets and steps to me, touching my hip. "You like the idea of me, but not the real me?"

"And what's the idea of you?" I argue back, leaning into his touch. Why, I don't even know. I should be angry, but I can't be because it's my fault too. If I wanted to reach out to him, I could have. I was the one who chose not to.

"The one where you don't really like what I do. The one where I am normal. I'm not normal, though. My demons are huge and my pain is worse." His hazel eyes lock onto my blue ones.

"That's the most you have ever shared with me."

"I don't like sharing," he says, pressing closer to me, so our bodies are now touching. "Come back to mine," he asks, almost pleading.

"I can't," I say, shaking my head.

I can, but it's not the smartest thing to do right now.

"Come back to mine," he asks again, more demanding this time. Leaning down, he kisses my neck and trails to my ear. "Come back to mine," he says again. This time it's whispered and breathy.

I'm as helpless as the girl who went down that rabbit hole.

As crazy as that cat that talks in riddles.

And as lucid as the red queen.

I look up at him. "Okay." The word leaves my mouth before I can stop it, and he smirks before his lips drop to touch mine tenderly.

Damn it all to hell. My resistance didn't last long. All it took was a touch and a few words, and I'm literally about to climb back in his bed.

"Why did you tell my mother you're my boyfriend?" I ask as he touches me.

"I wanted to see how it sounded on my lips." He kisses my lips again.

"And how did it sound?" I ask between touches and soft kisses that make me lose my train of thought.

"I'll let you know."

Chapter Nineteen

ROCHELLE

Marcus doesn't stop at my house to get my things before heading to his place. When we arrive, I see a light out front.

"Fuck," Marcus curses, then comes to a stop. It's then that I see it's Blaze leaning against his bike with his light on. When we get closer, he turns it off, kicks off his bike, and walks toward us.

Marcus turns to me. "Just wait in the car."

Words fail me as Marcus gets out. The light comes on in the truck and Blaze looks at me, his eyes narrowing as he walks over to Marcus.

"What the fuck is she doing here?" he asks.

Marcus' window is down slightly, so I can hear what they're saying.

"You don't get to tell me who the fuck I can bring to my house. Now, what the fuck do you want?"

Blaze's angry eyes turn to me. "Your friend is back on the drugs. Did you even know that?"

What the fuck!

I open the door and walk around to him. "I saw her yesterday. She's fine," I say defensively.

He scoffs. "No, she isn't. But it's *sweet* of you to think so." His lips turn up into a sinister smile.

"She's been good," I say back to him, clearly confused. I know she has. I've made a point of going to see her as often as possible. Tanika even said she was coming around tomorrow.

"She avoided me until she no longer could. The boys said she came over last night to get high." My hand covers my mouth. "Of course, they said no and kicked her out."

"Well, she isn't high, then."

"There are other places to get drugs, good girl."

Ignoring his words, I call her. Tanika answers straight away. Her voice sounds happy as she answers. I look back to Blaze, wondering if I should believe him or not.

But why would he lie about this?

"Tan."

"Yeah, babe."

"I have to ask you something."

"Umm…" She laughs. "Okay."

"Are you using again?"

Silence greets me, and my heart drops so hard in my chest I wonder if it will ever come back up to beat again.

"I tried. I was going to. But I didn't. I promise." Tanika starts crying into the phone, and I feel bad, but I'm so happy she's told me the truth, and even happier that she refrained.

"I'm going to her," Blaze says, walking away and getting on his bike.

"I can come to you. Or Blaze is." She doesn't speak. "Tan?"

"Blaze. Sorry, Rochelle, but I can't take your stare right now. I know you don't judge, but I still feel as if I judge myself when you are around. Blaze doesn't judge..." she pauses before she speaks again in a smaller voice. "I tried to be good, I swear."

"You're doing great. Blaze just left." His bike is loud as he pulls away. "Stay put until he gets to you, okay? Do you want to stay on the phone with me until Blaze gets there?"

"Yes."

"Okay, so how was your day?"

Her breathing becomes more even, and I can still hear the faint cry as she speaks, "No, tell me about yours, and why you are anywhere near Blaze." I turn to Marcus, who's on his cell. My eyes scan him from head to toe in appreciation, my heart beats fast as I admire him. He looks up, spots me, and winks before he goes back to his call.

My heart takes on a life of its own.

"I'm going to fuck Marcus tonight," I blurt it out.

Hazel eyes look back to me, mischief playing in them as he slides his cell back in his pocket and walks toward me.

"Oh my God, is he there?"

"Yep, right in front of me," I say as he leans forward and kisses my forehead. I close my eyes as his lips leave my skin and he walks around behind me.

"Okay, that's hot. I thought you hadn't spoken or seen him in ages?"

"I hadn't," I say, as I feel the ribbon belt of my dress come undone. Then he unzips the zipper over my ass and touches my bare ass when he sees I'm not wearing any panties.

"Blaze seemed happy that you weren't seeing him. I don't think he likes you all that much," Tan speaks. Her voice is sounding calmer. I look out to the night sky. No other lights are around us, and the only light we have is from the moon and my cell, which is glued to my ear, as he lives out in the middle of nowhere.

"I don't care what he thinks."

Tanika chuckles at my breathless words. "I know that as well."

Hands touch me and move around, circling my belly as the dress pools at my feet. Thank God it's strapless. I'm too afraid to move right now as I stand naked while the hands from this man are teasing me.

"I can hear his bike. Fuck. He's going to hate me."

"He doesn't hate you," Marcus says. Taking the cell from me, he stands behind me, one hand wrapped around my mid-section sneaking down to my bare pussy to touch my clit as he begins to speak. "He doesn't hate you. If he did, he wouldn't be there," he says, then hands the cell back to me, and in a whisper to me only he says, "Hurry up."

"Call me if you need me?" I tell her.

"Yeah, I will. And Roch?"

"Yeah." My breath comes out in bursts as he slips a finger in, his lips touching my neck.

"Thanks for asking and not just assuming."

"Of course." My eyes squeeze shut. "I love you," I say to her, but its Marcus' hand that freezes. My eyes pop back open, and his mouth pauses on my neck. "Have to go," I say back to her, hanging up the phone. "Marcus," I say, reaching for his hand to pull away, so I can turn to face him. He doesn't allow me, just starts moving again.

"Mmmm..."

"Why did you freeze just then?" I know why, but I want to hear him say it. I need to hear him say it.

"Let's not talk."

"Does that word scare you, Marcus? If I loved you, would that scare you?"

"It's just a word, it holds no meaning." Then he pushes in me harder, his mouth now sucking on my neck, his thumb circling my clit, and soon he's fucking me with his fingers. I arch and bend to give him every angle, my hand goes back and threads through his hair to keep me steady as he touches me, and soon I'm moving up and down to the beat of his fingers, wondering how I went so long without this. Without him.

He's so much better in real life than my dreams.

So much better.

I come all around his fingers, my body slumping back into him. He takes my weight and wraps both arms around my torso, holding me up.

"It holds great meaning," I say, once I get my words and thoughts back.

His grip becomes tighter at my words. "If you say so."

"I do." I won't back down from this.

He may know death, but I know life.

Maybe he needs to start living in the world a bit more.

"I didn't bring you here to talk about love, pretty girl. I brought you here to fuck you."

"Well, fuck me, then, pretty boy." I push off him and turn with my hand on my naked hip, the only thing I have on are my heels. He takes a menacing step toward me. His hands go to my hips, and he throws me over his shoulder as he turns and heads toward the house.

"My dress."

"You won't need that." He slaps my ass, making me giggle.

Marcus takes his steps fast as he goes to his bedroom. When we get there, he throws me on the bed and kicks off his boots one at a time, then reaches for his belt. When he pulls his shirt off, I sit up.

"What're the marks from?" I ask, not expecting an answer. But for some reason he starts to share.

"My mother used to let her boyfriends cut me or burn me for their entertainment."

My eyes go wide at his truths. "Oh my God."

"It was either I take it all, or I let them do it to Blaze." His clothes are fully removed, and he's standing there in all his naked glory.

"You love him."

"There you go with *that* word again." Marcus pushes me back and hovers over me. "If that is what you call love, then yes. But I will never repeat that. Think of that as the last bit of information you will get from me tonight. Now lay back and let me fuck you."

I do as he says while he kisses me, and when he does, I feel him hard and hot between my legs.

My hands go up to his hair and I pull, wrapping my legs around his waist, wanting him to just go in, but he doesn't. Instead, he slides up and down, rubbing my clit and taking this humping experience to an all-new level for me. I've dry humped but never naked. And I like it, but what I would like even more is him inside of me. Now.

"Marcus…" I moan, moving my hips farther down to feel him.

He stops as he reaches my entrance. His eyes fly open, and he looks at me. "Yes, pretty girl."

"If you aren't careful, I may fall for you."

His eyes shine, and I wonder exactly what he's thinking. "That would be a mistake." Then he pushes into me. I feel that it may be too late for that. That the mistake has been made and I'm falling. Falling from a cliff for a man I shouldn't be falling for, but I can't stop. And I'm afraid no one will be at the bottom to catch me.

I'll have to catch myself.

"Yes, I believe it would be," I murmur to him. I think he hears, but he doesn't respond. Simply pushes in harder and faster until we're both screaming and soon, very soon, we both fall.

"Will you stop," I complain, hitting him away as I wake up. We had sex two more times before I finally passed out, and now his cock is nudging my ass.

"I tried. It lasted…" he pauses, and I turn to see him looking at his watch, "… five hours."

Fuck, I've only had five hours of sleep.

"Happy birthday, birthday girl." He trails kisses all over me.

"Another year older," I mumble.

"Another year sexier," he says between kisses.

A doorbell rings, and he groans.

Getting up, he reaches for his pants, and I watch as he slides them on, looking back at me. He stares for the longest time, and then reaches down to kiss my lips. "Stay where you are, I'll be back." Marcus takes off, and while he's gone, I think about his words for a while. But soon realize I need to pee, so I quickly run to the bathroom, then climb back into bed just before he comes back in. When he does, he's holding a large box with a bag of food. I sit up.

"You're feeding me?" I ask, smiling.

He grins at my clapping and places the bag of food on the bed in front of me. I open it to find pancakes and hash browns, as well as many other things.

"I'm so hungry." I take a bite of a dry pancake, making him chuckle.

"Worked up an appetite, I see."

I nod. "You wouldn't let me sleep," I say between bites.

"I did for five hours." Marcus moves the food bag and drops another on my lap. It's big. I look up at him in question.

"Open it. I arranged it last night. One of my former customers works there." I tear open the box, and the familiar G that greets me when I see the box causes me to squeal. Tearing it open more, I reveal the perfect little black bag.

"This is way too much. I can't accept," I say while eyeing it, knowing I will never let it go. I've always wanted one, but it's so much money.

"It's yours. Accept it. I can't return it, and I don't look good in black," he jokes. My lips turn up into a full-on smile.

"You do look good in black. Sinful, actually. But this…" I say, looking back down at the gorgeous bag, "… this is huge. I can't let you waste your money on this for me."

"I have a lot of money, pretty girl. Death pays extremely well."

"So it seems," I say, putting it down to the side.

I reach for him, bringing him closer to me. "So, what are we?"

"We are whatever you want us to be," he says, then kisses my lips.

"You aren't going to sleep with anyone else?" I ask him.

"No."

"And I won't either, of course."

"Okay."

"You're fine with this?" I ask him to double-check.

Marcus brushes my hair back. "Yes."

"Perfect. Now hurry up and fuck me before I have to leave."

He pulls the blankets back. "Your wish is my command, pretty girl."

And he does just that.

Best birthday ever.

Chapter Twenty

MARCUS

"You what?" Blaze asks, shaking his head. "You want her? Really?" he asks as if he can't believe it.

"I do. Now shut the fuck up and tell me what you need."

Snow carries a body inside while I wait for Blaze to speak.

"I can't believe the man you're turning into. You don't fixate on a woman like this. What's wrong with you?"

"Last nerve, Blaze. Last fucking nerve," I say, shaking my head. "Now, tell me what you need."

"Fingerprints, that's it."

"Dispose of the rest?" Blaze nods as Snow steps out. As he passes, he slaps me on the back. "Heard you went back to that fine piece of ass. Smart choice, man. She is mighty fine." I shrug him off and walk inside.

The body is already on the steel table. Walking over to the iPod, I crank the music loud, zoning out as I start cutting. I don't need to cut the body to dispose of it. I have the cremator for that. Which usually has to have the body burn twice to turn the bones into ash, because sometimes the first go isn't enough. When I first started, we had to crush the bones. Now it's a lot easier and cleaner. But sometimes, just sometimes, I like to play with a body. Particularly the ones Blaze sends my way. Which doesn't happen all that often. But when they do, I zone out like I'm doing right now.

The dead are easy.

The dead don't complain.

The dead don't care if I cut them into tiny pieces so I can see what they're made of.

They don't care that I cut a hand off and hand it to someone else so they can access their phone.

They simply don't care.

They're dead.

And it's the reason I love this job so much.

But the dead also deserve respect.

No matter how vile or evil they are, their soul is gone, and their body is left. I take great pride in doing what I do—my cuts are flawless, precise, and the care I take is perfect.

For someone who is about to burn them that is.

They come to me in usually pristine condition, unless they don't have loved ones or were involved in a terrible accident. Their hair is combed, and they're dressed in their best outfits. It's the bad ones, or the homeless ones, or those who have no one that I take extra care of. Even the ones Blaze brings to me. I know he has his reasons, and I don't question them, but I still treat them respectfully.

I do it to help him, and I do it to cut.

I like to cut.

I love the sound of the saw.

Removing the first hand, I place it in a plastic bag and look up. When I do, Rochelle is standing there with Blaze next to her, a grin gracing his lips. Her eyes are wide, and there's fear evident in them. Removing the gloves, and not even bothering with the music, I walk to where she's standing. She steps back, and her hands go up as if warning me not to touch her.

"I know that person."

Fuck, of course she does.

Her eyes lift from him to lock on to me. "You look comfortable, more relaxed than I've ever seen you," she says while shaking her head. "How is that possible? How do you like that?" She nods, and I turn to see Blaze watching our exchange.

He's never inside. Ever.

"You had to bring her in, didn't you?"

Blaze shrugs. "She saw you… the real you." Blaze turns to her. "Tell him what you saw."

She does as if she's on autopilot. "You were smiling as you cut into him. You were smiling through your mask." Rochelle shakes her head. "I rarely get smiles like that." The music from the room thumps and she shakes her head. "I have to try to accept this side of you if I want you, don't I?" Then her eyes go back to the room, and she shivers. "He served me coffee. Creepy coffee guy, I used to call him."

"He was more than creepy," Blaze harrumphs next to us.

I turn, and without thinking, clock him one right in the fucking jaw. Hard.

Blaze falls backward and clutches where I hit him. "What the fuck," he screams, wiping the blood from his lip. "She asked to see you, so I brought her in," he mumbles, then he says something else as he walks out shaking his head, but I don't catch it.

Turning back to Rochelle, she's biting her bottom lip as she shyly looks up to me.

"I like you, Marcus, that is obvious. But this…" her eyes flick behind me, "… I don't like to see this."

"You don't have to see this. It's simple. Don't come here." My words seem harsher than I mean for them to be. "You don't have to come here," I say to her again, this time softer and with more care.

"I know. I was driving past, and I wanted to see when you were finished for the night." Rochelle steps back, and I know she's going to leave.

"I'll be finished in an hour."

She turns, giving me her back when she walks out. "I'll go home. See you after."

Rochelle doesn't give me a chance to respond, she leaves.

Walking back in, I turn the music off, my mood having significantly changed. Covering the body back up, I slide it to the cremator and push it in, letting it burn.

I would have spent up to an hour on that body.

Cutting. Spending time expelling my demons.

Now I can't even stand to look at it.

Walking out, I see her. She didn't leave like she said she was going to. She's sitting on the ground, much like where I first saw her that time she was here for her grandparents. I was shocked by her, a beautiful woman lying on the ground. She had all that hurt written on her face. So much so I had to take a deeper look. I had to know why, and what put that there. A girl as beautiful as her shouldn't carry such monsters around with her.

I watch as her eyes close the closer I get. She knows it's me because she doesn't move.

"I thought you were beautiful the first time I saw you. It's what pulled me to you," I tell her honestly.

Rochelle opens her eyes at my words. "I thought the same thing about you."

"That I was beautiful?" I smirk.

"No, that you were the most attractive man I'd ever laid my eyes on. And beyond that, you held something I was searching for that I didn't know I needed."

"What's that?"

"Death," she says, then sits up.

Chapter Twenty-One

ROCHELLE

Marcus looks at me as if he can't work out my words. Neither can I, but he doesn't need to know that. I understand only a fraction of why he's in my life, and why my pull to him is so intense.

He's the epitome of death—he works with it, and he lives in it. I had never been around or experienced something like that until that day I met him. I needed him, and that scares me.

"Death," he says, stepping closer. He offers me his hand and I take it. "They don't call me Reap for nothing." Marcus pulls me up and slams my body into his front. "Most women want me because they want the fear attached to me. They think it gives them something, being with someone who they can't contain or keep a hold on." His hazel eyes glisten as he stares at me. "You want me for me. I like that about you."

"You do?"

"I do," he says.

"You still scare me. That part of you…" I point in the direction of the crematorium, "…I hate."

"You don't need to like what I do. You simply need to like me. Isn't that the healthy thing to say in a relationship?"

I smirk at his words. "Relationship?"

"I'm fucking you. You're fucking me. This is what this is, right?"

Marcus' words make me pause. "I guess you're right."

"So how about we go back to mine and fuck?"

"Just what every girl wants to hear. You're such a romantic," I murmur against his lips as he kisses me.

Hands skim my body and claim me in places only he knows how I like to be touched. I moan as his hot lips connect with mine, while he slides in and out of me. I wonder if I will ever get sick of his touch, or ever not crave it as much as I do right now.

When he touches me, he brings anything but death. He brings fireworks that blow up so bright I can feel them wanting to escape into the darkened skies.

I'm falling in love with death.

I'm falling in love with Reap.

And I'm falling in love with Marcus.

I don't think he feels the same, though.

To him, I'm just someone who's here. Someone he likes to play with. I'm his new fascination. He hasn't ruined me yet, as he promised all those months ago. But I feel if I stay on this path we're on, he just may completely destroy me.

Marcus pushes my hair back and touches me with affection. He's always fucked me, and I never complain because I enjoy fucking him. But I can feel the shift, taste it, with each soulful kiss he gives me.

It's not just a sampling anymore.

It's more like a devouring.

My fingers thread through his, and I grip onto him for dear life as I come.

He kisses me harder, and soon my hands drop to the bed while he finishes.

Marcus' body is now on mine, our breaths heavy and our worry is slightly less.

Until.

"This won't be a long-term thing. You know that, right?"

Ruined.

He's ruined the moment.

"Why?" I question.

He pushes off of me and lays next to me, his hand touching mine ever so lightly that I want to reach out and grab it. Instead, I lay still. Perfectly still. Waiting for his answer.

"It's a right-now thing. And right now, we meet each other's needs, and I'm not going to lie and say you're like all the other girls, because we both know you're not. You are different, to me."

"Oh, how profound," I say with an eye roll while sitting up. "It's a rollercoaster of I want you, and then I can't have you." I reach for my outfit and he grips it, stopping me from putting it on.

"You want kids, am I wrong?"

I freeze at his words. "Yes, I do."

"This is why it's not long-term, pretty girl. I can't have kids." I gasp at his words and turn to look at him. He lets go of my clothes and sits on the bed naked, the sheet not covering him.

"Do you mean you don't want kids, or you can't have kids?" I ask, not sure what I've just heard. Before he can answer, my cell starts ringing. I look to it and see Tanika's name flashing. Usually, I wouldn't answer, but with the way she's been, I can't not.

"Hello."

Marcus looks at me, waiting.

"Roch, I need you to come."

"What?" I stand, trying to pull my clothes on as I listen to her.

"I need you to come. Please, come."

"Okay, okay, where are you? Tell me where you are."

I hear her gasping for breath.

"I'm on the town bridge. You need to come, Roch."

"I'm coming." Grabbing my keys, I run. My boob is hanging out, and I'm not fully dressed, but as I get in the car, it's the last thing I think of as I drive.

It takes me a total of ten minutes flying down the highway until I reach the town bridge. It's quiet, being late at night, but I spot her straight away.

Leaving my car, I run to her. She's standing on the edge, not quite on the railing, but her hands grip it with a force so tight her fingers are going white.

"Tan," I whisper carefully, coming up behind her.

She doesn't look at me straight away, but I can hear the pain in her soft cries.

"He found me. He found me." She lets go and hugs herself, then shudders. "This time I didn't get to run, Roch. I didn't get to run." She shakes, and I'm careful as I step closer to her. My hand goes to reach for her, but before I can, she pushes away so I can't touch her.

"Please come to me." My hands are outstretched, and she looks to them, then shakes her head.

"He touched me in all the wrong places." Tanika visibly shudders as she holds out her hands, showing me the bruises all over her arms.

"Tan," I say again, but she's in her own world now.

"He whispered what a dirty little slut I was. Then offered me this." She taps on her arm where I can see the injection area of a needle. "I couldn't say no. It was all I could hope for at that time, my hands were tied, and I needed an escape. It was an escape, Roch."

I hear a car door shut behind me, but I don't want to look. I'm too afraid to take my eyes away from her. She's a danger to herself right now, and I'm helpless to help her. I know this, but it won't stop me from trying.

"Tan, come to mine. You can come to mine and never leave if that's what you want."

"Tell Blaze I could have loved him. He's a good man."

"You tell him," I say while stepping closer. If I reach my fingers out now the tips will touch her.

The breeze picks up and floats her beautiful, long black hair over her face where it sticks in the tracks of her tears, but she doesn't seem to care.

"I won't be able to." She clutches at her chest like the pain is unbearable. "I'm broken now, so broken, Roch. I have no one."

"You have me."

Beautiful, sad eyes turn to me. "You're all I have."

Then it happens so fast that my heart rate skyrockets. She steps up, those beautiful, sad, haunted eyes look at me, and then she's falling. And before I know it, I'm going after her. My hands reach the edge, and before I can fall in to get her, hands clasp me from behind, lifting me up and pulling me back.

"Let. Me. Go," I scream, but it's no use.

Everything is silent.

Apart from the deafening sound of my breaths.

"Stop, pretty girl. Stop!"

I kick, but he won't let me go.

I need to get to her.

I have to help her.

How am I meant to do that if he won't let me go?

Sirens are heard in the distance, and I keep on struggling, trying to be set free, but his hold on me is too tight.

"I have to get her," I say, struggling, my legs and hands becoming exhausted. I collapse, but his hold doesn't let go.

"I got you," he whispers in my ear.

He does have me, but I don't have me right now.

I am drowning in that river under this bridge where her body is right now.

I'm drowning, and I can't get out.

I am floundering in a river of pain.

"Pretty girl."

I open my eyes to find the police standing in front of me. There are words being spoken, but I don't seem to hear them. I can't register anything. Everything hurts, but it's my heart that pains me the most.

Hands pull my shirt up, and I look down, realizing most of my breast has been out on display, but for some reason I don't even care.

Why would I care?

I can't care.

I can't feel.

When I look up again, ambulances are here, as well as a pair of angry eyes walking toward us.

Marcus's grip becomes almost painful as he holds me tight against his chest.

"Tell me that's not her." His voice is so angry.

My heart is too sore to care what he says.

"Brother," Marcus says.

Rough hands touch my chin and lift my face up to meet his. "You didn't save her? Who do you think you are?" Blaze spits in my face, but I don't even flinch. How can I? I don't care what he says or does. I just saw my best friend jump from a bridge because she was hurt. Hurt again.

Then, it's like something snaps and I manage to pull myself from Marcus' tight grip, and my fists are slamming into Blaze's chest.

"He got to her again, you prick. And you didn't protect her," I scream.

Marcus reaches for me again, but not before I slap Blaze in the face as hard as I can muster, but he doesn't even move.

Oh God, my hand burns.

"What's she talking about?" Blaze's eyes don't ask me the question they ask Marcus.

"He raped her. A-fucking-gain," I seethe, the words dripping like venom from my mouth. "And you were meant to protect her. You were meant to save her."

Blaze takes a step back, shakes his head, and before I can say anything else to hurt him the way I'm hurting, he's gone. The only thing left is the noise of his engine as he speeds away.

"I'm taking you home."

"No. I want to go to *my* home." I try to pull away, but Marcus holds me.

"You're wearing your underwear out in public, pretty girl. Let me take you home." I look down and see I only have on panties and my shirt, the latter just barely covering me. I didn't think clearly when I was leaving, I simply knew I had to get to Tanika.

"I want to go to *my* home. I don't want to go to your bubble where you make everything seem okay. Then you burst my bubble when I think it's all working." I take a deep breath. "Nothing is okay. Every damn thing is broken, and people are dying."

"People die, pretty girl, it's just the way of the world. We can't stop it."

"Trust you to say that. You love death. I bet you can't even wait till you die." We are standing on the bridge, the police and ambulance people are still milling around. Some know him from what he does, and it makes me even more uncomfortable.

"Death is inevitable. We can't stop it, and we should greet it as an old friend. It's not here to hurt us, it's here to set us free from this cage we live in."

"You're fucked," I say, shaking my head and walking to my car.

Marcus catches up with me, his hand catching my wrist and turning me around to face him. His body touches mine and he wraps himself around me. "I'll hold you all night, because I know that's what you need. All fucking night."

I'm too weak to tell him no.

To tell him he's everything I need and nothing I want.

Chapter Twenty-Two

ROCHELLE

Marcus does as he said he would. His arms never leaving me for long, and no matter how much I pushed him away, he would always come straight back, gripping me to him as if he needed it as much as I did. Maybe he does, I know I did.

Waking up the next day hurts, and all I want to do is to sleep again—there's no agony in the world of darkness.

So that's what I do. I only wake when a police officer comes to take my statement, or when Marcus feeds me, then I crawl back into bed.

The following day Marcus is still here, still in my house. I wake and know I have to move because I need to go to work.

I run on autopilot—find clothes, brush hair, apply makeup, get ready, leave.

"Are you going to work?" Marcus asks, walking in dressed, and holding two cups of coffee in his hands.

"I need to go to work," I reply, taking one and looking at the logo. "This is the coffee house of the guy's hand you were removing," I say, looking down at it. "Find any other suitable people in there today?"

"Pretty girl…" he warns.

"Whatever! I have to go."

"Tanika's body was found. She's coming to me tomorrow." I pause at the door, my keys now in hand. "I'll take care of her. Do you wish to see her?"

My hands sweat as they hold the coffee and keys. Words for some reason cannot leave my mouth.

"Rochelle…" *My name.* Marcus has never called me that before. It's always pretty girl.

Not looking back, not saying a word, I leave and head straight to work.

Martin is already there when I arrive. Which is a surprise, because he's never there before me.

"You're here," Martin says, surprised, while looking up over his glasses.

"You're in?" I ask, looking directly at the clock.

Martin shakes his head. "Dave has become quite painful. Seems he's worse than the men he was going after."

"What do you mean?"

"He destroyed my car last night. I had to call the police on him. Then I woke up to this." He pushes his cell toward me. There is a picture of his house on the screen, the words 'YOU'RE NEXT' are painted in red across the front. I shake my head and look up at him. The poor man is sweating profusely, his brows are furrowed, and worry is etched all over his face.

"Go to the police."

"I will. But, Rochelle, if you see him, I want you to stay as far away as you can, and call the police immediately."

"Yes, of course."

Martin nods, happy with my answer. "How was your weekend? It was your birthday, right?"

"My friend jumped off the town bridge and killed herself." I turn, taking his empty coffee mug to fill it when I hear him gasp.

Marcus doesn't wait at my car, instead he comes straight into the office the minute I finish at five. Martin looks up through his office entrance, then pays Marcus no attention once he sees who's here.

"I can get myself home," I tell Marcus, turning the computer off and reaching for my bag.

"I know you can, but I thought I'd prepare you. Your family is at yours, waiting for you."

A heavy sigh leaves my mouth. "I can't deal with them."

"You can come to mine," he says without missing a beat.

"Marcus."

"Mm-hmmm," he answers.

"You should stop now."

"Stop what?" he asks, clearly confused.

"You should stop helping. The more you do, the more I'm falling for you." I watch as his body goes rigid at my words. "See, you don't even know you're doing it. That's what makes it worse. And Marcus…" I say, stepping up to him like he does to me. "I can't take another heartache. You will destroy me."

"I would never—"

I don't give him time to answer fully, cutting him off as I walk past him and go straight to my car. Without looking back, I head home. My mother's out the front waiting for me when I arrive.

I look behind me wondering if I should reverse back out, when she knocks on my window, then opens my car door. "Why haven't you called?" She pulls me, and I get out of the car. Her hands wrap around my body as she holds me tightly to her. "The police stopped by again. Said something about an assault. Wanted to know if you had any information." I freeze at her words while Tanika's words from that night come back to haunt me.

"Roch," Kat yells from my door.

My mother hugs me tighter before she finally lets me go. "I'm here for you, you know that, right? And so is that man. He's here for you, too."

"Marcus?" I ask, confused.

"Yes, he was here before. He's been here all weekend." I can only nod as she starts walking with me to the house.

"What do you need?" my sister asks.

I look at Annabelle in her arms and take her. "Just this." Beautiful Annabelle smiles and slaps my face with her little hands. And then it hits me—Tan will never get to experience this.

And maybe, neither will I.

Marcus comes back, and I don't expect him. And when he climbs into my bed later that night, he wraps himself around me, and I cry. I sob until I no longer can, and when the tears stop, I turn to him.

Marcus brushes my hair from my face. "I don't like to see you hurting."

"Hurt is a part of life," I reply.

"I can make it go away. Even if it's just for a while, I can make it go away." He leans over and kisses my lips. "Do you want me to make it go away?"

"Yes," I answer almost desperately.

"Are you sure?"

"Yes," I respond, this time wrapping my hands around his head and pulling his lips to mine.

Marcus takes control, he always does. His lips scorch mine and his hands devour my body, stripping me bare with each touch.

One touch—legs spread.

Second touch—sliding in.

Third touch—euphoria.

My eyes bleed with love, and I know in that exact moment as he tries to take my pain away the only way he knows how, that I love him.

Dragging kisses along my neck, then biting, he pushes in harder, as if he can hear what I'm thinking.

"I love you," I whisper into his ear.

Marcus pushes in harder and fucks me faster, not saying a word in response. I didn't think he would, but for some reason I had to get it off my chest. I had to tell him.

Clinging to him, I let him take me. I give him what he needs while he takes all I have left. And it leaves me in a state of bliss with no thoughts running rampant in my head.

Marcus did what he said he would do, and I had to go and utter the words I never thought I would. When he comes, he stays on top of me, then looks down. Something has changed in his eyes, but I don't know what it is, and I don't want to find out either. Turning around, I pull the covers up and go to sleep.

I don't dream about death.

Instead, I dream of heartache.

This time I wake before Marcus does. His face is pressed against my pillow as he lightly snores. I reach for his curls, brushing them back. He moves but doesn't wake. One of his legs is under the sheet while the other is out, showcasing his perfectly sculptured ass. Reaching for my cell phone, I flick to the last pictures that were taken, which are of Tan and me from a few weeks ago. She was doing so well, so fucking well. And now? Now, I don't even know what to do or how to function in a world without her in it.

Death has many faces.

Some are beautiful.

Some are evil.

But they all lead down the same road.

Pain.

"I never told you about my mother." Marcus' eyes are open when I turn to look at him. He hasn't moved, he's simply watching me.

"No, not much."

"She was evil. We raised each other, my brother and I. To her, we were just a government paycheck so she could get high. I used to have to steal her money or steal her drugs to sell, so I could buy food for Blaze and me. She never cared. The most she bought us was one loaf of bread a week, that was when she remembered. And for two growing boys, a single loaf of bread? Well, let's just say, it doesn't last long." He breathes out harshly, and I turn fully to see him. "She was the first real death I witnessed, but not before she used me so she could get what she needed. Her friends, as she liked to call them, would pay her money to do things to us. Burn us. Make us scream. I took most of it, and Blaze would run. I would always tell him to run. The older he got, he stopped listening, and soon I stopped letting her get away with it."

"You were just kids," I say, shaking my head.

"She was dead in our trailer for over a week before we called someone. I loved her when she was peaceful, when she was asleep and with no words or motion left in her."

I just look at him, not really knowing what to say.

Marcus turns on his back and looks up to the ceiling. "I loved her, if that's even the correct word. She was beautiful, despite all her fucked-up ways. You remind me of her. It's why Blaze hates you so much. You look like her," he says it as if it's a good thing.

"I don't want to look like a woman who did that to you."

"I stopped seeing her in you the moment you opened your mouth. It's the hair… you have her hair." Marcus sits up, pushes my strawberry-blonde hair behind my ear. "If you died, pretty girl, I would keep you longer than a week. I now know what to do to prevent you from decaying."

"That's kind of fucked-up," I say, my nose turning up at his words.

"I did warn you… I am far from normal."

"Tell me what you see when you look at me?"

"I see a woman who has her claws in me so deep it hurts. That it's the first thing in this life I am scared of."

"And…" I say, climbing to sit on his lap.

"When I look at you…" he smiles, "… I don't see death. I see life."

"This is life. Can you feel it?" I ask, reaching between us and sliding him inside of me. His hands grip my hips as I start moving.

"I can feel your pussy."

"And…"

"The words you want to hear, I'm going to whisper in your ear."

He moves me faster with the help of his hands on my hips.

"That sweet pussy of yours that's milking my cock."

My breathing picks up a notch at his words.

"Yeah, you know the one. The one that's currently squeezing me so fucking tight that I'm about to come. But I won't. Do you know why?"

I shake my head.

"Because watching you come is the best thing since watching a body being torn apart. You have become my new favorite thing, pretty girl. If I were you, I wouldn't encourage it. My obsession has become something you may choose to regret."

Chapter Twenty-Three

MARCUS

Rochelle doesn't want to see the body. I take particular care when I prepare Tanika to be cremated. It's the most care I've taken in anyone I have handled. And in the end, as I watch Tanika burn, I wonder why. What is Rochelle doing to me? And why am I letting it happen?

The following weeks flow by, and not much changes. Except her. She changes. Something in her is gone, and I don't know exactly what. Not once does she bring up our relationship again or push for anything more. The words that she loves me also never leave her mouth again. It's as if she's been frozen in time and cannot escape.

Blaze ignores me as if I am the plague. He doesn't like Rochelle, and she doesn't seem to like him either. No matter how much Blaze dislikes her, I can't seem to stay away.

Rochelle sneaks up from behind me, wrapping her hands around my waist and snuggles into my back. "Let's stay in," she says.

I would usually say yes because I hate going out, but the clubhouse is throwing Blaze a party for his birthday, so I have to go. It's the one time of year I always give him. No matter what.

"Just an appearance," I reply, turning to her.

She's wearing something short, perfect for my hands to slide up and under to grip her ass.

"We can have more fun." Rochelle's hands slide down my body and she goes to touch the floor, but I reach for her and pull her back up. She distracts me with sex. It's her specialty, and she's good at it too.

"We will. After."

Rochelle stands, crossing her arms over her chest. "I don't like your brother."

"I know, and he doesn't like you either."

She shrugs her shoulders, throwing her hands up in the air. "Then why do I have to go?"

"Because you do nothing anymore, literally nothing," I say.

Rochelle bites her lip and looks down. "You never do anything either but work, so what's the problem?"

Stepping away from her, I take my keys and turn to her. "You're changing. I know why. But stop locking yourself away. You didn't die with Tanika," I say, and it's not until the last words leave my mouth that her eyes look up at me and anger is evident in them.

"A part of me jumped off that bridge with her," she says, walking over to me. "Now, if you're finished discussing this, let's go." She takes the keys from my hand and walks out of my house to my truck. She unlocks it and sits in the passenger seat as I lock up the house and follow her out. She hands me the keys and doesn't say a word as we drive.

I look at her and wonder why I've stuck around for so long. Why I haven't gotten sick of her. It's been months now, and not once have my eyes strayed. Not once have I wanted another woman more than I want her.

It's her.

Always her.

"I'm going to drink," she announces, as we pull up to the clubhouse. Rochelle jumps from my truck and waits for me to meet up with her before she goes any farther. Her hand reaches for mine and she clasps it, squeezing tight.

I've become her lifeline, and I don't know how to break that. Before me, she was her own lifeline.

Death has changed her. Seeing it, feeling it, has killed something inside her.

"You brought her? I told you not to bring her," Blaze says, as we walk toward him.

"She's right here, asshole." Rochelle pushes into my side.

Harper stands, smiling at us. "Hey, it's been too long."

"Sit, Harper," Blaze barks. "She isn't welcome here."

Rochelle ignores him and turns, looking up at me. "Drink?"

Before I can reply, a flash of blonde hair comes up behind Rochelle and pulls her strawberry-blonde hair backward, making her leave my side and fall to the floor. The blonde who was on my lap last time Rochelle was here jumps on Rochelle and punches her in the face. Hard. Rochelle gasps, covers her face, then in a split-second bucks the blonde off and flips her so she's on top. Rochelle's fast hands punch and she starts hitting, over and over again, until I reach for her, lifting her backward and off. The blonde who started it is lying on the floor crying.

"You stupid fucking bitch, you made me bleed," Rochelle screams, struggling to get free and go back to the blonde. I manage to keep hold of her when Harper walks over and helps the crying blonde up from the floor and walks her away.

Snow steps over with a beer in hand and passes it to a very angry Rochelle. She takes it as she calms in my arms.

"Girl, every time you come here, trouble follows you," he says, and gives her a smirk. "And… I'm sorry about your friend."

Rochelle's chest deflates, and I see the fight leave her.

Blaze pushes through and angry eyes land on Rochelle. "You have some fucking nerve."

"Me?" She points to herself while shaking her head. "I didn't even want to come, let alone be attacked from behind by some blonde maniac. Maybe you should control your bitches," she yells at him.

Everyone around us goes silent, and Blaze steps up to her, but I block his path, stepping in his way.

"I would calm down."

"You pick her?" he spits angrily.

"I'm not picking anyone. But you will watch what you say or do to her."

"I'll do no such thing. You're on my property now."

"It's in both our names. This is *our* place. I let you think you can have it."

Rochelle steps up from behind me. "Tell me, Blaze… tell me why you hate me?" She takes a long pull of her beer. She brushes up against me, and Blaze doesn't miss the action.

"You're changing him. I hate that you are."

Rochelle looks to me with her eyes pinched. "Am I?"

I don't answer her, because she is. I think she knows that too. I'm almost ready to walk through fire for her to make sure she's safe, and stand still as I burn.

"He won't answer you. He can't see it yet," Blaze says, looking between us. "But I see you. Your world is too perfect for him to fit in. How will you explain him to your friends? Your family?"

"My family loves him."

Blaze looks back at me, surprised. "You've met her family?"

I shrug.

Lips thin and squinted eyes look back at Rochelle. "I fucking hate you," he spits.

"Feeling's mutual, asshole. What Tan ever saw in you I will never know."

"Why she had you as a friend, yeah, who the fuck knows? You only cared for yourself, bitch," he throws back at her face.

Rochelle goes tight, her body rigid. But then fast as she can, she reaches up and slaps him across the face. Hard.

Blaze moves fast, grabbing his gun and pointing it directly at her head. She doesn't move.

"Prez," Snow says behind him. "Lower the gun."

"No, this bitch needs to know her place."

"Did you show Tan her place, too?" Rochelle eggs him on.

"No. I was nothing but good to her. Unlike you."

The gun doesn't lower.

"You know nothing about her. It wasn't you she called when she needed someone, it was me," she screams at him.

"It's because she loved you," Blaze says back to Rochelle.

"Lower the gun, Blaze," I say.

Rochelle doesn't even seem fazed anymore that the gun is in her face.

"Do it, I dare you. Do it."

"And make my brother hate me?" Blaze shakes his head and drops the gun. "Fuck off and don't bring her back again," Blaze says, as he walks away.

Chapter Twenty-Four

ROCHELLE

I manage to avoid Blaze for a good month after that night at the clubhouse. Marcus and I haven't changed, we see each other at least four times a week, and we can't keep our hands to ourselves for too long.

Everything with him is easy. It's nice. And *not* moving forward. I know that's also my fault. Something in me has changed. I guess death does that to you. You see the world in a different light. For me, I'm constantly seeing Tanika jump from that bridge. The nightmare wakes me when I'm by myself, and every time I close my eyes I dream of her.

Marcus helps those demons go away.

I'm becoming reliant on him.

I'm not sure how that makes me feel.

I love him, but I've pushed those feelings down because he's right. Love brings nothing but pain.

Leaving work, a man is leaning against my car. I should have gone an hour ago when Martin left. But tonight I'm not seeing Marcus because he's working, therefore I stayed back to finish up some things so I can leave early tomorrow.

My feet slow down when I notice who it is. Dave stands next to my car with a smile on his face as I get closer.

"Rochelle, right?" He straightens. I nod.

"Martin's left if you're after him. But I can give him a message if you like."

"Oh no, no message required. I actually came to see you."

"Me?" I ask, confused.

"Yes. I wanted to know if you would go on a date with me?"

"Oh," I shake my head. "Sorry. No. I'm seeing someone."

"Yes, Marcus, right?" He smirks at my shocked face. "I know things, but I could give you more than a man who works at a crematorium."

I'm sure he can, like the creeps for one.

Trying to step around him, a smile creeps up on his face, and I want to get away, I don't want to be near him. Looking around, there's no one in the area. It's after five and everyone has finished for the day. Damn it! I stupidly stayed back.

"I usually go for blondes, but there's something about you," he says, his head dropping to the side, assessing me. "I wonder what it is. I wonder if I'll know once I'm buried inside of you." My eyes go wide at his words, and I thread the keys resting in my hand through my fingers.

"You need to leave," is all I can manage to say.

Dave shakes his head. "No. No, I don't think I do."

"You do. You need to leave," I reiterate, not backing down. Men like this bastard like having power, but he doesn't know me, doesn't know I will fight to my last dying breath. I've had a shit year, so this guy can't make my life any worse.

Lights shine brightly and we both turn, then he looks back to me and smirks.

"I guess I will be off. Oh, and Rochelle… Tanika wasn't sweet, but I bet you will be."

Oh my God, his words make me freeze, and in doing so, it gives him enough time to step up to me, his hand coming up to my neck, locking tightly around it.

He licks my face and breathes heavily on me. "See, I knew you were going to be sweet."

A horn honks not far from us, and he lets go of my throat, backing away until he steps into a black car right behind mine.

The minute his car is gone, I get in my car and call Marcus, but he doesn't answer. I swear and start driving to his place. He has to be there, right? Because as I drive to his, I bypass his work and he isn't there. My hands shake as I drive, and tears are streaming down my face.

What did he mean?

What did he mean...

He couldn't have been the guy.

Could he?

Stepping on the gas, I speed up and pull into his driveway. We didn't arrange to see each other tonight, but right now I need him. I need him more than I've needed anyone for a long time.

I've been so numb. So numb, that right now I feel like I'm being slammed with all the emotions at once. And not one of them is good.

Pulling up at his house, I see he's not here. Where is he? Why isn't he here? I know he isn't a social man.

I call him again—there's no answer.

Hitting the steering wheel, I try to think of where else he could be. I should drive home, but I don't want to be by myself right now.

Pulling back out, I go to the one place I was told never to go to again. I don't stop on the way, and when I pull up to the front of the gigantic gates, which let me in, I spot his truck straight away. Taking only my keys with me, I walk in. It's not a party like the last few times I've been here, it's tamer, quieter. There're a few people sitting at a bar, Blaze not being one of them.

I look around for Marcus, and don't see him.

Harper spots me and waves me over.

"Oh God, you're here," she says in a tone that doesn't sound happy. But I'm not in the mood to dive into that right now, because I need to find Marcus.

"Yeah, look, I don't want to stay. I need to find Marcus. He isn't answering his phone."

"I know where he is."

Turning around, I see her, that same stupid-ass blonde. I don't even care what her name is.

"Where is he?" I ask, almost desperately.

She pulls the door open completely and it reveals she's naked. "Do you really want to know the answer to that?" Her eyebrows raise in question.

"Yes."

She steps out and points in. Stepping up closer to her, but not inside the room, I see him. He's asleep on the bed with no shirt on and a sheet covering his bottom half. I look up to her and know straight away she's won.

"He was in the mood, so was I. Didn't mean to hurt your feelings."

She did, of course, and she meant it because she's a cunt like that.

"You fucked him?" I ask, looking incredulously where he's lying asleep. Not a sound comes from him. Marcus looks so peaceful, so fucking beautiful. I hate him and love him all at once.

He's made me numb.

Or perhaps death has.

And those two? They are like twins.

I don't know who I am anymore.

Is it because of him?

"Come on, sweetheart, you do have eyes, right?"

My angry eyes fly to her, the blonde bitch. I want to pull her hair out, but I won't. I won't stoop to her level. Stepping away, a hand touches me, and I pull away.

"Rochelle," Harper says, as I turn to leave.

I run to my car and see Blaze standing at the entrance, watching me. Putting my car in reverse, I leave as fast as I can. My eyes fill with water as I head straight to my sister's house. It's the last place I can go to. My mother will ask too many questions, and I need to be with someone. Being alone right now isn't an option.

Wiping at my eyes, I manage to drive to Kat's house, which isn't too far from mine. And when I get out she comes over with Annabelle on her hip.

"Roch?"

"Can I stay tonight?"

"Yes. Of course."

I walk past Kat into her house. She's in the middle of cooking so she passes me Annabelle and I sit with her, playing on the floor.

"Do you plan to tell me why you're here and not with Marcus?"

"No."

"Okay. Did you guys have a fight?"

"No," I answer truthfully, pressing buttons on Annabelle's fake phone, which makes all kinds of whirring and dinging noises.

"How is it going with you two then?"

"Fine," I answer.

"Lord, Rochelle, tell me more. You've been so checked-out since Tan died. No one can talk to you without you giving them short, snippy words, and no one knows what to say to you."

"That's fine."

"Do you talk to him?" she asks.

I lean over and cover Annabelle's ears before I answer her, "We fuck."

"Oh, for fuck's sake," she says, then I smile and kiss Annabelle's cheek. "You love him though, right?"

"I think so."

"You either do or you don't."

"I love who he is with me. He helps me when he doesn't even know he's doing it."

"He lets you be silent," she says, as I look up to her. "I can tell straight away he isn't a man to push you for answers, or to give them." Kat's right about Marcus, he lets me be. "He would push you if he loved you. He would want you to be okay."

"I am okay."

"Why are you here, Rochelle?" She holds up her hands. "Not that I don't want you here. I do. I really, really do. But I won't be like Marcus because I need to know."

"A man came to my work today, he grabbed my throat and scared me. I don't want to be alone."

"Oh my God, how can you just say that so blasé." Kat shakes her head. "I'm calling the cops. You need to report this." And that's exactly what she does.

A man in uniform arrives quite quickly, and I recognize him. He coughs when he sees me and tells me he's sorry for my loss. Yet again. Then I give him all the information and he leaves. Kat has put Annabelle to bed, so it's just us now.

"Does Marcus know?"

"Know what?"

Her hand slaps my leg, and she pinches the skin as hard as she can. She's frustrated with me.

"Ouch."

"Yeah, that's right. You feel that."

"*I feel everything*," I scream at her. "I felt it the worst when Grandma and Grandpa died," I say to her, my voice still loud. "I felt it when his lips touched me, and I knew I was falling in love with a man who couldn't love me back, but I fell anyway." Taking a deep breath, I continue, "Then I felt it even worse… hell, it ripped my soul out… when she jumped. When I watched my best friend dive off a bridge because her demons were too big to handle. How do you think that felt?" I scream. Pushing her hand away, I stand. "And I feel it in the way he touches me, as if I'm his everything. So that's what I'm doing, letting myself get lost in the way he touches me. Letting myself lose myself in him. Because the pain… the pain of everything else is too much for me to bear."

"Rochelle, you need to end this. I don't know who you're becoming with him. You need to end it."

My phone rings, and I see his name come up on the screen, so I answer, "Hello."

"I'm home now. You were looking for me?"

"I'm coming over." I hang up and stand.

"You aren't staying?" Kat asks.

"No, I need him."

"No, no you don't. You need you."

"No, right now I need him," I say, walking out and going straight to him.

Chapter Twenty-Five

MARCUS

When she turns up, I'm expecting a war. Harper told me what Misha did, and I know things will be a battle, but Rochelle does the exact opposite. She falls into my arms, wrapping herself around me and starts tearing at my clothes. Hands are going everywhere, and I try to stop her, but she's on a mission. I don't see her every night, and when I do, we hardly speak. I like it like that. I like that words aren't needed as much anymore, and I also realize how selfish that is of me.

But I will take what I can from her.

Because soon she will crack, and when she does, I'll have to set her free. A woman like her shouldn't be tied to me. She has so much good, and I have none.

"Rochelle," I say, pulling her back. Her eyes flash with hurt before they're covered again in need.

"Since when do you call me that?" I've said it a few times, but she hasn't been paying much attention to what I say.

"What do you need?" I ask her.

She pushes up against me. "You. I just need you," she says, stepping back and removing her own clothing. I watch as she steps out of her skirt, leaving on her heels, so she can reach me. I've always liked her height, but with heels on she's closer to my head, making our kisses perfect.

She is perfect.

I am not.

Picking her up under her ass, I walk with her. Rochelle's kisses don't stop, and her hands won't stop roaming my body. I'm hard and I want in her, but first I need to take her to the only place I haven't had her—the pool. Stepping in, she stops what she's doing as the cold water hits her, and I stop on the step, depositing her on it. Stepping farther in, so my feet touch the ground, my chest is all that's exposed.

"The pool?" she asks.

Rochelle comes out here in the mornings sometimes to watch me swim, or late at night when I can't sleep and need the exertion of a good swim to exhaust me. She's fallen asleep multiple times on those lounge chairs.

"Do you plan to tell me the real reason you came looking for me?"

Surprise flashes on her face, and she slides forward until she wraps her sweet little body around mine. Her ass on the step brings her to the perfect position for me to slide into her when she is wrapped around me, and I do just that. Her head drops back, but her hands stay glued to me.

"No. Not at all," she says. It's then I notice marks on her neck. My hand touches the bruises, and she flinches but doesn't stop moving, sliding up and down my cock. Rochelle leans forward, her head coming into the crook of my neck, so I can no longer see her bruises, and she holds onto me tightly.

I grip on, lifting her and letting her move. She needs this more than I do right now. Usually, it's me needy with lust for her, but tonight it's all about her.

"You can have me," I tell her.

She shifts her hand to cover my mouth and doesn't stop moving. I can see her eyes vividly now, and hurt is evident in them, as she leans forward and bites her hand that covers my mouth as she comes. Then she slides off of me, and slides backward, putting distance between us.

"I can't really have you, though, can I?" Rochelle stands and walks back to the house, closing the door behind her. Getting out quickly, I follow her. She's already in my bed when I step into the room, her eyes are open as she lays there.

"What?" I ask her.

"I had another man's hands around my throat today. He told me I would taste sweeter than Tanika. How would he know that?"

I freeze at her words. What the fuck!

"Rochelle."

"Why are you calling me that?" Her eyebrows are pinched together.

"It's your name."

"Not for you, it isn't." And she's right, but I don't tell her that.

"Do you know this man?"

She nods. "Yes."

"How?"

Rochelle moves and pulls the blanket up to her chin. "He's a client. A private one of Martin's who I bumped into." She pauses. "I don't want to talk about this. I want to go to sleep."

"I have to work tonight, Rochelle."

"I'll just go to sleep, then." And she does, turning to give me her back and closing her eyes.

Walking out of the bedroom, I get dressed and go straight back to Blaze.

"Rochelle knows who he is," I tell him.

Blaze pauses his hand, which is up some girl's skirt, and turns to me. "What?"

"He threatened Rochelle. Told her she would taste sweeter than Tanika."

Blaze stands fast, the girl on his lap falling to the floor.

"Who the fuck is he?" he growls.

I smirk. "We're about to find out."

Chapter Twenty-Six

ROCHELLE

Marcus doesn't come back, and my sleep is awful. On and off I doze, never falling into a deep sleep. Those frightening eyes of Dave's stare at me, scare me, and then there's the dreams which consume me of that bastard touching her, of him hurting her.

When I pull myself out of bed, I feel worse than when I climbed into it. And Marcus isn't here to help me.

I should have said something to him last night, about the blonde. But I realized I needed him more than knowing what happened between them. So, I took him to remind him he has me, and I lost myself in his touch as I always do.

I love him based on kisses and lies.

Climbing out of his bed, I go into his closet, it's neat just like everything else in his house. He's always so clean. Everything's always so perfect. My hands grip on a neat pile of clothes, and I tear them down, tearing and ripping until it's not so perfect anymore. Not everything can be perfect. Sometimes you have to tear things down to build them back up.

"Do you plan on redecorating my whole room?" I jump, startled by his voice, and turn to find him and Blaze standing in the doorway. All I have on is a tank top and panties, but I don't care.

"Maybe," I say, looking between them.

"We have someone we want you to meet," Blaze says, then walks away.

Marcus continues to stand there, eyeing me. "You need to get dressed first and tie your hair up in a bun."

"Why?"

"Do the hair first, so it doesn't get on anything."

I sigh and do as he says—I'm on autopilot. A part of me knows the old me wouldn't take orders from Marcus like this, but I can't help myself. Once my hair's in a bun, I reach for my clothes, pulling them on.

"Is there a reason you were tearing my closet apart?"

It's been months now, months since we've been together, and I haven't asked for more.

He hasn't offered it either.

We are stagnant, going nowhere fast.

"No," I lie.

"Okay," he says, taking my answer as he usually does. There are times when he questions me, but it's never for too long, and then he gives up or doesn't care. I don't know which one is worse.

"Follow me."

We head downstairs, then out the back. We cross through some of his land before I see an old shed standing tall. Marcus doesn't stop or look behind as he opens the door, holding it open for me to pass through.

Stepping inside, the floor is white and clean. So extremely clean it's scary. Looking up, I see a chair. The chair reminds me of one you go and sit on at the dentist's office. But it's what is in that chair that makes me take a step backward until I hit a hard body.

"Rochelle."

There he goes again. Using my name. Why doesn't he call me pretty girl anymore?

"What…." The words get stuck in my throat, and I am unable to move.

"I told you not to bring her in here," Blaze says while shaking his head. "She should have left." His angry eyes meet mine.

Looking back to Marcus, his face is blank, as if it's normal to have a man gagged, and tied to a chair so he can't move.

"Do you want to leave?" Marcus asks.

"No," I answer truthfully.

He steps past me, happy with my answer, and walks over to Dave in the chair. I hate that I have to see him again, but I am happy it's not him in a position of power. That bastard creeps me out, and for a good reason. Dave's eyes look at me, and I can see he's pleading with me, but I don't have anything in me to give to him.

"He hired my boss to take you down," I tell Blaze, who looks up at me, shocked.

"That's interesting. So, you were behind the newspaper articles then?" Blaze asks while looking down at Dave. "I only fucked your wife once, and you know she wanted it. Plus, it was payment for all those fucking drugs you never paid for."

Dave starts thrashing in his seat, and Blaze smiles, looking over at me. "He would have lied, it's what Dave's so very good at. A lying, cheating, scumbag." Blaze shakes his head, and I turn to see Marcus dressed in a white coat, he's wearing gloves and a face mask.

"Did he do it?" I ask Blaze.

He leans down, takes the gag from Dave's mouth, and looks him in the eye. "Tell her."

"I knew she was yours, the second time. I marked her and told her my cock can go deeper than yours. Then I showed her. She screamed then," Dave says to Blaze.

What a mistake.

I lose all the contents of my stomach at his words.

I don't want to know. Really, I don't want to know any of the details.

"You should leave now," Marcus says through his mask.

"What do you plan to do to him?"

Marcus doesn't answer as he steps closer to a struggling Dave.

It's Blaze who answers, "He deserves everything he's about to get. And Rochelle…" I look up to Blaze, "… you were never here. And you know nothing of this place. Do you understand?"

I nod at his words.

"I need your words, Rochelle," he says.

"Yes."

"Good. Go home. You won't have to worry about him again." Then Blaze walks over to me, opens the door as Dave starts speaking his evil words about all the things he did to Tanika, and how much she liked it. The minute the air hits me, I can no longer walk. And as the door shuts behind me, I collapse onto the grass out the front. I can still hear Dave screaming awful things about Tanika, but, somehow, I can't seem to move my body. It's stuck in the position it is in.

Music blares and I know what's happening. I don't know exactly, but I have a pretty good idea.

The screams eventually fall silent, and the sky seems to grow darker.

Curling up in a ball, I lay there with the sun shining down on me, wondering what it would be like to live a different life. And how on earth did I end up here, lying out front while my lover is in a shed more than likely tearing apart a rapist.

All while I do nothing but twiddle my thumbs in the grass.

When the door finally opens, I'm still lying in the grass with my eyes closed and not wanting to move. The sun has started to set and I know, I just know, this isn't me. I have to change. I have to change all of this. Starting with the man standing above me.

"Déjà vu," I say.

Marcus walks around so he's standing in front of me, reaching down to help me up. When I stand, he picks me up as if I weigh nothing, and carries me back to the house.

"Is he dead?" I ask.

"Yes."

"Dave went back to Tanika the second time because he knew she was with Blaze, right?"

Marcus' eyes search mine as we reach the house. "Yes."

Pain radiates through me, and sadness hits me hard. "I miss her."

Marcus doesn't speak, just puts me in his bedroom and heads for the shower. When I manage to move, I head in too. His shower is large and open, and it has no glass doors.

"I'm going to go," I tell him.

Marcus nods, there's no fight in him. No asking me to stay.

Just a damn nod.

"Marcus…"

He turns that beautiful ass of his, leaving my view, and now stands before me, a man with scars and a face so hauntingly beautiful I have to remember to breathe.

"Do you love me?"

He picks up the soap, blinks a few times, and turns back again. Giving me no answer. I nod my head in acknowledgment and leave. He doesn't try to stop me. He doesn't even walk me out.

As I get in my car, I see Blaze standing in the dark near his motorcycle. He stubs out his cigarette and walks toward me, then leans down so he's at my window and looks me over.

"I hated you on the merit that you're too good. I can see it. You are too good for someone like my brother. Not that he isn't a great man," Blaze says. I don't speak. "You haven't experienced half the things in this life he has. He's walked through hell and never once looked back. He does that for people he loves. It's why I admire him so much." Blaze winks. "Don't tell him that, though."

I won't, because I think this is it.

I think I'm done.

I can't do this anymore.

Marcus had become a security blanket, one I no longer need. Well, one I have to stop needing.

"What I'm saying is, Marcus doesn't know good. You are the first good thing in his life that doesn't expect anything. Do you get what I'm saying?"

I do expect something from Marcus, and right now, I want something. I want him to tell me he loves me. And he didn't. So my heart, which is shattered, will slowly grow back to love again. Maybe I will love myself differently, but I need to grow it back and become whole once more.

Too much death, and not enough life.

Marcus is all about death.

I am not.

"I don't hate you, but I don't like you," he says, pushing back so his face is no longer near mine. "I couldn't protect her, but I can protect him. If you stay with him any longer, he will change, and he doesn't need to. Marcus is perfect just the way he is." I shake my head, confused by his words. "He will never love you. He vowed to never love another woman after our mother. You will be lonely with him, no matter how good you are. He is always in the dark. Always." Then he turns and walks off back to his bike, kick-starting it, and leaving me sitting in the driveway with no sign of Marcus and a hole the size of New York in my heart. He must know by now I'm no longer inside the house, and he hasn't come to stop me, or see if I am okay.

Maybe Blaze is right.

No, I know he is.

Marcus will never love me the way I love him.

And no matter how much I try telling myself it will be enough, it isn't.

Marcus told me he would only be with me.

Now that's a lie too.

Does he like her more than he likes me?

I shake my head as the jealousy of the blonde comes roaring into my head.

I'm not a jealous woman, and Marcus has turned me into a crazy person.

Chapter Twenty-Seven

MARCUS

"You lied to her," Blaze says later that night as he steps into the back house, his eyes falling to the source of the lie. Dave, who is not dead.

"It was necessary."

"Was it, though?" he asks. "You have a woman who, despite all of this…" he waves his hands around, "… still hangs around."

"You don't even like her."

"True. This is true. But I can see the way she looks at you."

"And how is that?" I ask, walking over to a passed out Dave, who is close to death.

"She looks at you as if you're her lifeline."

"I don't want to be anyone's lifeline," I mutter while shaking my head.

"I think you do," Blaze says.

Dave starts to stir. He's strapped to the chair, unable to move. He starts to make muffled sounds, then screams when the pain begins to take hold.

Blaze looks down on him and shakes his head. "Everyone thinks it's me who is the dangerous one and you're just the freak. But they don't really know it's you who's the dangerous one. And I feel even if she knew that as well, she'd still accept you."

"She's good," I tell Blaze, reaching for my favorite item—the saw.

Dave starts squirming.

"And you're evil. She will balance you out."

"Again… you hate her, that makes it hard," I tell him.

"I do, but I love *you*." My hand freezes at his words. "You protected me. Showed me what love is. You didn't even know you were doing it. I'd hear your screams when they would burn you. I never ran too far from the trailer. I had to know. Had to know they didn't kill you."

"They could never have killed me."

"They could have. You loved Mom, and you should have left several times. You didn't, though, because you wanted to protect me from *her*, Marcus. You stayed because you stay for broken things. And Rochelle is broken now."

"No, she isn't. She's hurt."

"If you say so. But also think about what you want." Blaze steps back as I put Dave's hand flat on the table, his screams are muffled as I start to saw each finger off individually. It's not long before he passes out. The area fills with blood again, mixing with what is already dried up from when we did his toes yesterday.

Blaze has instructed we give him the same pain he inflicted on Tanika. And short of shoving this saw up his ass, which I am still contemplating, this will do. Torturing him and stopping when he passes out, then restarting when he wakes again. Over and over until I have nothing left to cut off.

Then, if I feel generous, I might take this blade to his throat and finish the job.

"She wants kids," I tell Blaze, my blade sitting on Dave's stomach as we wait for him to wake.

Blaze steps back and shakes his head. "Fuck."

"Exactly," I groan.

"Well, you need to work out what you're doing."

The door pushes open, and Snow steps in. He's the only other one who knows about this place other than Blaze.

"I found these." Snow drops pictures and panties onto the floor.

Majority of those pictures are of Tanika, but a few are of Rochelle as well. Then I see ones where she's showering, and the curtain is not fully shut.

"Marcus," Blaze says, holding a photograph of Rochelle standing next to me. My arm's holding Rochelle possessively, and there's a look in her eyes that can only be described as love. She doesn't look at me like that anymore. She looks at me as if I'm a need to be filled.

She's lost in a world where I cannot pull her back from.

"Fuck," Snow says, moving a photograph on the floor.

It's one of Rochelle sleeping. *He was inside her house?* How the fuck was he in her house? Before I can stop myself, my saw is at Dave's neck, and as he opens his eyes, I watch as the life drains from them.

"Fuck. Really, Marcus?" Blaze shakes his head, picking up all the photographs. "Burn these when you burn him."

Chapter Twenty-Eight

ROCHELLE

"Oh, look, it's you again." I step back, my eyes narrow. Then I realize who it is. It's hard because I don't recognize her dressed in clothes.

The blonde.

The evil bitch.

Her cell phone dings, and she looks away from me then looks back with a smile. "Don't recognize me?" she asks with a hand on her hip.

Kat looks to us both. I can tell she's unaware of what's going on. I should have avoided this place, and from now on I know I will. But our food is on its way, and it's obvious the bitch works here. Just my luck.

"And you are?" Kat asks, clearly not happy being interrupted.

"I'm Marcus' other girl… hasn't this one told you?" blonde bitch says.

"No. No she hasn't because clearly you aren't relevant," Kat fires back.

The blonde, whatever her name is, which I don't really care, scrunches up her nose.

"Well, I was relevant to *him* the other night."

It was two nights ago now, and I haven't seen Marcus since.

"My guess is you're here annoying us right now in an attempt to get Rochelle to bite. For what reason, I don't know. Maybe you're jealous? Who knows? But if you don't go away, I will call your manager and get you the fuck fired," my sister says, then shoos blonde bitch with her hand, to which she scrunches up her nose and turns, leaving us.

I smile at Kat, but she doesn't return it. "Thanks."

"Oh, don't thank me. I want to know everything, and I want to know it now. So spill."

I tell her about the blonde bitch, and Kat shakes her head.

"You didn't ask him?"

"No."

"What did you do?"

"I went to yours, then I went to him. Fucked him until I fell asleep."

Kat's hand goes to her mouth and she mumbles something I don't quite hear. Then she says, "You fucked him? What the fuck is wrong with you? Wake up, Rochelle. Leave that fucking world you're in and wake the hell up." Kat stands and grabs my wrist, then starts walking toward the car. We don't even eat, but she left some money on the table before she dragged me out. We get in her car, and I don't question when she drives off. Kat stops at the cemetery, and I close my eyes.

"Oh no, you *are* getting out. Open those pretty blue eyes and get out." I hear her door slam, then she walks around to my side, opening the door and reaching in for me.

"I don't want to."

"No, you've been avoiding any sort of feeling. I can tell. Now get out and feel again."

I pull my hand back. "I like not feeling, it's easier."

"No, it's not. Now. Get. Out." Kat pulls me again until I'm out of the car, then she doesn't let go as we start walking. It's not long before the headstone registers in my brain, and I know whose it is straight away.

My grandparents.

I collapse to the ground, and tears start almost straight away. I haven't cried in so long because holding it in feels safer. Kat leaves me there until I can manage to calm my breathing, then she pulls me back up to her. We go to the wall of names. Tanika was cremated, so her plaque is on a wall with a few others, but I spot her name straight away, my fingers roaming over it as the tears blur my vision.

"You did nothing wrong. Tan had demons she thought she couldn't live with. She loved you, Rochelle."

I nod. I know Tanika loved me. I loved her too. No, love. Still do.

"I need to do something before I talk myself out of it," I say, standing and wiping my face.

"I'll take you to your car."

My hand grips the glass tightly, my breathing picks up as I watch Marcus Stone in action. I can see his skin glistening under the cold night as each stroke grows more powerful, one after the next. My eyes are glued to his body as he comes up for air. His strong jawline opening then closing with each powerful breath.

How can watching someone swim turn you on?

I'm not sure, but it can. Somehow it turns me on.

Bringing the glass to my lips, I take one more drink, finishing the contents and feeling the burn as it goes down. I need the liquid courage. I need it to face him.

Marcus turns, his strokes finally stop when he looks at me. The light from the kitchen is not helping to obscure me while I sit in the dark, stalking.

My breathing stops as his two powerful eyes lock on mine, his strong hand lifts and strokes his fingers through his hair. I'm helpless and can't help but watch as the muscles in his arm flex during the simple action. His hazel eyes narrow in on me.

"Rochelle…" Marcus says my name as easily as the water drips from his body.

It makes me even madder.

The drink in my hand feels like it could smash any second with the pressure I'm applying to the glass. He pushes himself out of the water, his body glistening as he comes to a stand not too far away from me. Reaching for a towel, he wipes his body. His hazel eyes, now darkening, lock on me when I don't answer him.

"I'm leaving you," I say with a smile when my breath doesn't hitch at those words.

"This is what you want?" Marcus asks.

No fight.

No argument.

Nothing.

"Yes. I'm leaving you," I say it more to myself this time. Perhaps to help me believe it.

He chuckles.

The asshole chuckles.

"Off you go, then."

With as much strength as I can muster, I throw my glass at him, just missing his head when he ducks out of the way. When he stands taller, I know that was a mistake. But I honestly don't care. I can't care anymore.

Pushing myself up from the lounger where I was reclining while working up the courage to tell him I am leaving, I step forward and come just under his chin.

Marcus is tall.

I hate that about him.

I hate a lot about him.

But then again, I also don't.

"Is that all you've got to say?" I arch an eyebrow.

Marcus arches one back. "Yes." Then he pushes past me, not caring that he almost knocks me over as he heads inside.

I follow. I shouldn't, but I can't help myself.

"You sleep with her… when I'm not here… in this house," I yell.

He halts, turns, and smirks. "I do," Marcus says, the towel now dropping. His swimwear is sitting low on his hips. "And I fuck her hard… all the ways you hate and I love." His lips turn up, waiting for me to say something in return.

"I hate you," I spit at him.

"I know you do."

"I hate you sooo much."

"That's okay. You can leave now."

"Is she coming over?" I yell.

Marcus turns, his hand touching the railing that leads up to his room.

I've never really lived here—I was simply a visitor. No one important. Just a person in this man's life. No one can penetrate him. I feel sorry for the person who finally does get through his impervious walls. They will either be very stupid or love him more than anyone else ever has.

"She will be now. I have steam I need to work off." He takes the steps two at a time and disappears, leaving me standing in the foyer with my hands clenched as I look around for my things. Luckily for me, I never moved out of my house. What a mistake that would have been if I had.

But worse, what a mistake Marcus was.

While rushing around and grabbing my things, I hear a ding. Looking over to the countertop, I see his cell light up. For some reason he doesn't have it locked, so I slide it open and up pops a girl's name.

Misha

I want you to spank me so bad, baby.

I gag, then throw his phone at the floor, hard enough that it shatters.

Fuck him and his cheating ass.

Picking up my bags, I walk to the door and step through, pushing it hard behind me so it slams. Again, fuck him and whatever he thinks.

My car is parked out the front where I left it when I arrived to break this nightmare off. I knew I'd have to make a quick getaway.

I need to get away from him.

He's poison.

Toxic.

A virus that has inserted itself in my system and won't leave, sucking me dry.

Now is my chance to extract that poison.

I have to for my own health.

For my own good.

Marcus Stone is not good for me, that much is obvious.

Throwing my bags in the car, I look back at his house, and when I look up, I see him standing on his balcony staring down at me. Marcus' hands are on the railing, his eyes locked onto mine.

"Fuck you," I say under my breath, as I walk around and get into my little red car.

The car creaks, and I wonder if it can hear my own heart doing the same.

The tears don't come, not until I'm almost home.

I feel everything. Everything.

And I want the pain to go away, but I won't allow it to.

I love a man who can't love me back. Marcus never made me believe that he could love me. I knew this, but it didn't stop me from falling in love with him anyway.

And fall I did.

My sister's sitting on my front steps when I arrive back at my house. Kat stands when she sees me, and I walk to her falling into her arms.

"You did it?"

I don't need to reply, she already knows. I manage to nod in her arms, and she squeezes me tighter. "Breaking your heart is the worst pain of all."

"He never loved me," I say, wiping my tears as I look up at her. "I knew it, but I stayed anyway. Hoping maybe it was possible."

"Yes. But, did you love yourself with him?"

That's the tricky part isn't it? Did I?

I was breaking when I met him, and I broke even more each day thereafter. Marcus didn't get the best of me, he got the broken part of me, and I did nothing to repair that.

Chapter Twenty-Nine

ROCHELLE

MARCUS MAKES NO ATTEMPT TO SEE ME. NONE AT ALL. I DIDN'T REALLY EXPECT him to, but as the weeks pass and I don't hear from him, I wonder if he even thinks of me, or if it's just my broken heart hoping maybe he does.

My soul's crushed, just as much as my heart was when I left his house.

I return to work and life goes back to where it was. Before my grandparents' death. Before meeting *him*.

I start to smile again, which is nice. It takes time, but eventually it comes, even though it's painfully slow. When I think of those whom I loved and lost, I don't break down at the drop of a hat anymore. Now, I smile and try to remember the good, and not get hung up with the bad. The bad is not a good place for me to dwell in.

Kat asked to move in with me. Her lease was up on her place, and she had been over at my house every day with Annabelle anyway. I was more than happy for her to move in. The company's nice.

Kat started dating.

I don't.

I won't.

Annabelle is my companion when Kat goes out, and thank God for my beautiful, toothy niece. She makes me smile on days when I'm not sure I can, or perhaps the truth is I don't want to.

"You need to date," Kat says, smiling as she slides on a red dress. "Get dressed, you're coming with me."

"Nope. No way," I reply while shaking my head and sitting my ass on the couch.

"Oh yes you are. Now get up."

"I don't want to do that speed date thing you do."

"This isn't that. I'm going out with a few friends to a club. You. Are. Coming."

"Nope," I say, crossing my arms over my chest.

"You haven't heard from Marcus since you broke up. It's been almost two months, Roch. Get dressed, it's time for another man to play with that heart of yours."

"I like not having my heart fucked around with, and I don't want that anymore if I can help it. Thank you very much."

Kat waves at me. "Please, you loved it." She throws a dress from her closet at me. "You can be pretty in red, too. Now get it on, it's a red party."

"Isn't it meant to be a white party?"

"No. Now slide it on and put your hair up. I have to leave soon, and the Uber is on its way."

"I don't want to go."

"If you come, I will clean for a month."

I jump at her words and start stripping, sliding on the dress, and heading off to change panties before I throw my hair up. When I walk out, she's wearing heels, and she dangles a pair off her fingers for me. "I knew that would work. You hate housework. Now, come on."

Of course, it would work, and she knows it. Honestly, I hate cleaning, cooking, you name it. Hate it. My goal in life is to live where I never have to cook again, I detest it *that* much.

Now that would be living.

"How long are we expected to stay out?" I ask as we both slide into the Uber.

"Don't even start the night off with that attitude," Kat answers with an eye roll.

"What?"

She points her finger in my face. "I know what you're doing, and don't. Relax, try to have fun. Have a few drinks and mingle. Mum has Annabelle and I need this."

"Are you meeting anyone?"

"No, but I hope to."

Kat's in a phase lately where she likes to go out. She never used to. Hardly went out before Annabelle, and now that Annabelle's over a year old she's started to go out more. If I don't watch Annabelle, our mother does. And it's not like Kat goes out often, just more times than we are used to from her. This is her second time this month, and I like to see her happy. It's as if she's discovering life again, and she's living it.

We come to a stop outside a club that is not in our area. I haven't been here before, as I prefer to stay local.

Getting out, there's a queue around the corner. Damn, I really don't want to wait in a line. Kat clamps her hand around mine and pulls me to the front of the queue. The bouncer smiles at Kat and instantly lets her in.

"When did you become miss popular?" I ask as we make our way down steps into a busy area full of people.

"One of the guys from my speed date owns this place. It's pretty cool, hey?" I can only nod at her words. "Okay, let's drink." Kat walks to the bar, buys two drinks, and turns around. "So, I know for a fact those guys over there…" she points to an area in the corner where a few guys are seated, "… are single. Any of them tickle your fancy?"

I look, even though I know I won't say yes. One guy with blond hair, the type I would usually go for, before *him* that is, takes my eye.

"That's Matt, by the way."

"I'm not interested."

"You want to turn into a lonely old cat lady?" she asks with an eyebrow cocked.

"No, I want to move on, but only when I'm ready."

Kat turns away with her drink in her hand. Then her hand grabs mine and she squeezes. I turn in her direction.

Then I see them.

Both of them.

They're walking to the booth area where all the guys are seated. Marcus stands behind his brother, Blaze. Marcus is just a fraction taller and just as big, but he doesn't look interested. Blaze, on the other hand, looks angry. A few guys straighten when they see them approaching, and they start talking, but my eyes don't leave him. Marcus is dressed in black jeans and a white shirt, and his hair is brushed backward, so his curls are not as strong or evident as they usually are.

Damn! I love those curls.

"I need to go," I say to Kat.

"Yes, okay, then. Sorry, I didn't know they would be here."

I don't reply to Kat, simply turn and start for the door. It's busier now, and it is hard to push through the people to get back to the front.

Suddenly, I'm pulled back, and I'm about ready to let go at Kat when I turn and see Marcus with his hand on me. "Pretty girl."

Something rushes toward my chest from the sound of that voice, suffocating me. Pulling my arm out of his grasp, he looks at me, shocked. "Why are you here?"

I scrunch my face at his words and turn to see Blaze talking with Kat, who's next to me. I can't hear what they're saying, but she's smiling. And Marcus, well, he looks serious.

"I was just leaving."

"You look good, pretty girl."

I laugh. Uncontrollable, crazy laughter, and wipe at the tears that burn in the back of my eyes.

"You are fucked, you know that? Fucked."

"Why did you leave, pretty girl?"

I step closer to him. "I chose to leave because loving you was making me become less and less like me."

Marcus looks at me like he can't believe the words that have left my mouth. I turn to Kat and see she's up on her tippy toes as she whispers to Blaze. Blaze's eyes go wide, and I reach for her. "We are leaving."

"Okay."

Pushing past Marcus, I walk out with Kat behind me and wave a cab down.

"We're really leaving?" Kat asks.

"Yes." Then I stop. "Do you want to stay?"

"No. Well, yes. But no."

Opening the cab door, I slide in, and just when I think she's going to follow, a pair of black jeans climbs in, and Marcus is sitting next to me, shutting the door with Kat standing next to Blaze.

"Get out."

"Where to?" the cab driver asks.

Marcus rattles off my address and the cab starts moving. When I look out the back window, Kat gives me a wave, smiling.

Fuck.

"You need to get out."

"No. It seems we need to talk."

"I don't want to talk to you." I pull my legs away from Marcus and make sure none of my body is touching him.

"You do. And I want to talk to you."

"You don't talk. So please don't act like you want to."

"I will, for you."

My head turns sharply to look at him, his hazel eyes already firmly on me.

"Lies," I spit at him.

"No. We need to talk."

"Then talk," I say, placing my hands in my lap with an eyebrow raised while waiting. The cab driver probably thinks we're crazy, but I don't care.

"I've missed you," he says, his face serious.

"Okay," is all that seems to leave my mouth at his words.

"Have you not missed me?" he asks. I watch as his hand moves closer to me.

I pull my leg away and narrow my eyes at him. "I don't give you permission to touch me. Do *not* touch me," I say as we come to a stop out the front of my house. I slide out and hear Marcus pay the cab driver before he also gets out. I don't want to invite him inside, so I stay on my stairs as he walks across to me. His eyes drink me in, and he stops just shy of me.

"I need permission to touch you now?" he asks.

I nod my head. "Yes. You lost that right when you stuck your cock in a blonde bitch's pussy," I say back to him.

His head shakes and he steps closer. "I did no such thing."

"I saw you with her. You didn't deny it, and then I saw the messages."

"Oh yes, thanks for smashing my phone," he says with his eyes narrowed.

"You're welcome," I reply, crossing my arms over my chest.

"I see you," he says, reaching for a piece of my hair. "You aren't so numb anymore."

I brush his hand away. "No thanks to you."

"I didn't make you numb, pretty girl. I didn't push you through it either, though."

Marcus is right, he was content with how we were.

So was I. Until I wasn't.

"You need to go," I say, taking a large step back.

"No. I didn't sleep with her. I haven't slept with anyone since I met you." Marcus steps closer, not caring that I'm trying to put distance between us.

"You lie."

Marcus shakes his head. "No. No, I'm not. No more kisses and lies, it's the truth."

"We c-could never work, we're t-two complete opposites," I say to him, my voice breaking.

I want him.

I want him so badly because my heart loves him.

I love this man.

"Opposites last. We will never get bored of each other."

"We don't want the same things," I say.

"I'll do anything you want as long as it involves you."

"What about kids?" I ask.

Marcus' face hardens, and he stops.

"What about kids?" I ask him again.

"I can't have kids."

"Why? Why can't you have kids?" I ask. He's told me this once before, but he never explained why.

"I have to go." Marcus steps back.

"This is why. This is why we will *never* work."

He pauses, and before he can turn or say another word, I spin around, unlock my door and walk inside my house, slamming the door behind me. Sliding down the door, I listen for his footsteps. He comes up the stairs and stops at my door, I wait for him to knock but it doesn't happen. A few breaths later his feet retreat, and I'm left on my floor wondering why my heart beats so fast for a man who can never love me the way I want to be loved.

It's really unfair.

Chapter Thirty

ROCHELLE

Having Marcus come back into my life when I was healing hasn't done me any good, it's fucked me over yet again.
 I still love him.
I still want him.
Despite his damn words.
And, is what he told me true? It can't be. I saw them together, and then the messages. He didn't deny it when I asked, he told me he was going to fuck her. So why lie if it's not true? It makes no sense. None at all.

"Blaze was angry that Marcus left with you," Kat says, sitting next to me the following day. She came home very late, smelling like smoke and alcohol.

"You friends with Blaze now?" I ask.

She harrumphs. "If you mean, do I want to sleep with him, then the answer is yes." She smirks. "But no, we haven't."

"You sound awfully sad about that fact," I say, shaking my head.

"I don't want to marry the man, I just want to sleep with him," she says while standing. "Anyway, it's you we should be talking about. Marcus left with you."

"Not by my choice."

"Do you want him?"

I shake my head. "Why are you asking me this?"

"It's a simple question. Do you want him?"

"Yes. Yes, of course I want him, but I will not be one of those stupid girls who goes back to her cheating-ass boyfriend."

"Fair enough." She shrugs. "Though Blaze did say he would never have fucked around on you." Then Kat walks off, leaving me hanging on her words.

Heading to my room, I get dressed, then drive out to see Blaze at the clubhouse. Because I know on the weekend that's where he will be, and so will she. Surprisingly, I am let in without anyone stopping me.

I spot blonde bitch straight away. She's dressed today—still slutty—sitting at a table with everyone else as they eat.

"Oh God, not you again. Thought we got rid of you."

"Tell me, are you always such a cunt?"

Snickers are heard around the table as her eyes narrow in on me. "Do you want me to hit you, bitch?"

"You tried that already. Pretty sure I won." I give her a wide smirk.

"Rochelle," Blaze growls from the end of the table. "You come in here and threaten my people? What the fuck is wrong with you?"

I ignore him completely and look at blonde bitch. "Did you really fuck him? Or, were you being a messy bitch?"

"Misha," Blaze says.

Oh, so that's her name.

"I may have." The bitch flicks her hair, and it does nothing but irritate the fuck out of me.

"You may have? Or you did?"

"Misha," Blaze says again, becoming annoyed.

I hear footsteps behind me, and a hand touches my hip. I know who it is without turning.

"Misha," Marcus says behind me.

Misha's eyes narrow in on me. "No, I didn't sleep with him. Not that I didn't try, though." Blonde bitch winks at Marcus.

"Pack your shit, Misha, and leave," Blaze says.

Misha's head whips around to Blaze. "You can't be serious… over her?" She points to me.

"Over you being a bitch. Now pack your shit."

"No," she says, crossing her arms over her chest.

"I could make you leave. You covered in a black bag might look good on you," Marcus says.

Blonde bitch's eyes grow worried, and she stands, letting the chair fall back on the floor and shouldering me as she walks past. Turning to leave, I don't even bother saying goodbye to anyone. I walk quickly, and as I go to get into my car, before I can open the door, Marcus reaches for me and turns me around to face him.

"Was there anyone else?" I ask.

"No, only you."

"What was the message about then? Remember, I read it on your phone."

"Misha always sent me messages. If you had looked properly, you would have seen I never replied to any of them."

"Have you ever slept with her?" I ask.

"Once. That was long before I met you."

"Why can't you have kids, Marcus?"

His hand lifts, and I watch as his muscles strain in his shirt. He looks everywhere but at me. "Will you come to my house?" he asks. "We can talk there."

"Maybe tomorrow," I reply while opening my car door and sliding in. He leans on the window and looks down at me.

"Tomorrow?"

"Yes, tomorrow, Marcus. You aren't the center of my universe anymore."

"Fair enough." Marcus steps back, giving me room to move. "Tomorrow, pretty girl."

I give him a simple nod and drive off.

It's late, raining, and I'm soaked as I knock on his door. I simply couldn't wait until tomorrow. I want answers now. I need them. At first, I don't think he's home, but his truck is here.

"Marcus," I yell, my hand banging on his door.

A light flicks on, and through the window in the door I watch as he comes down the stairs with no shirt, and only a pair of gray tracksuit pants hanging from his hips.

My body starts shivering when he comes to the door. He doesn't invite me inside, he just stares at me like he can't believe I'm here.

To be honest, neither can I.

"I want kids," I say to him. "Why can't you have kids?"

"You want to talk about this now?" he asks, running a hand through his hair.

"Yes. Why?" I wrap my arms around myself as the rain pours even harder.

"Come inside."

"No." I shake my head. "I don't want to be in your space, I simply want to know why. Now tell me, Marcus. Tell me, so I can walk away for good if I need to."

"You want to walk away?"

"I don't want to, but I will. I've sacrificed myself enough for you, even though I know you never asked that of me. But I did. I put away my needs because I wanted to be with you."

"I never asked you to."

"I know, and that makes it worse," I say, shaking my head. I'm freezing, my bottom lip is involuntarily quivering, but I'm not moving. I want my answer. "Tell. Me. Now."

"No," he replies.

I huff at his words and turn, walking back to my car. Before I can get there he turns me around, the rain's running down his face.

"Let me go." I pull away, but he makes a move for me again and I slip. When I do, I go down, pulling him on top of me so we're both wet. I struggle to move with him on me, but he doesn't budge. He looks down at me, and I see it then, the change in his eyes. Something is different.

"I told you about my mother. I don't want to bring children into a world where this is what happens to them. I would never wish that on any child."

"You think you will turn into her?"

He closes his eyes, water falling from his eyelashes. "I would never be her, but that doesn't mean I don't have her traits. I'm guarded like she was. I don't like people, which is exactly like her." He tells me how he feels.

"That doesn't mean you will be like her."

"I don't want kids, Rochelle."

A heavy sigh leaves my mouth, then I push at him. He gets up and helps me up too.

"That's it? I don't want kids and you walk away?"

"It's what has to be. I would never choose to be with someone who loves the dead more than he loves the living. But here I am, telling you I love you regardless. And here you are, telling me you won't give me what I need. What I want from life."

"You can have a happy life with me without kids, pretty girl."

I put my hands up while shaking my head. "But I don't want that. I want to know what it's like to grow a baby in my belly. I want to know what that unconditional love is like. It changed my sister, and I want the same thing. I saw what that love can do."

"My love can do that too," he says, his lips now in a thin line. I don't think he's realized what he's just said, but I certainly took notice.

"You love me?" I ask him, confused. He knows I love him, but not once has he told me he loves me. Every time I told him, I got nothing in return.

"Yes. Do you need written confirmation?"

"Well, yes."

Marcus reaches out and pulls me into his arms, then his hands start tearing at my clothes, and I let him.

"This doesn't solve our problem. I can't be with you if you don't want the same things as me," I say as he pulls my skirt from my body, then lifts my hands, taking off my shirt.

"I want whatever it is you want to make you happy."

"I want kids."

"Except that." Then he lifts me.

"No. It will never work unless we want the same things," I say as he walks us to his bedroom. My legs are wrapped around him as he holds me tightly to him. I can feel he's hard beneath me, but I won't act on it. I can't.

"I want you. Whatever comes with that, I will learn to accept."

"You will?"

Marcus places me on the bed and looks down at me, my hair a frizzy mess from the rain. His locks are sticking to his forehead, and he never looked so fucking good. His gray tracksuit pants are wet, revealing the outline of his hard cock, so he peels them off, standing naked in front of me. Hard and exceptional.

"As long as you are a part of the package, I think I can walk through this thing called life."

"Really?" I ask again.

"Yes. Now will you shut up so I can kiss you?"

"Tell me you love me again."

Marcus bends forward, his lips touching mine, and soft slow kisses begin to take over my mouth and own it as if it was always his. Pulling back, I look at him straight in the eyes. "Tell me, Marcus."

"Only for you," he says while pushing me back and climbing over me. "Only for you will I say those words…. I fucking love you, pretty girl, and I will until the day I fucking die. That I know for sure."

I smile. "And kids?"

"Can we start slow? We have time."

"Slow? As in how slow?" I ask breathlessly while he pushes my legs apart.

"How about you move in, then we talk more about the kids part. But I would like to be buried deep in you every night for the rest of my life."

"Sounds like a plan." I smirk as he reaches between my legs, touches my clit with his fingers, and rubs in a circular motion while he nips at my lips.

Chapter Thirty-One

MARCUS

She's asleep next to me while my hands roam her perfect body. Rochelle moans, and turns to face me.

"Did you ask me to move in with you last night?" she asks, smiling up at me.

"I think I did."

"Wowser! Who knew all I had to do was break my own heart for you to come to your senses?"

"It broke mine, too."

Rochelle's eyes go wide at my words. But I'm not going to lie to her, I was fucking lonely and desperate when she left. I didn't know I needed her that much until she was gone. I didn't know I wanted her so badly until I couldn't have her.

"Did you think this was how we'd end up?"

"We've only just started," I say, leaning into her, kissing along her bare neck, when her phone starts ringing. She moans, wanting to ignore it but knowing she can't. "I have to get it," she says when it rings again.

"Rochelle."

I hear a scream. Rochelle giggles at the sound of her screeching voice.

"It's my sister," she whispers. "Clearly, still drunk."

"So, I may be at your lover's brother's playhouse thing. Can you come get me?"

Rolling off her I get up.

ROCHELLE

I didn't want to come back here—I hate this place and the memories it holds of Tanika now. The gates open and I spot Blaze standing at the wooden door, holding it open as I slide out of my car.

"Déjà vu," he says.

"Yes, another one close to me I'll have to save from you," I say while walking up to him.

Blaze's lip quirks. "As long as you don't get this one killed, we'll be fine."

His words anger me, and I instantly want to strangle him.

How fucking dare he!

"This is my sister, and she will *not* have anything to do with you." I cross my arms over my chest.

"I haven't killed you because Marcus loves you. Don't make my brother hate me because I found the need to end you."

I hear Kat giggle and watch as she comes out. She leans on him and he takes her weight. "Rochelle, how come you never invited me here before? I love it."

"You shouldn't be here," I tell Kat.

Blaze turns to her. "Your annoying sister is right. Don't fucking come back."

Kat seems to straighten and sober all at once. "What the fuck?" Her eyes turn to angry slits as she steps up to Blaze. *Kat has a temper, a bad one.* "Did you really just say that?"

"Yes. Now fuck off."

Kat shakes her head, steps closer, and I watch as she grabs his cock, cupping it in her palm. "I'm going to break your fucking heart, Blaze, and you're going to enjoy every single moment of it." Kat smiles, and I know she means every word. She drops his cock and walks over to me threading her arm through mine as we turn and walk off. I flick a glance back over my shoulder to Blaze, and see him watching her with a look I can't quite read on his face.

Is that appreciation?

Loss?

Or is it hope?

I don't know, but I'm eager to find out.

Because Kat is going to do exactly what she said—she is going to break that man's heart.

She's vengeful like that.

This is going to be fun to watch.

If you would like to read Kat's story, it is available now in *Kisses and Warfare*.
Available now.

Escort

SKYE WARREN

Chapter One

THE CITY LOOKS BEAUTIFUL AT NIGHT, ITS ROUGH EDGES KISSED BY MOONLIGHT, bright neon lights full of hope. My Bugatti slices through the darkness, smooths over cracked downtown streets. The leather is warm on the steering wheel, the gears smooth under my control. Every muscle in my body hums with anticipation, the certainty that I'm going to get laid tonight. It's more than sex that gets me off. It's the journey. Discovering what makes a woman work. What holds her back and what lets her go.

I pull into the valet driveway and toss my keys to Alejandro, who has three kids at home and another one on the way. "Take care of her," I tell him, slipping a twenty into his palm.

"It's my pleasure," he says, giving the gleaming curves an admiring look.

She's gorgeous, this car. The first thing I purchased for myself once I was done scrabbling for scraps. Once I learned how to use my particular talents. Her form is both sleek and curvy, the kind of body that drives a man to his knees. But it's not the way she looks that I love best. It's the way she moves. The engine that has a mind of her own, sometimes sweet surrender, sometimes temperamental.

I love her best when she gives me a challenge.

L'Etoile is a luxury hotel with 24-karat gold chandeliers and white marble floors. A slice of European aesthetic in the center of Tanglewood's urban sprawl. It's garish and expensive, which suits me fine. It was founded in the '40s by a woman who claimed to be French nobility. In reality, she was the madame of a lucrative brothel.

That suits me fine, as well.

The front counter is carved with ornate scrolls and baby angels. A woman stands behind them. Jessica, her name tag says. I give her a winning smile, and her brown eyes widen. "Good evening to you. Is there perhaps a message left for me? Hugo Bellmont."

Her expression becomes soft, vulnerable. I should be very tired of this expression, especially when it comes so easily, but my male pride is a simple creature. It does not mind making women swoon, again and again.

"I… I can check for you." She looks around for a moment, almost dazed. As if it's never occurred to her that people might come to the desk for messages.

"You have my gratitude."

After some fumbling, her cheeks deeply pink, she locates a stack of envelopes in one of the little cubbies. There is one with black script that I can recognize as my name from here. "Here you are."

I think about what would be required to undress her, to take off her clothes and what remains of her defenses. Very little, but we would both enjoy the journey. Alas, she isn't my intended partner tonight.

Inside the envelope is a hotel key card, which leads to the penthouse.

I've been to a hundred penthouses inside the city. And several outside of it. Each one is its own brand of ridiculous luxury. That's part of the heavy price tag, the ridiculousness. Bathtubs that could fit a baby elephant. Private infinity pools. A helipad complete with exclusive helicopter usage. You don't spring for the penthouse unless you want to be wowed.

Somehow, I've never been to the penthouse in L'Etoile.

It's always eluded me. And haunted me.

It isn't the amenities that interest me. A bed made of solid gold. Draperies spun from a rare Chinese silkworm. Whatever they are I'm sure they're lovely, but it's the person who rents them I want to meet. My chest feels tight with anticipation. A heavy beat through my veins, because this is more than a client. This is someone who might have access to the current owner of this hotel.

I shouldn't get my hopes up, but hopes aren't under my control. They rise and rise, high enough that I have to turn my thoughts away from revenge. To something much more base. Sex.

There's a private elevator that leads only to the penthouse and the private rooftop gardens. It requires the key card to call it down. There are three buttons on the inside wood panel: L for lobby, P for penthouse, and R for the roof. There's also the silhouette of a bell. I suppose that's for if, in the space between the lobby and their suite, they decide they need champagne and strawberries delivered. I could call down for some. Or I could have brought some flowers. Props, you could say. Props to charm a lady, but I don't need them. Don't want them. I pride myself on making them feel like they're the most incredible woman I've ever met, because for one night, they are.

A soft chime signals my arrival. The doors slide open.

I was prepared for any type of penthouse decor. Something lush and antique to match the lower floors. Something modern and sleek to appeal to the upscale traveler.

What I'm looking at isn't a penthouse at all. Not one I've ever seen.

There's a lumpy corduroy sofa in front of a gilded brick fireplace. A pile of old books about to topple over on a side table that probably came from Ikea. Through the room I can see floor-to-ceiling windows that would have been the focal point, but they've been covered by drapes. That alone would not be remarkable, except for the string of star-shaped plastic lights that traipse across them. It takes me a moment to realize that my mouth is open. Shocked. I'm shocked, which is pleasant enough considering it's a novelty. How long has it been since something surprised me? And where is the object of that surprise? There is no woman to greet me. No seductress. No glamourous woman ready for the night of her life. God, what is that strange tightening in my chest? It feels like anticipation, deep and true, and it's been a lifetime since I felt that.

"Hello," I call, stepping into the suite.

There's a thump from the bedroom. A woman pops her head around the corner, all frizzy hair and wild eyes and plump pink lips. She wears a black dress with a startling high neck, lace on top, the kind that a matron would wear—but her skin is perfectly smooth, her eyes wide. This is a young woman. Younger than myself, her clothes an anachronism. Her expression? Pure relief. "Oh thank God."

She sounds so sincere that I have visions of an orgasm emergency. A deficiency so intense she had to dial a twenty-four-hour line to have it fixed. There's something undeniably hot about the idea of a woman in dire straits and me the only one who can help.

"Hugo Bellmont," I tell her, providing a small bow. "At your service."

And then I give her the smile. Not the megawatt one that I used downstairs. I give her the slow, suggestive one that lets her know every dirty thing that I'm thinking.

It isn't fake. It doesn't need to be. Not with her whispery curls that I'd love to feel in my fist. Not with the pale freckles across her nose that I'd love to track all the way down her body.

Her eyes are an interesting pale green. I want to look in them while I go down on her.

Every single dirty thought is in the smallest smile.

Except she disappears back into the bedroom. "In here!"

How unusual. I've never met a woman as hurried about her sexual requirements. She sounds worried, almost frantic, and I haven't even been here sixty seconds.

I follow her, feeling for the first time in years out of my depth. It's a nice feeling, a pleasant simmer in my veins. My steps feel lighter across the plush carpet.

At the threshold I barely have time to register the strange furniture. It's large and antique. Expensive but mismatched. As if they crammed an estate sale into one room.

The young woman is bent over a large dresser, her ass perfectly plump. I could fill my hands with her. Could press my new erection against the crease. Except it isn't a sexy pose.

Instead she seems to be looking *behind* the dresser.

"It's okay," she's saying, breathless. "Come out, sweetie. You can do it."

Based on the sweet tone of her voice and the cat dish I spotted on the way inside, I already know what I'm going to see when I peek over the top of the dresser. Sure enough, there's a fluffy cat with bright yellow eyes peering up at me.

I don't have much experience with cats. They were one level up from rodents where I grew up, useful for catching rats and underfoot in dark alleys.

However, my experience with pussies of a different sort translates just fine, because I can see exactly what's happened to the poor girl. She's backed herself all the way into a corner, made her body so small she can't possibly come out.

No matter how nicely her owner coaxes her, it won't work. It can't possibly. Something like this isn't solved with words; it's solved with a confident, calming touch.

I straighten enough to pull off my jacket. "If you'll allow me."

The woman glances back at me, her eyes going wide as she sees my forearms where I'm rolling up my sleeves. "What are you going to do?"

"I assume you wish me to retrieve the cat."

"Rescue her," she corrects. "Because you have long arms."

I've had women compliment my length before, but usually they're referring to a different body part. Nothing about this night is usual; maybe that's why I like it so much. "Happy to be of service."

"She's very nervous. She might scratch you."

"Wouldn't be the first time." I give her a small smile, and this time I'm rewarded by a pinkening of her cheeks. "Now if you would move aside. I require room to work."

She scoots herself around me, careful not to touch, sucking in her breath as she passes by me. Is she afraid of me? I don't think so. At least not the ordinary fear a woman might have of a man. Instead she seems wary, much like the cat that watches me from behind the dresser, nervous of the world and its unknowns, terrified of everything and nothing at all.

With both hands braced on the side of the dresser, I use all my strength to lift it. As I suspected it's an ancient piece, made back when they used solid wood for every beam and joint. It probably weighs a thousand pounds, which is why the woman didn't move it first. I manage to move it two inches farther from the wall, which isn't enough for a person to walk behind, but is enough for a cat. This one would probably wander out eventually, when she wants to eat, but I don't think my client will relax until she does.

So I return to the far end of the dresser, near the corner, and bend to look at the cat. She stares at me, her eyes almost glowing, unfathomable. "You're a beauty, aren't you?" I murmur.

No response. She doesn't even blink.

"I could talk to you for hours," I say, reaching down to stroke the top of her head.

She's soft and unexpectedly fragile beneath all that fur. It's almost like armor, the thickness of it. It makes her seem larger than she is. "I could talk for hours, and you still wouldn't trust me, would you? You won't believe a thing I say, so I'll just have to show you."

I don't change the cadence of my voice, not even as I reach below the cat and scoop her up, not even as I clasp her securely against my chest and pet her head. She curls against me with a faint purr of relief, her thick tail swishing back and forth in gratitude.

"Oh my God, thank you," the woman says, looking torn between snatching her cat away and coming near me. Quite a dilemma, she has. "I realized I couldn't find her thirty minutes ago, and then spent all this time looking, and then when I did find her she wouldn't come out." She stops herself, flushing. "Sorry, I babble when I'm nervous."

And it's adorable, but I know better than to tell her that.

"My assistance does come with a price," I say instead.

Her eyes widen. "Oh?"

"Your name. It's only fair now that I'm holding your pussy."

Oh, the color of her cheeks. They remind me of sunsets with wind from the west, the kind that herald good weather for sailors the following day. "Bee," she says.

"The kind that make honey?"

"No, Bea like Beatrix." She makes a face. "It was my grandmother's name."

I would love to say a name as unique as Beatrix while I pound into her, but it's clear she'd rather I called her by the nickname. Anyway, it suits her. Simple on the surface, a thousand meanings beneath. "It's a pleasure to meet you, Bea. And your cat," I prompt.

"Minette," she answers, her expression softening.

Upon hearing her name, the cat seems to realize she's been far too content in a stranger's arms. She pulls herself away, a little haughty, and leaps onto the floor. Only then, from the relative safety of two feet away, does she turn back to give me a warning hiss.

Then she swishes away with a walk I can only admire.

"I suppose I haven't made a friend," I say ruefully.

Bea grins. "Are you kidding? She didn't take a swipe at you. I'm pretty sure that means she loves you in Minette language. She doesn't like new people."

Why do you travel with a cat who dislikes new people? I suppose she could keep her locked up in penthouse suites around the country, wealthy enough to insist that her cat sit with her in first class instead of locked in steerage, but it still seems like a strange pet to travel with.

Come to think of it, the pet isn't the only thing strange. The old furniture. The young woman who's looking at me with a mixture of trepidation and hope.

"Is it possible..." I say, almost reluctant to ask, but needing to know. "That she doesn't meet a lot of people because she *lives* on the top floor of an exclusive boutique hotel?"

Green eyes blink at me, as wide as the ones that looked at me from behind the dresser. As if I've trapped her there. As if I'm the only one who can get her out. "Ah. Yes." She laughs a little. "What gave it away?"

A million things, but mostly the fact that Bea looks so skittish I think I could spook her if I move too fast. I nod toward a painting on the wall, which features a smaller version of Minette in pointillism. "I assume it's not standard concierge service to paint a masterpiece of the guest's pet. Though if it is you really have to mention that in the Expedia review."

She laughs, the sound light as air, making my chest feel full. "I'm guessing Olivier would rather paint her than clean her litterbox."

So she's on a first-name basis with the concierge. It means she's been living here for a while, most likely, which is interesting because she can't be older than twenty. The high-necked dress is strange for someone that young, but it's surprisingly sexy. It conforms to her figure, emphasizing her curves and making my blood run hot.

Her smile fades. "It's not a problem, is it? Me living here?"

As quickly as that, my profession fills the air like smoke. Like a bomb went off.

"It's no problem," I assure her. The agency will send me to a hotel room as easily as a client's high-rise condo. There's no difference as long as the credit card charge goes through.

She bites her lip, looking anywhere except the large antique bed. "Do you... I mean, did you want to just *start* or..."

"Perhaps let's go into the living room," I tell her, already leading the way, my hand light on her lower back. This is the way I picked up the cat, moving her before she really had to think about it, saving her from herself. "I would love to talk to you first."

And find out why this beautiful and nervous young woman hired an escort.

Chapter Two

There are ass men and there are breast men. I can appreciate a beautiful ass or a nice rack. The blood in my veins is red, after all. But what I really am, what drives me absolutely crazy, what seems obscene even though women walk around with them in full view, are freckles. There's something about them, the way they scatter over skin, the knowledge of the other places they must cover, that makes me hard as a rock. I have this primal instinct to map the constellations on Bea's body.

Her black dress covers more than it shows. The fabric reveals an hourglass figure that I would love to run my hands along, but we aren't close to that. And above the high neckline, that's where the freckles begin. Only a shade darker than her natural skin color, which is pale.

Pale enough to turn a charming pink whenever she's nervous.

"Thank you for coming," she says, pink all the way from the point of her nose to her neck. I would bet tonight's entire fee, which is sizable, that the pink extends across her breasts.

Everything about her is closed, her legs pressed together where she perches on the armchair, her lips clamped shut as if to keep herself from saying more. In contrast I'm a study in openness, my ankle slung over my knee, arm stretched across the top of the sofa.

"It's my pleasure," I assure her. "I'm touched that you trust me in your home."

She glances around, as if considering for the first time that she ought not have invited me inside. "We could get a room downstairs, maybe. Unless they're sold out."

"I'd rather be where you're most comfortable."

She gives a small laugh of embarrassment. "I'm not sure I'm capable of being comfortable."

"Shall we call down for dinner?" I offer, mostly because the opportunity to eat and drink and breathe will help soothe her. But also because it will give me more time with her, this woman who may hold the answers to my long-held questions.

"No, thank you."

"We could go out. I know a lovely bistro not two blocks away."

She shakes her head, almost stricken. "No."

Such refusal, this one has. Such determination.

Her eyes are wary, watching as I stroke the brocade fabric of the sofa leisurely. It's almost like she expects me to lunge at her, to rip her clothes away without any discussion. Of course, I would most enjoy that, if I thought she wanted me to do it.

My curiosity is a living, breathing presence in the room. I want to unravel her secrets. Why does the idea of leaving make her anxiety spike like a tangible blaze in the air?

I decide to go for frankness. "You're a lovely woman, Bea. It would be an honor to spend the evening with you, but I have to be honest. I don't usually work for clients as young as you."

A blink. "You don't?"

One shoulder lifts. "The CEO of a multinational corporation who realizes she's spent more time on work than building a social life. A divorcee who wants to experience pleasure without resentment. They are the usual, but I have a feeling those don't quite apply to you."

"Not exactly," she says, cheeks almost cherry pink.

The cat has found a perch on top of an old roll-top desk, her yellow eyes trained on me. I don't mind one female looking at me. Don't mind two. To be honest I have a bit of the exhibitionist in me, one of the many reasons I'm in the perfect profession. I know without looking that my shoes are perfectly shined, my bespoke suit conforming effortlessly to my body. Bea's green gaze, both nervous and curious, is the best foreplay I could want.

"I don't need to know what led you to call me, certainly not the details of your circumstances, but it would help if I knew what you expect out of our evening."

"Oh God," she says on a groan. "I'm screwing this up, aren't I? There's probably a secret handshake or something and I don't know it. You must think I'm insane."

I shake my head, slow and slight. "No secret handshake, I promise. There's only you and me, having a conversation about pleasure."

The word seems to take her aback. "Pleasure?"

"That's the nature of my business, yes." My body tightens, because it would be pleasure indeed to touch this woman. To kiss her. To make her moan for me.

Although I might have to rethink that plan, because the word *pleasure* might as well have been *medieval torture* based on the way Bea looks at me. "I thought we were going to have sex."

She sounds so forlorn it could break my heart.

Instead I laugh, a small huff of breath, because I can't afford to have a heart.

"Sex," I say, standing to full height, circling the scuffed oriental coffee table, standing behind her chair. "And pleasure. Pleasure and sex. They're interchangeable."

I brush my knuckles over the side of her neck, a demonstration. Her wild curls tickle my skin.

It's provocative, this. If she had agreed to dinner I would have started with small touches, a glance of my palm against the small of her back as I pulled out her chair, holding her hand while we talked over a glass of wine. Perhaps being so bold as to run a finger along the inside of hers, where it's more sensitive. She would shiver; her gaze would meet mine.

There's an order to these things. You can move fast or slow, but there's still an order.

"We can skip the pleasure part," she says, her voice high, her breathing faster. Her chest rises and falls in the black dress, made all the more alluring by how much it covers. She's a mystery. The black sky in the city. I have to work to see her secrets.

"No," I chide gently. "We focus on the pleasure. That's the point."

"What if—" Her breath catches as I drop the back of my hand over her collarbone, a reverse caress. That's what one does for a skittish creature like her. "What if I have a different point?"

"And what point would that be, my sweet Bea?"

"I want to lose my virginity," she says, so fast it comes out as a single word.

IWANTTOLOSEMYVIRGINITY. It takes my lust-warmed brain a full minute to comprehend. She's not only nervous, this woman. She's a virgin.

My hand freezes. I yank it away. "Pardon me?"

I can't have heard her correctly. There is no chance in hell that this beautiful young woman, as strange and interesting as she is, is a virgin. No chance in hell that I was the one tasked to be her first. I could not possibly spread her legs and thrust inside her, knowing that no one's ever been there. It would be a physical impossibility. Never. No possible way.

"It doesn't have to take long," she says, suddenly earnest. Almost begging me. "I don't need…you know…whatever you do for other women. I only want the sex."

My God. "You *are* insane."

A scrunch of her nose. "Well, you don't have to sound too surprised. It is what I requested when I called. The woman said that's what you do."

"I'm not taking your virginity." On some level I might have guessed this about her. If I had considered it even possible, I might have. Virgins don't hire me. They stammer and giggle and turn away from me, their protective instincts strong enough to send them in the opposite direction. So perhaps I can be forgiven for not recognizing this one, so forthright.

Bea frowns. "Is that a different department or something?"

She's mocking me. She's mocking me for being, well, prudish, and I feel strangely buoyant. I could float away with the absurdity of it. "Yes, it's a different department. The department of a frat boy who fumbles around in the dark."

"Are you seriously not going to do it?"

The irony is enough to flatten me, that this is a woman I might have pursued outside this job. She would have been too young for me, even if I weren't an escort and she wasn't my client. That wouldn't have stopped me from wanting her.

But in another incarnation, if I had been one of those fumbling frat boys, I would have followed this woman to the ends of the earth. That's a hypothetical scenario on multiple levels, but I'm good at hypotheticals, which is another reason I'm good at my job.

So good that I please every single client I've ever had.

Until this one, apparently.

"I'm seriously not going to do it."

A small line forms between her eyes. "Is it because I'm, you know. Not pretty enough?"

There are about a thousand ways that I'm beneath the woman in front of me. The fact that she might think I'm turning her down makes me want to flay my skin off.

Well, technically I am turning her down. "It's for your own good."

And then she makes a sound. Kind of like *ugh* but more annoyed.

"Look, I don't know what made you call to the agency, what made you think your first time should be a transaction instead of a meaningful experience, but I will not help you do it."

"Is this because I said no pleasure?"

I glare at her. "You must insist on pleasure. Regardless of who you're with."

"From a fumbling frat boy?" She sounds dubious. "It seems to me that if you were really concerned with making my first time pleasurable, you would be the one to do it."

There's only one thing I find sexier than freckles, and it's a sharp wit. I am ready to get on my knees for this woman, even as I know I should walk away. In short, I am screwed.

Chapter Three

THIS IS HOW WE END UP AT THE HOTEL RESTAURANT DOWNSTAIRS. I OFFERED TO take her out, would have preferred it, after the strangeness of our meeting. To text a friend of mine at the hottest restaurant in Tanglewood and secure a table for us.

It would have given me a sense of normalcy. Most of the women I see prefer to be courted before I take them to bed. And I enjoy courting them.

Beau Ciel has, predictably, a pretentious matre d'. Less predictably, Bea greets him with the smile of an old friend. "I'm sorry I didn't make reservations, Pierre."

Of course not, he tells her. *She needn't ever*, he tells her.

Then we are led to a private table, tucked behind heavy velvet curtains. The ceiling has been painted with a thousand stars on a dark background. It feels like looking up in a dream.

"You come here often?" I ask, keeping my voice casual.

She studies the menu like it holds the answer if she can only find it. I would bet that she knows every single item listed there. That she's tried them all. "Mostly by room service. I don't usually come down."

I warn myself not to ask how long she's lived in the hotel. It's too personal of a question, even for two individuals who are going to have sex. The only purpose would be to assuage my curiosity. It would not set her at ease. It would not seduce her. I must not ask.

"How long have you lived in L'Etoile?"

Damn.

The words are out before I can even comprehend them. I have only ever been charming with women. It is my one skill in life, discovered before I knew what I was doing, honed over the years. How has this one slip of a woman reduced me to a bumbling first date?

A faint flush touches her cheeks.

"You don't have to answer," I tell her, because she shouldn't answer.

"Ten years," she says, so soft I barely hear it. Then her eyes meet mine, the soft green of them like a fog I don't want to clear. "That's weird, isn't it?"

It's very, very weird. "Of course not. You must love it here."

She lifts one slender shoulder in a shrug. "It's safe," she says.

I swallow down every other question that comes to mind. She can't be much older than twenty. Ten years means she lived here since she was a child. There was no sign of a parent in that hotel suite. So who raised her there?

An image flashes through my mind, of the princess locked in a tower, her hair dropped out of the window for a prince to climb up. I have always been dramatic, mind. This isn't anything new. *Un rêveur*, my mother called me. Anyway, this girl could never be the princess from the story. Her hair is a wild mass of curls, completely unsuitable for climbing rope.

"Where do *you* live?" she asks, a challenge in her voice.

I understand that she's turning the tables, attempting to make me feel uncomfortable the way that she is uncomfortable. There is nothing personal about my living space, however. "A loft, in a recent development on the east side. Beige carpet. Granite counters. It is also safe."

Her lips twist, as if she's fighting a smile. "That sounds very…"

"Boring?"

"I was going to say normal."

I lean back in the chair, crossing one ankle over my knee. This is a conversation I'm comfortable with. The woman's curiosity about the life of a high-priced male escort. It doesn't bother me. It isn't even about me. They aren't asking about Hugo Bellmont, the man. They want the persona. That's all I have to give them, anyway.

"Did you expect me to have shag carpets and a mirror on the ceiling?"

She pauses, as if fighting with herself. In the end her curiosity must get the better of her because she blurts out, "Why would you have a mirror on the ceiling?"

"To watch you," I tell her, my voice low and blunt. "While you ride me. To see your beautiful ass move as you make yourself come, to turn you over, so that you can see mine."

Her mouth is open, eyes wide. I've shocked her. "Oh."

"But we aren't going to have sex in my boring loft with its boring walls. After we've eaten and enjoyed each other's company, I'm going to ask you to take me upstairs."

She makes a sound, like a squeak. I want her to make it again when I'm inside her.

"And you will say yes, Bea, won't you?"

"Maybe not," she says, but it's a thin rebellion. I can hear the arousal in her voice.

"You will, because you were curious about the pleasure. You didn't want it, which is interesting. Maybe sex without orgasms seems to you like your penthouse—safe. But I won't be safe, sweetheart. I will make you come so hard you cannot breathe."

Her pretty breasts rise and fall under the black dress. "That is—that is—"

Before she can tell me what that is, the waiter arrives. He unveils an expensive Bordeaux, which is on the house. I order the steak au poivre, medium rare, to give her time to get her bearings. She does not even glance at the menu as she orders for herself a blanquette de veau, in an accent more Parisian than my own. Interesting.

When the waiter takes our menus away, I busy myself with my cuff link. I have learned the art of foreplay, which extends outside of the bedroom. It starts right now, when I make her feel something only to retreat. The absence makes it sweeter.

Except she takes me by surprise. "Hugo," she says, almost tasting the name.

I look up at her, this fairy creature, at her wildfire hair and sea moss eyes. Her smile is all the more devastating because it's pointed at herself.

"You aren't even hungry, are you?"

My eyebrows go up. That isn't what I expected her to say. "Hungry? No. But I'm always willing to eat, especially food that is delicious and rare."

We aren't talking about food. "Don't you ever get tired of it?" she asks.

"Well, if you hadn't already told me, I would know now that you haven't had sex by the question alone. At least not good sex. If you had you would know the answer to that. We could eat all night, and I would never tire."

It's when we get to the creme brulee that I realize something has changed. The conversation is still foreplay, but we aren't talking about sex. Even in veiled terms. We're talking about childhood and dreams. We're talking about intimacy, which is all the more disturbing.

"It's the cars," I admit my weakness. "I would see them pull up night after night with rich men and beautiful women. These Porches and Bugattis. I knew that one day that would be me."

"And now that *is* you," she says, pride in her voice, as if anyone would consider being a prostitute a success.

"I suppose—" Suspicion narrows my eyes. "How do you know what I drive?"

She flushes a deep crimson. "I may have seen you out the window."

"Really?" I ask, because it's the right thing to say. It makes her feel charmed, but the truth is, I'm the one charmed by her. This sweet mysterious creature.

"I don't usually use that window," she says, the words rushing together. "It's too bright from the lights on that street unless I keep the drapes shut. But this time... well, I was over there."

"And?" I prod gently, because there's clearly more.

"And there was so much dust. I sneezed, and then the lamp fell over, and then Minette got so freaked out she ran behind the dresser and wouldn't come out."

I don't mean to laugh, but the image of this girl watching for me out the window like a nervous prom date is too adorable. "I'm sorry," I tell the hands that are hiding her face. "I'm really not laughing at you."

"I think you are," she says, her voice muffled.

"Bea. Bea, look at me."

Her hands finally drop, revealing this wry twist on her lips that I'm coming to recognize. "Are you done now?"

"Only getting started, darling. But I do have to ask, why do you live here? Besides the fact that it's safe. You must have money to go anywhere."

At some point in the meal there was a bottle of wine. It hasn't made me drunk, but there is a pleasant lightness to me. Any walls I might have had are gone.

The same might be true for Bea, because she leans close as if to tell me a secret. "Because I don't leave. I can't."

"Don't leave where?"

"L'Etoile."

"You mean you aren't allowed to move?" I understand what she's telling me, but I don't want to understand. This woman is so young, so full of life. How can she be imprisoned?

"No, I mean I don't leave the hotel. Like, to go to the grocery store. Or the park. Or anywhere."

Jesus. "How long has it been since you left? I mean, you weren't born here, were you?"

"No, I wasn't born here. I moved in when I was ten. I was... troubled, you know? The way only a rich kid can be." She laughs at herself, the sound hollow. "So my guardian, he got me a tutor who came every day. A therapist who came every week, for all the good that did."

I blow out a breath. So many years in the tower. "That's terrible."

She makes a face, self-deprecating. "Yes, it's a hard life, living in the penthouse."

"'I am a winged creature who is too rarely allowed to use its wings.'"

With a strange look she replies, "'Ecstasies do not occur often enough.'"

"So you can quote the Diary of Anais Nin, but you do not believe in pleasure?"

"It's not that I don't believe in pleasure," she says, her voice painfully earnest. "I'm sure it's very nice. But it isn't necessary tonight. Only the act itself."

"The act?" I'm taunting her, and it's only a little about foreplay.

"Fine," she says, speaking fast like she does when she's nervous. "Fine. I want to have sex with you. I want you to have sex with me. You know, the whole thing."

There's more she isn't telling me, and it feels important. I have never asked a woman her motives for hiring me before. It's never mattered. "Because you can't leave?"

"Yes, because I want to do this thing, and I need to do it *here*."

I glance behind her, at the many meals happening around us. There are women who look at me. And men. I am somewhat ostentatious with my suit and my assuredness. But even beside me, she shines. "And there has never been a man passing through the hotel that you have wanted? Someone sitting at the bar who bought you a drink?"

"There's you," she says softly, which isn't really an answer.

It's a distraction, and a successful one. Because for the first time in a long time, maybe ever, I want her. Not her body or her money. I want to unlock her secrets. "Then let's go upstairs, and we will see if we can make those ecstasies come more often."

※

Entering the penthouse, this time knowing that Bea lives here, is a revelation. Minette greets us with a plaintive meow, winding around our ankles as if we both belong.

There is a coatrack, beside the entrance, draped with a herringbone coat. A tightly wrapped umbrella sits in the base. I know without touching them that they won't be damp, despite the weather, because Bea didn't go outside today. She didn't go outside yesterday. How long has it been since she stepped foot outside this hotel?

"Do you want some coffee?" she asks in that too fast way. I'm not sure whether she's asking as a kind of date etiquette or whether she wants a reprieve, but I say what I always tell my clients.

"Yes, please. I would love some."

I follow her to the corner of the suite where a wet bar would be. It's been expanded, I see, to include a small two-range stove top with a wardrobe beside it that I assume serves as a pantry. It's still less than even a small apartment would offer, but much more utility than any ordinary penthouse suite. A gleaming mini-fridge must hold the meager contents of her food supply, when she doesn't order down for baked camembert or oysters.

What a life she leads, both decadent and desolate.

Her hands are shaking. The mug trembles for a beat too long against the metal plate of the fancy machinery, revealing her weakness. I take it from her, gently, setting it aside.

"Darling," I say, softly.

She gives a small shudder. It isn't quite a sob. That's the only warning I have before she crumples, not against anything, not on top of anything, it's more like she becomes suddenly small. Tiny. Like she's shoved herself behind a dresser in an effort to be invisible.

I wrap her in my arms before I can think better of it. That's what I'm here for, isn't it? To provide comfort with my body. That's all I am—my hands or my mouth. My cock. And if that makes me feel cold and paper-thin, it does not matter.

This woman, though, she seems to like me for my arms.

I stroke her back softly, murmuring words of assurance. In French, I realize belatedly, but it doesn't matter. She proved downstairs she could understand, and the language doesn't matter. Not for what we're doing here.

Her body feels impossibly slight in my grasp, like smoke that will disappear if I hold too hard. But her hair—God, her hair. It does not care that she is trying to make herself small; it's a perfect bronze cloud, tickling my nose, curling gently into my skin.

Her shoulders shake against me. The sound of her worry and her grief carve themselves into my skin, leaving marks I'm not sure will be gone by morning.

"Bea." I tilt her tear-stained face up with my thumb and forefinger. "Tell me what's wrong. Why have you called me here tonight? Why are you hurting?"

"I'm embarrassed," she says, her cheeks a deep red. "I mean, I know I should have gone downstairs to the bar. That makes way more sense than paying someone to have sex with me."

"Why didn't you?" I'm genuinely curious.

She speaks into my chest, her voice muffled. "I did. Five nights in a row, I wore this dress and went downstairs. Every night someone would send me a drink."

My voice is softer now. "Did you accept?"

"I tried to. I took a sip and gave them a smile when they sat down at the stool next to me. But it was too real somehow. Like they would expect something more than… you know."

"Sex," I say, with gentle encouragement.

"Sex," she repeats.

The word sends a soft breath of heat into my cock. God, this woman. Even hearing her say the word is enough to make me hard, what will it feel like to peel the black dress from her body? To hear her moans and sighs and a thousand other sounds?

"I have no expectation," I tell her. "Not even sex. If you want to sit with me and recite nursery rhymes, that is what we'll do. Or if you'd like me to leave. However…"

She looks at me, hope in her green eyes. "However?"

"However, it would be an honor to take you to bed tonight."

"Even though I haven't done it before?"

Especially because of that.

So much that it terrified me before, when she first told me. But I've had time to consider it over dinner, and besides the caveman-like effect it has on my body, how hard she makes me, it makes sense that I should be the one to do this.

One of those assholes at the bar, what if they don't make her come? What if they demand more from her than she wants to give? No, the way to make this good for her is to do it myself.

Even though I haven't done it before?

"Even though," I tell her, my voice grave.

She smiles, then, the parting of clouds. "My friend Harper said this would be a thousand times more awkward than a one-night stand, but it's not. It's easier. Is that wrong?"

"It's perfectly right."

I said it to reassure her, but I'm the one reassured when I stroke my thumb across her cheek. It feels perfectly right to bend my head and breathe in the faint smell of lavender. Perfectly right to press my mouth against her plush lips.

She opens her mouth with an acquiescent sigh, and I know she's still finding this easier. The men downstairs, none of them could have given her this. There's seduction in my movements, but confidence too. The kind of confidence that can only come knowing I can please her.

An entire city of men who would have had her, who would have been happy for the privilege of a single night, no money exchanging hands, and she paid for me.

I wasn't lying to her before. It will be an honor.

Chapter Four

Her freckles don't taste like anything. I know that, but I can't stop kissing them. Can't stop following the reckless trail across her cheek and below her jaw. I swear there's stardust in them, something elemental and bright. They singe my lips, my tongue.

She makes a sound of surprise, a strangled little gasp in her throat. "Is this regular? I thought it would be more like…"

"More like what?" I don't pause to give her time to answer. She must find the wherewithal even while I move my body closer to hers. Her hands flutter against my shoulders, not pushing me away, not pulling me close. They are confused, those hands.

"Like the movies."

That makes me stop. I pull back so I can look into her pale green eyes. Jade, I realize. They're the color of jade, the kind of stone you would hang on a gold chain. "What movies?"

This level of red, it's an emergency. Her cheeks burn. "You know."

"Do you watch porn, darling?"

"Only for instructional purposes," she says, too fast.

I do not laugh. I think I should get a medal for not laughing at this. "And what did you learn from the porn movies you watched?" I ask, quite seriously.

"Usually they…you know. The clothes come off."

Naturally I am desperate to know what sort of clothes came off. Was there a nurse's uniform? Or perhaps a man dressed as a burglar, come to tie her up? "Do you want to take off your clothes?"

"No," she says on a squeak.

Of course not. Because she isn't ready for that, despite the dubious education porn movies have given her. She's practically vibrating with nervousness. "Then you'll keep your clothes on. For now. For as long as you want them. You're safe with me."

Her eyes focus with puzzlement. "Safe?"

It's the reason she stays in this tower, this princess with red hair. Because it's safe. And that's what I must be, if I'm to be allowed to stay. "Safe," I say. "Tell me what you're thinking."

She looks reluctant, biting her lip.

"No matter what you say, I won't be angry. Cross my heart."

"I'm worried you aren't really aroused," she says, fast. "That you're faking it."

It's not the first time a woman has ever worried about that with me, but it *is* the first time I've been as desperate to get a woman naked. That she doubts me now is a great irony. "What makes you think that?"

"In the movies, they always show the—the—"

"You don't think my cock is hard?"

She flushes. "I mean, it doesn't have to be."

Now I can't help but laugh. A full belly laugh. When is the last time I had one of these? There are tears at the corner of my eyes. I turn her around, making her face the small countertop with its fancy espresso maker. She's right up against it, her tummy pressed to the curved stone ledge. Then I cover her with my body, my throbbing cock between her sweet ass cheeks, the only barriers her clothes and mine.

She stiffens with a small gasp. "That is—"

"Do you see what you do to it? You make it hard. So hard it hurts."

"I'm sorry."

"No, no," I murmur. "Never apologize for that. It's all a man can dream of, a woman making him so hard it hurts. Only letting him touch her over her clothes. Dying for a glimpse of bare skin."

She moans a little. "This isn't like the movies."

I press my lips to the small patch behind her ear. "No, it's not like the movies. This is real life, and that's why you called for me, isn't it? Because the movies were not real."

"Yes," she agrees, breathless.

"When the women come, and they squeal and shake, it isn't real. It isn't right. You know that, don't you? They fake it. You won't fake anything, darling." I turn her to face me, because for the first time, this is the right way. The only way.

"What if I don't—"

"You will," I assure her, which only seems to worry her more.

A shudder runs through her delicate frame, making her hair vibrate like dew drops on a pretty little flower. It only *looks* fragile; in truth it can withstand this earthquake. "It would be easier if it didn't feel so good," she says, her voice plaintive and pleasure-dipped.

"One day you'll tell me why you want sex so badly, without feeling anything."

"I won't," she says, but she's only cross with me because I'm rubbing gentle circles on her back, because it feels so damn good. She arches into my touch, the same way her cat would.

And then I move my hand lower, to the upper curve of her ass. It's a beautiful ass, which is saying something. I've seen more than my fair share. Enjoyed every single one of them, but the picture of her heart-shaped behind, from when she bent over the dresser, is emblazoned in my mind. So perfectly wrapped in black silky fabric, thick enough to ward most men away. I'm not most men. The challenge only makes it sweeter, as I stroke the slope of her, as I feel her gasp in response. I'm the first man to ever traverse this land, something I hadn't thought to find pleasure in. What a barbarian I am. A Viking, to find such deviant delight in taking a young woman's virginity. It has nothing to do with seduction, the palm I place on her, the squeeze I give her. That's pure indulgence on my part, knowing I am the first.

She shifts closer to me, making tiny sounds I'm not sure she hears. Her body is out of her control; it's in mine now. "I don't even know your favorite color," she whispers.

I laugh softly. "Red."

The color of my Bugatti.

"Mine's blue," she says, but she doesn't explain why.

I reach down to the lace hem of her dress, pulling the fabric into careless bunches, until I touch bare skin. It's a godsend, the satin of her. Like opening my mouth to the sky after years of thirst. With a firm grasp I hitch her leg up to my hip, spreading her. "Any other questions?"

Her eyes are hazy. I can see the struggle behind the green curtain, the valiant attempt to string words together as her body comes apart. "Favorite food."

"A tagine," I tell her, not adding that it's my mother's I dream about. The spice of it on a hot night, making me sweat in the dark. This isn't about revealing secrets, not truly. It's about making her feel like she knows me. I won't lie to her, but I won't rip apart my skin to set her at ease either.

That clears enough of the arousal from her eyes to ask, "A tagine?"

It makes me wonder what other foods she hasn't yet experienced, trapped in this gilded prison of hers. Even the richest of foods can be punishment if they're all she can eat. "A stew. Spicy. Do you like spicy food?"

"I don't know," she says, confirming my worst fears.

I want to book us a flight to Thailand or South Africa, to show her a thousand buildings and give her a million new tastes. Like most penthouse suites, this one is large—for a visit, not for a lifetime. "What's your favorite food, darling?"

She pulls back, looking me right in the eyes, proving that though she is untried, she is far from naive. "I haven't found it yet."

Her words travel straight to my groin, a challenge I'm desperate to accept. "You think these questions make it easier? We could talk for hours and hours, darling. And still you would be nervous."

"Then how do people do this?"

I grasp her small hand and place it flat on my chest. "These are your questions. So what do you wish to know?"

Awareness sparks in her eyes. She moves her hand in the smallest circle, testing, asking about the solidity of my body, wondering at the reality of this encounter. I can't let so eager a question go unanswered; I bend my head to capture her lips.

Her other hand flutters against my shoulder before settling there. A butterfly I must be careful not to spook if I want to enjoy its beauty. I dart my tongue against her lips, letting her think about the presence of it before delving into her mouth.

She startles for a moment, and I think, this is it. This was all I'll have of her, this taste. It's shocking the depth of my disappointment. I can walk away from any woman. We enjoy our time together. And then we part. I have never wanted more, never needed another taste like I do now.

She moans in sweet acquiescence.

I'm overcome with relief I don't want to examine, and I slide my tongue against hers in quiet insistence. The physical sensations are a tidal wave, they drown out any thoughts or worries. They sweep over the both of us, making her breath come faster. She's excited, and hungry, and needy, and so I can push aside the realization that I am, too.

If my response to her is stronger than I expected, so be it. I can use it to be a better tutor for her. Because that's what I am right now, as experienced as I am, with a virgin—her teacher.

I press my forefinger to the small furrow between her eyes. "You are thinking too hard. Feel, instead." To illustrate my point, I bite her plump bottom lip. It's only a small nip, but enough to make her jump. "Only feel."

Her eyes spark with a lovely rebellion. "Like this?"

I know what she's going to do before she leans forward, before her white teeth peek from between peach-colored lips. There are one, two, three seconds when I could jerk out of reach. And it wouldn't be awkward; I would be too charming for that. I would laugh and cajole and coax her into the most pleasure she's ever known.

It would be a beautiful performance, that. Instead I let her get close enough to hurt me, the sharp pain a brilliant counterpoint to the thrum of anticipation in my veins. It's only a pinch, but I have to close my eyes against the raw force of it.

"Yes," I say, and my voice is lower now. My accent thicker. "Like that."

"What else?" she whispers, and a dark current of arousal runs through me at the hope in her voice. It wasn't only me who was jaded, I realize. It was the women. The women who would call me, because they were tired of selfish, cheating men in their lives. I was happy to give them a reprieve from their loneliness, to take a reprieve from my own, but this is different.

Bea is full of hope, like a curved tendril of green splitting the earth in spring. She makes me want to breathe in deep, to stretch my limbs. To watch her rise.

What else? she asked. This is what else, my hand falling down her side to the indent at her waist. And lower, lower. She sucks in a breath, leaving only cool air against my collarbone.

And still lower.

My hand stops in the space below her stomach, well above her mound. A place that isn't on its own sexual, but a place a man would only touch if he's about to have sex.

"You have practice, yes? You touch yourself."

Her lips form a perfect "O" because of course she has. She isn't experienced, but she is curious. "That's not weird," she says, a little defensive. The voice of one who has to convince herself.

"But no. Very sexy, that's what it is. I would love to see it."

Her cheeks flame. "I couldn't."

"Maybe later," I say, and then I do something a little forward. I give her a wink. That would not be an introductory lesson on flirting, on foreplay, but I find myself out of my depth with this girl. As if I'm desperate to impress her, instead of a hired professional with a job to do.

She bites her lip. "Could I watch *you* do that?"

God, the mouth on her. She can't even say the words, but she manages to say them anyway. So much courage and so much fear. My body tightens with the image of her, leaning forward, lips parted, while I pumped my cock. I would become desperate, sweating and swearing, but still I would not come, not until she had looked her fill.

"It would be torture," I tell her honestly. "Exquisite."

She studies the top button on my shirt like it's an elaborate puzzle. It would be so easy to open it myself, without even removing my gaze from her. And it's so much sweeter to watch her struggle with herself.

Then she takes a deep breath, as if steeling herself.

Her small fingers brush against my chest through linen, uncertain with the stiff fabric. She pushes the button through the hole, tugging the fabric apart no more than a centimeter.

Another button and another.

She opens my shirt down to my navel before spreading it apart.

I look down, trying to imagine what I look like for her, dark hair and tanned skin. My body is acceptable. I work out enough to keep myself trim, to bulge a few muscles for the clients who like such things, but that is not my strong suit. There are weight lifters and ball players on the payroll for women who prefer men like that. Myself, I am tall and somewhat spare. It is my smile that makes them choose me, not my body, but Bea looks at me with awe.

"Do you like what you see?" I ask, my voice pure gravel.

I expect her to be demure, to shake her head and avert her eyes, what any well-behaved ingenue would do. Instead she meets my gaze with an impish smile. "Feeling insecure, are you?"

My laugh comes out full-bodied. It takes me by surprise. "A man does like to feel wanted."

"I do want you," she says with a candor I've come to admire from her. An eagerness I've already learned to crave. "But I'm not sure I should have you."

"Do you think I'll hurt you?" I don't think that's her worry, but I have to be certain. It would break me if she thought I would force her to do anything she didn't want to. "We can call the service right now. They can send someone else."

"No," she says, a little too loud, turning pink. "No, not that. It's just that I've spent so long here in these four walls. Seeing the same group of people. Doing the same things."

I hear the starvation in her words, the darkness that closes in on her. "You're afraid because I'm new. Because what we're doing is new. So we will only do what you've already done."

"Do you mean watch me…"

"Masturbate? *Oui*, I could watch that. I would gladly, but I would also love to make you come. It would be a feeling you've had before, only with my fingers instead of yours."

She likes that, I see the excitement brighten her eyes. Her fear recedes into the night. "Here?"

I look around at the small bar and the sofa beyond. "Where do you usually do it?"

"In bed."

My hand links in hers, and we go there together. This is the room where I began this journey, the dresser still slightly ajar from the wall. The mismatched furniture at odds with the sleekness of the penthouse suite. The bed neatly made in anticipation of what's to come, white ruffles in neat alignment. The thought of her wet and horny under this spread is enough to dampen a spot of precum on my boxers. Already my cock hurts with how long I've been hard, but I will wait as long as she needs. Forever, if that's what it takes to make her comfortable.

She turns off the lamp, and I let her, but only because she would normally do this in the dark. There is only the light spilling in from the doorway, barely enough to see her by.

I pull back the bedspread, messing up her ordered work. The sheets are cool beneath my palm, and I smooth them, smooth them, making them warm and ready.

When I turn back to face her, she looks up at me with luminescent eyes.

Every thought of teaching her, of tutoring her, of remaining aloof from her disappears from my head. There's only the need to kiss her and the physical movement to make it happen. Her lips yield under mine, softer now, quicksand, and I'm sinking.

This time when I touch her, she sighs into my mouth, a sound of infinite relief. I give in to my baser impulses and touch her plump ass, knead and mold her, and then it's my turn to sigh in relief. She is everything warm and vibrant in my arms.

I know a move for every situation, practiced and choreographed to maximize her pleasure, but it's clumsy hands that press her back to the bed, that lift her heavy lace dress in pursuit of ecstasy. I slide my palm up the inside of her thigh, and her hips lift, shocked and seeking.

"Spread for me, Bea."

She does, wordless, her eyes wide moons. There is enough mystery there to make me uncertain about my reception, but then I touch her—ah, there. And she's wet for me, drenched and swollen for my cock. It isn't my cock that she'll get though, only the stroke of my forefinger, making her cry out.

"Tell me what you feel."

"I feel wild," she whispers. "And so good. And it hurts. Why does it hurt?"

Beautiful. She's goddamn beautiful. "Because your body knows what it needs." I press my thumb in front of her clit, hovering there in the slickness. "Reach for it."

And then she does, lifting her body in a timeless rhythm. She doesn't need my lessons, that much is clear, not the way she writhes in relentless time, pressing her clit against me.

She could come this way, but I want more. Not only for her.

For me.

I slip my finger inside her. God, she's tight. She would be a vise around my cock, and I feel myself flex inside my pants. I have one knee on the bed, the other leg still planted on the floor. I'm bent over one of the most beautiful women I've ever seen, but I'm still fully dressed.

Part of me wants to open my pants and release myself. To slip inside her heat and take what she's already paid for. But something holds me back.

"Please," she whispers.

Then I'm helpless except to kiss her, to thrust my tongue into her mouth with the same steady gait as I slip my finger inside her. And still she fucks her body against my thumb, the friction making her gasp against my lips.

There is no longer a spiral to the top; she's hovered there, trapped in suspended agony.

Afraid, I realize with a terrible dread.

It's the first time I've ever wondered if I might not make a woman come. Her body is with me, but her mind is afraid. I bite her lip once more, and her attention focuses on me. "Nothing will happen to you," I tell her, even though I have no ability to protect her. No right. "I won't let anything happen to you. Let go for me, Bea. Let go."

She comes with a glorious rush of arousal, her body jerking in wild abandon. I pet her clit with firm strokes of my thumb through her orgasm, and then stroke her sex softly as she comes down, pressing kisses over her nose and across her forehead, telling her how beautiful she is, how sweet. My brave girl.

Everything is perfect, in this moment. Her body and its response to me. Even the fact that I'm rock-hard and suffering beneath my suit cannot mar this.

Until her gaze snaps to mine, and everything changes.

All the fear rushes back, tenfold. I see it march in like a thousand pinpoints of darkness, blotting out her bright arousal. And then she bursts into tears.

Chapter Five

Like most boys in Tangier I ran wild in the streets while my mother worked twelve-hour shifts. I swiped fruit from the backs of donkeys on their way into the market and learned to pick pockets from the men with glittering women. Almost a million people live between the city walls, speaking ten languages as commonly as the national Arabic, but for the poor son of a hotel maid, there was only the dust and the clamor and the dry burn of the sun. It was a rough existence, but also a joyful one. I didn't know anything else.

I knew early not to cry. There was no time with the caregiver with ten babies in the other room. And when I was older, there was always another boy to lash out. And so tears dried before they came out, even when my favorite street dog was run over in front of me, her leg twisted away, held to her only by flesh and tendon, part of her belly exposed. She lay whimpering in my arms until I used my pocket knife to end her suffering. And still I did not cry.

I don't know what to do with the sobbing young woman on the bed.

My throat feels tight. I've made women moan and scream and beg. Never this. "Did I hurt you? Was I too rough? Forgive me, Bea. I never meant to—"

"It wasn't that." She shakes her head, glancing at me with tearstained eyes, pleading. She wants me to understand, but I don't. Somehow my experience is failing me. My charm is failing me. If she wanted me to whisper to her in Italian on the rooftop, I could do that. If she wanted me to lick her pussy until her body went limp, I could do that. What is it she wants from me?

She buries her face in her hands, shoulders shaking, trying to muffle the sounds of her distress. "Just go. I'm okay. You can go."

There is no way that I can leave her like this. For a moment I stand there, helpless, still fully dressed, my arms outstretched as if to hold her, my cock still uselessly hard in my slacks.

There's a hard pit in my stomach that reminds me of that hot afternoon with the dog limp in my arms, frozen, frozen, the horror of knowing I could do nothing to help.

Except this isn't a packed dirt street in Tangier.

And I'm not a powerless little boy.

I lift her body into my arms, hearing her startled little gasp, and climb into the bed. With gentle determination I cradle her body in my arms. After a frozen moment, she buries her face against my chest. Only then can I breathe fully, knowing she's accepted my comfort, little though it is.

My words are useless now, all I have to offer her is my body. That's all I ever have, really. I rock her slowly, back and forth, holding her tight as her sobs slow and then stop.

"This isn't how you usually finish your dates?" she asks, her voice still thick from tears.

My heart squeezes that she's going for humor, that she's trying to make this more comfortable for me. "We finish with whatever you need."

She shudders her way through a sigh. "I'm sorry."

"Don't apologize to me. It tears a strip of skin from me when you do."

Her eyes meet mine, framed by damp lashes. "That makes me want to apologize more."

From somewhere I find the strength to laugh, a light thing, to let her know this is normal, even though it's not, it's not, it's not. I've never made a woman cry. *I've never been with a virgin before, either.* This was a terrible idea. What made me think I could do this? That because I can make a woman come, her body clench and convulse, that I should be trusted with her first time?

"Hey," she says. "I see you blaming yourself. But it wasn't you."

"I'm sure you cry also when room service arrives."

She gives a huff of laughter. "No, I'm sure that would freak Rene out."

"Consider me freaked out," I tell her, even though I'm relieved. Thirty seconds ago, she was bawling her eyes out. But this, a woman in need of laughter and reassurance, I can do.

She bites her lip. "I just didn't expect it to feel good."

"You must tell me where you learned these horrible ideas about sex."

"I mean, I knew about orgasms. I've seen them on movies and read about them in books. And I've given them to myself. But this was completely different. Like all my life I've been seeing water through thick glass and then one day I dive in."

"It makes you sad, this?"

"Yes," she whispers. "It makes me sad, thinking of all those days I never dipped a toe in. Because I was too afraid. That's the only reason."

"And you wonder what else you're missing."

"I *know* what else I'm missing, but that doesn't make the fear go away."

"Then what does?"

Her green eyes meet mine, a little fearful, a little wry. "Apparently, you."

Chapter Six

"AND YOU JUST LEFT HER THERE?"

The question comes from Sutton Cooper, the roughneck of our little group. The censure in his voice leaves no doubt as to his opinion on the matter. He may be a hard-ass, with a background roping steer and raising hell, but he has a hard line about treating women well.

Even if that only means making her breakfast after a night of no-strings sex.

"She paid for the night," I say blandly.

Christopher leans forward in the leather armchair, his eyes dark. They always see right through me. They see through everything. "Have you ever made a girl cry before?"

"But of course, that's why I'm the highest-paid escort in Tanglewood. Because I say sharp and insulting things that make the women cry."

Blue takes a sip of whatever new beer he's drinking. "Has Hugo been sarcastic before?"

"Only when he's upset," says Christopher, the bastard.

We're sitting at the Den, like we do almost every week. When we started there was only Blue and Sutton and me, starting with a handful of dollars in our pockets, determined to make something of ourselves. The Thieves Club, we called it, only half joking—our own Den of thieves. We weren't planning on robbing any banks, but every dollar we earn means taking one away from someone else.

Christopher runs a hand through his blond curls, the ones that can make any woman swoon. Some of the women in the room glance at him as he does it, the light from the amber fixtures glancing off golden strands. He's a veritable angel walking the earth—made hard from his fall.

"She must be something," he says. "For you to get shaken up."

"I'm not shaken up."

"So she wasn't something?" Blue says, crossing one booted foot over his knee. He wears only jeans and T-shirts and dusty black boots, in direct violation of the dress code. He wears enough suits running his security company, he says, when he would much rather be in army fatigues.

"She's beautiful, of course. All women are beautiful."

Christopher raises an eyebrow. "So she's ordinary?"

They're baiting me. I know they're baiting me, and still it works. "*Non*. She is perfection. Delicate and pale and covered in freckles. Everywhere, freckles."

"I do love freckles," Sutton says with a wistful sigh.

"And she has a smart mouth that presents itself at the most surprising times. When I think she will be most scared and cowering, that's when she tells me what's what."

Blue grunts, because he enjoys a woman with attitude. "Nice."

"And there's something about her—the strangeness of her staying in that hotel, for one thing. Her past. Her secrets. I want to unwrap them as much as I want to take off her clothes."

"Which is a lot," Christopher observes, his voice dry, but I'm not fooled.

He loves secrets as much as I do, with his neat suits and obsidian eyes. He was the last addition to the Thieves Club, one we never expected. But when he went into business with Sutton, he slid into our group as if there had always been a space waiting for him.

With his cold ambition, there is no one better suited to join us.

Plus he brings the most excellent brandy.

I take a sip, savoring the spice. "Most likely she won't call again. She will find some handsome traveler in the hotel bar, who will finally convince her to leave the safety of her little nest."

The thought turns the brandy sour in my mouth.

"Or not." Blue turns the amber beer bottle in his thick fingers, studying me. "If you really upset her that much she might be too afraid to try again. You might have fucked her up."

I choke on my next sip and set the crystal down. "Thank you for that."

"She's going to call again," Christopher says, raising his finger for the server. The Den has a full bar, of course, but we can bring our own liquor, especially if we have a special bottle. The brandy he brings for me. Obscure craft brews for Blue. His business partner, Sutton, prefers Patron.

He drinks only wine himself, the kind that must be purchased at auction.

There is terrible hope inside me at that, because Christopher is usually correct.

"Because she wishes to cry again?"

"This is a woman who has spent her whole life behind bars, essentially. Even if they are bars of her own making. She wants to feel something. That's why she called the first time. It's why she'll call again."

I turn to stare into the fire as the server attends to refilling our drinks. Absolute privacy is assured in the Den, but I still would not speak of Bea in front of a stranger. In fact I do not usually tell the Thieves Club about any of the women I'm with, but she's far from usual.

And of course there's the issue of L'Etoile, but I have no intention of telling anyone about that—not even these men. They don't need to know that I have a darker purpose for wanting to go back to the hotel, to get closer to the woman who lives there.

When we're alone again, I lean forward. "I want to see her again, which is enough to convince me that I shouldn't. I don't have feelings about my clients. I pleasure them, they pleasure me. That's all."

"It's clear this has gone beyond that already," Sutton says. He wears a white business shirt, rumpled from a day's use, the sleeves rolled up. They dress alike, he and Christopher, in their high-rise real estate office, but they could not be more different.

"And I'm worried that if I go again, I'll have sex with her. Of course I will. But how can I do that, knowing she cried when I only made her come? How do you take someone's virginity?"

"Don't ask me," Blue says.

He's the only one of us in a committed relationship. He loves his wife, who had a very rough childhood. Enough that he didn't take her virginity, even though they met as teenagers. I've met Hannah and she's impossibly sweet; it's heartbreaking to think of her hurt.

"No idea," Christopher adds, but I happen to know he holds a deep fascination with his stepsister. She's the reason he moved to Tanglewood, though he would not admit that.

Even Sutton puts up his hands. "Who wants that kind of responsibility?"

Mon Dieu.

"I am in very big trouble," I announce softly.

The group drinks in silent agreement.

Chapter Seven

THE NEXT SATURDAY NIGHT I COME PREPARED. THE PAPER BAG IN MY ARMS ISN'T about seducing her, at least not about having sex. I already know she will do that with me, but I want to seduce her in other ways. Her mouth and her mind. Maybe then I will be comfortable taking her body.

She opens the door, and her eyes widen. "What's this?"

"I told you I was bringing dinner," I say, stepping over the threshold and heading into the kitchen.

"I thought you meant takeout from downstairs."

"But no. Tonight I will cook for you my favorite meal." Inside this bag is everything I need: half a chicken that has been marinating overnight and roasted before arriving, vegetables, an onion, garlic. An array of spices from my pantry.

Her brow furrows. "A tagine?"

"You remember?"

She ducks her head and hides a shy smile. "I don't think I'll forget anything about that night."

It's rather uncomfortable, having a boulder sitting on my chest. I remove it by clearing my throat. "You can help me by chopping vegetables, if you'd like."

"Of course," she says, picking up an onion.

I take it away. "No need to make you cry so early in the evening. Start with the cauliflower."

That makes her laugh, and I feel myself relax. I have never cooked with a woman, certainly never a client, but we fall into a pattern of quiet preparation.

"Like this?" she asks, showing me the cherry tomatoes in quarters.

Her technique is clumsy, because this tiny kitchen leaves no room for cooking anything but the essentials. It reminds me of the way she kisses, all eagerness, no finesse. "Perfect," I say. "Keep going."

She flashes me a brief, nervous smile before turning back to work. My stomach feels lighter than it should, almost fluttery, and it takes me a moment to realize what this is: nerves. Dear God. She's turning me into a schoolboy.

It's perhaps with too much gusto that I break down the chicken, letting the slice of the knife break the strange tension in the air. The meat comes apart under my hands, tender and fragrant.

"Tell me about your day," I say, my tone coaxing. I need to get us back to solid ground. We are shallow and flirty, that's fine. But we will not be nervous. There is nothing more at stake here than a fun night together.

"I played for a while. And then—"

"Played what?"

"Oh." She makes an embarrassed face. "I forgot you didn't know. I'm a pianist."

I have to bite my tongue so I don't ask her to play for me. It's not her job to perform for me. It's mine to perform for *her*. Finished with the chicken I settle the pieces into the dish and wash my hands in the sink. "That's incredible. You play every day?"

A flush this time. "Yes, most days. It's my job actually, so…"

I pause with my hands under the warm water. It's not hard to believe that she's a concert pianist. She has the wild hair and the dreamy atmosphere. And certainly the wealth that would have afforded her the opportunity to train at a world-renowned music school.

But she does not leave this suite. How does a concert pianist work from home?

She fills in my questioning silence. "I have a video channel. You know, online."

First, there's shock. I turn off the water. This tentative creature exposes herself online? Perhaps not her body, but music is far more intimate than that. And then there's attraction, the kind that makes me want to watch every video she's ever posted. *Damn.* "That's incredible. Would it make you self-conscious if you showed me one of your videos?"

"No. I mean, yes, but not as much as what we did the other night. When I'm playing, that's when I'm the most comfortable. The most… me."

"After we've eaten," I tell her.

She looks more comfortable just talking about music. "I like this. The cooking thing."

"Here, add the vegetables." I hold the pan for her while she puts in carrots, zucchini, onions. On top of that I add the marinade, where they will simmer together on the stovetop before serving. Not a traditional terra-cotta dish, but I had to improvise with her small kitchen, doing most of the cooking at my home. "I cook almost every night. It's soothing."

She peers over my arm at the stew. "Why is it orange?"

"Paprika, is what gives it the color. Turmeric. Cinnamon. Ginger."

Her lips form an "O" and it's too much of an invitation, whether she means it or not. I touch my forefinger to her bottom lip, giving her the chance to pull away. Her eyes widen, but she doesn't move. I know without tasting them that my skin will taste like spices. Without breaking eye contact I push my finger inside, rubbing my finger pad along her tongue.

"Coriander," I murmur. "Cumin. Olive oil."

She sucks in a breath, which forms a seal around my finger. The pulling sensation almost brings me to my knees, strong enough, shocking enough that I pull away.

"What do you think?" I ask softly.

Her swallow is an audible surrender. "It's really good."

That makes me laugh, but only a little. "Really good? I'll have to try harder."

"I would die," she says, both solemn and playful in a way I'm learning is unique to her. "If it were any better, I wouldn't be able to handle it."

"Poof," I tell her, more playful than solemn. "You would expire on the spot."

Her smile is tilted. "You would do that to me?"

"I suppose you'll have to wait and see."

There are trolls who live under bridges, according to my mother. She was full of superstitions and stories. They were fun when I was small. They turned darker later. These trolls, they make you answer questions in order to pass. That's what I become during dinner, cajoling and curious.

I want to know everything about her, including when she started to play—she was three when she first read music, but she played from the moment her pianist mother sat her on her knee. She played from a young age, and then… and then there is tragedy. She does not tell me what it is, and I don't ask. That's beyond the scope of what we do here. Sorrow has no place here.

And under no circumstances will I make her cry—again.

"When did you begin your video channel?" The tagine turned out to be exceptional, despite her rather sad stovetop that heated completely uneven.

"A couple years ago." She takes a bite and closes her eyes, giving this little moan I don't think she knows she's doing. It's completely involuntary, that sound. Completely sexual.

When her eyes open again she looks a little dazed. "I was going through a dark time. Feeling very alone here, so I posted online thinking, maybe I would find another musician going through the same thing. It went viral on social media, and then I had these followers asking for more."

"You must have exceptional talent."

She looks shy, but of course she does. "There are so many talented musicians out there."

"Then what sets you apart?" I ask, half as a taunt, and half because I truly want to know. I see something incredible in her, something almost too sweet to be borne, but that does not mean the world will see it. In fact, the very opposite is usually true: the more rare and precious a gift, the more easily the world will dismiss it.

A helpless shrug is my only answer.

And then I cannot wait any longer. The tagine is only half gone, our plates almost empty but ready for second helpings, but I have to see her in her element.

The first thing when I get to the website she tells me is a picture of her. It's part of the header graphic, a picture of her with her hair a wild halo, the shadows falling dramatically around her, her eyes closed in ecstasy. *Climax,* my sex-ready mind supplies. That's how she will look during climax.

Of course, she isn't having sex in the picture. As the photo fades to black I can see the lace of another high collar. And the barest hint of her hands in motion. She's playing the piano. This has been sex for her. This is how a healthy young woman has managed to remain a virgin; not because she is sexless, but because she found a different sensual outlet for her body.

It's hard to tear my gaze away from that shot in the header. Distantly I recognize that it must have been taken by a professional photographer, the focus is too clear, the lighting too perfect, for anything less. There's a surprising streak of jealousy—that another man has been here, photographing her, admiring her, but I push that aside. All of this looks completely professional. The name across the top isn't hers, not precisely. A stage name. *Bea Sharp,* like the musical note. I have to blink once, twice, against the number of followers she has. This is more than an internet sensation. This is a real-life celebrity sitting beside me, blushing profusely.

"It's a little strange seeing someone look at it," the celebrity says, her skin a pretty pink. "Normally I can just pretend like no one really sees me."

Many thousands of people see her, the numbers prove. Millions actually. "This is incredible. You do this from here. Where is the piano?"

She gestures toward the other side of the suite. "The second bedroom. It was always the music room, but since the page has grown I have some lighting equipment and cameras."

My finger hovers over one of the videos. "May I?"

"You don't have to," she says, which doesn't answer the question.

"It's rather embarrassing how much I want to. But only with your permission."

She ducks her head in a picture of humble grace. My God, this woman. She is from a different time period, one with gowns and thrones. No wonder she lives at the top of the tower. So what would that make me? A court jester, I suppose. Someone to amuse her.

The video expands on the screen, focused on the piano. Only a little of her body is visible, a deep velvet dress that ends halfway down her forearms. Her nails are unpolished, neatly trimmed, square-tipped but delicate, strong and feminine. Her skin gleams in the bright light, highlighting the freckles across her skin, even there. I like to think that if I had seen this video first, I would have recognized her by her hands alone, both delicate and surprisingly strong.

On the screen she places her hands on the piano.

In real life she twines her fingers together, anxious and anticipatory.

Both of the actions make a knot in my chest, tight enough that it's hard to breathe. I can't take a breath until the first note reverberates through the air. Even through the pale phone speakers I can feel the depth of the sound. The undeniable rightness of them.

And then she plays, bringing to life Sia's *Chandelier* with a classical bent that I can only marvel at. I can feel her skill and her passion coming through every note. There is reckless abandon in the song, fear and grief and hope. "*Mon Dieu*," I breathe.

From the corner of my eye, in the single ounce of my body not focused wholly on the song being played, I can see Bea's fingers twitch in the same pattern they do on screen. She really is in her element with music. She's a goddess.

I set the phone down, letting it play between us.

The notes build something new between us, a kind of foreplay. When she looks at me, I can tell she feels it too. This time she isn't afraid. It isn't something to fear, the music.

"Bea," I murmur. "Come here."

She does not hesitate. In seconds she's in my arms, and I pull her firmly onto my lap. There's only a slight squirm, enough to make my cock throb, while she wonders whether I can support her. Why do women worry about that? There's nothing more fulfilling than holding her this way, than feeling her soft and supple in my arms while I hold her still for a kiss.

My lips touch hers with barely held restraint. *Don't devour her.*

The music is her tutor, this time, but it's also mine. It teaches us the rhythm to use as I nip gently at her bottom lip, as she shyly strokes her tongue against mine.

When she pulls back, she's breathing hard. Those pale green eyes are darker now, with passion, with confidence, and I am close to bursting.

"Wow," she whispers.

It makes me laugh a little, though it comes out unsteady. *Mon Dieu*, indeed.

You might think that I must woo every client, but most frequently it happens the other way around. Women tempt me and flatter me and please me, even when they are paying for the privilege. I have been treated to the finest chefs and flown in private jets. They wear beautiful lingerie and compliment me as if I might walk out the door if they don't.

Nothing has ever seduced me as much as this.

No one as much as her.

"Can we do it again?" she asks, a little playful.

Why did I think I could be the court jester for her? I would be the peasant, not even fit to set a foot in the same room. "I want to lick you," I tell her, fervent and true. "Kneeling before you while you play this song for me."

Her eyes widen, because she does not mistake my meaning. "I'm sure I couldn't keep playing."

"You'll have lots of practice first," I say, and I don't mean practice playing the piano.

I mean practice receiving pleasure from my tongue, her legs spread wide for me, her pussy wet and swollen from my caresses. I want her so well versed in this that she begs me with her subtle little moans, barely audible above the song. It's a physical pain, imagining her hips jerk against me as she climaxes, the singular vibration of the keys as she comes.

Her eyes have turned a beautiful shade of green, darker than jade. It makes me think of a smooth lake lit by a full moon, both opaque and luminescent.

"Again," I murmur.

Can we do it again? It's startling how much I want that. Not only to kiss her, but to hold her, to *see* her. There's a longing inside me to ask to see her again, even though it shouldn't matter if she books another Saturday night, shouldn't matter if it's her or any other woman. It's never mattered before.

This time she is the one to press her lips to mine, and it's that much sweeter. With her uncertainty and her eagerness. I have never experienced anything this wholesome. I certainly did not expect to find it in a client.

She does not move to open her mouth, nor open mine. There's only the press, somehow made more erotic by the chasteness. I surrender to it, surrender to *her*, glorying in the sensation of plump lips and feather breaths. The sensation of her trembling body in my arms, the shimmer of moonlight on water made real.

Her body shifts on my lap, barely an inch to the side. Enough to brush against my hard cock. I suck in a breath, shocked by the effort it takes not to come.

She barely touched me. She *didn't* touch me, not on purpose. There are so many layers of clothes between us, but I'm ready to come like a teenager.

Her eyes meet mine, wide and wondering. "Is that…"

"My cock. Say it. I want to hear you say the word."

A blush. "Right now?"

"If you want it inside you, you should be able to ask for it."

"Cock," she whispers.

I'm moved by her shyness and by how much she wants me. Moved by the sweet curiosity in her trembling voice. But not enough to let her off the hook. "Say *I want your cock*."

There's a longer pause this time. "I want your cock."

Jesus, my cock throbs in response. It hears her. It wants her right back. "Say *Make me come on your cock, until my pretty little cunt can't take any more*."

She sucks in a breath. "This is what you meant."

"What?"

"About desire."

"Haven't you felt it before, mon amie? Why did you call for me if not for desire?"

It's a question she has dodged before, her reasons. And she dodges it again. "Not like this. I wondered. I was curious, but I never felt it like this."

I force myself to observe her coolly, from a distance instead of like the slavering beast I feel inside. "Breathing hard, eyelids low. You're warm all over. Yes, this is what desire looks like. And I'm sure you'll be wet when I touch you, won't you?"

She exhales, a sound of acquiescence. "Make me come on your cock."

"Until?" Perhaps it is cruel of me. The knowledge isn't enough to make me stop. That's how badly I want to hear those words from her petal-pink mouth.

"Until my pretty little pussy can't take anymore."

Hearing the words from her lips is too much. I have to kiss her, and once I start, I can't stop. I'm tasting her, licking her, biting her. Her enthusiasm matches my own; she tugs at my shirt, my collar, trying to get closer. It's not enough, never enough.

There's a moment of indecision, when her knee comes up, blocking us. It's now that I should take us to the bedroom. Now that I should turn this frantic make-out session into a seduction. But my own need burns too hotly. I'm wild and untried, as if her inexperience has become my own. So I yank her onto my lap, harder, fully against me. And then she straddles me, her heat pressed right up against my cock. There's no slowing this down. No stopping.

She moves her hips against me, hesitant, curious. "Is this okay?"

"It's perfect. Do it again."

When she does, I'm the one who lets out a groan. *Mon Dieu*, her body is heaven. I'm torn between the places I want to touch her—to cup her face and feel her hair curl around my hand. To feel her breasts, maybe find the buttons hidden in the demure lace dress and bare her to me.

I decide on her hips, the better to rock her pussy against my cock. I'm throbbing and hurting, but all I want is for her to come. I show her the rhythm, and there, *there*, she learns it.

Her frantic little breaths flutter against my neck like a butterfly. Every muscle in my body strains against the need to throw her onto the table, the dishes and seduction be damned. There is self-control somewhere inside me, I don't *feel* it, but it must be there, because somehow I remain seated, barely, my whole body clenching, hips already fucking into nothing.

When she comes I feel her ecstasy wash over me like a balm. It doesn't feel *good*. That would be too ordinary for someone like Bea. It feels like I've been granted a reprieve.

I hold her against me as the tremors take her body, one hand keeping her hips flush against me, the other cradling her head against my shoulder.

Distantly I realize I'm muttering to her in Arabic. Strange, that. It's the language I used on the streets of Tangier. The one of familiarity and abandon. I'm alternately soothing her and cursing her, though I'm sure she can understand neither.

Slowly she stills. Her breathing evens out.

When she lifts her head there's a distinct echo of loss in my chest.

"Is this...okay?" Her pale green eyes are large now, still hazy from sex but with some worry seeping in. Perhaps she senses that I'm *not* okay.

Perhaps because I'm clenching her ass hard enough to leave fingerprint bruises.

It's an act of extreme hardship and heroism that I let go of her. I'm not entirely graceful as I shove her off my lap. Not entirely steady on my feet, but *mon Dieu*. My cock is as hard as iron in my pants, leaking against the black fabric, ready to explode.

If this were an ordinary relationship, I would take it out. Let her talented little fingers stroke me the way she plays the piano. Let her pretty lips taste me, but this isn't an ordinary relationship. I've had women blow me, of course. Many clients wish to. Some even want me like this, desperate and demanding. But they are experienced enough to ask for it. This woman, she's too innocent for the thoughts in my head. So I force myself to the bathroom.

I force out the words to say, *excuse me*, but I'm too far gone to be sure. They might be in English or French. Or in Arabic, the street language, the one I mumble in dreams.

Only in private do I lean my back against the door and pull down my zipper. There is infinite relief, letting my heavy cock fall onto my palm.

It only takes two strokes, remembering the spice on her tongue, the softness of her lips. The sweetness of her body in my arms. And I'm coming, spurting into my hand.

In the aftermath I can only stare at the gold-plated bathroom fixtures, the tile that is probably imported from Paris itself, with faded script and designs on every other piece.

I know I should not, but I have never been very wise. And so my head turns to the side, where I can see myself in the mirror. My hair is askew. My cheeks dark with passion. I look like a man who has been months without sex, years without it.

Like a man who has only just discovered what it is.

Chapter Eight

WHEN I RETURN THE DINING ROOM IS EMPTY. Except for the cat, who sits and watches me with judgment in her grey eyes. Does she smell Bea's desire in the air? Does she smell mine? Of course she does, she's a cat. Why do I care? I can't help but want her to like me, this scared little girl with razor-sharp claws.

I peek into the bedroom, but the white sheets are neat and tidy. I'm half tempted to check behind the dresser, as if Bea might have shoved herself into a corner.

And then the music starts.

Like the kind that came streaming over the internet, but far better than anything the tiny speakers in my phone could have reproduced. The sound draws me back through the living room to the other end of the penthouse.

I pause at the doorway, uncertain of my welcome.

Notes filter through the cracked doorway. More than anyone, I know that true privacy comes not from the body but from the mind. She might not want me in the room.

In the end it's my own need that decides me. I need to see her, to feel her. To make sure she's okay. We didn't do anything particularly traumatic. A dry humping session is practically adolescent, but I find myself strangely protective of her. Protective even from myself.

The door is silent as I push it open, revealing a room with a grand piano in the middle, lighting and video equipment all around the edges. There's a large black rectangle in the corner with a hundred silver switches on it, as if she's going to fly to the moon.

Bea sits at the piano, her eyes closed as her fingers dance over the keys.

The music stops.

Her eyes light up as she sees me, and I can finally take a deep breath.

"There you are," she says, a little playful.

I like her like this, relaxed. It's the music that makes her this way, but I like to think that it was me, too. Her orgasm, the one she wrung from my body.

"Here I am," I say, wandering into the room, careful not to step on any wires. "This is quite an elaborate setup. Do you know what all these machines do?"

A smile flickers at the edges of her lips. "It was either that or get a filming crew every day."

"You post every day?" I already know that I'll be checking her channel from home, a level of connection I've never had with any client before, never wanted.

"Most days."

"Do the other musicians mind? When you play their songs?"

"Some." A small shrug. "Now it's a big enough business that I can license the songs that I want to show. And before that…"

She plays a little song. It takes me a moment to realize it's the refrain from *Baby, One More Time* by Britney Spears. Considering why I'm here I can't help the smile that spreads. She's a dangerous woman, this one. Already beautiful and smart and shy. And now, funny?

Dangerous.

"Before that?"

"Before that I was lucky. This really huge artist saw one of my videos and she reposted it. Then it happened again with someone else. Next thing I knew I had these big PR firms contacting me, wanting me to do one of their client's songs as soon as it comes out."

I lean one hip against the piano, looking down at her. I'm the one above her but she's still the goddess on her glossy black bench. Lucky? That wasn't luck. That was her incredible talent and what must be serious business intelligence. "And if you don't like the song?"

"Then I don't play it. But that's not really the test. It's more about whether I think I can add something to the song, something to make it my own. I wouldn't just play the song as written. So if I don't feel it... on the inside, you know? If I don't have something to add, I won't take the deal."

"That's incredible," I tell her. "That you've built this empire in your spare bedroom. You can pick and choose what you play. Make it your own. I'm in awe of you."

A breathy little laugh that I feel all the way in my soul. "It feels like me alone in a room, most days. Which is the only reason I can do it."

So much isolation. Does it cost her something? I think it does, even if she doesn't know it. "Would you ever play in front of an audience?"

"Oh no," she says immediately. "I could never. Not only because I wouldn't leave, but… playing is private. The cameras aren't real people. They're just recording. Not watching."

An interesting distinction, but I'm not convinced. There are thousands of people watching those videos. Bea may tell herself she's alone, that she prefers it that way, but it hurts her. And for some reason I think I can help with this problem. A foolish idea, probably.

You're falling for her, asshole.

"Has it always been like this for you? Creating new songs from what you hear?"

She shakes her head. "I mean, I always heard the music in my head. I thought that was normal. My mom was the same way. She was a concert pianist." I hear the pride in her voice. "She played in Carnegie Hall."

"That's incredible."

A shaky breath moves her. "She died, when I was ten. My dad, too."

Everything inside me goes still. This is huge. An earthquake in the middle of afternoon tea. What she's revealing to me splits her world apart. It's splitting mine.

"It was…pirates, actually." This time her laugh is pained. Bitter. The kind that slices through my defenses. How many people has she told this to? Not many. Maybe no one. "They were on a yacht. A party with a hundred people but the pirates only took them."

"Why?" I breathe, but I already know the answer. It's folded around us. Money.

"They wanted a ransom. At least that's what they usually did, but something must have gone wrong. They usually would have only taken my mom, made my dad pay the ransom. But for whatever reason that day they took them both."

And they didn't come back. "Bea. You don't have to continue."

Her eyes are mournful. "But I do, because you do something to me. Make me feel open and vulnerable. Scared, but like I want to keep feeling it. How do you do that?"

You do that to me, too. I don't say it.

"They never found out exactly what happened on that boat. Probably my dad fought them. There was a struggle and both of them died that day, before they even asked for anything."

"I'm sorry, Bea." More sorry than I can put into words. More sorry than I thought I could feel for someone. On the streets of Tangier I saw more tragedy than should exist, but it moves me beyond bearing, her suffering.

She gives a little shake of her head. "Most of the time I don't think of it."

"Why now?" I ask softly.

She scrunches her nose. "This is embarrassing but I guess it's talking to you. I mean, using words. I go downstairs and chat with people but it's always on the surface. Anything deep, anything important, it happens through music."

"It's beautiful," I tell her, when what I mean is, *you're beautiful*.

"When they died I stopped speaking."

"You mean… entirely?"

"For a couple years, yeah. There were therapists and doctors. I could make a sound, if I was startled or scared. But I didn't form words. I already played piano before that, but after that it was the only way I would communicate. Anything I wanted to express, it happened here."

I understand that she means more than the piano. She means this room.

God.

Chords of longing and loneliness fill the air, her expression dark.

"Hotel California," I say softly.

Then her eyes brighten. "For you."

This one I recognize immediately. *Castle on a Cloud*. It's a song that's part of the Les Misérables musical. My face turns to stone, but inside there's a clamor.

The notes slow and then stop.

"Sorry. Was that weird? Because your name is Hugo. And the author was Victor Hugo." She looks crestfallen. "Of course that was dumb."

I force myself to speak through the chaos inside me. "Not dumb."

"Then why do you look like you're going to throw up."

Moving stiffly I manage to sit next to her on the bench. She scoots to the side to make room for me. "I'm sorry," I say.

"No, don't. I'm the one who can't interact with regular people."

"I hope you aren't categorizing me as *regular*," I tell her, managing to find some wry humor in this situation. I want to shut down, to push her away, but she opened herself up too far for that. "The truth is that my mother named me for that author."

Green eyes widen. "Did she?"

"I'm not sure why I'm named Hugo instead of Victor. Perhaps because it was easier to spell." Then I admit something that always pained *Mama*. "She couldn't read."

She couldn't read, so she never knew the irony of a book about a man starved enough to steal bread and a revolution he wouldn't need. About a whore who sacrificed for her daughter and a grand love she would never know.

"But she liked the story?" Bea asks, too innocent to realize that there was no one else on our street who could read either. No one knew the story, but *Mama* kept the large book as a sad little tribute to our French heritage. Only when I moved to America did I learn what it was about.

"She liked that it was long and important." Perhaps she thought it would help me become important, instead of an illiterate maid. I never knew what my father did for a living. My skin is darker than Mama's, my hair a rich black. So my father was probably native to Morocco, one of the transient workers who appeared and disappeared like ghosts haunting the harbor.

"I'm named after an author too," Bea says. "But her books were less long. Less important, too."

"Who?"

"Beatrix Potter." At my look of bemusement she explains. "She wrote Peter Rabbit. It's a children's book about a rabbit who gets into trouble."

"It sounds less tragic, at least."

She laughs a little, but sadly. "That's true. Will you come back next week, Hugo?"

I have the feeling this question is about more than money, but that's the only way I know how to answer. "Of course, darling. Call the agency and get on my schedule."

Chapter Nine

At the beginning I worked most nights. I shared a one-room apartment with Sutton, who arrived in Tanglewood more broke than myself. Every cent I earned went into investments, some throughout the city in real estate, others in the stock market. As my portfolio grew and my hourly rate got higher, I stopped working—except for Saturday nights.

Even with a large nest egg, the money I make in a single evening is worthwhile. My services are only for the elite women of the city, those who can afford to throw thousands of dollars at pleasure.

And I enjoy my time, usually.

The arrangement suits me, but not everyone is pleased. When a knock comes on my door Sunday morning, I know who it is before I check the security camera on my phone.

It is with great reluctance that I press the button to let her in.

I take a final swallow of espresso before I get up to meet her at the door. We exchange kisses on the cheek, superficial pleasantries before she attempts to stab me in the back.

"Come in," I tell her genially, because I have much experience with pretending.

Melissande gives me a dark look, because she knows this. "Beatrix Cartwright booked you again."

I stroll into the living room and recline on one of the over-plush leather sofas. Everything here is luxurious and modern and completely impersonal. The furnished loft was only going to be a stepping stone after moving out of Sutton's, but I've never seen any reason to leave.

"I thought you'd be pleased." This is a lie. Nothing has pleased her for many years.

She sits across from me, crossing her long slender legs, revealing the edge of her garters. Always dressed to impress, this woman. "Meanwhile the rest of your clients are clamoring for an appointment. This new girl is taking up all of your time."

"So give the night to someone else," I say, pretending my throat isn't tight at the thought of not seeing Bea again. But I've never minded who booked my time before. I'm not going to start now, especially when Melissande would see it for the weakness it is.

"Beatrix pays too well," she says, looking annoyed despite the fact that she makes a neat forty percent for doing nothing but taking phone calls.

"Then why are you here?"

"You know why. Because you need to work more nights."

"*Non*, I'm doing very well. You are the one who needs me to work more nights."

A sneer forms on her pretty lips. "Are you having trouble keeping it up more than once a week? There are medicines that can help with that."

It does not bother me, the insult. She used to be a whore before she became the madam. And like most women her hourly rates only went down and down. While mine only goes up. It is the curse of our genders, but I will not quibble over it. "I work Saturday nights. That's all."

At my quiet certainty, her face forms a pout. I'm sure that is effective on some men. Once it would have been effective on me, but I learned not to trust her a long time ago.

Her dark gaze takes me in, from my open collar to my fresh slacks to my bare feet. I am only beginning the day, still comfortable and crisp. Her eyes heat in that familiar way that once would have made the back of my neck warm. Now I'm left completely cold.

"Or perhaps I can remind you of what it felt like to have sex every night. Several times a night. You were quite skilled at that, once. Maybe that was only for me."

"I was fifteen," I say, my voice flat. "And horny."

Rage flashes in her eyes. "Don't be crass, darling."

I manage not to flinch when she says that. *Darling.* That's where I learned it, after all. A word to push someone away. "You know very well that I can leave you whenever I please and earn the same amount of money. More, probably."

She smiles, probably not realizing how cruel it looks. "Then why don't you?"

Melissande was a beautiful woman when I met her, in the finest designer clothes and with her glossy hair in curls. She had so much money, I could not have guessed that she was a prostitute for the wealthy men who came to the city. She took me into her penthouse suite and showed me what it meant to be a man—or at least what I thought it meant.

There was nothing keeping me in Tangier, so when she offered me the chance to come with her to America, I took it. Perhaps it should have alarmed me that we had to pretend I was her adopted son in the paperwork, but I was too eager to come. Too blindly in love.

My lips twist in a wry smile. "Perhaps because I still have feelings for you."

Her cheeks flush, most likely with anger. She hates to be the subject of pity. But what else can I feel for her? When I realized she only wanted to whore me out, it broke my heart. There are no feelings left in that organ now. No love and no warmth.

"I'll give you seventy percent," she says flatly.

"Thank you," I say. "I will be happy to accept seventy percent of what Beatrix pays for Saturday night. But no more than that. One night a week. That's all you get."

She narrows her eyes. "There's something different about this girl, isn't there?"

"Apparently she pays more," I say, my voice dry.

"No, something else. Is her pussy extra tight? She did mention her little problem. The virginity thing. I told her you would take care of that. Did it feel special, Hugo?"

It's been years since her digs could make me angry. And yet I feel it rising inside me now, the need to tell her not to talk about Bea. It would only give Melissande power.

"But no, I have not even fucked her yet."

Her eyes widen, her surprise real instead of manufactured. "Why not?"

"Perhaps because I'm making *her* fall in love with *me*. After all, I did learn from the best."

Chapter Ten

"D IM SUM," I TELL HER, TWIRLING THE LAST SIP OF WINE IN THE GLASS. We're having dinner again downstairs in Beau Ciel, because it's the only restaurant she can visit. *For now.* "They have dumplings with pork and lotus root. It comes fresh from the kitchen, still steaming as they bring it around to the tables."

It feels explicit to describe this food to her, especially the way her eyes have turned soft and sensual, the sage green she gives me when she's going to come. "Don't," she whispers.

"You pick one up with your chopsticks. Have you used chopsticks before? No matter, you can use your fingers. The dumpling will be soft and round, but tightly held. You can bring it to your lips and—"

She makes a squeak. There's no other word for the sound. Like a mouse. "I can't go. I want to, I mean I *really* want to, but it's not as simple as that."

"But no, I can have my car pulled around in two minutes flat."

"I would have a panic attack."

I can tell from the earnestness in her voice that she believes this. However I can also tell that she needs to overcome this, that she will never fully be living until she does. It's not only the fact of her existence in L'Etoile's marble walls. Perhaps another woman would be content here. It's the hunger in her eyes that becomes stronger every time I speak of a new thing she could experience if she left.

Bea must leave, and somehow I've made it my mission to have her do it.

"Is there something we could do for a panic? Perhaps a breathing technique. Or a medicine."

She's already shaking her head. "There's nothing."

I give her a dubious look. "How can you be sure? They have many advancements. And when is the last time you tried to leave?"

She picks at her steak. From here I can see that it's perfectly cooked. Juicy. And completely terrible to a woman who can have only this and a small menu besides. "It may have been a while but that's only because I learned my boundaries. I remember how it felt."

"And how was that?"

"Like dying."

That is no small feat to overcome, then. "Have I told you about the little shop off Fifth Street? They serve a green tea gelato pressed between two fresh lavender macarons."

Her eyes are darker again. It's the sex look. I've been dreaming about it. My nights are filled with moss and fog. I'm searching for something, for someone, but never satisfied.

"I'll have it delivered," she says.

I give her a look. "Non. You will have melting gelato and soggy cookies."

"You don't understand."

"So explain it to me. You must have some kind of doctor, yes? What does he say?"

"I have a psychologist, yes. She comes to visit me once a month."

"This time you will explain you wish to leave."

Her eyes narrow. "You're very bossy."

I take her hand from across the table. "I would not dare to boss you. I only want to help. The way you look at me, it seems like you want that, too."

She sighs. "Oh yes. Yes. But it's impossible."

Building an incredible celebrity without ever leaving this building, that's impossible. Hiring an overpriced escort to take her sweet virginity, impossible. This woman does impossible things.

A sudden stroke of inspiration has me sitting up straight. "What about a piano? Don't you wish to play on pianos other than your own?"

Her stricken expression is almost enough to stop me. Almost.

"Bellmont," comes a low voice behind me.

I turn, startled to recall that we aren't alone. There's Damon Scott, the proprietor of the Den. He's a powerful and dangerous man in this city. And apparently, one of the diners at Beau Ciel tonight.

My stomach tightens. I have been seen with my clients before. Of course I have. In some ways I am like an expensive crocodile leather purse. I am the toy breed dog they carry inside. Something to show how wealthy and fabulous they are. There is no shame for them, or for me, but Bea is different.

If they give her a snide look I'm not sure what I will do.

But the woman on Damon Scott's arm—I remember her name, Penny—she smiles at us. "Did I hear you mention pianos? We have a beautiful Bluthner grand in the library. I can't play but we keep it tuned in case someone else can."

Bea's lips form an O of undisguised longing. "That would be incredible, but... I really can't. I'm sorry."

Damon smiles genially, though he must remember my profession. And he must guess who Bea is to me. "It's perfectly fine. Anytime you wish to come, have Hugo bring you."

"Thank you," I tell him softly.

"A friend of yours is a friend of ours," Damon answers at the same volume.

I could not say what Bea is to me. A friend? A lover? But she is more than just a client, and I have not even taken her virginity yet. What will happen when I breach her hymen? It should be a purely physical act, but I'm discovering more and more that nothing is ever as simple as it seems with her.

"Bea is a very talented musician," I tell them.

"Oh, it must run in the family," Penny says brightly. All three of us stare at her for a surprised beat, and her lips twist. "Did I say something wrong?"

"How did you know?" I manage to ask, because Bea looks too shocked to respond.

Penny scrunches her nose. "Was I not supposed to say anything? I'm sorry. It's just that your father was so amazing. His work on computational lexicon is basically legend. I read his biography so I know about his wife and that he had a daughter. I shouldn't have said anything."

"No, it's fine," Bea assures her, recovering her voice. "Truly. I was only surprised because people don't usually recognize me unless they see my full name."

"You have his eyes," Penny says, as if offering a confession.

That makes Bea smile a little. "I know. And thank you for remembering him this way. It's really such a gift that you remember him for the good in his life instead of…"

Instead of his tragic death.

Damon clears his throat. "I'll see you at the Den, Bellmont?"

"Tomorrow," I murmur, unable to take my eyes from Bea's melancholy expression.

And then we are alone. "Who's your father?" I ask softly.

"Arthur Cartwright."

I know him immediately, though I never would have linked the tech magnate with

Silicon Valley origins to the timid young woman trapped in a tower in Tanglewood. "The inventor."

She nods. "The only thing he loved more than his work is my mother."

"I'm sorry," I say, knowing the memories are dark.

"I meant what I said. I'm glad that he can be remembered for the things he accomplished. I don't think I've lived up to the family name, anyway. Not with the way I'm stuck here. The way I panic at even the thought of going outside."

"We can go to the Den. I would stay with you every second."

She laughs, though the sound wrenches my heart. "It's impossible, Hugo."

I do not argue with words, but she knows my thoughts.

"Come upstairs," she offers, and my arguments evaporate into nothing. There is only her offer and the powerful knowledge in her eyes. *Tonight.*

Chapter Eleven

The first time I was in this bedroom I rescued her kitty. The second time I made her come. Both of those times I wanted to help Bea, but this time is completely different. It's my own need that drives me as I lead her by the hand to the bed. The need to undress her and feel her naked skin against my own. It's a wild animal inside me, this need. Gnashing and growling with hunger.

She's trembling. I feel the tremors where my hand holds hers. There's uncertainty in her eyes, enough to give me pause. Not enough to make me stop. I undress her with slow deliberation, undoing the small buttons at her back, then the zipper the rest of the way, revealing so much covered skin that I feel drunk with it.

Make this good for her.

I never have to remind myself of that. It's always my primary purpose. From the very beginning, sex has been a way to make a woman feel beautiful, feel pleasure. Only now does it seem like something else.

She wears a white lace bra, which I remove from her body an inch at a time, placing an almost chaste kiss to every inch revealed. Her white lace panties go next, but I don't kiss her there. Not yet. Not when she's looking at me like I'm going to ravish her, a little worried.

Desire beats a heavy drum in my veins. This time it's different because I want to touch her more than I want her to be touched. I want to fuck her more than she wants to be fucked. I want *her*…

More than she wants me.

I'm wild with this wanting, my hands too rough, my breathing harsh.

There's something primal about what's happening to me. It's out of my control, the way I push her back onto the bed, the way I slide between her legs, the way I push my cock against her. There are still clothes between us, but I have no intention of letting her grind against me to completion like we did in the dining room. The only way this ends is with me pulsing inside her wet heat.

"I'm nervous," she whispers, her eyes an opaque jade green.

"I won't hurt you."

There may not be any of my usual finesse, but I'll make her come hard enough to see stars. The way the ceiling of Beau Ciel lights up, pinpricks of white on a painted blue swirl.

She gives me a quick grin, full of mischief. "What if I hurt you?"

Mon Dieu, I'm already aching. How much more can I take? "You don't need to worry about me. You never need to worry. There's only your beautiful body."

And I need to feel her against me, naked and warm, so I pull back enough to unbutton my white dress shirt and push down my slacks. My boxer briefs are left, and I consider leaving them on for her comfort. But I'd rather she know what she's getting into.

So I strip completely, releasing my cock, heavy and dark with arousal.

Her gaze darts away, skittish now. And when she looks back at me, I have the sensation I had when her kitty looked up at me from behind the dresser. "I know I'm not who you would be with, not really, but I still want to make this good for you. If there's something I should do, you have to tell me."

My heart pounds. Not who I would be with?

Her hair curls wildly around her head, framing her pale face, decorating the pillow. Her lashes are the same copper color, fanning around those pretty eyes. Her eyebrows are a shade darker, two crescents I want to trace with my thumb. And then there's her nose. Should there be any allure to a nose? It's a utilitarian feature, not a form of seduction. But hers is small and curving up, a reminder of the innocence that brought me to her. Her lips are full and plush. I want to sink into them.

Not who I would be with?

If I wanted to be with her any more than this, I would expire on the spot.

"For that," I say, pressing a kiss to a cluster of freckles at the corner of her eyes, "I will have to make you come so hard you cannot think. There's no other solution to such a claim."

Her eyes widen. "What? No, you don't have to—"

"And when I'm licking you and drinking you down, lapping every drop with a hunger so great, you won't be able to doubt how much I want you, how beautiful I find you."

Her breath catches, which is better than self-doubt. I don't want doubt anywhere near her. Only the confidence she has when she plays at the piano, all the time.

I move down her body one constellation at a time, stroking her skin, pressing a quick kiss. Laving her with my tongue. Her freckles are pale on pale, almost an optical illusion. I can only see them under certain light, so I move her body as I go, lifting her hips, touching her so that she arches up toward my mouth. When I'm at the top of her sex, she presses her legs together.

I'm so starved for her. Can't she see that? But no, she's busy thinking of how she looks. Wondering if I like the bronze hair or the porcelain skin. It seems impossible that she doesn't know.

It almost seems impossible that she's real.

"Let me taste you, sweet Bea. I won't force you, but I want you bad enough that it hurts me inside. I'm imagining how you taste, how you'll feel on my tongue. The way you'll clench when you come. And it's a physical pain." I put a hand to my breastbone so she'll know where. There are barbs. "You are the most beautiful woman I've ever seen. Let me in."

Her eyes close briefly, as if in prayer. "How do you do this?"

"What?"

"How do you make me believe it?"

I want to say more, but then she opens her legs for me, and the sight is enough to render me speechless. The pain becomes a driving spear inside me, until I bend down and lick her deep at her core. She gasps a sound of shock and pleasure, so I do it again.

"You taste like sweetness and sex, Bea." I don't have the willpower to lift my mouth from her completely, so my words come out muffled, but I think she understands. Her hips press up, asking for more, and I run my tongue along the ridge of her sex. "My cock is as hard as it's ever been. I'm pressing it into the sheets for relief, but it doesn't help."

A soft moan. "Hugo."

I kiss an open-mouthed trail up to her clit. "And right here, this sweet bud. I've been dreaming about it and look at you. Even your sex is shy, hiding from me. Uncertain."

It needs to be reassured, like the woman beneath me, so I press my tongue flat against her bud. Her whole body goes tense and quivering, and I have to hold her down at her hips. She only has enough room to nudge her body up, up, up. I wait for her to realize this, to try it out, to feel the mind-melting pleasure of it. I'm not licking her at this moment; I'm letting her fuck my tongue.

"You're so beautiful," she murmurs.

I realize I've closed my eyes, the taste of her so incredible I want to memorize it. Because this won't last forever. How can it? She will move on to a man equal of her, and I will be left with a hollow loft and a cold madam. There's only now.

The corner of my lip kicks up. "Beautiful?"

She laughs a little. "Are you offended? But you are. You're handsome, too. And strong. I mean you have an actual six-pack. I thought those weren't even real."

The six-pack in question flexes against the mattress, as if showing off for her. Working out is something of a requirement for this profession. It's also a pleasant way to pass the time, but now it seems imperative, as if I've been lifting and running and swimming all these years for this.

"But you're beautiful, too," she says, soft and hurting.

I press one final kiss to her clit and am rewarded with a whimper. Then I climb up her body, my cock leaking a line of precum along the sheets. "I wish to be beautiful for you, if that's what you want. And handsome. And strong."

When I'm close enough, she traces two fingers over my lips which are still damp from her arousal. Her brow is furrowed in concentration, like maybe she's trying to memorize me too.

"Will you have sex with me now?" she asks, and I can't tell from her tone what answer she wants.

Somehow I find the condom in my wallet and tear the foil open, slipping the latex over my cock. "I think I'll die if I don't."

That makes her smile. "You're the only man I've ever wanted like this."

Those are the last words I hear before I notch my cock against her pussy and slide home. The pride wars with pleasure, a galaxy implosion in my chest. Her private walls stretch to accommodate me, but not far enough. It feels like a vise around my cock, and I shudder against the sensations.

Bea gasps and strains at the intrusion, her hands pushing weakly against my shoulders. Her hair in disarray, her face flushed. She's like wildflowers in full bloom across the valley. It makes me feel like the sun, beaming down on her, making her turn toward me.

"Too much," I say between gritted teeth.

It's not a question because I know I gave her too much and too fast. Her body trembles underneath me, struggling, maybe even in pain. I can't hurt her. *Mon Dieu*, I need to pull out.

Except that would be torture.

I drop my forehead to the pillow beside her, my body outside my control, my cock still hard and throbbing inside her. It's all I can do not to thrust again and again. "Forgive me."

She makes little panting noises. "I didn't know—"

"Didn't know what?" I ask, my jaw clenched hard, eyes shut tight. It's a terrible knot, our bodies together. Too tight for me to pull away. Pulled hard enough to hurt her.

"That it could actually be too big." A strange riff that might be laughter. Or maybe tears. "I thought it would always work. I mean it *looked* big, but what do I know?"

"It will work," I assure her, pressing a kiss to her temple even while my lower body pushes hard to stay inside her. "Once you have more experience. I'm so sorry for hurting you. I am an animal. A savage. A brute."

"I did ask for it," she offers weakly.

"Not like this." She wanted my patience and skill. She *paid* for it, but she's getting a side of me I didn't even know existed. I press my open mouth against her collarbone, tasting the salty sweetness of her skin.

A small sound, almost pain, but her lips are parted. There's pleasure in her eyes, and I think that maybe she likes me this way. Not the way I'm a steel rod inside her, but the way

I'm consuming her. And so I rock my hips gently against her, pressing my body against her clit.

Her hands unclench and fall back to the mattress. "So good."

It's like the scent of blood, the small proof of her pleasure. I'm a predator crouched over her, untamed, made ferocious by the taste of her. That's the only excuse for what happens next, when I hold her hips in place and find the angle that I know will release her entirely. And I pound into her swollen body with every ounce of my passion, no regard for her newly lost innocence.

In the reckless thrusts that follow I hit the place inside her body that makes her head fall back, her breasts push up, her legs open wider. "Oh my God."

Despite the intensity inside me, an unsteady laugh escapes me. "You are breathtaking. You are perfection. And I don't think I can ever leave your body."

For a moment she looks lost. "Is it always like this?"

In this moment there is only raw honesty. "It's never like this."

The thought terrifies me. This is supposed to be new for her, not for me. Never for me.

Then her lips are under mine, her body pliant and accepting, and I am lost. There's only the drive to make her come, fucking into her until she moans and stiffens. "Yes," I mutter. "Again."

There's a faint protest, I think. *You don't have to*, she says, but she does not understand how much I want this. So I show her, with the unrelenting drive into her body, against the place inside her that makes her legs shake. She comes again and again, drenching my cock with her pleasure, testing unused muscles that might make her sore tomorrow.

I can't think about tomorrow, when I definitely won't be inside her. Won't be in this large bed. Won't be breathing in the air around Bea.

So I fuck her until her eyes are hazy with orgasms.

The jade green clears slightly and she places a hand on my cheek, impossibly soft and not quite steady. "Aren't you going to?"

I don't know why I haven't already. I would have with any other woman, with any other *client*, after bringing her to climax a few times, if only to punctuate our evening. But I don't want this to end. As soon as I spill inside her I have to leave.

Ripping my body away from her is an acute pain, the cold air like razor blades on my cock. I grab one of the white pillows, feeling the abrasion of lace. There are two of them, enough to pad my beautiful girl as I turn her over.

"Oh," she says in lovely surprise.

There are a sprinkling of freckles coming down from her shoulders, like a shooting star fading into empty space. She's pale white down to her lovely ass, where she's peachy and flushed from my grasp. It's a beautiful sight, but I didn't flip her over to see this; I did it to hide myself.

"This will be an education," I murmur against her ear, my body covering her back. "That's why you wanted me, yes? Because of things I know. Things I can teach you."

Her moan is tortured pleasure. "Yes. Please. More."

I slide back into her as if her body was made for mine. She squeezes me in welcome, and it's enough to make me curse in Arabic under my breath. "My name," I tell her.

And thank the sweet Lord, she understands. "Hugo."

"Again," I say, reaching around to stroke two blunt fingers over her clit. She's slick and wet and warm, and I never want to leave this, never want to leave *her*.

"Hugo!" So low and breathy I feel the vibration in my cock.

"One more time, sweet Bea. For me. I want to feel you come like this."

Each one of my thrusts pushes out a little whimper from her, every strum of her clit makes her breath suck in. *Mon Dieu*, how am I going to last? Because I want one more.

I run the edge of my teeth along the curl of her ear and feel her shiver in response. "Do you know what it does to me? Having you like this? Helpless underneath me? I want to tear your pretty lace sheets into strips and tie you to the bedpost. I want to fuck you all night long, until we've made you come a hundred times. And even then it wouldn't be enough."

The words bring her close, but it's the bite of my teeth on her shoulder that sends her over the edge. She comes with a scream that makes me insane.

I want to come on her pale back, on her plush ass, on the pretty lace sheets. But I can't do that. This isn't about what I want. *This has never been about what I want.*

The pulse of her *chatte* is ecstasy on my cock, fierce even through the latex, and I come with sharp, bright-light bursts that seem to go on forever, longer than can be borne, until I collapse, wrung out on her sated body.

Chapter Twelve

I'M ALONE AT THE DEN THE NEXT DAY, BECAUSE WE AREN'T GOING TO MEET AGAIN until Sunday. I could have called the other men in the Thieves Club, but that would have meant admitting how much last night meant to me. How hard it was to leave her with a kind but reserved, *That was lovely, darling.* So when someone sits down at the armchair beside me, I'm startled.

Damon Scott looks out the window at the blur of cars and glint of sunlight. He does not ask permission before taking the seat, because he owns the place. Though I'm not sure he asks permission for anything, regardless. Except perhaps to his pretty lady friend.

We sit in silence in the way that only men can do. A woman would have asked me twenty question by now. And normally I could field them with charm and seduction. Right now I'm only fit to brood.

"Beatrix Cartwright," he says. "You didn't know?"

"That she was rich, yes. Not about her family."

"More than rich. She has one of the largest portfolios in the country. I knew she lived in Tanglewood but I never met her before last night."

"She doesn't get out much," I say, my voice bland because I don't wish to share the details of her personal struggle with this man, even if the information might be worth something to him.

"Because of her guardian? That's what I always assumed."

My curiosity is piqued despite myself. Her guardian. The missing link between when she lived in a mansion in California and when she was planted in a penthouse in Tanglewood. The person who must have raised her after her parents were killed.

Someone who must know the owner of L'Etoile.

"Who is she?" I ask, but it's impossible not to appear interested. Not when I've been searching for this for so long. I'm leaning forward in my chair, any pretense of being casual long gone. There is a burn in my body, like acid. It fills every inch of my skin, singeing me from the inside out. The fire is revenge.

Damon doesn't look surprised, as if he knew I would want to know. Perhaps he did know. He's that kind of man. Dangerous to someone who would cross him. "Her parents were both isolated. Both only children. There was no extended family to take her in."

"Her name." I'm gritting my teeth against demanding more, now, faster.

"It's a man, actually. I've met him a few times."

A man. Why does that make me uncomfortable?

Perhaps because he has her locked up in a damned tower, so afraid of men she had to pay one to take her virginity. Or perhaps because he let her hide herself from the time she was a child instead of helping her recover from her parents' death.

"Is he a member here?"

"Yes, although he does not come frequently. I could introduce you."

That would be... exceptional, considering I would no longer need to use Bea for that purpose. Would she find out? That depends on how much this guardian, this man, has done. "What would it cost me?"

Damon only smiles. He does not refute the claim that he will charge me something, because we both know that this is a place of business. "I'm not certain it's a price you're willing to pay."

"Ah, money. How crude."

"It *is* how I'm accustomed to doing business. I'm sure you know that."

"It's not the cost I was referring to, however. What if you had to choose between Beatrix and finding this person? What if you had to choose between Beatrix and revenge?"

I sit up straight. It's one thing for him to guess at my curiosity; another thing for him to know the source. Hearing her name makes a strange possessiveness rise in me. Possessiveness and pain, at the idea of losing her. "How the fuck do you know what I want with the owner of L'Etoile?"

"Do you know what I sell, Hugo?"

"People," I say, because Damon is known to own strip clubs in the city. Many of them. High-end ones. And he held a virginity auction in the Den once.

"And how would I sell people without information? That's the leverage I truly need to run my business. Which is how I know about the discreet inquiries you've made."

"Not discreet enough."

"I'm rather a special case, if you don't mind me saying so. Most people won't know."

"Well, I hope you don't plan on selling me to the highest bidder. I'm afraid my virginity is long lost."

"Lost early, if I had to guess."

"I'd rather you didn't. Guess, that is." I was fifteen when I lost my virginity, though it didn't feel like a loss at the time. It felt like I had won something—a beautiful, glamorous woman. "If you have information to sell me, then sell it. But don't think that you will leverage me, because I have enough people doing that."

"The beautiful Melissande."

Of course he would know her.

Perhaps I had been too young. At fifteen I had felt like a man. Had been built like one after working summers in the field. Mama had been gone two years before then. Breast cancer, caught far too late, and with far too little money to do anything about it. There had only been enough to buy Valium to ease her pain toward the end.

I had been young but I'd grown up early.

"Beautiful, indeed," I say grimly.

"I want her out of business," Damon says, his voice flat and final.

That's his price, I realize. It really won't be a sum of money I can pull from my investment accounts. It will be a person that I must sell in order to achieve my revenge. "Why?"

"Does it matter?"

"Perhaps."

"Would it make you feel better if I said there was a noble reason? That she is a danger to Tanglewood and the people inside it? That I care about this city more than money?"

"You are not a noble man."

He smiles. "No matter what Penny thinks, you are right. And so the real reason is much more simple than that. She's competition. And here is a way to get rid of her."

"I see." Melissande has done me no favors in this life, despite what she may think. I was too young to have sex with a woman in her late twenties, someone sophisticated and with an ulterior motive in bringing me to the states. She encouraged me to fall in love with her knowing I would be nothing but a pretty little commodity for her business.

But I also do not wish to harm her. There's a connection between us. She's the woman who took my virginity. And gave me a future in the process.

Damon's mouth twists in bitter understanding. "It's not so easy, is it?"

Hurting a person to further my own gains? Not easy.

Then again it was not easy for my mother to work eleven hours a day cleaning soiled sheets and toilets for rich gamblers in Tangier. It was not easy for her to trudge two blocks before dawn only to return after nightfall, her muscles trembling with exhaustion.

It was not easy when one of those gamblers followed her home.

"A name would not be enough," I say.

Damon nods, as if he expected that. "The means to ruin him."

I would only wish to ruin him if he's the man who pushed in the door when I was seven years old. The man who shoved me into the closet while my mother shrieked, blocked me in with a chair. The man who raped my mother on the floor while I watched from the crack in the door.

Once I meet the man, I'll know if he is the one. I would recognize him anywhere.

From the look on Damon's face, he knows what my answer will be. Which proves my deal with the devil is inevitable. I will trade anything for revenge.

Even Beatrix Cartwright.

Chapter Thirteen

The nice thing about only working one day a week means that I have most of the week for leisure. Walking the park that winds behind my loft. Painting. Reading. I thought that it was a fulfilling life. A sign of success that my bank account continues to grow through solid investments. And the Saturday nights have always been more about pleasure than work.

Today nothing seems to hold my interest. My books look empty and cold. The outside is a lonely place. This is Bea's fault. The world only looks colorful when she's near me, which is hardly any time at all.

Suddenly one day a week seems like not enough.

I'm looking through my phone, listless, before finally giving in. I pull up the video app so that I can view her page. There are so many videos here. So many days of her. It feels like a feast for someone who's been starving, even though I know it isn't real. Is this what her fans feel like? I scroll down to the comments.

There are many of only a few words: *Beautiful. Queen. Perfect soul.*

Many emojis as well. Hearts and music notes and faces that are crying, with happiness I think.

Other comments are more in-depth. *I love you so much, Bea. I'm your biggest fan and you're beautiful in every way. Follow me back PLS.*

And, *When are you going to go on tour?? I would love to hear you LIVE. #frontrow*

There are also some rather inappropriate ones that have me raising my eyebrows. If they are willing to say this in a public forum, I wonder what kind of private messages she gets. There was no reason for her to hire someone to take her virginity. There's no shortage of volunteers in the comments section.

But I know more than anyone that women don't hire me because there's no one else. They hire me because they want me to be the empty man, the one who can fuck them the way they want, not the way I want, the one who can act like I love them without feeling a thing.

And I'm good at being that man. Empty.

I scroll back to the top, where a new video has been uploaded since I looked at the page yesterday. This one is titled *Over the Rainbow*. I press the PLAY button and settle in to watch.

Most of the videos start with music. Only rarely does she say a brief piece before she begins. This time she begins speaking. "I met someone recently, someone who made me think that maybe there's more to life than what I knew before. Someone who makes me think there's somewhere else worth going."

My heart squeezes, because she must be talking about me. I can hear it in the husky bent of her voice, the way she speaks when my mouth is on her clit. Hungry and low.

"Most people would think he's happy. It feels like he's full of joy, but there's sadness, too. A part of him that longs for a world more colorful than this one."

How does she see inside me, like my skin is made of glass?

"And when I'm around him I long for that world, too. Have you ever met a person like that? A person who made you dream of more?"

There's a silence in which my mind fills in the answer. *You make me dream, Bea.* Because it's not as simple as one direction. It's what happens when we're together, the possibilities like sparks in the air, giving us a glimpse of what could be.

"I love doing the new songs for you, but I have this one on my mind. It's a classic song. I'm sure you've heard it before, but maybe today it will sound new to you like it does to me."

And then she plays the song in a slow, sultry, beautiful tune. It makes goose bumps rise on my arms, the deep sound of her breath coming through the small speakers. How does she do this?

By the time she gets to the end, there are tears in my eyes. I do not have the worry that other men have in Tanglewood. That other men had in Tangier, also. That I will not be properly masculine if I cry, but there is very little that can move me. A beautiful painting. A poem. I can enjoy them without being moved, but this is different. It's like she's singing to me, and my body responds as if she's touching me. I want to clench my hand in her wild hair. I want to press my lips against the rapid pulse at the base of her throat. God, she's perfect.

The notes end in a weighted silence. And then the video ends.

I feel the loss of her, acute and painful.

The video app gives me only a small pause before spinning into another one of her videos. And another, while I sit there, cold as a statue on top of a building, watching the city stream by. Eventually the app moves to play other musicians who share their work. And then pop music published by the major labels.

Still, I cannot bring myself to move.

The notes she played have embedded themselves in my head. It's all I can hear.

Until the phone buzzes in my hand. An incoming text. I glance down, detached from this ordinary world, disinterested, until I see Melissande's name. I try to ignore how much anticipation rises within me at the thought of seeing Bea again.

She booked the next three weeks.

A deep breath makes me realize I had been holding it, but for how long? Since I saw Bea perform that haunting melody? Or longer, since I left her bed? I text back, *Okay*, glad Melissande isn't here to see me. She would sense that something was wrong, no matter how well I try to hide it.

Your other clients will lose their minds.

My other clients will go back to their regular lives. They will find a nice man in a bar. Or finally approach someone they've had a crush on. There's nothing for them with me.

It's Melissande who's in danger of losing her mind. *I'm not giving you any more nights,* I type.

Three dots hover on the screen for a long time. Either Melissande is typing out something very long or she's doing a lot of erasing and starting over. In the end her message is brief: *I made you.*

That makes me laugh out loud, the sound echoing in the large loft. *Do you want me to thank you?* I type back, before adding, *Thank you, Melissande. For making me a whore.*

She'll read the sarcasm fine, because it's been a very long time since we were friends. A very long time since we were lovers. There must be fondness there, to make me reluctant to ruin her. I'm not in the business of ruining women. Usually I prefer to pleasure them. Could I make an exception for Damon Scott? Would I make an exception for revenge?

It is perhaps ominous that I don't know the answer myself.

Chapter Fourteen

In my loft I prepare a gourmet picnic with sliced meats and creamy cheeses. There are plump grapes and ripe strawberries. A baguette from the French bakery so fresh it crackles when I place it in the bag. Most of these items are easy to prepare. The only thing I make from scratch is a moist brioche with hints of orange and white chocolate, soft on the inside, the sugar caramelized on the outside. My mother taught me to make this.

She worked twelve hours a day in a hotel that cost more per night than she earned in a month. She did not have money for luxury or time for hobbies. But in the few minutes she had between waking and work, she loved to cook. Recipes handed down from her mother but spiced with what was available in the open-air markets of Tangier. There was ratatouille made with tomatoes and zucchini and bay leaf, but also couscous and ginger. French lentils with fava beans and cumin. She loved to try new things, both of us tasting from the pot while the meal simmered, heating the small room we shared.

I don't have her level of curiosity or wonder about cooking, but every meal I prepare is an homage to her. If you would have asked me if I loved my mother, I would have said yes. But I spent too much time fighting in the streets to be what you'd call a good son.

She was the one who let me out of the closet, limping and bleeding and crying too hard to speak. Even then I knew that the police would not help us against a rich American tourist. I cooked every day for her for a week, before she was well enough to return to work.

We did not speak of what happened that night. She didn't wish to, and I was too angry. Too selfish. Too busy fighting in the streets, thinking I would make something of myself in a city that hardly recognized me as human. But somewhere in my chest was the certainty that I would find that man.

After the cancer took her, it became my only purpose.

So when I met beautiful Melissande, when I found out where she came from—I knew she would be the way to revenge. She offered me the chance to come with her. It seemed almost miraculous, that I had fallen in love with a woman and could achieve my goal at the same time.

She kept me in a state of ignorant bliss in her bed for a year before revealing my purpose in Tanglewood. I would be a prostitute, catering to the wealthy men and women of society who wanted a dark-haired fallen angel in their beds. Someone with an exotic accent and very little inhibition.

That's when I learned that I could not have love and revenge.

There could only be one or the other.

My mind is in turmoil as the brioche cools on the oven, but I move with determination as I pack them with the rest of the picnic. We won't need Bea's tiny kitchen tonight, though I still hope to dine with her. The drive to the hotel is done in silence, without the usual joy I feel when driving the Bugatti.

I feel only a small amount of guilt for using my key card without being invited. It only takes me to the entrance. Once inside I knock on the wall and wait, a strange fluttering of nerves.

What if Bea isn't here? What if she *is* here but she doesn't want to see me? She isn't paying for tonight. There's nothing on the books with Melissande until tomorrow—our standing Saturday appointment.

From the elevator car I can see the empty living room. Soft voices filter through the closed bedroom door. "Hello? Is anyone home?"

The door opens, revealing a young woman with blonde hair with pink streaks. "Uh. Hi?"

Not Bea. For a moment I'm so thrown I wonder if I somehow found the wrong building. A different gaudy hotel established by the ex-owner of a French brothel. A different penthouse with an agoraphobic little ex-virgin. "Is Beatrix here?"

"Bea," the blonde says in a singsong voice. "Have you been holding out on me?"

Her voice comes from deep within the penthouse. "What?"

"There's a young Cary Grant at your door, so either L'Etoile has seriously upped their staffing game or you have been keeping very big, very sexy secrets." The young woman winks at me.

"Is there a baguette in that basket or are you just happy to see me?"

I laugh, as comfortable with flirting as she is. "Both, *naturellement*."

"A man to please all appetites," she says as Bea peeks around the corner, hair even more wild and dangerous than usual. It's untamable, that hair. Like the woman.

"Oh," she says, though it's more like a squeak. "Did we have an…"

Appointment, she means to say. "A date? But no, I wished to surprise you."

"You did surprise me." Her gaze slides to her friend, who's watching us with undisguised pleasure and interest. "Harper, this is… Hugo. And, Hugo…"

"Harper," I say with my best smile, which produces a blush. I recognize her faintly from the society papers, this girl who is related to Christopher from the Thieves Club. The stepsister that makes him scowl every time he says something about her.

"Ohhh my," Harper says. "Do you just go around smiling on the street, making people fall over and having cars crash around you? It's dangerous."

"*Non*, this one I reserve for private company." I turn to Bea, who looks torn. She's biting her lip, leaving indents in the plump flesh. Everything about her calls to me, but it's almost a relief that she's turning me away. I shouldn't be using her for information, shouldn't be trying to get close to her to find out more about the man who owns this hotel. "I can come back another time. You are clearly having a girls' night, and I'm the intruder."

I hid my disappointment rather well, I thought, but Bea still looks crestfallen. Crestfallen and beautiful in a black lace blouse that flutters around her elegant neck and jeans—a more casual look than she's ever worn for our dates. "Wait."

"I'm so out of here," Harper says, pointing a finger at me. "And I'm going to drag the details out of Bea, so you better make them worth our while. Dirty. Salacious. Shocking."

"I do aim to please," I say, my smile lazy. Of course I would love for the night to be dirty, but that depends on quite a lot. Like whether Bea will even speak to me after crashing her night.

It only takes a moment for Harper to grab her things—a model of phone that isn't available commercially yet and a handbag shaped like a panda. Then she leaves down the elevator, making promises to call Bea the next day.

As soon as we're alone Bea shakes her head, her smile both exasperated and fond. "She's never going to let up asking questions about you now."

"I'm sure we can give you plenty to tell. That is, if you wish to spend the evening with me."

"Of course I do." She pauses, as if to check herself. "But I didn't book this time with the agency. I thought you were coming tomorrow."

"This isn't through the agency," I say lightly, as if it's no big deal.

Of course it's a huge deal. When is the last time I spent time with a woman without being paid for it. The thought would disturb me, if I didn't have an ulterior motive for being here. It's not quite as much distance as money, but it's enough to keep this from meaning too much.

She looks at me, skeptical, uncertain. "So this is… what?"

"Why does a man spend time with a beautiful woman? It's a date, if you'll give me the honor. That's what this is."

I am not so worried about deceiving her, or at least, this is what I tell myself. She may not have paid for this night, but she understands the nature of this relationship. And soon enough, once she's gotten over her initial nervousness about sex, she will move on to a man more appropriate for her. Maybe one who will finally help her leave this tower prison of hers. I will merely be a distant memory to make her embarrassed.

Her green eyes are deep tonight, without the usual walls that keep her hidden. I can see her fear and her excitement. She looks impossibly innocent like this. "Do you want to come in?" she asks, a little shy.

"*Non*. I wish to take you outside."

Dismay. "You know I can't."

I make a noncommittal hum in my throat. "Whether you can or you can't, I won't ask you to set even one foot off the property. At least not tonight."

"Really?"

"But of course."

She narrows her eyes. "You know, it doesn't escape my notice that you're carrying a picnic basket. Where are you planning to spread that out? The lobby?"

All she gets is a half-smile. "You will have to trust me for that."

"Trust you?" she asks, so incredulous it would wound me, if I didn't know how deeply her fear of the outside runs. She doesn't trust anyone.

"You trust me with your body," I remind her. "With your most private places. With your pleasure. I'm only asking for a little bit more, *mon amie*. Trust me with tonight."

She takes a shuddering breath, which moves the lace at her throat. "Okay."

It moves me more than it should, her trust in me. Silently, urgently, I swear to myself that I won't betray that trust. She may never know my true interest in L'Etoile, but my feelings about her are pure. I like her. I respect her. And I will do nothing to make her doubt those things.

It takes only a little coaxing to bring her into the elevator.

Only when I press the UP button does she start to breathe faster. "What are you doing?"

"Taking us to the roof. There's a beautiful garden up there. I've seen it through Google Maps. And you have exclusive access to it. I'm shocked you don't spend all your time there."

"That's not… Part of the… Hotel." She's breathing faster now, close to panic.

I take her face between my hands, both gentle and firm. "It is part of the hotel. The same structure where you spend all of your time. You do not have to leave to see the stars."

"That's what windows are for."

My laugh comes out, surprised, unexpected. "*Non*."

"We can spread out the picnic on the carpet. It will be fun."

"Perhaps another time. Tonight we will dine in the night air and you will be fine."

She searches my eyes. "What if I'm not?"

Trust. That's what she's giving me right now, and the gift is worth more than a thousand nights. "I'll be with you every second, Bea. I won't let anything happen to you."

Chapter Fifteen

From the aerial view on my computer I saw the small greenhouse full of lush plants. The elaborate black iron table and chairs for dining. The expanse of wooden deck and brick walls. It's a beautiful space, meant to be enjoyed, meant to be lived in. The only person who comes up here is the caretaker. Not Bea, even though she's the only occupant of L'Etoile allowed to use the space.

The elevator doors begin to close behind me. I put my hand out to stop them. Bea looks at me with wide, unblinking eyes. Like a rabbit, I think. Too afraid to run away.

"Come here," I murmur.

A jerky shake of her head. "Can't," she says between gritted teeth.

"What will happen if you come?"

"I don't know." Her gaze darts behind me. The view is peaceful, but her expression is full of turmoil. Violence, even. The certainty is a blow to my stomach, making every muscle in my body clench. Because of what happened to her parents. Such a strange and random thing, to be killed by pirates.

And yet it wasn't random at all. They were targeted because of their wealth.

Which means she could be a target, too. No wonder she does not step foot outside. It's a wonder that she let me through the door that first night. My dismay only strengthens my decision to help.

"I imagine that if I tell you nothing will happen you don't believe me."

Her eyes plead with me, beautiful and haunted. "I do believe you, with my head. It's my body that doesn't seem to understand. It doesn't even let me come outside. I'm stuck here."

She means that she's rooted to the spot in the elevator, but it's more than that. She's stuck in this old hotel. Stuck in a life she was never meant to lead. Her parents were tech moguls and famous concert pianists. Their gifts should have been a privilege for Bea. Instead it's trapped her.

"What does your therapist say?" I don't wish to damage her, despite my own certainty that she needs to leave this place, that it's imperative for her. Life or death.

"I don't see her anymore."

"Why not?"

She mumbles at the marble floor of the elevator. "She wanted me to leave." Then she meets my gaze, almost angry. "She didn't understand. You don't, either."

"Explain it to me."

"I mean I physically can't move. My body won't let me."

I cock my head. "What if I move you?"

She shakes her head miserably. "I'll just freak out. Screaming. Crying. I've tried that before."

With who? I want to know who she trusted enough to take her outside, even if it failed. The same person who put her here in the first place? "If you scream, if you cry, I'll bring you back inside."

"You make it sound easy."

"Not easy." No one looking at her, the strain around her eyes, the tension in her body, could think this would be easy. "But you're strong enough to do it. With me, Bea."

I set down the picnic basket so that my hands are free. Then I move so that I'm facing her, my foot still blocking the door from closing. She stands in front of me, inside the elevator that she must have taken hundreds of times. Thousands of times. She knows this elevator too well, while a single step outside feels like a wild jump across oceans.

Her lower lip trembles, and I lean my head close, waiting for her to jerk back. There's every chance this won't work, that we'll end up having the picnic spread out on her bed.

She holds still as my lips press against hers, and I'm suspended in that moment. *Stuck*, that's the word she used. I'm not stuck, though. I'm floating. Free.

Our breaths come together, her skin flushed and fragrant.

Her hands are in mine. I could pull her out—one inch, two. I could carry her over this threshold, but I wasn't lying when I said she was strong enough. Strong enough to make the step herself.

A small swipe of my tongue over her bottom lip.

Then I move back, leaving only a moment between us. She sways toward me, wanting more. I surrender to her for a second, this time a kiss to the corner of her mouth. And then retreat again.

She comes closer, leaning toward me, her feet in the elevator.

"Bea," I say, gaze dark on hers. In my eyes I let her see every ounce of desire I have for her, which is more than I really should. It makes me naked, this look, more than if I stripped down to nothing.

Her lips part the slightest amount—an acknowledgement. A plea.

The kiss that follows is clumsy as she steps forward onto the hard wood, almost falling into my arms, caught by me, making a little panicked, pleased sound in my mouth.

Ding. The elevator doors close behind her.

I realize that I can't use her. Not tonight, anyway.

It means too much, that she would trust me this way. And so I hold her, safe and willing in my arms. Perhaps she feels the change in me, because she relaxes into my body.

Chapter Sixteen

WE FEAST ON CHEESES AND FRUIT, NOT QUITE ACKNOWLEDGING THE buildings that peak around us like mountains. She trusted me enough to stay on the roof, and for now that will be enough.

The sun sets in a glory of golden blue while she sips champagne, her gaze studiously on my own. I fill my own glass and take a drink, because I need the courage more than her. She's already the bravest woman I know. I'm the one wondering how I care about her so much after so little time. Wondering what I'll do when she's done with me.

I may have decided not to use her for revenge, tonight, but that does not mean I'll ask no questions. In fact I'm brimming with questions. Running over with them. I set the glass down carefully, wondering how much to ask. Needing to know the answers.

"Will you tell me now why you wanted to lose your virginity in this way? I know there's more you aren't telling me. More than loneliness." I suspected that from the very first night, a secret motivation that drives her, something close to desperation. It would have stopped a moral man from touching her.

Unfortunately for her I gave up any semblance of morality long ago.

She sighs, looking out at the city. Has she ever seen it without a panel of glass blocking it? A cool wind touches my skin. It gives her hair a sense of ceaseless motion, as if it's alive. "There is a reason. I mean, I was curious. I've always been curious, but when I turned twenty…"

At her pause I force myself to stay silent. This is her story; I have to let her tell it. But I do take her hand in mine, because that's what I'm here for, isn't it? My body and the comfort it can bring. It's all I have to offer.

Her hand squeezes back. "Someone proposed to me."

Shock tightens my stomach, though I don't know why I should be surprised. She's a beautiful, smart, extremely desirable young woman. Even trapped in her castle, she has suitors. There's a churning inside me, a strange mixture of jealousy and loss. *She was never mine.*

"What was your answer?" I'm pleased that my tone comes out light.

"I said I'd think about it, but I don't want to marry him."

Worry furrows her expression, and I feel myself grow hot from anger. "Are you afraid to tell him no?"

If there is someone threatening her I have no problem standing up to this faceless, nameless asshole. I may live a life of ease and luxury these days, in high-rise hotels and satin sheets, but I was a street mongrel once. I fought and scraped and clawed my way through Tangier's back alleys. A rich frat boy in Tanglewood will not stand a chance.

She looks away with a slight shake of her head, not quite agreeing, but not refuting it either. "This is going to sound weird, but I had this feeling that he only wanted me because…"

The final piece falls into place, making acid rise in my throat. "Because you're a virgin."

"I mean he didn't *say* that, but it felt like that was part of the reason. There's never been anything romantic between us. He's been with lots of women in the papers. So why would he propose to me unless there was something different about me."

There are many different things about Beatrix Cartwright, and they have nothing to do with the hymen that I took from her. But I do not point that out. If she doubts the motives of this man, then he is not worthy of her. "Have you told him that you are no longer a virgin?"

If he wanted her innocence, he might become angry when she tells him.

She seems to sense my concern. "He wouldn't hurt me."

"Then why not simply tell him no?"

"Our relationship is… complicated. I didn't want to hurt his feelings."

A sudden suspicion makes my blood pressure spike. "This man who proposed. Is he perhaps the same person who became your guardian when you were a child?"

She looks stricken. "How do you know about that?"

I force myself not to growl in frustration. "Someone must have done so. You were underage."

"Yes, he was my dad's business partner. And he became my guardian."

"And he wants to *marry* you?" This time I do not manage to sound light or calm. I'm furious.

"It's not like we were ever close. He didn't become a parent to me. He was more like… the money person. He was the custodian of my trust. And he made sure I had everything I needed."

If he had really done that, Bea would be able to leave this hotel. "He must be older than you."

A miserable shrug. "I suppose. That's not the reason I don't want to marry him, though. I just don't love him, you know? Not even as a guardian, really. And definitely not as a husband."

It's almost impossible to control my breathing. I'm like a bull, snorting and pawing at the ground. The image of anyone hurting Bea, coercing her, making her feel small—the red cape. "You don't need a reason to tell him no."

"I know that I can say no. That I *should* say no, but I think… once he finds out I'm not a virgin anymore, he'll lose interest. And that will be easier. That's why I called the service that first night. Why I wanted sex without the pleasure."

My stomach drops. "Who owns the penthouse suite, Bea?"

"He owns the hotel."

"So you have to marry him or he'll kick you out?" For any other heiress that wouldn't be a hardship, but for a scared young woman with anxiety and agoraphobia? Yes, that's a sufficient threat.

My blood runs hot, because only a true bastard would give her that choice.

"He didn't say that," she says, defensive.

"But you're worried that would happen."

"I'd rather avoid the problem."

And that sums up the reason she's still in the penthouse, why the biggest step she's taken in ten years is onto this rooftop. Because she wants to avoid fear instead of facing it. In some ways she's incredibly strong—the music she makes, the empire she's built from it.

Even hiring me, a stranger, to do intimate things with her, fighting years of isolation, took a strength most people don't have. In other ways she's still a scared little girl, trapped by her grief.

I brush the back of my fingers against her cheek, pushing aside the idea of this man trying to marry Bea, letting go for a few blissful moments the idea of revenge. Ignoring the knowledge that at some point, I'll be the problem Bea wants to avoid. Dread forms knots in my stomach, but it can't touch the immediacy of feeling her skin against mine.

She turns her face, pressing a kiss against my knuckles.

"Here?" I ask softly, giving her the option to retreat. It's the better part of valor, after all, and she's shown plenty of valor tonight. Being here on the roof is a new place to her, even if it's technically part of the building she's called home for over a decade.

She does not look away from my eyes, her green ones dark as emeralds in the final glory of dusk. "Something to remember this night."

Even she can feel the sands of time slipping away.

I lean close to her, pressing a kiss to the constellations across the bridge of her nose. Her eyes are closed, so I kiss one eyelid and then the other. She blows out a soft breath, still not looking at me, but *feeling* me. She's so attuned to me in this moment that she knows when my gaze lowers to her mouth. Her lips part, and I make her wait. Cruel, this. I make her wait while I study those plush pink lips. There's even the faintest spray of freckles over her lips.

When I kiss her I imagine I can taste them, these stars. They taste like woman and salt and something elemental to the universe, as if I'm taking sustenance from her. Nourishing myself with her flavor.

"Look up, Bea."

She looks at me, and that should be gratifying to me. It's not quite an accident that I ended up in a profession that amounts of exhibitionism with a different woman every night. They like to look at me, and I enjoy being looked at. But I want something different for her. Something better.

"Up," I say, giving her a tap on the chin.

Obediently her lashes lift. She looks up at the stars and lets out a shuddery breath. "How do people do this every day? They walk outside and they don't even worry? It seems impossible."

"You do things that are impossible," I tell her, tracing a finger lazily down her jaw. "You make beautiful music that millions of people want to watch."

And you make me dream of a different life than this.

Her eyes become wet with tears, but she does not look away from the dark sky. "Anything could happen. We're not protected out here."

And then despite my best efforts I cannot help but to think of her. Of my mother who could not even find safety in the small rooms we rented. "Safety isn't real, Bea. It's a dream."

A tear runs down her cheek. "Why would you say that?"

"I'm sorry," I say, immediately contrite. That isn't for her. That's only for me, the sense that I will never be safe, that I will never be enough. That I can never make up for being a scared little boy in the closet.

She shakes her head. "No, don't be. You're right. Oh God, you're right."

I can't convey to her all I wish to say—that she should be free, that she should be mine. Only one of those will come true. "No, I was foolish. But of course safety is real."

Except that I'm lying, and we both know it. Safety is a dream that only children have. Both of us grew up too soon, aware that everything we knew before would never come true.

Her eyes are as wide and as mysterious as the universe itself. She is a galaxy and a black hole, creation and destruction in one female-shaped body. "Dream with me," she says.

That's the only invitation I need. I lay her back on the picnic blanket, resting her head on my folded-up jacket. Unveiling her body to the moonlight has a sense of rightness, as if I've been waiting all my life to see her pale curves made luminescent, as if she's been waiting forever to be bared.

Sailors used the night sky to guide their path. That's what I become this night, finding my way over the slope of her breast to the tight point of her nipple, following down the flat of her stomach. They are signposts along the way, but my direction is the North Star. For this I must spread her legs with my hands, push her thighs apart and part the copper-colored curls.

The feel of her clit against my tongue is almost enough to burn. Too bright for mere mortals. I curl myself around her, letting her feel my desire, my devotion. She's the one who moves first, finding friction against my tongue. *Yes, mon amie. Take what you need. Fuck me.*

I don't have to say the words, because she's finding freedom underneath the stars. Finding safety in this shared dream, where she can rock her hips against my face, pulling her own orgasm to the surface.

Two fingers slide in easily. It's a little harder to fit the third, because she's still tight. Still untried, so I move her softly—easy, easy. I twist my fingers inside her to the same rhythm she's given me, because she is the one playing me. I may have arrived with my bedroom tricks and my sexual experience, but they were only an ordinary song. She's the one who turned it into something new, something beautiful. Something uniquely her own, the way she does at the piano every day.

She comes with a wild sound at the sky, her head thrown back.

There's something animalistic about her like this, naked and primal. It calls to something primal in me, and I tear off my clothes with an urgency that causes the bespoke shirt to rip. And I don't fucking care. All I need is to feel her against me, around me, underneath me. Nothing else matters.

I mount her with a need unlike anything I've ever known, barely tugging on a condom before I press inside her, expecting to find relief, surcease in the wet heat of her pussy. It only drives me higher, the swollen pressure, only makes me need more, feeling her dampness at the base of my cock.

She doesn't watch the night sky anymore. She's looking in my eyes, but her expression holds the same wonder, the same wariness. What does she see inside me? There's a vast emptiness there, too. Only she has the stars. Only with her is there ever any light.

"Once more," I tell her. "Come again, so I can feel you on my cock. That's how I want to come, Bea. Against my will, with your beautiful body forcing it out of me."

Her eyelids lower. "Make me."

So I angle her hips to receive my thrust in the right place and then drive home. It only takes a single thrust before she's panting, squealing, squirming to get away. It's too acute, this kind of pleasure, but the challenge can only be answered this way. Again and again. I fuck her until she comes with an almost guttural sound, grasping at my shoulders, clawing at them as if we'll never get close enough.

The pain would be enough to wake me from a dream, so I relish the red marks she leaves on my skin, proof that I must be awake even as an orgasm rips through my body like a shooting star, too fierce to be contained by my body, rushing out of me like a thousand fiery sparks. I convulse over Bea's body, collapsing onto her because she's the only relief I've found in a wide-open universe, the only light in a too-dark sky.

We're spread out on the seat cushions, which are the only thing separating us from cool, hard concrete. That and the dubious protection of my jacket as a blanket, but I've never been warmer. The residual heat between us simmers in the air. Bea rests her head on my arm, looking up at the stars. They're beautiful, I know. Luminous and ever-expanding, but I can't take my eyes off her profile. The faint constellations of her freckles glow a thousand times more.

Without the physical sensation the dread rushes back, gnawing and fierce. The realization that we have very little time left. Maybe only tonight. My hands tighten instinctively around Bea before I can catch myself. I release her, right away, pretending to run my hands down her arms, but she looks back at me with too much awareness.

"Is it difficult?" she asks, so soft I almost don't hear. "Doing this?"

My standard answer would be something charming and glib. Of course I do not mind having sex. It's the easiest job in the world. Something keeps me from giving her pretend, because it's not always easy. The sex is good, but the façade… it wears on me. Having to be someone else.

I don't want to do that with her. "Sometimes."

Her fingers draw lazy circles on my chest. "If you aren't attracted to a woman?"

"That's rarely a problem. I love women. Their bodies. Their hearts. Their minds. The way they're so wrapped up saving the world that it almost hurts them to focus on their own pleasure."

She looks skeptical. "There's never a woman you don't want to…"

"There's not much honor in my profession," I try to explain. "But if there's one part… a woman who doesn't feel beautiful. One who isn't attractive, according to what society tells her. Showing her that she deserves to be cherished is something worth doing."

"Is that what I am to you?" she asks. "A charity case?"

There's a wild thump in my heart. Surprise. "*Non.*"

"What am I then?"

"You're a gift."

Bea rests her chin on my shoulder, watching me with too much knowledge. "What about you?"

"I do feel beautiful," I say blandly, a small attempt at humor.

She gives me a shy smile. "You deserve to be cherished."

My stomach clenches, hard enough that I'm afraid the baguette and brie will make a swift return. It's no secret that women want me for the way I look, for the way I make them feel. No one wants what's inside. There's nothing here. A hollow space where a person might be.

I look up at the stars, counting them, distracting myself from the earnest woman, warm and willing in my arms. As if I won't dream of this later.

The tickle of her hair is my only warning. Her lips are warm and lush against my chest. Every muscle in my body tenses as she places another kiss, this one an inch lower. My cock does not mind that it has just been spent; by the third kiss it's already hard again.

Her lips are heaven alone, but the brush of skin as she moves over me drives me insane. The whisper of hair over my body makes me mad. "God," I groan. "What are you doing?"

"Can't you tell?"

She's halfway down the plane of my stomach, working across the ridges of my abs with clear appreciation. My cock flexes as if anticipating where she'll go next.

Down, down, down.

"You can't—" I'm panting now, almost incoherent. "You don't have to—"

Her smile is devilish, almost enough to make me come from the inherent feminine power within. "What did you tell me? It's rather embarrassing how much I want to."

My breath hitches. "Bea."

"But only with your permission."

This will be more than a blowjob. That much I know, because I want her more than air. I'm already moved by her belief in me. Humbled that she would give me her virginity, in every way. There won't be any recovering from her after this. "Please."

Before I've finished speaking the word her lips touch me. She tastes me with an innocence that makes me harder, the peach blush of her lips impossibly pale against the dark red arousal at my crown. First there is only a kiss, far too quick, the way you would buss someone on the cheek. Friendly but impersonal. She comes in again for a longer press, this one testing, unsure.

Only then does her tongue dart out, a small swipe that makes my hips jerk.

"Like that?" she asks, but she already knows. Her eyes sparkle with mischief.

"Devil woman," I say, cursing her in every language until her mouth returns. Her lips circle the head, and I lose all sense of words. There's only sensation—hot, wet, deep. An ocean so wide and dark that I would drown here. I never want to leave.

She is clumsy, at first, which only serves to emphasize the gift she gives me. The way her tongue explores me, darting and quick. The way she takes too much inside, her eyes going wide. I push her back gently, stroking her hair. "Go slow, *mon amie*. Be careful."

Someone must be careful with her, because I cannot. I'm reckless with her, this fragile flower, made of sunshine in a bottle. I'm spilling her everywhere.

It does not matter that she has no practiced moves to make me come. I'm close, from seeing her taste me, from feeling her mouth and her passion.

Except… *there*.

She touches her tongue against a certain spot and my eyes roll back. *God*, that was close. I almost came in her mouth, without warning, like the most crude sort of man. It must have been an accident.

And then she does it again.

My hips thrust into her mouth, without permission from me. "*Mon Dieu*," I mutter, panting, unable to see anything except stars.

When my eyes focus again I see her watching me. That's how she's doing this. Because she's watching me, gauging every reaction, weighing every touch. Figuring out what I like best, because she thinks I deserve to be cherished.

Desperation fills my chest, because eventually she'll find out the truth. I'm not worthy of her mouth, her body. I'm not worthy of anything.

She touches that place beneath my cock for a third time, and I lose control. Her hair is grasping me, or I'm grasping her hair, pulling her close. Pressure bursts from the base of my spine, turning every muscle in my body to pulsing stone. My mouth opens on a silent cry, the only sound a guttural surrender as my cock empties down her throat.

There's no reason for her to stay within my grasp, to let me pull at her and thrust into her mouth two more times, wringing out the most intense orgasm of my life. This is a base act, almost cruel the way I used her. I can't hate myself for it, because I would do it again.

She sits up, wiping her thumb across her bottom lip, looking both pleased with herself and self-conscious. "Was that okay?"

At this exact second I'm struggling to move my limbs or form words. It feels like a Herculean effort, putting together a complete sentence. "That was incredible. Come here."

I don't wait for her to snuggle in but instead pull her down, rolling on top of her with a burst of gratitude. My hand slides down her body, reveling in the way she twists and turns into my touch. Her body is wet and swollen, made ready for me.

The blowjob turned her on. That knowledge sits inside me, too powerful to resist. I slip my fingers inside, my thumb rough on her clit. I stroke her once, twice, three times. She comes with a soft exhalation, her body turning pliant, eyelids heavy as she sinks into sleep.

Through the walls I can hear the soccer games that Mr. Alami watches every night. From somewhere a baby cries. The windows don't close all the way. It smells like the smoke from the hookah lounge down the street. Our building is never quiet, never asleep, but no one came when Mama let out a short, surprised scream. They didn't come when I yelled at the man hurting her or when he hit me.

He's gone now. The bed stopped making that horrible creak. From the crack in the closet door I watched his shadow stand up and fix his clothes before he walked out the front door.

Mama's shadow got up much slower.

I can tell she's in pain by the way she's hunched over, by the sniffles she probably thinks I can't hear. She didn't come and move the chair locking me inside. Does she not know I'm here? Did she forget? I stay silent, my arms wrapped around my knees. I can tell my eye is getting big and swollen where he hit me, but it doesn't hurt. It doesn't feel like anything.

There's a high-pitched sound that I recognize as the pipes that are behind this wall. The shower is running, with its leaky spray and its hot water that runs out. *Mama.*

It feels like forever when she finally comes and lets me out.

I run to her, pressing my face against her warmth, her dress clean and soft—not the stiff uniform she wore home from the hotel, smelling of sharp chemicals, the one she wore when *he* came. *We have to call the police*, I tell her in French, my words too fast and too afraid.

She shakes her head, slow and sure. "*Non*. We call no one."

I have grown up for seven years on these streets. No one trusts the police, but this is something very bad. This is what they are supposed to protect us against. "He hurt you."

There is no mark on her eye. It was not that kind of hurt. "He's a powerful man. Very rich. Staying at the hotel in the top floor. The penthouse."

He may be very rich in the top floor, the penthouse, but he came into our rooms. "So he can do that and nothing happens to him?"

She looks away, hiding the tears. "Don't, Hugo."

Or maybe she's looking away because she does not want to see my tears. "You are wrong," I tell her, even though I'm afraid she's right. Rich men and women can do anything they want.

The sheets on the bed are still rumpled, the pillows fallen off. It's her bed, but I have crawled in at night to cuddle with her, when my cot in the main room feels too cold and sad. There's only one bedroom, and it has never bothered me, never felt too small or too poor until now.

On the floor there's something brown and flat. Something that does not belong.

I pick it up, feeling the very smooth material. Inside there is scribbled writing I can't read. And money. So much money.

Mama gasps, "What is that?"

She knows what it is.

I know how to pick pockets. This one would be a prize, but tonight I'm not interested in the pink and green slips of paper. I'm looking for something with a picture on it. A name.

There is nothing except for a matchbox with a design on it, like stars.

And the letters L'ETOILE.

Mama takes the wallet from me, very quick, the way she would do if I had taken something I shouldn't, if I had done something wrong. "We have to give it back."

"At least keep the money." I don't know what we will do with the money. Buy food or a better lock for the door. Maybe a knife so I can stop another man who tries this.

Her eyes become dark. "I do not want his money. I'm not a *kahba*."

For the most part Mama speaks French or the English she learned working at the hotel. That word is Arabic. It means the girls who stand on the streets. The ones who visit the lounge late at night and leave with American men. They would get to keep the money.

That's what I learn that night.

Chapter Seventeen

I WAKE UP WITH A RACING HEART, AS IF SOMETHING HAS GONE TERRIBLY WRONG.

Vaguely I remember the dream. The night I wish I could forget. The image of L'Etoile's logo stamped into my brain. Decades later, and I still have the same fucking nightmare.

A sound comes to me, keening that makes the hair on my neck rise. Heavy shadows in the past keep me in the dark longer than I should be. I blink against the too-bright moon, struggling to remember where I am. Hands are grasping at my arm. An urgency pounds in my skull, too hard and too fast.

"Oh my God, oh my God, oh my God."

The words filter through my blurry consciousness, making me snap to alertness. Beatrix. And she sounds like she did last night, afraid and trembling, only much worse.

My heart clenches when I look down at the sight of her. She's curled up into a ball, clinging onto my arm like it's a life raft in a wild ocean. Her wild hair sticks to the side of her face, her skin slick with sweat. "Oh my God," she whispers, her eyes squeezed shut.

"Bea, I'm here. I'm right here."

"It's not enough."

The words hit me like a ton of bricks, because of course it's not enough. I would never be enough. "I'll take you inside. Can you stand?"

We're only a few yards away from the elevator. The dining area and large concrete pots with plants in them block our path. She shakes her head, burying her head against me.

I would rather convince her to come with me, but her whole body shakes violently. Small sounds of distress are coming from her, as if she doesn't even register I'm here. I need to get her out of this situation and back where she feels safe—the penthouse.

She whimpers. "Hugo?"

Crouching over her, one hand on her arm, the other resting lightly on her head, I have never felt more helpless. This woman is suffering. It doesn't matter whether it's a physical punch in the stomach; it's clear she's hurt. And it's my fault. I'm the one who brought her here. "I'm going to carry you inside."

Her body relaxes only a fraction, but I'm in tune with her enough to feel it.

Which is also why my body is tied up in knots, my usual calm gone, any ability to seduce or reason with her disappeared into the early dawn. Anxiety clenches hard around my throat, as if we're connected, part of the same body.

That's how it feels when I lift her in my arms, when she curls herself into me—like I can finally take a breath. Her hair tickles my nose, curls itself around my face. It makes me pull her closer.

I press a kiss to her head, already striding toward the elevator. "Almost there, sweetheart."

"Sorry," she whispers. "Sorry. Sorry."

She's apologizing to me? *Mon Dieu.* "There's nothing to be sorry about."

The elevator takes approximately twelve years to make its way up, even though it's private for the penthouse suite. When the doors finally open I step inside and press the P button to return to her suite. We are now indoors, in a place that she's been herself many times, but she does not relax. Instead she clings to me even harder, her arms tight around my neck, her hands clenched in my wrinkled shirt, as if these familiar places have become new and scary.

"Almost there," I murmur on the twenty-four-hour ride down one floor.

The doors slide open, revealing the penthouse suite...that is full of people.

I recognize some of them as hotel staff. The head of concierge. Jessica from the front desk. A maid. And a man in a suit, directing them all with an angry and authoritative voice.

"Where are the police?" he demands, before turning toward us.

For a moment we stand there facing each other, this man who must control Bea's life. The one who's kept her in this tower, whether she sees it that way or not.

"Leave," he says to everyone else without breaking eye contact with me.

The room immediately clears, hotel staff filing past me and leaving the way they came, silent and obedient. Meanwhile I move deeper into the room. Past the stranger, to the bedroom. It's hard to let go of Bea's trembling body, but I lay her down on her rumpled sheets. This is where she should have been sleeping. Where she should have woken up, so that her body wouldn't be flushed and trembling.

"Don't go," she whimpers, grasping my arm.

"But no," I manage to say lightly. "I'm not going anywhere."

Her eyes meet mine, almost glazed from the terror she felt being on the roof. There's pleading in her eyes, whether because she still wishes to apologize or because she's worried I'll abandon her like this.

"Who are you?" a voice asks coldly.

Without letting go of Bea's hand, I turn to face the man in the suit. Only now, with Bea safely tucked in a place familiar to her, can I consider what I know. I thought I would know him immediately, on sight, this man from my nightmare. It seemed clear to me that I would, but now that I look at him I'm not sure.

The man in my dreams is ten feet tall with large muscles. He has a smile that's terrifying, but those are the imaginings of a scared little boy. Now that I'm a man, this one looks ordinary.

Is it him? Or is it merely some other rich asshole with ties to this hotel?

"I'm Bea's lover," I tell him, because I want him angry. Well, he's already angry. I want him frothing and helpless, the way I feel right now, unable to help the woman I care about.

"You're lying," the man says, his lip curled. "She doesn't have a boyfriend."

"Boyfriend? *Non.* I am her lover. Surely you understand the difference."

He snarls in a way that is almost, *almost* familiar. But his hair is peppered with white, his stance leaner than I remember. *Is it him?* "I don't know what kind of scam you think you're running, but this girl is under my protection."

"This *woman* does not need protection against me."

"I'll be the judge of that."

"Stop!" Bea is sitting up in bed, but only barely, holding up a hand as if to ward us both away. My heart breaks for her, that she needs to worry about this when she should be focused on herself. "Please, don't fight. Edward, what are you doing here?"

"Looking for you," he says, taking a step forward which I block with my body. He isn't getting near when she's in this state. He gives me a dark look but stays on his side of the bedroom. "Maria came to do turndown service and you didn't answer the door. She came in and you weren't here."

"I was on the roof," she says, sounding exhausted. I'm glad she's standing up for herself but it is sad that she needs to—against the man who was supposed to raise her.

"The roof," he says, looking even angrier. "You took her there."

Now I am the one exhausted. "Yes, and I can't bring myself to regret it even seeing what it did to her. She should not be locked up like this. It's killing her. Can't you see that?"

A muscle in his jaw ticks. "The only thing I see is a leech. That's what you are. You see a poor little rich girl and think it's your big payday. Well, you aren't getting a cent from her."

Of course I already have her money, but I don't want it. That's the irony of my life. Getting what I want and then wishing I had something else. "Are you any better? Wanting to marry a woman thirty years younger than you. One you've helped hide herself away."

It looks like a vein might pop out of his forehead. "She told you that?"

"I'm right here," Bea says, cross now. "And I can't believe you two are fighting over me like you're dogs and I'm a bone. I want to be alone now. I need to rest."

She does need to rest but not alone. Perhaps I can convince her to let me stay. All we have to do is get rid of this arrogant bastard with his Italian suit. I know that I can wrap her in her bubble—stifling though it is—and make her feel safe again. "I'll stay with you tonight."

And then the man gives me a look so imperious it looks exactly like it did when I was a child. "You are nothing but trash," he says, his voice the same from my memories. "That much is obvious from looking at you. Not to mention hearing you. I recognize the accent. Marrakesh?"

It's him. My heart pounds a war drum. "Tangier, actually."

"Yes, that sounds right." A smirk, which seals his fate.

And then I'm on top of him, taking him by surprise. I'm not seven years old anymore. He can't throw me off like I'm a pest to be disposed of. Can't lock me in the closet this time, not with my hands wrapped around his fucking throat. His eyes are wide, mouth open as he struggles to take in air.

"Paulette Bellmont," I say between gritted teeth. "Perhaps you remember her. She was a maid in a hotel. You stayed in the penthouse. Do you recognize my accent now?"

His mouth closes and opens, like a stupid fish. There are choking sounds.

"What are you doing?" Bea is beside me, tugging at my hands, not nearly hard enough to pull me away, *nothing* could pull me away. She looks shocked, horrified. Like I'm the monster instead of this asshole on the ground. "Let him go."

For a moment my fingers loosen. When Bea asks me to do something, I wish to do it. When she wants me, I wish to deliver. It goes beyond my regular desire to please women. Beyond any sense of professional duty. This is about Beatrix, a woman who I never deserved to even touch.

Much less love. God, I love her. In the riot of emotion inside me, this much is clear.

But I have been waiting my whole life to do this.

"You followed her home one night," I say, my voice hard, my hands tight around the neck beneath me, pleading with Bea with my eyes to understand. "She did not hear you. Perhaps because the street was busy and loud, like always. Or because she was tired from working for twelve hours straight."

Bea's rose-colored lips part in surprise. "What are you talking about? You know Edward?"

"You pushed your way in the door after her. Attacked her. The only thing you did not know is that she had a child living there. A small boy. Too weak to properly defend his mother."

"No," Bea whispers, horror in her green eyes.

Only then do I look down at the man whose skin has turned mottled red. I don't want to kill him—not yet, anyway. I want him to hear this, and the dead never listen. "You locked me in the closet."

I see the memory dawn in his red-rimmed eyes. Yes, he remembers now. There may have been other maids he hurt. Other women he followed home. But he remembers the screaming boy he trapped in the closet with a wood-worn chair, its hemp cords fraying, but its frame sturdy enough to hold me in.

"And then you raped her."

"She was nothing," he rasps, which is a fatal error.

Perhaps he sees that when I squeeze hard enough to take away his air. He makes a terrible sound, like the back of a car scraping against the road. His eyes roll back, and I'm looking forward to the moment he becomes silent. I did not plan to become a murderer for this, but at the moment the rage swirls around me like a firestorm. The only thing left to do is burn.

A soft crying sound prods at the edge of my consciousness. It's Beatrix, begging me to stop. "Please," she says. "Stop this. Hugo, please."

For a moment it seems that I can push aside her pleas as easily as I did before. As easily as this *Edward* pushed me aside when I was a child, but she is not a poor little rich girl no matter what he calls her. She's a woman, strong enough to call me back from the brink of madness.

Slowly my hands loosen, but they're made of cement. It feels like cracking to pry them away from where they've hardened. When they finally release I stumble back with the force of it.

Edward collapses on the floor, coughing and choking as he tries to breathe. As he tries to live.

Did I make a mistake? "A man like him deserves to die."

Bea kneels on the floor, her hands clasped together in futile prayer. Or maybe not so futile. She bent me to her will, after all. It makes me resent her, even while I recognize how much power she has over me. I would not change it if I could, but I hate that she wants me to let him be.

Her eyes are solemn. "A man like *you* doesn't deserve to be a killer."

Don't I? I hadn't thought I deserved anything at all. Definitely not the delicate woman who just pulled me off of my mother's rapist with the force of her will alone.

"Then he gets away with it," I say, my voice dull.

It had always been coming to this, hadn't it? Mama knew. Even then she knew.

The rich can get away with anything. Even now most would consider me a rich man. I could probably hurt a poor maid in this hotel and get away with it. How sick is that? I never would but it does not change the potential. How does it stop? How does it ever stop?

"No," Bea says, urgent. "We can tell the police. You witnessed it. We can—"

A short shake of my head. "That long ago? And my mother is dead now."

She gasps. "Did he...?"

"No," I say with a bitter laugh. "It was cancer who finished her off. But I'm not sure she ever really lived after he hurt her. She was far too busy looking over her shoulder for that."

"God." She looks at Edward like he's someone she's never seen before. "How could you?"

He has only recovered enough to get words out one at a time, coughing each one out, spitting it at her feet. "You. Believe. This. Piece. Of. Trash."

She stands up, holding herself with a remarkable poise considering only thirty minutes ago she was having an anxiety attack on the roof, curled into a ball. "I notice that's not a denial. Did you do it, Edward? Of course you did. I can see it in your face."

He snarls at her. "You. Fucked. Him."

I move to stand in front of her. She may not want my protection in this, but she's going to get it. "Don't speak to her that way. In fact don't speak to her at all. Be grateful she let you live, because she is the only reason you're able to take a breath right now. Be grateful and get the fuck out."

"You can't kick me out. I own this hotel."

"Actually," Bea says from behind me. "Your holding company owns the holding company which owns the holding company that owns this hotel. And my lease on the penthouse still stands. And I'm telling you to get out, too."

He narrows his eyes. "I can void your lease. You know that."

She takes a shuddery breath. "Then do it."

Slowly he picks himself up, looking like an old broken man. But when he stands up straight he stares down at us like we're trash. No, I'm the one he sees as trash. And he's right about that. "You don't want to cross me," he says to Bea. "I would have given you everything."

"No," she says softly. "You would have taken everything. That's what you do, isn't it?"

He gives me one final look—an appraisal, this look. As if considering the man who could have killed him. Weighing whether he would survive another fight. No, he wouldn't. Not even Bea could save him if he challenged me again. Nothing could save him if he hurts a single wild copper-colored hair on her head.

Perhaps he senses that because he turns and limps out of the room, keeping his head held high.

As soon as the elevator doors close behind him, I turn to Bea. "Are you all right?"

She holds up a hand as if I might hurt her, which makes me freeze. "I need you to go, too."

Shock is a thousand tons of bricks on my chest. They make it hard to breathe. Harder to speak. "I'm sorry, Bea. I didn't mean for that to happen in front of you."

"But you did mean for it to happen, didn't you? That's why you came last night, without me even having to pay. Not because you're interested in me, not because you're a friend. So that you could find out something about the owner of the hotel."

Shame is acid in my gut. "I care about you, Bea."

A small smile. "Is that the company line? The official response when a client is foolish enough to think she's special to you?"

"It's not a line. I care about you more than I should, more than I imagined was possible. More than I ever cared about a woman before. *Mon Dieu*, I let him go unharmed for you."

"You only had access to him because of me," she shoots back.

There's a tear down the center of me, its edges singed with guilt. The past and present. Revenge and a woman I can't ever have. "What will you do?"

She shakes her head. "I don't know. Look for somewhere else to live, most likely. Edward probably has his lawyers looking for a loophole in the contract right now. I mean, it's not going to be hard. They wrote the contract when my trust leased the penthouse."

"I'm sorry."

"No, you didn't do anything wrong. What you said… what happened to your mother… to *you*, it's horrifying. I can't believe that he… and well, somehow I'm not as surprised as I should be. He's always thought he was above the rules."

Relief suffuses me. She understands. "I knew he might have ties to this hotel, but that's all. I did not know for sure that he was the owner. It might have been a dead end, but that isn't why I came last night. I came because I wanted to see you."

She closes her eyes and takes a deep breath. When she looks at me again her eyes are clear. Poor little rich girl, he called her? How can you he look at her, standing here like a goddess, and think she is anything but strong? "I understand why you did it. More than you know." She has a sad little laugh. "I used to dream about getting my hands on the Somali pirates who killed my parents. Not that I would have been able to… you know, choke the life out of them."

"I stopped. I stopped for you." How could that not be enough? Why doesn't she? That was everything to me. My driving force. I gave up my past for her, for a chance at a future, and now I'm left with nothing.

Her eyes glisten with tears. "But I can't trust you. God, I barely *know* you."

"You do know me," I say, urgent. "What you said in the video… that was all true."

"You saw that?" She shakes her head, sad and lost. "I can't trust anything anymore. Not even myself. I thought Edward had my best interests at heart, even if he was a little pompous about it. But he was a monster all along. You need to go."

"What if he comes back?" What if he forces his way inside this penthouse? What if he pushes her down on the bed? Bile rises in my throat, knowing what he's capable of.

She shakes her head. "I can protect myself more than you think. More than he thinks."

"Let me stay. We don't have to do anything. We won't have sex or even talk if you're not ready for that. I'll sleep on the couch, but I'm not going to leave you alone."

"It's my decision," she says, and I can see her shutting down. I can see the walls come up around her like the marble walls of L'Etoile and the high windows. Like the private elevator that only she can use. "And if you don't listen to me, you'll be as bad as him."

Dread squeezes my heart. "I would never force you."

"Then go."

The Den is quieter in early afternoon, a steady hum of conversation instead of the raucous crowd. I'm surprised to see Sutton sitting in an armchair in front of the fire, a beer dangling from its neck, the glass beaded with condensation.

I sit down in the chair next to him. "A little early," I say, nodding toward the beer.

It's an invitation for him to tell me what's wrong. He takes a swallow before answering. "Needed a break from the office."

"Problems in paradise?" I ask, my voice light. The construction and real estate company he owns with Christopher does well. And so far there hasn't been conflict between the two men. I suppose it's only a matter of time. They're both strong-willed and stubborn, in their own ways.

"You could say that." Sutton leans forward and sets down the beer between his boots, studying the ground like it has the solution to life's problems. "There's this woman."

I groan. "No talk of women. Not today."

His eyebrows go up. "You love talking about women."

"Only good things. And I have no good things to say today."

He laughs. "Don't tell me Hugo Bellmont finally met his match. The virgin?"

She's not a virgin anymore, but I don't mention that. I'm sure he can fill in the blanks. I put up a finger for the cocktail waitress, because today we are drinking early. "Apparently you've met your match, too. Tell me about her."

"It's not like that. I mean, she's beautiful. Smart. Like crazy smart."

"Does she use words too big for you?"

He snorts, not bothering to argue the point. Sutton is basically a genius, he just hides it behind a Southern drawl. "That's not exactly the problem."

"Then what is it?" The waitress brings my brandy, and I take a sip.

"Christopher. She's his stepsister. Or at least they used to be. I'm a little hazy on the background except that I know there's something there."

I look into the fire so he can't see that it troubles me. There's history between Christopher and this Harper. And if it comes between them it will disrupt more than the company. It will disrupt the Thieves Club, a friendship I've come to enjoy greatly. "History is in the past, my friend. So what are you going to do about this?"

"The only thing I can do. The only thing I've ever done."

The answer is simple for a man as hard and ambitious as Sutton. "Go after her."

He nods. "I would prefer that it didn't interfere with business."

"I would have preferred that also, but here we are drinking at three in the afternoon."

We lapse into a contemplative silence. I didn't come here expecting to see anyone I knew. Sutton knows better than to push me when I don't want to talk. It doesn't happen often, but when it does it usually has to do with Melissande. And history. But history is in the past, as I said.

So what am I going to do about it?

The moments that follow are a brief reprieve, but in the back of my mind I know what I have to do. Revenge has been the thing that drove me for years. Now it will be something else, but no matter what I choose to do, I'll be left alone. That's all I deserve, really.

The waitress returns, this time with a note on her tray. *Hugo Bellmont*, it says on the front.

And inside: *Come upstairs.—D*

"I have been summoned," I say to Sutton, dropping the note on the small oak table between us.

He reads it with surprise. "What's your business with him? Do you need backup?"

It does feel good to have friends who would have my back, but he has his own problems. Problems of the female persuasion. And I need to solve this one myself. Need to solve it alone.

At the bottom of the stairs I pass by Penny, who is Damon's girl. I recognize her from around the Den and from our one meeting at Beau Ciel. "Good afternoon," I tell her with a small bow.

Her cheeks turn a little pink. It used to bring me pleasure that I could make any woman—even ones contented in their relationships—blush, but instead there's only emptiness. "Damon's waiting for you," she says, revealing that she knows more about his business than some people would suspect.

"*Merci*. And do you have any words of advice for me? He has quite a reputation."

"Don't believe a word they say. I mean, some of it's real but you'll never really know which parts."

"Very reassuring," I say drily. "You are a good match for him, to be sure."

She laughs. "He's a softie inside."

I'm still shaking my head, a small smile on my face, when I reach the top of the stairs. It is only such a ridiculous statement as Damon Scott being a softie that could make me laugh. It occurs to me that perhaps that's Penny's goal, to cheer me up against all odds. In which case she truly *is* a good match for the man who sits at a desk set far back in a dark room.

He does not look up when I enter but I know he hears me. There's nothing that happens in the Den that he doesn't know about. Maybe even in the whole of Tanglewood.

"Good afternoon," I say, neutral. "You asked for me?"

Of course he did not *ask*, it was a command. I do not take offense, not if he delivers what I need him to do. He looks up and sets his pen down. "Our deal. Do you still want it?"

I step farther into the room but don't bother to sit, not even when he inclines his head at the oversized leather chairs in front of the desk. This isn't a deal I want to sit for. "Melissande. You want her ruined. You haven't told me why and I don't imagine you will. But I agree to that."

"And in return I will ruin Edward Marchand. The owner of L'Etoile."

This is what it feels like to be torn in half, the halves pulled away completely. I'm two pieces now, the one from the past and the one adrift. "No."

One eyebrow rises. "No?"

Well, that's something at the least. I have managed to surprise Damon Scott. "Instead I wish for you to purchase the hotel for me. I will provide the money, but the owner may take some persuasion."

Damon leans back, pondering. "I have some knowledge of your portfolio. It's significant. Probably enough, but only barely. You won't have anything left."

And with Melissande ruined I won't be able to work in this town. At least not for the prices I normally command. She will do her best to blackball me and probably succeed.

It does not matter. I don't matter, not if it means Bea can be safe.

"Do we have a deal?" I ask, my voice even.

"Consider it done."

I set down a flash drive on his desk. It contains photographs I took in her office late last night of her ledger, written in her own handwriting. Names and dates and dollar amounts. The fact that she's a madam is well known in the underworld of the city. No cop would make a move on her for selling sex. Half of them are under her payroll. And the other half... well, she would be out within twenty-four hours and make it her mission to destroy them.

That's why I've circled the names of boys and girls I know to be under eighteen. It's a dark truth of the sex industry that this happens. When they don't have a good family, when the system fails them, it's the only way they survive. There are clients who prefer the young ones.

Which is one of the reasons Melissande wanted me all those years ago. She probably enjoyed that I worshipped her at the beginning, as well. But it wasn't long before she put me to work.

Damon nods. "A pleasure doing business with you."

No, I have experience with pleasure. This was something else. "You'll let me know?"

"It will take a couple days. I'll be in touch."

And this is how you make a deal with the devil. By selling the most valuable thing you have for the only person worth anything to me. Losing L'Etoile will be nothing to a man like Edward Marchand. It will not ruin him, not when he has a hundred other more valuable properties. Decades of searching for revenge, only to give it up in a single afternoon.

But it will mean freedom for Bea, which is the most important thing now. The only thing. I traded everything for her to feel safe, for her to never again tremble in fear.

Chapter Eighteen

I HAVE AN ENTIRE BOTTLE OF BRANDY SITTING ON THE COUNTER.
And beside it is a stack of papers that constitutes the signed and executed contract rendering me the new owner of L'Etoile. When Mama worked as a maid I looked at the hotel with awe, with anger, with distrust—but I never imagined I would own a place like it.

Now I am the proprietor.

Well, I won't become too comfortable with the title. I will have to face Bea soon so that we can transfer the title to her name. It won't matter if I promise never to evict her or coerce her into anything. Only when she owns her suite free and clear will she truly feel safe.

Not tonight, however. Tonight I plan to get very drunk. After spending all day at a lawyer's office, signing away almost every last cent I own, it seems the only fitting thing to do. At least I did not have to see Edward there. He signed the night before. Putting up quite a protest, Damon said, but in the end the Scott name held enough clout—and enough fear— in the city to convince him to sign. And Edward ended up fairly compensated for the hotel, something that I cannot help but dwell on tonight, with my bank account and investments depleted.

I reach for a glass as the door buzzes. Is it Melissande? I haven't heard from her, but I imagine that won't last. She will have some words for me once she realized what I've done. Unless Damon makes it hard enough for her that she has to leave Tanglewood.

My phone is open to Bea Sharp's page, where nothing new has been uploaded for a week. Her longest break, except for the one time she had the flu, one of the comments says— but even then she posted an update to let everyone know. The fans are in a frenzy about the absence, worried and dramatic, but none of it compares to the intensity of my own guilt.

I felt bad for making her cry the first night, but this is worse. I hurt her. Not her beautiful body but the tender heart inside. No wonder she kicked me out.

My finger flicks across the screen and the security app appears. I stare at the photo a long second, trying to blink away the mirage. It's dark outside, but the light clearly illuminates her upturned nose, her green eyes. Her copper curls. "Bea," I breathe.

She's here. Why is she here? *How* is she here?

I press the button to buzz her in the main door downstairs, but I don't wait for her to climb the stairs to my loft. Instead I'm out the door and running down to meet her, my heart pounding louder than my footfalls, hope a wild and unmistakable beat. I catch her up in my arms as she falls, trembling, afraid. "What are you doing?" I demand, my throat tight with fear for her. Not that she would be in danger in the world, but she will *feel* as though she is. Her body will undergo the same stress, the same reactions as if she were kidnapped by Somali pirates even if nothing happens.

"I took a cab," she whispers, her voice shaking.

"Mon Dieu." I don't wait for her to give me permission this time. I lift her up and carry her up the stairs, my stride fast and steady. Once we're inside the loft I shut the door and think about where to put her. Nothing about this place is what she's used to. Sleek modern furniture instead of embellished antiques. Crisp leather instead of thick brocade.

The bed, I realize. The white sheets on my bed aren't trimmed with lace, but they're close enough. No other woman has ever spent the night with me in the bed, but it feels completely natural that Bea would be there. I stride into the bedroom and set her down gently, pushing the hair back from her face. "Why did you do it, Bea?"

"I had to see you." Her lower lip trembles, and I'm terribly afraid she's going to cry.

"You could have called me. I would have come."

"No," she says, a little too loud. This is when I realize that she is more than afraid. She's perhaps tipsy. "I have to apologize to you. God, you had just seen the man who… And then I told you to leave."

She's definitely crying now, tears thick in her throat, fat drops on her copper lashes.

"You are killing me," I tell her honestly. "Don't cry."

Her lip trembles while she makes a valiant effort to stop. It isn't quite enough. "I couldn't stop thinking about your face when I asked you to go. And after everything you'd done. The picnic. You wanted me to get out of there, and I should have, a long time ago, and now I have to leave—"

"Shhh." I consider telling her about the sale of L'Etoile. I could show her the contract in the next room, but that will only raise questions of why Edward had been willing to part with it. The important thing is that she calm down now. I'll tell her about the hotel later. "Don't worry about that. Everything will work out. I promise, Bea."

"It's fine," she says, quite loud, and I realize she's more than tipsy. She's completely wasted. "I did it. Look! I'm outside the hotel right now and I'm not freaking out."

Except that she had to get drunk before she could come. And what happens when she sobers up? I'm afraid we're in for an even worse panic attack than before. "You amaze me," I tell her gently. "This is a beautiful first step. But right now I want you to go back with me."

She looks crestfallen. "Why?"

"Because I don't have a piano, and I want to hear you play." As I say the words I discover that they're true. This loft doesn't suit her. It's an impersonal husk, rather like myself. Even if she is able to leave L'Etoile on a regular basis, that penthouse is her home. And when she plays music, her soul.

She starts to cry again. "I do want to play. I do."

"And you will," I tell her. "Very soon."

"No." Her green eyes are deep reflective pools. "I haven't played since you left. How crazy is that? For years it was almost the only way I could speak. And then nothing."

I don't think it has anything to do with my absence. More likely she's terrified of being forced from her home after the confrontation with Edward. "You remember my Bugatti?"

She shakes her head, eyes wide. "Noooo."

Oh, she is an adorable drunk. I would enjoy the experience more if I didn't know how little time with her I have left. "You watched me arrive the first night," I remind her. "It's very pretty. Not as pretty as you, but still. Shall we take it back to L'Etoile?"

"Okay," she says. "I'll try not to throw up. The cab driver was not happy."

I decide to bring both the contract and the bottle of brandy with me. Something tells me I might need both of them before I'm done.

Chapter Nineteen

The next morning I wake up with a massive hangover and a pair of yellow eyes staring down at me. It takes me a moment to make the world stop spinning and orient myself.

Where the hell am I? The penthouse of L'Etoile.

What *is* that? Ah, that's right. The cat.

She's apparently warmed up enough that she's cuddling on my chest. Either that or she was plotting ways to kill me in my sleep. Gingerly I move the kitty aside and wander out of the bedroom.

A room service tray sits on the small table, filled with pastries and an omelet. I must have been sleeping very hard not to notice it arrive. And from behind the closed door I hear music playing. I believe the song is Breakaway by Kelly Clarkson, though it's been changed enough that I'm not sure. It's softer now, almost haunting. Feeling like an intruder I knock softly and step inside.

Bea sits at the bench looking impossibly fresh. Her hair is still dark and damp from the shower. I probably could have slept through an earthquake. Only vaguely do I remember working my way through the bottle of brandy while Bea played the piano beside me. There is an even hazier memory of singing Hotel California as a duet. We were both drunk, and now we're both hungover.

Though Bea's smile is too bright and too genuine. "Are you hungry?" she asks.

So apparently I'm the only one hungover. "No, thank you. Is it all right if I shower?"

"Of course. You don't have to ask me that."

Actually I do, because you'll soon be the new owner of this hotel. That's what I should say to her, but I can't quite bring myself to do it. Because I know that the sooner I say that, the sooner this ends. And she looks so lovely in a silk and lace robe. So lovely in her casual majesty. It makes me want to fall to my knees, to beg her to stay. But anything other than leaving would be a way to tie her down, to make her owe me. I need to give her the hotel, outright, without any strings attached or demands. And then I need to leave. I won't do to her what Edward did.

"I'll be back in a few minutes," I say roughly, because I need a cold shower and approximately ten thousand gallons of coffee before I'm ready to have that conversation.

In the bathroom I find a drawer with a couple unused toothbrushes wrapped in clear plastic, the kind the hotel probably sends up to forgetful travelers. I feel much better after I brush my teeth, but I need a shower. In the end I'm not quite self-flagellant enough to make the water cold. I make it hot instead, standing under the spray and letting it pound away some of the tension.

A sound catches my attention, and then a gust of cool air as the shower door opens.

Bea stands on the marble tile, looking shy and knowing at once in a gold silk robe. A virgin. A siren. I'm not sure my mind will ever wrap itself around her. I'm not sure I'd ever want to. I crave both parts of her, *all* of her.

"Can I come in?" she asks.

Already my body reacts to her, hardening, turning hot and eager. "There's nothing I want more, Bea. But I don't know if I can be gentle right now."

She tugs on the silk holding her robe together, revealing the glory of her body—pale skin and dusky nipples, high breasts with freckles across the slopes of them. Her belly narrows and then flares out again to hips I long to hold as I pound into her.

Between her legs her hair is a darker color, almost bronze. My cock throbs just looking at her.

The silk pools behind her, and she steps into the shower with me. "Then be rough."

It's been so long since I've had sex for only myself. Have I ever done that?

Have I ever touched a woman's breasts only to feel them in my hands? Have I ever sucked her nipples because I love the feel of her? Have I ever slid my fingers through her slit, blunt and greedy, because I needed to feel where my cock would be?

Bea gasps and arches, giving me better access to her pussy. "Whatever you want."

"Yes," I mutter, letting the need overtake me. For the first time. This is how she felt that night, being a virgin. It's the way I feel right now, doing this with her. I push two fingers inside her, slick from her arousal and the hot spray of the shower. "I want this."

She moans, leaning back against the tile. "Yes."

"I should prepare you more," I warn her. "You will feel this later."

"Make yourself feel good," she whispers, her eyes an unfathomable sea. She has depths I've never explored. Depths I never *will* explore, because I won't be here that long.

I'm here now, so I make it count, lifting her up against the tile wall, spreading her thighs wide, and notching my cock against her. My voice comes out as a growl. "Say it again."

Her head falls back, exposing her throat. "Whatever you want."

I thrust home, clenching my teeth against the ecstasy of her. She pulses around me, and it feels so good I want to make her do it again. "That's right," I say, my lids heavy. "Touch yourself, Bea. Come around my cock. I want to feel you."

She reaches down, whimpering as she finds her clit. It's too direct, I think. A little too harsh, touching herself while she's spread open and slick but I don't tell her to stop. It feels too good when her pussy grasps my cock like a fist. "Oh my God," she whispers.

Whatever you want. The words swirl around me in the hot steam, and for the first time I'm free. "Bite me," I gasp, because that's something I would not have asked for. I want it now.

She turns her head, making a delicate bite on my arm where I support us against the tile. Her hand moves faster on her clit, and I know she's close. Close, but I want more. Always more.

"Harder," I say, my teeth gritted.

She comes with a keening cry, biting down hard enough I see stars. I ride out her climax while her pussy squeezes my cock, and then I lose myself in her. I thrust into her, relentless and burning hot, turning her climax into a second and a third, until they string together in an endless litany, her voice echoing off the tile, her body wet and welcoming around mine.

I take her again and again, long after I should let her rest, only because I want to. *Whatever you want*, she says, so I pretend we have forever.

Chapter Twenty

We spend the rest of the day making love. I have had plenty of sex in my life—the passionate kind, the animalistic kind. The paid kind. There has been sex in my life but never love.

Which is why I force myself to leave the bed while she sleeps, to dress quietly, to write a note explaining that the deed will be hers. For such a large property it will require a visit to the lawyer to finalize the transfer, but I make it clear—it will be hers, outright. She owes me nothing. In fact, she most likely won't ever see me again.

Perhaps I could have been gone. I should have been.

Instead I find myself digging through the pantry for a can of tuna. I open it for the cat, who gobbles it almost faster than seems healthy, swallowing whole chunks of fish.

"Where are you going?" Bea stands in the doorway from the bedroom, holding the lace-trimmed sheet around herself like a toga. I suppose she could look nothing less than glorious, her body well-used, her hair even wilder than ever before.

"Home," I say, though the word is rather generous considering the emptiness of the loft.

She moves farther into the living area. "Oh."

"It's for the best," I say, managing a small smile for her. "I wrote out the details here, but you will be able to stay at L'Etoile. I made sure of that."

Her brow furrows. "What do you mean?"

It's only here that I realize the note was an act of cowardice. This woman has the strength to confront her worst fears. I can find some to tell her it won't be as bad as that. "I hope you continue to push your boundaries. To visit the rooftop garden or other places in Tanglewood. There are pianos all around the city for you. But you won't be forced to leave."

"You talked to Edward," she says, speaking cautiously because I'm sure she knows that if I confronted him a second time there would be no talking.

"I had a third party do it for me. He was convinced it would be in his best interest to sell the hotel. Which means you're free. You don't have to leave, except on your own terms."

A sense of peace flows out from her. "You did that for me?"

"I would do anything for you." Even leave.

Her gaze turns to the stack of papers. "Is that from Edward, then?"

"In a manner of speaking. Actually I purchased the property from him, because I had to make sure he would go through with it. I'll transfer the deed into your name as soon as the lawyer can arrange it. Then it will be yours."

"You mean I'm going to buy it from you?"

"No, Bea. It's a gift. There are no strings attached."

Her mouth drops open. "I could never accept a gift that big."

It has to be this way. For her, so she is never coerced into anything she doesn't want, never fearful of it. And for me, because I don't know how to offer anything but this. "It's already yours in all but name, Bea. The title is only to make sure you're safe."

She takes a step closer, standing right in front of me now. "I'm already safe. If you own L'Etoile then I'm safe here, with you."

I'm moved that she has such confidence in me. "I never want you to doubt it."

"I'll take the hotel from you if that's what you want. I would be happy to do that.

The building may be old and kind of, you know, gaudy, but I love it. And I love the people here."

"Good."

"But it will be a purchase. Not a gift."

I open my mouth to object, but to be fair, the woman probably has more money than God. Then why does it make me feel like I'm crawling out of my skin to accept? Like I'm losing far more than the woman I care about. "*Non.*"

"*Oui,*" she says, implacable.

I'm not above pleading, at least not with her. "Bea, you must understand how much I've come to care about you. It's not like the other women. They aren't even—"

For maybe the first time since I moved here I struggle for words.

She smiles a little. "I know."

That makes me pause. "You know?"

"You make your own kind of music. Not with your fingers on the keys. With your whole body. I thought I was just imagining it. After all, what did I know? I was a virgin. I don't know how it usually is between a man and a woman. But I know about music. You can't fake that kind of passion."

I breathe out in relief, that she understands what I could not find the words to say. There is too much in my past to love easily, or lightly, the grooves run too deep. I speak with my body instead, and in that language, Bea is an unexpected prodigy.

I give her a small bow. "In that case I accept your terms. You will buy the hotel."

"And I hope you will come visit me here."

My throat becomes tight. I would give almost anything to be with Bea, but I'm not sure I could handle being paid for the honor. Not anymore. "In a professional capacity?"

"If that's the only way I can have you, yes." She swallows hard. "But I'm going to be honest with you, even though it terrifies me. It terrifies me more than taking a cab to your loft, which was a lot. I want more than that. I want everything."

"Everything?" It seems impossible that I could have this. For so long I lived only for revenge. And for pleasure. I thought that would be enough until I met Bea.

She made me realize I want more than that. "What you said in the shower," I say, gruff.

Her lips twist into a secret feminine smile, and for the first time in my life I feel my skin flush hot. Am I blushing? *Mon Dieu.* She really has ruined me for anyone else. "I think I asked you to be rough with me."

"Something else," I say, though I'm dangerously close to being rough with her on the dining table. There is only one thing I want more than sex with her right now.

"That you should make yourself feel good," she says, letting the sheet fall away from her body.

"Minx," I say on a groan. "Witch. Siren. You said something else to me."

"Whatever you want," she whispers.

And then I take her in my arms. "Everything. *Mon Dieu,* I want everything with you."

She wraps her arms around my neck and gives me all of that and more. The fire in her wild hair, the freckles scattered across her body. The acceptance in her beautiful moss eyes. There is a whole universe waiting for us, and we find it one star at a time.

Chapter Twenty-One

THE NIGHT SKY STRETCHES TO INFINITY, BUT THE MOMENT IS ALMOST unbearably intimate. We are lying on the rooftop, naked but for a lace-edged sheet we stole from her bed. Bea's body is slung over mine, her hair a pleasant cloud of sensation against my neck. Her hand plays idly over my chest, tugging lightly at the springy hair, tracing down the muscles of my abs.

"Are you sad?" she asks. "About Edward?"

"He lost his hold on you. That's enough." It's more than whatever wealth he has in the world, actually. More precious than gold. Though nothing will ever be punishment enough for what he did to my mother. So I suppose it's fitting he gave up something priceless. "The truth is I feel more guilty than anything."

"About Melissande. Has she called you again?"

"No." I stare at the sky, which feels heavier when I think about her. "Not since I gave her a few thousand to start over somewhere else."

"What she did was wrong, Hugo. Selling children. You were a child, too, Hugo, when she took advantage of you. She didn't deserve your loyalty."

"Loyalty is a strange thing. It doesn't always need an excuse. In the case of Melissande, she took me from a place where I had no future and turned me into something women paid thousands of dollars to spend time with."

Anger flashes through Bea's green eyes, which are usually so calm. "She has no idea what you're worth. She never did."

Bemusement is a warm fire in my chest. "You are kind, *mon amie*."

"Yes, that's me. Kind and so incredibly selfless that I'm willing to spend my nights with the most sought-after man in Tanglewood, that I'm willing to have this body—" She walks her fingers down my abdomen. My cock is a predictable creature. It becomes hard beneath the blanket, despite the number of times I've taken her this night. "—bring me pleasure."

A small laugh. "If there's one thing I've taught you it's to appreciate pleasure."

"You taught me more than that," she says suggestively, and I know she's thinking of the rather athletic round of sex we had after our picnic of grapes and manchego.

I touch my finger to the bronze of her eyebrows, tracing them. "While you have learned your lessons well, there is still plenty more to teach."

"Oh?" she asks, her lips forming a perfect peach circle.

"I expect we will spend many nights on the rooftop."

She laughs. "I thought you were the one who wanted me to leave the hotel."

"*Oui*, but you have taught me things as well. For example, you taught me to appreciate staying between these four walls." It has been three days since I signed over L'Etoile to her. Since that time I have not left. There has been only sex and talking and the occasional break for delicious food. "Perhaps we will leave next week. Where would you like to go?"

She draws swirling circles on my skin. "There is an exhibit at the Tanglewood Art Museum I've had my eye on."

I think of the traveling exhibits. "The one with mummies?"

"No."

"The one about bugs in gemstones."

"No."

And then I groan. "It's the instruments of the Middle Ages, isn't it? That's a permanent exhibit, *mon amie*. Part of the original collection, I believe. It hurts my heart that you have not seen it."

"I know," she says, hiding her face against my chest.

"We will work up to it," I promise.

Naturally I don't mention that I know the director of the museum on an intimate level, that she was a regular client who was rather peeved when I told her I would no longer be working. Perhaps I could even arrange a private show of the instruments for Bea…if I made it worth the director's time. But no, we will attend the museum the old-fashioned way, with a ticket of admissions.

She shivers in my arms, still not quite ready to venture out. "Okay."

"I must tell you one of the most wonderful things about leaving your bed. It's thinking of all the delicious things to do to you when I return."

Her hand slips under the blanket. "Delicious?"

My breath catches when she touches somewhere particularly sensitive. "Yes."

My innocent ex-virgin has turned into a sex goddess. Her fist closes around my cock while her lips hover near my ear. "I do love the way you taste," she whispers.

I groan and press my hips up toward the night. "Please."

She moves down my body and takes me to heaven with her mouth, her hands. Her eyes, full of reckless confidence. This is how I want her—unafraid. The climax hits me, almost violent in its strength, making me choke out her name in a litany, "Bea Bea Bea."

It feels incredible, but nowhere near as good as it does to flip her onto her back. To turn the sly grin into an O of shocked bliss. We dine on the best food available in the city, in the world, but none of the flavors compare to the sweet salt of her arousal. The essence of this woman, which has become like sustenance. The taste that made me come awake, after so long spent in the dark.

Epilogue

Six months later

I SPENT MANY EVENINGS AT THE DEN BEFORE I MET BEA, BUT NONE OF THEM WERE A Saturday night.

Those were reserved for work.

Now I'm no longer a male escort. I suppose you could say I'm an investor now, though that word is rather boring. My modest fortune was restored when Bea purchased L'Etoile from me, and so I'm free to play with money like the Monopoly game. Though I consider my true profession to be pleasing Bea. That's something I find far more satisfying.

At first I thought we would focus on the museum, but then I realized another place would hold a far greater intellectual curiosity for her with its ever-changing population, its unique cross-section of the city. The Den. It also had a built-in support system. And so we visited a month after I moved into the penthouse, leaving quickly before she could succumb to panic.

And then we went again. And again.

The members of the Thieves Club were fascinated to meet the woman who had tied me down, but it was Penny who accepted Bea into her fold. For her part, Bea has flourished among a new group of people, like a flower that has survived in brittle, almost desert-like conditions, which has finally been given water.

I'm standing behind the curtain on the small stage set up in the ballroom. The Bluthner grand piano has been restored by craftsmen and expertly tuned, ready for Bea to play for the small crowd of the city's elite.

If she doesn't hyperventilate first.

She leans over a potted plant, heaving like she might throw up. It would be a waste of a beautiful roasted lamb I prepared for her, and it would not taste nearly as good on the way back up.

"*Mon amie*," I say softly, a little coaxing. "Come here."

She moans her refusal. "I can't do this. Why did I think I could do this?"

"Because you can do anything. This small show is only one small thing in a very large list."

"There's a *stage*," she says. "I've never been on a stage before."

"You have played for millions of viewers instead. You will do very well up there. And I'll be waiting in the eaves for you to return, to congratulate you." My tone makes it clear this congratulation would take a sexy form.

"Can we do that now?" she asks, hopeful.

Always ready, this one.

"But no, they are about to begin." I glance between the two heavy velvet curtains at the chairs filled with men in tuxes and women in glittering gowns. "Did you know that there was once a virginity auction on this very stage?"

"What?" Bea looks scandalized—and also curious, which I had hoped for.

"Yes, and now she returns as a guest." Tickets to this event were extremely sought after. The debut of the internet phenomenon Bea Sharp. "There she is on the front row. Next to Harper."

Avery James looks beautiful and composed, though the growling animal of a man beside her probably has something to do with it. No one in attendance would dare make even the smallest remark to shame her. Gabriel Miller would rip their head off.

"You know her?" Bea narrows her eyes. "Did *you* attend the auction?"

"Of course not. It was a Saturday."

She laughs softly, shaking her head. "Well done. You've successfully distracted me. Now all I can do is picture those two having sex."

"Very beautiful people, those two. I'm sure they are pleasant pictures. However, they're nothing compared to what you and I will look like after your show."

The corner of her lips turns up. "What will we look like?"

"This will be new. And impossible to describe. Much better if I show you."

She looks skeptical. "Something new?"

Our nights have been passionate and inventive. I have many tricks up my sleeve. That has less to do with my previous profession. It's Bea herself. Her body, her smile. Her music. She makes me dream up new ways to make love to her every night.

"Something new," I repeat, pointing to the curtains where Damon Scott appeared.

"Is the star ready to go on?" he says, but it's not really a question. I don't think he would look very kindly on her if he had to refund all of these people's money. So it's a good thing I don't doubt her.

Bea takes a deep breath and nods. "Let's do this."

I stand with her in silence, my arms around her, my lips against her temple, while Damon gives a stirring and awe-inspiring introduction. It includes her video-watched stats and the incredible artists who have praised her work. He finishes with, "Please welcome the luminous Bea Sharp to the Den tonight."

It's only with reluctance that I let her go, because she deserves to shine.

She deserves it as much as I deserve to witness it.

Her green eyes look back at me, filled with serenity that I knew would be there. When it comes to music there is nothing that makes this woman nervous. Not even the Den, which she has managed to visit a few times now. Not even this crowd of wealthy and powerful people, all of them watching her with wonder. There is only grace and confidence as she crosses the small stage and sits down on the bench.

Beyond the raised frame of the piano, I see Harper send a small wave to Bea. Behind her sits Sutton, a grave expression on his face. He hides it well, but it's clear how he feels about the vibrant young woman. Even less clear is how Christopher feels, though he does not seem to be in attendance tonight. There is sexual attraction, to be sure. Inappropriate between siblings, even if the connection was made through marriage and not biology. It remains to be seen whether there is anything more.

Bea takes a breath that I recognize from the countless times I've watched her play. Her fingers find the keys without her having to look down. This instrument may be new to her, but she knows the notes like they're parts of her soul. Like they're written on her skin.

And when she plays, the stars themselves come alight.

Thank you so much for reading Hugo and Bea's story!

Don't miss the brand new romance also about a heroine who loves music…

Liam North got custody of the violin prodigy six years ago. She's all grown up now, but he still treats her like a child. No matter how much he wants her.

"Swoon-worthy, forbidden, and sexy, Liam North is my new obsession."—*New York Times* bestselling author Claire Contreras

"Overture is a beautiful composition of forbidden love and undeniable desire. Skye has crafted a gripping, sensual, and intense story that left me breathless"—*USA Today* bestselling author Nikki Sloane

And if you want to read more about Harper and Sutton and Christopher, you'll love SURVIVAL OF THE RICHEST. Find out what happens in this scorching love triangle!

**Two billionaires determined to claim her.
And a war fought on the most dangerous battlefield—the heart.**

My story starts with a plunge into the cold water of Manhattan's harbor. A strong hand hauls me back onto the deck of the luxury yacht. Christopher was supposed to be my enemy. Instead he protects me with fierce determination.

That should have been my happily ever after, but then Sutton appeared–ruthless and seductive. He doesn't care that my heart belongs to someone else, because he's determined to win. No matter the cost.

It's an impossible choice, but I can't have them both.

Sign up for the VIP Reader List to find out when I have a new book release: www.skyewarren.com/newsletter

If you enjoyed ESCORT, you'll love the sexy virgin auction novel THE PAWN, available now! *There's one way to save our house, one thing I have left of value—my body.*

Join my Facebook group, Skye Warren's Dark Room, for exclusive giveaways and sneak peeks of future books.

Books by Skye Warren

Endgame trilogy & Masterpiece duet
The Pawn
The Knight
The Castle
The King
The Queen

Trust Fund duet
Survival of the Richest
The Evolution of Man

Underground series
Rough
Hard
Fierce
Wild
Dirty
Secret
Sweet
Deep

Stripped series
Tough Love
Love the Way You Lie
Better When It Hurts
Even Better
Pretty When You Cry
Caught for Christmas
Hold You Against Me
To the Ends of the Earth

Standalone Books
Wanderlust
On the Way Home
Beauty and the Beast
Anti Hero
Escort

For a complete listing of Skye Warren books, visit
www.skyewarren.com/books

About the Author

Skye Warren is the *New York Times* bestselling author of dangerous romance such as the Endgame trilogy. Her books have been featured in Jezebel, Buzzfeed, *USA Today* Happily Ever After, Glamour, and Elle Magazine. She makes her home in Texas with her loving family, sweet dogs, and evil cat.

Sign up for Skye's newsletter:
www.skyewarren.com/newsletter

Like Skye Warren on Facebook:
facebook.com/skyewarren

Join Skye Warren's Dark Room reader group:
skyewarren.com/darkroom

Follow Skye Warren on Instagram:
instagram.com/skyewarrenbooks

Visit Skye's website for her current booklist:
www.skyewarren.com